生死时代之双雄

（上册）

高 淳 著

图书在版编目（CIP）数据

生死时代之双雄 / 高淳著. -- 北京 : 中国文联出版社，2017.7

ISBN 978-7-5190-2901-2

Ⅰ. ①生… Ⅱ. ①高… Ⅲ. ①长篇小说－中国－当代Ⅳ. ①I247.5

中国版本图书馆 CIP 数据核字(2017)第 182325 号

生死时代之双雄

作　　者：高　淳

出 版 人：朱　庆

终 审 人：奚耀华　　　　复 审 人：王柏松

责任编辑：周小丽　　　　责任校对：潘传兵

封面设计：晓　攀　　　　责任印制：陈　晨

出版发行：中国文联出版社

地　　址：北京市朝阳区农展馆南里 10 号，100125

电　　话：010-85923036（咨询）85923000（编务）85923020（邮购）

传　　真：010-85923000（总编室），010-85923020（发行部）

网　　址：http://www.clapnet.cn　　　http://www.claplus.cn

E - mail：clap@clapnet.cn　　　zhouxl@clapnet.cn

印　　刷：虎彩印艺股份有限公司

装　　订：虎彩印艺股份有限公司

法律顾问：北京天驰君泰律师事务所徐波律师

本书如有破损、缺页、装订错误，请与本社联系调换

开　　本：710×1000　　　1/16

字　　数：755 千字　　　印 张：48

版　　次：2017 年 7 月第 1 版　　　印 次：2017 年 7 月第 1 次印刷

书　　号：ISBN 978-7-5190-2901-2

定　　价：99.00 元

中英参照迦陵诗词论稿

（上）

葉嘉瑩　著

南開大學出版社

图书在版编目(CIP)数据

中英参照迦陵诗词论稿：全2册：汉英对照 / 叶嘉莹著. —天津：南开大学出版社，2014.12

ISBN 978-7-310-04472-6

Ⅰ. ①中… Ⅱ. ①叶… Ⅲ. ①诗词研究—中国—文集—汉、英 Ⅳ. ①I207.2—53

中国版本图书馆 CIP 数据核字(2014)第 082082 号

南开大学出版社出版发行

出版人:孙克强

地址:天津市南开区卫津路 94 号　　邮政编码:300071

营销部电话:(022)23508339　23500755

营销部传真:(022)23508542　　邮购部电话:(022)23502200

*

河北昌黎太阳红彩色印刷有限责任公司印刷

全国各地新华书店经销

*

2014 年 12 月第 1 版　　2014 年 12 月第 1 次印刷

230×170 毫米　16 开本　63.125 印张　4 插页　840 千字

定价:128.00 元

如遇图书印装质量问题,请与本社营销部联系调换,电话:(022)23507125

謹以本書慶賀葉嘉瑩先生九十華誕

目 录

《中英参照迦陵诗词论稿》序言

——谈成书之经过及当年哈佛大学海陶玮教授与我合作研译中国诗词之理念

叶嘉莹

南开大学跨文化交流研究院最近拟出版一册我的《中英参照迦陵诗词论稿》，嘱我撰写一篇序言。我之《论稿》虽或者并无足观，但跨文化交流研究院之有意出版此一册中英参照之文稿的用意，则颇有可述者。原来南开大学跨文化交流研究院之成立与国家汉办/孔子学院总部之欲促进中外跨文化交流有着密切之关系。而谈到文化之交流则最为首要者自然应是对文化之深入的了解。其次则需要有对于不同文化之语文有确切掌握和译述的能力。我的这些文稿之所以入选，私意以为原来只是因为我曾经很幸运地与美国第一流大学中的第一流汉学家有过一段密切合作的经历。所以我想藉此机会把我过去的一些经历略加叙述以供从事跨文化交流的人们及海外孔子学院的教师们参考。

南开大学跨文化交流研究院拟出版的这一册中英参照本的《迦陵诗词论稿》所收录的六篇文稿，是从 1998 年哈佛大学亚洲中心（Harvard University Asia Center）所出版的一册《中国诗歌论集》（*Studies in Chinese*

Poetry）中摘选出来的。该书共收录有十七篇论文，是哈佛大学远东系教授海陶玮先生（Professor Hightower）与我多年来合作研究的成果。其中收录有海先生之论文四篇，我的论文十三篇（全部目录见附录）。我与海先生初识于1966年之夏，当时我是被台湾大学推荐将赴美国密西根州立大学（Michigan State University）作为交换教授的一个候选人，而海先生则是作为美国弗尔布莱特委员会（Fulbright Committee）的代表来举行面谈的一个甄选人。谁想到只因此一次晤面，我与海先生竟然结下了三十多年合作的机缘。据海先生后来相告，那一次面谈，他在众多的候选人中，只选了我一个人，而且他立即提出了要邀请我到哈佛大学做访问教授的提议。只不过因为台湾大学校长已与密西根州立大学签约在先，所以我必须去密西根州立大学。于是海先生乃退而求其次，邀请我在九月赴密西根州立大学任教以前，先到哈佛与他做两个月的暑期合作研究。在这一次合作研究中，我们完成了两篇文稿，一是海先生所撰写的《论陶渊明的饮酒诗》（*Tao Qian's "Drinking Wine" Poems*），一是我所撰写的《谈梦窗词的现代观》（*Wu Wenying's 'Ci': A Modern View*）。海先生的论文是先由他写为初稿，经过讨论后写成定稿；我的论文是由我先写出来定稿，经过讨论后由他译成英文。就当我们这两篇文稿完成时，恰巧美国的高级学术团体理事会（American Council of Learned Society），将于1967年元月在北大西洋的百慕大岛（Bermuda Island）举办一个以"中国文类研究"（Studies in Chinese Literary Genres）为主题的会议，与会者都是西方有名的汉学家，如英国牛津大学的霍克斯（David Hawkes）教授、美国耶鲁大学的傅汉思（Hans Frankel）教授、加州大学的白芝（Cyril Birch）教授、哈佛大学的韩南（Patrick Hanan）教授、康奈尔大学的谢迪克（Harold Schedick）教授。还有不少著名的华裔西方学者，如刘若愚、夏志清、陈士骧诸教授。当时海先生就把我们暑期合作所完成的两篇文稿也提交给了会议的筹办人。完成此一暑期合作计划后，我就离开哈佛去了密西根州立大学。及至次年（1967）元月，海先生原曾

邀我先到哈佛大学与他见面后，再一同飞往百慕大，只因我订机票时正值波士顿大雪，飞机无法降落，所以我只好自己一个人由密西根飞去了百慕大。在会议中见到海先生，他说他本来在哈佛为我安排了一个欢迎会，只可惜我这位主客没有到场。百慕大会议中，诸位来开会的汉学家在正式会议中虽必须使用英文发言，但也大多会说流利的中文，一起参会，相谈甚欢[①]。会后，我就又飞回了密西根，而海先生则坚嘱我在1967年暑假与密大交换一年期满后不要再接受延续的聘约，而邀我以访问教授的名义赴哈佛。于是1967年7月我就如约又回到了哈佛大学。这一年我除教学外，与海教授又合作完成了两篇文稿，一篇是海教授撰写的《论陶渊明诗中之用典》（*Allusion in The Poetry of Tao Qian*），一篇则是我所撰写的《论常州词派的比兴寄托之说》（*The Changzhou School of 'Ci' Criticism*）。文稿完成后，已是学期结束的时候。我本应立即离开哈佛返回台湾才是，但当时外子已经以探亲名义来到美国，两个女儿也已于前一年由外子嘱我携来美国，外子之意盖因他曾受台湾白色恐怖之累，被他所任职的台湾海军军法处囚禁过三年以上之久，他是坚决不肯回台湾的。于是海先生乃极力劝我留在哈佛，也不要回台湾了。而我却坚意要返回台湾。关于这种去留之争，我在《中国诗歌论集英文版后记》一篇文稿中已曾叙写，该文已收录在本书的《附录》中，此处就不再赘叙了。总之，海先生既留我未成，他就又提出了一个建议，要我写一个研究计划，他要为我争取一笔研究补助，以备我下次再来哈佛与他合作之用。当时我写的就是有关王国维及其文学批评的一个研究计划。这个计划写成后，我就回了台湾。及至次年1969年春，他把邀请函寄给我后，却因种种原因我未能获得美国签证，其后乃经由海先生之介绍转去了加拿大的温哥华，并且于1970年春获得了不列颠哥伦比亚大学亚洲系的终身教授聘约。而海先生之介绍我到加拿大任教，原来也是为了我自加来美更

---

① 此次会议中之论文，后由加州大学白芝教授编成一册论文集 *Studies in Chinese Literary Genres*，于1974年由加州大学出版社出版。

It contains the famous article with her bold and insightful reassessment of Wu Wenying's *ci*; the English version, "Wu Wenying's *Ci*—a Modern View", translated by Professor James R. Hightower, appeared in the *Harvard Journal of Asiatic Studies* as well as in *Studies in Chinese Literary Genres* (ed. Cyril Birch, Berkeley, 1974). This book of *ci* criticism set new trends in the study of *ci* in China with its innovative methods of inquiry and analysis. Through Professor Hightower's translation of her other essays, for example, her ground-breaking study of traditional *ci* hermeneutics, "The Changzhou school of *Ci* criticism" (*Chinese Approaches to Literature*, ed. Adele Rickett, Princeton, 1978), Professor Yeh's scholarship has come to occupy a significant place in Western sinology as well.

In the past few years, Professor Yeh began an ongoing collaborative project with Professor Miao Yue of Sichuan University on the history of *ci* poetry. The first volume of *Lingxi cishuo* (*Ci Criticism from Spirit Stream*) was published in 1987 (Shanghai Guji). It contains critical essays by these two eminent *ci* scholars on important poets and topics of *ci* poetry from the genre's origins in the Tang through the end of the Song dynasty. It is a veritable treasure trove for scholars and students of Chinese poetry. The second volume will cover the later imperial period. When completed, this work will be the most comprehensive critical study of *ci* poetry extant, and a standard reference in the field.

Yet another subject of Professor Yeh's wide-ranging intellectual interests is the life and oeuvre of the late Qing scholar-intellectual Wang Guowei. In *Wang Guowei jiqi wenxue piping* (Hong Kong, 1980), she wrote extensively and with critical acumen on Wang's intellectual development and the cross-currents of traditional Chinese thought and Western philosophy influencing his literary theory and criticism. Professor Yeh herself has been very receptive to contemporary Western literary theory, and

方便于与他合作研究之故。所以我在接受了加拿大的聘约后，当年暑期就又回到了哈佛大学与海先生继续了我们的合作研究。那时我的工作主要是完成有关王国维及其文学批评的研究，而海教授则因为与我合作的缘故，而引发了他对于宋词研究的兴趣。白天我与他一起读词，晚间则我一个人留在哈佛燕京图书馆继续我对王国维的研究写作，海先生甚至向图书馆争取到了我晚间在图书馆内使用研究室工作的特权。所以此一阶段我们合作的工作进行得极为顺利，而且在 1970 年的 12 月，我们曾共同应邀赴加勒比海的处女群岛（Virgin Islands）参加了一次有关中国文学评赏途径（Chinese Approaches to Literature）的国际会议，我所提交的就是由海先生协助我译成英文的《论常州派比兴寄托之说》的文稿。当时来参加会议的学者，除了欧美的多位名教授以外，还有日本的吉川幸次郎教授。会议余暇，在谈话中他们问起了我有什么诗词近作，我就把 1968 年夏我所写的《留别哈佛》三首七律写出来向大家求正。一时引起了吉川教授的诗兴，他次日上午就写出了三首和诗。美国威斯康辛大学的周策纵教授也立即写了三首和诗，一时传为佳话。有人把这些诗抄寄给了美国的顾毓琇教授，顾教授竟然也写了三首和诗。诸诗都已被收录在中华书局出版的《迦陵诗词稿》中，读者可以参看。当时吉川教授的和诗中曾有“曹姑应有东征赋，我欲赏音钟子期”之句，表现出想要邀我赴日本的心意，而我因初到加拿大任教，要用英语教学，工作甚重，而且有老父在堂，不敢远行，所以未能赴日本讲学。吉川先生的愿望，直到十三年后才由九州大学的冈村繁教授完成。而自此以后，我的词学研究遂引起了北美学术界的注意[①]。其后，1990 年加州大学的余宝琳（Pauline Yu）教授与哈佛大学的宇文所安（Stephen Owen）教授曾联名向美国高等研究基金会（American Council of Learned Society）申请专款补助，于 1990 年 6 月在美国缅因州举办了一次专以词学为主题的会议。我所提交

① 此次会议中之论文后由 Adele Austin Rickett（中文名李又安）编成一册论文集 *Chinese Approaches to Literature from Confucius to Liang Ch'i-ch'ao*，由普林斯顿大学于 1978 年出版。

的一篇论文《从我对王国维境界说的一点新理解谈王词之评赏》（*Wang Guowei's Song Lyrics in Light of His Own Theories*），这也是我与海先生合作的又一篇成果。在这次会议之后，美国耶鲁大学的孙康宜教授曾经写了一篇题为《北美二十年来的词学研究——兼记缅因州国际词学会议》的文稿，发表于台湾的《中外文学》第二十卷第五期。文中曾提到“论词的观点与方法之东西合璧，这方面最具代表性的学者非叶嘉莹教授不作他想”，又说叶氏“论词概以其艺术精神为主。既重感性之欣赏，又重理性之解说，对词学研究者无疑是一大鼓舞”。孙教授的过誉，使我愧不敢当，而这一切若非由于海先生之协助把我的论著译成英文，则我以一个既没有西方学位又不擅英语表述的华人，在西方学术界是极难获致大家之承认的。我对海先生自然十分感激，但我深知海先生之大力协助把我的文稿译成英文，其实并非由于他对我个人的特别看重，而是由于他对西方学人之从事中国诗歌之研著者，原有他的一种极为深切的关怀和理念，下面我就将对海先生的理念略加叙述。原来早在1953年海先生就曾在美国杜克大学（Duke University）所出版的一册《比较文学》（*Comparative Literature*）刊物上发表过一篇题为《中国文学在世界文学中的意义》（*Chinese Literature in the Context of World Literature*）的文稿，在那篇文稿中海先生曾特别提到，古典中国文学的历史比拉丁文学的历史更久远，而且古代的文言文，即使在白话文出现已久后也仍然是一种重要的文学语言，两者可以并存而不悖，不像拉丁文学的古今有绝大的歧异。以中国文学传世之久、方面之广，所以中国文学在世界文学中是占有重要之地位的。而要想研究中国文学，就需要彻底了解中国文学。研究文学的西方学者想要知道的是，他是否会在中国文学中找到任何可以补偿他学中文之一番心血的东西，同时他也想有人以他所熟悉的东西向他讲解。海先生还以为，“中国文学值得研究在于它的内在趣味，在于它的文学价值”，又说，“一些最令人心折的文学批评是出自批评家对文学作品所作的语文分析，把语文分析用到文学研究上，使我们领悟语文和文学的基本问题，语文是如何发挥作用产生文学效果的”。更说，“这种透彻的中文研究只能由那些彻底精通中文的人来做”。海先生还以为，“中国学者一般缺乏中国以外其他文学的良好训练”，所以“我们所需要的是把一些西方研究方法用到中国文学研究上，才能使西方读者心服口服地接受中国文学”。而毫无疑问，海先生与我的合作正是按照他的理念来做的。他在合作中一方面要我把中国诗歌的语文作用对他做详细的说明和讲解，另一方面也介绍我读一些西方的文学理论著作。在我与他合作的第一年，他就介绍我去读勒内·韦勒克（Rene Wellek）及奥斯汀·华伦（Austin Warren）合著的一册《文学之理论》（*Theory of Literature*）。我当时还曾翻译过其中之一章《文学与传记》（*Literature and Biography*），并对中英对译之事发表了一些看法（此篇译文曾被台湾大学学生刊物《新潮》于1968年发表）。我非常感谢海先生对我的协助，后来我自己更去旁听了不少西方文学理论的课，并曾经引用西方文论写过一些诗词评赏的文字。其中的一篇长文《论词学中之困惑与〈花间〉词之女性叙写及其影响》被海先生见到后，他非常高兴，立刻就提出要与我合作将之译成英文。我前面所提到的那篇于1990年提交给美国缅因州词学会议的《从我对王国维境界说的一点新理解谈王词之评赏》的文稿，就也是经海先生协助而译成英文的。只不过自从1974年我利用暑期回国探亲，及1977年回国旅游，又自1979年回国教学，更自1981年赴成都参加杜甫学会的首届年会以后，就被四川大学的前辈教授缪钺先生相邀每年到川大与他合作撰写《灵谿词说》，于是我与海先生的合作就一连停顿了数年之久。海先生后来在英文版的《中国诗歌论集》中曾经提到，他的本意是计划与我合写一系列论词的文稿。后来这个论词的系列著作是由川大缪钺先生与我合作撰写的《灵谿词说》一书完成了。不过海先生还是把我在《灵谿词说》中所撰写的《论苏轼词》与《论辛弃疾词》两篇文稿译成了英文，而他则已曾与我合作完成了《论柳永词》与《论周邦彦词》两篇文稿。另外他又曾协助我把我的《论晏殊词》、《论王沂孙词》和《论陈子龙词》也都先后译成了英文。遗憾的是当我于上世纪 90 年代初写成了《从艳词发展之历史看朱彝尊爱情词之美学特质》一篇论文时，他的视力已经极度衰退。本来他对我的这一篇文稿甚感兴趣，以为我在此一文中所提出的朱氏爱情词的“弱德之美”是指出了词之美感的一种更为基本的特质。他曾经把我在此文中所举引的朱氏之《静志居琴趣》中的九首爱情词都翻译成了英文，并鼓励我把这九首英文译词和我的那篇论朱氏爱情词之美学特质的中文稿，提交给了 1993 年 6 月在耶鲁大学举办的一个以“女性之作者与作品中之女性”为研究主题的学术讨论会。可惜的是海先生终因视力下降未能完成这一篇文稿的英译。其后有一位我在温哥华的友人陶永强先生中英文俱佳，曾经选译过我的一些诗词，出版了一册题为 *Ode to The Lotus*（《叶嘉莹诗词选译》）的集子。他曾有意要把我那篇论朱彝尊爱情词的长稿译成英文，后来终因我的文稿太长和他的工作忙碌，未能完成。海先生当年颇以他未能完成这一篇长文的译稿为憾，而我则更因为自己当年忙于回国讲学及与川大缪先生合作，未能及时与他合作完成此一长篇文稿的英译而深感歉憾。2001 年我被邀到美国哥伦比亚大学客座讲学期间，曾利用春假的机会到康桥去探望一些老朋友，与海先生及赵如兰、卞学鐄夫妇有过一次聚会，那时海先生与他的一个孙女在康桥附近的地方同住，视力已经极弱。此次相晤以后，我每年圣诞假期都会以电话向他致候。及至 2005 年圣诞，我给他打电话一直无人接听，我想他可能被儿女们接往他的故乡德国去住了。及至 2006 年 2 月，我忽然收到了哈佛大学韩南（Patrick Hanan）教授一封电邮，说海先生已经于 1 月 8 日在德国去世了，哈佛大学将为他举办一个追悼会，希望我能去参加，并且说他将在仪式中提到海先生与我的合作，他以为在北美汉学界中，像海先生与我这样有成就的学者能在一起合作研究，是一件极为难能可贵的事。我收到韩南教授的信后，曾写了一封回邮，表示了我对海先生深切的怀念和哀悼。只可惜路途过远，我当时正在天津南开讲学，未能及时赶去参加海先生的追悼会，至今仍深感歉仄。海先生之大力协助我把一些论诗词的文稿译成英文，并非只为了个人之私谊，而是由于作为一个研究中国诗词的汉学家，他有几点极深切的理想和愿望：其一是西方汉学家要想研读中国诗词，首先需要有大量英译的文本；其次是中国诗词在中国独有的语文特质下，也需要有精通中国语文特质和中国诗词之美感的华人学者的密切合作。尤其是“词”这一种文体，其美感特质更为窈眇幽微，一般而言西方学者对此更深感难于着力。但一般学者大多追求一己的研究成果，很少有人能具有像海先生那样的胸襟和理想，愿意与一个如我这样的既无西方学历又不擅英文表述的华人学者合作。我对海先生既深怀感激，更对他的胸襟志意和理想深怀景仰。他去世后，我未能赴哈佛参加他的追悼会，这使我对他一直感到愧歉，所以愿藉此机会把我们合作的经过和他与我合作的理念略加叙述，也算是我对他的感念之一点补偿。同时我也想海先生与我合作之理念或者也可以提供给今日从事跨文化交流的工作者们一点参考，故而不惮繁琐历叙海先生与我合作之经过如上，但愿我们的合作经验或者也有一点可供参考之处。

最后我还要做一点说明，就是何以本书只称为“中英参照本”，而不称为“中英对照本”的原因，那是因为以论文而言，中西方的思维方式既有不同，中文和英文的句式和文法也有很大的差异，要想把中文与英文并列在一个页面上对照列出，那几乎是一件不可能的事。至于有些小诗可以对照刊出，则是因为诗歌往往可以把一句做为一个单位，则每句中之原意虽经英译之颠倒，但每句之情意仍可大致保留不变。而论文之论说则往往因中西文法不同与思维方法之异，要做很大的调节和改变，而且海先生原是一位重视整体之意旨的学人，其个别之诗词的译文虽极为讲求切当，但在论述时则不愿受中文语法之拘执，这也是我何以只称此书为“中英参照本”的重要原因，乃在此略加说明如上。

本书第一版乃从《中国诗歌论集》的十七篇论文中摘选六篇而成，本版则将本人的十三篇论文全部收入。

Preface to the Chinese-English Cross-Referencing Edition of *Jialing's Collected Essays on Shi and Ci Poetry*: The Book's Inception and Ideas Behind my Joint Study and Translation Projects on Chinese Poetry with Professor Hightower

Author: Chia-ying Yeh

Translator: Teresa Yu

Nankai University's Institute of Cross-Cultural Studies recently launched the publication of a Chinese-English cross-referencing edition of my book *Jialing Shici Lungao* (*Jialing's Collected Essays on Shi and Ci Poetry*). I was asked to write the preface. While my book may not have much to recommend itself, the purpose behind this publication is worth mentioning. The Institute was established to help fulfill the mandate of the Hanban/Confucian Institute Headquarters in promoting cultural exchange between China and the rest of the world. Two important criteria in such an exchange would be a deep understanding of the cultures involved, a good grasp of the two languages and the ability to translate from one to the other. My essays have been selected because I was fortunate enough to have worked closely with a first-rate sinologist from a first-rate American University. I would like to share some of my experience in this endeavor with those who work in cultural exchange and those teaching in Confucian Institutes overseas.

The upcoming cross-referencing edition of *Jialing Shici Lungao* includes 6 articles taken from *Studies in Chinese Poetry*, a book published in 1998 by the Asian Center of Harvard University. There are altogether 17 articles in the book, the result of years of collaboration between me and Professor Hightower from the Department of East Asian Languages and Civilizations at Harvard. Of the 17 articles, 4 of them are by Professor Hightower and the other 13 written by me (See the appendix for a complete list of the articles). I first met Professor Hightower in the summer of 1966. I was then a candidate for a Faculty Teaching Exchange Program between Taiwan National University and Michigan State University. Professor Hightower was at the time a member of the Fulbright Committee that oversaw the selection. Who could have imagined that the meeting during this selection process would sow the seeds of 30-odd years of collaboration between us? Professor Hightower later told me that I was the only one he had chosen among all the candidates. Right after the selection, he said he wanted to invite me to Harvard as a visiting Professor. However, I had to go to Michigan State because my university had a prior agreement with them. Professor Hightower then suggested that I go to Harvard to work with him for two months that summer before I started teaching at Michigan State in September. During that time, we completed two papers. Professor Hightower wrote one paper titled "Tao Qian's 'Drinking Wine' Poems" and I wrote another one titled "Wu Wenying's *Ci*: A Modern View". With Professor Hightower's paper, he first provided the draft, which we discussed together before it was finalized. With my paper, I came up with the final draft for our discussion, after which he translated the article into English. At about this time, the American Council of Learned Societies was organizing a conference called "Studies in Chinese Literary Genres" which was scheduled to be held in January 1967 on Bermuda. Those who would be attending were all well-known sinologists such as Professor David Hawkes (Oxford), Professor Hans Frankel (Yale), Professor Cyril Birch (University of California at Berkeley), Professor Patrick Hanan (Harvard) and Professor Harold Schedick (Cornell). There would also be other famous Chinese scholars from the West such as Professors James Liu, C. T. Hsia, and Professor Shih-hsiang Chen. Professor Hightower then submitted our two articles to the conference organizing committee. Having completed our joint summer projects, I went on to teach at Michigan State University that fall.

Professor Hightower had wanted me to meet him at Harvard in January, 1967 before we flew together to Bermuda. But there was a big snow storm in Boston when I was trying to book my flight ticket. I therefore had to fly to Bermuda from Michigan by myself. Professor Hightower told me at the conference that he had organized a welcome party for me at Harvard. Unfortunately, as the guest of honor, I was unable to attend. At the Bermuda Conference, all of the sinologists had to present their papers in English, but most of us were able to speak fluent Chinese. We had a very enjoyable time chatting and discussing. After the conference, I flew back to Michigan State. Professor Hightower urged me not to renew my one-year contract with Michigan State at the end of the term. Instead, he invited me to Harvard as a visiting Professor.

I therefore went back to Harvard in July 1967. Other than teaching, I spent my one year there collaborating again with Professor Hightower and we completed another two papers together. The paper Professor Hightower wrote was called "Allusion in the Poetry of Tao Qian". The one I wrote was titled "The Changzhou School of *Ci* Criticism". At the end of the semester I was supposed to leave Harvard and return to Taiwan. However, at this time, my husband had already come to the U.S. on a visitor's visa. He had also bid me earlier to bring our two daughters to the U.S. Because my husband had suffered persecution under the White Terror in Taiwan, being sentenced to prison for more than three years by the Taiwan Naval Military Court where he had worked, he was strongly against us going back to Taiwan. Professor Hightower then tried to persuade me to stay at Harvard. But I was quite determined to go back. I have detailed the story behind this struggle over whether I should go back or not in the Afterword of *Studies in Chinese Poetry*. It is also included in the Appendix of this book, so I will not repeat myself here.

Unable to persuade me to stay, Professor Hightower suggested that I write a proposal for a research grant to cover for a future joint project in my next visit to Harvard. The proposal I wrote was on Wang Guowei and his literary criticism. I then returned to Taiwan. The following year, in the spring of 1969, he sent me another invitation letter. For various reasons, however, I was unable to obtain an American visa this time. Through Professor Hightower's introduction, I eventually secured a position at the University of British Columbia, and received my tenure there in the spring of 1970. Professor Hightower had facilitated my getting a position in Canada because it would make it easier for us to collaborate on a regular basis. Therefore, the summer after my appointment in Canada I went back to Harvard again to work with him. My focus at the time was to complete my study on Wang Guowei and his literary criticism. Because of our collaboration, Professor Hightower became interested in researching on Song *ci* poetry. During the day, we read *ci* poems together. In the evening, I would stay behind at the Harvard-Yenching Library to write on Wang Guowei. Professor Hightower even arranged a special privilege for me to use the study room at the library in the evening. During this time our work together went very smoothly. In December 1970, we also attended an international conference called "Chinese Approaches to Literature" held on the Virgin Islands. The paper that I presented there was titled "On the Changzhou School and its Allegorical Interpretations" which Professor Hightower had translated for me. Other than many well-known scholars from North America and Europe, Professor Yoshikawa Kojiro from Japan was also at the conference. In the spare time between presentations at the Conference, I was asked if I had recently written any *shi* or *ci* poems. I responded by showing everyone three seven-character regulated verses titled "Taking Leave of Harvard" which I had written in the summer of 1968. That sparked an interest in Professor Yoshikawa, who wrote three poems in response the next morning. Professor Chow T'se-tsung from the University of Wisconsin immediately wrote three other poems in reply. The whole event was very much talked about afterwards. Someone later sent a copy of all these poems to Professor Ku Yu-hsiu in the U.S. and she surprisingly also responded with three poems of her own. All of these poems can now be found in *Jialing Shici gao* (*Jialing's Shi and Ci Poetry Collection*, Zhonghua Books Publishing Press). At the time, Professor Yoshikawa expressed the wish to invite me to Japan, as he says in one of his poems, "Lady Cao should compose a *fu* on journeying east, I wish to show my appreciation as Zhong Ziqi." I was, however, unable to make the long trip to lecture in Japan because I had just started teaching in Canada. My workload then was heavy, having to teach in English. I also had an elderly father at home so I dared not travel too far. Professor Yoshikawa's wish was finally fulfilled 13 years later by Professor Shigeru Okamuri of Kyushu University. From then on, my work on *ci* poetry began to attract the attention of North American academics. In 1990, Professor Pauline Yu (California at Irvine) and Professor Stephen Owen (Harvard) jointly applied for a grant from the

American Council of Learned Societies to cover for a special conference on *ci* studies. It was held in June that year, in Maine. The paper I presented then, titled, "Wang Guowei's Song Lyrics in the Light of His Own Theories", was yet another collaboration between me and Professor Hightower. After the conference, Professor Sun Kang-I (Yale) wrote an essay titled "Twenty Years of *Ci* Studies and the International Conference on *Ci*". (See Taiwan's *Zhongwai Literary Monthly,* vol. 20. No. 5). The essay mentions that "The scholar who most exemplifies a joint East-West approach to the study of *ci* has to be Professor Yeh Chia-ying and no other." It also says that "Yeh's discussion focuses on *ci* poetry as an art form. Her response and analyses are both affective and cognitive. For those engaged in *ci* studies, it is a huge encouragement." Professor Sun's compliments were too generous. Yet none of this would have been possible without Professor Hightower's help in translating my articles into English in the first place. For someone like me who does not have a degree from the West and who cannot express herself well in English, it would not have been easy to gain recognition in western academia. I am, of course, most grateful to Professor Hightower. On the other hand, I am deeply aware of Professor Hightower's larger intent to help render my articles into English. He was not placing the emphasis particularly on me. Rather, he was motivated by a deep concern and certain ideas he had long held regarding research on Chinese poetry by western scholars. I shall now try to explain some of his ideas.

As early as 1953, Professor Hightower had written an article titled "Chinese Literature in the Context of World Literature" for *Comparative Literature*, a journal published by Duke University. He points out in the article that, compared with Latin literature, Chinese classical literature has had an even longer history. Unlike Latin, which is a great departure from modern western languages, the Chinese classical language (*wenyan*) continues to be an important literary language even after the emergence of the modern Chinese vernacular. The two, in fact, continue to co-exist. Both for its scope as well as its long history, Chinese literature has an important place in World Literature. In order to do research in Chinese literature, however, one must understand it thoroughly. A western scholar engaged in literary study would want to find out first if there is anything in Chinese literature that would compensate for all his years of hard work learning the language. While he is already familiar with the language, he would also like to have someone explain to him how it actually works. Professor Hightower thought that "Chinese literature is worth studying for its intrinsic qualities and its literary value." He also said, "Some of the most impressive literary criticism has to do with the way critics analyse the language in the texts. When language analysis is used in literary study, it helps us understand the basic connection between language and literature, specifically how language can be utilized to create literary effects." He went on to say that "This kind of in-depth study of the Chinese language could only be done by those who are highly proficient in the language." Professor Hightower also thought that "Chinese scholars normally lack good and proper training in other foreign literatures." Therefore, "we need to apply western research methods on Chinese literary studies. Only then could a western reader accept Chinese literature whole-heartedly." Without doubt, Professor Hightower's collaborations with me were based exactly on such ideas. On the one hand, when we were working together, he wanted me to explain to him in detail how the Chinese language actually functions in poems. On the other hand, he would suggest that I read some works on western literary theories. The first year that we worked together, he introduced me to Rene Wellek and

Austin Warren's *Theory of Literature.* At the time, I even translated one of its chapters—"Literature and Biography"—and expressed some of my views on rendering English into Chinese. My translation was later printed in the 1968 issue of *New Waves*, a journal published by Taiwan University students. I was very grateful for Professor Hightower's help. Later on, I attended a number of classes on western literary theories and even applied some of these theories in my writings on *shi* and *ci* criticism. One of them, a longer paper titled "Ambiguity and the Female Voice in *Huajian* Songs" interested Professor Hightower so much that he immediately proposed to work with me in translating it into English. A paper I mentioned earlier which I submitted to the *Ci* Conference in Maine titled "Wang Guowei's Song Lyrics in Light of His Own Theories" was also translated into English by Professor Hightower. However, after a series of visits to China (a family visit in the summer of 1974, a tour of the country in 1977, a return to teach there in 1979, and my attendance at the first Du Fu Annual Conference in Chengdu in 1981), I eventually accepted the yearly invitation from Professor Miao Yue (Sichuan University) to go to Chengdu to work on a joint book project, *Lingxi Cishuo* (*Spirit Brook —Essays on Song Lyrics*). As a result, my collaboration with Professor Hightower was suspended for several years. Professor Hightower mentions in *Studies in Chinese Poetry* that he had originally planned to write a series of articles on *ci* poetry with me. This, in effect, was later realized in the book *Lingxi Cishuo*, jointly written by Professor Miao Yue and me. Sill, Professor Hightower wanted to translate two of my articles in this book ("On the Song Lyrics of Su Shi" and "On Xin Qiji's Song Lyrics") into English. Other than these, his other earlier renditions of my articles on *ci* into English include: "The Song Lyrics of Liu Yong", "The Songs of Zhou Bangyan", "An Appreciation of the *Ci* of Yan

Shu", "On Wang Yisun and his Songs Celebrating Objects" and "Chen Zilong and the Renascence of the Song Lyric". Unfortunately, by the time I have finished writing the article "The Special Aesthetic Qualities of Zhu Yizun's Love Lyrics in the Context of the Development of Sensuous *Ci* Poetry", Professor Hightower's eyesight had seriously deteriorated. He did, however, show a great deal of interest in this article. He also thought that when I pointed out that Zhu's love lyrics express a "beauty of passive virtue," I was identifying a most fundamental quality in *ci* aesthetics. He rendered all the 9 love lyrics of Zhu Yizun's which I have cited in my article. He also encouraged me to submit my article in the original Chinese together with his translations of the 9 poems to a Seminar on "Female Literary Writers and the Feminine in Literary Works". The Seminar, held in June, 1993, was organized by Yale University. Unfortunately, because of his failing eyesight, Professor Hightower was eventually unable to complete his translation of the article. A friend in Vancouver, Mr. T'ao Yung-ch'iang, who excels both in English and Chinese, had once translated some of my *shi* and *ci* poems which were published in a collection titled *Ode to the Lotus*. He, too, showed interest in rendering my article on Zhu Yizun into English. However, he was eventually unable to complete the work because the article was too long and he was too busy himself. Professor Hightower had expressed regret back then for not completing the translation of this long article. And I, for my part, also lamented the fact that I was too busy working and lecturing in China. As a result, I missed the opportunity to work with him in time to complete the translation.

In 2001, as a guest lecturer at Columbia University, I went to see some old friends at Cambridge during the spring break. There, I met Professor Hightower, Ju-lan Chao and her husband Pien Hsueh-huang. Professor

Hightower was living with a grand-daughter of his near Cambridge at the time. His eyesight was extremely weak then. After this meeting, I continued to greet him every year at Christmas on the phone. When I called him again at Christmas in 2005, there was no one answering the phone. I thought his children must have taken him back home to live in his native Germany. Then, in February, 2006, I suddenly received an e-mail from Professor Patrick Hanan of Harvard University. He said that Professor Hightower had passed away on January 8 in Germany. Harvard had organized a memorial service for him. They wished that I could attend. He also said that he would mention my collaboration with Professor Hightower during the service. The fact that two accomplished scholars like Professor Hightower and I had collaborated together was, according to Professor Hanan, something very special in the sinology field in North America. I immediately wrote back to Professor Hanan, expressing my remembrance and deep condolences. At the time, I was lecturing in Nankai, a long distance away. I was unable to make it to the memorial service for Professor Hightower. I still feel deeply sorry and unhappy about this today.

Professor Hightower had given me great assistance in rendering my articles on *shi* and *ci* poetry into English. This was, however, not only due to our personal friendship. More importantly, it was because he had certain deeply held ideas and wishes as a sinologist researching on Chinese poetry. First of all, a western sinologist interested in studying Chinese poetry would require a large number of *shi* and *ci* texts in English. Secondly, given the very unique characteristics of the Chinese language, he or she would need the help and close collaboration of a Chinese scholar who is thoroughly familiar with the language's distinctive qualities as well as the special aesthetics of *shi* and *ci* poetry. This is especially so in the case of *ci*. As a poetic genre, it requires a particularly subtle aesthetic sensibility to appreciate, making it even harder for a western scholar. Most scholars are keen on their own research. Very few of them would have the magnanimity, the vision, nor the willingness of Professor Hightower to work with a Chinese scholar who has no training in the West, and who is not adapt in expressing herself in English. I am not only grateful to Professor Hightower. I also admire deeply his generosity, ideal and aspirations. I was unable to attend his memorial service at Harvard after his passing, for which I have always felt a certain unease and regret. Now that I have the opportunity to describe briefly the history of our collaboration and the ideas behind it, it is in a sense my way of remembering him. I hope that those who are engaged in the work of intercultural exchange would find this detailed history of our collaboration and some of the ideas behind it useful.

Finally, a word about why our book is called a “Chinese-English cross-referencing edition” and not simply a “Chinese-English edition”. It is quite possible sometimes to put two language versions of the same short poem side by side. If each line of the poem is seen as a unit, the general emotive meaning of each line may be retained while the two versions may not match perfectly. This is not the case in the translation of articles. Since Chinese and English differ both in rhetoric as well as syntax, it is quite impossible to put two articles side by side for direct comparison. Professor Hightower was, as a scholar, more concerned with the overall meaning and significance of any article that he is working with. While he always followed each line of a poem closely in his translation, he was unwilling to be hampered by Chinese grammatical structures when rendering expositional and analytical prose. For this reason, I have decided to call this a “Chinese-English cross-referencing edition”.

附录五种：

1. 海陶玮先生英文版《中国诗歌论集》序言（*Preface*）
2. 叶嘉莹《中国诗歌论稿》前言（*Foreword*）。此文之中文稿曾收入《迦陵杂文集》，题为《中国诗歌论集》英文版后记
3. 英文版《中国诗歌论集》全集篇目
4. 海陶玮先生逝世后哈佛大学韩南教授致叶嘉莹之电邮及叶嘉莹之覆信

海陶玮先生英文版《中国诗歌论集》序言

Preface

These essays are the result of a collaborative effort that goes back nearly thirty years. The name assigned to each is that of the person who wrote it in the first place; the version presented here was arrived at after extensive consultation and rewriting. Our acquaintance dates from 1966, when I was a member for the Taiwan Fulbright Committee interviewing candidates for a grant to go teach in the States. The sole successful candidate was Yeh Chia-ying, then Professor at National Taiwan University and Furen University, of which she was a 1945 graduate when it was still in Beijing and where I was also a student under some of the same teachers in 1942, though we did not meet at that time. She spent a couple of summers and then a year at Harvard as Visiting Professor before accepting an appointment at the University of British Columbia. After that we continued to work together sporadically summers until 1979 when I was able to spend a year at the University of British Columbia as Senior Killam Fellow. For the past six years we have met for a month or more every summer. For travel and research grants that enabled us to meet summers we are grateful to the Harvard-Yenching Institute, the Harvard East Asian Research Center, and the Social Sciences and Humanities Research Council of Canada.

Our intention at first was to write a comprehensive account of the song lyric during the Song period, each of us dealing with a chosen group of poets. Such a project was actually carried out by Professor Yeh in collaboration with Professor Miao Yue of Sichuan University and published in 1987 under the title *Lingxi cishuo*, and some of Professor Yeh's contributions to that volume appear here in an English language version. We have extended the range beyond the Song dynasty and outside the song lyric genre to bring together all that we have written jointly on Chinese poetry. Many of these essays have appeared in various scholarly journals and come with the kind of annotation expected in such. They are reprinted here in their original form and make no reference to translations and works on the same subjects that have appeared subsequently. The issues with which we have been concerned are those confronted by critics of poetry of whatever literary tradition, and though we cannot pretend to recreate Chinese poetry in another language, we do claim that our translations are—on one level—accurate, and we hope that what we supply in the way of exegesis will make it more accessible to English language readers.

James R. Hightower

叶嘉莹《中国诗歌论稿》前言

Foreword

The essays collected here represent a collaborative effort over many years, beginning in 1966. Not every year afforded an opportunity to work together, and during those years each of us engaged in other projects. There is no unifying theme in these studies beyond our common interest in Chinese poetry.

My acquaintance with Professor Hightower began in Taibei in 1966 when I was a candidate for a Fulbright grant to teach at Michigan State University, which had an exchange program with National Taiwan University, where I was teaching Chinese poetry. Professor Hightower was a member of the screening committee chaired by Professor Liu Chonghong. After the interview, as the successful candidate, I was invited to Professor Liu's house for dinner, where Professor Hightower was also a guest. Talking to him I discovered he had an excellent knowledge of Chinese poetry, and we found much in common to discuss. We continued our talk in the taxi Professor Liu had ordered to take us to our respective dwellings, and Professor Hightower asked me whether I would like to come to Harvard where we could work together. I was delighted with the prospect of collaborating with an informed Westerner who shared my interest in Chinese poetry and gladly agreed, supposing that sometime in the future there would be an opportunity to go to Harvard. I was surprised the next day when Professor Liu's secretary called to say that on the preceding evening, instead of going directly home, Professor Hightower had returned to Professor Liu's house to propose that I should go to Harvard instead of Michigan State. This unexpected development put me in a difficult position, for the president of Taida, Qian Siliang, in proposing me a year earlier for a Fulbright grant, had specified Michigan State. I went to the chairman of my department, Professor Tai Jingnong, for advice. He said the department could choose someone else to go to Michigan State in my place. I carried that proposal back to President Qian. He was adamantly opposed to the idea, for he had agreed with Michigan State that I was to be the person, and he could not go back on his word. I then asked Professor Liu to convey my regrets to Professor Hightower. But he turned out to be quite as stubborn as President Qian and came up with a compromise: I would leave Taibei two months early and spend the summer in Cambridge before taking up my duties at Michigan State. And that is what I did, arriving in Cambridge with my two daughters in July 1966.

That summer we worked on Tao Yuanming, whose poetry Professor Hightower had translated, and Wu Wenying, on whom I was writing a critical essay. We conducted our sessions in English, since that was the language I would have to use in teaching coming fall. He was very considerate in helping me find the appropriate vocabulary and correcting my grammar. It not only contributed to my ability to carry on a conversation, it even made it possible for me to lecture in English on Chinese poetry when I got to Michigan State. I was also influenced by his systematic and logical approach to the problems we were studying together and learned something of Western methodology. The summer passed all too quickly, but it laid the foundation for a long-term collaboration. Before I left, we agreed that I would return to Harvard the following summer.

In July 1967, I was back to take up where we had left off. This time we were better acquainted and less restrained in expressing divergent views, and the resulting lively arguments usually ended in both of us modifying our original opinions. It was educational and good fun. That summer we had adjacent offices on the second floor of the Harvard-Yenching Library. Outside our windows was a large maple tree that caught the light of the sun morning and evening, casting an ever-changing pattern of light and shade. Whenever I raised my head from my work there it was, its leaves dancing in the breeze. Then as autumn came on, we watched the leaves as they gradually turned yellow and red. With winter the tree lost its leaves, and its branches were covered with snow. When I arrived that summer, I was looking forward to a long year's stay, but the time slipped away even as I watched the tree undergoing its annual transformation. The maple was putting on its autumnal colors in September of the second year when the academic year at Taiwan National University was about to begin, and I prepared to return to Taibei. Professor Hightower wanted me to stay, but I had to go back as I had promised before getting a two-years' leave. Furthermore, although my two daughters had accompanied me to America and my husband had since joined us, my father was alone in Taibei, and I wanted to look after him. At Professor Hightower's suggestion, I wrote up a research project in anticipation of my return to Harvard the following year.

Before my departure I wrote three poems, "On Taking Leave of Harvard". The third is addressed to Professor Hightower:

About to go, I deeply feel my host's concern;

When fine wine is scarce, pour it carefully.
With good books on the table we forget the time.
The stately tree puts on its changing hues.
Reluctant or impatient, stay or leave, someone's hurt.
We have studied together, debated past and present.
I'll try to make this song convey my parting thoughts:
Clouds in the eastern sky, the ocean is deep.

The first line is to express appreciation of my host's kindness. In the second the metaphor of the rare wine in short supply represents the happy time of working together now nearing its close. It involves an allusion to Tao Qian, the poet whose works he had translated. Line 3 is in appreciation of the riches and convenience of the Harvard-Yenching Library, and line 4 brings in the maple tree and its seasonal changes as a measure of the too rapid passage of time. Line 5 alludes to a line from Tao Qian, "Once drunk, I withdraw, indifferent to whether I stay or go," turning it around to reflect my host's wish to have me stay and my determination to go. Line 6 is a reminder of our discussion of matters old and modern, and our occasional disputes. Lines 7 and 8 deal directly with my departure, which took place shortly after I wrote this poem.

During the year that I was back teaching at Taida, Professor Hightower made arrangements for me to come to Harvard the following year on a research grant, but when I applied for a visa for my father to accompany me, it was not only refused, the re-entry visa in my own passport was canceled, on the grounds that it was U.S. policy to discourage emigration from Taiwan. Letters from Professor Hightower to the Taiwan consul and the State Department were to no avail. He then recommended me for a position that had opened up at the University of British Columbia, thinking it would be easier for me to enter the United States from Canada, and in July 1969 I flew to Vancouver, where I was joined by my husband and two daughters, who had spent the year in the States. After the initial year's appointment as visiting professor, I was given tenure at UBC, where I continued to teach until my retirement in 1990. After the first year I was able to bring my father, then almost eighty years old.

My relationship with Harvard was re-established in the early 1970's, when as a Landed Immigrant I was provided with Canadian papers, and I regularly spent summers in Cambridge, except 1976 and 1977 when I used the summer vacation to visit relatives in China. And beginning in 1979 I lectured in various Chinese universities. In 1982 I started work on Chinese lyric poetry with Professor Miao Yue of National Sichuan University. The resulting volume was published in 1987 under the title *Lingxi cishuo.*

After 1987 I again came to Cambridge every summer to work with Professor Hightower. In the early 1970's he developed an interest in Song writers of lyric poetry, and among our joint productions were his articles on Liu Yong and Zhou Bangyan. After my article on Wu Wenying we brought out my studies of the Changzhou School and Wang Yisun. All of these were originally published in the *Harvard Journal of Asiatic Studies.* It was after that I worked with Professor Miao Yue on the *Lingxi cishuo*, which was conceived as a study tracing the historical development of the *ci* form, and so we dealt with poets in chronological order, from the Tang and Five Dynasties through the Song, dividing them between us according to our individual preferences. Two of my essays, the ones on Su Shi and Xin Qiji, were reworked for the present book, providing two examples of the so-called "heroic songs" to match the "soft and sentimental" poets, Liu Yong and Zhou Bangyan, treated by Professor Hightower. The essays in *Lingxi cishuo* were composed in a traditional Chinese style; more recently I have been influenced by my reading in current literary theory. And this is reflected in my publications during the past few years. Three of these, on Chen Zilong, Wang Guowei, and the *Huajian* songs, appear here in English-language versions. They represent a shift in direction from the individual poet to the aesthetics and theory of the Chinese song lyric. Aside from these, the articles on Yan Shu and Li Shangyin were written earlier, when I tended to emphasize a more subjective appreciation of poetry. They belong in the Chinese tradition of criticism, and from the western point of view are lacking in logical rigor. The traditional Chinese attitude is that the function of poetry is to rouse the reader's (or hearer's) emotions. My own education was of the traditional sort, and it is reflected in my early writing about poetry. The two essays included here prevent any claim to consistency in the critical approach elsewhere adopted, but they serve to show how my own thinking has evolved. Appended to this volume are two essays on Wang Guowei's character and his suicide. These are not covered by the book's title, but they are included for their relevance to my analysis of his song lyrics. It is also something Professor Hightower and I worked on together. In 1968 when I was about to go back to Taiwan, I suggested as a topic for a future collaboration a study of Wang Guowei's literary critical writings. Over the next few years it grew into a 490-page volume, published in Hong Kong in 1980. Subsequently my understanding of Wang Guowei's terminology evolved further and is represented in the article included here on Wang Guowei's own song lyrics. The two pieces appeared here can serve as background studies that contribute to our understanding and appreciation of his poetry.

We would like to express our thanks to the institutions and individuals that have supported our studies. There have been grants from the Harvard East Asian Research Center, the Social Sciences and Humanities Research Council of Canada, and the Harvard-Yenching Institute. We are also indebted to the Harvard-Yenching Library and the Library of the University of British Columbia, where the staff put at our disposal the resources of those rich repositories of Chinese materials. I want personally to thank the Assistant Librarian of the Chinese Collection of the Harvard-Yenching Library, Ms. Hu Jiayang. She not only provided me with the reference materials I need, but also met me at the airport at inconvenient times and arranged for my living accommodations every year when I arrived for a summer in Cambridge. We are both grateful to Dr. Chen Shanmu and his wife, Chen Xiaoling, for typing and proofreading our manuscript. It has taken over two decades to get this book out, and without the timely help from such friends it would still be languishing in bits and pieces.

《中国诗歌论集》英文版后记

这一册书内所收录的，是哈佛大学远东系教授海陶玮先生（James R. Hightower）与我多年来陆续合作所完成的15篇文稿。其时间跨度自1966年暑期开始，至今年1994年暑期为止，前后盖已有28年之久。在这28年间，我们并不一定每年都有合作的机会，所以书中所收录的论文也并没有一个可以贯穿终始的主题和体系，不过大体上都是有关中国诗歌之评赏和理论的一些论述，所以乃名之为《中国诗歌论集》。

我与海先生相识于 1966 年的春夏之交。当时美国的弗尔布莱特（Fulbright）委员会委托海先生在台湾邀谈和甄选一些将去美国任教的台湾学者，我那时正在台湾大学担任诗选及杜甫诗等课的教学，台湾大学与美国密西根州立大学有一项交换计划，每两年由两校互派一个教授到对方的学校讲学。而台大的钱思亮校长则自 1965 年暑期便已与密大商定，将于 1966 年派我赴密大讲授中国古典诗歌。所以我当时就自然也成为了被海先生所邀谈的众多候选者之中的一员。记得那次邀谈是由美国弗尔布莱特委员会在台负责的台大历史系教授刘崇鋐先生主其事。邀谈后我退出到外面另一个房间，刘教授的秘书吴女士随后就追出来对我说，今晚刘教授邀你和一些友人在他家中晚餐。当晚我应邀而去，发现海先生也在座中，我与海先生遂得有更多交谈之机会。谈话中我发现海先生对中国古典诗歌之学识甚为渊博，有不少共同的话题可以讨论，所以晤谈甚欢。临行时，刘教授叫了一辆计程车先送我回家，再送海先生回他的住处。在车上，海先生问起我是否愿去哈佛与他合作之事，我想如能与对中国旧学学识如此渊博之人共同合作，当然是一件幸事，就表示了乐于接受的意愿。原以为将来或可有机缘至哈佛一做访问，岂知刘教授的秘书吴女士第二天就给我打来了电话，说海先生送我抵家后并未乘车回他的住处，却令计程车立刻又折返到刘教授家中，向刘教授提出了要请我去哈佛的要求，而这却使我陷入了一个两难的处境，因为台大钱校长原是一年前就与我约定了要派我去密大交换的。于是我就去见台大中文系主任台静农先生商谈解决的办法，台先生说如我不去密大，中文系可以派另外的人去密大。我想这是个解决难题的办法，就立即又去见钱校长商谈此事，而钱校长则坚持不肯同意，因他在一年前便已与密大商定了派我去，如何可以临时改变。我想钱校长的坚持也甚为有理，遂将不能应海先生之邀请的困难告知了刘教授，请他代我向海先生致歉。但海先生的邀请之意也极为诚恳和坚持。最后商定了一个解决之道，就是我提前两个月出国，先至哈佛与海先生合作研究，然后再于 9 月转往密大任教。于是我遂于 1966 年暑期来到了哈佛大学。

当时我们合作研究的主题，一是陶渊明诗，海先生为撰写人；一是吴文英词，我为撰写人。我们的讨论主要是以英语进行的。海先生为人极为恳切真诚，每当我的英语有辞不达意或语法不正确之时，都随时给我指正，这使我无论在英语会话或用英语表述中国诗歌之能力方面，都获得了很大的进步。此外在研讨问题时，海先生所表现的西方学者之更为理性且更富于逻辑性之思辨的方式，也给了我很大的影响，两个月的时间虽短，但却奠定了我们以后长期合作的基石。

9 月初，我离开哈佛往密西根州立大学任教，临行前，海先生就已经与我约定了明年暑期再返回哈佛客座讲学的邀请，所以 1967 年 7 月，我就又回到了哈佛大学。这次已经是我与海先生的第二次合作，我们既已较前更加熟识，所以在讨论问题时，我们也就可以更加坦诚相对，遇有意见不同之时，我们也往往可以互相争议而不以为忤，而且因此反而更增加了共同研读之乐。那时我们在哈佛燕京图书馆的二楼上，各有一间研究室。我的研究室窗外恰巧面对着一棵高大的枫树，不仅朝暮阴晴各有不同的光影，而且我来时正值夏季，窗前是一片浓密的树荫，每当读写之暇，偶然抬头一望，便可见一片翠色的繁枝密叶，随风起舞。其后秋天来到，又眼见其逐渐染成一片黄赤缤纷的彩色的图画。最后严冬来到，木叶尽脱，又被覆盖上了满枝晶莹的白雪。初来时，原以为一年的时间很长，谁想一年的光阴转眼就过去了。当第二年我窗前的枫叶再度染上秋色的时候，已是深秋 9 月，台大即将开学，在我将要离开哈佛大学前，海先生曾坚意要把我留下来。而我则坚持要返回台湾，其原因之一是因为我来美之前已对台大做出了两年后回去的承诺；其原因之二则是因为那时我的外子和两个女儿都已来了美国，只有老父一人只身在台，所以需要我回去照顾。于是海先生遂又坚持要我写了一篇研究计划，以为一年后再度来美合作的准备，我当时曾经写了三首《留别哈佛》的七言律诗，第三首就是与海先生告别之作，诗是这样写的：

临分珍重主人心，酒美无多细细斟。
案上好书能忘晷，窗前嘉树任移阴。
吝情忽共伤留去，论学曾同辨古今。
试写长谣抒别意，云天东望海沉沉。

首句表示我对主人海先生的感激之意，次句写研读合作之乐已近尾声，而因主人所研究之对象陶渊明以饮酒为名，故以“酒美”为喻。三句写哈燕图书馆藏书之富与阅读之便，使人耽读而忘倦。四句写窗前嘉树之美景与光阴推移之速。五句用陶渊明“曾不吝情去留”之句，反衬今日主人力加挽留而我则坚意归去的去留之争。六句写研讨时共商古今或时有争论的合作研究之真谊。七、八两句则正写告别之意。于是在写了这首诗不久之后，我就回台湾去了。

次年接到了哈佛寄来的聘书后，我就去台湾的美国领事馆办理接我父亲一同来美的手续。谁知美国领事馆不仅不给我父亲签证，还把我护照上原有的多次出入美国的签证取消了。几经周折，甚至我已来到温哥华后，都未能获得签证，于是遂经由海先生介绍，被加拿大不列颠哥伦比亚大学亚洲学系主任蒲立本（E. G. Pulleyblank）教授聘往该系任教。而且只教了一学期后，于次年春就给了我终身聘约。那时我已全家移来北美，上有将近八旬的老父，下有一个读大学和一个读高中的女儿，而外子则尚未找到合适的工作，为了使生活早日安定下来，我遂决定接受了加拿大的终身聘约，而以后与哈佛大学的关系，遂只是不定期来短期访问的性质了。

本来早在 70 年代初期，我还曾保持每年暑假都来哈佛访问并与海先生继续合作，直到 1974 年及 1977 年我两次利用暑假去大陆旅游探亲，又从 1979 年开始陆续赴大陆各地讲学，更自 1982 年开始了与大陆四川大学缪钺教授共同合撰《灵谿词说》的研究计划，于是我遂一连数岁没有再来哈佛。直到 1987 年《灵谿词说》一书之文稿全部完成后，我才又开始了经常利用暑期前来哈佛与海先生共同合作研究的工作。海先生自70年代初期开始，原来也已对宋词之研读，产生了浓厚的兴趣。在那一时期的合作中，海先生曾经撰写了《论柳永词》与《论周邦彦词》两篇长稿，而我则曾继《论吴文英词》之后，又撰写了《常州词派》及《王沂孙之咏物词》等文稿。这些论文都已在哈佛大学《亚洲学报》发表。其后我应承了中国四川大学缪钺教授的邀请，共同撰写《灵谿词说》，而缪先生之意则是要撰写一部有词史之性质的著作，于是我遂依时代之先后撰写了论述唐五代及两宋之词人的文稿多篇。本书中所收录的《论苏轼词》及《论辛弃疾词》二文，就是其中两篇的压缩和改写。我们之所以选录了这两篇文稿，是因为海先生已写了《论柳永词》与《论周邦彦词》两篇文稿，都是属于所谓“婉约”一派的作者，所以现在乃又选入了两篇属于所谓“豪放”一派的作者，以为对比。不过，因为此二文原是发表在《灵谿词说》一书中的作品，所以我所采用的乃是较近于中国传统的写作方式。而在《灵谿词说》一书出版以后，我曾又尝试摆脱中国传统之约束，而结合了近年来我所阅读的一些西方文论，写作了另外多篇作品，本书中所收录的《论陈子龙词》、《论王国维词》和《论〈花间〉词中之女性叙写及其影响》等文稿，就是其中的一部分。事实上我近年的研读兴趣已经逐渐从对于个别词人的评赏，而转向了对于词之美学特质与词学之理论的探讨了，并已曾以中文刊印了《中国词学的现代观》及《词学古今谈》等书，本书中所选录的虽只是很少的几篇，但已经显示出来我的近作与旧作之间，已有了很大的差别。除此之外，本书中还收录了我所撰写的《论晏殊词》与《李商隐〈燕台〉四首》二文，这是我较早期的两篇文稿。当时我所采取的乃是全然以主观之感受为主的评说方式。这种评说方式，从西方学术界衡量论文的标准来看，虽然缺少理论和架构，但这实在乃是真正属于中国式的一种评说方式，因为从春秋时代开始，孔子教他的弟子们读诗，其所重视的就是所谓“兴于诗”的一种兴发感动的作用。我幼年时所受的是传统教育，所以我早年所写的说诗文字，乃大多是属于这一类的作品。本书收录了这两篇文稿，也许使得全书之风格更显得不相一致，但另一方面却更为真实地反映出了我在诗词研读方面所走过的不同的历程。此外本书还附录有两篇关于王国维之性格与他的自沉之悲剧的文稿及一首词的评赏，表面看来，这几篇之性质与其他诸篇论诗词之作的性质完全不同，但本文却实在代表了我与海先生合作研究的一段过程。原来我在 1968 年将要离开哈佛返回台湾之际，海先生曾要我提出一篇研究计划，我所提出的研究主题，就是《王国维及其文学批评》。其后此一研究成果之中文部分，已早由香港中华书局于 1980 年出版为一册专书，并曾经广东人民出版社及台北桂冠图书公司，先后商得原出版者及作者之同意，于 1982 年及 1992 两年予以再版。至于英文部分则迄未发表，而我个人对于王氏《人间词话》所提出的"境界"之说，则已逐渐有了更为深刻的新的体会和理解，遂于 1989 年重新写了一篇《从我对王氏"境界"说的一点新理解谈王词之评赏》的文稿，现在已收录在本书之内，至于我旧日所写的有关王国维之性格特色与治学途径的部分文稿，则不仅代表了我与海先生合作研读的一段过程，同时也提供了研读王氏之词与词学的一些重要资料和背景，所以乃决定将之附录于本书之后了。正因为本书既包括了时间、空间、风格、内容各方面都有很多不同的作品，所以我遂不得不写此《后记》略述其原委及经过如上。

最后我要感谢多年来给我研究补助的一些机构，依时代先后而言，60 年代曾给我补助的是哈佛燕京学社（Harvard-Yenching Institute），70 年代曾给我补助的是哈佛东亚研究中心（Harvard East Asian Research Center），80 及 90 年代曾给我补助的是加拿大社会人文科学研究理事会（Social Sciences And Humanities Research Council of Canada）。没有他们的赞助，我们的研究是无法继续下来的。此外我也要对不列颠哥伦比亚大学亚洲图书馆（Asian Library of U.B.C.）及哈佛燕京图书馆（Harvard-Yenching Library）中许多友人表示感谢，他们曾在查找资料方面，给了我很多方便和协助。特别是哈佛燕京图书馆中文负责人胡嘉阳女士，她不仅在图书馆查阅资料方面曾给我很多协助，更曾在我旅居哈佛期间，在生活方面给了我很多照顾。还有不列颠哥伦比亚大学亚洲学系的陈山木博士及其夫人陈小玲女士，他们曾协助我打字并校读了多篇文稿。没有这些机构的支持和友人们的协助，这册书是难以完成的。在此即将成书付印之际，我愿对他们表示最诚挚的感谢。

1994 年 6 月写于康桥哈佛大学

英文版《中国诗歌论集》全集篇目

Contents

海陶玮先生逝世后哈佛大学韩南教授致叶嘉莹之电邮及叶嘉莹之覆信

海陶玮先生逝世后哈佛大学韩南教授致叶嘉莹之电邮

Dear Prof. Yeh:

I am sure that by now you have heard the sad news of Bob Hightower's death (January 8, in Germany). I expect there will be a memorial service at Harvard, perhaps this fall. In the meantime, I and a number of my colleagues here are preparing a "memorial minute" for the Faculty of Arts and Sciences at Harvard. It will focus mainly on Bob's scholarship and teaching. I would like to say something about your collaboration with him, which has always struck me as remarkable in our field—a case of two senior, established scholars working closely together on a common topic. Could I possibly persuade you to write just a few lines on your collaboration that I could use? If so, please email them to me.

It's a long time since we last met. I hope you are continung well and active.

With best wishes

Pat

叶嘉莹之覆信

Dear Prof. Hanan:

I am very sad to hear the news of Bob Hightower's death, the last time I saw him was five years ago, when I visited Cambridge I invited him and Iris Pien to have dinner together. I usually phone him during Christmas season every year, but last time there was no one to answer the phone. I thought that he might have moved to some where to stay with one of his children, but never thought that he passed away so suddenly.

Sure I will write some thing about our enjoyable and successful collaboration during the last decades of last century. I will send it to you as soon as possible.

I am still ok, right now I am staying at Nankai university, and going to visit Taiwan on February 22, I will be back to Vancouver early in April.

With best wishes.

Chia ying

Florence 2006.2.2

旧诗新演

——李义山《燕台四首》

前言

庄子的“得鱼忘筌，得意忘言”，渊明的“好读书不求甚解，每有会意，便欣然忘食”，这二位古人对言语文字所取的态度，乃是我这天性疏懒而又颇耽于自得其乐的人所最为欣赏的。虽然有时为了求得鱼，也不得不用到筌。但结网制筌毕竟只是一种手段而已，得鱼才是最大的欣喜和最终的目的。何况有些时候，我们所觅取的材料又确实不够结成一面完整的网或制出一具完整的筌来，而山辉川媚之闪耀的光彩中，则似乎又确可必信某一条溪流中之蕴有无数锦鲤珍鲂，于是乎当临川羡鱼而又结网无方之际，我这懒于结网而又急于得鱼之人，乃颇想把制不成的筌或网一手抛开，而亲自跃入水中去做一番摸索探寻的尝试了。虽然这种尝试可能颇为大雅君子所不取，而且这种探寻也并不见得有必然得鱼的把握，但即使不能捕得一条鱼，而只要我们确实能在水中抚触到活泼的鱼之生命自我们手指间滑过的一种感觉，也就应该是足可使人欣喜的了。

我国旧诗的遗产中，就一直存留着有一部分徒然令人对之兴临川之叹，而又苦于无结网之方的作品，于是在无可奈何之馀，似乎便只有亲自跃入水中去试作摸索探寻之一法了。可是我之为人一方面虽然颇有任性大胆的狂想，而另一方面却又颇有悖礼犯禁的顾忌，所以很想为自己这种不尽合法的尝试找到一个可援的先例，以资为辩护之依据。因之乃想到了在我国旧小说中既早有史话演义一类的作品，在新小说中也不乏古事新编一类的尝试。这两种写作的态度就不尽拘执于史实之考证，其发言叙事都有着由改写者可以自由操纵掌握的一种推演发挥的馀地，虽然旧日的史话演义，不免有着以听众或读者为对象之欲求其取悦于大众之目的，而近代之古事新编也有着以时代现象为背景之欲以之讽刺现实之作用。而我今日之要推演某些旧诗，而给予一些新的诠释和解说，则只是自己入水摸鱼的一点抚触的心得而已，取材和用意与前二者都迥然并不相类。但是对于不尽拘执于材料之整理和考证，而有着推演和发挥之自由的一点，则是颇为相同的。因之乃揉合了历史演义与古事新编之两种命名的办法，为这种新尝试起了一个新名字，名之曰“旧诗新演”。因略叙写作之动机及命名之源起如上。

春

风光冉冉东西陌，几日娇魂寻不得。
蜜房羽客类芳心，冶叶倡条遍相识。
暖蔼辉迟桃树西，高鬟立共桃鬟齐。
雄龙雌凤杳何许？絮乱丝繁天亦迷。
醉起微阳若初曙，映帘梦断闻残语。
愁将铁网罥珊瑚，海阔天宽迷处所。
衣带无情有宽窄，春烟自碧秋霜白。
研丹擘石天不知，愿得天牢锁冤魄。

夹罗委箧单绡起，香肌冷衬琤琤珮。
今日东风自不胜，化作幽光入西海。

夏

前阁雨帘愁不卷，后堂芳树阴阴见。
石城景物类黄泉，夜半行郎空柘弹。
绫扇唤风阊阖天，轻帷翠幕波洄旋。
蜀魂寂寞有伴未？几夜瘴花开木棉。
桂宫流影光难取，嫣熏兰破轻轻语。
直教银汉堕怀中，未遣星妃镇来去。
浊水清波何异源，济河水清黄河浑。
安得薄雾起缃裙，手接云軿呼太君。

秋

月浪衡天天宇湿，凉蟾落尽疏星入。
云屏不动掩孤嚬，西楼一夜风筝急。
欲织相思花寄远，终日相思却相怨。
但闻北斗声回环，不见长河水清浅。
金鱼锁断红桂春，古时尘满鸳鸯茵。
堪悲小苑作长道，玉树未怜亡国人。
瑶琴愔愔藏楚弄，越罗冷薄金泥重。
帘钩鹦鹉夜惊霜，唤起南云绕云梦。
双珰丁丁联尺素，内记湘川相识处。
歌唇一世衔雨看，可惜馨香手中故。

冬

天东日出天西下，雌凤孤飞女龙寡。

青溪白石不相望，堂中远甚苍梧野。
冻壁霜华交隐起，芳根中断香心死。
浪乘画舸忆蟾蜍，月娥未必婵娟子。
楚管蛮弦愁一概，空城舞罢腰支在。
当时欢向掌中销，桃叶桃根双姊妹。
破鬟倭堕凌朝寒，白玉燕钗黄金蝉。
风车雨马不持去，蜡烛啼红怨天曙。

这四首诗真是使人读后对之深感无可奈何的作品。其一是因为他所闪放的一种深幽而冶艳的光彩，使人对之有无穷的眩迷；其二是因为他所含育的一种无可把捉的意蕴，使人对之生无穷的想象。面对如此幽微窈眇的诗篇，我们所见的只是一片心灵之光影与彩色的闪烁，一切言筌在这种光彩中都早已成为糟粕。这种作品好像是一种在梦幻中的心灵之呓语，原来就不属于人类理性之解说分析的范畴之内。如今我却妄想要迈越过人类理性的拘限，而进入一位作者心魂深处的梦魇里去探寻，则其不免于没顶丧生而终然无获，正该是必然的结果。但我却仍然愿意跃入这一条绵渺幽深的水中去一作探寻的尝试，一则是因为我无法抵御其美与不可知的双重之诱惑；再则我在前面已经说过，我原不敢存必然得鱼之望，只是想亲自体验一番摸触追寻的欣喜而已。

关于这四首诗，前人也曾对之作过结网制筌的尝试。在我以一己之体验为演绎之前，我愿先把有关的一些材料略作简单的介绍。首先我们该提到的，乃是与这四首诗有关的一则悲哀的插曲，一个最早为这四首诗所眩惑了的女子柳枝的故事。据义山《柳枝诗序》云：“柳枝，洛中里娘也。父饶好贾，风波死湖上。其母不念他儿子，独念柳枝。生十七年，涂妆绾髻未尝竟，已复起去。吹叶嚼蕊，调丝擪管，作天海风涛之曲，幽忆怨断之音。居其旁，与其家接故往来者，闻十年尚相与，疑其醉眠梦物断不娉。余从昆让山，比柳枝居为近。他日春曾阴，让山下马柳枝南柳下，咏余《燕台》诗。柳枝惊问：'谁人有此？谁人为是？'让山谓曰：'此吾里中少年叔耳。'柳枝手断长带，结让山为赠叔乞诗。明日，余比马出其巷，柳枝丫鬟毕妆，抱立扇下，风鄣一袖，指曰：'若叔是？后三日，邻当去溅裙水上，以博山香待，与郎俱过。'余诺之。会所友有偕当诣京师者，戏盗余卧装以先，不果留。雪中，让山至，且曰：'东诸侯取去矣！'明年，让山复东，相背于戏上，因写诗以墨其故处云。"有不少人把这一则故事与《燕台》诗比附立说，将二者混为一谈，且根据《燕台四首》所提及的一些地名，对柳枝为东诸侯取去以后的踪迹大加猜测。其实，关于柳枝的事，除了这一篇序文以外，我们所知道的并不多，一切猜度都只是假想。而且据义山《柳枝诗序》，是义山写《燕台》四诗在前，而与柳枝相遇在后，《燕台》诗中当然不该混有柳枝的事迹。我以为与其将《柳枝》与《燕台》四诗比附立说去猜测其悲欢离合的时与地之踪迹，倒不如透过义山笔下柳枝对《燕台》四诗之赏爱，去看义山自己对《燕台》诗所自许的某种境界，该更为真实可信。第一，我们先看一看义山对柳枝为人的一段描摹叙写。义山笔下的柳枝，所过的乃是"吹叶嚼蕊，调丝擪管"的生活，所爱的乃是"天海风涛之曲，幽忆怨断之音"的曲调，寥寥几笔，所勾画出的乃是何等幽美迥绝的心魂。我们再看柳枝初闻人咏义山《燕台》诗时，所发出的"谁人有此？谁人为是"的重复迫切的询问，其声气口吻中，所表现的乃是何等心弦被撼拨震动着的惊喜，以及未遇义山前的"涂妆绾髻未尝竟"的无以为容的寥落的情怀，与义山约见时的"手断长带"、"丫鬟毕妆"、"以博山香待"的一份倾迟奉献的心意，这是义山笔下所叙写的柳枝。然而语云："同声相应，同气相求。"我们往往可以从一个人所爱的对象中去认识一个人，这在大体上是不错的。虽然有时也不免有失误，如孔子之圣尚不免于有"以言取人失之宰我，以貌取人失之子羽"的可能，但有一点必然可信的，就是我们自己所塑造的爱之偶像，一定为我们自己心灵之所爱慕和向往则是必然的。辑本《李义山诗辨正》，张采田曾云："柳枝为义山第一知己，此文极力写之，有声有色，是最用意之作。”义山所最用意写的，正不仅是柳枝，而实在乃是义山自以为其知己相感的某种属于义山自我的心灵之境界。“天海风涛之曲，幽忆怨断之音”，这岂非正是义山所为诗的风格？不得知爱的寥落，与既得知爱的奉献，这岂非正是义山所用情的态度？所以我以为与其把这篇序文与《燕台》诗比附去猜测柳枝之事迹，倒不如从这篇诗序来体认义山所向往之某种境界，进而去了解《燕台》诗，或者反而更有助益。

除去这一则有关的故事外，关于《燕台》四诗之时、地与人，还有不少其他的猜测。以人而言，大别之约有以下数说：

一、燕台，唐人惯以言使府，必使府后房人也。（中华书局本《玉谿生诗笺注》卷五，页三七《燕台》诗注）

二、其“学仙玉阳东”时，有所恋于女冠欤，其人先被达官取去……以篇中多引仙女事，故知女冠。（同前）

三、据序语是先作《燕台》诗后遇柳枝，是两事也。然艳情大致相同，艳词每多错互……终不能辨其是一是二矣。（同前卷五，页三九《柳枝》诗注）

四、燕台，用燕昭故实，唐人例指使幕……《燕台》诗四章，盖皆为杨嗣复而作。（中华书局本张采田《玉谿生年谱会笺》页七一，开成五年谱）

五、义山与燕台相见在人家饮席，其人已先为人后房矣。（《玉谿生年谱会笺》附《李义山诗辨正》页四六八。观此则是竟直以“燕台”为人之代名矣）

六、此四诗乃对宫嫔飞鸾、轻凤二人之哀悼，诗中桃叶、桃根等句，表明卢氏等乃系姊妹。（商务本苏雪林《玉溪诗谜》，页八七至九一，与宫嫔恋爱的关系，追悼章）

七、商隐诗之隐僻者，有些似为讽刺贵主，亦似为讽刺女冠，抑又似为讽刺宫妾，如……《燕台》诗四首。（新亚学报抽印本，孙甄陶《李

商隐诗探微》)

以地而言，则有以下诸说：

一、其人先被达官取去京师，又流转湘中矣……玉阳在东，京师在西，故曰东风、西海也；玉阳在济源县，京师带以洪河，故曰浊水、清波也。曰石城，曰瘴花，曰南云，曰楚弄，曰湘川，曰苍梧，皆楚地之境，故知又流转湘中也。(《玉谿生诗笺注》卷五，页三七，《燕台》诗注)

二、统观诸诗（按：指《燕台》、《柳枝》、《谑柳》、《赠柳》、《河内》、《河阳》、《石城》、《莫愁》诸作），似其艳情有二：一为柳枝而发，一为学仙玉阳时所欢而发，《谑柳》、《赠柳》、《石城》、《莫愁》，皆咏柳枝之入郢中也；《燕台》、《河阳》、《河内》诸篇，多言湘江，又多引仙事，似昔学仙时所恋者，今在湘潭之地，而后又不知何往矣。……但郢州亦楚境，或二美堕于一地，不可细索矣。(同前卷六，页二，《河阳》诗注)

三、开成五年杨嗣复出为湖南观察使，冬贬潮州刺史……“木棉”，点潮州；“瑶琴”四句“楚弄”“南云”云云，喻嗣复自湘贬潮；四章，义山赴湘，嗣复已去之事。(《玉谿生年谱会笺》页七六、七七，开成五年谱)

四、《燕台》诗次章第一段说现在到曲江离宫去走走……三章第三段，言宫禁虽严，但外人可以从小苑进去。(《玉溪诗谜》页八八、八九，与宫嫔恋爱的关系，追悼章)

五、石城……蜀魂……瘴花……木棉……南云……云梦……湘川……青溪……楚管蛮弦，这许多可指实的地方色彩，是不妨认为诗中女主人是在南方的。假如再检查诗中北方地方色彩如“济河水清黄河浑”，就知道北方地名偶亦采用一二。再诗题“燕台”更是标准的北方。所以诗中忽南忽北，正是原作者故弄狡狯，无意将谜底告人。(文学杂志社《诗与诗人》第一集劳榦《李商隐燕台诗评述》，页五五)

再以四诗春夏秋冬之章法言，则有以下诸说：

一、首篇细状其春情怨思；次篇追叙旧时夜会；三篇彼又远去之叹；

四篇我尚羁留之恨。(《玉谿生诗笺注》卷五，页三六《燕台》诗注）

二、首章，记义山与杨嗣复相见，及文宗忽崩嗣复渐危之事；次章专记杨贤妃安王溶事；三章嗣复至湘约义山赴幕之事；四章义山赴湘嗣复已去之事。(《玉谿生年谱会笺》，页七六、七七，开成五年谱）

三、盖其人春间与义山相见即为人取去，夏间流转金陵，至秋又赴湘川，曾约义山赴湘，及冬间赴约，而其人又不知转至何处矣。诗所以分四时写之。(《玉谿生年谱会笺》附《李义山诗辨正》)

以上诸说不过就手边所有的几种书略举其大要而已，然其说法之纷纭杂乱已可概见一斑，甚至于同一家之说法亦不免于先后之矛盾歧出，则其所说之完全出于一己之臆度与假想可知，守着这些不可据信的材料，正如治丝益棼，不过徒增困惑而已，原来就无法编出一面完整的网来，则我们何如把它暂时抛在一边，亲自跃入水中去做一番摸索探寻的尝试呢！

第一点我们所当探寻的当然乃是《燕台》四诗中的人物究竟何指的问题。在中国旧诗中，人物之所指有几种可能，其一是其人确为实有且确可实指的，如乐天诗中之小蛮樊素，小山词中之莲鸿蘋云；其二是其人虽属实有，然而信据不足无法确指者，如端己词“四月十七”的“别君”，“那年花下”的“初识”，白石词“肥水东流”的“相思”，“淮南皓月”的“感梦”；其三是其人并非实有，不过诗人泛为香艳之辞者，如南朝之宫体，五代之令词；其四是其人虽亦并非实有，然而亦并非泛为香艳之辞，乃全属于托喻之作，如曹子建之“南国佳人”，阮嗣宗之“江滨二妃”；其五是其人亦非实有，然既非泛为香艳之辞，亦非有心托喻之作，而但为心中某种缠绵惆怅之情的一种自然之流露，如正中词之“花前失却游春侣”，六一词之“纵有远情难写寄”，以上五种乃是一时所想到的作品中人物之所指的几种可能性。至于读者对作品中人物所当取的态度，则当然最好乃是知之为知之，不知为不知。其果然有所确指者，则读者自当细加研读以求其究竟何指，至其本不可确指者，则读者如果强做解人横加附会，那就有时不免会陷于欺妄和误谬了。义山的《燕台》四首，观其恍惚错综的叙写，无一句落实之语，则其人物之属于不可确指，乃是不容置疑的一件事，只是此四诗中之人物又究竟属于不可确指中的哪一类呢？观其深悲切至之语，则此四诗必非泛泛之艳辞；然而若迳谓其虽不可确指而确为实有，则此四诗又不似端己与白石诸词之单纯显豁；若谓其但为托喻之作，则此四诗又不似子建、嗣宗二诗之喻言可想；若但谓其只为心中惆怅缠绵之情的自然流露，则此四诗之章法井然，自春徂秋，也决不同于正中、六一的流连光景惆怅自怜的一时抒情之作。要想解说这一类难于归属的作品，我以为有两点基本观念，乃是读者所应当具备的，其一是承认其难于归属的多种可能，从而欣赏其由多种可能所暗示的丰美幽微的含蕴，而根本不必妄图加以拘限的归属；其二是承认诗歌本身之价值与作品中所写之人物对象并无必然之关系。先就其意蕴之丰美来说，此四诗有极真实深切之感受，其使人心动神迷之处，恍如出于真实体验之情事，此其一；此四诗又有极复杂错综之象喻借比，完全不为任何真实情事所拘限，似全为象喻之作品，此其二；此四诗更充满了一种惆怅哀伤之致，似全为作者心灵中低徊悱恻之情的自然流露，此其三；然而如前所言，此四诗之周密精致，又不同于一时的抒情偶然之作，而似乎确实当有更深入的取义，此其四。我们欣赏这一类的作品，实在最好是同时承认这多种的可能，不受任何拘限地去体会作者内在最窈眇之心魂与外在最精美之艺术的一种最敏锐的结合。这种作品原来就不属于理念的有限的解说之内，它的不可指说正是它的好处所在，如果要对这一类作品加以指实的解说，那反而将是对其丰美幽微之含蕴的一种斲丧和损害了。再就诗歌本身之价值与所写之人物对象并无必然之关系而言，这种道理实在是极为浅显易明的，举个最通俗的例子来看，譬如酒之与水，其差别乃在于本身之品质是什么，而并不在于其所倾注的容器是什么，如果是酒则即使只盛起一杯来，也必然是酒，如果是水，则即使盛起一缸来也依然是水，如果撇开本身的品质，而单就其所倾注的对象来讨论酒与水的价值，这种误植重点的衡量，其错误乃是显然可见的。义山诗的好处，原来就在于其所具含的一种窈眇幽微的迥异于人的品质，如同《西溪》之潺湲无奈，如同《锦瑟》之哀怨无端，像这种无奈无端的情意，原是与诗人之生命深相结合着的一种品质，则我们又何必将那种与生命结合着的品质强加分割，而将之拘限于某一个并不确知的狭隘的对象之中呢。所以我以为这四首诗中所叙写的对象，如果确实有可以指明的足够的证据，可以使我们在理性上有更清楚的认知的满足，不仅品味了酒的滋味还认知了酒的容器，那当然很好，否则，如果我们把酒的滋味丢开不尝，而只在隔靴搔痒地猜测容器的形状，那岂非是一种舍本逐末劳而少功的愚执之举。因此我以为对于义山这四首诗，我们与其妄加猜测义山诗外之“人”，倒毋宁细加品味去体认义山诗中之“我”了。

第二点我们所当探寻的，则当是《燕台》四诗中的地域问题。在这四首诗中，义山所提到的有着地域性的名物，大约有十余处之多，而且南北杂举，既无系统，又不一致，因此劳榦先生乃说：“诗中忽南忽北，正是原作者故弄狡狯。”关于这一点，我以为当从几方面去看。因为地域或方位的指述，在中国诗中原可以有多种意义：第一种为写实性的，如杜甫《绝句四首》之“窗含西岭千秋雪，门泊东吴万里船”二句，其“西岭”与“东吴”便都是写实性的地域和方位；第二种是用典性的，如杜甫《奉送严公入朝》一诗之“南图回羽翮，北极捧星辰”二句，其“南图”与“北极”，便是用的庄子《逍遥游》大鹏之将图南，与《论语·为政》众星之拱北辰的典故；第三种是象喻性的，如张衡《四愁诗》之“泰山”“东望”、“桂林”“南望”、“汉阳”“西望”、“雁门”“北望”，其中之诸地名与诸方位便都是象喻性的，并不实指任何一地，不过列举四方艰险之地，以表现一种无所不至的追寻与终然不见的艰阻而已。有了这几点基本的认识，再来看义山《燕台》四诗，就会发现其中许多地名及方位，原来都只是用典或象喻，而并非实指，如其举“济河”与“黄河”之取其清浊之对比，举“南云”与“楚弄”之取其绵渺之哀思，举“石城”与“苍梧”之取用石城莫愁与舜死苍梧之故实，凡此种种，如果我们不肯仔细体味原诗的取义，而妄加指实，那当然会不免于误谬百出而迷乱自失了。

第三点我们所当探寻的乃是《燕台》四诗中时节的问题。这首诗分明标举出春夏秋冬四时，当然应当有其所以如此标举的取义，只是如果按旧说之便据此实指为某些情事发生之时间与季节，则就又不免近于刻舟求剑的迂执了。在中国诗中的时间与季节也有写实与象喻两种可能，如《诗经·豳风·七月》一篇，其一年四季十二月之叙述，当然乃全属写实之纪事；至于如繁钦《定情诗》之自日旰、日中，直写到日夕、日暮，则就并非写实之笔，而完全乃是一种无尽之期待的时间性之象喻了，因为时间性的推移，原来就可以在诗中造成一种久远而循环不已的感觉，这不仅是在象喻性的诗歌中，可以感受其明显的效果，即使在写实性的诗歌中，如《豳风·七月》一篇，我们之所以能对它所叙写的生活民俗得到如此强烈的周遍的感受，也未始不是由于它对时间的循环不已的叙述所造成的效果。至于在象喻性的诗歌中，则自屈子楚骚之往往以“春”“秋”“朝”“暮”的对举暗示时间性的永恒周遍之感，降而至于民歌俗曲之往往以四时十二月的重叠排比，来写无尽的爱恋相思，则更是一种常见的表现方法了。义山《燕台四首》之标举四时，我以为也不可过于拘执实指，而当从其所造成之整个的永恒周遍之感来做体认，从而领会这一位“荷叶生时春恨生，荷叶枯时秋恨成”的诗人，他所表现的一种“身在情长在”的经春历秋的整个一生的深情极怨，这似乎才是一种更有意义的探寻的角度。

最后还有一点也是我们所当探寻的，那便是这四首诗之标题“燕台”二字的取义何指的问题。在义山诗集中有不少无题之作，也有不少取诗歌中首句中二字为命题的虽有题而实近于无题之作。此四诗既标名“燕台”，自不同于一般无题之作，而燕台又非首句或全诗中任何一句中曾经出现过的字样，则此标题自又不同于一般取首句中二字为题的近于无题之作，然则如此说来，是此二字之标题之必当有所取义，乃是无疑的了，至于其取义为何，则冯浩注云："燕台，唐人惯以言使府。"这话实在是不错的，义山在《梓州罢吟寄同舍》一诗中，就曾经有"长吟远下燕台去"之句（按：义山于大中五年柳仲郢镇东蜀之时曾被辟为节度书记，迄大中十年柳仲郢内征为吏部侍郎府罢之时，恰为五年，义山此诗前有"五年从事霍嫖姚"之句，可以为证，是"长吟远下燕台去"固正指梓州府罢之事也）。所以"燕台"可以指"使府"该是无可疑的。只是如果因此就臆测为义山与使府后房有恋爱之事如冯浩注之所云云，那就未免想入非非了，张采田《会笺》即曾严驳冯氏之说以为不可信，可是张采田却又因燕台指使府之一念，而联想及于杨嗣复之自湖南观察使贬为潮州刺史之事，而谓义山此四诗乃专为杨嗣复而作，且牵附及于文宗之崩，武宗之立，以及杨贤妃欲立安王溶之种种情事，字比句附，较之冯注尤为牵强，岑仲勉《玉谿生年谱会笺平质》也早已辨其同样为不可信（见台湾中华书局《玉谿生年谱会笺》附岑仲勉《平质》页二三〇）。那么这四首诗究竟何指呢？我以为关于《燕台》二字之命题，可以分作两层来看：其一、燕台确指使府，义山终生不遇，托身幕府，历依天平、兖海、桂管、武宁、东川诸幕，这种寄人趋走的生活，必多抑郁辛酸之感。像杜甫在成都依故人严武之幕，两代世交，而杜甫在其《宿府》、《遣闷》、《简院内诸公》等作品中，尚不免有"已忍伶俜十年事，强移栖息一枝安"，"胡为来幕下，只合在舟中"及"白头趋幕府，深觉负平生"等愤怨的话，则义山于其一生之历依诸幕之辗转漂泊的生活以及依违恩怨的感情之间必当更有许多悲苦难言之情事，这是可以想见的，而义山一生仕宦之生活，则舍此栖托幕府之一片辛酸以外，又更别无较幸运之机遇，然则义山《燕台四首》岂非很可能有着对其整个之一生的自叙自慨之意，此其一；再则燕台原来又指燕昭王之黄金台，欲以延天下之贤士者，后人为诗往往用之以慨其不得知遇之悲，如李白之《行路难》，即曾有"昭王白骨萦蔓草，谁人更扫黄金台，行路难，归去来”之句，然则义山之以燕台命题除自慨其幕府生活之醉辛以外，岂非更可能有其自伤不遇的失志莫偶的悲怨之情在。何况义山幼而孤寒，对仕宦之幸蹇，自会比别人有更为重视的心理，而义山与令狐父子及其岳父王茂元之间的一段恩怨，虽然见仁见智，有着许多不同的解说和看法，然而一则为世交之谊，一则为翁婿之情，其间的猜嫌误会必有许多难言之痛，也是可以想见的，而义山平生所遇到的不幸又不仅仕宦一途而已。义山早年丧父，中年丧偶，都是在最为需要的时候失去了最大的依傍，其心灵上当然也都曾受到极大的挫伤。此外从义山诗集中许多缠绵悱恻的写恋爱的诗篇来看，纵使其中有一部分作品可能为别有寄意的托喻之作，然而一位多情善感的诗人如义山，他在感情方面之曾经有过一些伤心蚀骨的苦恋的经验，更是大有可能的，凡此种种不幸的挫伤失意，都可归之于广义的命运之不偶，把平生命运之不偶结合于平生羁栖幕府的一世的酸辛，如果从这种角度对《燕台四首》作一种象喻性的深入的体认，而不必字比句附地强加穿凿，也许反而不失为一条可以探寻个中真意的新途径。

其一　春

这是《燕台四首》的第一首诗，以春为标题，从萌发着的生意，与醒觉着的追寻写起，正象喻着一个有情之生命的诞生之开始。开端“风光冉冉东西陌”，仅只七字便已写出春日之无限风光。而且义山笔下的春光并不像一般人所写的只是一片万紫千红的坚凝而浓重的颜色而已。义山所写的春光是流动的、娇柔的、飘飞在人的眼前身畔，而几乎可以随时抚触得到的。所以义山不曰“春光”而曰“风光”，“春光”二字较为呆滞，而“风光”二字则较为活泼轻灵。再继之以“冉冉”二字的形容，这两个叠字无论在声音或意义上，都予人以一种轻柔荡漾的感觉。“风光”

而加之以“冉冉”，于是而叶底微风之轻拂，水面波光之闪烁，天边云影之流移，一切光与色皆于春风骀荡中，以其新鲜之生意向人飘飞舞动而来。更承以“东西陌”三个字，于是而东阡西陌之上，远近四方之间，无处而不有此冉冉之风光，无处而不有此飘飞之生意矣。如果以之与北宋词人欧阳永叔的“候馆梅残，溪桥柳细，草熏风暖摇征辔”，及秦少游的“柳下桃蹊，乱分春色到人家”诸句相较，虽然同样是写春光的无处不在，则永叔与少游二人的形容较为具体，色泽亦较为浓重，似乎全以官能视觉的感受为主。而义山之“风光冉冉东西陌”一句，则轻柔绵渺，别有恍惚迷离之致，其感受乃不全出于官能之视觉，而隐然更有着诗人心魂深处的一种幽微窈渺的跃动在。所以继之乃曰：“几日娇魂寻不得。”从上一句冉冉风光带给诗人的心灵的震触，到下一句对“娇魂”的惘惘地追寻，这正是极自然的感发和承应。因为一位多情锐感的诗人，面对此轻柔绵渺迷离恍惚之风光，其内心深处自会有一种难以言说而又无从填补的空虚怅惘之感。冯正中词说：“河畔青芜堤上柳，为问新愁，何事年年有。”晏同叔词说：“细草愁烟，幽花怯露，凭阑总是销魂处。”柳永词说：“草色烟光残照里，无人会得凭阑意。”这种面对春天的青芜、堤柳、细草、烟光，而使人惆怅魂销的感觉，是极难加以解说和分析的。所谓“物色之动，心亦摇焉”。而尤以春日之纤美温柔所显示着的生命之复苏的种种迹象，最足以唤起诗人内心中某种复苏着的若有所失的惘惘追寻的情意。然而“自古皆有死，莫不饮恨而吞声”，千古以来，竟然没有一个诗人在这种追寻中获得过满足。所以说“几日娇魂寻不得”，“娇魂”正不必确指，只是诗人某种追寻的象征，“魂”字可见其窈眇，“娇”字可见其纤柔，“几日”者，可见其追寻已非一日而终然竟无所得，这正是有感情有理想的诗人千古之所同悲。然而“余心所善，九死未悔”，纵使追寻无获，而无奈此情难已。所以接下去乃说：“蜜房羽客类芳心，冶叶倡条遍相识。”这两句正写其一片追寻的辛苦和情意。“蜜房羽客”自然是指蜜蜂而言。朱鹤龄注此句引郭璞《蜂赋》云“亦托名于羽族”，所以义山乃称蜂曰“蜜房羽客”，一方面固然有其出处来历，一方面又予读者以一种极新颖极鲜明的感受。从此句末三字“类芳心”来看，则义山原以之拟诗人之“芳心”。所以称之曰“羽客”者，“客”字既可收拟人之效果，而羽化登仙的凌虚御空之联想，则读之更可使人感到一份上下飞翔求索的深情，和一份悠扬飘举的褊褼的神致。而又于其上加以“蜜房”二字，不仅切合蜜蜂之取喻，而“蜜”字之甘美芳醇，“房”字之闭藏深隐，也都可使人想到诗人“芳心”之蜜爱深情。义山另一首《二月二日》诗有句云：“花须柳眼各无赖，紫蝶黄蜂俱有情。”人非太上，孰能忘情，情之所钟，正在我辈，像眼前的紫蝶黄蜂一样，随冉冉之风光而飘飞起舞，以全生命的本能追求寻索着的，正是诗人的一片多情缱绻的“芳心”。至于下一句“冶叶倡条遍相识”，这一句如果只从字面以传统的道德眼光来看，不免竟会觉得义山用字过于浮艳轻薄。因为从《易经·系辞》的“冶容诲淫”，以及“倡”字之多与“倡伎”“倡优”等字连用，一般人对“冶”字和“倡”字，早就先存了一个偏颇的成见，而“遍相识”三个字似乎也容易使人想到用情之浪漫不专。其实这七个字才正是义山极严肃极沉重地道出其追寻之殷勤辛苦的一句诗。“冶”字“倡”字如果摆脱掉陈腐的成见来看，是何等色泽鲜明精力饱满的字样。“冶”字之美，“倡”字之盛，万紫千红之缤纷多彩，长条密叶之披拂多姿，岂不皆可从这两个字中想象得之……至于“遍相识”三个字，则更是全心奉献和追寻的表现。“余既滋兰之九畹兮，又树蕙之百亩。畦留夷与揭车兮，杂杜衡与芳芷。”早自屈子就曾经对百卉群芳有过如此深情遍爱的愿望。其实屈原和义山所写的原来就都并不真指客观之实物，而只是他们自己内心中，一种对完整周遍而无终极的爱之向往。每一片在春风中舒展着的娇美的花叶，每一根在春风中款舞着的袅娜的枝条，都曾引起诗人深切的怜爱，都曾唤起诗人怅惘地追寻。然而“众里寻他千百度”，何处才是诗人所萦心系梦以寻求的那一缕“娇魂”呢？

于是在深情苦想之中，诗人也仿佛果真曾经若有所见，所以乃有“暖蔼辉迟桃树西，高鬟立共桃鬟齐”之句。“暖蔼”七个字，义山真是把春光的一片迷惘娇慵之感写得恰到好处，所以不曰“暖日”，不曰“和风”，不曰“淑气”，而曰“暖蔼”，前面三个词语都过于现实，过于拘狭，而“暖蔼”一辞则不但兼有了前三者的意义，而且“蔼”字更别有烟蔼迷濛之致，这是最能表现春光之特色的。所以中国的诗人写到春天的景物，往往加一“烟”字，如“烟光”、“烟柳”、“烟花”，这真是极好的形容。“蔼”字有烟字之意，而更富于和柔温暖之感。“暖蔼”二字自可令人联想到和风淡宕暖日生烟之种种景象。至于“辉迟”二字则写日光之光影迟迟。昔杜审言《早春游望》诗有句云：“淑气催黄鸟，晴光转绿蘋。”杜甫《江畔独步寻花》亦有句云，“春光懒困倚微风”，又曰：“桃花一树开无主，可爱深红爱浅红。”今如将义山之“暖蔼辉迟”四字，与下面“桃树西”三字合看，则淑气微风之中，日影晴光乃正在深浅桃红之上慢转轻移。这真是何等令人痴迷的景色。在此痴迷之中，乃恍惚见有人焉立于桃树之下，而更不形容此人之容饰衣装，乃但着以“高鬟”二字，一则此人原在迷离恍惚之中，故不得详为叙写。再则“高鬟”虽仅二字，然发型之样式实在最足以代表一个女子的身份、地位和个性。如果以此句之“高鬟”与前所引《柳枝诗序》之“丫鬟毕妆”相较，则“丫鬟”之发式更富于青春活泼之感。而“高鬟”之发式则更富于端丽成熟之美，且别有高贵矜持之意态，至于以“高鬟”与“桃鬟”相比，则是诗人故弄恍惚之笔，夫彼桃树既无毛发何得有鬟？而曰“桃鬟”者，方其恍惚痴念之中，人既如花，花亦似人，于是而高枝之上之万朵繁花，乃竟真如美人头上之簪花高髻矣。中间着以“立共”二字，就文法言之，曰“共”，分明该是二物；而就感觉言之，则“立共”二字之密切亲近，乃竟使人有二者合一之感。义山此句运笔极妙，曰“高鬟立共桃鬟齐”，恍兮惚兮，如幻如真，方见是花而又疑为是人，于是在暖蔼辉迟之中，在桃树繁花之下，乃仿佛真如有一位高鬟拥髻的佳人，且颇可想见其含睇宜笑的风致矣。而紧接着这一份乍睹还疑的惊喜，义山却忽然笔锋一转，写下了

“雄龙雌凤杳何许？絮乱丝繁天亦迷”，这真是使人心伤望绝极尽凄迷惨切的两句话。“雄龙雌凤”四字，“雄”与“雌”是一层对举，“龙”与“凤”是又一层对举。早自屈子《离骚》就曾经有过“两美其必合兮”的祝愿，太白《梁甫吟》也曾经有过“张公两龙剑，神物合有时”的信心。因为唯有当“雄龙”与“雌凤”能相遇相合的世界，才是圆满无憾的。然而义山在这二句诗中所发出的却是“杳何许”的茫无所见的苦觅悲呼。没有鸣高桐的彩凤，也没有翔九天的神龙，更遑论彩凤与神龙的结合相遇？人世间所有的只是黯淡绝望中的一片残缺的憾恨。而况冉冉之风光欲老，羽客之芳心虽在，而高鬟之花蕊将残，茫茫天地之间，到处是濛濛的飞絮，到处是惘惘的游丝，所以义山接下去便说了“絮乱丝繁天亦迷”的话。如此不得相遇的深悲，如此莫能补赎的长恨，天若有情，固亦早已为之意惘情迷。云谁不信，则此乱絮繁丝便可为天人之同证。

写情至此，原已更无余地，然而义山最善于以其缠绵宛转之笔写缠绵宛转之情，于是遂又有“醉起微阳若初曙，映帘梦断闻残语”之言。像再世的宿缘，像前生的梦魇，永远无法忘怀，也永远无法解脱的。清醒时固然是絮乱丝繁的迷惘，而即使在醉里在梦里也一样在心魂之中盘旋萦绕着的，这是何等缠绵深切，何等凄迷哀怨的一份感情。首句“微阳”，朱鹤龄注云：“夕阳也。”此二字盖遥遥与后之“初曙”相对，“微阳”是真，“初曙”是幻；次句则以“梦断”与“残语”相对，“梦断”是真，“残语”是幻。已是微阳欲入，而犹疑为初曙方生；已是梦断难留，而恍闻其叮咛细语。这二句之中有多少对所追怀思念者的痴迷苦想，有多少对已残破消逝者的震悼哀伤。而其写醉起梦醒时的恍惚之感又复何等真切传神。至于“映帘”二字则为两句相结合之关键所在，映于帘上者，正为首句所写之微阳，而见此映帘之微阳者，则次句犹闻残语之梦断之人。昔杜甫《梦李白》诗有句云：“落月满屋梁，犹疑照颜色。”思之而至于入梦，入梦而至于梦醒之时于帘际微阳梁间落月之中，犹仿佛如闻其细语如见其颜色，则怀念之深自可想见。只是杜甫所写乃是实境实情，义山所写则似不必实指，而只是其内心中一直缠绵悱恻着的某种情意。深情如许，所以继之乃曰："愁将铁网罥珊瑚，海阔天宽迷处所。"上一句接写其永无休止的寻觅与追求之辛苦，下一句又依然落于永难偿获的失望与落空的悲哀。姚培谦《笺注》引本章云："珊瑚生海底盘石上，海人先作铁网沉水底，贯中而生，绞网出之。"曰"铁网"，曰"沉水"，曰"贯中"，曰"绞网"，其用心之深切，致力之勤劳，立意之坚毅，与夫珊瑚之珍贵与难得，皆可想见。然而珊瑚纵使难得，而海人终以其深切勤劳与坚毅毕竟得之。我今日虽有一如海人之殷切勤毅之心力，然而面对此茫茫大海渺渺长空，何处有我所欲觅求之鲜红似血之珊瑚？何处是我可以把自己千丝情缕所织成的铁网抛下的所在？"将"者，以手将持之意，空持此千丝之铁网，而四顾苍茫，除寂寥空漠之外，更无所有。昔孟浩然诗有句云："迷津欲有问，平海夕漫漫。"这种失望落空之后的怅惘迷失，其苦痛真是不可言喻的。所以于上一句开端着一"愁"字，诗人所愁的正就是下句"迷处所"的痛苦的迷失。而中间更加上了"持铁网"的辛勤，"罥珊瑚"的希望，"海阔天宽"的茫茫的追寻，如此一气贯下，才更使人觉得"迷处所"的堪为愁恨。（"天宽"之"宽"字一作"翻"，二者相较，作"宽"字可与海阔之"阔"字相呼应，似更可以加深其寂寥落空之感；而作"翻"字则可使人想见广海之上海天相接之处的一片汹涌翻腾，似亦大可加深其迷惘不安之苦。朱鹤龄注本作"翻"，冯浩注本作"宽"，二者难断其优劣，今兹所说暂从冯本。）

以下接云"衣带无情有宽窄，春烟自碧秋霜白"，则全写伤心绝望之后的悲苦无奈。古诗云："相去日已远，衣带日已缓。"在睽隔失望之中，不知别愁之多少，但觉衣带之渐宽，生命有尽，而相思无尽，当带孔频移，其宽窄有如此明显之变化时，又安能不令人自觉心惊不已。以一个多情的生命，面对着如此无情地日日向人诉说着生命将终的渐宽之衣带，这是宇宙间何等无可挽赎的极恨深悲。然则此宇宙间更复何有乎？则春烟自碧，秋霜自白。无论其为三春之暖日生烟，无论其为九秋之冷露凝霜，春烟之碧自是迷濛无奈，而秋霜之白则更复冷漠无情。着一“碧”字，一“白”字，颜色何等分明，感受何等真切。又着一“自”字，有一任彼自碧自白之意，口吻亦何等无奈。由此而从春到秋，诗人之生命乃尽消蚀于烟之迷濛与霜之冷漠之中。这种消蚀，其痛苦乃一如遭遇到研磨擘裂一样，所以接下去乃说：“研丹擘石天不知，愿得天牢锁冤魄。”冯浩注引《吕氏春秋》曰，“石可破也，而不可夺坚；丹可磨也，而不可夺赤”，这是何等贞毅的一种情操。然而如果反过来看，则纵使有石之坚，而无奈已遭擘裂；纵使有丹之赤，也无奈已遭研损，这对石之坚与丹之赤来说，是何等深重的折辱和伤毁。然则谁实为之？孰令致之？倘所谓天道，是耶非耶？困惑哀怨之极，所以乃说“天不知”也。至于下句“天牢”云云，朱鹤龄注引《汉书》曰，“戴筐六星，六曰司灾，在魁中，贵人之牢”，又引孟康曰：“贵人牢曰天理，即天牢也。”冯浩注则引《晋书·志》云：“天牢六星，在北斗魁下，贵人之牢也。”又曰：“贯索九星，贱人之牢也，一曰天牢。”是天上星宿之间原有“天牢”之名称，而世传之天牢有二：一为戴筐六星在北斗魁下，为贵人之牢；一为贯索九星，为贱人之牢。（详见《史记·天官书》、《汉书》及《晋书·天文志》）至于义山之用“天牢”一辞，则当但取其人间天上永远被羁锁的一种象喻，原不必有贵贱之区分。至于所羁锁者为何，则含情莫展，屈抑难伸之冤魄也。观义山之用字，真所谓情深意苦，所以冤而曰冤魄。则其悲憾冤恨之深，固已是至死难消，牢而曰天牢，则此恨不仅长留于人世，更将且长羁于天上矣，又复于此句开端加以“愿得”二字，义山之长留此恨乃竟直欲誓以永矢弗谖，深情苦恨，至此而极矣。

继之以“夹罗委箧单绡起”，则山穷水尽之时，忽作柳暗花明之笔。春光既老，朱夏将临，义山乃将此一份春去夏来之感，全从衣饰与肌肤之感觉写出，因为唯有身体之感受才是最真实最亲切的感受，所以人们说到对某一件事的认识与了解时，往往用“体”会、“体”验等字样。而季节寒暖之变，当然更以身体之感受最为敏锐。《论语》中记载，有一次孔子的弟子曾皙说到春天，第一句说的就是“暮春者，春服既成”。把厚重而黯淡的冬衣脱卸下来，换上夹罗的春袍，闪着使芳草都生妒的春天的颜色，这是何等轻快鲜明的一种感受。至于春去夏来之际，则把夹罗的春袍又脱卸下来而换上了单绡的夏服，衣袂飘然，微风轻拂，这又是另一种褊褼轻举的情调。以善于铺叙著称的北宋后期的大词人周邦彦在写到夏天来临的时候，就往往先从衣服之感受写起。如其《琐窗寒》的“单衣伫立”，《六丑》的“单衣试酒”，都可为证。而这种感受如果从女性写起，当然就会显得更纤细而柔美。所以义山接下去就说：“香肌冷衬琤琤珮。”“香肌”自当指女性而言，其下着一“冷”字，苏东坡《洞仙歌》词有句云：“冰肌玉骨，自清凉无汗。”这是在炎夏中，一种专属于女性所特有的静美丰柔中的清凉的感觉。而义山更于其下加了“琤琤珮”三个字。辛稼轩《江神子》词写一个“宝钗飞凤鬓惊鸾”的女子，也曾更饰之以“珮声闲，玉垂环”的描写。因为如此才能使这个女子更有风姿和情致。义山所云“琤琤”者，正此闲闲之珮声也。如果我们向更远一步去推想，则姜白石《念奴娇》咏荷花词，曾有句云：“三十六陂人未到，水珮风裳无数。”然则义山笔下的如花之人，于其琤琤之珮声间，岂不亦似更有无边之寂寞在。于此而再回顾前一“冷”字，则知此一字所写者，亦当不仅但为冰肌玉骨之清凉而已，更当有于琤琤之珮声间，所映衬之一份心魂寂寞的凄寒在。如果有人在此蓦然作拦截式的诘质，问我此女子为作者之自喻抑为作者所怀思向往之人？则我将应之曰观此处之口气似以近于自喻为是。若再诘之曰既自喻为女子，则前此高鬟立于桃树下之女子岂不曾释为所思之象喻乎？则我又将应之曰然，盖以诗人往往在一篇作品中既以某一象征为自喻，又以之为他喻。此亦不乏例证，洪兴祖《楚辞补注》于《离骚》“恐美人之迟暮”一句，即曾注曰：“屈原有以美人喻君者，‘恐美人之迟暮’是也；有喻善人者，‘满堂兮美人’是也；有自喻者，‘送美人兮南浦’是也。”《史记·屈原贾生列传》说：“其志洁，故其称物芳。”无论是以之喻称自己，或喻称所爱之对象，皆同此理。读者也大可不必对义山诗中所引喻之美人过事苟求确指。至于末二句“今日东风自不胜，化作幽光入西海”，则为全篇深悲极怨之总结。标题曰“春”，而春去难留，逝者如斯，到“东风无力百花残”的时候，一切誓愿，都成虚语；一切追寻，都归枉然。所以说“今日东风自不胜”，谓时至今日，东风自无力稍作留春之计，则唯有含恨从此长逝而已。昔李后主有词云：“林花谢了春红，太匆匆，无奈朝来寒雨晚来风。胭脂泪，留人醉，几时重？自是人生长恨水长东。”义山之“化作幽光入西海”，亦是长恨东流到海之意，只是义山更工于窈渺幽微之想象，故其出语亦较之后主更为奇诡凄迷。自篇首之冉冉风光，经篇中无数深情苦恨之怅惘追寻，乃今日东风无力，风光将老，则此长逝之春，究竟何所归往乎？此一问，可分三点作答：一则其逝也既如光影之迅疾而丝毫不可挽留掌握，故曰“光”；再则其逝也又更含有如许难以言说之苦恨深情，使其果然而化为光影，则此满怀长恨而永逝之光，其必为“幽光”无疑；三则此绵绵长恨之所汇聚，唯海之辽阔深邃可以象之，此所以此幽光之必入于“海”也，而春日之风则东风也，随春光之永逝，为东风所吹送，而携长恨以俱往者，其非“西海”而何？故曰“化作幽光入西海”也。古今多少写春归的诗人词客，如后主的“流水落花春去也，天上人间”，山谷的“春归何处？寂寞无行路”，清真的“春归如过翼，一去无迹”，稼轩的“是他春带愁来，春归何处？却不解带将愁去”，虽然这些词句也各有各的佳处所在，然而唯义山此二语最为悱恻凄迷。朱鹤龄注本评此句云：“所谓幽忆怨断之音也”，读之唯令人徒唤奈何而已。

其二　夏

此章标题为《夏》。说到夏，一般人所想到的多半是炎夏、盛夏、盛暑、骄阳等一类字样。因为在人们的印象中，夏日一直是炎热的，强烈的，喧嚣的。而义山这一章诗所写的夏日，却与此迥然相反。义山所写的夏乃是阴暗的，凄清的，寂寞的。在前言中我曾经说过，一篇作品中最重要的并不在作者感情的对象是什么，而在于作者感情的本质是什么。现在我们更得一例证，就是一篇作品最重要的并不在其所写的主题是什么，而在于作者对此主题所得的感受是什么。杜甫写夏的诗，如其在华州所写的《夏日叹》、《夏夜叹》，在夔州所写的《火》、《热》、《毒热》诸作，他笔下的夏乃是“朱光彻厚地”，“峡中都似火”的极酷烈的夏日，这一方面固然因为杜甫所写的夏日乃是特别炎热的夏日，而另一方面也因为杜甫的天性原来就属于阳刚的明朗而强烈的一型，所以喜欢从强烈鲜明的一面着笔的原故。因此甚至当他自己写到自己的感情时也往往用“热”字来形容，如其《赴奉先县咏怀》的“叹息肠内热”，《铁堂峡》的“回首肝肺热”，皆可为证。而义山写到自己的感情时，他所用的则是“春蚕到死”、“蜡炬成灰”等一类字样。因为义山的性格一直就属于纤柔而抑郁的一型，一直就缺乏着健康和明朗的色泽，而布满着残缺怅惘的憾恨。所以本章虽标题是《夏》，而义山却完全不从夏日之炎热繁盛的一面着笔。开端：“前阁雨帘愁不卷，后堂芳树阴阴见”。一起便予人以一种阴沉晦暗的感觉。“帘”而“不卷”，已使人有“庭院深深深几许，云窗雾阁常扃”的一种深杳凄迷的感受。而“帘”字上更加一“雨”字，义山另一首《重过圣女祠》诗有句云：“一春梦雨常飘瓦。”则在此垂帘之外，于檐前瓦际的雨丝飘飞雨声淅沥之中，帘内之人的梦魂之随淅沥之雨声以共其飘飞萦想，殆可想见。所以乃更于“不卷”二字之上加一“愁”字，长垂不卷的帘，与长存不解的愁，正复互为因果。帘因人之愁而不卷，人因帘之垂而益愁，在雨中闭锁的重帘，也就正象喻着在雨中闭锁的深愁。而此句首二字之“前阁”则更与下一句之“后堂”相映照，二句相呼应，有其相反的一面，也有其相成的一面。自其相成的一面来看，则后堂之“阴阴”更加深了前一句“雨帘”“不卷”的阴沉晦暗的感觉。是其时虽为朱明的炎夏，而无论其为“前阁”，为“后堂”，乃并皆不能予人以一丝光明温暖之感，则此阁与堂中之人的寂寞忧伤可想。而若自其相反的一面来看，则树而曰“芳树”，如陶渊明诗所写的“孟夏草木长，绕屋树扶疏”，则亦自有其欣欣然之一片生机在。而“阴阴”二字，除阴暗之感外，亦自有其浓密繁茂的另一意义在。结尾着一“见”字，是堂中之人虽无光明与温暖可言，而隐约可见于堂外者，则芳树垂阴、叶繁枝茂，乃正当欣欣向荣之日。彼亦一生命，此亦一生命，堂内有情之生命寂寞如斯，而堂外无情之生命则清阴若此。当此二种不同之生命相面对时，一个锐感的诗人，往往会产生一种极悲哀寂寞而内心又充满跃动的难以述说的感情。义山这二句诗就全从生命之相反的两面下笔，来写这一种微妙而难以言说的感觉。写炎夏而全从阴暗着笔，这是第一层相反；写阁内之人着一“愁”字，写堂外之树却偏偏着一“芳”字，这是第二层相反。在这种对比中，生命黯惨不幸的一面因了与生命繁盛美好的一面相映照的原故，一方面对美好者既倍增怀思向往之情；一方面对自己的黯惨悲苦也更加深了憾恨不幸之感。所以下面义山就更加明切地举出了另外两个相反对比的象喻：“石城景物类黄泉，夜半行郎空柘弹。”叫做“石城”的所在，在中国历史上最著名的两处：一指金陵之石头城而言，《文选》左思《吴都赋》云：“戎车盈于石城。”李善注引刘渊林曰：“建安十七年城石头。”五臣注云：“石城，石头坞也，在建业西，临江。”吕延济曰：“石头城中置府库军储，故云：‘盈于石城。’”这一个石城，是因其为六朝的都城而出名；又一石城则指湖北竟陵之石城而言，为晋羊祜之所筑，北周置石头郡于此，王应麟《地理通释》云：“三面墉基皆石造，正面绝壁，下临汉江，石城之名本此。”这一个石城则是因一个女子而出名。《旧唐书·音乐志》云：“石城在竟陵。莫愁乐者出于石城乐。石城有女子名莫愁，善歌谣，因有此歌。”石城既有不同之二地，则义山这一章诗中的石城究竟何指呢？朱鹤龄、姚培谦二家注皆引《乐府·莫愁乐》及《唐书·音乐志》为言（见前），冯浩《笺注》云：“石城……楚地之境。”张采田《会笺》亦云：“石城，楚地。”是诸家之说皆以为义山此诗中之石城乃指女子莫愁所在之石城也。关于这一点，我以为是可信的。因为义山还有另二首标题《石城》和《莫愁》的诗，也同样用的是这一故实。只是义山屡屡用之又何所取义呢？冯浩以为乃指义山所恋之女子“流转湘中”而言。张采田则以为乃指杨嗣复之出为湖南观察使而言。关于冯氏之说，张氏曾讥其诬义山以“万里浪游，窥人后房”，其说为不足信；至于张氏自己的说法，则字比句附以为义山《燕台》四首全指杨嗣复之迁贬而言。其说实更为牵强拘执，也一样不足信。撇开这些徒乱人意的说法不谈，就诗论诗，我以为此二句诗所给读者的感受，似正与前二句相承而下。同样是从相反的两面着笔，以加深表现美好之生命与受挫伤的悲哀。而且从这种感受来看，不但可以使这首诗得到恰当完满的解说，同时更可与“石城”、“莫愁”诸作相互为证，看出义山经常用这一故实的取义。第一我们该注意的乃是石城的女子名字叫做“莫愁”，这正是与义山所要写的悲愁的一个明显的对比。义山往往用莫愁的故事为无愁而美好的一种生命的象喻。《古乐府·莫愁乐》云：“莫愁在何处，莫愁石城西，艇子打两桨，催送莫愁来。”这首诗所表现的是何等轻捷愉快的欢欣之感。所以义山在《莫愁》一诗中就曾经说：“若是石城无艇子，莫愁还自有愁时。”虽然是具有美好的生命如莫愁者，而当她如果受到挫伤，不能得到与她的美好的生命相配合的事物时，她的生命就将充满哀愁而不复欢愉了。至于《石城》一诗“石城夸窈窕，花县更风流”二句，则以石城窈窕之女子莫愁为女性美好之象喻；而以于河阳县遍树桃李花之诗人潘岳为男性美好生命之象喻，这也正是我相信此章诗中之“石城景物类黄泉”一句，是指莫愁所在之石城的缘故。因为在这一句诗之后，次句的“夜半行郎空柘弹”义山就依然又用了潘岳的典故。《晋书》载：“潘岳美姿仪，少时尝挟弹出洛阳道，妇人遇之者皆连手萦绕，投之以果，满车而归。”至于义山之用“柘弹”二字，则极写其所挟之弓弹之美。冯注引《西京杂记》云：“长安五陵人以柘木为弹，真珠为丸，以弹鸟雀。”可以为证。现在如果将这二句诗合起来看，则上一句是说：石城之景物美好，乃有“艇子打两桨，催送莫愁来”之欣愉之生活，而今石城之景物竟然凄惨阴暗有类黄泉，则虽有美好之生命如莫愁者，又岂能乘艇子以嬉戏长度其欣愉之生活乎？其不可得，所可断言者也。次一句则言潘郎虽美姿仪，且挟有柘木之美好之弓弹，行于洛阳道，妇女往往掷果盈车，然而如果以夜半而出行，则如《史记·项羽本纪》所说的“衣锦夜行”，谁知赏爱者乎？故曰“空柘弹”也。“空”者徒然落空之意。有美莫赏，世无知爱之人，则丰容姿致之美，臂弓腰箭之能，并属徒然矣。“夜半”二字原只是托喻的虚写，冯注云“此四句皆夜景”已嫌过于拘实，至于三色批本《义山诗集》，朱彝尊氏竟评此句云：“不眠无聊，戏以自解”，则更是无聊的妄说了。此二句遥遥与首二句相承，皆从生命之美好与生命之受挫伤的不同的两面为相对之叙写。这正是诗人心灵深处求美满而不得，而又不甘心自弃的一种无可消融之悲苦的流露。前人之解说者，不肯从诗人感情之基本状况求解，而徒务于事迹之摭拾比附，遂往往自掘坑堑，陷于扞格不通之地。所以冯注就曾表示其不解，说：“石城二字，与石城、莫愁之作又相类，何欤？”其实如果从诗人感情之本质求解，则义山这几首诗原不必尽指一人一事，只是其内心深处所蕴蓄着的某种生命被挫伤的痛苦，以及对美好与完整之向往追求而终不可得的悲哀，则原来又正自有其基本上的一脉相通之处，这正是这几首诗颇为相类而又不能以相同之事迹为笺注解说的缘故。

以下接言“绫扇唤风阊阖天，轻帏翠幕波洄旋”（朱注作“渊旋”，冯注作“洄旋”，后者较为习见易解，故从冯注作“洄旋”）。此章首四句由夏景转入痛苦之象喻，至此再荡开笔墨重写夏景。“绫扇唤风”，原为夏日常见之景，“绫”字写扇之精美，扇摇而风生，然而义山不用“摇”字而用“唤”字，一则摇扇之手，其姿态恍如有所召唤之貌；再则下面接言“阊阖天”，此处用一“唤”字，则天人之间仿佛一若有所呼唤感应之意；三则用“唤”字可收拟人之效，使读者对扇与风之关系生更亲切活泼之想象。至于“阊阖天”三字，“阊阖”者，天门也，朱鹤龄注及姚培谦注并同。此处义山用之，一则如前所言，乃取天人之间一份呼求感应之意，二则写有风之来高远自天，昔杜甫有诗云“天清风卷幔”，必是高风清远，悠然而至，然后才可以飘帷荡幕，使之波动洄旋。此所以下一句接之以“轻帷翠幕波洄旋”也。如果只是绫扇之风，则帷幕岂能为其所飘动乎？“帷”字上着一“轻”字，使人想见其质地之柔软单薄；“幕”字上着一“翠”字，使人想见其颜色之鲜朗明丽。而“轻”与“翠”二字，又正所以唤起下面之“波”字。“轻”字使人想见“波”之动态；“翠”字使人想见“波”之颜色。至此而帷幕动摇之际，乃直如波影之洄旋矣，故曰“波洄旋”也。这两句义山似只是写夏日生活之一种情景，虽然在“绫扇唤风”“帷幕洄旋”之精微细致的描写中，亦别有寂寞无聊之感在，然除此而外，则似并无深义可求。可是这二句却极富于轻灵活泼之诗感。语云：“无用之为用大矣”，这种荡开笔墨的点染，非有敏锐之诗感及欣赏之馀裕者不能为。这正是义山诗虽在极悲苦中仍能不失其可赏玩之美感与诗意的一大原因。这二句既纯从夏日之情景作悠然的点染，下二句义山遂又掉转笔锋，对残春作送别的回顾，重新写其一贯的无休止的深情苦觅的怅惘追寻。于是乃又有“蜀魂寂寞有伴未？几夜瘴花开木棉”之句。“蜀魂”自是指蜀望帝之魂魄化为子规的故事。此在义山诗中往往用之。如其《井泥》一首之“蜀主有遗魄”，《锦瑟》一首之“望帝春心托杜鹃”，就都是用的此一故事。朱鹤龄《锦瑟诗注》引《蜀王本纪》云：“望帝使鳖灵治水，与其妻通，惭愧，且以德薄不及鳖灵，乃委国授之。望帝去时，子规方鸣，故蜀人悲子规鸣而思望帝。”又引《成都记》云：“望帝死，其魂化为鸟，名曰杜鹃，亦曰子规。”然则，“蜀魂”者原来乃是一个失去了国也失去了家的，满怀着感情上的愧疚隐痛的寂寞的魂魄。而暮春之日，鸣声凄切动人归思的杜鹃鸟，则相传正为此一怨苦哀伤之魂魄所托化。于是在子规啼血送春之际，再加上此一悲剧故事的联想，因而每一声鹃鸟的哀啼，遂都成了这一永怀憾恨之魂魄的寂寞悲哀之呼唤。如果从其哀啼之悲苦来推想，则其欲寻得一侣伴之安慰的需求，当是何等激切。以如此挚切的需求之心，他应该获得他所欲寻求的才是；然而如果从其哀啼之终于不止来推想，则他之悲寻苦觅又似乎终于未曾得到报偿。所以义山乃用疑想不定的口吻，写下了“有伴未”三个字。这种不定的口吻，正表现了诗人冀其能得而又虑其终然未得的无限同情和关爱。至于“几夜瘴花开木棉”一句，则是上一句“蜀魂寂寞”的陪衬。“木棉”，据姚培谦注引《吴录》云：“交址有木棉树，高大，实如酒杯，中有棉如絮，可作布。”孙光宪《菩萨蛮》词云：“木棉花映丛祠小，越禽声里春光晓。”郑因百先生《词选》注此句云：“木棉产热带，吾国广东等处有之，高可十丈，其花红色，种子亦有纤维，可供纺织。知木棉树之高、花之红，乃知‘映’字‘小’字之妙。”我们现在也可引申这一注解来说明义山这两句诗。“知木棉树之高、花之红，乃知在其映衬下之‘蜀魂’之益增‘寂寞’。”杜甫《登楼》诗云：“花近高楼伤客心。”高处的花，原来予人的意象就更为鲜明，而且易于引人作高远的向往，再加之以红艳的颜色，如火之燃烧，如血之凝聚的，则其所象喻着的，应该是何等深挚浓烈的一份追寻向往的情意。更何况木棉的产地在热带，提起木棉，就自然会引人发生“热”的联想，又加以“瘴花”的“瘴”字，更加重了郁蒸炎热的感觉，而“木棉”的“棉”字也会引人想到一份绵密绵远的情意。如此说来，则上一句寂寞悲哀的蜀魂，纵使终然未能有伴，而在下一句所写的如同在高处燃烧着的血一般红的瘴花的映衬下，其泣血以追寻的深情苦恋乃更为可哀，也更加无法弃绝了。冯浩注云：“木棉花红，借比炎暑。”虽然木棉的开花乃在暮春并非炎暑，只是木棉之产地及颜色则确乎能予人以一种炎热之感，因之义山此句也就更有以之映衬此章“夏”之主题之另一作用在了。至于前云“蜀魂”，后曰“瘴花”，并不属于同一之地域，则正为我在前言中所说的，义山这四首诗中的地名，原来就多为借喻之辞，并不需要加以牵附或确指的又一证明。

以下接云，“桂宫流影光难取，嫣薰兰破轻轻语”，则于长期之追寻怀想之中，仿佛如有所见之意。义山在这四首诗中，有不少地方表现了这种“如见”的情境，然而却又都是“来如春梦”“去似秋云”一般的难于逼视或捕捉。那么这种情境究竟果然是属于生命中所实有？抑或只是出于诗人心灵中之某种假想呢？我的意思以为这两种情形都有可能。以人生实有之经历言之，如大晏《木兰花》词即曾有过“燕鸿过后莺归去，细算浮生千万绪，长于春梦几多时，散似秋云无觅处”的慨叹。人生多少美好的感情，当一旦情随事迁之后，在回忆中所残存的便只是一缕如云烟似的逼取便逝的痕影了。这是义山之所以把这种情境写得分明如见而却又恍惚难得的一个原因；再则如以诗人假想中之境界言之，此种境界既出现于诗人之想象之中，则其必为诗人理想中所确信所深爱之一种境界，可以断言者也。是此境界既原非实有，却又因了怀此信心与爱意者之向往，而时时萦回心上如在目前，虽则渺远难寻，而却又分明如见。如王国维在其一首《蝶恋花》词中就曾说“忆挂孤帆东海畔，咫尺神山，海上年年见，几度天风吹棹转，望中楼阁阴晴变”的话。海上神山，分明如见，而天风吹棹，幻变难寻，这是义山之所以把这一种情境写得如此恍惚而又如此分明的又一原因。从义山的诗来看，在现实生活中义山该确曾经历过一种苦恋的情感，这是不可讳言的事实。然而另一方面，义山天性中似乎也生来就抱有一种对理想中某一不确知之完美境界之向往。而其诗作中，也就往往交揉着这种现实与理想之双重的追寻和憾恨。这也是我一直以为欣赏义山诗该从其感情之本质着眼，而不必强加区分或牵附的又一缘故。因为在义山诗中，我们经常可以见到这种交揉着理想与现实的如梦如真的追寻或憾恨之情的流露，而其情事则是并不必也不可确指的。这两句“桂宫流影光难取，嫣薰兰破轻轻语”，就写得极尽分明而又恍惚之能事。“桂宫”，朱鹤龄及姚培谦注皆云：“月宫也。”俗传月中有桂树，且为嫦娥所居之所，故曰“桂宫”。义山之所以不称之为“月宫”而称之为“桂宫”者，则因为如果直称为月，则明白拘限但指天上之明月而已，而如果称之为“桂宫”，则“庐家兰室桂为梁”，除指天上之明月外，更可使人发人间居室美好之想，而如此也就造成了义山诗中的既恍惚又真切莫辨其为真为幻的效果。“桂宫”而曰“流影”，则曹植有诗云，“明月照高楼，流光正徘徊”，“流影”二字固当指明月流泻之光影而言。而月之光影则虽可望见而不可把捉者也，故继之乃云“光难取”也。流光倾泻，映鬓投怀，而持拥无从，都归空幻，只此一句，已经表现了多少如我前面所说的“海上神山，分明可见，而天风吹棹，幻变难寻”的境界。如果必欲对这一句加以现实明白的诠释，则此句所写自当为深宵月夜之景色。而次一句之“嫣薰兰破轻轻语”，则此月色朦胧中之所闻见也。至于所闻见者为何？则从“轻轻语”三个字来看，大似其中有人呼之欲出矣。所以冯浩《笺注》就真以为实有其人云：“言月光流转，难见其貌，惟微笑私语，吹气如兰。”喜欢从外表形迹去对义山诗作狭隘的私情一面的比附探索的人，自然会有这种浅俗的说法。然而可注意的是义山自己并未尝作此径直浅俗的叙写。如果从字面来看，则此七字实极幻变之妙。一般说来，“嫣”字多用以状容颜之姣美，而“薰”字则多指气味之芳郁，“嫣”与“薰”二字连言，这是一种极巧妙的结合。至于其结合之方式，则如温飞卿一首《菩萨蛮》词中的“双鬓隔香红”一句的“香红”二字一样，乃是一种视觉与嗅觉的错综的结合。“嫣”字下用一“薰”字，则不仅香气醉人而已，其嫣然之容色乃亦大有使人薰然如醉之意矣。若欲追问义山此二字所写的嫣然姣美而又薰然醉人者究为何物？则此二字之下，岂不是明明说了“兰破”两个字吗？“兰破”当指初放之兰花而言。用一“破”字把兰花之展瓣伸蕊含苞乍破的情景，写得极生动而真切。至于下面的“轻轻语”三个字，如果从其对于前面四个字的承应而言，则此三字仍以指初破之兰花为是，实不必直指为“微笑私语”之真有其人也。若曰既是兰花如何能有言语？则古人岂不有“花如解语”之言乎？“轻轻语”者，在微风轻拂中，彼初破之兰花的嫣然而且薰然的醉人之色与香之动摇飘拂恍如有语也。此二句若谓为但指夏夜明月微风中之花影幽香固亦原无不可，然而如果从义山一向所惯写的某种属于心灵的杂有追寻与怅惘之情的境界来看，则亦大有可说：前一句“桂宫流影”是恍如有见的引人追寻的境界，“光难取”则是毕竟难寻的怅惘，既是难寻，便当断此追寻之一念，而“嫣薰”七字遂又另作一层转折，极写某一种使人情移心醉的欲罢不能谁能遣此的境界，既是深情难遣，因之乃有下二句“直教银汉堕怀中，未遣星妃镇来去”之言。相爱至深，相思至苦，此情所感，即使如天边云汉之远，亦直当使之堕我怀中，这是何等坚毅诚挚的一份情意。至于下一句之“星妃”，朱鹤龄及姚培谦注皆云：“星妃，谓织女也。”承上句“云汉”而言，则“星妃”指云汉边织女之说，当属可信。“镇来去”之“镇”字，则有终久长然或时而常常之意，如义山《无题》诗“益德冤魂终报主，阿童高义镇横秋”之“镇”字有长久之意，而其《独居有怀》一诗之“蜡花长递泪，筝柱镇移心”之“镇”字则为常常之意，此句“镇来去”之“镇”字，似以作“常”字解较胜。至于上面的“遣”字则为遣使之意，二句合看，意谓我之精诚所感，既直可使天边云汉堕我怀中，则云汉侧之星妃织女亦当长为我有，不可使之如传说中牛郎织女之故事，一年始得一度相逢，既来复去，使之常在离别相思之痛苦中也。这二句最使人感动的乃是“直教”与“未遣”两句所表现的执着坚定的口吻。纵使如云汉之遥，星妃之远，而以我之深情苦恋之一份心意，遂终信其必有长相归属聚首无分之一日，这是何等坚贞诚挚的信心和爱意。

以下陡接“浊水清波何异源，济河水清黄河浑”二句，则无情之现实，蓦然将所有一切美好的想象一击而全部归于破灭虚空。昔曹子建有诗云：“君若清路尘，妾若浊水泥，浮沉各异势，会合何时偕？”清浊异质，趋向难同，永无相偕之日，这是命定的悲剧，任谁也无法挽回的。冯浩注引《战国策》曰：“齐有清济浊河。”义山用之，盖但取其清浊之对比而已。至于此二水之在于何地，则似并不重要，而冯浩《笺注》则既以《燕台》四诗为义山学仙玉阳东有所恋于女冠之作。乃引此二句为证云：“玉阳在济源县，京师带以洪河，故曰浊水清波也。”其说似过于穿凿附会。屈复《意笺》就只说“水源之清浊既异，流亦不同，比其终不相合也”，所说极是。这二句诗紧接在前二句的一片期望和痴想之后，乃愈显得现实之隔绝的残酷无情。然而现实所能隔绝的只是物质的躯体而已，至于心灵上那一份深情苦恋的情意，却是永远没有任何事物可以将之加以隔绝的，因之义山接着就又写了“安得薄雾起缃裙，手接云軿呼太君”的两句呼求向往的话。无论经历了多少艰阻，无论遭遇到多少挫伤，一颗追寻期待的心，则终始不易。韩冬郎有诗云：“此生终独宿，到死誓相寻。”相思若此，则安得而有一日真能亲接目睹其翩然之临莅乎？义山此二句就全从假想中之临莅着笔。“缃裙”之“缃”字，姚培谦注引《韵会》云：“缃，浅黄色。”“云軿”二字冯浩注引《真诰》云“驾风骋云䡖”，又曰：“辎軿，妇人车有障蔽者。”“太君”二字，冯浩注云：“指仙女。”此二句盖将所思之对象假想为一仙女，而想象其来临之情景。裙而曰“缃裙”，一则缃之为色可予人一种柔美之感觉；再则有此颜色之描写，乃使人有恍如目睹之真实。而又于其上着以“薄雾”二字，一则状裙之既轻且薄恍如云雾之轻飘；再则可使人想见神仙之飘渺，恍如云雾之朦胧。至于下句之“云軿”自当指仙女所乘之车，杜甫《送孔巢父》诗有句云：“蓬莱织女回云车，指点虚无引归路。”彼仙女既然降自云霄，所乘者自当是云车，“霓为衣兮风为马”，“乘回风兮载云旗”，这在想象中当是何等飘逸的神致，而义山却在“云軿”二字上加了“手接”两个字，感觉何等亲切，情意何等殷勤，恍惚中乃别有真实之感。何况又在“云軿”二字下加了个“呼”字，于是在其以手亲接之际，乃更伴随有口中的低唤。此种情景该是何等可使人欣喜安慰的境界。然而我们却不要忘记在这二句开端，义山原来曾写了“安得”两个字。“安得”者，谓如何方能得致如此之境界乎？是终于未尝得也。王静安有词云：“蜡泪窗前堆一寸，人间惟有相思分。”义山这二句所写的原不是果然得见的欢愉，而只是历经艰苦挫折而终于无法磨灭的一点刻骨的相思而已。

其三　秋

此章开端“月浪衡天天宇湿，凉蟾落尽疏星入”两句，全从秋宵静夜之景色写起，凄清真切，而又不仅为一静态之景物而已，更包括了动态的时间之移转，而隐寓诗人长夜之无眠与夫怀思之深切。首句“衡天”一作“冲天”，“冲”字似过于强劲，与诗中所写秋宵静谧之感觉不合。故私意以为作“衡”字较佳。按“衡”字通“横”，有横布之意。“月浪衡天”者，谓明月之流光似浪，横布于天也。“天宇”者，《说文》云：“宇，屋边也。”引申有四方边宇之意。“天宇”自当指四方之天边而言。“天宇湿”者，谓如水之月光流布于天，于是而四方之天际皆恍如有被此流光沾湿之感也。“月浪衡天”四字仍只是平平叙写而已，益以“天宇湿”三字，则秋月之澄明朗澈，秋空之广远高寒，光波之流泻倾布，皆直如在人目前矣。而此句之佳处尚不仅在写景之真切生动而已，而更在此种景色所象喻之一种高远凄寒之境界。这是在义山诗中常可体验到的一种境界，如其《霜月》一诗之“初闻征雁已无蝉，百尺楼高水接天。青女素娥俱耐冷，月中霜里斗婵娟”。在此种境界中的诗人，该负荷着多少孤寂凄寒之感。而下一句之“凉蟾落尽疏星入”，则写在此孤寒之境界中所经历之时间之悠久漫长。“凉蟾”自然仍指天上之明月而言，盖月中传有蟾蜍，秋宵之凉月，故曰“凉蟾”。“落尽”两个字，写月之由落到尽的一段时间之感觉，写得极好。有此二字，天上之一丸凉月乃逐渐由中天而西斜而终至完全沉没了。而月光也由流波之四布而逐渐移转消褪，而终至完全隐去了。在这一段漫长的时间之感内，诗人所承受着的无可温慰的孤寒与无可挽回的消逝的双重之悲感是可以想见的。而义山笔下所写的却只是“月浪”、“天宇”、“凉蟾”而已，并未尝着叙写人事之一字。直至“疏星入”三字，才隐然有自天上转向人间之意。冯浩注云：

"月既落，则星光入户。"星光在天上，诗人在户内，此"疏星入"三字，不仅写出了明月已经完全落尽以后之又一凄寒之景象，使读者益觉时间之久长，景物之寥寂，而且此凄寒之感更直自天上逼向人间，是诗人虽欲无愁，有不可得者矣。所以下面乃全从人事着笔，写出了"云屏不动掩孤嚬，西楼一夜风筝急"的一个长夜无眠的人物。"云屏"，义山诗中屡用之，其《为有》一首云："为有云屏无限娇，凤城寒尽怕春宵。"冯浩注引《西京杂记》云："昭仪上赵皇后物，有云母屏风。"义山《嫦娥》诗亦有句云："云母屏风烛影深，长河渐落晓星沉。"知义山诗中往往以"云屏"或"云母屏风"写居室之精美与长夜之寂寥，以及屏内人哀怨之幽深，此句亦然。曰："云屏不动掩孤嚬"。"嚬"者，颦眉之意，愁怨之貌。太白《怨情》有句云："美人卷珠帘，深坐颦蛾眉，但见泪痕湿，不知心恨谁。"云屏深掩，独坐孤颦，不着一哀怨字样，而哀怨自深。"云屏"而曰"不动"者，言屏风之镇长深掩，不动不移，正以之写愁怨之幽深之终于不解也。至于下一句之"风筝"，冯浩注云："吹之牵之，使远去也。"似以"风筝"为纸鸢之俗名，而姚培谦注引杜诗注云："风筝，谓挂筝于风际，风至则鸣也。"则"风筝"盖檐间铁马之类，当从姚注为是。"西楼一夜风筝急"七字，当与上句合看，是在云屏深掩之中的独坐孤嚬之人，已听尽西楼一夜之风动筝鸣也。而其下又着一"急"字，则风声与筝声之凄紧哀切可知。此一句之七字，正为孤嚬之人长夜之所闻，而开端二句，自"月浪衡天"直至"凉蟾落尽"十四字，则孤嚬之人长夜之所见。上下合看，乃更觉"云屏不动掩孤嚬"一句哀怨之深切。而其不动与深掩之中，更蕴含了多少对此孤寂凄寒之境界一意承受负荷的坚贞的心力。

在这种承受与负荷中，相思与苦怨同样深切，所以诗人接下去就写了"欲织相思花寄远，终日相思却相怨"的两句话，相思之情假如果然可化为可见之具象，则其必为色香绝艳之花朵殆无可疑，于是当相思至极而无可寄托之时，乃直欲将所有的相思之情尽化为一丝一缕以编织出象喻着相思的美艳的花朵，而投寄于以全生命怀恋着的远人。然而音尘阻隔，纵有欲织之心而无投寄之所，清真词有句云："怨怀无托，嗟情人断绝，信音辽邈"，在无情的隔绝之下，无尽的相思乃尽化为无边的怨怀，所以说"终日相思却相怨"也。由相思而转为相怨，其原因乃同出于一份无法泯灭的深沉的爱意，除非能做到无爱，才能做到无怨，然而这是抱此爱心之人永远无法做到的。所以用"相思"与"相怨"互为呼应，"相思"见爱之挚切，"相怨"见爱之悲苦，而其上又加以"终日"二字，于是诗人之感情乃始终辗转于挚切而痛苦的爱恋中，永无脱解之时矣。其下"但闻北斗声回环，不见长河水清浅"，则所写者乃是在此种感情之辗转中的光阴之流逝，以及人间天上永远无法迈越之一种隔绝的象喻。关于北斗之回环，原来就代表着光阴之流逝。或以之纪一岁之迁替，如孟浩然《田家元日》诗之"昨夜斗回北，今朝岁起东"，或以之纪长夜之渐深，如《古乐府·善哉行》之"月没参横，北斗阑干"。义山此诗自"月浪衡天""凉蟾落尽"写起，原不过写一夜之间的不眠相思之苦而已，而北斗之回环，则不仅一夜之间，其方位每时而不同，一年之间其方位亦每日而不同，着此一句，于是诗人所写的相思之苦，遂更有自一夜如此而扩及到夜夜如此之意。义山另一首《嫦娥》诗有句云，"碧海青天夜夜心"，这是何等孤寂哀苦，何等恒久不灭的相思。而义山更在"北斗"与"回环"之上，分别加了一个"闻"字与一个"声"字，是北斗之回转乃竟可于耳中分明闻见其声，把光阴流逝之感觉写得如此真实，而相思之悲苦也就因之而更加深切了。而义山却更在此句之下紧接了一句"不见长河水清浅"，"长河"，自指天上之银汉而言，自古以来，这横亘中天的银汉，就一直是有情人被阻隔的象征。魏文帝《燕歌行》有句云："星汉西流夜未央，牵牛织女遥相望，尔独何辜限河梁。"义山《西溪》一首亦有句云："人间从到海，天上莫为河。"而今则不仅天上为河而已，此横亘中天之一水，更且永不见其有清浅之时。于是这种无法迈越的阻隔就成了永恒的定命了。而此句之"不见"二字又遥遥与上一句之"但闻"

二字相呼应，“但”者，徒然仅只之意，谓徒仅闻北斗回环之声，一任相思之悲苦若此，一任光阴之流转如斯，而终于不见横亘之长河有清浅之日，则人之悲苦，时之转移，都于此永恒之睽隔无丝毫之补赎矣。这真是心断望绝极哀苦的两句话。

其下“金鱼锁断红桂春，古时尘满鸳鸯茵”，则写一切美好之事物的同归不幸之遭遇。姚培谦注云：“金鱼，鱼钥也。《芝田录》：‘门钥必以鱼，取其不瞑目，守夜之意。’”按，钥谓门户之键锁也，见《方言》。锁钥而取鱼之状，则长夜不瞑的看守，使被扃锁者将永无可以遁逃之隙；鱼而为金，则坚刚牢固，被扃锁者更永无可以将之破毁之时，于是被键锁者遂真将闭绝终生，无复得见天光之一日矣。至于“桂”而曰“红”，又曰“春”，一般多以为桂树秋日始花，其实不然，亦有春日作花者。王维《鸟鸣涧》诗云“人闲桂花落，夜静春山空”，可以为证；又，一般多以为桂树之花多为黄、白二色，其实亦有红色者，李时珍《本草纲目》云：“花有白者，名银桂；黄者名金桂；红者，名丹桂。有秋花者，春花者，四季花者。”可见“桂”之可以为“红”，亦可以为“春”，而义山之用“红”与“春”则取此二字所象喻之颜色与时节之美好而已，初不必考其品种也。夫以如此美好之颜色，生当如此美好之时节，而金鱼之钥乃将其美好之生命一举而锁断终身，于是这一树红桂之春遂命定要在幽暗闭锁之中自开自落，永远不会有看到光明，永远不会有得到知爱的日子，这是何等可憾恨的美好之生命的悲剧。次句“尘满鸳鸯茵”，则义山又标举出另一无生命的美好之事物的悲剧。朱鹤龄注：“茵，褥也。”又引《西京杂记》云：“飞燕为皇后，其女弟上遗鸳鸯茵。”鸳鸯原为美满幸福之象，而茵褥亦令人生温柔旖旎之想，如温飞卿词所写的“暖香惹梦鸳鸯锦”，这才是鸳鸯茵所当有的情境。而今义山竟于其上用了“古时尘满”四个字，“鸳鸯茵”而为尘土所沾蔽，已是对此美好之事物的毁废不珍，沾“尘”而至于竟“满”，则其毁废之甚可知，又加以“古时”二字，则其毁废直乃自古而然，曾未尝一得珍爱之日，这是何等可惋惜的不幸的遭遇。于此再回顾上一句，则有生的红桂之春，固已是终生锁断；无生的鸳鸯之褥乃竟亦自古沾尘，在如此充满悲剧性的宇宙之内，人类之难逃此相类似之命运，自然也是必然的了。所以义山在下面接着就写了两件人世间的悲剧："堪悲小苑作长道，玉树未怜亡国人。"朱鹤龄注引《南史》云："文惠太子求东田起小苑。"这句诗里的小苑，并不必指文惠太子所起的小苑，义山只是泛指一些精美的园林宫苑而已。而一切美丽的宫苑，似乎也都注定了必然有归于荒芜败落的下场。早自阮籍《咏怀》就曾经有过"繁华有憔悴，堂上生荆杞"的慨叹，此种盛衰兴亡之变，原是自古而然的。只是唐代自安史之乱以后，这种变化，更是尤其显然可见，因此引起诗人的悲慨也就更多。如杜甫《曲江》诗的"江上小堂巢翡翠，苑边高冢卧麒麟"，《哀江头》的"江头宫殿锁千门，细柳新蒲为谁绿"，盖皆慨旧时苑囿之败废荒凉者也。义山自己的一首《曲江》诗，也曾有"望断平时翠辇过，空闻子夜鬼悲歌"之句，则更是写得凄凉哀切无限深悲。盖义山此诗原在慨文宗之重修曲江亭馆而旋有甘露之变；世变惊心，原非泛泛的叙写可比。高步瀛先生《唐宋诗举要》注义山《曲江》诗曾引《旧唐书·文宗纪》云："太和九年冬十月，内出曲江……上好为诗，每诵杜甫《曲江行》（按：当是《哀江头》）云：'江头宫殿锁千门，细柳新蒲为谁绿。'乃知天宝以前曲江四岸皆有行宫、台殿、百司、廨署，思复升平故事，故为楼殿以壮之。……十一月……中尉仇士良率兵诛宰相王涯……等十馀家，皆族诛。"又引《资治通鉴·唐纪》曰："十二月甲申敕罢修曲江亭馆。"又云："安史乱后，曲江亦日就芜废，起二句（按：指"望断平时翠辇过"二句），言巡幸久旷，夜鬼悲歌，状当时曲江之荒凉也。"此外如白居易《勤政楼西柳》之"半朽临风树，多情立马人，开元一株柳，长庆二年春"及刘禹锡《杨柳枝》的"花萼楼前初种时，美人楼上斗腰支，而今抛掷长街里，露叶如啼欲恨谁"，虽然不明咏宫苑之荒废，但也同样是这一份盛衰的悲慨。义山此诗之"小苑作长道"当然不必拘指为安史乱后唐代之宫苑，既不必是通夹城的花萼楼，也不必是近曲江的芙蓉苑。然义山以宫苑之荒废取为诗中之象喻，则未必不有其身经目睹之一份时代之阴影在也。“小苑作长道”者，谓当年之离宫禁苑，乃一旦竟成为来往之长街矣。人世间原没有一件事物是可以恒久保持其完整美好而不变的，所以下面接下去又说“玉树未怜亡国人”。姚培谦注引《陈书》云：“后主制新曲，有《玉树后庭花》。”陈后主既为亡国之君主，后庭花更是一向被目为亡国之歌谶，玉树亡国之人，自当是指如同陈后主一样倾覆败亡的人。可注意的是，义山却于其间加了“未怜”二字，此二字须与上一句之“堪悲”二字合看，其意盖谓可悲者乃在此小苑之竟为长道，而不在彼玉树亡国之人也。何则？“小苑作长道”并不确指，乃是千古由盛而衰一切美好之事物皆不得保全的共同的象喻；“玉树亡国人”则仅为一个朝代的一个君主而已，何况陈后主之败亡，更有其由于自取的咎责在。《人间词话》曾经说：“政治家之眼域于一人一事，诗人之眼则通古今而观之。”“小苑作长道”是千古的兴亡悲慨，“玉树亡国人”则是一人的得失成败。曰“堪悲”，曰“未怜”者，意谓宇宙之可悲者，乃在凡一切美好之事物之终归于毁废，而非仅只某一人某一事之堪为怜惜而已。如此我们方能体会得出“未怜”二字原来并非真的不怜，而是有更超过于此种哀怜的更为永恒深切的悲痛在。于此再回看前二句之锁断的红桂之春，尘满的鸳鸯之茵，乃知义山所见之世界，原来乃是整体的绝望堪悲，并不仅限于一人一事而已。

下面“瑶琴愔愔藏楚弄，越罗冷薄金泥重”，则与第二章《夏》之“绫扇唤风阊阖天，轻帷翠幕波洄旋”二句，有异曲同工之妙。都别具一种富于美感与诗意的笔墨荡漾之致。只是此二句似乎更有较深之意味可求。“愔愔”，姚培谦注引《左传注》云：“愔愔，安和貌。”朱鹤龄及冯浩注引嵇康《琴赋》云：“愔愔琴德，不可测兮。”《文选》李善注引《韩诗》曰：“愔愔，和悦貌。”又引《声类》曰：“和静貌。”是“愔愔”本写琴音之安柔和美，而义山却于“愔愔”二字之下又写了“藏楚弄”三个字，朱鹤龄注及姚培谦注并引《琴历》云：“琴曲有《蔡氏五弄》，又有九引，九曰楚引。”按：弄原为曲调之意，楚弄或楚引，盖谓楚曲楚调之意。而自屈子之《离骚》以来，楚音楚调似乎就一直代表着一种忧愁幽思的音调。其后如陶渊明之诗，有标题为“怨诗楚调”者，而其诗中又有“悲歌”之语，是楚调原为悲怨之音。义山所谓“瑶琴愔愔藏楚弄”者，盖谓听其琴音虽外若安柔和美，而实含有忧愁幽怨之思。这种揉杂反衬的句法，写出了多少人世间外若美好而中含苦痛的境界和心情。至于下面的“越罗”一句，则也同样是一种揉杂反衬的象喻。姚培谦注引《唐书》云：“越州土贡，花文宝花等罗。”夫越地所产之罗，其质地原以轻软绵薄为美。质地既薄，自多寒冷之感，故曰“冷薄”。至于“金泥”，则当为薄罗上以金屑涂饰之花纹。朱鹤龄注引《锦裙记》云：“惆怅金泥簇蝶裙。”金之色彩既予人以富丽秾艳之思，金之质地亦予人沉实凝重之感，而今轻罗之上乃着以金泥之涂饰，则金之富丽与罗之凄冷为一层对比，金之沉重与罗之轻软为又一层对比，以彼轻罗之软，对此金泥之沉重，有多少负荷之感；而以彼轻罗之冷，对此金泥之附着，又当有多少亲切之情。义山此二句所表达出的人心中之一种极错综复杂的情意，原不是可以言语说明的。我之解说只是勉力说明对此种不可解说之境界的一点个人感受而已。假如像冯浩的《笺注》，必指此二句为“想其人之夜起弹琴”，以及“弹琴时之服饰”，则未免死于句下，大为辜负了义山一片幽微深曲的情意。至于下二句：“帘钩鹦鹉夜惊霜，唤起南云绕云梦。”则一方面既与上二句相承，使此种复杂反衬之情境更得荡漾之致，一方面则用此“霜”字回头重点本章标题之“秋”字。先说“鹦鹉”二字，夫鹦鹉之为鸟，一则毛色美丽，能供人愉悦爱赏之玩；二则灵性慧黠，能效人语言婉转之声；三则多豢养于闺阁园亭之中，能令人生旖旎繁华之想，如温飞卿《南歌子》词之“手里金鹦鹉，胸前绣凤凰，偷眼暗形相，不如从嫁与，作鸳鸯”，晏同叔《玉楼春》词之“朱帘半下香销印，二月东风催柳信，琵琶旁畔且寻思，鹦鹉前头休借问”，这种多情旖旎的风光，才是鹦鹉所当处的环境。然而义山却于“帘钩鹦鹉”四字之后用了“夜惊霜”三个字，于是前四字的旖旎温柔遂与后三字之孤寂凄寒造成了极强烈鲜明的对比，而隐隐与前面一串表示复杂反衬之情意的句子相呼应。至于“帘钩”二字亦不仅写鹦鹉栖息之处所而已，更且为由鸟而转至人，由帘外之凄寒转至帘内之绮梦的一个过渡的桥梁。有此二字，于是诗人之笔乃可以由鹦鹉之夜惊霜而转移至南云之绕云梦了。朱鹤龄注引《陆机赋》云“指南云以寄钦”，又引《高唐赋序》云：“昔者楚襄王与宋玉游于云梦之台，望高唐之观。”义山笔下的“南云”，我以为乃是一种热情怀思之梦的征象。云的绵柔飘渺，正如一片绵远的怀思，或一片渺茫的梦境。至于云而必曰“南云”者，则因为在中国诗人一般的意念中，“北”字所引起人的联想乃是寒冷孤绝，而“南”字所引起人的联想则是热烈多情。假如怀思的梦果然像一朵云的话，那么“南云”所象喻的梦，当然该是更为热情更为绮丽的一份梦境。何况下面又着以“绕云梦”三个字，从朱鹤龄注所引宋玉的《高唐赋》来看，则“云梦”二字原暗示有一段多情旖旎的高唐之梦的故实在。其实如果撇开这段故实不谈，只从义山所用的字面来看，自其梦魂所象喻的南云，到其梦魂所萦绕的云梦，这种字面的呼应，便已经足以引起人无限的怀思遐想了。至于这句开端的“唤起”二字，屈复《意笺》云“‘南云绕云梦’谓方在高唐梦中，乃鹦鹉惊霜而动帘钩遂惊醒也。”昔金昌绪《春怨》诗有句云：“打起黄莺儿，莫教枝上啼，啼时惊妾梦，不得到辽西。”苏东坡《水龙吟》词亦有句云：“梦随风万里，寻郎去处，又还被莺呼起。”义山此句之“唤起”二字，当然亦大有可能为梦境被惊醒呼起之意。只是我个人读这首诗却一直有着与这种解说并不相同的另一份感受。我以为“唤起”乃是“引起”之意，不仅不是把梦惊破，而且正是把梦引起。我更以为此处“南云”其象喻的梦境，并非真实睡梦中之境界，而只是诗人心魂所萦想的一种如痴如梦的境界。我之所以作此想者，一则这一首诗从开端的“月浪衡天”、“凉蟾落尽”以及“一夜风筝”、“北斗回环”诸句来看，则诗人所写者，终夜之久并无成眠入梦之事。既未尝入梦，则如何能有梦被惊醒之可能？再则如屈氏所说“方在高唐梦中”云云，其说既不免于拘狭落实，且颇近于平浅鄙俗，与义山《燕台》四诗全以象喻之笔法写诗人心魂间一种窈眇幽微之境界的作风并不相合；三则如果依我之所解说，“唤起南云”为引起一份如“南云”一般绵邈的怀思梦想，则与上一句之鹦鹉惊霜乃造成了另一鲜明之对比。我们试看义山这一首诗中所写的种种境界，无不暗含有对比之意味，如红桂春之竟遭锁断，鸳鸯茵之自古沾尘，与夫小苑之变为长道，瑶琴之暗藏楚弄，都是以缺憾或悲哀来反衬美满与幸福之不能长保。而现在这两句则是用另一种反衬的笔法以南云之绕云梦的温柔绵渺来反衬鹦鹉之夜惊霜的寂寞凄寒，以表现虽在悲凄孤寂的绝望中，却终于无法泯灭其对幸福与美满之追求和向往的一点未死的心魂。所以用“唤起”二字，其意若云正是因为眼前所有的只是凄寒，才更引起诗人对眼前所没有的温馨的追寻和怀想。千回万转，欲罢不能。这样体会这两句诗，岂不较之直释为睡梦之被鸟啼惊醒为更有深意。

下面的“双珰丁丁联尺素，内记湘川相识处”二句，就正是承继着前面的一份追寻怀想之情而接写下去的。按:“珰”为耳上之珠饰，见《风俗通》；“尺素”则为书简之意，见《文选·饮马长城窟行》。“双珰丁丁联尺素”，自当指尺素之书简内附有丁丁之一双耳珰之意。惟是此事果为实有乎？抑或仅为对多情相知之境界之一种向往乎？冯浩《笺》云:“尺素双珰，诗中屡见，盖实事也。钱氏（按：指钱木庵）谓女郎寄来；或谓义山寄与；未知孰是？有寄必有答，彼此同之矣。”朱鹤龄注云:“即前诗玉珰。”朱氏所云，盖指义山另一首《春雨》诗之“玉珰缄札何由达，万里云罗一雁飞”二句而言。如果从这二句来看，大似义山欲寄与而无从之意。然而如果从这一章的“双珰丁丁联尺素”二句来看，则又大似女郎寄来之意。此所以冯注虽指为“实事”，而又终不能确定其事实究竟如何之故。其实寄物投赠之事只是相爱之深相思之切的一种表示而已。从《诗经》的“投我以木桃，报之以琼瑶；投我以木李，报之以琼玖”，其投赠之物，就已经并不完全是实指了。其后张衡《四愁诗》的“美人赠我金错刀，何以报之英琼瑶”；“美人赠我金琅玕，何以报之双玉盘”；“美人赠我貂襜褕，何以报之明月珠”；“美人赠我锦绣缎，何以报之青玉案”，一连四章，更是全属托喻。此外如洛水赠珠，汉皋解佩的故事，则更衍为神话之传说。义山诗中屡见“尺素”“双珰”之字样，虽然可能为实有之情事，然而义山用来所表示的却已并非仅只外表的一件事实而已，而是象喻着某种全心交托付与的一种相思相爱的情意。所以“珰”而曰“双珰”，更以“丁丁”之音，状其灵巧精美，而更联以尺素之书，则其所显示之情意的深切可知。至于下一句之“内记湘川相识处”，承上句而言，当然该是尺素书中的言语。韦庄词有句云：“记得那年花下，深夜，初识谢娘时。”晏几道词亦有句云：“记得小蘋初见，两重心字罗衣。”可见当爱情发生之时，那初识的一段使我们全心被撼动的日子，是何等难以忘怀。所以无论睽隔多么久远，而当日湘川相识之情事则依然历历如新，而今日书中，亦仍以其深情苦想而琐琐忆及。至于“湘川”二字，冯浩及张尔田皆以为实指，冯氏曰：“是其人先至湘川，及义山抵湘，得一相识，而其人又他往，故屡以此事追慨”；张氏曰：“‘双珰’二句，记其人私书约我湘川相见。”虽然这种说法并无充分的证据以证其必为实指，但我们也没有充分的反证以证其必非实指。只是我以为“湘川”二字，除了把它看成地名之实指外，在文学表现的艺术上，还可以更有其他的作用。其一，“湘川”之“湘”字，与相识之“相”字声音相同，如此就收到了一种音乐性的重沓呼应的效果，更增加了情意之绵密深切的一份感觉。如同李白《长相思》一诗之“长相思，在长安”二句，就也是接连用了两个“长”字以唤起一种相思之绵长悠远的感觉。其二，“湘川”之地名所使人联想到的乃是湘灵二妃娥皇、女英泣竹成斑的一段哀怨的故事，以及死后化为湘水之神的一段神话的传说，因此“湘川”二字遂同时给予了读者以一份相思哀怨的情调，和一份不尽属于人间的幻想的意味。如此则即使湘川二字为实有之地名，而在诗歌之表现艺术上，也早已带上了若干象喻的色彩了。晏同叔有词云：“闻琴解佩神仙侣，挽断罗衣留不住。”纵使有双珰尺素的解佩的情谊，纵使是湘川相识的神仙的侣伴，然而也终于有相离相失的一日。从义山的诗句来看，这二句就该正是写相离失后的怀思。既然是一切美好的都终将失落，于是乃有结尾二句“歌唇一世衔雨看，可惜馨香手中故”的叹息。姚培谦注云：“衔雨看，应是泪雨。”“歌唇”自当指所思者之歌唇，李后主词云“一曲清歌，暂引樱桃破”，此所谓“歌唇”也。能面对如此之歌唇，固真当可以忘忧者矣。然而乃满眼衔如雨之泪而对之者，就前二句双珰尺素的别后怀思来看，则此歌唇盖当为记忆中之歌唇，并非眼前所实有。“衔雨”者，则今日含泪之相忆也。然而义山乃于此着一“看”字，于是此歌唇在记忆中遂有如见之真实。惟其在记忆中之歌唇有如见之真实，是以不能忍泪之如雨也。再则义山于此又重用对比之法，以加强一切幸福美好之事物之终必归于憾恨不幸之结局的永恒性的悲剧之感，所以歌唇之美乃承之以雨泪之悲者也。而义山之苦恨深悲至此犹未能尽，遂又更承之以下一句之“可惜馨香手中故”。朱彝尊评曰：“末句即指尺素。”然则此“馨香”二字盖当指寄书者手泽之芳香也。陆放翁《菊枕诗》有句云：“人间万事销磨尽，只有清香似旧时。”到了人世的一切都已销磨净尽，而只剩下当年的一缕馀香的时候，固已足以使人肠断魂销。而义山乃更进一步地说出了“馨香手中故”五个字。是并此一缕残馀之香气又岂能常相保有乎？更无奈者，则是此馨香之渐故乃即在珍惜者的手上掌中。以如此不可尽的深情，面对如此不可返的消逝，这是人世间何等可哀痛憾惜的情事。夫然后知开端所下“可惜”二字之悲痛的深切沉重。而“馨香”二字所代表之一切美好幸福之象喻，与“手中故”三字所显示的纵使有多少深情也无从补赎的长恨深悲，则又岂是朱彝尊评语所云“当指寄书”的实指所可拘限得住的？义山有诗云：“姮娥捣药无时已，玉女投壶未肯休。何日桑田俱变了，不教伊水向东流。”这种无已的深情，这种东流的长恨，何日桑田能变而伊水能西，如可赎兮，人百其身。

其四　冬

这是《燕台四首》的最后一章，也是四首中写得最为绝望的一章诗。开端“天东日出天西下，雌凤孤飞女龙寡”，只两句，就写尽了万古以来人世间的无常与缺憾的深悲。首句“天东”“天西”是何等鲜明的对比，才曰“出”便曰“下”，是何等匆遽的无常。孟子曰：“见其生不忍见其死。”而这句诗所给予我们的感受，则是方见其生即见其死，如此强烈不稍假借地展示着俯攫向人间的无常的巨灵之掌，这是多么使人恐惧战怖的一种认知。李白《拟古》诗云：“长绳难系日，自古共悲辛。”挥戈的鲁阳，追日的夸父，写下了千古以来在无常中作绝望之挣扎者的悲剧。义山这一句诗的“天东日出天西下”，就是把这一绝望无常的自古悲辛表现得极鲜明具体的七个字。我们看他从“天东”蓦然接到“天西”的口吻之斩截，以及其用上声马韵的“下”为韵字，所表现的声调之高亢，都在在表现出了对此一无常之断然无可挽赎的战怖和深悲。在中国诗中，写无常之哀感的作品很多，而写得如此简截具体使人震撼的，则并不多见。而义山这句诗的好处，还并不仅在其予人的一份震撼而已，更在其与标题之“冬”字的一种相关连的呼应。“天东”，“天西”，“日出”，“日下”，一日之迟暮如此，一岁之迟暮亦然，那是所有光明温暖和生机的终结的消逝，古诗云：“浩浩阴阳移，年命如朝露。”义山这一句的七个字，强烈地使人感受到了生命无常的绝望的深悲。而次一句的“雌凤孤飞女龙寡”则强烈地使人感受到人生永无圆满之日的缺憾的极恨。“雌凤”与“女龙”，义山于此又用了另一种强调的对比手法。“雌”与“女”是性别之相同，“凤”与“龙”是种类之相异，凤之雌者既孤飞，龙之女者亦长寡，这种异类而同命的不幸，正显示着世间所有不同族类的共同的憾恨。于是这种缺憾乃不复为某一特殊之不幸，而成为了千古有生命者之共同的不幸，因而下面义山就更切近地写出了有生之物中的属于人类的悲剧："青溪白石不相望，堂中远甚苍梧野。"朱鹤龄注引《古今乐录》云："神弦歌十一曲，五曰白石郎，六曰青溪小姑，'青溪白石'正指此也。"按《青溪小姑曲》云："开门白水，侧近桥梁，小姑所居，独处无郎。"又《白石郎曲》云："积石如玉，列松如翠，郎艳独绝，世无其二。"我们看《青溪曲》中所写的水侧桥边表现的是何等风神；而《白石郎曲》中所写的"积石如玉，列松如翠"更是何等坚贞秀美的资质。世果有如此之独处的小姑与如此绝艳的郎君，固真当永结为同生并命之侣伴，然而义山却在"青溪白石"四字之下用了"不相望"三个字。遂使原当属于同生并命之侣伴终生睽隔永无相见之日，所以下面遂更承接了一句："堂中远甚苍梧野。"姚培谦注引《礼记·檀弓》云："舜葬于苍梧之野，盖二妃未之从也。"舜与娥皇、女英二妃死生离别之事，在中国文学中一向都被目为最具代表性的悲剧故事。其原因约有以下数端：一则人世间之离别恨事原可分为生离与死别二种，或则万里相思，或则终生抱恸，而舜与皇、英二女之离别，则是从生离转为死别的兼有双重性质的悲剧；再则舜葬九嶷之山，《山海经》云："南方苍梧之丘，苍梧之渊，其中有九嶷山，舜之所葬。"郭璞注云："山在今零陵营道县南，其山九溪皆相似，故云九疑。"李白《远别离》云："九疑联绵皆相似，重瞳孤坟竟何是。"按《史记·项羽本纪》云："舜目盖重瞳子。"此孤坟自当指帝舜之坟，是皇、英二女与帝舜之离别乃不仅由生离转为死别而已，更且孤坟野葬，并其埋葬之地亦复不可确知，人间憾恨，孰甚于此；三则《述异记》云："昔舜南巡而葬于苍梧之野，尧之二女娥皇、女英追之不及，相与恸哭，泪下沾竹，竹上文为之斑斑然。"李白《远别离》又有句云："苍梧山崩湘水绝，竹上之泪乃可灭。"然而山川不改，竹泪长存，则此死生离别的永恒的隔绝失落之恸乃真将亘古而不灭矣；义山所用"苍梧野"三字，原来乃深含如许悲苦绝望之情在。然而义山又于其上着以"堂中远甚"四字。"远甚"者，谓其隔绝之远尤有过之也。于是帝舜与皇、英二女之隔绝的悲剧遂重见于人世之画堂中矣。李白《远别离》诗云："海水直下万里深，谁人不言此离苦？"而韦庄《浣溪沙》词乃云"咫尺画堂深似海"。是寻常人世之咫尺画堂，其隔绝之苦乃真有甚于苍梧之远，而其离恨亦真有过于海水之万里者矣。

在"青溪"与"白石"不相望的隔绝中，其足以冻彻心魂的孤寂凄寒不言可知，故其下乃云："冻壁霜华交隐起，芳根中断香心死。""壁"字自当是环堵四壁之意。所以张采田《玉谿生年谱会笺》乃云："冻壁句，点景。"其意盖以为"冻壁霜华"乃冬日居室中之实景。而私意以为义山《燕台四首》原非写实之作，此句亦当不仅指现实之屋壁而已，而当指精神感情上一种孤寒隔绝的境界：用一"壁"字者，正取其环阻而隔绝之意；用一"冻"字者，则取其凄清寒冷之感。曰"冻壁"，则诗人遂完全处于彻骨之凄寒的环锁之中矣。而又曰"霜华交隐起"，将此一闭锁之凄寒更写得如此悱恻迷离，而且真切如见。"交"者，写霜华之浓密交杂；"隐"者，写霜华之朦胧隐约；"起"字则写霜华结壁之渐积渐厚。这是一种在凝静幽美中逼人走向死亡之境界。在此境界中，乃更无有情之生命可以延续生存。所以下句乃曰："芳根中断香心死。""根"字之植根何等幽邃；"心"字之衷怀何等深切；"芳"字、"香"字，何等美好芳醇。然而以如此美好的生命之根株乃竟然中断；以如此芳醇之衷怀的心蕊，乃竟致死亡，若使美好之事物尽皆下场如此，则天下更有什么可以使人期待信赖的希望？故曰："浪乘画舸忆蟾蜍，月娥未必婵娟子。""浪乘"之"乘"字诸本皆同，唯冯浩注本作"秉"字，当系误字。"蟾蜍"盖指月而言，冯注引张衡《灵宪》曰："姮娥托身于月，是为蟾蜍。""画舸"者，画船之意，《方言》曰："南楚江湘凡船大者谓之舸。""乘画舸"而"忆蟾蜍"，诸家皆无解说。私意以为此盖为诗人之一种假想，原不必有什么出处故实。至于其引发此种假想之故，则约有二因：一则旧传有人曾乘槎至天河见牛女而后返，载《博物志》及《荆楚岁时记》。既有人可乘槎而至天河，则安见无人可乘舟而至月宫乎？此其联想产生之一因；

再则月光如水，流波似浪，前于说第三章时，曾引义山霜月诗“百尺楼高水接天”之句，亦可作此句注脚。“水”字正指如波之月光，水既“接天”，则乘此流波岂不正可直抵月宫，此所以生此联想之又一因。如诚然有画舸可乘，则于明月之流波中，岂不真欲作直泛月宫之想，故曰“乘画舸”“忆蟾蜍”也。至于其上着一“浪”字，则虚枉落空之意，如虚语曰浪语，空信曰浪信，徒作泛舟至月宫之想，而实不可得，故曰“浪乘画舸忆蟾蜍”也。且也，纵使直抵月宫得见月娥，又果能如我所想象期待之美好乎？则又殊未可断言者也。故曰“月娥未必婵娟子”也。从前我的一位老师曾写过两句词说：“谁信今朝花下见，不如夙昔梦中来，空花今后为谁开。”是说所追求的梦想终于在现实中完全破灭之堪悲。至于义山此二句诗，则更有双重之悲感在。一则此梦想原来就并无实现之可能；再则于未曾实现此梦想之前，固早已知其必归于破灭之下场。人生而有此双重悲感的认知，于是此封锁于冻壁霜华中的心魂，遂更无温暖复苏之望矣。

继之以“楚管蛮弦愁一概，空城舞罢腰支在”，则写哀愁一例，妙舞终销的悲慨。此二句中，曰“管”，曰“弦”，曰“舞”，原该是何等歌舞欢乐的场面。然而无论其为“楚管”，为“蛮弦”，却总是一概的哀愁，其所以然者，一则听歌之人心中有愁，则无论其所闻者为管为弦乃全成为有愁之曲；再则，一弹三叹，慷慨馀哀，凡一切足以使人入耳动心的歌曲，原来就都含有可发人哀愁的因素在；三则，义山此句原来乃更象喻着有欢乐都虚惟哀愁永在的深悲，故有“愁一概”之言。至于次句的“空城舞罢”，舞而至于罢，固已是生命中一段美好活动的终结，其上又着以“空城”二字，昔鲍照《芜城赋》有句云：“边风急兮城上寒，井径灭兮丘陇残，千龄兮万代，共尽兮何言。”则其可哀者乃不仅为一人之舞罢而已，乃更含有千龄万代同归空灭之深哀。何况就此句之“空城舞罢”四字之口吻言之，大似舞者纵然未罢之时，亦不过舞向空城而已，如此则舞罢是第一层可哀，城空是第二层可哀，未罢之前的舞向空城是第三层可哀。而义山却于此重重的幻灭之后偏偏写了“腰支在”三个字。昔陆放翁有《咏梅》词云：“零落成泥碾作尘，只有香如故。”纵使赏爱无人，纵使生机都尽，然而惟梅花的一缕香气，惟舞者的一段腰支，却是抵死难销的，虽然，纵有如此坚贞之资质，却又终于抵不过人间冷漠与无常的磨损，此梅花之所以终于成泥作尘，舞者之所以终于空城罢舞。义山这七个字真是万转千回道尽了所有有情者的极恨深悲。既然一切美好的生命都无法逃免被磨蚀毁损的不幸，于是乃有下二句之“当时欢向掌中销，桃叶桃根双姊妹”的叹息。欢乐之终销，已是可哀之事，而更为使人感到无可奈何的乃是义山所用的“掌中”二字，《西厢记》写张生对莺莺之痴恋，有句云：“我得时节手掌儿里奇擎，心坎儿上温存，眼皮儿上供养。”擎向“掌中”，是何等珍爱的情意，然而欢乐之终销却并未尝因此一份珍重爱惜的情意而能作稍久之延长。于此义山乃更着以一“向”字，于是欢乐乃竟向珍爱者之掌中眼见其销亡矣。这是何等可伤痛的事。至于所销亡之欢乐的象喻为何？则下一句之“桃叶桃根双姊妹”也。《古今乐录》云：“晋王献之妾名桃叶，其妹曰桃根，献之尝临渡歌以送之。”苏雪林女士以此句为实指，所以在其《玉溪诗谜》一书中说：“桃叶桃根表明卢氏等乃系姊妹。”以为乃指宫嫔飞鸾、轻凤二姊妹而言。而顾翊群之《李商隐评论》则驳苏氏之说以为绝不可信。（苏氏之说详见其所著商务出版之《玉溪诗谜》；顾氏之说则详见其所著中华诗苑印行之《李商隐评论》。）盖以《燕台》四诗原来就不是可以事实求证的写实之作。如果真的以猜谜式的办法来说诗，一则既不能使读者心悦诚服；再则似乎也未免辜负了作者的用心，过于浅之乎视义山了。所以私意以为此二句仍当以象喻说之。在中国诗词之作品中，桃叶桃根之典，一般多用之以为离别之象喻。如辛弃疾《祝英台近》之“宝钗分、桃叶渡，烟柳暗南浦”，吴文英《莺啼序》之“记当时短楫桃根渡，青楼仿佛，临分败壁题诗，泪墨惨淡尘土。”无论其所用之字面为“桃叶”抑为“桃根”，而其为写离别之情则一也。义山继上句“欢向掌中销”而承以“桃叶桃根”云云者，盖亦取其与所欢离别之意也。至于义山之并列“桃叶桃根”，且标明白“双姊妹”，其意实并不必指现实中之果有此一双姊妹也。然而竟故作如此之说者，一则欲以之加强其美好可珍爱之感觉，着一“双”字，乃令人于直觉上弥觉价值之倍增；再则欲以之显示销亡之净尽，纵使有一双之多，而竟无一个可以存留，终不免于双双失落之痛，故曰“桃叶桃根双姊妹”也。义山之着此一“双”字，用笔既重，致慨亦深，而销亡失落之恨，乃真成无可挽赎者矣。

继之曰“破鬟倭堕凌朝寒，白玉燕钗黄金蝉”，如承接上面的“欢向掌中销”来看，此二句所写，自当为记忆中所欢者之容饰。朱鹤龄、姚培谦并引《古今注》云：“堕马髻，今无复作者，倭堕髻，一云堕马之馀形也。”（冯浩注本作“矮堕”，“矮”字当系误字）是“倭堕”乃妇女髻形之一种。温飞卿《南歌子》词有句云“倭堕低梳髻”，则其髻形当有低垂欲堕的娇慵之态，所可想见者也。而义山又于其上着以“破鬟”二字，“破”者，残破不整之意，如词人所谓“云鬟乱”或“鬓云残”者也。至于“凌朝寒”则当为清晓凌晨之意，而着以“朝寒”二字，一则可使凌晨的感受更为鲜明；再则言外亦似有一份“罗衾不奈五更寒”和“楼头残梦五更钟”的好梦难留欢会终销的凄寒之感在。至于下面的“白玉燕钗黄金蝉”，则全从女子之饰物着笔。“白玉燕钗”四字，朱鹤龄及姚培谦并引《洞冥记》曰：“元鼎元年，起招仙阁，神女留玉钗以赠帝，至元凤中发匣，有白燕升天，宫人学作此钗，因名玉燕钗。”“黄金蝉”三字，朱注引韩偓诗“醉后金蝉重”曰：“黄金蝉亦首饰。”此二句自表面看来，若谓为但写回忆中所欢者之容饰，自亦原无不可。而义山之佳处则在其恍惚之叙写中别能引人象喻之想。其中，上一句“破鬟”之“破”字，虽为鬓云残乱之意，而义山不用“残”“乱”字样，而用一“破”字，盖“破”字不仅予人之感觉更为强烈鲜锐，且言外亦似更蕴有无限残缺破灭之悲。更接以下面的“凌朝寒”三字，则以残缺破灭之悲，当此五更凄寒之候，其意境与义山另一首《端居》诗的“只有空床敌素秋”句颇为相似。当一切都归于残缺破灭之时，而欲以此空虚孤寂的哀痛之心，面对周围“朝寒”或“素秋”所象喻的侵袭的寒意，这是何等难以禁受的悲苦，故此句乃于“朝寒”二字上着一“凌”字，《端居》诗乃于“素秋”二字上着一“敌”字，则其心灵所感受到的寒意的酷烈，抵御的悲辛，不言可知。至于下一句之“白玉燕钗黄金蝉”，除其字面所标举的饰物之名以外，就感觉而言，“玉”字与“金”字所象喻的资质何等美好；“白”字与“黄”字所显示的色彩何等鲜明。如果以之与上一句合起来看，则髫鬟虽破，朝寒虽苦，而金蝉玉燕之美质难消，此亦为义山诗中常见之境界，如其《落花有感》之“落时犹自舞，扫后更闻香”，《咏灯》一首的“皎洁终无倦，煎熬亦自求”，凡其所写，盖皆以美好之资质面对折磨破损的深哀。如果从“白玉燕钗黄金蝉”的美好，来回看“破鬟倭堕凌朝寒”的残破与寒冷，我们当更可体会出义山此二句于表面字句所写的髫鬟容饰之外的更深一层的意境。然而凡此种种，无论其所写者为现实之情境，或者为非现实之情境，总之朝寒破梦，欢乐全销，所剩下的只有淋击在耳边心上的一片风雨，以及以全生命燃烧垂泪的一支红烛而已，而消逝的往昔，时空的艰阻，则是永远无法迈越的了。故曰“风车雨马不持去，蜡烛啼红怨天曙”也。如果以之做实解，则此二句盖写窗外之风雨凄寒，窗内之红烛啼泪的一种破晓前之情景。而义山用字之妙，乃于“风”字下着一“车”字，“雨”字下着一“马”字。夫风雨狂骤，其所象喻者原当为摧伤与阻隔，而义山却以其深情苦恋之心将原本象喻着摧伤阻隔的风雨，想像为突破阻隔的车马，这是何等使人感动的想象。而义山又于其下接以“不持去”三字，是诗人虽有如此多情之痴想，而凡一切消逝破灭者终不复返，则纵使风之疾速如车，雨之奔驰如马，然而终不能载此相思苦恋之人持之以赴其所思之地也。从如此风雨阻隔的现实，转入如彼车马奔驰的痴想，又从如彼情痴的狂想，再跌入如此终于无可冲破的现实阻隔之中。而长宵欲曙，烛泪啼红，于是诗人所有的遂只剩了一份长隔永逝的沉哀了。晏殊《撼庭秋》词有句云：“念兰堂红烛，心长焰短，向人垂泪。”如果把一支燃烧的红烛作为生命的象喻，则其以自己心血所煎熬出的一点光明之闪烁，不过都化成了点点泣血的红泪，而步步走向死亡而已。而窗外的曙光，就正是蜡烛生命将终的讯号。陶渊明《闲情赋》就曾把蜡烛作为生命及感情之象喻，而慨叹说：“悲扶桑之舒光，奄灭景而藏明。”无论是何等美好的生命，无论有何等闪烁的心焰，当扶桑舒光，晓风送曙的时候，面对着生命将终的死亡之讯号，一切都已无可挽留补赎，其中心之深悲极怨可知，然而逝者莫返，则所馀者亦惟有泣血的哀啼而已。故曰“蜡烛啼红怨天曙”也。义山以此一句为《燕台》四诗之总结，从首章的“风光冉冉东西陌”之生意的萌发，经过多少深情苦恋的向往追求，缠绵往复，最后却只落得一片啼红的临终的哀怨。义山这四首诗真是写尽了宇宙间所长存的某一种长怀憾恨的心灵之境界。这种境界该是只可以相类似的心灵去感触探寻，而并不可也不必以某一人或某一事加以拘限之解说的。

信有姮娥偏耐冷，休从宋玉觅微辞。
千年沧海遗珠泪，未许人笺锦瑟诗。

这是我从前所写的一首小诗，原意是为自己的某些旧诗作辩解，但标题却写的是《题义山诗》，现在就录在这里，借用为本文的结束，以说明义山的某些诗篇之原不可以作指实的解说。以前的各家笺注既然并不足以完全采信，而我个人的推演则更属愚妄的徒劳。想要得鱼的人，还是自己跃入水中亲自作一番探寻的尝试吧。

馀论

原来当我开始说《燕台四首》之时，本打算把这四首诗解说完了就加以结束。但是就在我即将结束之际，却忽然收到了台北友人为我寄来的一册第三十一期《现代文学》，这一期本来是詹姆斯·乔埃斯（James Joyce）都柏林人（Dubliners）研究专辑，但在这一专辑之后，却更附有一组评介法兰兹·卡夫卡（Franz Kafka）的译文。卡夫卡原是我所偏爱的一个近代的西方小说家，正如李义山一直是我所偏爱的一个古典的东方诗人。只是因了时空相距之遥远，以及生活与思想之背景的迥异，使我从来未曾把他们二人联想到一起加以比较过。但是这次却因了台北友人寄书来正值我写义山诗的时间的巧合，我蓦然发现到这二位作者之间，竟然有着某一些相似之处，现在就把我偶然想到的几点略述于后，虽标名《馀论》，实在只是一段曼衍的卮言而已。

第一，我以为一般出色的文学家，其成功之因素，重要者大约有以下数项：一则是以生活体验之过人的深广取胜；一则是以其写作技巧之过人的功力取胜；再一者，则是以其本然所禀赋的一种迥异于常人的心灵取胜的。义山与卡夫卡之成为出色的文学家，无疑的主要乃是由于最后一项因素。梁景峰译的一篇《卡夫卡简介》（原载于德国出版的《现代文学家》，著者为 Dr. Toni Meder），文中曾引用卡夫卡自己的日记，说他自己把创作视为"我梦幻般的内在生活之表现"，又说他的小说"并不能以理性去领悟，光是个内容概要是没有多大作用的，惟有竭尽心力去体会卡夫卡作品中之象征性和语言造型，才能启开其文学性而推究之"。义山的《燕台四首》，也正是属于这一类的作品，他所写的同样只是一种梦幻般的内在生活，读者并不能以理性去了解，而只当以心灵去追踪体悟其内在的象征性，以及其外在的语言之艺术性。卡夫卡简介一文中所提供的欣赏卡夫卡的途径，也正是欣赏义山诗所可取的途径，这一点他们二人是相同的。

其次，则是卡夫卡与李义山都极善于把真实生活之体验，揉入其自己充满梦魇的心灵之幻想中。所以他们的作品往往既非纯粹的写实，也非纯然的幻想，更不是出于理性的寓言或托喻。奥斯汀·华伦（Austin Warran）在其《法兰兹·卡夫卡》一文中就曾经说："卡夫卡的世界，既不属于一般以官能感受的人，也不属于狂妄的梦想者，更不像斯威夫特的《格列佛游记》那样，用蹊径分明的方法把怪诞的事件安全地覆置于最初的假想事件之中，卡夫卡的世界，其真实与假想是被移放在更切近更易感的关系之中。”这一点义山与卡夫卡也极为相似，义山的某些诗篇也同样既不是但以官能的感受叙写现实，也不是但以狂妄的梦想制造幻境，更不像一般传统的作者之写寓言或托喻之作有心的安排，他的作品也正如卡夫卡一样，乃是真实生活在其梦魇之心灵中的反映。而就在这样经过反射的变态的映像中，读者从不同的角度可以得到许多不同的感受，而且可以赋予不同的意义。而他们的作品也就在这种多面的感受和解说中，显示了他们所独有的一份神秘之感，这一点他们两个人也是相同的。

其三，就读者对他们的态度来说，卡夫卡与李义山也有着某些相似之处。陆爱玲译的爱德文穆尔的《卡夫卡论》，文中说：“假如有人承认他的优点的话，他便毫无选择馀地的要把那些优点列于首席。另一方面也有许多人觉得他无甚优点，且认为竟有如许读者尊他为相当有天才的作家是不可思议的。”李义山在读者群中所得到的遭遇也大致相同。一般说来，赏爱义山诗的人，就都会对之有极大的偏爱，而不能赏爱他的人，则往往对之加以轻视或诋毁。我以为这种情形乃同由于一个原因，就是他们的作品乃大半属于心灵之感受，所以要想欣赏他们的作品，似乎就不得不先预备有一颗与他们相类似的心灵，然后才能进入到他们的属于心灵之梦幻的境界中，作较深入的体会和欣赏。而也就是这种心灵的契合之感，使某些读者对他们的作品，自然而然地产生了无可选择的偏爱。然而另一些读者对他们的作品却只想从理性上去认知，拿着一根固定的丈尺做刻板的衡量，不得其门而入，不见宗庙之美百官之富，当然不免会对他们加以轻视或诋毁了。这种评价的悬殊，他们二人也是大致相同的。

其四，西方与东方的批评界，似乎同样有着一个极易陷入的相类似的窠臼。西方人之喜爱从作品中发掘宗教的意义，正如东方人之喜爱从作品中寻找仕隐穷达的托意。这一点卡夫卡与李义山所遭致的情形也是相类似的。爱德文穆尔与维拉穆尔合译的卡夫卡的《城堡》（*The Castle*），其序文中就曾建议把这本小说看作一种“现代的《天路历程》（*Pilgrim's Progress*）”，以为《城堡》和《天路历程》同样是一个宗教的寓言，有些人甚至把《城堡》视为天国的象喻。这正如有些笺注义山诗的人，喜欢把义山的许多诗都解作为令狐氏父子而作的一样。虽然卡夫卡的思想确有其宗教的背景，而义山的一生也确与令狐父子有很密切的关系，但是他们的作品都决不是这些狭隘的观念可以限制得住的。奥斯汀·华伦的《法兰兹·卡夫卡》一文，就曾经说：“卡夫卡没有供给这些作品以概念上的略图，因为他的小说都不需要这些图表……我们不必按系统地想城堡就是天国。”又有一些人喜欢从作者的身世立论，如同卡夫卡的一些读者，他们往往以他与他父亲相对立的关系来当作解答他的《蜕变》（*Metamorphosis*）、《审判》（*The Trial*）等一些作品的锁钥；而笺注义山诗的人也喜欢把他的诗与生平事迹比附立说。然而作者的生平毕竟不是作品的本身，陈绮红译的爱利克·海勒的《卡夫卡之世界》，文中就曾经批评这种说法的偏失，以为“那就如同说，如果有不同的父亲，卡夫卡就是不同的人一样……这种心理学对一件艺术品的解释之贡献，就如同鸟类解剖学对测量夜莺的歌声一样。”华伦与海勒的开明通达的见解，不仅可用以作为欣赏卡夫卡的南针，也同样可用以作为打破东方传统之笺注义山诗的某些偏执的借镜。

以上是略举我个人一时联想所及的卡夫卡与义山的某些相似之处。当然，真正说起来，他们二人的作品实在是迥然相异的，不仅他们所用以表达的形式和语文不同，他们所生的时代与环境也有着悬殊的差异。一个远生于唐代宪宗元和七年即公元 812 年的中国诗人李义山，如何能与一个晚到公元 1883 年才诞生于西方布拉格（Prugue）的犹太小说家卡夫卡放在一起相并而论？就思想背景而言，卡夫卡曾经受过德国哲学家尼采和丹麦存在主义神学家齐克果（Kierkegaarol）的很深的影响，这是义山梦也未曾梦到过的。因此卡夫卡的作品中，自然而然流露着一种宗教与哲学的意识，而义山则纯然只是一位诗人而已；卡夫卡的作品中，有着西方宗教原罪之感的沉重的负荷，而义山诗中所有的则只是一颗敏锐的心灵对人世间无常与缺憾的锐感深悲；卡夫卡作品中所表现的世界，往往是一个爱和同情和了解完全枯竭了的世界，而义山作品中则仍保留有对爱、同情和了解的期待和信赖；因此卡夫卡的意境往往使人陷入于绝望到濒临于疯狂的地步，而义山的作品则始终有一种滋润的诗意，即使面对悲苦，也仍能保有一份欣赏的馀裕。然而我们毕竟从远在卡夫卡千馀年前古东方的一位诗人的作品中，发现了两者之间的一些相似之处，则某一类型之心灵之可以超越时空而存在，而且可以其所独具之映现世界表现自我之方式，突破时空的束缚与隔阂，造成一线相通之感，这种心灵的力量是多么使人震惊和讶异的。

最后，我要说明一点，我对卡夫卡偏爱虽深，但我对于西方的文学批评理论则所知并不多。现在竟把卡夫卡与李义山强拉在一起相提并论，完全只因为如前所言的一种机会的巧合。自知不免浮浅谬误，好在本文并非庄论，如今只是从本来为了得鱼而跃入的一条水中，一时见猎心喜，又游向一段短短的支流而已。

Li Shangyin's "Four Yantai Poems"

Zhuangzi said, "when you've got the fish, forget the net; when you've got the sense, forget the words", and Tao Yuanming said of himself that he liked to read without insisting on too exact an understanding, but whenever he found something to his liking, he was so delighted he would forget his meals. These are attitudes toward poetry that I find very sympathetic, being by nature careless and given to self-indulgence. Still, if you want to catch a fish, you can't help using a net; but even so, the net is only a means to the desired end. And sometimes you can't find anything to hand that will serve as a net, while you are convinced that beneath the shimmering mountain light on the surface of that stream there must be any number of lovely fish swimming in the current. At such a time, someone like me, too lazy to make a net and too eager to have the fish, will abandon the idea of fishing with a net and simply jump into the water to try to catch a fish bare-handed. Not the sort of thing a proper gentleman would do, and what's more, there is no guarantee you will catch any fish. But even if you don't catch any, the contact with a living, wiggling fish slipping through the fingers should in itself be a source of pleasure.

Among Chinese poems of the past there are some that inspire the feeling of standing by a stream without a net, where you have no choice but to jump in the water and see what you can catch with your bare hands. Now while I am rather given to wild impulses, on the other hand I am timid about offending against propriety, and so before embarking on this not altogether orthodox experiment, I am looking for a saving precedent to justify it. Two occur to me: there is a kind of traditional Chinese novel known as Historical Stories Elaborated, and in modern fiction there are the Old Tales Retold. Their authors are not completely tied to ascertainable historical fact; there is room for free manipulation and expansion as they unfold their stories. However, neither provides an exact analogy: the traditional writers of historical narrative wrote to entertain their readers, and modern retellers of old tales use a historical setting to criticize modern conditions. What prompts me to elaborate on an old poem and provide a new interpretation is just the personal satisfaction of getting into the water and feeling the fish; my goal and my material are both quite unlike theirs. The only similarity is in having a bit of freedom to elaborate and develop my materials and not simply shuffle them about. So I am combining the two names and calling my experiment a new elaboration of an old poem. Here is the poem, in four parts:[1]

Four Yantai Poems 燕台四首

Spring 春

Breeze-light spreads along the east-west paths,	风光冉冉东西陌
The lovely ghost has long been sought in vain.	几日娇魂寻不得
Winged guest of the honey cell—like the sensitive heart,	蜜房羽客类芳心
Alluring leaves, seductive twigs—I know them all.	冶叶倡条遍相识
Warm mist-light lingers west of the peach tree	暖蔼辉迟桃树西

Where a tall hair-knot stands level with the peach hair-knot.	高鬟立共桃鬟齐
Dragon male and lady phoenix somewhere far away,	雄龙雌凤杳何许
Catkins flying, gossamer drifting—even Heaven loses track.	絮乱丝繁天亦迷
Arising drunk, when fading sunlight like early dawn	醉起微阳若初曙
Shines on the curtain of the broken dream—the voice still audible.	映帘梦断闻残语
Despair of catching the pink coral with a net of iron:	愁将铁网罥珊瑚
The sea is broad, heaven vast, and the place not to be found.	海阔天宽迷处所
A girdle has no feeling, but it grows tight or loose,	衣带无情有宽窄
Spring mist greens itself, and autumn frost is white.	春烟自碧秋霜白
Cinnabar can be ground, stone split, but Heaven doesn't notice—	研丹擘石天不知
Would there were a Heaven-jail to confine the tormented soul.	愿得天牢锁冤魂
The lined silk gown is packed away, the thin brought out,	夹罗委箧单绡起
Tinkling pendants against the cool of fragrant skin.	香肌冷衬琤琤珮
Today the east wind has no strength to stay,	今日东风自不胜
Transmuted somber light sinks in the Western Sea.	化作幽光入西海

Summer 夏

Outside the hall, rain; the curtain left down for grief;	前阁雨帘愁不卷
On the back room sweet trees cast thick shade.	后堂芳树阴阴见
The Stone City scene is like the Yellow Springs:	石城景物类黄泉
At midnight the young man walks with useless bow.	夜半行郎空柘弹

A silken fan summons a breeze from Heaven's gate,	绫扇唤风阊阖天
The thin curtain and green drapes billow in swirls.	轻帏翠幕波洄旋
The Shu ghost is still—has he a companion now?	蜀魂寂寞有伴未
Tropical flowers open night after night on the panha tree.	几夜瘴花开木棉
Cassia palace pours down light, the rays are hard to catch;	桂宫流影光难取
Seductive fragrance when the orchid opens; soft, soft words.	嫣熏兰破轻轻语
Even make the Milky Way fall into the breast,	直教银汉堕怀中
Don't make the Star Lady always come and go.	未遣星妃镇来去
Are the sources forever other for muddy stream and sparkling waves—	浊水清波何异源
The clear water of the Ji, the turbid Yellow River?	济河水清黄河浑
How to conjure up the golden skirt out of the light mist,	安得薄雾起湘裙
Lay hand on the cloud carriage and call to the Great Princess?	手接云軿呼太君

Autumn	秋
Moon waves traverse the sky, the eaves of the sky are wet;	月浪衡天天宇湿
The chill toad has dropped away, sparse stars come in.	凉蟾落尽疏星入
The mica screen, unmoving, covers the lonely frown,	云屏不动掩孤嚬
All night in the west house the wind-harp is quick.	西楼一夜风筝急
One longs to weave a love flower to send afar,	欲织相思花寄远
To the day's end yearning and bitter too.	终日相思却相怨
The only sound she hears is the Dipper turning,	但闻北斗声回环

She never sees the Long River flow clear and shallow.	不见长河水清浅
The golden fish locks up the red cassia spring,	金鱼锁断红桂春
Ancient dust covers the lovebird bed.	古时尘满鸳鸯茵
One can deplore the little park made a long road,	堪悲小苑作长道
But jade trees do not pity the deposed king.	玉树未怜亡国人
Soothing jasper zither holds a Chu melody,	瑶琴愔愔藏楚弄
Silk of Yue is cool and thin, heavy with gold appliqué	越罗冷薄金泥重
The parrot by the curtain hook, alarmed by night frost,	帘钩鹦鹉夜惊霜
Calls up south clouds to circle cloud dream.	唤起南云绕云梦
Paired dingling earrings along with the letter	双珰丁丁联尺素
That tells of the Xiang River rendezvous.	内记湘川相识处
Through rain I see singing lips all my life long—	歌唇一世衔雨看
Alas the sweet perfume grows old in the hand.	可惜馨香手中故
Winter	冬
The sun comes up in the eastern sky and sets in the sky's west,	天东日出天西下
Lady phoenix flies alone, woman dragon is solitary:	雌凤孤飞女龙寡
Greenstream and Whitestone out of each other's sight,	青溪白石不相望
The hall is farther even than Cangwu Plain.	堂中远甚苍梧野
Frost flowers rise on the icy wall in crisscross relief,	冻壁霜华交隐起
Snap short the sweet root, and the fragrant heart dies.	芳根中断香心死
Vain to ride a painted boat, recalling the Toad—	浪乘画舸忆蟾蜍
The Moon Lady may not be so very beautiful after all.	月娥未必婵娟子

Southern pipes, southland strings are all of them sad; 楚管蛮弦愁一概
In the empty town when the dance is done the dancer's waist remains. 空城舞罢腰支在
Onetime happiness melts in the palm of the hand, 当时欢向掌中销
Peach Leaf and Peach Root are a sister pair. 桃叶桃根双姊妹
Undone, down-the-back locks match the early morning's chill, 破鬟倭堕凌朝寒
White jade swallow pin, yellow gold cicada clasp. 白玉燕钗黄金蝉
Wind carriage and rain steeds will not take you there; 风车雨马不持去
The wax candle weeps red, grieved that the sky grows light. 蜡烛啼红怨天曙

Reading these four poems leaves you with the feeling that they are somehow out of reach. They emit a mysterious, dazzling emanation; they harbor elusive ideas that stir up ineffable visions. In the face of poetry as subtle and mysterious as this, all we can see is a flash of magic light, a brightly colored burst of flame. In this radiance the net of words can catch only the dregs. The poetry is like the psychic language of a dream that lies outside the reach of logical analysis and explanation. To probe the depths of a poet's soul and search out his secrets would seem foredoomed to failure, but I am willing to make the attempt, for I cannot resist the attraction of unknowable beauty; and at least I will have the pleasure of trying.

Critics before me have essayed to fish in these murky waters, and I would like first of all to give a summary of what they found. I will begin with the tragic episode associated with these poems, the story of the girl Willow Branch, who was the first to be bewitched by them. Li Shangyin wrote a set of poems about her, introduced as follows:[2]

Willow Branch was the name of a girl who lived in Luoyang. Her father was a well-to-do merchant who perished in a storm on the lake. Her mother neglected the other children to lavish her care on Willow Branch. At seventeen she could never sit still long enough to finish her makeup or do up her hair. She would blow on a leaf or nibble on a flower; pluck strings or finger a reed to play a song of the wind in the sky and the waves on the sea, tunes of secret memories and deepest passion. Neighbors and friends long in touch with the family knew she had been this way for the past ten years and so would not consider a marriage contract with her, believing her to be intoxicated with her dream world.

My cousin Rangshan lived near Willow Branch. One spring day Rangshan dismounted under the willow tree south of her house and recited my "Yantai" poems. Willow Branch asked in surprise, "Whose is that? Who wrote it?" Rangshan said, "That was written by a young man of my home town, my cousin." Willow Branch tore a piece off her long sash, tied it in a knot, and asked Rangshan to give it to the cousin in return for a poem.

Next day I rode with him into her lane. Willow Branch had put her hair up and made up her face. She stood by the gate, a sleeve raised against the wind. Pointing, she said, "Is that your cousin? Three days from now the girls in the neighborhood are going to splash their skirts in the river.[3] I will be waiting with my incense burner for you to go with me." I said I would.

But it so happened that some of my friends whom I was supposed to accompany to the capital left early and took my luggage as a joke, so as it turned out I did not stay. That winter Rangshan came and reported that she had been married to a lord of the east. Next year Rangshan went back east again. When we parted at the Xi River, I wrote these poems to inscribe on the wall of her old dwelling.

This story has sometimes been quoted as throwing light on the subject of the "Yantai" poems, and commentators have looked there for place names that would provide a clue to where the "nobleman of the East" had taken Willow Branch. The fact is, we know nothing whatsoever about Willow Branch apart from what the preface tells us; and the preface is to the Willow Branch Quatrains, not to the "Yantai" poems, which Willow Branch heard before Li Shangyin met her, so nothing in those poems could have any reference to her. A more productive use of the preface is to notice what Li Shangyin says about Willow Branch's appreciation of those poems as a clue to what he expected of them himself.

First is his characterization of Willow Branch. He depicts her as a girl who "blows on a leaf or nibble on a flower, plucks strings or fingers a reed." She likes a "song of the wind in the sky and the waves on the sea, tunes of secret memories and deepest passion." In these few lines he has sketched a reclusive and unworldly spirit. Her reaction to hearing Li Shangyin's "Yantai" poems was to ask, "Whose is that? Who wrote that?"—a repeated and insistent question, revealing the surprise and pleasure of one whose heartstrings have been touched. Before she met him, she never finished her makeup or tying up her hair, the negligent attitude of a girl who has no one she loves. To make her appointment with Li Shangyin she tears a piece off her sash; to meet him she has put her hair to rights; she will bring her incense burner; she is wholly at his disposal. Such is Li Shangyin's account of Willow Branch.

Like responds to like, similars seek one another out; a person may be known by the one he loves. Of course one may err, but this is generally true, and surely the model one imagines as the ideal object of one's affections must be a faithful reflection of what one admires. Zhang Caitian remarked that Willow Branch was the one who best understood Li Shangyin, as she is so vividly portrayed here, in this very deliberate description.[4] Li Shangyin was not just describing Willow Branch, he was actually describing how that person would feel who really understood his own soul, the kindred spirit who best appreciated his poetry. "A song of secret memories and deepest passion"—are not these precisely the qualities of Li Shangyin's poetry? Negligent when not knowing herself loved, and surrendering herself completely when finding her lover—is this not exactly Li Shangyin's attitude toward love? It seems to me that it is better to use this preface to the Willow Branch poems to understand the kind of effect Li Shangyin was trying for in his poetry, particularly what he imagined the ideal reader of his "Yantai" poems to be, rather than look there for information about Willow Branch.

There are other hypotheses about these poems. I will summarize them under three heads: time, place, and person. First, the person:

1. The word *yantai* in Tang times was a term of respect for a Provincial Governor; its use as the title of the poems has led to the conclusion that their subject is a lady in the Governor's household.[5]

2. The frequent mention of female Immortals in the poems is the basis for the speculation that, when Li Shangyin was studying Taoism in Yuyang East, he may have had an affair with a Taoist nun, who was taken away by a high official.[6]

3. Since there is some wording in common with the "Willow Branch" poems, and since the "Yantai" poems are also love poems, it may be that there is some connection with the girl Willow Branch.[7]

4. The four poems were all written for Yang Sifu.[8]

5. When Li Shangyin met the girl Yantai at a party, she was already someone else's concubine.[9]

6. The poems are a lament for the Palace Ladies Feiluan and Qingfeng.[10]

7. The poems are satirical, directed against the palace concubines.[11]

There are five theories about the setting:

1. After being taken away to the capital by the high official, the girl wandered off to the south.[12]

2. There are two love affairs involved: one, with Willow Branch, in the south, and one with the Taoist nun in Yuyang, who perhaps also went south.[13]

3. The southern place names are symbolical of Yang Sifu's banishment to the south.[14]

4. Chang'an place names make the capital the setting.[15]

5. Mostly southern place names means a southern setting; the northern places are deliberately misleading.[16]

About the implication of the four seasons:

1. The first poem gives delicate form to his spring feelings and painful longings. The second recounts a night-time meeting of the past. The third regrets that she is far away. The fourth is the sorrow of the poet that he is still detained.[17]

2. The first records the meeting of Li Shangyin and Yang Sifu, and the gradual decline in Sifu's fortunes on the sudden death of Wenzong. The next is devoted to the affair between the Imperial Concubine Yang and Prince Rong of An. In the third, Yang Sifu arrives in Xiang and invites Li Shangyin to join his staff there. In the fourth, Li Shangyin goes to Xiang, but Sifu has already left.[18]

3. They met during the spring but someone took her away. During the summer she went to Jinling and by autumn was in Xiangchuan, where she invited Li Shangyin to join her. He arrived in winter, but she had gone someplace else, he knew not where.[19]

This is a bare summary of the interpretations I have at hand, but it is enough to show how various and muddled they are. Sometimes the same critic includes mutually contradictory explanations, and it should be obvious that they all are the product of the critics' own imagination. To try to reconcile these conflicting views is rather like trying to unravel a skein that just gets tangled worse the more you fiddle with it. You will never make a net out of it, and I propose to throw the whole thing away and go jump into the water to see what I can catch bare-handed.

The first thing to decide about the poems is whom they are concerned with. In traditional Chinese poetry there are several possibilities: it may be a real, identifiable person, as Bai Juyi's Xiaoman and Fansu,[20] or Yan Jidao's Lian, Hong, Ping, and Yun.[21] Or the person may be real enough, but there is no external evidence to establish the identity, as in Wei Zhuang's lines "On the seventeenth of the fourth month, just a year ago today, I left you,"[22] or the one he first got to know "that year under the blossoms",[23] or Jiang Kui's imprudent love "where the River Fei flows east".[24] The third possibility is that the person is just a romantic figment of the poet's imagination, as the women in Palace Style poetry or the Five Dynasties songs. A fourth possibility is that the person, while inexistent, is not so much a product of the poet's romantic feelings as an allegorical figure, as in Cao Zhi's "There is a lovely lady in the South,"[25] or Ruan Ji's two beauties on the River's shore.[26] The fifth is more elusive. There is no such person in real life, but she is not a romantic ideal, nor allegorical, but only a natural effusion of a deep-seated longing in the heart, as Feng Yansi's "The trees are in bloom, but 1 have lost my companion of spring walks"[27] or Ouyang Xiu's "Even though I long for someone far away, it is hard to write to her".[28]

With these five possibilities, in any given poem the proper attitude of the critic, it seems to me, is to say so if you know which it is, but if you can't decide, admit you don't know. If the person is identifiable, the identity should be established, but if it can't be established, it is irresponsible and misleading to guess. Given the vague, confusing manner of the four "Yantai" poems, there is no single line that corresponds to reality, so there can be no question that the person is unidentifiable. But which of the categories of unidentifiable is appropriate here? The passionate intensity of the language precludes the "romantic figment of the poet's imagination", but if we just say it is a real but unidentifiable person, these four poems still are not simple and obvious like the examples from Wei Zhuang or Jiang Kui. And if allegories, they are also not at all like the ones by Cao Zhi and Ruan Ji. There remains the "natural effusion of a desperate longing in the heart", and here too there is an obvious difference between these four poems organized around the seasons and the short lyrics of Feng Yansi and Ouyang Xiu.

It seems to me there are two essential attitudes to have in mind in approaching these poems that are so refractory to classification: one must constantly remember that there are many possibilities of interpretation, and be prepared to appreciate all the lovely, subtle suggestions generated by these ambiguities without limiting the poem by arbitrarily excluding some.

The rich suggestiveness of the poems is responsible for the impression of an extremely real and intense emotion. They move and dazzle the reader as profoundly as though they were inspired by the poet's real experiences. These poems also employ extremely complex metaphors and symbols, quite unrelated to any real event, as though they were wholly symbolical. In addition, they are filled with intense sorrow and unhappiness, as though they were a spontaneous outpouring of uncertainty and despair from the poet's heart. But their density and polish make them unlike casual lyrics, and they seem to have some deeper implication. To appreciate these poems we had best acknowledge that there are many possibilities and accept them as a most ingenious amalgam of the poet's deepest feeling and his most refined technical skill. Poems of this kind are not subject to logical exegesis, and it is precisely there that their excellence lies; to explain the poem by looking for a referent in the real world is to destroy its rich, subtle suggestiveness.

One must recognize that there is no necessary correlation between the value of a poem and the persons and objects in it, and resist the temptation to lend it an adventitious value by forcibly relating it to external events socially recognized as important. Wine is distinguished from water by its nature, not by the container it is served in, and the container does not determine the value of its contents.

The beauty of Li Shangyin's poetry is in the complexity and subtlety that distinguish it from that of all other poets: the uncontrollable flowing waters of "West Stream",[29] the unaccountable grief of "Inlaid Zither"[30]—feelings as irrepressible and inexplicable as these are something deeply embedded in the poet's life. How can we dissect out these qualities so intimately bound up with the poet's life and tie them down to some narrowly defined topic that we cannot even be sure of? Therefore, if we can bring convincing evidence that identifies the subject of any of these four poems and that yields the satisfaction of a clearer understanding of the poetry—appreciate the container as we enjoy the wine—that is fine, but if we can't do that, it is surely getting the priorities mixed when we fail to appreciate the flavor of the wine while making a wild guess at one remove about the shape of the container. So instead of making unverifiable guesses about the identity of the subject of these poems, I propose to try to discern the "I", the persona assumed in them by the poet.

The next problem demanding investigation is the setting of the poems. There are more than ten regions named or invoked, helter-skelter, without order or system, inspiring Lao Gan's remark, "In the poems it is one time north and then abruptly south; the author was being deliberately misleading."[31] It seems to me that there are several appropriate ways to approach the problem, as places and directions in Chinese poetry generally have various meanings. They can be literal, as in Du Fu's quatrain,

The window frames the West Range snows of a thousand autumns; 窗含西岭千秋雪
At the gate is moored East Wu's myriad-miles-boat.[32] 门泊东吴万里船

where West Range and East Wu are places and directions that correspond to reality. Or they can be part of an allusion, as in Du Fu's poem to Yan Wu,

From his southward plan he wheels his feathered wings, 南图回羽翮
To the Northern Apex he offers a star's service.[33] 北极捧星辰

Here the "southward plan" alludes to the giant roc in *Zhuangzi* that moves to the south;[34] the "Northern Apex" is the Pole Star; the allusion is to the *Analects* passage that says, "The one who rules by virtue is like the Pole Star: it holds its place and all the stars are subservient to it."[35]

Another possibility is a symbolical use as in Zhang Heng's "Fourfold Sorrow", where Mt. Tai / look to the east, Guilin / look to the south, Hanyang / look to the west, Yanmen / look to the north, are all used symbolically as part of a series listing the obstacles to be found in the four directions.[36] No literal sense of place or direction is intended, but it implies that there are obstacles everywhere, in all directions.

When we approach the "Yantai" poems with these possibilities in mind, we notice immediately that many of the directions and place names are parts of allusions or are merely symbolical, without referring to any real place. When the "Ji River" and "the Yellow River" are contrasted for their respectively clear and muddy water, or the "south cloud" and "Chu tune" as representing yearning for something far-off, or "Stone City" for its association with Nevercare and "Cangwu" as the place where Shun died, in all these cases we will go hopelessly astray if we are too ready to look for a location on an itinerary instead of carefully evaluating the function of the term in the context of the whole poem.

The time of year is obviously significant, since each of the four poems carries as its subtitle one of the four seasons. However, if you follow one of the old interpretations that looks for a correspondence between the seasons and the development of one of the poet's love affairs, you will find yourself at sea with no landmarks to take your bearings from. The seasons appear in Chinese poetry in two different uses: they may have literal or a symbolical meaning. In the *Shijing* poem that unfolds the twelve months of the agricultural year[37] it is obvious that any mention of a season is to be taken literally. But Fan Qin's poem "Stilling the Passions",[38] as it moves from sunrise to midday to sunset and evening, is not recounting the passage of time for one day; instead, this sequence symbolizes endless waiting. The passage of time in this poem creates the effect of an endlessly repeated cycle, and such an effect is not limited to symbolical poetry, for in straightforward realistic poetry we can also get the feeling of an endlessly repeated cycle, as in that same *Shijing* poem just mentioned, where the farmer's annual round of labor, harvest, and rest is also perceived as always recurring. This symbolical use of a temporal cycle is a common one, from the repeated occurrence of words like "spring", "autumn", "morning", "evening", in the Qu Yuan poems, where it suggests the sense of time's inexorable passage, to the constant mention of the four seasons and the twelve months in popular poems and ballads about eternal love.

The same four seasons in Li Shangyin's "Yantai" poems should be understood, I think, from the general impression they give of continuity and universality, and from that we should try to understand this poet who wrote

When the lotus leaves grow my spring sorrow grows; 荷叶生时春恨生
When the lotus leaves decay my autumn sorrow is complete.[39] 荷叶枯时秋恨成

Through the seasons he invokes the intense emotions of one who "will always feel while his body lasts."[40]

There remains one more point to be considered: the significance of the title "Yantai". There are a number of poems in Li Shangyin's collection headed "Untitled", as well as several more that take their title from the first two words of the first line that are also in effect "untitled". The "Yantai" poems do have a real title, one that is not just a couple of words lifted from the text of the poems, and it can reasonably be expected to mean something, but just what it means is by no means obvious, as the divergent suggestions by the commentators demonstrate. Feng Hao says, "It was commonly used in Tang times for a provincial governor's office." That is undeniable, and Li Shangyin himself used the term in that sense in the poem "On the Closing of the Zizhou Office, a Poem for my Colleagues":[41] "Singing long, I am going far away from the office."[42] So there is no doubt that *yantai* has this meaning. However, to jump to the conclusion that Li Shangyin was involved in a love affair with one of the governor's concubines, as Feng Hao goes on to speculate, is pure invention. Zhang Caitian energetically rejects Feng Hao's story as unacceptable, but then he makes up one of his own. His point of departure is the same: *yantai* is an administrative office. Remembering that Yang Sifu was demoted from his position as Imperial Overseer of Hunan to be Prefect of Chaozhou, he wants to take these four poems as written specifically for and about Yang Sifu, supposing him to have been a potential patron of Li Shangyin's. He drags in the death of the Emperor Wenzong, the accession of Wuzong, and even the affair of the Imperial Concubine Yang, who wanted to make Prince Rong of An the successor to the throne. By making every word and every line refer to these events, he is even more arbitrary than Feng Hao. Cen Zhongmian thoroughly refuted his arguments.[43]

So what are the "Yantai" poems about? Starting with the title, there are two levels to be distinguished: First, *yantai* definitely means "an administrative office". Unsuccessful in his career, Li Shangyin was secretary in military headquarters successively at Tianping, Yanhai, Guiguan, Wuning, and Dongchuan. This unsettled, rootless life must have led to feelings of depression and bitterness. Even Du Fu, when he was serving in the headquarters of his friend Yan Wu, whose father had also been his own father's friend, could feel frustration and resentment at his position, judging from poems where he wrote:

Ten years endured, alone and neglected	已忍伶俜十年事
No choice but to take a secure perch on one branch.[44]	强移栖息一枝安

Why do I come to the office here?	胡为来幕下
The right thing is to be on a boat.[45]	只合在舟中

White-haired, I humbly serve at headquarters	白头趋幕府
Too well aware I have wasted my life.[46]	深觉负平生

By comparison Li Shangyin's life was considerably more trying, as he was shifted from post to post, depending on the caprice of his superiors. And outside his life as an official, with the trials associated with working in a military headquarters, there was no compensatory good fortune. It makes it reasonable to take the four "Yantai" poems as written to commiserate his own unfortunate life.

There is another meaning of the words *yantai* that supports such a reading, from the allusion to the Gold Terrace of King Zhao of Yan, who welcomed talented and worthy men from the whole world. Poets frequently refer to King Zhao when complaining that they have found no such welcome in their own times; for example, Li Bai's lines:

Vines grow around King Zhao's white bones	昭王白骨萦蔓草
Who now sweeps out his Gold Terrace?	谁人更扫黄金台

The way is hard to find—let me go home.[47] 行路难，归去来

Besides complaining about the bitterness of his life as a secretary at headquarters, Li Shangyin's title also strongly suggests his disappointment and regret at never finding an appreciative patron. Poor and orphaned young, he was especially vulnerable and took the vicissitudes of official life more seriously than others might do.

His involvement in the partisan conflict between his one-time patrons of the Linghu family and his father-in-law Wang Maoyuan, however it is interpreted—and there are all sorts of different ways of looking at it—must have been a source of distress to him, given the suspicions and misunderstandings inherent in such a situation of conflicting loyalties. His misfortunes did not all come from his career as an official. He lost his father at an early age and his wife died in his middle years, depriving him of the support he most needed at critical periods of his life. These experiences too must have left their scars. Further, there are the many poems about unhappy love. Even if some of them were intended to be political allegories, it is unlikely that a poet as sensitive as Li Shangyin could have been immune to such experience, and he certainly writes with a profound understanding of the feelings roused by frustrated love.

All of these disappointments and misfortunes can be subsumed under the inclusive concept of an unlucky life—he was a man born out of his time. If you combine Li Shangyin's experience of bad luck with the bitterness of a lifetime spent in a military camp, and consider the "Yantai" poems from this perspective and attempt a deeper understanding in symbolic terms, refraining from forcing every line and every word into a narrowly conceived frame of reference, it should be possible to discover a new path to their real meaning.

Spring

This first poem with the title "Spring" invokes the budding, germinati g life-force and in the first line creates perfectly the atmosphere of a spring day: "Breeze-light spreads along the east-west paths." Li Shangyin's spring is not the standard one of massed, striking colors; it is fluid rather, tender, trembling, practically tangible. Instead of the usual, static term "spring light" or "spring scene", he writes the dynamic "breeze light". The next word, *ran ran*, translated "spreads", is really an adverb with connotations of billowing lightness. Combined with "breeze light", it brings all the fresh new life of spring dancing before one's eyes—the leaves stirring in the moving air, the slow passage of clouds on the horizon, the whole panorama of light and color in the spring breeze. The concluding words "along the east-west paths" really serve to extend the observed phenomena to every point of the compass: east and west—and north and south, near and far—everywhere. It is interesting to compare this line with other poems that evoke the feeling of ubiquitous spring. Ouyang Xiu writes:

Beside the high house the plum-blossom is past	候馆梅残
And willows by the brook bridge are thin.	溪桥柳细
The grass smells sweet; the breeze is warm that shakes my bridle.[48]	草熏风暖摇征辔

And Qin Guan:

On the peach path under the willow trees	柳下桃蹊
The spring scene spreads to every house at random.[49]	乱分春色到人家

Both poets are describing the spring visible everywhere, in concrete terms, with rich colors, emphasizing sensuous perception. Li Shangyin's line is softer, more diffuse, with an effect of vagueness, of indirection. Its effect is not wholly through the senses; there is a subtle movement from the depths of the poet's heart, leading naturally to the next line: "The lovely ghost has long been sought in vain." The stirring in the heart generated by the advent of spring prompts the disheartening search for the "lovely ghost". For this delicate, vague, confusing, uncertain spring scene acts on the sensitive poet to produce a feeling of emptiness and melancholy, hard to express in words and impossible to alleviate. Feng Yansi's song has the lines,

Green weeds on the riverbank, willows on the dyke	河畔青芜堤上柳
Make me ask, why this sorrow	为问新愁
Comes again, year after year?[50]	何事年年有

And Yan Shu,

Fine grasses, worry about the mist,	细草愁烟
Hidden flowers, fearful of the dew:	幽花怯露
In transports I lean on the balustrade.[51]	凭阑总是销魂处

And Liu Yong,

The grass color and mist-shine in the twilight—	草色烟光残照里
No one can know my feelings as I lean on the balustrade.[52]	无人会得凭阑意

It is hard to explain and specify why these features of the spring scene—the green vegetation, willows on the dyke, mist-light—rouse such feelings of sadness. Liu Xie wrote, "A movement in nature, and the heart flutters";[53] and especially the signs of rebirth in the gentle warmth of springtime revive in the heart of a poet feelings of striving after something lost. But, "from the first there has always been death; we must all swallow our regret and hold back our sobs."[54] The poet never lived who found his quest fulfilled, and this is the sense of the line, "The lovely ghost has long been sought in vain." There is no need to specify who or what the lovely ghost is; it symbolizes the object of the poet's quest: mysterious and elusive as a ghost, yet something delicate and soft. The quest has gone on for a long time, "many days", and without success—a source of sorrow for the idealistic and sensitive poet. However, "what my heart finds good, I shall never regret though I die."[55] Though the search be unsuccessful, he will not relinquish his desire. This leads to the next couplet, which expresses the bitterness and the passion of the quest:

Winged guest of the honey cell—like the sensitive heart,	蜜房羽客类芳心
Alluring leaves, seductive twigs—I know them all.	冶叶倡条遍相识

The "winged guest of the honey cell" is of course the honeybee.[56] From the concluding words of the line it is clear that it is being compared with the heart of the poet, literally, "fragrant heart". The word "guest" reinforces the personification of bee as man, and the immediate association with "winged person" is the Taoist immortal who soars through space. This contributes to the emotion-laden vision of a questing flight and a soaring, fluttering, spiritual journey. The preceding "honey cell" not only goes with the bee, but also with the sweetness and fragrance of the honey; the enclosed and hidden cell is a reminder of the sensitive heart of the poet. In another springtime poem Li Shangyin wrote,

Flower-beard and willow-eyes, both beyond control,	花须柳眼各无赖
Purple butterfly and yellow bee, each with feeling.[57]	紫蝶黄蜂俱有情

Only a man of the highest type can be free of emotion,"it is just on people like us that emotion weighs heavy."[58] Like the bee or the butterfly rising to dance with the advent of spring, their whole life devoted to unceasing search—such is the emotion-laden, sensitive heart of the poet.

The next line, read in the traditional moralistic way, could be understood as a piece of frivolity on Li Shangyin's part. For the adjectives "alluring" (*ye*) and "seductive" (*chang*) have erotic connotations: "An alluring appearance invites wantonness,"[59] and *chang ji* and *chang you* are defined as "prostitute, entertainer". The concluding words of the line, "I know them all", seem at first to reinforce this kind of association with promiscuous love. In fact, Li Shangyin is portraying in all seriousness the earnestness and toil of the quest. If we can rid ourselves of the stereotyped associations of the words *ye* and *chang*, we will see how fresh and forceful they are. *Ye* first of all means "beautiful", and *chang* also has the meaning "flourishing, plentiful". Their function is to conjure up the riot of colors, the waving, leafy branches of the springtime trees. And the words "I know them all" convey the wholehearted commitment to the quest. Qu Yuan expressed a similar emotional predilection for flowers,

I grow nine fields of orchids	余既滋兰之九畹兮
And plant a hundred acres of cattleyas,	又树蕙之百亩
Bed *liuyi* and *jieche*,	畦留夷与揭车兮
Edged with angelica and asarum.[60]	杂杜衡与芳芷

Of course neither Qu Yuan nor Li Shangyin was writing about literal flowers, but rather used them to symbolize the feeling of the attraction evoked in their hearts. Every lovely flower petal unfolding, every graceful branch dancing in the spring breeze, rouses in the poet a melancholy yearning. But having "looked for her in the crowd a thousand hundred times,"[61] where is that lovely ghost he seeks that is so bound to the poet's heart and dreams?

Caught up in these painful emotions, it seems to the poet that he really does see someone:

Warm mist-light lingers west of the peach tree	暖蔼辉迟桃树西
Where a tall hair-knot stands level with the peach hair-knot.	高鬟立共桃鬟齐

The languid, bemused feeling induced by a spring day is concentrated in the words "warm mist". The usual phrases—"warm sun", "mild breeze", "mild air"—are all too specific, too limited. "Warm mist" implies all the others and adds the indistinct vagueness that best characterizes a spring scene. It is often invoked by poets, who write "mist-shine", "misty willows", "misty flowers". The word *ai* has the same meaning as *yan* but is milder and warmer. The words "warm mist" conjure up a vision of mist softly billowing in the gentle breeze under a warm sun. The "light lingers", that is, the rays of the sun move gradually. Du Shenyan's "Early Spring Outing" has the lines,

The mild air prods the yellow birds,	淑气催黄鸟
Clear sunlight rotates the green cress.[62]	晴光转绿蘋

And Du Fu in one of his quatrains writes,

Lazy in the springtime, I lean against the breeze.	春光懒困倚微风
No one owns all the open peach blossoms	桃花一树开无主
I love the deep pink and I love the delicate pink.[63]	可爱深红爱浅红

When we read the rest of Li Shangyin's line "west of the peach tree" in this context, we see the sunlight slowly turning, moving through the light and deep pinks of the peach blossoms in this soft, warm air—a dazzling vision. In the midst of this vision, we are dimly aware of someone standing under the peach tree. In the obscurity, the face, the clothes are not clearly discerned; all we are given are the words "tall hair-knot", but that suffices to show it is the figure of a woman. The term *gao huan* contrasts with *ya huan* "hair done up in two buns", where the associations are with youthful exuberance. The style of hairdo indicated by *gao huan* becomes a more mature, graceful beauty, with connotations of aristocratic reserve. In Li Shangyin's line it is set off against "peach hair-knot", turning the tree's crown of blossoms into a stylized hairdo and at the same time appropriating the quality of the flowers to the woman who stands beside them, a deliberate confusion of the two embodiments of beauty. They "stand together", and though logically there must be at least two separate entities, the effect of their juxtaposition is to make us feel that they are joined into one. The line blends illusion and reality: we see a tree in bloom and think it might be a woman, until in the warm mist and shifting light it looks as though there really was a lovely woman standing there, hair piled up on her head and a suggestion of a smile in her eyes. On top of this illusion comes an abrupt turn:

Dragon male and lady phoenix somewhere far away, 雄龙雌凤杳何许
Catkins flying, gossamer drifting—even Heaven loses track. 絮乱丝繁天亦迷

lines full of pain and disappointment. Male and female, dragon and phoenix, both make a pair—"the two fair ones must come together," Wu Xian promised Qu Yuan,[64] and Li Bai wrote,

Lord Zhang's two dragon swords— 张公两龙剑
Divine objects that must sometime join.[65] 神物合有时

A world where male dragon and female phoenix can meet is the only satisfactory one, but Li Shangyin says they are "somewhere far away", with no hope of finding one another. There is no gaudy phoenix that sings on the tall phoenix tree, nor a divine dragon that soars through the sky, so how can they meet? We can only regret the imperfection of this human world, filled with gloomy disappointment. Especially when spring is passing, and though the honeybees' sweetness endures, the topknot of peach blossoms will fade, and everywhere is the wildly flying willow fluff, the drifting gossamer, so that even Heaven loses its bearings. Heaven, if capable of feeling, must be disappointed and disturbed at their frustration and helpless grief. The flying catkins and drifting gossamer are there as common witness for Heaven and man.

There would seem to be no way of developing this pitch of feeling any farther, but Li Shangyin is very good at introducing unexpected turns, and here he writes,

> Arising drunk, when fading sunlight like early dawn 醉起微阳若初曙
> Shines on the curtain of the broken dream—the voice still audible. 映帘梦断闻残语

It is like the karmic debt of a former life, or its nightmare: something never to be forgotten and never to be free from. To a person cold sober the sight of flying catkins and drifting gossamer is upsetting enough, but in a state of drunkenness, half awakened from a dream, how much more profound the impact, how much more shattering the reaction.

Zhu Heling glosses *wei yang* (faint sunlight) as "evening sunlight"—i.e., sunset. The words stand in contrast with *chu shu*, "early dawn". Sunset is the reality; dawn, illusion. In the next line there is a similar contrast between "interrupted dream" and "lingering words"; the broken dream is reality, the still audible voice illusion. Sunlight comes into the room and one is uncertain whether it is not from the rising sun, as one seems indistinctly to hear the faint sound of the solicitous voice. In these two lines are concentrated the bitterness toward the one remembered and the racking grief for what is shattered and vanished; they effectively convey the confusion of awakening from a dream, still in a state of drunkenness.

"Shines on the curtain" links the two lines: The one who sees the pale sunlight on the curtain is the same one who arises drunk from the broken dream and hears the still audible dream-voice. Du Fu wrote in his poem "Dreaming of Li Bai":

The setting moon floods the rafters	落月满屋梁
And I imagine it shines still on your face.[66]	犹疑照颜色

You think of someone until he comes into your dream, and the intensity of this thought is shown by the fact that you seem still to hear the voice or see the face, in the sunlight on the curtain or in the moonlight on the rafters. The difference in the two poems is that Du Fu was writing about something that happened, whereas Li Shangyin is not necessarily writing about a real event, but only a certain feeling of pathos.

Despair of catching the pink coral with a net of iron:	愁将铁网罥珊瑚
The sea is broad, heaven vast, and the place not to be found.	海阔天宽迷处所

The first line continues the theme of the pain of a never ended seeking and pursuit; the second is likewise the disappointment at something irretrievably lost. The *Herbal* says, "Coral grows on the bottom of the sea.... To obtain coral, first they prepare iron nets which they sink to the bottom. When the coral grows through the nets,... they haul it out with ropes."[67] This gives an idea of what effort it costs, what determination is required to harvest the coral, the value of which is measured by its inaccessibility. But though it is hard to come by, through their unremitting efforts the men of the sea do ultimately get coral. The poet, however, for all that he is prepared to make a similar effort, has no way of knowing where in all this vast, uncharted ocean he is to look for the blood-red coral he wants to find. Where shall he cast his iron net, woven of a thousand strands of his own feelings? Net in hand he looks out over the expanse of blue and sees nothing but empty desolation. Meng Haoran writes,

> I would like to ask for the uncertain ford, 迷津欲有问
> But the level lake stretches out and out in the evening.[68] 平海夕漫漫

In the face of futility and disappointment, grief and loss are beyond the power of words to express. The word "despair", which begins the first line of the couplet, is linked with the words "the place is not to be found" in the second, the pain of being lost. In between comes the desperate labor with the iron net, the hope of snaring the coral, the search extending over the broad sea, under the vast sky,[69] and then the sorrowful realization that the place is not to be found.

> A girdle has no feeling, but it grows tight or loose, 衣带无情有宽窄
> Spring mist greens itself, and autumn frost is white. 春烟自碧秋霜白

These lines convey the despair that follows disappointment. Already in the first of the "Nineteen Old Poems" we see what grief does to the waist:

> Every day you go farther away, 相去日已远
> Every day my girdle grows looser.[70] 衣带日已缓

In the midst of separation and disappointment we have no measure of grief, but as we become aware of the gradual loosening of our belt, and as we shorten it, we realize that a life may end, but the longing for the absent person does not end. It is a painful irony that a sentient being must be reminded of his pain by this inanimate object. The world of nature is indifferent: spring mist takes on the green color of spring, autumn frost brings its own white; the soft, concealing mist is there on its own terms, and the cold frost is indifferent. The green mist and the white frost are presented distinctly, and the feelings are equally sharp. The addition of the word "itself" puts the process outside human control, leaving the observer helpless. Moving from spring to autumn this way encloses the poet's life between the obscuring mist and the chill frost.

Cinnabar can be ground, stone split, but Heaven doesn't notice—	研丹擘石天不知
Would there were a Heaven-jail to confine the tormented soul.	愿得天牢锁冤魂

Stone and cinnabar are taken as symbols for constancy in *Lüshi chunqiu*: "Stone can be split but you cannot take away its hardness; cinnabar can be ground, but you cannot take away its redness." If you turn it around and say "stone may be hard, but it can be split; cinnabar may be red, but it can be powdered"—this is to violate their hardness and redness. And who would do it, or have it done? What we call the Way of Heaven—is there such a thing?[71] In an extremity of bafflement and grief, the poet writes, "Heaven doesn't notice".

"Heaven's Jail" has traditionally been identified with two different constellations, one known as the "Nobleman's Jail", the other as the "Commoner's Jail",[72] but in Li Shangyin's poem it is used as a symbol for an eternal confinement; there is no place here for class distinctions, on earth or in Heaven. What is shut up is the tormented soul, oppressed and with no vent for its feelings. If it is a tormented soul, it must be sensitive to its suffering, and to such a degree that even death seems to offer no relief—it must endure through this life and continue afterwards in Heaven's jail. The line begins with a wish, or a desperate vow, "would that", as though the poet were expressing a resolve to accept his suffering through all eternity.

The lined silk gown is packed away, the thin brought out,	夹罗委箧单绡起

Tinkling pendants against the cool of fragrant skin. 香肌冷衬琤琤珮

Just when the spring scene begins to decline, the poet turns our attention to the change of season: when the willow trees are covered with green and the first trees are in full bloom, spring is nearly past and summer approaches. All the feelings about this transition are roused by recalling the change of garments called for by the weather turned warm. Our whole body responds to seasonal changes, and what we wear is determined to some degree by our body's needs. When Confucius' disciple Zeng Xi spoke of spring, it was in such terms: "At the end of spring, when our spring clothes are all done"[73]—when the dark, heavy winter clothes are put off for the lined silken robes of spring, shining with all the colors of spring—what a feeling of lightness and freshness! Then as summer comes on the lined spring robe is changed for the unlined summer gown, with sleeves that lift in the gentle breeze—it creates a sensation of billowing lightness. Zhou Bangyan frequently used such associations as a way of suggesting this particular change of season, for example,

Standing a long time in my unlined gown,[74] 单衣伫立

or

Wearing an unlined gown I try the wine.[75] 单衣试酒

This kind of sensitivity seems especially appropriate when attributed to a delicate and beautiful woman, and Li Shangyin's next line invokes such a figure:

Tinkling pendants against the cool of fragrant skin. 香肌冷衬琤琤珮

The expression "fragrant skin" is used only of women; that it can be "cool" is also asserted by Su Shi:

Ice flesh and jade bones— 冰肌玉骨
Of course she is cool and does not sweat.[76] 自清凉无汗

Such delicacy and refinement could only be attributed to a woman. But Li Shangyin's line contains also the words "Tinkling jade pendants". In Xin Qiji's song about the River Spirit,

Her pendants sound idly, jade circlets hang from her belt,[77] 珮声闲，玉垂环

this is what lends her style and appeal. Li Shangyin's word "tinkle" is precisely this slow, languorous sound. If we push it a step farther, we get the lines in Jiang Kui's song about the lotus:

In all the ponds where no one ever comes, 三十六陂人未到
Countless water-pendants, wind robes.[78] 水珮风裳无数

But there is even more loneliness in the tinkling pendants of Li Shangyin's flowerlike lady. When we look again at the word "cool" we realize that it applies not only to her skin, but also to the feeling of lonely chill in her heart. Now if someone wants to interrupt at this point and ask whether this lady is an allegorical figure for the poet himself, or is the someone he is yearning for, I would reply that, judging from the tone of these lines, she would seem to stand for the poet. But if the poet is presenting himself in the guise of a woman, then why did I explain the woman with the tall hair-knot in the third couplet as being the object of his desire? Well, a poet will sometimes use the same symbol in one poem for himself and for another person. In the "Li sao", for example, on the line "I fear the Lovely One will come too late," Hong Xingzu comments, "Qu Yuan takes the 'Lovely One' as a figure for his prince, but elsewhere the lovely ones that fill the hall stand for good men. In the line, 'They see off the lovely one at the southern bank,' she stands for the poet himself."[79] In his "Biography of Qu Yuan", Sima Qian says, "His aim was pure, and so he appeals to fragrant objects."[80] Whether Qu Yuan was choosing a symbol for what he admired or one for himself, the principle is the same. Likewise, we cannot demand consistency from Li Shangyin in his use of symbols.

The last couplet is a fitting conclusion to the disconsolate grief of the whole poem:

Today the east wind has no strength to stay,	今日东风自不胜
Transmuted somber light sinks in the Western Sea.	化作幽光入西海

Spring has gone and there is no holding it back. "The east wind has no strength and all flowers have faded,"[81] all one's hopes and vows are proven fruitless, the pursuit has been in vain, and all that's left is regret for what is gone forever. Li Yu wrote,

The orchard trees have lost their spring pink	林花谢了春红
All too soon	太匆匆
To the inevitable cold rain mornings and the evening wind.	无奈朝来寒雨晚来风
Tears through rouge	胭脂泪
That kept me on to be drunk—	留人醉
When again?	几时重
Man's life is one long grief, as long as the river flows east.[82]	自是人生长恨水长东

Li Shangyin's last line "Transmuted somber light sinks in the Western Sea" is another version of Li Yu's last line, only more subtle in its imagery and so more unusual and disturbing in its language. From the opening line "Breeze light spreads ..." through the emotion-laden, melancholy quest to "Today the east wind has no strength," the scene grows old and spring departs, forever out of reach. Where has it gone?

It has gone like the rapidly passing days that cannot be grasped, and so the word "light"; if it really has been transformed into light, then the light must be "somber" to convey the bitter feeling with which its passage is viewed. And finally, the accumulation of enduring sorrow can appropriately be symbolized by the vast expanse and depth of the ocean, and so this somber light must sink into the sea. Since the spring wind is an east wind, it must naturally blow the spring light away into the Western Sea, along with its burden of regret.

Poets have long written about the departure of spring:

Flowing water, falling flowers—spring is gone	流水落花春去也
On earth as in Heaven.[83]	天上人间
Where has spring gone to?	春归何处
A lonely road where no one walks[84]	寂寞无行路
Spring has gone, as on passing wings,	春归如过翼
Gone without a trace[85]	一去无迹
Here's another spring brought sorrow back.	是他春带愁来
Where does spring go?	春归何处？
It simply does not know to take sorrow with it.[86]	却不解带将愁去

All these lines from songs are good, but Li Shangyin's two lines are the most moving and the most hopeless.

Summer

One's first association with summer is heat, but Li Shangyin's summer day is altogether different. For him it is the shade, the quiet, the stillness that matter, and here is another illustration of the principle that the important thing in a poem is the author's feeling, not the thing that he takes for his subject. In his poem about summer, Du Fu describes a summer day in such terms as "red rays pierce the thick earth"[87] or "In the gorge everything seems on fire."[88] This could be because the days were particularly hot, or because with his sturdy straightforward disposition, he liked to write unambiguously and strongly. He even applied the word "hot" to his own feelings: "I sigh and my bowels are hot inside,"[89] "Looking back, my liver and lungs are hot."[90] When Li Shangyin writes about his feelings, it takes a different turn: "Spring silkworms spin out their thread until they die, / The wax candle turns to ash before its tears are dry."[91] His is a more delicate and a more melancholy disposition. He lacks the robust clarity of Du Fu, avoiding the direct and the obvious, projecting instead the misery of frustration and disappointment. So he does not emphasize the heat of summer, but begins,

> Outside the hall, rain; the curtain left down for grief; 前阁雨帘愁不卷
> On the back room sweet trees cast thick shade. 后堂芳树阴阴见

It leaves an impression of gloom, of obscurity. The curtain not rolled up reminds you of the lines,

> The courtyard is deep, deep, how very deep; 庭院深深深几许
> Cloudy windows, misty halls always locked.[92] 云窗雾阁常扃

with its suggestion of seclusion and cheerlessness. In Li Shangyin's line it is a “rainy curtain”. In another poem he writes “All spring a long dream-rain drifts over the tiles.”[93] One can imagine how the sound of the rain that drifts over the roof blends with the dreamy ruminations of someone inside the lowered curtain. And when the word “out of grief” is added to the “not rolled up”, the unopened curtain is paired with the unrelieved grief that is the reason it has been left so long untouched. The person is unhappy, and so the curtain stays down; and because it remains down, the person is even more unhappy; being shut up inside the curtained room becomes a symbol for being enveloped in unhappiness.

The opening words “the (front) hall” of this line make a link with the first of the next, “the back room”, providing both a contrast and a similarity. As counterpart, the “thick shade” intensifies the feeling of dark and gloom invoked by the drawn curtain. Although the season is summertime, there is no feeling of warmth or brightness, in front of the house or in back—the loneliness and depression of its inhabitant can be imagined. By way of contrast, the trees are “sweet smelling”; there is a trace of the joyous vitality implicit in Tao Qian’s lines,

In early summer when the grasses grow	孟夏草木长
And trees surround my house with greenery.[94]	绕屋树扶疏

And the “thick shade” yields, besides its feeling of darkness, the sense of rich, lush vegetation. The line ends with the word “appears, is seen” (omitted in the translation), implying the presence inside the room, where warmth and light are lacking, of someone who dimly perceives that outside the room the leafy branches of sweet trees are casting their shade on this day of joyous burgeoning. Here are two modes of being: the sentient one inside the room is still, quiet; outside, the insensate life of the pure shade. The sensitive poet reacts to such a contrast with profound sadness and loneliness, his heart filled with inexpressible feelings, and these two lines are Li

Shangyin's reaction to these contradictory modes of being, his attempt to express the inexpressible. The first contrast comes in writing about summer wholly in terms of shade; the next is between the grief inside the room and the sweet shade outside. Illuminating the gloomy, unhappy side of life with that lush beauty doubles the attraction of the beautiful and intensifies the feeling of regret and unhappiness.

The next couplet contains a further set of contrasting images:

The Stone City scene is like the Yellow Springs:	石城景物类黄泉
At midnight the young man walks with useless bow.	夜半行郎空柘弹

There are two places in Chinese history associated with the name Stone City.[95] One is Jinling (Nanjing), famous as the capital of the Six Dynasties.[96] The other is Jingling, in Hubei,[97] associated with a singing girl, Nevercare.[98] Which Stone City was the one Li Shangyin intended? All the commentators take it to be Nevercare's city, and I see no reason to disagree, for Li Shangyin has two other poems using this allusion, one called "Stone City", the other "Nevercare".[99] But what were his associations with Nevercare? Feng Hao claims it was a girl he loved who was wandering about in that region. Zhang Caitian thinks it refers to Yang Sifu, who was demoted there as Imperial Overseer of Hunan, and he has criticized Feng for slandering Li Shangyin as someone who would travel a thousand miles to get a glimpse of someone else's wife. But Zhang Caitian wants to make every line of the "Yantai" poems refer to Yang Sifu's demotion, and his explanation is even more forced. Leaving aside these attempts that only confuse the issue, and sticking to the poem itself, it seems to me that this couplet is a continuation of the first one: it intensifies the contrast between two aspects of life, the good life and the tragedy of humiliation. Not only does this yield a reasonably coherent interpretation of the poem, it also brings it into line with the two poems “Stone City” and “Nevercare”, showing consistency in Li Shangyin’s use of this allusion. He always used it as a symbol for the good life, and the name “Nevercare” itself is a contrast to the tragic tone of the poem. The “Nevercare Song” goes,

Where does Nevercare live?	莫愁在何处
Nevercare lives west of Stone City.	莫愁石城西
A pair of oars propels the boat	艇子打两桨
That brings Nevercare to me.[100]	催送莫愁来

It is a joyous, light-hearted song, but Li Shangyin’s poem “Nevercare” has the lines,

If there had been no boat in Stone City	若是石城无艇子
Nevercare would have been unhappy for a time.[101]	莫愁还自有愁时

So even someone like Nevercare, who had a good life, would have been unhappy if kept from what was a proper part of that life. In Li Shangyin’s “Stone City” are the lines,

In Stone City they boast of the shy fair one,	石城夸窈窕
In Flower County lives the most romantic one.[102]	花县更风流

The shy beauty of Stone City, Nevercare, the symbol of female loveliness, is joined with the poet Pan Yue, the symbol of the handsome man, who planted flowering peach and plum trees everywhere in Heyang County. This the reason for taking the Stone City of the “Yantai” poem as the one associated with Nevercare, for the next line alludes to a story about Pan Yue. It occurs in his *Jin History* biography: “Pan Yue was of handsome appearance.... When young he used to go out in the streets of Luoyang with his pellet crossbow, and when women saw him, they would make a circle around him, holding hands, and then throw fruit into his carriage, which would be full by the time he got home."[103]

Now if we read the two lines of Li Shangyin's couplet together, we get, for the first line: The Stone City scene was lovely, as when Nevercare joyously set out to row her boat to her lover, but today it is gloomy and sad as the Yellow Springs of the netherworld. Today the carefree life would be unattainable even for Nevercare. The next line says that handsome though Pan Yue may be, and however fine his *zhe*-wood bow,[104] if he goes through the streets at midnight, no girls are going to recognize him and fill his carriage with their tokens of admiration—it does no good to wear brocade in the dark, as Xiang Yu remarked.[105] Hence his skill with the bow is to no purpose; it is as wasted as the young man's looks. The "midnight" is symbolical; it is already taking it too literally to say, as Feng Hao does, that it belongs to the night-time imagery of all of the first four lines, and Zhu Yizun's comment that "Sleepless and at loose ends, he seeks distraction in sport"[106] is wholly irrelevant.

There is also a distant connection with the first couplet, in that in both there is a contrast between the good life and life's frustrations; in his inmost being the poet seeks beauty and perfection, but in vain; and one senses his inconsolable bitterness at what he cannot willingly resign himself to. The commentators on these lines have been unwilling to look for the sense in the underlying feelings of the poet, inventing instead arbitrary connections with "what actually happened" and ending up caught in a tangle of contradictions.[107] If we simply follow the logic of the poet's emotional nature, we do not have to look for the particular person or event he was thinking of, but only the bitterness generated by life's frustrations, and the unhappiness created by the unconsummated search for beauty and perfection. This is the single thread running through this series of poems that gives them their unity, not some common episode that can be looked to for a guide to understanding time.

With the next couplet we are back to the summer setting:

A silken fan summons a breeze from Heaven's gate, 绫扇唤风阊阖天
The thin curtain and green drapes billow in swirls.[108] 轻帏翠幕波洄旋

A fan stirring a breeze is common enough in summer; that the fan is "silken" prettifies the fan. Instead of saying the fan "stirs" a breeze, Li Shangyin writes "calls, summons"; the word is appropriate, first, because the motion of the hand holding the fan makes a summoning gesture, and second, because of the following words, "Heaven's gate". It seems as though a response was expected from Heaven, implying a connection between man and Heaven. And finally, the word "summons" personifies the fan, creating in the mind of the reader a more lively impression of the relation between fan and breeze.

The words *chang he* by themselves mean "Heaven's gate"; and the added word "Heaven" goes on to suggest a distant source for the breeze—from the heavens above, as in Du Fu's line, "A pure wind from the heavens billows the curtain."[109] It must be pure and come from a great height, if it is to fill the curtains and make them flutter. In Li Shangyin's next line we find the curtains similarly agitated, and we wonder, how can the current of air generated by a hand-held fan cause such a commotion? But the curtains are light; the material must be thin and soft. The drapes are green, a fresh, bright green. And both "light" and "green" are appropriate to the word "billows" (a noun in the Chinese); they are light, gentle billows, and fresh green in color. As the curtains are filled with air, they turn and seem to make waves. The couplet seems merely to present a summer setting, but in the delicacy and refinement of the description there is an undercurrent of loneliness and boredom. Beyond this, it seems to me there is no deeper meaning. However, there is a wealth of pure poetry. As the ancients says, the useless has a great deal of use. To work at all, this sort of spontaneous fine writing demands an acute poetic sensibility. It is what keeps Li Shangyin's poetry, even when it is wholly lugubrious, from losing the poetic quality and sense of beauty that we appreciate.

These two lines present a picture of a purely summer setting, but in the next couplet Li Shangyin pays a parting tribute to departed spring and reverts to the never-ending melancholy pursuit, the bitter search, fraught with deepest feeling:

The Shu ghost is still—has he a companion now?	蜀魂寂寞有伴未
Tropical flowers open night after night on the panha tree.	几夜瘴花开木棉

The Shu ghost refers of course to the legend of King Wang of Shu whose ghost turned into a cuckoo. It is frequently alluded to in Li Shangyin's poetry—"The ruler of Shu has a lingering ghost";[110] "King Wang's spring heart is lodged in the cuckoo."[111] There are two versions of the story: "The Emperor Wang put Bie Ling ('Turtle Spirit') in charge of waterways. He had sexual relations with Bie Ling's wife. Overcome by shame and convinced that he was morally inferior to Bie Ling, he turned his kingdom over to him. When the Emperor Wang left, the cuckoo was just then singing. Consequently the people of Shu find the song of the cuckoo sad, recalling the Emperor Wang."[112] The other version specifies the Emperor's reincarnation as a bird, without giving the reason: "When the Emperor Wang died, his soul was transformed into a bird; its name was the cuckoo."[113]

The Shu ghost, then, is one that has lost home and country, a guilty, silent ghost, filled with secret sorrow. And, according to the legend, the cuckoo that sings during the last days of spring, rousing people's sad thoughts of home, is the incarnation of this unhappy ghost. If you associate this tragic legend with the cuckoo's sobbing song as it bemoans the departure of spring, every note becomes a sad, lonely cry of the tormented ghost. And from the perception of its misery, you realize how desperately it needs the consolation of a companion. With the need so imperative, he should have found what he was looking for, but since the sad cry never changes, we must believe that the grievous, bitter search will never be rewarded. Hence Li Shangyin ends his line with a question: Has he a companion, or not? The uncertainty shows the poet's sympathy for the unfortunate victim, hoping he may have found someone, but not believing it has happened.

The next line is the counterpart to this one. The panha is a tall tree with a red flower, native to Annam; it also grows in Southern China. The bright red flowers in the tall panha tree emphasize the loneliness of the Shu ghost. As in Du Fu's poem, "Flowers near the tower pain the traveler's heart."[114] Flowers at a height seem brighter; they catch the eye and carry our thoughts off into the distance. When they are red like flames or clotted blood, the rich associations give all the more impetus to the pursuit of thoughts and feelings that lead into the distance. "Panha tree" makes us think at once of the warmth of the south, and here the association of steamy warmth is reinforced with "tropical flowers". The component *mian* of the word panha *mu mian*, suggests, through its homophone *mian*, vast distance, "*mian yuan*". If the lonely, grieving Shu ghost is never to have a companion, its tearful search is all the more pathetic against the background of burning, blood-red blossoms high up above, and all the more desperate. Feng Hao notes that the red of the panha flowers is a reminder of the heat of summer, and although the tree blossoms toward the end of spring (and not during the height of summer), it is a tropical plant after all, and the color does carry the suggestion of flame and heat, so it is appropriate to a poem about summer. That the ghost belonging to Shu (in Western China) is paired with "tropical flowers" is no problem. As I said before, the places named in these poems are used symbolically, and there is no need to try to connect them with Li Shangyin's travels.

Cassia palace pours down light, the rays are hard to catch;	桂宫流影光难取
Seductive fragrance when the orchid opens; soft, soft words.	嫣熏兰破轻轻语

After a long time of seeking and ruminating, it seems as though here is a suggestion of a discovery. In several places in these four poems we encounter such a tentative manifestation, and every time it "comes like a spring dream" and "departs like a morning cloud",[115] elusive and hard to approach. Are they the poet's real experiences, or something he imagines? Both are possible, it seems to me. As real experiences they could be like the lament in Yan Shu's song,

After swallows and geese have gone, the orioles leave too.	燕鸿过后莺归去
Carefully count the thousand myriad threads of this floating life:	细算浮生千万绪
How much longer than spring dreams,	长于春梦几多时
Scattered like autumn clouds nowhere to be found.[116]	散似秋云无觅处

How many of one's lovely feelings change with circumstances, until looking back all that is left is a shadowy film of mist that vanishes as one draws near. This is why Li Shangyin can write about such things so vividly and yet leave it indistinct and unfathomable. If we express it in terms of the poetic imagination, since it is a world created by the poet, it certainly must be something the poet believed in and was deeply attached to. It may not have existed in reality, but because of his inclination to cherish and believe in it, it remains entangled in his heart and as though present to his eyes, at once indistinct and inaccessible, yet clearly visible. Wang Guowei wrote in a song,

I recall hoisting a lonely sail off the eastern seacoast:	忆挂孤帆东海畔
These fairy isles close at hand	咫尺神山
That appear in the sea, year after year.	海上年年见
How often has the sky wind blown my boat about	几度天风吹棹转
As the palaces change in sun and shade.[117]	望中楼阁阴晴变

Those fairy mountains in the ocean, as plain as if before the eyes, become transformed and inaccessible as the wind blows on the boat. This is how Li Shangyin can present a state of feeling as simultaneously vague and crystal clear.

From Li Shangyin's poems, it is undeniable that he must have experienced in real life a painful love affair. On the other hand, in his nature was also an inclination toward a world of perfect beauty that logically he could have no certain knowledge of. In his poem he was constantly fusing the yearning and the regret attached to these two things. This is why I insist that to appreciate Li Shangyin's poetry you must concentrate on the feeling and not insist on distinguishing particular incidents or making irrelevant connections. Because in his poetry we constantly see this fusion of imagination and reality, half dream and half real, and it is neither necessary nor possible to specify which it is. This couplet is a perfect example of this combination of complete clarity and indefinite vagueness.

"Cassia palace" is the palace in the moon, from the legendary cassia tree in the moon; it is where Chang'e lives. If Li Shangyin had written "moon palace", it would limit the meaning to just that; but "cassia palace" could also be a real palace on earth, one with cassia wood rafters.[118] The result is an ambiguity that makes it impossible to decide between reality and illusion.

"Pours down light" should refer to the light coming from the moon, as in Cao Zhi's poem,

The bright moon shines on the tall house,	明月照高楼
The light pouring down lingers long.[119]	流光正徘徊

Since moonlight is visible but not palpable, he can say "the rays are hard to catch". The light pours down on one's head and breast, but there is no way to hold it in the arms; it is empty, illusory. In this one line is much of the feeling of Wang Guowei's lines that I quoted earlier, and of which I said, "Those fairy mountains in the ocean, as plain as if before the eyes, become transformed and inaccessible as the wind blows on the boat." If you insist on a clear and realistic explanation of Li Shangyin's line, it must be a scene late at night, and the next line should describe what appears indistinctly in the moonlight. And what is to be seen? From the "soft, soft words" it seems as though someone is there, and Feng Hao assumes it is a real person: "It says that the figure is barely visible in the flowing moonlight, and there are only the words whispered with a smile and an orchid fragrance wafted by the air." This is the kind of superficial comment to be expected of someone committed to looking for narrowly private feelings in this poetry. However, it is worth noticing that Li Shangyin himself never writes this sort of straightforward banality. The seven words of this line are extraordinarily ambiguous. The word "seductive" is usually used to describe a pretty face, and "fragrance" of course is a sweet smell; to put the two together is a most unusual combination. Wen Tingyun makes a similar union of sight and odor in his line, "Paired hair-knots keep apart fragrant reds,"[120] meaning the red flowers in her hair. With "seductive fragrance", it is not only the fragrance; the seductive appearance is also intoxicating. And if you ask what it is that intoxicates with its beauty and fragrance, the next words "the orchids open" make it clear. The word "bursts open" is most effective for suggesting the precise moment when the swelling buds split open to expose pistils and stamens (and release their fragrance). The "soft, soft words" with which the line concludes can still refer to the newly opened orchids; there is certainly no need to assume someone is actually present who smiles and whispers, as Feng Hao would have it. But how can orchids talk? A poem that says "If flowers knew how to speak"[121] suggests that the idea has occurred to someone. Touched by the faint breeze, the newly blossoming orchids with their intoxicating beauty and fragrance sway as though they were speaking. It is perfectly possible to take the couplet as simply presenting the moving shadows and hidden fragrance of the flowers brushed by a breeze on a moonlit summer night. But if we refer to Li Shangyin's practice of creating a poetic ambience that includes a sense of seeking and melancholy that is purely subjective, we may infer here that the light pouring down from the cassia palace creates a setting that inspires a quest for something lacking, and the "rays hard to catch" mark the depressing realization that it is not easy after all. Since it is so hard, the quest should perhaps be abandoned, but a new level is reached in the "seductive fragrance" line, which presents a realm so entrancing, so intoxicating that it is impossible to relinquish, impossible to put out of the mind, and this indelible feeling leads directly to the next couplet:

Even make the Milky Way fall into the breast,	直教银汉堕怀中
Don't make the Star Lady always come and go.	未遣星妃镇来去

A love so intense, a yearning so bitter, would make the object of such dedicated emotion fall into the poet's breast, though as far away as the Milky Way in the sky. The "Star Lady" is the Spinning Girl, the star on the edge of the Heavenly River (the Milky Way). Taken together the two lines mean: a love so pure it could even make the Milky Way fall into my arms, can also keep the Spinning Girl always at my side, not separated from her lover all year long except for a single night's meeting, so that she is always languishing in her loneliness. The most effective words in these lines are the "even make" and "don't make", with their connotations of something absolutely definite and determined. They suggest that the poet's heart is so filled with unfailing love that he believes there must surely be a day of reunion, with no more separation, and that this will be brought about by the force of his sincerity and faith.

Abruptly, the next couplet:

Are the sources forever other for muddy stream and sparkling waves—	浊水清波何异源
The clear water of the Ji, the turbid Yellow River?	济河水清黄河浑

wholly devoid of emotion, reduces all those lovely imaginings to emptiness. There is a Cao Zhi poem with the lines,

You are like the dust of the clean roadway,	君若清路尘
I am like the mud in the ditch:	妾若浊水泥
Floating or submerged, each differs in state.	浮沉各异势
United, how long can they stay together?[122]	会合何时偕

Clean and muddy, two different states, their goals can hardly be the same, and they can never be joined; this is a tragedy decreed by fate, inescapable. Qu Fu's comment on the line is unquestionably correct: "The streams are clear or muddy from their different sources, and they do not flow together. It is a figure for an eternal separation."[123] These lines, coming directly after the wishful daydream of lines 11-12, emphasize the cruel indifference of the reality of separation. But what can be separated in reality is only the physical body; the love that belongs to the spirit can never be cut off by any physical obstacle. And so the yearning appeal of the final couplet:

How to conjure up the golden skirt out of the light mist,	安得薄雾起湘裙
Lay hand on the cloud carriage and call to the Great Princess?	手接云軿呼太君

No matter how many the difficulties encountered, the obstacles traversed, the yearning, expectant heart first and last will not fail. As in Han Wo's poem,

In this life to the end I may sleep alone,	此生终独宿
But I swear I will search for you until I die.[124]	到死誓相寻

Given a love like this, how is the real manifestation, the sudden before-the-eyes appearance to be achieved? Li Shangyin does it through a purely imaginary encounter. The object of his longing is presented as a fairy girl, a female immortal, coming to this imagined meeting. Her skirt is of a pale yellow stuff, one thinks of it as soft and fine; "golden" has a different set of associations, but just by specifying a color for the skirt the poet makes the apparition seem real. The "light mist" makes the skirt, too, light and diaphanous as the billowing mist, while at the same time conjuring up the vision of a fairy creature hovering indistinct in the mist. The "cloud carriage" must be the carriage in which she is riding; a similar expression occurs in Du Fu's poem,

The Weaving Maiden from Fairyland wheels her cloud carriage;	蓬莱织女回云车
Pointing into space, she leads the way back.[125]	指点虚无引归路

A cloud carriage is the expected vehicle for an immortal who descends from the clouds—"Rainbow for robes, the wind for steeds,"[126] "Riding the whirlwind, bearing cloud pennons"[127]—this is the way poets imagine the arrival of spirits. By adding the words "Lay hand on", reinforced by the word "call", Li Shangyin introduces a touch of immediacy and brings a feeling of reality in the midst of this insubstantial vision: a hand stretched out to touch the carriage, a cry of recognition; an occasion for rejoicing, of reassurance. But we must not forget the opening words "How to conjure up…" How can such a thing be realized? So it never really happens. Wang Guowei writes,

Wax tears by the window grow an inch—	蜡泪窗前堆一寸
In his life man's lot is only longing.[128]	人间惟有相思分

It is not happiness achieved that Li Shangyin is writing about; it is the bone-cutting longing that is left after the experience of trouble and ineradicable failure.

Autumn

The poem opens with an autumn night, chill and clear:

Moon waves traverse the sky, the eaves of the sky are wet,	月浪衡天天宇湿
The chill toad has dropped away, sparse stars come in.	凉蟾落尽疏星入

It is not a wholly static scene; there is the movement of time, and also the implication that the poet is sleepless through the long night, preoccupied with his longing. The rays of the moon are perceived as waves that spread out across the sky.[129] The "eaves of the sky" is the horizon; that they are wet continues the conceit of moonlight as waves, flowing across the sky and depositing their moisture on the horizon. The line effectively realizes the bright autumn moonlight spreading out and saturating the vast, chill heavens until it seems to drip off at the edges. But the excellence of the line is not only in conveying the reality of the scene, but also in the remote, chilly ambience the scene symbolizes, an ambience occurring frequently enough in Li Shangyin to suggest that he was painfully familiar with its cheerless solitude. For example in the poem "Frosty Moon",

When we hear the migrant ducks, the cicada is gone.	初闻征雁已无蝉
From the hundred-foot-high hall the water touches the sky.	百尺楼高水接天
Green Girl and White Lady can both bear the cold,	青女素娥俱耐冷
Flaunting their beauty in moonlight and frost.[130]	月中霜里斗婵娟

The next line measures out the time that has slowly passed in this desolate setting. The "chill toad" is the common metonymy for the moon, the toad traditionally belonging to its fauna. It is chill, appropriately enough, on this autumn night. It has "dropped away", giving the impression of a completed unit of time: the round, cold moon has slowly descended from the zenith to disappear in the west, and the waves of light that saturated the cosmos have gradually diminished and died out. We can only imagine what feelings of inconsolable loneliness and irretrievable loss oppressed the poet through this long night. And yet there has so far been not a single word about human affairs—only moonlight, the eaves of the sky, the chill toad. But with the last words, "sparse stars come in", we begin to move from the sky to the human realm. Feng Hao's comment is, "Once the moon has set, the starlight comes into his door." The starlight is in the sky; the poet stands in his doorway. It is another chill, lonely scene in the starlight after the moon has set, and it makes us notice again the passage of time, but now the chill and loneliness have moved from the sky to penetrate the human world, unavoidably involving the poet. With the next couplet we are firmly on the earth:

The mica screen, unmoving, covers the lonely frown,	云屏不动掩孤嚬
All night in the west house the wind-harp is quick.	西楼一夜风筝急

Here someone is sleepless through the long night. Li Shangyin often uses the words "mica screen", as in the poem "Because",

Because behind the mica screen she is lovely beyond compare,	为有云屏无限娇
In Phoenix Tower the cold is past and she dreads spring nights.[131]	凤城寒尽怕春宵

and in "Chang'e",

Behind the mica screen the candle shadows are deep.	云母屏风烛影深
As the Long River slowly drops, the morning stars drown.[132]	长河渐落晓星沉

In these poems the mica screen is associated with elegant quarters and the loneliness of a long night, with a grief-stricken person hidden behind the screen. In the "Yantai" poem she is frowning, the visible evidence of her unhappiness. Li Bai's quatrain "Unhappiness" presents a similar scene:

The palace lady rolls up the pearl curtain.	美人卷珠帘
Sitting hidden inside, she knits her moth brows.	深坐颦蛾眉
One sees only the wet marks of tears	但见泪痕湿
And does not know for whom her heart's pain.[133]	不知心恨谁

In Li Shangyin's poem the fact of her unhappiness is conveyed without using a single word that makes it explicit. The screen is unmoving, it has long been in place untouched, hiding someone; and this serves to suggest long-hidden unhappiness that has never been assuaged.

The "wind-harp" (*feng zheng*) is probably the wind chimes that hang under the eaves and tinkle when the wind blows, though commentators have suggested a literal stringed *zheng* placed outside that also makes a sound in the wind.[134] This line should be read as going with the preceeding one: the person sitting with a lonely frown inside the screen has been listening all night long to the wind in the chimes. The line ends with *ji* (quick, urgent), suggesting her sadness at the jingle of the chimes in the insistent wind. The first couplet described the scene observed by the unhappy person behind the screen; this second couplet tells the sounds to be heard, and we are even more aware of the pathos of "The mica screen, unmoving, covers the lonely frown," stoical strength of this single-minded acceptance of desolate solitude.

Longing and resentment are both clearly apparent in the next couplet:

One longs to weave a love flower to send afar	欲织相思花寄远
To the day's end yearning and bitter too.	终日相思却相怨

If love could be changed into a visible object, it would have to be a flower of perfect color and fragrance, and when the love is great and has no outlet, one might well wish to convert it into a flower-pattern that would symbolize the love in every thread, and send it to the distant beloved. But in the absence of news, even if you wanted to weave such a token, there would be no place to send it. Zhou Bangyan writes,

No place to dump my heart's load of care;	怨怀无托
The one I love is gone for good, alas,	嗟情人断绝
Too far for letters.[135]	信音辽邈

When the letter brings no response, the inexhaustible longing turns into boundless resentment, and this is the burden of Li Shangyin's line. The yearning turns into resentment, and the source of both is a profound love of which there is no eradicating. The only way not to feel resentment is not to love, something forever out of reach of the person susceptible to love. So the yearning and the resentment are inseparably linked. The yearning shows the intensity of love, and the resentment shows its pain. "To the day's end" puts no limit to the conflicting feelings, alternating between the intensity and the pain, for there is never any relief, to the end of time.

> The only sound she hears is the Dipper turning, 但闻北斗声回环
> She never sees the Long River flow clear and shallow. 不见长河水清浅

These lines symbolize the passage of time and the insurmountable barriers that keep people apart, agitated by such feelings as those. The Dipper revolves with the passage of time. It can record the lapse of a year's time, as in Meng Haoran's poem,

> Last night the Dipper turned to the North, 昨夜斗回北
> This morning the year begins in the East.[136] 今朝岁起东

It can also mark the slow passing of the long night, as in the old *yuefu*,

> The moon sets, the Triad is aslant, 月没参横
> The North Dipper declines.[137] 北斗阑干

Li Shangyin's poem began with the night sky, but the first couplet was concerned only with the unhappy longing on a sleepless night. The Dipper's turning in this line is not just what it does on one night; the position of the Dipper in the night sky at any given time changes from day to day throughout the year. The force of this line is to extend the bitter longing from one night to the next: every night is like this. His "Chang'e" quatrain ends with the line,

> Green sea, blue sky—night after night in her heart,[138]

and here is the same lonely bitterness, the never-assuaged longing. By making the turning Dipper audible, the poet intensifies our awareness of the passage of time and, in so doing, deepens the pain of longing. The "Long River" of the next line is the Heavenly Han River, the Milky Way, which traditionally flows across the sky and separates the two lovers, the Spinning Girl and the Herdboy, as in Cao Pi's poem,

The starry Han flows west, the night is not yet done,	星汉西流夜未央
Herdboy and Spinning Girl gaze at one another far apart.	牵牛织女遥相望
What have they done to be separated by that River?[139]	尔独何辜限河梁

and Li Shangyin's poem, "West River":

On earth let it flow into the sea	人间从到海
And let there be no River in the sky.[140]	天上莫为河

But now it is not just making a river in the sky; this stream that flows all the way across the sky never runs clear and shallow but makes an impassable barrier destined to last for all eternity. In this line the words "never sees" match the "only hears" of the preceding line; *dan* also means "in vain"; she vainly (only) listens for the sound of the Dipper turning. Surrendered to the bitterness of longing, to time slipping away, and never once seeing the Long River of the sky run clear and shallow, leaves no slightest glimmer of hope for a reprieve from this eternal separation—two lines of utter disappointment and heartbreaking grief.

The golden fish locks up the red cassia spring,	金鱼锁断红桂春
Ancient dust covers the lovebird bed.	古时尘满鸳鸯茵

Here all lovely things come to a wretched end. Yao Peiqian comments, "The 'golden fish' is a fish-shaped lock; a door lock is in the shape of a fish because a fish never closes its eyes, according to the *Zhitian Record*." So a lock in fish form is one that is forever on guard, leaving no way to slip through the door it fastens. Made of metal, it is hard and secure against any attempts of the one locked up to break out. Locked up here is to be confined for life, with no hope of seeing the light of the sun. "Red cassia spring": it is generally held that the cassia tree blooms in the autumn, but actually there are varieties that bloom in the spring, as Wang Wei's line proves:

People are idle, the cassia petals fall,	人闲桂花落
The night is still, spring hills are empty.[141]	夜静春山空

Though cassia flowers are mostly yellow or white, there are also red ones.[142] Cassia flowers may be red, and they may appear in the spring, but Li Shangyin is using these epithets as evocative of beauty, not to suggest a specific variety of cassia tree. For all the beauty of flower and season, the golden fish locks it all up, and this red springtime tree is shut away in the dark to bloom and wither alone, out of sight of any who might appreciate it—such is the tragedy of beauty wasted.

The next line introduces yet another lovely, lifeless object as a source of distress, the "lovebird bed". *Yuanyang* are mandarin ducks, always in pairs, symbols of conjugal felicity, and *yin* is a mattress. The *Western Capital Miscellany* says that when Flying Swallow was Empress, her younger sister presented her with a love-bird quilt and a love-bird mattress.[143] The connotations are apparent in Wen Tingyun's line, "The warm incense provokes a dream under the lovebird brocade."[144] But in Li Shangyin's line the lovebird bed is neglected; it is covered with dust, and not just covered, but "filled"; furthermore the dust is "ancient". Something valuable has been long neglected and never put to its proper use. If we look back at the preceding line, it is the animate red cassia spring that is locked up for all time; here the inanimate lovebird bed has been collecting dust for a long time. Living in a tragic world, man can hardly escape a similar fate. Two occasions of human tragedy come in the next couplet:

One can deplore the little park made a long road, 堪悲小苑作长道
But jade trees do not pity the deposed king. 玉树未怜亡国人

The "little park" evokes a palace garden with lovely trees; it does not have to allude to a specific park.[145] It seems that all beautiful parks are destined to revert to wasteland. As early as Ruan Ji poets were lamenting,

The luxuriant flowers must fade, 繁华有憔悴
In the hall thorns and willows grow.[146] 堂上生荆杞

There have always been vicissitudes of this sort, but after the An Lushan rebellion such sights were more common than earlier in the Tang, and the poets' laments became more frequent. Du Fu, for example:

Kingfishers nest in the little hall by the water, 江上小堂巢翡翠
The qilin lies beside the high grave by the park.[147] 苑边高冢卧麒麟

And,

Palaces on the waterway: a thousand gates are locked; 江头宫殿锁千门
Slender willows, new reeds—for whom do they green?[148] 细柳新浦为谁绿

These are scenes of parks neglected and gone to ruin. Li Shangyin also wrote a poem on the Serpentine that expresses the desolation more intensely:

I keep looking for the royal carriage that used to pass, 望断平时翠辇过
Listen in vain at midnight for the ghost's sad song.[149] 空闻子夜鬼悲歌

Li Shangyin probably wrote his poem to lament the Sweet Dew assassinations, shortly after the Emperor Wenzong had restored the palaces on the Serpentine. This was a poem written as a reaction to a catastrophic event and not as a casual composition. Gao Buying, in commenting on this poem, quotes the *Old Tang History*: "In winter, the tenth month, the ninth year of Taihe (814), the court made an excursion to the Serpentine.... The Emperor was fond of poetry and someone recited the Du Fu poem 'On the Serpentine'[150] with the line, 'Palaces on the waterway: a thousand gates are locked,' from which it was clear that formerly there were palaces and other buildings on all sides of the Serpentine. Thinking to restore conditions of those happy times, he had storied palaces built to realize them... In the eleventh month, the Army Chief Qiu Shiliang led troops to punish the Prime Minister Wang Ya ... and a dozen others. All were put to death along with their entire families."[151] Gao Buying adds a line from the *Comprehensive Mirror*, "On the *jiashen* day of the twelfth month construction of the pleasure palaces on the Serpentine was halted by Imperial order,"[152] and comments, "After the An-Shi Rebellion the Serpentine fell daily into greater neglect. In his poem Li Shangyin says the Emperor's visits have long been omitted. The sad song of the night-time ghost represents the desolation of the Serpentine Park at that time."[153]

Bai Juyi also wrote,

Half-decayed, the tree in the wind,	半朽临风树
Filled with grief, the man on horseback.	多情立马人
One willow tree from Kaiyuan times,	开元一株柳
In this spring of Changqing two.[154]	长庆二年春

And Liu Yuxi's song "Willow Boughs",

When planted in front of Flower Calyx House	花萼楼前初种时

Palace ladies upstairs compared slender waists. 美人楼上斗腰支
Today cast out in the long thoroughfare 而今抛掷长街里
Dew on leaves like tears, blaming whom?[155] 露叶如啼欲恨谁

Though not directly about the desolation of the park, this too is a lament over the decay from former prosperous times.

Li Shangyin's "little park made a long road" need not be specifically identified with the palace grounds after the An Lushan Rebellion, nor need it be Flower Calyx House, nor Hibiscus Garden in the Serpentine. On the other hand, using a decaying park as a symbol in his poem does not exclude a specific personal experience on the part of the poet. The sense of the line is that a park at one time belonging to a detached palace has become the site of a thoroughfare. No place is secure from change, however beautiful or protected.

In the following line the allusion is specific. It was the Last Ruler of the Chen Chen Houzhu, the king of a doomed state, who had the song "Jade Tree Flowers in the Back Court" (*Yushu houting hua*) composed,[156] a song always regarded as belonging to the music of a fallen state. Jade trees and a deposed king should refer to the Last Ruler of the Chen, or to someone overthrown and destroyed as he was. Notice that Li Shangyin includes the words "do not pity" (*wei lian*) which match "one can deplore" (*kan bei*) of the preceding line; so what is deplorable is the park become a highway, not the deposed ruler. And why? Because the garden has no specific referent, it is a symbol for all that is beautiful and cannot be preserved, the eternal round of flourishing and decay. The deposed king with his jade trees is only one individual person, who is considered to have been responsible for his own downfall. Wang Guowei remarks, "The man of affairs' field of vision is focused on a single individual or a single event; the poet's vision encompasses past and present."[157] The little park becoming a highway is the tragedy of rise and fall through the centuries; the jade tree of a deposed ruler refers to the fate of a single individual. One is to be deplored, the other is not to be pitied: the implication is that what is regrettable is the ultimate destruction of beauty, not the fate of one man or the outcome of one affair. In this sense we can understand that "does not pity" is not really indifference; it is rather subordinated to an all-encompassing eternal lament that transcends this kind of pity. Looking back at the preceding couplet, where the red cassia spring is locked off and the lovebird bed is covered with dust, we can see that the world as Li Shangyin saw it was filled with disappointment and sadness; it was not just a unique episode or the fate of a single person.

The next couplet,

> Soothing jasper zither holds a Chu melody, 瑶琴愔愔藏楚弄
> Silk of Yue is cool and thin, heavy with 越罗冷薄金泥重
> gold appliqué.

works the same way as the lines from "Summer": "A silken fan summons a breeze from Heaven's gate, / The thin curtain and green drapes billow in swirls." But there is a deeper meaning to be found in these two lines. The expression *yin-yin*, "soothing, pleasing", is well attested in musical contexts, especially zither music.[158] Li Shangyin connects it with "Chu melody",[159] and Chu music ever since Qu Yuan and the "Li sao" has been sad music.[160] The line "Soothing jasper zither holds a Chu melody" suggests that although the zither music superficially is soothing, there is in it an undercurrent of sadness and despair. This combination of conflicting feelings can apply to any number of situations where externally everything is fine but where someone is secretly consumed with bitterness. The following line likewise contains a complicated and contradictory image. Yue silk is a lightweight, patterned material produced in the eastern region of Yue,[161] used for summer clothing and hence thought of as "cool and thin". The "gold appliqué" is a flowery design painted on with a suspension of gold powder.[162] The color of gold has associations of richness and beauty, while the thing itself is solid and heavy. The application of this rich, heavy substance on the soft light cloth creates a contrast between the density of gold and the coolness of silk: gold is heavy and gauze is light. The weight of the one against the fragility of the other creates a feeling of oppression, and the gold liquid permeating the cool silk suggests an intimate contact. These lines carry a most involved and complicated emotion not wholly subject to logical analysis, and this is only an attempt to give expression to my own reaction. Feng Hao's is altogether too confined to a literal understanding of the two lines: "One imagines she has got up at night to play on her zither," and "the clothes worn while she is playing". This does less than justice to the subtlety and depth of the lines.

The next couplet develops this complicated, involuted emotional tone and, through the word "frost", recalls and emphasizes the "autumn" of the title:

The parrot by the curtain hook, alarmed by night frost,	帘钩鹦鹉夜惊霜
Calls up south clouds to circle cloud dream.	唤起南云绕云梦

The parrot is a bird whose gaudy plumage is a source of pleasure to its owner; it is an intelligent bird that can mimic human speech; and as it is often kept in a woman's apartment or garden, it has romantic associations, as in Wen Tingyun's lines,

A parrot on her hand,	手里金鹦鹉
Embroidered phoenix on her breast,	胸前绣凤凰
She secretly steals a glance at him.	偷眼暗形相

"Best we get married　　不如从嫁与
And be a pair of lovebirds."[163]　　作鸳鸯

And Yan Shu, in his "Spring in the House of Jade",

The red curtain half-lowered, the incense burnt out,　　朱帘半下香销印
The east wind of the second month prods the willow.　　二月东风催柳信
The lute laid aside, thinking of him—　　琵琶旁畔且寻思
Don't say it aloud in front of the parrot.[164]　　鹦鹉前头休借问

It is in such romantic settings that the parrot has a place. But Li Shangyin's parrot is "alarmed by night frost"; the pleasantly romantic associations that go with a parrot in a lady's chamber are in violent contrast with the chill and loneliness of a frosty night. It subtly recalls the complexity and contradictions of the preceding couplet. The "curtain hook" not only serves to locate the parrot, it also leads from the bird to its owner, making a bridge between the outside chill and the dream inside the curtain; through these words we move from the parrot overtaken by night frost to the southern clouds encircling cloud dream. Zhu Heling takes "Cloud Dream" as referring to the Terrace at Cloud Dream (*Yunmeng zhi tai*) of the Song Yu "Gaotang Rhapsody",[165] and Zhu Heling invokes a line from a Lu Ji Rhapsody for the term "south cloud".[166] I believe that "south cloud" is used symbolically for a dream of passionate yearning. The softness and indefinite contours of a cloud fit the nature of vague longing or of an indefinite dream world. "South" is associated in Chinese with warmth and passion, as against the cold and isolation of "north", and if a yearning dream is in some way cloud-like, the dream symbolized by a south cloud should be a dream more passionate and more resplendent. If we follow Zhu Heling and understand the "Cloud Dream" as an allusion to the Terrace at Cloud Dream of the "Gaotang Rhapsody", the suggestion of an erotic dream is obvious. For the moment, I will leave this reading aside to consider the words of the poem. From the south cloud that symbolizes the dreaming poet to the cloud-dream it circles around, the associations summoned up by the words themselves are already infinitely suggestive and far-reaching. The opening words of the line, *huan qi*, are subject to two readings. Qu Fu says, "'South clouds circle Cloud-dream' means that in the midst of his (erotic) Gaotang dream, he is rudely awakened by the parrot which was disturbed by the frost and is shaking the curtain-hook."[167] In support of this one could recall Jin Changxu's "Spring Grievance" quatrain,

Drive away the oriole	打起黄莺儿
Don't let him sing in the tree.	莫教枝上啼
Singing, he disturbed my dream	啼时惊妾梦
Before I got to Liaoxi.[168]	不得到辽西

Also Su Shi's song to the tune "The Water Dragon Sings", in which he writes,

I dreamt I went with the wind a thousand miles	梦随风万里
Looking for where you have gone,	寻郎去处
But came back, called out of my dream by the oriole.[169]	又还被莺呼起

It is a perfectly possible reading of Li Shangyin's line, to take *huan qi* as "roused from sleep". But I have the feeling that this line is to be understood differently. I would take *huan qi* as *yin qi* "to invoke", and I would understand the kind of dream symbolized by "south cloud" as not the dream of sleep, but a dream-like world of fantasy created by the poet's brooding imagination. My reasons for taking it this way are: first, this whole poem, with all its imagery of night-time, from the first line on, invokes a sleepless night, leaving no place for a dream that one is to be awakened from. Further, Qu Fu's reading is a narrowly literal one, and a bit vulgar to boot. It accords ill with Li Shangyin's practice in all four poems of using symbolism to present an uncertain, subtle state of mind. Finally, my reading of the line makes it a contrast with the preceding one, like the pairs of contrasting elements we have noticed all through this poem: the red cassia spring which is locked off, or the lovebird bed covered with dust, the little park turned into a highway or the jasper zither playing a sad melody. In all of them a flaw or sadness is injected into something perfect or fortunate which cannot be prolonged. And here the contrast is between the loneliness and chill of the parrot alarmed by the night-time frost and the gentleness and indefiniteness of the south cloud enveloping a cloud-dream, so that even in the face of the disappointment of grief and loneliness, the stubborn urge toward the pursuit of happiness and perfection persists. With the words "calls up" it is as though the poet said, just because the present is so barren, it rouses the yearning and the search for the sweetness that isn't there. Understood in this way, these lines carry considerably more meaning than simply explained as being awakened from a dream by a bird call.

The next couplet continues the theme of longing and searching.

Paired dingling earrings along with the letter	双珰丁丁联尺素
That tells of the Xiang River rendezvous.	内记湘川相识处

The earrings should be an enclosure in a letter, but is this to be understood literally, or as an indication of an emotional involvement? Feng Hao says, "A letter and earrings appear frequently in his poetry; it probably is an actual occurrence. Qian Mu'an says a girl sent them, or perhaps Li Shangyin sent them; it is not clear which it was. But a gift requires an answer, so it's all the same." Zhu Heling says, "They are the earrings of the earlier poem," probably referring to the poem "Spring Rain":

Jade earrings in a sealed letter, how to deliver them?	玉珰缄札何由达

Through a thousand miles of cloud-gauze a single goose flies.[170] 万里云罗一雁飞

From these lines one would assume it was Li Shangyin who had no way to send his letter with the earrings, but from the "Yantai" line it seems it is something sent by the girl. This is why Feng Hao was unable to decide just how the supposed event took place. Sending a present is in practice only a way of showing affection for someone one loves, and in poetry the mention of such a gift is not always intended to be taken literally, as in the *Shijing* poem,

She gave me a peach 投我以木桃
I responded with jasper... 报之以琼瑶……
She gave me a plum 投我以木李
I responded with chalcedony,[171] 报之以琼玖

and it is obvious that the presents exchanged in Zhang Heng's "Fourfold Sorrow" are based on the *Shijing* poem and are completely symbolical.[172] Besides these, there are the gift of pearls by the Luo River[173] and the girdle pendant taken off at Han'gao, in purely legendary stories.[174] The earrings in a letter in other Li Shangyin poems may well have been real, but putting them in a poem is not just to record something that happened, it is to symbolize a love wholeheartedly shared. So the earrings are a pair, and the delicate sound they make (*ding-ding*) embodies their artistry and beauty; that they are sent in a letter implies the depth of the affection they were meant to show.

The following line is closely connected; in fact, it should be the contents of the letter "that tells of the Xiang River rendezvous." There is a Wei Zhuang song that goes,

I remember that year under the blossoms 记得那年花下

Late at night 深夜
When I first got to know Miss Xie.[175] 初识谢娘时

And Yan Jidao also writes,

I remember when first I saw Xiaopin 记得小蘋初见
There were two double hearts on her dress.[176] 两重心字罗衣

So unforgettable is that first impression on meeting someone whom one begins to love. No matter how long the separation has been, the feelings of that time of first acquaintance on the Xiang River remain forever new, and in this letter today those deep feelings are recalled in bitter detail. Both Feng Hao and Zhang Caitian take "Xiang River" as a reference to an actual place. Feng says, "Here the person went first to the Xiang River and when Li Shangyin arrived there, he got to know her; then she went somewhere else. He repeatedly reverts to this episode." And Zhang Caitian, "This couplet records the letter from that person inviting him to a meeting on the Xiang River." Aside from its specific meaning as a place name the Xiang River occurs in literary writings with other uses. The word *xiang* is homophonous with "one another", and it can serve as a pun on that word, making a sort of musical reinforcement in the right context, deepening the reader's perception of a close association with someone, just as the component *chang* in Chang'an works in Li Bai's *yuefu* "Always Thinking of You", "Always thinking of you, (always) in Chang'an,"[177] where the repeated *chang* intensifies the feeling of the long duration of "always thinking of you". Then there is the association with the place where the two wives of Shun spotted the bamboo with their tears, grieving for their lost lord. So the reader also gets a suggestion of grieved yearning, along with something of the legendary and supernatural, for the two ladies became the guardian spirits of the Xiang River after their death. In this way the occurrence of the words

"Xiang River" in a poem already carries a symbolical coloring. Yan Shu writes,

Understanding me, the divine companion took 闻琴解佩神仙侣
off her pendant;
Her robe tore in my hand, not to be held back.[178] 挽断罗衣留不住

Though the friendship was marked by the gift of a girdle pendant or earrings in a letter, and even if the companion was a goddess whose acquaintance one made by the Xiang River, still there must come a time of separation. In Li Shangyin's poem these two lines are concerned with the feelings after parting, and again it is the loss of all that is fine and lovely. Everything is concentrated in the lament in the final couplet:

Through rain I see singing lips all my life long— 歌唇一世衔雨看
Alas the sweet perfume grows old in the hand. 可惜馨香手中故

The "rain" should be a rain of tears;[179] the "singing lips" are those of the person longed for. Li Yu's lines,

One clear song 一曲清歌
Momentarily breaks open the cherry lips,[180] 暂引樱桃破

make a perfect gloss on "singing lips". As long as they are there to be watched, one can forget his cares. But seen through eyes blinded by a rain of tears, invoked perhaps by the letter from someone far away about a meeting long ago, these lips must belong to a singer remembered from the past; it is a vision, seen vividly in spite of the tears, not an actual presence.

Here again a contrast is introduced that strengthens the feeling of the tragedy of the inevitable end of happiness in frustration and grief: the beauty of the singing lips leads to the misery of a flood of tears. And this is not all: the sweet perfume grows old in the hand. Zhu Yizun thinks this refers to the letter of line 17, making the perfume the fragrance from the hand of the one who wrote the letter. There is a couplet in Lu You's poem "Chrysanthemum Pillow" (*ju zhen*):

All human affairs ground to a powder,	人间万事销磨尽
Only the pure fragrance is as it was of old.	只有清香似旧时

When all is vanished and only a fragrance remains as a reminder of the past, that already is a moving experience. Li Shangyin goes a step farther: the fragrance itself grows old. This one surviving vestige of the past cannot be preserved, even when held closely in the hand of the one who values it. This is the final human tragedy; seeing what you love vanish beyond recall before your very eyes.

The last line begins with the lament "alas". What is being deplored is something far deeper than the letter which Zhu Yizun believed to be the source of this unhappiness. It is a lasting sorrow, an unhappiness there is no assuaging. In another poem Li Shangyin wrote,

Heng'e mixes the elixir and will never give up,	姮娥捣药无时已
Jade Girl plays tosspot and does not stop.	玉女投壶未肯休
When will this imperfect world change?	何日桑田俱变了
Don't let the Yi River keep flowing east.[181]	不教伊水向东流

Despite their devoted dedication, the regret is as unchanging as the eastward flowing river; no price would be too great if this unsatisfactory world could be turned upside down and remade nearer the heart's desire.

Winter

Of the four poems, "Winter" is the most despairing. The first two lines express the eternal human tragedy of impermanence and imperfection:

The sun comes up in the eastern sky and sets in the sky's west, 天东日出天西下
Lady phoenix flies alone, woman dragon is solitary. 雌凤孤飞女龙寡

The eastern sky paired starkly with the western sky, the sun rising and then at once setting, convey the breakneck speed of the passage of time. In another context Mencius said, "Having seen them alive, you cannot bear to see them dead,"[182] and the feeling one gets from this first line is that no sooner have you seen it rise than you see it expire, and this brings a frightening realization of the helplessness of man at the mercy of impermanence. As Li Bai wrote,

Even with a long rope it's hard to tie up the sun— 长绳难系日
It has always made us sad and bitter.[183] 自古共悲辛

Lu Yang brandished his spear to make the sun turn back,[184] and Kuafu ran his race with the sun;[185] they are part of the ancient hopeless struggle against the passage of time. The seven-word line of Li Shangyin expresses perfectly the ancient bitterness at this impermanence against which there is no appeal. We see the abrupt conclusion implied in the sun's sudden passage from the eastern sky to the sky's west. Lots of Chinese poems bemoan the inexorable passage of time, but such a stark, concrete line is rare. The line is good not only because it is moving, but also because it is an appropriate echo of the poem's title. Just as the day goes to its end from sunrise to sunset, so too the year comes to its end; it is the final extinction of light and warmth and growth.

Eternally the seasons change, 浩浩阴阳移
The years of our lives are like the morning dew 年命如朝露

—so goes the old poem.[186] Li Shangyin's line is a powerful evocation of the hopeless grief at impermanence, and his next line is an equally strong evocation of the pain at the eternal incompleteness of human life. Here the emphasis is on a different comparison: lady phoenix and female dragon—they are of the same sex but are creatures of a different kind. The phoenix flies without a mate, the dragon is alone, different species but alike unhappy, representing the grief common to all, whatever their disparate allegiance. The disappointment is no longer anything special; it becomes the unhappiness shared by all. It is given a more specifically human application in the next couplet:

Greenstream and Whitestone out of each other's sight,	青溪白石不相望
The hall is farther even than Cangwu Plain.[187]	堂中远甚苍梧野

"Whitestone Boy" is the fifth of the eleven "Songs for Spirit Strings", and the sixth, "The Little Lady of Greenstream". The sixth song reads

White water before the gate	开门白水
Near to the bridge	侧近桥梁
Where Little Lady lives	小姑所居
All alone without a lover.[188]	独处无郎

The fifth:

Piled-up stones like jade,	积石如玉
Ranked pines like blue feathers:	列松如翠
The boy is most handsome,	郎艳独绝
Not another in the world like him.[189]	世无其二

In both stanzas the setting is idyllic, and it seems fitting that the little lady and the handsome boy should be united as lifelong companions. But in Li Shangyin's poem they are "out of each other's sight"; the two who are meant for one another are separated and given no occasion to meet—"The hall is farther even than Cangwu Plain."

According to the *Record of Rites*,[190] Shun was buried on the Plain of Cangwu, where his two wives could not follow him. Their grief when he died is often referred to in Chinese poetry. There are several features of the story that are invoked. In the first place it involves two kinds of separation: while the absent person is still alive, it is harder to accept the fact of long separation, but his death adds yet a further source of grief. Shun was doubly absent from his wives, for he died while separated from them. Further, Shun was buried on the Hill of Nine Doubts, which the *Seas and Mountains Classic* locates in the south, among the Cangwu hills on the Gulf of Cangwu.[191] It is so named because the nine gullies on the mountain are indistinguishable from one another,[192] as Li Bai writes in his ballad on the grief of Shun's wives,

The Nine Doubts run together, all alike;	九疑联绵皆相似
In which one is he of the odd eyes buried?[193]	重瞳孤坟竟何是

So not only did Shun die separated from his wives, to be buried in the wilderness; even the site of his grave was uncertain—an added source of grief. The *Record of Strange Things* (*Shu yi ji*), relates, "Of old, when on a southern tour, Shun was buried in the wilds of Cangwu, and Yao's two daughters E'huang and Nüying (his wives) were unable to get to him. They wept together, and their tears ran down and wet the bamboo. From this the bamboo has had spotted markings."[194] Hence Li Bai's ballad,

When Cangwu mountain falls and the Xiang River flows no more,	苍梧山崩湘水绝
The tear marks on the bamboo only then will vanish.[195]	竹上之泪乃可灭

But hills and stream do not change, and the tear marks on the bamboo endure, and even so the pain of this eternal separation will never vanish. So much sorrow and hopelessness are conveyed by the words "Cangwu Wilds".

The line begins with "The hall is farther even…", laying emphasis on the distance; the tragic separation of Shun and his wives is re-enacted in a present day setting. Li Bai's ballad again,

> The ocean's waters straight down a myriad *li* deep— 海水直下万里深
> Who would not say this separation is bitter?[196] 谁人不言此离苦

And one of Wei Zhuang's songs,

> The nearby painted hall is remote as the sea.[197] 咫尺画堂深似海

It is worse being cut off from this everyday, nearby painted hall than from distant Cangwu, and the pain of separation is greater than if it were over a myriad miles of ocean water. One can understand the heart-piercing loneliness felt by the residents of Greenstream and Whitestone separated and out of sight of one another.

This leads to the next couplet,

> Frost flowers rise on the icy wall in crisscross relief, 冻壁霜华交隐起
> Snap short the sweet root, and the fragrant heart dies. 芳根中断香心死

The "walls" must be the four walls of a dwelling, and Zhang Caitian comments on the line, "It details the setting," implying that the frost on the icy walls is the actual situation inside the room on a winter day. For me these are not descriptive poems, and this line should not just describe the poet's room; it serves to create an atmosphere of cold and isolation. The word "wall" suggests a space enclosed and cut off; "icy" adds the feeling of desolation and chill. It locks the poet wholly in a circle of bone-piercing cold. The line continues, “frost-flowers in crisscross relief”, rendering this encircling cold sharply visible. “Crisscross” implies the thickness and complexity of the frost lines, and their amorphous quality is suggested by “blurred” (the translation has “in relief”). The verb “rise” makes the growth of frost a process of gradual accumulation. In such an environment no sensitive being could survive, as the next line so unequivocally states, “Snap short the sweet root, and the fragrant heart dies.” A “root” grows deep underground, and the heart is the receptacle of deep feelings. The one is “sweet”; the other, “fragrant”—so aromatic and pure, and yet the root of this lovely life is prematurely cut off, the calyx of this aromatic sensibility is destroyed. What else in this world can one hope for, in a world where all beauty ends like this?

And so it continues:

Vain to ride[198] a painted boat, with the Toad in mind—	浪乘画舸忆蟾蜍
The Moon Lady may not be so very beautiful after all.	月娥未必婵娟子

The Toad is the moon, identified with Chang’e by Zhang Heng in his star catalog.[199] The “painted boat” is glossed as the term used in the South for a large boat.[200] The commentators have nothing to say on this line. I take it as the poet’s own invention, for which no allusion need be sought. There are two possible sources of inspiration for it: the old story about someone who rode a raft to the Heavenly River (the Milky Way) and saw the Herdboy and Spinning Girl before returning.[201] If it is possible to get to the Milky Way on a raft, why not ride in a boat to the moon? Another possible suggestion is the resemblance of moonlight to water. I have already cited the line, “From the hundred-foot-high house the water reaches the sky,” where the word "water" implies wavelike moonlight. If it reaches the sky, why not ride on it in a boat straight to the moon? And if it was a real painted boat floating in the moonlight, it could easily inspire the fantasy of drifting off to the moon. The word *lang*, "in vain", conveys the futility of the dream of floating to the moon on a flood of moonlight, or the pointlessness of the association. But even if you could get there, how do you know that Chang'e, the lady in the Moon, is really so beautiful as we imagine?

I once had a poetry teacher who wrote the lines,[202]

Who'd have thought today's meeting under the blossoms	谁信今朝花下见
Is not so good as the visit dreamed last night?	不如夙昔梦中来
After this, for whom will the futile flowers open?	空花今后为谁开

It is a lament for a realized dream shattered by reality. In Li Shangyin's couplet there is a double lament, first at the impossibility of realizing the dream, and then at the fear that its realization would end in disillusionment. For a man with this double awareness, whose spirit is shut up inside frosty, cold walls, there is truly no prospect of a renewal of warmth.

Southern pipes, southland strings are all of them sad;	楚管蛮弦愁一概
In the empty town when the dance is done the dancer's waist remains.	空城舞罢腰支在

Music and dance are ordinarily occasions of pleasure, but now they are all sad, no matter whether or not the pipes and strings are of the south, because the heart of the listener is melancholy and for him all tunes are sad. There is an element of sadness in all moving music—"three sighs for every plucked string, a lingering grief from strong emotion."[203] When Li Shangyin says all music is sad, he is expressing the constancy of grief, the vanity of all pleasure. "In the empty town the dance is done," and all the lovely movement of life is over. The “empty town” evokes Bao Zhao’s Rhapsody, “The Deserted City”, with the lines,

The frontier wind is sharp, it is cold on the wall.	边风急兮城上寒
Walls and paths obliterated, mounds and dikes leveled,	井径灭兮丘陇残
A thousand years, a myriad generations,	千龄兮万代
All is finished, what’s there to say?[204]	共尽兮何言

It’s not just the end of one person’s dance that gives rise to grief; it extends to the common fate of myriad generations of dancers. If we focus on the words, “In the empty town when the dance is done”, it seems that before it was finished, there was no one in the town to watch, giving yet another layer of regret: it is sad that the dance is over, sad that the town is empty, even sadder that there was no one to watch when the dance was performed. On top of it all come the words, “the dancer’s waist remains”. The effect is similar to the concluding line in Lu You’s song celebrating plum blossoms,

Battered into mud, ground into dust—	零落成泥碾作尘
All that’s left is their fragrance.[205]	只有香如故

Though their life is finished, a trace of fragrance remains from the exquisite blossoms, and though no one is left to appreciate her skill, the dancer’s supple waist is still a reminder of what she once was. Even if there is no one to appreciate her, even though its life is over, still the plum blossom’s fragrance, the dancer’s waist, persist to the end. However, even such durable attributes are ultimately unequal to human indifference and time’s attrition. This is why the plum blossoms end up as mud and dust, why the dancer finally stops dancing in the empty city.

There is no way to salvage beauty from eclipse and destruction, and the next couplet laments,

Onetime happiness melts in the palm of the hand,	当时欢向掌中销
Peach Leaf and Peach Root are a sister pair.	桃叶桃根双姊妹

It's the words "in the palm of the hand" that make lost happiness unbearable. A passage in "The Western Chamber" describes Zhang's infatuation with Yingying:

If I could get her, I would hold her tenderly in the palm of my hand,	我得时节手掌儿里奇擎
A warm spot in the depths of my heart,	心坎儿上温存
Serve her as the apple of my eye.[206]	眼皮儿上供养

To "hold her tenderly in the palm of my hand" is an impulse of true love; but joy will end, and not even such love will prolong it the least little bit. On top of this, Li Shangyin has added the word "towards": the joy vanishes in the true love's hand even as one watches.

The next line gives a clue to the nature of the vanished joy. Peach Leaf and Peach Root were two sisters, concubines of Wang Xianzhi of the Jin. The elder was named Peach Leaf; the younger, Peach Root. He wrote a song for Peach Leaf as she left to cross the river.[207] On the strength of this allusion, an attempt has been made to identify Peach Leaf and Peach Root with two Imperial Concubines that Li Shangyin was supposed to have had an affair with.[208] These, however, are not autobiographical poems subject to that kind of interpretation, and I prefer to take the lines symbolically. In Chinese poetry the Peach Leaf/Peach Root allusion is always used to symbolize separation. For example, Xin Qiji's song *Zhuyingtai jin* begins,

The jeweled clasp is divided	宝钗分
At Peach Leaf Ford;	桃叶渡
Misty willows hide Southbank.[209]	烟柳暗南浦

And Wu Wenying's "Oriole Song Prelude",

I remember short oars crossing Peach Root Ford. 记当时短楫桃根渡
It may have been in the green house 青楼仿佛
I wrote the poem on the broken wall, 临分败壁题诗
The tearful ink now sad and faded under
the dust.[210] 泪墨惨淡尘土

Both poets use Peach Leaf and Peach Root, together with the river crossing, in poems of parting, and in Li Shangyin's poem the names most likely have this connotation. In making them sisters, he is not necessarily suggesting that they were girls he knew. The word "pair" emphasizes their beauty and value by doubling it, at the same time doubling the loss now that they are irrevocably vanished.

After this couplet, the next must be understood as a memory of the pleasure occasioned by someone's makeup:

Undone, down-the-back-locks match the early
morning's chill, 破鬟倭堕凌朝寒
White jade swallow pin, yellow gold cicada clasp. 白玉燕钗黄金蝉

"Down-the-back-locks" is a kind of woman's hairdo; Wen Tingyun's "Southland Song" refers to it.[211] It should be a casual, appealing coiffure of hanging locks, from the name. In Li Shangyin's poem it is qualified by the words "undone, unloosed hair-bun", hence not put in order, uncombed. (The usual terms in song-poetry are "in disorder" and "disheveled".) In the rest of the line, the word *ling* means "match" as is clear from the context. "Morning chill" invokes the association of sleeping alone, common in this setting: "The thin coverlet is not proof against the Fifth Watch cold."[212] "A dream in the upstairs bedroom broken by the Fifth Watch drum."[213]

The second line of the couplet is not just a list of jewelry worn by women, for each item has its associations. *The Record of Contacts with the Otherworld* recounts a story.[214] In the first year of Yuanding (115 B.C.), a female divinity left a jade hairpin as a present for the Emperor. It was kept in a box until the Yuanfeng period (80-75 B.C.). When the box was opened, a white swallow flew up to the sky. Imitations of this hairpin worn by the palace ladies were accordingly called "jade swallow pins". There is nothing wrong with regarding these two lines as simply recollections of the appearance of a lover of long ago. But it is the strength of Li Shangyin that his casual descriptions are capable of rousing further associations. In the first place, the choice of the much stronger word *po* in place of the usual *luan* or *san* for hair that is disheveled carries implications of total ruin, damage beyond repair. Then the rest of the line places this feeling of desolation in the early morning hours. It reminds one of another line by Li Shangyin, "Only the empty bed to withstand white autumn."[215] Just when everything is going to ruin and the lonely suffering heart faces the surrounding morning cold of white autumn that symbolizes the insistent, numbing thoughts, it is hard to bear the bitterness and pain. That gives the force of the word "to match" which has the same function as "withstand" in the line just quoted; one seeks to hold at bay the invasive cold.

We might consider the associations with the objects named in the second line of the couplet. "Jade" and "gold" are fine materials; the colors "white" and "yellow" are fresh and bright. Their enduring beauty contrasts with the disordered hair, the bitter morning cold. This sort of contrast is common in Li Shangyin's poetry, like the fallen petals:

While falling they are dancing still, 落时犹自舞
Swept up, they still smell sweet.[216] 扫后更闻香

Or the lamp,

White and pure, unwearied to the end,	皎洁终无倦
Burnt out with its own seeking.[217]	煎熬亦自求

It is the destruction of something intrinsically beautiful that rouses distress. If we look back from the beauty of the "white jade swallow pin, yellow gold cicada clasp" to the preceding line, "undone, down-the-back-locks match the early morning's chill," we can appreciate a little better the significance attached to these ornaments.

To sum it up: it doesn't matter whether he was writing about an actual experience or an imagined one. The shattered dream, the morning cold, all joy gone—all that's left is the sound of the wind and the rain dripping, in the ears and in the heart, and the weeping red candle burning its life out. And the past is past, separated by time and space, irrevocably lost.

Wind carriage and rain steeds will not take you there;	风车雨马不持去
The wax candle weeps red, grieved that the sky grows light.	蜡烛啼红怨天曙

If you read it as a description of reality, then these lines create a scene just before daybreak, with the cold wind and rain outside the window and the red candle weeping its tears inside the room. The words "carriage" and "horse" supplied after "wind" and "rain" are an example of Li Shangyin's poetic skill. For as wind and rain drive hard, one associates with them the idea of breaking down, of isolating, cutting off; but he transforms them into a vehicle that could break through the barriers that separate, an original and effective figure. But then he ends the line with "will not take you there". What is lost is lost for good; even though the wind is swift as a carriage and the rain drives like horses, they still cannot bring this sorrowing man to the place he longs for. The fact of rain as an obstacle is transformed into the fantasy of a dashing carriage, and this wild fantasy is brought up short by the reality of an unpassable obstacle. The long night approaches dawn, the candle weeps its red tears, and all that's left is the despair of an enduring separation. Yan Shu writes, .

I remember the red candle in Orchid Hall,	念兰堂红烛
Long the heart and short the flame,	心长焰短
Shedding tears in our presence.[218]	向人垂泪

If you take a burning candle as a symbol of life, it burns its own heart's blood to produce a brief flame, changing into blood-red tear-drops as it progresses toward extinction and death. And the light of dawn outside is the signal for the approaching end of the candle. Tao Yuanming used the candle as a symbol for both life and feeling in his "Stilling the Passions" Rhapsody,

I grieve that with the spreading rays from the sun-tree	悲扶桑之舒光
Its light will be covered, its brilliance hidden.[219]	奄灭景而藏明

No matter how fine the life, or how brilliant its heart's flame, the rising sun and the morning breeze are its death warrant, with no stay of execution and no reprieve—such is the tragedy. But what is gone is gone for good, and all that remains is grief. In truth, "The wax candle weeps red, grieved that the sky grows light." An appropriate concluding line to these four "Yantai" poems!

From the "Breeze light spreads along the east-west path" of the first stanza through all the emotional upheavals and evocations of the past, the labyrinthine involvements, we reach this scene of ultimate grief, mourned by the candle's red tears. The poet has in truth explored all corners of the realm of pent-up chagrin. It is a realm accessible to any sympathetic reader, who need not and indeed should not try to understand it by looking for identifiable persons or specific incidents. Some time ago I wrote a quatrain with the title Li Yishan:

Heng'e had to endure more than her share of cold,	信有姮娥偏耐冷
Don't look for hidden meanings in Song Yu.	休从宋玉觅微辞
For a thousand years pearl tears remain in the blue sea,	千年沧海遗珠泪
No need to explain the Brocade Zither poem.	未许人笺锦瑟诗

As I wrote this, Li Shangyin's poetry was only the ostensible subject, for what I had in mind was my own old-style poetry and how I should like it to be read, but it makes an appropriate conclusion for this essay, which seeks to make just this point. The efforts of earlier exegetes do not inspire confidence, and my own speculations are also ineffectual. Anyone who wants to catch the fish had better jump into the water and try looking for them himself.

Notes:

1. Feng Hao, *Yuxisheng jianzhu*, 5.34a-36b. This is the basic text used for references to Li Shangyin's poetry; it is cited as *Works*. Others used for commentaries on the "Yantai" poems are: Zhu Heling, *Li Yishan shi ji*; in bibl, Qu Fu, *Yuxisheng shi yi*; Yao Peiqian, *Li Yishan shi ji* (not available to the translator).

2. Feng Hao, 5.37a-38b.

3. Jian qun, referring to the Third Month Shang Si purification ceremony (Feng Hao, 5.31a).

4. Zhang Caitian, *Li Shangyin shi bianzheng*, in *Yuxisheng nianpu hui jian*.

5. Feng Hao, 5.37a.

6. Ibid.

7. Feng Hao, 5.38b-39a, note on "Willow Branch" poem. After pointing out that the "Yantai" poems where written before he met Willow Branch, he still concludes that "it is impossible to decide whether they belong together or not".

8. Zhang Caitian, p. 71.

9. Ibid., p. 468.

10. Su Xuelin, *The Secret of Li Shangyin's Poetry* (*Yuxisheng shi mi*), pp. 87-91.

11. "From the circumlocutions in his poems generally, it seems that some are directed against the ruling class, some satirize Taoist nuns, and some the palace concubines, as the four 'Yantai' poems". Sun Zhentao, "Exploring the Obscurities of Li Shangyin's Poetry".

12. Feng Hao, 5.37a.

13. Feng Hao, 6.2b. He is considering a group of poems together besides *Yantai*: "Willow Branch", "Jesting with Willow", "For Willow", "Henei", "Heyang", "Stone City", and "Nevercare".

14. Zhang Caitian, pp. 76-77: "In the fifth year of Kaicheng [840], Yang Sifu went out to Hunan as Regional Commissioner and in the winter of that year was banished to Chaozhou as Prefect.... Panha suggests Chaozhou.... The four lines starting with 'jasper zither', 'Chu songs', and 'southern clouds' are metaphors for Sifu's banishment from Xiangnan to Chaozhou.... In the fourth poem Yishan has gone to Xiang, but Sifu has already left".

15. Su Xuelin, pp. 88-89: "The first section of the second poem says that at present he has gone to the detached palace in the Serpentine for a walk.... In the third section of the third poem it says that although the palace is closely guarded, an outsider can get in through the little garden".

16. Lao Gan, "A Critical Account of Li Shangyin's 'Yantai' poems", *Zhonguo de shehui yu wenxue* (*Wenxing congkan*, vol. 40), pp. 44-45:

"Shicheng, the Shu ghost, panha flowers, southern cloud, Xiangchuan, Qingxi, Chu pipes, and Southern Barbarian strings, all these could indicate real places and the things associated with them. Hence there is nothing against reading it as the girl being in the south. We also find a couple of northern place-names, and the title of the poem itself is a northern place. So the sudden shifts from north to south are deliberately misleading on the part of the author, unwilling to reveal his secret".

17. Feng Hao, 5.36b.

18. Zhang Caitian, pp. 76-77.

19. Ibid., p. 471.

20. For Fansu, see Bai Juyi's preface to his poem, "Unable to Forget" (*Bu neng wang qing yin)*, *Baishi changqing ji* (*SBCK* ed.) 70.15b. Xiaoman and Fansu are mentioned together in his poem "Arising Late on a Cold Day…", ibid., 67.19b-20a.

21. These four names occur repeatedly in Yan Jidao's songs, e.g., to the tune "Magnolia Flower", nos. 82, 83, *Quan Song ci* (hereafter *QSC*), p. 233; to the tune "Immortal by the Stream", no. 3, *QSC*, p. 222.

22. To the tune "Taoist Nun", (*Nü guan zi*) *Tang wudai ci* (hereafter *TWDC*), p. 110.

23. To the tune "Lotus Leaf Cup" (*He ye bei*), *TWDC*, p. 118.

24. To the tune "Partridge in the Sky", no. 20, *QSC*, p. 2173.

25. Cao Zhi, "Untitled poem No. 4", *Cao Zijian ji* (*SBCK* ed.) 5.4a.

26. Ruan Ji, *Ruan Bubing Yonghuai shi zhu*, p. 3.

27. Feng Yansi, to the tune "Picking Mulberry Leaves" (*Cai sang zi*), *TWDC*, p. 242.

28. Ouyang Xiu, to the tune "The Butterfly Loves Flowers", no. 46, *QSC*, p. 128.

29. "Sadly I watch the waters of the West River / Flowing, flowing, —and what can you do?" "West Stream". (*Xi xi*) *Works* 4.27a.

30. "Inlaid Zither" (*Jin se*), *Works* 4.28a-b.

31. See note 16.

32. Du Fu, "Four Quatrains", no. 3, *Jiujia jizhu Dushi* 26.26c, p. 409 (cited as *Works*).

33. "Presented to His Excellency Yan as He Left for Court", ibid., 23.17, p. 374.

34. *Zhuangzi* 1.

35. *Lun yu* 2/1.

36. Zhang Heng, "*Sichou shi*", *WX* 29.12b.

37. *Shijing*, no. 154, *Qi yue*.

38. Fan Qin, *Ding qing shi*, *Yutai xinyong* (*SBCK* ed.) 1.15a-16a.

39. "End of Autumn, Alone on the Serpentine", *Works* 6.24a.

40. Ibid.

41. *Zizhou ba yin ji tong she*, *Works* 4.40b.

42. In the fifth year of Dazhong (851), when Liu Zhongying was military governor of East Shu, Li Shangyin was made his secretary. It was just five years later, the tenth year (856), that Liu Zhongying was summoned by the court to be vice-president of the Board of Civil Office, and the office under his administration in Zizhou was closed. In the same poem Li Shangyin says, "For five years I served Huo Qubing" (i.e., Liu Zhongying), showing that the word *yantai* in this poem refers to the Zizhou office.

43. Cen Zhongmian, *Yuxisheng nianpu huijian pingzhi* (appended to Zhang Caitian), p. 230.

44. Du Fu, "Passing the Night at the Office" (*Su fu*), *Works* 26.13, p. 405.

45. "Expressing a Grievance: Presented to His Excellency Yan" (*Qian men cheng Yan Gong ershi yun*), *Works* 26.1.4, p. 405.

46. "Written on the Third Day of the First Month on Returning..." (*Zheng yue san ri gui xi shang you zuo...*), *Works* 26.22, p. 407.

47. Li Bai, "It is a Hard Road to Travel" (*Xing lu nan*), *Li Taibai shiji*

jiaozhu (Shanghai Guji, 1980), 3.204 (hereafter cited as *Works*).

48. To the tune "Treading the Sedge" (*Ta suo xing*), no. 19, *QSC*, p. 123.

49. To the tune "Viewing the Ocean Tide", (*Wang hai chao*), no. 3, *QSC*, p. 455.

50. To the tune "The Magpie Treads the Branch" (*Que ta zhi*), *TWDC*, p. 232.

51. To the tune "Treading the Sedge", no. 78, *QSC*, p. 99.

52. To the tune "Phoenix in the Phoenix Trees" (*Feng qi wu*), no. 62, *QSC*, p. 25. The translation follows the quotation of the variant reading in *Yuezhang ji* (*Song Liushi mingjia ci* ed.), 19b.

53. *Wenxin diaolong* (Wang Liqi ed.) 10 / 120 / 1.

54. Jiang Yan, "Rhapsody on Regret" (*Hen fu*), *WX* 16.26b.

55. "Li sao", *Chuci* (*SBCK* ed.) 1.14b.

56. Zhu Heling cites the expression "winged race" (*yu zu*) from Guo Pu's "Bee Rhapsody" (*Huang feng fu*) (*Quan Jin wen* 120.6b), which may well have inspired Li Shangyin's kenning, one that nonetheless strikes the reader as fresh and original.

57. "The Second of February" (*Er yue er ri*), *Works* 4.36a-b.

58. *Shishuo xinyu* (*SBCK* ed.), 3A.10a: "The sage forgets about emotion, the lowest types haven't got so far as emotions; it's just on people like us that emotion weights heavy."

59. *Yijing*, *Xici* vol. 1,VIII: *ye rong hui yin*.

60. "Li sao", *Chuci*, 1.10b.

61. Xin Qiji, to the tune "Green Jade Table" (*Qing yu'an*), no. 57, *QSC*, p. 1884.

62. Du Shenyan, "To Match a Poem by Assistant Lu of Jinling...", *Tangshi sanbaishou xiangxi*, p. 13.

63. Du Fu, "A Solitary Stroll Looking for Flowers on the Riverbank"

(*Jiang pan du bu xun hua*), *Works* 23.3E, p. 369.

64. "Li sao", *Chuci*, 1.36b.

65. Li Bai, "Song of Liangfu" (*Liangfu yin*), *Works* 3.211.

66. Du Fu, "Dreaming of Li Bai" (*Meng Li Bai*), *Works* 5.10A, p. 79.

67. The *Bencao Herbal* (*SBCK* ed.) 4.37a.

68. "Written in the Early Cold on the River" (*Zao han jiang shang you huai*), *Meng Haoran ji* (*SBCK* ed.) 4.9a.

69. Zhu Heling's edition writes *fan* for *kuan*. *Kuan* works to reinforce *kuo* and emphasizes the associations of loneliness. *Fan* takes one to the horizon, where the sea pulses under the sky, emphasizing its uncharted restlessness. The readings are equally good, but I have followed Feng's text.

70. *WX* 29.1b.

71. Sima Qian's question in his "Biography of Boyi and Shuqi", *Shiji* 61.2125.

72. Zhu Heling quotes the *Han History* "Essay on Astronomy" (*Tian wen zhi*) (*Han shu* 26.1275): "Of the six stars in the Basket (*Dai kuang*)... the sixth is called 'Controls Disaster'; it is in The Leader (*kui*), the Jail of the Nobility (*Gui ren zhi lao*)". Meng Kang's commentary: "The Jail of the Nobility is called 'Heaven's Justice' (*Tian li*), it is Heaven's Jail". The "Essay on Astronomy" in the *Jin History* has a different explanation: "The six stars in Heaven's Jail are below the Leader star of the Dipper; it is the Nobleman's Jail" (*Jin shu* 11.291). "The nine stars of the Rope (*Guan suo*) are the Commoner's Jail...; some say it is Heaven's Jail". (Ibid. 11.294. These and all subsequent reference to the Standard Histories are to the Beijing, Zhonghua punctuated edition.)

73. *Lun yu* 11/24.

74 To the tune "The Lattice Window is Cold" (*Suo chuang han*), no. 2, *QSC*, p. 595.

75. To the tune "Six Kinds" (*Liu chou*), no. 80, *QSC*, p. 610.

76. Su Shi, to the tune "Song of the Immortal in the Cavern" (*Dong xian ge*), no. 117, *QSC*, p. 297.

77. Xin Qiji, to the tune "River Spirit" (*Jiang shen zi*), no. 150. *QSC*, p. 1897.

78. Jiang Kui, to the tune "Niannu is Charming" (*Niannu jiao*), no. 39, *QSC*, p. 2177.

79. *Chuci* 1.7a.

80. *Shiji* 84.2482.

81. Li Shangyin, "Untitled Poem" (*Wu ti*), *Works* 3.4.

82. Li Yu, to the tune "The Crow Caws at Night" (*Wu ye ti*), *TWDC*, p. 224.

83. Li Yu, to the tune "Waves Scour the Sand" (*Lang tao sha*), *TWDC*, p. 231.

84. Huang Tingjian, to the tune "Qingping Music" (*Qingping yue*), no. 47, *QSC*, p. 393.

85. Zhou Bangyan, to the tune "Six Kinds", no. 80, *QSC*, p. 610.

86. Xin Qiji, to the tune *Zhuyingtai jin*, no. 75, *QSC*, p. 1882.

87. Du Fu, "Lament on a Summer's Day" (*Xia ri tan*), *Works* 3.15, p. 56.

88. "Three Poems on the Heat". (*Re san shou*), *Works* 28.21b, p. 433.

89. "From the Capital to Fengxian District ..." (*Zi jing fu Fengxian xian yong huai*), *Works* 2.16, p. 37.

90. "Iron Hall Gorge" (*Tie tang xia*), *Works* 6.6, p. 91.

91. "Untitled Poem", *Works* 3.48a.

92. Feng Yansi, to the tune "The Magpie Treads the Branch", *TWDC*, p. 238. (Also attributed to Ouyang Xiu.)

93. "Another Visit to the Temple of the Goddess" (*Chongguo Shengnü ci*), *Works* 3.36b.

94. Tao Qian, "On Reading the *Seas and Mountains Classic*" (*Du*

"Shanhai jing"), *Tao Yuanming ji* (*SBCK* ed.) 4.18a (hereafter, *Works*).

95. Or "stone wall". The walls around Chinese cities were ordinarily of earth and brick, and a wall of stone would be quite distinctive. Since all cities were walled, the term applies indifferently to the wall or to the city it contains.

96. Li Shan, commenting on the line "War chariots fill Stone City" from Zuo Si's "Rhapsody on the Capital of Wu" (*WX* 5.16a); "In the 17th year of Jian'an (212) they built a wall of stone", and Liu Kui (ibid.): "The stone wall was along the River, on the west side of Jianye".

97. It was founded by Yang Hu of the Qin dynasty, and became the site of Stone Prefecture (*Shi tou jun*) under the Northern Zhou. The name "stone wall" comes from the fact that the foundations on three sides were all of stone, and the fourth side was a sheer cliff overlooking the Han River. (Wang Yinglin, *Tongjian dili tongshi* [*Xuejin taoyuan* ed.] 13.6a-b.)

98. "'Nevercare Music' comes from 'Stone City Music'. There was a girl in Stone City named Nevercare who was a good singer, and she is the source of this song" (*Old Tang History* [*Jiu Tang shu*], ["Essay on Music" *Yinyue zhi*] 29.1065).

99. *Works* 5.93a, 39b.

100. *Yuefu shiji* (*SBCK* ed.) 48.4a.

101. *Works* 5.39b.

102. *Works* 5.39a.

103. *Qin History* 55.1507.

104. The adjective "of *zhe*-wood" (omitted in the translation), which Li Shangyin supplies for the pelletbow, serves to emphasize its quality. Feng Hao attributes to the *Miscellany of the Western Capital* (*Xijing zaji*) the quotation, "The aristocrats of Chang'an have pelletbows of *zhe*-wood, and using pearls for pellets, they shoot sparrows". The line is missing in the *SBCK* ed. of the *Miscellany*.

105. *Shiji* 7.315.

106. Zhu Yizun, interlinear note in Zhu Heling's edition, C. 22a.

107. It made difficulties for Feng Hao, who asks, "What has this Stone City to do with the Stone City in the poems 'Nevercare' and 'Stone City Song'?"

108. For *hui xuan* "to swirl", Zhu Heling's text writes *yuan xuan* "the pool revolves", a combination that does not yield much sense in this context.

109. Du Fu, "Pained by Spring" (*Shang chun*), *Works* 28.2B, p. 424.

110. "Mud in the Well" (*Jing ni*), *Works* 2.4a.

111. "Inlaid Zither" (*Jin se*), *Works* 4.28b.

112. Quoted by Zhu Heling from *Basic Annals of the Kings of Shu* (*Shu Wang benji*), in his commentary on "Brocade Zither", A.1b.

113. Quoted by Zhu Heling from the *Records of Chengdu* (*Chengdu zhi*), ibib.

114. "View from the Tower" (*Deng lou*), *Works* 21.42, p. 353.

115. Bai Juyi, *Works* 12.25b.

116. To the tune "Magnolia Flowers" no. 57, *QSC*, p. 95.

117. To the tune "The Butterfly Loves Flowers", *Renjian ci*, p. 39.

118. At least such a building has been proposed in poetry: "The Lu's house had orchid roof with rafters of cassia". (Song attributed to Xiao Yan, Emperor Wu of the Liang, *Yutai xinyong* 9.3b).

119. Cao Zhi, "Sevenfold Sorrow" (*Qi'ai shi*), *WX* 23.15a.

120. Wen Tingyun, to the tune "Bodhisattva Barbarian" (*Pusa man*), *TWDC*, p. 56.

121. Bai Juyi writes in the second of his two quatrains "Mountain Loquat Flower" (*Shan pipa*), *Works* 14.12a.

122. Cao Zhi, "Sevenfold Sorrow", *WX*, 23.15a.

123. Feng Hao, committed to a reading of the poems as concerned with Li Shengyin's love affair with a Taoist nun when he was studying Taoism in

Yuyang, finds the significance of these lines in the place-name, Yuyang being in Jiyuan xian. His reading is hopelessly forced.

124. Han Wo, "A Parting" (*Bie xu*), *Xiang lian ji* (*SBCK* ed.) 12a.

125. Du Fu, "Seeing off Kong Chaofu…", *Works* 2.1, p. 21.

126. Li Bai, "A Dream Excursion on Mt. Tianmu" (*Meng you Tianmu yin liubie*), *Works* 15.899.

127. The Nine Songs, "Lesser Master of Fate" (*Shao SiMing*), *Chuci* 2.19b.

128. To the tune "The Butterfly Loves Flowers", *Renjian ci*, p. 22.

129. The variant *chong tian* "dash against the sky" for *heng tian* "traverse the sky" suggests too violent an image for the quiet autumnal tone that pervades the whole poem.

130. Li Shangyin, *Works* 5.1b-2a.

131. *Works* 5.9b.

132. *Works* 6.20a.

133. Li Bai, *Works* 25.1483.

134. Feng Hao's gloss suggesting that it is a word for "kite" should be rejected as making no sense. Yao Peiqian interprets it correctly as "wind chimes".

135. To the tune "A Chain Undone" (*Jie lian huan*), no. 10, *QSC*, p. 597.

136. "The Farmer's New Year's Day" (*Tian jia yuan ri*), *Meng Haoran ji* (*SBCK* ed.) 1.13a.

137. "Fine!" (Shan zai!) (*Shan zai xing*), *Yuefu shiji* 36.9b.

138. *Works* 6.20a.

139. Cao Pi, "Song of Yan" (*Yan ge xing*), *WX* 27.19b.

140. *Works* 4.27a.

141. "Bird-call Rapids" (*Niaoming jian*), *Wang Youcheng ji* (*SBCK* ed.) 3.12a.

142. "Those with white flowers are called Silver Cassia (*Yin gui*); with yellow flowers, Golden Cassia (*Jin gui*); with red flowers, Cinnabar Cassia (*Dan gui*). Some bloom in autumn, some in spring, and some in all four season" (*Herbal Conspectus Bencao gangmu*, p. 1932).

143. *Xijing zaji* 1.6b, quoted by Zhu Heling.

144. To the tune "Bodhisattva Barbarian", *TWDC*, p. 56.

145. As Zhu Heling seems to imply by quoting the *History of the Southern Dynasties*, "The Heir Apparent Wenhui asked for the fields to the east to build a little park" (*Nan shi* 44.1100).

146. "Song of Sorrow" (*Yong huai*), *WX* 23.3a.

147. "The Serpentine", (*Qujiang xing*), *Works* 19.30, p. 307.

148. "Lament by the Serpentine" (*Ai jiang tou*), *Works* 2.20, p. 43.

149. *Works* 1.35b.

150. The lines quoted are really from Du Fu's poem *Ai jiang tou*, not *Qu jiang xing.*

151. *Tang shu* 17B. 561, 562.

152. *Zizhi tongjian*, p. 7921.

153. Gao Buying, *Annotated Anthology of Tang and Song Poetry* (*Tang Song shi juyao*) 5.46b.

154. "The Old Willow West of Qinzheng Mansion" (*Qinzheng lou xi lao liu*), *Works* 19.16b. Kaiyuan (713-741) and Changqing (821-824) are reign periods.

155. *Liu Mengde wenji* (*SBCK* ed.) 9.10a.

156. *Chen shu* 7.132, quoted by Yao Peiqian.

157. *Renjian cihua*, p. 47.

158. "Gently soothing, the virtue of the zither is unfathomable", from Ji Kang, "Rhapsody on the Zither", *WX* 18.21b, cited by Zhu Heling and Feng Hao.

159. For *nong* meaning "tune, song", see *Qin li* (*Yuhan shanfang ji*

yishu ed.) 1a, where "Cai's five tunes" (*Cai shi wu nong*) is the first entry under "Zither tunes" (Qin qu), (Zhu Heling, Yao Peiqian).

160. For example, Tao Qian's "Sorrowful Poem in the Chu Mode" (*Yuan shi chu diao*), *Works* 2.10a-b.

161. Yao Peiqian quotes *Tang shu* to the effect that the local tribute from Yue included thin silk with a flower pattern.

162. Zhu Heling quotes a line from the "Record of a Brocade Skirt" (*Jin qun ji*), "Melancholy appliquė clustered-butterfly skirt". The line is not to be found in either the *Shuo fu* or *Tangdai congshu* editions of the "Record".

163. To the tune "Southland Song" (*Nan ge zi*), *TWDC*, p. 47.

164. To the tune "Magnolia Flower (*Mu lan hua*), no. 60, *QSC*, p. 96.

165. *WX* 19.1a: "Of old King Xiang of Chu went on an outing with Song Yu to Cloud Dream Terrace".

166. Lu Ji, "Thinking of My Family" (*Si qin fu*), *Lu Shiheng wenji* (*SBCK* ed.) 1.10b: "I send my respects by the south cloud".

167. *Yuxisheng shiyi* 2.10b.

168. *Three Hundred Tang Poems*, p. 281.

169. No. 3, *QSC*, p. 277.

170. Li Shangyin, *Works*, 5.46a.

171. *Shijing*, no. 64/4.

172. "She sent me a gold inlaid knife / How requite it? / A fine piece of jasper. / She gave me a gilded jade. / How requite it? / A pair of jade plates. / She gave me a sable robe. / How requite it? / A full-moon pearl. / She gave me a piece of brocade. / How requite it? / A green jade stand" (*WX* 29.12a).

173. The Goddess of the Luo River offered her pearl earring to Cao Zhi; see his "Rhapsody on the Goddess of the Luo" (*Luo shen fu*), *WX* 19.15b.

174. Zheng Jiaofu met two supernatural girls who gave him the pearls they were wearing as girdle pendants. The story is attributed to *Hanshi*

waizhuan by Li Shan in his commentary on Zhang Heng's "Rhapsody on the Southern Capital", *WX* 4.2b. It is not in modern texts of *Hanshi waizhuan*.

175. To the tune "Lotus Leaf Cup" (*He ye bei*), *TWDC*, p. 118.

176. To the tune "Immortal by the River" (*Lin jiang xian*), no. 7, *QSC*, p. 222.

177. Li Bai, *Works* 3.244.

178. To the tune "Wine Spring" (*Jiu quan zi*), no. 57, *QSC*, p. 95.

179. Yao Peiqian's comment.

180. Li Yu, to the tune "A Bushel of Pearls" (*Yi hu zhu*), *TWDC*, p. 221.

181. "For Someone Far Away" (*Ji yuan*), *Works* 6.31b.

182. *Meng zi* 1A/7.

183. Li Bai, "After an Old Poem" (*Ni gu shi*), *Works* 24.1375.

184. Lu Yang, his battle unfinished at sunset, waved his spear at the sun, which obediently retreated three stages (*Huainan zi* [*SBCK* ed.] 6.1b).

185. Kuafu lost his race and died of thirst. See *Seas and Mountains Classic* (*Shanhai jing*)… [*SBCK* ed.] B.81a).

186. "Nineteen Old Poems", no. 13, *WX* 29.6b.

187. Zhu Heling quotes the *Record of Music, Ancient and Modern* (*Gu jin yue lu*) for the titles, perhaps from the quotation in *Yuefu shiji* 47.5a-b, or from Huang Shi's reconstruction in *Huangshi yishu kao*, vol. 26, p. 23b.

188. *Qingxi Xiaogu qu*, *Yuefu shiji* 47.7a.

189. *Baishi lang* ibid. 47.6a.

190. *Liji* 2.7a-b.

191. *Seas and Mountains Classic* B.86b.

192. According to Guo Pu's commentary, ibid.

193. "Far Away from You" (*Yuan bie li*), *Works* 3.191. Shun was supposed to have had eyes with double pupils, according to Sima Qian (*Shiji* 7.338). "Odd eyes" is a paraphrase.

194. *Shuyi ji* (*Sui'an Xushi congshu* ed.) A.4b.

195. *Works*, 3.191.

196. Ibid.

197. "Sands of the Washing Stream" (*Huan xi sha*), *TWDC*, p. 111.

198. The reading *bing* in Feng Hao's text is a misprint for *cheng*.

199. "Heng'e subsequently escaped to the moon: this is the Toad". (*Ling xian*, fragments collected in Yan Kejun, *Complete Houhan Prose* [*Quan Houhan wen*] 55.5b, quoted by Feng Hao.)

200. *Fang yan* (*SBCK* ed.) 9.4a.

201. *Bowu zhi* (Beijing: Zhonghua, 1980), p. 111.

202. Gu Sui (1898-1960). I am quoting the lines from memory.

203. No. 5, "Nineteen Old Poems", *WX* 29.3b.

204. *WX* 11.13a.

205. To the tune "Fortune Teller" (*Bu suan zi*), no. 49, *QSC*, p. 1586.

206. *Xi xiang ji*, p. 22.

207. *The Record of Music, Ancient and Modern* 22a (also quoted in *Yuefu shiji* 45.10b) identifies only Peach Leaf, but the line in one of the "Peach Leaf" songs, "Peach Leaf is tied to peach root", inspired someone to add a sister (explicitly identified as such in *Liuchao shiji* A.132), or so Feng Hao suggests. Li Shangyin elsewhere alludes separately to Peach Root ("Apricot Flower" [*Xing hua*], Works 2.15a) and Peach Leaf ("Singing girl" [*ji xi*], Works 5.25b).

208. Su Xuelin, pp. 87-91. Her arguments are strongly criticized by Gu Yiqun, *A Critical Study of Li Shangyin* (*Li Shangyin pinglun*) (Taibei: Zhonghua, 1958), pp. 80-81.

209. To the tune, *Zhuyingtai*, no. 75, *QSC*, p. 1882.

210. Wu Wenying, to the tune "The Oriole Sings" (*Ying ti xu*), no. 167, *QSC*, p. 2908.

211. Wen Tingyun, to the tune "Southland Song" (*Nan ge zi*) *TWDC*, p. 47. Both Zhu Heling and Yao Peiqian quote *Notes on Ancient and Modern*

(*Gu jin zhu, SBCK* ed,) B.6b for the terms *wo duo ji* and *duo ma ji*, neither of which is described.

212. Li Yu, to the tune "Waves Scour the Sand" (*Lang tao sha*), *TWDC*, p. 231.

213. Yan Shu, to the tune "Spring in the Jade House" (*Yulou chun*) no. 136, *QSC*, p. 108.

214. *Dong ming ji*, in the anonymous Song collection *Supplemental Aids to Conversation* (*Dong ming ji*, *Yueyatang congshu* ed.) 1.13b-14a (quoted by Zhu Heling and Yao Peiqian).

215. "At Leisure" (*Duan ju*), *Works* 6.28b.

216. "Moved by Falling Petals—to match a poem by Graduate Zhang" (*He Zhang Xiucai luohua yougan*), *Works* 6.23b.

217. "The Lamp" (*Deng*), *Works* 3.18b.

218. To the tune "It Shakes the Courtyard in Autumn" (*Han ting qiu*), no. 48, *QSC*, p. 94.

219. *Xian qing fu*, *Works* 6.5b.

论词学中之困惑与《花间》词之女性叙写及其影响

一

“词”这种文学体式，自唐、五代开始盛行以来，以迄于今盖已有一千数百年之久。在此漫长之期间内，虽然“江山代有才人出”，曾在创作方面为我们留下了无数多姿多彩而且风格各异的作品，但在如何评定词之意义与价值的词学方面，则自北宋以迄今日却似乎一直未能为之建立起一个完整的理论体系。虽然在零篇断简的笔记和词话中，也不乏精微深入的体会和见解，然而却因为缺乏逻辑性的理论依据，因此遂在词学的发展中为后人留下了无数困惑和争议。至其困惑之由来，则主要乃是由于早期词作之内容既多以叙写美女与爱情为主，而此种伤春怨别的男女之情，则显然不合于传统诗文的言志与载道之标准，在此种情况下，自然使得一般习惯于言志与载道之批评标准的士大夫们，对于如何衡量这种艳歌小词，以及是否应写作此类艳歌小词，都产生了不少困惑。即如魏泰在其《东轩笔录》中，即曾载云：“王安国性亮直，嫉恶太甚。王荆公初为参知政事，闲日因阅读元献公（晏殊）小词，而笑曰：'为宰相而作小词，可乎？'平甫（王安国字）曰：'彼亦偶然自喜而为耳，顾其事业岂止如是耶？'时吕惠卿为馆职，亦在座，遽曰：'为政必先放郑声，况自为之乎？'平甫正色曰：'放郑声，不若远佞人也。'吕大以为议己，自是尤与平甫相失也。"[①]从这段记载来看，小词之被目为淫靡之"郑声"，且引起困惑与争议之情况，固已可概见一斑。于是在此种困惑中，遂又形成了为写作此种小词而辩护的几种不同的方式，如胡仔在其《苕溪渔隐丛话·前集》即曾载云："晏叔原（几道）见蒲传正云：'先公（晏殊）平日小词虽多，未尝作妇人语也。'传正云：'绿杨芳草长亭路，年少抛人容易去，岂非妇人语乎？'晏曰：'公谓"年少"为何语？'传正曰：'岂不谓其所欢乎？'晏曰：'因公之言，遂晓乐天诗两句云"欲留年少待富贵，富贵不来年少去"。'传正笑而悟。"[②]这是将词中语句加以比附，而推衍为他义的一种辩护方式。又如张舜民在其《画墁录》中，曾载云："柳三变既以词忤仁庙，吏部不敢改官。三变不能堪，诣政府。晏公（殊）曰：'贤俊作曲子么？'三变曰：'只如相公亦作曲子。'公曰：'殊虽作曲子，不曾道"针线闲拈伴伊坐"。'柳遂退。"[③]这是将词句分别为雅正与淫靡二种不同之风格，而以雅正自许的一种辩护方式。再如释惠洪在其《冷斋夜话》中，曾载云："法云秀关西铁面严冷，能以理折人。鲁直（黄庭坚）名重天下，诗词一出，人争传之。师尝谓鲁直曰：'诗多作无害，艳歌小词可罢之。'鲁直笑曰：'空中语耳。非杀非偷，终不至坐此堕恶道。'"[④]这是以词中语句为"空中语"而强为自解的一种辩护方式。这几段话，从表面看来原不过只是宋人笔记中所记叙的一些琐事见闻而

① 魏泰《东轩笔录》卷五，第 337 页，见《笔记小说大观》第 28 编，册一，台北新兴书局 1979 年版。

② 胡仔《苕溪渔隐丛话·前集》卷二十六，第 178 页，人民文学出版社 1962 年版。

③ 张舜民《画墁录》，引自许士鸾《宋艳》卷五，见《笔记小说大观》第 28 编，册四四，第 6203 页，台北新兴书局 1979 年版。

④ 释惠洪《冷斋夜话》卷十，见《笔记小说大观》，第 22 编，册一，第 642 页，台北新兴书局 1979 年版。

已，而且其辩解既全无理论可言，除了显示出在困惑中的一种强辞夺理的辩说以外，根本不足以称之为什么“词学”，但毫无疑问的，中国的词学却也正是从这种困惑与争议中发展起来的。即以我们在前面所引用的这几则笔记而言，其中就也已然显露出了后世词学所可能发展之趋向的一些重要端倪。

我们先从前面所举引的《苕溪渔隐丛话》中的一则记叙来看，蒲传正所提出的“绿杨芳草长亭路，年少抛人容易去”二句词中的“年少”两字，就其上下文来看，其所指自应是在“长亭路”送别之地，“抛人”而“去”的“年少”的情郎，这种意思本是明白可见的，可是晏几道却引用了白居易之“富贵不来年少去”二句诗中的“年少”，从文字表面上的相同，而把“年少”情郎之“年少”，比附为“年少”光阴之“年少”，其为牵强附会之说，自不待言。至于晏几道之所以要用这种比附的说法来为他父亲晏殊所写的小词做辩护，主要当然乃是由于如我们在前面举引《东轩笔录》时所提出的当时士大夫之观念，认为做宰相之晏殊不该写作这一类淫靡之“郑声”的缘故。而谁知这种强辩之言，却竟然为后世之词学家之欲以比兴寄托说词者，开启了一条极为方便的途径。清代常州词派的张惠言，可以说就是以此种方式说词的一个集大成的人物。而此种说词方式一方面虽不免有牵强比附之弊，可是另一方面却有时也果然可以探触到小词中一种幽微深隐的意蕴，因此如何判断此种说词方式之利弊，自然就成为了词学中之一项重大的问题。其次，我们再看前面所举引的《画墁录》中的一则记叙。关于晏殊与柳永词的“雅”“俗”之别，前人可以说是早有定论，即如王灼在其《碧鸡漫志》中，即曾称美晏词，谓其“风流蕴藉，一时莫及，而温润秀洁亦无其比。”又曾批评柳词，谓其“浅近卑俗，自成一体……予尝以比都下富儿，虽脱村野，而声态可憎。”①可见词是确有雅俗之别的，于是南宋的词学家张炎遂倡

① 王灼《碧鸡漫志》卷二，《词话丛编》册一，第32-34页，台北广文书局1967年版。

言“清空骚雅”[①]，提出了重视“雅词”的说法。而一意以“雅”为标榜的词论，至清代浙派词人之末流，乃又不免往往流入于浮薄空疏，于是晚清之王国维乃又提出了“词之雅郑，在神不在貌”[②]之说，因此如何判断和衡量词之雅郑优劣，自然也就成为了词学中之一项重大问题。最后，我们再看前面所举引的《冷斋夜话》中的一则记叙，黄山谷所提出的“空中语”之说，虽然只是为了替自己写作小词所做的强辩之言，但这种说法却实在一方面既显示了早期的小词之所以不同于“言志”之诗的一种特殊性质，另一方面也显示了早期的士大夫们当其写作小词时，在摆脱了“言志”之用心以后的一种轻松解放的感情心态。不过，词在演进中并不能长久停留在早期的小词的阶段，因此我在 1987 年所写的《对传统词学与王国维词论在西方理论之光照中的反思》一篇长文中，遂曾尝试把词之演进分为了“歌辞之词”、“诗化之词”与“赋化之词”三个不同的阶段。[③]早期的小词，原是文士们为当日所流行的乐曲而填写的供歌唱的歌辞，这一类“歌辞之词”，作者在写作时既本无“言志”之用心，因此黄山谷乃称之为“空中语”，这原是可以理解的。不过，如我在《传统词学》一文中所言，这类本无“言志”之用心的作品，有时却反而因作者的轻松解放的写作心态，而于无意中流露了作者潜意识中的某种深微幽隐的心灵之本质，而因此也就形成了小词中之佳作的一种要眇深微的特美。其后这类歌辞之词既逐渐“诗化”和“赋化”，作者遂不仅在作词时有了抒情言志的用心，而且还逐渐有了安排和勾勒的反思，那么在这种演进之中，后期的“诗化”与“赋化”之词，是否仍应保持早期“歌辞之词”的特美？以及对“空中语”所形成的词之特质与特美，究竟应该怎样加以理解和衡量？这些当然也都是词学中的一些重大问题。透过上面的叙述，我们已可清楚地看到一个有趣的现象，那就是中

---

① 张炎《词源》卷下，《词话丛编》册一，第 208 页，台北广文书局 1967 年版。
② 徐调孚《校注人间词话》第 19 页，香港中华书局 1961 年版。
③ 叶嘉莹《中国词学的现代观》，第 5-8 页，岳麓书社 1990 年版。

国早期的词学原是由于当日士大夫们对此种文体之困惑而在强辞辩解之说中发展起来的。这种现象之形成，私意以为主要盖皆由于早期之小词乃大多属于艳歌之性质，而中国的士大夫们则因长久被拘束于伦理道德的限制之中，因此遂一直无人敢于正式面对小词中所叙写的美女与爱情之内容，对其意义与价值做出正面的肯定性的探讨，这实在应该是使得中国之词学，从一开始就在困惑与争议中被陷入了扭曲的强辩之说中的一个主要的原因。

而也就在早期的艳歌小词使士大夫们都陷入了困惑与争议之中的时候，中国词坛上遂出现了一位以其天才及襟抱大力改变了小词之为艳歌的作者，那就是“一洗绮罗芗泽之态”、“使人登高望远”、“指出向上一路，新天下耳目”[①]的作者苏轼。但苏词的出现，却不仅未曾解开旧有的困惑和争议，而且反而更增添了另一种新的争议和困惑。即如陈师道在其《后山诗话》中，即曾云“退之以文为诗，子瞻以诗为词。如教坊雷大使之舞，虽极天下之工，要非本色”[②]，胡仔在其《苕溪渔隐丛话·后集》中，也曾引有一段李清照词论中评苏词的话，说苏词乃是“句读不葺之诗耳”，而词则“别是一家”[③]，于是在苏词的向诗靠拢，与李清照之向诗宣告背离之间，遂使中国之词学更增加了另一重新的困惑和争议，而且事实上苏氏在创作方面所做出的开拓，与李氏在词论方面所做出的反思，对于早期之词在艳歌时代为这种文体所树立的宗风，以及这种宗风所形成的特殊的美学品质，也都未能有明确的体会和认知。而也就正因其无论是在词之创作方面，或词之评说方面，都未能从理论方面来解答词之美学特质的根本问题，因此遂使得婉约与豪放的正变之争，以及婉约中的雅郑之争，与豪放中之沉雄与叫嚣之别等种种问题，遂一

① 见王灼《碧鸡漫志》及胡寅《酒边词序》，味闲轩藏版汲古阁校选《宋六十名家词》第二集，第五册，第 2 页。

② 陈师道《后山诗话》，见《笔记小说大观》第 9 编，册六，第 3671-3672 页，台北新兴书局 1979 年版。

③ 胡仔《苕溪渔隐丛话·后集》卷三三，第 254 页，人民文学出版社 1962 年版。

直成为了词学中长久难以论定的困惑和争议。于是在这种种困惑与争议之中，遂又有人想把合乐而歌的小词比附于古代的诗、骚和乐府。王灼在其《碧鸡漫志》中，即曾云："古歌变为古乐府，古乐府变为今曲子，其本一也。"[①]王炎在其《双溪诗馀·自序》中，也曾云："古诗自《风》、《雅》以降，汉魏间乃有乐府，而曲居一，今之长短句盖乐府之苗裔也。"[②]胡寅在其《酒边词序》中，也曾云："词曲者，古乐府之末造也。古乐府者，诗之傍行也。诗出于《离骚》、《楚辞》，而《离骚》者，变风变雅之怨而迫，哀而伤者也。"[③]而《诗》之变风变雅及《离骚》、《楚辞》等作品，既都可以有比兴寄托之意，于是中国的词学遂又从溯源与尊体的观念中更发展出了一套比兴寄托之说。这种说法的形成，本来也同样是出于对词之被目为艳歌而受到轻视的一种反弹，与本文前面所举引的宋人笔记中那些强辩之说，同不免于有牵强比附之处。不过，对美女与爱情的叙写，既在诗骚中原曾有比兴寄托之传统，而且词之发展到了南宋的时代，在一些咏物之作中也确实有了比与喻的用意，因此到了清代常州词派张惠言等人的出现，其所倡导的以比兴寄托来说词的风气，乃开始盛行一时。于是自此以后遂又引起了如何判断其所说之是否为牵强附会的另一场困惑和争议。到了晚清另一位词学家王国维的出现，乃直指张惠言之说为"深文罗织"[④]，于是王氏自己遂又提出了其著名的"境界"之说，但王氏对其所标举的"境界"一词之义界，却也仍然未能做出明确的理论说明，于是遂又引起了近人的更多的困惑和争议。对于一种已经流行了有一千数百年以上之久，而且其间曾经名家辈出的重要文类，我们却竟然至今日仍然陷入在困惑与争议中，而不能对如何衡定此种文类的意义与价值做出溯源推流的理论性的说明，这实在不能不说是一项

① 王灼《碧鸡漫志》卷一，《词话丛编》册一，第32页，台北广文书局1967年版。

② 王炎《双溪诗馀·自序》，见《宋元三十一家词》，册三，第1页，光绪十九年王鹏运四印斋汇刻本。

③ 胡寅《酒边词序》，见味闲轩藏版汲古阁校选《宋六十名家词》第二集，第五册。

④ 徐凋孚《校注人间词话》第58页，香港中华书局1961年版。

亟待我们做出反思和检讨的重要问题。

关于中国的词学之所以从一开始就陷入了困惑与争议之中的主要原因，私意以为实在乃是由于在中国的文学批评传统中，过于强大的诗学理论妨碍了词学评论之建立的缘故。如我在数年前所写的《传统词学》一篇论文之所言，“所谓‘词’者，原来本只是在隋唐间所兴起的一种伴随着当时流行之乐曲以供歌唱的歌辞。因此当士大夫们开始着手为这些流行的曲调填写歌辞时，在其意识中原来并没有要藉之以抒写自己之情志的用心，这对于诗学传统而言，当然已经是一种重大的突破，而且根据《花间集•序》的记载，这些所谓‘诗客曲子词’，原只是一些‘绮筵公子’在‘叶叶花笺’上写下来，交给那些‘绣幌佳人’们‘举纤纤之玉手拍按香檀’去演唱的歌辞而已。因此其内容所写乃大多以美女与爱情为主，可以说是完全脱除了伦理政教之约束的一种作品，这对于诗学传统而言，当然更是另一种重大突破。”[①]因此要想真正衡定词这种文类本身的意义与价值，我们自不能忽视《花间集》中对于美女与爱情之叙写，所形成的词在美学方面的一种特殊的品质，以及此种特殊的品质在以后词之演进和发展中，所造成的一种特殊的影响。关于《花间集》之重要性，早在陈振孙之《直斋书录解题》中，已曾称其为“近世倚声填词之祖”[②]。近人赵尊岳在其《词籍提要》中也曾谓：“盖论词学者，胥不得不溯其渊源，渊源实惟唐五代，当时词人别集莫可罗致，则论唐五代词者，舍兹莫属。”[③]虽然早在《花间集》编订以前，自隋唐间宴乐之开始流行，社会上原已出现过两类配合这种乐曲而创作的歌辞：一类是市井间传唱的俗词，如后世敦煌石窟中所发现的曲子词可以为代表；另一类则是当时文士对这种新文体的尝试之作，如刘禹锡、白居易诸诗人所写作的《忆江南》、《长相思》等作品可以为代表。只不过前一类的曲

① 叶嘉莹《中国词学的现代观》第4-5页，岳麓书社1990年版。

② 陈振孙《直斋书录解题》卷二一，第582页，商务印书馆1939年版。

③ 赵尊岳《词籍提要》，《词学季刊》第三卷，第三号，第55页，台北学生书局1967年影印本。

子既未经编订流传，且又过于俚俗，因而遂未曾引起当时作者的重视；至于后一类刘、白等诗人之作，则又因其与诗之风格过于相近，并不足以为“词”这种新兴的文学体式树立起什么特定的宗风。因此乃必待《花间集》之出现，这种新兴的文学体式，才开始形成了自己所特有的一种品质和风貌，而且在五代以迄宋初的词坛上，造成了风靡一世的极大的影响，甚至当词之演进已经“诗化”和“赋化”以后，这种由早期《花间集》中的歌辞之词形成的一种美学方面的特质，在那些风格已经完全不同的作品中，也仍然有着潜隐的存在。因此要想厘清中国词学中的困惑和争议，我们所首先必须面对的，实在应该就是《花间》词究竟含有怎样一种美学特质的问题。如我们在前文之所言，这一册词集中所收的作品，原来只是“绮筵公子”为“绣幌佳人”所写作的香艳的歌辞，其内容既多以叙写美女与爱情为主，因此其所形成的美学特质，当然就必然与其所叙写之内容，有着密切的关系，而对美女与爱情的叙写，则无论是在道德传统或是在诗歌传统中，却一贯是被士大夫们所鄙薄和轻视的对象。所以也就正当这种特殊的美学特质形成期，这种美学特质却在意识观念上，立即就受到了士大夫们的否定的裁决，因此遂将这一类以叙写美女与爱情为主的小词，目之为“艳歌”、“末技”，讥之为“淫靡”、“郑声”。然而有趣的则是，尽管这些士大夫们在意识观念上将这一类“艳歌”的小词，予以了否定的裁决，可是他们却又敌不过这一类小词的“美”的吸引，而纷纷加入了写作的行列，直到南宋的陆游，在他写作小词时仍存有这种矛盾的心理，因此他在《渭南文集》的《长短句序》一文中，就曾经自叙说：“乃有倚声制词，起于唐之季世。……予少时，汩于世俗，颇有所为，晚而悔之。……今绝笔已数年，念旧作终不可揜，因书其旨，以识吾过。”[①]这种矛盾的心理，在当时不仅存在于作者之中，就连宋代著名的词学家王灼，在其专门论词的《碧鸡漫志》一书的序文中，就也

① 陆游《渭南文集》卷一四，第 34 页，《陆放翁全集》册一，商务印书馆“国学基本丛书”本 1933 年版。

曾自叙说："乙丑冬，予客寄成都之碧鸡坊妙胜院，自夏涉秋。与王和先、张齐望所居甚近，皆有声妓，日置酒相乐，予亦往来两家不厌也。"他所写的《碧鸡漫志》五卷，就都是当时饮宴听歌后所写的有关歌曲的见闻考证。而当他二十年后要将所写的这五卷《碧鸡漫志》付之刊印时，却忽然自我忏悔说："顾将老矣，方悔少年之非，游心淡泊，成此亦安用？但一时醉墨，未忍焚弃耳。"[①]这与陆游自序其词所表现的既曾经耽溺，又表现忏悔，而又终于付之刊印的矛盾心理，简直如出一辙。那么，又究竟是由于什么样的因素，才使得这些艳歌小词具有如此强大的吸引力，竟使得当日的士大夫们乃甘冒礼教之大不韪，虽在极强烈的矛盾和忏悔中，也终于投向了对这类小词之创作与评赏的呢？关于此一问题，我们所可能想到的最简单且最明显的答案，大约可归纳为以下两点：其一可能是由于小词所配合来歌唱的音乐之美，如我在《论词的起源》一文之所考证，隋唐间新兴的此种所谓"宴乐"，原是结合有中原之清乐、外来之胡乐，及宗教之法曲而形成的一种新的乐曲，而"词"则正是配合这种集合众长之新乐而演唱的歌辞，则其音声之美妙，自可想见。[②] 这当然很可能是使得当日的士大夫们纷纷愿意为这种新兴的乐曲来填写歌辞的一项重要的因素。其次则可能是由于当日的士大夫们，在为诗与为文方面，既曾长久的受到了"言志"与"载道"之说的压抑，而今乃竟有一种歌辞之文体，使其写作时可以完全脱除"言志"与"载道"之压抑和束缚，而纯以游戏笔墨做任性的写作，遂使其久蕴于内心的某种幽微的浪漫的感情，得到了一个宣泄的机会，这当然也可能是使得当日的士大大们纷纷愿意为此种新兴的乐曲来填写歌辞之另一项重要的因素。而黄山谷之所以用"空中语"来为自己写作的小词做辩解，就正可以证明了当日士大夫们，在写作这一类小词时，所感到的被从"言志"与"载道"之束缚中解放出来的一种轻松的心理状态。以上所提出的两点因素，

① 王灼《碧鸡漫志·序》，《词话丛编》册一，第17页，台北广文书局1967年版。
② 叶嘉莹《论词的起源》，《灵谿词说》第1-26页，上海古籍出版社1987年版。

本应是对于士大夫们何以甘冒礼教之大不韪而投身于小词之写作的两个最明显且最简单的答案，而除去这两点表面的因素以外，私意以为小词之所以特具强大之吸引力者，实在更可能由于经过了写作和评赏的实践，这些士大夫们竟逐渐体会到了这一类艳歌小词，透过了其表面所写的美女与爱情的内容，竟居然尚具含有一种可以供人们去吟味和深求的幽微的意蕴和情致。只不过这种意蕴和情致，就作者而言既非出于显意识之有心的抒写，就读者而言也难于作具体的指陈和诠释，有些词学家如常州词派的张惠言，可以说就是对此种幽微之意蕴颇有体会的一个读者，但他却犯了一个最大的错误，就是想把这种幽微的意蕴，都一一加以具体的指述，于是遂不免陷入于牵强比附之中而无以自拔了。至于《人间词话》的作者王国维，当然也是对小词中这种幽微深隐之意蕴颇有体会的一位读者，所以他一方面虽批评张惠言的比附之说为“深文罗织”，但另一方面却也曾经用“成大事业大学问”之“三种境界”来评说晏殊等人的一些小词。他之较胜于张惠言者，只不过是未曾将自己的说法指称为作者之用心而已。总之，小词之佳者之往往具含有一种引人生言外之想的幽微深远之意致，乃是许多词学家的一种共同的体会。只不过他们却都未能对小词之所以形成此种特殊品质的基本原因，做出任何理论性的说明。我在 1988 年所写的《传统词学》一文中，虽曾对词在演进中由歌辞之词转化为诗化之词再转化为赋化之词的经过历程，及各类词之风格特色都做了相当的探讨，并曾做出结论说：“以上三类不同之词风，其得失利弊虽彼此迥然相异，然而若综合观之，则我们却不难发现它们原有一个共同的特点，那就是三类词之佳者莫不以具含一种深远曲折耐人寻绎之意蕴为美。”[①]我更曾在 1986 年所写的《迦陵随笔》中，举引过若干词例，用西方之符号学、诠释学和接受美学等理论，对张惠言与王国维二家之好以言外之想来说词的方式，做过相当理论性的研述。[②]但

① 叶嘉莹《中国词学的现代观》第 9 页，岳麓书社 1990 年版。
② 叶嘉莹《中国词学的现代观》第 70、79、94 页，岳麓书社 1990 年版。

对于词之何以形成了此种以富于深微幽隐的言外之意致为美之特质的基本原因，也未曾做出溯本穷源的探讨。近年来我偶然读了一些西方女性主义文学批评的论著，当我透过他们的某些观点来反思中国小词之特质时，遂发现中国最早的一册词集《花间集》中对于女性的叙写，与词之以富于幽微要眇的言外之想的意致为美的这种特质之形成，实在有着极为密切的关系。而中国词学之所以长久陷入于困惑之中，一直未能为之建立起一个理论体系，也正与中国士大夫一直不肯面对小词中对美女与爱情之叙写，对之做出正面的肯定和研析有着密切的关系。因此下面我遂想借用西方女性文论中的一些观点，来对中国小词之特质之所以形成了以幽微深隐富于言外之意致为美的基本原因，略做一次溯本穷源的探讨。

二

谈到西方女性主义的文学批评，那原是伴随着西方的女权运动而兴起的，带有妇女意识之觉醒的一种新的文学理论。一般人往往将之溯源于 1949 年西蒙•德•波瓦（Simone de Beauvoir）之《第二性》（*The Second Sex*）一书之刊行。在此书中，波瓦曾就其存在主义伦理学的观点，提出了两个重要的概念：那就是女性是男性眼中的“他者”（the other），是“被男性所观看的”（being looked at）。而在这种情况下，女性遂由“人”的地位被贬降到了“物”的地位。①波瓦的这种观念，当然代表了一种强烈的女性自我意识之觉醒。于是到了 20 世纪 60 年代后期与 70 年代初期，遂有大量的有关女性意识之书刊相继出现，即如李丝丽•费德勒（Leslie Fiedler）在其《美国小说中的爱与死》（*Love and Death in the*

① Simone de Beauvoir, *The Second Sex*, tr. by H. M. Parshley, Harmondsworth Press, 1972.

American Novel）一书中，就曾指出了男性作者在其文学作品中所叙写的女性形象，对于女性有着歧视的扭曲。[①]又如费雯·高尼克（Vivian Gornick）和芭芭拉·莫然（Barbara K. Moran）所合编的《在性别主义社会中的女人》（*Women in a Sexist Society*）[②]，以及凯特·密勒特（Kate Millett）所写的《性别的政治》（*Sexual Politics*）[③]等书，这些著作的重点主要就都在于要唤起和建立一种可以和男性相对抗的女性意识。到了70年代后期，乃有艾琳·邵华特（Elaine Showalter）所写的《她们自己的文学》（*A Literature of Their Own*）[④]，以及桑德拉·吉伯特（Sandra Gilbert）和苏珊·葛巴（Susan Gubar）所合著的《阁楼中的疯妇》（*The Mad Woman in the Attic*）[⑤]等书相继出现，其后吉伯特与葛巴又于80年代中期合力编成了一部厚达两千四百余页的《诺顿女性文学选集》（*Norton Anthology of Literature by Women*），于是紧随在女性意识之觉醒及对文学中女性形象之探讨之后，遂更开始了对于女性作者及女性文学的介绍和批评，而且蔚然成为了一时的风气。而与此相先后，则更有露斯文（K. K. Ruthven）之《女性主义的文学研究概论》（*Feminist Literary Studies: An Introduction*）[⑥]与特丽·莫艾（Toril Moi）的《性别的 / 文本的政治：女性主义文学理论》（*Sexual/Textual Politics: Feminist Literary Theory*）[⑦]，以及艾琳·邵华特的《女性主义诗学导论》（“Towards a Feminist Poetics”, in Women Writing and Writing about Women）[⑧]和玛吉·洪姆（Maggie

---

① Leslie Fiedler, *Love and Death in the American Novel*，NewYork: Stein and Day, 1966.

② Vivian Gornick & Barbara K. Moran, *Women in a Sexist Society: Studies in Power and Powerlessness*, New York, Basic Books, 1971.

③ Kate Millett, *Sexual Politics*, New York: Double Day, 1970.

④ Elaine Showalter, *A Literature Of Their Own: British Women Novelists from Bronte to Lessing*, Princeton: Princeton University Press, 1977.

⑤ Sandra Gilbert and Susan Gubar, *The Mad Woman in the Attic: The Woman Writer and the Nineteenth Century Literary Imagination*, New Haven: Yale University Press, 1979.

⑥ K. K. Ruthven, *Feminist Literary Studies: An Introduction*, New York: Cambridge University Press, 1984.

⑦ Toril Moi, *Sexual/Textual Politics: Feminist Literary Theory*, London & New York: Routledge, Chapman and Hall, Inc., 1988.

⑧ Elaine Showalter, “Towards a Feminist Poetics”, in *Women Writing and Writing About Women*, ed. by Mary Jacobus, London: Croom Helm, 1979.

Humm）的《女性主义文学批评：作为当代文学批评家的妇女》（*Feminist Criticism: Women as Contemporary Critics*）[①]等书相继问世。于是女性主义文学批评，乃逐渐脱离了早期的女性与男性相互对立抗争的狭隘的观念，而发展成为了一种由女性意识觉醒所引生的新的文学批评理论的建立。本文由于篇幅及作者能力之限制，对于西方的这些女性主义的文学理论自无暇做详细之介绍，而且本文也并不完全套用西方的模式来评说中国的词与词学，但无可否认的则是任何一种新的理论出现，其所提出的新的观念，都可以对旧有的各种学术研究投射出一种新的观照，使之可以获致一种新的发现，并做出一种新的探讨。一般说来，无论中西的历史文化，在过去都曾长久地被控制在男性中心的意识之下，因此当女性意识觉醒以来，遂在短短的几十年间，就对世界上各种社会经验及文化传统都造成了强烈的震撼。我个人作为一个中国古典诗词的研究工作者，遂在西方女性主义文论的观照中，对于中国小词中之女性特质，以及此种特质在词学中所引起的许多困惑的问题，也有了一些新的体认和想法。下面我就将把个人的这一点新的体认和想法，略做简单的叙述。

首先我们所要提出来一谈的，乃是《花间》词中的女性形象之问题。中国旧传统之文评家，往往将诗词中所有关于女性的叙写都混为一谈，因此过去之说词人才会将小词中关于美女与爱情的叙写，或者任意比附于古代之风骚，或者推源于齐梁之宫体，或者等拟为南朝乐府中的西曲及吴歌。然而事实上则这些不同的文类中，虽同样有关于美女与爱情的叙写，但其所形成的美学之特质与作用，显然有着极大的区别。关于这方面，我觉得西方女性文论中对于文章中女性形象的论述和探讨，似乎颇有可以提供我们反思之处。早在 60 年代，李丝丽·费德勒（Leslie Fiedler）在其《美国小说中的爱与死》一书中，就曾提出了男性作者所写之女性往往将之两极化了的问题。费氏以为男性作者所写之女性，总

① Maggie Humm, *Feminist Criticism: Women as Contemporary Critics*, Brighton: Harvester, 1986.

是或者将之写成为美梦中之女神，或者将之写成为噩梦中之女巫[①]，而这两类形象，当然都并不是现实中真正的女性。其后在 70 年代又有苏珊・格伯曼・柯尼伦（Susan Koppeiman Cornillon）编辑了一本论集，题名为《女性主义者所看到的小说中之女性形象》（*Images of Women in Fiction: Feminist Perspectives*），其中收有 21 篇论文，都严格地批评了文学作品中女性形象之不真实性[②]。后来在 80 年代，玛丽・安・佛格森（Mary Anne Ferguson）在其《文学中之女性形象》（*Images of Women in Literature*）一书中，则更将文学中之女性形象详细地分成了三大部分：第一部分为"传统的妇女形象"（traditional images of women），在此一部分中，佛氏曾将女性分为五种类型：其一为妻子（the wife）之类型，其二为母亲（the mother）之类型，其三为偶像（woman on a Pedestal）之类型，其四为性对象（the sex object）之类型，其五为没有男人的女性（women without men）之类型。这五种类型之身份虽然各有不同，但事实上却都是作为男性之配属而出现的，即使在没有男人的女性之类型中，也是作为因没有男人而被怜悯被异视而出现的。这些传统的形象在早日的文学作品中，早已成为固定的类型（stereotype），不仅在男性作品中存在，即使在女性作品中也难以脱去这种限制。不过自女性的意识开始觉醒以后，于是文学中遂有了另外的女性类型之出现，这就是佛氏书中的第二部分，所谓"转型中之女性"（women becoming）。这一类型的女性形象，主要在努力脱除旧有的定型的限制，试图表现出女性真正的自我，写出女性自我的真正生活体验，和自我真正的悲欢忧乐，成为自我的创造者（self-creators）。另外，佛氏在书中的第三部分，还提出了所谓女性的"自我形象"（self-images）。这主要是由于近年来有不少女性的日记和书信被发现和整理了出来，不过因为内容和性质的杂乱，

① Leslie Fiedler, *Love and Death in the American Novel*, New York: Stein and Day, 1966, p.314.

② Susan Koppeiman Cornillon, *Images of Women in Fiction: Feminist Perspectives*, Ohio: Bowling Green University Popular Press, 1973.

还有待于进一步的研究和探讨。[①]

以上我们虽然对西方女性主义文论中有关女性形象之论著，做了简单的介绍，但本文却并不想把关于《花间》词中女性形象的讨论，套入到西方的模式之中。这一则因为东西方之文化背景原有着明显的不同，我们原难将西方之模式做死板之套用；再则也因为他们的探讨乃大多以小说中之女性形象为主，这与我们所要探讨的《花间》词中的女性形象，当然也有着极大的差别；三则更因为西方女性主义之文论，原与西方之女权运动有着密切的关系，而本文之主旨，则只是想透过《花间》词中的女性叙写，来对小词之美学特质一加探讨，而全然无意于女权之运动。但我却仍然对他们的论点做了相当的介绍，我的目的只是想透过他们对女性形象之身份性质之分析的方式，也对中国诗词中之女性形象之身份性质一加反思，并希望能藉此寻找出《花间》词中之女性叙写与词之美学特质的形成究竟有着怎样的一种关系而已。

在中国诗歌中关于女性的叙写，当然并不自《花间》词为始，即如为《花间集》写序的欧阳炯，就曾把这一类写美女与爱情的作品，推溯到前代的乐府与南朝的宫体诗，而后世之以溯源与尊体为说的词学家，其不惜将小词比附于《诗》、《骚》，则更已如前文之所述，他们的这些说法，从表面看来似乎也都有可以成立的理由，因为自《诗经》、《楚辞》以下，降而至于南朝乐府中之吴歌、西曲和齐、梁间的宫体诗，以至于唐人的宫怨和闺怨的诗篇，其中本来早就有了大量的对于美女与爱情的叙写，这原是不错的。盖以男女之情既为人性之所同具，爱美而恶丑也为人性之所同然，因此若只从其叙写美女与爱情的表面情事来看，则所有这些作品自然便都有着可以相通之处，但值得注意的则是，虽然同样是叙写美女与爱情的作品，为什么却只有“词”这种文类中的一些作品才特别富于一种引人生言外之想的要眇宜修之特质？我以为这才是最值得我们去探讨的一个重要问题。关于此一问题，私意以为西方女性文论

① Mary Anne Ferguson, *Images of Women in Literature*, Houghton Mifflin Co., 1986.

中对作品中女性形象之身份性质的讨论，似乎颇可以给我们一些启发。在中国的文学史中，虽然早自《诗经》开始，就已经有了关于美女与爱情的叙写，但事实上各种不同时代、不同体式的文学作品中，其所叙写之女性形象之身份性质，以及其所用以叙写之口吻方式，却原有着极大的差别。以下我们就将对这些差别稍加论述。

《诗经》中所叙写的女性，大多是具有明确之伦理身份的现实生活中之女性，其叙写之方式，亦大多以写实之口吻出之，这是一类女性的形象。《楚辞》中所叙写之女性，则大多为非现实之女性，其叙写之方式，乃大多以喻托之口吻出之，这是又一类女性的形象。南朝乐府之吴歌及西曲中所叙写之女性，则大多为恋爱中之女性，其叙写之方式则大多是以素朴的民间女子自言之口吻出之，这是又一类女性的形象。至于宫体诗中所叙写之女性，则大多为男子目光中所见之女性，其叙写之方式乃大多是以刻画形貌的咏物之口吻出之，这是又一类女性之形象。到了唐人的宫怨和闺怨诗中所叙写的女性，则大多亦为在现实中具有明确之伦理身份的女性，其叙写之方式则大多是以男性诗人为女子代言之口吻出之，这是再一类女性之形象。如果以词中所叙写之女性形象与以上各文类中之不同的女性形象相比较，我们就会有一种奇妙的发现，那就是词中所写的女性乃似乎是一种介乎写实与非写实之间的美色与爱情的化身。我这样说，也许有一些读者不免会对此产生疑问，盖以如我们在前文所言，《花间集》中所选录的作品，既原是“绮筵公子”为“绣幌佳人”而写的“文抽丽锦”的歌辞，因此其中所写之女性，自然应该乃是那些当筵侑酒的歌儿酒女之形象。如此说来，则此一类女性形象自当是现实中之女性。可是这一类女性却又并无家庭伦理中之任何身份可以归属，而不过仅只是供男子们寻欢取乐之对象而已。而《花间集》中的作品，就正是出于那些寻欢取乐的男性作家之手，因此其写作之重点乃自然集中于对女性之美色与爱情之叙写，而“美”与“爱”则恰好又是最富于普遍之象喻性的两种品质，因此《花间集》中所写的女性形象，遂以现实之女性而具含了使人可以产生非现实之想的一种潜藏的象喻性。如果以这一类女性形象与我们在前文所提到的其他文类中的女性相比较，则《诗经》中所写的现实生活中之女性，可以说基本上并不是什么象喻性，即使后世的说诗人可以据之为美刺讽喻之说，也只是后加的一种比附，而并非其所写之女性形象之本身所具含的特质。这是我们所当注意的第一点区别。至于《楚辞》中所写之女性，则大多本出于作者有心之托喻，而有心之托喻，则一般皆有较明白之喻旨可以推寻，这与《花间》词中之本无托喻之用心，而本身却极富象喻之潜能的女性形象，当然也有很大的不同。这是我们所当注意的第二点区别。再就吴歌及西曲中的女性而言，则此类乐府歌辞本出于民间，且观其口吻盖多为女子之自述：如果以之与《花间》词之出于男性文士之手的作品相比较，则前者之所叙写乃大多为现实的女性之情歌，并无象喻之色彩，而后者则由于乃是男性作者对其心目中之"美"与"爱"的叙写，因而遂具含了某种象喻之色彩。这是我们所当注意的第三点区别。更就宫体诗言之，则宫体诗中所写之女性乃大多是被物化了的女性，作者在叙写之时，很少有主观感情之投入，可是《花间》词中所写的女性则正是爱情所投注的主要的对象，因此宫体诗中的女性遂只为一些美丽的被物化了的形象而已，而《花间》词中的女性则因为有着爱之投注，而具含有一种象喻的潜能，这是我们所当注意到的第四点区别。再就唐代的宫怨与闺怨之诗言之，则私意以为此类怨诗似可分别为二种不同之情况：一种怨诗所写者乃属于现实生活中女性所实有的空虚寂寞之怨情，另一种怨诗所写者则是假托女性之怨情来喻写男性诗人自己不得知遇的悲慨。前者之所写，与《诗经》中的思妇弃妇之性质似乎颇有相近之处，后者之所写，则与《楚辞》中的托喻之性质似乎也颇有相近之处。而此二种情况则与我们前面所言及的《花间》词中所写的现实中之女性而却具含有引人生象喻之想的，介乎写实与非写实之间的女性形象都并不相同，这是我们所当注意的第五点区别。

以上是我们透过西方女性主义文论中对文学作品中女性形象之反

思，所可能见到的在《花间》词中所叙写的女性形象，与其他文类中所叙写的女性形象的一些重要区别。而这当然是形成词之特别富于引人生言外之想的象喻之潜能的一项最主要的因素。

其次我们所要提出来一谈的乃是《花间》词中之语言的问题。关于词与诗之语言的不同，前代的词学家当然也早曾注意及之。所谓“诗庄词媚”之说，固久为论词者之共同认知。至于词与诗在语言形式上的明显差别，则主要当然乃在于诗之句式整齐，而词则富于长短参差之变化。即如清人笔记就曾载有一则故事，说清代的学者纪昀博学而好滑稽，一日偶然在扇面上题写了唐代诗人王之涣的一首七言绝句，原诗是：“黄河远上白云间，一片孤城万仞山。羌笛何须怨杨柳？春风不度玉门关。”而纪氏却漏写了首句最后的“间”字。当有人指出其失误时，纪氏乃戏谓其所写者原非七言之绝句，而为长短句之词，于是乃对之重加点读为“黄河远上，白云一片。孤城万仞山。羌笛何须怨？杨柳春风，不度玉门关。”[①]如果从内容所写的景物情事来看，则二者本来原可以说是完全相同，可是却因其句式之不同，后者遂显得比前者更多了一种要眇曲折的姿态。可见词之语言形式的参差错落，乃是造成其与诗之语言的性质不同的一个重要原因，但二者之区别，又不仅在形式之不同，即如《王直方诗话》曾载苏轼与晁补之及张耒论诗之言，晁、张云：“少游（秦观）诗似小词，先生（苏轼）小词似诗。”[②]元好问《论诗绝句》也曾引秦观《春日》诗中的两句而评之云：“‘有情芍药含春泪，无力蔷薇卧晚枝’，拈出退之《山石》句，始知渠是女郎诗。”[③]可见词之语言与诗之语言的分别，除了形式方面的差别以外，原来也还有着性质方面的差别。秦观诗之被评为“女郎诗”，又被评为“诗似小词”，都足以说明“词”较之于“诗”乃是一

① 笔者幼时闻先伯父狷卿公讲述如此，经查，未见出处。

② 见郭绍虞校辑：《宋诗话辑佚》卷上，第97页，哈佛燕京学社出版，《燕京学报》专号之十四，1937。

③ 元好问《论诗绝句》之二十四，《元遗山诗集笺注》册下，卷十一，第8b页，台北：广文书局影印道光蒋氏藏版，1973。

种更为女性化的语言。那么究竟怎样的语言才是女性化的语言呢？关于此点，西方的女性主义文论的一些观点，也有颇可以供我们反思参考之处。原来西方的女性主义文评之重点，开始原在对文学作品中女性形象之探讨，其后遂转向了对于女性之作品之探讨，于是他们遂注意到了女性作品中的女性语言之问题。关于女性语言（female language）的讨论，最初他们也是站在两性对立的观点来看待的。他们以为一般书写的语言，都带有男性的意识形态，这对于女性遂形成了一种压抑。所以法国的女性主义文评家安妮·李赖荷（Annie Leclerc）在其《女性的言说》（“Parole de Femme”）一文中乃尝试专以写作实践写出一种自己的语言，而不欲被限制在男性意识的界限之中。[①]此外卡洛琳·贝克（Carolyn Barke）在其《巴黎的报告》（“Reports from Paris”）一文中，也曾指出法国女性文学的一个重要论题，乃是如何去发掘和使用一种适当的女性的语言。[②]至于所谓女性语言的特色，则在英国任教的一位女性主义文评家特丽·莫艾在其《性别的/文本的政治：女性主义文学理论》一书中，曾指出一般人的看法，总以为男性（masculine）所代表的乃是理性（reason）、秩序（order）和明晰（lucidity），而女性（feminity）所代表的则是非理性（irrationality）、混乱（chaos）和破碎（fragmentation）。[③]不过莫氏自己却又提出说她本人反对这种男性与女性的对分法。她以为我们必须停止这种把逻辑性、观念性和理性认为是男性的分类法。这种争议之由来，私意以为主要都是由于西方女性主义文评之源起与女权主义运动有密切之关系的缘故。因此当他们讨论到女性语言时，遂往往将之牵涉到两性在社会中之权力地位等种种方面之问题。不过，我们现在却不想从生理的性别来讨论男性之语言是否较之女性之语言，更为逻辑性与更为理念

① Annie Leclerc, “Parole de Femme”, in *New Feminisms: An Anthology*, ed. by Elaine Marks & Isabelle, The University of Massachusetts Press, 1980, pp.79-86.

② Carolyn Barke, “Reports from Paris: Women’s Writing and the Women’s Movement”, in *Signs* 3, Summer 1978, p. 844.

③ Toril Moi, *Sexual/Textual Politics: Feminist Literary Theory*, London & New York: Routledge, Chapman and Hall, Inc., 1988, p.160.

性之问题，也不想把女性语言与男性语言相对立而讨论其优劣的问题。我们现在只是想借用西方女性主义文论中的一些观念，来探讨《花间》词之语言所形成的某种美学特质之问题。

如果从西方女性文论中所提出的书写语言带有男性的意识形态的一点来看，则中国传统文学中的言志之诗与载道之文等作品，当然便该毫无疑问的都是属于所谓男性的语言。因为中国儒家的教育一向以治国平天下为其最高之理想，所以在中国的诗文中遂一向充满了这种想法的意识形态，朱自清先生在其《〈唐诗三百首〉指导大概》一文中，就曾指出了唐诗中的一种主要意识形态，说："在各种题材里，'出处'是一重大的项目，从前读书人唯一的出路是仕，出仕为了行道，自然也为了衣食，出仕以前的隐居、干谒、应试（落第）等，出仕以后的恩遇、迁谪，乃至爱民、爱国、思林栖、思归田等，乃至真个归田，都是常见的诗的题目。"①而在中国旧传统的社会之中，则女性既根本没有仕的机会，因此这种以"仕隐"与"行道"为主题的作品，当然乃是一种男性意识的语言。可是《花间集》小词的出现，却打破了过去的"载道"与"言志"的文学传统，而集中笔力大胆地写起了美色与爱情，而且往往以女子之感情心态来叙写其伤春之情与怨别之思，是则就其内容之意识而言，《花间》词之语言，固当是一种属于女性化之语言。何况在语言之形式方面，如我们在前文之所曾论述，词之语言与诗之语言的主要差别，固原在诗之语言较为整齐，而词之语言则更富于长短错落之致。而如果从西方女性主义所提出的两性语言之性质方面的差别来看，则毫无疑问，诗之语言乃是一种更为有秩序的明晰的，属于男性的语言，而词则是比较混乱和破碎的一种属于女性的语言。也许有些人会认为混乱而破碎的语言形式，相对于明晰而有秩序的语言形式，乃是一种较为低劣的语言形式，可是中国的小词却大力地证明了这种混乱而破碎的语言形式，不仅不是一

① 见《朱自清古典文学论文集》册下，第357页，台北：远流出版公司1982年版。

种低劣的缺点，而且还正是形成了词之曲折幽隐，特别富于引人生言外之想之特美的一项重要的因素。即如为《花间》词树立宗风的一位弁冕全集的作者温庭筠，他的词之所以备受后人推崇，认为有屈骚之托意的主要原因，事实上就正在于他所使用的语言，无论就内容意识方面而言，或者就外表形式方面而言，都恰好是带有最强烈的女性语言之特色的缘故。温词既大力描述女子的衣饰之美与伤春怨别之情，又经常表现为混乱破碎不连贯的章法和句式。所以讥之者如李冰若之《栩庄漫记》乃谓其往往“以一句或二句描写一简单之妆饰，而其下突接别意，使词意不贯，浪费丽字，转成赘疣，为温词之通病”[①]。而赏之者如陈廷焯之《白雨斋词话》乃称其“意在笔先，神余言外……若隐若见，欲露不露，反覆缠绵，终不许一语道破。匪独体格之高，亦见性情之厚”[②]。可见温词之所以特别具含有引人生言外之想的潜能，固正由于其所使用之语言，无论就内容意识而言，或就外表形式而言，都是最富于女性化之特色的缘故，因此我们自然可以说词之女性化的语言，乃是形成了词之特别富于引人生言外之想的象喻之潜能的另一项重要的因素。(关于温词中所写的女性的姿容衣饰之美，以及其句法中之看似扞格不通之处，之所以易于引人生言外之想的缘故，我在《温庭筠词概说》及《温庭筠〈菩萨蛮〉词所传达的多种信息及其判断之准则》二文中，已曾就其“客观”与“纯美”，及符号学中之“语码”等理论，做过相当详细之析论，兹不再赘。[③]只不过本文所提出的其所写的容饰之美在意识方面之属于女性化之语言，以及其句法之破碎在形式方面之属于女性化之语言，乃是更为触及到词之根本特质的一种看法而已。)

以上我们既然从西方女性文评中所提出的“女性形象”与“女性语言”两方面，对词之所以形成其幽微要眇具含丰富之潜能的因素，做了

① 李冰若《栩庄漫记》，见《花间集评注》第16页，上海：开明书店1935年版。

② 屈兴国：《白雨斋词话足本校注》册上，第20页，济南：齐鲁书社1983年版。

③ 见《迦陵论词丛稿》，第1-37页，上海古籍出版社1980年版；《中国词学的现代观》，第78-83页，岳麓书社1990年版。

相当的探讨；但事实上这其间却原来存在着一个重大的问题，那就是西方女性文评之所谓“女性语言”，本是指女性作者所使用之语言而言的，可是《花间集》中所收录的十八位词人，却清一色的都是男性的作者，于是《花间》词特质之形成，遂在除去我们已讨论过的两项因素以外，还应再增入一项更为重大的因素，那就是由男性作者使用女性形象与女性语言来创作所形成的一种特殊的品质。关于此种特殊之品质，私意以为西方女性文评近年来所提出的一些观念，似乎也有颇可以供我们参考之处。原来西方的女性文评，近年来已逐渐脱离了早期的女性与男性互相对立抗争的狭隘之观念，而发展成为了一种由女性意识之觉醒，从而引生出来的新的文学批评理论之建立，而其中最值得注意的一个理论观念，就是卡洛琳·郝贝兰（Carolyn G. Heilbrun）在其《朝向雌雄同体的认识》（*Towards Recognition of Androgyny*）一书中，所提出的“雌雄同体（androgyny）之观念。这个字原是古代的一个希腊语，其字原乃是结合了andro（男性）与gyn（女性）两个字而形成的一个词语，本意原指生理上雌雄同体的一种特殊现象，但郝氏之提出此一词语，本意指性别的特质与两性所表现的人类的性向，本不应做强制的划分，因此就郝氏之说而言，此“androgyny”一词，也可将之译为“双性人格”。郝氏之提出此一观念之目的，是想从一种约定俗成的性别观念中，把个人自己真正的性向解放出来。郝氏在书前序文中，曾经引用批评家汤玛斯·罗森梅尔（Thomas Rosenmeyer）在其《悲剧与宗教》（*Tragedy and Religion*）一书中的话，以为希腊神话中的酒神戴奥尼萨斯（Dionysus）既非女性，亦非男性。或者更好的说法应说戴奥尼萨斯所表现的自己，乃是男人中的女人，或女人中的男人。[①]郝氏更曾引用心理学家诺曼·布朗（Norman C. Brown）在其《生对死：心理分析的历史意义》（*Life Against Death: The Psychoanalytical Meaning of History*）一书中的话，以为犹太神秘哲学的宗教家就曾提出说上帝具有双性人格的本质；东方道家哲学的老子，在

① Carolyn Heilbrun, *Toward a Recognition of Androgyny*, New York: Norton & Co. 1982, p.xi.

《道德经》中也曾提出过“知其雄，守其雌”的说法；而诗人里尔克（Rilke）在其《给一个青年诗人的信》（“Letters to a Young Poet”）中，也曾认为男女两性应密切携手，成为共同的人类（human beings）而非相对之异类（as opposites）。[①]从以上所征引的种种说法来看，郝氏的主要之目的原不过是想要证明，无论是在神话、宗教、哲学和文学中，“双性人格”都该是一种最高的完美的理想，因此女性文评自然也应该摆脱其与男性相抗争的对立的局面，而开创出一种以“双性人格”为理想的新的理论观点。是则郝氏虽然反对社会上因约定俗成而产生的把男女两性视为相对立的观念，但其出发点却实在仍是以此一观念为基础的。至于本文之引用郝氏之说，则与现实社会中男女性别之区分与对立全无任何关系，而不过只是想借用其“双性人格”之观念，来说明《花间》词的一种极值得注意的美学特质而已。

所谓“双性人格”或“阴阳同体”之说，如果从医学和生理方面来理解，则我们之使用此一词语来讨论《花间》之小词，自不免会使人感到怪异而难以接受。但若就美学之观点言之，则《花间》之小词却确实具含了此种“双性人格”的一种特美。虽然《花间》词之作者并未曾有意追求此种特美，但却由于因缘之巧合，乃使得《花间》词的那些男性作者，竟然在听歌看舞的游戏之作中，无意间展示了他们在其他言志与载道的诗文中，所不曾也不敢展示的一种深隐于男性之心灵中的女性化的情思。关于男性在意识中之潜隐有女性之情思，本来50年代的心理学家荣格（C. G. Jung）就曾提出过此种说法。[②]而近年有一位美国西北大学的教授劳伦斯·利普金（Lawrence Lipking）在其1988年出版的《弃妇与诗歌传统》（*Abandoned Women and Poetic Tradition*）一书中，则更曾从诗学之传统中，对男性之潜隐有女性化之情思，做了深细的探讨。

---

① Carolyn Heilbrun, *Toward a Recognition of Androgyny*, New York: Norton & Co. 1982, p.xi., pp.xvii-xviii.

② *The Collected Works of C. G. Jung*, translated by R. F. C. Hull, Vol.9, Part Ⅱ, Bollingen Foundation, Inc., 1959, pp.1-42, “Aion: Phenomenology of Self”.

不过利氏所谓“弃妇”，并非狭义的只指被弃的妻子，而是泛指一切孤独寂寞对爱情有所期待或有所失落的境况中的妇女。利氏自谓促使他撰写此书的动机之一，乃是因为他读了西蒙·德·波瓦的《第二性》一书中的“恋爱中之妇女”（Women in love）一节，于是才引起了他对于此一主题的思考。利氏以为诗歌中之有弃妇的叙写，可以说是与诗歌之有历史同样的悠久。他曾举古希腊的诗人欧威德（Ovid）所写的《一组女人的书信》（*Epistulae Heroidum*）为例证，此一组书信乃是欧氏假托古代有名的女人——从希腊神话中的奥特塞（Odyssey）的妻子潘尼洛普（Penelope）到希腊的女诗人莎孚（Sappho）之名而写作的一系列的爱情的书信，信中所表现的都是她们对所爱的远方之人的情思。利氏以为此种在诗歌中所表现的弃妇思妇之情，无论在任何文化中都是普遍存在着的，而“弃男”的形象则很少在文学作品中出现。因为社会上对男女两性有着不同的观念，诗歌中写到女性之被弃似乎是一件极自然的事，但男性之被弃则似乎是一件难以接受之事。而男人有时实在也有失志被弃之感，于是他们乃往往借女子口吻来叙写，所以男性诗人之需要此一“弃妇”之形象实较女性诗人为更甚。因此“弃妇”之诗所显示的遂不仅是两性之相异性，同时也是两性之相通性。①利氏之所言，当然有其普遍之真实性，而此种观念验之于中国传统之诗歌，则尤其更有一种特别之意义。因为在中国传统社会中，除去如利氏所提出的，男女两性因地位与心态不同，故男子难于自言其挫辱被弃，乃使得男性诗人不得不假借女性之口以抒写其失意之情以外，在中国旧日的君主专制社会中，原来还更存在有一套所谓“三纲五常”的伦理观念。“五常”一般多以为指“仁、义、礼、智、信”五种常德，此与本文所讨论之主题无关，姑置不论；至于“三纲”则是指三种不平等的人际伦理关系，也就是“君为臣纲，父为子纲，夫为妻纲”。在这种关系中，为君、为父与为夫者，永远是高

① Lawrence Lipking, *Abandoned Women and Poetic Tradition*, Chicago: University of Chicago Press, 1988, pp.xv-xxvii.

高在上的掌权发令的主人，而为臣、为子与为妻者，则永远是被控制支配的对象。不过此“三纲”中，“父子”乃是先天的伦理关系，所以“弃子”的情况，不仅发生得比较少，而且复合的机会也比较多；可是“君臣”与“夫妻”则是后天的伦理关系，其得幸与见弃乃全然操之于高高在上的为君与为夫者的手中，至于被逐之臣与被弃之妻，则不仅全然没有自我辩解与自我保护的权力，而且在不平等的伦理关系中，还要在被逐与见弃之后，仍然要求他们要持守住片面的忠贞。在此种情况下，则被逐与见弃的一方，其内心所满怀的怨悱之情，自可想见。而也就正由于这种逐臣与弃妻之伦理地位与感情心态的相似，所以利普金氏所提出的男性诗人内心中所隐含的“弃妇”之心态，遂在中国旧社会的特殊伦理关系中，形成了诗歌中以弃妇或思妇为主题而却饱含象喻之潜能的一个重要的传统。曹植《七哀诗》中之自叹“当何依”的“贱妾”，以及《杂诗》中之自叹“为谁发皓齿”的“佳人”[①]，可以说就都是此一传统中的明显的例证。

当我们有了以上的对于东西方诗歌中“弃妇”之传统的认识以后，再来反观这些在歌筵酒席间演唱的歌辞，我们就会发现这些歌辞所写的，原来大多乃是寻欢取乐的男子们对那些歌伎酒女们的容色与恋情的叙写。这种恋情盖正如利普金氏在其《弃妇》一书中所提到的，如同 11 到 13 世纪间法国南部、西班牙东部和意大利北部所流行的，一些抒情诗人们所写的恋歌（troubadour）一样，总是男子们在爱情的饥渴中寻求得一种满足后便扬长而去，而女子们则在一场恋情后留下了绵长的无尽的怀思。[②]中国小词中所写的恋情也正复如此，这在早期的敦煌曲中便已可得到证明。即如《敦煌曲子词》中的两首《望江南》“莫攀我”及“天上月”，这两首词中所写的“恩爱一时间”及“照见负心人”，所表现的就都是一些歌伎酒女们对那些一度欢爱后便抛人而去的情人们的怨意和

① 见《曹集诠评》卷五，第 41 页，及卷四，第 28 页，上海：商务印书馆 1933 年版。

② Lawrence Lipking, *Abandoned Women and Poetic Tradition*, Chicago: University of Chicago Press, 1988, p.xviii.

怀思。[1]只不过那些敦煌曲子所写的很可能就是那些被弃的歌伎酒女们的自言之辞，所以其词中所表现的就只是一份极质朴的女性的怨情；可是《花间集》的作者则是男性的诗人文士，因此当他们也尝试仿效女子的口吻来写那些相思怨别之情的时候，就产生了两种极值得注意的现象。其一是他们大多把那些恋情中的女子加上了一层理想化的色彩，一方面极写其姿容衣饰之美，一方面则极写其相思情意之深，而却把男子自己的自私和负心以及由此而引起的女子的责怨，都隐藏起来而略去不提。于是在他们的作品中之女子遂成为了一个忠贞而挚情的美与爱的化身，而不再是如敦煌曲中的充满不平和怨意的供人取乐和被人遗弃的现实中的风尘女子了。这是第一点值得注意之处。其二则如我在前文所言，由于“逐臣”与“弃妻”在中国旧社会中伦理地位之相似，以及“弃妇”之词在中国诗歌中所形成的悠久之传统，因此当那些男性的诗人文士们在化身为女子的角色（persona）而写作相思怨别的小词时，遂往往于无意间就竟然也流露出了他们自己内心中所蕴含的，一种如张惠言所说的“贤人君子幽约怨悱不能自言之情”。这种情况之产生，当然可以说是一种“双性人格”之表现。而由此“双性人格”所形成的一种特质，私意以为实在乃是使得《花间》小词之所以成就了其幽微要眇，具含有丰富之潜能的另一项重大的因素。

除去以上所提及的种种因素以外，最后还有一点我想要加以说明的，就是男子之假借女子之形象或女子之口吻来抒写其仕宦失志之情，原不自小词为始，但何以却只有小词才形成了其独特的要眇幽微之特质？关于此一问题：本来我在前文论及诗歌中女性之形象时，已曾将小词中女性之形象，与其他诗歌中女性之形象之性质的不同，以及由此而产生的美学效果的不同，都做过一番比较和讨论。我以为一般而言，大多数诗歌中所写之女性形象，约可分别为两大类：一类是具有明确之伦理身份的现实中之女性；另一类则是并无明确之伦理身份的托喻中之非现实的女

① 见《敦煌曲子词集》卷上，第44页，上海：商务印书馆，1956年修订版。

性，而小词中所写的女性，则似乎乃是一种介于写实与非写实之间的、美色与爱情的化身。而这种介于写实与非写实之间的，并无明确的象喻之意义的女性形象，却似乎较之那些有心托喻具有明确之象喻意义的女性形象，具含了更丰富的象喻之潜能。关于此种现象之形成，私意以为当代法国的一位女学者朱丽亚·克里斯特娃（Julia Kristeva）所提出的一些理论，似乎也颇有可供我们参考之处。克氏是一位关心女性主义文评，然而却不被女性文评所拘限的、学识极为渊博的女性学者。她自称她自己所建立的学说为解析符号学（semanalyze），是针对传统符号学（semiotics）在诠释近代一些诗歌时所面临的不足，因而创立出来的一种新说。克氏主要的论点在于要把符号（sign）的作用分为两类：一类是符示的（semiotic），另一类是象征的（symbolic）。克氏以为在后者的情况中，其符表之符记单元（signifying unit）与其所指之符义对象（signified object）间的关系，乃是一种被限制的作用关系（restrictive function-relation）。而在前者之情况中，其能指之符记单元与所指之对象中则并没有任何限制之关系。克氏以为一般语言作为表意的符记，其作用大抵是属于象征的层次，也就是说其符表与符义之间的关系，乃是固定而可以确指的；可是诗歌的语言，则可以另有一种属于克氏所谓的符示的作用，也就是说其符表与符义之间的关系，往往带有一种不断在运作中的生发（productivity）之特质，而诗歌之文本（text）遂成为了一个可以供给这种生发之运作的空间。在这种情形下，文本遂脱离了其创作者的主体意识，而成为了一个作者、作品与读者彼此互相融变（transformer）的场所。[①]克氏生于保加利亚，于1966年来到法国巴黎，当时她只有二十五岁。带着她东欧的学术思想背景，立即投入了西方学术思想菁英的

① Julia Kristeva, *Revolution in Poetic Language*, translated by Margaret Waller, New York: Columbia University Press, 1984, chapter I. “The Semiotic and the Symbolic”, pp.19-106，并请参看于治中先生《正文、性别、意识形态》一文，见《中外文学》十八卷一期，第151页，台北：《中外文学》月刊社，1989年1月。关于“transformer”一词，见于克里斯特娃所著 *Semiotike: Recherches Pour une Semanalyse*, Paris: Seuil, 1969, p.10.

活动之中，这种双重学术文化的融会，使她所本来具有的卓越的才智得到了极大的发挥，她的学识之渊博与思辨之深锐都是过人的。本文因篇幅及笔者能力之限制，对于克氏之说自无法做详尽的介绍。我现在只不过是想断章取义地借用她所提出来的“符示”与“象征”两类不同的符号作用之区分，来说明《花间》小词中，由于“双性人格”之特质所形成的一种幽微要眇的言外之潜能，与传统诗歌中那些有心为言外之托喻的作品之间的一些差别而已。

就传统诗歌中有心托喻的作品而言，其用以托喻的符表，与所托之意的符义，可以说乃是完全出于作者显意识之有心的安排。即如屈原在《离骚》中所写的“美人”，与曹植在《七哀》诗中所写的“弃妇”，就该都是属于克氏所说的“象征的”作用之范畴。也就是说其符表之符记单元与其所指之符义对象之间，是有着一种明白的被限定之作用关系的。虽然洪兴祖的《楚辞补注》曾经提出说“屈原有以美人喻君者……有喻善人者……有自喻者”[①]，指出了三种不同的喻意，但“美人”之为一种品德才志之美的象喻则是一致的，而且这种喻意可以说乃是明白可晓的所有读者的一种共同认知；至于曹植《七哀》诗中的“贱妾”，以及《杂诗》中的“佳人”，则是中国诗歌中女性之形象，已由单纯的“美”之象喻，融入了“君臣”与“夫妇”之不平等的社会伦理之观念以后的一种喻意，以不得男子之赏爱的女子喻托为仕宦失志的逐臣，这种喻意可以说也是明白可晓的所有读者的一种共同认知。像这种情况，其文本中的符记单元与其所喻指的符义对象之间的关系，自然是属于一种由作者之显意识所设定的被限制了的作用关系，也就是克氏所说的“象征的”作用之关系。可是《花间》小词中所写的女性之形象，就作者而言，则当其写作时原来很可能只是泛写一些现实中的美丽的歌女之形象，在显意识中根本没有任何托喻之用心，可是却由于我们在前文所曾述及的“女

① 洪兴祖：《楚辞补注》，第3页，台北：广文书局1962年版。

性形象”、“女性语言”及“双性人格”等因素，而使之具含了一种象喻之潜能。像这种情况，其文本中的符记单元，则如克氏所云只是保持在一种不断引人产生联想的生发的运作之中，而并不可对其所指的符义对象，做出任何限制性的实指，也就是说这种作用乃是属于克氏所说的一种“符示的”作用之关系。像这种充满了生发之运作的活动而却完全不被限制的符记与符义之间的微妙的关系，当然是使得《花间》小词虽然蕴含了丰富的象喻之潜能，而却迥然不同于有心之托喻的一个重要的原因。

三

以上我们既曾透过西方女性主义文学批评的一些论点，对《花间》小词之何以特别具含有一种要眇幽微的言外之潜能的种种因素，做了相当理论化的论述。现在我们就将以这些论述为基础，回过头来对本文开端所曾提出的中国词学中的一些困惑之问题，结合实例来做一番反思的探讨和说明。首先我们将举引《花间集》中的几首小词来略加比较，以为评说立论之依据。下面就让我们先把这几首词抄录下来一看：

二八花钿。胸前如雪脸如莲。耳坠金环穿瑟瑟。霞衣窄。笑倚江头招远客。（欧阳炯《南乡子》

倭堕低梳髻，连娟细扫眉。终日两相思。为君憔悴尽，百花时。（温庭筠《南歌子》）

晚逐香车入凤城，东风斜揭绣帘轻。慢回娇眼笑盈盈。　消息未通何计是，便须佯醉且随行。依稀闻道太狂生。（张泌《浣溪沙》）

春日游。杏花吹满头。陌上谁家年少足风流？妾拟将身嫁与一

生休。纵被无情弃，不能羞。（韦庄《思帝乡》）

以上我所抄录的四首词，可以看做是两相对比的两组作品。第一和第二两首是一组对比，主要都在写一个美丽的女性形象。不过，其叙写的口吻，却有着明显的不同。第一首乃是纯出于男子之口吻的对一个他眼中所见的容饰美丽的女子的描述；第二首则出于女子之口吻的对自己之容饰及情思的自叙。至于第三和第四两首则是另一组对比，主要都在写外出游春时对一段爱情遇合的向往和追寻。第三首是写一个男子在游春时对一个香车中的女子的追逐；第四首则是写一个女子在游春时对一个风流多情之男子的向往和期待。如果从表面所写的情事来看，则无论是前二首所写的美色，或者后二首所写的爱情，固应同属于被士大夫们所鄙薄的不合于传统道德观念的淫靡之作，但温、韦二家之词，在后世词学家中却一直受到特别的推重。至其受推重之原因，则是由于他们认为这两家的词特别富于深微的言外之意蕴，令人生喻托之想。[①]我们现在就把这四首词略加比较和讨论，看一看究竟是什么因素，使得同样是叙写美女与爱情的小词竟有了优劣高下之分。先就前两首言，欧阳炯所写的“二八花钿，胸前如雪脸如莲”，与温庭筠所写的“倭堕低梳髻，连娟细扫眉”，虽在表层意义上同属于对女子的美色之描述，但在本质上却实在有着很大的差别。欧词所写的乃是男子之目光中（male gaze）所见到的一个已经化妆好了的美丽的女子，是男子眼中的一个既可以观赏也可以欲求的他者（the other）。像这种对美色的描述，除了显示出男子的一种充满了色情的心思意念之外，自然就更没有什么可供读者去寻思和探求的深远的意蕴了。可是温词所写的则是一个正在化妆中的女子的自述，如果结合着中国文化背景中之所谓“士为知己者死，女为悦己者容”的观念来看，则在此一女子之“梳髻”和“扫眉”的容饰中，自然便也

① 张惠言《词选》谓温词为“感士不遇”，有“《离骚》初服之意”，又谓韦词为“留蜀后寄意之作”，北京：中华书局1957年版。

蕴含了想要取悦于所爱之男子的一份爱意和深情。何况紧接在此二句之后的就是“终日两相思”的叙写，则其在“梳髻”与“扫眉”之中就已蕴含了此“相思”之情，更复从而可知。而且“低梳”与“细扫”，所叙写的是何等柔婉缠绵的动作，“倭堕”与“连娟”所描述的又是何等容态秀美的风姿。而结之以“为君憔悴尽，百花时”。“为君”一句，既写出了“衣带渐宽终不悔，为伊消得人憔悴”的用情之深挚，而“百花时”一句，则更呼应了开端的“梳髻”“扫眉”两句之“为悦己者容”的期盼，而表现了一份“欲共花争发”的“春心”。综观全词，即使仅就其表层意义所写的容饰与怀春的情事而言，我们也已经可以清楚地感受到了其用字的质地之精美，与其句构的承应之有力。这一份艺术效果，便已迥非欧阳炯一词之粗浅轻率之可及。何况若更就其深层的意蕴而言，则不仅其所写的“女为悦己者容”的情意，可以在文化传统上引起一份“士为知己者死”的才志之士之欲求知用的感情心态方面的共鸣，而且其所写的“梳髻”、“扫眉”之修容自饰的用心，也可以令人联想到《离骚》中屈原所写的“余独好修以为常”的一份才人志士的修洁自好的情操，何况“扫眉”一句所暗示的蛾眉之美好，与画眉之爱美求好的心意，在中国文化中更有着悠久的喻托之传统。于是温庭筠的这一首小词，遂在其所写的美女之化妆与怀春的表层情意以外，更具含了一种可以引人生言外之想的深层意蕴之潜能。这一份深微的意境，当然就更非欧阳炯之只写出男子的色情之心态，而更无言外之余蕴的作品之所能企及的了。

其次，我们再看后二首词。张泌的“晚逐香车入凤城”一首，乃是以一个男子口吻所写的，在外出游春之际偶然见到了一辆香车上的一个美女，于是遂对之紧追不舍的一段浪漫的遇合；韦庄的“春日游”一首，则是以一个女子口吻所写的，在外出游春之际因见到繁花盛开而希望有所遇合的一份浪漫的情思。二者之情事虽然并不全同，但其皆为由春日所撩动而引起的一份男女之恋情，则是相同的。也就是说就表层的意义而言，二词之所写者固皆为男女之春情，但若就其深层的本质而言，则二者间实在也有着很大的差别。张泌之词与前面所举引的欧阳炯之词相近，同是写一个男子之目光中所见到的一个美丽的女子，一个可观赏也可以欲求的他者。只不过欧词还停留在观看凝视的阶段，张词则已展开了追逐的行动。至于韦庄之词则与前所举引的温庭筠之词相近，同是以一个女子口吻所写的对于一个男子的期盼和向往。不过温氏那首词的风格表现得纤柔婉约，而韦氏这首词的风格则表现得劲直矫健，即以其开端而言韦词之“春日游”所表现的一种向外的游赏和追寻之主动的心态，就已经与温词所表现的在闺中“梳髻”、“扫眉”而坐待之被动的心态有了明显的不同。不过，尽管二者间有着如此的分别，但在具含有言外的较深之意蕴的一点，则是相同的。只是它们之所以具含有较深之意蕴的因素，却又不尽相同。温词之佳处在于其文本中所使用的一些语言符号，随时可以唤起我们对文化传统中之一些符码的联想。而韦词之佳处则在于其文本自身中所蕴含的一种字质和句构中的潜力。不过，我这样说却并不是为之做出绝对的区分，因为温词除予人符码之联想外，同样也仍表现有字质和句构的潜力；而韦词除表现有字质和句构的潜力以外，同样也仍可予人符码之联想。我所说的只不过是一种相对的比较而已。关于温词由文本所可能引生的言外之意蕴，我们在前面既已做了相当的探讨，现在就来让我们对韦词也一加探讨。

韦词之第一句“春日游”，虽只短短三个字，但事实上却已掌握了全首词的生命脉搏。“游”字自然已显示了外出游赏和追寻的主动心态，而“春日”两个字则更已明白暗示了其外出追寻的诱因与目的。因为“春日”既是万物之生命萌发的季节，也是人类之感情萌动的季节，所以开端的“春日游”一句虽只三个字，却实在已传示了全词之由诱因到目的之整个脉动的方向。至于次句的“杏花吹满头”，则是进一步以更为真切有力的笔法来叙写由“春”之诱因所引发的追寻之情志的旺盛和强烈。先就“杏花”而言，一般说来，不同品类的花都各自有其不同之品质，也都可以引起人们的不同的感受和联想，所以周敦颐才会说“菊，花之隐逸者也；牡丹，花之富贵者也；莲，花之君子者也。”[①]至于杏花之为花，则一般对之虽并无一定的评断，但证之于文士们在诗词中对杏花之描述，如“红杏枝头春意闹”，“一枝红杏出墙来”[②]等句之所叙写，则杏花以其娇红之颜色与繁茂之花枝，所给予人的自应是一种充满生命力的春意盎然的撩动。何况韦词在“杏花”之下还接写了“吹满头”三个字，则此撩人春意之迎头扑面而来，乃真有不可当之势矣。而且这种“不可当”之势，还不仅是一种意义上的说明和认知而已，而是在其所使用的“吹”字与“满”字等字质之中，直接传达了一种极其充盈饱满的劲力。而这种劲健直接的表现，就正是韦词的一种特色。于是紧接着这种劲健直接的春意撩人的不可当之势，此一被春意撩动的女子，乃以毫不假饰的极真挚的口吻，脱口说出了“陌上谁家年少足风流？妾拟将身嫁与一生休”的择人而欲许身的愿望。然后接下来还更以“纵被无情弃，不能羞”两句，表明了对这种许身之不计牺牲、不计代价的，全然奉献而终身不悔的一份决志。而且这种决志也不仅只是在意义上的一种说明而已，同时还有自“陌上”以下两个九字句一个八字句的长句之顿挫抑扬，以及“妾拟将身嫁与”一句中运用的几个舌齿的发音中，用韵律、节奏和声音，直接传达出了此一许身之决志的坚毅无悔的情意，给予了读者一种极为直接的感动。综观此词，即使仅就其表层意义所写的自春意的萌发，到许身的愿望，再到无悔的决志，其劲健深挚的感人之力，无论就感情之品质或艺术之效果而言，便已都决非张泌《浣溪沙》词以轻狂戏弄之笔墨所写的调情之作品之所能比。何况若更就其深层之意蕴而言，则韦词所表现的感情之品质，其坚贞无悔之心意，乃竟然与儒家之所谓“择善固执”的品德，及楚骚之所谓“九死未悔”的情操，在本质上有了某些暗合之处。这种富含潜能之意蕴，当然就更非张泌所写的

① 周敦颐《爱莲说》，见《周濂溪集》卷八，第139页，上海：商务印书馆，《国学基本丛书》1937年版。

② 宋祁《玉楼春》，见《全宋词》册一，第716页，北京：中华书局1965年版；叶适《游小园不值》，见《千家诗》，第131页，香港：广智书局，未著出版年月。

“佯醉随行”之浅薄轻佻的调情之作所能企及的了（关于韦庄此词之详细论述，请参看江苏古籍出版社1986年出版的《唐宋词鉴赏辞典》所收拙撰之评说）。

透过以上四首词的两两相比较，我们已可清楚地见到，虽然同样是叙写美女与爱情的小词，但其间却果然是有着深浅高下之区分的。也就是说早期的艳歌小词为“词”这种新兴的文类所树立起的一种特殊的美学品质，乃是特别易于引起读者的言外之联想，且以富于此种言外之意蕴为美的。而此种特殊之品质，与评量之标准的形成，则与早期艳歌中之女性叙写，如温词中之“梳髻”、“扫眉”的形象和语码，以及韦词中之许身无悔的口吻和情思，结合有极为密切的关系。因为正是这些女性的叙写，造成了一种潜隐的双性之性质，也才造成了这类小词的双层意蕴之潜能。而这实在是我们要想探讨中国词学，所当具备的一点基本的认知。有了这一点认知以后，我们就可以对旧日词学中之一些使人困惑的问题，来依次一加探讨了。

首先我们要提出来一谈的乃是以“比兴”说词的问题。关于此一问题，我在多年前所写的《对常州词派比兴寄托之说的新检讨》一篇长文中，已曾有过详细的论说，在此并不想对之再加重述（见《迦陵论词丛稿》）。我现在只不过是想就本文所提出的一些论点，对之再加一些补充的说明。首先我们应该认识到的，乃是早期《花间》的小词，本来大都是文士们为歌伎酒女所写之艳歌，本无寄托之可言。至其可以令人生寄托之想，则是由于这些艳歌中所叙写的女性之形象，所使用的女性之语言，以及男性之作者透过女性之形象与女性之语言所展露出来的一种“双性人格”之感情心态，因此遂形成了此类小词之易于引人生言外之想的双重或多重之意蕴的一种潜能。此种潜能之作用，则是如本文在前面所引述的克里斯特娃氏之所说，其作用乃是“符示的”，而并不是“象征的”。其符表与符义之间的关系乃是不断在生发的运作中，而并不可加以限制之指说的。清代常州词派张惠言所犯的最大的错误，就在于他想把自己由此种符表之生发运作中所引生的某种联想，竟然直指为作者之用心。所以常州派后起的一些说词人，为了想补救张氏之失，乃对读者之以联想说词的方式，做了一番更为深细的探讨。在这些探讨中，私意以为周济与陈廷焯二人所提出的两段话最为值得注意。周氏在其《宋四家词选目录序论》中，对于有关读词者之联想，曾提出过一段极妙的喻说，谓："读其篇者，临渊窥鱼，意为鲂鲤。中宵惊电，罔识东西。赤子随母笑啼，乡人缘剧喜怒。"[①]周氏的这段话，如果透过我们前面所引的克里斯特娃的说法来看，则周氏所谓"随母"之"母"，与"缘剧"之"剧"，自当是指其富含有生发之运作的文本。至于随之而"笑啼"、"喜怒"的"赤子"和"乡人"，则是经由文本中符记之生发运作而因之乃引生出多种之感发与联想的读者。但此种感发与联想又不可以作限制的指实的说明，所以周氏乃将之喻比为"临渊窥鱼"和"中宵惊电"，虽然恍惚有见，然而却不能指说其品类之为鲂为鲤，其方向之为东为西。至于陈廷焯则将此种难以指说的深隐于文本之符示中的生发运作之潜能，名之以为"沉郁"，而且对之加以解说云："所谓沉郁者，意在笔先，神余言外，写怨夫思妇之怀，寓孽子孤臣之感。凡交情之冷淡，身世之飘零，皆可于一草一木发之。而发之又必若隐若现，欲露不露，反复缠绵，终不许一语道破。"[②]这段话之可贵，我以为乃正在于陈氏曾"一语道破"地点出了"怨夫思妇之怀"与"孽子孤臣之感"之相类似的感情心态。这种体会其实已经触及到了我们在前文所曾提出的"双性人格"之说。只不过在陈廷焯之时代当然还没有所谓"双性人格"的说法和认知，因此陈氏乃将小词中此种由女性之叙写而引生的"符示的"生发运作之关系，与传统诗歌中之有心喻托的"象征的"被限制的符表与符义之关系，混为了一谈。不过陈氏却也曾感到了小词之引人联想的作用，与传统诗歌中可以指说的喻托之意，又显然有所不同，于是遂又对之加上了一段"若隐

① 周济：《宋四家词选目录序论》，第 1b 页，台北：广文书局影印滂喜斋刊本，1962 年版。
② 屈兴国：《白雨斋词话足本校注》上册，第 20 页，济南：齐鲁书社 1983 年版。

若现”、“欲露不露”的说法。综观周、陈二氏之说，当然都不失为对小词之富含感发作用与多层意蕴之特质的一种体会有得之言。至于他们所犯的错误，则就其明显之原因言之，乃是因为他们都受了张惠言的比兴寄托之说的影响，因此遂将读者所引发的偶然之联想，强指成了作者有心之托喻。而如果就其更根本的内在之原因言之，则实在乃由于他们对小词中之女性叙写所可能造成的双性人格之作用之未能有清楚的认知。按照他们的意思来看，则小词之所以有深浅优劣之分，原来乃是由于作者在创作意识中便有着根本的差别。一则有心写为喻托之作，一则但为淫靡香艳之辞。但事实上原来却并非如此。因为就《花间》之小词言之，其所写者本来大都是绮筵绣幌中交付给歌女去唱的艳词，本无所谓喻托之意。至于其中某些作品之竟使读者产生了言外之想则我们在前文中虽已曾就其字质、语码、句法、结构等各方面，都做了分析和说明，但事实上其中却还有一个更为重大也更为基本的原因，我在当时所未曾提及的，那就是其叙写口吻与心态的不同。温庭筠与韦庄的两首词，其叙写之情思乃皆出于女性之口吻，代表了一种女性的心态。而欧阳炯与张泌的两首词，其叙写之情思乃皆出于男性之口吻，代表了一种男性的心态。如果将此两类词一加比较，我们就会发现前者之所以特别富含有一种言外之双重意蕴，实与男性之作者假借女性口吻来叙写女性之情感所形成的一种双性人格之作用，有着密切的关系。至于后者则直接以男性之作者，用男性之口吻来写男性对美色之含有欲念之观看与追求，则纵然此一类作品虽或者也可以写得生动真切，但却毕竟也只是单层的情意，而缺少了一种言外之双重意蕴的特美。

关于此种双重意蕴，我们在前面所举引的四首词例中已做了相当的探讨。透过温、韦二家的两首词，我们已经清楚地看到，这些词中之“低梳髻”、“细扫眉”，及“将身嫁与一生休”等，我们所称为字质、语码、句法、结构等各方面引人产生言外之联想的因素，实莫不与我们所提出的女性之叙写及双性之人格有着密切的关联。因此“女性”与“双性”

实当为形成此类小词之美学特质的两项重要因素。写到这里，有些读者也许会产生一个疑问，那就是以男性之作者直接用男性本身之口吻所写的艳歌小词，有时岂不是也可能同样富含有一种言外的意蕴深微之美？举例而言，即如韦庄的《菩萨蛮》五首、《女冠子》二首，以及《谒金门》（空相忆）一首等作品，就都是直接用男性口吻所写的作品。但这些作品却迥然不同于欧阳炯与张泌二词之浅率轻狂，而写得极为深婉沉挚。关于此种情况之产生，私意以为其间实有一点极可注意之处，那就是这些词虽然是用男子之口吻所写的作品，但其所表现的情意之深挚绵长，乃与前所举之欧阳炯及张泌二词之把女子视为可观看与可追求之“他者”的轻狂之态大异其趣，反而大有近于用女子口吻所写的女性的执著和无尽的怀思。此种现象之形成，遂使我想到了本文在前面所曾举引过的劳伦斯·利普金的一些说法，利氏不仅以为男性与女性对待爱情的态度有所不同，男性往往在满足其爱情之饥渴后便扬长而去，而女性在经历了爱情后，则往往便对之留下无尽的怀思；利氏更以为男子是要透过对女子的了解和观察，才能学习到被弃掷和失落以后的幽怨之情。[①]因此我们可以说凡男性之作者用男性口吻所写的相思怨别之词，其所以有时也同样能具含一种言外的意蕴深微之美，固正由于其在表面上虽未使用女子之口吻，然而在本质上却实在已具含了女性之情思的缘故。如此，我们当然更可证明《花间集》中之艳歌小词，其美学特质乃是以具含一种双重的言外深微之意蕴者为美，而《花间》词之女性叙写及其所蕴含的双性之人格，则实为形成此种美学特质之两项最基本且最重要之因素。至于传统词学家之所以往往将本无比兴寄托之艳歌，强指为有心托喻之作，造成了牵强附会之弊，就正因为他们对此种由女性与双性形成的特质，未曾有明确之认知的缘故。不过从另一方面言，则后世之词也果然有一些有心为比兴喻托的作品，这类词之性质与《花间》一派词当然已有了

① Lawrence Lipking, *Abandoned Women and Poetic Tradition*, Chicago: University of Chicago Press, 1988, p.xix.

很大的不同，但却实在仍是《花间》词之特质的影响下之产物，关于此种情况，我们将留待后文论及《花间》词之特质对后世之影响时，再加探讨。

其次我们所要讨论的乃是词学中之所谓“雅”、“郑”的问题。如我们在前文所言，《花间集》中所收录的本都是歌筵酒席的艳歌，就其所写之美女与爱情言，固当同属于淫靡之“郑声”，然而就前所举之四首词例来看，则其间又果然有着优劣高下之不同，所以王国维在《人间词话》中乃提出了“词之雅郑，在神不在貌”之说。至于其“雅”、“郑”之分的标准，则王氏以为乃在其“品格”之高下，因此王氏遂又曾提出了“永叔、少游，虽作艳语，终有品格”之说。[①]但既然同是“艳语”，则品格高下之依据又究竟何在？王氏对此虽并无理论之说明，可是我们却也不难从王氏另外的几则词话中窥见一些消息。第一点值得注意的，乃是王氏之论词也同样注意言外之感发，即如其曾将晏、欧等人的一些写爱情的小词，拟比为“成大事业大学问者”的“三种境界”，又以“诗人之忧生”及“诗人之忧世”来评说冯延巳和晏殊的相思怨别之句。[②]而冯延巳及晏、欧诸家之令词，则正是自《花间》一派衍化出来的被北宋评词人视为艳歌小词的作品。可是这些作品又竟然可以使读者产生极高远的超乎艳歌以外的联想，这当然可能是使得王氏提出了“词之雅郑，在神不在貌”以及“虽作艳语，终有品格”之说的一个重要原因。第二点值得注意的，则是王氏论词虽然也推重引人产生言外之联想的小词，可是却对于被常州词派所推重的也足以引人生言外之想的温庭筠的词，有着不同的歧见，以为温词虽然“精艳绝人”，却并无“深美闳约”的言外之丰富的意蕴。[③]这种歧见之产生，私意以为乃是由于常州派《词选》的作者张惠言，与《人间词话》的作者王国维，二人对于小词之所具含的

① 徐调孚：《校注人间词话》，第 19 页，香港：中华书局 1961 年版。
② 徐调孚：《校注人间词话》，第 15-16 页，香港：中华书局 1961 年版。
③ 徐调孚：《校注人间词话》，第 6 页，香港：中华书局 1961 年版。

可能引起言外之联想的因素，有着不同的体认之故。张氏好以比附为说，所以重在小词中可以用于比附的文化语码，如“画眉”之可以引人联想到《楚辞》中的“众女嫉余之蛾眉”，“深闺”之可以引人联想到《楚辞》中的“闺中既已邃远”之类。而王氏所重视的则是作品本身之感发的品质所可能引起的读者之联想，温词则一般说来较缺少直接之感发，且王氏又极不喜字面之比附，这很可能是王氏不认为温词有“深美闳约”之意蕴的一项重要原因。王氏所重视的是作品本身之感情品质所可能引起的感发之联想，即如他在词话中所举引的晏、欧等词中所写的某些感情之品质，与“成大事业大学问者”或诗人之“忧生”、“忧世”者的感情之品质在基本上可以有相通之处之类。所以王氏在另一则词话中，乃又曾提出过“故艳词可作，唯万不可作儇薄语”的重视感情品质之说。[①]值得注意的则是，所谓“儇薄语”的作品，大都乃是男性作者用男性口吻所写的，视女性为“他者”的作品。而另一方面则凡是用女性口吻所写的词，或者虽用男性口吻而却是具含有女性之情思的作品，一般说来则大多不会有“儇薄语”的出现。经过以上的讨论，我们就会有一个奇妙的发现，那就是凡是可以引人产生深微或高远的超乎艳歌以外之联想的好词，其引发联想之因素，无论就文化语码方面而言，或者就感发之本质方面而言，原来都与小词中之女性叙写，以及作者隐意识中的一种双性的朦胧心态，有着密切的关系。如“画眉”与“深闺”之类的语码，其有合于“美人”之喻托，固自应属于“女性”之叙写。至于就感发之本质而言，则王国维所提出的“不可作儇薄语”之说，也足可使我们想到王氏所赞美的“虽作艳语，终有品格”的好词，必然不会是男性作者直接用男性口吻所写的，视女性为“他者”的轻狂之作，而当是男性作者用女性口吻所写的，或者虽用男性口吻但却具含有女性之情思的作品。这类作品则显然都含有一种“双性”之性质。这是我们对于《花间》一

① 徐调孚：《校注人间词话》，第 67 页，香港：中华书局 1961 年版。

派之艳歌小词的所谓“雅”、“郑”之分，所当具备的一点最基本的认识。至于当小词演化为长调以后，则所谓词之“雅”、“郑”的分别，自然也就随之而另有了一种新的性质，也另有了一种新的评量标准。不过，其性质与标准虽然有了不同，但却也仍然受有《花间》词之特质的极大的影响。关于此种情况，我们也将留待后文，论及《花间》词之特质对后世之影响时，再加探讨。

以上我们既然对《花间》一派小词之“比兴”与“雅郑”的问题，都做了相当的探讨，现在我们就将再对此类作品之被目为“空中语”，以及“空中语”之价值与意义，也一加探讨。如我们在前文所言，《花间》之词既大多为歌酒间之艳歌，因此在本质上遂与“言志”之诗，有了一种明显的区分，也就是说诗歌之写作对作者而言，乃是显意识的一种自我之表达，可是词之写作则往往只是交付给歌女去演唱的一时游戏之笔墨，与作者本身显意识中的情志和心意，本无任何必然之关系。因此黄山谷在为自己所写的艳歌小词做辩护时，乃将之推说为“空中语”，这种说法，在黄氏本意不仅是对自己所写的美女与爱情之词的一种推托，而且对此类并非言志的游戏笔墨之艳词，也含有一种轻视之意。所以一般而言，北宋人在编选诗文集时，往往并不将小词编入正集之内，其不视之为严肃之作品的轻鄙之态度，自可想见。然而殊不知小词之妙处，乃正在其并不为严肃之作，而为游戏笔墨的“空中语”。下面我们便将对此种“空中语”之价值与意义，结合我们在前面所提出的“女性”与“双性”之特质，略加论述。

关于“游戏笔墨”的“空中语”之所以能在小词中产生一种微妙的作用，我以为其主要的因素约可分为以下的几点来看。第一点微妙的作用，乃在于这些“空中语”恰好可以使作者脱除了其平日在写作言志与载道之诗文时的一种矜持，因而遂在游戏笔墨中，流露出了一份更为真实的自我之本质。所以王国维在《人间词话》中，乃曾提出说：“五代北宋之诗，佳者绝少。而词则为其极盛时代，即诗词兼擅如永叔、少游者，词胜于诗远甚。以其写之于诗者，不若写之于词者之真也。”[①]这是可注意的第一点。第二点微妙的作用，乃在于小词之所以为“空中语”，还不同于其他戏弄的笔墨，小词之为“空中语”，乃是在自我从显意识隐退以后，更蒙上了一层女性之面目的作品。因此遂使其脱除了显意识之矜持以后的自我之真正本质，与作品中之女性叙写于无意中融成了一种双性之特质。这是可注意的第二点。至于第三点微妙的作用，则更在于以其为“空中语”之故，遂使作者隐意识中之真正本质，与其小词中之女性叙写之融会，乃完全达成了一种全出于无心的自然运作之关系。而这也就正是何以小词中所写的美女，与传统诗歌中所写的有心托喻之美女，在符表与符义之运作关系上，遂产生了极大之不同的一个基本原因。我们在前文所举引的克里斯特娃之说，就曾将符表与符义之关系，分别为“符示的”与“象征的”两种不同之作用。有心托喻之作中的美女，其符表与符义之间的关系，乃是属于“象征的”作用关系，是一种可以确指的被限制了的作用关系。可是这种“空中语”的小词中所写的美女，则恰好因其本为并无托意的“空中语”，因此其符表中之女性叙写，乃脱离了所谓“象征的”关系中之固定的限制，而成为了一种自由运作的“符示的”关系。克氏以为在此种关系中，文本遂脱离了其创作者所原有的主体意识，而成为了作者、作品与读者彼此互相融变的一个场所。而就“空中语”的小词而言，则更因其创作者既本来就缺少明确和强烈的主体意识，而其对美女与爱情的叙写，又如此富含女性与双性所可能引生的微妙的作用，因此这类“空中语”的小词，遂于无意间具含了如克氏所说的融变的最大的潜能。这是可注意的第三点。而这种“空中语”之微妙的作用，当然是造成了小词之双重性与多义性之特质的一个重要的因素。不过，词之发展却很快地就超越了歌辞之词的“空中语”的阶段，而在文士们的写作中逐渐走向了“诗化”和“赋化”的演进。在此种演

---

① 徐调孚：《校注人间词话》，第 45 页，香港：中华书局 1961 年版。

进中，词遂脱离了所谓“空中语”之性质，而成为了具有明显的主体意识之叙写和安排的作品。但值得注意的则是，虽然这些“诗化”和“赋化”之词的性质及写作方式已与早期《花间集》的歌辞之词有了很大的不同，可是《花间》词所形成的一种双重与多义为美的特质，却仍然对这些“诗化”与“赋化”之词的优劣之评量，具有极大的影响。下面我们就将从《花间》词之女性叙写所形成的双性特质，对后世词与词学之影响方面，也略加探讨。

谈到词之演进，私意以为其间曾经过几次极可注意的转变：其一是柳永之长调慢词的叙写，对《花间》派之令词的语言，造成了一大改变；其二是苏轼之自抒襟抱的“诗化”之词的出现，对《花间》派之令词的内容，造成了一大改变；其三是周邦彦之有心勾勒安排的“赋化”之词的出现，对《花间》派令词的自然无意之写作方式，造成了一大改变。如果从表面来看，则这三大改变无疑的乃是对我们前文所曾论及的《花间》词之女性语言、女性形象，以及由自然无意之写作方式所呈现的双性心态的层层的背离。因此下面我们所要探讨的，自然就该是当词之发展已脱离了《花间》词之女性与双性之特质以后的这些不同的词派，其美学特质之标准又究竟何在的问题了。关于此一问题，私意以为有一点极可注意之处，那就是当词之发展已脱离了《花间》词之女性叙写以后，虽然不再能完全保有《花间》词之女性与双性的特质，但无论柳词一派之佳者，苏词一派之佳者，或周词一派之佳者，却都各自发展出了一种虽不假借女性与双性，然而却仍具含了与《花间》词之深微幽隐富含言外意蕴之特质相近似的，另一种双重性质之特美，而这种美学特质之形成，无疑地曾受有《花间》词之特质的影响。王国维曾云“词之雅郑，在神不在貌”,这种脱离了女性与双性之后的多种方式的双重性质之美学特质的形成，可以说正是《花间》词之特质的一种“在神不在貌”的演化。下面我们就将对柳词苏词与周词所发展出来的这些各自不同的双重性质之特点，分别略加论述。

首先，我们将从柳永之长调慢词对《花间》派令词之语言所造成的转变说起。如我们在前文论及《花间》词之语言特色时所言，就其语言形式来看，《花间》令词所使用者乃是比较混乱和破碎的一种属于女性化之语言形式，也就是说是句子短而变化多的一种语言形式。即以《花间集》中温、韦二家所最喜用的《菩萨蛮》一调而言，全词一共不过只有八句，但却换了三次韵，每两句就换一个韵。而这种参差跳跃的变化，事实上却正是造成了如陈廷焯所称美的“发之又必若隐若现，欲露不露，反复缠绵，终不许一语道破”之富于言外之意蕴的一个重要的因素。可是柳永之长调慢词，则势不得不加以铺陈的叙述，因此柳永乃以其善用“领字”，长于铺叙，为世所共称。而如果从我们在前文所引用之西方女性主义对两性语言之差别的说法来看，则这种以领字来展开铺叙的语言，无疑地乃是一种属于明晰的、理性化的、有秩序的男性的语言。此一变化，遂使得柳词失去了短小之令词的“若隐若现”、“欲露不露”的富含言外之意蕴的女性语言之特点而变为了一种极为显露的、全无言外之意蕴的现实的陈述。所以温庭筠《菩萨蛮》词所写的“鸾镜”、“花枝”、“罗襦”、“鹧鸪”等关于女性的描述，乃使读者可以生无限言外托喻之想；而柳永《定风波》词所写的“暖酥消，腻云亸，终日厌厌倦梳裹”和“针线闲拈伴伊坐”等关于女性的描述，乃不免为人所讥了。不过，柳永除去此一类被人讥为“俚俗”、“媟黩”的作品以外，却实在还更有一类被人称为“言近意远”、“神观飞越”、“一二笔便尔破壁飞去”的佳作[①]，而所谓“破壁飞去”，事实上其所赞美的便应该仍是一种富于言外之意蕴的特点。那么柳永在以其领字铺叙变小词之错综含蓄为浅露之写实以后，又是怎样达成了另外一种“破壁飞去”之特点的呢？关于此点，我以为主要盖在于柳永在写相思怨别的作品中，竟然加入了一种秋士易感的成

① 周济《介存斋论词杂著》，第 2b 页，见《宋四家词选》附录，台北：广文书局影印滂喜斋刊本，1962 年版；龙榆生《唐宋名家词选》，第 89 页，“集评”引郑文焯与人论词遗札，上海：古典文学出版社 1956 年版。

分，而对此种悲慨，柳氏又往往不做明白的叙说，却将之融入了对登山临水的景物叙写之中，于是相思怨别之情与秋士易感之悲既造成了一种双重之性质，景物的叙写与情思的融会又造成了另一种双重之性质，于是遂形成了其“破壁飞去”的一种特美。何况秋士易感之悲与美人迟暮之感，在基本心态上又有着极为相似之处，所以柳永的这一类词虽以男性口吻作直接之叙写，但在其极深隐的意识深处，却实在也仍隐含有一种双性之性质。这正是柳永的这一类词之所以“言近意远”，引人感发联想的一个重要缘故。从柳永的这两类词，我们自可看出虽然其长调慢词对《花间》令词之语言，曾造成了一大改变，但《花间》令词所形成的以富含言外之意蕴为美的美学之要求，则即使在柳词中也仍然是判断其优劣的一项重要的准则（关于柳词之详细论说，请参看《灵谿词说》中拙撰《论柳永词》一文）。

其次，我们将再看苏轼自抒襟抱的“诗化之词”对《花间》派令词之内容所造成的改变。如我们在前文所言，《花间》词内容所叙写者，乃大多以美女与爱情为主，而苏词则以“一洗绮罗芗泽之态”著称[①]，一变歌辞之艳曲，而使之成为了可以抒写个人之襟抱与情志的另一种形式的诗篇。其后更有南宋辛弃疾诸人之继起，于是词学中遂产生了婉约与豪放二派之分，且由此引发了无数之困惑与争议。要想解答这些困惑和争议，私意以为我们实应先对柳词与苏词之关系略加叙述。从苏轼平日往往以己词与柳词相比较的一些谈话来看，苏氏对柳词盖有两种不同之态度。一方面是对柳词之所谓“俚俗”、“媟黩”之作的鄙薄，另一方面则是对柳词之所谓“神观飞越”之作的赞赏。关于此两方面之关系，早在《论苏轼词》一文中，我对之已曾有相当之论述，兹不再赘。[②]至于本文所要做的，则是将柳、苏之关系放在本文所提出的《花间》词之女性叙写所形成的词之美学特质中，再加一番更为根本的观察和探讨。如

① 胡寅：《酒边词序》，味闲轩藏版汲古阁校选《宋六十名家词》第二集，第五册，第2b页。
② 见《灵谿词说》，第191-228页，上海古籍出版社1987年版。

前文之所述，柳词之被人讥为俚俗媟黩者，主要原因实并不在其所写之内容之为美女与爱情，而在于其所使用之语言形式，使之失去了《花间》词之语言在写美女与爱情时所蕴含的双重意蕴之潜能。至其被人称赏为“神观飞越”者，也不在其所写的单纯的秋士易感之悲，或景物之高远而已，而在其能将二者相融会，且在基本心态上隐含有一种双性的性质，因此遂产生一种富含双重意蕴之美。至于苏轼对柳词，则是只从表面见到了其淫媟之失，与其超越之美，但却对其所以形成此种缺失与特美之基本因素，也就是对其是否具含言外双重之意味的一种美学特质，未曾有真正的体会和认知，因此苏词所致力者主要乃在一反柳词的淫媟之作风，而以自抒襟抱“一洗绮罗芗泽之态”者为美，而对其是否具含双重意蕴的一点，则未曾加以注意。因此苏轼对词之开拓与改革，乃造成了一种得失互见的结果。而在苏词之影响下，对后世之词与词学，遂形成了几种颇为复杂的情况，因此我们对之就也不得不略费笔墨来做一点较详的论述。

先从词之写作一方面而言，此一派“诗化”之词的得失，约可分为以下三种情况：一类是虽然改变了《花间》词之女性叙写的内容，然而却仍保有了《花间》词所形成的以双重意蕴为美的词之美学特质者；另一类则是既改变了《花间》词之内容，也失去了词之特美，然而却由于其“诗化”之结果，而形成了一种与诗相合之特美者；再一类则是既未能保有词之特美，也未能形成诗之特美，因之乃成为了此一类词中的失败之作品。关于第一类之作品，我们可以举苏轼与辛弃疾二家词之佳者为例证：即如我在《论苏轼词》一文所曾析论过的《水调歌头》（明月几时有）、《念奴娇》（大江东去）、《八声甘州》（有情风万里卷潮来）诸作，以及在《论辛弃疾词》一文中所曾析论过的《水龙吟》（举头西北浮云）（楚天千里清秋）、《摸鱼儿》（更能消几番风雨）诸作，可以说就都是具含有词之多重意蕴之美学特质的“诗化”以后之词的佳作之代表（见《灵谿词说》）。至于第二类之作品，则如张元幹《贺新郎》（梦绕神州路）、陆游《汉宫春》（羽箭雕弓）及张孝祥《六州歌头》（长淮望断）诸作[①]，虽然缺少言外深层之意蕴的词之特美，但其激昂慷慨之气，则颇富于一种属于诗的直接感发之力量，故亦仍不失为佳作。至于第三类之作品，则如刘过《沁园春》（斗酒彘肩）（玉带猩袍）（古岂无人）诸作[②]，则但知铺张叫嚣，既无词之意蕴深微之美，亦无诗之直接感人之力，是以陈廷焯在其《白雨斋词话》中，乃谓刘过之所学但为"稼轩皮毛"，并对其《沁园春》诸词，讥之为"叫嚣淫冶"[③]，像这一类作品，其为失败之作，自不待言。透过以上的例证，我们已可看出词在"诗化"以后，固仍当以其能保有词之双重意蕴者为美。至其已脱离词之双重意蕴之特美者，则其上焉者虽或者仍不失为长短句中之诗，而其下焉者则不免流入于粗犷叫嚣，岂止不得目之为词，抑且不得目之为诗矣。由此可见是否能保有词之双重意蕴之特美，实当为评量"诗化"之词之优劣的一项重要条件。而如我们在前文所言，《花间》派令词之所以形成其双重意蕴之特美，主要盖由于其女性叙写所形成的一种双性人格之特质。至于"诗化"之词，则既已脱离了对美女与爱情之内容的叙写，那么其双重意蕴之特美的形成，其因素又究竟何在？关于此一问题，私竟以为"诗化之词"之仍能保有双重意蕴之特美者，其主要之因素，盖有二端。一则在于作者本身原具有一种双重之性质。在这方面，苏、辛二家可以为代表。就苏氏言，其双重性格之形成，主要乃在同时兼具儒家用世之志意与道家超旷之襟怀的双重的修养。就辛氏言，其双重性格之形成，则主要乃在其本身的英雄奋发之气与外在的挫折压抑所形成的一种双重的激荡。而更值得注意的，则是苏词的儒、道之结合，和辛词的奋发与压抑的激荡，主要盖皆由于在仕途中追求理想而不得的挫伤。如果按照我们在前文所引的利普金氏的"弃妇"心态而言，则苏、辛二家词之双重意蕴之

① 见《全宋词》册三，第1073、1588及1688页，北京：中华书局1965年版。
② 同上，第2142-2143页。
③ 屈兴国：《白雨斋词话足本校注》上册，第110页，济南：齐鲁书社1983年版。

形成，当然也与这种男性之欲求行道，与女性之委曲承受的双重心态有着密切的关系。因此苏、辛二家词乃能不假借女性之形象与口吻，而自然表现有一种双重意蕴之美，此其一。二则在于其叙写之语言，虽在“诗化”的男性意识之叙写中，但却仍表现出了一种曲折变化的女性语言的特质。在这方面，辛词较之苏词尤有更高之成就。所以苏词有时仍不免有流于率易之处，因而损及了词之特美。而辛词则虽在激昂悲慨的极为男性的情意叙写中，但却在语言方面反而表现了一种曲折幽隐的女性方式的美感。我以前在《论辛弃疾词》一文中，对辛词之艺术手段，曾有过颇为详细的讨论，以为其对古典之运用，“乃造成了一种与使用美人芳草为喻托的同样的效果”；而且在语法句构中又能极尽骈散顿挫的各种变化，更善于将自然之景象与古典之事象及内心之悲慨交相融会[①]，因此遂能以豪放杰出之姿态，却达成了一种如陈廷焯所说的“发之又必若隐若现，欲露不露，反复缠绵，终不许一语道破”的女性语言之特美。因此遂使得这一类“诗化”之词，具含了一种双重意蕴之美，而这也正是诗化之词中的一种成就最高的好词。

以上我们既然从词之写作方面，对“诗化”之词的得失优劣做了简单的论述。现在我们就将从词学方面，对“诗化”之词所引起的困惑和争议，也一加论述。我们首先要讨论的，乃是所谓“本色”与“变格”的问题。如本文在前面所言，早期《花间》词之特色，既以对美女与爱情之叙写为其主要之内容，从而遂形成了一种以“婉约”方为正格的传统之观念。而苏轼对词之内容的开拓，自然是对《花间》传统的一大变革，如果从这方面来看，则此种目苏词为变格之观念，本来无可厚非。不过，如我们在前文之所论述，《花间》词中同样以叙写美女与爱情为主之作品，既已有优劣高下之分；“诗化”之词在“一洗绮罗芗泽”之后的作品中，也同样有优劣高下之分。是则就苏词在内容方面之开拓改革而

① 见《灵谿词说》，第424-429页，上海古籍出版社1987年版。

言，虽可以有“变格”之说，但在优劣之评量方面，则所谓“本色”与“变格”之别，实在并不应代表优劣高下之分。世之以“本色”与“变格”相争议者，便因其未能认清所谓“本色”的婉约之词，并非以其婉约方为佳作，而主要乃在于婉约词中对女性之叙写，往往可以形成一种双重意蕴的美学特质，而其下者则一样可以沦为浅率淫靡。至于所谓“变格”的豪放之词，则其下者固可以沦为粗犷叫嚣，而其佳者则同样也可以具含一种深微幽隐之双重意蕴的词之特美。这是我们在词学的本色与变格之争议中，所当具有的一点基本的认识。

接着我们所要讨论的，则是女词人李清照所提出的“词别是一家”之问题。李氏之说，就文学中之“文各有体”的基本观念而言，当然是不错的。只不过李氏对“词”之“别是一家”的认识，却似乎是只限于外表的区分，如“协律”、“故实”、“铺叙”等文字方面的问题，而对于词之最基本的以深微幽隐富于言外意蕴为美的一种美学之特质，则未能有深入之认知。缺少了此种认知，遂不仅影响了其词论之正确性与周密性，而且也影响了李氏自己之词作，使其未能将自己所本有的才能做出更大和更好的发挥。现在我们就将透过李氏自己的词作，来对其词论一加检讨。如我们在前文所言，早期的《花间》词原以女性之叙写为主，是中国各种文类中最为女性化的一种文类。不过值得注意的则是，这种使用女性的语言，叙写女性的形象，富有女性之风格的文体，最早却是在男性作者的手中发展和完成的。至于女性的作者，则不仅以其性别的拘限，不能在以仕隐出处为主题的，属于男性语言的诗歌创作中，与男性作者一争长短；而且在极为女性化的文体“词”之创作中，更因其所叙写者多为男女相思怨别之情词，遂因而在传统的礼教中受到了更大的禁忌。即以李清照言，就曾因其在自己的词中对于夫妻间之爱情有较为生动真切的叙写，尚不免遭到词学家王灼所说的“自古缙绅之家能文妇女，未见如此无顾藉”[1]之讥评。私意以为李清照本有多方面之才华，如其诗、文各体之作，皆有可观，且无丝毫之妇人气，而独于其词作则纯以女性之语言写女性之情思，表现为“纤柔婉约”之风格，此种情况之出现，盖皆由于李氏心目中之存有“词别是一家”之观念，有以致之。而李氏在当时妇女中，无疑地乃是敢于使用此种“别是一家”之文体来直写自己之爱情的一位勇者。本来以女性之作者，使用女性之语言和女性化之文体，来叙写女性自己之情思，自然应该可以在其纯乎纯者之女性化方面，达到一种过人的成就。而且以李氏之喜好与人争胜之性格言，在这方面也必有相当之自觉。关于此点，我们在其极为女性化的尖新而生动的修辞方面，也可以得到证明。不过可惜的则是李氏乃只知其一，不知其二；只知词之以女性化为好的一面，而忽略了词之佳者更需具有双性化方为好的另一面。不过，李氏在显意识中虽并没有词之佳者以具含双性之意蕴为美的观念，但在隐意识中李氏却实在具含了双性之条件。那就因为李氏所出生的家庭，既是传统士大夫的仕宦之家，而且以李氏在诗、文等各方面之成就而言，也足可证明其幼年必曾接受过很好的传统的教育。而所谓“传统的教育”，所诵读者自是充满了男性思想意识之典籍，这我们从李氏所写的诗文中，也可以得到充分的证明。因此在李氏之词作中，乃出现了另一类超越了单纯的女性而表现出双性之潜质的作品。清末的沈曾植在其《菌阁琐谈》中论及李氏之词时，就曾将之分别为“芬馨”与“神骏”两类，云：“堕情者醉其芬馨，飞想者赏其神骏，易安有灵，后者当许为知己。”[2]其所称赏的“神骏”一类，私意以为就当是我在前文所提出的蕴含有双性之潜质的作品。如其《渔家傲》（天接云涛连晓雾）一首，可以为此类之代表作。只可惜这一类作品传下来的不多，这一则固可能是由于当日编选易安词者搜辑之未备，再则也很可能是由于李氏自己之限于“词别是一家”之观念，故其所写之词乃以偏

① 王灼：《碧鸡漫志》卷二，第4b页，见《词话丛编》册一，台北：广文书局1967年版。
② 沈曾植：《菌阁琐谈》，见《词话丛编》册十一，第3698页，台北：广文书局1967年版。

于“芬馨”者为多，而偏于“神骏”者则少。是以沈氏之言就词之美学特质来看，固属甚为有见，但就易安言，则或者未必许为知己也。这也就是我在前文何以提出说，李氏只知其一，未知其二，遂使其“词别是一家”之论，乃但及于外表的音律文字之特色而未能触及词之美学本质，因而遂限制了李氏自己之词的成就，使其才能未能得到更大和更好的发挥的缘故。这是我们对李氏“词别是一家”之论所当具的一点认识。

其三，我们将再看一看周邦彦的“赋化之词”对《花间》派令词之写作方式所造成的改变。从表面来看，这一次改变固仅在于写作方式之不同，但如果更深入一点去看，则我们就会发现这一次改变，实隐含有对词之双重与多重之意蕴的深微幽隐之特质的一种潜意识的追求。如我们在前文所言，当柳词以理路分明之铺叙的男性之语言，改变了《花间》一派小词之婉曲含蕴的女性之语言以后，遂使得柳词中对女性与爱情的叙写，失去了《花间》一派令词之幽隐深微的多重意蕴之美，而不免流入于俗俚淫靡。苏轼有见于此，遂致力于内容之开拓改革，想藉此以挽救柳词之失。不过苏词之“诗化”，基本上乃是以男性之作者来直接叙写男性之思想和情志，因此除非如苏、辛二家在男性思想和情志的本身质素方面，原就具有双重之性质，否则乃极易因缺乏双重意蕴之美，而不免流入于浅率叫嚣。一般词学家之往往将苏、辛一派词目为“变格”而非“本色”，其“一洗绮罗芗泽”之内容方面的改变，固为一因；其缺少了双重意蕴的词之特美，实当为另一更重要之原因。只不过一般人对于更为重要的次一原因，却并没有明白的反省和认知，于是遂单纯地以“婉约”和“豪放”作为了“本色”与“变格”的区分。在此种情况下，一方面既要保持词之“婉约”的“本色”，一方面又要接受词之由小令转入长调的文体之演化，而且还要避免柳永之直接铺叙所造成的缺少余蕴的浅俗之失，因此遂有周邦彦一派“赋化”之词的兴起，想从写作方式方面来加强词之幽隐深微的特美，以避免柳词对《花间》词女性化之语言加以改变后，所造成的浅俗淫靡之失，以及苏词对《花间》词女性化之内容加以改变后，所造成的粗犷叫嚣之失。于是所谓“赋化”之词在写作方式方面的改变，乃大多以加强词之幽微曲折之性质者，为其改变之主要趋向。即以周邦彦而言，周济即曾称：“美成思力，独绝千古。”又云：“钩勒之妙，无如清真。”[①]此外陈廷焯亦曾称周词之妙处乃在其“沉郁顿挫”，以为“顿挫则有姿态，沉郁则极深厚。”[②]可见以“思力”来安排“钩勒”，以增加其“姿态”之变化，及意味之“深厚”，乃是所谓“赋化”之词在写作之方式上所致力的重点。至于就周邦彦之词而言，则我在《论周邦彦词》一文中已曾对周词做过不少的论述。约言之，则其以思力为安排钩勒的特色，大略可分为以下三点：其一是在声律方面好为拗句，及创用“三犯”、“四犯”甚至“六犯”之曲调以增加艰涩繁难之感。其二是在叙写方面好用盘旋跳接之手法，以增加词之曲折幽隐之性质。其三则是往往以有心之用意写为蕴含托喻之作。关于以上三点，我在论周词一文中，曾分别举引其《兰陵王》（柳阴直）、《夜飞鹊》（河桥送人处），及《渡江云》（晴岚低楚甸）诸词为例证，分别做过详细的论说（见《灵谿词说》），兹不再赘。

而自周词之写作方式出现以后，南宋诸词人遂不免多受有周词之影响，因而乃造成了赋化之词在南宋之世盛极一时之风气。即以南宋著名之词家如姜夔、史达祖、吴文英、周密、王沂孙、张炎诸人而言，虽然成就不同，风格各异，但就其写作之方式而言，则实在可以说莫不在周词的影响笼罩之中。这种现象之出现，当然自有其外在的社会之因素，即如南宋之竞尚奢靡与结社吟词之风气，当然就都有助于此种以安排勾勒取胜的写作方式之流行，而除此以外，私意以为实在也有词在发展方面的本身内在之因素的存在。盖以如我在前文所言，自小令之衍为长调，此固为词之发展的必然之趋势，长调之需要铺陈，此亦为写作上必然之

① 周济：《介存斋论词杂著》，第3a页，见《宋四家词选》附录，台北：广文书局影印滂喜斋刊本，1962年版。

② 屈兴国：《白雨斋词话足本校注》上册，第74页，济南：齐鲁书社1983年版。

要求，而过于直率的铺陈则不免使婉约者易流于淫靡，豪放者易流于叫嚣，此亦为一种必然之结果。在此种情形下，“赋化”之词的出现，从表面看来虽只是一种写作方式的改变，但实质上却原带有一种想要纠正前二类词之缺失的一种作用。如此说来，自然就无怪乎周词之写作方式，会对南宋词人造成如此重大之影响了。而在词学方面，则与此种写作方式相应合者，乃有张炎之《词源》，与沈义父之《乐府指迷》两种论词专著之出现。综观二书之要旨，如其论句法、字面、用事、咏物，以及论起结、论过变、论虚字等，盖莫不属于如何安排的写作技巧方面之事，而其所以如此重视写作技巧之安排，主要目的又在避免柳词一派之淫靡与苏、辛一派之末流的叫嚣，所以张、沈二家之词论，于重视安排技巧之余，乃又提出了对于“雅”之要求。而南宋词论之所谓“雅”，乃是特别重在句法与字面之雅，这与本文前面所举引的王国维之所谓“词之雅郑，在神不在貌”之针对五代北宋词所提出的论点，实在已有了很大的不同。因此张、沈二家之词论，其想要挽救词之末流的淫靡与叫嚣之失的用心，虽然不错，但可惜的是他们只见到了外表的语言文字，而未能对其何以造成了词之末流的淫靡与叫嚣之失的根本原因，也就是缺少了词之以富于引人生言外之想的双重意蕴为美的一种美学的特质，未能有深刻之反省与认知，因此一意致力于安排之技巧与避俗求雅的结果，遂形成了另外一种得失互见的偏差。其佳者固可以藉写作技巧之安排，使其原有之情意更增加一种深微幽隐的富于言外意蕴之美，至其下者则因其本无真切之情意，因而遂但存安排雕饰之技巧，乃全无言外之意蕴可言。而且此一类词之深微幽隐之意致，既大多出于有心安排之写作技巧，因此如果用我们在前文所举引的克里斯特娃的解析符号学之说来加以反思，我们就会发现此类词中的符表与符义之间的关系，乃是属于克氏所谓被限制了的“象征的”作用之关系，与《花间》一派歌辞之词的深微幽隐的引人生双重意蕴之想的，属于“空中语”之全然不受限制的自然生发和融会的所谓“符示的”作用关系，其间有了很大的不同。而如果以《花间》词所树立的美学特质而言，则词之美者自当以具含后者之作用关系者，较具含前者之作用关系者尤为可贵。在此种差别中，私意以为对此类赋化之词的衡量，遂有了另一层更为深细的标准。也就是说，能在有心安排之写作技巧中，表现有意蕴深微之美者，固是佳作；但如果其符表与符义之间的作用关系过于被拘限，则毕竟不能算是第一流的最好的作品。举例而言，周济在评周密之词时，就曾谓其词如“镂冰刻楮，精妙绝伦”，但虽“才情诣力，色色绝人，终不能超然遐举”。又在评王沂孙之词时，谓其“思笔可谓双绝”，“惟圭角太分明，反复读之，有水清无鱼之恨”。[①]于是周济在其《介存斋论词杂著》中，乃又提出了从“有寄托”到“无寄托”之说，谓：“初学词求有寄托，有寄托则表里相宣，斐然成章。既成格调，求无寄托，无寄托，则指事类情，仁者见仁，知者见知。”[②]也就是说学词之人虽可以从有心安排的写作技巧下手，以求其富含幽微深远的言外之意蕴，但却同时又要超出有心安排所形成的符表与符义之间的被限制了的作用关系，而使之达到一种可以脱除拘限的自由的作用关系，如此方为此一类赋化之词中的最高之成就。而如果以此种标准来衡量，则私意以为周邦彦与吴文英二家之词，实在极值得注意。周词之佳者以“浑厚”胜，虽是以有心安排之写作技巧为之，然而却能“愈勾勒愈浑厚”，不仅泯灭了安排的痕迹，而且具含了一种错综变化“令人不能邃窥其旨”的“沉郁顿挫”的意蕴。[③]这自然是在“赋化之词”中的一种可注意的成就。至于吴词之佳者，则能于艰涩沉郁中见飞动之致。所以周济之赞美吴词，乃称“其佳者，天光云影，摇荡绿波，抚玩无斁，追寻已远。”又云“梦窗每于空际转身，非具大神力不能。”[④]况周颐也曾赞美吴词，谓“其芬菲铿丽之作，中间隽句艳字，莫

---

① 周济：《宋四家词选目录序论》，第 2b 页；《介存斋论词杂著》，第 4b 页，见《宋四家词选》，台北：广文书局影印滂喜斋刊本，1962 年版。

②《介存斋论词杂著》，第 2a 页。

③ 见《宋四家词选目录序论》及《白雨斋词话足本校注》，第 74 及 76 页，同前。

④《介存斋论词杂著》，第 3b 页。

不有沉挚之思，灏瀚之气，挟之以流转，令人玩索而不能尽。”[①]这自然也是“赋化之词”中的一种可注意的成就。总之，“赋化之词”虽是以有心安排之写作技巧，改变了《花间》词之“空中语”的以自然无意为之的写作方式，但此类词之佳者，其仍以具含一种深微幽隐难以指说的双重或多重之意蕴为美的衡量标准，则是始终未变的。因此周济所曾提出的“临渊窥鱼，意为鲂鲤。中宵惊电，罔识东西”的一种词所特具的微妙之感发的作用，遂不仅可以适用于“歌辞之词”的佳者，也同样可以适用于“赋化之词”的佳者了。于是词学中之“比兴寄托”之说，遂也从五代北宋之本无托意而可以引人生比附之想的情况，转入为一种纵有喻托之深意，而却以使人难于指说为美的情况了。

透过以上的论述，我们已可清楚地见到，词在不断的演进中，虽然曾经过了三次重大的改变。但无论是柳永的长调之叙写对《花间》令词之语言的改变；苏轼的诗化之词对《花间》令词之内容的改变；或周邦彦的赋化之词对《花间》令词之写作方式的改变，尽管他们的这些改变，已曾对《花间》词之女性叙写与双性心态做出了层层的背离，可是由《花间》词之女性叙写与双性心态所形成的，以富含引人联想的多层意蕴为美的一种美学特质，则始终是衡量词之优劣的一项重要的要求。过去的词学家们之所以会对于词之雅郑的问题，词之比兴寄托的问题，词之本色与变格的问题，词在诗化与赋化以后当如何加以评赏和衡量的问题，张惠言与王国维二家说词之以不同的方式重视言外之感发的问题，不断地产生种种困惑与争议，私意以为盖皆由于旧日的词学家，不敢正视《花间》词中之女性叙写，未尝对之做出正面的美学特质之探讨的缘故。希望本文透过西方女性主义文评，对于中国之“词”这种特别女性化之文类的美学特质之形成与演变，所做出的一番反思，对于解答旧日词学中的这些困惑与争议的问题，能够提供一点帮助。

---

① 况周颐：《蕙风词话》卷二，第 48 页，《蕙风词话·人间词话》，香港：商务印书馆 1961 年版。

关于中国文学批评之有待于西方理论的补充和拓展，早在20世纪60年代，当我撰写《从比较现代的观点看几首中国旧诗》一文时，就早已有了此种认知。[①]其后在70年代初，当我撰写《王国维及其文学批评》一书时，更曾在书中第二篇之第一章，对此一问题做过相当理论性的探讨。[②]不过，不久以后我就注意到了有些青年学者在盲目引用西方理论来评析中国古典诗歌时，往往会因旧学根底之不足，而产生了许多误谬和偏差，因此我遂又撰写了《关于评说中国旧诗的几个问题》一篇文稿，想对此种偏差加以劝导和纠正。[③]其后自80年代初，我与四川大学缪钺教授合撰《灵谿词说》以来，遂久久不复引用西方之文论。然而时代之运转不已，就目前世界情势言，中国之古典文学批评确实已面临了一个不求拓展不足以更生自存的危机。因此近年来我遂又接连写了几篇在西方理论之观照中，对中国传统文学批评加以反思的文稿。[④]这些文稿如果从传统的眼光来看，也许会不免被目为荒诞不经，而如果从现代的眼光来看，则似乎与西方理论也并不完全相合，而我的用意则本是取二者之可通者而融会之，而并非全部的袭用，所以我不久前在《论纳兰性德词》一篇文稿中，就曾写有“我文非古亦非今，言不求工但写心”两句诗[⑤]。而我现在则更想引用克里斯特娃的两句话来作自我辩解，那就是：“我不跟随任何一种理论，无论那是什么理论。”[⑥]

1991年9月3日完稿于哈佛燕京图书馆

原载1992年2月台湾出版之《中外文学》第二〇卷第九期

---

① 见《迦陵论诗丛稿》，第240-275页，北京：中华书局1984年版。

② 见《王国维及其文学批评》，第122-145页，香港：中华书局1980年版。

③ 见《中国古典诗歌评论集》，第109-159页，香港：中华书局1977年版。

④ 见《中国词学的现代观》，台北：大安书局1988年版。

⑤《论纳兰性德词》，见《中外文学》第十九卷第八期，第30页，台北：《中外文学》月刊社1991年出版。

⑥ 所引克氏之语见于《语言之意欲》(*Desire in Language*)一书，ed. by Leon S. Roudiez, trans. by Thomas Gora, Alice Jardine & Leon Roudiez, New York: Columbia University Press, 1980, p.1.

附记

本文写作之动机盖始于 1990 年之春，当时我在温哥华曾举行过一次标题为“词中之女性与女性之词人”的系列讲演。其后于暑期中乃开始动笔写作，而未几即应台湾清华大学之聘，赴台讲学。又曾赴大陆参加辛弃疾词学术会议，琐事忙碌，遂将写作搁置。直至 1991 年春假，倏惊光阴之易逝，乃决定利用春假期间闭户不出，陆续以将近二周之时间，完成文稿之大半。乃不慎在来往旅行途中，先后将已写成之文稿，及补写成之文稿两度遗失，遂致一直拖延至 1991 年 8 月底始将全稿完成。借用一句《圣经》上的话来说，这一篇文章对我而言，可以说乃是“死而复活，失而又得”的，故谨为此记，以为个人两次遗失文稿的不慎之戒。

作者谨识

Ambiguity and the Female Voice in 'Huajian Songs'

Every generation of poets since the ninth century has left us many examples in a variety of styles of the literary form known as *ci*, or song lyric, but despite their repeated efforts to come to terms with what was recognized by the tenth century as a new verse form, critics failed to develop a logically consistent theory of interpreting and evaluating this poetry. Their comments, buried in their critical notes and random jottings, are not without insights, but they do not add up to a coherent theory of *ci* and how it should work. As a result, studies of the early song lyric leave many unresolved problems. One source of uncertainty comes from the content of the early songs, most of which were concerned with love themes: spring yearnings, pangs of separation, and the like, which clearly deviated from the standards of conventional poetry, whose function was to express a poet's aspirations and to inculcate lessons of morality. As a result, traditional critics, conditioned by a critical standard that required high seriousness and moral instruction in poetry, were at a loss to judge these sometimes erotic songs—or even to decide whether anyone should be writing such poetry. These uncertainties are reflected in such anecdotes as the following:

Wang Anguo was an outspoken person with an intense hatred of evil. When his brother Wang Anshi was first put in charge of the government, he happened to be reading the short songs of Yan Shu and asked, laughing, "Is it all right for a Prime Minister to write songs?" Wang Anguo answered, "He just wrote them as a diversion. This was not the only thing he could do, was it?" At the time Lü Huiqing was in office and was also present. He quickly interposed, "The first thing for a governor to do is to get rid of licentious songs—how can he possibly write them?" Anguo turned a serious face and said "Better than getting rid of licentious songs is to stay away from flatterers." Huiqing took the remark personally and henceforth was estranged from Wang Anguo.[1]

This exchange shows that contemporary song lyrics were regarded as being of the kind condemned by Confucius as licentious ("the songs of Wei and Zheng"); it also shows the uncertainty and conflicting opinions involved. These uncertainties inspired different ways of defending the practice of song writing.

Yan Jidao had an interview with Pu Chuanzheng and said, "My late father [Yan Shu] may have written many songs, but he never used the language of women in them." Chuanzheng quoted the lines,

Green willows and sweet grass on the way-station road;	绿杨芳草长亭路
It is easy for [a] youth to abandon a person.	年少抛人容易去

Isn't that the voice of a woman?"

Yan Jidao asked, "What do you understand by the word 'youth'?"

"Isn't it her lover?"

"If that's the way you take it, how would you read Bai Juyi's couplet,

> I wanted to detain youth until I became rich and famous; 欲留年少待富贵
> Riches and fame never came, but youth has gone." 富贵不来年少去
>
> Chuanzheng laughed, having got the point.[2]

This is simply taking lines out of context and forcing another meaning from the occurrence of the same word in a wholly different poem. Another example:

> After Liu Sanbian (Yong) had offended the Emperor Renzong with a song, the Board of Personnel did not dare give him a promotion. In frustration Sanbian went to the Prime Minister, Yan Shu, who said, "Do not you, sir, write songs?"
> "Even as your Excellency writes songs."
> "I may write songs, but I never wrote [such a line as] 'Idly sewing, she nestles close to him.'" Whereupon Liu withdrew.[3]

Here song lyrics are clearly divided into two classes, refined and licentious, with the refined variety being tolerated. Another example:

> The monk Fa Yunxiu of Guanxi was a man of iron countenance and the utmost strictness, able to compel others by force of reason. At the time Huang Tingjian was well known throughout the country, and whenever he produced a poem or a song, people strove to copy and spread it. The monk once said to him, "Writing a lot of poems does no harm, but you should stop writing erotic songs." Huang Tingjian laughed, "They are just idle words; it's not killing anyone, or stealing. They hardly deserve to be judged as the road to perdition."[4]

Characterizing song lyrics as "idle words" is a rather forced piece of self-exoneration, and all these stories are, superficially anyhow, no more than gossip current in Song times. Aside from demonstrating a readiness to exploit the confusion by forced interpretations, they hardly constitute what one might call a theory of *ci*. However, there can be no doubt that theories of *ci* developed from precisely this confusion and these disputes, and already in the episodes just quoted we can see the beginnings of the directions taken by later *ci* critics. Let us first take the anecdote recounted by Hu Zi. In Yan Shu's couplet,

> Green willows and sweet grass on the way-station road;
> It is easy for [a] youth to abandon a person,

the word "youth" (*nianshao*), in the immediate context of "way-station" (*changting*, traditional place of parting when someone is leaving for a long journey) and "abandon" (*pao*, lit., "cast away") and its object, "a person" (*ren* is not really ambiguous here, for its use in song, "a certain person", commonly refers to the speaker), is certainly an individual young man, not the abstraction "youth"; and obviously he is the girl's lover. To quote the line from Bai Juyi, where "youth" is contrasted with "success", as providing a clue to the interpretation of Yan Shu's line is wholly unconvincing. The reason Yan Jidao was willing to go to such lengths to defend his father's practice of song-writing is obviously because upper-class literati considered writing songs about love a frivolous and inappropriate activity for a prime minister. But it could hardly have been predicted that such examples of forced interpretation would pave the way for later *ci* critics, anxious to rescue song as a legitimate verse form, to apply to song the critical criteria traditional in the interpretation of classical poetry. The critical practice of Zhang Huiyan of the Changzhou School marks the culmination of the method. Although vulnerable to the charge of being a misreading and out-of-context interpretation, this technique can still sometimes reveal a hidden suggestion in a song, and so it needs to be examined more closely.

The distinction between "refined" and "licentious" (or "vulgar") was confirmed early by critics. Wang Zhuo, who praised Yan Shu's songs as "romantic and refined": "they were unmatched by any of his contemporaries, nor could anyone equal them for freshness and purity," said that Liu Yong's songs were "shallow and vulgar": 'it's a special style of his own... I have compared them to a rich fellow who may have left the countryside but still has detestable manners."[5] Clearly there is a difference between refined and vulgar in song lyrics, and we find the Southern Song songwriter and critic Zhang Yan using such terms as "pure and refined (*qing kong*), like 'Li sao' and the Ya,"[6] in commending the songs he esteemed. And the late Qing dynasty Zhexi School of *ci* writing made refinement the single critical standard, inevitably tending toward the superficial and the trivial. In reaction, Wang Guowei declared that "refinement or vulgarity in song comes from the spirit, not the content."[7] This distinction has continued to be an important criterion for judging song lyrics.

Finally, I would like to refer back to the deprecatory remark attributed to Huang Tingjian in defending his erotic songs as "just idle words". He was referring specifically to his own songs, but his remark reflects an essential difference between early song lyrics and traditional *shi* poetry, which was supposed to be serious and moral. It also reflects something of the attitude of those early song writers, their feeling of relief at being free of the expectations that attended the writing of *shi* poetry. Song lyric, however, as it developed did not long remain as it was in this early period, and these lyrics written to a given tune for performance by entertainers were followed by songs written as just another form of poetry, not always intended even to be sung.[8] For the early lyrics, written to a popular tune, it is understandable that their authors would regard them as just a diversion, "idle words" as Huang Tingjian said. But even as the poets experienced freedom from the constraints of more didactic verse, it sometimes allowed them to reveal their own secret and even unconscious concerns, creating the subtle suggestiveness we find in the best of these songs.

Later on, the song lyric developed a greater similarity to *shi* poetry, as poets began to use it as a vehicle for self-expression and eventually came to write elaborately structured compositions with a deliberately allegorical content. This historical development poses a problem for *ci* critics: do these evolved versions of *ci* retain the aesthetic qualities of the earlier lyrics written to be sung? And how is the characteristic beauty generated by those songs written for diversion to be understood and evaluated? These are important questions. We can observe an interesting phenomenon in the confusion and forced attempts of the early poets to defend *ci*. The fact that most of these early songs were love songs required some sort of rationalization, for upper-class men were constrained by moral conventions, and none of them ventured to face up to the fact that the subjects of the songs were women and love. Unable to deal directly with the issue of their meaning and value, critics from the very beginning were trapped in a specious defense when the songs were attacked as immoral.

Just when upper-class writers were being attacked for their love songs, one of China's great poets appeared on the scene, who would transform the song lyric through his genius into a vehicle for serious poetry. This was Su Shi, who "washed away the silken garments and perfume," who "made his readers climb high and gaze afar," who "pointed out the road to the heights and renewed the eyes and ears of all the world," as his admirers have said.[9] But Su Shi's song lyrics did nothing to resolve existing disagreements among critics; instead they added a new element of conflict. Chen Shidao (1053-1102) said, "Han Yu wrote poetry (*shi*) that was like prose, and Su Shi wrote songs that were like *shi* poetry. It is like a dance by Master Lei in the Music Academy: he may be the finest artist in the world, but this is not his proper role."[10] And Hu Zi quotes Li Qingzhao's criticism of Su Shi's songs,

"His sentences are just uneven *shi* lines; song is quite another skill."[11] Su Shi's shift toward *shi* and Li Qingzhao's repudiation of the change as a contamination brought a fresh source of confusion to *ci* criticism. In fact, neither Su Shi's innovations nor Li Qingzhao's reflections on the nature of *ci* cast much light on the style of the early love songs or on their aesthetic quality, nor could either provide rational answers to the basic questions about the aesthetic nature of those songs. Consequently confusion persisted through the disputes about whether the orthodox tradition was to be found in refined songs or heroic ones and which of each variety was correct—an enduring legacy of uncertainty. There were those who wanted to associate these lyrics written for a musical setting with the ancient classical *shi*, *sao*, and Music Academy Songs (*yuefu*). Wang Zhuo said, "The ancient songs evolved into Music Academy Songs, which then evolved into our modern songs—essentially they are all the same."[12] And Wang Yan said, "The old *shi*, from 'Guofeng' and 'Ya' on down to the *yuefu* of Han and Wei are all alike songs. Our contemporary *ci* (long and short lines) are the descendant of *yuefu*."[13]

Hu Yin is more specific: "*Ci* songs are the latest version of the old *yuefu*, and *yuefu* are an offshoot of *shi*. *Shi* derives from the 'Li sao' and '*Chuci*'; the "Li sao", like the degenerate poems of a period of decline in the *Classic of Songs*, is angry and violent, sad and hurt."[14] Since "degenerate Feng and Ya" as well as the "Li sao" and *Chuci* were all subject to allegorical interpretation, *ci* were also considered to be subject to such readings by conservative critics seeking to make *ci* respectable. This development was rendered suspect by the view that *ci* were merely love songs, in effect condemning allegorical readings as forced. But the tradition that treated the love themes in the *Classic of Songs* and the "Li sao" as allegorical went unchallenged: in Southern Song times allegory frequently underlay songs that ostensibly were written as odes celebrating objects, so the interpretations proposed by Zhang Huiyan and his school were widely accepted for a time, thereby introducing a new source of conflict and confusion—are these interpretations valid or are they forced? By late Qing times Wang Guowei could characterize Zhang Huiyan's theory as far-fetched and fanciful.[15] He himself proposed his famous *jingjie* theory, a new concept that he never successfully explained, and which added to the confusion and the disputes among modern critics of *ci*. We are left with the problem of constructing, on a historical basis, a coherent method of understanding and evaluating this particular kind of poetry.

Disputes about the nature of the song lyric were present from the beginning and were the consequence of the Chinese tradition of literary theory which emphasized the moral-didactic function of literature to the neglect of aesthetic considerations, leaving no room for the development of an aesthetic appreciation of *ci*. For *ci* originated as the lyrics sung to the melodies popular in Sui-Tang times. When poets of the educated class began to write their own verses for those tunes, they had no intention of using them to express their own feelings and aspirations: that in itself was a break with the traditional expectation of Chinese poetry. As the "Preface" to the *Huajian ji* put it, those "song words by poets" were written by "gentlemen at the party" on "sheets of figured paper for lovely ladies of the silk-curtained chambers" to sing while "raising their delicate jade-like hands to beat the rhythm with fragrant sandalwood castanets." Not surprisingly, the songs were largely about those lovely ladies and their loves—another radical departure from the moralistic tradition.[16]

Now, if we want to arrive at a just estimate of the meaning and value of the *ci*, we cannot neglect these love songs in *Huajian ji*, first as a special category in the aesthetics of *ci*, and next as a conditioning influence on later *ci* as the genre developed. Chen Zhensun early recognized the importance of *Huajian ci* when he said they are "the ancestor of our contemporary lyrics written to music."[17] And recently Zhao Zunyue, "If you are going to talk about *ci*, you must go back to its origins; and that is in Tang and Five Dynasties, and since there are no collections of *ci* by individual writers of the period, there is no way to get at the *ci* of Tang and Five Dynasties if you neglect this book."[18] In the ninth century, however, before the compilation of that anthology, popular tunes were in circulation, and lyrics for them were composed. Some were rustic songs like those preserved on Dunhuang manuscripts. A few were the tentative experiments of established poets like Liu Yuxi and Bai Juyi, who wrote words for tunes like "Remembering the Southland" (*Yi jiangnan*) or "Always Thinking of You" (*Chang xiang si*). The rustic songs were never carefully recorded for circulation (indeed, their preservation was quite accidental, having been written by semiliterate scribes on the backs of manuscripts), and their language was anything but elegant, so they never attracted the notice of the literary world.

As for the second kind of song words, those composed by poets like Bai Juyi and Liu Yuxi, because they were so similar to their *shi* poetry, they did not establish a new literary entity. It was only with the appearance of *Huajian ji* that *ci* achieved widespread recognition as a new genre with its own special characteristics and began to exert an influence that continued well after *ci* had developed into other channels. So if we want to dispel some of the confusion that has plagued *ci* studies, we should begin with that anthology and examine the aesthetic qualities that underlie its songs. We should expect a close connection between the content of those songs—lovely ladies and their loves—and their aesthetic quality. But there was no place for such themes in Confucian morality, so that even as this new genre was being created, this particular aesthetic property was categorically rejected in the minds of the educated classes. As a result, these songs, which took beautiful women and love as their theme, were looked on as minor verse and criticized for being erotic and vulgar. Interestingly enough, however, though these same upper-class literati may have consciously dismissed these love songs, they were unable to resist the attraction of their beauty and frequently joined the ranks of the songwriters. Right down to Lu You in the Southern Song this contradictory attitude is apparent. In the "Preface" to the song lyrics in his *Weinan Collection* he said, "Words written for a tune began to appear at the end of the Tang.... When I was young, misled by the fashion of the time, I also wrote some, which I later came to regret.... Today it is already some years since I stopped writing them, but there is no way to hide what has been done, so I record the fact to acknowledge my error."[19]

This contradictory attitude was present not only in the writers of songs but also in the "Preface" to the *Biji manzhi* (*Green Cock Notes*) of the famous *ci* critic Wang Zhuo: "In the winter of 1145 (*yi chou*) I was visiting the Miaosheng Temple Garden in Green Cock suburb of Chengdu. From summer into fall of that year Wang Hexian and Zhang Qiwang were living nearby. They both kept singing girls, and every day they gave wine parties. I never wearied of my intercourse with the two."

The five chapters of his *Green Cock Notes* are a record of what he learned about entertainment songs he heard at their parties. Twenty years later, when he was about to have his book printed, he suddenly confessed his error: "But I grow old and regret my youthful mistakes. My errant heart is now at peace, so what's the use of producing this book? It's just that I cannot bear to cast into the flames these drunken scribblings from a time long past."[20]

This is the same psychological pattern of addiction followed by repentance and then the ultimate release for publication of the offending verses that we saw in Lu You's "Preface". But what was the enormous attraction that led upper-class gentlemen to violate the prohibitions of Confucian moral teachings and, despite contrition and the glaring contradiction involved, still surrender themselves to the enjoyment, the writing, and finally the publication of those songs?

The simplest answer would include two factors: first, the attraction of the music itself—the tunes for which the lyrics were written and sung. The so-called "banquet music", *Yan yue*, that became popular in the ninth century was originally a blend of a type of Chinese music, *Qing yue*, with an imported Central Asian music and Buddhist hymns (*Fa qu*).[21] It may well have provided the incentive for the literati to supply lyrics to these catchy new tunes. Second, the literati could have seen in songwriting a chance to escape the long imposed compulsion to write didactically and express only socially acceptable aspirations. Composing the lyric for a popular song gave them the opportunity to write playfully and give vent to any secret romantic feelings they may have been harboring. When Huang Tingjian defended his song lyrics as words "written in idleness", he could have been expressing the feeling of liberation experienced by the poets of his time at escaping the restrictions imposed by Confucian morality.

In addition to these two obvious, if hypothetical motives for writing songs in defiance of propriety, I believe there is another reason for their great attraction, derived from the poets' experience of composing and interpreting *shi* poetry, through which they gradually came to realize that, under their surface content of love and beautiful women, these love songs could carry a subtle meaning that readers might look for and respond to. This suggested meaning did not come from the poet's conscious effort, and so the reader would not be led to a simple and unambiguous interpretation of the text. When critics like Zhang Huiyan forced these subtle suggestions into a definite allegorical interpretation, they fell into the trap of allegorizing poetry that was written with no allegorical intent. It was their mistake to think they could find a single specific referent for each subtle hint; in short, they were looking for something that was not there. To sum up, the best of these songs continually arouse in the reader subtle and far-reaching associations beyond the immediate sense of the words, something recognized by some *ci* critics, though none of them tried to form a coherent theory explaining the source of this peculiar quality.

Recently, after reading in feminist literary theory, I realized first, that there is a close connection between the way women are presented in the songs in the *Huajian ji* and the suggestive power of the language of those songs, and second, that there is a connection between the long failure of *ci* critics to come up with a rational system of interpretation of *ci* and their reluctance to confront the subject matter of these songs in their studies.

Historical cultures east and west have long developed under the dominance of male-centered concepts. During the past few decades the emergence of a female self-consciousness has brought profound changes in social and cultural attitudes in societies all over the world. It is from this perspective that I have been able to look at this special form of Chinese poetry, the song lyric, and see connections that have been obscured. I have no intention of trying to apply the whole of feminist literary theory indiscriminately to Chinese song lyrics, but I do believe that some of the problems connected with their nature, development, and interpretation are illuminated when regarded in the light of those studies.

First, there is the question of the female image in *Huajian* songs; traditional critics viewed the women in all forms of poetry indiscriminately and either interpreted the women and love affairs in song lyrics as allegory, or dismissed them as variants on the erotic themes found in Palace Style verse or in the amorous dialogues of the Wu Ballads. These same themes, however, served vastly different aesthetic functions in the *Huajian* songs. The difference can be illuminated by Leslie Fiddler's observation in *Love and Death in the American Novel*: women as portrayed by male writers generally oscillate between extremes of the divine figure of a vision and the witch of a nightmare, neither of them real.[22] Mary Ferguson identified five versions of the female image devised by male authors: the Wife, the Mother, the Woman on a Pedestal, the Sex Object, and finally, Women without Men. What all five have in common is a male perspective, even Women without Men, where a woman, if not an object of commiseration, is distinguished as a category only by the absence of the male. They were established early on as stereotypes in literary works, and not only in those written by men. Women writers, too, found it difficult to escape these limiting concepts.[23]

When we turn to the female image in *Huajian* songs, obvious differences in the Chinese cultural background prevent any mechanical application of such patterns. I am concerned here with the aesthetic quality of the female image in the song lyric, and this requires some attention to the specifically Chinese attitudes that determined the form taken by that image. Before the *Huajian ji* was compiled in the ninth century, there was already a considerable body of poetry in which love and women figured prominently. Given that love between men and women is a part of human nature, the theme of love in the several kinds of poetry over the centuries appears on the surface to be the same thing. But that leaves us with a question: why is it that *ci* have a special kind of suggestiveness rarely found in other verse forms? Let us consider the differences in the way the themes of women and love are used in Chinese poetry of different periods.

The women that appear in the poems of the *Classic of Songs* are for the most part presented in a realistic manner as occupying a definite place in the social structure. This is one kind of female image in Chinese poetry. The descriptions of women in *Chuci* are for the most part not realistic and have an allegorical flavor—this is the second kind of female image. Women as depicted in the folk songs of the Southern Dynasties (the Wu Ballads and the Western Ditties) are women in love, mostly presented through their own words in a plain vernacular language—the third kind of female image. The women in the Palace Style poems appear as seen through the eyes of male poets, depicted in the same precise language of the Ode Celebrating an Object (*yongwu shi*)—the fourth kind of female image. The lonely palace ladies and neglected wives of the Tang poets are also realistic descriptions of women who occupy a definite place in the social structure presented by a male poet speaking for the woman—the fifth kind of female image.

When we compare the image of the woman in the Song Lyric with these five, we make an interesting discovery: these women embody a beauty and a love that is neither wholly realistic nor completely idealized. This may seem to contradict what has already been said of the *Huajian* songs, that they were composed for singing girls to perform, and hence the female image in them should reflect the singing girls who performed them at the party, and that image should be realistic, since the girls were presumably present. But those girls, by their profession, were outside the normal social structure, where the roles defined by family relationship—mother, wife, elder sister, aunt, daughter-in-law—provided the identifying labels. Socially they existed only as objects sought by men looking for diversion, and it was precisely those men who wrote the songs. Naturally they focused on describing the woman's beauty and her feelings, both loaded with an established symbolism, as in "Li sao". Consequently, realistic description of the female image in *Huajian* songs contains a latent symbolism, provoking a reading that is not at all realistic.

The realistically presented female image in the *Classic of Songs* mostly lacks any symbolic quality. That exegetes were able to make it the vehicle of praise or censure was simply a forced interpretation imposed on the text for doctrinal purposes, not from any latent suggestion of symbolism in the image itself.

In "Li sao" the female images were for the most part deliberately symbolic constructs of the poet himself and had readily identifiable referents, wholly unlike the *Huajian* songs, which were written with no thought of creating allegory and only latent symbolism.

The Wu Ballads and other folk songs presented a female image in the woman's own words, and they remain realistic love songs with no symbolic overtones, while *Huajian* songs, written in a woman's voice by male poets, carry a man's perception of her beauty and love that gives them their symbolic flavor.

Palace Style poems treat the female image as an object seldom affected by any subjective emotion on their author's part, whereas in *Huajian* songs the feeling of love are centered on the female image, which thereby gains symbolic potential.

The Tang Dynasty poems about disappointed palace ladies and lonely wives can be further divided into two types: one which realistically depicts the feeling of a woman who is bored and lonely, the other in which the woman's feelings are the vehicle for expressing the male poet's own unhappiness at a lack of recognition. The first of these has some resemblance to the *Classic of Songs* poems about lonely women and divorced wives; the latter are closer to the *Chuci* allegorical figures. Neither resembles the *Huajian* songs with their realistically presented female image that still invites a symbolic interpretation.

The next problem is the language of the song lyric compared to that of *shi* poetry. *Ci* critics have long noticed the difference; an axiom of *ci* criticism has been "*Shi* is vigorous, *ci* dainty." The obvious prosodic difference is that *shi* lines are of regular length, while *ci* characteristically uses unequal lines. The point is neatly illustrated by an anecdote from Qing times. Ji Yun, a scholar of great learning who also enjoyed a joke, once inscribed on a fan the heptameter quatrain of the Tang poet Wang Zhihuan:

The Yellow River ascends in the distance among 黄河远上白云间

the white clouds.	
A strip of a lonely town, mountains ten thousand feet—	一片孤城万仞山
No need for the barbarian flute to complain about the willow trees;	羌笛何须怨杨柳
The spring wind does not cross Jade Gate Pass.	春风不度玉门关

In writing it, Ji Yun inadvertently omitted the last word in the first line (*jian*, "among"). When someone pointed out the mistake, he jokingly insisted he was not writing a heptameter quatrain but a song lyric with irregular lines. Repunctuated, it would read

Yellow River ascends in the distance,	黄河远上
One strip of white cloud,	白云一片
A lonely town, ten thousand foot mountains	孤城万仞山
No need for the barbarian flute to complain—	羌笛何须怨
Willow trees in the spring wind	杨柳春风
Do not cross Jade Gate Pass.[24]	不度玉门关

The words of the two versions are identical, but with the change in meter the second has acquired an increased subtlety and indirection, demonstrating that one source of what one perceives is the irregularity of line length in the song lyric.

But the difference is not only one of form. Wang Zhifang records an exchange between Su Shi and two of his friends, Chao Buzhi and Zhang Lei, who say, "Qin Guan's *shi* poems are like songs, while your songs, sir, are like poems."[25] And Yuan Haowen criticizes a couplet from a poem by Qin Guan in a quatrain:[26]

"The sensitive peony holds spring tears	有情芍药含春泪
The listless rose lies on the evening branch."	无力蔷薇卧晚枝

Take any line from Han Yu's "Mountain Stones"	拈出退之山石句
And you realize this is a woman's verse.	始知渠是女郎诗

So there is a difference in language that goes beyond the obvious prosodic difference in the two forms. Taken together, these criticisms of Qin Guan's poetry as "women's verse" and as "like song lyrics" suggest that the language of song is feminized.

And just what is "feminine" language? Feminist literary criticism makes several points that may be of use here. As feminist critics shifted their attention from the image of women in literature to writings by women, they focused on their language, primarily by contrasting it with male language. It was generally regarded as being characterized by irrationality and chaotic fragmentation, as against the reason, order, and lucidity of typically masculine writing. This sort of polarization was not universally adopted by feminist critics and I have no intention here of comparing masculine and feminine language in terms of physiological differences in the sexes, nor in judging the merits and shortcomings of the two languages.

There can be no question that didactic prose and traditional Chinese poetry, written to express the writers' aspirations and feelings, reflect masculine attitudes in a male-dominated society and can be viewed as being written in masculine language as defined in feminist criticism. The highest ideal of that society was always the Confucian theory of government, and traditional Chinese prose and poetry fit this ideological frame. Zhu Ziqing spelled it out in his "Preface" to the *Three Hundred Tang Poems*: "The topics for a great majority of the poems have to do with the poet's official career. For the educated men of former generations the only possible career was public service: to serve as an official was a moral obligation. Of course it also provided a good livelihood. Before holding office there was living in obscurity, seeking interviews, taking the civil service examinations (and passing or failing), and then after getting an office, being noticed favorably, promoted or cashiered—all this, right down to compassion for the people, patriotism, dreams of country life, or returning to the farm (and sometimes actually doing it)—these are the constant topics for poetry."[27]

For women in traditional Chinese society there were no such opportunities. Any writing about a career as an official or about fulfilling one's public duty had to be in the language of masculine concerns. But the song lyric of the *Huajian ji* broke out of the literary tradition that demanded that poetry be moral in intent and express the aspirations of the poet. Instead, the *Huajian* poets boldly used their skill to write about feminine beauty and love, presenting a woman's feelings about the passing of spring or the pain of parting. Hence, in terms of content and attitudes, the *Huajian* songs required a more feminine kind of language. As pointed out earlier, the meter of *shi* poetry is regular, while that of *ci* is irregular; the language of *shi* is predominately coherent, a characteristic of male language according to feminist critics, while *ci* language is relatively disorganized and fragmentary. Some might feel that a fragmentary, disorganized language is intrinsically inferior to one that is clear and structured, but the song lyrics of *Huajian ji* demonstrate that instead of being an inferior vehicle for poetry, this chaotic, fragmented kind of language explains why these songs so effectively evoke such rich trains of associations outside the words of the poem. For example, the songs of Wen Tingyun, given pride of place in the *Huajian* collection, owed their appreciation by later critics to the perception that they alluded to Qu Yuan and the *sao* poems; in fact, it is because the language of his songs is strongly imbued with the special quality of women's language. As he describes a woman's beauty through her attire and her feelings in a situation usually implied rather than specified, he typically employs a chaotic and fragmented syntax and structure. It is something criticized by Li Bingruo: "He takes one line or two to describe a simple ornament and then follows with something wholly unconnected, so that the sense of the poem is not continuous. His lavish use of fine words turn into redundancy and excrescencies. These are his constant faults."[28] Critics who praise him call attention to the special quality of his songs to inspire readings that go beyond the words themselves, as Chen Tingzhuo: "The idea is there before he writes, and the poet's vision goes outside the words, ... half-hidden, half disclosed, about to appear but not appearing, back and forth, inextricable, not to be broken loose with one word. It not only marks a high point in style, it also shows a depth of character."[29]

So it is clear that praise for Wen Tingyun's language, whether from the content or from its form, is a result of the peculiarity of a feminized language. We may conclude that this is an important source of the potential of *ci* to evoke interpretative readings.[30]

In borrowing the concept of a female language from feminist critics, we are left with a question: their "female language" refers to the language used by women writers. But the eighteen poets represented in the *Huajian ji* are all men. Hence there is still another source of the special quality of *ci* besides the two already considered, one created by the fact that it is male writers who are employing a female language to portray a female image. Here again I believe we can find a useful hint in recent feminist criticism. Carolyn Heilbrun applies the term *androgyny* to a bisexual personality, liberated from the bonds of gender-oriented attitudes, who can give free expression to his/her own sexual inclinations.[31] My own use of the term is focused more narrowly on the ambiguity resulting from male poets' practice of assuming a female persona to write about the woman in love. This androgynous component in the *Huajian* songs introduces another element of ambiguity, which I believe contributes significantly to their capacity for multiple readings. It should be made clear that the poets were not deliberately assuming the role of a woman in their songs as, for instance, Qu

Yuan was in parts of the "Li sao". It was simply the circumstance that allowed the male poets who composed these songs for what after all was only a song-and-dance performance to give expression to feminine feelings from deep within their masculine unconsciousness—feelings that they could never have expressed or even suggested in their formal, moralistic, and socially sanctioned compositions.

The Jungian idea of feminine feelings deeply hidden in the male psyche has been explored by Lawrence Lipking in his *Abandoned Women and Poetic Tradition*. He finds that the theme of the abandoned woman is as old as poetry itself in the West. Rejected men, on the other hand, as a result of the different social attitudes toward men and women, rarely appear as figures in literary writing. Abandoned women are to be expected, but it is harder to accept that a man should be cast off. That is not to say it never happened, but when it did, one way for a man to express his feelings was to use the voice of a woman. Consequently the abandoned woman presented in such poems is an amalgam of the two sexes.[32]

What Lipking says has special significance for traditional Chinese poetry and song lyrics, for in traditional Chinese society male and female attitudes differed sharply. Enshrined in the old autocratic Chinese society were the so-called Three Bonds, the three unequal social relationships: prince and minister, father and son, husband and wife. Prince, father, and husband always occupy the higher place of authority; minister, son, and wife are objects of control. Of the three relationships, that of father and son is determined from birth; examples of disinherited sons are rare and still permit reconciliation. But prince and minister or husband and wife are relationships not ordained from the start; favor or disgrace are in the hands of the superior ruler and husband. It is not within the power of the dismissed minister or divorced wife to initiate a reconciliation or indulge in self-justification. After being dismissed from an unequal relationship, they are still expected to maintain a one-sided loyalty and faithfulness. Under such circumstances—being arbitrarily dismissed or divorced—they must feel resentful and aggrieved. Because the position of divorced wife and dismissed minister are so similar, their feeling must also be similar. The aspect of the cast-off woman hidden in the heart of the male poet, postulated by Lipking, belongs to the Chinese tradition of poetry and song, making the divorced wife and lonely woman potential symbols. For example, in his "Sevenfold Lament" Cao Zhi complains, in a woman's voice, "On what can your poor concubine rely?" and in an untitled poem he has a "lovely lady" say, "For whom do I sing and smile?"

With this as background, let us now take a look at Chinese songs as actually performed by singing girls at parties. By and large, the immediate concern of the songs is the appearance and the feelings of the girls themselves. The feeling of abandonment can be direct and unambiguous, as in the early popular songs found in Dunhuang, for example, the two to the tune "Yearning for the South" (*Yi jiangnan*):

I

Don't break me	莫攀我
Breaking me is too selfish.	攀我太心偏
I am the willow by the Qujiang pond,	我是曲江临池柳
This one breaks me, that one breaks me	这人攀了那人攀
For a moment of love.	恩爱一时间

II

The moon in the sky	天上月
Like a silver ball far away.	遥望似一团银
The night drags on past midnight, the wind grown stronger.	夜久更阑风渐紧

Blow away the clouds by the moon for me　　为奴吹散月边云
So it will shine on his fickle face.[33]　　照见负心人

These songs express quite directly the pain and the resentment these girls feel toward the men who abandon them after a night of love.

It may well be that these are the compositions of the girls themselves, and that what we read is simply a straightforward statement of their feelings. But the authors of the *Huajian* songs were educated male poets, and when they tried to imitate the voice of a woman who felt those painful emotions, two things occurred. First they imposed a patina of idealization on the infatuated girls by emphasizing the beauty of their person and attire, by insisting on the intensity of their feelings, and by avoiding any mention of their lovers' selfishness and inconstancy, all of which were the cause of the unhappiness. As a result, the girls become the embodiment of beauty and of a love that is enduring. This is not the attitude in the two Dunhuang popular songs, which portray the girls of the pleasure quarters realistically as dissatisfied and resentful at being at the service of men's pleasure and then cast aside.

The second point to notice is the parallel situation of the dismissed minister and the divorced wife in Chinese society, and the established poetical tradition of taking the latter as a symbol of the former. So when the educated male poet assumed the persona of a woman to record her feelings in a song, he could unconsciously reveal his own inmost feelings, "the secret sorrows that the worthy gentleman cannot speak out," as Zhang Huiyan put it.[34]

This situation can be called the product of androgyny, and it is this special effect created by androgyny that, it seems to me, is the secret of the subtle suggestive power of *Huajian* song lyrics.

Finally, there is another point I would like to discuss. The practice of using a female image and a woman's voice to express the disappointments a male poet feels in his official career did not begin with the song lyric, so why is it that we find this subtle suggestive power only in song? Earlier I contrasted the female image in song lyrics with its occurrence in *shi* poetry, where it produces different aesthetic effects. Generally speaking, the female image in most poetry can be divided into two types, one a realistically presented woman with a clearly defined social status, and the other, an allegorical figure. But the women in song lyrics seem to fall between the real and the ideal embodiment of beauty and love. They have no definite symbolic significance, but compared with the deliberately allegorical figures, they are vastly richer in symbolic potential.

To see how this occurs, I believe some ideas of the critic Julia Kristeva may be of use. Her theory of semanalysis distinguishes a semiotic function from the simply symbolic. In everyday language the signifying unit serves to identify a signified object and functions restrictively: this is the relationship of symbolism. In the language of poetry this relationship between signifier and signified is sometimes not unambiguously fixed. This more fluid semiotic relationship creates a situation in which the signifying unit becomes a continuously productive center generating associations in the reader's mind without ever limiting them to a specific object. This concept, it seems to me, finds its application in those *Huajian* song lyrics, with their potential for interpretation in ways that could hardly have been deliberately intended by their authors.[35] I propose to apply these theoretical considerations to four examples of *Huajian* song lyrics:

To the tune "South Town" (*Nan xiang zi*) by Ouyang Jiong:

At sixteen, with a flower pin in her hair	二八花钿
Breast like snow, face like lotus—	胸前如雪脸如莲
Jade dangles from a golden circle in her ear,	耳坠金环穿瑟瑟

Her colorful dress is tight. 霞衣窄
Smiling she leans on the jetty waving to the voyager. 笑倚江头招远客

To the tune "Southland Song" (*Nan ge zi*) by Wen Tingyun:

She brushes her hair in falling-down-style 倭堕低梳髻
And delicately traces drawn-out eyebrows. 连娟细扫眉
All day long thinking of one another, 终日两相思
For you I am wholly haggard 为君憔悴尽
Now in flower blossom time. 百花时

To the tune "Sands of the Washing Stream" (*Huan xi sha*) by Zhang Mi:

Toward evening I chased her carriage into Phoenix town. 晚逐香车入凤城
The east wind lightly lifted the brocade curtain, 东风斜揭绣帘轻
She slowly turned charming eyes and demurely smiled. 慢回娇眼笑盈盈

No way to send a message, what to do? 消息未通何计是
Just play drunk and follow her: 便须佯醉且随行
Faintly I hear her say, He's too crazy. 依稀闻道太狂生

To the tune "Thinking of God's Realm" (*Si di xiang*) by Wei Zhuang:

Out on a spring day 春日游
My head covered with blown apricot blossoms. 杏花吹满头
What young man on the path 陌上谁家年少
Is romantic enough 足风流
That I could marry myself to him 妾拟将身嫁与
My whole life long, 一生休
And even if, heartless, he left me, 纵被无情弃

Never be ashamed? 不能羞

These four songs can be grouped into pairs of contrasting types. The first pair both describe a beautiful woman, but with an obviously different tone. The first one describes a girl as seen through the eyes of a man, while the second employs a woman's voice to describe how she makes herself up and what her feelings are. The third and fourth, another contrasting pair, essentially recount a romantic encounter during a spring outing. The third depicts a young man actively chasing after a woman in a carriage; the fourth expresses the hopes of a girl who is looking for a young man she might love. On the surface, all four songs are about love and beautiful women, topics despised as licentious and immoral by the educated classes. The songs by Wen Tingyun and Wei Zhuang have been esteemed, however, by even the sternest critics, who have found hidden meanings to redeem the ostensible subject.[36]

Using these examples I hope to show what led traditional critics to their interpretations and, at the same time, to find a basis for judging songs on the subject of romantic love. Compare the opening lines of Ouyang Jiong's song with the first two lines of Wen Tingyun's: "At sixteen, with a flower pin in her hair / Breast like snow, face like lotus," and "She brushes her hair in the falling-down-style / And delicately traces drawn-out eyebrows." Superficially, both are describing feminine beauty. But Ouyang Jiong presents a woman already made up, as seen through a man's appreciative eyes, an attractive and desirable "other". This sort of description of beauty shows the object of male sexual fantasy but fails to suggest any deeper implication. What Wen Tingyun describes is a woman in the process of making herself up, and if we bring in, from the Chinese cultural background, the idea "the gentleman will die for the man who truly understands him, just as a woman will make herself beautiful for the one who loves her," then the description of a woman carefully brushing her hair and painting her eyebrows can easily suggest that she is doing it out of her deep feeling to please her lover. The suggestion of her motive is reinforced by the next line, "All day long thinking of one another." The expressions "brushing" and "delicately tracing" emphasize the concentration and care she puts into the operation; the carefully traced eyebrows and the fashionable style of her hairdo imply her wish to appear stylishly elegant. And then the concluding lines, "For you I am wholly haggard / Now in flower blossom time." They bring something of the feeling of Liu Yong's poem:

Never mind my girdle is growing loose—	衣带渐宽终不悔
She's one worth getting haggard for.	为伊消得人憔悴

That the season is spring reminds us that it is her springtime heart that inspires her to make herself beautiful—like the flowers—for the man who takes pleasure in her appearance.

Looking at the whole poem, we can admire the beauty of its diction and the effectiveness of its structure, even when we limit ourselves to the surface meaning. The effect of its artistry goes far beyond anything to be found in Ouyang Jiong's superficial, straightforward lyric. If we probe a bit more deeply, we will recognize that there is not only the analogy between a woman making herself beautiful for her lover and the officer ready to sacrifice himself for the ruler who appreciates him, but also a parallel between the details of the woman's makeup and the attributes claimed by the protagonist of the "Li sao": eyebrows long drawn-out are surely the "moth[-antenna] eyebrows" her rivals were jealous of and are reminiscent of Qu Yuan, who claimed that "I am alone in my love of refinement," that prototype of the man of principle dedicated to self-improvement and to keeping himself pure. Added to this is the long-standing literary tradition that makes the penciling of moth-eyebrows the symbolic gesture of an allegorical figure. As a result this song of Wen Tingyun's, despite its obvious subject, has a suggestive power that carries well beyond the range of Ouyang Jiong's flirtatious girl.

Of the second pair of song lyrics, Zhang Mi's is a romantic episode recounted in a man's voice: out for a spring stroll, he sees a pretty girl in a carriage and chases after it, unwilling to give up the pursuit. The song by Wei Zhuang is also concerned with a springtime outing, this one recounted in a woman's voice. In this time of blossoming flowers she is full of hopes for a romantic encounter. The episodes in the two poems are not exactly the same, but both involve the romantic feelings stirred by a vision of the opposite sex. But for all their superficial similarity of subject, if we look a bit more closely there is a great and obvious difference. Zhang Mi's song is closer to that of Ouyang Jiong: both show a woman as seen through a man's eyes, an "other", attractive and desirable. Ouyang's observer does not go beyond a closely focused gaze, while Zhang Mi shows the man in active pursuit. There is also a resemblance between Wei Zhuang's song and Wen Tingyun's: both express in a woman's voice their inclination toward and hopes for a man. Yet Wen Tingyun's is subtle and indirect, while Wei Zhuang's female voice is forthright and resolute. From its opening line Wei Zhuang's song is focused on the out-of-doors and a man's purposeful search, in sharp contrast to Wen Tingyun's boudoir scene, its occupant engaged in her toilette and passively waiting. But granted this difference, the two songs are alike in suggesting implications beyond the words. However, the source of those implications is not the same. The beauty of Wen Tingyun's song comes from his use of code words, terms rich in associations, while Wei Zhuang gets his suggestive force through style and syntax. He too can employ code words, but here I am emphasizing the contrast with Wen Tingyun.

Wei Zhuang's first line consists of only three words, "Spring day's outing" (*chun ri you*), which establish the tenor of the whole poem. The word "outing" sets the mood of an excursion outdoors in search of something to appreciate, and "spring day" suggests what it is one goes outside looking for. Spring is, after all, the season of blossoming and growth, when human desires too are stirred. So these first words establish the direction toward which the whole poem is drawn.

The second line, "My head covered with blown apricot blossoms", takes us a step in that direction, with a striking floral image of the abundance and force of the seductive power of spring to elicit human desires. Different flowers have different characteristics, evoking different emotional associations. Zhou Dunyi wrote, "The chrysanthemum is the recluse among flowers. The peony is the rich man, lotus the gentleman."[37] There is no such definite characterization of apricot blossoms, but from its occurrences in poetry and song we can gather that the pink, densely covered branches of the apricot stimulate an awareness of the irresistible life force of spring: "Pink apricot branches, and spring thoughts stir," "Spring fills the garden and can't be contained, / A branch of pink apricot stretches over the wall" (which usually implies a flirtatious woman).[38]

This association is reinforced by the words "blown to cover my head", for here the stimulus for spring thoughts is not to be ignored. That this force is indeed irresistible is conveyed by "full, covered" (*man*), with the implication of "completely, wholly". This display of strength, this forthrightness, is a characteristic of Wei Zhuang's songs.

Now, directly exposed to this irresistible impulse of spring, the girl is stirred by spring feelings, and she expresses in her own voice, and without false modesty, her desire to find on the path a man worthy of her lifelong devotion. And she concludes, "Even if, heartless, he left me, I would never be ashamed." She does not consider the cost or reckon it a sacrifice, determined that she will never regret it. This resolve is not only expressed in her words, it is reinforced by the structure of the three long, cadenced lines beginning with "on the path", two lines of nine and one of eight characters, through the use of alliteration, rhyme, tonal patterns, and rhythm, underlining her resolve and the strength of feeling behind it.

Taken as a whole, this song vastly surpasses Zhang Mi's playfully presented flirtation, both in depth of feeling and in artistry of construction. On another level Wei Zhuang's song evokes further resonances. The idea of a commitment that knows no regret is expressed by the Confucian injunction to "choose the good and stick to it." It is reminiscent of Qu Yuan's "Though I should die nine deaths, I would have no regrets." Associations of this sort lie well outside the capacity of Zhang Mi's song.[39]

From this comparison of the two pairs of song lyrics we can see obvious differences between songs concerned with identical (or similar) subjects and situations in depth and in quality. This is why some of the love songs of the early period have a special aesthetic quality that enables them to arouse associations not apparent in the words of the text, a quality that sets them apart from the others. This special quality was closely connected with the formation of standards for evaluation, with the use of the female voice, and with the use of code words (Wen Tingyun) or emotional tone (Wei Zhuang). It is precisely this female narrative voice which creates ambiguity and suggests another level of understanding. Once recognized, it provides the basis for an investigation of a whole series of difficulties that have troubled *ci* critics.

Perhaps the first source of confusion was the application to the song lyric of the old Han Dynasty allegorical interpretation of the poems in the *Classic of Songs*.[40] Of course there should be no question of deliberate allegory in the songs in *Huajian ji*, given the circumstances of their composition and performance. That these songs could be subjected to such interpretations was made possible because their male authors, in writing about a female image and in a woman's voice, took on what we might call an androgynous character. Their verses could then suggest to some readers the possibility of double or multiple meanings. Zhang Huiyan's mistake was to think he could explain the associations aroused by the effect of a semiotic relationship as a deliberate effort by the author of the poem. Later Changzhou critics, attempting to rectify his error, suggested a more subtle approach. Of them, Zhou Ji and Chen Tingzhuo show a better understanding of what occurs in these readings.

Zhou Ji proposed a series of apt metaphors for the suggestive power of the song lyric: "To read these lyrics is like standing by a pool to watch the fish and guess it might be bream or perhaps a carp; or a sudden lightning flash at night, leaving you uncertain whether it was in the east or in the west; or, an infant that laughs or weeps as its mother does, or a rustic fellow who feels joy or anger as they are mimed on the stage."[41]

Considered in the light of Kristeva's idea of semiotics, the images of infant and mother, or playgoer and play, are apt analogies for the continuous flow of suggestion between signifier and signified. The infant's tears or laughter, the rustic's anger or joy, are analogous to the multitudinous emotions elicited by the action of the signifier in the text. But these feelings and associations are not to be limited by insisting on a specific referent, as Zhou Ji indicated in the image of the fish seen in a pool, of whose identity one cannot be certain, and the lightning flash one perceives but whose direction one cannot determine.

Chen Tingzhuo gave the name "deep and dense" (*chen yu*) to this hidden potential of a text: "What I mean by 'deep and dense' is the idea before it is written down, a tone beyond the words. The pangs of the unmarried man and the lonely woman are what the poem describes, but it contains the feelings of the disinherited son or the minister in disfavor. The indifference of friends, a wasted life—all can be implied by a tree, a blade of grass, but the suggestion must be half-hidden, half-apparent, almost but not quite revealed, a delicate balance, never to be resolved by a single word."[42] What is important in this explanation is, I believe, Chen's realization of the connection between the "pangs of the unmarried man or the lonely woman" and the feelings of the disinherited son or the minister in disfavor. This understanding is consistent with my earlier comments on the effect of the androgynous mode, a concept which was, to be sure, not current in Chen Tingzhuo's time. In consequence, Chen confused the generative semiotic effect of the female voice in the song with the limited symbolic function of the same device when used allegorically in traditional Chinese poetry. At the same time, Chen sensed that the way the song lyric aroused associations was not the same as that demanded by the symbolism in standard poetry, carefully insisting that it is "half-hidden, half apparent, almost but not quite revealed."

Both Zhou Ji and Chen Tingzhuo succeeded in appreciating the special quality of associative richness in the song lyric. Their mistake comes from following Zhang Huiyan's allegorical interpretations to the point of attributing the ideas aroused in the reader's mind by the text to an allegorical intent on the part of the author. A more fundamental error is their inability to recognize clearly the androgynous effect created by the female voice. From their point of view, the relative complexity and worth of a song is determined by the creative consciousness of the poet as he writes: he might be writing deliberate allegory but he might also be simply making an erotic song. But that is not the way it works. If we stick to the songs of the *Huajian ji*, they were written for entertainment, with no suggestion of allegory. But for reasons I have already examined, some of those songs nevertheless suggest to sensitive readers ideas not explicit in the text. Another even more important factor must be considered; namely, the tone of the narrative voice and the attitude conveyed by it. In the lyrics by Wen

Tingyun and Wei Zhuang, the feelings are presented in a feminine tone representing a woman's attitude. The two songs by Ouyang Jiong and Zhang Mi use a masculine tone that represents a man's attitude. Comparing these two pairs of songs, we discover that the reason the former are richer in suggestion is closely connected with the fact that a male poet is practicing a sort of androgyny. The male authors of the latter pair of songs use a masculine tone to depict the male desire to see or pursue a pretty girl. Compositions of this sort may be lively and realistic, but they function on only one level and lack suggestiveness and multiple meanings.

This "androgyny", the male poet writing in a female voice, evokes a richer ambiguity than the other devices—texture, code words, syntax, structure. Androgyny and the female persona are two important elements in the aesthetic quality of the Short Song.

This leaves us with the problem of how to account for the unquestionably powerful effect of equally evocative song lyrics written by male poets in their own voice—Wei Zhuang's series to the tune "Bodhisattva Barbarian" (*Pusa man*) for example, or one of his "Taoist Nun" (*Nü guan zi*) songs. However, these songs are altogether more serious and convincing than the two by Ouyang Jiong and Zhang Mi examined earlier. Where those verses present woman as "other", an object to be admired or pursued, the tone being essentially frivolous, the poet's voice in Wei Zhuang's songs presents a woman's enduring feelings, although they are attributed to a male persona. Lawrence Lipking has argued not only that the attitude toward love is different in the two sexes, the man ready to leave as soon as his sexual needs are satisfied while the woman is left longing, but also that men are able to experience the sadness of abandonment and rejection only through their observation and understanding of women's feelings.[43] Thus, song lyrics in which a male poet speaks in a masculine voice to convey love-longings and the pangs of separation can also suggest something beyond the surface meaning of the text precisely because an essentially feminine attitude is being expressed. This permits the conclusion that the two most basic elements contributing to the special aesthetic quality of the love songs in *Huajian ji* and their capacity to suggest subtle meanings are the female voice and its androgynous character.

Failing to recognize this point, traditional *ci* critics were led to perceive intentional allegory in love songs where it is certainly absent. However, many of the song lyrics of later times were actually allegorical in intent, and though they are quite unlike *Huajian ji* songs, they were subject to their influence. The matter of this influence is a subject I shall take up later.

Here I want to pursue the contrast of proper (*ya*) and licentious / vulgar (*zheng*). All *Huajian* songs were entertainment songs, and where they take as their subject the loves of pretty girls, they ought automatically to fall into the category condemned by Confucius as licentious. But as we have seen from our four examples, there are degrees and gradations; not all love songs can be dismissed out of hand, as Wang Guowei observed. Of Ouyang Xiu's and Qin Guan's he said that "though they are love songs, they still had stature."[44] Wang Guowei never said in so many words just what determines "stature", but from his numerous random remarks we can get a good idea. In the first place, he always emphasized the suggestive power of song lyrics, saying of the songs of Feng Yansi that the poet is concerned about life and of Yan Shu that he is concerned about the state of the world.[45] The short songs of Yan Shu, Ouyang Xiu, and the others he admired are directly descended from the *Huajian* school and were regarded by Northern Song critics as love songs. But these same love songs can arouse associations far removed from their sentimental content, providing grounds for Wang Guowei's assertion that the spirit, not the content, determines whether a song is proper or licentious, and that even a love song can have moral stature.

Though Wang emphasized the suggestive power exerted by his

preferred songs, he did not share the Changzhou School's enthusiasm for the songs of Wen Tingyun, despite their power. While granting that "for sheer lushness they are unsurpassed", for him they "lacked the deeper beauty which comes from a richness of meaning."[46] Where he differs from Zhang Huiyan is in his concept of the source of the associative capacity of those songs. Zhang was fond of talking about allegory, and so emphasized the presence of cultural code words that could be associated with allegorical interpretations (as "painting eyebrows" makes one think of Qu Yuan's "all the women were jealous of my moth eyebrows," or "deep inside the women's quarter" is reminiscent of his "Far, far away in the women's quarter, the king does not wake up.") But Wang Guowei was more aware of a quality within the text of the poem itself, and Wen Tingyun's songs are relatively lacking in this appeal to the emotions.

In another critical remark about *ci* Wang wrote, "So one may write love songs, but one must never write frivolously," emphasizing the importance of emotional content in *ci*.[47] We might notice that those songs that deserve censure as "frivolous" mostly view woman as "other" and are written in a man's voice, while those written in a woman's voice and those written in a man's voice with feminine feeling cannot be so labeled. This, I believe, is the basic perception underlying the refined/vulgar distinction.

After the Long Song (*man ci*) evolved, this distinction persisted in a new form, requiring new critical standards. The influence of the *Huajian* songs, however, remained strong, a point to which I shall return in discussing their later history.

Next I want to consider the attitude toward *ci* as "words written in idleness" (*kong zhong yu*) expressed by Huang Tingjian, this of course in contrast to *shi* poems written to express one's inner concerns and hence self-consciously focused on the poet's feelings. *Huajian* songs were written at a party for female entertainers to perform, and were, from the poet's point of view, verses composed in an idle moment, nothing serious. Although Huang Tingjian was talking about his own love songs, his remark can be understood as involving a dismissive attitude toward all verse lacking the high seriousness demanded of *shi* poetry. When the Northern Song men of letters compiled their collected works, they never included their song lyrics; such frivolous poems were not a part of their serious work. They could not have realized that the value of *ci* lay precisely in their lack of seriousness, their being written in idleness for distraction.

There are three sources for the ambiguity generated in song lyrics. The first is the poet's freedom from the obligation to write seriously of his feelings and inculcate a moral message, leaving the possibility that something of his true character will be revealed. As Wang Guowei observed, "Very little of the *shi* poetry of the Five Dynasties and Northern Song is first-rate, while this is the period when song lyrics were at their most flourishing. Of the poets who excelled in both genres, like Ouyang Xiu and Qin Guan, their song lyrics greatly surpass their *shi* poems because what they wrote in *shi* lacks the veracity (*zhen*) of their songs."[48]

The second is the use of a female voice, creating an androgynous quality in which the male poet's own nature is unconsciously fused with the female persona of his song. This in turn is reinforced by the third source, the unselfconscious nature of this amalgam of the poet's own self and the female persona, which makes it especially productive of ambiguity. Since this effect is not deliberately concocted, it is at once spontaneous and variable and thus a basically different kind of relation between signifier and signified. Its function is semiotic, not symbolic as in deliberate allegory, which is limited to a specific referent. The semiotic function of the *Huajian* lyrics is a fluid and continuously productive force, free of the limitations of symbolism. As Kristeva puts it, the text is then independent of its author's intent and produces a field in which there is continuous interaction between author, text, and reader. Precisely because *Huajian* song lyrics were written in idleness, with no deliberate commitment on the part of their male authors, and in a female voice, they have great potential for multiple interpretations. That they were casual compositions contributed to the subtlety and rich ambiguity of *Huajian* lyrics. However, song lyric soon evolved beyond that stage, becoming more like *shi* poetry—subjective and deliberately constructed. Despite the difference, great as it was, the special aesthetic quality that characterized *Huajian* songs continued to exert enormous influence, particularly in the critical evaluation of *ci*.

The first transformation of the *Huajian* song lyric came with the changes in prosody and diction in the Long Song as written by Liu Yong. The second was Su Shi's deliberate use of *ci* as a vehicle for the poet's personal feelings, which opened up a new range of subject matter. The third was the appearance of the architectonic *ci*, discursive songs constructed with poetic artifice and often deliberate allegorical intent, which completely abandoned the light, improvisational tone of the early songs. These developments would seem to have been at the expense of those elements in *Huajian* lyrics found to be most productive of ambiguity—the female voice and image, and the undercurrent of androgyny. However, these later *ci* still share with those earlier songs a multilayered suggestiveness that attests to a continuing influence, even while they dispensed with those features that were responsible for ambiguity in the *Huajian ji*. It remains to examine more closely how ambiguity arose in the songs of Liu Yong, Su Shi, and Zhou Bangyan.

The typical *Huajian* lyric was short and choppy and had few run-on lines, much like the eight-line songs to the tune "Bodhisattva Barbarian" with its four different rhymes, in which the disjointed syntax often leaves a good deal to the reader's imagination. By their very length Liu Yong's Long Songs were discursive, allowing room for introductory, connective, and subordinating words (*ling zi*), in the use of which he excelled, and giving his songs the more explicit, logical structure characteristic of the masculine voice. To this extent his songs have lost the suggestive power derived from a female voice, retaining only an unambiguous, straightforward narrative content. It was such explicit descriptions of women as "The soft cream melted, glossy cloud-hair undone, / Idle all day long, / too bored to comb or tie up her hair" or "Idly sewing, she nestles close to him" that made Liu Yong vulnerable to critics. If these songs were criticized as vulgar or erotic, he also wrote others praised as "familiar language that carries a deeper meaning, a spiritual view soaring afar"[49] or "In a couple of brush strokes the dragon breaks free from the wall and flies away."[50] The object of that praise must have been the very quality of suggesting another, deeper meaning. But how did he achieve such effect with an explicit narrative style? I believe that in writing about the yearning and the sorrows of parted lovers he introduced the sensibility of the disappointed official, although not explicitly: blended into the description of a scene viewed from a height or while standing by a riverbank was the grief of disappointment, creating an ambiguity between love-longings and frustrated ambition. The admixture of feeling and description produced yet another ambiguity, thus producing evocative power characteristic of *ci*. It succeeds because the easily provoked sadness of the disappointed official is psychologically very similar to that of a woman concerned with the passing of time. Deep in the poet's mind is a hidden ambiguity that elicits these associations in the reader.[51] Despite differences in language and style, *Huajian* songs provided a standard critics applied when they praised later *ci* for their evocative quality.

Let us next consider the changes wrought in the content of *ci* when Su Shi turned to songs as a vehicle for expressing his own feelings and aspirations. Critics noted with approval that he avoided the earlier preoccupation with themes of women and love, and, after Xin Qiji and other

Southern Song songwriters provided the models, the so-called Heroic Style (*haofang*) became a label used by critics to mark these *ci* as a new type, distinct from the old "devious-evocative" (*wanyue*) songs. The terms brought, however, more confusion than clarity. To understand this confusion it is necessary to return to the relation between the songs of Liu Yong and those of Su Shi. Su Shi expressed two contradictory judgments of Liu Yong's songs, disdaining the ones considered vulgar and erotic but praising those with evocative power.[52] Critics objected not so much to the content of these "vulgar, erotic" songs as to their language, their vernacular vocabulary and discursive style, which deprived them of the subtlety and ambiguity of the *Huajian* songs on the same subjects. And the songs with evocative power achieved their effect not by simply depicting the grief of the frustrated official or by describing a scenic spot but by combining the two in a fundamentally ambiguous unity.

In Liu Yong's songs Su Shi saw only their superficial eroticism or, alternatively, their evocative beauty, unaware of the source of that beauty and having no real conception of ambiguity as the source of that aesthetic quality. He was determined in his compositions to avoid the erotic flavor of Liu Yong's songs, believing that his own owed their value to the absence of such topics. Whether or not ambiguity was involved was not his concern; so Su Shi's revolution in song writing produced good consequences as well as bad.

Songs written under Su Shi's influence developed in a rather complicated way, as did the views of *ci* critics. Such songs were of three sorts: first, those that retained the evocative ambiguity of *Huajian* songs while avoiding their feminine subject matter; next, those that lost their evocative power along with the *Huajian* subject matter but still achieved the kind of beauty appropriate to *shi* poetry; and finally, those that no longer had the characteristic subtlety of *ci* and failed to meet the standards of *shi*. Su

Shi and Xin Qiji provide examples of the first. These *ci* demonstrate the presence of ambiguity in songs written after Su Shi's innovation.[53] An example of the second, the *ci* that have lost that quality, is Lu You's "Written on First Coming to Chengdu from Southern Zheng" to the tune "Spring in the Han Palace" (*Hangong chun*):

Feathered arrows, carved bow—	羽箭雕弓
I remember I called my hawk on the old ramparts	忆呼鹰古垒
To intercept the tiger on the plain.	截虎平川
When I returned at evening, playing the flute,	吹笳暮归野帐
Snow weighed down the black tent at my campsite.	雪压青毡
Dripping drunken ink—	淋漓醉墨
Look at the dragon snakes Flying down onto the thick paper!	看龙蛇飞落蛮笺
People are disappointed Expecting of me	人误许
A poet's feeling and a general's strategy	诗情将略
For our time.	一时才气超然
What has sent me back south?	何时又作南来
I see the herb market at Chongyang	看重阳药市
A mountain of lanterns on New Year's Eve.	元夕灯山
In flower blossom time a place where a myriad men rejoice,	花时万人乐处
Hats askew, they drop their whips.	欹帽垂鞭
Hearing the song, I am moved at past ideals	闻歌感旧
And sometimes still	尚时时
Let fall a tear in my cup.	流涕尊前
Just remember,	君记取
There are great deeds to be done—	封侯事在

Achievements are not at Heaven's whim. 功名不信由天

That this poem lacks subtlety and suggestiveness is in part due to the limitations of this particular song pattern; nearly half the lines are in a 4-beat meter and even the few longer lines are followed by a succession of fours. Read straight through, it has vigor but lacks nuance. Not only is the syntax close to *shi* poetry, it also has the rhythmic feel of prose, a weakness also observable in the lyrics to this tune written by other poets.[54] Other examples of such *shi*-like song lyrics are those of Zhang Yuangan, to the tune "Congratulating the Groom"[55] (*He xin lang*), and Zhang Xiaoxiang, to the tune "Six Provinces Song" (*Liuzhou getou*).[56] Though lacking the evocative quality of *Huajian* songs, their vigor and impassioned feeling gives them the force of the *shi* poetry of direct statement.

The third kind of *ci* is represented by Liu Guo's song for Xin Qiji to the tune "Spring in the Qin Garden" (*Qinyuan chun*).[57]

For a bottle of wine, a shoulder of pork 斗酒彘肩
To cross the River even in wind and rain— 风雨渡江
I would be glad to do it. 岂不快哉
But Bai Juyi of Mt. Xiang 被香山居士
Together with Lin Pu 约林和靖
And old Su Dongpo, 与东坡老
When I was about to go, urged me to stay. 驾勒吾回
Su said, West Lake 坡谓西湖
Is just like Miss West 正如西子
Making herself up before the mirror. 浓抹淡妆临镜台
The other two 二公者
Turned their heads and paid no attention, 皆掉头不顾
Absorbed in their cups. 只管衔杯

Bai said, Fly-From-India Mountain	白言天竺飞来
Is like a picture	图画里
With soaring pavilions scattered about.	峥嵘楼阁开
I love the two east-west valleys	爱东西双涧
Where the surging waters turn,	纵横水绕
And the North and South mountains	两峰南北
With clouds stacked above and below.	高下云堆
Lin Pu said, I don't agree.	逋曰不然
There is a hidden fragrance floating in the air—	暗香浮动
Better first go to Mt. Gu to look for the plum trees.	争似孤山先探海
Let's wait until the weather clears to cross;	须晴去
It won't be too late to visit Xin Qiji then.	访稼轩未晚
Tarry here for now.	且此徘徊

In this playful, superficial poem the words attributed to those earlier poets extolling West Lake scenery are all quotations, sometimes slightly modified, from their poems. The song itself is an exercise in the form of an apology for not paying a visit to Xin Qiji. This sort of verse deserves Chen Tingzhuo's criticism of Liu Guo as able only to imitate the "skin and hair" of Xin Qiji.[58]

After the innovations introduced by Su Shi, except for aberrations of this sort, *ci* were still being written with the same ambiguity that gives the form its characteristic quality. And here we have a useful criterion for judging these later *ci*, by observing how far they preserve the quality that essentially defines the genre. As we have seen, *Huajian* songs derived that quality from the use of a female voice by a male poet who thereby assumed an androgynous nature. These later *ci* also owe their ambiguity to a quality in their authors, this time not of gender but of something generated by a conflict. This conflict can be of two different sorts. One is typified by Su Shi, the other by Xin Qiji. In Su Shi the conflict was between his dedication to the Confucian ideal of public service and his dedication to a Taoist yearning for emancipation. For Xin Qiji the conflict was the stress created by outside circumstances that thwarted his patriotic ambitions.

It is worth noting that the combination of Confucian and Taoist ideals in Su Shi's songs and the note of stress in Xin Qiji's in both cases resulted from frustration in the pursuit of an ideal in their official careers. Referring back to Lipking's psychology of the rejected woman, we can see how the songs of these male poets, striving to do their duty, suggest the feelings of the aggrieved woman. Consequently, there was no need to borrow a female persona to create ambiguity. Further, the narrative language they employed, though conveying a masculine consciousness, had, nonetheless, a devious, vacillating quality associated with feminine language. This aspect is especially prominent in Xin Qiji's songs, while those by Su Shi sometimes lapse into a facile directness that diminishes their value as *ci*. Though Xin Qiji's have all the ardor and passion of the male voice, the syntax demonstrates the indirect, secretive manner of expression characteristic of the female voice, resulting in an effect analogous to the allegorical use of the beautiful woman/fragrant flowers trope in Qu Yuan. Furthermore, in syntax and stanza structure he brings the changes on all the devices of the prose stylist. He is especially skillful at combining allusion and natural scenery with personal feeling.[59] The result is masculine ardor clothed in feminine language well characterized by Chen Tingzhuo: "As it comes out, always half-hidden, half-revealed, almost exposed yet not exposed, it is inextricably interwoven, never allowed to become explicit."[60] Truly, this stage in the development of *ci* produced some of the finest examples of the genre.

These new *ci* were the source of further confusion among critics, who became newly concerned about the "authentic type" (*ben se*) of song now that there was a "deviant form" (*bian ge*). *Huajian* songs developed a soft, fluent style regarded as the style appropriate to the content. But a revolution occurred when Su Shi opened up the range of subjects for *ci*, and it was natural to regard his songs as belonging to a deviant form. As we have seen, however, those *Huajian* songs about pretty girls were of two different kinds, some good and some less so. Likewise, songs written after Su Shi's campaign to "flush out the silk and perfume" included good ones and bad ones, so that although they could be classified as "deviant" in content, the terms "authentic" and "deviant" could not be used to establish criteria for a value judgment. Those who employed "authentic type" and "deviant form" as categories of relative value failed to recognize that what made some *Huajian* songs outstanding was not their "soft, fluent style", but their use of the female voice and image in songs that were soft and fluent, suggesting the multiple meanings that mark their excellence, while inferior songs lapse into shallow extravagance. As for the deviant form as represented by the heroic mode (*haofang*), the inferior songs decline into boisterous clamor, while the best ones get their value by suggesting multiple meanings.

Next I want to consider Li Qingzhao's dictum that "*ci* is a different form"—different, that is, from *shi* poetry. She was of course quite right: *ci* is a distinct genre of poetry. But she was apparently basing her statement on content and purely formal considerations—tonal pattern, rhyme, allusion—without being aware of the aesthetic value of ambiguity and suggestion. This affected not only the accuracy and generality of her concept of *ci*; but also her own practice as a *ci* poet, preventing her from pushing her talent to even greater achievement. Let us consider Li Qingzhao's songs in the light of her own pronouncements about the genre.

Huajian songs constitute the most feminized genre in Chinese literature; yet, this use of female language to present a female image, so rich in female psychology, was developed by male poets. Women poets were at a double disadvantage: conventional restrictions on women excluded them from public office and thus deprived them of the theme so prominent in poetry written by men, the conflict between serving and retiring, so they could not compete with male poets on their own ground. And in writing *ci*, that most feminine of verse forms whose subject was most often love and disappointment in love, they were faced with an even greater handicap: the traditional moral code. Some of Li Qingzhao's most moving songs, about her love for her husband, opened the way to the sort of denunciation expressed by the critic Wang Zhuo: "Since antiquity, among the educated women of good family there has never been one so shameless as this."[61]

Li Qingzhao showed a versatile talent in literary composition: her *shi* poetry and her prose writings in several forms include first-rate specimens, but in none of them is there the slightest hint that the writer is a woman. It is only in her *ci* that she writes in the person and language of a woman, and there she achieves the grace and delicacy she thought proper to the genre, no doubt a reflection of her conviction that *ci* is a different form. Among women of her time she was certainly the boldest in using this form of poetry indirectly expressing her own feelings of love. For a woman to express a woman's feelings in women's language in the most feminine of verse forms should, from a purely feminist point of view, produce an unprecedented effect. Moreover, she was of an argumentative disposition and should have had some self-awareness in this area. Regrettably, her understanding of the function of the female image in *ci* was limited to recognizing that it was a good thing. What she failed to realize was that its effect came from its androgynous character. But if she was not consciously aware of it, her upbringing would have prepared her; she grew up in a family of officials with traditional upper-class values, where, as her *shi* poetry and prose prove,[62] she received a thorough classical education. And a classical education meant mastering a corpus of works that incorporated a wholly masculine set of ideas and values.[63] So among her *ci* are some that transcend the purely feminine and betray a hidden androgyny. The Qing Dynasty critic Shen Zengzhi discerns two kinds in Li Qingzhao's *ci*, one he labels "perfume and powder" (*fen xin*) and the other, "spiritually outstanding" (*shen jun*). The first are much appreciated by sentimentalists, he says, the second by people of imagination. "If her spirit has awareness, she will see in the latter her understanding readers."[64] The songs he characterizes as spiritually outstanding are surely the suggestive ones in which I discern a kind of androgyny: for example, Li Qingzhao's song to the tune "The Fisherman Is Proud" (*Yu jia'ao*).[65]

The sky touches cloud-waves trailing morning mist;	天接云涛连晓雾
The Milky Way is about to turn as a thousand sails dance.	星河欲转千帆舞
My soul in a dream draws near God's place	仿佛梦魂归帝所
And I hear heaven's voice	闻天语
Earnestly ask where I am going.	殷勤问我归何处
I say, the road is long, alas, and the day is late.	我报路长嗟日暮
In poetry startling lines come hard.	学诗谩有惊人句
On a ninety-thousand-mile wind the phoenix really soars.	九万里风鹏正举
May the wind not stop	风休住
While it drives my tattered sail to the Fairy Isles.	蓬舟吹取三山去

Unfortunately, few such songs by Li Qingzhao have come down to us, perhaps because the early collections were incomplete or because, inhibited by her concept of *ci*, she wrote many "perfume and power" songs and few like this one.

Next I would like to consider the innovation introduced by Zhou

Bangyan. On the surface it looks to be no more than stylistic, but on another level it shows an approach that is different from the subtle ambiguity I have postulated as the essential quality of *ci*. The need to incorporate the softness and fluency of the Short Songs with the Long Song as developed by Liu Yong, while avoiding his lack of subtlety, led to the development of the architectonic form in the hands of Zhou Bangyan and his followers. They increased the depth and ambiguity of *ci* on the stylistic side while avoiding both the shallowness and extravagance of Liu Yong's followers and the crude boisterousness that followed in the wake of Su Shi's rejection of a feminine content. The most important tendency of their stylistic innovations was to strengthen the devious, subtle quality of *ci*.

In his architectonically structured songs Zhou Bangyan used three different techniques, involving the deliberate manipulation of stanza structure, syntax, and prosodic elements. First, there are the rough meters; here, he uses three, four, or even six different musical modes to create a medley of tunes that give the effect of dissonance and complexity. Second are the revolving displacements and discontinuities in the text, which emphasize the indirect, suggestive quality in his songs. And third are his allusions to contemporary events in a way that deliberately suggests allegory. An example of his devious style is the song to the tune "Prince of Lanling"; deliberate allegory appears in "Clouds across the River".[66]

Later Southern Song *ci* writers could hardly escape Zhou Bangyan's influence, and it was the period when the architectonic *ci* flourished. Though they differed in style and achievement, all the well-known writers—Shi Dazu, Wu Wenying, Zhou Mi, Wang Yisun, Zhang Yan—derived their technique from him. There were of course external social reasons for this phenomenon: the Southern Song tendency toward extravagance and the writing of *ci* in social gatherings both contributed to the circulation of this sort of carefully constructed composition.[67] But beyond this there was, I believe, another reason, a tendency inherent in the form itself as it developed from the lyrical Short Song to the more discursive Long Song. From its very length the Long Song requires that its author be discursive. Too much direct elaboration inevitably inclines the soft, fluent style toward extravagance and the heroic style toward bombast. Consequently, though Zhou Bangyan's architectonic style seems to be only a stylistic innovation, it brought with it a way of avoiding these weaknesses and was understandably a strong influence on Southern Song *ci* writers.

Two Song critics responded to the new style. Zhang Yan and Shen Yifu were preoccupied with the technical elements that were the concern of the writers of architectonic *ci*: syntax, vocabulary, allusion, transition, opening and closing lines, grammatical particles—all matters of technique in composition. Their chief object was the avoidance of the extravagance associated with Liu Yong's school and the bombast of the followers of Su Shi. Their ideal was *ya*: "elegance, refinement".[68] Their determination to avoid the faults of the songs of some of their contemporaries was not misplaced, but by limiting their view to prosodic and verbal matters, they failed to see the real reason for the superficiality of many Southern Song *ci*. Successful practitioners of the art could use the techniques to increase the complexity and subtlety of their inspiration and so give their compositions greater suggestive power, but others, lacking the inspiration in the first place, could only manipulate techniques. The successful *ci*, those rich in suggestive ambiguity, were produced by the conscious application of technical skills; as a consequence of this self-conscious process of composition, these *ci* are characterized by a contrived symbolism that contrasts with the vague, ill-defined, and hence more suggestive code words that we find in *Huajian* songs and which belong to Kristeva's category of the semiotic. If excellence is defined solely in terms of the aesthetic qualities perceived in *Huajian* songs, then the architectonic *ci* is inferior. The best of them, however, set a new standard of depth and refinement; although, because of their too-circumscribed symbolism, they lack the resonance of the semiotic and cannot be placed among the very best of the genre.

Elsewhere, on the subject of allegory, Zhou Ji said, "Apprentice writers of *ci* should try for allegory, for with allegory surface meaning and deeper implications reinforce one another, resulting in a good composition. Once the style is mastered, one should seek to dispense with allegory. When there is no deliberate allegory, then ... the implications are up to the reader: the benevolent will perceive benevolence; the wise, wisdom."[69] Which is to say, the apprentice *ci* writer may begin by deliberately employing the techniques of composition to try to imbue his *ci* with resonance and suggestive power, but he should transcend the deliberately assigned and therefore limited relation between signifier and signified and strive for an unrestricted, free relationship; only then will this architectonic *ci* reach the highest form.

Judged by this standard, I think the *ci* of Zhou Bangyan and Wu Wenying certainly deserve consideration. The best of Zhou's *ci* are outstanding for their density and richness; and though the effect is achieved by conscious artistry, the more he sketches in details, the denser they become. Not only does he obliterate all traces of his artistry, but his *ci* contain profound suggestions of a complexity that prevent readers from immediately apprehending his meaning—a notable achievement.

In Wu Wenying's best songs difficulty and obscurity appear in an extreme form. Zhou Ji said, "The good ones are like the light of the sky or the shadows of clouds on the green waves—one never tires of toying with them; but when you chase after them, they are far away." "He is always turning around in space—it takes great spiritual force to do it."[70]

Although the product of a self-conscious artist, in contrast to the relaxed, more spontaneous *Huajian ci*, the architectonic *ci* shared the suggestiveness and ambiguity that is the mark of excellence in all *ci*. This suggestive ambiguity so praised by Zhou Ji could appear in both the Five Dynasties and Northern Song *ci* and the Southern Song architectonic *ci*; and though the earlier ones involved no deliberate attempt at allegory, the associations aroused led critics to assume it was present. The same assumption held for the later ones, which were written to carry multiple meanings that, in turn, remained vague and ambiguous.

Through the three stages of *ci* development—Liu Yong's narrative Long Song, Su Shi's transformation of the content of the short lyric, and the change in style brought by Zhou Bangyan—the female voice and androgyny of the *Huajian* songs were abandoned; but the capacity for multiple meanings always remained an important ingredient of the best *ci*. The problems of evaluation that concerned *ci* critics—the contrast between elegant/refined and vulgar/erotic, the presence of allegory, the authentic type and the deviant form, the different approaches of Zhang Huiyan and Wang Guowei to the interpretation of ambiguity in *ci*—all caused continual conflict. I believe it was the result of the unwillingness of traditional critics to confront the phenomenon of the female voice in *Huajian* songs and examine its aesthetic effect. I hope these remarks will be of some help in dispelling those conflicts.

Notes:

1. Wei Tai, *Dongxuan bilu*, in *Biji xiaoshuo daguan* 5.37.

2. Hu Zi, *Tiaoxi yuyin conghua qianji* 26. 178.

3. Zhang Shunmin, *Hua man lu*, quoting Xu Shiluan, Song Yan, in *Biji xiaoshuo daguan* 6.6203.

4. Shi Huihong, *Lengzhai yehua*, in *Biji xiaoshuo daguan* 1. 642.

5. Wang Zhuo, *Biji manzhi*, in *Cihua congbian* 1. 83, 84.

6. Zhang Yan, *Ci yuan*, in *Cihua congbian* 1.259.

7. Xu Tiaofu, *Jiaozhu Renjian cihua*, p. 19.

8. In *Zhongguo cixue de xiandai guan*, I proposed three stages in this development: first the lyrics set to music and intended for performance, then lyrics composed as another form of poetry, and finally, the elaborate deliberately constructed *ci* for which I am here borrowing Gao Yougong's term "architectonic" (see "The Aesthetic Consequences of Formal Aspects of *Ci*", paper read at the Conference on *Ci*, "Song Lyrics", Joint Committee on Chinese Studies, ACLS-SSRC, York, Maine, June 1990).

9. Wang Zhuo, 1.85; Hu Yin, Preface to *Jiubian ci*, in *Song liushi mingjia ci* (*Jiguge jiaoxuan ben*) 2/5.2b.

10. Chen Shidao, *Houshan shihua*, in *Biji xiaoshuo daguan* 6.3671-a.

11. Hu Zi, *Hou ji* 33.254.

12. Wang Zhuo, 1.74.

13. Wang Yan, Preface to *Shuangxi shiyu*, in *Song Yuan sanshiyi jia ci* 3.1.

14. Hu Yin, 2/5.2b.

15. Cf. Wang Guowei, in Xu Tiaofu, p. 58.

16. See Yeh Chia-ying, *Zhongguo cixue de xiandai guan*, pp. 4-5.

17. Chen Zhensun, *Zhizhai shulu jieti* 21.581.

18. Zhao Zunyue, "Ci ji ti yao" in *Ci xue jikan* 3.3.55.

19. Lu You, *Weinan wenji*, in *Lu Fangweng quanji* in *Guoxue jiben congshu* 14.34.

20. Wang Zhuo, Preface 1.67.

21. Miao Yue and Yeh Chia-ying, *Lingxi cishuo*, pp. 1-26.

22. Leslie Fieldler, *Love and Death in the American Novel*, p. 314.

23. Mary Anne Ferguson, *Images of Women in Literature*, pp. 21-398.

24. I have been unable to find the textual source for this anecdote, which I got from my uncle and teacher Ye Tingyi, styled Juanqing.

25. Remark collected by Guo Shaoyu in *Song shihua jiyi*, in *Yanjing*

xuebao zhuanhao 14, A.97.

26. Yuan Haowen, *Lunshi jueju*, verse no. 24 in *Yuan Haowen shiji jianzhu* 10.2b.

27. Zhu Ziqing, *Gudian wenxue lunwen ji* 2.357.

28. Li Bingruo, *Xuzhuang man ji*, quoted in *Huajian ji pingzhu*, p. 16.

29. Chen Tingzhuo, *Baiyuzhai cihua zuben jiaozhu* 1.20.

30. See Yeh Chia-ying, *Jialing lunci conggao*, pp. 1-37. Also cf. Yeh Chia-ying, *Zhonguo cixue de xiandai guan*, pp. 78-83.

31. Carolyn Heilbrun, *Toward a Recognition of Androgyny*, p. xi.

32. Lawrence Lipking, *Abandoned Women and Poetic Tradition,* pp. xv-xxvii.

33. *Dunhuang quzi ciji* 1.44.

34. Zhang Huiyan, *Cixuan xu*, in *Cihua congbian* 5.1617.

35. See Julia Kristeva, *Revolution in Poetic Language*, pp. 19-106.

36. Zhang Huiyan, 5.1609, 1611, says of Wen Tingyun's *ci*, "They express the frustration of a gentleman unappreciated", and of Wei Zhuang's, "They were written to give vent to his feelings after he was stranded in Shu".

37. Zhou Dunyi, "Ai lian shuo", in *Zhou Lianxi ji* (*Guoxue jiben congshu* ed.) 8.1319.

38. Song Qi, *Yu lou chun*, in *QSC*, 1.716; Ye Shaoweng, *You xiaoyuan bu zhi,* in *Qian jia shi* (Hong Kong; Guangzhi shuju), p. 131.

39. For an analysis of this *ci* of Wei Zhuang, see my entry in *Tang Song ci jianshang cidian.*

40. See Vol. II, "The Changzhou School of '*Ci*' Criticism".

41. Zhou Ji, Preface to *Song sijia cixuan*, p. 16.

42. Chen Tingzhuo, 1.20.

43. Lipking, p. xix.

44. Wang Guowei, p. 19.

45. Ibid., pp. 15-16.

46. Ibid., p. 6.

47. Ibid., p. 67.

48. Ibid., p. 45.

49. Zhou Ji, p. 2b.

50. Zheng Wenzhuo, quoted in Long Yusheng, *Tang Song mingjia ci*, p. 84.

51. See the chapter on Liu Yong in Yeh, *Lingxi cishuo*, pp. 129-160.

52. I have discussed this point in *Lingxi cishuo*, pp. 198-206.

53. Su Shi, Xin Qiji.

54. For a detailed account of lyric songs by Lu You, see ibid., pp. 379-400.

55. *QSC* 2.1073.

56. Ibid., 3.1686.

57. Ibid., 3.2143.

58. Chen Tingzhuo, 1.110.

59. See chapter 9 on Xin Qiji in *Lingxi cishuo*, pp. 424-429.

60. Chen Tingzhuo, 1.20.

61. Wang Zhuo, 1.88.

62. *Li Qingzhao ciji jiaozhu*, pp. 101-182.

63. Shen Zengzhi, *Junge suotan*, in *Cihua congbian*, 1 1:3698.

64. Ibid.

65. *QSC* 2.927.

66. For a discussion and exegesis of both *ci*, see *Lingxi cishuo*, pp. 289-329.

67. See ibid., pp. 547-548.

68. Zhang Yan, 1.229-232, 255-261; Shen Yifu, *Yuefu zhimi jianshi*, in *Cihua congbian* 1.278-280.

69. Zhou Ji, p. 13b.

70. Ibid.

大晏词的欣赏

谈到文学的欣赏，原是颇为主观的一件事。譬如口舌之于五味，滋味既异，嗜好亦别，强人同己，固属无谓的多事，然而美芹献曝，略述个人品味之所得，或者也尚不失推己的一份诚意。因此，我想略谈一谈关于大晏词的欣赏。

在北宋初年的词坛上，晏殊、晏几道父子和欧阳修是并称的三位作者。而一般读者对这三位作者的爱好，则以小晏为最，欧阳次之，而爱好大晏者则最少。大晏之所以不易得人欣赏的原因，我以为有两点：其一是因为大晏词的风格过于圆融平静，没有激情，也没有烈响，既不能以色泽使人眩迷，又不能以气势使人震慑，正如其词集名中“珠玉”二字，只是一奁温润的珠玉，虽然澄明纯净秀杰晶莹，然而自有些人看来，却会觉得它远不及一些光怪陆离、五色缤纷的琼瑰更足以使人目迷心动，这是大晏词之不易得人欣赏的第一个原因；至于另一个原因，则是由于大晏的富贵显达的身世，在一般人心目中，似乎都根深蒂固地存在着一种“穷而后工”的观念，而大晏在这方面却不能满足一般人对诗人之“穷”的预期，和对诗人之“穷”寄以同情的快感，这是大晏词之不易得人欣赏的第二个原因。宛敏灏君在《二晏及其词》一书中对大晏的一些词作甚至讥之为“富贵得意之余”的“无病呻吟”。宛君于二晏之身世、作品，搜罗考订极详，对小晏亦赞扬备至，而独于大晏的一些词作不能欣赏，因而颇有微词。昔蒋弱六之评杜甫《陪郑广文游何将军山林》“万里戎王子”一首云：“见遗于无意搜罗之人不足怪，遗于搜罗已尽之人为可恨耳。”[①]看到宛君“无病呻吟”的话，我真不得不为大晏仕途之幸而叹息其不幸了。

我以为想要欣赏大晏的词，第一该先认识的就是大晏乃是一个理性的诗人，他的圆融平静的风格与他的富贵显达的身世，正是一位理性的诗人的同株异干的两种成就。诗人的穷与达，原来并没有什么“文章憎命达”、“才命两相妨”的必然性，而大半乃是决定于诗人所禀赋的不同的性格。一般说来，诗人的性格约可大致分为两种：一种是属于成功的类型，而另一种则是属于失败的类型。属于成功的一型，就性格而言，可以目之为理性的诗人；而属于失败的一型，则可目之为纯情的诗人。《人间词话》之评李后主词云：“词人者，不失其赤子之心者也。故生于深宫之中，长于妇人之手，是后主为人君所短处，亦即为词人所长处。”又说：“主观之诗人不必多阅世。阅世愈浅，则性情愈真。”这些话，就纯情的诗人而言，是不错的。因为纯情的诗人，其感情往往如流水之一泻千里，对一切事物，他们都但以“纯情”去感受，无反省，无节制，无考虑，无计较。“赤子之心”对此种诗人而言，岂止是“不失”而已，在现实的成败利害的生活中，他们简直就是个未成熟的“赤子”。此一类型之诗人，李后主自是一位最好的代表。而破国亡家，也正为此一类型之诗人的典型的下场。“天以百凶成就一词人”，对此一类型的诗人而言，其“百凶”之遭遇与其“纯情”之作风，也正为同株异干的两种必然之结果。至于理性的诗人则不然，他们的感情不似流水，而却似一面平湖，虽然受风时亦复縠绉千叠，投石下亦复盘涡百转，然而却无论如何总也不能使之失去其含敛静止、盈盈脉脉的一份风度。对一切事物，他们都

① 语见杨伦《杜诗镜铨》卷二引蒋弱六评语。

有着思考和明辨，也有着反省和节制。他们已养成了成年人的权衡与操持，然而却仍保有着一颗真情锐感的诗心。此一类型之诗人，自以晏殊为代表。《宋史·晏殊传》记载云：“仁宗即位，章献明肃太后奉遗诏权听政。宰相丁谓、枢密使曹利用，各欲独见奏事，无敢决其议者。殊建言：‘群臣奏事太后者，垂簾听之，皆毋得见。’议遂定。”又载元昊寇边时，“陕西方用兵，殊请罢内臣监兵，不以阵图授诸将，使得应敌为攻守；及募弓箭手教之，以备战斗。又请出宫中长物助边费，凡他司之领财利者，悉罢还度支。”从这些事，我们都可以看出晏殊的明决的理性。他的识见与谋虑，都可说得上是将相之才，而决不是一个“长于妇人之手”，未经阅世的“赤子”。然而自其《珠玉词》来看，晏殊又确实是一个资质极高的诗人，由此可知事功方面的成就原无害于一个理性的诗人之为真正的诗人，而《珠玉》一集的价值，也决不该因其富贵显达的身世而稍有减损。我将“理性”二字加诸于“诗人”之上也许会有人颇不谓然，因为诗歌原该是缘情之作，而情感与理性则又似乎有着釐然迥异的差别。这就一般人而言，也许是对的，因为一般人的理性乃但出于一己头脑之思索，但用于人我利害之辨别，此种理性之为狭隘与坚硬，而与感情之格格不能相容，自是显然而且必然的事。然而诗人之理性则有不同于此者，诗人之理性该只是对情感加以节制，和使情感净化升华的一种操持的力量，此种理性不得之于头脑之思索，而得之于对人生之体验与修养。它与情感不但并非相敌对立，而且完全浸润于情感之中，譬若水乳之交融，沆瀣之一气，其发之于心亦原无此彼之异与后先之别。是理性既可以与情感相成而非尽相反，则诗歌虽为缘情之作，而诗人则固可以有理性之诗人了。

作为一个理性的诗人，我以为大晏的词有着几点特色。而第一点该提出来说明的，则是大晏《珠玉词》中所表现的一种情中有思的意境。如前所述，理性既可以与情感如水乳之交融，则《珠玉词》的情中有思的意境，便正为此种交融了的理性与情感的同时涌现。在一般人的诗作与词作中虽然也不乏表现思致的作品，但大晏与他们不同的，则是一般人所表现的思致多出于有心，而大晏则完全出于无意，譬如酌水于海，其味自咸，这和有心要泡一杯盐水的人，自然有着显著的差异。如大晏最有名的一首《浣溪沙》词之“满目山河空念远，落花风雨更伤春，不如怜取眼前人”，这三句词从表面看来，所抒写的只不过是“伤春”、“念远”的情感，丝毫也看不出有什么思致在其间。而大晏也确实未尝有心于表现什么思致，只是读这三句词的人，却自然可以感受到，它所给予读者的，除去情感上的感动外，另外还有着一种足以触发人思致的启迪，这种启迪和触发，便正是大晏的情中有思的特色之所在。即以这三句词而言，如“满目”一句，除“念远”之情外，它更使读者想到人生对一切不可获得的事物的向往之无益；“落花”一句，除“伤春”之情外，则更使人想到人生对一切不可挽回的事物的伤感之徒劳；至于“不如怜取眼前人”一句，它所使人想到的也不仅是“眼前”的一个“人”而已，而是所该珍惜把握的现在的一切。大晏在另一首《玉楼春》词中也曾有句云：“不如怜取眼前人，免使劳魂兼役梦。”由此一句之重复使用，我们更可以体认出来，大晏之所屡次提到的“眼前人”，实在只是表现了大晏的一种明决的面对现实的理性。这种种联想与体认，在读者亦并不需深思苦想而后得，而是当读者感受词句中的一份情感之时，便已同时感受到其中的一份思致了。那便因为如前文所言，这一份思致乃是由大晏对人生感受体验而得，而并非由头脑思索而得，它原即在情感之中，而并非在情感之外，所以其表现于词亦全属无心，而决非有意，因之这一份思致也就只宜于吟味和感受，而并不宜于辨察和说明。如我之所解释，自不免有牵藤附葛、坠坑落堑之嫌，不过，大晏词之易于引起读者一些有关人生的哲想，则是不可否认的事实。王国维先生在《人间词话》中，对大晏的《蝶恋花》词之“昨夜西风凋碧树，独上高楼，望尽天涯路”三句，便也曾经既许之为诗人“忧生”之词，复喻之为“古今成大事业、大学问者”之“第一境”，这两段话，本文不暇详说，我不过引来证明以哲想解说大晏词并非自我作古。而其所以易于使读者生此种联想的缘故，便正因为大晏的词有着一种情中有思的特色。这种特色，加深也加广了大晏词的意境。如果以大晏与他的儿子小山相较，那么像小山的一些名句，如“当时明月在，曾照彩云归”（《临江仙》），“今宵剩把银釭照，犹恐相逢是梦中”及“舞低杨柳楼心月，歌尽桃花扇底风”（《鹧鸪天》）诸句，虽然其“清壮顿挫，能动摇人心”（黄庭坚《小山集序》）之处，大晏自有所不及，然而如只就情中有思这一点而言，则小山词之意境，实在远较乃父为狭隘而浅薄。其原因便在于小晏所表现的悲欢今昔之感与歌酒狎邪之词，乃但为人生之一面，而其所触动者亦但为读者之感情而已；至于大晏，则其所触动者已不仅为读者之感情，而且更触动了读者有关整个人生的一种哲想，因此，大晏词乃超越了其表面所写的人生之一面，而更暗示着人生之整体。宛敏灏君在《二晏及其词》一书中，曾举大晏《憾庭秋》词之“念兰堂红烛，心长焰短，向人垂泪”三句，与小晏《破阵子》词之“绛蜡等闲陪泪”及《蝶恋花》词之“红烛自怜无好计，夜寒空替人垂泪”三句相比较，以为“向”字尚不及“陪”字之深，更不敢望“替”字矣。殊不知小晏之“陪”字、“替”字虽佳，然而其“陪”人、“替”人垂泪者，仍不过只是一支蜡烛而已，而大晏之“心长焰短，向人垂泪”二句，则使读者所感受的实在已不复仅是一支蜡烛，而同时联想到的还有心余力绌的整个的人生。虽然这在大晏也许未尝有此意，而其特色却正在使读者能生此想。故就情感言，小晏自较大晏为秾挚，然而如就思致言，则小晏实不及大晏之深广，而此种差别也正是理性的诗人与纯情的诗人的主要区别之所在。大抵纯情的诗人，对于人生只有入乎其内的真切的感受；而理性的诗人，则除感受外，更有着一份出乎其外的澄明的观照。唯其为“入”，故所失在狭；唯其能“出”，故所长在广。唯其但得之于“感受”，故其所表现者，有情而乏思，而其意境亦较浅薄；唯其能得之于“观照”，故其所表现者，情中乃更复有思，而其意境亦较深刻。除以上所举各例证外，则如大晏另一首《浣溪沙》

词之“无可奈何花落去，似曾相识燕归来”，《喜迁莺》词之“花不尽，柳无穷，应与我情同”，《少年游》词之“莫将琼萼等闲分，留赠意中人”诸作，或者表现了圆融的观照，或者表现了理性的操持。这种特色，正为大晏之所独具。欣赏大晏词，如果不能从他的情中有思的意境着眼，那真将有如入宝山空手回的遗憾了。

至于大晏词的第二点特色，我以为则该说是他所特有的一份闲雅的情调。《汉书·司马相如传》云：“相如时从车骑，雍容闲雅，甚都。”大晏的闲雅，就正有着这一份雍容富贵的风度。而这一份风度，在我国诗人的作品中，是极为罕见的。其所以罕见的缘故，当然是因为一般诗人们都未尝有过如大晏的显达的身世，因之也未曾有过如大晏的雍容闲适的生活；而有大晏之身世与生活者，则又未必有如大晏的诗人的资质。这种美具难并的机会既不多，因此大晏的闲雅的风格，乃成了他所独有的一种特美。大晏生当北宋真、仁两朝的太平盛世，自十四岁以神童应试擢秘书省正字，仕至宰相，其显达之身世，已具见史传的记载，本文对此不拟再加详述；至于大晏的诗人的资质，则可从他的词作中所表现的锐感与善感得到证明。如其《破阵子》词写少女神情之“疑怪昨宵春梦好，元是今朝斗草赢，笑从双脸生”，及《菩萨蛮》词写黄葵之“高梧叶下秋光晚，珍丛化出黄金盏”，“擎作女真冠，试伊娇面看”，这些词句都具有极鲜明的意象，也给予读者极强力的感染。这是唯有一个锐感的诗人才能具有、才能给予的。又如其《玉楼春》词之“陇头呜咽水声繁，叶上间关莺语近”，《踏莎行》词之“春风不解禁杨花，濛濛乱扑行人面”诸句，则凡耳目所及，写得万物都若有情。这更是唯有一个善感的诗人才能感受、才能抒写的。以这种锐感、善感的资质，无论其所遭之境遇之为穷为达，都无疑地该不失为一个真正的诗人，只是因境遇之影响而形成的风格或者不免将要有所不同而已。大晏的境遇是富贵显达的，因之怀着“穷而后工”的成见，想要在大晏的词中寻找孤臣孽子，落魄江湖的深悲幽怨的人，当然不免要感到失望。但大晏的诗人的资质，却毫不曾因此而减损，他的闲雅的风格，就正是他的显达的身世与他的诗人的资质所相浑融、相调剂而结成的佳果。这一类风格闲雅的作品，在他的词集中最可举为代表的是那一首《清平乐》，现在把这一首词抄在后面：

金风细细，叶叶梧桐坠。绿酒初尝人易醉，一枕小窗浓睡。紫薇朱槿花残，斜阳却照阑干。双燕欲归时节，银屏昨夜微寒。

在这一首词中，我们既找不到我国诗人所一贯共有的伤离怨别、叹老悲穷的感伤，甚至也找不到前面第一点所谈到的大晏所特有的情中有思的思致。在这一首词中，它所表现的，只是在闲适的生活中的一种优美而纤细的诗人的感觉。对于这种词，我们不当以“情”求，也不当以“意”想，而只当单纯地去体会那一份美而纯的诗感。语有之云：“无用之为用大矣。”想在诗歌中寻找情感和意义的人，在大晏这种闲雅的作品中，自将无所收获。然而譬之醇醪甘醴，饮之者原不必要求得解渴之功用，更不可抱有解饥之目的。醇醪甘醴的好处，原只在它所给予人的一股甘美芳醇的味道，同样地，大晏的此种作品，其佳处亦仅只在于它所给人的一种闲静优美诗意的感觉而已。

大晏词的第三点特色，我以为该说是他的词中所表现的伤感中的旷达的怀抱。陆机《文赋》云：“遵四时以叹逝，瞻万物而思纷。”对于任何一个人来说，当“日月逝于上，体貌衰于下”的时候，都或多或少免不了会产生时移事去、乐往哀来的伤感，更何况是一个锐感善感的诗人，所以诗人们都或多或少有些伤感的作品。大晏对此当然也并不能例外。虽然宛敏灏君曾经以为大晏的一些伤感之作只是“无病呻吟”，但我却并不这样想，因为伤感之产生，原不必定要有什么人事上的剧变大故，而仅只自然界的盛衰代序便已足可令人体会到无常的可悲了，而无常对人类的威胁，则又是无分穷达与贵贱的，因之诗人对无常的威胁所感受的深浅，实在并不在其身世之穷达，而只在其感觉之锐钝。大晏正是一个锐感的诗人，所以他的身世虽达，而他在词中所流露的一份“无常”的伤感，却是与其他不达的诗人同样真实也同样深切的。只是诗人之伤感虽同，而其伤感的情调则不尽同，即以与大晏的作风最相近的冯、欧两家来与之相较，其间也颇有不同之处。我以为在正中的伤感中，有着执著的热情；在六一的伤感中，有着豪宕的意兴；而在大晏的伤感中，所有的则是一种旷达的怀抱。我们现在试举大晏的几首词来看：

> 时光只解催人老，不信多情。长恨离亭。滴泪春衫酒易醒。梧桐昨夜西风急，淡月胧明。好梦频惊。何处高楼雁一声。（《采桑子》）

> 秋露坠。滴尽楚兰红泪。往事旧欢何限意。思量如梦寐。　人貌老于前岁。风月宛然无异。座有嘉宾樽有桂。莫辞终夕醉。（《谒金门》）

> 湖上西风斜日，荷花落尽红英。金菊满丛珠颗细，海燕辞巢翅羽轻。年年岁岁情。　美酒一杯新熟，高歌数阕堪听。不向尊前同一醉，可奈光阴似水声。迢迢去未停。（《破阵子》）

在这几首词中，《采桑子》的“时光只解催人老”，“滴泪春衫酒易醒”与《谒金门》的“往事旧欢何限意，思量如梦寐”，这几句所表现的自然都是伤感之情，然而《采桑子》的末一句“何处高楼雁一声”，却结得如此其超脱高远，《谒金门》的末二句“座有嘉宾樽有桂，莫辞终夕醉”，则又结得如此其通达放旷。至于《破阵子》一词之“湖上西风斜日，荷花落尽红英”，与“可奈光阴似水声，迢迢去未停”，所表现的自然更是极真切的无常的哀感，然而大晏却偏偏在中间加上了“美酒一杯新熟，高歌数阕堪听”的慰安。由这些词句，我们可以看出大晏在现实的无常的悲苦中，虽然也不免于伤感，然而他却既有着安于现实的达观，也有着面对现实的勇气。若以之与冯、欧二家相比，则正中所表现的执著，如其“一晌凭阑人不见，鲛绡掩泪思量遍”，“日日花前常病酒，不辞镜里朱颜瘦”（《鹊踏枝》）诸句，对悲苦的现实只不过有执著的热情；六一所表现的豪宕，如其“尊前百计得春归，莫为伤春眉黛蹙”，“直须看尽洛城花，始共春风容易别”(《玉楼春》）诸句，对悲苦的现实只不过有遣玩的意兴；而大晏在旷达的情怀中，却隐然有着处置的办法。这一种伤感中的旷达的怀抱，是大晏这一位理性诗人的性格与修养的最好表现。所以大晏的伤感，在他的词作中，既没有形成凄厉之音，也没有发为决绝之词。伤感，在他的《珠玉词》中，只是给那些温润的珠玉染上了一种淡淡的凄清的情调。这一份凄清的情调，使得他的温润的珠玉更加了一份纤柔婉秀，因而教人看了也更加觉得眩目怜心。这正是《珠玉词》的风格上的又一种特美。

至于大晏词第四点特色，则是昭昭在人耳目尽人皆知的两种好处，这就是写富贵而不鄙俗，写艳情而不纤佻。关于这两种好处，前人述及之者甚多，我现在随便摘录两条作为佐证：

> 晏元献公虽起田里，而文章富贵，出于天然。尝览李庆孙《富贵曲》云：“轴装曲谱金书字，树记花名玉篆牌”，公曰：“此乃乞儿相，未尝谙富贵者，故余每吟咏富贵，不言金玉锦绣，而惟说其气象。若‘楼台侧畔杨花过，帘幕中间燕子飞’，‘梨花院落溶溶月，柳絮池塘淡淡风’之类是也。”故公自以此句语人曰：“穷儿家有这景致也无？”(吴处厚《青箱杂记》)
>
> 柳三变既以词忤仁庙，吏部不放改官。三变不能堪，诣政府。晏公曰：“贤俊作曲子么？”三变曰：“只如相公亦作曲子。”公曰：“殊虽作曲子，不曾（一作会）道‘彩线慵拈伴伊坐’。”柳遂退。（张舜民《画墁录》)

以上两则，分别说明了大晏不鄙俗和不纤佻的两种好处。这两种好处虽是截然不同的两件事，但我以为它们却是出于一个共同的原因，那就是写其精神而不写其形迹。一般说来，人们对事物感受的态度，约可分为两种：一种是以感官去感受的；而另一种则是以心灵去感受的。以感官去感受的人，所得的大多是事物的形体迹象；而以心灵去感受的人，则所得的大多是事物的气象神情。即以富贵而言，譬如现在有两个人，一同进入了金张之第，则以感官去感受的一个人，其所见者乃但为金玉锦绣诸富贵之物质，而以心灵去感受的一个人，则其所见者乃为博大高华的富贵之气象。又如以艳情而言，方二人携手并肩之际，以感官去感受的一人，则其所感者但为相携相并之双手与双肩，而以心灵去感受的一人，则其所感受者，实在已不复是身体上的相并相携，而乃是精神上的深合密契。也许那一种气象上的博大高华之感，也是经由物质上的金玉锦绣而来，而那一种精神上的深合密契之感，也是经由形体上的相并相携而得，只是对于以心灵去感受的人而言，那些感官上的感受，实在只是一些无足轻重的接触的媒介而已。所谓“得意忘言，得鱼忘筌”，既然已经得到了心灵上的感受，则那些感官上的物质与形体，便已被遗忘而不复存在了。这其间的取舍，丝毫没有勉强与造作，而纯出于自然。大晏之不用金玉之字，不为纤佻之语，那正因为大晏的天性是近于后者的缘故。现在我们试举他一些写富贵与写艳情的词作为例。写富贵者，如其《浣溪沙》之“小阁重簾有燕过，晚花红片落庭莎，曲栏干影入凉波”，《踏莎行》之“翠叶藏莺，朱帘隔燕，炉香静逐游丝转”，《玉楼春》之“朱簾半下香销印，二月东风催柳信，琵琶旁畔且寻思，鹦鹉前头休借问”，这些词句，皆所谓不言金玉而自有富贵气象者，正如《能改斋漫录》所载晁无咎云：“知此人不住三家村也。”至于写艳情者，如其《诉衷情》之“此情拚作，千尺游丝，惹住朝云”，《踏莎行》之“樽中绿醑意中人，花朝月夜长相见”，《破阵子》之“多少襟怀言不尽，写向蛮笺曲调中，此情千万重”，若以这些词句与柳永《定风波》之“彩线慵拈伴伊坐”，《菊花新》之“欲掩香帏论缱绻”诸作相较，则大晏正所谓“虽作艳语，终有品格”，因为大晏所唤起人的只是一份深挚的情意，而此一份情意虽然或者乃因儿女之情而发，然而却并不为儿女之情所限，较之一些言外无物的浅露淫亵之作，自然有高下、雅鄙的分别。而其形成此一差别的缘故，则正是因为一者是写其心灵上的感受，而一者则是写其感官上的感受。所以大晏之不屑于琐琐记金玉锦绣，喋喋叙狎昵温柔，大部分该是由于他的天性使然，至于他的富贵显达的身世和环境，当然也有着颇大的影响，但如果以为他之写艳情而不纤佻，乃是如宛敏灏君所说的，只是由于“观瞻所系”的有心的规避，那就未免浅之乎视大晏了。

除以上四点特色外，我还想作两点补充的说明。其一是《珠玉词》中有一部分祝颂之词，这是最为不满大晏的人所据为口实，而对之加以诋毁的。祝颂之词之易流于俗恶，自是不可讳言的事实。大晏位居台阁，应制唱酬之间当然免不了有一些祝颂之作。这些词在《珠玉词》中自非佳作。然而我却以为若以大晏之此类作品，与其他一般人的祝颂之作相较，则大晏仍有他的可喜之处。如前文所言，大晏所写之事物及情感，多以气象神情为主，而不沾滞于形迹，所以大晏所写的祝颂之词，也绝没有明言专指的浅俗卑下之言。他只是平淡然而却诚挚地写他个人的一份祝愿，且多以大自然界之景物为陪衬，而大晏对自然界之景物又自有其一份诗人之感觉，所以大晏所写的祝颂之词，不但闲雅富丽，而且更有着一份清新之致。如其祝寿词之《蝶恋花》：“紫菊初生朱槿坠。月好风清，渐有中秋意。更漏乍长天似水，银屏展尽遥山翠。　绣幕卷波香引穗。急管繁弦，共庆人间瑞。满酌玉杯萦舞袂，南春祝寿千千岁。”又如其歌颂天子之《拂霓裳》：“笑秋天，晚荷花缀露珠圆。风日好，数行新雁贴寒烟。银簧调脆管，琼柱拨清弦，捧觥船，一声声、齐唱太平年。”这些词虽然并没有什么深远的含意，然而在感觉与情致方面也并非全无可取之处。何况在人之一生中有些欢乐美好的日子和生活，原也是值得歌颂的，我们又何可一概诋之为俗恶。这是我对大晏词要补充说明的第一点。

至于另一点我要补充说明的，则是在《珠玉词》中有一首风格颇为例外的作品，那就是大晏题为《赠歌者》的一首《山亭柳》词。现在把这首词抄在后面：

> 家住西秦。赌博艺随身。花柳上，斗尖新。偶学念奴声调，有时高遏行云。蜀锦缠头无数，不负辛勤。　　数年来往咸京道，残杯冷炙谩消魂。衷肠事，托何人。若有知音见采，不辞遍唱阳春。一曲当筵落泪，重掩罗巾。

大晏词的风格，一向都表现得圆融平静，而这首词却偏偏写得声情激越、感慨悲凉；大晏词一向都不曾加冠标题，而这首词却偏偏有个《赠歌者》的题目。这两种例外的情形，同时发生于一首词之上，这是颇可玩味的一件事。要想解答此一问题，我想我们该对大晏的性格和生平有更进一步的认识。大晏在词作中所表现的闲雅的风格和旷达的怀抱，确实显示出了他的一份理性的修养——平静而有操持。然而在史传中，对他的性格却也有着另一面的记载。《宋史·晏殊传》云："殊性刚简……累典州，吏民颇畏其悁急。"又欧阳修之晏殊的神道碑序亦云："公为人刚简。"而《四库提要》评其《珠玉词》则云："殊赋性刚峻，而词语特婉丽。"大晏确实有着理性的操持，这是不错的；大晏也确实有着刚峻的个性，这也是不错的。而他在词中所表现的婉丽，就正是他的刚峻的个性透过了理性的操持所达到的一种矛盾的统一、复杂的调合的境界。所以他的词有澄明之美，而无单调之失，有圆融之美，而无颟顸之病，正如日光七色之融为一白。这正是大晏词的一贯的风格。惟是日光若经折射，则仍可见其七彩的本色；同样的，大晏在遇到拂逆挫折时，也往往会表现出他的另一面的刚峻的性格，而且极为激动。如《宋史·晏殊传》载其为枢密副使时，曾"上疏论张耆不可为枢密使，忤太后旨。坐从幸玉清昭应宫，从者持笏后至，殊怒，以笏撞之，折齿，御史弹奏，罢知宣州"。又《画墁录》云："张（先）议事府中，再三未答，晏公作色，操楚语曰：'本为辟贤，会贤会道"无物似情浓"，今日却来此事公事。'"我们对大晏这一面刚峻激动的性格有了认识后，再来看这一首《山亭柳》

词，就会觉得这首词中所表现的感慨激越，不但并非例外，而且正是必然的意中之事。这首词虽然题名为《赠歌者》，然而郑骞《词选》却认为它乃是“借他人酒杯，浇胸中块垒”之作，又说：“此词云‘西秦’、‘咸京’，当是知永兴军时作，时同叔年逾六十，去国已久，难免抑郁。”这是一段极有见地的话。大晏自十四岁以神童擢秘书省正字，至五十四岁罢相以前，在仕途上都可说是顺利而且得意的。但自五十四岁罢相后，则出知外郡将近十年之久，而以永兴为最远。又据《宋史·晏殊传》云其罢相乃由于“孙甫、蔡襄上言：‘宸妃生圣躬为天下主，而殊尝被诏誌宸妃墓，没而不言。’又奏论殊役官兵治僦舍以规利。坐是，降工部尚书、知颍州。然殊以章献太后方临朝，故誌不敢斥言；而所役兵，乃辅臣例宣借者，时以谓非殊罪。”是晏殊既以非其罪的罪名被罢相，又出知外郡既久，这种种拂逆挫折，使他在词作中露出了刚劲激动的另一面性格，原该是极自然的一件事。只是这一首《山亭柳》词，还有另一点值得我们注意的地方，那就是它的题目是《赠歌者》。从大晏晚年的遭遇与这首词中所表现的感情来看，谓为浇自己胸中块垒之作，当是无可置疑的事，只是为什么他一定要借他人之酒杯，找一个《赠歌者》的题目呢？关于这一点，我以为则该是仍然由大晏一贯的理性的修养所使然。王国维《人间词话》云：“尼采谓一切文学余爱以血书者。”同样是滴满鲜血的作品，有些人则喜欢将自己血淋淋的伤口显示给别人看；但有些人则不然，他们宁愿将自己的伤口隐藏起来，而把他们所滴的鲜血、所受的伤害，都只藉着一件不相干的故事，做间接的叙述，这正是作为一个理性的诗人的特色。他们常想保有一份感情上的余裕，因此，大晏也藉《赠歌者》的题目，先把感情的距离推远了，然后才能无所顾忌地将他的感慨抑郁藉着别人的故事而发泄出来。同时我还以为这首词的题目并不是由臆想加上去的，而该是确有一位歌者，而此歌者之身世，则曾唤起了大晏的深切的共鸣，于是郁积已久的情怀乃因之一泄而出。这种机会正是可遇而不可求的，因此，我们在大晏其他的词作中，并不容易看到这一种感慨激越的情调，这正因为大晏不容易遇到这样可以借端发挥的好题目的缘故。而毫无假借地揭露自己的创口，则又是大晏所断乎不肯做的。明乎此，我们就可以知道，这首风格例外的作品，不但不能使大晏的理性的诗人的基础动摇，而且反更多了一层有力的证明。这是我所要补充说明的第二点。

最后我想模仿王国维先生引词人自己的词句评词的办法，为此文作一结束。大晏的词，圆融平静之中别有凄清之致，有春日之和婉，有秋日之明澈，而意象复极鲜明真切，这使我想起了大晏《少年游》的几句词，因仿王国维先生之言曰：“霜前月下，斜红淡蕊，明媚欲回春”[①]，同叔语也，其词品似之。

① 按此三句词，见晏殊《少年游》词“重阳过后”一首。

An Appreciation of the 'Ci' of Yan Shu

The judgment of a work of literature is to some extent a subjective matter, much as an individual's enjoyment of food depends on his own palate and experience; tastes notoriously differ, and there is no need to insist that everyone share one's own preferences. But, like the old peasant who recommended the flavor of fresh celery and the warmth of the spring sun on the back to the Emperor, I will pass on my honest opinion about the value of Yan Shu's songs.

Among song writers at the beginning of the Northern Song, Yan Shu (991-1055), his son Yan Jidao, and Ouyang Xiu are commonly mentioned together. Most readers consider Yan Jidao the best of the three, fewer would choose Ouyang Xiu, while Yan Shu has the fewest admirers. There are two reasons why Yan Shu's songs are not easily appreciated: first, his style is smooth and unruffled: there is no strong emotion, no striking language—neither colors to dazzle nor vigor to impress. His songs are like the title under which they are collected, "Pearls and Jade" (*Zhu yu ci*), smooth and polished as jade and pearls; they may be pure and refined and crystalline, but in the eyes of most readers they are not so splendid or interesting as a multi-colored piece of jasper.

Another impediment to the appreciation of Yan Shu's songs is the fact that he was highly successful in his public career. Many people feel that great poetry can only be written by a poet who has experienced hardship and poverty, and Yan Shu fails to fulfill their expectations. In Wan Minhao's book on the *ci* of Yan Shu and Yan Jidao, Yan Shu's songs are dismissed as the groans of a rich man who has nothing wrong with him.[1] Mr. Wan's study is a thorough one, and while he is unstinting in his praise of the son, he finds little to appreciate in the father. As Jiang Ruoliu once remarked in another context,[2] to be overlooked by someone who is not looking for you is nothing to complain of, but to be rejected after careful scrutiny is truly distressing. Mr. Wan's remark makes me sigh at Yan Shu's misfortune in being so fortunate.

To appreciate Yan Shu's songs one must first of all recognize that he is an intellectual poet, a rational poet. It is not necessarily true that "poetry is incompatible with success in life"[3] or that "talent and luck do not go together",[4] but a man's character does have something to do with shaping his career, and we can divide poets into two large groups: those who were successful in their extra-poetic lives and those who failed. In terms of temperament, among the successful will be found the rational, intellectual poets, while the failures will include the poets of pure feeling. Wang Guowei said of Li Yu, "He was a poet who never lost his child-heart. That he was born in the seclusion of the palace and raised by women was a handicap to him as the ruler of the state, but it was his great advantage as a poet.... The subjective poet needs no wide experience of the world. The less his experience, the more genuine his own nature."[5] This is certainly true of the poet of pure feeling. The emotions of such a poet are like the unimpeded flow of water. He reacts emotionally to circumstances, unreflecting, without control or afterthought, uncritically. Of such poets it is not enough to say that they never lost their child-heart; in the world of practical affairs they simply remain children. Li Yu is an excellent example, and "Kingdom ruined, family finished" is the classic end of this kind of poet. "Heaven takes a hundred disasters to make one poet"—for poets like this the disasters that are his lot and the pure feeling of his poetry are but two sides of the same coin.

It is otherwise with the intellectual poet. His emotions are more like a placid pool than flowing water: the wind may raise thousands of ripples; cast a stone in and it will sink in a little whirlpool, but nothing will make it lose its essential stillness, its limpid beauty. The intellectual poet is always reflecting on his experience, trying to understand it, or examining his own feelings and keeping them under control. He has developed an adult's standards of behavior while preserving a poet's sensitivity. Yan Shu is representative of this kind of poet.

When the Emperor Renzong (1023-1063) came to the throne as a child of thirteen, the government was left in the hands of his adoptive mother, the Empress Zhangxian. The Minister Ding Wei and the Commissioner of Military Affairs Cao Liyong both wanted exclusive access to the Empress to present their memorials. The situation called for tact and a thorough grasp of the intricacies of court politics. When no one ventured to decide the matter, Yan Shu proposed that the Empress listen to all memorials from behind a screen, so that no one would get to see her individually.[6]

On another occasion he had to deal with a military crisis. The Xixia under the leadership of Yuan Hao (Li Nangxiao) were making incursions along the Shanxi border. Yan Shu requested that the generals be allowed to operate without interference by the Palace Commissars and that tactics not be prescribed from the court, so they would be free to respond to the movements of the enemy. He proposed that bowmen be conscripted and trained, that palace luxuries be curtailed to aid those defending the borders, and that other government agencies apply directly to the treasury for all their income.[7]

These proposals show Yan Shu to have had a clear, incisive mind and a good grasp of the situation. The measures he proposed were those of a statesman and a general—certainly he was not just a ladies' man, nor was he a child with no experience of the world. Yet his songs show a real poetic talent. Practical accomplishments did not keep him from writing good poetry, nor was the value of his poetry diminished by the fact that he was successful and well-off.

Some may object to the label "intellectual" or "rational" for a poet, since poetry is supposed to rouse feeling, and feeling is diametrically opposed to intellect. This may be true if you think of intellect as the rationally calculating part of the mind, when it stands as the antithesis of feeling. But this is not a poet's rationality. For the poet, reason serves only as a restraint exercised over feeling, a controlling force that both refines and enhances feeling. It is not a matter of ratiocination, but of education and experience of life. Far from being antithetical to feeling, it is in fact steeped in feeling; the two are perfectly compatible, indistinguishable even as they arise simultaneously in the heart. Poetry may well be an emotional creation, but a poet may be a rational, intellectual writer.

Yan Shu's songs, as the product of an intellectual poet, have several characteristic features. The first is feeling that holds a thought. It is a mixture of two perfectly blended elements. Although there is no lack of poems and songs by other writers that convey an idea, what is different is that theirs give the impression that it was done deliberately, whereas his songs seem to achieve it quite unconsciously. A cup of water from the sea is salty without any intervention; or you can make a cup of salt water by adding salt to fresh water. In Yan Shu's songs the reader is not confronted with an Idea, something the poet holds up for his consideration and approval. For instance, the lines in his famous song to the tune *Huan xi sha* (Sands of the Washing Stream) (No. 17, p. 90):[8]

Hills and rivers fill the eyes: vain to think of what is far away.	满目山河空念远
When flowers fall in wind and rain we grieve the more for spring—	落花风雨更伤春
Best love the one that's here right now.	不如怜取眼前人

On the surface, these lines express an emotional response to the passing of spring in a place far from home, with no intellectual content whatsoever; it seems certain that Yan Shu was not consciously trying to express a thought. But the reader gets something in addition to the feeling, a stimulus or an invitation to a thought. In the first line, besides the emotion roused by "vain to think of what is far away", the words lead the reader to reflect on the things in life that lie out of reach and which we long for in vain. The second line stirs feelings of regret at the passing of spring and at the same time invites us to think of all loveliness as irrevocably gone. And the last line makes us think not only of "the one that's here right now", but of the precious fleeting moment we should cling to. Yan Shu uses the same line in another song to the tune *Mu lan hua* (Magnolia Flower) (No. 56, p. 95):

Best love the one that's here right now	不如怜取眼前人
And not ask too much of your soul in dreams.[9]	免使劳魂兼役梦

We can take the repeated line "the one that's here right now" (*yan qian ren,* "the person before your eyes") as representing Yan Shu's awareness of the necessity of facing reality.

Associations and inferences of this sort demand no profound reflection. The reader is aware of the implication at the same time he is moved by the emotional content of the poem. As suggested earlier, this intellectual content derives from Yan Shu's experience of life: it is not produced deliberately by reflective thought but originates in the emotions and is not merely tacked on. It follows that this intellectual content can appropriately only be felt and savored. It does not really lend itself to analysis and elucidation. My sort of exegesis is open to the objection that it is forced and trumped up, but Yan Shu's *ci* undeniably do suggest reflections about the human condition. Wang Guowei, for instance,[10] remarked that the poet showed weariness of life in the lines, from the song *Que ta zhi* (Magpie Treads the Branch) (No. 23, p. 91):

Last night the west wind withered the green trees.	昨夜西风凋碧树
Alone I climb the high stairs	独上高楼
And gaze down the world's-end road.	望尽天涯路

Of the same passage he said elsewhere,[11] "This is the first experience of one who has done great things, who is greatly learned." I shall not stop to elucidate Wang Guowei's comment here,[12] having quoted it only to show that I am not the first to find an element of philosophy in Yan Shu's *ci*. That his songs owe their characteristic depth and significance to this factor is apparent when we compare them with those written by his son Yan Jidao, who surpasses him certainly in the qualities praised by Huang Tingjian:[13] "refined strength of phrasing" that "agitates the heart", as in the lines:

The moon of that night is there still	当时明月在
Which once shone on the Bright Cloud going home.	曾照彩云归

To the tune *Lin jiang xian*
(Immortal by the River), No. 7, p. 222

Tonight I keep shining the silver lamp on her	今宵剩把银钎照
Fearful lest this encounter might be a dream.	犹恐相逢是梦中

To the tune *Zhegu tian*
(Partridge in the Sky), No. 24, p. 225

We danced the moon down from the peak of the willow house 舞低杨柳楼心月
And sang the air to the end under the peach blossom fan. 歌尽桃花扇底风

(Ibid.)

But the son's verse is both narrower and shallower, lacking the intellectual component found in Yan Shu. For Yan Jidao's songs are preoccupied with "song, wine, and dalliance", "grief and joy, then and now"; they present only one aspect of human life, and appeal only to the reader's feelings. It is because Yan Shu's songs involve the reader's whole philosophy of life that they go beyond the limits of a given situation and suggest the entire human predicament.

Wan Minhao argued that Yan Jidao had a better command of diction than Yan Shu, quoting these lines in support of his view, first by Yan Shu:

I remember the red candle in Orchid Hall 念兰堂红烛
The heart was long, the flame short 心长焰短
Shedding tears for someone. 向人垂泪

To the tune *Han ting qiu*
(It Shakes the Courtyard in Autumn), No. 48, p. 94

and by Yan Jidao:

The crimson candle joins me in idle tears 绛蜡等闲陪泪

To the tune *Po zhen zi*
(Break the Ranks), No. 173, p. 246

The red candle is sorry but has nothing to suggest 红烛自怜无好计
And through the cold night drips futile tears for me. 夜寒空替人垂泪

To the tune *Die lian hua*

(Butterfly Loves Flowers), No. 15, p. 224

He claims that the word *xiang* (in *xiang ren* "for someone") is less effective than *pei* (in *pei lei*, lit., "accompanies my tears"), and especially is weaker than *ti* (in *ti ren* "for me"). That is all very well as far as these two words are concerned, but it overlooks the fact that in Yan Jidao's poems, what sheds tears is nothing more than a candle, while the figurative language of Yan Shu's "The heart was long, the flame short" leads the reader by a process of association from the burning candle to human life, where "the heart is ready for more, but the strength is lacking". Yan Shu may have had no intention of arousing such an association, yet it is the peculiar characteristic of his to make such reverberations accessible to his reader. So we may grant Yan Jidao the greater emotional content, while insisting that Yan Shu is a more profound, more intellectual poet.

Precisely here lies the difference between the poet of feeling and the poet of intellect: one responds passively to life, registering experience as pure feeling; the other does not simply experience reality, but contributes a ray of understanding to his experience. The response of the former suffers from its narrowness, whereas the latter has the advantage of breadth. Where the response is purely emotional, the poetry conveys feeling but lacks thought, making it superficial; the one who can illuminate his subject will combine thought with feeling and achieve greater depth. Consider these lines by Yan Shu:

The flowers will fall for all you can do　　无可奈何花落去
And the swallows that look familiar return.　　似曾相识燕归来

To the tune *Huan xi sha*

(Sands of the Washing Stream), No. 9, p. 89

The flowers don't give out　　花不尽

The willow lasts forever— 柳无穷
They should be just like my feelings. 应与我情同

To the tune *Xi qian ying*
(The Oriole Flies for Joy), No. 45, p. 94

In both passages observing seasonal change is not simply an occasion for emotional response. The poet perceives a pattern, a contrast or a repetition, that provides a rational basis for the emotion. Or the following lines, which suggest rational control of the feelings:

Don't share these carnelian blossoms casually, 莫将琼萼等闲分
Keep them for the one you love. 留赠意中人

To the tune *Shao nian you*
(Youthful Diversions), No. 49, p. 94

It is this combination of feeling and idea that is Yan Shu's trademark, and a reader must recognize it to truly appreciate his poetry. Otherwise, you will find no treasure in his "Pearls and Jade".

Another quality of Yan Shu's poetry is a certain quiet elegance of tone, the sort of aristocratic bearing the provincials admired in Sima Xiangru's demeanor. It is something that seldom finds expression in Chinese poetry, chiefly, no doubt, because few poets lived the life of refined luxury that Yan Shu enjoyed, and men who did live such a life lacked his talent for poetry. Yan Shu lived under the peaceful reigns of Zhenzong (998-1022) and Renzong. The chronicle of his promotions, from the time he passed his examinations as a child prodigy of fourteen and received the post of Collator in the Chancellery until he became Prime Minister thirty years later, is recorded in his biography and does not need to be reviewed here. His songs attest to the sensitivity and insight of his poetic talent. He portrays a girl's psychology:

You might suspect she had a nice spring dream last night,	疑怪昨宵春梦好
But it was winning the flower competition this morning	元是今朝斗草赢
That spread the smile on her cheeks.	笑从双脸生

To the tune *Po zhen zi*
(Break the Ranks), No. 135, p. 108

or apprehends the yellow hollyhock:

The autumn scene is late under the phoenix tree leaves—	高梧叶下秋光晚
The rare plant transformed into golden cups.	珍丛画出黄金盏

To the tune *Pusa man*
(Bodhisattva Barbarian), No. 117, p. 105

You can pick a blossom for a golden wine-cup	摘承金盏酒
When you wish me a long long life,	劝我千长寿
Or I can hold it up as a Taoist nun's cap	擎作女真冠
And try it on you to see how pretty you look	试伊娇面看

To the tune *Pusa man*
(Bodhisattva Barbarian), No. 116, p. 105

There is a fresh vision in these lines that conveys something of the poet's delight in the flower (and the occasion), a sensitive perception effectively translated into a verse.

Yan Shu has an ear and an eye for nature and can write as though it were capable of human feeling:

From the Longtou the water voices gurgle	垄头呜咽水声繁
Behind the leaves soon the orioles will be chattering.	叶下间关莺语近

To the tune *Mu lan hua*
(Magnolia Flower), No. 64, p. 96

The spring breeze has not learned to keep the willow fluff	春风不解禁杨花
From pelting the pedestrians in the face.	蒙蒙乱扑行人面

To the tune *Ta suo xing*
(Treading on the Sedge), No. 82, p. 99

Anyone with such sensitivity and insight is a poet, whether a failure or success in everyday life, though his experience of life will naturally affect the tone and style of his poetry. Yan Shu enjoyed a successful career, and there are no themes of banishment and frustrated ambition in his songs. If you are committed to the belief that to be a poet one must first be a failure, you will be disappointed at not finding such themes in his poetry, but their absence does not diminish his poetic endowments. The quiet elegance of his poetry is the product of his experience and temperament. It is best illustrated by a song to the tune *Qingping yue* (Qingping Music) (No. 32, p. 92):

The autumn wind stirs	金风细细
And one by one the leaves fall from the phoenix tree.	叶叶梧桐坠
It's easy to get drunk on green wine	绿酒初尝人易醉
And nap soundly by the little window.	一枕小窗浓睡
Blue myrtle and Rose of Sharon both are faded	紫薇朱槿花残
The setting sun shines on the railing	斜阳却照阑干
The pair of swallows are ready to leave.	双燕欲归时节
There was a bit chill last night inside the silver screen.	银屏昨夜微寒

We look in vain here for the usual stereotypes of Chinese poetry—sorrow in parting or grief at separation, lament on growing old and complaint about poverty—nor is there the effect peculiar to Yan Shu of an idea conveyed through feeling. All we have is a poet's subtle aesthetic perceptions. In poetry of this sort we should seek neither emotion nor idea, but attempt only to savor the unadulterated poetic impulse. As Zhuangzi put it, "Great is the usefulness of the useless!" Poetry is like a vintage wine: you do not drink it to quench your thirst. The excellence of a poem like this is the aesthetic experience itself.

The third characteristic of Yan Shu's songs could be described as an embracing perspective. Lu Ji said of the poet,[14] "He sighs at the passing of the seasons, and is pensive as he regards the complexity of Nature." Everyone to some degree feels the approach of old age when he is made aware of the flight of time, of the evanescence of happiness, of the decline in human affairs, and the poet is more responsive than most of us. The poet also puts his feelings into verse. Where Wan Minhao dismissed Yan Shu's poems of feeling as "moaning when he was not sick", I would understand them differently. What moves one emotionally need not be some great human tragedy; even the natural sequence of flourishing and decay will suffice to make one feel the sadness of impermanence. And in human terms, the threat of transience makes no distinction between the rich and the poor, the success and the failure. Likewise the intensity of the poet's reaction to that threat has nothing to do with his station in life but depends on his sensitivity. Yan Shu's response can be every bit as intense as that of a poet who did not enjoy his privileged position in society. Poets may react similarly, but the tone of their reaction will vary. If you compare Yan Shu's songs with those of Feng Yansi and Ouyang Xiu, the two poets most nearly like him in style, the difference is apparent. Feng Yansi responds to grief with stoical resolution, Ouyang Xiu is exuberant and refuses to be depressed by it, and Yan Shu brings a broad view that puts the unhappiness in perspective.

Let us take a look at a few songs by Yan Shu.

To the tune *Cai sang zi* (Picking Mulberry leaves) (No. 41, p. 93):

All that spring is good for is to make us old.	时光只解催人老
I don't think I'm so very sensitive,	不信多情
But still I always grieve at the parting place	长恨离亭
When tears fall on the spring gown and wine has no effect.	滴泪春衫酒易醒
Last night the west wind was sharp in the phoenix tree,	梧桐昨夜西风急
The pale moon shone clear.	淡月胧明
I kept waking up from a dream of her:	好梦频惊
Above a tall building somewhere, the call of a wild goose.	何处高楼雁一声

To the tune *Ye jin men* (Visiting the Golden Gate) (No. 1, p. 87):

Autumn dew falls	秋露坠
Dripping out the red tears of the southern orchid.	滴尽楚兰红泪
Past affairs, the old joys—	往事旧欢何限意
All like a dream.	思量如梦寐
One's face has aged since last year	人貌老于前岁
But breeze and moonlight are just as they were.	风月宛然无异
A guest at the table, cinnamon wine in the glass	座有嘉宾樽有桂
We must not fail to get drunk tonight.	莫辞终夕醉

To the tune *Po zhen zi* (Break the Ranks) (No. 5, p. 88):

On the lake the west wind and slanting sun	湖上西风斜日

The lotus have dropped all their pink petals.	荷花落尽红英
Tiny pearl-buds in the bed of golden chrysanthemum.	金菊满丛珠颗细
The sea swallow leaves its nest on light wings—	海燕辞巢翅羽轻
Every year, the same feelings.	年年岁岁情
A cup of the new wine.	美酒一杯新熟
A few stanzas of a wild song to listen to.	高歌数阕堪听
If we don't get drunk together on this bottle,	不向尊前同一醉
Whatever shall we do about time like water	可奈光阴似水声
Slipping off into the distance without stopping?	迢迢去未停

Some of these lines ("All that spring is good for is to make us old," "When tears fall on the spring gown and wine has no effect," "Past affairs, the old joys—/ All like a dream") express feeling. Others invoke something high and far-off ("Above a tall building somewhere, the call of a wild goose") or invite uninhibited abandonment ("A guest at the table, cinnamon wine in the glass, / We must not fail to get drunk tonight"). On the other hand, there are lines that show acute sensitivity to the transience of things:

> On the lake the west wind and slanting sun
> The lotus have dropped all their pink petals.
>
> Whatever shall we do about time like water
> Slipping off into the distance without stopping?

But the sadness is tempered by "A cup of the new wine, / A few stanzas of a wild song to listen to." Yan Shu was sensitive to the fact of impermanence, but he had the courage to face reality and accept it.

In contrast, Feng Yansi's attitude toward suffering was simply to bear it with fortitude.

For long she leans on the rail, but he does not appear. 一晌凭阑人不见
With a bit of silk she wipes her tears, and keeps on thinking. 鲛绡掩泪思量遍

To the tune *Que ta zhi*
(Magpie Treads the Branch), No. 1, p. 234[15]

Watching the flowers every day, I drink too much; 日日花前常病酒
It's all the same to me the mirrored face is thin. 不辞镜里朱颜瘦

(same tune), No. 2, p. 234

Ouyang Xiu's unconcern in the face of painful reality is only playful high spirits:

After all your drinking and scheming you've got spring back— 尊前百计得春归
Don't knit your brows now lamenting spring. 莫为伤春眉黛蹙

To the tune *Yu lou chun*
(Spring in the Jade Mansion), No. 86, p. 134

Watch until all of Luoyang's blossoms fall, 直须看尽洛城花
Then you can easily bid spring farewell. 始共春风容易别

(same tune), No. 75, p.132

Yan Shu's broad perspective gives him a way of coping; his songs are a perfect demonstration of the character and self-discipline of an intellectual poet. There are no shrill cries, no despair. Emotion in the *Zhu yu ci* is only a delicate shading on the smooth surface of pearls and jade, a nuance of color that adds a special beauty.

The fourth characteristic of Yan Shu's songs is his ability to describe luxury without being vulgar and write about love affairs without seeming either coarse or frivolous. Critics have frequently remarked on these qualities. For example, Wu Chuhou (late 11th century) wrote,[16]

> Although His Excellency Yan Yuanxian [Yan Shu] came from the country, he was a natural aristocrat in letters. On reading the lines in Li Qingsun's "Song of the Rich Man":
>
> Fine bound songbooks written in letters of gold
> Trees and flowers named on plaques of jade,
>
> he commented, "This is the beggar's view, someone with no firsthand knowledge of upper class life. When I write on such subjects, I never directly mention gold or jade, brocade or embroidery. I just speak of their effects. For instance,
>
> On the path by the pavilion the willow flowers are past,
> Between the curtains the swallows fly.[17]
>
> In the pear blossom park the spreading moonlight
> Across the willow-fluff pond the flowing wind[18]
>
> Do you think such scenes exist for the poor?"

Zhang Shunmin (late 11th century) tells the following anecdote:[19]

> When Liu Sanbian [Liu Yong] had offended the Emperor Renzong by one of his songs, the Ministry of Civil Appointments would not give him a promotion. Dissatisfied, Sanbian went to the office to complain. Minister Yan said, "Sir, you write songs?" Sanbian said, "Like your Excellency, I, too, write songs." The Minister said, "I may write songs, but I never wrote such a line as 'Languidly holding her needlework she nestles close to him.'" Whereupon Liu withdrew.

Because he disliked both vulgarity and impropriety, Yan Shu avoided them by describing the spirit, not external appearance.

Generally speaking, there are two ways of reacting to experience: one way simply registers the perceptions of the senses and is content with external appearances; the other is through the mind, which penetrates through the superficial appearances of a situation to the underlying essentials. If someone enters a rich man's house and simply records what his senses tell him, then it will be the gold and jade, the brocade and embroidery, that he sets down. But if he reacts with his mind, then what he perceives will be the aura of wealth, and this will have to be conveyed more indirectly. In the matter of sensuality, two people going hand in hand can be described in terms of their physical contact, or, from another kind of perception, in terms of the feeling of closeness. Of course, the sense of affluence and luxury in the first case comes initially from the visible objects of luxury; in the second it is the evidence of physical contact that lets one infer the intimacy between the couple. But for the one who perceives essences, the evidence of the senses is unimportant except as an intermediary. Like Zhuangzi, when you catch the fish you can forget the net, and when you have the idea you can forget the words. Once you have grasped the essencc of a situation, you are no longer aware of the evidence provided by the senses; it is a spontaneous process, not something deliberately contrived. Yan Shu avoided the words "gold" and "jade" not as a matter of policy, as the anecdote would seem to suggest, but because his reaction led him to the essentials underlying appearance.

Here are some examples of how he presented a luxurious setting in his songs:

A swallow passes by the double curtains of the little hall, 小阁重帘有燕过

Late pink petals fall on the courtyard grass;	晚花红片落庭莎
Reflection of a curving bannister in the cool water.	曲栏干影入凉波

To the tune *Huan xi sha*
(Sands of the Washing Stream), No. 12, p. 88

Green leaves hide the orioles	翠叶藏莺
Red curtains keep out the swallows	朱帘隔燕
Incense from the burner slowly pursues twisting gossamer.	炉香静逐游丝转

To the tune *Ta suo xing*
(Treading on the Sedge), No. 82, p. 99

The red curtain half lowered, incense burned out.	朱帘半下香销印
A second-month east wind brings an urgent message to the willow.	二月东风催柳信
Beside her lute, lost in thought—	琵琶旁畔且寻思
Don't ask in front of the parrot.	鹦鹉前头休借问

To the tune *Mu lan hua*
(Magnolia Flower), No. 60, p. 96

In these passages Yan Shu manages to suggest luxury without flaunting the appurtenances of wealth. "You know this is not someone living in a three-family village," as Chao Buzhi put it.[20]

Right now I would like to be	此时拚作
A thousand-foot strand of gossamer	千尺游丝
To hold fast the Moving Cloud.	惹住朝云

To the tune *Su zhong qing*
(Telling How I Feel), No. 66, p. 97

Green liquor in the cup, and someone she loves　　樽中绿醑意中人
Always together beneath the flowers,　　花朝月下长相见
in the moonlight.

To the tune *Ta suo xing*
(Treading on the Sedge), No. 81, p. 96

So much love beyond telling　　多少襟怀言不尽
Is written into the words of the song—　　写向蛮笺曲调中
This feeling a thousand thousand times.　　此情千万重

To the tune *Po zhen zi*
(Break the Ranks), No. 3, p. 88

It is lines like these, which create the feeling of sensuality without the impropriety of Liu Yong's "Languidly holding her needlework she nestles close to him" or "She wants to draw the fragrant curtain and talk of love." The feelings Yan Shu evokes are those of real love, not mere erotic dalliance. His verse is never indecent, and although his worldly position and circumstances undoubtedly played some part in determining his standards of taste, his natural delicacy and refinement kept him from writing vulgar or obscene verse. Wan Minhao was surely less than generous in asserting that he was only inhibited by what others might say.

In Yan Shu's "Pearls and Jade" there are a certain number of congratulatory songs that provide good material for looking for something to criticize. It is a kind of verse that easily becomes empty and fatuous. As a minister of state, Yan Shu naturally had to write poems to order on social occasions, and these are certainly not among his best. However, compared with the congratulatory songs written by his contemporaries, Yan Shu's have some redeeming features. As in his other songs, he does not descend to the obvious; he manages to introduce some subtlety and conveys a mood rather than simply presenting the subject's excellencies for admiration. He offers his congratulations soberly and with restraint, most often against a background of natural description, about which he retains his poet's sensitivity. The result is congratulatory poetry that is refined and graceful, but which still manages to be fresh and original. For example, to the tune *Die lian hua* (Butterfly Loves Flowers) (No. 107, p. 103):

Purple chrysanthemums begin to bloom when Rose of Sharon declines.	紫菊初生朱槿坠
The moon is nice, the breeze fresh.	月好风清
Gradually the feel of full autumn—	渐有中秋意
The nightwatches grow longer, the sky is like water.	更漏乍长天似水
The silver screen is spread to show the green of far-off hills.	银屏展尽遥山翠
The embroidered curtain rolled in waves, the incense ash grows,	绣幕卷波香引穗
Quick pipes, massed strings.	急管繁弦
Everyone loves this old man.	共庆人间瑞
Fill the jade cups full, whirl dancing sleeves.	满酌玉杯萦舞袂
The southern spring congratulates his long, long life.	南春祝寿千千岁

Or one celebrating the Emperor, to the tune *Fu nishang* (Brushing the Rainbow Robe) (No. 114, p. 105):

We smile to see the autumn sky	笑秋天
Evening lotus with round strung dew-pearls,	晚荷花缀露珠圆
The breeze and the sun are nice.	风日好
Several rows of new geese stuck onto the cold mist cloud.	数行新雁贴寒烟

On silver reeds blow crisp woodwind notes,	银簧调脆管
On jasper frets pluck clear strings.	琼柱拨清弦
We offer a flowing bowl,	捧觥船
With one voice sing of this age of peace.	一声声齐唱太平年

Neither of these songs is particularly profound or subtle, but they are not wholly without merit in evoking a response in the reader. When one thinks of how many happy occasions need celebrating, over a lifetime, one can hardly disparage all such songs as vulgar or common.

One final point: There is one song in "Pearls and Jade" that is in a different style from the others. It is to the tune *Shan ting liu* (Mountain Pavilion Willow) and carries the subtitle "To a Singer" (No. 123, p. 106):

She hails from Qin in the west	家住西秦
And takes her chances with the skills she has.	赌博艺随身
In the entertainment world	花柳上
She ranked with the best.	斗尖新
Sometimes she equaled Niannu's virtuosity	偶学念奴声调
And on occasion could stop the marching clouds.	有时高遏行云
Her reward—any amount of Shu brocade;	蜀锦缠头无数
Her efforts were not wasted.	不负辛勤
For some years now she's worked the capital road	数年来往咸京道
Wearing out her soul for heeltaps and poor fare.	残杯冷炙谩消魂
To whom can she confide	衷肠事
Her heart's pain?	托何人
If a real connoisseur would choose her	若有知音见采
She would willingly sing the Spring Song to the end.	不辞遍唱阳春

A song at the banquet, and her tears fall 一曲当筵落泪
She keeps wiping her eyes on a silken kerchief. 重掩罗巾

In his other songs Yan Shu's style is smooth and placid, but in this one he writes with strong feeling. None of them has a subtitle, but this one is carefully labeled "To a Singer". It is interesting that one song should be exceptional in two different ways, and some explanation seems called for. First we need to amplify a bit what has already been said about Yan Shu's disposition and his career. The quiet elegance and the balanced perspective of his songs show clearly the rationality which he cultivated: everything tranquil and under control. But his biographer mentions another side of his character: "He was forceful and incisive, and in his assignments as prefectural governor the officers and people were somewhat fearful of his temper and impatience."[21] Ouyang Xiu uses the same terms, "forceful and incisive" (*gang jian*), to characterize him,[22] and the Siku editors[23] echo it with "Yan Shu was endowed with a forceful and rugged disposition, but his written style was particularly graceful and lovely." To keep a forceful and rugged disposition in check, Yan Shu certainly must have exercised self-control, and the "graceful and lovely" language of his songs is the result of a forceful nature showing through, conflicting elements held in balance, a complex amalgam. Consequently they can be limpid without being monotonous, smooth without being insipid.

Let me suggest an analogy: White sunlight contains the seven colors of the spectrum, and when it passes through a prism, the colors appear. The complexity of Yan Shu's character likewise was revealed only under special circumstances. When he was involved in difficulties, he could be provoked to the point where the forceful, rugged component of his nature appeared. His biography tells a story[24] about the time he was Assistant Court Commissar of Military Affairs. He had memorialized against making Zhang

Qi commissar, against the wishes of the Empress Dowager. He was ordered to follow her to palace. His servant was late in bringing his ivory tablet of office, and Yan Shu struck the servant with the tablet, breaking his teeth. Another anecdote[25] tells how Zhang Xian, a fellow poet-official, insisted on discussing business in Yan Shu's home. Yan Shu would not respond to his remarks and finally flushed and said in his southern accent, "I got you an appointment because you could write 'There's nothing so strong as love',[26] but now you come here to talk business."

Once we have recognized these elements of forcefulness and irritability in Yan Shu's character, we should not be surprised at the passionate complaint of the "Mountain Pavilion Willow" song. Although the subtitle specifically says "To a Singer", Zheng Qian suggested that with it Yan Shu is "borrowing a winecup from someone else to drown his own sorrows."[27] He also comments, "Since the song mentions 'Qin in the west' and the 'capital at Xian', it should date from the time he was in charge of the Yongxing District, when he was over sixty and had long been out of the court and found it hard not to be depressed." This is very perceptive. From the time Yan Shu was recommended as a child prodigy at age fourteen and was appointed collator by Shenzong until he was dismissed as minister when he was fifty-four, his career was as successful as one could wish. But during the nearly ten years after his dismissal until his death in 1055 he was given provincial assignments, of which the one in Yongxing was the farthest away from the court. The reason for his dismissal, according to the *Song History*,[28] was an accusation that in the grave inscription he was ordered to write for the Imperial Concubine Li he failed to mention the fact that she was the real mother of the Emperor Renzong; and that he had used conscripts to repair a building for his personal profit. But, in the words of the *Song History*, "Since the Empress Dowager Zhangxian was ruling, Shu did not dare state the truth (that she was not the Emperor's real mother), and it was one of the perquisites of a minister to make use of conscript labor for private purposes. Contemporaries felt that Shu was not at fault."

The frustration of having been dismissed for offenses for which he was not to blame and left in exile for such a long time prompted him to express the forceful, irritable side of his character in a song. But this song has another peculiarity already noted: it is "To a Singer". If, as seems likely, the song expresses his own feelings during his later years of exile, why did he "borrow someone else's winecup to drown his own sorrows"? It seems to me that this can be considered another sign of Yan Shu's rational self-control. Wang Guowei quoted Nietzsche, "The literature I love is all written in blood."[29] Some authors, having written in their own fresh blood, want to point out the still dripping wound. Others prefer to keep the wound out of sight and make up a story to account for the painful event. This is the characteristic method of the intellectual poet, who prefers to maintain a distance from his emotions, and that is why Yan Shu chose to write "To a Singer", separating himself from his feelings by attributing them to someone else, so that he could write without inhibition.

At the same time, I do not believe that this subtitle is a convention, something concocted for the purpose; there must have been a singer. The singer's situation elicited a response in the poet that released his long-harbored feelings.

This sort of encounter is not something that can be arranged, and it is not easy to find another song that is comparably unrestrained in expression, for such a perfect occasion may never have happened again. And since Yan Shu was not one to flaunt his wounds without such a disguise, the fact that this uncharacteristic poem is unique in his collection is further confirmation that he was indeed an intellectual poet.

In conclusion I would like to imitate Wang Guowei by quoting a *ci* poet's own verse as a critical evaluation of his poetry. Yan Shu's songs have a touch of melancholy under the placid surface, the sharp clarity of the autumn sun along with the spring sun's mild warmth. This and the freshness and appropriateness of his images make one think of his lines:

In the frost, under the moon　　霜前月下
The slanting pinks, pale petals　　斜红淡蕊
Fresh and charming enough to bring back spring.　　明媚欲回春

To the tune *Shao nian you*
(Youthful Diversions), No. 50, p. 94

Notes:

1. Wan Minhao, *Er Yan ji qi ci*, p. 166.

2. Jiang Ruoliu, commenting on the third of Du Fu's ten poems "You He Jiang jun shan lin", *Dushi jingquan* 2.8a.

3. Du Fu, "Tian mo huai Li Bai", *Du Fu yinde*, in vol. 2, 20/25.

4. Li Shangyin "You gan", in *Li Yishan shi ji* (*SBCK ed.*) 6.18b.

5. Wang Guowei, *Renjian cihua*, pp. 197-198.

6. *Song shi* 70.1b-2a .

7. Ibid.

8. All references to Song *ci* are to Tang Guizhang, *QSC*. The no. refers to the number in sequence of any author's *ci* in that collection, followed by a page reference.

9. In a dream one's soul is supposed to make journeys to a distance o see another person; such dream trips are considered dangerous or fatiguing. For example, see Du Fu's "Dreaming of Li Bai", in *Du Fu yinde*, p. 79, 5.10

10. *Renjian cihua,* p. 202.

11. Ibid., p. 203

12. The author has discussed Wang Guowei's *ci* criticism in her *Jialing tan ci*, pp. 1-11.

13. Huang Tingjian, Preface to *Xiaoshan ci*, p. 1.

14. Lu Ji, *Wen Fu, WX,* 17.1b.

15. References for Feng Yansi are to Lin Dachun, *TWDC*.

16. Wu Chuhou, *Qingxing zaji* (*Bai hai*), 5.1b-2a.

17. This couplet is not in any of the poems collected in *Yan Yuanxian yiwen* (vol. 17 of *Song ershi jia ji*).

18. Ibid., 7b, "Untitled Poem".

19. Zhang Shunmin, *Hua man lu* (vol. 2 of *Bai Hai*) 1.30b.

20. Chao Buzhi, quoted in Wu Zeng, *Nenggaizhai man lu* (*Cihua congbian*, vol. 1) 16.1a.

21. *Song shi* 6.3b.

22. Ouyang Xiu, *Ouyang Wenzhonggong ji*, p. 74.

23. *Siku quanshu zongmu Hiyao* 113. 1a.

24. *Song shi* 6.3b, 6.2a.

25. *Hua man lu* 1.33a-b.

26. A line from Zhang Xian's song to the tune "A Clump of Flowers", no. 22, p. 61.

27. Zheng Qian, *Ci xuan*, p. 24.

28. *Song shi* 6.3a.

29. *Renjian cihua*, p. 198.

论苏轼词

一

> 揽辔登车慕范滂，神人姑射仰蒙庄。
> 小词余力开新境，千古豪苏擅胜场。

在《宋史》苏轼的传记中，开端就记载了他早年时代的两则故事。一则是说，当他十岁时，“父洵游学四方，母程氏亲授以书，闻古今成败，辄能语其要。程氏读东汉《范滂传》，慨然太息。轼请曰：‘轼若为滂，母许之否乎？’程氏曰：‘汝能为滂，吾顾不能为滂母耶？’”又一则则是说他长大之后：“既而读庄子，叹曰：‘吾昔有见，口未能言，今见是书，得吾心矣，”此二则故事，本来都出于苏轼之弟辙为他所写的《墓志铭》中，这两段叙述可以说是极为扼要地表现了苏轼之性格中的两种主要的特质。一种是如同东汉桓帝时受命为清诏使，登车揽辔，遂慨然有澄清天下之志的范滂一样，想要奋发有为，愿以天下为己任，虽遇艰危而不悔的用世之志意；另一种则是如同写有《逍遥游》和《齐物论》中之“大浸稽天而不溺，大旱金石流而不伤”的“姑射神人”与“栩栩然”

超然物化的“梦中蝴蝶”之寓言的庄子一样的，不为外物之得失荣辱所累的超然旷观的精神。记得以前我们在论柳永词的时候，曾经述及柳永之平生，以为柳氏乃是在用世之志意与浪漫之性格的冲突矛盾中，一生落拓，而最后终陷入于志意与感情两俱落空之下场的悲剧人物；然而苏轼则是一个把儒家用世之志意与道家旷观之精神，做了极圆满之融合，虽在困穷斥逐之中，也未尝迷失彷徨，而终于完成了一己的人生之目标与持守的成功的人物[①]。苏氏一生所留下的著述极多，他的天才既高，兴趣又广，各体作品都有杰出的成就。其中所保留的三百余首小词，在他的全集中所占的比例并不大，此在东坡而言，可以说仅是余力为之的遣兴之作而已。然而就在这一部分余力为之的数量不多的小词中，却非常有代表性地表现了他的用世之志意与旷观之襟怀相结合而形成的一种极可注意的特有的品质和风貌，为小词之写作，开拓出了一片广阔而高远的新天地。这种成就是极值得我们注意而加以分析的。

本来，早在我们论欧阳修词的时候，就已曾经提出来说过，北宋的一些名臣，既往往于其文章德业以外，有时也耽溺于小词之写作，而且在小词之写作中，更往往于无意间流露其学养与襟抱之境界。这种情形，原是歌词流入文士之手，因而乃逐渐趋于诗化的一种自然之现象。在此一演变之过程中，早期之作如大晏及欧阳之小词，虽然也蕴含有发自于其性情襟抱的一种深远幽微之意境，但自外表看来，则其所写者，却仍只不过是些伤春怨别的情词，与五代时《花间集》中的艳歌之词，并没有什么明显的区分。一直到了苏氏的出现，才开始用这种合乐而歌的词的形式，来正式抒写自己的怀抱志意，使词之诗化达到了一种高峰的成

① 苏轼之思想于儒道二家以外，其后亦受有佛家之影响。盖苏轼之性情超旷，才识过人，故能撷取诸家思想之与自己性情相近者，使之皆成为自己修养之一部分。就苏氏之见，盖以为儒、释、道三者，在相异之中亦有相同之处，虽相反，而可以互相为用。苏辙在其所撰《老子解》之跋文中，即曾引苏轼之语云：“使汉初有此书，则孔子、老子为一；使晋宋间有此书，则佛老不为二。”（见《丛书集成》本《老子解》）苏轼在其自己所写之《祭龙井辩才文》中，亦曾以为虽然“孔老异门，儒释分宫”，然而“江河虽殊，其至则同”。当其为人所用，则可以“遇物而应，施则无穷”。（见《苏东坡全集·续集》卷十六）此种融汇运用之妙，盖正为苏氏一己学而有得之言也。

就。这种成就是作者个人杰出之才识与当时之文学趋势及社会背景相汇聚而后完成的一种极可贵的结合。如果说晏、欧词中所流露的作者之性情襟抱，其诗化之趋势原是无意的；那么在苏轼词中所表现的性情襟抱，则已经是带着一种有意的想要开拓创新的觉醒了。苏氏在给鲜于子骏（侁）的一封信中，就曾经明白提出来说："近却颇作小词，虽无柳七郎风味，亦自是一家。"（见《东坡续集》卷五《书简》）其有心要在当日流行的词风以外自拓新境的口气，乃是一望可知的。如果我们想要对苏轼在词的写作方面，从开始尝试到终于有了自成一家之信心的过程一加考查，我们就会发现他的这一段创作历程，大约是从熙宁五年（1072）到元丰二年（1079）之间的事。在苏轼的早期作品中，似乎并没有写词的记录。苏轼抵杭州任在熙宁四年冬，而据朱彊邨编年龙榆生校笺之《东坡乐府笺》，其最早之词作乃是由次年春以后所写的《南歌子》、《行香子》及《临江仙》等一些游赏山水的短调小令。至于其长调之作，则首见于熙宁七年秋移知密州时所写的一首《沁园春·赴密州，早行，马上寄子由》。[①]自兹而后，其词作之数量既日益增多，风格亦日益成熟。其在密州与徐州之所作，如《江城子·乙卯正月二十日夜记梦》的一首悼亡词，及另一首《江城子·密州出猎》词，和《水调歌头·丙辰中秋欢饮达旦，大醉，作此篇，兼怀子由》词，与《浣溪沙·徐门石潭谢雨道上作》五首叙写农村的词。仅只从这些作品在词之牌调后面各自附有种种不同的标题来看，我们便已经可以清楚地见到苏轼之想要以诗为词的写作的意念，以及其无意不可入词的写作之能力，都已经得到了很好的实践的证明。他给鲜于子骏的那封信，就正是他对自己此一阶段之词作已经达成了某一种开拓的充满自信的表示。经历了此一阶段的由尝试而开拓的

① 按：苏轼此词，元好问曾疑为伪作，见《元遗山文集》卷三十六中之《东坡乐府集选引》云："绛人孙安常注坡词，……删去他人所作……五十六首，不可谓无功。然尚有可论者，……如'当时共客长安……袖手何妨闲处看'（即此词这下半阕）之句，其鄙俚浅近，叫呼炫鬻，殆市驵之雄，醉饱而后发之，……而谓东坡作者，误矣。"元氏之言，盖由其素日推尊苏词，故尔不欲以此等浅率之句属之苏轼，然苏词并非绝无浅率之笔，此意当于下一节详之。且自孙安常以来，历代编选校注苏词者，多仍以此词属之苏氏。元氏之说，并无确据，似仍以从众为是。

创作的实践，苏轼的诗化的词遂进入了一种更纯熟的境界，而终于在他贬官黄州以后，达到了他自己之词作的质量的高峰。而在此高峰中，有一点最可注意的成就，那就是苏轼已经能够极自然地用小词抒写襟抱，把自己平生性格中所禀有的两种不同的特质——用世之志意与旷达之襟怀，作了非常完满的结合融汇的表现。即如其“莫听穿林打叶声”之一首《定风波》词、“照野弥弥浅浪”之一首《西江月》词、“大江东去”之一首《念奴娇》词、“夜饮东坡醒复醉”之一首《临江仙》词，以至将要离黄移汝时，他所写的“归去来兮”之一首《满庭芳》词，便都可以说是表现了此种独特之意境的代表作品。

经过前一节的概述，我们对于苏轼在小词方面由初期之尝试而逐渐开拓的发展，以及后期之能成功地使用此一形式来表达自己的性情襟抱中的某些主要的特质，从而形成了自己独特之意境与风格的过程，可以说已经有了简单的认识，下面我们便将对于促使其如此发展的某些外在与内在之因素略加分析。如我们在前文所言，世所流传的苏轼的词作，是从神宗熙宁五年他出官杭州以后才开始的，那时的苏轼已经有卅七岁。关于此一情形，可以引起我们两点疑问：其一是苏轼早年是否对于词之写作全无兴趣？其二是如果有兴趣，又何以晚到将近四十岁才开始着手于词之写作？关于此二问题，我们可以从苏氏全集的其他作品中，找到一些答案。苏轼在黄州时曾经给其族兄子明写过一封信（见《东坡续集》卷五《书简》），其中曾提到说：“记得应举时，见兄能讴歌，甚妙。弟虽不会，然常令人唱为何词。”[①]从这段叙述，可见苏轼盖早在赴汴京应举的时候，就已经对当时流行的传唱的歌词有了兴趣。本来以像苏轼这样多才而富于情趣的一位诗人，来到当日遍地歌楼酒肆、到处按管弹弦的繁华的汴京，若说他竟然完全不被这种流行的乐曲和歌词所引动，那才是一件决不可能的事。所以苏轼在其与友人的书信及谈话中，

① 按：此句原文如此，苏轼之意，盖谓自己虽不能歌，然常令人唱为任何歌词而听之也。

都曾多次提到当时作曲的名家柳永，这便是苏轼也曾留意于当日传唱之歌词的最好的证明。不过，值得注意的是，苏轼在当时却并未曾立即致力于词的写作，我以为那是因为当日的苏轼还正是一个满怀大志的青年，初应贡举，便获高第，而且得到了当日望重一时的名臣欧阳修的不同寻常的知赏，因此当日苏轼所致力去撰写的，乃是关系于国家治乱安危之大计的《思治论》和《应诏集》那些为朝廷谋深虑远的《策略》等论著，在这种情形下，他当然无暇措意于小词之写作。如此一直延续到神宗熙宁四年，虽然其间苏轼曾经先后因母丧及父丧两度返回眉山守制家居，而且当其再度还朝时，神宗已经任用王安石开始变行新法，但苏轼之慨然以天下为己任的心志则仍未改变。他既先后给神宗写了《议学校贡举状》和《谏买浙灯状》等疏状，更陆续写了两篇长达万字以上的《上皇帝书》和《再上皇帝书》，因此遂招致忌恨，有御史诬奏其过失（见苏轼墓志铭），乃请求外放，通判杭州。而苏轼致力于小词之写作，就正是从他到达杭州之后开始的。我认为此一开始作词之年代与地点，对于研究苏轼词而言，实在极值得注意。因为由此一年代，我们乃可以推知，苏轼之开始致力于词之写作，原来正是当他的“以天下为己任”之志意受到打击挫折后方才开始的。而就地点而言，则杭州附近美丽的山水，又正是引发起他写词之意兴的另一因素。本来，如我们在前文所言，“用世之志意”与“超旷之襟怀”原是苏轼在天性中所禀赋的两种主要特质。前者为其欲有所作为时用以立身之正途，后者则为其不能有所作为时用以自慰之妙理。苏轼之开始写词，既是在其用世之志意受到挫折以后，则其发展之趋势之终必形成以超旷为主之意境与风格，就原是一种必然之结果。只不过当他在杭州初开始写词时，尚未能纯熟地表现出这种意境与风格的特色，而仍只是在一种尝试的阶段。由杭州时期所写的一些令词，到他转赴密州时所写的“早行，马上寄子由”的一首长词《沁园春》，苏轼都还免不了有一些学习模仿和受到别人影响的痕迹，而其中最值得一提的则是欧阳修和柳永。原来早在我们写《论欧阳修词》一篇文稿时，在结尾之处便已经引过冯煦之《蒿庵论词》的话，说欧词“疏隽开子瞻”。盖欧词之特质，固正如我们在以前之所论述，原在于其具有一份遣玩之意兴，而且欲以之作为遭遇挫折忧患后之一种排解之力量。而苏轼早期在杭州通判任内所写的一些游赏山水的令词，其性质便与欧词的此一种意境及风格甚为相近。盖欧、苏二人皆能具有古代儒家所重视的善处穷通之际的一种自持的修养，不肯因遭遇忧患而便陷于愁苦哀伤，如此就必须常保持一种可以放得开的豁达的心胸，而在作品中，便也自然形成了一种比较疏放的气势。而这也正是冯煦所说的“疏隽”的特色，而由此更开拓出去的苏轼，他在不以穷通介怀的修养方面，既与欧公有相近之处，而且在早年应举时，又曾特蒙欧公之知赏，而欧公原来本极喜欢写制小词付之吟唱，是以苏轼必曾对欧阳修之词，留有深刻之印象，此在苏轼之词作中，固曾屡屡及之。即如其《西江月》（三过平山堂下）一首，其所咏之平山堂既原为欧公当日之所修建，而其词中之所谓“仍歌杨柳春风”一句，更指的就是欧阳修当年写的《朝中措》（平山栏槛倚晴空）一首中的“手种堂前垂柳，别来几度春风”的词句；再如苏轼的《木兰花令》（霜余已失长淮阔）一首，更是在题目中便已经注明是“次欧公西湖韵”，而其中所写的 “佳人犹唱醉翁词”，也指的就正是欧阳修当年所写的《玉楼春》（西湖南北烟波阔）一首歌咏颍州西湖的词句。（按：《玉楼春》即《木兰花令》，为同调之异名）从这些例证，我们不仅可以见到苏词之曾受有欧词之影响，而且还可以见到这种影响之作用，主要盖可以归纳为两点特质，一点即是如欧阳修在《朝中措》一词中所表现的“平山栏槛倚晴空，山色有无中”之疏放高远的气度；另一点则是如欧阳修在《玉楼春》一词中，所表现的“西湖南北烟波阔，风里丝簧声韵咽”之遣玩游赏的意兴。而苏轼早期所写的一些游赏山水的令词，就正表现了他所受到的这两点影响的痕迹。即如其熙宁五年在城外游春所写的“昨日出东城，试探春情”的一首《浪淘沙》词，其所表现的主要便是一种游赏遣玩的意兴。而其熙宁六年过七里濑所写的“一叶舟轻，双桨鸿惊，水天清影湛波平”的一首《行香子》词，则其所表现的又隐然有一种疏放的气度。而以上这两类风格，便恰好正代表了苏轼得之于欧阳修的两点主要的影响。不过苏轼之性格又与欧阳修毕竟有所不同，欧之放往往仅是借外景为遣玩的一种情绪方面的疏放，而苏之放则往往是具有一种哲理之妙悟式的发自内心襟怀方面的旷放。所以欧词之内容仍大多只是以写景抒情为主，而极少写及哲理或直抒怀抱之句；而苏词则于写景抒情之外，更往往直言哲理或直写襟怀。即如其《行香予》（一叶舟轻）一首下半阕所写的“君臣一梦，今古虚名”数句，及《虞美人》（湖山信是东南美）一首下半阕所写的“夜阑风静欲归时，惟有一江明月碧琉璃”数句，前者是哲理性的叙述，后者则隐然喻现了一种开阔的襟怀。像这两种意境，便不仅是欧阳修词中所少见的，也是《花间》以来五代、宋初各家词作中所少见的。所以苏氏早期的词，虽然也流露有曾受过欧词影响的痕迹，然而同时也已经表现了将要从欧词之“疏隽”，发展开拓出另一条更为开阔博大之途径的趋向。以上可以说是从早期的苏词中所可见到的欧词对苏词之影响，以及二人间之继承与开拓的关系。下面我们便将对柳永词及苏轼词之间的关系，也略加探讨。我们以前在论说柳永词的时候，本来也曾提到过苏轼对柳词之特别注意，以及苏轼对柳词之两种不同的评价。根据苏轼自己的作品和宋人笔记中的一些记述来看，苏轼对当时词人作品的关心和论评，实在以有关柳永的记述为最多，而且往往欲以自己之所作来与柳词相比较。即如我们在前文所引苏轼在《与鲜于子骏书》中所说的“虽无柳七郎风味，亦自是一家”的话，其欲以自己之词作与柳词相比较的口吻，就是显然可见的。再如我们以前在《论柳永词》一文所举引的宋人笔记的记述，说苏轼在玉堂之日，曾问幕士自己之所作比柳词何如的故事（见俞文豹撰《吹剑续录》）。这些记述都表现出苏轼对于柳永的词，实在非常重视，所以才斤斤欲以自己之所作与柳词相比较。至于苏轼对柳永之评价，则可以分别为正反两种不同的意见。先从反面的观点来看，即如《词林纪事》卷六引《高斋诗话》所记载的秦观自会稽入京见苏轼。苏轼举秦之《满庭芳》（山抹微云）一首中之“销魂，当此际”数语，以为秦氏学柳七作词，而语含讥讽之意。（按：此一故事，又见于《御选历代诗余》卷二五及叶梦得《避暑录话》卷下，所引述者大旨相同，已详《论柳永词》一篇中，兹不再赘。）从这些记述来看，都可见到苏轼对于柳词的某些风格，是确实有不满之处的。可是值得注意的是，另一方面则苏轼对柳永之词却也曾备致赞扬。我们在以前《论柳永词》一文中，便曾经引述过赵令畤之《侯鲭录》、吴曾之《能改斋漫录》及胡仔之《苕溪渔隐丛话》所转引之《复堂漫录》等诸宋人之记述。皆谓苏轼曾称美柳词《八声甘州》（对潇潇暮雨洒江天）一首中之“渐霜风凄紧，关河冷落，残照当楼”数句，以为其“不减唐人高处”。（可参看《论柳永词》一文，兹不再赘。）总结以上之记述，我们可以把苏轼对柳词之态度，简单归纳为以下三点：其一是对柳词极为重视，将之视为相互比并的对手；其二则是对柳词中的淫靡之作也表现了鄙薄和不满；其三则是对柳词中之兴象高远之特色，则又有独到的赏识。基于此种复杂的态度，因此柳词与苏词之间，就产生了一种颇不容易为人所体会的微妙的关系。首先就苏轼对柳词之重视而言，当仁宗嘉祐二年，苏轼初来汴京应举之时，盖正为柳词盛行于世到处传唱之际，此种情形必曾予青年之苏轼以极深刻之印象。因此当苏轼后来也着手开始写词之时，他所写的第一首长调《赴密州，早行，马上寄子由》的《沁园春》词，就留下了明显的曾受柳词影响的痕迹。即如该词上半阕所写的“孤馆灯青，野店鸡号，旅枕梦残。渐月华收练，晨霜耿耿，云山摛锦，朝露漙漙”数句，便与柳永的羁旅行役之词中铺叙景物的手法和风格甚为相近。这种情形，无论其出于有心之模仿，或无心之影响，我以为都是一种可以谅解的极自然的现象。因为一般说来，由写诗而转入写词之尝试的作者，习惯上往往多是先从小令开始，即使高才如苏轼者，对此也并非例外。此盖由于小令之声律与近体诗较为接近，习惯于写诗之人，对小令之声律便也更易于掌握。所以苏轼最早所写的词作，原来也是与欧阳修之疏隽的风格相接近的、表现有高远疏放之气度和游赏遣玩之意兴的令词。及至他后来要尝试长调慢词之写作，而慢词之声律及铺排既迥然不同于近体诗和短小的令词，如此则在未能熟练地掌握慢词之特色与手法之际，若想找一个足资参考借鉴的作者，则苏轼所熟悉的一位曾予他以极深之印象的慢词的作者，当然就是柳永。所以他的第一首长调的《沁园春》词，就不免流露了柳词之影响的痕迹。不过以苏轼之高才，自并非柳永之所能局限，何况以他的旷逸之天性。对柳永的一些淫靡鄙俗之作又本来就有所不满，因此他遂又想致力于变革柳词之风气而独辟蹊径，自成一家。在这种开径创新的拓展中，苏词之最值得人注意的一点特色，就是其气象之博大开阔，善写高远之景色，而充满感发之力量。即如其《赤壁怀古》一首《念奴娇》词开端之“大江东去，浪淘尽、千古风流人物”数句及《黄州快哉亭》一首《水调歌头》词开端之“落日绣帘卷，亭下水连空”数句，以及《寄参寥子》一首《八声甘州》词开端之“有情风万里卷潮来，无情送潮归”数句，凡此之类，盖皆有如前人评苏词之所谓“逸怀浩气，超然乎尘垢之外，”大有“使人登高望远，举首高歌”之意味。故后人往往称苏词为“豪苏”，而称柳词为“腻柳”，以表示二人之风格之迥然相异，而殊不知二人风格虽异，但苏词中此等兴象高远之笔致，却原来很可能正是有得之于柳词之启发和灵感。苏轼之赞美柳永的《八声甘州》（对潇潇暮雨洒江天）一首词，举出其中的“渐霜风凄紧，关河冷落，残照当楼”数句，以为其“不减唐人高处”，就正是对此中消息的一点泄漏。因为柳词这几句的好处，原来就正在于其所写的景象之高远和富于感发之力量，而这也就正是苏词对之称赏有得之处。而且柳词中表现有此一类气象与意境之作，还不仅限于此词之此数句而已。即如以前我们在《论柳永词》一文中，所曾举引过的《雪梅香》（景萧索，危楼独立面晴空）一首，《曲玉管》（陇首云飞，江边日晚）一首，及《玉蝴蝶》（望处雨收云断）一首，这些词便也都是极富于此种高远之兴象的作品。盖柳词中虽然有不少为乐工歌伎而写的淫靡之作，但另外却也有不少极富于高远之兴象，表现了一己才人失志之悲慨的作品。所以柳词中可以说本来就含有两类不同性质的作品，苏轼所鄙视的是柳永前一类作品，而其所称赏者，则是柳永的后一类作品，只不过柳词常把这种兴象高远的秋士之慨，与缠绵柔婉的儿女之情结合在一起来抒写，因此遂往往使一般人忘其高远而只见其淫靡了。而苏轼则具有特别过人的眼光，能见到柳词中这一类意境之“不减唐人高处”。此种赏鉴之能力，一方面固然由于苏轼之高才卓识果有过人之处，另一方面也由于此种高远之气象与苏轼开阔超旷之天性也原有相近之处的缘故。但同时此种天性却又正是促使苏轼的词向着另一条途径发展，终于形成了与柳词全然相异之另一风格的主要因素。此种关系，看似微妙，但却也并不难于理解。盖正如上文论及欧词与苏词关系时之所言，欧词与苏词的同中有异，其故乃在于欧词之放，仅为借外景遣玩时情绪之疏放，而苏词之放，则为发自内心襟怀的具有哲理意味的旷放。是则造成欧、苏两家词风不同的主要因素，原即在于苏氏天性中所具有的一种超旷之特质。现在我们又论及柳词所写高远之兴象，虽与苏词有近似之处，但两家风格乃迥然相异，其主要之区别，便也仍在于二人天性之不同。柳词所写景物虽极高远，但多为凄凉、日暮、萧瑟、惊秋之景，其景与情之关系，乃是由外在凄凉之景，而引起内心中失志之悲，这当然是由于柳永自己本来就是一个落拓失志的词人之故。至于苏轼所写的高远之景象，则使人但见其开阔博大，而并无萧瑟凄凉之意，其景与情之关系，乃是作者天性中超旷之襟怀与外界超旷之景物间的一种即景即心之融汇。而且柳词在写过高远的景物以后，往往就又回到其缠绵的柔情之中，但苏轼则常是通篇都保留着超旷之襟怀与意兴。所以苏轼虽然也曾从一部分柳词“不减唐人高处”的意境和气象中获得启发，但却并未为其所限制，而终于蜕变成与柳词迥异的超旷之风格。总之，苏轼与柳词之关系，也正像他与欧词的关系一样，早期作品中虽曾受到若干影响，而却终于突破局限，而开拓出自己的道路，至其开拓之主要方面，则是以其天性中超矿之精神为本质的一种超旷之风格。在这种继承与开拓之关系中，我们既看到了词这种文学体式，在本身发展方面之一种要求开拓的自然趋势，也看到了北宋时到处演唱歌词的社会背景对一位多才且兴趣广泛的作者的影响，更看到一位具有特殊禀赋的诗人，如何发挥其本身禀赋之特质，因而突破前人之局限，而开拓出自己的一条途径来。英雄既足以创造时势，时势也可以成就英雄，在词之发展史中，苏轼就正是这样一位天性中既具有独特之禀赋，又生当北宋词坛之盛世，虽然仅以余力为词，而却终于为五代以来一直被目为艳科的小词，开拓出一片高远广大之新天地的重要的作者。

二

道是无情是有请，钱塘万里看潮生。
可知天海风涛曲，也杂人间怨断声。

在前一节中，我们已曾论到苏轼天性中盖原禀赋有两种不同之特质：一种是儒家用世之志意，另一种则是道家超旷之精神，前者是他欲有所为之时的立身之正途，后者则是他不能有为之时的慰解之妙理。苏轼之开始致力于词之写作，既是在其仕途受挫折以后，则其词之走向超旷之风格，便自是一种必然之结果。何况我们以前在论欧阳修词时，还曾提到过“观人于揖让，不若观人于游戏”的话，一般人作词之态度既不像作诗之态度那样严肃，因此当其写词之时，反而也就更能摆脱了在严肃的文学作品中之有意为之的拘束，而往往可以更加自然地流露出自己天性中之某些特质。所以苏轼的词作，乃较之其全集中之其他体式的文学作品，更为集中地表现了这种超旷之特质。当然，苏轼词中原不仅只有超旷的一种风格（关于苏词中的其他风格，我们将留到下节再加讨论），不过超旷乃是苏之所以异于其他诸词人的主要特色。关于此一特质，也有人以豪放称之，且将之与南宋之辛弃疾并称，以为苏、辛二家乃两宋豪放词人之代表作者。其实苏、辛二家之词风原不尽同，王国维在其《人间词话》中曾云："东坡之词旷，稼轩之词豪"，这是极有见地的话。盖辛词沉郁，苏词超妙，辛词多愤慨之气，苏词富旷逸之怀。虽然二人皆有其能"放"之处，而其所以为"放"者，则并不相同。一般说来，辛词之放是由于一种英雄豪杰之气，而苏词之放，则是由于一种旷达超逸之怀。这便是我之所以舍弃"豪放"二字而以"超旷"称述苏词的缘故。如果说苏词中也有表现为英雄豪杰之气者，则最为众所熟知的一篇作品，自当推其《江城子》（老夫聊发少年狂）一首为代表。然而如此词之风格者，在苏词中实在并不多见，所以此种风格乃但能视之为苏词多种风格中之一种，而不能将此种风格视为苏词之主要特质也。至于其主要风格之超旷的特质，则一般人的认识对之也各有不同。以下我们就将略举几家重要的说法来一作参考。最常为众人所引用的，如胡寅之《酒边词序》云："眉山苏氏，一洗绮罗香泽之态，摆脱绸缪宛转之度，使人登高望远，举首高歌，而逸怀浩气，超乎尘垢之外。"又如王若虚《滹南诗话》卷中云："盖其天资不凡，辞气迈往，故落笔皆绝尘耳。"再如周济《宋四家词选目录序论》云："东坡天趣独到处，殆成绝诣。"更如刘熙载《艺概》卷四云："东坡词颇似老杜诗，以其无意不可入，无事不可言也。"又云："东坡词具神仙出世之姿。"以上诸说，大抵皆为对苏词超旷之特质的有见之言，而且各种观点也都有可供发挥阐释之处。但本文既因篇幅及体例之限制，故不拟在此更为推演，且凡此诸说既为一般读者之所共有的感受，则亦不需本文于此再费笔墨来述说人所共见之言。现在我们在引述诸说之后，所要提出来讨论的，乃是在这些说法中，过去也曾有两点颇引起过一些人们的疑问和争议。其一是苏词既是"一洗绮罗香泽之态，摆脱绸缪宛转之度"，是否这便表示了苏轼为人之"不及情"的有情无情的问题；其二则是苏词既是"天趣独到"、"逸怀浩气，超乎尘垢之外"、"具神仙出世之姿"，有如此超旷之襟怀与意境，然而却也有人从苏词中见到了其“寄慨无端”之处，与“幽咽怨断之音”的问题。以下我们就对此二问题一加讨论。

先谈苏轼之是否“不及情”的问题。王若虚之《滹南诗话》卷中即曾载：“晁无咎云：‘眉山公之词短于情，盖不更此境耳。’陈后山曰：‘宋玉不识巫山神女而能赋之，岂得更而后知？’是直以公为不及情也。呜呼，风韵如东坡，而谓不及于情，可乎！”本来，自五代以来，词既然是在歌筵酒席间传唱的歌词，所以几乎历代词人之作品中，都或多或少地曾经留有一些为歌儿舞伎写作的歌词，此在苏轼也并非例外。不过，在苏轼的这一类作品中，却表现了几点与别人不同之处。其一是苏轼虽然也为一些美丽的女子填写歌词，但其中却大多是为友人之姬妾、侍儿而作，因此很少有私人一己之感情介入其间；其二是在苏轼的笔下，即使同样是写美女，也不同于一般俗艳之脂粉，而别具高远之情致。即如其赠赵晦之吹笛侍儿的《水龙吟》（楚山修竹如云）一首词，其开端数句写笛之材质，便已可见苏轼之健笔高情。至其结尾数句之“嚼徵含宫，泛商流羽，一声云杪。为使君洗尽，蛮风瘴雨，作霜天晓”数句，写侍儿之吹笛，则更复寄兴高远，直欲以笛音胜过人间贬谪蛮风瘴雨之苦难矣。再如其为王定国歌儿柔奴所写的《定风波》（常羡人间琢玉郎）一首词，其上半阕结尾“自作清歌传皓齿，风起，雪飞炎海变清凉”数句，既写得矫健飞扬，后半阕结尾“试问岭南应不好，却道，此心安处是吾乡”数句，也写得旷达潇洒。如此之类，是虽写歌儿舞伎，而并不作绮罗香泽之态者也。至于苏轼自己赠伎之词且写得颇为有情者，则前后盖有两度，第一次是当苏轼自杭州通判移知密州经过苏州时所写的《醉落魄·阊门留别》一首词，其下半阕之“离亭欲去歌声咽，潇潇细雨凉吹颊。泪珠不用罗巾浥，弹在罗衫，图得见时说”诸句，写得极为凄婉。再有则是苏轼将要自徐州移知湖州时所写的《江城子·别徐州》一首词，其中有“为问东风余几许，春纵在，与谁同”及“欲寄相思千点泪，流不到，楚江东”之句，写得也极为婉转缠绵，而且这两度的离别之作，都不仅只写了一首词而已。前者在《醉落魄》之前，还写有一首《阮郎归》（一年三度过苏台）的词，后者则在《江城子》以后还写有一首《减字木兰花》（玉觞无味）的词。从这四首词来看，苏轼所写都并不是泛泛的赠伎之作，而该是果然有惜别之情的作品。盖当时苏轼正在仕途受到挫折流转各地之时，而从他在《醉落魄》一词前半阕所写的“旧交新贵音书绝，惟有佳人，犹作殷勤别”的话，和《江城子》词开端之“天涯流落思无穷”之句来看，是苏轼既满怀失意流转之悲，而此两地之怜才红粉乃如此殷勤惜别，则苏轼对之自然亦复不免有情，只是尽管是如此有情的作品，苏轼在《减字木兰花》一首词的结尾之处，也还是写了“一语相开，匹似当初本不来”的超解之辞；而且在前半阕的结尾处，也还写了“学道忘忧，一念还成不自由”的话，则其不欲为此多情之一念所拘缚，而欲获致心灵上超解之自由的意愿，也还是隐然可见的。古人有云：“太上忘情，其下不及情，情之所钟，正在我辈。”苏轼固未能全然忘情，更绝非不及情者，然其高旷之资禀，则又使其不欲为情之所拘限。他曾写有送陈令举的《鹊桥仙·七夕词》一首，云：“缑山仙子，高情云渺，不学痴騃牛女。凤箫声断月明中，举手谢时人欲去。　客槎曾犯，银河波浪，尚天风海雨。相逢一醉是前缘，风雨散、飘然何处。”陆游跋苏轼此词（见《渭南文集》卷廿八）曾云：“昔人作七夕诗，率不免有珠栊绮疏惜别之意。惟东坡此篇，居然是星汉上语。歌之，曲终，觉天风海雨逼人。”盖苏轼天资既高，襟怀又旷，故其用情之态度乃能潇洒飘逸，如天风海雨。像他在《八声甘州》一词中所写的“有情风万里卷潮来，无情送潮归”，飘然而来，倏然而逝。刘熙载《艺概·词概》曾云：“东坡词在当时鲜与同调，不独秦七、黄九别成两派也。晁无咎坦易之怀，磊落之气，差堪骖靳，然悬崖撒手处，无咎莫能追蹑矣。”其所谓“悬崖撒手”者，就正指的是苏轼之用情，有一种倏然超解的意境，固不必以世俗之见对之作有情无情之争论也。以上是我们就苏词之超旷是否便尔“不及情”一点，所做的讨论。

其次，我们再谈苏词在超旷之特色中，是否也有“寄慨无端”之处及“幽咽怨断之音”的问题。本来清代之陈廷焯在其《白雨斋词话》卷一中，即曾谓词至东坡“寄慨无端，别有天地”。近人夏敬观则曾将苏轼词分为两类，云：“东坡词如春花散空，不着迹象，使柳枝歌之，正如天风海涛之曲，中多幽咽怨断之音，此其上乘也。若夫激昂排宕，不可一世之概，陈无已所谓：‘如教坊雷大使之舞，虽极天下之工，要非本色。’乃其第二乘也。”（见《唐宋名家词选》引《吷庵手批东坡词》，至其所引陈无已云云，则见于陈师道之《后山诗话》）本来，如我们在前文所言，苏词之以超旷为其特质，原为一般读者之所共见；只是一则既有人对此超旷之特质各有不同之体会，再则有人对于词中是否可以表现超旷之风格各有不同之意见，要想说明此种复杂之情况，首先我们就不得不对苏词本身超旷风格之复杂性略加探讨。原来伴随着苏词之超旷的特质而同时出现的，也还有一些粗旷率易的弊病。即以其早期之作品言之，如其任杭州通判时所写的《风水洞作》一首小令《临江仙》词，其开端之“四大从来都偏满，此间风水何疑”两句，用佛教之以“地水火风”为“四大”之说，来写风水洞，全无真正之感发及情意，就已不免有粗率之病。再如其自杭州赴密途中所写的第一首长调《沁园春》词，其下半阕之“当时共客长安，似二陆初来俱少年。有笔头千字，胸中万卷，致君尧舜，此事何难。用舍由时，行藏在我，袖手何妨闲处看。身长健，但优游卒岁，且斗尊前”诸句，便亦不免有粗率之病。此盖由于苏轼之才气过人，故为文下笔之际，乃有时不免有率易之处。昔周济在《介存斋论词杂著》即曾云：“东坡每事俱不十分用力，古文、书、画皆尔。”又云：“人赏东坡粗豪，吾赏东坡韶秀，韶秀是东坡佳处，粗豪则病也。”而世人之读东坡词者，乃竟有人专赏其放旷而近于粗豪浅率之作，如此者自非苏词之真正赏音。而又有些读者，其胸中先有一成见，以为词之传统必须以柔媚婉约为主，因此乃对苏词抱有一种成见，以为此非词之本色。陈师道《后山词话》即曾云：“退之以文为诗，子瞻以诗为词，如教坊雷大使之舞，虽极天下之工，要非本色。”据蔡絛《铁围山丛谈》卷六载“太上皇在位，时属升平，手艺人之有称者”，以下乃列举棋、琴、琵琶诸艺人，然后曰：“舞有雷中庆，世皆呼之为雷大使。”是则雷大使本为当时著名之舞人，舞艺极天下之工。而陈师道（后山）认为“非本色”者，其意盖以为舞者皆当为妙龄之女子，今以男子而舞，则虽舞艺极工，亦非本色矣。如此之论，乃是想要把词一直保留在晚唐、五代以来之柔媚的传统之中，以为超旷之风格，非词中所宜者。若此之说，盖昧于任何一种文体，在历史的演进中，都必有其更新拓展之自然趋势，故其所见乃不免有偏狭之处。至于夏敬观以陈后山所拟之为“雷大使之舞”者为苏词之第二乘，而以其“如天风海涛之曲，中多幽咽怨断之音”者为第一乘，则是又将苏词的超旷之特质分为二类。一类为全然放旷，“激昂排宕”之近于粗豪者，为第二乘；另一类则是如“天风海涛之曲”具有超旷之特质，却并不流于粗豪，而“中多幽咽怨断之音”者，为苏词之上乘。私意以为夏氏之言实甚为有见。盖苏词于超旷之中乃偶或确有幽咽怨断之音的流露，也就是陈廷焯所说的“寄慨无端，别有天地”之处。而苏轼却又能将其幽怨的悲慨，写得如“春花散空，不着迹象”，所以乃不易为一般人之所察觉耳。盖如前文所言，苏轼在天性中既原禀有“欲以天下为己任”的“用世之志意”，也同时禀有“不为外物得失荣辱所累”的“超然之襟怀”，所以当他在仕途受到挫折时，虽也能以超旷之襟怀，作为自我解脱与安慰之方；然而究其本心，则对于用世之志意却也并不曾完全放弃。这只要我们一看苏轼平生之事迹，就可以得到具体的证明。苏轼一生屡经迁贬，但他无论流转何方，也无论在朝在野，他都未曾放弃其系心国事、关怀民瘼的志意，而且无论对己对人，他也都一直做着一种“与人为善”的努力。他在知密州任内之祈雨救灾，在知徐州任内之治平水患，在知杭州任内之浚湖筑堤，在疾疫流行时之广设病坊，甚至在晚年流迁惠州时还曾率众为二桥，以济病涉者。而即使他当年经历了九死一生的乌台诗狱，贬到黄州，受人监管不得签书公事之时，他还曾研思著述，不仅为世人留下了许多篇极好的诗、词、文、赋，还曾研读《易经》、《论语》，开始了《易传》与《论语说》之写作[①]。其后当元祐之际他再度入朝，也并未曾因为以前曾以直言系狱，便改变他立言忠直的作风。他的“欲以天下为己任”的“用世之志意”，丝毫也未曾因为忧患挫折而有所改变。则苏轼之决未全然忘情于世，从可知也。至其立身之态度，则有他写给友人的两封书简，颇可以作为参考。一封是当他贬官黄州时，给李公择写的信，其中有云：“吾侪虽老且穷，而道理贯心肝，忠义填骨髓，直须谈笑于死生之际，若见仆困穷，便尔相怜，则与不学道者大不相远矣。”又一封信，则是当他在元祐年间，与朝中旧党论政不合，想要请求外放时写给杨元素的信，其中有云：“昔之君子，惟荆是师（按：荆指王安石），今之君子，惟温是随（按：温指司马光），所随不同，其随一也。老弟与温相知至深，始终无间，然多不随耳。致此烦言，盖始于此。然进退得丧，齐之久矣，皆不足道。”（《续集》卷六《书简》）我以为从这两封信，我们很可以看到，苏轼在立身之道上，既有其坚毅之持守，而在处得失之际时，又有其超旷之襟怀。此二封书简可谓同时流露了他所禀赋的双重特质，也表现出这两种特质对于他而言，乃是既相反又相成，可以互相融汇而为用的。他的词既大多写于宦途失意流转外地之时，所以表面看来乃大多以超旷之风格为其主调，然而究其实，苏轼则决非忘怀世事无所关心的人，他与某些不分黑白是非，只求独善其身，更且自命为高士的人物是完全不同的。所以在苏轼词中，虽以超旷为其主调，然而其中却时而也隐现一种失志流转之悲。即以其最著名之词作为例，如其中秋夜怀子由的那首《水调歌头》，开端之：“明月几时有，把酒问青天。不知天上宫阙，今夕是何年。我欲乘风归去，又恐琼楼玉宇，高处不胜寒。起舞弄清影，何似在人间。”郑文焯曾称此词，谓其“发端从太白仙心脱化，顿成奇逸之笔”，其飘逸高旷之致，诚不可及。

① 苏轼在黄州写《上文潞公书》云：“到黄州，无所用心，辄复覃思于《易》、《论语》，……作《易传》九卷，又自以己意作《论语说》五卷。”（见《经进东坡文集事略》卷四十四）。

然而其中却实在也隐然表现了他自己内心深处的一种入世与出世之间的矛盾的悲慨，而这种悲慨，却又写得如“春花散空，不着迹象”。相传神宗读此词，至“琼楼玉宇”数句，曾以为“苏轼终是爱君”。读词者固无妨有此一想，然若指实其为有不忘朝廷的忠爱之意，则反似不免有沾滞之嫌矣。再如其赤壁怀古之一首《念奴娇》，其开端数句“大江东去，浪淘尽、千古风流人物”，其气象固然写得极为高远，结尾的“人间如梦，一尊还酹江月”两句，语气也表现得甚为旷达。但事实上则在“公瑾当年”之“谈笑间、樯虏灰飞烟灭”，与自己今日之迁贬黄州、志意未酬而“早生华发”的对比中，也蕴含着很多的悲慨。而世人乃有因见其“人间如梦”之外表字样，便评讥之以为消极者，若此之类，盖与另一些但赏其粗豪之作，便以为积极者，同其肤浅矣。至于苏轼在黄州所写的一些小令之作，如其《沙湖道中遇雨》的一首《定风波》词，他所表现的在“穿林打叶”之风雨声中“吟啸徐行”的自我持守的精神，以及“回首向来萧瑟处，也无风雨也无晴”之超然旷达的观照，则更是将其立身之志意，与超然之襟怀做了泯没无痕的最好的融汇和结合。但事实上则在其“穿林打叶”的叙写中，又岂没有他对自己在人生之途上所遭受的挫折和打击的悲慨。再如后来在元祐年间，他既曾因与朝中旧党论事不合，请求外放，出知杭州，两年后又被召还朝，曾写有“寄参寥子”一首《八声甘州》词，全词是：“有情风万里卷潮来，无情送潮归。问钱塘江上，西兴浦口，几度斜晖？不用思量今古，俯仰昔人非。谁似东坡老，白首忘机。　记取西湖西畔，正春山好处，空翠烟霏。算诗人相得，如我与君稀。约他年、东还海道，愿谢公、雅志莫相违。西州路，不应回首，为我沾衣。”这首词，我以为实在是苏词中最能代表其“天风海涛之曲，中有幽咽怨断之音”的一篇作品。此词开端二句写万里风涛，气象开阔，笔力矫键，外表看来似乎极为超举，然而在其“有情”、“无情”与夫“潮来”、“潮归”之间，却实在也隐含有无穷感慨苍凉之意。其下继以“问钱塘江上”至“俯仰昔人非”一段，写古今推移之中，人间的盛衰无常,便正是对前二句所透露的感慨苍凉之情意的补述和完成。而却于此种悲慨之后，突然转入“谁似东坡老，白首忘机”二句，乃脱身一跃而起，若此等处，真所谓“悬崖撒手”、“他人莫能追蹑”者矣。及至下半阕，则自“记取西湖西畔”以下三句，换笔写记忆中难忘之西湖美景，意致清丽舒徐，正可见周济所称述的苏词的“韶秀”之美。而后接以“算诗人相得，如我与君稀”二句，写苏轼自己与参寥子二人间之交谊，在前面的“春山好处，空翠烟霏”之美景的衬托之下，这一份“诗人相得”之情，真是千古所稀，今日读之，犹使人艳羡不已。而其下“约他年、东还海道，愿谢公、雅志莫相违”二句，则苏词之笔锋又再度转折，用东晋谢安之虽受朝寄而不忘东山归隐之志的故事以自喻。这正是中国古代士大夫之将入仕的用世之志意，与归隐的超旷之襟怀相结合的一个很好的典型。而且也正因为有此超旷之襟怀，入仕时方能不为利禄所陷累，而保持住清正之持守。至于就谢安而言，则他入仕以后既曾以其侄谢玄等淝水克敌之功，官至太保，然而却也曾因功高见忌而出镇新城，乃造泛海之装以自随，欲循江路归隐东山，而未几乃遇疾不起，东归之志，始终未就。苏轼用此谢安之故事以自喻，“东还海道”既有暗指重返杭州与参寥子再聚之愿望，同时也表现了自己此度再次蒙召入朝，也正如当日谢安之既有用世之心也怀出世之志，而未知他日此双重愿望与志意之能否成就，言外自有无穷恐惧志意终违之悲慨。结尾三句“西州路，不应回首，为我沾衣”，则仍用谢安之故事。盖谢安在新城遇疾之后，重返都城建康之时，乃舆病入西州门（故址在今南京市西）。安卒后，其甥羊昙行不由西州路。一日醉中不觉过州门，乃悲感不已，痛哭而去。东坡用此故事，虽改为宽慰之辞，曰“不应回首，为我沾衣”，然究其实，则岂不因苏轼心中正有此生死离别之悲感之故欤？综观此词，则一起之开阔健笔，确如天风海涛之曲，而前片结尾之“白首忘机”亦大有超旷之怀，然而中间几度转折，既有今古盛衰之慨，又有死生离别之悲，更虑及于入朝从政之忧危，知交乐事之难再。百感交集，并入笔端。夏敬观谓其“中有幽咽怨断之音”，良非虚语也。

总之，苏轼之词，虽以超旷为其主调，然其超旷之内含却并不单纯。其写儿女之情者，是用情而不欲为情所累，故当观其入而能出之处；其写旷逸之怀者，则又未全然忘情于用世之念，故又当观其出中有入之处；至其偶有失之粗豪浅率者，则是高才未免于率易之病，固当分别观之也。

三

捋青捣麨俗偏好，曲港圆荷俪亦工。
莫道先生疏格律，行云流水见高风。

在前两首绝句的讨论中，我们既曾提出了苏轼天性中原禀赋有用世之志意与超旷之襟怀两种特质，以及此二种特质在其词之写作中，所形成的“如天风海涛之曲，中多幽咽怨断之音”的特殊而可贵的风格。这种风格可以说是苏轼词中最高的成就和最重要的主调，也是他天性中之本质在词中的自然流露。而另外我们在第一首绝句的讨论中，则还曾提到过苏轼对词之写作，原是带着一种有意想要开拓创新之觉醒的。苏轼在词之发展方面的成就，就正是他的足以开拓的天性之资禀，与他的有意为之的开拓的理念相互结合所获致的一种成果。而当时北宋词坛的一般作者，却并没有能够完全接受和追随他的开拓。这一则是因为别人既没有像苏轼一样过人的资禀，再则也因为别人并没有像苏轼一样的开拓之理念的缘故。所以陈师道《后山诗话》乃谓“子瞻以诗为词”，又曰：“虽极天下之工，要非本色。”这正是当时一般人对苏词的看法。直到由北宋转入南宋的杰出女词人李清照也依然保持这种看法，所以李清照虽然在其诗作中也曾写出过像“至今思项羽，不肯过江东”和“木兰横戈好女子，老矣不复志千里，但愿相将渡淮水”之类的豪壮的句子，但在她的词中，却决没有此种风格的作品。这便可见其天性中纵然也未尝没有可以为词做出开拓的本质，但在理念中却缺乏此种开拓之觉醒，总以为词应该“别是一家”，所以对于苏词才会有“皆句读不葺之诗耳”的讥评。而苏轼之于词，却是既具有为之开拓的资质，也具有意欲为之开拓的理念的一位作者，既然具有此一理念，所以在苏词中，除了由其本质所形成的超旷之主调以外，他便也还曾做过各种不同风格的多方面的尝试。简单举些例证来看，即如他的一首《江城子》（老夫聊发少年狂）词中所写的“会挽雕弓如满月，西北望，射天狼”和他的另一首《南乡子》（旌旆满江湖）词中所写的“诏发楼船万舳舻”及“帕首腰刀是丈夫”，其豪放之致，在词中便是一种明显的开拓。此外，如其为李公择生子而写的《减字木兰花》（维熊佳梦）一首词，其中的“多谢无功，此事如何著得侬”，和他的另一首为迎紫姑神而写的《少年游》（玉肌铅粉傲秋霜）词，其中的“谁能借箸，无复是张良”诸作，则都是以游戏笔墨写的嬉笑谑浪之辞。再如其赠润守许仲涂的另一首《减字木兰花》（郑庄好客），则更以妓女之名字嵌入词中，全词八句，分别以“郑容落籍，高莹从良”八字为句首，则是以词为文字游戏矣。更如其另一首《减字木兰花·送东武令赵昶失官归海州》词，其开端之“贤哉令尹，三仕已之无喜愠”，则又将经书《论语》之句融入小词之中；又如其在泗州雍熙塔下所作的两首《如梦令》（水垢何曾相受、自净方能净彼），则是以小词写名理禅机。至于其《浣溪沙·徐门石潭谢雨道上作五首》，其“麻叶层层檾叶光”及“捋青捣麨软饥肠”等句，则又以乡俚之语写田野农家风物，表现得极为朴质自然。而其作于燕子楼之《永遇乐》“明月如霜”，则又以“明月如霜，好风如水”，“曲港跳鱼，圆荷泻露”，及“紞如三鼓，铮然一叶”一系列骈偶之句，来写静夜之景色，又表现得极为工整清丽。他如其《卜算子》（缺月挂疏桐）一首写孤鸿之幽意深远；《水龙吟》（似花还似非花）一首，写杨花之柔致缠绵，则不仅有随物赋形之妙，且对南宋之咏物词也具有相当之影响。总之，苏轼对于小词之写作，是不仅有杰出之成就，也有广泛之拓展的。以上，我们不过只是简单举引一些例证，便已经足可以见出其内容及风格之多采多姿之一斑了。苏轼自己对于他在词中的拓展，也颇为自负，而这种自负之意，又可以分为两个不同的阶段：第一个阶段是当他由杭州通判转知密州及徐州之际，这时他对词境的拓展，已有了初步的成就，这种自负之意曾表现于他给鲜于子骏的书简中，所谓“亦自是一家”者是也；第二个阶段则是经过了黄州的贬谪，他在元祐年间又再度入朝的时候，这时他已曾写出了不少名篇杰作，完成了他所特具的超旷之风格的最高成就。宋人俞文豹《吹剑续录》所载，他在玉堂之日，曾问幕士自己作的词比柳永何如？当幕士回答说：“柳郎中词，只好十七八女子执红牙板唱‘杨柳岸晓风残月’；学士词，须关西大汉执铁板唱‘大江东去’”时，苏轼曾经“为之绝倒”（参看本书《论柳永词》第三节）。其自负之意亦复如在目前。至于我们对于苏词所作出的开拓，应该采取怎样的态度，则我以为可以将之主要区分为后人可以学习及后人不可以学习的两类来看待。先谈后人不可以学习的一类，那就是我们在前一首绝句之讨论中所曾经提出的，苏词中之以超旷为主调，但在其“天风海涛之曲”中却又含有“幽咽怨断之音”的作品。这一类词，是苏轼的用世之志意与其超旷之襟怀相融汇所达成的最高境界，是后世既无其学问志意更无其性情襟抱的人无论怎样也无法学习到的。这是在苏词之开拓中，所表现出的一部分最可宝贵的成就。再谈后人可以学习的一类，则我以为苏词对后世之影响，可以说是功过参半的。先就其有功的一方面而言，则苏词之“一洗绮罗香泽之态”，确实有使天下人“耳目一新”之功。这在与苏轼同时代的一些词人，虽然尚未能完全接受，而对以后南宋之词人，则形成了相当大的影响。即如胡寅为向子湮写《酒边词序》，即曾言：“芗林居士步趋苏堂而哜其胾者。”黄昇《花庵词选》论陈与义之词，亦曾云“识者谓其可摩坡仙之垒也”。唐圭璋《宋词三百首笺注》于叶梦得词，亦曾引关注之言，谓“其合处不减东坡”。其他如张元干的豪壮之篇，朱敦儒的闲放之什，便也都留有受到苏词之影响的痕迹。至于张孝祥之为词，则更是有意学苏的（谢尧仁《张于湖先生集序》可以参看）。而其中最值得注意的一位重要的作者，自然便是被后人与苏轼并称的南宋词坛上最伟大的作者辛弃疾。本来我们在前一首绝句的讨论中也曾提出过辛弃疾来与苏轼相比较，不过在那一篇的讨论中，我们的重点是在于要说明两家的不同之处。唯其苏、辛有相似之处，所以才要分辨出其中相异之差别，这与我们论及苏轼与柳永之关系时，曾提出二人在兴象高远之一点有可以相通之处，也是因为柳、苏二家之风格迥异，所以才要在其相异之中分辨出可以相通之处的道理一样。这正是有才识的大作家之善于汲取及变化的本领，也是论文学之演进者所不可不注意的观察角度。如果说苏词得之于柳的，是其兴象高远之启发，那么辛词所得之于苏者，则正是苏轼在词之开拓中所表现的“无意不可入，无事不可言”的魄力和眼界。不仅凡是以上我们所举出的苏词在开拓中所完成的各种意境与风格。辛词无不有之，而且辛词还更曾以其纵横不世之才，抑塞难申之气，突破了苏词的范畴，完成了他自己的更为杰出也更为博大的成就。纳兰成德《渌水亭杂识》卷四即曾云：“词虽苏、辛并称，而辛实胜苏。”周济《介存斋论词杂著》亦云：“世以苏、辛并称，苏之自在处，辛偶能到，辛之当行处，苏必不能到。”关于苏、辛同异之详细差别，我们只好等到论辛词时再加细述，这里只好从略了。总之，苏词之开拓，对于南宋辛弃疾诸人之影响，是极为重大的。《四库全书提要》即曾谓词之演进，“至柳永而一变，至轼而又一变，遂开南宋辛弃疾等一派”。这自然是苏词影响后世之有功的一面。至于其有过的一方面，则我以为主要乃当归过于其率意之笔及游戏之作。关于苏词之用笔率易之病，我们在前一首绝句之讨论中，已曾举例说明，且曾引周济《介存斋论词杂著》之言，谓：“东坡每事俱不十分用力，古文、书、画皆尔，词亦尔。”此言实甚为有见。至其所以然者，则我以为一则盖由于苏轼之才大，他人所千思百虑而不可得者，苏轼乃可以谈笑得之，故有时乃不免有率意之病；再则亦由于苏轼之性情超旷，遂尔不甚斤斤于形迹，故有时乃不免有脱略之处。这是造成苏词之有时不免率易之笔的两个主要原因。至于其好为游戏之作，则如本文前面所举例证中，其为李公择生子而作的一首《减字木兰花》词，便不仅词句谐谑而已，词前小序中亦曾有“乃为作此戏之，举坐皆绝倒”之言。其另一首为迎紫姑神而写的《少年游》（玉肌铅粉傲秋霜）词，词前小序亦曾有“乃以此戏之”之言。再如其在泗州雍熙塔下所作的两首《如梦令》小词，词前小序便亦有“戏作《如梦令》两阕”之言。此外，如其赠润守许仲涂之一首《减字木兰花》词，则词前小序虽无“戏作”字样，然其“以‘郑容落籍，高莹从良’为句首”之语，乃是说明此词要以妓女之名字嵌入句首，则其为游戏笔墨，亦复可知。从这些词例，足可说明苏轼之好以游戏笔墨来写作小词。至其所以然者，则我以为主要亦可归纳为二因：一则因为苏轼之性情坦率乐观，富有风趣，故好为游戏之作；再则也因为词之写作，在当时本来就未尝被视为严肃的作品，这可以说是造成苏词中多有游戏之作的主要原因。以上我们所谈到的率易之笔与游戏之作两点，就苏词本身言之，本不过为大醇之小疵，未足深病。盖凡属天资禀赋属于超放一型之天才，其创作便常不免如长江大河之挟泥沙以俱下。古人有云：“江海不择细流，故能就其深。”这一类天才之小疵与其大醇的飞扬博大之成就，常是结合而不可分的，而另一种属于粼粼清泚一型之才人，每当有所写作，必字斟句酌而后出者，则虽无泥沙之渣滓，而往往也就难成其为泱漭之洪流矣。所以就苏轼本人而言，若将其小疵与大醇相较，则他的这些小的疵病，原是可以谅解的。只不过若就其对后世的影响而言，则有一些庸俗浅薄之辈，对苏词之佳处所在，往往并不能真正欣赏了解，而只能以浅拙之笔写一些粗率之作与游戏之辞，自以为源于苏轼，则始作俑者，苏轼亦不能辞其咎矣。

以上我们既对苏词多样风格之开拓及其得失功过，做了简单的说明，另有一点，我们也要讨论的，则是苏词往往有不尽合律之处的问题。胡仔《苕溪渔隐丛话》后集卷卅三引晁无咎评本朝乐章之语，即曾云：“东坡词，人谓多不谐音律。”陆游亦曾云：“世言东坡不能歌，故所作乐府词多不协律。晁以道谓：‘绍圣初，与东坡别于汴上，东坡酒酣，自歌《阳关曲》’，则公非不能歌，但豪放，不喜剪裁以就声律耳。”（见《历代诗余》卷一百十五《词话》宋二）从这些叙述来看，苏轼词之多有不合律之处，盖原为人所共见之事实。至其所以多不协律之原因，则有两种不同的说法。一则以为“东坡不能歌”，故其词多不协律；又则以为苏轼非不能歌，惟因性情豪放，故“不喜剪裁以就声律耳”。兹先就苏轼是否能歌的问题来谈，则本文第一节中，曾引苏轼致其兄子明的一封信，其中谓：“记得应举时，见兄能讴歌，甚妙。弟虽不会，然常令人唱为何词。”据此可知苏轼青年时代本不能歌。至于晁以道所谓苏轼曾歌《阳关曲》云云者，则已为绍圣年间之事，距离其嘉祐年间初赴汴梁应举之时，盖已有将近四十年之久。我们以前也曾谈到苏轼之尝试为小词，是从熙宁年间出为杭州通判以后才开始的。方其致力小词之写作时，可能也曾学习吟唱之事。苏轼在贬谪黄州时，曾写有《哨遍》一词，前有小序云：“陶渊明赋归去来，有其词而无其声。余既治东坡，筑雪堂于上。人俱笑其陋，独鄱阳董毅夫过而悦之，有卜邻之意。乃取《归去来词》，稍加檃括，使就声律，以遗毅夫，使家僮歌之，时相从于东坡。释耒而和之，扣牛角而为之节，不亦乐乎？”从这段话来看，苏轼既能檃括《归去来词》“使就声律”，又可以“释耒而和之”，已足可见到苏轼自从事小词之写作以来，盖早曾习为声律吟唱之事，则其词之偶有失律之处。决非由于不能歌或不知律的缘故，这是我们所可断言的。再则词之是否谐律，与作者之是否能歌也并无必然之关系，故此一说法可谓根本不能成立。其次再就苏轼之“不喜剪裁以就声律”之问题言之，则苏词其实大部分都是合乎声律的，偶有少数不合律之处，不过以天才恣纵，如晁无咎所云“横放杰出，自是曲子中缚不住者”，故不屑于斤斤计较而已。关于其不合律之现象，则我们可以举两则例证来说明两种不同的情况。其一是《水龙吟·次韵章质夫杨花词》，其最后的十三个字的长句之句逗该如何点读问题。其二则是《念奴娇·赤壁怀古》词，下半阕换头以后之“小乔初嫁了，雄姿英发”二句，每句字数之多少与音调之平仄，都与正格之格律不合的问题。先谈《水龙吟》词，此词结尾处的“细看来不是杨花点点是离人泪”十三字长句，按一般格律，原当将之标点为“细看来不是，杨花点点，是离人泪”，也就是每句字数为五、四、四的停顿，而且最后一个四字句应该是一、三的读法。但一般选注苏词者，却大多将此一句标点为“细看来不是杨花，点点是离人泪”，也就是七、六的停顿，而七字句是三、四的读法，六字句是三、三的读法。像这种情形，表面看来，虽似与一般格律不合，但这其实只是后人对苏词之标点的不同，并不能说是苏词不合格律，盖此一十三字长句之平仄，依格律，其平仄声调应是“｜——｜｜＋—＋｜｜｜——｜”（“—”代表平声，“｜”代表仄声，“＋”代表平仄通用）。苏轼此结尾十三字长句之平仄，与格律完全相合，决无不谐平仄之处。至于标点之不同，则因古人诗词之读法，原有以声律为准之读法与依文法为准之读法二种。一般说来，讲解时可依文法为准，而吟诵时则应依声律为准。一般苏词选注本将此句断为“细看来不是杨花，点点是离人泪”，是依文法的断句。但依声律，则仍可将此句读为：“细看来不是，杨花点点，是离人泪。”在“是”字下的停顿可视为“逗”，不视为“句”。而“点点”二字，则既是对“杨花”之描述，也是对“泪”之描述。明白了这种情形，就可知此句本该依声律标读，“点点”二字，亦可标于“杨花”之下。如此不仅不会有文法不通之感，且由于音节之顿挫，乃更可见其情意的曲折深婉之致。若此者，当然并非苏词之不合律，而只是后人标读的不同。另外在苏词中还有些别的长句，也有类似情形，读者可自己寻绎得之，因篇幅所限，就不再更为辞费了。至于另一则例证《念奴娇·赤壁怀古》词，其下半阕换头以下之“小乔初嫁了，雄姿英发”二句，据万树《词律》，于此调之用仄韵者，仅收辛弃疾之“野棠花落”一首为正格及苏轼此词为别格，且加有按语曰：“《念奴娇》用仄韵者，惟此二格止矣。盖因‘小乔’至‘英发’

九字，用上五下四，遂分二格。”盖在辛氏之《念奴娇》（野棠花落）一词中，此换头以下之两句，乃是“行人曾见，帘底纤纤月。”其断句为上四下五，为一般习用之常格也。但苏词与辛词格式相异者，原来还不仅只是两句之断句字数不同而已，其平仄之声调也并不相同。辛词这九个字的声调是“———丨—丨——丨”，而苏词这九个字的声调则是“丨——丨丨———丨”，二者相比较，除开端首字之平仄往往可以通用之外，其主要之差别盖在后五字之声调，辛词是“—丨——丨”，而苏词则是“丨———丨”，且将第一字之“丨”声（即“了”字）断入上句。如此，则表面看来，苏词便与辛词所代表之《念奴娇》常格，就同时既有了断句之不同，又有了平仄之不同的双重差异。这正是苏词之所以留给读者一个“不谐音律’之印象的主要缘故。不过这种判断并不完全正确。首先我们该注意的是苏之时代在前，而辛之时代在后，虽然辛词《念奴娇》之格式在后世较为通行，因此被万树《词律》认为正格，但我们却不该仅据此格便认定苏词为不谐律，而当看一看与苏轼同时或较早之作者，他们所写的《念奴娇》的格式是怎样的。如此我们就会发现，原来苏词的平仄才是当时通行的格式。举例来看，即如北宋中叶的名臣韩琦有一位门客，名叫沈唐，曾写有一首《念奴娇》（杏花过雨），其换头以下的两句是“多情因甚，有轻离轻拆”（见《全宋词》），后五字之平仄便是“丨———丨”。又如与苏轼同时之黄庭坚，也曾写有一首《念奴娇》（断虹霁雨），其换头以下此二句是“晚凉幽径。绕张园森木”，后五字之平仄亦同。如此便可见当时之《念奴娇》词，本有此一格式，是则苏词之平仄，原无所谓“不谐律”之处也。至于其断句之问题，则此处九字一气贯下，原来也是一个长句，中间句逗亦未始不可微有变化。即如沈唐之“多情因甚有轻离轻拆”，及黄庭坚之“晚凉幽径绕张园森木”，如果我们读时在沈词之“有”字下略顿，或在黄词之“绕”字下略顿，都未尝不可。只不过苏词所用之“了”字，是个语尾助辞，遂使此一九字长句于此处截然断开，反而失去了原来之欲断还连的曲折婉转之致，如此而已。实在也不能说是什么严重的“不谐律”。再有一点值得注意的是，就在苏轼写了前一首《念奴娇·赤壁怀古》以后不久，他还曾写了另一首题为《中秋》的《念奴娇》（凭高眺远）。换头以下的两句是“举杯邀月，对影成三客”，则其断句及平仄又完全与《赤壁怀古》一首不同，而反与辛词之“野棠花落”一首全同，而这一体式，则在苏词以前反而未曾见有别家如此写过。是则此二体式究以何者为正格，或当时传唱之《念奴娇》本有此二体式，或者反而是后世流传所谓“正格”者，才是由苏轼所变化创制而出，亦未可知。盖此二首《念奴娇》词皆为苏轼在黄州所作，当时他既然已经能够把陶渊明的《归去来辞》檃括以就声律，则在词调中小作变化，原来也是可能的。除以上所讨论的被一般人认为不合律的两则明显的例证以外。其他本来还有一些每句字数多少等问题，即如苏轼曾写过几首《满江红》词，其下半阕之第七句，即有时作七个字，有时作八个字，如其题为《怀子由作》的一首《满江红》（清颍东流）此句为“衣上旧痕余苦泪”，是七个字一句，而其题为《正月十三雪中送文安国还朝》的另一首《满江红》（天岂无情），则此句为“不用向佳人诉离恨”，是八个字一句。盖词既原为合乐之歌辞，故于拍板缓急之间，知音律者往往可于其中加入衬字（词中加衬字者，自敦煌曲即已有之，惟不若后世元曲用衬字之习见而已）。苏词“不用向”一句，其“用”字即可视为衬字。此自为词中可以有的变化，而不得谓为“不谐律”也。除去此种情形外，还有词句中用骈用散的问题，即如苏轼在其所作一首《永遇乐·寄孙巨源》，开端之“长忆别时，景疏楼上，明月如水。美酒清歌，流连不住，月随人千里。别来三度，孤光又满，冷落共谁同醉”，九句一气贯下，全为散行。而其另一首为燕子楼作的《永遇乐》（明月如霜），则开端之“明月如霜，好风如水，清景无限。曲港跳鱼，圆荷泻露，寂寞无人见。紞如三鼓，铮然一叶，黯黯梦云惊断”，同样的九句，却变为两句骈、一句散的三度重复，而因此遂造成此同调二词在风格及吟诵间有了很大的差别。若此等者，盖所谓才人伎俩，变化无方，固全非不谐律也。只是在此九句中有一个五字句，平仄及顿挫小有不同。前一首之“月随人千里”是“｜———｜”，后一首之“寂寞无人见”是“｜｜——｜”。前一首为三、二之顿挫，后一首为二、三之顿挫。在大同中有小异，若此者则是大才之人不斤斤于小节之表现。总之，苏轼词就寻常格律来看，是确实有些“不谐律”之处的，不过，经过我们的分析，便可以了解，苏词虽有“不谐律”处，但确都掌握了基本的重点，若此者，我以为并非由于苏轼之不熟悉音律，反而正是已熟于律然后能脱去其束缚之表现，所谓“曲子中缚不住者”是也。此正如李白之于律诗，往往突破外表声律及对偶之限制，而却掌握了保持声律之优美平衡的某种本质上的重点。此亦正如骑车技术之高妙者，方能在车上做出不守常规之种种表演，而却掌握了平衡的重点，所以才不致跌落地上。至于一般无此高妙之技术者，则最好依守常规，不可胆大妄为，以免跌致血流骨折之下场。近人为词者，也有些不遵格律，平仄句法任意妄写之人，则其作品使人读之根本无法上口。盖诗词原为美文，音律之美为其最重要之一种质素，苏轼纵有不合一般外表格律之处，然而却自有其自己所掌握的韵律之美的基本质素。近人则破坏旧有格律之后，并不知且不能掌握自己的韵律之美，遂成为拗涩槎枒，不可卒读。若此者，固不得引坡公为例而自我解嘲也。

1984 年 6 月写于成都

On the Song Lyrics of Su Shi

The biography of Su Shi in the *Song History*[1] begins with two anecdotes of his early life. When he was nine years old, while his father was away from home pursuing his studies, his mother was responsible for teaching him. When they read the biography of the Eastern Han public servant Fan Pang, who, with his mother's approval, sacrificed himself for his principles, Su Shi sighed in admiration and said, "Would you permit me to act as Fan Pang did?" His mother said, "If you are capable of doing what he did, could I fail to act as Pang's mother did?"

Another passage records his reaction, as a grown man, to reading *Zhuangzi*: "I used to have such ideas but had no words to express them. Now I have discovered them in this book."

Both of these stories are taken from the grave inscription composed by his younger brother, Su Zhe. They illuminate two basic strands in Su Shi's character. When appointed Executor of the Emperor's Purifying Edict, Fan Pang took his responsibilities literally and resolved to cleanse the state of corruption, and like Fan Pang, Su Shi was committed to the Confucian ideal of service, taking the whole world as his responsibility, at whatever cost to himself. At the same time he found a kindred spirit in Zhuangzi, who wrote of those enlightened men who rose above the affairs of the world, who created the parable of the butterfly dream, and who invented the genii that did not drown when the world was inundated by flood waters nor suffer from heat that melted metal and stone. Unlike Liu Yong, who was torn between his desire to serve and his inclination toward romance and dissipation, only to be disappointed in both, Su Shi achieved a harmonious combination of Confucian dedication to service and Taoist detachment. Even in misfortune and exile he was never reduced to doubt and indecision, and in the end he maintained his integrity and achieved his own goals in life.

His literary output was enormous. His talent matched his broad interests, and he wrote outstanding pieces in every genre. His three-hundred-odd song lyrics constitute a small part of his collected works and might be dismissed as casual compositions done on the spur of the moment. Yet these casually composed song lyrics are remarkably representative of the unique quality of his literary works generally. In them he expresses simultaneously his determination to serve and his disposition to be detached; they are also notable for opening up a vast new realm for this verse form.

Several high officials of the Northern Song sometimes indulged in the composition of song lyrics and, while writing them, unconsciously disclosed something of their personality and inner feelings. This was part of a gradual development that came to permit a verse form originally regarded as appropriate only for love songs to be used by educated, literary men for many of the themes proper to formal *shi* poetry. Though the Short Songs of Yan Shu and Ouyang Xiu subtly suggest a deeper reflection of the poet's feelings, what they wrote was not obviously different from the love songs of the *Huajian ji*. With Su Shi, lyrics set to music came to serve as the direct expression of the poet's own feelings. This remarkable achievement came about through the combination of one man's genius with the social background and the literary currents of the times. Granted that this tendency for the song lyric to function as a vehicle for the individual poet's feeling was already present in the songs of Yan Shu and Ouyang Xiu, and even more obviously so in the earlier Li Yu, with Su Shi it was deliberate, bringing a new awareness of the possibilities. In a letter to Xianyu Zijun, he said very clearly, "Recently I have been writing song lyrics. They may not have the flavor of Liu Yong's, but this is my own way of doing it."[2] This is a clear statement of his intention to establish a new approach to the current fashion of song writing. The period from the time when he first began writing song lyrics until he evolved his own distinctive manner lies between the years 1072 and 1079. In his earlier writings there is no mention of writing songs. He took office in Hangzhou in the winter of 1071, and his earliest songs date from the next spring:[3] "Southern Song" (*Nan ge zi*, *QSC*, p. 293), "The Spreading Fragrance" (*Xing xiang zi*, *QSC*, p. 303), and "Immortal on the River Bank" (*Lin jiang xian*, *QSC*, p. 286). These are all Short Songs. His first Long Song is "Spring in the Qin Garden" (*Qinyuan chun*, *QSC*, p. 282), written in the winter of 1074, when he was transferred to Mizhou. It bears the title "En Route to Mizhou, travelling early, sent to Ziyou".[4] Thereafter the number of songs grows daily, and their style matures rapidly. There is "River Town" (*Jiang cheng zi*, *QSC*, p. 300) in memory of his wife, another to the same tune with the title "Going out Hunting at Mizhou" (*QSC*, p. 299), "Water Music" (*Shuidiao getou*, *QSC*, p. 280), and the five stanzas to the tune "Sands of the Washing Stream" (*Huan xi sha*, *QSC*, p. 316) describing rural village life. The various descriptive titles following the tune title show Su Shi's intention to write song lyrics on *shi* poetry subjects, and these examples demonstrate his ability to use such topics for a song. The letter to Xianyu Zijun is a statement of his confidence in the innovation he was already practicing at this stage.

Su Shi's song lyrics developed rapidly after these first experiments and reached their high point after his exile to Huangzhou. The most notable feature of these songs is that Su Shi was already using their form quite naturally to express the two concerns that preoccupied him—his desire to serve and his inclination toward detachment. For example, songs to the tunes "Stilling Wind and Waves" (*Ding feng bo*, *QSC*, p. 288), "West River Moon" (*Xijiang yue*, *QSC*, p. 284), "Niannu is Charming" (*Niannu jiao*, *QSC*, p. 282, translated below), "Immortal by the Riverbank" (*Lin jiang xian*, *QSC*, p. 287), and "Fragrance Fills the Courtyard" (*Man ting fang*, *QSC*, p. 278) all show this characteristic combination of contrary impulses.

I would like next to consider the influences, both external and from within himself, that led to this development in Su Shi's songs. When he began writing them, around 1072, he was thirty-seven years old. Had he no interest in such poetry before then, one wonders, and if he did, why didn't he try his hand at writing songs? The answer is to be found in a letter he wrote earlier, while still in Huangzhou, to his cousin Su Ziming: "When I went up for the civil service examinations, I remember you sang ballads very beautifully. Although I could not sing, I always had someone perform some song or other for me."[5] It is inconceivable that a sensitive poet like Su Shi could have been oblivious to the ubiquitous music of the flourishing entertainment establishments of the bustling capital. Clearly, he had a taste for popular songs even then. There is further evidence of his interest in the frequent mention in his letters and conversations, as recorded by contemporaries, of Liu Yong, the most popular songwriter of the time. But it is significant that he made no effort to write songs himself. I believe it was because he was at that time a serious young man with high aspirations, one who placed next to the top in his examination and won the unqualified admiration of the famous minister Ouyang Xiu. What Su Shi then devoted his writing to were proposals for government action and essays on the nature of government. He had no time for such frivolities as song writing. During the two periods of mourning after the death of his parents, first his mother and then his father, he was back in Meishan managing family affairs; and after his return to duty at the court when Wang Anshi was inaugurating his Reform Policy, Su Shi still held to his ideal of taking the empire's affairs as his personal responsibility. He presented the Emperor Shenzong with the memorials "Considerations for Judging Candidates for the State Schools" and "Protest at Buying Zhejiang Lanterns", and wrote successively his two ten-thousand-word memorials. All this activity roused suspicion and resentment in the bureaucracy, and the Imperial Censor submitted a slanderous memorial castigating his errors. He then requested a provincial assignment and was made Governor of Hangzhou. It was soon after his arrival in Hangzhou that he began to write song lyrics.

The time and the place are both significant, for it was in 1071 that his ambition to make a significant contribution to government policy was checked, and Hangzhou, with its scenic setting, served to rouse his interest in song writing. The determination to serve and the inclination toward detachment were both ingrained in his character. A career as a court official was the way to be of use to the world, and when that path was blocked, he found consolation in detachment and began to write songs. However, the song lyrics he began to write in Hangzhou were not yet an unmixed expression of those feelings; he was still experimenting with the form. The Short Songs he wrote before his transfer to Mizhou all show the influence of earlier poets, chiefly Ouyang Xiu and Liu Yong.[6] Ouyang Xiu's songs are characterized by their playful tone, which dispels the pain of frustration;[7] the Short Songs celebrating excursions in the countryside Su Shi wrote soon after his arrival in Hangzhou are similar in tone. Of course, Su Shi and Ouyang Xiu shared the Confucian belief in self-control in any situation, and they were unwilling to let themselves fall into depression because of their troubles. This determined optimism shows up in their songs as a sort of free and easy tone. Besides their similarity in temperament, Ouyang Xiu's early recognition and patronage of the candidate Su Shi and his own indulgence in song writing made it inevitable that his songs would make a strong impression on the younger poet, who refers to Ouyang Xiu frequently in his songs. In the one to the tune "West River Moon" (*Xijiang yue*, *QSC*, p. 285) the Mount Ping Hall it celebrates was built by Ouyang Xiu, and the line "They still sing about the spring wind in the willow trees" alludes to Ouyang's song to the tune "*Chao zhong cuo*" (*QSC*, p. 122), with the lines "The trailing willows I planted before the hall, How many times has the spring wind passed through?" Another example, his song to the tune "Magnolia Flower" (*Mulanhua ling*, *QSC*, p. 283), carries the note, "Using the same rhyme as Master Ouyang's 'West Lake'", and in it the line "Pretty girls still sing the Old Tippler's songs" refers to Ouyang's song on West Lake to the tune "Spring in the Jade Mansion" (*Yulou chun*, an alternative title for "Magnolia Flower", *QSC*, p. 133).

These examples not only show Su Shi acknowledging Ouyang's influence, they also reveal the nature of that influence: the attitude of airy detachment conveyed in Ouyang's line, "I lean over clear emptiness on the balustrade on Mount Ping, the mountain suspended between being and non-being" and the mood of relaxed enjoyment in "Misty waves spread out north and south on West Lake, the sound of pipes and strings carried in the breeze." These attitudes are prominent in all of Su Shi's Short Songs about landscape scenery. An example is the one to the tune "Waves Scour the Sand" (*Lang tao sha*, *QSC*, p. 327) written in 1072 on an excursion out of the city:

Yesterday I went out east of the city	昨日出东城
To look for signs of spring.	试探春情
Pink apricot blossoms hung thick over the wall	墙头红杏暗如倾
With a host of buds inside the fence not yet open,	槛内群芳芽未吐

But spring was there already.	早已回春
Fragrant dust is laid on the pretty path,	绮陌敛香尘
Snow no longer falls in the village up ahead.	雪霁前村
The Lord of Spring works hard and doesn't neglect his job:	东君用意不辞辛
I imagine the spring light some place	料想春光先到处
Has already blown the plum blossoms into flower.	吹绽梅英

He is concerned here only with appreciating the early signs of spring. In the one written in 1073 to the tune "The Spreading Fragrance" (*Xing xiang zi*, *QSC*, p. 303) on visiting Seven Mile Shoals, where Yan Guang (Han Dynasty), unwilling to serve at court, retired to fish, he describes the setting, hills on both sides enclosing the stream. The tone is one of detachment:

The leaf-boat is light	一叶舟轻
The oars startle the wild swan.	双桨鸿惊
Sky and water are clear, the waves still, the reflections deep.	水天清，影湛波平
Fish overturn the water-plant mirror,	鱼翻藻
Egrets dot the misty isle.	鹭点烟汀
Over the sandbank the stream is swift:	遇沙溪急，
Frosty stream runs cold	霜溪冷，
Moonlight stream flows bright.	月溪明
Layer after layer, like a picture,	重重似画
Folded like a screen.	曲曲如屏
Consider the past:	算当年，虚老殿陵
Yan Guang grew old in vain;	
To serve your ruler is but a dream.	君臣一梦

Then and now it's all an empty name. 今古虚名
Only the far-off hills endure, 但远山长，
Hills obscured by clouds, 云山乱，
Hills clear at dawn. 晓山青

The first stanza clearly shows Ouyang Xiu's influence. However, the differences in the two poets' characters are also revealed in their songs. For Ouyang Xiu, a relaxed, carefree mood was inspired by an external scene, which provided emotional release. For Su Shi, dissipating care came not just from appreciating nature but from philosophical understanding, from within himself. Ouyang Xiu's songs seldom have philosophical content or make a direct emotional statement, but both qualities are common in Su Shi's songs. The lines "To serve your ruler is but a dream, / Then and now it's all an empty name" make a statement about human affairs; and when he writes in "The Beautiful Yu" (*Yu mei ren*, *QSC*, p. 306) "At midnight the wind is still and I am ready to go home, / Only the moonlight shimmering on a green glass river," he is subtly conveying his feeling of loneliness. He differs from not only Ouyang Xiu in this respect; earlier song writers from the *Huajian* collection seldom wrote in this way.

Thus, even Su Shi's early songs depart from his models and, despite the unmistakable influence of Ouyang Xiu, open up a wider channel for the development of the song lyric. The other major influence on Su Shi's songs was the contemporary Liu Yong, about whose extremely popular songs he expressed contradictory opinions. Liu Yong is the song writer he mentioned most frequently, both in his own writings and in the conversations and anecdotes recorded by his contemporaries, and it is with Liu Yong's songs that Su Shi most often compared his own: "I may not have Liu Seventh's flair, but I do my own thing" conveys the tone. His frequent mention of Liu Yong's songs suggests how important they were to him, yet his own critical estimate of those songs was sometimes derogatory, as when he remarked contemptuously of a line in one of the lyrics written by his follower Qin Guan ("My soul melts at this occasion"), "You've learned to write songs from Liu Yong." Such comments lead us to believe that Su Shi has a low opinion of at least some of Liu Yong's songs. On the other hand, he also sometimes gave them unstinting praise, as when he says of these lines from the song to the tune "Eight-Rhymed Ganzhou Song" (*Basheng Ganzhou*, *QSC*, p. 43) that they are worthy of the best of the Tang dynasty poets:[9]

The frosty wind turns sharp,	渐霜风凄紧
River and hills are desolate.	关河冷落
The last rays of the sun shine on my window	残照当楼

These various judgments permit the following inferences: Su Shi took Liu Yong seriously as an equal. He felt distaste and contempt for his erotic songs, but he had nothing but praise for the evocative imagery and panoramic descriptions in some of his lines. This mixed attitude resulted in a subtle relationship between the song lyrics of the two poets, one that readers have not always grasped. In 1057, when Su Shi first came to Bianliang for the examinations, Liu Yong's songs were being sung everywhere and must have made a strong impression on him; their influence is apparent in his first Long Song, subtitled "Setting out early on horseback for Mizhou, I sent this off to Ziyou" and written to the tune "Spring in the Qin Garden" (*Qinyuan chun*, *QSC*, p. 282):

The dim light of the lamp in the lonely tavern	孤馆灯青
The crowing cock at the country inn	野店鸡号
Breaks the traveler's pillow dream.	旅枕梦残
The moonlight's luster fades,	渐月华收练
Dawn frost glitters,	晨霜耿耿

Cloudy mountains spread their brocade,	云山摛锦
Morning dew hangs heavy.	朝露漙漙
There is no end to the roads of the world	世路无穷
But this toilsome life has its limit.	劳生有限
Petty concerns like this, and joy is always rare.	似此区区长鲜欢
My little song is done	微吟罢
And I rest in the saddle, silent,	凭征鞍无语
Reflecting on a thousand things past.	往事千端
When we were both staying in Chang'an, young men	当时共客长安
Like the Lu brothers first come to the capital,	似二陆初来俱少年
A thousand words on the tips of our pens	有笔头千字
Ten thousand volumes in our heart.	胸中万卷
To make a perfect ruler of our sovereign—	致君尧舜
Nothing hard about that!	此事何难
Employed or let go is a matter of the times,	用舍由时
Whether to act or withdraw is up to us.	行藏在我
Hands in sleeves, why not watch from the sidelines?	袖手何妨闲处看
As long as our health holds	身长健
Let's finish out our lives in idleness	但优遊卒岁
And enjoy a drink when we can.	且斗尊前

The tone and structure of the first stanza closely resemble the description of scenery in Liu Yong's songs about his journeys from one post to another. Whether through deliberate imitation or unconscious influence, it is perfectly understandable that Su Shi should sometimes have written like this.

For a poet accustomed to writing *shi* poetry and just starting to experiment with song lyrics, it is natural to begin with Short Songs, because the prosody of the Short Song is similar to *shi*. Su Shi's first attempts at Short Songs were influenced by Ouyang Xiu. Long Songs have an altogether different prosody and structure, and here it was Liu Yong to whom he turned for a model.

But a talent like Su Shi's could not be constrained by the bounds set by Liu Yong's sometimes erotic and unrefined song; hence his determination to create a style of his own. What one most notices in these songs is their expansiveness of spirit, their skilled depiction of vast panoramas, and their strength of feeling. This is all concentrated in the opening lines of many of his Long Songs:

As the Great River flows east	大江东去
Its waves have washed away the heroes of a thousand ages.	浪淘尽、千古风流人物

(*QSC*, p. 282)

and

The brocade curtain rolled up in the setting sun,	落日绣帘卷
Below the pavilion the water merges with the sky.[10]	亭下水连空

(*QSC*, p. 279)

and

The compassionate wind from a thousand miles brings the tide in	有情风、万里卷潮来
And, ruthless, sends it back again.[11]	无情送潮归

(*QSC*, p. 297)

Such passages as these are replete with implications that seem to "make one climb high and gaze afar, lift the head and sing aloud," deserving the critic's praise: "full of overflowing feeling and bursting with energy, they soar above the dust and the dirt."[12] Hence the epithet "Heroic Su" applied to Su Shi, with the damning contrast of "Creamy Liu", which emphasizes the enormous difference in style between the two, but ignores the fact that Su Shi's songs most probably owed the excellence of their evocative images and panoramic views to Liu Yong's innovation. Su Shi's appreciation is obvious in his comment on Liu Yong's lines,[13] "The frosty wind turns sharp, / Rivers and hills are desolate, / The last rays of the sun shine on my window," as not inferior to the best in Tang poetry. For their excellence in describing a scene lies in the strength of their evocative imagery, and it was precisely this feature that Su Shi appreciated and by which he profited.[14] Although many of Liu Yong's songs were on love themes and written for performance by professional singers and courtesans, many others, like these admired by Su Shi, reflected his disappointment as a man whose abilities were not given scope. It was in response to these different kinds of songs that Su Shi expressed such contradictory opinions. Because Liu Yong often combined the themes of the disappointed official with the tender longings of romantic love, critics usually dismissed him as a writer of erotic songs. It took someone like Su Shi to see that Liu Yong could write poetry equal to the best of the Tang poets. At the same time, it is not hard to understand why Su Shi's open, expansive nature moved his own song lyrics in a different direction.

The typical scene in Liu Yong's songs is autumnal, isolated, depressing, lit up by the setting sun. The melancholy setting evokes the disappointment of Liu Yong's frustrated career. The scenes in Su Shi's panoramic songs, however, reveal a spaciousness, a grandeur, that conveys nothing of melancholy or loneliness. They are an expression of the poet's own expansive nature. When Liu Yong has described a scene, he always comes back to his romantic attachments, while Su Shi continues the detached tone throughout the poem. Though inspired by that aspect of Liu Yong's songs he felt to be a sign of poetic talent, Su Shi was not limited by it and created a poetry with a new kind of panoramic feeling.

Su Shi's relation to Liu Yong is similar to his relation to Ouyang Xiu in that his earlier song lyrics are strongly influenced by both of them. He then frees himself to open up his own path, writing in an expansive style that expresses his own nature. In this alternation between borrowing and innovation, we can see a tendency to break away from established styles; we can also see how a society where popular songs were ubiquitous influenced a writer of many talents and wide interests and how an extraordinarily gifted poet exploits his talents to transcend his predecessors and create a style of his own. The times shape a genius even as the genius puts his imprint on the times. In the development of the song lyric, Su Shi was the genius born into a period when popular song flourished. Although songs were only a small part of his literary work, he was able to transform the song lyric, regarded since the Five Dynasties as merely sentimental or erotic, into a verse form with a greatly enlarged range equal to that of traditional *shi* poetry.

Song lyrics give more insight into some aspects of a poet's nature than can be had from his more formal writings, just as how a person acts when at play is more revealing than his behavior on formal occasions. From the beginning, writing song lyrics was regarded as a pastime not requiring the same serious commitment as *shi* poetry. Released from such expectations, a poet could give free rein to his own natural inclinations. Certainly Su Shi's songs display more of his expansive, untrammeled nature than the rest of his literary works—not that all his songs are in that mode, but this is the quality that distinguishes them from those of his predecessors. Critics have traditionally labeled it the "heroic" (*haofang*) mode, a term they also applied to the songs of Xin Qiji as the other Southern Song representative of the style. In fact, their styles are anything but identical: as Wang Guowei has perceptively noted, Su Shi's songs are expansive (*kuang*), while Xin Qiji's are heroic (*hao*).[15] Xin Qiji is profound, where Su Shi is transcendent. Xin Qiji's songs are filled with indignation; Su's are unrestrained. However, both poets can achieve release, though they accomplish it in different ways. For Xin Qiji comes from a heroic disposition, whereas in Su Shi it is the result of his emancipated nature. It is for this reason that I use "expansive, untrammeled" rather than the traditional term "heroic" to characterize Su Shi's songs. Of course some of them deserve the epithet "heroic", the best known being "Hunting in Mizhou" to the tune "River Town" (*Jiang cheng zi*, also called *Jiang shen zi*, "River Spirit", *QSC*, p. 299):

An old man for the moment moved by youthful madness	老夫聊发少年狂
Pulls Brown with his left	左牵黄
Carries Black on his right,	右擎苍
In brocade cap and sable furs	锦帽貂裘
He gallops around the slope with a thousand riders.	千骑卷平冈
They call the whole city to follow the Prefect	为报倾城随太守
To watch Master Sun shoot the tiger himself.	亲射虎，看孙郎
His courage still swells when he's had a drink;	酒酣胸胆尚开张
If his hair's a bit frosty at the edges	鬓微霜
What does it matter?	又何妨
When will they send Feng Tang	持节云中
To Yunzhong with the pardon?	何日遣冯唐
He will bend a carved bow like a full moon	会挽雕弓如满月
And looking off to the northwest	西北望
Shoot the Heavenly Wolff	射天狼

The hunting party becomes an excuse for the poet to offer his services in his country's defense, half facetiously. The theme of the old general is a common one; he is still vigorous and eager to fight while languishing in retirement or disgrace. If it is intended to express the poet's own aspirations, it should be taken metaphorically; Su Shi was not a military man.

The poem depends on several allusions; the one to Feng Tang is the most important to its understanding. Feng Tang defended the disgraced general (and governor) Wei Shang and persuaded the Han Emperor Wen to pardon him. He was dispatched to Yunzhong with the pardon restoring Wei Shang to his position as Governor of Yunzhong. "Brown" and "Black" in lines 2 and 3 are for "brown dog" and "black falcon", part of the hunting scene. Master Sun (line 7) is Sun Quan, the third-century ruler of the state of Wu, who shot a tiger from horseback. Lines 7 and 8 occur in reverse order in the text. The Heavenly Wolf is a constellation. In the "Nine Songs" (*Chuci*) the line "I draw a long arrow and shoot the Heavenly Wolf" is simple hyperbole; here it stands for China's enemies in the northwest. Su Shi did not write many such songs, and so the term "heroic", appropriate enough in this case, will not do to characterize the whole corpus. Critics, however, have found other aspects of his songs to emphasize. Hu Yin's is the most common: "Su Shi…swept away the silk and perfume and discarded the cloying, ingratiating manner [of *Huajian* songs] to make one scale the heights and gaze afar, lift up the head and sing aloud to vent the exuberance one feels, transcending the dirt of the world."[16] And Wang Ruoxu: "His inborn talent was extraordinary, the force of his language explosive. Whatever he wrote was out of this world."[17] Zhou Ji: "Su Shi went where no one can follow. His was perhaps the supreme achievement [in song writing]."[18] Liu Xizai: "Su Shi's songs are like Du Fu's *shi* poetry, where no idea was excluded, no subject not to be used." "Dongpo's songs are replete with the bearing of a holy immortal leaving the world."[19] All are cognizant of the expansive, untrammeled quality of Su Shi's song lyrics and add something more to our understanding.

There is no need to pursue further what every reader can perceive for himself. However, there are a few doubtful points that call for discussion. One is whether the absence of the sort of love theme that had been prominent in earlier songs means that Su Shi was indifferent to love. The view that Su Shi's songs did not include love themes because he had no such feelings was directly expressed by Chao Wujiu: "he had no experience of love"; and implied by Chen Shidao: "Song Yu could write the rhapsody about the Goddess of Witches' Mountain without ever having met her, so why is it necessary to have the experience before you can know about a thing?"[20]

From the beginning song lyrics were written for performance by entertainers, and every poet who contributed lyrics for popular tunes wrote at least some sentimental love songs. Su Shi was no exception, but with a difference. Although he wrote lyrics for girls to sing, they were mostly for the maids and concubines of his friends, where there was no place for his own feelings. Even these songs involving pretty girls avoid the paint-and-powder descriptions common to love songs and instead convey something of Su Shi's own spirit of lofty detachment: for example the one for someone's flute-playing maid, to the tune "The Water Dragon Sings" (*Shuilong yin*, *QSC*, p. 277):

On a Chu mountain among the tall bamboos, cloudlike,	楚山修竹如云
One remarkable spire emerged above the thousands.	异才秀出千林表
Dragon whiskers trimmed a bit,	龙须半翦
Phoenix breast slightly swelling,	凤膺微涨
Jade flesh smooth and round.	玉肌匀绕

Huainan trees shed their leaves 木落淮南
Rain clears over Yunmeng. 雨晴云梦
The moon is bright, the breeze gentle. 月明风袅
Since Cai Yong is no more 自中郎不见
And Huan Yi is gone 桓伊去后
It's lain neglected 知孤负
No telling how many autumns! 秋多少

I've heard tell, the Prefect of Lingnan 闻道岭南太守
Deep inside the inner court 后堂深
Has Green Pearl, young and charming. 绿珠娇小
Behind the gauze window she learned to play 绮窗学弄
The first stanzas of "Liangzhou" 梁州初遍
And not quite all of "Rainbow Robe", 霓裳未了
Shaping *sol* and damping *do* 嚼徵含宫
Holding *re* and sustaining *la* 泛商流羽
And a single note to the cloud's peak. 一声云杪
To help her master wash away 为使君洗尽
The foreign wind and miasmal rain of exile 蛮风瘴雨
She plays "Dawn in the Frost Sky". 作霜天晓

The song begins with a fanciful account of the source of the material the flute was made of (bamboo), an austere opening for a song on a traditionally erotic theme, and closes with its imagined cleansing effect on the oppressive atmosphere of Lingnan in the south where her master was serving in what amounted to foreign exile.

Another example is the song written for one of Wang Dingguo's singing girls, Rounu, on their return from the south. It is to the tune "Stilling Wind and Waves" (*Ding fengbo*, *QSC*, p. 290):

I've always admired the handsome young fellow	常羡人间琢玉郎
Who deserves to have a creamy girl from Heaven.	天应乞与点酥娘
Passing through her white teeth his song	尽道清歌传皓齿
Would raise a breeze	风起
And make snowflakes fly to cool the burning sea.	雪飞炎海变清凉
On her return from a thousand miles away	万里归来颜愈少
She looks even younger.	
When she smiles	微笑
Her smile carries the plum fragrance from the south.	笑时犹带岭梅香
When I ask, wasn't it bad down there in Lingnan?	试问岭南应不好
She says	却道
Wherever my heart's at ease, that's my homeland.	此心安处是吾乡

Though addressed to the girl, the song begins by congratulating Wang Dingguo on having had this lovely singer with him to temper the heat with her singing. It closes with the girl's philosophical acceptance of the hardships of exile, happy to be wherever her master is. These examples show that Su Shi could write songs for a performer without introducing a *Huajian* scene of a woman making herself up.

There are two songs written for a courtesan that are distinct from those for the maids and concubines of his friends, and they do have an erotic content. The first, to the tune "Drunk and Disorderly" (*Zui luopo*, *QSC*, p. 310), was written when Su Shi passed through Suzhou on his way to a new post in Mizhou. It bears the title "Remembering a Parting":

Weathered face, greying hair,	苍颜华发
When will I ever get to go back home?	故山归计何时决
Old friends newly rich write no letters	旧交新贵音书绝
Only a pretty girl bothers to say goodbye.	惟有佳人
	犹作殷勤别
As I start to leave, her song becomes a sob.	离亭欲去歌声咽
A drizzling rain blows cold on her cheeks.	潇潇细雨凉吹颊
Don't wipe away the tear-pearls	泪珠不用罗巾浥
That splash on your silken skirt—	弹在罗衣
We can talk about them when we meet again.	图得见时说

The song closes with a nice twist, turning from the present sad parting to a future reunion.

The second song is the tenderly affectionate one, to the tune "River Town" (*Jiang cheng zi*, *QSC*, p. 299), written when Su Shi was about to leave Xuzhou for a new post in Huzhou:

A homeless exile at the world's end, filled with yearning,	天涯流落思无穷
I met you, all too briefly.	既相逢、却匆匆
Holding hands, lovely, you picked a fading flower	携手佳人 和泪折残红
Prompting me to ask, how much is left of spring?	为问东风余几许
And even if spring delays Who will be here to share it?	春纵在、与谁同
In the third month the surging water in the Canal is high.	隋堤三月水溶溶
Unlike the migrating wild geese	背啼鸿、去吴中

I head south	
And turn to look at Pengcheng.	回首彭城
The clear Si flows into the Huai,	清泗与淮通
But the thousand tears of longing I shed	寄我相思千点泪
Will never get so far	流不到、楚江东
As Chu River east!	

That these songs are not just exercises on the conventional theme of lovers parting but reflect the poet's own experience is reinforced by two other songs he wrote in Suzhou and Xuzhou, which suggest an identity of sorts for the girls addressed in them. The first, written in Suzhou before "Remembering a Parting" above, is to the tune "Master Ruan's Come Home" (*Ruan lang gui*, *QSC*, p. 298), and in Long Yusheng's edition,[21] it is introduced by a note recording the circumstances: "Three times in one year I have passed through Suzhou. This last time on my way to Mizhou I was asked, 'Will you come this time?' She was very pretty, and the Prefect, Wang Guifu (Hui) , congratulated me, asking me to write this song."

At a Party in Suzhou

For the third time this year I visit the Governor of Suzhou	一年三度过苏台
And always he gives me a feast.	清尊长是开
The pretty maid asks and insists on knowing—	佳人相问苦相猜
"Will you come this time or not?"	这回来不来
I'm still susceptible	情未尽
But old age comes on apace.	老先催
Life is really pretty funny—	人生真可咍
Who will plant the peach trees another time?	他年桃李阿谁栽
Master Liu is getting white-haired.	刘郎双鬓衰

The other was written in Xuzhou and, like the "River Town" lyric, to the tune "Magnolia Flower, Short Version" (*Jianzi Mulan hua*, *QSC*, p. 312):

Parting at Peng Gate

The jade wine cup has no flavor	玉觞无味
It holds the thousand tears of a pretty girl.	中有佳人千点泪
I have studied the Way to forget sorrow	学道忘忧
But one thought and I am no longer free.	一念还成不自由
Today we have yet to see	如今未见
The flowers in East Garden as they scatter.	归去东园花似霰
One word of comfort for us both:	一语相开
Let it be as though I never came.	匹似当初本不来

These four songs for singing girls seem to reflect a genuine feeling of personal loss. We can see that despite his own cares when he was being transferred from place to place, Su Shi still had room for tender feelings when saying farewell to a talented girl who offered him sympathy. But even in songs like these, which show emotional involvement, he can conclude on a note of release, and clearly express the wish for freedom from the bonds of attachment: "I have studied the Way to forget sorrow" and "Let it be as though I never came." It has been said, "Best is to forget feeling, the worst is not to feel at all; but we are just the ones in whom feeling is concentrated." Certainly Su Shi was not one to forget feeling completely, nor was he unable to feel. But his expansive nature kept him from being the slave of his feelings.

Invited to write a song at a farewell party for Chen Lingju on the evening of the Seventh Day of the Seventh Month, the time of the annual meeting of the Herd Boy and the Spinning Girl crossing on the bridge of magpies that only once a year joins their constellations, Su Shi produced

"Evening of the Seventh" to the tune "Immortal on Magpie Bridge" (*Que qiao xian*, *QSC*, p. 294):

Evening of the Seventh

The Immortal of Mount Gou	缑山仙子
High-minded as the remotest cloud	高情云渺
Will not imitate the stupid Boy and Girl.	不学痴牛騃女
The sound of his phoenix flute breaks off in the moonlight.	凤箫声断月明中
With raised hands he takes his leave of us here.	举手谢时人欲去
He came on a raft to cross	客槎曾犯
The ripples of the Milky Way	银河微浪
Still carrying Heaven's wind, the ocean's rain.	尚带天风海雨
Our meeting for a drink together was ordained.	相逢一醉是前缘
When wind and rain are dispersed	风雨散
He will float away who knows where.	飘然何处

Lu You adds a note, "Formerly poets writing on the Evening of the Seventh would always suggest a bedroom scene and a sorrowful parting. But exceptionally this song of Su Shi's keeps the astronomical setting. After reading it one feels the force of the heavenly wind and the ocean rain."[22]

Su Shi could adopt a carefree attitude in dealing with the emotions, as epitomized in his lines about the Qiantang tidal bore: "The compassionate wind from a thousand miles rolls in the tide / And ruthless, send it back again." Liu Xizai wrote, "Few in Su Shi's time wrote songs in his manner. Qin Guan, Huang Tingjian both took a different path. Chao Wujiu with his straightforward, relaxed nature and heroic spirit sometimes keeps pace with him, but can never follow when he takes his wild leaps into space."[23] This applies especially to the way Su Shi deals with the theme of love by reaching for a sudden release. It is not the common dichotomy of feeling versus indifference.

It is generally recognized that the distinctive quality of Su Shi's song lyrics is their exuberant tone, but the term "exuberant" covers a wide variety of songs and is variously understood by different critics. There are even those who, perceiving its presence, deny that it properly belongs in the song lyric. Readers with preconceived notions assume that, since songs traditionally emphasized delicacy and subtlety, Su Shi was temperamentally unqualified to write them. Chen Shidao, for example, in remarking that Su Shi wrote song lyrics as though they were *shi* poetry, was implying that his was not the right talent for song writing.[24] This is to assume that song lyrics should always remain in the Tang/Five Dynasties tradition, which allows no place for exuberance. But as long as any literary genre continues to be productive it will change with time.

The modern critic Xia Jingguan recognizes that exuberance is the distinctive quality of Su Shi's song lyrics, but he makes a useful distinction between those that are straightforwardly exuberant and those in which there is an undercurrent of sadness, a suggestion of discontent.[25] It is the latter, more complex songs that represent Su Shi's greatest achievement in the form. The uncomplicated ones can be too direct, too obvious: for example the opening lines of an early song to the tune "Immortal by the River" (*Lin jiang xian*, *QSC*, p. 286), written in Hangzhou on the occasion of a visit to the so-called Wind and Water Grotto:

The four elements are always everywhere	四大从来都遍满
No doubt air and water are here as well.	此间风水何疑

He applies the Buddhist concept of the four elements—earth, water, fire, and air—to the name of the grotto, but it is an obvious and hardly inspired association. Another example is in the second stanza of the song he wrote for his brother, to the tune "Spring in the Qin Garden", while en route to Mizhou from Hangzhou. Again, this is too obvious, the result no doubt of his extraordinary facility at versifying. Zhou Ji remarked, "Su Shi never exerted all his strength on anything he wrote (prose, essays) or did (calligraphy, painting) it was all the same...People praise Su Shi as unrestrained; I would praise his refinement. That is where his excellence lies, in refinement; it is his weakness that he was unrestrained."[26]

Su Shi's best songs display his characteristic exuberance, but they are more subtle, and within the exuberance there lurks a suppressed feeling of sadness, even desperation. Given his abiding ambition to take the world as his responsibility, even his contrary inclination toward detachment and avoidance of worldly ties could not make him give up the hope of being of use to the world, though it did provide consolation in the face of frustration and disappointment. This is amply demonstrated by the events of his checkered career. He was frequently transferred or exiled in disgrace, but wherever he was, whether at court or in the provinces, he never ceased to worry about the affairs of the country or to feel concern for the hardships of the common people. He always strove to do what lay within his power. As Prefect of Mizhou he organized disaster relief and conducted public prayers for rain; in Xuzhou he took charge of controlling flood waters; as Governor of Hangzhou he dredged the lake and built a causeway. When the plague struck, he set up shelters for the afflicted. Even when exiled in his old age to Huizhou, he still led the people to construct two bridges for those unable to ford the river. When he was banished to Huangzhou for writing poems judged seditious, he was not permitted to put his name to official documents, so he devoted himself to study and writing. Many of his best poems, song lyrics, essays, and rhapsodies, as well his commentaries on the *Confucian Analects* and the *Classic of Changes*, were composed then. Later, when he was recalled to court, he never changed his outspoken, straightforward conduct, although earlier it had landed him in prison. The checks and frustrations never made the slightest difference in his determination to be of service to the world. Obviously he never completely forgot his involvement in public affairs.

He expressed his attitude toward a career in two letters to friends. One was written to Li Gongze from exile in Huangzhou: "Though I am old and in straits, I have reason in my heart, loyalty in my bones, and I can laugh in the face of death. If you look at me with pity because I am in trouble, you are not much different from someone ignorant of philosophy."[27] The other letter, to Yang Yuansu, was written during the Yuanyou period when he was at odds with the conservative party's policy and was considering a request for a provincial assignment: "The worthies of yesterday would have only [Wang Anshi] for their leader. Today's worthies will follow no one but [Sima Guang]. The person followed is not the same, but the following is. I am a good friend of Sima Guang, and we have never had a falling out, but there's lots I don't follow him in. That is probably the cause of all the gossip. However, promotion and dismissal, success and failure have long been all the same to me and are not worth talking about."[28]

These passages show that in his public career, Su Shi held firmly to his principles and, at a critical moment, was able to rise above worldly concerns. They also show that his contradictory ruling passions—to serve and to withdraw—were also complementary, the latter serving as a resource when the former was frustrated. Most of his song lyrics were written in exile from the court in provincial posts, and their tone is most frequently one of detachment. Su Shi, however, was not a man to be indifferent to or lose interest in public affairs. He was not like those who make no distinction between good and bad, black and white, and seek only what is good for themselves while claiming to be high-minded and without worldly ambition.

In the songs he wrote in exile, underlying the dominant tone of exuberance there is sometimes a current of sadness and disappointment: here, for example, is his most famous one, written for his brother Ziyou to the tune "Water Music" (*Shuidiao getou*, *QSC*, p. 280):

How many times has the moon shone full?	明月几时有
Lifting my cup I ask the blue sky,	把酒问青天
In the palaces and towers of Heaven	不知天上宫阙
What season is it tonight, I wonder.	今夕是何年
I would like to ride there on the wind,	我欲乘风归去
But I fear I could not stand the cold	又恐琼楼玉宇
Of those crystal domes and jade halls on high.	高处不胜寒
I rise and dance and make my shadow move—	起舞弄清影
How much nicer it is here on earth!	何似在人间
Over vermilion chambers	转朱阁
Through curtained windows	低绮户
Shining on the sleepless—	照无眠
The moon should not be blamed.	不应有恨
But why always full when friends are separated?	何事长向别时圆
Men are happy or sad, apart or together	人有悲欢离合
The moon is dim or clear, waxing or waning:	月有阴晴圆缺
In this world perfection seldom comes.	此事古难全
I only hope that we can live long	但愿人长久
And both enjoy the moon's beauty, though a thousand miles apart.	千里共婵娟

Zheng Wenzhuo said of this song, "It takes off from Li Bai's heart of an Immortal and creates a most amazing poem."[29] It is unsurpassed for unworldly detachment; yet it reveals the inner conflict between his wish to serve and the attraction of retirement although with a subtlety that only hints at the underlying pain. There is a story that when the Emperor Shenzong read this lyric as he came to the lines "I fear that I could not stand the cold / of those crystal domes and jade halls on high," he exclaimed, "Su Shi loves me after all."[30] Such an understanding may suggest loyalty to the court, but this is a limited interpretation.

Another example is "Red Cliff, Thinking of the Past" to the tune "Niannu is Charming" (*Niannu jiao*, *QSC*, p. 282):

As the Great River flows east	大江东去
Its waves have washed away the heroes of a thousand ages.	浪淘尽、千古风流人物
There west of the ancient wall	故垒西边人道是
Is Zhou Yu's Red Cliff, people say, of the Three Kingdoms.	三国周郎赤壁
Wild rocks, tumbling clouds,	乱石崩云
Threatening breakers strike against the cliff	惊涛拍岸
Rolling up a thousand mounds of snow,	卷起千堆雪
Mountains and river like a painting.	江山如画
So many heroic men there were then!	一时多少豪杰
Think back to that far-off year when Zhou Yu	遥想公瑾当年
Had just taken Xiao Qiao to wife,	小乔初嫁了
A man of noble bearing, in his prime:	雄姿英发
Feather fan and black turban.	羽扇纶巾谈笑处
While he talked and laughed	
The ashes of his enemy's fleet flew as the flames died out.	樯橹灰飞烟灭
For these spirit journey into the past	故国神游
You can laugh at me for being sentimental	多情应笑
With my too-soon grey hair.	我早生华发

Man's life is like a dream—	人生如梦
Pour another libation into the river moonlight.	一尊还酹江月

The song's opening lines contain a vast panorama and the final couplet, a feeling of liberation. But the contrast between Zhou Yu, relaxed and cheerful as he wins a great victory, and Su Shi, banished in disgrace to Huangzhou, his ambition frustrated, his hair turning gray, is stark. It inspires sadness, especially when we recall the circumstances under which the song was composed. Misled by the implied indifference of "life is but a dream," readers have criticized the song as pessimistic, but this reading is just as shallow as the one that praises the bombastic songs as optimistic.

Some of the Short Songs Su Shi wrote while in Huangzhou unobtrusively blend his two conflicting impulses into an effective amalgam, like the one to the tune "Stilling Wind and Waves", (*Ding fengbo*, *QSC*, p. 288). It is introduced by the note:

On the seventh of the third month on the road to Sand Lake we ran into rain. Our rain gear had been sent ahead, and my companions were in a state of consternation. It did not bother me, and in a little while the sky was clear again. Thereupon I wrote this:

Don't listen as it passes through the woods pattering on the leaves.	莫听穿林打叶声
Let's whistle and sing and walk slowly.	何妨吟啸且徐行
With bamboo staff and hempen sandals we are better off than on horseback.	竹杖芒鞋轻胜马
Who's afraid?	谁怕
A shower is just a part of life.	一蓑烟雨任平生
The cool spring breeze blows us sober.	料峭春风吹酒醒
A bit chill	微冷

Over the hill the setting sun greets us.	山头斜照却相迎
Look back there where the shower was—	回首向来萧瑟处
We are going home	归去
Where there's neither wind nor rain nor shine.	也无风雨也无晴

The injunction to ignore the pattering rain drops and make no haste comes from one who believes in self-control, and the expansive detachment with which he views the shower as it passes comes out in the concluding line. But as he described the unexpected rain, he must have been painfully aware of the analogy to the setbacks he had suffered in his official career.

Two years after his service as Governor of Hangzhou, he was recalled to the court. To the tune "Eight-Rhymed Ganzhou Song" (*Basheng Ganzhou*, *QSC*, p. 297), he wrote a song lyric addressed to the monk Can Liaozi:

The compassionate wind from a thousand miles	有情风
rolls in the tide	万里卷潮来
And, ruthless, sends it back again.	无情送潮归
On the bank of the Qiantang I ask,	问钱塘江上
Over Xixing landing,	西兴浦口
How many times have the sun's rays gone down?	几度斜晖
No use thinking of today and yesterday—	不用思量今古
In a moment the men of old are no more.	俯仰昔人非
Who is there like old Dongpo	谁似东坡老
White haired and indifferent to the world's intrigues?	白首忘机
I remember once on the west bank of West Lake	记取西湖西畔
Just when spring hills were at their best	正春山好处
Azure sky, floating mist—	空翠烟霏

I reckon of poets who met	算诗人相得
There've been few like you and me.	如我与君稀
I promise one time	约他年
I'll come back east by boat	东还海道
And hope that Master Xie's high hope will not fail.	愿谢公雅志
	莫相违
On the Xizhou Road	西州路
You need not look back	不应回首
And shed a tear for me.	为我沾衣

There is no constancy in human affairs, now or ever, he says. But then, after this depressing thought, the tone suddenly changes: he can at least be indifferent to the vain pursuit of worldly advantage. This sort of unexpected alternation of mood is characteristic of Su Shi. In the second stanza, when he reminisces about the unforgettable beauty of West Lake scenery, we see the kind of refinement Zhou Ji praised. This setting for the meeting of the two poets makes the event even more rare and to be treasured. The last lines introduce a final twist by alluding to the Jin dynasty statesman Xie An, who was called to court duty (like Su Shi on this occasion) but never forgot his hope of retiring to his home on East Mountain. He has always stood as the classic example of the gentleman who accepts his duty to serve without forgetting his hope to withdraw someday, and so remains immune to the corrupting attractions of reward and rank. In Xie An's case, he incurred the jealousy of his colleagues after the victory at the Fei River, Xincheng, and was sent off to administer Xincheng. He planned to go back to East Mountain by boat, but got sick and died without ever fulfilling his desire. Su Shi is using the allusion to suggest that his own desire to return east to Hangzhou and see his friend is frustrated by the duty to obey the summons to serve, and that he may become, like Xie An, the victim of intrigue, his hope of retiring being perhaps unfulfilled by the time he dies. The final lines continue the Xie An allusion. After Xie An fell ill in Xincheng, he came back to the capital at Jiankang and entered through the Xizhou Gate. After he died, his nephew Yang Tan would not use that gate out of respect for his admired uncle. But one day he got drunk and inadvertently went through the gate. When he realized too late what he had done, he wept inconsolably. Su Shi incorporates the story into words of condolence: you won't have to weep for me; but the very mention of the possibility, even to deny it, brings to mind the fear that he will in fact never return and will never get to see his friend again.

Again, the song opens with a powerful panorama, and the first stanza concludes with a self-confident assertion of independence. In between there are several shifts and an acknowledgment of the vicissitudes of human life, the dangers of public service, the difficulty of the reunion of friends—"It holds a note of hidden sorrow and disappointment" as Xia Jingguan put it.

In short, though exuberance characterizes most of Su Shi's songs, the tone is more complex. When he writes love songs, Su Shi refuses to be bound by his emotions, always leaving himself a way out. When he writes of freedom and release from care, he never completely forgets his ideal of service. And when he sometimes strays into the obvious, it is the price of his enormous facility in versifying.

Su Shi was a great innovator who exerted a major influence on the development of the song lyric. In the earliest stage of his song-writing activity he had already begun to break with tradition: "I have a style of my own."[31] The second stage in his development dates from the time of his return to court after his exile in Huangzhou. During this period he wrote several of his most famous songs, having perfected the exuberant style that characterizes his best compositions. That he was well aware of his accomplishment is illustrated in the following anecdote: he had asked someone to compare his songs with those of Liu Yong. "Liu Yong's songs are a sixteen-or seventeen-year-old girl with red castanets singing 'Morning breeze and waning moon over the willow bank.' Your Excellency's songs require a frontiersman with iron clapper singing 'The Great River flows east.'" Su Shi is supposed to have said, "You have it exactly right."[32]

In judging Su Shi's innovations, we should distinguish between those successfully adopted by later writers and those not subject to imitation. The latter comprise his finest song lyrics, blending his Taoist inclinations and his urge to play an active role in the affairs of the world. These songs are the product of Su Shi's own personality, of his education and experience, and could not readily be duplicated.

Not all of the innovations that influenced later writers were beneficial. Su Shi expanded the range of the song lyric beyond the traditional boudoir scenes and love laments of the *Huajian ji*. In this his influence was felt more by writers of the Southern Song than by his contemporaries,[33] the most notable being that greatest of Southern Song songwriters, Xin Qiji, whose name is commonly linked with his. There can be no doubt that he profited from Su Shi's extension of the range of subjects treated in song lyrics, but also that he surpassed even the innovator and went on to greater achievements.[34]

On the whole Su Shi's influence on Southern Song song writers was beneficial. But there was another side that stemmed from his frequently casual attitude toward composition in all his writing. I have suggested that it came from an unequaled facility to compose poetry effortlessly, resulting sometimes in superficiality. He liked to write jokingly: for example, the song to the tune "Magnolia Flower, Short Version" (*Jianzi Mulan hua*, *QSC*, p. 312) congratulating Li Gongze on the birth of a son, which he introduced with "Written as a joke; everyone present fell down laughing." Another, to the tune "Youthful Travels" (*Shaonian you*, *QSC*, p. 324), on the "Goddess of the Privy", also has the note "Written as a joke", as do the two lyrics to the Tune "Like a Dream" (*Rumeng ling*, *QSC*, p. 311). Another, written for Xu Zhongtu to the tune "Magnolia Flower, Short Version" (*QSC*, p. 312), is not specifically labeled "a joke". The poem itself, a conventional congratulatory verse, was written on the back of a petition requesting the release of two prostitutes from their contract, according to the author's note. Taken together, the first words of the eight lines of the song make the sentence "Zheng Rong has left the brothel, Gao Ying is getting married," using the names of the girls mentioned in the petition. Such an acrostic is obviously not meant seriously. These examples demonstrate Su Shi's readiness to write frivolous songs. His playful, cheerful disposition inclined him toward such sport, and, of course, songs were not at the time considered serious literature. His few compositions of this sort hardly count as a flaw in his total output, although they did set an unfortunate precedent for less talented writers, who could excuse their frivolity and vulgarity by appealing to Su Shi.

Notes:

1. *Song shi* 338.10801.

2. *Dongpo xuji* (Letters), *Sibu beiyao* 19.58a.

3. Zhu Qiangcun, ed., Long Yusheng, comp., *Dongpo yuefu jian* 1.1a-4a.

4. Ibid., 1.29b.

5. *Dongpo xuji* 5.23b-24a.

6. The debt to Ouyang Xiu was noticed by Feng Xu, *Hao'an lun ci*, *Cihua congbian*, vol. 4, p. 3585.

7. See Yeh Chia-ying, *Lingxi cishuo*, pp. 112-113.

8. See *Cilin jishi* (quoting *Gaozhai shihua*) 6.179.; and Ye Mengde, *Bishu luhua* 3.1b-2a.

9. Recorded by several Song writers, e.g., Zhao Lingzhi, *Houjing lu* in *Biji xiaoshuo daguan*, p. 1053; Hu Zi, *Tiaoxi yuyin conghua* 32.665, quoting *Fuzhai manlu.*

10. To the tune "Water Music" (*Shuidiao getou*), *QSC*, p. 279.

11. To the tune "Eight-Rhymed Ganzhou Song" (*Basheng ganzhou*), *QSC*, p. 297.

12. Hu Yin, Preface to *Jiubian ci* in *Song liushi mingjia ci* (Jiguge ed.) 25.2b.

13. To the tune "Eight-Rhymed Ganzhou Song" (*Basheng ganzhou*), *QSC*, p. 43.

14. These are not the only lines in Liu Yong's song lyrics with this sort of setting and atmosphere. Other examples are in the songs to the tunes "Fragrance of Plum Blossoms in the Snow" (*Xue mei xiang, QSC*, p. 13); "Jade Butterfly" (*Yu hudie*, *QSC*, p.40); and "Crooked Pipe of Jade" (*Qu yu guan*, *QSC*, p. 17).

15. Wang Guowei, *Renjian cihua*, *Cihua congbian* vol. 5, p. 4250.

16. Preface to *Jiubian ci*; see note 12 to this chapter.

17. Wang Ruoxu, *Hu'nan shihua*, *Lidai shihua xubian*, p. 517.

18. Zhou Ji, *Song sijia cixuan Mulu xulun*, *Cihua congbian* 2.1643.

19. Liu Xizai, *Ci gai*, *Cihua congbian* 4.3690-3691.

20. Quoted by Wang Ruoxu, *Hu'nan shihua.*

21. *Dongpo yuefu jian* 1.24a.

22. Lu You, *Lu Fangweng quanji* 28.171.

23. Liu Xizai, *Ci gai*, p. 3692.

24. Chen Shidao, *Houshan shihua*, *Biji xiaoshuo daguan* 6.3671-3672.

25. Xia Jingguan, *Qu'an shoupi Dongpo ci*, quoted by Long Yusheng, *Tang Song mingjia ci xuan*, pp.12-17.

26. Zhou Ji, *Song sijia cixuan Mulu xulun* 2.1633.

27. "Yu Li Gongze shu", *Dongpo xuji* 19.16a.

28. "Yu Yang Yuansu shu", ibid., 6.10a.

29. Zheng Wenzhuo, *Dahe shanren cihua, Cihua congbian* 5.4321.

30. *Dongpo ji waiji*, quoted in *Dongpo yuefu jian* 1.41b.

31. In the "Letter to Xianyu Zijun"; see note 2 to this chapter.

32. Yu Wenbao, *Chuijian xulu,* in *Shuo fu*, no. 3, vol. 24, p. 1716.

33. Noticed by many critics: Hu Yin, Preface, of Xiang Ziyin; Huang Sheng, *Zhongxing yilai juemiao cixuan*, in *Hua'an cixuan*, p. 167, of Chen Yuyi; Tang Guizhang, *Songci sanbaishou jianzhu*, p. 118, of Ye Mengde. There are also traces of his influence in the lyrics of Zhang Yuangan and Zhu Dunru; Zhang Xiaoxiang deliberately tried to imitate Su Shi; see Xie Yaoren, *Zhang Yuhu xiansheng ji xu*, pp. 1-2.

34. Nalan Chengde, *Lushuiting zashi*, in *Biji xiaoshuo daguan*, no. 8, vol. 16, p. 386; also cf. Zhou Ji, *Jiecunzhai lunci zazhu* in *Cihua congbian*, vol. 2, pp. 1633-1634.

论辛弃疾词

少年突骑渡江来，老作词人事可哀。
万里倚天长剑在，欲飞还敛慨风雷。

曾夸苏柳与周秦，能造高峰各有人。
何意山东辛老子，更于峰顶拓途新。

幽情曾识陶彭泽，健笔还思太史公。
莫谓粗豪轻学步，从来画虎最难工。

一

辛弃疾一向是我所极为赏爱的一位词人，不过多年来当我撰写论词之文字时，对于辛词却一直未敢轻易着笔，其主要原因盖有二端：一则辛词之数量既多，方面又广，如此则在论评之时，势必极难加以概括之介绍，乃迟迟不敢着笔，此其一；再则辛词之各种好处与特色，大多警动鲜明，昭昭在人耳目之间，前人之称述评介辛词者，既已有甚多之著作，所以我也就不想更为狗尾续貂之举，此其二。故多年来我遂未尝一论辛词。但现在我与四川大学缪钺教授合撰《灵谿词说》一书，在对个别词人加以论说之外，更希望在编排次第方面能具有一种词史之性质，如此则辛弃疾这一位两宋词人中之大家，当然就在必须加以论说之列。本来缪钺教授在多年前已曾写过一篇《论辛稼轩词》的文章，收入于其《诗词散论》一书之中，但此次分配《灵谿词说》之撰写工作时，缪先生却坚意要我承担撰写论辛词之任务，此自为前辈对后学加以督奖之意，所以我也就只好勉为其难，对辛词尝试一加论述。

辛词之传世者，共有六百首以上之多，为两宋词人中作品数量最多的一位作者。至于其内容的方面之广与风格的变化之多，则早在南宋时代，辛氏的一位友人刘宰在其《贺辛待制弃疾知镇江》一文中，就曾经对其词有过“驰骋百家，搜罗万象”的赞美（见刘宰《漫塘文集》卷十五）。而较辛氏时代稍晚的另一位南宋词人刘克庄，在其所写的《辛稼轩集序》中，对于辛词也曾有过“大声鞺鞳，小声铿鍧，横绝六合，扫空万古。……其秾纤绵密者亦不在小晏、秦郎之下”的称誉（见《后村先生大全集》卷九十八）。自此而后，对辛词之称美者，可谓代不乏人。直至近代，对辛词之研究致力最勤、成果最丰的一位学者邓广铭先生，在其《略论辛稼轩及其词》一文中，于论及辛词时，亦曾谓：“就辛稼轩所写作的这些歌词的形式和它的内容来说，其题材之广阔，体裁之多种多样，用以抒情，用以咏物，用以铺陈事实或讲说道理，有的‘委婉清丽’，有的‘秾纤绵密’，有的‘奋发激越’，有的‘悲歌慷慨’，其丰富多彩也是两宋其他词人的作品所不能比拟的。”（见邓广铭著《辛稼轩词编年笺注》）面对这样一位伟大的作者，我自己固深恐才力浅薄，对其多方面之成就难以做周遍之介绍，则势将不免于“以有涯逐无涯”之叹。因此就颇想做一次将“万殊”归于“一本”之尝试，将辛词之丰枝硕果姑置不论，而尝试对其所以形成此伟大之成就的本质之根源略加探讨。

本来就诗歌之创作言之，在中国之传统中，固一向以言志抒情为主，故首重内心之感发。所以我在《王国维及其文学批评》一书中，于论及《人间词话》境界说与传统诗说之关系时，便曾提出说："感发作用实为诗歌的主要生命之所在。"因此内在的作者的感物之心的本体之资质，以及外在的感心之物的生活中的现象与遭遇，自然便是形成诗歌中感发之生命，以及影响其质量之深浅厚薄、广狭高下的两项重要因素。先就作者的感物之心的资质对作品风格之影响的重要性而言，早在刘勰的《文心雕龙·体性》篇，便曾说过："贾生俊发，故文洁而体清；长卿傲诞，故理侈而辞溢；……安仁轻敏，故锋发而韵流；士衡矜重，故情繁而辞隐"的话，将作品之风格与作者之品质，一一作了相互之印证。所以王国维在其《人间词话》中，于论及辛词时，便也曾提出说："东坡之词旷，稼轩之词豪。"又说："无二人之胸襟而学其词，犹东施之效颦也。"就把苏、辛二家词之风格，与苏、辛二人之品质襟抱也做了相互结合的品评。可见把作者的感物之心的资质作为基础，来从事诗歌的品评，在中国文学批评中原具有悠久之传统。这种品评的基础，当然是不错的。只不过我以为在这种品评的标准中，还须做出一点重要的分别，那就是作品之风格中所显示的作者之性情襟抱，原来还可以分别为偶然之反映与本体之呈现两种不同的层次。举例而言，即如北宋初期词坛上之晏殊及欧阳修这两位重要的作者，我以前在论述此二家词时，就曾经提出说，晏殊词中所表现出的"圆融的观照"，与欧阳修词中所表现的"豪宕的意兴"，固皆为其性情襟抱之一种流露和反映。只是像晏殊所写的"无可奈何花落去，似曾相识燕归来"及欧词所写的"直须看尽洛城花，始共春风容易别"诸词句，就其情意言之，却实在仅不过是一种伤春怨别光景流连的偶发之情而已，而并不是晏、欧二人之性情襟抱中之志意与理念的本体之呈现。可是在中国诗歌之传统中，则第一流之最伟大的作者，其作品之所叙写者，却往往也就正是其性情襟抱中志意与理念的本体的呈现。

即如屈原作品中之高洁好修的向往追求，陶潜作品中之任真自适的信念持守，杜甫作品中之忧国忧民的忠爱缠绵，他们所写的诗歌，无论是什么题材和内容，往往都表现有这一种与其生命相结合的性情襟抱的本体之呈现，而并不仅只是流连光景的偶发之情而已。而这也就正是最伟大的作家与一般作家的区分之所在。盖以一般之作者不过以其性情才气为诗而已，但真正伟大之作者则其所写乃并不仅为一时才气性情之偶发，他们乃是以自己全部生命中之志意与理念来写作他们的诗篇，而且是以自己整个一生之生活来实践他们的诗篇的。此在诗人中之屈原、陶潜、杜甫，便都是很好的例证。但在唐、宋词人中，则我们便很难找到这样的作者。这一则固然因为词在初起时，原只是歌筵酒席间供歌儿酒女吟唱的曲子，与传统之诗歌之被视为有“言志”之严肃目的者，本来就有所不同。再则也因为自温庭筠以来，一些逐弦吹之音为侧艳之词的作者，他们本身原来也就缺乏一种如屈原、陶潜、杜甫诸人之精诚光伟，可以将人格与作品相互结合为一体的品质和情操。因此，如果以词与诗相比较，我们就会发现，在词的作品中，一向缺乏两种品质，其一是作者在写作时根本就缺乏一种以全心力去投注的精神，其二则是在作品的内容中也缺乏一种崇高伟大的志意和理念。关于第一种情况，即如我们在前面所举引的晏殊与欧阳修二位作者，他们虽有相当的学养和襟抱，但他们对词之写作却是都视之为游戏笔墨，仅以余力为之，而并不曾将之作为可以抒写襟抱，表现自己之志意与理念的一种文学形式，故其词中所表现的，乃往往但为一种偶然的情意之感发，虽然也可以引起读者深远之联想，但与诗歌中屈、陶、杜诸公之以全心力投注于写作，且在作品中表现出某种志意与理念的本体之呈现者，则毕竟有所不同。这种区别自是明白可见的。至于第二种情况，则如词人中之南唐后主李煜，其写词之态度，虽可视为全心力与感情之投注，然而李氏所具有者，实在仅为一种真纯深挚之情，而并无志意与理念之可言，故其词之佳者，虽然因其情感之深锐，而往往可以引发人类心灵中某些共鸣之感受，但如果以之与诗歌中之屈、陶、杜诸公相比较，则其在襟抱学养方面之欠缺，自然也是明白可见的。至于号称“以诗为词”的苏轼，对词之意境虽然有所开拓，一洗绮罗香泽，而表现了浩气逸怀，然而私意以为苏词中之意境，实在仍不可以称之为如我在前文所言的生命中志意与理念的本体之呈现。因为如我在《论苏轼词》一文中之所言，苏氏天性中盖原禀具有两种不同之资质，一则是欲以天下为己任的儒家用世之志意，另一则是超然于物外的道家放旷之襟怀。前者可以说是其欲有所作为时的立身之正途，后者则是其不能有所作为时的自慰之妙理。而苏氏之从事于词之写作，既是在其仕途受到挫伤以后，故其词中所表现者，乃大多以放旷之襟怀为主。而且苏氏原是一个长于“出”，而并不执著于“入”的人，故其词中乃极少有生命中志意与理念的本体之呈现。而他虽然也有意于开拓词境，但如果将他的词与他的诗文相比较，则苏轼之于词实在仅不过是以余力为之，而并非全力的投注。这种种情况，当然也都是我们在读苏词时，可以明白感受到的。可是我们现在要讨论的这一位词人辛弃疾，则是不仅将其全部才力都完全投注于词之写作，而且更是如我们在前文所言，乃是在其作品中，表现有一种生命中之志意与理念的本体之呈现的一位作者。所以我们如果说要想在唐、宋词人中，也寻找出一位可以与诗人中之屈、陶、杜相拟比，既具有真诚深挚之感情，更具有坚强明确之志意，而且能以全部心力投注于其作品，更且以全部生活来实践其作品的，则我们自当推崇南宋之词人辛弃疾为唯一可以入选之人物。而凡是此一类作者，其所写作的诗篇，都必然是光彩耀目千古常新的。其所以然者，还不仅是由于其人格与性情之精诚光伟足以表现出一种道德伦理方面的价值而已，而且更因为他们的作品既是其全生命中之志意与理念的本体之呈现，所以就诗歌中之主要质素的感发作用而言，这一类作品所具有的感发力量，就也必然会有一种最为精诚充沛的表现，这正是辛弃疾这一位词人在两宋词坛上何以能“屹然别立一宗”，而且表现出过人之成就的一个最基本的原因，而这也正是我们要想欣赏和评价辛词时，所首先应当具有的一点最基本的认识。

不过，辛弃疾与屈、陶、杜诸公在其感物之心的精诚投注之品质上虽有相近之处，然而辛弃疾之性情志意毕竟与屈、陶、杜诸公有着许多不同，而且他们所经历的外在的感心之物的生活中的现象与遭遇，也有着很大的差别，因此我们要想真正体认到辛词中之特殊的品质和成就，就还必须要将辛弃疾的性情志意与其所生活之环境遭遇互相结合起来，做更进一步的探讨。

二

据《宋史·辛弃疾传》之记述及邓广铭先生《辛稼轩年谱》之考证，则辛氏盖生于宋高宗绍兴十年（1140），也就是金熙宗之天眷三年，他的出生地山东历城，在当时已经沦陷了有十余年之久。其祖父辛赞是一个具有强烈民族观念的老人，虽因宋室南渡之时以族人众多未能脱身南下，遂仕于金，但却把他民族忠义的观念，完全传给了他的孙子——幼年的辛弃疾。据辛氏在其《进美芹十论劄子》中追叙其少年时之生活，即曾谓：“大父臣赞……每退食，辄引臣辈登高望远，指画山河，思投衅而起，以纾君父不共戴天之愤。尝令臣两随计吏抵燕山，谛观形势。”所以忠义之心与事功之志，对于辛弃疾而言，实在可以说是自其少年时代便与他的生命一同成长起来的。当绍兴三十一年（1161）金主亮起兵南侵之际，辛弃疾已经二十二岁。当时中原各地义军蜂起，有农民名耿京者，起兵山东，节制山东河北忠义兵马，发展至数十万之众。辛氏原来也尝纠集义士有二千人之多，至是遂率其众投隶耿京，为掌书记。因劝耿京决策南向，耿从之，遂于绍兴三十二年（1162）正月奉耿京命与贾瑞等奉表南归。时值高宗巡幸建康，辛、贾二人乃亲蒙召见，且分别授官，完成了使沦陷区之义军得与南宋朝廷相联合之任务。然而谁料到就当辛氏离开山东奉表南下之时，耿京竟然被其部下之汉奸张安国所叛杀。当辛弃疾诸人自建康北返，还至海州之时，听见了此一意外的不幸消息，于是辛氏当即率领一部分人马直趋虏营。时张安国方与金军将士庆功酣饮，辛氏乃率众直入虏营，缚张安国上马。金兵追之不及。辛氏乃一路以不眠不休之精神直趋行在献俘，斩张安国于市。其后二十年，当辛弃疾被谗劾放废，在带湖闲居时，曾自筑室日“稼轩”，其友人洪迈为之作《稼轩记》，还曾追述及辛氏此一段少年时意气风发之往事，谓其“壮声英概”，可以使“懦士为之兴起”（见《洪文敏公集》卷六）。但辛氏此一壮举，其可称述者却原来还不仅只是其“壮声英概”的豪气与胆略而已。如果我们更深入一层去看，就会发现在此一事件中，原来乃是结合有辛氏的深远之谋略与宏伟之度量的。盖辛氏在其后来所进献之《美芹十论》中，于《详战》篇曾论及沦陷区义军之形势，在篇末曾提出两点应注意之事项。其一是起义者多为农民，但“锄犁之民，寡谋而易聚，惧败而轻敌”，所以不能“坚战而持久”；而一些“豪杰可与立事者”，则又由于“东北之俗，尚气而耻下人”，因而“不肯俛首听命以为农夫下”。可是这些豪杰之士之“思一旦之变，以逞夫平昔悒怏勇悍之气”，则又有时还更“甚于锄犁之民”，只是“计深虑远，非见王师则未易轻发”。从这些议论，我们就可见到辛氏当年之所以能以其过人之才略，且已纠众有二千人之多。乃竟甘心归附于农民的义军领袖耿京，而且劝说耿京奉表与南宋王师相联络，原来本是有其极深远的战略性之识见的。至于其能甘心下人之度量，当然也是极可称述的。而这一切谋略与度量，实在又都源于他的一心想要收复中原的志意之急切。是则当其擒缚张安国献俘行在，决心南来之际。对于他全心所冀望的收复中原之理想，固当原以为是即可付诸实践的指日可期之事业，而其所有的“壮声英概”的勇略，也当都是源于此一坚强之信念。因此，辛氏在南渡以后不久就接连献上了《论阻江为险须藉两淮疏》和《议练民兵守淮疏》，又先后献上了《美芹十论》和《九议》，在这些疏论奏议中，辛弃疾对于敌我双方在政治、军事、经济各方面之形势，都作了切实详尽的分析，充分表现了辛氏对于作战的全部理论和收复中原的通盘计划，真是千百年以下读之，仍然可以使人为之奋发兴起。只可惜这些建议与谋略，始终未被南宋朝廷所采用，而终于在他六十八岁那年。在南渡的四十五年以后，怀抱着满腔未得一用的忠义和谋略而赍志以殁了。辛弃疾晚年在落职家居时曾经写过一首题为“有客慨然谈功名，因追念少年时事，戏作”的《鹧鸪天》词。说：“壮岁旌旗拥万夫，锦襜突骑渡江初。燕兵夜娖银胡䩮，汉箭朝飞金仆姑。思往事，叹今吾，春风不染白髭须。却将万字平戎策，换得东家种树书。”对于他自己当年深入金营擒获张安国千里献俘渡江南来时之壮志之未能完成，表现了很深的悲慨。辛弃疾在南渡以后的四十五年中，曾经遭受过多次的谗毁和摈斥，放废于林泉间者，前后有将近二十年之久。但其用世之心与恢复之志，则始终没有改变。即使只是短期的被起用，他也莫不奋发振起，以其过人的才略，思欲有所建树。即如其在乾道八、九年间（1172—1173）出知滁州时，就曾施行了宽征薄赋收招流散的政策，表现出在短短期间内便足以振衰起敝的治绩。其后在淳熙年间（1174—1181），当他在江西、湖北、湖南诸地任职为提点刑狱、安抚使及转运副使的任内，更曾先后完成了平盗、赈饥、创建飞虎军之种种事功，处处表现出他是一个既关心国家，也爱护百姓；既有识见，又有干才的具有豪杰之气的栋梁之材。据史书上的记载，谓其在湖南安抚使任内，一方面既为朝廷讨平了盗贼，而另一方面则也为百姓请命，奏上了《论盗贼劄子》，对于“残民害物”的官吏提出了批评，说“夫民者国之根本，而贪浊之吏迫使为盗”，因此建议朝廷说：“欲望陛下深思致盗之由，讲求弥盗之术，无徒恃平盗之兵也。”又自己表白了惩治贪吏的决心，说：“臣孤危一身久矣，荷陛下保全，事有可为，杀身不顾。况陛下付臣以按察之权，责臣以澄清之任，封部之内，吏有贪浊，职所当问，……自今贪浊之吏，臣当不畏强御，次第按奏。”史又载其在湖南创置飞虎军营之时，议者曾以聚敛上闻，孝宗降金牌止之，而辛氏接受金牌后竟藏而不发，反督令监办者“自官舍神祠外，应居民家取沟匾瓦二”以救其缺瓦之急，乃使飞虎营克日建成，“雄镇一方，为江上诸军之冠”。史又载其在江西安抚使任内，因当地大饥，乃下令榜通衢曰：“闭粜者配，强籴者斩。”又“尽出公家官钱银器，召官吏、儒生、商贾、市民各举有干实者量借钱物。……责领运籴，……期终，自至城下发粜”，于是量船遂“连樯而至”。时信州守谢源乞米救助，幕属不从，弃疾曰：“均为赤子，皆王民也。”即以米舟十之三予信州。从这些事迹的论述，我们对辛氏之志意、才识、胆略之不凡自可想见。然而辛氏却也常在谗摈的忧惧之中。在《论盗贼劄子》中，辛氏即尝自言云：“臣生平刚拙自信，年来不为众人所容，顾恐言未脱口而祸不旋踵。”果然就在赈饥后的当年，辛氏就被台臣王兰所论劾，谓其“用钱如泥沙，杀人如草芥”，遂被免官落职。于是辛氏便在江西上饶带湖附近，购地治宅。其自作上梁文，有“抛梁东，坐看朝暾万丈红。直使便为江海客，也应忧国愿年丰”及“抛梁西，万里江湖路欲迷。家本秦人真将种，不妨卖剑买锄犁”之语。其忧国之志之难以或忘，而且自比于汉代罢废家居之飞将军李广的心情，是可以想见的。辛氏此一度罢官家居，竟然被闲废了差不多有十年以上。及至绍熙三年（1192），再被召赴福建为提点刑狱，不久又受命兼任福建安抚使。这时的辛弃疾虽然已经是年过半百，然而其平生欲建立功业、收复中原之壮志则未尝稍减。于是在绍熙五年（1194），他遂又创置了备安库。据史书记载，谓其在福州任职时，每叹曰：“福州前枕大海，为贼之渊，……帅臣空竭，缓急奈何。”遂为备安库积镪至五十万缗。又欲“造万铠，招强壮，补军额，严训练”。于是遂再被论劾，谓其“残酷贪饕，奸赃狼藉”，遂再度被罢官家居，筑室于铅山县之期思市。适旧居上饶之带湖毁于火，乃正式迁居于铅山。这一次被罢废，又闲居了八年以上之久。乃至宋宁宗嘉泰三年（1203），再被起用知绍兴府兼浙东安抚使之时，辛弃疾已经是六十四岁的老人了。但他一上任又立刻上疏奏陈“州县害农之甚者六事”（见《文献通考》卷五《田赋考》）。其后于嘉泰四年（1204）至开禧元年（1205）差知镇江府时，仍屡次遣谍至金，侦察其兵骑之数，屯戍之地，将帅之姓名，帑廪之位置。并欲于沿边招募土丁以应敌，并造红衲袄万领备用。这时距离他当年的南渡来归，已有四十三年之久，所以他在此时所写的一首题为“京口北固亭怀古”的《永遇乐》词中，即曾写有“四十三年，望中犹记，烽火扬州路”的句子，表现了对于当年甘冒烽火艰危而南渡来归之壮志的追怀难忘。又在此词之结尾，写了“凭谁问，廉颇老矣，尚能饭否”的句子，表示了虽在垂老之年，也仍然想要据鞍上马冀求一用的未死的雄心。可惜不久他就又受到言官的论劾，谓其“好色贪财，淫刑聚敛”，遂再度被罢官家居。这时的辛弃疾已经是六十六岁的年纪了。其后身体乃日渐衰病，虽然又曾被诏命进封了一些官职，而辛氏则亦曾屡次上章求免，终于在开禧三年（1207）致仕以后不久，怀抱着满腔未能实践之壮志和历尽挫伤的悲慨而病死在铅山了。以上是我们根据《宋史·辛弃疾传》以及邓广铭先生的《辛稼轩年谱》对辛氏生平所作的极简单的介绍。至于其时代背景和南宋政局的情况，则都未暇详加叙述。因为我们的用意，原来就并不是要作历史的介绍，只不过由于感心之物的外在境遇，既原来也是形成诗歌中感发生命之一项重要因素，而尤其是像辛弃疾这样一位将全生命中之志意与理念都表现于其诗篇，且以全部生活来实践其诗篇的作者，要想对其作品有深入之了解，则我们对于其感心之物的种种外在因素，当然就更需要具备有相当之认识，因此我们才不得不在此对其生平之重要事迹加以简单之介绍。

三

由上两节所叙写的辛弃疾这一位作者的感物之心的资质，及其感心之物的遭遇来看，我们已可以认识到，辛弃疾实在不仅只是一位有性情、有理想的诗人而已，他同时也还是一位在实践方面果然可以建立事功的，有谋略、有胆识、有眼光、有手段、有才华，而且有权变的英雄豪杰式的人物。而他整个生命的重心，则是他的心心念念不忘收复中原的志意。这其间自然有他对于国家的一份忠义之心，也同时有属于他自己的一份故乡之念。所以他的这一份志意乃是极其深挚而且强烈的。只可惜他在南渡以后却遭受到了不断的谗摈和摧抑，遂终于未能实现其志意成为收复中原的一位英雄，而却只落得成为了南宋词人中一位伟大的作者，这对辛弃疾而言，当然决非其自己之本意。不过，我在前面却也曾说过，辛弃疾之于词，乃是以其全心力之投注而为之的。那就因为他在事功方面既然全部落空，于是遂把词之写作，当做了他发抒壮怀和寄托悲慨的唯一的一种方式。所以徐釚在《词苑丛谈》卷四《品藻二》即曾引黄梨庄之语曰："辛稼轩当弱宋末造，负管、乐之才，不能尽展其用，一腔忠愤，无处发泄，……故其悲歌慷慨抑郁无聊之气，一寄之于词。"因此辛弃疾在词一方面之成就，实在可以说乃是他的收复中原之志意在现实方面失败以后所转化出来的一种一体两面之结果。这当然是我们在欣赏辛词时所当具有的一点最基本的认识。不过，值得注意的则是，辛词之感发生命的本质，虽以英雄失志的悲慨为主，然而他的词却又在风格与内容方面表现出了多种不同样式与不同层次的变化。关于这种由一本演为万殊的变化，私意以为其演化之情况盖有几点特色。第一，我们该注意到的是，辛词中感发之生命，原是由两种互相冲击的力量结合而成的。一种力量是来自他本身内心所凝聚的带着家国之恨的想要收复中原的奋发的冲力，另一种力量则是来自外在环境的。由于南人对北人之歧视以及主和与主战之不同，因而对辛弃疾所形成的一种谗毁摈斥的压力，这两种力量之相互冲击和消长，遂在辛词中表现出了一种盘旋激荡的多变的姿态，这自然是使得辛词显得具有多种样式与多种层次的一个主要的原因。第二，我们该注意到的，则是辛词中之感发生命，虽然与当日的政局及国势往往有密切之关系，但辛氏却绝不轻易对此做直接的叙写，而大多是以两种形象做间接的表现。一种是大自然界的景物之形象，另一种则是历史中古典之形象。这种写法，一则固然可能由于辛氏对于直言时政有所避忌，再则也可能是由于辛氏本身原具有强烈的感发之资质，其写景与用典并不仅是由于有心以之为托喻，而且也是由于他对于眼前之景物及心中之古典本来就有一种丰富的联想及强烈的感发。这自然是使得辛词显得具有多种变化与多种层次的另一个重要的原因。辛弃疾曾经写过一首题为《过南剑双溪楼》的《水龙吟》词，足可以作为例证来说明我们前面所提到的辛词中的几种特质。全词是：

举头西北浮云，倚天万里须长剑。人言此地，夜深长见，斗牛光焰。我觉山高，潭空水冷，月明星淡。待燃犀下看，凭栏却怕，风雷怒，鱼龙惨。　　峡束苍江对起，过危楼、欲飞还敛。元龙老矣，不妨高卧，冰壶凉簟。千古兴亡，百年悲笑，一时登览。问何人又卸，片帆沙岸，系斜阳缆。

这首词可以说就是辛弃疾结合了景物与古典两方面的素材，把内心中之两种互相冲击的力量，表现得极为曲折也极为形象化的一首好词。要想了解其好处何在，我们首先便要对这首词的题目略加说明。题中的“南剑”，乃宋代州名，古为七闽之地。汉武帝元封年间于此置南平县，唐高祖武德三年于此设延平军，肃宗上元元年改为剑州。宋太宗太平兴国四年因蜀有剑州，乃加“南”字以别之，称南剑州，治所在今福建南平市。据《南平县志》所载：“双溪楼在府城东，又有双溪阁，在剑津上。”又载：“剑津一名剑溪，又名龙津，又名剑潭，城东西二溪会合之处。昔时有宝剑跃入潭，化为龙，故名。”（以上所叙分别见《南平县志》卷一之《历代沿革表·第二》，卷四之《名胜志·第六》及卷三之《山川志·第四》）以上是有关此词题目之地理背景的记述。至于所谓“宝剑跃入潭，化为龙”之说，则又牵涉到一则历史故事。盖据《晋书·张华传》所载，谓当时斗牛间常有紫气，张华闻豫章人雷焕妙达象纬，询之，焕曰：“宝剑之精上彻于天耳。”又问在何郡，焕曰：“在豫章丰城”。华乃补焕为丰城令。到县掘狱屋基，得一石函，内有双剑，一曰龙泉，一曰太阿。焕遂送一剑与张华，留一剑自佩。及张华被诛，失剑所在。焕卒后，其子华为州从事，持剑行经延平津，剑忽于腰间跃出，坠水，使人没水取之，不见剑，但见两龙，各长数丈。没者惧而返。须臾，光彩照水，波浪惊沸，于是失剑。（见《晋书》卷卅六《张华传》）以上是有关此地的历史上的传述。对此词题目中的地理和历史的背景都有了认识以后，我们就可以对词一加评析了。先看开端两句，首句之“西北浮云”，既可以为眼前之景物，亦可以喻指沦陷之中原；次句之“长剑”，既可以指有关此地之历史传说，亦可以喻示作者想要恢复中原之壮志。而曰“举头”，则把遥远的“西北浮云”也就是所喻指的沦陷的乡国之恨，写得何等真切分明。曰“倚天万里”，则又把传说中之神剑，也就是所喻示的作者的壮志，写得何等雄杰不凡。即此二句，也已经足可见出辛词的层次之深曲及其感发之强烈了。以下“人言此地，夜深长见，斗牛光焰”三句，则既是紧扣住题目写有关“南剑双溪楼”之历史故实，是上冲斗牛的神剑之光焰难销，也是作者的收复中原之壮志的慷慨长存。以下“我觉山高，潭空水冷，月明星淡”三句，则蓦然由前三句所表现的高扬激昂而转入了另一种空寂凄冷的情调，这种转变，一方面既是写作者由冥想中的有关此地的往昔之神剑之传说，折返到了现实的此地的眼前之景象；另一方面则也象喻了作者由自己理想中的收复中原之壮志，跌入了现实中的被摈斥和冷落的不足以有为的现实的境遇。举头仰视则是月明星淡的冷漠无情，低头下望则是水冷潭空的凄寒空寂，然则昔日上冲斗牛的神剑之精华今日乃究竟何在？作者的收复中原之壮志又究竟何日得偿？以辛弃疾之感情志意的深切坚强，当然决不是一个轻言放弃的人，于是下面的“待燃犀下看，凭栏却怕，风雷怒，鱼龙惨”数句，乃写出了他想要有所追寻的心意，和在追寻时所可能遇到的危险和阻碍。盖当年之神剑既传说是跃入潭中，所以辛弃疾乃用“待燃犀下看”一句，写出了他想要到潭水中去寻神剑的愿望。而由此一句，遂又引出了辛弃疾对于另一则古典的联想。原来在《晋书》的《温峤传》中，曾记述有一则故事，说温峤曾由牛渚矶经过，其地“水深不可测，世云其下多怪物，峤遂燃犀角而照之。须臾，见水族覆火，奇形异状，或乘马车着赤衣者”云云。不过，辛弃疾在此处用温峤“燃犀”之典故，与前面所用的张华“神剑”之典故，其用典之方式与作用则并不尽同。前面的“神剑”之典故，是用其整个故事为全词之骨干，以切合题意而唤起全篇之感发，此处用“燃犀”之典故，则不过取温峤曾见水中有水族鱼龙精怪之一义而已。而此数句亦有二层含意，表面是写欲向深潭中寻觅神剑的艰难不易，而暗中却也喻示了辛弃疾自己如果想要实践收复中原之壮志所可能遇到的谗阻和迫害。而且“风雷”、“鱼龙”诸字样，原来也颇易于引起读者有关政治性之托喻的联想。盖早在唐代李白之《远别离》一诗中，即曾有过“雷凭凭兮欲吼怒”及“君失臣兮龙为鱼”等诗句，前者可以喻当政者之威权迫害，后者可以喻朝廷形势之变化无常，辛弃疾词与李白诗所托示之喻意当然并不相同，但“风雷”、“鱼龙”等字样之可以引起政治托喻之联想，则是相同的。以上是此词之前半阕。其所叙写的景物之形象与古典之形象，已经喻示了作者之壮志与现实境遇之冲击，并且做了多种层次的对比。至于下半阙过片之“峡束苍江对起，过危楼、欲飞过敛”几句，第一层意思固是正面写南剑双溪楼所在之地理形势。我们在前文已经根据《南平县志》介绍过，说双溪楼“在剑津上”，而剑津也就是“剑潭”，为“城东西二溪会合之处”。据《延平府志》卷二《山川一》之记叙，谓：“西溪源出长汀县，东流至顺昌，与邵武溪合流，……至沙溪口与沙县溪合流四十里至剑潭，与东溪接。”又谓：“东溪源出浦城、崇安、松溪三县，凡五派合流，会于建宁城下，南流一百二十里至剑溪，遂合流而下，俗呼丁字水，又名南溪。”辛词所云“峡束苍江对起”，就正是写西溪及东溪二水在此峡口会合之形势。而观夫前所引《延平府志》有关二水之叙述，则东、西两溪既曾汇纳沿途诸水而合流，是则其水势必极为澎湃汹涌，而在此地骤然为山峡所约阻，则两水相对流入时，其相互冲击排荡的力量之强大自可想见，故曰：“峡束苍江对起，过危楼、欲飞还敛。”这几句，不仅极为生动真切地写出了在双溪楼上所见的两水会合之激荡的形势，而且承接着上半阕，也正好把前片所喻示的作者的恢复之壮志与现实谗阻之矛盾，做了一个极为形象化的总结。是则“欲飞还敛”者，固是眼前之水势，而同时也就正是辛弃疾内心中的激荡悲愤的情怀。所以下面的“元龙老矣，不妨高卧，冰壶凉簟”三句，作者乃从前面托喻的隐藏的阴影中，正式出现到读者的面前。可是在这种由隐而显的承接中，辛弃疾却又并不接着前面的激荡的情怀做叙写，反而转变为一种悠闲平静的笔调，写出了“高卧”和“冰壶凉簟”的句子，因而乃给了读者更多寻思的余味。而且在此处辛弃疾却又用了一则典故，原来“元龙”乃是三国时代“名重天下”的陈登的字，据《三国志》卷七《陈登传》及裴松之注引《先贤行状》之记述，陈登之为人盖“深沉有大略，少有扶世济民之志”，曾任广陵太守，“明审赏罚，威信宣布”，曾经平定海贼，围攻吕布，以功加封为伏波将军，年三十九病卒。其后许汜与刘备并在荆州牧刘表座上，共论天下人物。许汜曰："陈元龙湖海之士，豪气不除。"备问汜："君言豪，宁有事耶？"汜曰："昔遭乱，过下邳，见元龙，元龙无客主之意，久不相与语。自上大床卧，使客卧下床。"备曰："君有国士之名，今天下大乱，帝王失所，望君忧国忘家，有救世之意；而君求田问舍，言无可采，是元龙所讳也，何缘当与君语？如小人，欲卧百尺楼上，卧君于地，何但上下床之间耶？"辛弃疾用这一则典故，盖有几层取意。其一是陈登与许汜的对比，陈登有扶世济民之志，而许汜则求田问舍，但求个人之安居，所以辛氏在另一首《水龙吟》（楚天千里清秋）词中，便也曾说过"求田问舍，怕应羞见，刘郎才气"的话，表示了对于只求个人安居而不关心国家安危的如许汜之类人的鄙弃，也暗示了辛弃疾自己之不求个人安居，而一意以收复中原为职志的用心。这本该是辛弃疾用此一典故的本意。可是在这一首词中，辛氏在使用此一典故时，却又更加了一层转折之意。盖当年之陈元龙，本以扶世济民为己志，不求个人之安居，而现在则以陈元龙之志意来自比的辛弃疾，则已经年华老去，壮志难成，是则也不妨但求个人之安居矣。词中的"冰壶凉簟"，就正表示在炎夏中有清凉之饮料与凉爽之竹席的舒适安乐的生活。而"高卧"两个字，则是辛弃疾在把这一则典故加以转化应用时一个表示反讽之意的关键。因为在《陈登传》中，陈氏之高卧上床，本是表示对于但求个人安居的许汜之轻视，因而也显示着陈登之不求个人安居的志意之远大。可是此处辛氏之"不妨高卧"一句，则是断章取义，把"高卧"转化成了一种无所事事的闲居的形象。以原来表示壮志的字样来表示闲居，这正是辛氏在反讽中所透露的、对于自己的壮志无成的嘲笑和悲慨。于是下面的"千古兴亡，百年悲笑，一时登览"三句，辛弃疾遂将典故中的古人、古事，与现实的今人、今事，做了一个综合的总结。得剑的张华，燃犀的温峤与高卧的陈登，都已经在历史中消逝，而人间之盛衰兴亡，其推演循环，乃正复沧桑未已。而自沦陷区归正南来的辛弃疾，其当年突骑渡江的壮声英概，与今日屡遭谗摈的感慨哀伤，无论其为悲为笑，盖亦皆将在历史之长流中消逝无存。个人一世之百年，与历史兴亡之千古，相较起来，自然微不足道，而辛弃疾却偏偏在今日双溪楼的一时登览之中，对历史上的千古兴亡与自己个人的百年悲笑，在景物与典故的相互生发之联想中引起了触绪纷来的平生万感。只不过辛氏却又并未明写其感慨，而只写了“一时登览”四个字，把感慨都留在言外，未加说明。关于这种言外之慨，我们可以引用辛弃疾另一首《水龙吟》（楚天千里清秋）词中的“江南游子，把吴钩看了，阑干拍遍，无人会、登临意”数句，来互相参看。其所谓“登临意”，就正可以作为此词“一时登览”的注脚，而其所谓“江南游子”所表现的南来以后的失志之悲，也正可以作为此词开端的“西北浮云”一句所表现的对沦陷之中原的难以或忘的说明。至其所谓 “吴钩”，则又恰好与此词之“长剑”相应合。而且我们在前面还曾引用他那一首《水龙吟》词中的“求田问舍，怕应羞见，刘郎才气”数句，来作为对这一首词中的“元龙老矣，不妨高卧”数句之为反讽的说明。是则此二首《水龙吟》词，就其感发生命之本质言之，固皆为其平生志意与理念的本体之呈现。只不过“楚天千里清秋”一首，其慷慨激昂之气多为正面之流露，而此词则颇多幽隐曲折之致，且曾使用反讽之笔法。所以在“楚天千里清秋”一词结尾，辛氏乃明白写出了自己的悲慨，说：“可惜流年，忧愁风雨，树犹如此。倩何人唤取，红巾翠袖，揾英雄泪。”而在这一首词中，则不仅“一时登览”之句，未明言自己的悲慨，而且在最后的结尾，也只以悠闲淡远之笔，写了一幅眼前的景物之形象，说：“问何人又卸，片帆沙岸，系斜阳缆。”此三句，在一方面固可以视为紧承着上一句之“一时登览”而来，是写登览中所见的眼前之景象，而另一方面则在此词前面之多重喻示的衬托中，此结尾三句就也提供给了读者更深一层的喻托之联想。盖“卸帆”、“系缆”，原都是表现船之停泊不再前进的形象，也喻示了南宋朝廷之耽溺于眼前之苟安，不再想收复中原的一种颓靡的心态。何况辛弃疾还对于系缆的船，用了“斜阳”两字的形容，而“斜阳”两字，在辛词中则往往有喻示渐趋衰亡的南宋国势之含意。即如其另一首著名的《摸鱼儿》（更能消几番风雨）一词，其结尾之处的“休去倚危栏，斜阳正在，烟柳断肠处”三句，便是很好的例证。罗大经《鹤林玉露》卷一即曾云：“斜阳烟柳之句，比之‘未须愁日暮，天际乍轻阴’者异矣。在汉、唐时，宁不贾种豆种桃之祸哉!”许昂霄《词综偶评》亦云：“结句即义山‘夕阳无限好，只是近黄昏’之意，斜阳以喻君也。”这些说法，都可以与此词之“系斜阳缆”一句相参看。

本来辛弃疾的好词甚多，但因篇幅的限制，我们无法多加选说。不过，我们前面既曾将其“楚天千里清秋”一首《水龙吟》词，与这一首“举头西北浮云”的《水龙吟》词，作了约略的比较；而如果我们再将他的“更能消几番风雨”的《摸鱼儿》词参照来看，则《摸鱼儿》词开端的“更能消几番风雨”一句，便也正可以与其另一首《水龙吟》词中的“可惜流年，忧愁风雨”相参看；而《摸鱼儿》词中的“天涯芳草无归路”一句，则也可以与另一首《水龙吟》词中的“休说鲈鱼堪脍，尽西风、季鹰归未”数句相参看；还有《摸鱼儿》词中的“脉脉此情谁诉”一句，亦可以与另一首《水龙吟》词中的“无人会，登临意”二句相参看。至于就我们现在所讨论的这一首《水龙吟》词而言，则除了“斜阳”一句可以与《摸鱼儿》词中的“斜阳”一句相参看以外，还有这首《水龙吟》词中的“凭栏却怕，风雷怒，鱼龙惨”数句，与《摸鱼儿》词中的“蛾眉曾有人妒”一句，所喻托的既同样是对于谗摈的忧惧，是则其情意固亦有相似之处。所以我在前文中就曾经提出来说，“辛词之感发生命的本质”，原以“英雄失志”的悲慨为主，只不过由于一则其感发生命中原来就具古有两种互相冲击的力量，此二种力量又往往因时地境遇之不同而可以有彼此间迭为消长的变化的情况，故其词之风格乃发展为多种不同之情调与面貌；再则其词中藉以表现感发生命的各种触引喻托的媒介，或用眼前之景物，或用历史之古典，也各有性质不同之形象，何况当他用典故时，其使用之态度与方法，又有正反宾主之各种变化，这当然是使得辛词表现得曲直刚柔多采多姿的另一个原因。就以本文所提到的这两首《水龙吟》词及一首《摸鱼儿》词而论，其所蕴含的感发生命之本质虽然是一贯的，然而其风格面貌，却已经表现了各自不同的变化。其“楚天千里清秋”一首《水龙吟》词，自眼前现实之景物起兴，当下就承接了“献愁供恨”和“江南游子”诸句，对自己的感情作了直接的抒写；可是这一首“举头西北浮云”的《水龙吟》词，则通篇大多以景物与古典之形象为喻示，直到“元龙老矣”三句，才在古典中显出了自己的影子，而却还用了反讽的笔法，并未作直接的抒写。何况开端的“举头西北浮云，倚天万里须长剑”的雄杰的气势和口吻，也与结尾处的“卸帆”“系缆”的闲淡的笔法和口吻造成了另一种反讽的对比。所以这一首词的幽隐曲折的变化，较之“千里清秋”一首的慷慨激昂，便已经在风格上有了很大的不同，只不过其开端之“长剑”的形象还保留了一些“慷慨激昂”的气势。可是他的《摸鱼儿》“更能消几番风雨”一词，则通篇都是以暮春之景色及女子之哀怨为喻托之形象，于是遂在风格上便又表现了一种幽咽缠绵的风貌，所谓“百炼钢”化为“绕指柔”，才人伎俩乃真有不可测者矣。希望我们对于这一首“举头西北浮云”的《水龙吟》词所作的讨论说明，以及我们把这一首《水龙吟》词与另一首“楚天千里清秋”之《水龙吟》词和《摸鱼儿》“更能消几番风雨”一词所作的一些比较，可以为辛词的一本万殊的特色，提供给读者一点小小的参考。而这一首《水龙吟》词中的“峡束苍江对起，过危楼、欲飞还敛”三句，我以为也恰好可以作为对辛词之感发生命中的两种冲击力量的极为形象化的说明。这正是我何以在辛弃疾那么多首著名的好词中，却单单只选取了这一首词来作为说明其一本万殊之特质的例证的缘故。

四

以上三节，我们既分别对于辛词感物之心的内在本质与其感心之物的外在遭遇，以及其一本万殊的特色，都已经作了相当的分析和说明，现在我们就将对辛词在词史中之地位以及其在艺术方面的特色，也略作简单之介绍。本来以前我们在论述五代及北宋诸家之词时，对于词之发展已曾有过相当之论述。大体说来，自五代之温、韦、冯、李，以迄北宋初年之晏、欧，曾被我们目为词之发展的第一阶段。在此一阶段中，其发展情况乃是歌筵酒席之艳曲因经过文士之插手写作，而逐渐转为具有鲜明个性之新体歌诗的过程，形式上虽然一直承袭着唐、五代以来短小之令词的体式，然而在内容方面即已经有了作者之性情襟抱的隐然的流露。其后则柳永与苏轼之相继出现，可以目之为词之发展的第二阶段。在此一阶段中，其发展之情况表现为两方面的开拓：一则是柳永在形式方面的开拓，将俗曲慢词的音调带入了文士手中，使得词在篇幅、声律及叙写之层次手法各方面，都得到了很大的拓展；另一方面则是苏轼在内容方面的开拓，一洗五代以来之艳词的绮罗香泽之态，而表现为一片天风海雨之才人旷士的浩气逸怀。这两方面的开拓当然都是极为可贵的，也都是极有发展余地的。至于以后秦观与周邦彦之相继出现，则可以目之为词之发展的第三阶段。秦观词之成就，主要盖在其精微柔婉之特质，故能使抽象之情思与具象之景物作出一种更为锐敏也更为深切的结合；至于周邦彦词之成就，则早已被历代词评家目之为北宋集大成的作者，而其最可注意的则是周之以赋笔为词，一变五代以来诸作者之但重直感的叙写，而将着重钩勒的思索安排的手法带入了词的写作之中，于是遂为南宋后来之姜夔、吴文英、王沂孙、张炎诸作者开启了无数法门。在以上我们所叙及的几个发展阶段中，自晏、欧、柳、苏以迄秦、周诸家之相继出现，北宋之词坛真可谓高峰迭起，各有独具之特色与过人之成就。不过值得注意的则是，柳、苏二家在第二阶段所造成的不同方面之拓展，到了第三阶段却只剩下了以柳词之影响为主流的秦、周等作者，而苏词之突破绮罗香泽的在意境与风格方面的拓展，则并未曾得到应得的反响和继承。这其间实在牵涉到了一个极值得重视的问题，那就是直到今天也仍然时常引起争议的，词之为体是否应以婉约方为正宗的问题。关于这个问题可以说自从苏词一出现便已经引起了论议。即如我们在论说苏词时，便曾经引过苏氏致鲜于子骏（侁）的一封信中所说的“自是一家”的话，也曾引过陈师道《后山诗话》谓苏词“虽极天下之工，要非本色”的话，还曾引过俞文豹《吹剑续录》中所载苏之幕僚将苏词与柳词作比较，谓苏词“须关西大汉执铁板唱‘大江东去’”的话，凡此种种说法，都足可说明苏词之开拓在当日之不被目为正统。这种观念之形成，自然由于词在初起之时原只是当筵侑酒之妙龄少女所唱的艳歌，为了适合这种演唱的场合和人物，所以才形成了词要以婉约为正宗的传统观念。不过艳歌之内容既不免淫靡浅俗之病，所以自士大夫染指写作以来，此种艳歌乃逐渐转化为可以供士大夫抒写个人情意的一种新的韵文形式。这在词之发展中，自然是一种进步的现象。如此，则因作者个性之不同与环境之不同，于是在非绮席歌筵的背景中，或在个人特殊之遭遇下，自然便也可能会写出一些并非属于婉约的作品。所以即使早在五代及北宋之初，也已有一些雄健激昂的作品出现了。即如后蜀鹿虔扆为悼念前蜀灭亡所写的《临江仙》（金锁重门荒苑静），南唐后主李煜在亡国后所写的《浪淘沙》（帘外雨潺潺），宋初范仲淹在边防戍守时所写的《渔家傲》（塞下秋来风景异），这些词就都并不是全属于婉约的作品。所以《谭评词辨》卷二即曾称鹿词《临江仙》为“哀悼感愤”，称李词《浪淘沙》为“雄奇幽怨”，称范词《渔家傲》为“沉雄似张巡五言”。是则就词之发展而言，固早具有拓出雄健悲慨之词风的可能性，只不过鹿虔扆、李煜诸人之写出此类作品，却并非有意要写为变调来对词之意境加以拓展，他们的这些词都只不过是在某种特殊情况中自己感情的一种自然流露而已。至于真正有心要开拓词境。并对此一意念带有明白之自觉的，自然要以北宋之伟大天才苏轼为最重要的一位作者。所以就词之演进而言，苏词之开拓原为一可供发展的大有可为之途径。然而苏词之拓展却并未能引起同时代作者普遍的共鸣，私意以为其主要之原因盖有以下数端：其一是由于词要以婉约为主的传统观念之拘限；其二是由于北宋直到末期仍充满了歌舞淫靡的社会风气；其三则是由于词在苏轼手中虽表现了词在诗化以后的很高的成就，但同时却也显示了词在诗化以后的一些缺点。即如我们以前在论说苏词时，便曾提出过苏词之佳者虽有时如“天风海涛之曲，中多幽咽怨断之音”，然而有时却也不免有“失之粗豪浅率者”。这种情形之出现，一方面固由于苏氏之性格超放，又复天才过人，写作时往往并不需精心为之结撰，故不免有下笔率意之处；而另一方面则也由于词与诗之特质原有不同，苏轼在词之发展中既曾使之达到了诗化的高峰，而且乃是以写诗之余力为词，因此在写词之际有时遂亦不免以诗笔为之，因而乃不免有失之粗豪率易之处（关于此种情形，我在论说陆游词时亦曾约略及之，可以参看）。总之，正是由于以上的一些因素，遂使得苏轼对词之拓展在当时并未被北宋之词人所普遍接受。其后经过了靖康之难与北宋沦亡的世变，于是早自五代以来便已经隐伏在鹿虔扆与李煜诸词作中的由世变之刺激而形成的雄健悲慨之词风，乃得在南宋之词坛上再度出现。只不过五代之时所流行的只是短小的令词，所以鹿虔扆、李煜诸人的雄健悲慨之词风，便也只是表现于小令之中而已；及至南宋之时，则长调之慢词既已经流行甚久，因此南宋词人之雄健悲慨的词风，便也在长调之中开始大量出现。即如以前缪钺教授所曾论说过的张元干、张孝祥，以及我所论说过的陆游，还有我们现在正在论说的辛弃疾，以及较辛氏稍晚的刘过、刘克庄诸人，便都是属于表现有这一类词风的重要作者。如果我们对这种发展演进之情况略加注意，我们就会发现用小令来写雄健悲慨的作品，较易得到成功；而用长调来写雄健悲慨的作品，则往往不免会有流于质直浅率之弊，而失去了词所应具有的一种曲折含蕴的特美。关于此种属于词体之特美，王国维在其《人间词话》中便早曾说过“词之为体，要眇宜修”及“诗之境阔，词之言长”的话。缪钺教授在其《论词》一文中，也曾说过“诗显而词隐，诗直而词婉”及“诗尚能敷畅，而词尤贵蕴藉”的话（见于上海古籍出版社刊行之《诗词散论》）。所以词中虽然也可以写雄健悲慨的内容，但其叙写之笔法却一定要有曲折含蕴之美。此在小令之体式言之，则其篇幅既短，故写之者乃必须将其雄健悲慨之情意尽力压缩于此短小之形式中，如此则自然容易产生一种含蕴曲折之深致。而且小令之句式节奏往往与五、七言诗之形式相近，因此以诗笔为词者，在写作小令方面也就比较易于得到成功。至于慢词之长调，则篇幅既然增大，因此就不得不在叙写时多所铺陈，而且长调中又往往杂有四言、六言等近于散文之句式，所以用此一形式来写雄健悲慨之情意，稍一不慎，乃往往不免有一泻无余缺乏曲折含蕴之美的遗憾。关于这种情况，我以前在论说陆游词时，便曾经举出其《汉宫春》（羽箭雕弓）一首来加以讨论过，以为此词“写得过于浅率质直，缺乏委曲含蕴之美”，又说“这首词一口气读下来，便只感到一种气势，而缺少含蕴”。其实这种现象不仅陆游词为然，就是南宋其他一些以长调来写豪放之壮词的作者，如张元干、张孝祥、刘过、刘克庄诸人，也都或多或少表现有此同样的缺乏曲折含蕴之美的遗憾。而其中唯一的一位写豪放之壮词但却并没有质直浅率之弊的作者，则自当推我们现在所正在讨论的辛弃疾。辛氏乃是一个能以英雄豪杰之手段写词而却表现了词之曲折含蕴之特美的一位杰出的词人，他在词中所做出的开拓和成就，不仅超越了北宋的苏轼，而且也是使得千百年以下的作者一直感到难以为继的。世之论词者每以苏、辛并称，此就其开拓词境突破传统而言，两家固有相近之处，而且辛词之有此开拓突破的勇气与眼光，也可能是因为受了苏词的启发和影响。不过，苏、辛二家对传统之都能有所开拓突破之一点虽同，但其开拓突破以后所表现的风格特色，以及其所以能达成此种开拓突破的因素，则并不尽同。苏轼对词境之开拓突破，主要盖由于其才气与胸襟之超迈过人，本非“绮罗香泽”之所能拘限。而且苏轼对于写作，又一向有“行乎其所当行，止乎其所不得不止”的一种独立开创之精神，这正是苏词之所以能对词境做出了极大之开拓的主要原因，故苏词风格之特色乃在其时时有超旷飞扬之致。至于辛弃疾对词境之开拓突破，则主要盖由于其志意与理念的深挚过人，也原非“剪红刻翠”之所能拘限，更加之其平生的不凡与不幸之遭遇的相互冲击，则更是造成其词之意境得以突破传统的另一重要原因。所以辛词对传统之突破，可以说乃是斯人与斯世相结合而造成的必然的结果，正如前人评阮籍诗所说的“遭阮公之时，固应有阮公之诗也”，我们也可以说“遭辛公之世，固应有辛公之词也”。故辛词风格之特色，乃在其处处有盘旋郁结之姿，这与苏词之但凭天赋之才气胸襟而突破传统，其本质上原是有相当不同的。而且如我在前文对辛氏之介绍，辛弃疾原来还并不仅是一个有性情、有理想的诗人而已。他同时还是一位在实践方面果然可以建立事功的有谋略、有度量、有识见、有手段，且有权变的英雄豪杰式的人物。只是他在建立事功方面的理想既然全部落空，遂在侘傺失志之余，乃不仅将其平生之志意与理念一皆寄托于词之写作，而且还将其平生之英雄豪杰的胆识与手段也都用在了词的写作之中。而值得注意的则是，辛词虽然一方面以其英雄豪杰的志意与理念突破了词之内容意境的传统，另一方面更以其英雄豪杰的胆识与手段突破了词之写作艺术的传统，可是就其词之本质言之。却又同时保有了词之曲折含蕴的一种特美，这两种相反而又相成的现象，既是辛词最值得注意的特色，也是辛词在词之发展中所完成的最为不可及的过人的成就。对于辛词之英雄豪杰的志意与理念，我们在前面既已曾有所论述，因此现在我们对其英雄豪杰式的艺术手段便也将略加介绍。关于辛词之艺术手段，历来论词者早已曾对之有过不少论述，此自非本文之所能遍举，如果博中取约，举其最为重要者言之，则私意以为辛词之艺术手段大概可以分为语言方面与形象方面两个重点来略加讨论。第一，先就语言方面言之，则辛词既能用古又能用俗，在词史上可以说是语汇最为丰富的一位作者，而尤以其用古方面最为值得注意。因为词之兴起既本是源于里巷之俗曲，所以五代、宋初之词原来极少使用古典者，及至诗人苏轼与赋家周邦彦在词坛上相继出现，始稍稍在词中使用古典，但周氏之用古典多只限于以唐人之诗句为主，苏氏之用典亦远不及辛氏之多而且广。早在刘辰翁之《辛稼轩词》序（《须溪集》卷六）中，论及苏、辛二家对词之开拓时，便曾谓："词至东坡，倾荡磊落，如诗如文，如天地奇观，岂与群儿雌声学语较工拙；然犹未至用经、用史，牵《雅》、《颂》入郑、卫也。自辛稼轩前，用一语如此者必且掩口。及稼轩横竖烂熳，乃如禅宗棒喝，头头皆是。"其后清代吴衡照之《莲子居词话》亦曾云："辛稼轩别开天地，横绝古今，《论》、《孟》、《诗·小序》、《左氏春秋》、《南华》、《离骚》、《史》、《汉》、《世说》、选学、李、杜诗，拉杂运用，弥见其笔力之峭。"刘熙载在其《艺概·词概》中，亦曾谓："稼轩词龙腾虎掷，任古书中理语、廋语，一经运用，便得风流，天姿是何夐异。"由以上所引述之评语，可见辛词之佳处，固不仅在其能融汇运用古人之辞语及故实，而尤在其能用之而可以"头头皆是"、"笔力甚峭"，而且可以将古语赋予鲜活之生命力，所谓"一经运用，便得风流"。即以其曾在岳珂《桯史》中被认为"微觉用事多"的《永遇乐》（千古江山）一词而言，陈廷焯在其《词则·放歌集》卷一中对此词之使用古典便曾大加赞美，说："稼轩词拉杂使事，而以浩气行之，如五都市中百宝杂陈，又如淮阴将兵，多多益善，风雨纷飞，鱼龙百变，天地奇观也。岳倦翁讥其‘用事多’，谬矣。”再如论词最反对用典的王国维，在其《人间词话》中，对辛词用典极多的《贺新郎》（绿树听鹈鴂）一词，便也曾大加赞美，谓其“语语有境界”。又如其《贺新郎》（凤尾龙香拨）一首，题为“赋琵琶”，本是一篇属于咏物之作，通首皆用有关琵琶之故实，然而却能不落入南宋一般咏物词之刻划沾滞之窠臼，而写得精力饱满，慷慨动人。陈霆在其《渚山堂词话》卷二中便也曾赞美此词，谓：“此篇用事最多，然圆转流丽，不为事所使，的是妙手。”陈廷焯之《白雨斋词话》亦曾赞美此词，谓其“运典虽多，却一片感慨，故不嫌堆垛”（关于咏物词，请参看拙作《论咏物词之发展及王沂孙之咏物词》一文）。另外，如我们在前文所举引的辛氏之《水龙吟》（举头西北浮云）一首词，便也是辛词之借用古典为生发而写得感慨万千的一篇佳作。而且辛弃疾之用古，还不仅只是用古典之故实而已，他有时还喜欢模拟古书之风格，或者完全袭用古书之辞句。陈模《论稼轩词》即曾谓辛词《贺新郎·送茂嘉十二弟》一首“全与太白《拟恨赋》手段相似”；又谓其《沁园春·止酒》一首“如《宾戏》、《解嘲》等作”。再如其《水龙吟·用些语再题瓢泉》一词之仿《天问》与《招魂》；《水调歌头》（我志在寥阔）一词之仿《九章·抽思》而用“少歌”。又如其《卜算子》（一以我为牛）一词之用《庄子》；《水调歌头》（长恨复长恨）一词之用《楚辞》；及另一首《水调歌头》（四座且勿语）之杂用《礼记》、《诗经》、《晋书·陶侃传》及左思、谢灵运、鲍照、杜甫诸家诗句；还有《踏莎行》（进退存亡）一首之杂用《周易》、《诗经》及《论语》之成句，凡此诸例，皆可见出辛弃疾写词之具有英雄豪杰的胆识与手段，其突破传统不主故常之开拓与变化，固更有过于苏轼者。所以《四库全书总目提要》之论辛词，乃曾谓：“其词慷慨纵横，有不可一世之概，于倚声家为变调。”冯煦在《宋六十家词选例言》中，亦曾谓：“稼轩负高世之才，不可羁勒。能于唐、宋诸大家外，别树一帜。”又云：“自此以降，词家遂有门户主奴之见。”于是世之论词者，乃莫不称辛词为“豪放”，而将之与“婉约”一派相对举。但辛词之风格虽有英雄豪燕之手段，但却又并非“豪放”二字之所能尽，所以刘克庄论辛词乃又有“公所作，大声镗鞳，小声铿鍧；横绝六合。扫空万古；其秾丽绵密处，亦不在小晏、秦郎之下”之言（见《后村大全集》卷九十八《辛稼轩集序》）。夫辛词中之亦有“不在小晏、秦郎以下”的“秾丽绵密”之作，斯固然矣；但辛词之真正佳处，却毕竟仍在其所独具的一份英雄豪杰之气。即以其为世所盛称的特具婉约之致的《摸鱼儿》（更能消几番风雨）及《祝英台近》（宝钗分）诸词而言，其潜气内转寓刚于柔的手段与意境，便已绝非小晏、秦郎之所能及。而辛词之更为难得之成就却还不在其能以英雄豪杰之气写入伤春怨别的这些小词之中而已；其更可注意者，乃是他即使在“别开天地，横绝古今”、“牵《雅》、《颂》入郑、卫”的“大声镗鞳”的作品中，却也仍保有了词之曲折含蕴的一种特美，虽然极为豪放，但却绝无浅率质直之病，这才是辛氏最为了不起的使千古其他词人皆莫能及的最为可贵的成就。而辛词之好用古典突破传统的作风，却恰好也就正是造成了他的雄奇豪放之词同时也仍能保有词之曲折含蕴之特美的一个主要原因。盖辛词之用古典，约可归纳为以下几种作用：一则既可以使之避免直言之质率；再则又可以将一己之感情推远一步，造成一种艺术之距离；三则更可以藉用古典而唤起读者许多言语之外的联想。于是辛词之驱使古典的雄奇豪放之作风，乃造成了一种与使用美人香草为喻托的同样的效果，这正是辛词使用古典的妙处之所在。然而其所以能达致此种妙处，则首在辛氏之有博学熟诵的修养，所以才能在使用古典时左右逢源而没有牵强堆砌的弊病；次则也因为辛弃疾自己内心中原具有一种强烈深挚的感发之力量，所以才能在使用古典之时，对古人、古事、古书、古语，也都赋于了充沛鲜活的生命，这种手段，自然是辛词中最值得注意的一点艺术特色。而辛词在语言方面的艺术手段之过人，还不仅在其善于用古而已，即是对俗语之使用，辛词亦自有其独到之处。本来用古典原非词之传统所有，故尔善用古典乃成为辛词最大之成就与开拓；然而用俗语则为词之传统所本有，盖词之兴起既是源于里巷之俗曲，所以早期之词如敦煌所发现之唐写本曲子，其中就含有大量之俗语。只不过自从文人诗客着手为这些曲子填写歌词以来，俗语遂在文士词中开始逐渐减少。直至柳永在词坛上出现，乃因其往往为歌伎、乐工填写市井中所流行的慢曲，于是俗语遂又在柳词中大量出现，因而也就形成了在词中使用俗语的一时风气。即如黄庭坚、秦观、周邦彦诸家，便都在词中保留有不少使用俗语之作；即使是号称以诗为词的苏轼，在其词中也同样有一些使用俗语的作品。所以辛词之用俗语，在词之传统中原不能算是一种独创的开拓。不过，词人之用俗语者虽多，而如果以辛词与其他词人之作品相比较，却也仍有一些值得注意的特色，这我们只要对辛词所用俗语之性质及其效果略加注意，便可见到其不同之处。

原来一般作者之在词中使用俗语者，大约有二种情况：其一是以俗语写男女调情之词者，柳永就是往往写有此类作品的一位词人，此固早为读词者之所共知，故不须再赘；至于北宋其他名家之作，如黄庭坚《归田乐引》（对景还消瘦）一首之“看承幸厮勾”及“冤我忒捫就”之类；秦观《品令》（幸自得）一首之“须管啜持教笑”，及“又也何须胳织”之类；周邦彦《青玉案》（良夜灯光簇如豆）一首之“轻惜轻怜转唧嘈”及“把我来僝僽”之类，他们所用的俗语便可以说大多都是勾栏瓦舍中男女欢爱的调情之辞。这是宋词中最常见的一种俗语的用法。除去此一类调情性质的俗语以外，其次则还有一类用于游戏笔墨之俗语，苏轼词中就有不少属于这类性质的作品，即如其《如梦令》（水垢何曾相受）及（自净方能净彼）二首中之“轻手、轻手”与“我自汗流呀气”之类；又如其《南歌子》（师唱谁家曲）一首之“借君拍板与门槌”及“不见老婆三五、少年时”之类，便都是属于游戏性质之使用俗语。以上两类之用俗语者，虽有时也能写得生动活泼、表现出一种真切如话的情趣，然大体言之，则无论其为调情性质或游戏性质之使用俗语，却毕竟都缺少一种严肃深挚的情意。至于辛词则虽然也有用俗语的游戏之作，然而除了这些一般性质的游戏之作以外，辛词之用俗语者却还表现了另外两种特色：一种是藉俗语抒写了对农村生活的一份亲切质朴的感情；另一种则是藉俗语之游戏性质表现了自己的一份嘲讽和悲慨。即如其题为“戏题村舍”的《鹧鸪天》（鸡鸭成群晚未收）一词，题为“夜行黄沙道中”的《西江月》（明月别枝惊鹊）一词，以及题为“村居”的《清平乐》（茅檐低小）一词，这些便可以说都是属于前一种用俗语表现了对农村生活的一份质朴亲切之情的作品；再如其题为“齿落”的《卜算子》（刚者不坚牢）一词，题为“遣兴”的《西江月》（醉里且贪欢笑）一词，以及题为“苦俗客”的《夜游宫》（几个相知可喜）一词，这些便可以说都是属于后一种用俗语表现了自己的一份嘲讽和悲慨的作品。这些词就辛氏而言，固决非其精心结撰的重要之作，但惟其因为他在浅俗游戏的作品中却也表现了真切深挚的情意，有时还可以表现出一种反讽的作用，于是辛词之用俗语遂也就造成了言语浅俗而意境却并非浅俗的艺术上之双重效果，这自然也是辛词在语言方面另一点值得注意的艺术特色。至于辛词中每好以“老子”自称，则原来亦为山东之俗语，而此种自称之辞，自亦原非词中传统之所有。盖词在初起本为不具个性之艳歌，故甚少自称之辞，其有之者，则多为以女子口吻自称的曰“奴”、曰“妾”之辞；即使有以男子口吻自称者，亦不过简单以“我”字自称而已。至苏轼“曲子中缚不住者”始有以“老夫”自称之语。辛弃疾之自称为“老子”，盖亦曾受有苏轼之影响，只是苏氏之自称“老夫”，不过仅表现了一份疏放而已，至辛氏之自称“老子”，则似乎更多了一份以乡音自慨的失志之悲。盖辛词之以“老子”自称，原来乃是始于其被劾罢官退居带湖以后，即如他在带湖闲居时所写的《水调歌头》（寄我五云字）与（白日射金阙）

二首，就曾屡有“老子政须哀”及“老子颇堪哀”之语，其以乡音俗语自慨的情意，自是明白可见的。而辛词在语言方面的艺术手段，还不仅是其在语汇方面之既能用古、又能用俗的两点特色而已，还有一点我们也该加以叙及的，那就是辛词在叙写之语法方面的变化多姿。先就其句法之骈散顿挫而言，即如我们以前在论陆游词时，曾经举引过陆氏的《汉宫春》（羽箭雕弓）一首词，谓其“过于浅率质直”，其故盖由于此一词调多为成排之四字句，所以容易形成一种气势而缺少含蕴，如陆词之“忆呼鹰古垒，截虎平川”及“看重阳药市，元夕灯山”诸句，都是一个领字带出两个四字偶句，因此便显得质直浅率，一泻而出，缺少了一种曲折含蕴之美；可是辛弃疾的《汉宫春》（亭上秋风）一词，在此等排句之处，所写的则是“记去年袅袅，曾到吾庐”及“甚风流章句，解拟相如”等句，都是以一个领字带起了两个声律虽相偶而辞意则并不相偶的句子，于是在其声律之骈与辞意之散的矛盾间，也就增加了一种曲折含蕴之美。而且陆游之《汉宫春》词结尾，所写的乃是：“君记取、封侯事在，功名不信由天。”全用直言，遂尔了无余味；而辛词之《汉宫春》词结尾，所写的则是：“谁念我、新凉灯火，一编太史公书。”既用的是问语的口气，又结合了眼前“新凉灯火”的背景与千年前“太史公书”的悲慨，于是辛氏此词遂给予了读者无穷的感慨深思之余味。在此种比较以下，则辛、陆二家之两首《汉宫春》词，其深浅曲直之差别岂不显然可见。此外，辛词在语言方面之骈散顿挫变化多方之例证甚多，又有用问答之句法者，用古文之句法者，而且这种语言句法方面之变化，还往往影响及其所使用之词调在风格方面也产生了相应的改变。即如《踏莎行》之牌调，晏殊所写的“细草愁烟”与“小径红稀”诸词是何种情调？辛氏用经语所写的“进退存亡”又是何种情调？再如《永遇乐》之牌调，苏轼所写的“明月如霜”一词是何种情调？辛氏所写的“千古江山”又是何种情调？所以范开之《稼轩词序》乃谓：“故其词之为体，如张乐洞庭之野，无首无尾，不主故常；又如春云浮空，卷舒起灭，随所变态，无非可观。”此固由于辛氏感发之本质之深挚过人，而其对语言文字之驱使运用之艺术手段，则实在才是使得辛氏不仅为一位忠义奋发的英雄豪杰，同时还是一位伟大词人的主要缘故。

其次，再就形象方面来谈一谈辛词之艺术手段。本来诗歌之重视形象化之表现，固早为一般人之所共知的老生常谈，我以前在《迦陵论诗丛稿》与《迦陵论词丛稿》二书所收之诸篇论文中，也曾多次讨论到形象与情意之关系的种种问题。约而言之，则形象之范畴既可以指自然界之一切物象，亦可以指人世间之一切事象。至于形象之来源，则既可以取之于现实中所有之实象，亦可以取之于想像中非实有之假象，更可以取之于古典中历史之事象。而形象与情意之关系，则既可以有由物及心的属于所谓“兴”的关系，也可以有由心及物的属于所谓“比”的关系，还可以有即物即心的属于“赋”的关系。以上所提到的种种区分，其实都只不过是在文学批评理论中为了立说方便而制定的一些名目而已；至于真正想要衡量一首诗歌的优劣，则事实上这些理论上之名目，却都并不能作为衡量之标准。因为无论是使用属于任何一种范畴、任何一种来源或任何一种关系的形象，都同时既有成为好诗的可能，也有成为坏诗的可能。而真正使一首诗歌成为好诗的基本因素，则主要实当以其形象与情意相结合时所传达出来的感发生命之质量为衡量之标准。因此现在我们对于辛词中之形象，便也将舍弃一切枝节，而专对其所传达之感发生命的质量一作探讨。一般而言，要想在诗歌之形象中传达出一种感发的力量，则首在具眼，次在具心，三在具手。具眼，所以才能对一切事物有锐敏之观察而掌握其鲜明之特色；具心，所以才能对所观察接触之事物引起真切活泼的感发；具手，所以才能以丰美之联想及切当之言语来加以表达。而辛弃疾就正是在以上三方面都具有过人之禀赋的一位作者。举例而言，即如其“青山欲共高人语，联翩万马来无数”（《菩萨蛮》）

之写山势；“昨日春如十三女儿学绣”（《粉蝶儿》）之写春光；“望飞来半空鸥鹭，须臾动地鼙鼓”（《摸鱼儿》）之写江潮；“春已归来，看美人头上，袅袅春幡”（《汉宫春》）之写节物。凡此诸例，辛氏对各种形象莫不写得鲜明真切，充满了生动活泼的感发之力量，则其在使用形象方面的艺术手段之不凡，固已可以概见一斑。不过，以上诸词例，若就辛词整体而言，却实在还并不是他的最具代表性的作品。因为如我在本文前面所言，辛氏之所以异于其他词人者，原来乃在于他的词中有一种志意与理念的本体之流露，而辛氏在使用形象方面的艺术手段，自然便也应该以其能藉用形象而传达出其志意与理念的作品方为最具代表性的佳作。本来我在前文已曾举过辛氏的《水龙吟》（举头西北浮云）一词，来说明辛词中以两种互相冲击之力量为主的一本万殊之变化。只不过那一首词中所用的大多为古典，古典中虽也具含有历史之事象，但总体说来，则历史之事象所予人之印象仍不免以抒情叙事为主，而并非单纯对形象之描绘。而且我们在那一首所讨论的重点乃在辛词之感发生命中两种互相冲击之力的特质，而并不在其对形象之描绘的艺术手法。因此我们现在便将再举另一首词例来对辛词中描绘形象的艺术手法及其与感发生命之传达的关系也略加探讨。我们先把这首词抄录下来一看：

沁园春　灵山齐庵赋，时筑偃湖未成

叠嶂西驰，万马回旋，众山欲东。正惊湍直下，跳珠倒溅；小桥横截，缺月初弓。老合投闲，天教多事，检校长身十万松。吾庐小，在龙蛇影外，风雨声中。　争先见面重重，看爽气、朝来三数峰。似谢家子弟，衣冠磊落；相如庭户，车骑雍容。我觉其间，雄深雅健，如对文章太史公。新堤路，问偃湖何日，烟水濛濛。

这首词是辛弃疾第二次被弹劾罢官后在铅山闲居时之所作。本来我

们在前文论及辛词万殊一本之物色时，已早曾提出过辛氏词中经常具含有“欲飞还敛”的两种互相冲击之力量，而其罢废家居以后所写的一些词中，则更表现有一种闲而不适的抑塞难平之气。因此，辛氏之词在表面看来，其内容虽有写壮怀之词，写闲居之词，写农村之词，写嘲讽之词，种种性质不同的作品，但究其实，则辛氏之关怀国计民生，一心想要恢复中原的志意与理念，则一直是其贯穿于万殊之中的一本，只不过写之于词的面目不同，其曲折隐显的层次变化也各有不同。现在就让我们从辛氏这一首罢废闲居的描绘山川景物的作品中，看一看辛氏如何在对景物形象的描述中传达了自己的理念和志意。在这首词中，辛氏用以描述景物之形象而传达出自己内心中一种感发之作用者，大约可归纳为以下几种手法：其一是由其在描绘形象时所用之状语及述语而传达出一种感发之作用者，如其“惊湍直下，跳珠倒溅”二句中所用之形容词、动词及副词，便不仅真切生动地写出了惊湍流泻水珠飞溅的景象，而且还表现了一种激动腾跃的力感。如果我们试将这两句词与王维在《辋川集》中所写的“跳波自相溅”一句诗相比较，我们就会发现他们所写的景象虽然颇为相似，然而王诗的写法则似乎仅为视觉上的冷静客观的描述，而辛词的写法则似乎在客观景象以外，还传达了作者内心中一种强烈的感受和兴发。这种由状语及述语对形象所做的生动真切的描述而传达出作者内心中强烈感发的写法，正是辛词在形象描写中的一大特色。其二是辛词往往将静态的形象拟比为动态的形象，即如此词开端的“叠嶂西驰，万马回旋，众山欲东”数句，辛氏乃将静态之群山拟比为回旋奔驰之万马，而谓其有“欲东”之势。如此便不仅描绘出了众山的形象和气势。同时还表现出了作者自己的一份沉雄矫健的精神气魄。像这种拟比之描述，自非具有如辛氏之英雄豪杰眼光与手段，不易达成此种感发之效果，这正是辛词在形象描写中的另一点特色。其三则是辛词也往往将具体之形象拟比为一种抽象之概念，即如在此词中的“争先见面重重，看爽气、朝来三数峰。似谢家子弟，衣冠磊落；相如庭户，车骑雍容。我觉其间，雄深雅健，如对文章太史公”数句，作者就是用自己对历史上人物与文章之概念来描状和拟比外在之景物的。要想说明此数句中感发之意境，我们就不得不先对此数句中历史之古典略加介绍。原来其“爽气”、“朝来”二句所用的乃是《世说新语》中的典故，据《世说新语·简傲》篇载云：“王子猷作桓车骑参军，桓谓王曰：‘卿在府久，比当相料理。’初不答，直高视，以手版拄颊云：‘西山朝来，致有爽气’。”至其“谢家子弟”一句，用的则是《晋书》中之典故。据《晋书·谢玄传》载云：“谢安问：‘子弟亦何豫人事？而正欲其佳。’玄答曰：‘譬如芝兰玉树，欲使其生于庭阶耳’。”至其“相如庭户”二句，用的则是《史记》中的典故，据《史记·司马相如列传》载云：“相如之临邛，从车骑，雍容闲雅甚都。”而其“雄深雅健”数句用的则是韩愈的话。韩氏称美柳文，曾谓其“雄深雅健似司马子长”（见刘禹锡《刘梦得文集》卷廿三《唐故柳州刺史柳君集纪》）。本来辛氏此词下半阕自“争先见面重重”一句以下，全写作者眼前当面所见之群山，而辛氏乃完全不从山之实象着笔，却用了一连串得之于古典中的抽象的概念，于是遂把自己平日读书所得的学养襟抱，一并都投入了对山的描述之中，因此遂使得既无知觉又无感情的山，也竟然有了人的品格和修养，而产生了一种强大的感发的力量，这自然更是辛词在形象之描述中的另一点值得注意的特色。以上我们从这一首《沁园春》词已经举出了辛词在描述形象时所使用的三种不同的艺术方式；但这首词的真正感发的重点却还并不仅在这些分散的描述，而更在他把形象与抒情叙事完全结合在一起，所写的“老合投闲，天教多事，检校长身十万松。吾庐小，在龙蛇影外，风雨声中”数句，这才是辛氏这一首词中真正传达出他的志意与理念的画龙点睛之笔。在这数句词中，“老合投闲，天教多事”二句，乃是全词中唯一直接抒写情意之处。本来我在以前论陆游词时，曾经说过陆词多用直笔故不免质率之失的话，但辛氏此二句却不仅无质率之失，且有画龙点睛之妙。此盖正如钟嵘《诗品·序》所谓:“若专用比兴,患在意深,意深则文踬;若但用赋体,患在意浮,意浮则文散。”所以曲直隐显之笔,总要相互映衬生发,方能获得既富于感发而又不失之于浅率的效果。何况此二句词虽是直写情意,但却是反讽的语气,暗示了作者之不甘投闲置散的心情;而下句之“检校长身十万松”,则又把此一份不甘投闲置散的心情结合着眼前的景物做了极为形象的叙写,遂于言外表现了极深重的悲慨。而其感发之作用则主要乃在辛氏于“十万松”之名物形象之上所用的“长身”两字的形容词,以及“检校”两字的动词。盖“检校”乃检阅军队之意,“长身”乃将松拟人之语。曰“检校长身十万松”,是直欲将十万松视为十万长身勇武的壮士之意,则辛氏自憾不能指挥十万大军去恢复中原的悲慨,岂不显然可见。而此词开端之将群山拟比为回旋奔驰之万马的想像,则又正与此句之将松树拟比为十万大军的想像互相映衬生发,遂使此词传达出一份强大的感发之力量。至于下面的“吾庐小,在龙蛇影外,风雨声中”几句,则表面一层乃是承接以上所写的“叠嶂”“惊湍”和“十万松”的背景,点明题目中的“灵山齐庵”也就是“吾庐”的所在之地,为上半阕词的一大总结。“龙蛇影”是写“十万松”的枝干盘虬之影;“风雨声”则是写“惊湍”的流泻喷溅之声,仅就此对形象之绘影绘声而言,这两句词便已极为工妙。然而辛词之佳处却还不仅只此一点而已,这两句词的更可注意之处,实在还更在其言外之另有深一层的喻托意,那就是“龙蛇影”及“风雨声”实在也象喻了外在的一种迫害和侵袭的阴影及威力。而这种对外在的迫害的危虑,则正是与辛词之豪壮的志意理念所经常结合在一起,无论是在其所谓“豪放”之词,或所谓“闲适”之词中都经常出现的各种画面之下的底色。像这种结合着形象而表现了一种志意理念,且隐含着多种情意的叙写,如此词之“检校长身十万松”及“龙蛇影外,风雨声中”诸句,当然是辛词之艺术手法中的一种极高的成就。

以上我们对辛词的《沁园春》(叠嶂西驰)一首词,可以说已经大体都作了评赏和说明。但读者一定会注意到我们原来却还遗漏了“小桥横截，缺月初弓”及“新堤路，问偃湖何日，烟水濛濛”数句未加评说。其所以然者，盖因为前面的一大段评说，我们的重点乃在于阐述辛词中对形象之叙写所传达的感发之力量，而“小桥横截”与“新堤路”数句，则在形象之叙写中并未曾传达出什么强大的感发的力量，这正是我们在前面一段对此数句未加评说的缘故。不过，这几句词却也具有另一种供我们探讨的价值，那就是辛弃疾在罢官闲居后，在上饶带湖及铅山瓢泉两处购地置产的规划和心情。本来我们在前面评赏辛词之《水龙吟》（举头西北浮云）一首词时，已曾屡次谈到辛弃疾轻视对于三国时代“求田问舍”全无救世之意的许汜，以及将许汜与陈登和刘备相对举的或正或反的种种深意。是则辛氏之一心想要恢复中原重返故乡之本意，自是可以想见的；其原来并没有想要在江南购地置产之用心，也是可以想见的。然而辛氏却毕竟在江南购置了产业，这对于一心想要恢复中原的辛弃疾而言，实在是一个绝大的讽刺和悲剧。而其所以竟然不得不如此者，则一在于深感到被谗摈之无奈，二在于有见于欲恢复之无望。不过，其购地置产之用心虽出于无奈与无望，可是当他规划安排起来时，却又做得极为有声有色。这种情况我以为一则是由于辛弃疾原是个英雄豪杰式的人物，因此不仅当他用兵论战之时，有他的英雄豪杰式的眼光与手段，就是在他购地置产之时，也同样有他的英雄豪杰式的眼光与手段。这自然是使得他在购建之规划中做得有声有色的一个主因。再则也因为辛弃疾确实是对于山川花鸟一切大自然的景物都有着一份深厚的赏爱之情，所以当他建置房产时，遂在取景布置方面常不惜投入很多心力，这自然是使得他在购地置产之时做得有声有色的另一个原因。三则更由于辛弃疾之购地置产既本就含有一份无奈与无望的悲慨，因此他遂将对于山水的安排当作了英雄失志以后的一种安慰和寄托，这自然也是使得他在建置规划中做得有声有色的又一原因。因此，辛弃疾在建置方面的规划虽大，然而却与南宋其他一些大官们之竞尚奢华豪侈的情况，原是有很大不同的（可参看拙文《论咏物词之发展及王沂孙之咏物词》一文对于南宋奢靡之社会风气的叙述)。这我们只要看一看辛词中对带湖和瓢泉两处建置的描述就可以得到证明。即如其《沁园春》(三径初成)一词所写的:“东冈更葺茅斋,好都把、轩窗临水开。要小舟行钓,先应种柳;疏篱护竹,莫碍观梅。秋菊堪餐,春兰可佩,留待先生手自栽。”又如其《水调歌头》(带湖吾甚爱)一词所写的:“东岸绿阴少,杨柳更须栽。”还有其题为《检校停云新种杉松戏作》的《永遇乐》一词所写的:“投老空山,万松手种。”又有其题为《停云竹径初成》的《蓦山溪》一词所写的:“斜带水,半遮山,翠竹栽成路。”更有其题为“新开池戏作”的《南歌子》一词所写的“涓涓流水细侵阶,凿个池儿,唤个月儿来。”凡此诸例,都使我们既可以看到辛弃疾在建置时对景物之安排规划的眼光与手段,与其他竞尚华奢的豪富之家的果然有所不同,也使我们又可以看到辛弃疾在布置景物时,也曾经付出了自己一份辛勤的劳动。像这一类对安排景物的叙写,从个别词句看来,虽未必有什么强大的感发的力量,然而就辛词之整体看来,则是既表现了辛弃疾对山川花木的赏爱之深情与安排布置的眼光和手段,同时也隐含有罢官家居后寄情山水的一份无奈与无望之悲慨。我们在本文所讨论的《沁园春》(叠嶂西驰)一词中所写的“小桥横截,缺月初弓”与“偃湖何日,烟水濛濛”几句,就也同样正表现了辛弃疾在景物安排中的这些委曲的情意。“缺月初弓”是写其眼前所见的横截水上的小桥形象,“烟水濛濛”则是写他想像中尚未建成的偃湖的形象。而在这种对景物的赏爱和安排之中,辛弃疾却原是隐含有极深的无奈与绝望之悲慨的。这在本词之上半阕所写的“检校长身十万松”和“龙蛇影外,风雨声中”诸句,便都足可为之证明。而在这种罢官家居的生活中,辛弃疾所最为向往而且经常提起的一位古人,则是东晋时辞官归隐的陶渊明。台湾的陈淑美在其所写的《辛稼轩与陶渊明》一文中,曾经统计过辛词中之述及陶渊明之姓名、诗、文及引用个别辞句者,共有七十余处之多(见台湾《中外文学》1975 年第 4 卷第 6 期)。而且辛氏既曾在带湖之居用陶之《归去来兮辞》中的“植杖”之句以名其亭;

又曾在瓢泉之居用陶之《停云》诗以名其堂，还在一首《水龙吟》词中写有“老来曾识渊明，梦中一见参差是。觉来幽恨，停觞不御，欲歌还止”的句子，这正因为在陶渊明的内心深处，原来也蕴蓄有一种“欲有为而未能”的幽恨。陶渊明在其《杂诗十二首》的第二首中，就曾写有“岁月掷人去，有志不获骋。念此怀悲凄，终晓不能静”的句子。而这种“幽恨”既正是隐蓄在陶诗深处的底色，也正是陶诗之所以最能引起辛弃疾之共鸣的一个基本原因。不过，陶渊明实在不仅只是一位具有真淳深挚之情的诗人，他同时还是一位具有通观妙悟的哲人，因此他遂能透过深隐的幽恨而终于达到了一种“俯仰终宇宙，不乐复何如”、“此中有真意，欲辨已忘言”的自得的境界。而辛弃疾毕竟是一位想要建立事功收复中原的英雄志士，因此他与陶渊明在“幽恨”方面虽有近似之处，但却一直不能达到陶渊明的俯仰自得的境界。辛弃疾乃是终生都挣扎在“天远难穷休久望，楼高欲下还重倚”的悲慨痛苦之中的。这种悲慨和痛苦的由来，就正如我在前文所言，乃是由于他一方面既在南渡以后不断受到谗毁和摈斥，而另一方面他对于自己的强烈深挚的想要恢复中原的理念和志意则又始终无法弃置。所以我在前文就曾经说过，这两种冲击的力量乃是辛词之感发生命中的万殊之中的一本。不过辛氏在词中却很少对他的志意理念作直接的说明，他总是把他内心中的志意和悲慨结合在他得之于古典中的感发或景物中的感发来作形象的表现。因此，他在词中所传达出来的，才真正是一份感发的生命，而不像其他所谓豪放的词人之但为浅率质直的豪放的言辞而已。本文虽然对辛词之艺术手段提出了语言及形象两个重点，但读者却也切不可误会为只要多用古典及形象便可写出好词。辛词之所以好，乃是因为辛弃疾内心中首具一种沉挚的理念和志意，无论是对古典还是对景物的观赏，他都能随处引起感发，这才是辛词之所以能胜于其他所谓豪放的词人，同时也异于其他词人之堆砌刻划地使用古典和景物的形象而独能在词中既传达出一份强大的感发力量，并且还具有一种曲折含蕴之特美的主要缘故。不过这种区别却并非只用简单的概念化之语言所能说明，因此本文才不得不在叙写中举出了《水龙吟》（举头西北浮云）和《沁园春》（叠嶂西驰）两首词例来作较为具体的分析和讨论，遂造成了文字篇幅过长的结果，这一点还希望能得到读者的谅解。

至于辛词之不易学步，则世人对之固早有定论。陈廷焯《白雨斋词话》卷一即曾云："稼轩一体，后人不易学步。无稼轩才力，无稼轩胸襟，又不处稼轩境地，欲于粗莽中见沉郁，其可得乎？"周济《介存斋论词杂著》亦称辛词："才情富艳，思力果锐。南北两朝，实无其匹。"又云："后人以粗豪学稼轩，非徒无其才，并无其情。稼轩固是才大，然情至处，后人万不能及。"这些评语都是极为有见之言。盖辛词之佳处及其所以不易学之故，乃在于非知之难，行之为难；非行之难，而有之为难也。本文的析论就正是试图从不同的角度对辛词之"所有"所作的探讨。不过辛词之方面甚广，本文虽长，仍只是扼要言之而已。至于辛词中偶有仿效他人风格之作，如其《丑奴儿近》（千峰云起）一首之题为"效李易安体"；《玉楼春》（少年才把笙歌盏）一首之题为"效白乐天体"；《河渎神》（芳草绿萋萋）一首之题为"效《花间》体"等，盖皆一时兴到之戏作，并非辛词之本色，故不具论。此外辛词中亦偶有失之浅拙或失之嵯岈者，则是英雄豪杰偶尔不顾细行之作，亦不须苛论求之也。

1986年3月，写毕第一、二、三节于加拿大之温哥华，同年6月，写毕第四节于成都。

On Xin Qiji's Song Lyics

Xin Qiji has left a corpus of over six hundred song lyrics, more than any other song writer of the Song Dynasty. Their variety, both in content and style, earned the admiring comments of his contemporaries,[1] and since then there has never been a time when his songs were not appreciated.[2] It is a daunting task to try to give a comprehensive account of a poet of such versatility; instead I propose to look for the unity underlying the diversity to try to discover the ultimate source of his inspiration before examining in detail a few of his songs.

In China, poetry is traditionally defined as the expression of the poet's thoughts and feelings; hence, it originates in the heart. Since the strength of a poem comes from its evocative effect, it will be measured by the nature of the poet's feelings, the quality of his heart as he is moved by some external stimulus. This was early noted by Liu Xie: "Jia Yi's intelligence is apparent, and so his poetry is clear and the style is transparent. Sima Xiangru was proud and exuberant, and so the description in his Rhapsodies is extravagant and his vocabulary prolix...Pan Yue was light-hearted and clever, and so his points stand out and his rhythms flow. Lu Ji was sober and serious, and so his feelings were complex and his style devious."[3]

Wang Guowei also linked the character of a poet with his poetry: "Su

Shi's song lyrics are expansive, Xin Qiji's are heroic...To try to imitate the songs of those two poets without their kind of heart is like Xishi's ugly neighbor trying to look like her by frowning as she did."[4]

This long-standing tradition, which makes the poet's character the basis for judging his poetry, has a certain validity, but a distinction should be made between an incidental, spur-of-the-moment response to some external stimulus and a fundamental, enduring preoccupation that shapes a poet's style and reveals his character. For example, Yan Shu's lyrics reflect his comprehensive outlook, and Ouyang Xiu's express his enduring capacity for enjoying life, for making the most of things; in both cases they surely reflect the poet's own nature. When Yan Shu writes (*QSC*, p. 89)

The nothing-to-be-done-about-it flowers have fallen	无可奈何花落去
And the seemingly familiar swallows are back again	似曾相识燕归來

and Ouyang Xiu (*QSC*, p. 132)

You should watch the Luoyang flowers to the end	直须看尽洛城花
And then it will be easier to say goodbye to the spring breeze.	始共春风容易别

they are only expressing a momentary reaction to the evanescence of a spring scene. These lines give no clue to any of the enduring concerns of either poet. But the greatest of China's poets continually reveal in their poetry their inner nature and their dominant concerns: Qu Yuan's pursuit of purity and refinement, Tao Qian's integrity, which he maintained by trusting his own instincts, Du Fu's overriding patriotism and his Confucianism—these show up in their poetry whatever the topic, for these were not just passing feelings stirred by some occasional event or scene but lifelong preoccupations. This is what sets off a truly great poet from the rest. For most poets their words are the product of temperament and talent. A truly great poet, however, puts his lifelong aspirations and ideals into his poems, which then become a faithful reflection of what he was. This is exemplified in the poetry of Qu Yuan, Tao Qian, and Du Fu, but more difficult to find in the song lyrics of Tang and Song poets. The song form, from its origin associated with parties and entertainment, was not thought suitable for the serious expression of a poet's aspirations. Further, from Wen Tingyun on there was no song writer of the stature of those poets who could achieve this perfect blending of man and poetry. As a result, compared with *shi* poetry, song lyric was lacking in two respects: first, no song writer put his whole heart into his lyrics; and second, songs failed to express any great aim or idea. Yan Shu and Ouyang Xiu were both men of integrity and education; song writing was a diversion they practiced in their spare time, not a medium for expressing their deepest feelings and aspirations. Their song lyrics record only reactions to an immediate situation, and while they may arouse far-reaching associations in the reader's mind, they cannot compare with the poems of those writers who put all their hearts into their poetry.

Among song writers one might think of Li Yu as an exception, since he did write about his feelings in his songs, but he did so without evoking a philosophy of life; the best of them, although they arouse sympathy for his plight at the loss of his kingdom and his freedom, still fail to convey an awareness of anything beyond his personal loss. There is also Su Shi, who enlarged the scope of the song lyric to include topics hitherto reserved for *shi* poetry. In spite of the power and feeling in his songs, their conceptual scope still falls short of expressing his lifelong ideals and aspirations. Though he aspired to a life of public service, he was temperamentally attracted to the Taoist ideal of detachment from the world, and when his official career was checked by court intrigues, he could console himself by withdrawing. It was only after being frustrated in his career that he turned to writing songs, and their dominant tone was one of expansive freedom. Moreover, because Su Shi was not an introspective person, very few of his songs reveal a commitment to any single determining aim or philosophy. Compared with his *shi* poetry and prose writings, his songs were obviously not the focus of his literary activity, though he did deliberately work to enlarge their range.

Xin Qiji, on the other hand, put all his poetic energies into writing song lyrics that did express his aspirations and philosophy. He is the one song writer who can be put alongside Qu Yuan, Tao Qian, and Du Fu in possessing a strongly held goal in life, a poet who poured all his heart's strength into his poetry and whose life does not belie his work. It is poets like this whose poetry remains fresh and arresting after thousands of years. Philsophical and ethical values are intrinsic to their character, and their poetry embodies their lifelong aspirations and ideals. The moving power of such poetry derives from its wholly honest expression of character. In this, Xin Qiji is unique among Song Dynasty song writers, and we must recognize this fact if we are to appreciate his song lyrics.

Xin Qiji was born in 1140[5] in Licheng (modern Shandong Province), which had already been under the control of the invading Jurchen for more than ten years. Because of his many dependents, his grandfather, Xin Zan, though an ardent patriot, was unable to follow the Song Court when it fled south. He took office under the Jin but inculcated his own patriotic feelings in his grandson. Xin Qiji was twenty-one when the Jin undertook an expedition against the Southern Song. There was a widespread uprising among the Chinese population in Jin-occupied territory; and a Shandong peasant, Geng Jing, became leader of a force that grew to more than 100,000 men. Xin Qiji himself recruited some 2,000. He put them at Geng Jing's disposal and was made his secretary. He advised Geng Jing to make contact with the Song, and in 1162 was sent south to lead a delegation to offer allegiance to the Song court. The Song Emperor Gaozong was temporarily in Jiankang where he received the delegation and bestowed official titles on them, making them responsible for uniting Geng Jing's rebel forces with the Song armies.

While the delegation was still in Jiankang, however, Geng Jing was killed by a subordinate, one Zhang Anguo. Hearing the news on his return, Xin Qiji led a band into the Jin army camp where Zhang Anguo was being feted for his deed, seized him, and carried him away, never stopping until the traitor was delivered to the Song court, where he was summarily executed. This exploit gives a measure of Xin Qiji's courage and dedication to the cause of regaining China's lost territory. In a memorial he submitted later[6] he discussed the conditions for local uprisings in occupied territory. It was mostly the peasants who rebelled, he observed, but though easily recruited, they were without a plan of action, and were easily dispersed when facing regular troops. The gentry, on the other hand, which included men of ability and resolve, were not inclined to accept the leadership of their social inferiors. Even more than the peasantry, they dreamed of an opportunity to give vent to their suppressed anger. Aware of consequences, however, they would not act without military support from the Song. Xin Qiji's analysis shows his understanding of the social and psychological factors to be reckoned with in any attempt to overthrow the Jin. He had acted on that understanding when he put himself and his 2,000 recruits under the command of the peasant leader Geng Jing. His overriding concern was always the recovery of the territory lost to the invaders.

After his move to the South he continued to submit memorials to the throne advising military action against the Jin, always taking political and economic factors into account. But none of his proposals was accepted by the Song court, and he was repeatedly dismissed from office. Some of his frustration and disappointment is reflected in the song: "Written in Jest after a visitor had been excitedly talking about great deeds, and I recalled the days when I was young" to the tune "Partridge in the Sky" (*Zhegu tian*, *QSC*, p. 1943).

When 1 was young I had ten thousand men under my colors, 壮岁旌旗拥万夫
Brocade-shirted cavalrymen just crossing the River. 锦襜突骑渡江初
Yan troops carried their silver quivers at night, 燕兵夜娖银胡䩮
Han archers let fly their golden arrows at dawn. 汉箭朝飞金仆姑

Remembering the past 追往事
I lament the present me. 叹今吾
My white beard gets no color from the spring wind. 春风不染白髭须
1 would be glad to trade my ten-thousand-word pacification plan 却将万字平戎策
For the gardeners' guide of the man next door. 换得东家种树书

During his forty-five years in the South, nearly twenty of which he spent in banishment to the countryside, repeatedly slandered and demoted, he never lost his desire to serve or his hope of recovering the lost territory. During his brief intervals in office, he was indefatigably active, applying his extraordinary abilities in his effort to accomplish something. As Prefect of Xuzhou from 1172 to 1173, he reduced taxes and resettled refugees, demonstrating that it was possible, in even a short time, to reverse the trend toward disorder. Later, from 1174 to 1181, when he held various offices in Jiangxi, Hubei, and Hunan, he succeeded in putting down banditry, relieving famine, and organizing a Flying Tiger Brigade, at once combining compassion for the people and devotion to the national cause. His were not just good intentions; he put them into practice. In a memorial he wrote as Pacification Officer in Hunan, he criticized corrupt officials whose extortions forced people into banditry and concluded, "I venture to hope that Your Majesty will ponder the cause of banditry, and when you look for a way to put an end to it, will rely not only on force to suppress the bandits."[7] He also declared his determination to expose official corruption and abuse of power wherever he found it, regardless of consequences.

The *Song History* records[8] that when he established a camp for his Flying Tiger Brigade, it was reported to Xiaozong that he was using tax money for the purpose, and the Emperor issued a "metal placard" to stop it. But Xin Qiji concealed the placard instead of posting it. He ordered that from every house, with the exception of official buildings and temples, two tiles should be contributed, so that the barracks for the brigade was completed.

There was a famine in Jiangxi while he was Pacification Officer there. He posted a notice in the streets: "Those who hoard grain will be banished; those who appropriate grain will be executed." He also took all the cash and silver vessels from the official residence and ordered the officials, the gentry, the merchants, and the townspeople to raise funds or goods according to their means to pay for grain shipments. As the grain transport boats kept coming, one after the other, the Prefect of the neighboring district (Xinzhou) asked for help for his own starving people, but Xin Qiji's staff refused. But he responded, "All children are the ruler's subjects," and sent a third of the grain boats to Xinzhou.[9]

These stories attest to an understanding, ability, and courage that were out of the ordinary, yet Xin Qiji was constantly harassed by slander. In his memorial on measures against banditry, he wrote, "I have always been stubborn and self-reliant, and people have not always tolerated me, so I fear

I will get into trouble before the words have left my mouth."[10] And sure enough, in the same year in which he succeeded in relieving the famine, he was impeached by the Censor Wang Lin, who accused him of "spending money as though it were dirt, killing people as though they were weeds." As a result, he was relieved of his office. He then bought land and built a house near Lake Dai in Jiangxi. On its completion he wrote, "To the east / I sit and watch the red dawn across the sky. / Though banished to rivers and seas, I still worry and hope for a good year.../ To the west / The roads are uncertain through a myriad miles of rivers and lakes. / Born to be a general, like him of the Qin clan / Doesn't keep me from selling my sword to buy plow and hoe."[11] He has carried his worries for the country into retirement with him: the tone is one of bitterness and frustration rather than resignation. It is easy to see how he could compare himself with the Han dynasty general Li Guang, native of Qin, whose talent for a distinguished career as a general was inborn.

He spent some ten years out of office, until 1192, when he was recalled to be Inspector of Prisons in Fujian and not long afterward Pacification officer of Fujian. He was over fifty at the time, but his resolve to reconquer the north was undiminished. In 1194 he created a "security arsenal". Because Fujian bordered on the ocean, it was vulnerable to pirate raids, and Xin Qiji felt the need to prepare for emergencies. He collected weapons and some 500,000 strings of cash for his arsenal. He also wanted to make 10,000 helmets, and recruit men to fill out the army quota, and he instituted a strenuous military drill. Again he was impeached on the charges of cruelty, greed, extortion, and corruption, and relieved of office.

He built a new house in Qisi in Qianshan district and when his house by Lake Dai burned, made his home there for the next eight years. In 1203 he was again recalled to be Prefect of Shaoxing commandary and Pacification Officer for the Zhedong region. Now sixty-four years old, he kept trying to perform his duties as a public servant. On assuming office, he immediately sent in a memorial enumerating the six things most harmful to farmers of the region; the very next year he was transferred to Zhenjiang Prefecture. During the next two years he dispatched spies to find out the military strength of the Jin, what places were fortified, the names of their generals, and the sites of their arsenals. He also intended to recruit men from the border region for a defense force and had a thousand red uniforms made for their use.

It was now forty-three years since he had escaped from the north, as he recalled in a song, "In Beigu Pavilion at Jingkou, Remembering the Past", to the tune "Always Having Fun" (*Yong yu le*, *QSC*, p. 1954): "Forty-three years and I still remember looking back at the beacon fires on the Yangzhou road." The song concludes, "Who will ask for me? / Lian Po is old now, / Can he still eat meat do you think?" Even in old age he had the unquenchable desire, like Lian Po, to leap into the saddle and prove he could be of service. But he was once again impeached for being "lecherous and greedy, extorting taxes and reckless punishments," and dismissed, age sixty-six. His health declined and he died the next year 1207, his lifelong ambition unfulfilled.

This biographical sketch, based on his biography in the *Song History* and on Deng Guangming's "Chronobiography", gives some of the historical background necessary to understanding and fully appreciating the song lyrics of this great poet, who was also a statesman and a man of action very much involved in his country's confrontation with a foreign invader. It conveys some idea of the nature and sensibility of the man and of the events to which he responded emotionally. He was not only sensitive and intelligent, he was resourceful, courageous, far-sighted, and adaptable. The central concern of his entire life, fueled by patriotism and reinforced by homesickness for a native place occupied by alien invaders, was his determination to recover China's lost territory. It became a veritable obsession. Frustrated by repeated misinterpretations of his actions and by downright slander from his political opponents, he failed in his ambition to become the heroic leader who recovered the northern half of his country. Instead, he became the greatest song writer of the Southern Song. Into his song lyrics he poured his pent-up feelings, and they carry the burden of his disappointment. So, in a sense, he owed his achievement as a poet to his failure in the world of action.

Not all the six hundred-odd song lyrics that survive are in the same style or on the same theme, nor were all his conflicts internal. As a refugee from the North obsessed with the idea of recovering his homeland, he was misunderstood by southerners, who saw things differently and anyhow preferred peace to war. Although he was sensitive to political conditions and changes in government policy, these were not matters he could write about directly. References to them in his songs take two forms: one uses the natural world as an analogy to political events; the other draws upon historical analogs introduced by way of allusion. Circumspection could have been a reason for choosing this mode of expression, but it was also something that came naturally to him. In the natural world he found it easy to see symbols of his own passionate feelings, and the knowledge of history and literature that filled his well-stocked mind provided countless similarities to his own situation without his having to consciously look for them. What he saw and what he had read became imbued with his own passionate feelings and provided an inexhaustible source of inspiration, adding to the variety and complexity of his songs. For example:

Visiting Double Stream Tower
at South Sword
to the tune "The Water Dragon Sings"

(*Shuilong yin*, *QSC*, p. 1896)

I look up at the floating clouds in the northwest.	举头西北浮云
I would need a sword that stretched a thousand miles into the sky.	倚天万里须长剑
People say that right here	人言此地
Late at night you can always see	夜深长见
A light flashing up to the stars.	斗牛光焰
But I feel the hills are high	我觉山高
The pool empty, the water cold.	潭空水冷
The moon is bright, the stars pale.	月明星淡
I thought to light a rhino horn and go down to look	待燃犀下看
But leaning on the rail I was afraid	凭栏却怕
Of wind and thunder angry,	风雷怒
Fish and dragons cruel.	鱼龙惨
Rising walls confine the Blue River	峡束沧江对起
As it passes the precarious tower,	过危楼
About to take flight, receding again.	欲飞还敛
Chen Deng is old now	元龙老矣
And might as well retire	不妨高卧
With a cold drink and a cool bed.	冰壶凉簟
The ups and downs of a thousand years	千古兴亡
The joys and sorrows of a lifetime—	百年悲笑
I see them all from here	
Where I've climbed for the view.	一时登览
Who is it I wonder lets fall	问何人又卸
A sail at the sandbank	片帆沙岸
To tie up in the setting sun?	系斜阳缆

Here Xin Qiji brings together scenic description and historical allusion, infusing them with the conflicting feelings in his own heart to create a complex poem. To begin with the title: "South Sword" (*Nanjian*) is a Song Dynasty district, variously named, but always including the word *jian* ("sword") as an element, for legend says that it was here that a sword once sprang into the pool and changed into a dragon.[12] Behind the legend is an allusion to the biography of Zhang Hua in the *Jin History*.[13] He asked a Yuzhang man, Lei Huan, reputed to understand such things, about a purple emanation in the sky between the constellations Herd Boy and Dipper, and was told, "It's the spirit-essence of a sword in Fengcheng in Yuzhang rising up into the sky." Zhang Hua then appointed Lei Huan Prefect of Fengcheng, where he dug up a stone casket containing a pair of swords. He sent one to Zhang Hua, keeping the other for himself. When Zhang Hua was executed, the sword was lost. Lei Huan's own sword was inherited by his son. He was wearing it when he passed through South Sword, and the sword leapt from its scabbard and fell into the water. A man dispatched to dive into the pool to recover the sword reported that he saw no sword but a pair of dragons, each several yards long. In a little while the pool was filled with light and the water boiled and bubbled. After that the sword was seen no more.

This is the legend connected with the place, and it explains some of the song's implications. The "floating clouds in the northwest" in the opening line can be taken as part of the scene viewed by the poet, but it is at the same time a reference to the lost territories, once the heartland of China. The long sword could be suggested by the legendary swords associated with the place and also refer to the poet's resolve to reconquer the North. He looks up (1iterally, "I lift my head") to see the clouds, a look that registers as a symbolic expression of his resolve. The hyperbolic dimensions of the long sword (borrowed from Song Yu's "Big Words") are a measure of the magnitude of the task he has set himself. Already in this first couplet we are faced with the complexity of the poet's inspiration.

The next three lines bring in the legend ("people say") associated with the place, which is signaled by the title of the poem—the emanation from the dragon-sword flashing up to the heavens, another symbol for the poet's determination. The following three lines recall us to the present scene: the hills, the pool, the moonlight. But the pool is empty, the water cold, the stars dimmed by the bright moonlight, and we are reminded of the actual situation of the poet, who has no real hope of carrying out his grandiose project. When he looks down into the pool, the magic sword no longer flashes its light up to the stars; likewise, his hopes for the recovery of his homeland must also fade. But Xin Qiji was not one to surrender easily. To seek out the sword in the pool, he imagines taking a rhinoceros horn lamp, a magic device mentioned in the biography of Wen Qiao in the *Jin History*,[14] who used it to illuminate the murky water of a pool, thus revealing the strange creatures lurking there. From this story only the lamp is borrowed for its property of revealing what lies hidden in the depths. That so exotic an instrument is necessary suggests the difficulty of the search. The reminder of unlooked-for dangers lying in wait under the murky waters is also a warning of the unscrupulous attacks Xin Qiji can expect if he continues to pursue his policy of reclaiming the North. "Wind and thunder angry, / Fish and dragons cruel" readily symbolize the political dimensions; this from the similar language used by Li Bai: "The august canopy [that is, the sky] will not, I fear, light up my loyal integrity, / Thunder gathers, about to roar its displeasure… / Prince loses his minister, dragons become fish,"[15] where the thunder represents the ruler's anger and the fish/dragon transformation symbolizes the shifting power structure of the court. The scenic setting in the first stanza and the invoked allusions mirror the irreconcilable conflict between the poet's own obsessive desire and his present circumstances.

The second stanza begins with what appears to be a straightforward description of the site of Double Stream Tower at South Sword: "Rising walls confine the Blue River / As it passes the precarious tower, / About to take flight, receding again." This fits well with the description in local gazetteers of the rapids in the ravine where the two rivers come together.[16] For all that these lines are a vivid and accurate description of the view from the tower, coming after the highly allegorical first stanza, the turbulent waters of the colliding streams provide a dramatic correlative of the poet's internal conflict.

The next three lines abandon symbolism for straightforward statement: "Chen Deng is old now / And might as well retire / With a cold drink and a cool bed." The mood of agitation has changed to one of calm resignation. A new allusion is introduced, one that enriches and gives resonance to the line "Chen Deng is old now." Xin Qiji is invoking a famous character of the Three Kingdoms period whose career was similar to, yet significantly different from his own. Chen Deng is characterized in his biography[17] as a man with great ambitions, who aspired to maintain order in the world and help the people. He distinguished himself as an enlightened but strict governor, and gained recognition for suppressing the pirates who had been raiding the coast and for leading a force against a rebel before dying at the age of 39. Once his name came up in a discussion between Liu Bei and Xu Si, who said, "Chen Deng was a rough fellow; he could never get rid of his overbearing manner." When Liu Bei commented, "You must have some reason for saying that he was overbearing," Xu replied, "Some time ago, during the troubles, I passed through Xiapi and visited him. He did not treat me like a guest and went a long time without speaking to me. And [at night] he lay on a great, raised bed and made his guest sleep on a low bed." Liu Bei said. "You have the reputation of being a patriot. Today the empire is in disorder and the emperor has lost his place. One would expect you to be concerned for the state and forget your private affairs, thinking instead about how to save the world. But you shop for land and inquire about real estate topics one would not choose to discuss. This is what Chen Deng was avoiding. Why should he talk to you? If it were I, I would recline in a hundred-foot-high mansion, leaving you to lie on the ground. It's not just a difference between a high and a low bed."

There are several implications in this allusion as Xin Qiji uses it. First, there is the contrast between Chen Deng and Xu Si, the one wanting to save the world, the other concerned for his own comfort. Xin Qiji refers to this conversation in another song to the tune "The Water Dragon Sings" (*QSC*, p. 1869), expressing his contempt for Xu Si's self-interest at a time of national crisis. But here, in comparing himself with Chen Deng, whose ambition to save the world and whose contempt for selfish interest he shared, he introduces a contrast. Chen Deng died at 39 after great accomplishments. When Xin Qiji writes "Chen Deng is old," it is he himself who is old, his aspirations disappointed: this modern Chen Deng might as well give up and, like Xu Si, look to his own comfort, with a cold drink and a cool mat to temper the summer's heat. For the sense of "retire" he has chosen the phrase "to recline on high" (*gao wo*), recalling the language of the speech of Liu Bei, "recline in a hundred-foot-high mansion," with the ironic effect of reducing Chen Deng to the likes of Xu Si. Originally the elevated bed of Chen Deng signified the distance between the patriot and the self-serving Xu Si, but now has become a symbol for his own enforced idleness, which lies at the heart of the poem. To transform an expression that conveyed heroic resolve into a symbol for idle repose is a supreme irony whereby he at once mocks and deplores his own failed ambition. "The ups and downs of a thousand years / The joys and sorrows of a lifetime—/ I see them all from here, / Where I've climbed for the view." These lines bring together antiquity and the immediate present. Zhang Hua and the sword he acquired, Wen Qiao with the rhinoceros horn lantern, and Chen Deng on his high perch have all vanished into the past. Compared with the rise and fall of dynasties over the centuries, a human lifetime is short, and he cannot expect his own life to last long enough to ensure the survival of the present dynasty, with its precarious hold on a remnant of its former territory. As he stands today on Double Stream Tower, the poet's own life experiences, the events of the past, the scene before his eyes, and the historical associations all come together to stir up these latent feelings. But he does not spell out what the feelings are; he merely states that all are present as he looks. The feelings are left outside the words. What they might be can be inferred from another lyric to the same tune (*QSC*, p. 1869):

On Climbing Shangxin Pavilion
in Jiankang

Clear autumn in a thousand miles of southern sky,	楚天千里清秋
The water follows the sky line, endless autumn.	水随天去秋无际
Distant peaks as far as the eye will reach	遥岑远目
Offer grief, supply regret	献愁供恨
Jade hairpins, snail coifs	玉簪螺髻
Declining sun on the upper story.	落日楼头
In the sound of the last wild goose	断鸿声里
The wanderer in the Southland	江南游子
Examines his blade of Wu steel	把吴钩看了
And beats the railing with his fist.	栏杆拍遍
No one understands what he feels up here.	无人会登临意
Don't tell him that perch makes a fine dish.	休说鲈鱼堪脍
Never mind the west wind	尽西风
Is this Zhang Han going to quit?	季鹰归未
Anyone out for himself	求田问舍

Is going to have to be ashamed to see	怕应羞见
Liu Bei's determination.	刘郎才气
Alas the flowing years!	可惜流年
My troubles are like wind and rain—	忧愁风雨
Even the trees suffer.	树犹如此
Who's there, red kerchief in green sleeve,	倩何人唤取
to call	红巾翠袖
To wipe away the hero's tears?	揾英雄泪

The concluding lines of the first stanza convey something of his frustration and pent-up anger as he gazes out toward his lost homeland. He is the wanderer in the south, cut off from his native place and unhappy that he cannot fulfill his burning desire to drive out the invaders. These lines can serve as a commentary on the "floating clouds in the northwest", reminding us of his never-forgotten hope of returning. The "blade of Wu steel" has its analog in the long sword of our poem, just as the lines "Anyone out for himself / Is going to have to be ashamed to see / Liu Bei's determination" underline the irony of "Chen Deng is old now / And might as well retire." These two songs are both inspired by the same obsessive desire, but in the second one it is expressed directly, while in the earlier one it emerges more subtly, even ironically. The second poem concludes with a direct outpouring of feeling: "Alas the flowing years! / My troubles are like wind and rain—/ Even the trees suffer. / Who's there, red kerchief in green sleeve, to call / To wipe away the hero's tears?" The implication of the second and third lines is that the storm of slander and political attacks he has suffered have aged him, even as the wind and rain wear down the trees Huan Wen planted.[18]

In the poem with which we are concerned there is no straightforward expression of what the poet feels. The concluding lines are relaxed, almost casual, simply presenting what the poet sees from his lookout: "Who is it I wonder lets fall / A sail at the sandbank / To tie up in the setting sun?" Of course, in the context of the preceding densely textured lines it carries wider implications. A boat that drops its sail and ties up at a mooring has completed its journey and will go no farther, today at least, even as the Southern Song court stays anchored in its policy of appeasement and has ceased to move against the northern invaders. The boat is tying up as the sun sets, a perfect symbol for a declining dynasty, an image also used in the concluding lines of another song to the tune "Tickle the Fish", (*Moyu er, QSC*, p. 1867), and since there are other parallels between it and the two songs to the tune "The Water Dragon Sings", I shall quote it in its entirety:

How many more times can I endure wind and rain,	更能消几番风雨
Spring going away so soon?	匆匆春又归去
Who loves spring always fears the flowers bloom too early,	惜春长怕花开早
And now it's worse with fallen reds past counting.	何况落红无数
Spring, stay a while!	春且住
I'm told	见说道
There's no way home through the sweet grasses to the horizon.	天涯芳草无归路
Too bad spring won't talk.	怨春不语
I suppose all we've got	算只有殷勤
Is the faithful spiderweb in the painted eaves	画檐蛛网
All day long catching flying willow fluff.	尽日惹飞絮
The Long Gate Palace affair—	长门事
She was wrong to expect a happy end.	准拟佳期又误
Someone was jealous of moth eyebrows.	蛾眉曾有人妒
Even with a thousand of gold to buy Xiangru's	千金纵买相如赋

poem,

Who was there to share secret longings?	脉脉此情谁诉
Don't you girls dance!	君莫舞
Don't you see	君不见
Yang Guifei, Zhao Feiyan—both turned to dust?	玉环飞燕皆尘土
Idle sorrow is bitterest of all.	闲愁最苦
Avoid a high balcony	休去倚危栏
When the sun setting	斜阳正在
Over misty willows	烟柳断肠处
Breaks the heart.	

The concluding lines, beginning with "Avoid a high balcony, " use the same image of the setting sun to symbolize a dynasty in decline.[19] The very first line, "How many more times can I endure wind and rain", should be put alongside "Alas the flowing years, / My troubles are like wind and rain." The line "Who was there to share secret longings" alludes to the neglected Empress Chen of the Han Emperor Wu; Xin Qiji has availed himself of the accepted allegorical use of the neglected woman for a rejected minister, namely himself. It helps us to understand what preoccupies the poet when he says "No one understands what he feels up here." Juxtaposing "There's no way home through the sweet grasses to the horizon" and "Don't tell him that perch makes a fine dish. / Never mind the west wind / Is this Zhang Han going to quit?"[20] underlines his yearning and despair at being cut off from his homeland. "Someone was jealous of moth eyebrows," with the established allegorical implication of slander by jealous colleagues at court, illuminates the "But leaning on the rail I was afraid / Of wind and thunder angry, / Fish and dragons cruel."

Nearly all his songs reflect the dominant passion of his life, the desire to recover his lost homeland, and the despair he felt when his efforts were frustrated. These two elements are present in varying proportion as circumstances changed, and the whole corpus of his songs has a remarkable variety of tone and form. He employs symbolism and allegory, and introduces different settings: he draws upon a wealth of historical antecedents and applies allusions from the whole range of Chinese writing with a tremendous range of nuance, objective and subjective, literal and ironical; taken together, it all contributes to the ever-varied, multifaceted complexity of these songs. Although the three lyrics we have been considering revolve around the same theme and, read together, can be used to reinforce and illuminate one another, each has its own style and manner. The first relies wholly on scene, symbol, and allusion; everything is achieved by indirection. The poet himself appears only as the reflection of a historical figure (Chen Deng) used ironically, an irony reinforced by the contrast between the heroic ambition of the opening lines, with the gigantic sword, and the anticlimactic, placid, resigned tone of the concluding scene of the boat tying up at the end of its journey. The second starts with landscape, moves to the poet himself ("the wanderer in the southland") who is grieved by the scene, and then continues with his feelings. There could be no sharper contrast than the subjective cry of despair of the second song, though both have basically the same theme. The third takes as its material the lament for the passing of spring and the grief of an abandoned woman used allegorically—yet another form of indirection. Truly Xin Qiji was a consummate artist. These three songs can perhaps give some idea of the infinite variety he achieved in a corpus of over six hundred song lyrics.

It remains to consider the stylistic aspects of Xin Qiji's song lyrics. Originating in the popular songs composed by performers, the form evolved in the hands of educated, upper-class poets to become a new genre of lyric poetry, and it was further expanded through the innovations of Liu Yong and

Su Shi. The lyrics became longer and more elaborate and admitted a vastly expanded list of possible subjects, which displaced the earlier exclusive concern with beautiful women and love themes. A further development came with the long, elaborately constructed architectonic song lyric. It is noteworthy that, although Liu Yong's influence continued in the songs of the writers of architectonic lyrics, Qin Guan and Zhou Bangyan, they remained unaffected by Su Shi's break with the love song tradition. This brings up the question that has bothered critics ever since: should the song lyric be used for other subjects? Should it admit the strong, masculine "heroic" style at all? A few poets before Su Shi had provoked a reaction against this sort of writing, which was considered not only different but somehow inappropriate, an attitude also fostered by the origins of the song as a form for female performers. On the other hand, their sentimental and erotic content was also subject to criticism, and as upper-class gentlemen became involved in their production, it is understandable that their songs began to include their personal concerns. And as soon as song lyrics were written in circumstances other than drinking parties, they began to reflect the situation and feelings of the individual poets. Even before the Song Dynasty we occasionally find spirited, masculine song lyrics, such as the one by Lu Qianyi to the tune "Immortal beside the River" (*Lin jiang xian*, *Huajian ji*, p. 415) lamenting the fall of the Former Shu, Li Yu's lament for his country to the tune "Waves Scour the Sand" (*Lang tao sha*, *Quan Tang Wudai ci*, Shanghai Guji 1986, p. 478), and Fan Zhongyan's frontier song to the tune "The Fisherman's Pride" (*Yu jia ao*, *QSC*, p. 11). None of these belongs to the feminine type, as noted by critics.[21] So although the possibility of heroic subjects for song lyrics was there already, these pieces were the product of an individual poet's response to a particular situation and do not represent a deliberate attempt to extend the range of the song lyric. Of course, Su Shi holds the place of self-conscious innovator, and it was he who demonstrated a new way of writing song lyrics that others could follow. That his example elicited no great response from his contemporaries can be explained by three factors: the tradition that songs should be feminine, the decadent atmosphere of the entertainment world, and the shortcomings inherent in the song lyric used as a form of *shi* poetry, despite Su Shi's obvious achievements. These faults are not apparent in his best lyrics, but the shallowness and roughness of others are in part due to his facility in versifying, which could result in carelessness and a lack of focus. Another factor was the difference between *shi* and lyric: if you write the latter as though it were the former, it will not have the quality that one expects and appreciates in song lyric.[22] For these reasons, Northern Song song writers did not adopt Su Shi's innovation.

The fall of the Northern Song created a situation like that experienced by Lu Qianyi and Li Yu, and inspired a new generation of song writers to write on patriotic themes. What Lu Qianyi and Li Yu wrote were Short Songs, but the song writers of Southern Song had access to the Long Song with its enormously expanded possibilities. The most important practitioners were Zhang Yuangan, Zhang Xiaoxiang, Lu You, Liu Guo, Liu Kezhuang, and, above all, Xin Qiji.

It is easier to write effective Short Songs on patriotic themes or laments for the fall of a state, as Lu Qianyi and Li Yu did, than to write equally good Long Songs where the scope for exposition is broader. They tend to become straightforward narrative and cease to work as song lyric, which relies on subtlety and indirection for its effects, qualities that set it apart as a genre distinct from *shi* poetry.[23] When a large subject has to be compressed into the limits of a Short Song, the poet is forced to use suggestion and indirection. Furthermore, the lines of Short Songs are comprised mostly of five or seven beats, a rhythm familiar in *shi* poems and hence readily employed by poets trained in that form. Long Songs require elaboration and frequently use four-and-six-beat lines, the basic rhythm of prose. As a consequence, the poet is apt to lapse into straightforward narrative.[24] This is a fault shared to some degree by nearly all Southern Song writers of the so-called heroic songs. The outstanding exception is Xin Qiji. He was able to combine subtlety and indirection with heroic themes in songs that preserve the distinctive character of the form. In this he not only surpassed the innovator Su Shi but set a standard seldom matched in succeeding centuries.

His name is often linked with Su Shi's, for both of them opened up new possibilities in the song lyric form, and no doubt Xin Qiji's vision and inspiration owed something to Su Shi's example. But for all that they had in common, they differed in style as in their motive for breaking with tradition. For Su Shi it was his towering genius, his self-sufficient superiority that would not be constrained by the delicate femininity of the *Huajian* tradition of song. His independence of spirit let him "do what he had to do and stop only when he had to," lending a characteristic quality of unrestrained exuberance to his song lyrics. For Xin Qiji it was his ideals and his dedication to a cause that set him apart. No more than Su Shi could he be limited to the traditional themes of song, and from his adventurous past and the continuing frustrations of his career he drew upon material outside the previous range of song lyric. His songs were very much the product of his individual character and the times he lived in, like Ruan Ji's, of whom Shen Deqian said,[25] "Given Ruan Ji's times, you should expect Ruan Ji's poems." The result was a body of poetry quite different from Su Shi's. And besides being a sensitive and widely read poet, Xin Qiji was at the same time a man of action—daring, resolute, and resourceful—someone capable of strategic planning, someone who had performed heroic deeds. When the achievements he had dreamed of all came to nothing, he poured his lifelong hopes and aspirations, together with his disappointments and frustrations, into his song lyrics, imbuing them with his heroic spirit. As a result he not only transcended the traditional limits of what could be expressed in song, he also revolutionized traditional poetic techniques. But at the same time he preserved the indirection and suggestiveness that constitute the special quality of the form. It is his success in combining these contradictory elements that is the most notable aspect of his songs.

It remains to consider the technical devices he used to get his effects. This is a subject with which traditional critics have been much concerned, and I shall limit myself to only two features, vocabulary and allusion.

Of all song writers Xin Qiji employs the richest vocabulary. He draws upon both literary and vernacular languages, but it is his exploitation of the resources of literary language that is most unusual. Originating in anonymous popular song, the language of early song lyrics was basically vernacular, and early Five Dynasties and Song song writers made little use of the literary language. Su Shi, and following him Zhou Bangyan, began on occasion to introduce literary vocabulary into their song lyrics, Su Shi sparingly and Zhou Bangyan chiefly in lines borrowed from Tang poets. Su Shi did not draw upon the *Confucian Classics* or the *Histories*,[26] whereas Xin Qiji quotes from the *Confucian Analects*, *Mencius*, the *Classic of Songs*, *Zuo Zhuan*, *Zhuangzi*, *Shiji*, and *Han Shu*.[27] He also takes words and phrases from earlier poets, from Qu Yuan to Li Bai and Du Fu, making these borrowed words part of the seamless fabric of his own verse and giving them new life.

Some critics have objected to Xin Qiji's use of allusion as excessive,[28] but others recognize that these allusions contribute significantly to the effect of the poem.[29] Even Wang Guowei, the great opponent of allusion in song lyric, had only praise for "Congratulating the Groom" (*He xin lang*, *QSC*, p. 1914), a song that is filled with them.[30] Another lyric to the same tune with the title "On the Lute" (*QSC*, p. 1890), an ode belonging to the category of verses celebrating an object, is filled throughout with allusions to lute lore.

However, rather than fall into the sort of lifeless description common in Southern Song ode, it is full of life and emotion.[31] Another example in which allusion helps create an outstanding poem is his "Visiting Double Stream Tower at South Sword" quoted earlier, to the tune "The Water Dragon Sings".

In addition to his allusions to passages in earlier literature and events of the past, Xin Qiji occasionally likes to imitate the styles of earlier writers in his songs, incorporating words and phrases from their work.[32] The song to the tune "The Water Dragon Sings" (*QSC*, p. 1894), for example, imitates the "Heavenly Questions" and the "Summons to the Soul", and the one to the tune "Water Music" (*QSC*, p. 1932) imitates the "Shao ge" stanza of "The Outpouring of Sad Thoughts" (one of the "Nine Declarations") and "The Fortune Teller". He uses the *Zhuangzi*,[33] and in two other lyrics (both to the tune "Water Music") he uses *Chuci*, *Liji*, *Shijing*, *Jinshu*, *Zuozhuan*, and poems by Bao Zhao and Du Fu.[34] In another lyric ("Treading the Sedge") whole lines are taken from *Yijing*, *Shijing*, and *Lunyu*.[35] These examples show how far Xin Qiji's practice departed from that of conventional song writers.[36] It contributed to the label "heroic style", which critics applied to his song lyrics, in contrast to the "smooth and gentle" songs of the *Huajian* tradition. Although his songs do have a heroic quality, however, the term dose not begin to cover their range and variety. As Liu Kezhuang said, he is not inferior to Yan Jidao or Qin Guan in delicacy,[37] but his excellence still lies in his uniquely heroic tone. It is evident even in those songs generally held to be "smooth and gentle", where the reserve strength and inner convolutions, the firmness beneath the softness, are beyond anything Yan Jidao or Qin Guan could manage. An example is the song to the tune "*Zhuyingtai jin*" (*QSC*, p. 1882):

Late Spring

The jeweled pin was divided	宝钗分
At Peachleaf Ford	桃叶渡
Where misty willows shaded the Shore of Parting.	烟柳暗南浦
She fears to climb the stairs.	怕上层楼
Out of ten days, nine days of rain.	十日九风雨
Broken-hearted as each red petal flies—	断肠片片飞红
No one else cares.	都无人管
Who will tell the singing oriole to stop?	倩谁唤流莺声住
From the flowers in her hair	鬓边觑
She takes one to divine the day of his return,	试把花卜归期
Puts it back, then counts again.	才簪又重数
The lamp outside the thin curtain grows dim.	罗帐灯昏
In a dream she sobs,	哽咽梦中语
"It was the spring brought sorrow here.	是他春带愁來
Where did spring go when it left	春归何处
That it failed to take sorrow with it?"	却不解带将愁去

Another, to the tune "Tickle the Fish", is translated above as "How many more times can I endure wind and rain…"

It is not only his success in infusing these songs of separation and lament for spring with his heroic spirit; most notable is that his truly heroic songs still preserve the indirection and suggestiveness characteristic of song lyric at its best: they can be heroic without being obvious or shallow. This is what sets him apart from all other song writers. His fondness for allusion, also a break with tradition, contributed to his success in preserving the aesthetic excellence peculiar to the form. It works in several ways: it avoids the obviousness of straightforward statement, it provides a way to distance his own feelings, and it inspires associations outside the words of the poem. These allusions function like the beautiful women and fragrant flowers in the "Li sao".

Xin Qiji was able to make such effective use of allusion because the enormous range of his reading and his tenacious memory put the whole of Chinese cultural history at his disposal; he did not have to consult encyclopedias or stop to ferret out apposite references—they were there when he needed them. His allusions never seem contrived or far-fetched; they are a seamless part of the texture of his poem. The strength of his inspiration lends freshness and vitality to the men and events to which he refers.

His supreme mastery of the resources of language extends well beyond the artistic exploitation of allusion; he also drew upon the resources of colloquial speech. Popular song had always been based on the vernacular language, so this was not an innovation that can be credited to him. But once song lyrics began to be written by literary men, their language became increasingly literary. Liu Yong's songs owed some of their great popularity to his use of easily intelligible language, and though critics found him vulgar, his example made the practice fashionable for a time; spoken-language locutions and vocabulary appeared in the lyrics of Huang Tingjian, Qin Guan, Zhou Bangyan, and even Su Shi, whose song lyrics were more like *shi* poetry. So, such elements in songs were nothing new. Still Xin Qiji's application had significant differences. In earlier song lyrics purely colloquial lines were used, appropriately enough, for dialogue, specifically the flirtatious talk of lovers. This is common in Song Dynasty songs.[38] Vernacular vocabulary was also used for playful effects,[39] although such colloquial lines add liveliness and verisimilitude at the expense of seriousness and depth. Xin Qiji also uses the colloquial playfully, but in his songs it serves two other functions. First, it conveys the intimate feeling of village life, as in the song to the tune "Partridge in the Sky" (*Zhegu tian, QSC*, p. 1924):[40]

On a Country House, Written in Jest

Evening flocks of geese and chickens still running about,	鸡鸭成群晚不收
Mulberry and hemp grown up to the rooftop:	桑麻长过屋山头
Why shouldn't I envy them—	有何不可吾方羡
They lack everything, but are content with enough to eat.	要底都无饱便休
The new willow trees	新柳树
The old sandbar	旧沙洲
Last year's brook flows over there.	去年溪打那边流
They say, Here we raise our children	自言此地生儿女
And they marry either Jin or Zhou.	不嫁金家即聘周

Colloquial language also gives an ironic turn to his worries, as in "Losing Teeth" to the tune "The Fortune Teller" (*Bu suan zi*, *QSC*, p. 1945):

Anything hard won't last;	刚者不坚牢
The soft is hard to grind down.	柔者难摧挫
If you don't believe it, look into my mouth:	不信张开口角看
The tongue is there, the teeth have dropped out.	舌在牙先堕
Already I was missing two side-chambers	已缺两边厢
And now a gap in between.	又豁中间个
You young fellows better not laugh at an old man—	说与儿曹莫笑翁
Here's a dog hole for you to go in.	狗窦从君过

and in another to the tune "West River Moon" (*Xijiang yue*, *QSC*, p. 1944):

Drinking I look for fun and laughs	醉里且贪欢笑
Where would I find time for sorrow?	要愁那得工夫
Of late it struck me—those books of the ancients	近来始觉古人书
Have not a word of truth in them.	信著全无是处
Last night I fell down drunk beside a pine tree.	昨夜松边醉倒
And asked, just how drunk am I?	问松我醉何如
It moved, to help me up, I thought	只疑松动要来扶
So I pushed it with my hand and said, Go away!	以手推松曰去

These songs are not among Xin Qiji's important ones, but even here he shows genuine feeling, and sometimes irony, combining frivolous language with feelings that are not frivolous to achieve an artistic result.

He is fond of using the term "old fellow" (*lao zi*) for himself, a Shandong colloquialism not previously a part of the vocabulary of song lyric. In the *Huajian* tradition, where the speaker's voice was usually that of a woman, the terms commonly used for the first person were *nu* (your slave) or *qie* (concubine), or, for a man's voice, simply the pronoun *wo* (I). It was Su Shi, as always unbound by convention, who first called himself *lao fu* (old man), and this probably influenced Xin Qiji in his choice of "old fellow" for himself. But for Su Shi the term served only as an informality, while "old fellow", with its connotation of a village rustic, provides Xin Qiji with a way of emphasizing his disappointment; it begins to appear after his dismissal and retirement to Lake Dai, as "This old fellow must grieve for the country" (to the tune "Water Music", *QSC*, p. 1871), where he is clearly using the self-deprecating label to convey his response to being rusticated.

His artistry in language goes beyond employing both colloquial and archaic vocabulary. He also varies the syntax in a multitude of ways. Earlier, I criticized Lu You's song to the tune "Spring in the Han Palace" (*QSC*, pp. 1587-88) as too straightforward, the result of the prosy monotony of too many four-beat lines called for by the tune pattern: the lines "I remember calling to my falcon by the old fort. / To cut off the tiger on the plain" and "I saw the herb market on the Double Ninth, / The lantern hill at New Year's", in both of which a single verb ("remember", "saw") governs two parallel four-word phrases. But Xin Qiji's lyric for the same tune varies the syntax of these same two lines: "I recall last year it was blowing gently / When it reached my hut," and "With such poetic lines / He could match Xiangru." The tonal pattern of these two couplets is the same, but the grammatical structure is altogether different, and the contrast between the parallelism of tonal pattern and the varied syntactical structure makes for sinuosity and density. Lu You concludes his lyric with "You must remember, heroic deeds lie before us / Achievements don't come from Heaven." This is direct statement, with no overtones or implications beyond the words. Xin Qiji's lyric concludes, "Who thinks of me, in the new chill by the lamplight / With a volume of the Grand Historian's book?"—lines filled with the suggestion of sadness and resignation, the man of action reduced to reading about the exploits of historical figures. Comparing these two lyrics to the same tune by the two poets provides a clear demonstration of the qualities that set Xin Qiji apart. By mingling different styles and syntactical structures, he achieves variety and puts his own imprint on the lyrics he wrote for tunes that conventionally called for quite different treatment. There are many examples of this combination of parallel and unmatched in Xin Qiji's lyrics. Typically, the tune "Treading on the Sedge" inspired lyrics like these two by Yan Shu:

To the tune "Treading on the Sedge"
(*Ta suo xing*, *QSC*, p. 99) 踏莎行

On the narrow path the reds are few, 小径红稀
In fragrant suburbs green is everywhere. 芳郊绿遍
The high pavilion barely shows through the covering trees. 高台树色阴阴见
The spring breeze has not learned to keep the willow fluff 春风不解禁杨花
From pelting the pedestrians in the face. 濛濛乱扑行人面

Green leaves hide the orioles, 翠叶藏莺
Red curtains keep out the swallows. 朱帘隔燕
Incense from the burner slowly pursues twisting gossamer. 炉香静逐游丝转
Awake after a sad dream, and sober now 一场愁梦酒醒时
As the slanting sun shines into the deep deep courtyard. 斜阳却照深深院

To the same tune (*QSC*, p. 99)

Fine grass and sorrowful mist— 细草愁烟
A hidden flower fears exposure. 幽花怯露
Everywhere is something to touch her as she leans on the railing. 凭栏总是销魂处
The sun is high over the deserted courtyard. 日高深院静无人
From time to time swallows fly by in pairs. 穿帘海燕双飞去

The girdle on her silken dress is loose 带缓罗衣
The fragrance fades from the orchid incense. 香残蕙炷
The sky stretches far, the long road farther still. 天长不尽迢迢路

The drooping willow only knows to provide the spring wind	垂杨只解惹春风
And is of no use for holding back the wanderer.	何曾系得行人住

Contrast these with Xin Qiji's version (*QSC*, p. 1921), a cento of lines from the *Classics*:

Get ahead or retire, survive or fail,	进退存亡
Advance or hide, employed or rejected—	行藏用舍
Just let this little fellow learn farming, like Fan Xu.	小人请学樊须稼
Behind a rustic gate one can take his ease.	衡门之下可栖迟
When the sun goes down, the cows come home.	日之夕矣牛羊下

He left Duke Ling of Wei	去卫灵公
And ran into the Marshall Huan	遭桓司马
He was a man of the four directions.	东西南北之人也
Changju and Jieni plowed as yoke-mates—	长沮桀溺耦而耕
Why was Confucius so unsettled?	丘何为是栖栖者

Every line of this lyric is taken from texts as dissimilar as the *Conversations of Confucius*, *The Classic of Songs*, *The Classic of Changes*, and the *Book of Rites*, yet it reads like an independently created composition, though a full understanding requires an awareness of the original context of the several names.

A less obvious contrast is provided by two lyrics to the tune "Always Having Fun," one by Su Shi. These are both major poems and require a close reading. Su Shi's song has the title "In Xuzhou, On Climbing Swallow Tower after a Dream" (*QSC*, p. 302). An alternative version has the title "After Spending the Night in Swallow Tower in Dreaming of Panpan":

Bright moon like frost　明月如霜
Gentle breeze like water,　好风如水
Scene of perfect purity:　清景无限
Leaping fish in the winding stream,　曲港跳鱼
Round lotus leaves dripping dew,　圆荷泻露
All deserted, no one to see.　寂寞无人见
Like the roll of the third watch drum　紞如三鼓
A single leaf rustles,　铿然一叶
Shattering the murky dream cloud,　黯黯梦云惊断
In the expanse of night, lost past seeking.　夜茫茫重寻无处
Wide awake, I pace around the little garden.　觉来小园行遍

The weary traveler at the world's end　天涯倦客
Whose road home lies in the hills.　山中归路
Stares his heart out for his old garden.　望断故园心眼
Swallow Hall is empty—　燕子楼空
Where is its lovely lodger now?　佳人何在
Only swallows in the locked hall.　空锁楼中燕
Past and present are both like a dream　古今如梦
From which there is no awakening—　何曾梦觉
The old happiness, the new sorrow—that is all.　但有旧欢新怨
Another time someone　异时对
Wakeful at night in Yellow Tower　黄楼夜景
Will heave a sigh for me.　为余浩叹

Xin Qiji's is entitled "At Beigu Pavilion in Jingkou, Remembering the Past" (*QSC*, p. 1954):

Rivers and hills thousands of years of history　千古江山
The heroes nowhere to be found.　英雄无觅

Where Sun Quan once dwelt—	孙仲谋处
Dance pavilion and song terrace	舞榭歌台
Their glamor all	风流总被
Rain-swept, wind-blown away.	雨打风吹去
The sun slants over the shrubbery	斜阳草树
In everyday lanes and roads	寻常巷陌
Where Liu Yu, they say, used to live.	人道寄奴曾住
One can imagine in those days	想当年金戈铁马
Bronze spears, iron cavalry	
Strong as tigers, swallowing up a myriad leagues.	气吞万里如虎
In the Yuanjia period the halfhearted effort:	元嘉草草
The sacrifice to Heaven on Wolf Lair Hill	封狼居胥
Earned only a distraught glance to the north.	赢得仓皇北顾
It was forty-three years ago	四十三年
I still remember seeing	望中犹记
The beacon fires on the Yangzhou road.	烽火扬州路
I cannot bear to turn my head	可堪回首
Toward Bili's temple,	佛狸祠下
The cacophony of sacred crows and altar drums	一片神鸦社鼓
Who will ask it of me—	凭谁问
Old as he is	廉颇老矣
Can Lian Po still eat a man's meal?	尚能饭否

It is his mastery of the craft of writing, his artistry in the use of language, his readiness to experiment that gives Xin Qiji preeminence among song writers.

I would next like to discuss the question of imagery in Xin Qiji's lyrics. Images in themselves do not provide a criterion for judging poetry, except insofar as they contribute to a poem's emotional impact. The term "image" can refer to something perceived in the natural world or to a human situation. An image can be derived from actual experience or from the imagination, or even from a historical account one has read. An image can be variously related to feeling: it may provide the poet's inspiration, or he may imbue the image with his feeling, or he may equate the two by direct description. These distinctions belong to the realm of literary theory and are of no use in the practical matter of finding in imagery a criterion for judging the excellence of a poem, for any of these relationships can occur in both good and bad poems. Essentially the value of a poem is measured by the amount of emotional vitality conveyed by the combination of imagery and feeling, and it is this which I propose to investigate in Xin Qiji's song lyrics. The power of conveying feeling through imagery comes from the eye, the heart, and the hand. That is, the poet needs an eye that can discern the rare, or the special quality of what he observes; a sensitive heart that responds with vivid emotion to what he experiences; and the technical skill to give these feelings expression through apposite words rich in associations. Xin Qiji was a poet admirably equipped with all three—eye, heart, and hand. Here, for example, is his description of a range of hills:

The green hills want to talk with the recluse: 青山欲共高人语
A myriad horses come pell-mell, past counting. 联翩万马来无数
(*QSC*, p. 1881)

Or the spring scene:

Yesterday spring was like a thirteen-year-old girl 昨日春如十三女
learning embroidery, 儿学绣
The flowers bursting out from every branch. 一枝枝不教花瘦
(*QSC*, p. 1919)

Or a tidal river:

In the distance half a sky of egrets come flying 望飞来半空鸥鹭
And in a moment earth-shaking thundering drums. 须臾动地鼙鼓

(*QSC*, p. 1868)

Or a seasonal outing:

Spring is back 春已归来
And on pretty girls' heads you see 看美人头上
Twisted spring ribbons. 袅袅春幡

(*QSC*, p. 1921)

All these images are presented clearly and precisely, and inspire a responsive feeling in the reader. They demonstrate an extraordinary technical mastery.

However, these examples are not from the most representative of his lyrics. In his best poems the imagery also conveys his obsessive concern for the nation's loss of its northern territory and his inability to prod the government into taking action. The point is illustrated in a song lyric written when he had retired to Mount Qian after being dismissed from office a second time. It is to the tune "Spring in the Qin Garden" (*QSC*, p. 1934):

Written at Qi Lodge in Lingshan
Before Work on Yan Pond was Finished

Tiered cliffs race off to the west, 叠嶂西驰
Ten thousand horses wheel, 万马回旋
And the mountains are poised to go east. 众山欲东
Unpredictable, the downward dashing rapids 正惊湍直下
Kick up pearl drops to splash in the face. 跳珠倒溅
A little bridge cuts across: 小桥横截
A new moon's arching bow. 缺月初弓

For an old man to retire is the right thing to do.	老合投闲
Heaven has made this busybody	天教多事
Inspector of ten myriad stalwart pine trees.	检校长身十万松
My hut is small—	吾庐小
Outside, their snake and dragon shadows,	在龙蛇影外
Inside, the sound of wind and rain.	风雨声中
They come jostling forward one by one to show their faces.	争先见面重重
In the fresh morning air I see three or so,	看爽气朝来三数峰
Looking distinguished,	
Like the young men of the Xie clan	似谢家子弟
In official caps and robes,	衣冠磊落
Or Xiangru seen arriving at the courtyard door,	相如庭户
dignified among his attendants.	卓骑雍容
It makes me feel as though	我觉其间
I were reading a powerful passage	雄深雅健
In the book of the Grand Historian.	如对文章太史公
By the new dike path	新堤路
of Yan Pond	问偃湖何日
When will the misty water be ready?	烟水濛濛

The tension between two contradictory impulses characteristic of Xin Qiji's songs is more prominent than ever in the ones he wrote when in involuntary retirement, and it dominates this one, where his impatience with idleness is treated ironically. On the surface the song shifts between violence and repose: mountain scenery is presented through images of military action, expressions of heroic feeling abruptly give way to resigned acceptance of retirement in the country, and throughout the tone is one of sardonic irony. Yet through these incompatible elements there runs the unifying theme: the poet's concern for his country and its people, and his single-minded determination to recover the North, expressed deviously through the many devices at his command. In this lyric, ostensibly describing mountain scenery, we can see how he conveys his complex feelings about his situation, choosing his imagery to that end.

He uses three methods. The adjectives and verbs create the effect of strong feeling: for example, "the downward dashing rapids / Kick up pearl drops to splash in the face," where the lively picture of the drops of water flying off the rapids creates a feeling of agitated movement. It is instructive to compare these lines with one from a quatrain by Wang Wei:[41] "Leaping waves splash together." Both depict rapidly flowing water, but Wang Wei's is a coolly objective description, while Xin Qiji's lines suggest the agitation roused in the poet's breast by the scene. This method of choosing adjectives and verbs that go beyond a simple description of nature to reflect strong emotion is an outstanding characteristic of Xin Qiji's lyrics.

The second method is his use of personification and metaphor to transform a static scene into one of dramatic activity, as in this lyric's opening lines: "Tiered cliffs race off to the west, / Ten thousand horses wheel / And the mountains are poised to go east." Here the unmoving cliffs have become a herd of horses dashing across the plain. The description carries something of the poet's own ardent, heroic spirit as he constructs a physical setting for his poem.

The third method is his constant practice of conveying a flight of fancy through images, as in the lines about the mountains:

> They come jostling forward one by one to show their faces.
> In the fresh morning air I see three or so,
> Looking distinguished,
> Like the young men of the Xie clan

In official caps and robes,
Or Xiangru seen arriving at the courtyard door, dignified among his attendants.
It makes me feel as though
I were reading a powerful passage
In the book of the Grand Historian,

who, of course, is Sima Qian. In these lines Xin Qiji translates his feelings about historical individuals and literary style into similes for scenic objects.

To show how these lines achieve their effect, it is necessary to explain the underlying historical allusions. There is a passage in *New Specimens of Contemporaty Conversations*.[42] Wang Ziyou was General Huan's adviser. Huan said, "You have been here in office some time now, and I should be making plans for you." At first Wang said nothing but looked straight up, stroking his cheek with his tablet of office. Then he said, "The western hills come in the morning bringing refreshing air." This reply, implying indifference to personal advancement and contempt for the one in authority, is recalled in Xin Qiji's song by the words *shuang qi* ("fresh air") and *zhao lai* ("the morning brings").

In the *Jin History* biography of Xie Xuan, an anecdote has Xie An asking him, "What do you expect of young men that should all be good?" Xie Xuan answered, "Like the orchid or the magic mushroom or the jade tree which one would like to have growing in the courtyard."

The biography of Sima Xiangru in the *Historical Records* says, "Xiangru came to Linqiong with mounted attendants, looking dignified and refined, very sophisticated."[43]

The phrase "strong and elegant style" was used by Han Yu of Liu Zongyuan's prose, also referring to Sima Qian's style.[44]

The entire second stanza applies to the hills before his eyes, but there is not one word of direct description. Instead, he uses a string of personifications and metaphors embedded in allusions drawn from the resources of a well-stocked memory to endow the inanimate and insensate hills with life and human personality.

The impact of this lyric comes not so much from these skillfully employed rhetorical devices as from accompanying emotional charge with which the poet has invested them. His own predicament and his feeling of helpless frustration are ironically conveyed in the lines, "For an old man to retire is the right thing to do. / Heaven has made this busybody / Inspector of ten myriad stalwart pine trees. / My hut is small—/ Outside, their snake and dragon shadows, / Inside, the sound of wind and rain." An underlying tone of bitterness permeates this jocular account of the poet's situation: a man used to marshaling troops is cashiered and living in involuntary retirement. He imagines the forest of pine trees he sees through the window of his modest dwelling transformed into an army of stout soldiers which Heaven has put in his charge. The only direct statement of feeling in the whole poem is ironic: "For an old man to retire is the right thing to do." It was pointed out earlier that Lu You tends to the obvious by expressing everything directly, but this line, the key to the poem, avoids the obvious through irony. The nuance and suggestiveness of Xin Qiji's lyrics are results of the interaction of the direct and the devious. Here he transforms the present scene into a concrete embodiment of his discontent by making the trees into soldiers, by applying the adjectives "stalwart" to them, and by casting himself as the "Inspector". We sense the feelings of a man who yearns to lead an army of real soldiers to expel the invader. We recall the opening lines of the poem, where the hills are transformed into galloping horses, and can understand that for the poet these are the mounts for his troops; but then this vision of frenzied activity dissolves into the drab reality of "my hut is small", and the hills, rapids, and trees are reduced to their actual status as scenery, alluded to in the title. Those "snake and dragon shadows" belong to the twisted trunks and branches of the pine trees, and the sounds of wind and rain are the noise of the splashing rapids of line 4. The images invest the scenery with an emotional charge, but they carry a further association that is even more potent by suggesting the overshadowing threat of court intrigue. It is this threat that continually combines in Xin Qiji's song lyrics with his heroic aspirations; and not only in the heroic ones, it is also present as the recurrent background in the so-called "idle diversions". This capacity for bringing together images and symbols suggests his dedication to an ideal, the characteristic mark of his finest lyrics.

In several of the remaining lines of this lyric, although the imagery does not directly contribute to the emotional impact, it still calls for some comment, since the effect depends on a knowledge of biographical background. After being relieved from office, Xin Qiji had plans to buy land and build a residence on two sites: Shangrao near Lake Dai and Mount Qian near Piao Spring. Earlier, in discussing the lyric to the tune "The Water Dragon Sings", I mentioned the contempt expressed by Liu Bei for Xu Si, who was more concerned with buying land and living comfortably than in saving the country, a distaste Xin Qiji endorsed. At first he had no intention of ever settling down to live in the South. For him to buy land in the South on which to build represented a major disappointment, a concession that he saw no immediate prospect of a return. What drove him to this realization were the slanderous charges he was helpless to refute and the hopelessness of his cause. In his frustration he turned all his energies to this new undertaking, as was his nature in anything he did. Just as his poetry shows a strong feeling for nature, he put a great deal of thought into the choice of a building site. It became for him something that provided comfort and distraction from his great disappointment. His building plans were on a correspondingly large scale, not that he was competing with the ostentatious extravagance of Southern Song high officials.[45] We can see his attitude toward landscape architecture in his lyrics, for example, in this one to the tune "Spring in the Qin Garden" (*QSC*, p. 1868):

And there on the mound to the east is my thatched study	东冈更葺茅斋
Well placed so the window opens to the water.	好都把轩窗临水开
I will need a little boat to go fishing,	要小舟行钓
But first I must plant willow trees	先应种柳
And move the bamboo hedge	疏篱护竹
So it won't obstruct the view of plum blossoms.	莫碍观梅
Fall chrysanthemums make a feast,	秋菊堪餐
Spring orchids will do for a nosegay—	春兰可佩
They wait to be planted by the master himself.	留待先生手自栽

and in another, to the tune "Water Music" (*QSC*, p. 1871):

The east bank lacks green shade	东岸绿阴少
I must plant some willow trees.	杨柳更须栽

and in "Written in Jest, after Tao Qian's 'Hovering Clouds'", to the tune "Always Having Fun" (*QSC*, p. 1910):

For my old age, on the bare hills	投老空山
A myriad pine trees I planted myself	万松手种

and in "The Bamboo Path at Hovering Clouds Just Finished", to the tune "Over the Mountain Stream" (*QSC*, p. 1910):

It angles across the water	斜带水
And half hides the hill,	半遮山
Green bamboo planted to finish the path.	翠竹栽成路

and "Written in Jest on Digging a Pond", to the tune "Southern Song" (*QSC*, p. 1922):

The dashing stream narrows as it reaches the steps;	涓涓流水细侵阶
I will make a pool welcome the moon.	凿个池儿唤个月儿来

In all these landscaping projects his goal was aesthetic; it was not display and certainly not an attempt to compete with the extravagances of the wealthy. They also reveal how much attention he paid to an activity that was becoming a surrogate for his life as a public official. For all that he had a taste for natural beauty and obviously took pleasure in choosing a site for his dwelling and rearranging the surroundings to create an aesthetically pleasing whole, these activities can hardly have compensated for his dismissal from office and the loss of any chance to carry out his great ambition to lead an army against the invaders of his country. That he never forgot the danger threatening his country is apparent in the images he chooses in describing a scene (as in the lyric for "Spring in the Qin Garden" translated above).

In his retirement he found a congenial predecessor in the fourth-century poet Tao Qian, whom he mentions, quotes, or alludes to more than seventy times.[46] He borrowed the phrase "I plant my staff" to name a belvedere, and "Hovering Clouds", the opening words of Tao's poem so titled, for his hall. In the lyric to the tune "The Water Dragon Sings" (*QSC*, p. 1931), he writes:

In my old age I have come to love Tao Yuanming;	老来曾识渊明
In my dreams I can almost see him.	梦中一见参差是
Awake with my hidden sorrow	觉来幽恨
I put down my cup	停觞不御

And when about to sing, I stop. 欲歌还止

Xin Qiji must have discerned in Tao Qian another like himself, who "wanted to act and was not able", in Zhu Xi's words.[47] Tao Qian wrote: [48]

Days and months will cast a man away. 日月掷人去
His cherished goal he never will attain. 有志不获骋
I ponder this and sadness fills my heart, 念此怀悲凄
Until the break of day I cannot rest. 终晓不能静

Such lines must have struck Xin Qiji as an accurate statement of his own feelings. But Tao Qian could take a philosophical view of the world and achieve a degree of detachment from its troubles. He could lose himself in books: "A glance encompasses the ends of the universe—/ Where is there any joy if not in these?"[49] and in scenery: "In these things is a fundamental truth / I would like to tell, but lack the words."[50] Xin Qiji was, at heart, a man of action who aspired to great deeds; whatever the similarity, his hidden sorrow was more intractable, and he never achieved Tao Qian's acceptance of his lot. All his life he struggled with a lasting sorrow. "Heaven is far and hard to get to, so don't gaze too long. / This tower is high and I am ready to go back down, but still I linger," as he wrote in the lyric to the tune "All the River is Red" (*Man jiang hong*, *QSC*, p. 1953).

In his lyrics, however, Xin Qiji seldom made direct mention of the concerns ever-present in his heart—the slanderous attacks of politicians, the plight of his country, his lost homeland—but they found expression in allusions to analogous situations he found in history. As a result, what we get from his lyrics is a genuine poetic effect that other poets writing in the so-called heroic mode failed to achieve through an overt display of heroics. Of course, allusion and imagery are not a formula for producing good poetry. The excellence of Xin Qiji's poetry derives from his resolve, which he never relinquished, so that whatever the historical allusion, whatever the scene, it became emotionally colored by his obsessive concern. It is this that sets him apart from other writers of heroic lyrics and distinguishes him from those poets who self-consciously pile up allusions and images. The difference, however, is not adequately conveyed by such a general statement, and I hope the two examples I have presented in some detail will demonstrate the point more convincingly.

Critics early remarked that Xin Qiji's poetry is not easily accessible. Chen Tingzhuo said as much: "Later readers have not found it easy to learn to grasp Xin Qiji's style. Without his genius, his idealism, his emotional capacity, without experience of his situation, how can we hope to grasp his subtle obscurities?"[51] Zhou Ji likewise emphasized the unique qualities that put him beyond the reach of imitators.[52]

In this essay I have tried to indicate where the difficulties in Xin Qiji's lyrics lie and to point out how they contribute to making his poetry great. He wrote a great many lyrics of extraordinary variety, and I have touched on only the most important aspects. I have said nothing about those imitating the style of other poets, and it is hardly necessary to single out the ones that are crude, obvious, or otherwise below his usual standard. At his best—and his best lyrics greatly outnumber the inferior ones—he is without equal among the hundreds of Song Dynasty lyricists.

Notes:

1. His friend Liu Zai wrote, "He has run through all the philosophers and collected a myriad images" (*Mantang wenji* [Jiaye Tang ed.] vol. 5, p. 1). Liu Kezhuang, a younger contemporary, was even more effusive: "The great tones reverberate, the small notes tinkle; he traverses the six directions, goes

through a myriad years..., yet for delicacy and refinement he is not inferior to Yan Jidao or Qin Guan" ("Preface to *Xin Qiji's Collected Works*" in *Houcun xiansheng da quanji* 98.2b).

2. Deng Guangming, the modern scholar who has made the most intensive study of Xin Qiji, writes, "No other song writer of the Song Dynasty can compare with Xin Qiji for multiplicity of subject and variety of styles. He used the form to express his feelings, to celebrate objects and as a vehicle for narrative and philosophy. Some songs are subtle and refined, some are delicate and graceful, some are an impassioned call to heroic action, some are plaintive laments."

3. Liu Xie, *Wenxin diaolong zhushi*, p. 309.

4. Wang Guowei, *Renjian cihua jiaozhu*, p. 31.

5. *Song shi*, p. 12162.

6. In *Xin Jiaxuan shiwen chaocun*, p. 23.

7. Ibid., p. 36.

8. *Song shi*, pp. 12163-12164.

9. Ibid.

10. *Xin Jiaxuan shiwen chaocun*, pp. 36-37.

11. Ibid., p. 39.

12. *Nanping xianzhi*: "Lidai yan'ge biao" 2.1a-1b; "Mingsheng zhi" 6.5a; "Shanchuan zhi" 4.15b.

13. *Jin shu* pp. 1075-1076.

14. Ibid., p. 1795.

15. *Li Bai ji jiaozhu*, p. 191.

16. *Yanping fuzhi* (1873 ed.), "Shanchuan zhi" 1.10a-b.

17. *San'guo zhi jiaozhu*, *Wei zhi*, p. 239.

18. Alluding to *Shishuo xinyu*, Yu Xin, in his rhapsody "The Withered Tree" (*Ku shu fu*), quotes Huan Wen: "Long ago I planted willow trees. They grew lush south of the Han River. Today when I see them, they are bare and

desolate beside the river pool. When this has happened even to the trees, how can a man withstand the passage of time?"

19. Critics have frequently noticed this symbolic use of the setting sun; cf. Luo Dajing, *Helin yulu* vol. 1, p. 12, and Xu Angxiao, *Cizong ouping* in *Cihua congbian*, vol. 5, p. 1587.

20. The autumn wind reminded Zhang Han of perch, a seasonal delicacy, which he had enjoyed as a young man in his hometown, and he immediately resigned from his office and went back (*Jin shu*, p. 2384).

21. See *Tanping cibian* in *Cihua congbian*, vol. 11, p. 4019.

22. See the chapter on Lu You in *Lingxi cishuo*, pp. 390-391.

23. The point has been made by Wang Guowei, p. 48; and Miao Yue, *Shici sanlun*, p. 3.

24. See the discussion of Lu You's song to the tune "Spring in the Han Palace" (*Han gong chun*, *QSC*, p.1588) in *Lingxi cishuo*, p. 391.

25. Shen Deqian, *Shuoshi cuiyu quanping*, p. 131.

26. See Liu Chenweng, "Preface to the *Collected Songs of Xin Qiji*", in *Xuxi ji* (*Yuzhang congshu*) 6.9a.

27. Wu Hengzhao, *Lianziju cihua* (*Cihua congbian*, vol. 7), 1.6a-b.

28. For example, Yue Ke, *Ting shi*, of the song to the tune "Always Having Fun" (*Yong yu le*, *QSC*, p. 1954), p. 38.

29. Chen Tingzhuo, *Ci ze*, *Fangge ji*, vol. 1, pp. 166-167, contradicting Yue Ke's objection.

30. *Renjian cihua*, p. 151.

31. Both Chen Tingzhuo, *Baiyuzhai cihua* (*Cihua congbian*, vol. 11) p. 3791, and Chen Ting, *Zhushantang cihua* (ibid., vol. 1), p. 314.

32. Chen Mo, *Lun Jiaxuan ci,* notes that the entire song "For Twelfth Cousin Mao Jia" to the tune "Congratulating the Groom" (*He xin lang*, *QSC*, p. 1914) is in the manner of Li Bai's "Imitation of the Rhapsody on Sorrow", and "One Giving up Wine" to the tune "Spring in the Qin Garden" (*Qin yuan*

chun, *QSC*, p. 1915) is like Ban Gu's "Response to a Guest's Jest" or Yang Xiong's "Deflecting a Sneer" (quoted from Deng Guangming, *Jiaxuan ci biannian jianzhu*, p. 563).

33. "The Fortune Teller" (*Bu suan zi*, *QSC*, p. 1946).

34. All in "Water Music" (*Shuidiao getou*, *QSC*, p. 1913).

35. "Treading the Sedge" (*Ta suo xing*, *QSC*, p. 1921).

36. This was noted by the Siku editors, *Siku quanshu zongmu tiyao*, vol. 40, p. 641, and Feng Xu, *Hao'an lun ci* (*Cihua congbian*, vol. 11), p. 3685.

37. *Houcun xiansheng da quanji* 98, "Preface to Xin Jiaxuan's collection."

38. Examples can be found in Huang Tingjian's "*Gui tian le yin*" (*QSC*, p. 407), Qin Guan's "*Pin ling*" (*QSC*, p. 468), and Zhou Bangyan's "*Qing yu'an*" (*QSC*, p. 622).

39. Su Shi, "*Ru meng ling*" (*QSC*, p. 34) and "*Nan ge zi*" (*QSC*, p. 293).

40. Other examples are the ones to the tune "West River Moon" (*Xijiang yue*, *QSC*, p. 1899) and "Qingping Music" (*Qingping yue*, *QSC*, p. 1885).

41. Wang Wei, *Wang Mojie quanji jianzhu*, p. 193.

42. *Shishuo xinyu* (Shanghai: Guji, 1983), p. 406.

43. *Shiji*, vol. 9, p. 300.

44. Liu Yuxi, "A Note on the Collected Works of Master Liu, Once Tang Dynasty Prefect of Liuzhou", in *Liu Yuxi ji jianzheng*, vol. 1, p. 514.

45. See "On Wang Yisun and His Songs Celebrating Objects" (in the second volume) for a discussion of the taste for extravagance in Southern Song times.

46. See Chen Shumei, "Xin Jiaxuan yu Tao Yuanming", *Zhongwai wenxue* 4.6(1975), 4.

47. Zhu Xi, *Zhuzi yulei*, quoted in *Tao Yuanming ziliao huibian*, p. 75.

48. "Untitled Poem", No. 2 in J. R. Hightower, *The Poetry of Tao Qian*,

p. 187.

49. "On Reading the Seas and Mountains Classic", ibid., p. 229.

50. No. 5 of "Twenty Poems after Drinking Wine", ibid., p. 130.

51. *Baiyuzhai cihua*, in *Cihua congbian*, vol. 11, p. 3819.

52. *Jiecunzhai lunci zazhu*, ibid, vol. 5, pp. 1626-1627.

惨结秋阴，西风送、霏霏雨湿。凄望眼、征鸿几字，暮投沙碛。试问乡关何处是，水云浩荡迷南北。但一抹、寒青有无中，遥山色。

天涯路，江上客。肠欲断，头应白。空搔首兴叹，暮年离拆。须信道消忧除是酒，奈酒行有尽情无极。便挽取、长江入尊罍，浇胸臆。

——宋·赵鼎《满江红》

动荡岁月里人性的挣扎与救赎

——《生死时代之双雄》序

朱辉军

“双雄”？竟然指的是两个做过汉奸的家伙，他们怎么能被称作“雄”！

带着巨大的疑问，时常还怀有一些抵触情绪，我逐页阅读完高淳的新作《生死时代之双雄》。

那是在“风雨如磐暗故园”的年代，江南小镇赵家镇的百姓们过着度日如年的艰难日子。裁缝的儿子赵宏伟、拳师的儿子赵驹，一个懦夫，一个恶棍，都被父亲送去日本留学。由此开启了他们那屈辱而又悲壮的人生历程。

优秀小说要写出人的命运，特别是在极端状况下的命运，那是最考验人性，也是最能体现人性的时空。

战争就是人类的极端状况之一。

伟大的抗日战争尽管已经过去了80年，但还是有许多值得我们深入发掘和全面展示的地方。以往一些作家艺术家对战争的处理，往往有这么几个阶段：最初是讴歌英雄的阶段，然后就有反其道而行之，有的甚至以嬉戏玩闹的方式来游戏历史。这些艺术处理，都有其片面性。讴歌英雄的，往往粉饰历史，在英雄的传奇里冲淡战争的残酷和荒谬；暴露战争的，往往走向颠覆历史，甚至将敌人也写得富有人性；而戏说历史的，则彻底将历史的真相给消解了。这些年，我们读过的作品，或看过的影视中，类似的情况还少吗？

并不是说本书就十分客观全面了，但在总体把握上，作者是辩证地来认识和处理其笔下的人物的，尤其通过两个汉奸从堕入深渊到逐渐觉醒这样一个特殊的视角，来展现抗日战争的严酷与复杂，显示了作者的独特眼光和独具匠心。

小说最可贵之处，是写出了人的复杂性。

两个主人公，无论出身、经历，还是禀赋、性格，都完全不同。为什么却不约而同地走上了出卖灵魂之路呢？这里确实有环境的逼迫。唯物主义者从来认为是环境决定人生。赵宏伟留学日本归国，却毫无用武之地，只能做个小学校长。如果没有那场战争，他也就是小镇上一介书生而已，却偏偏让日寇获悉了他的留日经历，在刀枪的威逼下，他一步步走向深渊。而赵驹比他更惨，因为得罪土匪、黑帮，在日本各地逃窜，回国后也只能四处流浪，到处被匪徒特别是国民党特务追杀，于是卖身投靠了日寇。读着他们的堕落历程，真是倍感愤怒而又深觉无奈！

环境固然决定个人命运，但每个人的选择却是不同的。这两个家伙，骨子里都相当懦弱，就算武艺高强的赵驹，其实内心深处也是胆小鬼，而且都自私、自欺并欺人。小说关于赵宏伟与赵驹的描绘，其实也从一个特殊视角触及了中国国民性中的顽疾。正是这些顽疾，使一些国人在关键时候，陷入泥潭而不能自拔。小说借游击队员小秦之口，义正词严地怒斥赵宏伟道："我是真恨你们这些汉奸，日本人为什么打中国能打得那么厉害，占中国能占得那么快？还不都是因为有你们这些卖国贼在帮着他们！他们的武器再厉害，军事素质再过硬，可是来到中国，人生地不熟，语言又不通，如果没有你们给他们引路、翻译、提供情报，他们能在中国节节胜利、势如破竹吗？要是中国人个个都不怕死，不当汉奸，齐心抗敌，日本人又岂能占我们国土一寸！现在，你的相好被日本人抓走了，这完全是你的报应！你给老虎带路，老虎来了却吃掉了你的女人，活该！"这番话说得真是掷地有声，代表了所有正义之士的心声！

那这两个家伙又是怎么幡然悔悟过来的呢？是侵华日军的惨无人道，是周边百姓的自发反抗，是共产党游击队的英勇奋战，使他们灵魂深处残存的良知受到了深深的触动。而最主要的，则是小秦提到的，赵宏伟的恋人王秀珍被日军不断骚扰和凌辱，在赵驹那里，则是其恋人庄丽云之家业被日寇侵吞，最终惨遭毒手。这样的缘由似乎不怎么纯洁，更谈不上高尚，但我以为这恰好符合赵驹和赵宏伟的实际。历史深处的真实并不总令人振奋和激越。

于是文弱的赵宏伟趁乱手刃日酋竹内，并在最后关头引爆游击队留下的炸药与日军同归于尽；而勇猛的赵驹则如入无人之境，连连射杀日本官兵，自己也遭日军乱枪扫射，血洒疆场。他们都是在生死关头，完成了自己灵魂的拯救和升华。

这么两个被迫做过汉奸的普通书生，最后都置生死于度外，义无反顾地站到了坚决抗击日寇的立场上，可见日寇的侵华战争是多么的不得人心，多么的违背潮流！作者从这么一个特殊的角度，展示了日寇必败、中国必胜的历史必然性。而这样的处理，截然不同于我们先前所接触过的，因此也显示了作者的不同凡响。

对游击队员姚志的艺术处理让我一直很矛盾，甚至困惑。他是一个孤儿，从十六岁起开始参加战斗，一直都在不停地打仗，跟土匪打，跟军阀打，跟国民党打，跟日本侵略军打。作者最初并未直接表现他，而是通过他的战友，还有汉奸，特别是由日寇的嘴里，间接表现出来的。渡边在回答竹内大佐时是这么说的："金钱美女与高官厚禄，他都视如粪土；皮肉之痛与濒死之苦，他都不屑一顾。他的生命，就像是全部用忠诚与信仰打造而成的，除此之外别无他物。这样的人，我这一生，也很少见过。"渡边说，"我们割他的皮肉、剁他的脚趾，他连哼都不哼一声；我们每隔一个月就会将他全身的骨头重新打断一遍，可是他连泪水都没有掉过一滴；最残忍的那一次，是我们割去了他的生殖器，当他醒来的时候，我们让他看着狼狗在他的面前吃掉了他的生殖器，但是他的脸上却仍然没有一丝恐惧。这样的人，的确是真正的勇士。"竹内也痛苦地承认："这样的人，是不可征服的。"——然而，就这么一个英勇不屈、视死如归的壮士，却在阴毒的山本不断折磨下，最终叛变了！这令我大吃一惊，姚志的选择完全与赵驹、赵宏伟的选择逆反了。细细琢磨，作者的处理有其良苦用心，一方面充分揭露了日寇在中华大地上除了暴行之外，还有各种险恶奸诈的手段和方式，另一方面也揭示了精神的崩塌、信念的动摇，必定会导致灭顶之灾！

而王秀珍和庄丽云的遭遇，则是那个年代千千万万中国女性的一个缩影。

她们一个是江南小家碧玉，一个是北国大家闺秀；一个身处穷乡僻壤，一个久居喧嚣都市，身世、家境、教养等都有着巨大差异，唯一的共同点就是秀外慧中，然而美貌和贤淑并未给她们带来好运，反而厄运连连。王秀珍被强征为慰安妇，庄丽云则屡遭日本商会的暗算，最后都未逃脱日军的魔掌。柔弱的两个女子，却坚决放弃苟且偷生，而选择以死抗争，让多少须眉为之汗颜！

这些小人物的浮沉，固然与他们自己的遭际有关，但主要取决于那个暗无天日的世道。他们人人都有一笔伤心事、一本血泪账。赵驹沦为乞丐后结识的几位中，孔仁全家老少，都被地主恶霸逼死；孟义的新婚妻子，被英国人拐卖到了南洋做妓女；朱理的一条胳膊，是在军阀互斗的战场上被炮弹给炸飞的；黄道那才一岁的儿子，则被青帮的人给剁成了肉泥。大家虽然来自五湖四海，但脸上流的是一样的泪。地主、洋人、军阀、黑帮，他们的身上负了多少中国人的血债？可是又有谁能去向他们要回一个公道？起先他们逆来顺受，但日寇的惨绝人寰使他们终于忍无可忍，便奋起反抗。可无组织的抵抗，最终只能是以悲剧收场。读来令人唏嘘而又扼腕。

侵华日军方面，赤木的奸诈、山本的残暴、渡边的阴险，都被作者描绘得跃然纸上。其中那个当地最高指挥官竹内大佐，是一个颇值得玩味的人物。这个双手沾满中国人民鲜血的恶魔，居然在听赵宏伟讲课时，流露出别样的感觉来。赵宏伟在课堂上用日语讲了一个世外桃源的故事，竹内觉得这就是说给他听的。这个故事真的是太美妙了，让他感到了难言的惬意与舒畅。竹内忽然开始十分向往没有战争的生活，他忽然发现了那种生活的美妙，他很想可以坐在自己家乡的花园里，喝喝清酒，吃吃寿司。为什么要出来打仗，为什么要向往权力，这些真的是对人生之美莫大的践踏。竹内的这些感受应该是十分真切的，可见战争机器对人性的摧残和扭曲，是多么的深重。

小说对所涉及的主要人物，都做了真实而又大胆的描绘，让我们见识了以前少有见到的他们的真正面目。有的人物，如小秦、短毛等，尽管只是寥寥数笔，也性格鲜明，栩栩如生。如果拍成电视剧，应该会引人入胜，扣人心弦。

由此说说小说的艺术表现。

给人留下极其深刻印象的，是其心理描写十分出色。赵宏伟的卑微、怯弱、逢迎，赵驹的犹疑、烦闷、焦灼，都被刻画得入木三分，深切展现了他们附逆时期心灵的撕痛和灵魂的煎熬。正因为有这样充分的心理依据，才使他们后来的人性觉醒和自我拯救显得顺理成章，为人们所理解。

与之相关的是几段梦境，描摹得都很有特点：

“心音又来梦里找赵宏伟了。她拉着他的手，走过了一道又一道门，每一道门的后面，都是一个风光迥异的季节。春红夏绿，秋黄冬白，每一个季节里，都生长着一些赵宏伟似曾相识的故事。每一个故事里，都布满了赵宏伟和心音的影子。这个梦好长，每一个季节都有赵宏伟一生那么长。每一道门过去，赵宏伟和心音就像是重新又相识相爱了一次。大半个梦走下来，赵宏伟和心音就像是已经相爱了几生几世，而他们却还没有厌倦，依然充满好奇地期待着下一道门之后的缠绵悱恻与依依不舍。直到他们迈入了最后一道门，横在他们跟前的，是一个没有季节没有颜色的悬崖。只要他们再往前走几步，就会一起掉进那悬崖下的无底深渊中。心音说，我们一起跳，我们一起跳。赵宏伟说，不要，不要。心音忽然就放开了赵宏伟的手，自己往前跑了去，大笑着，跳下了悬崖。悬崖下传来了一声巨响，赵宏伟背后的那一道道门开始纷纷倒塌。烟尘四起，五彩碎尽。终于，‘轰隆’一声，赵宏伟脚下的地也塌了，他猛地就掉进了一条冰河里。河水刺骨，冰得他周身发麻僵硬，而他不能呼吸，不能呼吸！”

这一段对梦境的诡异、迷离展示得十分精彩，而关于门、季节与悬崖的隐喻，也十分精妙。

赵驹因得罪日本黑帮头子而被追杀，虽侥幸逃脱，但也噩梦不断，其中一个是：“梦中，自己仍在东京夜晚的街道上奔跑，没命地奔跑。街上空无一人，鸦雀无声，星光暗淡，路灯残损。自己的喘息声与跑步踏地声交叠在一起，震耳欲聋，幽深似鬼。身后，始终有一个看不清脸的杀手在紧紧地追赶自己，他越追越近，越追越近，自己拼尽了全力也没办法再跑快一点点。终于，杀手追了上来。黑暗中，他的刀尖抵住了自己的喉头。自己拼命地抗拒着。但是，那寒气如霜的刀尖，还是在一点一点地深入自己的喉咙。很痛，很冷。忽然，街上一道光掠过，自己看清了他的脸。他竟然就是自己。他怒吼一声，用力将刀一插。自己就吓得醒了过来。”这段梦境与赵宏伟的完全不同，说明了二者的性格反差，但两人内心的忧惧与惶恐，却又异曲同工。

全书的互文、对比及比喻都运用得十分精妙，显示了作者驾驭这种复杂题材的能力。赵宏伟与赵驹的部分经历交叉，因此互为观照，同时也互为对比。王秀珍与庄丽云的遭遇，既互为对照，又互为补充。而各种精到的比喻及象征等，俯拾即是，显示了作者的深厚功力。

小说的语言十分讲究，生动而鲜活。比如写赵驹父亲生前最后一次打拳，“龙形虎步，啸声震天，拳破南山，脚碎北海。疾时赛雄鹰，徐时如磐石。掌开梅花千万朵，腿似铁桩地根生。进则如狮扑，退则似山固。追风降龙九天中，摧金伏虎地狱里。万马奔腾劲，千钧一发力。吞吐山河英雄气，横扫雷霆将军意。四书安天下，八极定神州。开天辟地豪杰情，沧海横流壮烈心。”很有些古代武侠的感觉，用在赵三牛身上，实在是再贴切不过了。

有许多段落简直可以当作诗歌来读。像“风萧萧，雨飘飘。鸿雁浩渺出天际，马踏冰霜道别离。相思千番却无语，哭到泪干此生虚。人影灭，夕阳血，情意绝，烟花碎”这样的句子，感情诚挚，词句优美，令人回味无穷。

虽然作者试图在叙事方式上也做一些探索，包括视角转换，现实与回忆交织等，但这种探索并不成熟，尤其是第二部赵驹的自述，与前后两部无法有机统一，使全书的结构和整体艺术效果都受到了一定损害。创新精神可嘉，但还是要看实际效果。不知作者与读者对此以为然否？

有谁能想到：这么一部繁复深刻厚实的长篇小说，是出自一位重度残疾的80后青年作者之手？

作者高淳，1984年出生于北京，现居江苏常熟。因久病而只有初中学历，但在学生时代，就曾先后获得过“常熟市十佳好少年”“常熟市精神文明十佳标兵”等荣誉称号。初中期间因先天性肌迟缓症而重度残疾，生活完全不能自理。但他凭着顽强的毅力，不仅完成了初中学业，而且自学走上了文学创作道路。

1996年年仅12岁的高淳就开始正式发表文学作品。2002年起专心致力于文学创作。他曾经参加过鲁迅文学院培训中心的四年函授学习，并被评为培训中心高级班优秀学员。作品有诗歌、散文、小说，散见于各类报刊。

2005年加入常熟市作家协会。2009年25岁的高淳花四年的时间完成了一部长达151万字的长篇小说《风逝》，当时托人请我为之作序。我既为他的坚忍不拔、自强不息的精神所感动，也为他优美的文笔、横溢的才华所折服。通读全稿后，我真切地感到这部“作品展开了当代社会的生活长卷，宛如新时代的清明上河图”。这一评价获得了广泛的认同。这次他转向历史，绘就了一幅如油画般凝重浓烈的历史长卷，同样令我大为叹服，便特别认真地细读了他的这部新著，也特别认真地写下了上述文字。

是为序。

2017年5月20日于北京副中心大方居

目 录

第一部

赵宏伟的荒唐人生

一九三八年。

又是一年秋天。

赵家镇上的人都在说，日本兵就要来了。而众所周知，县城里的国军上个月就已经跑光了。

人们都很害怕。虽然镇子上的人谁都没亲眼见过日本兵，但是大家都知道日本兵个个都是吃人不吐骨头的魔鬼。如果不是这样，为什么那么多中国的土地都已经叫日本兵给占了呢？如果不是这样，那些守城的王八蛋国军为什么上个月就纷纷逃跑了呢？所以，日本兵一定是极其可怕的，大家都想。三个月前县城里的国军还向赵家镇上的百姓许诺过，他们要来赵家镇上布防建工事，决不允许鬼子踏进赵家镇半步，现在看来全是扯淡。

镇子上人心惶惶，小孩害怕，女人害怕，男人也害怕。有人提议，镇上自建一支保安队，但是立即就遭到了人们的集体否决。人家国军的正式装备都挡不住日本兵前进的步伐，你一支连枪都没有的保安队能干啥？军阀混战的那几年，镇上不是也自建了一支大刀自卫队吗？有个屁用，人家散兵游勇一过来，朝天乱放了几枪，自卫队的队长就吓得尿了裤子。据说，那个队长请那队散兵游勇的排长吃饭的当晚，连自己的老婆都让人家给睡了，而他连屁都没敢放一个。当然了，这也只是镇子上的一个已经久远了的传说。并没有人去向当年的那个队长求证虚实。但是从此以后，镇上的人们就都在心底里达成了一个共识：这个镇子上的男人，全是窝囊废。有一位前清的老秀才，满腔悲凉地写下了两句诗：江南多才子，水乡无英雄。当时，有一些小

伙子就不服气，去对老秀才说，那些兵痞来的时候，我们也都是想要出去砍他们的，我们可不怕死。老秀才就问，那你们怎么没砍呢？小伙子们都纷纷委屈地说，是家里的爹娘不许。是他们的爹娘，把他们给拦在了家里。老秀才就仰天长叹，说，连家里的爹娘都不敢反抗，我江南无人矣！

不管老秀才的话是否有以偏概全之嫌，他都说出了人们长久以来对江南男人的一个普遍看法。而且他又是在赵家镇兵痞事件之后表明的看法，大家也就都不得不承认他言之有理。只是苦了镇上的女人和孩子，生逢乱世，这镇上的江南男人连砍人都不敢，这日子过得可真是提心吊胆哪！现在日本兵又要来了，连蒋介石的正规军都打不过的日本兵就要来了，这日子还叫人怎么过呀！

有人就提出来，要不就逃吧。大家思索片刻，一个个眉头又都拧成了连环锁。都是世世代代吃喝拉撒在这块土地上的人，凭啥要给日本人让地方？唉，都怪国运不济呀。多少年了，这老百姓的日子是一天不如一天，屋漏还偏遭连夜雨，这日本人还来趁火打劫，想想还真是不如死了算了。再说了，怎么逃啊？去大后方的路上又是兵又是匪的，其凶险程度可一点儿也不比日本兵来了差。去年，不就有两户人家，是在逃往大后方的路上遭了难吗？一户是遇上了土匪，一户是遇上了国军。遇上国军的那户还好，就是钱没了，女儿成了残花败柳。遇上土匪的那户可就惨了，不光钱财被洗劫，妻女被糟蹋，最后还全家丢了性命，被灭了门。你说叫人怎么逃啊！

这时，有人轻轻地说了一句：听说，日本人不杀良民。

大家沉默了几秒钟。

你个汉奸坯子。一个年轻人愤怒地说。

大家又都沉默了几秒钟。

安静里，只有远远的几声犬吠。秋高气爽，万物肃杀。

赵宏伟站在后院里，看着金灿灿一树的桂花，不禁深深地吸了一口气。浓郁的清香从他的鼻子里蔓延到了整个身体。他觉得自己的精神仿佛好多了。近来，连学校里也都已经乱作了一团，老师不来教书，孩子不来上课，偌大的一个赵家镇小学，每天上课铃一响，各个教室里空空荡荡。兵乱还未至，学校里已是一片荒芜的景象。这让赵宏伟忧心忡忡。他忧的不光是眼前，还有那可以预见的明天，又或者还有其他更多的说不清道不明的东西。

而现在，似乎也只有自家后院里种着的这棵桂花树，还能给人以一丝淡淡的安慰。金秋送爽，桂花绚烂一树。不管风吹雨打，每年花香总会如约而至。平淡里孕育着一股坚韧的恒久。不管再苦再难，明年花开时，清香还会来，赵宏伟想。

赵宏伟是江庆县教育局正式任命的赵家镇小学校长。想当年，父亲弥留之际，还仍然在为他这个不肖子的前程担忧，而今想来，赵宏伟仍觉心酸。人生至困，无非就是树欲静而风不止，子欲养而亲不待。但是想想，父亲也幸亏是走得早，不然见到时局如此动荡，日子过得定会是更惊更怕。日本人一来，不知还会遭什么罪。唉，赵宏伟不禁长长的一声叹息。

一些同事临走前也劝赵宏伟走。虽说县政府当初下了令，说是没有命令，政府工作人员一律不准撤退，违者一律撤职，但是现在县政府自己都已经撤了，教育局长也不知是带着哪个小老婆已经奔重庆去了，你一个小小的小学校长还守在这里干啥？不是找死吗？赵家镇上的一些人家，也都已经踏上了逃难的路程。日本人就要来了，不管逃难路上会碰上兵还是碰上匪，总比不逃待在这里碰上日本人强吧？但是赵宏伟就是不走。

赵宏伟是这样想的，万一国军很快就又打回来了，到时候县政府一查，他赵宏伟私自撤退，那不撤了他的职才怪呢。人家局长逃是人家局长的事，没有人会去追究局长的责任。但是他赵宏伟只是一个小小的小学校长，上面要是真的追究下来，那他可是连一丝辩白的机会也不会有的。这就是官大和官小的区别。排长当了逃兵会被枪毙，但是蒋介石当了逃兵有谁敢动他？事情就是这样简单。

赵宏伟从后院踱回了后屋。他正莫名地有些感慨，一抬眼，就又看见了放在后屋墙角的那两坛酒。那两坛酒的外面，很仔细地包着一层旧报纸，那些旧报纸都已经旧得又黄又脆。这种旧，此刻让赵宏伟的心里很不舒服。他立马就去拿了几张新报纸过来，要换掉那些旧报纸。旧报纸上弹起的灰尘，让赵宏伟重重地打了一个喷嚏。

裹在旧报纸里的两个酒坛，依旧干干净净、光光亮亮，一点儿也没有饱经风霜的模样。赵宏伟觉得这也真是一件很值得感慨的事情。或许只有人和纸，才是最经不住岁月磨砺的吧，他不禁想道。他记得差不多二十年前，自

己面对着这两坛酒，内心也曾发出过如此的感慨，而那时，自己刚二十岁。而今，自己的双脚已快要踏进不惑之年的大门了，但依旧是在尘烟里孤舟横渡。唯有这两坛老酒如旧。不，那隔着坛子都能闻得出来的酒香，仿佛是更芬芳了。赵宏伟的心里愈觉萧索。

这两坛老酒，是赵宏伟的父母在一八九八年冬天的时候，为赵宏伟埋下的状元红。那一年，戊戌变法失败，六君子慷慨就义。赵家镇上的那位老秀才在听到六君子的死讯之后，坐在镇上大街的街口，痛骂了慈禧一整天。不过好在也没人管他。那一年的冬天特别冷，赵家镇的街面上，都常能看到积水结成的薄冰。而赵宏伟，就是在这样的一个冬天里，呱呱坠地的。他父亲赵宝贵是在他出生的这一天，亲自去县城最好的酒坊里买的酒。他买的两坛是酒坊里最好的酒。回家后，他就用老婆郑玉梅事先裁好的大红纸，将原本就已经是密封好了的两个酒坛子又仔细地包了起来。红纸与红纸间，用糯米粘住。埋之前，他还特地将其中一坛酒捧到郑玉梅和刚生下来的孩子面前，对郑玉梅说，你闻闻，多香，等孩子长大了，考上了状元，我们一起喝。郑玉梅就高兴地对孩子说，儿子，听到了没有，你爹盼着你中状元呢，你要快快长大，中了状元，去见皇上。

赵宝贵就将两坛酒埋在了自家后院的地里，傍着那棵桂花树。他希望花借酒香，酒借花香，一切都吉祥如意。此后的许多岁月里，赵宝贵和郑玉梅都觉得，这院里的桂花树下，是全家最惬意的地方。

赵宝贵是赵家镇上有名的裁缝。连县里的许多富户，都喜欢找赵宝贵去做衣服。因此，赵宝贵一家的日子倒也一直是过得颇为宽裕。但这裁缝，毕竟是一份下人做的活计，跟路边卖油条的地位没什么两样，尤其是在这小小的赵家镇上。赵宝贵也曾听说省城的名裁缝是要比卖油条的高一等的，但那不是省城吗？所以，从他老婆郑玉梅被老中医确诊怀孕的那天起，他就暗暗做了一个决定：若是生女儿，就传她手艺；若是生儿子，就一定要让他读书，中状元、中进士，哪怕就是个举人，也比秀才好。

赵宝贵请了老秀才——就是那个大骂慈禧的老秀才给赵宏伟开蒙，教他读书。赵家镇上近几十年来，也就只出了这么一个秀才。虽然赵宝贵经常怀疑这个老秀才的思想属于康梁一派，但是他想，这个老秀才，总不至于会将赵宏伟教成一个反贼吧。而他赵宝贵能给儿子请到的最好的老师，也就只有这个老秀才了。赵宝贵对儿子的希望，就全押在这个老秀才身上了。

赵宏伟倒也的确是聪明伶俐，老秀才教得尽职尽责。赵宏伟五岁就会背唐诗，一背一大串。赵宝贵走在路上都觉得很有面子。老秀才原本打算在赵宏伟七岁的时候，教他背《史记》，但是赵宏伟七岁还没到，清廷就下了一道谕旨，宣布正式废除科举。听到消息的那一天，赵宝贵和老秀才都感到了万念俱灰。怎么会这样呢？怎么会这样呢？老秀才和赵宝贵相互诘问，就好像这道谕旨是他俩下的一样。

半年后，老秀才就劝赵宝贵：还是送孩子去县里的新式小学堂念书吧，大清是不会再有状元了，这孩子聪明，别耽误了孩子。赵宝贵很沮丧，说，不能当状元了，再念书有个什么用，还花掉我的钱。老秀才就说，你看着吧，这个乱世的明天，就决定在两种人手里，一种是拿枪的人，一种是读书的人，康有为他当年要是成功了，就是万世的英雄。

赵宝贵就送赵宏伟去县里念了小学，念完初等小学又念高等小学，后来，还送他去省城念了中学。当然，那时早已是民国。而赵宏伟在新式学堂念书的同时，也并没丢了四书五经、经史子集。与民国时接近全盘西化的课程安排不同，当时清末的新式学堂里，仍然有不少孔孟儒学的课程。但是当时在县里的小学堂里教授经典的几位先生，其学问见识俱在赵家镇的老秀才之下。所以赵宏伟只要一放假或一有空，还是会跟学问高深的老秀才学习，在他那里读些高深的古书，学些高雅的古事。赵宝贵觉得这样也不错，他隐隐地想，毕竟世道这么乱，天知道哪天会不会又恢复科举呢？什么都不一定的。但是当然，不能再给老秀才正式的学费了，只能偶尔稍微意思一下。老秀才倒也不在乎钱，老秀才说，我在乎的是人才。康熙一朝为什么国富民强？就是因为朝中人才济济！

郑玉梅是在辛亥革命那一年，难产死的。生产前，老中医说一切都好，肯定会母子平安。当然，也可能是母女。郑玉梅在那段大着肚子的时间里，总是喜欢去后院的桂花树下坐坐。她总是跟赵宝贵说，不管这世道有多乱，只要能把那乱挡在家门外，家里的日子就还是好的。就像这棵桂花树，和埋在桂花树旁边的两坛酒，任凭它外面风雨飘摇，这花该开的还是会开，这酒该香的还是会香。也别说，有时候站在那埋酒的地方，赵宝贵还真的是会闻到一阵隐隐的酒香。也不知是幻觉，还是那地底下的酒坛子漏了。但想想，

那酒坛子那么好，也没人去动过，怎么可能会漏呢？所以，他觉得，这酒是真香。他想，要不怎么说酒香不怕巷子深呢？想必真正的好酒，埋得深也是不怕的吧？

但是郑玉梅却死了。孩子生不下来，血也止不住，接生婆急得满头大汗，老中医一脸羞愧，无地自容，并且束手无策。郑玉梅在最后的时间里，告诉赵宝贵，她是多想在赵宏伟长大了娶媳妇的那一天，喝上一口埋在那桂花树旁的状元红。

说完，她就咽了气。赵宝贵号啕大哭。

民国终于还是来了。溥仪退位。赵宝贵给赵宏伟剪了辫子，赵宏伟也帮赵宝贵剪了辫子。赵宝贵将两条辫子都埋在了郑玉梅的坟旁边。他说，玉梅呀，你不孤单，我们一家人还在一起呢。

一九一八年冬天，第一次世界大战结束。但是这看起来和赵家镇也并没有什么紧要的关系。而对赵宝贵一家来说，这一年则发生了两件很紧要的事情。第一件，是儿子赵宏伟终于中学毕业了。中学毕业了的赵宏伟无事可做，只好待在父亲的裁缝铺里给父亲当帮手。赵宏伟原本是想去外面的大城市里上大学的，但是上大学要花的那个钱，当时的赵宝贵是实在负担不起，所以赵宏伟也只好将此念作罢。而没学可上了的赵宏伟，又只是个百无一用的货色。这让赵宝贵郁闷不已。他当年送儿子去上洋学堂，是希望儿子长大了可以做国家栋梁的。就算科举无望，但是和状元差不多的国家栋梁总还是要努力去当的。要是早知道他中学毕业只能来裁缝铺帮忙，那还要他去读书干什么呢？还不如教他做个像自己一样的好裁缝呢。所以，赵宝贵对老秀才就颇有怨言，觉得老秀才骗了他。其实老秀才也是个可怜人，早年是赵家镇上有名的富户，哪知道后来儿子染上了鸦片，最后家财散尽，一家人死的死，逃的逃，就只剩下了老秀才一个人。所以赵宝贵也不好意思去跟老秀才要个说法。

赵宝贵家发生的第二件事，则是一件天大的喜事。一九一八年初冬的一天，赵宏伟的一个远房叔叔死了。这个远房叔叔无儿无女，也无妻室，一辈子就喜欢捧戏子。临死前，他就将一大笔财产留给了赵宏伟。

赵宏伟兴高采烈地向父亲提议，用这些钱，可以开一家绸缎庄了。父亲抬手就给了他一记耳光。没出息！父亲骂道，我送你读了这么多年的书，就是为了让你在这小小的赵家镇上开一家小小的绸缎庄？

其实在发财之后，赵宝贵和赵宏伟都在心里有了一个同样的想法：上大学的钱有了。但是，两人又都心存着一个同样的顾虑：上完了大学，会不会仍和现在上完了中学一样没用？两人都不知道。当然，赵宏伟其实是可以选择上职业学校的，但是赵宝贵和赵宏伟对此都觉得很不屑。君子不器，若只想学谋生的技艺，又何必还要花钱去学校里学？家里的亲爹一身裁缝的好本领，跟自己亲爹学不就成了。父子两人都把问题憋在心里，从没当面交流过。两人都觉得很彷徨。

后来，赵宝贵终于有了想法，赵宝贵的想法，就是想去县里，给儿子买一个官当当。反正自己当初送儿子上学就是因为想让儿子当状元，而自己想让儿子当状元的目的就是想要儿子当官，那么家里现在既然已经有钱了，何不干脆就一步到位，为儿子买下一片锦绣前程？反正买官卖官这种事情古已有之，想来现在及将来定也不会灭绝。哪怕只是买个小官也好，总比平头百姓强。只要送儿子上了道，往后儿子定能成事。但是他又拿不定主意。一来他不知这官究竟该怎样买，他以前只见人家这么干过，自己却从未参与其中，不谙门道；二来，他心底里觉得这民国的政府也实在是乱得可以，万一送儿子当官不成，反而送儿子进了一个危巢、贼窝，他这当父亲的岂不是悔之晚矣？思来想去，赵宝贵觉得还是去问问老秀才比较好。毕竟，老秀才也是看着赵宏伟长大的。

老秀才问赵宝贵，你知道赵三牛的儿子赵驹，中学毕业后去了哪儿吗？赵宝贵问，哪儿？

日本。

去那鬼地方干吗？

宝贵呀，赵三牛看得比你长远。中国的未来，必定还是需要一场大革命的，要革命，就必须要有懂革命的人出来领头，他赵三牛，就是想让儿子当这个头。

说得太远了吧？他赵三牛不就是开了家破镖局吗，一个江湖中人，还能懂革命？

他不懂革命，但他懂帮会。有时候，是可以用帮会的道理来解释党派的问题的。你想想看，他儿子若从日本学成归来，那他赵三牛再出几个钱给他

儿子买一个官当当，他儿子在官场上岂不是会平步青云？留学生总比中学生要高贵些。

老秀才，你现在说话越来越像我们老百姓了。

已经是民国了，我本来就只是一个小老百姓，只可惜年轻时以为自己不是。听我的，趁现在有钱，送宏伟去日本，他是个聪明的孩子，待在这小小的赵家镇上太可惜了。或许，你可以让他成为第二个康有为，或者第二个孙中山。日本和中国有很多相似的地方，他们已经富强了，而我们，还需要有人领导我们走向富强。就让宏伟去日本，学学他们的富强之道吧！

赵宝贵听得热血沸腾。

回家后，他将老秀才的话又对赵宏伟说了一遍。赵宏伟一脸疑惑的神情。但是，日本他还是愿意去的。以前他是知道家里条件不够，不敢想，但是现在，家里有钱了。

事情定了下来，父子两人都很高兴。

郑玉梅死后，赵宝贵常常会独自站在桂花树下发呆。他有时也会用力地嗅嗅，想再嗅到当年那酒香混合着桂花香的味道。只可惜，桂花香倒还是年年都有，酒香他却是再也没能闻到。赵宏伟长大后，就笑着对父亲说，爹，酒埋在地下呢，再香，也是不可能闻得到的呀。赵宝贵说，不，那些年，我经常可以闻到从地底下飘出来的酒香，只是你娘走后，我的鼻子就不大灵了。再也闻不到酒香的赵宝贵，时常就会觉得自己和那没有了酒香陪伴的桂花香一样孤单。他以前从来就不知道，原来香味也会让人憔悴。

看多了父亲呆站着的模样，赵宏伟有些心酸。一九一九年春节里的一天，赵宏伟就动手，将埋在后院地里的那两坛酒给挖了出来。泥土翻开的那一瞬间，酒香四溢，沁人心脾，赵宏伟还以为是自己不小心把坛子给弄破了呢。他赶紧将坛子捧出来一看，好好的，都还是好好的呢。原来，这酒真的是隔着坛子就能闻得到香啊。这真是好酒中的好酒！况且，是埋了二十年的老酒。只可惜，包在酒坛子外面的大红纸，是早已经烂了。赵宏伟听父亲说过，那包酒坛子用的大红纸，都是母亲在怀着他的时候，亲手裁的。虽说这不是什么大事，但红纸毕竟全烂了。只有老酒如故。不，或许是芬芳胜往昔。这真是让人忧伤无语。

赵宏伟想，自己就要去日本了，在离开前，敬爹和娘一碗，也算是了了娘临死前的愿望，也希望爹能再闻一闻那一股当年的酒香，一慰心酸。谁知，赵宝贵一回来，看见了这两坛酒摆在桌上，就傻了。他呆若木鸡，而后勃然大怒。

赵宏伟觉得很委屈。赵宝贵用抹布一遍又一遍地擦拭着两个酒坛子，他用力地嗅着酒的香，仔细地反复检查两个酒坛子的封口，就怕赵宏伟弄坏了封酒坛口的蜡。赵宏伟说，爹，我没弄坏，我还想等你回来，一起开坛子呢。

赵宝贵的泪就下来了，一滴滴全滴在了酒坛子上。儿子啊，你不懂，这状元红，是只有在儿子考上状元或是娶媳妇的那天，才能开的呀。

爹，我错了，您别生气，我这就把它们埋回去。

赵宝贵长叹了一声，摇了摇头。算了，外面的红纸也都烂了，再去埋它干什么呢。这也是天意，就把它们放在你娘以前经常待的后屋吧，让你娘也闻闻它们的香。不要放在摆牌位的灵台旁，不吉利。过几年，等你回来，做了大官，娶了媳妇，我们爷儿俩再一起好好喝这状元红。

好，爹。

一九一九年五月四日，五四运动爆发。而赵宏伟就是在这一天，登上了东渡扶桑的轮船。

江庆县下面共有八个镇，而赵家镇就是这八个镇里头最大最好最发达的一个镇。从地理位置上来说，赵家镇是最紧贴着江庆县城的，所以日军只要占了赵家镇，江庆县城就等于是门户大开。

日军沿着赵家镇大街直奔江庆县城而去。这一天，家家户户门窗紧闭，连狗都不敢叫一声。空旷的镇子上，就只有日军靴子踏地的声音和枪械碰撞的声音。当然，偶尔还有几句日本话。日本人看上去也不轻松。

下午的时候，从南城门方向传来了密集的枪声，枪声持续了大概半个多小时。赵家镇上的人后来才知道，这一天，鬼子在南城门口遭遇了新四军游击队的伏击。鬼子死了十三人，伤了六人，还死了一个汉奸翻译官。新四军游击队也死了七个人，一名游击队员被俘虏。

赵宏伟躲在家里，瑟瑟发抖。他怕得要死。他相信其他人也一定是和他一样的。不然，赵家镇大街上的日军已经走了好久，为什么街上还是连一条

狗都没有？根本就没人敢出门。

赵宏伟想起前几天，自己还衣冠楚楚地要求学校里的老师和学生，能上课的尽量照常来上课，能教书的尽量正常来教书。自己说的时候，说得大义凛然，仿佛外面天打雷劈也不能动摇他教书育人的壮志雄心。但是现在看来，自己也就是个软蛋，彻头彻尾的软蛋。赵宏伟觉得自己很对不起老秀才，老秀才直到临死前还期盼着他赵宏伟有朝一日能成为康有为式的人物。老秀才这辈子就只知道康有为。唉，想这些干什么呢，赵宏伟不禁自叹。他蹲在后屋里，看看墙角那两坛自己新包好的酒，又看看屋里灵台上父母的牌位，觉得自己真是愧对列祖列宗。他现在有些后悔自己当初没听同事的劝，要是一早就跟他们一起逃了，哪还会像今天这样担惊受怕。他就是舍不得父亲给他买来的这个校长。他本来就一事无成，要是再把这校长的职位给弄丢了，就真是连死都没脸去死了。

外面的天渐渐暗下来了。赵宏伟去厨房拿了两个冷馒头吃。他不知道今天晚上赵家镇上还有没有人敢烧火做饭。反正他赵宏伟是不敢。这么想着的时候，他就又想到了隔壁的秀珍母女。她们孤儿寡母的，在家不知要不要紧？他心里有些担心她们娘儿俩，但是也无计可施。他现在要是出门去看秀珍，不小心引来了日本兵就完了。按理说，他在日本待了那么多年，对日本人很了解，是不应该怕日本人的。他甚至还很会做日本料理，他当年做出来的寿司，心音可是赞不绝口的。去年南京沦陷后，几个侥幸从南京城里逃出来的人，后来都疯了，他们是被吓疯的。他们都说，南京城里的死人是堆成了山，堆成了海，南京城里的血是流遍了地，流遍了天。老人、小孩、妇女，统统都要被杀，良民、刁民都一样要死。女人被开膛剖肚，挖出生殖器官；小孩被刺刀挑起，像牛排被叉子贯穿；男人被活活烧死……没有人知道南京到底死了多少人。那就是一座鬼城。你说，这样的军队，可怕不可怕？怕，才是一个正常人的反应。

赵宏伟用纸包了六个冷馒头，揣在了怀里。等到天更暗了一些，他听听外面没有什么动静，就壮了壮胆子，从后门溜了出去。他开门和关门都用了最小的声音。巷子里安静得可怕。他像做贼一样，溜到了隔壁秀珍家的后院墙角旁。他轻轻地敲了敲秀珍家的后门，没想到声音听起来还是这样大，大得简直让人害怕。小巷子里只有恐怖的风声。

是我，秀珍。赵宏伟轻轻地喊。他太恨自己的声音了，这么静的环境里只有他一个人的声音，他简直就像个怪物。

是我，秀珍，赵宏伟。赵宏伟又轻轻喊了一声。他打算喊完这声里面再没动静他就走，别不小心把日本兵招来那可就惨了。

他正准备走，听见秀珍家的后门里面有动静了，好像是桌椅被搬走的声音。宏伟哥，你等一下，秀珍在里面说。赵宏伟听明白了，这后门原本是被秀珍用桌椅堵着呢。他这时忽然才觉得，其实这后门的风险，是一点儿也不比正门小。他真后悔自己这一次的出门。偌大的赵家镇上，一片空静死寂，此刻却被他弄出了这样清晰的一片动静来。而且这动静，在死寂中是愈发显得扎耳。他怕得要死。他真怕自己会引来什么害人害己的后果。

后门开了。秀珍怯怯地站在门口，问，宏伟哥，什么事？

哦，没什么，今天大家都没出门，我想你和小菊可能都没有准备吃的东西，就给你们带了几个馒头来，是冷的，只能将就一下了。今天可千万别生火什么的。这几天你和小菊都别出门，吃的用的我给你们送来。还有，最近不能出去做事，那洗衣服的差事丢了就丢了吧，而且最近也不会有人要洗衣服。这些钱你拿着，拿着，别推。先挨一段日子。不说了，我走了，你把门窗都关好。你多小心。

赵宏伟轻轻地跟秀珍告了个别，看着秀珍把门关好了，才转身走开。他像贼一样又溜回了自己的家里。他尽量不去想秀珍那可怜的眼神。他觉得，当时秀珍的眼神里，甚至是有一种希望他能留下来保护她们母女的意思。但是他不能。虽说现在是非常时期，她们母女两个无依无靠地躲在家里是一件很可怜也很危险的事，但是秀珍毕竟是个寡妇，而且今年才二十七岁，他不想被人背地里说闲话。秀珍也是因为相信他，才没有逃的。前段时间，秀珍还特地来问过他，问他逃不逃。他说我不逃。她就问，日本兵不可怕吗？他就说，我在日本待了那么多年，你看见我身上少了块肉吗？于是，秀珍就也决定不逃。因为逃难的路上有兵和匪，而且赵宏伟也不走，所以她就觉得她和小菊逃也未必就比不逃来得更好。赵宏伟哪里会告诉秀珍，他不是不怕，他是舍不得校长这个职位。他想到这里，就愈发觉得自己对不起秀珍。秀珍从小到大都那么信任他，前段时间，别的孩子都不来学校上课了，就她秀珍，还相信他赵宏伟的话，让小菊天天照常来上课。赵宏伟觉得自己真不是

个东西。他恨哪，他恨自己怎么小时候就没有去学武练枪，生逢乱世，真是当个土匪都比当个校长强啊。

赵宏伟面向西天佛祖的方向，跪了下来，虔诚地磕了三个响头。他默默地说，佛祖保佑，不要让赵家镇受南京被屠之苦。

赵宏伟是在一九二六年的春天回国的。那时，江庆县还是五省联军总司令孙传芳的地盘，主张联俄联共的孙中山早已去世，轰轰烈烈的北伐还没开始。中国比他出国前更乱了。但是当然，这一切跟他都没有什么关系。他是在日本收到了一封父亲托人寄来的书信，才回的国。赵宏伟的家里，出了大事。

一伙土匪烧了赵宝贵的裁缝铺子，还砍掉了赵宝贵的右手。据秀珍她爹王树忠说，这一定都是赵三牛那个王八蛋干的。

事情的起因说来话长。赵三牛家的威远镖局以前在江南一带也是颇有名望的。从赵三牛的曾祖父开始，威远镖局就是赵家镇上的一块响当当的牌子。附近有什么富贵人家要押运些什么重要的家当，都会来找威远镖局帮忙。在那个冷兵器为主的时代，赵三牛的父辈们因为有祖上传下来的厉害武功八极拳撑腰，生意倒也做得有声有色。但是这镖局的祖业传到赵三牛手里的时候，赵三牛却是倒了霉。时代变迁，晚清末年，连土匪都已经端起了长枪短枪。他赵三牛八极拳打得再好，有个屁用。在赵三牛连失了两次镖之后，镖局的生意便一落千丈。到张勋复辟的那年，威远镖局里已只剩两个镖师。所以，赵三牛的前半生，倒也是值得同情的。

赵三牛的儿子叫赵驹。赵三牛鉴于晚清的时势，并没有教赵驹练那祖传的八极拳，而是让儿子一门心思读书。读完了初小读高小，读完了中学去留学。赵宏伟后来在东京，还跟赵驹做了几年同学。但是赵宏伟并不喜欢赵驹，正如赵宝贵也不喜欢赵三牛一样。后来的事实说明，赵宝贵的不喜欢是有道理的。就在赵驹东渡扶桑的那一年，赵三牛审时度势，和附近玉山上的一伙土匪，结成了一家。他教土匪们打拳，土匪们给他高昂的工钱。土匪们有了厉害的八极拳撑腰，队伍是日益强壮，而收入也自然是芝麻开花节节高。土匪的收入一高，赵三牛也就重新富贵了起来。但是赵三牛也和土匪们说好了，兔子不吃窝边草，抢哪里也别抢赵家镇。因此，赵家镇上的人，也就都睁一只眼闭一只眼，没人去县里揭发赵三牛。

赵宝贵也不是存心想揭发赵三牛。一切都是个意外。一次，他去县长家里为县长夫人量大衣的尺寸，就听县长的夫人说了一件最近县里发生的惨案。说的是一户人家让玉山上的土匪给洗了。不光钱财洗尽，人命洗光，那户人家的两个才满十三岁的闺女，还被土匪们给糟蹋了。那两个闺女，原本还在一起为生病的娘煎药呢。赵宝贵听得凄惨，一时义愤填膺，忍不住就骂了一句，赵三牛你个畜生。赵家镇上的人都知道，赵三牛入的就是玉山帮。赵宝贵自知失言，连忙说些别的话。但县长夫人却是留了心眼。几天后，赵宝贵就被县里抓了起来，要他说出他那天骂的那句话的意思。赵宝贵本来不想出卖赵三牛，但是他又一想，这怎么能叫出卖呢？说出赵三牛来那是替天行道啊。何况赵宝贵再不说，警察就要对他用刑了。于是赵宝贵就做了一回英雄，把赵三牛的事情都给说了出来。后来县长派人去赵三牛的家里一搜，还真就搜出了不少赃物来。于是赵三牛被抓了起来。

当时，赵驹早就从日本回来在县政府里当差了。赵驹拿着一大盒金条去找了一次县长，对他说，听说您马上就要离开江庆县了，要去省城，在省城交际和铺路，花销一定是不小的，家父希望这盒金条能助您一臂之力。而听说即将到来的江庆县长，素来与您不睦，您又何必收拾好了玉山帮这个烂摊子，给敌人一个白白捡来的政绩呢？

于是几天之后，赵三牛就又从牢里大摇大摆地走了出来。虽然赵家镇上的人都不清楚赵三牛究竟是怎么出来的，但是大家一想到他那个在县政府当差的儿子，就也自然能猜到个八九分。大家都骂民国政府，说和晚清也没什么两样。王树忠那时就对赵宝贵说，宝贵，你要当心了。

果不出所料，几天后，玉山帮就又下了一次山来。这一次，他们冲进了赵家镇，直奔赵宝贵的裁缝铺而去。他们一把火将裁缝铺烧了个干干净净，还剁掉了赵宝贵的右手，然后扬长而去。王树忠出来为赵宝贵说了两句话，也被打折了腿，不过好在那条腿后来让医生给接好了。

事情就是这样。赵宝贵本不想让儿子知道这些事，但是一来，他现在没了右手，日常生活很是艰难，二来，手没了，他也不能再做裁缝了，家中固然还有不少积蓄，但终究断了财路，有坐吃山空之忧，不能再长期往日本寄钱了。思来想去，赵宝贵最后就还是听了王树忠的建议，让赵宏伟回家

来吧。

赵宏伟知道了这一切之后，怒不可遏，当时就想去找赵三牛父子算账，但是被赵宝贵和王树忠给拦了下来。赵宝贵说，让你回来，不是叫你去惹事的，赵三牛不对我们赶尽杀绝，我就已经是谢天谢地了，你还去惹什么事。王树忠也说，是啊，宏伟，人家政府都不管，你去能有什么用？你又不是腰里有枪的军官，讲得再有理人家也不会理你。

就在赵宏伟又哭又恨的时候，一个小小的声音在门外喊了一声：宏伟哥哥。

赵宏伟泪一抹，回头一看，是王树忠的独生女儿，王秀珍。那时的王秀珍才十四岁。

秀珍妹妹，这次回来得急，我忘了给你带糖了。赵宏伟上次回来看父亲，给了秀珍一盒日本糖果，临走时，答应了秀珍，下次回来会再送给她一盒。赵宏伟还是拿秀珍当小孩子看的。

宏伟哥哥，我不要糖了，你要听你爹的话，不要出去。秀珍说。

赵宏伟抹了一把泪，说，我知道的。

赵宝贵说，秀珍你真乖。

赵宏伟对王树忠说，忠叔，您为我爹受了伤，以后您家里有什么粗活重活，只管叫我，我来给您帮忙。

秀珍小手一拍，说，好哇。

江庆县全境沦陷。

半个月过去了，天气越来越凉。今年赵家镇上没有人过中秋节。秋天的凉就愈是显出了萧索。

江庆县全境共驻扎了日军三千八百余人，是一个联队。大半个联队的兵力都屯在县城，剩下的兵力就都分散驻扎在江庆县下面的八个镇子上。镇子小一点，屯的兵就少一些，镇子大一点，屯的兵就多一些。

因为赵家镇是江庆县下面的几个镇子中最大最重要的一个镇，所以日本人就将一支四五百人的大队留在了赵家镇上。这支大队人数只有正常大队的一半，是打剩下来的，但是据说其战斗力极强，非一般大队可比。镇政府重新开张，当然，里面坐的最高长官，是这支大队的大队长，少佐渡边次郎。

渡边次郎要求赵家镇上的居民恢复正常的生活秩序。但是没人敢信他的话。渡边的大队进驻赵家镇的第一天，一个铁匠舍不得丢在铺子里的东西，去收拾了一下，结果不小心就撞见了两个日本兵。当时也是不巧，铁匠的手里刚好拿着一把榔头。两个日本兵就向他端起了枪，对他喊了两句什么。铁匠听不懂，人也吓傻了，就站在那里一动也不敢动。然后，枪就响了。铁匠死了。日本兵也拍拍屁股走了。铁匠的老婆也不敢上街去收尸。两天以后，才有两个老头上街去抬走了铁匠的尸体。那时，铁匠的血已流干。榔头却还紧握在他手里。

半个月来，一直是赵宏伟在给秀珍母女送吃的送喝的。有时候，他看着小菊望着他时的那副模样，就会不禁心疼。小菊还不到八岁，长得跟秀珍小时候是一模一样。赵宏伟记得，他第一次去日本前，还陪秀珍玩了一天跳绳。那时，秀珍还不到八岁。秀珍是个可怜的孩子，她还小时，她娘就得肺痨死了。所以赵宏伟从小就对秀珍很好。但是那时的他并没有想到，厄运会一直缠着秀珍。秀珍的男人，在小菊很小的时候，也是得了肺痨，最后死了。那段时间，秀珍的模样是任谁见了都会掉泪。所以，赵宏伟觉得，无论如何，他都不能再看着她们娘儿俩受什么苦。

今天，赵宏伟在秀珍的后院里坐了一会儿。秀珍的脸上抹着一些灶灰，她无助地望着赵宏伟，问，宏伟哥，这日本人还会在赵家镇上杀人吗？

赵宏伟说，不会的，铁匠那天是拿着家伙，大家误会了，所以才出了事。

秀珍说，可也不能随便开枪啊。那不是不拿我们当人吗？

赵宏伟低着头，不说话。

娘，我怕，小菊突然说。

秀珍就搂了搂小菊，说，不怕，小菊不怕，有宏伟伯伯在呢，不怕。说着，秀珍自己却是流下了泪来。

对不起，我当初该让你们逃的。赵宏伟说。

秀珍摇摇头说，不，这里是我家，离开了家，去哪儿都是要怕的。

赵宏伟鼻子一酸。

宏伟伯伯，你留下来陪我们吧，不要走，我们怕，我娘昨晚做梦还喊你的名字呢。

小菊，你乱说话。秀珍脸一红，要打小菊。

赵宏伟就抱住了小菊，不让秀珍打她。小孩子不懂事乱说话，你怎么能当真，还打她。赵宏伟说。秀珍就红了脸低着头，也不敢看他。

小菊乖，伯伯要出去给你找好吃的，找到了就回来，好不好？赵宏伟逗小菊。

小菊就懵懵懂懂地点了点头。

赵宏伟将小菊还给秀珍，说，给小菊的脸上也抹一点儿灰。

秀珍惊恐地看着赵宏伟。赵宏伟说，没事，我只是看别人也都这么做，所以才嘱咐你。他不敢告诉秀珍，当年的玉山帮，就连小女孩都不放过，更不用说现在的日本人了。

这样的日子，何时才是个头哇，赵宏伟心里不禁叹道。

县城里又发生了几次枪战。日本人还放了迫击炮。赵宏伟后来才知道，那是共产党的新四军游击队在劫狱，他们想救出那个被俘虏的同志。但是他们没有成功。

人们终于还是陆陆续续地上街了。不是因为别的，是因为各人家里能吃的都已经吃光了，不得不出来。该干活的还干活，该卖东西的还卖东西，只有这样，大家才能继续生活下去。况且，在铁匠事件之后，日本人再没有在赵家镇上杀什么人。大家彼此安慰：只要我们当个良民，日本人是不会拿我们怎么样的。

秀珍也重新开始出去给人家洗衣服了。虽然赵宏伟不同意，但是秀珍坚持要去。她还把他那天给她的钱也都还给了他。自从秀珍的爹和男人相继离世之后，秀珍就过着吃了上顿没下顿的苦日子。赵宏伟时常想接济她，但她都不要。前段时间接受他送吃的，那是因为秀珍家里的确是一点儿存粮都没有。她只要三天不出去洗衣服，小菊就会饿肚子。但是现在大家都上街了，一切又恢复了正常，她秀珍又怎么还会待在家里，等着赵宏伟去接济她呢？秀珍就是这样的一个女子。赵宏伟有时也会为她感到心痛，但也无可奈何，唯有自责不已。他总是觉得，自己是欠秀珍的。

赵宏伟最近除了担心秀珍和小菊之外，也很担心自己。他现在隐隐有种不好的预感，全赵家镇都知道他赵宏伟是在日本留过洋的，万一日本人也知道了，来找他干什么，那他就惨了。他很后悔自己当初怎么就没想到这一点。现在想什么也都晚了。只能乞求上天保佑，让国军快点打回来吧。

赵宏伟去找方远梦。赵宏伟有时候就觉得，这全赵家镇，只有方远梦是他的朋友。方远梦是外乡人，他是在九一八事变发生的第二年，来到赵家镇。方远梦是个很瘦小的男人，不认识他的，第一眼看见他绝不会相信他是个纯正的东北人。但是相识久了，你就会真的感受到，他的心像东北的土地一样，深厚而辽阔，绵长而悲怆。赵宏伟欣赏这样子的人。他不喜欢像自己一样畏首畏尾、缩手缩脚的江南男人。

方远梦是赵家镇小学的副校长，是赵宏伟一手提拔的。赵宏伟倒也不是想培植自己的党羽，老秀才从赵宏伟小时候起就教育他，君子周而不比，小人比而不周。赵宏伟是看方远梦是个人才，又懂俄语，不想埋没了他。这世道，好人靠正常途径是很难有出头之日的。自然，方远梦也是一直很感激赵宏伟的知遇之恩的。

赵宏伟敲了门，方远梦过了好一会儿才来开的门。赵宏伟一进门，就闻到了一股消毒药水的气味，就问，怎么有股药水味？

哦，昨天上房修瓦，下来的时候不小心摔了一跤，擦破了手臂，我正在给自己上药呢。

你小心些。幸亏是你自己有药，不然你现在上医院，日本人见你有血，不查你才怪。

是啊是啊，我大意了。来，坐。

赵宏伟在方远梦的家里坐了下来，心里才算安定了一些，就像是一个在孤舟渡河的人，终于找到了一个伙伴。大撤退的时候，方远梦也没走。他对赵宏伟说，赵家镇上还有许多孩子没走，有孩子的地方，怎么可以没有一个老师留下来？于是，在那段时间里，他和赵宏伟一起，给剩下来的孩子上课。他们又教国文又教算术，有了个伴，倒也是不觉得累。这更让赵宏伟觉得此人难得。

赵兄，今天怎么想起来我这里？方远梦给赵宏伟倒了一杯水，也坐了下来。

赵宏伟沉吟了片刻，说，方兄，你是从东北过来的，我想问问你，对现在的时局，有何看法？

现在的形势，中国是万分危难，但是日本人想要征服中国，最终只是一场痴心妄想。

怎么说？

日本人以为，他们还能让成吉思汗和努尔哈赤的事迹在中国重演一遍，但是他们忘了，时代已经变了。我们已经连自己的皇帝都不要了，又怎么可能向一个外人的皇帝俯首称臣？世界潮流，浩浩荡荡，顺之者昌，逆之者亡，日本人连这么简单的道理都不懂，又怎么可能会不败呢？

赵宏伟默默点头，但眉头依然是紧锁的。

赵宏伟今天来，想问的和想听的，其实不是这天下事，他对中国的明天，其实不是很感兴趣。他想问的，其实是：这日本人在赵家镇上还会乱杀人吗？他们真的会随便糟蹋妇女吗？他们真的会把小孩当羊一样烤吗？但他知道，这些话问出来，是可笑的。他也知道自己可笑，但他就是怕。他就是盼着有人能给他一些否定的答案，那样他或许就能摆脱一些恐惧的纠缠。他每天夜里都怕得想哭，但他又不敢哭，枉为七尺男儿。老秀才若在天有灵，也一定会唾弃他的。

方兄，那接下来，你打算怎么办？赵宏伟又问。

我们既然选择留在了这赵家镇上，就一定要为赵家镇的百姓做一些事。方远梦大义凛然地说。

赵宏伟心中一惊。怎么，难道？赵宏伟又惊又疑，不敢开口。

方远梦就笑了。赵兄，瞧你怕的，想哪儿去了，我们老百姓又没枪又没炮，我总不至于会傻得想要去杀日本人。杀得了日本人去杀那是勇敢，杀不了日本人去杀那叫送死，是愚蠢。我虽不才，总还不蠢。

赵宏伟就笑了起来。

看样子，日本人是会在赵家镇上待很长一段时间了，方远梦说。我想，这么长一段时间，孩子们总不能一直在家待着。我们既然是老师，就要负起一个老师的责任。我想我们可以选个地方，继续给孩子们上课。荒什么也不能荒了孩子的学习不是？他们才是中国明天的主人。特别在现在这种时候，我们更要让孩子们知道，他们是中国人，中国才是他们的爹和娘。我们要给孩子们讲岳飞，讲文天祥，讲邓世昌，这样，我们中国人的火种，才会生生不息！

赵宏伟听着方远梦慷慨激昂的话，心里却还是在担心着自己的种种。小菊可怜的样子忽然又出现在了他的眼前，他觉得心痛不已。他知道秀珍和小菊都需要他，但是没办法，他和她们，今生注定了只能是邻居。因为他，不能对不起已经死去了的心音。

心音的全名是藤田心音。她是一个比樱花还要纯洁而浪漫的少女。赵宏伟至今，也无法将心音和那些入侵中国的日本兵想象成同一个国家的子民。

初到东京的赵宏伟，日语讲得很不地道。他从踏上日本国土的那一刻起，才发现自己在国内学校里学到的那点儿日语，简单粗糙得可怜。虽然一到日本，他就去了一所专门教授中国留学生日语的学校里学习，但是语言这东西，毕竟不是临时抱佛脚就能学好的。况且他来日本也不是为了学日语的，他还要正正经经地去上日本的大学，所以他学日语的时间很紧。不过好在他是一个江南人，日语的发音方式和吴方言的发音方式很接近，而且他赵宏伟也的确是天资聪颖，所以在正式进入大学一年以后，他的日语就突飞猛进到了近乎纯正的水平。这里面，被歧视以后引起的发奋之志，起了重要的决定作用。

到了日本才知道，日本人看不起中国人，对中国人不屑一顾。比如，他们并不会当面嘲笑你是个中国人，甚至也不会在背后对你指指戳戳，但是，他们会觉得，你根本就不在“人”这个群体的行列里。给一个普通人吃残羹剩饭是对一个人的羞辱，但是给一个中国人吃残羹剩饭那简直就是大发慈悲。就是这么个意思。这种感觉你抓不住，握不牢，但是它时时刻刻就在你的身边游动、浮沉，向你挤压。就像是你周围的空气，不管你乐不乐意，你都必须要吸它入你体内。以前，赵宏伟从不懂得这种感受。他至此，才懂得了老秀才一生的愤怒与哀怨，他至此，才懂得了老秀才为何要他东渡扶桑。国家是百姓的脊梁，国若不强，百姓又怎能挺起腰板做人？

赵宏伟在学校里一心发愤读书。这引来了赵驹的嘲笑。赵驹油滑而放浪，赵宏伟本来就不喜欢他。但是到了东京，赵宏伟遇上赵驹，就想又是同乡又是同学的，也是难得的缘分，不如交个朋友算了。然而道不同终究不相为谋，赵驹喜欢吃喝嫖赌，在异国他乡仍然不改本性。赵宏伟不想跟着他去，也跟不起。毕竟赵驹的钱多，自己的钱少。这样一来二去，两人的关系

就又疏远了。赵驹在赵家镇的时候就一直被公认为不如赵宏伟聪明，现在到了东京，看赵宏伟又嫌弃他，心里就也开始看不上赵宏伟了。他想，聪明有个屁用，没钱就是个废物，死书呆子。于是，渐渐地，两人又形同陌路。这些事情对他们两个人来说，都很不重要。就像是你素不相识的一个陌生人，忽然靠近了你，然后又有些厌恶地走开，这除了会让你稍微觉得有点儿不舒服以外，对你一点儿影响也不会有。那时的赵宏伟是根本不会想到，将来有一天，他会深切地后悔，后悔自己没有与赵驹结成兄弟。

刻苦读书的赵宏伟也是稍微赢得了一些日本同学的尊重。这种感觉是很美妙的。人家本来十分看不起你，但是到了跑道上，你却远比他们出色，他们只能诧异地看着你回首向他们微笑，看着你把他们给的耻辱化作动力，一跃千里。这种美妙简直令人陶醉。就是在这个时候，一个叫藤田武的日本同学，开始和他产生了友谊。

据藤田武说，他的祖上，其实也有汉人的血统。中国明朝的时候，一批倭寇——藤田武说的是“一批日本武士”——来到了温州，劫掠了一批女子回到了日本。其中一个女子后来流落街头，就遇上了当时还是一名乞丐的藤田家的祖先。当然了，那时他们藤田家还没有“藤田”这么个姓，日本的平民百姓有姓，是明治维新以后的事情了。两人后来结为夫妻，生下了儿女一群。藤田武说，如果不是那名中国女子，一个乞丐，恐怕终身也难有子嗣。虽然赵宏伟听了这个故事觉得心里有点儿不是滋味，但是毕竟，人家藤田武是在向他示好，并没有恶意。

赵宏伟和藤田武学的都是机械。赵宏伟本来是想学医的，但是老秀才的一番话打消了他的这个念头。老秀才说，你要学医的话干吗要去日本呢？待在赵家镇上跟老中医学学不就行了？要学就要学机械，学工业，那样才能为国家之振兴尽绵薄之力，因为中国现在缺的就是工业。于是赵宏伟就学了机械。藤田武也曾问过赵宏伟，你这样优秀，毕业以后会留在日本吗？赵宏伟不假思索地就说，不会，我要回国去。藤田武就问，那你们那里，有工厂吗？要是没有工厂，你岂不是英雄无用武之地？赵宏伟一想，赵家镇上还真没有工厂，江庆县城里也没有。但是他还是斩钉截铁而骄傲自豪地说，有，我们那里有工厂。藤田武就没有再说什么。

藤田武喜欢和赵宏伟手谈。赵宏伟以前一直觉得自己棋艺不精，但是碰上了藤田武，才发现自己原来也还不差。他就不禁有些得意地想，毕竟中国才是围棋的故乡啊。有时候赢的次数太多了，赵宏伟也会觉得不好意思，就故意输个一两次，让藤田武乐乐。赵宏伟有时就会很惋惜地想，可惜你藤田武不是中国人哪，否则，我们一定会成为好兄弟的。

事情的转变发生在赵宏伟手头拮据的这一年。那时，赵宏伟收到家里寄来的钱，全部被贼给偷了。警察局抓不到贼，赵宏伟就只好发电报回去，重新问家里要钱。但是由于各种原因，这封要钱的电报在国内传递的路上竟耽搁了两三个月。赵宏伟迟迟收不到回音，还以为家里暂时有困难，也没敢催。直到后来才知道是让电报给耽误了。当时，赵宏伟欠了房东两个月房租，房东已决意要赶赵宏伟走。赵宏伟无计可施，不敢跟人家耍横，就想着去找赵驹借钱。他那时还不知道赵驹已是麻烦缠身。但是他又觉得自己去向赵驹借钱是件很丢脸的事。他一向是看不起赵驹的，是不愿与他同流合污的。俗话说得好，饿死事小，失节事大，他赵宏伟，是绝不会为了五斗米而折腰的。

于是他赵宏伟就被房东赶到了大街上。

就在他一筹莫展之际，藤田武出现了。他得知了事情的原委，就对赵宏伟说，宏伟君，这种事情，你一早就可以来找我的。藤田武家里是开旅馆的，这赵宏伟早就知道，可是一来，他知道旅馆的价钱不便宜，二来，他也是不想跟藤田武发生金钱上的关系，他在日本好不容易有了个挺不错的日本朋友，他不想让这个朋友成为他的房东。但是现在他没了栖身之所，别无选择，也只好求助于藤田武了。藤田武倒是很高兴，他说，帮助朋友，是一个武士应有的品德。

藤田武以一个极其便宜的价格将旅馆里的一间不错的房间租给了赵宏伟，而且还允许赵宏伟先欠两个月房租。赵宏伟心花怒放。而藤田武的父亲也没有反对藤田武的决定。藤田武的母亲在很早以前就死了。赵宏伟没有想到，就是藤田武的这个善意的帮助，将几个人同时推上了一条悲剧之路。

赵宏伟第一次看见心音，是在旅馆后面的樱花树下。美丽的樱花在风中凋落，绚烂死去，一个漂亮的少女蹲在树下，快乐地捡拾着花瓣。赵宏伟后来才知道，她就是藤田武的妹妹，藤田心音。那一年，心音十七岁。看见她的第一眼，赵宏伟就想起了黛玉葬花。但是他又知道，这样明朗的少女，不

会是林黛玉一样的病人。

那一天的后来，赵宏伟问，你捡这些花瓣来做什么呢？心音灿烂地一笑，然后说，这样啊。说着，她便将手里的花瓣往天上一抛。刹那间，花雨缤纷，阳光美丽。心音在花雨中欢笑。

临走时，她问，你叫什么？

他说，木村太郎。你呢？

藤田心音。

赵宏伟的心里就咯噔一下，想，不会这么巧吧？

方远梦想好了，就在赵宏伟和他的家里轮流办课堂，继续把学生们的课上下去。赵宏伟对于办课堂没有意见，他甚至还想，等将来哪天国军光复了，这说不定还是小功一件呢。但是，赵宏伟凭直觉判断，这件事，肯定不会很顺利。

县城里最近没有发生枪战，太平得很。倒是县城的日军总部里有几个鬼子，出来惹了些事。他们在县城里的老酒坊那儿，糟蹋了几个大姑娘，然后还用刺刀捅死了一个姑娘的爹。这件事产生了一个很严重的后果，那就是县城里，家家户户又重新关窗锁门，开始了尽量大门不出二门不迈的死城生活。这让县城日军联队总部里的最高长官联队长竹内中佐很伤脑筋。几天之后，他就做出了一个重要的决定，枪毙捅死老头的那个日本兵。他还真的就是在广场上枪毙了一个日本兵。但是后来有人发现，这个兵的嘴里没舌头。也就是说，这个被毙了的，很有可能是个中国人。但是人们又能怎么样呢？真的能去跟日本鬼子较真吗？他们能把那几个糟蹋姑娘的日本兵给阉了吗？别去送死了，能活着就不错了。于是，人们还是重新又走出了家门，渐渐地又一次恢复了正常的生活秩序。没办法，人活着，不能不生活。那些王八蛋国军走的时候又没给老百姓留下枪，想反抗，难道还能拿着菜刀去反抗？忍着吧。

赵宏伟很庆幸，赵家镇上太平无事。他天天祈祷着，渡边那个王八蛋能治军从严，以德服人。赵宏伟不是真的相信祈祷，只是觉得，祈祷了，心里的害怕会暂时减轻一些。

但是这一天，赵宏伟家的门，还是被人敲响了。

打开门，门外站着一名中年日本军官。军官的后面站着两个拿长枪的日本兵。在军官的旁边，还站着一个微微地弯着腰的人，他身上没穿军装，只头上戴了一顶皱巴巴的日本兵帽子。赵宏伟几乎不敢相信自己的眼睛。这是谁？这不就是赵驹吗！

“你好，请问你就是赵宏伟先生吗？”日本军官用日语问。

“是的，太君，他就是。”赵驹点头哈腰地代替赵宏伟回答。

赵宏伟暗自为赵驹感到悲哀。这么多年过去了，他赵驹看样子是已经当了汉奸，日语说得却还是那么生硬而粗糙，甚至还有了点儿东北口音的味儿，什么东西。赵宏伟暗骂。

“赵宏伟，多年不见，怎么，不认识老朋友了？”赵驹挺起了腰，笑哈哈地对赵宏伟说。

“哪里哪里，多年不见，赵兄别来无恙？”赵宏伟也笑哈哈地说。

日本军官看样子听不懂汉语。他疑惑地看了看赵驹。

“哦，忘了介绍，这位，就是大日本皇军驻赵家镇部队的最高长官，大队长渡边少佐。”赵驹用他那恶心的日语向赵宏伟介绍，“而我，现在是渡边先生的翻译官。”

从看见渡边的第一眼起，赵宏伟的心里就打起了鼓，但他依旧要求自己保持镇定，保持风度，保持腰杆笔直的姿态。有时候，本来没事，你要是一慌，事就来了，他对自己说。

“太君，请。”赵驹自作主张，请渡边进了门。赵宏伟只好让开，连拒客于门外的权利都没有，可能这就是被占领的悲哀，赵宏伟想。

两个日本兵在门外站岗。赵宏伟在关门的时候，看见远处有一些乡邻在对着他这边张望，并且还伴有一些指戳，赵宏伟心下一紧。他放弃了关门，将门大敞着。

渡边坐在正屋里的太师椅上，看了看木讷地站着的赵宏伟，说，赵先生，请坐。

赵宏伟犹豫了一下，没有坐。

你听不懂太君的话吗？他叫你坐。赵驹说。

赵宏伟犹豫着坐了下来。

你也坐，渡边对赵驹说。

谢谢太君。赵驹坐下。

赵先生，听说你也是从日本留学回来的？渡边问。

赵宏伟想了一想，然后点了点头。

那真是太好了，想不到在这小小的赵家镇上，也有我们大日本帝国的学生。相信以后，我们一定会合作愉快的。渡边说。

赵宏伟呆愣着，不明白，也不敢想。他全身本来就已很僵硬了，这时，更像是成了个木雕。渡边看赵宏伟没反应，不禁就疑惑地望了望赵驹。

喂，赵宏伟，太君在跟你说话呢，难道你现在听不懂日语了？

多年没听，生疏了。赵宏伟生硬地用汉语说。

太君说，要跟你合作。

赵兄，你可真幽默，我一没钱二没权，只是一个混日子过的穷书生，哪有什么可跟日本人合作的？赵兄你快别开我的玩笑了。

赵宏伟，我就知道你是个滑头。

这时，渡边插话了。他问赵驹，你们在说什么？为什么不讲日语？赵驹就向渡边汇报了一下情况。

渡边就面向了赵宏伟，说，赵先生，今天我们来呢，只是想请你继续担任赵家镇小学的校长，把学校重新开起来，方便孩子们念书，并没有什么别的意思。

赵宏伟顿了一顿，不敢表现出自己的疑惑。他问赵驹：就是这事？

废话，不然你以为你还能有什么用。赵驹不屑地说。

赵宏伟略微舒了一口气。

渡边笑着说，赵先生，我们是很有诚意的。本来，我们是想让孩子们都去县城里的学校里上学的，请你也去县城里当校长，但是，县城里的学校现在暂时都被用作了兵营，所以就只能暂时让孩子们都集中到赵家镇上的学校里来上课，也只好暂时先委屈一下赵先生你了。但是你放心，我们大日本皇军是不会亏待朋友的，一切顺利的话，过段时间，竹内中佐就将正式任命你为江庆县的教育局长。

赵宏伟不敢接话。教孩子没问题，孩子反正是要教的，但是日本人的任命，他是万万不能要的。一要，那就是铁板上钉钉的汉奸了。

我只是一个老百姓，我什么职务也不要，教孩子念书可以，但是我只会以一个普通老师的身份去教。赵宏伟对赵驹说。

赵驹翻译了一下。

渡边的眉头微微皱了一下，但是很快又舒展了开来。他和颜悦色地说，赵先生，我听我的翻译官说，你的日语水平和他是差不多的，为什么你今天一句日语都没有讲过？

赵宏伟心里狠狠地“呸”了一声。我跟赵驹差不多？我呸，他也配！赵宏伟心里骂道。

哦，多年不讲，生疏了，生疏了。赵宏伟又用汉语说。

渡边就站了起来，在屋里转了一圈。他沉吟片刻，然后说，赵先生，我们邀请你，就是看重你会讲日语的才能，因为我们要在学校里教孩子们讲日语，让他们了解我们大和民族的优秀文化，要他们热爱我们大日本帝国的一草一木。没有一个会日语的老师，我们怎么教他们呢？赵先生，我们知道你是会讲的，你不要谦虚。

赵宏伟脑袋里嗡的一下。他想，上当了，完了。他脸白得没了半点血色。

他沉默不语。事实上他此刻头脑里也的确是空白一片。他不想死，他也不想当汉奸。他该怎么办？此刻，他宁愿自己是个哑巴。

喂，赵宏伟，你怎么不说话？赵驹问。

哦，我、我身体不大舒服。赵驹，麻烦你告诉太君，日语我现在是真不会说了，我不能干误人子弟的事对不对？那样也是辜负了皇军的信任。请皇军还是另请高明吧。医生说，我要在家长期静养，不能劳碌，不能劳碌。

赵驹将赵宏伟的话翻译了一遍。

渡边阴冷地笑了笑。赵先生，我们是不会另请高明的，今天你既然不舒服，那么我们就先告辞了。但是三天后我们会再来，希望到时候，你已经考虑清楚，究竟是要做我们大日本皇军的朋友，还是做我们大日本皇军的敌人。

说完，不等赵宏伟回话，渡边就径自往大门口走了去。赵驹赶紧跟了上去。赵宏伟也跟了上去，想表示一下欢送。

到了大门外，渡边回头又对赵宏伟说，赵先生，相信你是个聪明人，我们后会有期。说着，他向赵宏伟伸出了一只手，是握手的意思。赵宏伟犹豫

了一下，也就伸出了手跟他握了一下。

这时，赵宏伟看到，秀珍正站在一个很远的地方，惊恐地看着他。

就在赵宏伟在藤田家的旅馆里安顿下来的同时，赵驹已是被人逼得走投无路。事情的起因是这样的，赵驹喜欢嫖妓，以前没出过什么事，但是这次却出了意外。他去了一个比较高档的场所，想玩几个高级货，但是他的口音却出卖了他。人家不做中国人的生意，于是赵驹就耍起了横。他以为这里也是他爹的地盘呢。他要霸王硬上弓。他打了人家日本妓女两个耳光。于是，他就触怒了一个地头蛇——山本。山本发誓一定要弄死赵驹。赵驹东躲西藏，惶惶不可终日，而他武功高强的爹又远在海的另一边。他叫天天不应，叫地地不灵，万般无奈之下，最终选择了放弃学业，仓皇出逃。开始，大家听说，他逃去了北海道。后来又有人说，赵驹已经回了国。不管哪种说法更准确，总之，大家都觉得赵驹是罪有应得。每个洁身自好的中国留学生，都以赵驹为耻。而赵宏伟，在得知了赵驹的倒霉遭遇后，更是绝口不再提他跟赵驹是同乡的事。他怕山本找不到赵驹，会找到他来向他问赵驹的消息。不过还好，赵驹走后，一切也都风平浪静，就好像根本没发生什么事一样。

藤田武将藤田心音介绍给赵宏伟的时候，赵宏伟掩饰住了自己的尴尬。心音诧异地问，你不是叫木村太郎吗？

藤田武摸摸自己的脑袋，感到莫名其妙。

赵宏伟风度翩翩地说，看见你，一时起了调皮的心情，就给自己取了一个日本名字。其实我是一个中国人，你会看不起一个身为中国人的我吗？

心音天真地说，当然不会，你是我哥哥的朋友，也就是我的朋友了。她对藤田武说，哥哥，你的这个朋友说话真有趣。

藤田武笑了，说，宏伟君是一个优秀的人，他并不像一般的中国人。

赵宏伟虽然觉得藤田武此话有贬低中国人之嫌，但是想想也算了，人家也不是故意的，而且是在说你的好话。

但是藤田武的父亲却是个高傲而寡言的人，有时候进出旅馆，赵宏伟碰到他，向他礼貌地问一声好，他也是爱理不理的，眼神里流露着一股不屑。时间久了，赵宏伟知道他并不像他的儿女那样好相处，进出旅馆的时候，就多了一丝忐忑的心情。想想，毕竟是在异国他乡，处处不得不看别人的脸色，赵宏伟觉得很孤独。

有时候，藤田武跟赵宏伟手谈，心音就在一旁观战。她总是看得很认真，有时不懂还会问。赵宏伟就充当了她的老师。她渐渐地对赵宏伟产生了敬佩。赵宏伟心中很是得意。

不知是从什么时候起，赵宏伟总觉得，和藤田武单独在一起总像是少了些什么。多年以后赵宏伟才明白，孤独中的男子是不可以接近少女的，一接近，你就会中毒。

一次，赵宏伟问藤田武，你是怎么看待今天的中国和日本的？

藤田武想了想，就有些尴尬。他说，我知道，我们日本从占了你们的台湾岛开始，对中国做了很多不友好的事情，但是，那些事，不是我们老百姓想出来的，也不是我们老百姓做的，甚至有些军人，他们也只是在遵守服从命令的原则。希望你能明白。

我们明不明白，恐怕不会对时局有丝毫的影响。

是啊，宏伟君。总之，我希望我们能一直是朋友。

我也这么希望。

其实赵宏伟是想问，你以后会不会去当兵？但他后来一想，这么问很傻。时局这么乱，一切想不到的都可能发生，一切不情愿的也都可能成真，这种事情又有什么好问的。他从一开始就没准备和藤田武做一生的朋友，因为他远比藤田武谙熟世事沧桑。中日一开战，夫妻也会变仇敌，更何况区区的朋友之情。但是近来赵宏伟在孤独中倍觉多愁。想想藤田兄妹对他这么好，也真是不敢想象反目的那一幕。他很苦恼。老秀才从小就教育他，千金易得，朋友难求。现在他有了一个朋友，但可惜却是个日本人。真是自古忠义难两全。

友谊的烦恼倒还在其次。现在最令赵宏伟发愁的，是他一见到心音就会很开心。他隐隐感到这不是个好苗，但是心音却还是喜欢跟着他们出去玩，甚至有时候藤田武不在，心音也会要赵宏伟出去陪她散散步。赵宏伟很想拒绝，但是到头来却总是喜出望外，他甚至还为了取悦心音，而去学习了日本料理。他无数次地指责自己卑鄙，也无数次地要自己看清自己的现在与将来，要自己不要越陷越深。但他越是这样，就沉得越快。毕竟，在此之前，

他还从来没有如此喜欢过一个女孩子。在有些事情上面，理智与忠告是无能为力的。

这一年秋天的时候，赵宏伟和心音两个人彼此确定了对方对自己的好感。心音又害羞又快乐，粉红的嘴唇里含了好多话，却又都藏在嘴里。只有喜上眉梢，分外妖娆。赵宏伟不禁又想起了第一次见到她时的模样，人在花中笑，花在笑里飘，令人心醉。

然而，赵宏伟依然不知道自己的明天究竟会怎样。跟与藤田武的友情一样，赵宏伟也从未想过，他跟心音的爱情会延续到天长地久。他知道心音不是这么想的。她是天真的，一拥有爱情，她就以为他会像她的眼睛一样对她不离不弃，直到生命的终点，少女总是那么天真而浪漫。而赵宏伟却现实而多思，他当然也是真心爱她的。天知道爱情为什么就是那样不知不觉地就发生了，弄得人措手不及，而又丝毫无招架之力。真心相爱的感觉是美妙的，但是这样的美妙落在了这样的一个时局之中，就近乎是成了一场恶作剧。赵宏伟头痛不已。

冬天下了雪，心音快乐地将雪堆成了一个小人。这是一种没有国界的游戏，赵宏伟暗自感叹。他感受着雪落在脸上冰凉而痒痒的感觉，这与他在赵家镇上享受到的冬天并没有什么两样，但是这又毕竟不是故乡的雪。他在雪里留恋着现在，又怀念着过去。心音在他面前快乐地飞舞，他的时间在彷徨里止步。他将她的小手焐在自己的手心，他的心里举棋不定。他说，心音，我爱你。心音说，我也爱你，宏伟君。

他就吻她，吻得那样热烈而不顾一切，就好像，希望两个人可以永远停在这一刻，让时光把他们变成石头。

事情终于还是败露了。那是在夏天，赵宏伟和藤田武都即将面临毕业。心音织了一顶帽子送给赵宏伟，赵宏伟将它放在自己的房间里。结果一不小心，被心音的父亲发现了。老人的怒火可以烧掉整个房间。

赵宏伟被撵出了这座旅馆。老人果断而干脆。赵宏伟甚至还没有来得及交这个月的房钱。这是一个给赵宏伟留下了多少美好回忆的地方啊。可是顷刻之间，他就因为一顶爱的帽子，又成了一条无家可归的丧家之犬。自怜在他的心里并没有占据多少地盘，他的自责，同老人的怒火一样，声势浩大。他从一开始就知道，自己不该和一个日本女子恋爱，更何况，这个女子又是藤田武的妹妹、旅馆老板的女儿。现在好了，他又流落街头了。他觉得爱情真是个害人的东西。这一次，他不知道该找谁帮忙。

幸亏这是在夏天，在街角上睡一晚也不是很难。他很幸运，白天，他就找到了一个房东。人家还以为他是一个离家出走的日本青年。房租不是很贵，赵宏伟又安顿了下来。他睡下时，就又想起了心音。他很喜欢那顶帽子，这辈子还是第一次有女孩子送他东西，况且又是心音亲手织的，还织得那么精致。可惜这顶帽子已经被那个暴跳如雷的老头给没收了。赵宏伟后悔自己当时的大意。他心里对心音充满了歉疚，又伴着一些说不出的伤心，然后他觉得很累，就昏昏然地睡了过去。

当藤田武站在赵宏伟面前时，赵宏伟还没有想好该怎样面对他。藤田武脸色发灰，赵宏伟猜不出他的态度。

宏伟君，你以后打算留在日本吗？

不会。

那你为什么要和我的妹妹恋爱？难道你想让她跟你回中国吗，还是你真的像我父亲所说的，仅仅只是在欺骗她？

不是的，不是的。赵宏伟连忙说。他想说，我是真心爱她的，但是又一想，是啊，藤田武说得没错，难道我想带他回中国去吗？如果不是，那我又干吗要跟她恋爱呢？

赵宏伟愧疚地低下了头。

宏伟君，你真是太让我失望了！你竟然这样对待我的妹妹！

赵宏伟以为藤田武要打他，但是藤田武只是愤怒地转身走了。赵宏伟跌进了一团令人窒息的黑暗里。

几天后，赵宏伟还在彷徨里打转。心音却突然出现在了他的面前。我终于找到你了，为什么你不来找我？心音幽怨地说。

赵宏伟转头看着别处，无法回答她，也无法面对她。

宏伟君，你放心，我是不会向我的父亲屈服的，我们的人生，要由我们自己来安排。

心音，是我太无能了。

不，你是一个优秀的人。哥哥说，我和你是没有未来的，因为在我和你之间，还有一场两个国家之间的仇恨，但是我并不这样认为。你并不讨厌日

本，而我也并不讨厌中国，我们藤田家族的身上，本来也流有中国人的血。政客们的事情，和我们又有什么关系呢？

是的，心音。赵宏伟激动地抱住了心音。

我想过了，谁也不能阻止我们在一起。你要是愿意留在日本，那很好；要是你不愿意留在日本，那也没关系，我愿意跟你去中国。总之我们要在一起，你说好吗？

好，好，太好了。心音，我爱你。

心音笑得像孩子一样天真。

赵宏伟几乎流出了眼泪。

但是之后，赵宏伟就一直再没看见心音。他找藤田武问，藤田武叫他滚开。赵宏伟说，我没有欺骗心音，我要带她回中国。

你说什么？你再说一遍！

我说，我爱心音，我没有骗她，我要带她回中国。

混蛋！你居然要带我妹妹去中国！你这不是害她是什么？她天真是她的事，但我们不能任由她一直傻下去！你滚！

你不要这么粗鲁，我发誓，我一定会好好对待心音的，我对她是真心的。

你要讲道理，好，那我跟你讲道理。宏伟君，你说你爱心音，那我问你，心音跟你回了中国，你能让她过上跟现在一样条件的生活吗？请你坦诚地回答。

赵宏伟默不作声了。

你回答！

不能。

很好，你还需要我告诉你心音在哪里吗？

赵宏伟流泪了。他问：如果我是英国人，你们是不是就不会反对心音跟我在一起了？

是的。

你以前还说你不会歧视中国人。

我没有歧视中国人，但你们落后是事实。难道我要看着我的妹妹去过猪狗的生活而不表示反对，才能显示我人格的高尚吗？简直是荒谬！

赵宏伟无言以对。

他的泪，滚烫得像火。

宏伟君，其实你也并非毫无选择。凭你的才干，留下来，待在日本，根本就不会有人把你当成一个中国人，那样，我父亲或许才能重新考虑你跟心音的事。那样，我也才能为你说几句话。你仔细想一想，我说的对不对？

赵宏伟把泪一抹。

谢谢你的忠告，你说得没错，但我是不会留在日本的。

为什么？我是真不明白！

就是为了，不要再有中国人，会像我今天这样，为了祖国而流泪！

赵宏伟拂袖离去。

这一年冬天的时候，赵宏伟本来准备要回国了。可是，好久不见的藤田武，却突然主动来找赵宏伟。

我知道你要回去了。

你有什么事？

事实上，是父亲让我来找你的。

怎么？

我曾经在你最困难的时候帮助过你，所以，希望你也能无私地帮助我们一次。

你们要我做什么？

很简单，让心音死心。

赵宏伟终于又见到了心音。心音已瘦得变了样子，但是见到赵宏伟的那一刻，心音的眼里还是像星星一样放出了光彩。

你来了，你终于来了！你知道吗，父亲终于同意我们的事了！

对不起，心音，我要走了，我是来向你告别的。

什么？告别？

心音还没从惊喜中缓过神来，就被赵宏伟说得糊涂了起来。

我要一个人回中国去了。

什么？难道你不带我一起走吗？

不，对不起，心音，其实我在家乡，已经有未婚妻了。

赵宏伟说着，脸一阵一阵地抽搐。

什么？

对不起！我在家乡，已经有未婚妻了！

——啊！

只听见心音一声惨呼，赵宏伟扭头就跑。

赵宏伟一边跑，一边想，我就要走了，就让心音恨我、忘了我吧！从头到尾，就是我不对！让我被雷劈吧！

真的下起了雷雨，赵宏伟在雨中狂奔，他向着有闪电的地方跑去，但是闪电总在他遥不可及的高空中劈斩，他根本就触不到死亡的边。他的泪就在雨里横流。他在雨里咆哮，像个疯子一样。他想，藤田武是对的。

然而赵宏伟并没有马上回国。他忽然像是被什么拖住了后腿。在斩断了与心音的一切之后，他却突然无法果断离开这个地方。就好像，他只要一走，他的人生里就会出现一个洞，一个黑得看不到边的洞。他换了一个新的住址，在居酒屋里做起了杂役。他不是不想回去了，他是想，知道心音安好之后，再走。

但是心音的消息一直没有传来。他也无法再去面对藤田武。他与藤田武已彼此厌恶。自从藤田武让他用谎言撕碎心音的爱之后，他已无法再在藤田武的面前保持平静。他牵挂着心音，就像牢记着自己欠下的一笔债。

是居酒屋里的一份旧报纸，让他知道了心音后来的故事。心音在一九二五年的春天，嫁给了一位影楼老板的儿子。新婚当晚，心音割腕自杀。未死。心音醒后，神志不清，成了疯子。丈夫愤而与其离婚。

丢下报纸，赵宏伟离开了居酒屋，又去了一次心音的家。她的家还在，依然是原样。他希望里面的人也没换。敲开门，是心音父亲苍老的脸。这张脸在见到赵宏伟的第二秒，就扭曲成了一块可怕的伤疤。“中国人，可恨的中国人！我要杀了你！我要杀了你！”

还是藤田武跑出来制止了老人的暴行。

赵宏伟的脸上流着血，藤田武给他擦了一擦。赵宏伟忽然发现，自己和藤田武，还是有过真的友谊的。只是太多外在的东西，撕裂了人们善良的情感。

藤田武带着赵宏伟，去见了见心音。心音已认不出赵宏伟。她头发凌乱，口角流涎，手里抓着一顶帽子。仔细一看，正是那时她给他织的那顶帽子。藤田武说，只有拿着这顶帽子，她才会平静。

赵宏伟跪下来抱着她，流泪喊着她的名字，但她什么也不明白。

窗外秋叶飘零。

藤田武说，心音疯后，他曾去找过他，但他早已搬走了。

赵宏伟说，心音，你醒醒，你醒醒，我是赵宏伟。

藤田武说，没想到会变成这样。

赵宏伟说，心音，我骗你的，我没有未婚妻，我没有未婚妻！你看看，是我呀！

藤田武突然流泪了，他说，宏伟君，你别喊了。

赵宏伟突然仰天笑了起来，他对藤田武说，这是一个多么俗套的故事啊，地位差距，情人分离，藤田武，你以前在学校的舞台上，也是演过罗密欧的！

藤田武掩面，说，你不要再说了。我也是没有办法。重来一遍，事实依然会如此。

心音！心音！赵宏伟哭喊。

心音毫无反应。

此时，只听门外“咚”一声，很沉闷。藤田武跑出去一看，他的老父亲，倒在地上。

藤田武的父亲去世了。老人下葬的那天，心音跑去了她以前和赵宏伟常去的那座桥上，投了河。据目击者说，她投河前，嘴里一直在念着赵宏伟的名字，还说，我们一起跳，我们一起跳。

心音的尸体是第二天被捞到的。她的表情很安详，嘴角甚至还挂着一丝微笑。她的手里始终抓着那顶帽子。

赵宏伟晕了过去，醒来的时候，身边空无一人。他对墙坐了很久，唱了一首家乡的歌。他觉得自己应该陪着心音去死，况且心音临跳前也是这么喊的。但是，他终究觉得万万不可如此。

他陪藤田武办完了心音的后事。那顶帽子，也随着心音入了土。赵宏伟原本是想留那帽子做个纪念的，但是藤田武说，给心音吧，她更离不开它。

赵宏伟和藤田武一起喝了一夜的酒。日本的清酒是很好的，但是终究比不上家乡的酒，赵宏伟想。

藤田武说，我还是不明白，中国那么大，多你一个不多，少你一个不少，为何非要回去？

赵宏伟醉眼蒙胧地说，如果每一个学有所成的中国人都不再回国，那么中国怎么会富强起来？如果中国不能富强起来，那么像赵宏伟和心音一样的故事，又怎么会停止？

藤田武哈哈大笑，说，你是个傻瓜，但我敬佩你。来吧，让我们再干一杯，从明天起，我们不再是朋友。

赵宏伟说，我知道我对不起你们一家，如果你要我切腹，我会照做的。

藤田武又笑了，说，告诉你个秘密，其实我的父亲，在台湾奉命杀过很多反抗的中国人，后来他退伍了，回到日本，每天晚上都会做噩梦。他讨厌中国人，不是真的瞧不起你们，是害怕，怕中国人会找他索命。他怕得一生都没有安宁过。

说完，藤田武又是将一杯清酒一饮而尽。

妹妹，是哥哥害了你呀！是哥哥要赵宏伟骗你的！藤田武扔掉酒杯，跑出屋去，向着夜空大喊。

赵宏伟一脸泪水，我恨战争，他说。

第二天酒醒起来，赵宏伟摸到了地上冷冰冰的血。他大惊，一看，藤田武昨夜已剖腹，血流了一地。

赵宏伟安葬了藤田武。站在无花的樱花树下，他又想起了第一次见到心音时的情景。樱花在风中飞舞，心音在花间欢笑。

赵宏伟本打算为心音守坟一年，权当赎罪，但是一九二六年春天的时候，赵宝贵的信，就来到了赵宏伟的眼前。

赵宏伟在藤田一家的坟前坐了一天一夜，最后站起来，说，别了，日本。

赵宏伟紧锁着眉头，在屋里走来走去。他现在很想离开赵家镇，但是离开已经成为不可能。从占领赵家镇的那天起，日军就在赵家镇的各个出入口设立了关卡。更何况，渡边已经盯上了他赵宏伟。

方远梦也很为赵宏伟担心。他说，他愿意帮助赵宏伟离开赵家镇。但是赵宏伟却摇了摇头，说，算了吧，万一走不掉，又多搭上你一个。方远梦欲言又止。

渡边终于还是又来了。这一次，他看见赵宏伟在院子里煎药。赵驹捂了捂鼻子，就说，赵宏伟，你在干吗呢？

报告太君，我在煎药。赵宏伟笑嘻嘻地说。

渡边看见赵宏伟笑嘻嘻的，就觉得他很友善，但是赵驹却听出了意思来。

给谁煎药呢？赵驹问。

瞧您说的，当然是给我自己啦。

你？你得了什么病？

肠痨，肠痨。

狗日的，怎么上次没听你说呢？

我说了，怎么没说，我说我身体不大舒服嘛。

好哇，赵宏伟你要滑头是不是？告诉你，别敬酒不吃吃罚酒。

渡边这时插话了，问他们在说什么。赵驹禀报了一番，渡边眉头一皱。他问赵驹，肠痨是什么？

赵驹就问赵宏伟。赵宏伟就说，是不停地肚子痛，拉肚子，一个时辰就得拉个两三次。

赵驹说，你装病。

赵宏伟说，不信你去问医生。

渡边在屋里坐了下来。他沉吟了一会儿，就从包里掏出了一张卷好的纸来。他慢慢地展开纸，对赵宏伟说，你看，这就是竹内中佐给你的委任状，你现在已经被正式任命为江庆县的教育局长了，我们大日本皇军，是说话算话的，对待朋友，我们也是坦诚而慷慨的。

赵驹说，赵宏伟，你听见没有，你走运了。

赵宏伟说，不知刚才这位渡边太君，他在说什么？

你想尝尝三八大盖的枪子儿是不是？赵驹没有耐心了。

赵宏伟把煎好的药倒在碗里。他想，大不了，头掉了碗大个疤。

赵局长没有夫人？渡边问。赵驹翻译。

没有。

没有儿女？

没有。

那么双亲呢？

都已不在了。

哦，那真是太可惜了。渡边说。

赵宏伟却想，我是真走运，有了就惨了。

渡边站了起来，在屋里转悠了起来。像在自己家里走动一样。赵宏伟咕咚咕咚地喝完了药，放下了碗，就看见渡边往后屋里走了去。他心里忽然一紧，连忙就也跟了上去。

渡边在后屋里看到了一个灵台，灵台上是两个牌位。问了赵宏伟，他说这就是他的父亲和母亲。渡边感到深深的惋惜。他正愁眉不展，忽然鼻子一动。他闻到了一股酒香。

他找来找去，就找到了放在这间屋子角落里的那两坛东西。坛子外面还包着赵宏伟前不久新换上去的干净报纸。

渡边鼻子嗅着，就蹲下来，将脸凑到了那两坛酒前面，样子有些滑稽。好浓烈的酒香！渡边不禁赞叹。

这是我父母的遗物。赵宏伟赶紧用汉语说。

赵驹却对渡边说，他说这是上好的酒，名叫状元红。

哦，听说过，听说过，原来就是这种酒，让我看看。渡边说着，就捧起了一坛酒，一边在手里转动一边嗅。

太君，这是我父母的遗物，不是什么好东西，请放下它。赵宏伟又说，声音里已透出了紧张。

赵驹又向渡边翻译：太君，赵局长请您打开它，尽情喝个够。

哦，是吗，赵局长真是太客气了，这怎么好意思。渡边笑着说，抱着那坛酒就是站了起来。

不，太君，请你不要动这酒！赵宏伟口气里已带了大不敬的怒。

赵驹说，太君，赵局长让您快尝尝，您千里迢迢地来到咱们江南，一定得尝尝这有名的状元红。

好，谢谢，那我就不客气了。渡边一把就撕掉了裹在酒坛外的报纸。

“住手！”

赵宏伟，终于用了日语。

渡边一听，就知道赵宏伟的日语水平，远在赵驹之上。

“赵局长，我们终于可以直接对话了。”渡边笑眯眯地说。

赵宏伟脸色死白。

赵驹哈哈笑了起来，说，赵宏伟，早告诉过你了，别敬酒不吃吃罚酒，你怎么就听不懂我善意的暗示呢？赵驹用力地拍了两下赵宏伟的脸，说：你也不想想，你家的这两坛老酒，赵家镇上谁不知道？全镇上上下下，哪家的状元红有你家这两坛年头长？四十年了呀，你个老光棍，也真不容易。皇军已经给足你面子了，快跟皇军问个好吧！

赵宏伟的嘴唇哆嗦了起来。

“把酒放下。”他努力平静地用日语对渡边说。

渡边笑了笑，说：“没有人可以命令大日本皇军。”

“这是我家的酒，请把它放下。”赵宏伟又说。

“好吧，既然是赵局长的命令，那我照办。”渡边笑着说。

说完，渡边就是一松手。“啪”的一声，酒坛在地上摔了个粉碎。酒液流了一地，奇异的酒香顿时溢满了全屋。

“请问，是这样放吗？”渡边摊开了双手，笑眯眯地问赵宏伟。

赵宏伟的牙齿，咬出了声音。

渡边哈哈大笑。赵驹也跟着笑。

酒液在地上四处流淌，像碎掉的河。奇香扑鼻，仿佛呼吸也会令人醉去。而渡边就在酒水里行走，像在用酒洗着他鞋底的泥。渡边又往地上吐了一口痰。

赵宏伟紧握着拳，向前迈了一步。赵驹赶紧拔出了别在腰里的驳壳枪，指着赵宏伟，紧张地问，干什么？

赵宏伟顿了顿，深吸了一口气，然后松开了紧握的拳，说，地弄脏了，我想收拾收拾。

渡边挥了挥手，让赵驹放下枪。

赵宏伟蹲了下来。一块酒坛子的大碎片里还盛着一汪干净的酒，赵宏伟小心地捧起这块碎片，将碎片里的酒倒进了嘴里。他将酒慢慢地咽了下去，然后又深深地吸了一口屋里的空气。突然，他的眼睛红了。但是他依旧蹲在地上，没有站起来。只有两行泪，从他的眼里淌了出来。他只是默默地捡拾

着地上的碎片。

“低贱的中国人。”渡边摇了摇头说。“不过，这酒还的确是香得很哪，我实在是很想尝尝看。”渡边说着，也深吸了一口气，陶醉地闭了闭眼，然后睁开眼，大踏步地又向剩下的那坛酒走了过去。

“慢着。”赵宏伟站了起来，“你们的要求，我答应。”

“我没太听清，你再说一遍。”渡边转回身来，说。

“你们的要求……我答应。”赵宏伟失魂落魄地说。

渡边就哈哈大笑了起来。“这就对了，这才是一个聪明人该说的话。”渡边说。

贱骨头。赵驹说。

渡边还是向剩下的那坛酒走了过去。

赵宏伟喊了起来：“太君——”

渡边却只是轻轻踢了那酒坛一脚，说：“总有一天，你会自己跑到我嘴里来。”

说完，便和赵驹扬长而去。

屋里，只剩下了失魂落魄的赵宏伟和那满屋芬芳的酒香。这酒香，就像是从四十年前起，就已准备好了今日的忧伤。这忧伤，在满屋下雨。

赵宝贵断手之后，心情一直很抑郁，而且还要日夜担心，就怕赵三牛不会善罢甘休。但是，日子一天天过去了，赵三牛倒也没有继续跟他赵宝贵过不去。想来，赵三牛也就是想杀鸡儆猴，吓吓那些想跟他作对的人吧。

赵宝贵终于还是振奋了起来。但是赵宏伟却依旧是长久地皱着眉。赵宝贵以为赵宏伟是一心仍惦记着报仇，便不时拿一些话来劝他，但赵宏伟却依旧是一副委靡不振的样子，走在街上，都像是一只斗败了的公鸡。

赵宝贵又怎会知道，儿子的梦中，一直立着一座日本女孩的坟。有时从梦中醒来，赵宏伟的眼角仍流着泪。而眼前的现实，又比他曾经想象过的更逼仄。他回国已有一段时间，却还没找到工作，这跟他曾经的设想是大相径庭。整个江庆县上什么工厂都没有，也没有任何跟工业或者机械有关的行业。铁匠铺倒是有的，但那应该也是和赵宏伟的专业没有什么关系的。本来，在日本，赵宏伟的打算是，学成归国后，就去上海或者广州等较先进的城市，找到一家工厂，为其工作，为国工作。但是，现在父亲一只手没了，自己需要留在父亲身边，留在赵家镇。这样，他的所学，就成了屠龙之术，啥用也没有。他在日本时所坚持的回国，似乎越来越有了一层荒诞的色彩。

老秀才的脑子已经有些糊涂了，但是赵宏伟他还认得出。赵宏伟去看他，他还高兴地跟赵宏伟说，宏伟呀，要革命了，要革命了。赵宏伟只有一声叹息。

赵宝贵并不了解儿子在日本多年到底学了些什么东西。他也不懂何为机械和工业。当年，他也就是听老秀才说这是好东西，是济世经邦的本事，才让赵宏伟去学的。在他的想象中，赵宏伟是应该要得到县长的亲自重用的。但是，赵宏伟回国后，却居然连一个铜板也没挣到，这实在是出乎他的意料，也让他有些丈二和尚摸不着头脑。他想去跟老秀才谈谈，老秀才却只是说，宝贵呀，要革命了，要革命了。赵宝贵一拍大腿，长长地“唉”了一声。

王树忠的腿好了以后，终究还是落下了一点瘸的毛病。赵宏伟说话算数，王树忠家里有什么重活累活，他都抢着干。王树忠有时就会开玩笑说，我这条腿，断得还真值。有时候，空下来，赵宏伟还会陪秀珍跳跳绳，踢踢毽子。秀珍的睫毛很长，已经有了个美人的模样，性子却还是像孩子一样。

赵宏伟回国的第二年，即一九二七年，赵家镇上发生了一件大事。一天清晨，人们在赵家镇的大街上发现了赵三牛破碎的尸体。而一个多月后，赵驹也成了县政府通缉的要犯。事情的发生既出人意料，又大快人心。大家以为，民国政府终于要整顿山河了。

而这些事情，都不是赵宏伟干的，这让赵宏伟不禁有些遗憾。真相很快便大白于天下，原来，是赵三牛色胆包天，居然睡了玉山帮大当家的小老婆，事情败露之后，赵三牛被土匪在胸口处三刀六洞，然后五马分尸。而赵驹，则是在赵三牛死后，被现任县长发现了他与玉山帮的关系，且现任县长又听说了他行贿前任县长的事。那前任县长和现任县长可是死对头哇。于是，新账旧账、公仇私怨聚在一起，现任县长便决定枪毙了赵驹，以儆效尤。赵驹提前得到消息，连夜便逃往了东北。赵宏伟不禁觉得赵驹真是可怜，在日本的时候就闯祸，到处逃命，回了国，得意了没多久，就又开始了亡命天涯，真是人贱命衰。

南昌起义爆发后，原来被调来剿灭玉山帮的国民党部队又被撤了回去，听说被国民党调去剿灭共产党了。玉山帮继续在江庆县一带猖獗了一段时间。那几年里，百姓的日子很不好过。直到后来，玉山帮被招安，入了国军，江庆县才算是消了匪患。但是，兵患却是更重了。可不是，老百姓都说，连玉山帮都能入的国军，跟匪又还有什么两样？当然，这些都是后话了。

赵宏伟终于找到了一份工作，就是在赵家镇小学里教书。赵宝贵对此自然是觉得大失所望，不过总还不算丢人。赵宝贵现在很后悔当初送儿子去了日本。当初如果不是送儿子去日本读书，而是给儿子买了个官做，说不定儿子现在早已是平步青云。但是看看现在，自己用给儿子买官的钱送儿子去日本读了书，儿子学成归来后居然既没当上官也没捞到钱，这可真是有苦没处诉了。早就觉得日本不是个什么好地方了，赵驹去了日本，回来当了个逃犯，自己的儿子本来是个状元的坯子，去了日本，回来竟然只做了个普普通通的教书匠，由此更可见，日本是个倒霉地方。赵宝贵在家里总是这样不停地唠叨。当然，在外面，他还是很要面子的。

老秀才生了病，快要被镇上的人遗忘了。不过好在还有赵宏伟一直去看看他。老秀才见到赵宏伟，就像是见到了儿子。他总是时而清楚，时而糊涂。他开始频繁地回忆过去，向往曾经的年轻。他告诉赵宏伟，他当年就差那么一点儿，便可以考上举人了，可惜时运不济，辛苦半生，最后什么也没捞到。他说，他治家也没治好，前半生光顾着自己的功名，忽略了教子育子，害得儿子沾上了鸦片，最后自己成了一个断子绝孙的笑话。他还说，康有为的失败其实是可以预料的，维新派手里没兵啊，没兵怎么会成功，书生闹革命，十个人来九个败。

老秀才是在九一八事变发生的那一年去世的。九一八事变发生的消息传来时，老秀才的脑子正好很清醒，他义愤填膺，思来想去，却也无计可施。最后只得手书了两句诗：中国不可欺，南北多豪杰。写完，他突然就吐了血。这一躺下，他就再没起来。老人临终前，赵宏伟坐在他的旁边，老人感动得热泪盈眶。他握着赵宏伟的手，说，小时候，我该教你读《武经七书》的，那样，你一定比康有为强，也不至于现在只能当个教书匠，宏伟，老师错了。说完，老人就闭了眼。赵宏伟心里感慨万端，想，老秀才，终究还是这样痴。想完，赵宏伟就哭了出来。

赵宏伟将老秀才最后写的那两句诗烧了。诗上还带着血。他把这两句诗记在了心里。

赵宏伟是在秀珍十六岁的时候，突然发现秀珍已经是个大姑娘的。他教秀珍写大字的时候，开玩笑地握住了秀珍的手，说，今天这么冷，你的手要和笔杆子冻在一起啦。秀珍的脸却红了，手还被他握着。他开始还想笑，忽然瞥见了秀珍微微起伏着的胸部。此刻他心里奇怪地一热。在此之前，他从未发现，其实秀珍的身上，已经有了女人的美。他的脸也腾地一红。他赶紧放开了她的手。

他还像往常一样，经常去秀珍家里帮他们做这做那，但是却已不太愿意和秀珍单独在一起。秀珍还像往常一样喜欢跟着他，喜欢和他说话，可他却莫名不想再这样。而他却发现，秀珍在越长越漂亮。他觉得自己真是愧为人师。

可是最后，他最担心的事还是发生了。一天，赵宝贵笑嘻嘻地找他去谈话。那一年，秀珍十七岁。赵宝贵笑了一会儿，开口就问他：儿子，你看秀珍这姑娘怎么样？赵宏伟的头皮霎时一紧，问：什么怎么样？赵宝贵一乐，说：瞧你这脑子，平时的聪明劲儿上哪去了？当然是问你秀珍的模样和人品怎么样啦。

都很好哇。赵宏伟说。

赵宝贵乐得一拍手，刚要再说话，赵宏伟问：爹，你问我这个做什么呢？

赵宝贵就哈哈笑，说：儿子，你那点心思，我和秀珍她爹能不明白？都这么多年了，你还打着光棍儿，不就是在等秀珍吗？虽然我和树忠不是读书人，但是青梅竹马这种事情，我们还是懂的。不过树忠以前一直都觉得秀珍还小，你呢，那时也还没工作，我也不好主动去说。但是现在不同了，秀珍也长大了，你都快老了，我们要抓紧了。

爹！赵宏伟莫名地愤怒了。你都在说什么呀！

赵宝贵愣了。旋即，他就将儿子的这个反应理解成了不好意思。哦，是的，这个事情我这个当爹的可能不该这么坦白地跟你说，但是我们老百姓办事不就图个干脆明白吗？不兴扭扭捏捏那一套。而且，儿子你放心，秀珍她

爹都告诉我了，说秀珍也同意这事，你别担心！

“我喜欢的不是秀珍！”赵宏伟大声说，“爹，你们全弄错了！”

赵宝贵以为自己弄错了。他的笑还僵在脸上，就像一堆不知该怎么死去的野花。

赵宝贵要赵宏伟再说一遍。赵宏伟就又说了一遍。

赵宝贵开始焦躁。他站起来，来来回回地踱着步。

“那你喜欢的是谁？”赵宝贵问。

“我没喜欢的。”赵宏伟说。

“上次问你，你不是这么说的，你说，‘反正是有喜欢的了’，是不是？”

“我、我是骗你的。”

“兔崽子，你现在还在骗我呢是不是？”

“我没有！”

“你真不喜欢秀珍？”

“真不喜欢！”

“唉！”

赵宝贵重重地坐了下来，脸上的皱纹，纵横得像一片树林。

赵宏伟在院里蹲着，心里乱得慌。从王树忠和秀珍的眼神里，他其实早已看出了一些讯息，但是，他想，他只要一直做像一个大哥的样子，事情总不至于发展到这一步。但是他想错了。他总不能去告诉所有人，他喜欢的那个姑娘早已死了，而他决定终身不娶，以示忠贞。大家会当他是傻子的。

赵宝贵后来又找赵宏伟谈了一次话。他在确定了赵宏伟心中确实别无他人之后，就劝赵宏伟把秀珍给娶了吧。他说，秀珍这闺女是真不错的，知根知底，秀外慧中，赵家镇上，没有哪家的姑娘比她更好了。但是赵宏伟坚决不肯。他在心里说，心音，你安息吧。赵宝贵说，你快三十了！还要不要让我抱孙子了！赵宏伟就跪了下来，说，爹，算我不孝，强扭的瓜不甜，你就让我错这一次吧。赵宝贵突然就流泪了。赵宏伟走了出去。

两天后，赵宏伟在秀珍家的后院外，听到了秀珍嘤嘤的哭声。王树忠在骂她：“都是你，自作多情，把我这张老脸都给丢光了！”赵宏伟心如刀绞。

他不再去秀珍家里帮她干活了。但是比邻而居，总是要抬头不见低头见的。这一天，赵宏伟不小心，还是碰到了秀珍。“宏伟哥哥。”她还是叫他。

“哎。”他应了一声，踌躇半晌，才说：“秀珍，是你呀。”

秀珍眼圈忽然就一红，她轻声说：“是我，宏伟哥。”

他知道，他不会再叫她妹妹了。他蓦然觉得人生好重，重得什么都难免会被压碎。

秀珍十八岁的时候，王树忠招了一个上门女婿。小伙子一穷二白，无父无母，但人不错，又精神又勤快，比赵宏伟强得多。第二年，秀珍便有了小菊。

而变故，就发生在王树忠给小菊摆满月酒的那一天。当时赵宏伟已被内定为赵家镇小学的校长人选。玉山帮的大当家的带着一批人马，忽然就来到了王树忠家里。他们来的目的很简单，就是要掳了秀珍去做压寨夫人。此次事件与江湖恩怨无关，完全就是因为玉山帮的大当家的在去年赶集的时候，在人群中多看了秀珍一眼。大当家的去抱秀珍，秀珍不从。秀珍的丈夫上前去拼命，被人一棍打晕。秀珍被绑了起来，丢上了马背。赵宝贵、赵宏伟、王树忠一起上前去救，大当家的发了怒。他一枪打在了赵宝贵的肚子上，赵宝贵流血倒地。王树忠拿了菜刀一瘸一瘸地冲上前，眼看一刀将要劈下，却被大当家的一枪爆了头。秀珍尖声大哭。赵宏伟尿了裤子。大当家的大笑着，踢着赵宏伟。大当家的去亲秀珍。秀珍大喊“宏伟哥救我”。赵宏伟突然爬起来，拿过王树忠手里的刀，就朝大当家的冲了过去。大当家的冷冷一笑，正要朝赵宏伟开枪，突然远远的一声枪响，大当家的倒下了。远处一大队人马杀到。正是为首的那人开枪打了大当家的。大家后来才知道，这是玉山帮的三当家的，大当家的外甥。两队人马立刻交上了火。三当家的带来的人多，因此，一场短暂的激战之后，大当家的带来的那批人就死的死，投降的投降，全部被制服了。战斗平息以后，三当家的下马，看大当家的还没死透，就又补了两枪。补枪前，大当家的问为什么。三当家的说，我们都想被招安，就你不想，你说你能不死吗。杀死了大当家的，三当家的放了秀珍，向大家喊：乡亲们，不要怕，我们是国军，我们来帮你们剿匪了。

赵宝贵被送到医馆的时候，已经奄奄一息。一番抢救，拖了大半天之后，还是走了。临走前，不只担心赵宏伟究竟能否当上校长、送出去的钱会不会白花，还很为赵宏伟的光棍生活感到痛心疾首。赵宏伟除了流泪，什么也不会。最后，赵宝贵无限遗憾地说了一句：“可惜啊，我和你娘，都没能

喝上你的状元红。”说完，他就走了。

赵宏伟哭到第二天，才发现自己的裤裆里，还是满满的尿臊味。虽然父亲走时没有说，但是他知道，他的这一尿，让父亲丢尽了最后的老脸。他觉得，自己此生，已不配再喝状元红。

赵宏伟最终如愿当上了校长。而秀珍的丈夫此时已染上了肺痨。赵宏伟用踏实而光彩的工作成绩逐渐抹去了他当年尿裤子的一幕。赵家镇上的大人们教育孩子的时候都会说：你要好好读书，长大了像赵校长一样，被县长表彰。

秀珍的丈夫死后，赵宏伟帮她料理了她丈夫的后事。看她哭得伤心，他觉得，自己就是她在这世上除小菊以外最后的亲人了。

而他一直像保护自己的眼睛一样保护着那两坛状元红。每次看到那两坛状元红，他心里都会悲酸不已，怅惘难禁。有时候，他也会后悔当初没有娶了秀珍。那样，至少父亲在世时，就能和他一起畅饮那两坛状元红了，娘地下有知，也定会欣然而笑。而今，却什么都完了。只有漫长的人生还没完，动乱的时局还在乱。

谁也不知道明天究竟会怎样，谁也不确定明天自己是否还会活在世上。

赵宏伟走在街上，感觉到了一种异样。走在他前面的人都像是在避开他，而走在他后面的人又都像是在看他。人们的目光敏感、多疑而诡秘，就像一条条荆棘，在他身边缠绕、舞动。他有些不寒而栗，就像自己突然闯入了一片陌生的森林，而事实上他和他们都或深或浅地相识。终于，他敏感的耳朵听到了一个后生的议论：“嗨，知道吗，他当了汉奸了。”这句话说得略响，好多人吓得愣了一愣。后生反应过来，拔腿就跑。其他不相干的人也加快了脚下的步伐，在街道两旁鱼贯来去。只有赵宏伟还愣在原地，仿佛池塘里的一条死鱼，又仿佛人喉咙里的一根鱼刺。他不知自己的存在有何意义。天上突然下起了雨。秋深雨凉，赵宏伟无处可藏。

他到现在也没有想起来，自己那天喝下去的那一口状元红究竟是什么味道。他光顾着喝了，居然没有品味酒的味道，他觉得自己真是糟蹋了那一口好酒。珍藏了四十年的一坛宝贝，就这么成了洗地水，他觉得自己已经不需要再有什么想法了。思考就是对于自己的嘲笑，所以他现在已决定如行尸走肉一般地活。生命里除了苦，又哪来的什么香。

秀珍问，宏伟哥，你真的给日本人做事了？

赵宏伟说，是的。

为什么？

不为什么，我就是怕。

怕什么？

你别问了。总之，我现在是汉奸了。对不起，秀珍。

干吗跟我说对不起？

没啥。秀珍，你别跟小菊说我是汉奸。

怎么会呢，宏伟哥，你不是汉奸，我知道的。

不，我是。

不，你不是。

赵宏伟突然就哭了起来。他哭得瑟瑟发抖。秀珍愣在那里。赵宏伟转身跑回了屋里，抱起剩下的那坛状元红，想要用力地摔下去，最终却还是没能摔。他想起，父亲说过的，要考上了状元，或者娶媳妇的那天，才能开的。他想，苍天哪。

游击队又去县城里劫狱了。听说这次游击队的死伤比较惨重。赵家镇上的一些小伙子都有了去参加游击队的想法，他们都说，看，人家共产党多讲义气，这就叫同生共死，值！

入冬了。学校重新开了课。老师不足，日本人就又去强征了一些有文化的人来充当教师。学生不够，日本人就一家一家去督促。赵家镇小学总算又是被弄出了一片繁荣的景象来。

但是方远梦没有来。从渡边向外宣布赵宏伟为皇军效力开始，赵宏伟就没再见过方远梦。他也不敢去找他。他哪还有脸见方远梦呢？算了，还是希望方远梦远走高飞吧。别重蹈他的覆辙了。赵宏伟想。中国这么大，已经连一块太平的地方也没有了，真是叫人怎么办哪。

渡边现在对赵宏伟倒是很有礼貌。用渡边的话来说，那就是“我们现在是同事”了。虽然赵宏伟深感此话不敢担当，但还是努力装出了一副受宠若惊的嘴脸来。渡边去学校听赵宏伟讲了几堂课，赵宏伟跟学生们讲的是明治

维新，渡边听后深感满意，连说“这就是我们帝国培养出来的人才”。虽然赵宏伟现在走在路上有时也会被人丢臭狗屎，但是他想，我尽力了。

渡边只零零碎碎地会讲几句中国话，是个汉语白痴，但是他对中国的历史文化却是颇为了解。他知道三国，知道儒学，还知道李白，甚至还略懂一些八卦。所以他跟赵宏伟之间也不能说是一点共同语言也没有。渡边是在发现赵宏伟会下围棋之后，才跟赵宏伟熟络起来的。渡边是个棋痴，但是水平不高。赵宏伟感到很奇怪，渡边说他来中国之后一直就没有碰到过对手，但是赵宏伟第一局就赢了他。他还以为自己会不会遭殃，谁知渡边狼颜大悦，对赵宏伟是赞不绝口，一定要他再陪他下。赵宏伟只好舍命陪豺狼。赵宏伟还真就纳闷了，日本人的棋艺都这么差，居然能在战场上节节胜利。但是现在想什么都属多余了。国军回来，汉奸也是要被一起枪毙的。反正他是完了。

最令赵宏伟伤心的，是小菊现在见了他要躲。赵宏伟知道这不是秀珍教她的。学校里的学生，现在谁不视赵宏伟为贼伙匪类？小菊怕他也是对的。还是离他远一点的好，赵宏伟想。不然小菊就该被别的孩子欺负了。人就是这样一种奇怪的动物，总是阵营分明，非友即敌，连小孩子也是这样。敌人的朋友就是敌人，这就是一条绝妙的真理。这么想着，赵宏伟就又落泪了。他是一直拿小菊当女儿的呀。现在却成了这样。不过也好，不过也好，他哭着想。

晚上做梦，他又梦见了爹和老秀才。爹骂他：你个尿裤子的窝囊废！老秀才骂他：你个没出息的吴三桂！赵宏伟哭着吓醒，大喊：“我不是——”黑夜里，他的声音是那么可怕，就像狼嚎一样；这声音又是那么孤独，就像旷野里的一簇鬼火。他真怕自己会引来巡逻的日本兵。你就是，他狠狠地对自己说。

渡边改造了镇政府里面的几排房屋，将它们建成了坚固的牢房。他不仅建了几间正式的审讯室，而且在许多牢房里也装上了刑架。他说，这样一来，不仅可以增加牢房里的恐怖气氛，而且，要审的人太多时，那些有刑架的牢房还可以充当临时审讯室。有些腿被打断了的犯人，每次将他们从牢房里拖到审讯室里，都要费很大力气，如果能直接在牢房里给他们上刑，那就省事多了。渡边并不愿意将自己抓到的每一个抗日分子在第一时间就直接送去江庆县城，他更愿意让自己带着满意的审讯结果去见竹内。这让赵宏伟倍觉感慨，原来升官发财之心真的是没有国家之别和行业之分的。赵宏伟甚至还在下棋的时候提醒了渡边一句：适当的时候，还是要送些功劳给上司的。渡边闻言心情极佳，点头赞许，大有视赵宏伟为诸葛亮的意思。赵宏伟顿时感觉和渡边关系又近了一层。他想，死了以后真是没脸埋在中国地上了。

赵宏伟又和赵驹打了几次照面。很奇怪，赵驹一直都没有再为难赵宏伟。有时候，他还会很友善地跟赵宏伟打招呼。这令赵宏伟疑窦丛生。但是转念想想，自己现在怎么说也是个局长了，可能人家拍拍自己的马屁也很正常吧。但是再一想又悲意万丈：自己和赵驹，现在是一丘之貉了。

赵宏伟现在连上街买根油条都不能尽如人意。卖油条的老张不敢收他的钱，他就只好去老李那里买，老李倒是收他的钱，但是给他的油条却是臭的。油条居然可以是臭的，这令赵宏伟自己都觉得讶异。但是老李嘿嘿地笑，赵宏伟也不好把油条吐出来，不然大家就真的会把他当成没事找事的恶霸了。赵宏伟看老张一眼，老张羞愧地低下了头。接连几天，赵宏伟吃到的都是臭油条，他才开始明白这玩意儿是专门为他特制的。他痛苦地想，自己真是活该。吃就吃吧，他总是一边嚼，一边想，觉得能让群众从他身上收获一点报仇的快感，那他也就算是鞠躬尽瘁了。谁让他是个软骨头呢。

这天，赵宏伟出门的时候刚好碰上秀珍和小菊。不知为何，自从赵宏伟当上汉奸以后，他出门时偶遇秀珍母女的概率便低了许多。一方面，这令他颇为伤感和遗憾，另一方面，他却觉得庆幸。小菊一个劲儿地往秀珍身后躲，秀珍反复地将小菊拉到前面来。秀珍说，小菊，快叫宏伟伯伯。小菊就是不叫。秀珍终于生气了。你叫不叫，你再不叫娘要打你了。小菊害怕地要往家里走。秀珍去拉小菊。赵宏伟尴尬极了，觉得是自己连累了小菊，他又莫名感到心酸，想哭也没脸哭。秀珍，你别吓孩子，别吓孩子。赵宏伟尴尬地说。

秀珍终于抱住了小菊。“小菊乖，这是你宏伟伯伯呀，快叫。”

小菊轻轻地却说了一句：“他是坏蛋。”

“啪”一声，秀珍打了小菊一个耳光！

“秀珍你干什么！”赵宏伟大惊失色，一个箭步冲上去，就将哇哇大哭

的小菊给抢了过来。他抱着小菊，责怪秀珍："你怎么能真的打孩子呢！"

秀珍的眼泪却也刹那流了出来。她慌忙地擦着泪水。赵宏伟心里顿时五味杂陈。小菊在赵宏伟的怀里一边哭，一边挣扎。赵宏伟突然才意识到小菊是不要他抱。他慌忙放下了小菊。小菊哭着跑回了屋里去。秀珍也没有去追。

"对不起，宏伟哥。"秀珍眼圈红红地，说。

赵宏伟无地自容。"是我对不起大家，是我对不起大家。"他说。

秀珍突然说："宏伟哥，你带我们走吧！我们一起逃吧！"

赵宏伟愣了一会儿，什么也说不出来，突然，转身就走了。

他走得像跑。

跑得飞快。既不知是要跑去哪里，也不知为何要跑。

是啊，逃吧，逃吧，还留在这里干什么？难道真的要给日本人做狗？难道真的要等着国军回来枪毙自己？可是怎么逃，往哪逃呢？自己现在已经被日军宣传成了一个合作典范，就差到处去做投降演讲了，自己又能往哪逃呢？又真的逃得了吗？一个又一个想法在赵宏伟的脑里流过，像风一样凉，像水一样清澈而哀伤。奔跑中的赵宏伟，就像是在逃脱自己的追赶。他越跑，被自己追得越紧。他想去学开枪。打死渡边，打死自己，那样，至少小菊就不会说他是坏蛋了，秀珍也不会哭了。这狗日的战争啊！

赵宏伟一个人在酒馆里喝闷酒的时候，就看见了赵驹。很奇怪，赵驹也是一副沮丧透了的神态。赵宏伟莫名就向赵驹挥了挥手。赵驹看见了他。赵宏伟惊讶于自己的堕落，他现在是真想和一个资深汉奸喝顿酒。赵驹走了过来，友善地笑笑，问：一起吧？赵宏伟点头。赵驹就手一挥：小二，上菜！

赵驹喝了那么多酒，却一点儿也不醉。赵宏伟觉得奇怪透了，赵驹现在和在渡边身边时，简直判若两人。"赵兄，看来心里是有什么不痛快？"赵宏伟谨慎地问。

"没啥，今天被渡边揍了一顿，还好没打脸。"赵驹一笑，说，"以后，你也会有这个待遇的。"

赵宏伟的心里就有些不舒服。"他干吗打你？"

"有情报显示，赵家镇上潜伏着共产党，渡边要我查，我查不出什么东西来，他就揍我喽。”赵驹说。

赵宏伟酝酿了一下字句，说：“伴君如伴虎嘛。”

赵驹笑了起来，拍拍赵宏伟肩膀，说：“你还真是有文采。”

赵宏伟笑笑，喝起了酒来。两个人不再聊天，各喝各的。赵宏伟觉得自己真是要闷得发疯了。

这么多年不见，我一回赵家镇上，就帮着渡边拉你下了水，你恨不恨我？赵驹突然问。

赵宏伟一时难以回答。扪心自问，在做汉奸这件事上，他还真没恨过赵驹。但是，说出来就不大合适了。

你恨吧，反正这些年，我做下的坏事也有天那么高了，不在乎再多你那一点点。赵驹边喝边说。有时候，我觉得人的命真是天定下的，你想拧也拧不过它。你知道吗，其实我从小就妒忌你，赵家镇上的人都知道赵宏伟是最有出息的孩子，却从来都没人拿我赵驹当回事，就算我再好，有你在，我永远是第二。就算现在也还是这样。我想让你跟我一样当汉奸，可是你就算当了汉奸，也还是比我高一级，你说这叫什么事，哈哈哈。

赵兄你喝醉了。

我没醉，我其实就是想跟你说说我的心声，不然我觉得我就要爆炸了。做日本人的狗是不容易的，刚才你说得对，伴君如伴虎，小日本只要不高兴，想拿我们怎么样就怎么样，我们还不敢不伺候他。想我当爷的那些年，也没这么嚣张过。我怨我那个没出息的爹，要不是他惹出那么多事，我现在可能连县长都当上了，起码在民国的政府里还有一席之地。我知道他当年也是走投无路才跟了土匪，可他干什么真的就把自己当成了一个土匪呢！赵驹竟然流起了泪。

小时候，镖局里的师傅说，不嫖不赌不是男人，我就学着去嫖去赌，可是等我嫖赌出了滋味来以后，爹又说我是辱没了门楣。几百年了，朝廷一直在告诉我们，满汉一家，要君君臣臣，我们就学着去做奴才，可等我们学会当奴才了，皇帝却突然没有了，你说这都是些什么事。

刚到东北那几年，我就只能靠要饭度日。你不会懂的，你没和狗一起吃过东西。那些年里我没赌过钱，也没嫖过妓，我每晚做梦都会看见我的爹。我总会想起小时候，爹把他碗里的肉省下来给我吃的样子。那时的爹

真好。我在要不到饭的时候，就总是想要回到小时候。那时候，我再怎么说也还是个正正经经的少爷。终于有一天，我看见了渡边。那时，我还在他的背后吐过他一口口水。那时的我，还是一个多么像样的中国人。

可是有一天，我饿疯了，我真的饿疯了。要是有人肯让我吃他身上的肉，我也一定会去吃的。我去找一个女人，那个女人很漂亮，也很善良，她每次在街上看见我，都会给我两个馒头。而我总是很怕被她看见。如果那天我不是饿疯了，就不会想要去找她，绝对不会。到了她家门前，她家的门却没有关。屋里传来一阵阵她的哀号。我冲进去一看，竟然是渡边带了三个鬼子，正在侮辱她！那个女人大喊着我的名字，要我救她。两个鬼子朝我端起了枪。我用日语说，冷静，冷静，我只是来要饭的，我只是来要饭的。鬼子将信将疑，我抓起了桌上的两个馒头，就去角落里吃了起来。那个女人拼命地喊着我，拼命地喊着我。而我只当什么也没看见，什么也没听见。我饿极了，我只要吃馒头。等一切都结束了，渡边穿好了裤子，我看见他在摸枪。我就冲上去，跪在他面前，用日语说，把这个女人留给我吧，就像赏赐一个乞丐，就当是可怜一条狗。说完，我还去舔了渡边的鞋。渡边高兴地哈哈大笑，就收起了枪，一挥手，对其他人说，走。可是渡边他们刚出门，那个女人就抄起了一把菜刀，疯了一样地冲出了屋去。我追出去，拼命地抱住了那个女人，对她说，活着就好，活着就好！可那个女人终究还是大喊了起来。渡边回过头来的时候，我就知道全完了。那个女人中了两枪，浑身是血地死在我怀里。临死前，她微笑着说，赵驹，我以为，你会救我的。而我，却已经没脸再告诉她，我爱她。

最后，我终于来到了渡边的身旁。我帮他杀死了无数个抗日分子。有时我也会觉得奇怪，我为什么要帮他？是为了吃饱吗？是为了识时务者为俊杰吗？我想都不是。也许从我说出活着就好这句话的时候，我就已经是和渡边蛇鼠一窝了。我只有和日本人在一起，才能忘了自己是个中国人，我只有忘了自己是个中国人，才能忘了那个给过我馒头的女人。这听起来是很荒谬，但你早晚会明白的。今天的我，明天的你会懂得的。这些年来我一直盼着有人来杀我，可我却还一直活着，我自己都无法理解这是为什么。也许你觉得我说的是疯话，可你早晚也会懂得的。你会懂得的。

赵驹眼圈红红地一直说着话。赵宏伟心里乱成一团。曾经的他是多么仇恨赵驹这个畜生，可是今天却莫名想引他为知己。而最终，他却在赵驹的诉说里战栗不已。他能有几分懂得赵驹，就有几分恐惧自己的未来。他又想起自己今天的冲动，那种想要一枪崩了自己的冲动！

赵宏伟，你知道吗，其实当年，烧你家铺子的主意是我爹想出来的，但是砍你爹的手，是我吩咐的。

赵宏伟憋足了劲，一拳打倒了赵驹。而赵驹还在地上笑。笑得赵宏伟心惊胆战。赵宏伟骑到了赵驹的身上，用力地揍他。而赵驹不还手。酒楼里的客人都跑光了。赵驹拿出了枪，对着自己的脑袋，说，老天爷，快来取我的命吧！

“砰、砰、砰——”赵宏伟在赵驹的身旁，连开了三枪。开完枪，他自己也瘫倒了。

又是一个寂静无声的夜。

赵宏伟在梦里又想起了心音，那个早已久远了的少女。那时的他们多么明朗而欢乐，纵然明知前路多坎坷，但是眼前依旧是春花灿烂。在他们常去的那座桥上，心音还在微笑，而他还在诵诗。诗是唐诗，那些令心音迷醉的故事，他已讲了一遍又一遍，而她总也听不厌。他将采来的野花送给她，她高兴地将花插在头上，问他漂不漂亮。他将折的纸飞机投入河中，她说人的生命就像这纸的飞翔一样短暂，一入水，就到了天堂。春暖秋凉，昼云夜星，夏花散去流水不息，冬雪落尽芳菲又生，和心音在一起的日子那么美好，那么短，在梦里却又是那么永恒。从梦里醒来，赵宏伟惆怅不已。时光荏苒，他已老去，而她，已永远定格在了过去，那个纯真浪漫的少女。

赵宏伟花了很长时间忘掉了这个梦。微痛的惆怅却越来越浓。心音离开人间已有十几年了，但是每每想起她来，却还宛如近在昨天。时光带走了太多的纷扰，一些最纯粹的东西反而历久弥新。比如她的爱，比如他的软弱。是的，他觉得是自己的软弱构成了整个悲剧的核心。怪谁都是借口，自己才是罪魁祸首。爱情就是两颗心的不离不弃，自己不想走，谁也赶不走。而他当年，却要心音对他死心。那个在当年无比合情合理的逻辑，在今天想来，却总是会令他泪流满面，自恨不已。而他每多恨自己一分，他的梦就更深一层。他总是会在梦里陷入回忆，这种双倍的痛楚无人会懂。几乎令他对睡眠

都有所恐惧。但是在这恐惧里，又满含着无尽的迷恋。他的爱，只有在痛苦的梦里还活着。或许这就是梦的魔力。

而他忽然又想起了那个喝醉了的赵驹。他恨赵驹入骨，而在今天，却又莫名不希望他死。他甚至还能微微有些懂得赵驹的痛苦，这令他不禁在夜里起了惶恐。因为懂得即意味着类同，他在懂得他，也即正在成为他。这是一个令人恐惧的逻辑。而他赵宏伟却已踏进了这个逻辑，难以自拔。他忽然又想，假如自己当年真的娶了心音，那么今天又会是怎样一幅景象呢？他也不敢想。他只能痛恨战争。他痛恨这场无比该死的战争，就像痛恨自己此刻无限纷乱而惶惑的内心。

外面突然响起了一连串的枪声，声音很近，好像就来自赵家镇上的大街。突兀而恐怖的枪声在静夜里分外令人惊心动魄，远胜晴天霹雳那样的吓人。赵宏伟觉得整个赵家镇上更安静了。原本可能还有人在做梦，现在好了，连梦也没了，能不安静吗。赵宏伟连大气也不敢出，又侧耳倾听了一会儿，再没什么动静。他突然决定，出去看看。

一个人站在门外，忽然才深感冬夜彻骨的冷。路灯微明，夜色澄清。如果不是这一片乱时乱地，此刻多像一首陶渊明的诗，但田园终究只是一个虚构，近在眼前的只有长城内外。站在家国沦丧之处，白发又何止三千丈，更何况他已是一个变节之人，什么笑谈渴饮匈奴血之类的词句，他是连吟也没有资格再去吟的。思虑至此，他又更感悲凉。自小读的是忠义之书，最终却立了个无节之身，真是多活何益。

几个日本兵小跑而过，赵宏伟认出了其中一个是渡边队伍里的兵，就想叫他来问一问。这个兵比较好说话，在日本也就是个贫民的儿子，在中国杀了人之后才有了一些做人的自信。

这个兵匆匆忙忙地告诉他，今夜玉山上的新四军游击队又袭击了江庆县监狱，有人看见一个受伤的瘦小男人逃到了赵家镇上来。说完，这个兵又提着枪跑了。

赵宏伟在空旷里又站了一会儿，觉得有些无聊，就想要回去了。转回身，看见秀珍家紧闭着的门，心里又是莫名一小阵感伤。他摇摇头，想要赶走心里那些没用的多愁善感。觉得还是以前老秀才说得对，江南的男人都太细腻了，细得都没了英雄气。还是燕赵之地多豪杰呀，赵宏伟想。他推开门，心里忽然一个激灵，顿住了。他傻站在那里，额上沁出了汗。他退了两步，又走了两步，左右一看，最后，把门一关，向小巷子里走了去。

没错，他想到了方远梦，那个瘦小而慷慨的东北汉子，说他是共产党，谁都会信。可他以前竟然从来没往这上面想！他小心而急促地走着路，心里七上八下，乱作一团。他也不知自己怎么会突然就想到了方远梦头上，他也不知自己现在为何要去找方远梦，找到了又会怎样，等等。他现在就像是在被自己的直觉和本能指挥。他要找到方远梦。日本人说那个人逃到了赵家镇上，如果那个人真是方远梦，那么方远梦此刻除了自己的家，根本无处可去。

临近方远梦的家了。路上一片黑暗。这条巷子里没有路灯，赵宏伟只能凭着微弱的月光和记忆中的经验摸黑前行。他越走越慢，越走越慢。自从降日之后，方远梦似乎就已和他绝了交，没有再来找过他一次。他现在去找他，他会怎样对待他？骂他是狗？扇他耳光？都有可能。他该怎么向他解释呢？说自己就是因为舍不得一坛酒，所以才当了汉奸？这不是笑话吗！他赶紧又摇了摇自己的头。都什么时候了，还想这些乱七八糟的。日本人抓不到人，很快就会开始挨家挨户地搜查，要快，要快。他赶紧又加快了脚步。

静夜里响起了狗吠的声音，一些喧闹开始远远地升腾了起来。日本人已经在开始入户搜查了。赵宏伟在漆黑中来到了方远梦的家门前。他停了步，一刹那忽然有些害怕：如果方远梦不是共产党呢？毕竟只是直觉，把直觉弄成笑话的大有人在。而他也不明白，为什么他是那么希望方远梦是共产党。如果他不是，赵宏伟想，自己会绝望的。

赵宏伟的手碰到了门上。这时，他的脚踩到了一团东西。赵宏伟差点摔了一跤。他仔细一摸，是个人。方兄，方兄，是你吗？是你吗？赵宏伟急促地低声问。

那个人痛苦地哼了一声。赵宏伟立马知道了，是方远梦。

钥匙，你门钥匙在哪里，快。

赵宏伟开了门，抱起方远梦，就进了屋。

狗日的，慢慢查，慢慢查，别那么早过来。赵宏伟大汗淋漓地祈祷。

空旷的夜幕下，一切都是那么模糊不清，风声鹤唳。

“咚咚咚！”猛烈的拍门声。

吵什么吵！来了！

赵宏伟穿着睡衣，草草地披着一件棉大衣，开了门。

门刚开了条缝，就被人从外面一脚踹开。几个日本兵一拥而入，把赵宏伟都撞翻在了地上。

“混蛋！你们想干什么！”赵宏伟用日语大声怒喝。

进来的几个日本兵都愣了一愣，停止了行动，转回了身来。一个日本兵问：“你是日本人？”

赵宏伟从地上爬了起来，捡起了掉在地上的大衣，拍了拍灰，重新披在身上，说：“不是。”

“混蛋！”那个问话的日本兵大怒，端起枪就对准了赵宏伟。

赵宏伟迎着枪口走上去，用日语问：“你不认识我吗？”

那个日本兵疑惑地愣着。

赵宏伟又问其他人：“你们不认识我吗？”

日本兵们面面相觑。

“你敢用枪指着我？”赵宏伟问那个端枪指着他的日本兵。

那个日本兵左看右看，迟疑地放下了枪。“混蛋！”赵宏伟怒喝一声，挥手就给了这个日本兵一个耳光。

全体日本兵都举起枪来，对准了赵宏伟。

“把你们长官叫来！”赵宏伟怒喝。

一个日本军官被叫了进来。赵宏伟一看，是竹内身边的一个中尉，北川。

“哎，怎么是赵局长？”北川有些意外，忙对周围的兵说：“快放下枪，快放下枪！”

“北川阁下，我记得竹内中佐那天跟我说过，我只要成了大日本皇军的朋友，那皇军就会像对待家人一样地对待我，是不是？”

“是，是，那天我也在场。”

“那你看看，今天他们是在干什么？踹开我的门，把我撞翻在地，未经允许进来乱跑，还居然说不认识我，并且用枪指着我！你们就是这么对待家人的？你们是这么对待朋友的？前两天竹内中佐还要我写一篇大东亚共荣的文章去发表，你们这样叫共荣？我写出去岂不是要被人笑话死！”

“赵先生，非常对不起，是我的手下做错了！”北川说着，就扇了那个刚才去报信的日本兵两个耳光。

北川手里牵的狗叫了两声。

“赵先生，今天因为有突发情况，一个共产党要犯逃窜进了赵家镇，路上还留下了血迹。我们正在沿路搜查，所以才找到了这里来，请您体谅我们的工作。”

“嗯，逃犯是一定要抓的。”

“这个……赵先生，我记得您好像不是住在这里的。是吗？”

“对，我家是不住在这里，这里是我一个朋友的家，他最近去了乡下，要我给他看家，这不，我只能两头待着。真是忙死了。今天晚上我来晚了，还发现这里丢了一只鸡，是活的鸡，你让我怎么向朋友交代？你们不要光想着捉抗日分子，我们这些留下来的良民，人身安全和财产安全你们也是要保护的对不对？小偷小摸的那种罪犯，你们也要查查，对不对？这样我们才会信赖你们皇军嘛。”

“是，是，赵先生丢的鸡我们一定会查。”

“好，那谢谢了。你们走吧，我就不送了。”

北川却没动。他手里牵的狗又叫了两声。

赵宏伟转身，径自往屋里走去。

“等一等，赵先生——”北川喊道。

赵宏伟转回了身来，“怎么，北川阁下，还有事？”

“这个……疑犯的血迹一直延伸到这条巷子里，而您这里……我们还没搜查。”

赵宏伟双手叉了腰。“怎么，这条巷子里有血迹就说明疑犯一定在这条巷子里？店里有苹果就说明这家店后面一定种苹果树？你们这是什么逻辑！”

“不好意思，我们不能放过任何一个可疑的地方。”

“你们怀疑我？”

“不是，绝对不是，但是还是请您配合我们的工作。毕竟，中国有句话，叫清者自清。”

赵宏伟走到了屋前的大水缸旁，一只手肘往缸沿上一搁，另一只手不耐烦地仍叉着腰。他说："好吧，那你们搜吧。搜得仔细点，不要再来打扰我第二次。"

"谢谢赵先生。"北川一挥手，"快，搜！"

日本兵涌进了各屋。北川的狗也跟着一个日本兵去了屋里。

赵宏伟打了一个喷嚏。

"赵先生，屋外冷，进屋去吧。"北川说。

"不用。"赵宏伟说着，把披在身上的大衣穿了起来。他的一只手肘，仍搁在缸沿上。

各屋都搜完了，日本兵纷纷报告说没有找到。牵狗的那个日本兵也报告，各处都没有发现。

牵狗的绳又回到了北川的手里。北川走到赵宏伟面前，立正，敬了个礼，说，对不起，打扰了。

这时，狗却走到了赵宏伟的跟前，在水缸的旁边转起了圈。狗在赵宏伟的跟前闻了又闻，终于，叫了两声。

"这小东西，鼻子还真灵。我喜欢。"赵宏伟高兴地说着，蹲下来，摸了两下狗头，然后，从大衣口袋里掏出了一大包东西来。看得出，这包东西已开封。赵宏伟从这包东西里掏出了一把什么来，放到了狗鼻子底下，狗立即快乐地叫了两声，大口地吃了起来。

"这是什么东西？"北川马上问。

赵宏伟笑着，也拿了一把，给了北川，说："没闻出来吧？要不怎么说，人不如狗呢。这是五香牛肉干，我最喜欢吃了，被这小东西发现了。"

赵宏伟一边说，一边又喂了狗一把。狗吃得快乐极了。

屋里透出的光照在水缸上，缸里的水波光粼粼。但是天毕竟是黑的，灯光毕竟不够亮，没人能从水里看见缸底。

北川退后两步，一只手放在了腰里别的枪上。他冲一个貌似心腹的日本兵使了个眼色。这个兵揣摩了一下，就去屋角的地上捡了一根很长的柴，将柴伸进水缸里，搅了起来。只有水声微微。柴也搅动得十分顺畅、毫无阻碍。那个兵扔掉了柴，向北川摇了摇头。北川十分沮丧。

"北川阁下，你在怀疑我的人品？"

“不，不，对不起，这只是我的工作，我是一名军人，必须严厉地对待一切细节。请谅解！请谅解！”

赵宏伟把牛肉干全倒在了地上。他站起身来，疲倦极了地说，好了，北川阁下，您也别道歉了，我也理解你们的工作，我们是朋友嘛，但是我真的已经累了，你们走吧。

这时，一名日本兵进来向北川报告，在另外的一条巷子里，又发现了大量的血迹。北川连忙就带人撤了。临走时，他的狗还对那些地上没吃完的牛肉干依依不舍。

关上了大门，赵宏伟双腿发软，一屁股坐在了地上。

夜渐渐又恢复了平静。

赵宏伟关掉了各屋的灯光，然后跑回了大门前，将耳朵贴在大门上，听着外面的动静。直到确信外面的确平静下来以后，他才长长地舒了一口气。他跑回到了大水缸前，用力抱住了水缸，开始了艰难的挪动。

终于搬开了水缸。赵宏伟在黑暗里摸着地，终于，他摸到了一个凹陷处。一块石板被掀了开来，地面上赫然出现了一个入口。赵宏伟走了下去。

到了地下室，赵宏伟点亮了一盏煤油灯。昏暗的火光一闪一闪，墙上的人影左右摇曳。方远梦就躺在墙角。

赵宏伟扶方远梦坐了起来。方远梦痛得低哼了一声。赵宏伟看见方远梦衣服上的血又像是多了一些，就说，方兄，我想重新看一看你的伤口。方远梦点了点头。

解开了方远梦的衣服，果不出赵宏伟所料，血没止住。包扎伤口的布条，已经都被血浸透了。赵宏伟一阵六神无主。子弹是从靠近肩膀处的锁骨下方进入的，从背后的肩胛骨处穿出。骨头肯定是碎了，但不知伤没伤到肺。三八大盖射出的子弹有几分阴险的味道，子弹既飞得特别的稳和准，以至于一枪出去有时都能打穿两个人，又不失凶狠的杀伤力，在战场上宛如一个犀利的幽灵。不过也好在这枪射出的子弹穿透力强，近距离作战时，第一个中枪的人被子弹打穿，子弹不会留在人的体内。要不然，让赵宏伟此刻去哪里找医生来给方远梦开刀取子弹？

方兄，我再给你上点药吧。赵宏伟说。

方远梦点了点头。

赵宏伟小心翼翼地解开了布条，方远梦痛得颤抖了起来。看着那血肉模糊，赵宏伟手都软了。但是他必须镇定。他把剩下来的白药一半全敷到了方远梦的伤口上，敷好后，他又重新给他包扎。这一次他包得要好一些，不像刚才第一次，急急忙忙包得那么仓促那么乱。给方远梦穿好了衣服，他又将剩下的一半白药全给方远梦吃了下去。他只希望这样能管用。

谢谢你。方远梦有气无力地说。

方兄，你要撑住。赵宏伟说。其实他原本想对他说，你撑过了今晚，明天我会想办法给你找医生，但他没说出口。这个承诺是不能轻易说的，毕竟，他去哪儿找医生呢？别伤没治好，让人给先告到了日本人那儿去，那就全完了。可是看着方远梦这伤势，怕是性命堪忧。赵宏伟想说说不出话，只能站了起来，焦躁地来回走着。

赵兄，你不用担心，以前更重的伤我都受过，没大碍的。方远梦说着，却忍不住咳嗽了起来。

不行。赵宏伟看见，方远梦咳出了血来。“方兄，你们游击队有没有信得过的医生？知不知道在什么地方，我去给你请来。”

方远梦笑了笑，摇了摇头。

赵宏伟迟疑了一下，说，方兄，你是不是信不过我？我是不会出卖你们的。

方远梦笑了，说，赵兄哪里的话，日文我也略知一二，刚才你在上面说的话我也听懂了一些，你还是我认识的那个赵宏伟，我怎么会信不过你。只是医生在山里，你们一出一进，一旦暴露，就会连累包括你在内的许许多多人，我方远梦担不起这个责。

“可是你……”赵宏伟话还没说完，方远梦就又咳了起来。赵宏伟赶紧去扶直了方远梦的身子，让他好咳一点。

有白药就行，有白药就行。方远梦有气无力地说。

赵宏伟不再与他争辩。他只能自己想办法了。

对不起。方远梦说，前段时间，我一直误会了你，以为你是真的投敌了。

赵宏伟放开了方远梦，蹲着，沉默了良久，说，你没误会，我是真的投敌了。

“怎么会……”方远梦疑惑地说。

赵宏伟搂着自己的头，说，你别问了，我也不知道该怎么回答你，总之我投降是真的，可我并没有做伤害中国人的事情，我也不想这样，可我没办法，我想我可能是怕死，我是个懦夫。日本人要我教学生日文，我教了，可我没教他们忘记自己是个中国人，我教他们明治维新和工业强国，我想这些日本的事情，他们学会了，对中国也是好的。我没想过要当亡国奴，真的。还有我写的那些大东亚共荣的文章，是日本人逼我写的，我也不敢不写，可我写的全是屁话，没一句是真心的。我想一个真心爱国的人，总不至于看了我几篇文章就会变成汉奸了吧，是不是？我不是在为自己辩解，可我真是这么想的。我也知道我做的不对，可我也没办法。我不知道该怎么说。算了，算了，我就是在为自己辩解，不说了。

“赵兄……”

赵宏伟沉默着。长久，他听到了方远梦的一声叹息。

“你知道竹内他们，为什么喜欢拿你当一面旗，到处去招摇，而不去捧那同样是投降者的伪县长和伪镇长吗？”

“为什么？”

“现任的江庆县伪县长和赵家镇伪镇长，本来都是财主。财主投敌不稀奇，文人投敌，才是动摇民心之举呀。”

赵宏伟不敢看方远梦。

算了，方远梦说，赵兄，事事岂能尽如人意，但求无愧我心。

方远梦问，对了，你怎么会刚好来找我？赵宏伟说，不是刚好，是有个鬼子告诉我，受伤逃到了镇上来的，是个瘦小的男人，于是我第一个就想到了你。

为什么是我？

也许你不会信，但是，我希望是你。如果真的不是你，那我会感到非常遗憾，那我就会觉得自己更像一个十足的汉奸。如果我有一个朋友，我希望他能是个共产党。你可能不会明白，但事情就是这样。

我明白。方远梦说。

赵宏伟就勉强地笑了笑。

方远梦看着赵宏伟，忽然费力地挪动着一只手，去口袋里掏出了一张照片来。给，你看，他说。

赵宏伟拿过了照片，照片上是一个人。这个人叫姚志，方远梦说，他就是我们一直在想方设法营救的同志，我们在鬼子内部本来有一个内应，他已查清了姚志所在的具体位置，这次行动我们本来有十成的把握成功的，可是谁知却中了鬼子的埋伏，原来我们的内应早已暴露，鬼子是欲擒故纵，在等我们去送死呢。

你怎么敢告诉我这些？赵宏伟问。

方远梦笑了笑，说，我也想让你明白，你是我的朋友，我相信你。

赵宏伟忽然就感动了。他眼圈一热，说，有朋友真好。

方远梦微笑着，又咳了起来。

我去给你炖鸡。赵宏伟说。

鸡？

就是你养的那只，我把它给弄死了，鸡血洒到了另一条巷子里，想要引开日本人的注意力，你不要怪我。

方远梦就笑了，说，怪不得，你刚才跟日本人说，我家丢了鸡，原来是这样，真有你的。

赵宏伟也明朗地笑了。他感觉真好，就像是一双冻僵了的手，忽然又被焐热了。有朋友真好，他想。

爬出地窖，黎明已在前方。

赵宏伟买了两串鞭炮，一盒火柴，往赵家镇西边的一个出入口走去。到了这个出入口，日本人盘查，赵宏伟说，我要去乡下看亲戚。日本人问，带鞭炮和火柴干什么？赵宏伟说，给亲戚家的小孩买的，乡下孩子，喜欢这个。

出了赵家镇，赵宏伟租了匹马，直奔玉山而去。自从玉山帮被招安之后，玉山就成了一座荒山。直到去年，大家才知道玉山上有了一支共产党的游击队。这支队伍不小，据说有五百个人五百条枪。他们训练有素，神出鬼没，杀伤力极强。一早就沦陷了的青梅县里的小鬼子，可着实是吃了游击队不少的苦。青梅县的鬼子一直都想剿灭这支游击队，可是苦于玉山地形复杂、山势险峻，他们实在是攻不进去。就算再怎么用炮轰，没轰对地方，也不管用。青梅县的鬼子曾经组织了两次大围剿，结果游击队员一个没抓到，鬼子自己倒是被土制地雷和手榴弹给炸死了一百多个，可谓损失惨重。百姓无不暗暗高兴。

赵宏伟在山脚下，大喊了几声“我是汉奸赵宏伟”，一点动静也没有。他马术不太好，一路上几次差点从马上摔了下来，此时已精疲力竭。他看看日头又已落西，心中愈发焦躁。他策马奔上了半山腰，大喊了几声“大日本帝国万岁”，还是一点动静也没有。寂静里，他反倒像是听到了两声狼叫。没听说过江南有狼，但是这年月，啥也不一定。他怕了起来。

赵宏伟下马，在一处空旷的地方，点燃了鞭炮。“噼里啪啦”的一串完了，又点一串，跟放枪似的。他看看周围，还是人影子也没有。他感到绝望了。忽然，他后脑被什么一击，眼前一黑，就昏了过去。

醒来，发现自己被绑在一张椅子上。他欣喜若狂，“嗯嗯”叫着，才发现嘴被堵上了。一个年轻人走到了他面前，拿掉了他嘴里的布条。

“你们是不是游击队？”赵宏伟问。

“怎么，狗汉奸，知道自己是送死来了？”年轻人鄙夷地说。

“我要见你们队长，或者政委，快，有要紧事！”

年轻人终于还是去叫来了政委。赵宏伟跟政委说明了来意。他说，要么你们想办法，把方远梦运出来，要么你们想办法，把医生送进去，总之要快，白药没用，方远梦还在流血，再拖就完了。

政委将信将疑地看着赵宏伟。赵宏伟说，我要想害你们，就不会一个人来了，而且我也不是要你们出大队伍，就是出个医生，是去救人，救人哪！快！

政委把烟摁灭，对年轻人说，松绑。

最后决定，还是医生进去比较容易。方远梦受了枪伤，一定过不了检查。赵宏伟被蒙眼带下了山。他带着医生上马，疾奔赵家镇而去。

医生化装成老农，将工具箱藏在干牛粪里，混进了赵家镇。赵宏伟随后也跟了进去。

手术在半夜里进行。赵宏伟就在大门后面把风。他的心一直提在嗓子眼

上，汗一直流个不停。汗被冬夜的风一吹，冷到心里，让人不禁更惊更怕。一方面他担心医生能不能救活方远梦，一方面他又担心鬼子会不会再度搜查。毕竟，没找到人，日本人是不会善罢甘休的。

太阳爬起来了，医生也从地窖里钻了出来。医生说，别的没什么了，接下来就是需要吃些消炎药，中药太慢，最好是能有磺胺，但磺胺是管制药品，不容易弄到。

赵宏伟说，这个容易，我来。

说完，他就去厨房里，拿菜刀，在自己的手臂上划了一刀。

刀刚划过肌肤的时候，他没感到痛。他忽然又想起了当年那个在强盗面前尿裤子的自己。他忽然又想，有朋友真好。

赵宏伟谎称自己被铁钉弄伤了手臂，在医院里骗到了磺胺。日本人也没有怀疑他。

过了春节，方远梦康复得差不多了。医生回到了山里。方远梦以做生意为掩护，继续着他的各种活动。赵宏伟不再经常去方远梦那里了，自己是个显眼而尴尬的人物，跟谁来往多了都不好。他在中国人眼里是个汉奸，在日本人眼里又是一条不能被完全信任的狗，所以无论他跟谁亲近，都只能给人带来很多麻烦。

赵宏伟依旧一直去老李那里买油条吃，虽然老李卖给他的油条一直是臭的，并且连炸臭油条的锅都是老李特地弄的另外一口，但是每当他看见自己吞下油条后街坊邻居们满足的笑，他就会觉得自己的表演真是物有所值。直到有一天，他又准备再一次地啃着臭油条招摇过市的时候，秀珍出现了。秀珍一把扯掉了他的油条，甩在街上。她指着老李的鼻子说，你太过分了！老李轻蔑地瞟了瞟呆若木鸡的赵宏伟，又瞧了瞧义愤填膺的秀珍，一边继续炸那些正常的油条，一边半死不活地说：“狗东西自己犯贱，小骚货还不舍得了。来，一起下油锅！”一根生油条又下了锅。

秀珍脸红了，又羞又愤，说不出话来。她一把将老李炸好的油条全扫在了地上，然后拉着赵宏伟就跑。赵宏伟跟着她跑，也不知究竟要跑去哪里。跑了很久，到了一条僻静的巷子里，才停了下来。

“我今天才听人说，老李卖给你的油条里都掺了鸡粪，你难道吃不出来吗？”秀珍义愤地问。

“我吃出来了。”赵宏伟木讷地说。

“那你还吃！”秀珍惊讶了。

赵宏伟欲言又止，忽然背转身，就大口地呕吐了起来。他一直以为那是馊面，没想到居然是鸡粪。真是报应，他想。他吐得胆都要呕出来了。也好，杀鸡儆猴，这样往后就没人那么情愿当汉奸了，他说。

秀珍的眼泪就掉下来了。“宏伟哥……”

“秀珍，你别管我，以后离我远一点。”

秀珍脸一白。

“不是，我是说，离我近了，我会连累你。对不起。”

“我不管。”

赵宏伟忽然就尴尬了起来。对话忽然就有了些其他的意思。赵宏伟急于要摆脱这个意思。这个意思他还从没认真想过。子曰三思而后行，没思透的事情他赵宏伟是不干的。

“我先走了。”赵宏伟说着，转身就要走。刚转身，秀珍却突然是从身后抱住了他。她哭着说：“宏伟哥，我们一起走吧！”

赵宏伟的思想停顿了。众多的意思挤在一起，而他连分辨的勇气也拿不出来。他都感觉到了秀珍的热，而他的脸，却还是夜一样的凉。

赵宏伟像个女人一样，挣脱了秀珍的拥抱。秀珍看着他，他看着秀珍。此时此地，寂静像河一样流淌。

“秀珍，我一直当你是我妹妹。”赵宏伟说。

秀珍泪如雨下，一转身，就跑了。

其实，原本想跑的是他。他觉得人生真是奇怪。

渡边知道了赵宏伟前段时间要磺胺的事，就旁敲侧击地试探了赵宏伟几次，都被赵宏伟给混过去了。渡边问，你知道玉山吗？赵宏伟说，近在咫尺，有什么不知道的。渡边问，那你知道玉山上有共产党吗？赵宏伟说，有吗？我只知道玉山上以前有个玉山帮，个个恶贯满盈，想来，那山上也不会有什么好鸟。渡边问，听说，你以前被玉山帮吓得尿过裤子？赵宏伟说，是的。渡边问，那你今天还心有余悸吗？赵宏伟说，只要有太君撑腰，我就无

所畏惧。渡边一笑，说，好，大日本皇军，喜欢勇敢的人。

渡边在的时候，赵驹总是一副趾高气扬、仗势欺人的样子，像极了一条狗。而渡边不在的时候，他就总是一副郁郁寡欢的模样。在渡边的眼里，这就是奴隶的本性，主人不在，就不敢放肆。但是在赵宏伟看来，赵驹却是在极聪明地生存。这令赵宏伟万分矛盾。他在同情他的仇人，他在他的仇人的身上，找到了同病相怜的感觉。这是让人难以接受的。

赵驹抓到了几个在半夜里起来刷抗日标语的人。赵驹给了他们一把枪，说，我数一二三，大家一起开枪，你们要是把我打死了，你们就无罪了。赵驹数到二的时候，就一枪打死了那个拿枪的人，然后，谁去捡枪，就打死谁。几个人在赵驹的枪下都没有尊严地死去了。赵驹看着尸体，哈哈大笑，说，又是大功一件。

赵宏伟确信，在渡边的眼里，竹内比中国人更可恶。比如，在江庆县大办奴化教育，这原本是渡边的谋略，但是事成之后，功劳却都归了竹内。渡边曾在一次酒醉之后对赵宏伟说，你要记住，今天你能成为我们大日本皇军的座上宾，这全是拜我所赐，与竹内那头猪无关。他说，竹内是个连自杀都不敢的懦夫，而军部的人居然以为竹内是个智者，这都是什么世道。

赵宏伟有时也会在渡边的面前说说赵驹的坏话。这令渡边十分满意。奴才之间的相互嫉妒与使坏，是对主人地位的最好肯定，赵宏伟深谙此理。只有让主人对奴才百分之百放心，主人才不会以为奴才有什么二心。赵宏伟相信赵驹也是在这么干，只不过，赵宏伟想，赵驹的嫉妒应该是真的。

渡边也曾谈起过赵驹的归顺之路。渡边说，当年，在东北，有一个疯女人，拿着一把菜刀，想要攻击我，是赵驹帮我拦住了她。那时，赵驹还只是一个乞丐。疯女人咬赵驹手臂的时候，我就朝她开了枪。我是特意对准她的胸部开的枪，她的胸部原本是那么美丽，简直就不应该属于一个奴隶的身体，我很想知道，它们中弹以后会是什么样。结果令人感到十分恶心。但我喜欢这种恶心。哈哈，那个女人临死前捏着赵驹的手，对他说了两句话，我很好奇，就问赵驹，她说了什么。我不懂中文，但是我想赵驹是懂日文的。赵驹回答我说:“她说，我恨日本人。”我真是开心透了，一个人临死前仍对你恨之入骨，却又不能动你分毫，这种感觉有多美妙，你可能这辈子都不会懂。我来中国，要的就是这种快感。我问赵驹，你懂日文？赵驹抱着尸体，没有回答我。我想，他也一定是在为这个女人感到惋惜。本来，他也是可以享用到她的。那一刻，我忽然很奇怪地对这个男人心生了一丝怜悯。毕竟，一个再坚强的武士，心中也是有柔情的。我又问，你在哪学的日语？赵驹终于放下了尸体，回答我说，他曾在日本留过学。我更好奇了，就问，那你怎么会在这里要饭？他忽然就哭了，像一个真正的懦夫一样痛哭流涕。他说，千仇万恨，一言难尽。然后，他就脱下了自己的破衣服，裹住了那个死女人的裸体，抱起她走了。我喊着问他，你要抱她去哪里？他远远地说，剁了喂狗，给太君解气。我原本还想提议让我来亲自动手，但赵驹早已跑得没影了。真是大大的可惜。

第二次遇见赵驹，是因为在我的辖区里发生了一件凶案。两个日本军人被人杀害了，而在凶案现场，还躺着一个昏死过去的赵驹。赵驹醒来后，说，是有人袭击了他们三人。他用日语向那两个日本军人乞讨的时候，就有人袭击了他们。但他没看清凶手的模样。我并不完全相信赵驹，就把赵驹给关了起来。之后的半年内，又有几场凶案发生，死者均为帝国的军人。终于有一天，我破了案，抓住了四名凶手，他们都是中国武当派的道士。这令我觉得十分好笑，道士也杀人？中国真是不可救药了。我起初很怀疑赵驹也是他们中的一员，但是没想到那几个道士对赵驹的尚在人间感到极度的气愤与遗憾。原来他们本来也想杀了赵驹的。那个疯女人死的时候，远处有两个目击者。赵驹帮助皇军的英勇举动在愚昧的中国人心中成了罪恶的行径。他阻止别人向皇军发动攻击，就等于是向冥顽不灵的中国人发动了挑衅。事情传开后，没有一个中国人再愿意施舍给他一个馒头，于是他就只好向日本人乞讨，但这却只为他招来了更多中国人的愤怒。终于，那几个道士，对他动了杀心。听完凶手们的陈述之后，我十分同情赵驹。我不仅立即释放了赵驹，还试图邀请他担任我的翻译官。但是他似乎已对亲近我们大日本皇军有了疑虑和恐惧，我知道，都是那些不友好的中国人给闹的。我说，你不用害怕，有了我们皇军做靠山，没人再敢对你伸拳头。他说，他还是想回去坐牢，牢里有吃有喝，只要不被判死刑，就很好。我说，你好歹也是在我们大日本的学校里深造过的，怎么能说出这种不知羞耻的话来呢？我说，你不要怕，我们皇军，现在正需要你这种对中日友善有高度认识的翻译人才，你就别推辞了，你怎么能当乞丐呢？中国这么埋没人才，所以才这么落后，中国这么落

后，所以才这么埋没人才，难道你不懂吗？我是伯乐。但他还是不肯。我烦了，就拿起一把枪，塞到他手上，然后我握住了他的手和枪。我用他的手向那四个道士开了枪。四个道士的脑袋全开了花。然后，我叫手下把四具尸体和一个赵驹一起丢出了宪兵队本部。半个月后，赵驹就成了我的翻译官。他虽然办事能力不足，但心狠手辣还是有的，对我们大日本皇军也忠心可嘉。

渡边还说了很多赵驹归顺之后的事情，意思都大同小异，在说明赵驹是怎样一条偶有缺点但仍不失为出色的狗。渡边说，他在初见赵驹的那一刻，从赵驹的眼里看见了两股东西：桀骜与软弱。这两种气质他都非常喜欢。前者应该存在于武士身上，而后者应该存在于女人身上。而他，只要掌控了赵驹的软弱，就能使用赵驹的桀骜。渡边说，有时候，操纵人才能让他获得和玩弄女人同样猛烈的快感。而这些快感，在日本国内，他连碰都碰不到。他说，他感谢这场战争，让他得到了太多他在日本国内根本就得不到的幸福。

赵宏伟耐心地听他说这说那。他一直装出十分钦佩且感兴趣的样子，而他的心在滴血。就是这么个畜生，就是这么个魔鬼，就是这么个在日本国内可能连正经老婆都娶不上的日本垃圾，在中国的土地上横行无忌，为所欲为。在日本，他可能要什么没什么，但是战争却给了他武力，给了他权力，让他在中国要什么就有什么，想怎样就怎样。他体内的垃圾越多，破坏力就越强，破坏力越强，在战争中建功立业的机会就越大。战争将一个畜生装扮成了英雄，军国主义让一个魔鬼成了楷模。而这一切，又都只源于中国的羸弱。羸弱的国人构成了羸弱的国家，羸弱的国家又养育了羸弱的国人。祸根在哪，似乎是个可以讨论上几百年的话题。但这清谈空谈，可能本身也就是民族祸根之一。自强不息，这句话中国人说得最早，但可能懂得最晚。就像他赵宏伟，四书五经和西学革命学了一肚子，但又有什么用呢？还不是在任人宰割。道理学进了肚子里，却没学进心里，有个屁用。赵宏伟想。

渡边带着赵驹，去赵宏伟的家里，给他颁了两次奖状，都是什么良民楷模之类的东西。第二次送渡边出门的时候，秀珍正好从外面回来。秀珍吓得在她家门前站定了。渡边笑眯眯地扫了她一眼，点了点头，然后便和赵宏伟说了再见，带着赵驹走了。赵宏伟站在渡边刚才站的地方，回头去看秀珍。秀珍毕竟才二十七岁，正是花好果熟之时。她惊魂未定，恰如风吹过后，一枝微颤的艳丽桃花。赵宏伟深信，刚才渡边看到的，就是这样的一个她。赵宏伟心里一慌，额头沁出了汗来。

必须尽快将秀珍和小菊送去大后方。最好能去重庆。赵宏伟开始日夜焦虑于这个问题。简单地送她们母女出赵家镇是没用的，外面依然到处是日本人和土匪。不是有消息传回来吗，去年日本人来之前，逃出去的那些人家里，有十多户半路上去见了阎王，还不如留着不走活得长一些呢。而且她们孤儿寡母的，去大后方的路上，最好要有人护送。不得不承认，生逢乱世，女人长得漂亮，真是一个累人害己的大麻烦。但是再麻烦，这麻烦也是必须要解决的。他一早就向秀珍承诺过，要一辈子照顾好她们母女的，像一个称职的哥哥或者伯伯一样。

有了上次进出赵家镇的经验垫底，赵宏伟确信，带她们混出赵家镇去不是问题。问题在于，他不能一路上陪着她们。别说他只是个文弱书生，陪着她们也保护不了她们，单就他是个远近闻名的汉奸这一点来说，他就不能站在她们的旁边祸害她们。赵宏伟想，自己的名字，恐怕都已经上了重庆那边的锄奸名册了，哪还能带着人去投奔重庆呢？真是要命啊。

其实，就算渡边没有多看秀珍那一眼，赵宏伟也已经在考虑要将秀珍母女送走了。秀珍已经说了两次了，要和他一起走。且不说他要不要走，他觉得，秀珍和小菊，已经是必须要走的了。他承认，自己当初对日本兵的估计是幼稚了一点。他把兵临城下的日本兵都想象成了藤田武，或者差一点的藤田武，而藤田武是不可怕的。但是藤田武只是藤田武，其他人不是藤田武，侵略者更不是他赵宏伟预想中的那个样子。他们不讲道理，不知廉耻，只有贪婪，只有残暴。日本兵都是来自日本的老百姓，但是他们一旦成了侵略者，就不再是原来的老百姓，就好比牛成了牛魔王，牛魔王就不再是牛一样。这真是一个很有趣的逻辑。赵宏伟有时也会想，藤田武当年若没有死，今天也成了侵略大军里的一员，他藤田武还会是当年的那个藤田武？他赵宏伟若去侵略别人，是否也会如同魔鬼一般？战争实在是个罪恶的东西。渡边的驻扎让赵宏伟逐步看清了战争的可怕和被奴役的黑暗，他越看清，就越为自己当初不走的决定悔恨不已。重要的不是他自己没走，而是他当初居然没送秀珍母女走。这真是一个天杀的决定。他觉得当初的自己，脑子里真是进了鸡粪。扪心自问，这么多年来，他是早已将秀珍和小菊当成了自己最后的

亲人，他一直拿小菊当亲生女儿看待，拿秀珍当亲妹妹看待，不，简直比亲妹妹还要更近，几乎接近于妻子。当然还不是妻子。有谁会让自己的妻女或妹妹待在沦陷区呢？自己真是对不起她们，赵宏伟痛苦地想。

北川升了大尉，赵宏伟送了一份厚礼祝贺他。赵宏伟一直很害怕北川会在某次不经意的回想之中重新发现些什么，或者对他赵宏伟当日的不敬耿耿于怀，而伺机报复，但是这些都没有发生。与渡边那种痴迷于在战争中获取乐趣的人不同，北川似乎只是个敬业的人。他做一切，仅仅只是出于敬业。当然，他所敬的业，是战争。赵宏伟有时也会想，如果换一个环境，北川可能会是一个优秀教师，或者一个忠实的管家。而从事这些职业，你的忠诚与负责，绝对不会为你换来仇恨与子弹。但北川是个日本鬼子，赵宏伟希望他死。他死了，就没人会再记起那一天的大搜查了。

自从救了方远梦之后，赵宏伟开始变得有些神经过敏。附近有鬼子跑过，他都要暗暗吓一跳，就怕是自己暴露了，鬼子要来抓自己，甚至有许多个半夜，他会被猫叫吓得魂不附体。他每次一害怕，就想要去见方远梦。一见方远梦，他就又会变得大义凛然。他觉得自己活得很难受。

方远梦说，这么久了，我们一直都还没有救出姚志，我们对不起同志。赵宏伟说，为了救姚志，你们已经死伤了那么多同志，这样做合算不合算？方远梦说，要是这么说，那一定是不合算的，但革命不是买卖，生死无法算账，姚志在牢里天天受着鬼子的折磨，难道我们就任其深陷苦海？赵宏伟说，你们有没有做好一种准备，那就是万一有一天，姚志叛变，那么你们游击队的大本营，还有你，就都会被日军一锅端了？方远梦说，准备也是有的，但是至今为止，我们都还安然无恙，就说明姚志没有叛变，而他只要一日不叛变，鬼子对他的折磨就一日不会停，你说我们要是不去救，怎能安心？赵宏伟说，那你又有没有想过，姚志是否还活着？方远梦叹了口气，说，我只能说，起码可以肯定，在我们上次行动之前，姚志还活着。赵宏伟说，县城里的鬼子有大半个联队，你们救不出人来的。方远梦无语。

是的，赵宏伟知道，那个人，游击队是救不出来的。怎么可能呢？除非共产党能夺下江庆县城。大半个联队的鬼子啊，装备精良的鬼子，靠游击队，怎么救？根本就是以卵击石，况且共产党在鬼子内部的内应已经死了。赵宏伟想，那个姚志，怕是要有罪受了。只要他一天不投降，就一天不会逃脱生不如死的折磨。老虎凳，长竹签，小刀割肉。赵宏伟想想就觉得腿软。有句话不太仁义，但是赵宏伟还是在心里说了：姚志，你还是早死早投胎吧。

但是赵宏伟还是会经常想起那个自己仅在照片上见到过的姚志。有时候是在洗着碗，有时候是在看着书，那个人的模样，忽然就会浮上他的心头。影像时而清晰，时而模糊。这个让他觉得很可怜的人，更令他有一种深深的惭愧。一种所有的自我辩解都被无形中瓦解了一样的感觉。揭去种种理由的外衣，他能看到自己的卑微和羸弱。同样是个人，人家是宁死不屈呀！他赵宏伟，真的是怕渡边会连摔他两坛酒吗？不，他怕的是，渡边在摔完了酒之后，会来摔他的脑袋！他赵宏伟，是个真懦夫哇。赵宏伟有时会祈祷：姚志，要是你还没死，就撑着吧，撑到小鬼子投降的那一天。那一天会有吗？赵宏伟不知道。

上次拒绝秀珍之后，就更不容易看见秀珍了。偶尔看见，秀珍总是羞得低头就走。赵宏伟是喊也不是，不喊也不是。他从未想过事情会变成这样，但是细想想，又发现这好像是早晚的事。也许这样的事情早就该发生了，只不过是迟来了太多年而已。他的耳边仿佛又响起了当年他拒婚后秀珍那伤心的哭声，虽然是隔着院墙，但那伤心还是淅淅沥沥地，打湿了他半截人生。他对秀珍真的没有半点男女之意吗？也未必。秀珍很漂亮，而他赵宏伟也不是圣人。只不过，赵宏伟要从一而终，心音已为他而死，他若再娶，他觉得天地不容。

而现在，他觉得秀珍终于是要远离他了。没有什么具体的原因，他就是有这种直觉。男人也是有直觉的，特别是对于一个细腻的男人来说。她已亲近了他那么多年，而他已拒绝了她那么多年，一切，也许该到尽头了。有时候扪心自问，他也的确是有些自私自利。自从秀珍的男人去世以后，他一直以替秀珍赶走那些狂蜂浪蝶为己任，但是却真的从未想过，要给秀珍重新再好好找一个男人。秀珍一直没再找男人，是因为她心里有人。而他明知她的情况，却放任这种情况自然生长，这不是自私是什么？不是害她是什么？他既不想拥有她，却也不舍得她属于别人。

而现在，他的直觉告诉他，一切都要结束了。秀珍已不会再和他亲近了，而他也无法再待在秀珍的身边了。按理说这是好事，他可以不用再为自

己的卑琐自责不已了。腾出地方来，给某个真心实意爱秀珍的好男人一个位置，这是他赵宏伟早就该做的人。现在这么晚了才做，都只能算是赎罪了。可是莫名，他心痛不已。想到也许将来有一天，他只能在秀珍的千里之外向她遥望呼喊，他的心，就会痛得像被撕开了一样。也许自己是爱她的，他有时也会想。但是那又能怎么样呢？他已经是个在民族大义上愧对祖宗的人了，在对待秀珍的问题上，已是自私、阴暗了那么多年，又何必还要让自己再做一个背叛初恋、忘情忘义的人呢？赵宏伟觉得，人生有很多问题，真是剪不断，理还乱。

秀珍很久没和赵宏伟说话了，而赵宏伟也很久没能看到秀珍那双水汪汪的大眼睛了。他忽然开始明白，心音死后的这十几年里，自己并未感到太多深入骨髓的孤单和绝望，也许，就是因为他的身边还有秀珍环绕。而现在，秀珍却不能再和他如常相处了。一切都是天意弄人。赵宏伟忽然很想告诉秀珍，他离不开她，他想天天看到她。

而领悟总是迟到的。深情总是来临在结束的前夜，或者说，只是因为知道已到了结束的前夜了，那情才会蓦然深邃了许多。赵宏伟已想到了送走秀珍母女的方法了。这个方法就是方远梦。方远梦的背后有游击队。用游击队的通道送秀珍母女走，没有比这更好的方法了。虽然赵宏伟觉得这种请求是有些公器私用的意思，但是他也别无选择了。没什么比秀珍和小菊的安全更重要了。他救过方远梦，方远梦一定会答应的。虽然要人回报是一种很无耻的行径，但是他希望方远梦能理解他的爱与焦虑。

方远梦答应了，说一定会尽快想办法。赵宏伟欣喜若狂，差点想抱抱方远梦。但是欣喜过后，他的心里又是一片深深的怅惘。他想：秀珍，我真的要送你走了。

生逢乱世，秀珍这一走，他是真不知自己此生还会不会再见到她，忽然，真的好想吻一吻她。想想这一切，令他潸然泪下。

春深了，花花草草都有了一丝蓬勃的意味。而赵家镇和江庆县城在日军的统治之下就像两座坟墓，一小一大，死气相依。周边更有小冢几座，荒上添凉。

重庆来的锄奸队刺杀了江庆县的伪县长，大家拍手称快。而赵宏伟是又喜又怕，喜的是国军的影子终于回来了，怕的是自己将会是下一个以儆效尤的对象。他开始惶惶不可终日，朝不保夕的恐惧像乌鸦一样天天在他的头顶盘旋、聒噪。他走路不敢走小道，太阳升起前和落下后都不敢出门。半夜里睡着睡着，都会突然吓醒，就好像有枪顶到了他的脑门上一样。他现在是又怕日本人，又怕国民党，里外不是人。但是冷静下来想想，这又是他从投降的那天起，就已经预料到了的结果。只是现在这天真的来了，他的恐惧远超出了他的估计。他还甚至幻想过，万一有一天锄奸队来找到他了，他一定要告诉他们他曾救过共产党的事，看能不能换一个不杀之恩。但是转念一想，他又觉得，自己是幼稚了。你跟国民党讲你救过共产党，不是自己给自己加一条死罪吗？看来这一劫，他是逃不过了。

但是在死之前，他有一件事情必须要做好，那就是安顿好秀珍母女。伪县长遇刺的那一天，赵宏伟就去敲了秀珍的门。他知道事情一下子变紧急了，也就顾不得什么礼义廉耻了。秀珍开门看见是他，表情很惊讶。赵宏伟没等她开口，自己只管说了起来。秀珍，你听我说，我对不起你，当初我就不该让你和小菊留在赵家镇上，日本人是疯狗，谁也不知道哪天哪家就会遭殃，我们只能任人宰割，所以我觉得你说得对，还是走吧，你和小菊都走吧。具体的事情我正在安排，一有消息就告诉你，你做好准备。记住，这些天不管会发生些什么事，你都不要犹豫，必须要走，知道吗，记住了。

你来就是跟我说这些？

是啊。

不，我不想走了。说着，秀珍就要关门。

赵宏伟急了，一把推住了门。怎么，怎么不想走了呢？赵宏伟急得声音都变了。

“别人都能在这里待下去，我和小菊为什么就不可以？”

“可是、可是你那天不是还说……”

赵宏伟话说了半句，秀珍的脸忽然就红了，然后她的眼圈也红了。赵宏伟不知该怎样把话说完，在原地呆若木鸡。秀珍赌气地又说了一句：“反正我不想走了。”然后，“嘭”的一声，就关了门。

赵宏伟想拍门再叫她出来，但是又怕动静闹太大。他在她门前走来走去，抓耳挠腮，最后发现有路人在看他了，他才只好回了自己的屋里。这可

如何是好哇，他想。

烦恼中，他又略感欣慰。秀珍和他这样赌气，就是还没拿他当外人哪。她那闹别扭时的小女儿情态，甚至有三分更像是撒娇。赵宏伟这样一理解，反倒还乐了起来，觉得秀珍对他是真好。想完，他就给了自己一耳光。都什么时候了，还想这些？赵宏伟呀赵宏伟。他懊恼地想。

不久之后，竹内决定，提拔赵家镇的镇长去担任江庆县的县长。此时渡边提议，让赵宏伟卸去可有可无的江庆县教育局长一职，出任稍有实权的赵家镇镇长。竹内说好，还进一步建议，要将赵宏伟这个合作典型，宣传到江北去。要是能宣传到华北，就更是好上加好了。竹内说，中国人素以文天祥之流自勉，现在就要让他们看看，他们的读书人，已都成了我们的狗。

镇长就职仪式的当天，渡边讲了好一通话。北川还代表竹内，向赵宏伟赠送了礼物。礼物是一件青花瓷，据说原本是属于江庆县城里的某个富户的。而它现在居然到了赵宏伟的手里，就好像是赵宏伟去抢的一样。真是造孽呀，他想。

突然，枪响了。一颗子弹从赵宏伟头顶飞过。几乎是贴着头皮过去的，赵宏伟都感觉到了那颗子弹的滚烫和头发似被烧焦的恐怖。北川对他大喊了一声“卧倒”，然后赵宏伟痴痴呆呆地就被推倒在了地上。那件精美且昂贵的青花瓷，在地上摔了个粉碎。

枪战持续了好几分钟。两名刺客，最终被北川击毙。日军只伤了两个小兵。赵宏伟惊魂甫定，从地上爬起来，看着台下台上一片的狼藉。他发现自己的手上全是血，原来是被瓷器的碎片给割破了。他忽然感到一阵眩晕，差点从台上一头栽下去。

“赵镇长，您受惊了，刺客已被我们击毙。经验证，此二人正是重庆锄奸队成员。”北川说。

赵宏伟悲怆地想，你们两个傻呀，渡边就在我旁边，打他比打我要有用得多呀。

血从他手上滴下，他一点也没感到疼。

春风里的寒意，有时也胜过匕首的锋利。

赵家镇小学依旧由赵宏伟负责。从小孩子到大孩子，赵宏伟都要教他们日文，甚至有些已经高小毕业了的学生，日本人又让他们回赵家镇小学去念书。日本人根本不跟他们讲学历，也不是真心搞教育，其实就是办了个日语奴化培训班。有时候站在学校的大门外，回首往事，赵宏伟会唏嘘不已。他小的时候，赵家镇上没有小学，县城里才有；县城里没有中学，省城里才有。后来，镇上开始有了小学，初小高小齐全，县城里也有了中学，女子念书也成了常见的事，省城里还建起了大学，真是上了个新台阶，赵宏伟觉得国家还是有希望的。毕竟，再怎么年年打仗、民不聊生，只要人才能出来，国家就不会真的垮掉。泱泱大国，千千万万个读书人里，出十个二十个诸葛亮那肯定是没问题的。这就是赵宏伟以前的中国发展观。虽然他没能如父亲所愿当上什么光宗耀祖的长官，也没能如自己在日本时的所愿成为中国工业建设队伍里的一员，而只是做了个小小的教书匠，他倒也不觉得很委屈，也没什么太大的遗憾。毕竟，孔子从政不成，不也是教书才教出了名堂来吗？赵宏伟再怎么说也是念四书五经长大的，圣人伟岸的事迹是铭记于心的。忠孝节义，赵宏伟是死了也不敢忘的。

但是，赵宏伟当初又哪能想到，多灾多难的中国会被一个小小的日本给祸害到了今天这个地步呢？在日军的炮火面前，教育兴国不就成了个屁吗？更别说渡边现在是在大力搞教育亡国了。赵家镇虽小，但模范的力量是无穷的，这星星之火，一旦燎原，可就真有了亡国亡种的意义。而他赵宏伟又居然是这亡国亡种行动里的一分子，不，甚至可以说是模范部分的主要负责人，这都叫什么事！对国不忠，对祖宗不孝，对国人不仁也不义，他还能算是个人吗？赵宏伟痛苦地想。

赵宏伟是真觉得自己对不起所有人的，也包括对不起他自己，对不起他一生信奉的忠孝节义。要说做个中国人也真难，圣人既教人忠，又教人不要愚忠，这忠和愚忠的差别在哪里？君为轻，民为重。于是，反清复明到了康乾盛世就成了逆天下之举。而到了慈禧老佛爷的年月里，反清又成了顺应民心之动。可是，你让小小的一个个人，在历史的洪流里，又哪能那么容易看清民心所向呢？又不能去一个一个地问。而只要一步错，忠就会成为奸，奸就会成为忠。赵宏伟有时是真觉得，圣人除了留下了一堆废话，啥也没留下。就是那些狗屁圣人，拖了中国的后腿。而今，国、共、日并存，一个人，如果不能像陶渊明那样隐居，就必然要有所选择，有所投奔。但是，究竟选择哪一边呢？赵宏伟是真不知如何是好。他只知道，他是真恨日本人。不为别的，就为那些惨死的老百姓。君为轻，民为重，谁伤了天下百姓，谁就是全民公敌。

赵宏伟向渡边争取到了开中文课的权利。赵宏伟说，这些孩子长大了光会日文不会中文有什么用呢？就好像你渡边长官，想办事身边还总得带着个翻译，多麻烦哪。要为大东亚共荣事业奉献人才，那中文必须也要教，不然教了他们日文也是白教，对大日本皇军将来的事业一点用也没有。

渡边一开始并不情愿。但是赵宏伟说，我是忠言逆耳，这个问题早晚会被大家想到的，但是如果是被竹内中佐先想到了，这以后要有再大的功，也都不是你渡边队长的了。渡边立即说，赵镇长真是忠心可嘉，就照你说的办。

当初刚开始教日文的时候，孩子们都很不配合。当然，赵宏伟自己也是不想配合的。但是天天耗着，教学毫无进展，日本人是要生气的。他们一生气，学生或老师就都会遭殃，遭殃的都是无辜的。所以赵宏伟最终还是决定动员学生配合，就像一个实至名归的汉奸应该做的那样。他苦口婆心地对孩子们说，学一门外国话没有坏处，会不会讲日语跟爱不爱国没有什么关系，学了日语就一定要给日本人当狗吗？那要是学了英语、法语、德语、俄语呢？就是给英国人、法国人当狗吗？那么那些会中文的日本翻译，难道就是中国人的狗了吗？当然不是。两者一点关系也没有。我们大唐时那么鼎盛，日本那时候拿我们当天皇拜，现在为什么反过来了？他们强了，我们弱了，他们要我们拿他们当皇帝拜了，这里面是有道理的。我们就是要学这里面的道理，知道一个国家怎样才会走向失败，怎样才会走向胜利。所以，我教你们明治维新什么的，你们都要认真学。师夷长技以制夷，这就是你们跟我学习的目的。当然，有日本人在场的时候你们不要乱说话。不然，他们会乱打乱杀。

赵宏伟一有机会就向他的学生阐明他的这套道理。而他的确也是这么想这么做的。后来他救方远梦的那次，他也给方远梦说了一回。他是真觉得自己说得不错。学生们在他的影响下， 开始慢慢配合他了。他们学日文，学日本历史，为了应付检查，偶尔还喊喊天皇万岁。渡边视察了几次，很满意。

而学生们还是不喜欢赵宏伟。有一次，小菊就是因为喊了赵宏伟一声“宏伟伯伯”，随后就被别的孩子吐了口水。所以，赵宏伟还是十分痛恨自己的汉奸身份的。

这一次，渡边终于批准了让他赵宏伟在学校里重开国文课，赵宏伟心里兴奋万分。好像这国文课只要一开，他汉奸的罪名就能轻了许多似的。但是开课第一天，一个高小的学生就问他：我们长大了要是不当翻译，那学中文又有什么用？

“你说什么？”赵宏伟觉得自己是不是听错了，或者这位同学他说错了。赵宏伟觉得，他该问的是：我们长大了要是不当翻译，那学日文又有什么用？

但是那位同学又重复了一遍同样的话。

赵宏伟颓然了。

他真的，在给日本人教出好学生来。

赵宏伟遇刺的消息一传开来，街坊邻居纷纷扼腕叹息，都说可惜了那两个刺客了，为了杀一条狗白搭上了两条好命。北川建议赵宏伟住进镇政府，或者在家门前设立岗哨，都被赵宏伟拒绝了。北川说，您现在毕竟是赵家镇的镇长了，跟教育局长那种虚衔不同。赵宏伟说，现在这镇长，难道就不是虚衔？北川说，当然不是，我们皇军是有诚意的，我们当然要保护好我们的朋友。赵宏伟手一挥，说，我不怕，他们要锄奸，让他们来锄。渡边就在一旁嘿嘿一笑，说，很好，赵镇长代表体现了我们大日本皇军的英勇无畏精神，这非常值得宣传，近朱者赤，和我们在一起待久了，懦夫也会变成勇士。赵宏伟胸闷无比。

赵宏伟遇刺事件上报的那一天，秀珍来敲赵宏伟的门。敲门声急促而恐慌，以至于赵宏伟在开门前都没想到会是秀珍。秀珍大大的眼睛里满是激动与悸动，微红的眼角似还有着未干的湿痕。她看见了赵宏伟，却又说不出话来。赵宏伟说：“秀珍，你怎么来了？”秀珍张了张嘴，却又闭了上去。她的嘴唇颤抖了一下，伸出手，似乎是想要摸一摸赵宏伟的脸，但是却又缩了回去。一股剧烈的痛苦从她的脸上爬过。赵宏伟忽然一阵心痛。“你怎么了，秀珍？”赵宏伟轻声问。

“我看到报纸了，有人要……要杀你，是不是？”

“……是。”

“那……你没事吧？”秀珍的声音，弱得像一捧捧不住的水。

“没事，你瞧。”赵宏伟乐呵呵地说着，从上到下地拍打着自己的身体，以示自己安然无恙。

秀珍难过地低下了头。“……没事就好。”她说。

两人相对无言。

赵宏伟忽然又想起了子弹从自己头上飞过的一刹那。那一刹那，他的头发都被蹭掉了一些。他心里一热，突然忍不住说：“秀珍，能再看见你真好。”说得都有些莫名其妙。

秀珍抬起头，有些疑惑地看着他。他又说了一遍，说得一片痴傻。她忽然就笑了，破涕为笑，欲笑还带雨。她用她那水汪汪的大眼睛笑他，似是笑他说得痴，似是笑他想得傻。他也笑。两人都笑得山花烂漫，天光绚烂。笑完，他眼圈一红，她蓦然泪如雨下。

赵宏伟拉住了秀珍的手，说，秀珍，我们一起走吧，去重庆。

秀珍梨花带雨，点点头，说，嗯。

她紧紧地将头依在了他的胸前。他都感到了她泪的滚热。一刹那，他忽然很想吻她。但他知道，这一定不是真的。

快要到夏天了。时光在不知不觉中漏走，一转眼，赵家镇已沦陷半年有余。

剩下来的那一坛状元红，依旧被赵宏伟保管得很好。酒坛外纤尘不染，酒坛内芳香馥郁。赵宏伟也曾想过，要让它重新入土。以前就想过，两坛子酒都在时就想过，但莫名又觉得很无聊。就好像一个婴儿已经出世，你为了要让他少见一些这世上的污秽，就想把他重新塞回娘肚子里，这样做是十分可笑也很无聊的。酒为什么越陈越香？那香，就是用无尽的悲欢酿成的。而这无尽的悲欢，又只有裸露的岁月里才有，或者可以说，是无情的时光流逝中唯一的财富，也或者可以说，是霜刀雪剑里最珍贵的宝物。所以，赵宏伟常想，这状元红，不该是一种太陈太香的酒。不管是洞房花烛的欢喜，还是金榜题名的荣光，都只有在人年少时大驾光临，才足够点亮一个人一生心情的火炬。来得太晚，那心早已被失败浸透，被失望磨烂，被无尽的悲欢沉浮炼得如铁似铜、泡得锈气弥漫，那迟来的欢喜和荣光，又还有何欢喜与荣光可言？所以，状元红，是越陈，越香，便越苦。错过了年少时最美的时光，它便成了一坛失意之酒。而再失意，人也要在遗憾里继续走下去。这就是人活着的无奈之处。晚清动荡，新起旧亡，制度变革消灭了赵宝贵第一个为儿子开酒坛的理由，而心音的香消玉殒，又在赵宏伟的心里把第二个开酒坛的理由带进了阴森的坟墓。当然理由都是人自己找出来的，但是藏在理由背后的某些东西，恐怕穷尽某个人的一生，也未必能于废墟之中重新建立起来。这样就令人陷入了彷徨。而赵宏伟已彷徨半生。在这半生里，他苦乐不醒，宠辱难惊，浑浑噩噩，自惭形秽。有时候，他也想，也许有一天，他会将剩下来的这坛酒一饮而尽，而那一刻，他一定会泪流满面，就好像他喝下的将必然不是酒，而只是一坛几十年的尘。这想象令人心灰意冷、颓废不堪。

而他依然精心保存着这一坛酒，就像保护着自己的眼睛，仅剩了的一只眼睛。

方远梦给赵宏伟带来了好消息，说游击队经过慎重考虑，已经答应了赵宏伟的请求，愿意送秀珍母女去大后方。但是最近路上鬼子查得紧，得过一阵子再走。赵宏伟心情激荡，千恩万谢，说，游击队仗义，我记住了。

方远梦在伤病期间，其实也曾劝说过赵宏伟弃暗投明。不一定要投奔共产党，只要不当汉奸就好。毕竟，当汉奸终究是个祸国殃民的差事。但是赵宏伟每次都闭口不言，他心事重重，举轻若重。比如，他会想，我来教学生日文和日本历史，起码还能告诉学生们，师夷长技以制夷，但是我一走，换个人来，说不定真就只会教孩子们喊天皇万岁了，而孩子们一变坏，到最后罪魁祸首又总会算在我这个开创者身上，我不能毁了孩子们，也不能毁了我自己，不要像姜维一样，计谋了一半人去事空，留下千古遗憾。他又想，我要不当汉奸了，就必须得逃，要逃，不能一个人逃，起码得带上秀珍母女，不然日本人一定会拿平日里和他最亲近的人开刀。但是带着秀珍母女逃，必须要有个说法，自己是个光棍，人家是个寡妇，这么结伴一逃，人家会怎么说？玷污了自己的名节事小，毁了人家的名节事大。再说了，一个汉奸，能往哪逃，不要走到半路上就让人给毙了，那就全完了。如此种种，他日思夜想，辗转反侧，难以成眠，最终还是觉得先安于现状再说吧。慢慢来，也许

会有办法。虽然当时秀珍已早就向他表露过了想要一起逃的愿望，但是他始终认为，那只是她一时的激动之语。很多事情和问题，女人想不到的，男人一定要想到，不然一定会害人害己，他认为。

然而孩子们并不怎样明白赵宏伟的苦心。随着教学的不断深入，孩子们逐渐分成了两派，一派越来越讨厌侵略者，一派越来越想到日本去。而这两派又都有讨厌赵宏伟的理由。这个情况赵宏伟原本并没察觉，是他争取到国文课重开以后，他才认识到的。那些崇日媚外的学生，既令赵宏伟心痛不已，又让他自责无尽。他开始认识到，事情的发展总是会有些出人意料的地方的。他开始发现，自己一切的思来想去，全是个屁。孩子们怎么可能明白明修栈道、暗度陈仓的道理？他把一切都想得太理想了。

方远梦也曾警告过赵宏伟，如果有一天，他真的做出了什么不利于中国人的事情，那么每一个有良知的中国人，都不会放过他。赵宏伟知道方远梦其实也是矛盾的。他赵宏伟今时今日作为一个汉奸典型，影响深远，动摇民心不浅，已很难说是还没有做出什么不利于中国人的事情。但他赵宏伟又的确是救过方远梦，也从心里敬佩共产党的新四军游击队。这就让他自己和别人都觉得十分为难。所以，当方远梦答应帮他去向游击队请求特殊帮助时，他赵宏伟就已经有了一种来自灵魂深处的惭愧，觉得自己真是恬不知耻。自己好不容易有一点对得起人家的光辉地方，现在还被自己拿来当筹码，要人家做出回报。而游击队居然答应了，赵宏伟在听到确切答复的那一刻，心里的复杂味道真是说也说不出。

赵宏伟在这里做了一个手脚。这个手脚不太干净，甚至有些卑鄙，但他个人认为是情有可原、值得原谅的。那就是他欺骗了秀珍，他骗她说，他会跟她一起去重庆。其实他根本就没有这么打算过。正如他之前所考虑过的那样，种种想法都证明，他不能和她一起走。但是他若不那么骗她，他知道，她肯定不会走。从情感上来说，她一定不愿离开他，从赌气上来说，她也一定不会听他的话。所以只有像现在这样，告诉她，他离不开她，他要跟她一起走，她才会真的听他的话。虽说日军占领赵家镇都这么久了，赵家镇上一直还算很太平，但是赵宏伟忘不了渡边看秀珍的那一眼。那一眼咸湿而腌臜，充满了那种只有男人才能一眼洞穿的渴望。那是一种凶猛的雄性力量，凶猛到足以将一座高山踏平；那是一种践踏的欲望，就好像是只有最残忍的破坏，才能给破坏者带来灵魂上的阵阵快感。赵宏伟很怀疑，也许渡边在踏上中国土地的第一刻，眼里射出的就是这样的一种目光。这是一种能令所有聪明人胆战的目光。赵宏伟知道秀珍不笨，他就怕她太天真。

但是，秀珍真的没有发觉他是在骗她吗？他也并不真的确定，毕竟，是从小到大一直相伴在一起的两个人。他对她说“能再看见你真好”时，他还并没想到要骗她。秀珍并没有像他前段时间伤心时所想的那样，不再理他、不再亲近他、拒他于千里之外，但是，送她和小菊走，却已是真真切切地来到了大家的眼前。只等游击队的行动了。而这一别，也许真的是此生不会再见了。赵宏伟泪流不止。

初夏，花开得像云一样轻盈。

竹内很快就要被提拔为大佐，调往南京了。渡边忧愤异常。当年他和竹内一样大，而今竹内步步高升，他却依然只能当一个残破大队的大队长，这真是让人心灰意冷。但渡边又绝不是个甘心淡泊的人，他加大了拍竹内马屁的力度，也扩大了人际活动的范围，只希望能早日步竹内的后尘，成为中佐，领导起战斗力非凡的江庆县日军联队。渡边是真希望这场战争能一直打下去，一直打到他坐上将军的位置，那样他也就算对得起他的祖宗了。

竹内在临走前，希望能去赵家镇小学听一堂赵宏伟讲的日文课。毕竟这个颇得上头欣赏的教育计划实施至今，他竹内本人还从未到学校里去视察过一回。这样他去了南京也不好吹牛，而且在职业感情上，他也觉得颇为遗憾。于是，渡边就着手安排起了竹内的听课视察事宜，力求务必要让竹内乘兴而来，满意而归。赵宏伟被渡边喊去谈话。虽然赵宏伟已贵为镇长，但本质上还是被渡边呼来喝去的东西。渡边对赵宏伟说，联队长亲自前来，讲课内容务必振奋人心，要知道，竹内中佐，不，竹内大佐，必将是皇军明日的名将之花。赵宏伟腰一挺，说，哈依。

没有其他同学在的时候，小菊已经愿意重新喊赵宏伟一声“宏伟伯伯”了。这是最令赵宏伟激动涕零的事情。就像女儿肯重新认他了一样。从以前到现在，他一直不敢在别人面前对小菊太好。因为小菊毕竟不是他生的，他对她太好，万一镇上的人以为小菊是他生的，那不仅对秀珍死去的男人来说是个侮辱，对秀珍和小菊来说也是个麻烦。人言可畏，不得不防。而他当了

汉奸以后，就更不用说了，镇上的人在背后说了秀珍什么，他都知道，甚至还有孩子，在学校里骂过小菊，说她是野种。那一天，赵宏伟是真想挥手打那个骂人的孩子，但他终究没下得去手。孩子都是无辜的，他们不懂事，错的只有大人。小菊泪汪汪地看着赵宏伟，赵宏伟也没有去安慰她。他对她好，就是最大的不好，他想。那一刻小菊的失望与委屈，他懂。

面对小菊时，赵宏伟总有些莫名的悲怆。他也说不上什么原因。他有时候就是会暗想，要是小菊真是自己的孩子，那该多好。毕竟，他是个四十岁的老男人了呀！他有一腔的父爱，有柔软的心肠，但他却无妻无子。小菊就算再可爱，他也不能堂而皇之地抱着她去逛大街，给她买糖吃，给她做新衣服穿。他必须要恭恭敬敬，严严肃肃，为人师表，让镇上的人都说他好。这活着是多累呀！

这一天，小菊却突然问赵宏伟："宏伟伯伯，日本真的是个很美的地方吗？"

赵宏伟说："是的。"

"那我们为什么不做日本人呢？"

"因为别人的地方再好，也不是我们自己的家。日本人来我们的家里，也不是帮我们种花的，他们是来抢了我们的东西，拿回去装点他们自己的家的。"

"哦。"

"小菊，伯伯这段时间给你们上的课，你不要当真，伯伯是在唱大戏呢。以后不管到了哪里，都要记住，自己是个中国人，中国人永不服输。"

"哦。"

"……小菊……"赵宏伟搂着小菊，心里一酸，差点流下了泪。我真是造孽呀，他想。

赵宏伟一个人在酒楼上喝闷酒。

近来收到的都是一些不好的消息，重庆开始遭受日军飞机轰炸，汪精卫开始大展宏图，戴笠的锄奸队撤出了江庆县，转去支援上海军统站。而这支锄奸队的撤退据说也和赵宏伟有关，就是因为上次他们刺杀他没成功，反而还死了两个人，他们觉得这太亏了，为了一个小角色牺牲了两名骨干，所以才决定转道奔赴上海。这让赵宏伟捶胸顿足地难受，为什么每一件遗臭万年的事情都跟他有关？他已经背负了那么多的骂名，为什么现在连锄奸队的离开都和他有关？但这又是事实。他觉得太痛苦了。事实上，他个人觉得自从秀珍与他重修旧好之后，他对生死已经置之度外了。要不是锄奸队的那一枪，秀珍也不会那么快地重新接受他的存在，而秀珍既然答应了离开赵家镇，那么他死不死、何时死就已经都不是那么重要了。汉奸迟早是要死的，也必须要死，否则国家的抗战没有胜利的可能，这一点他赵宏伟一早就深知。而能死得没有牵挂，便已是大幸福。因为他已为秀珍和共产党建好了通道，他不怕自己死后，秀珍母女会被困在赵家镇。

锄奸队一走，江庆县的日军和卖国狗都更猖狂了，老百姓日子更不好过了。大家恨赵宏伟，却也没人敢动他。连军统都打不死的人，必是福大命大，一般人又怎能打死他？大家都说。赵宏伟深陷在矛盾的煎熬里。没有人再来杀他，他固然是庆幸的，但是正因为他的不死，却让家乡再一次失去了自卫与反击的利刃，他又的确是成了助纣为虐的恶棍。他以前从未想到过自己会落入今天这样的困境，这种困境，与生死无关，却比生死抉择都来得更重要，更让人难以取舍，一切都像个谜一样无解，却又阴魂不散，萦绕不去。他该怎么办？他该怎么办？

微醉的时候，他又看见了赵驹。他还以为自己是看花了眼，但是赵驹却向他走了过来，在他的桌旁坐下。他认识到这是真的，这让他更郁闷了。他此时此刻最不想看见的就是赵驹。本来他一个人坐在这里喝酒买醉，不一定会有多少人认出他来，现在好了，两大汉奸聚首，不令人瞩目也难了。

赵驹让伙计赠送了两盘牛肉上来。赵驹边吃边说，赵镇长，看样子你这喝的不是高兴酒，也不是怡情酒哇。

赵宏伟一抱拳，说，见笑，见笑。

赵驹喝了一杯酒，说，你这个人就是矫情，日子都过得这么滋润了，还喝什么闷酒？

我怎么滋润了？

还不是？你当了镇长，又大难不死，锄奸队现在又滚出了赵家镇，你不该大笑特笑吗？

你难道不也该笑吗？锄奸队一走，你也高枕无忧了，可是我看你今天，

喝的也不是什么高兴酒吧？

我从来没有在乎过锄奸队，军统早晚会被特高课灭掉的，杀我也不是白杀的。我不高兴，是因为我升官升得没你快。

你不是就要出任江庆县警察局局长了吗？

黄了，渡边给按下来了。

为什么？

渡边说，他离不开我这个人才。

他是怕会失去了当主人的乐趣吧？

想不到你能悟出这一层，看来你也是深有体会了。当初我怎么说的？我说，你早晚会和我一样的。

谢您吉言，这份祝福就不必了。

不过也不要紧，你知道吗，内部消息，渡边也马上要升中佐了，到时会担任江庆县日军联队的副联队长一职，我跟着去，也不会吃亏。

哦，渡边就要离开赵家镇了？

是的。

太好了。

你也别高兴得太早，北川会来赵家镇接班，担任大队长。听说北川不太喜欢你？你的日子要难过了。

不会，我和每位太君的关系都不错。

同伙面前，就不要装大爷了。

赵驹嘿嘿地笑着，甩给赵宏伟一脸的轻蔑，然后仰脖喝酒。一杯下肚后，用手一抹头发，满脸的志得意满状，一只膝盖却在不停地哆嗦。赵宏伟在某本西洋书上看到过，抖膝盖是人撒谎或者紧张时的动作。这令赵宏伟顿时困惑不已。赵驹此刻撒了什么谎吗？赵驹有什么需要紧张的吗？赵宏伟觉得，都没有。赵驹喝着酒，吃着肉，眼神是那么傲慢与不可一世，腰上的枪锃亮，为他更添了几分威武与强壮。怎么看，此刻的赵驹都是赵宏伟记忆里原来的那个赵驹，镖局的大少爷，风流的浪荡子。与上次跟他赵宏伟在酒楼里聚饮时的那个赵驹不一样，那个赵驹的眼里是含着热泪的。正是那种热泪，才让赵宏伟没能狠下心来把子弹往他身上打。但是今天的赵驹却又是饱含着平日里恃强凌弱的风采。只不过他平日里不抖膝盖而已。这让赵宏伟不禁觉得赵驹是个谜。赵宏伟喝了一小口酒，不说话，就听赵驹扯东扯西。赵驹说，汪精卫的事情将来一定会是个历史谜团，天知道他和蒋介石之间究竟是怎么回事，说不定汪精卫就是蒋介石的第二套方案，要不然戴笠为什么没在能下手的时候对汪精卫下手？也可能，是因为蒋介石原本平白无故不好除掉汪精卫，知道汪有了当汉奸的心，就故意放他去当，然后汪就成了全民公敌，蒋要宰汪就成了天经地义，这种内幕谁能说得清呢，是不是？总之都不是什么好东西。赵驹说，我们小时候的书，真的都是白念了，儒家要我们当忠臣，道家要我们绝圣弃智，佛家就更不用说了，三国教了我们权谋，唐僧教了我们改过，红楼教了我们痴情受苦，最有用的一本水浒，也就只是教了我们乱从上起，两千五百年了，从来就没人教过我们，要是有一天皇帝不在了，我们究竟该给谁卖命。赵驹又说，本来这几天，大家都是可以乐一乐的，东北派了一个四五十人的慰安团过来，先去了江北，接下来就要来江南，哪知道往这边过来的时候，半路上碰上了一架不知道是从哪里蹿出来的国民党飞机，把那个慰安团给炸了个稀巴烂，你说国民党有病是不是，有日本人不炸去炸那些比劳工还惨的女人，你说他们的抵抗对日本人究竟还有个啥用？能胜利才怪！

赵驹滔滔不绝地说着，两盘牛肉就快见底。他唾沫飞溅，笑容四溢，偶尔有人向他投来厌恶的目光，他便总是不可一世而充满挑衅地向那人一瞪。瞪完，他由内而外地舒畅。听着赵驹的口若悬河，赵宏伟越来越感到寒意刺骨。他忽然开始领悟到，赵驹的东拉西扯，或许和他平日里的东想西想、反复思量没什么两样。大家都是在用脑子里无用的空转，来麻痹心底里疼痛的神经，遮盖住眼前刺目的一切。当然在赵宏伟的心里还有另一个声音一直在对他说：赵驹就不是一个入流的东西。赵宏伟感到这本身就是一种悲哀。

“赵驹，我们的下场最后都会是一样的。”赵宏伟喝了口酒，突然说。

“我知道。”赵驹不假思索地说。

“那你说说看，我们现在，为什么还要在这里为了一些无益的事，说一些无益的话？”

赵驹一笑，说：“不为无益之事，何以度有涯之生？”

赵宏伟无言以对，眼前忽然差点一黑。

而赵驹却开怀大笑，笑得四座皆惊。他威武极了，环视了一圈，遂无人

敢动。

赵驹叫来了第三盘牛肉。他吃了两块，又开始说话，说这说那。赵宏伟突然觉得自己已经失去了听这个人说话的勇气。他越是说得滔滔不绝、宛若家常，赵宏伟就越觉得人活着可怕。这是一种十分奇怪的感觉，就好像一个人明明已经死了，却还在照常吃喝拉撒，吹拉弹唱；人生已经绝望而死亡，生命却还没有结束，尸体依然要活得朝气蓬勃、自强不息，这是怎样的一种恐怖。又或者这的确只是赵宏伟的个人感觉，赵驹也许并不觉得自己恐怖。那么，真正令赵宏伟感到可怕的，也许就是他在觉得恐怖的那一刻，真的是拿自己当成了赵驹。

就好像，在赵驹之谜的深处，躺着的，却是他赵宏伟的尸骨。

赵宏伟从口袋里掏出了钱来，放在了桌上。他向赵驹一抱拳，说，您慢用，我先告辞了。说完，转身就走。

赵驹还在他背后醉醺醺地大喊：喂，赵镇长，别走哇，我还有话没说完呢，渡边说，你个老光棍，该不会是不喜欢女人吧，哈哈哈。

赵驹的笑声在后面余音绕梁，赵宏伟难受得都想要吐了。他走出酒楼，一看天空，那天是蓝得那么深，没有半点阴暗，光芒万丈，照得人心里一阵发慌。

再过几天，就是端午了。方远梦已捎来了消息，五月初六晚上带秀珍母女出赵家镇。方远梦最后又征求了赵宏伟一次意见：你是不是确定要送她们去重庆？

然而这一回，赵宏伟没有马上回答。他短暂地陷入了一阵犹豫之中。以前方远梦也问过他这个问题，他总是回答得毫不犹豫。当然是去重庆了，有哪里会比临时首都更安全呢？虽说第一批逃去武汉的人都后悔死了，说早知蒋介石还要再撤，就不瞎耽误工夫了，当初直接奔重庆就得了，但是赵宏伟想，重庆总不会再失守了吧？临时首都总不是说改就能改的，定了，就必定会严防死守的吧？想当年，赵构退到了临安，也就没有再退了。但是现在，日军又开始轰炸重庆了！真是怎么办才好哇！焦土抗战，焦他个屁，赵宏伟莫名悲愤地想。老蒋想学俄罗斯当年对付拿破仑的那一套，生搬硬套，结果是自己给自己下了套，赵宏伟想。赵宏伟现在实在是无法再果断地向方远梦说出“重庆”两字，行动已近在眼前，他必须马上做出决定。

其实再仔细想想，赵宏伟也觉得自己当初的考虑不周。送秀珍母女去了重庆，然后接下来呢？她们的生活会怎么样呢？秀珍依然要靠给人家洗衣服来维持生计吗？维持得了吗？听说重庆那里的物价高得很，有些老百姓已经连粥也喝不上了。另外，重庆那里是没有日本人，也没有土匪，可是恶霸与豪绅呢？那应该是不会少的。大家都在说，前方吃紧，后方紧吃，那么重庆那里的政治风貌和社会环境是可想而知的。而这些问题他以前居然都没有认真地考虑到。他的头“嗡”一下地就大了。

最后，赵宏伟还是说，对，重庆。算了，人算不如天算，你想得再多再周全，也不如世事变化得又快又出奇。就去天子脚下吧，再不好，总是国家的心脏。赵宏伟想。

方远梦说，好的。

赵宏伟觉得，自己其实是很对不起方远梦的。自己已经在请人家共产党帮忙了，其实骨子里却又并不十分信任人家，不然，他为什么没想过要把秀珍母女送去延安呢？他不知道方远梦是否想到过这个问题，他希望他没想到过。

赵宏伟有时还是会想起那个姚志。方远梦已经有很久没有再说起那个姚志了，最后一次说起时，也只是一声叹息。江庆县里也已经很久没有再发生过正式的枪战了，一切都太平得很。有传说，玉山的游击队已经垮掉了。但是赵宏伟知道游击队没垮。之所以这么长时间以来，游击队都一直不再有什么行动，赵宏伟猜，一定是因为共产党在日军内部的那个内应已经死了的缘故。没有了内应，再和日本人打，那就等于是瞎子斗老虎。所以，赵宏伟觉得游击队的确是不要动的好，安全第一，他自己就一直是秉承着这么个宗旨在生存。姚志应该没有叛变，不然，日军早上玉山剿灭游击队了。玉山是个地形复杂、山势险峻的地方，以前国民党的剿匪部队声势浩大、一本正经地剿了玉山帮好几次都没能将玉山帮剿掉，可想而知玉山是个多么好的堡垒雄关。没有内部的人带路指道，外面的人根本进不去，进去了也是送死。所以有些玉山上的游击队员，和日军交战时受了伤，是宁死也不愿当俘虏的，就怕会有个万一。但是很不幸，姚志逃也没逃成，死也没死成，就成了被日军天天活活折磨的俘虏。姚志被捕后，赵宏伟相信玉山上游击队的部署一定会

有所调整的，毕竟谁还没有个万一呢？但是一旦姚志开口，部署再怎么与以前不同，姚志也总还是能猜出个几分来的，毕竟以前是自己人嘛。这也是游击队一直在营救姚志的一半原因，赵宏伟想。然而日军至今仍未攻山，赵宏伟心中对姚志的仰慕开始深重了起来。那该是怎样钢筋铁骨的一个人哪！日军的手段，赵宏伟在镇政府里渡边建的普通审讯室里也见识过，那都不是人能干出来的事啊！更不用说县城里的高级审讯室了。日子越是长一天，赵宏伟心中对姚志这个人的敬仰便莫名的深重一分，他对自己的憎恶也就越是浓烈一成。有时候，他憎恶自己和可怜自己，就跟憎恶赵驹又可怜赵驹一样。一个在敌人的胯下自我麻痹而自甘堕落的人，有多么的可憎又可怜！

当然，姚志也可能已经死了。虽然方远梦嘴上没说，但是赵宏伟猜，他心里也已有了这个准备。大半年了，天天酷刑，谁能受得了哇？姚志之所以还没开口，多半是因为，他已无法再开口了。

方远梦一直没有再向赵宏伟透露过姚志的其他信息，赵宏伟猜，其实当初方远梦给他看姚志的照片并告诉他姚志的事情，这本身一定是违反纪律的。不管姚志事件在当时游击队行动失败的情况下是否仍具有不可透露性，单就他赵宏伟是个汉奸来讲，方远梦就不该告诉他那么多真实的事情。但是方远梦是条北方汉子，豪迈的背后是单纯，他面对赵宏伟的救命之恩与尴尬身份，选择了不以政治标准画线的肝胆相照，他用坦露这次行动的原委与事件核心人物的情况的方式，向赵宏伟表达了他真诚的友谊与真诚的信任，这对于一名潜伏人员来说，其实是犯罪的行为。但他就是告诉了赵宏伟。赵宏伟是被方远梦感动了的。什么是朋友？就是人家信任你，毫无顾忌地将他的秘密和他的性命一齐放在你的手上，然后对你说“你是我的朋友，我相信你”。这也许就是所谓的义气。义气，有时或许是能够超越政治立场的，赵宏伟想。但是在民族大义上，他又是否真的没有对不起方远梦呢？他不敢想。

赵宏伟忽然下了个决心：在秀珍走后，他，一定要报答方远梦。共产党安插在日军内部的眼睛不是瞎了吗？这只眼睛，他可以当。

竹内将于六月初二离开江庆县，奔赴南京。于是，他确定将于六月初一赴赵家镇小学听课。同时，竹内决定，将尽快把县城里的学校都给空出来，不再作兵营，还给孩子们，以减轻赵家镇小学的负担。渡边提醒赵宏伟，学生一旦转移至江庆县城，那么你赵宏伟也是有可能要跟着被调去江庆县城的。去了县城以后干什么呢？那就要看你这次公开讲课给竹内留下的印象好不好了，要是讲得好的话，那么除了铁定会担任县城里的小学校长或中学校长以外，再担任个副县长也是有可能的。你毕竟已经是镇长了，去了县城，总不能反而让你没了政府职位吧？必定是会让你更上一层楼的。你只要表现好，皇军一定不会亏待你的。

副县长？副县长？赵宏伟的脑子像是陷入了一个停顿。副县长的下一步会是什么？县长。县长的下一步会是什么？什么都有可能。这难道就是传说中的步步高升、锦绣前程？赵宏伟心里一阵恍惚。自从东洋留学归来，赵宏伟就一直徘徊在一个大丈夫无用武之地的低谷之中，聪明好学在一个已经不再是学生了的人的身上成了一件多余的装饰品。他既不能用他辛苦学来的西学为国家的机械工业做出什么贡献，也不能用他自小就背熟了的孔孟之道为天下兴亡出一计一策，他前半生的努力好像就是为了让他的后半生看起来更加无用和更加可笑。赵宝贵对儿子的希望和老秀才对弟子的梦想，在赵宏伟的身上就像是两块令人痒得睡不着觉的巨大皮癣，想找一点对症治疗的药又找不到，挠又挠不好。挠多了会出血，不挠又痒得慌。最终好不容易当上了个区区小学的校长，还是花钱托关系买来的。赵宏伟在漫长的人生里，日复一日地感受着自身的荒唐与可笑，简直都快要麻木了。社会地位与金条银票的双重缺失，几乎已让赵宏伟的下半生步入了一个和他的上半生截然不同的深重泥潭里，那里不仅没有众人真心的赞扬与仰慕，还充满了个人深切的自卑与失落，令他时时刻刻不得不承认自己的人生是个可悲的笑话。而举目四望，那些大字都不识几个的军阀、财主，却都活得金玉满堂、活色生香。枪杆子一指，要啥有啥。赵宏伟是羡慕得两眼生疮。

而日本人一来，就让他当了局长，还委他以重任，树他为典型，令他频频上报，让他发言出声，这简直就是千里马碰上了东洋伯乐呀！赵宏伟又像是重新收获到了他学生时代所惯常享有的那些骄傲与荣光。那种出类拔萃而又鹤立鸡群的美妙感觉，在他东洋毕业以后他就再也没有占有过了。那是一种多么令人上瘾的感觉呀！他都已经四十岁了，大半辈子都过去了，功名利禄，早已是让他望穿秋水、饥渴难耐、两鬓斑白。细想想，他的投降，开

始时固然是无奈、恐惧所致，但后来，他难道又真的没半分企图？他自己也不敢对自己撒谎。而今，他已是赵家镇的镇长，明天，还可能是副县长、县长，后天，甚至还可以是省长！只要他能选定主子，一忠到底，将来必定要啥有啥。

赵宏伟给了自己一个耳光。自己这都是在想啥呢？自己是在想着要当卖国贼吗？老秀才从小就教给他的那些英雄好汉都去哪儿了？苏武、岳飞、杨家将、文天祥，他们当年要是都识时务者为俊杰，哪里还来的什么千古英名啊！圣贤有云，饿死事小，失节事大呀！

赵宏伟用一颗愧对国家民族的心，惩罚自己饿了一天肚子。晚上实在饿得忍不住了，还是出去买了三个肉包子吃。

赵宏伟在镇政府里行走也有一段时间了，政府院子后面的审讯室和牢房，他是不去的，只偶尔经过几次，每次经过，都是心惊胆战。随着赵家镇日渐太平，镇政府里也没什么人好关，可是只要一有人被关进来，那审讯室里必是惨叫不绝。赵宏伟有一次好奇，探头往审讯室里看了一眼，吓得直想把自己的眼珠子抠出来。日本人正在给犯人拔指甲，犯人拒绝回答一次就拔一次，拔一次，犯人就惨叫一次，等到犯人的十根指头都血淋淋了，犯人已昏死过去三次，每次都被日本人用烙铁烫醒。审讯室里总是充满了浓烈的血腥味和焦煳味，赵宏伟一经过就想吐。

死掉的犯人和从犯人身上割、拔下来的东西，都会被日本人丢在牢房后面的垃圾场里，由专人定期处理。那是整个政府院子里最臭最恶心的地方，也是全镇最惨最恐怖的地方，赵宏伟从来不去那里，每次都是远远地绕过。纵然是远远地绕过，也依旧会有无数的绿头苍蝇围扑而来。竹内也曾提醒过渡边，要注意镇政府的卫生问题，不要弄得如此肮脏不堪。渡边却不以为意，他说，这里不是后方，是战场，身为军人，在战场上哪还有空去考虑干净不干净的问题？中国有句俗语，不干不净，吃了没病。

赵驹去了县城的靶场。据说，只要条件允许，赵驹每周都会去一次靶场。赵驹的枪法，在渡边的大队里是有名的。北川有一次想要和赵驹在枪法上一决高下，而赵驹居然没有输，给渡边挣足了面子。后来，渡边就定下了一条规矩，只要是赵驹想开枪，子弹管够。就算没有靶场，赵驹也一样要练枪，有时他干脆就拿死刑犯练。当然了，是不是死刑犯，随渡边高兴。渡边看着赵驹拿活人练枪，赞叹不已，经常会由衷地鼓掌。就像猎狗，表现得越出色，猎人越是感到由衷的欣喜。这样的一个赵驹，想要去当竹内手下的警察局长，渡边又怎会放行。所以，从这个角度来看，其实是该赵宏伟嫉妒赵驹才对。赵宏伟的名分比赵驹大，但在渡边的眼里也就只是一面旗而已。旗倒了不会死，猎狗跑了才是心头之痛。

赵宏伟能感受到赵驹骨子里对他的轻蔑。这种轻蔑从何而来？也许是他看穿了赵宏伟的处境，也许是他看穿了赵宏伟的人品。赵驹捧赵宏伟的那些话，在赵宏伟听来都像是在挖苦他。但是赵驹的挖苦又似乎并不是为了抬高他自己，而只是为了进行一个嘲笑的游戏。在这个游戏里，一切严肃的都会被分解成可笑，一切冠冕堂皇的都会被解释成荒诞不经。赵宏伟感到很难受。他感到这样一个俯视的角度应该理所当然地是由他来占据的，但是莫名其妙的，他却成了被俯视的对象。而更荒唐的，是他居然很在乎，他和赵驹，究竟是谁才有资格去俯视谁。他感到了自己的堕落。

赵驹要赵宏伟去见他。赵宏伟只能赶去了靶场。到了靶场，日头已经西斜。赵驹以一个雕塑般的姿势一动不动地站着，手举着枪，歪着头，瞄准着前方，却又迟迟不开枪。日光为他拉下了一条细长的黑影，黑影在不平的地上像是被人给揍了个坑坑洼洼。

赵宏伟从背后走过去，问，你找我有什么事？

赵驹不开口，也不动，依旧端着枪。

赵宏伟耐着性子，就像憋着尿一样地等着。等了一会儿，赵驹终于说，来了？

废话。赵宏伟想。

赵驹放下了枪，长长的枪管戳在地上，就像一根造型独特的拐棍。他依旧没有回转身来，而是面朝着夕阳，就像有些诗人喜欢干的那样。

方远梦是你什么人？赵驹问。

赵宏伟顿时一惊。是我朋友。他说。

他是干什么的？

以前和我一样，也教书，教算术，现在在贩鸡。

贩鸡？

是的。

生意好不好？

还行。

听说你经常去他那里玩？

是的。我们是好朋友。

哦。好朋友。

赵驹一动胳膊，又抬起了枪，瞄准着前方。

来，也去拿一把枪，咱俩比比。赵驹说。

赵宏伟就去拎了一条枪过来。

枪口瞄准着前方，但是赵宏伟知道自己一定打不准。没开枪之前，是个人拿眼睛瞄都能瞄得准，但是真开了枪，枪一抖，子弹往哪飞，就真的是只有有本事的人才能掌控得了。所以赵宏伟知道自己此刻的瞄准很可笑，也很像是在做戏，但是他又的确是不想输给赵驹。

“砰”一响，赵驹打碎了一个瓶。“砰”一响，赵宏伟浪费了一颗子弹。

“知道吗，上海军统站的副站长叛变了，全站的人都被捕了。从江庆县刚过去的锄奸队也在拒捕时死光了。”

“是吗，那是好事。”

“你真的这么想吗？”

“砰”，又一枪，赵驹又打碎了一个瓶。赵宏伟放下了枪，说：“你什么意思？”

“有学生告诉渡边，你让他们当着日本人的面喊天皇万岁，背着日本人说‘我是中国人’。”

“教育要一步一步来，你现在让我教他们说‘我是日本人’，他们也不信哪。”

“这话你得去跟渡边说。”

赵宏伟生气了，“渡边他不相信我还干吗要我当镇长，叫他另择贤能！”

“谁告诉你，渡边让你当镇长就一定会相信你？”

赵宏伟觉得自己就要漏气了。“我问心无愧！”他说。

赵驹放下了枪，长叹一声，“最好不要说这句话，会被祖宗笑死的。”

赵宏伟干瘪了下去。

“知道渡边为什么不相信你吗？”

“为什么？”

“就因为你的手上，从来没沾过中国人的血！”

赵驹说完，朝天又放了一枪。

“你……究竟是不是汉奸？”赵宏伟颤抖着问。

“我不是谁是！”赵驹说完，端起枪，朝天乱放。

夕阳照得人眼花缭乱。

心音又来梦里找赵宏伟了。她拉着他的手，走过了一道又一道门，每一道门的后面，都是一个风光迥异的季节。春红夏绿，秋黄冬白，每一个季节里，都生长着一些赵宏伟似曾相识的故事。每一个故事里，都布满了赵宏伟和心音的影子。这个梦好长，每一个季节都有赵宏伟一生那么长。每一道门过去，赵宏伟和心音就像是重新又相识相爱了一次。大半个梦走下来，赵宏伟和心音就像是已经相爱了几生几世，而他们却还没有厌倦，依然充满好奇地期待着下一道门之后的缠绵悱恻与依依不舍。直到他们迈入了最后一道门，横在他们跟前的，是一个没有季节没有颜色的悬崖。只要他们再往前走几步，就会一起掉进那悬崖下的无底深渊中。心音说，我们一起跳，我们一起跳。赵宏伟说，不要，不要。心音忽然就放开了赵宏伟的手，自己往前跑了去，大笑着，跳下了悬崖。悬崖下传来了一声巨响，赵宏伟背后的那一道道门开始纷纷倒塌。烟尘四起，五彩碎尽。终于，“轰隆”一声，赵宏伟脚下的地也塌了，他猛地就掉进了一条冰河里。河水刺骨，冰得他周身发麻僵硬，而他不能呼吸，不能呼吸！

赵宏伟一下子醒了过来。他喘着气，坐了起来，才发现自己已浑身是汗。黑茫茫的夜里，他听着窗外夏虫的声息，忽然感到了梦结束了的孤独。一种人烟寂灭的难受，像河水一样漫过了他的脖颈，慢慢淹没了他的头顶。他的心憋得好难受，两行清泪，流过他的嘴角，流进他的嘴里。他忽然发现人生最无用的就是流泪。你就是把泪流成了河，你心里的难受，泪也带不走一点点。而窗外的夏虫依然在鸣叫，叫得这夜更显枯寂。枯寂得就像是在人的生命里，已经没有了许多许多年的人烟，枯寂得叫人喘不过气来。

赵宏伟忽然就觉得很对不起秀珍。他终究还是不爱她。或者说，有些爱，却终究还是不能爱到梦里。这或许就是人生的无能为力。

从靶场回来以后，赵宏伟就想偷一把枪。这个愿望非常强烈，以致他寝食难安。很早以前，他也曾向渡边提出过要枪的请求，但是渡边并没答应。你一个文职人员要什么枪？是不是信不过我们皇军，还是另有企图？所以，赵宏伟也就一直没再动过这个要枪的念头。上一次在酒楼里他赵宏伟对赵驹动了枪，这令渡边十分恼怒，赵宏伟能明显感受到渡边对他提高了戒心，这更是令赵宏伟在渡边面前不敢再多看枪一眼。但是现在，要枪这个强烈的愿望又从他的心里冒了出来，而且怎么样也压不下去。以前，他不敢要枪是怕引来性命之忧，而现在，要枪已成了他保命的必需。

赵宏伟可以肯定，渡边是派人跟踪了他。仔细一回想，还真是有那么一些蛛丝马迹。他心里直懊悔，平时言行太不注意。也不知渡边现在究竟是知道了他多少秘密的事。要是真把方远梦给暴露了，那他的罪孽可就大了。而且秀珍她们还没被送出去，这可如何是好？自己本来还想帮着方远梦打听打听姚志的事情，这下可好了，能不暴露就已是万幸了。

那么赵驹是什么意思呢？看样子，他也并不是想要为难他赵宏伟。而且，赵驹的谈话，多少好像是有点通风报信的意思。赵宏伟彻底迷惑了。难道赵驹是军统？难道赵驹是共产党？不可能。赵驹的手上，沾了不知道多少国共两党抗日人士的血，他不可能是潜伏人员。那么赵驹又为什么要提醒他赵宏伟呢？赵宏伟解释不了了。

不管是日本人还是亲日的中国人，对赵驹的统一评价都是：心狠手辣、血债累累。从某个角度上来说，其实赵驹比赵宏伟更具日中合作的典范性质。只不过因为赵驹年轻时的名声太臭，学识也不好，所以渡边才不立他为汉奸榜样。赵驹是日本人身旁最出色的鹰犬，这一点在日军内部毫无争议。但是，唯一有一点，是让大部分日本鬼子无法理解而颇感困惑的，那就是：赵驹从不强奸女人。

从跟随日本人的那天起，就从不。

端午节，天气不是很热。除了粽子、黄酒、黄瓜、黄鳝、黄鱼、黄泥蛋，赵宏伟还做了很多菜，弄了满满一大桌。小菊高兴得直拍手，秀珍直说不要烧了，不要烧了，怎么吃得掉。

赵宏伟兴高采烈，说，吃，吃。

赵宏伟此刻心里的想法其实很复杂。这顿饭，是他难得和秀珍、小菊在一起吃的团圆饭，况且又正值端午佳节、出逃前夕，可以说是三喜齐聚。而秀珍也的确就是这么想的。赵宏伟心里却明白，这是他最后一次和秀珍、小菊在一起吃饭了。他骗秀珍，说为了掩人耳目，她们必须要明天先走，他得晚几天再动身，到了重庆再会合。秀珍轻易地相信了他的话。赵宏伟心里酸酸的。他不禁觉得，中国人的吃饭真是一件意义极其丰富的事情。

赵宏伟不停地给秀珍和小菊夹菜，说，尝尝我的手艺，看看我是不是宝刀未老。小菊塞得嘴里满满的，呵呵笑。小菊啃着鸡腿，说，要是天天都有这么多好吃的，那就太好啦。赵宏伟摸摸小菊的头，说，小菊要是喜欢，伯伯以后天天给你做这么多好吃的。小菊说，好哇。

秀珍说，傻孩子，娘啥时候把你养成了一个小馋鬼。

小菊呵呵笑，赵宏伟和秀珍也笑。秀珍给赵宏伟倒酒，赵宏伟问，你东西都收拾好了吗？秀珍说，都收拾好了。赵宏伟点点头，然后起身，去屋里拿出一个盒子来，交到了秀珍的手上，说，这个你拿着。

秀珍拿着沉甸甸的盒子，不禁问，这是什么？一边就打开了盒子。一看，是五根金条和厚厚的几沓法币。你这是干什么？

是这样的，这些钱你先帮我拿着，你知道，我太显眼了，走的时候身上带着这些一定不方便。你先帮我把这些东西带出去，小心拿好。以后到了重庆，你也别给人洗衣服了，我也不抛头露面了，我们就拿这个做本钱，一起做点小生意，相信维持温饱是不会有问题的。

赵宏伟一口一个“我们”，一口一个“一起”，向秀珍描绘着未来的美好蓝图。听他的言下之意，到了重庆之后，就是要跟秀珍和小菊在一起过日子了。秀珍听着听着，不禁就有些羞涩了起来，一直低着头，嫣然而笑，没说好，也没说不好。倒是小菊，高兴得拍起了手来，说，好哇，好哇。

“宏伟哥你放心，这些钱我一定帮你拿好，不会有事的。到了那边，我们……我们一起好好过下去。”秀珍开心而欢喜地说。

赵宏伟将杯中的酒饮尽，依然笑着，心里却说，秀珍哪，我在骗你，以后你只要少恨我一些，我就死也瞑目。

赵宏伟又喝了一碗酒，看着对他深情了半生的秀珍，忽然心里涌起了一

股难以名状的热流，热得他直想流泪，热得他只想喝醉。他蓦然有了一个冲动：那坛状元红，今日不开，更待何时？

他果断地站了起来，心中激情澎湃。然而，一阵小小的头晕恰逢其时地袭击了他。不是酒的作用。年纪大了，近来又倍觉寝食难安，头晕一下也很平常。莫名其妙地，他的激情顿时烟消云散。

宏伟哥，你怎么了？秀珍关切地问。

哦，没什么，想去拿个碟子，一时有点头晕，现在又不晕了。

我去拿，你坐着。

赵宏伟就又坐了下来。赵宏伟呀赵宏伟，不能让秀珍她陷太深，不然，几天之后，真相大白之时，你让她情何以堪？他对自己说。今天你和她喝了状元红，明天，她会恨你一生一世，这头晕来得正是时候哇，不要孟浪，不要孟浪。

秀珍拿来了碟子。赵宏伟的眼神不经意与她一撞，她又喜又羞。借着酒劲，赵宏伟想，秀珍真美。他看不够似的看着她。人是真奇怪，越想好了要断情断义了，那情义却反倒浓得像个梦似的，他想。秀珍拍拍他，说，宏伟哥，你醉了。他说，嗯，我醉了。秀珍就笑了，说，嘿嘿，你装醉，哪有醉鬼知道自己醉的。

秀珍，还记得你小时候我教你唱过的那支歌吗？“长亭外，古道边，芳草碧连天——”

记得呀。“晚风拂柳笛声残，夕阳山外山——”

娘，这支歌我也会唱，你教过的。“天之涯，地之角，知交半零落——”

三人笑着，一起唱了起来。

歌声袅袅，欢情无痕。

一壶浊酒尽余欢，今宵别梦寒。

余音散尽，赵宏伟说：秀珍，来生我一定一早就娶你。

五月初六，天有些阴。

上午，赵宏伟很小心地去了一次方远梦那里。他很确信后面没有尾巴。自从被赵驹提醒之后，他每次去方远梦那里都得在路上磨蹭好长时间，他又不敢告诉方远梦，日军已在注意他们的关系。他怕说了，方远梦会要求他疏远他。起码在秀珍的事办好之前，赵宏伟是不允许这种情况发生的。方远梦疏远他了，谁还能帮他？

一路上赵宏伟看见有不少日本兵在街上贴告示，他也没有心情去看。该死的鬼子，肯定又是在征钱征粮，吃死他们。他恨恨地想。

见到了方远梦，赵宏伟没有寒暄。虽然这并不符合他一直以来讲话之前必先寒暄的处世风格，但是他今天心里莫名乱得很，已无所谓自己该是怎样的一个自己才对。他觉得连讲话都是自己的一个巨大负担。他无言地将一封信交给了方远梦，嘱咐他说，到了重庆后，请将此信交给秀珍。方远梦一琢磨，点头说好。方远梦放好了信，说，路上有好几天，我不能保证，能帮你把谎圆上。赵宏伟说，你尽力吧，谎话要是半路上穿帮了，你就提前把这信给她，我想她会懂的。

赵宏伟莫名感到了累极了地坐着，就像全身没一处不是锈了一样。这和他昨天的想象完全不一样。他本来以为，今天该是斗志昂扬的一天，今天该是意气风发的一天。

怎么了，你身体不舒服吗？方远梦不禁问。

赵宏伟仔细感受了一下自己身体的感觉，还真是没病。他叹了一口气，沮丧透了地说，方兄，一切都拜托了。

赵宏伟告辞了。虽然他极不想再走动，但是理智告诉他，此地不宜久留，关键时刻，不要惹出什么是非来。

走在回家去的路上，赵宏伟垂头丧气。他也很不明白自己，大功将成，何以不喜反愁？

走着走着，赵宏伟忽然觉得有些不对。哪里不对？路上有些乱。

一队日本兵在挨家挨户敲门，门开了，他们就询问。太远了，也听不清日本人在问些什么。有些人家被问完了以后就直接关上了门，有些人家被问完了以后，就会从屋里走出来一个或大或小的姑娘，跟在这队日本人的队伍后面。这队日本兵的态度看上去很友善，但是被问的人家和那些姑娘，却都是满脸又惊又疑又怕又无奈的神色。路上有些老太婆在窃窃私语。有的人在赶着回家。一些菜叶在地上被人踩来又踩去，一条死鱼躺在路中间，也没人去捡。赵宏伟看看天，还是阴的。

又走过了一条街。赵宏伟又看到了另外的一队日本兵，在做着同样的事情。两队日本兵人都不多，一队才十来个，可是赵宏伟莫名觉得，好像是有几百个鬼子在逛街。他的心莫名紧了。他想问问人，是怎么回事，可是他既不方便去问日本人，也不方便去问中国人。

他看到了几个老太婆憎恨他的目光，就只好低着头，继续走。

终于找到了一个贴有告示的墙角，赵宏伟迫不及待地看了起来。是日本人的征工启事。说是日本人有大量的军服军被需要清洗，但是没有人手，所以要在本地征一批短工，短工必须是十四到三十五岁之间的女性，无论有空与否，见到告示，即去当地镇政府报到，报酬丰厚，洗完这批被服，即可完工回家。任何人不得借故推托，孕妇可以不参加。另外，女工一律不准在脸上涂灰抹黑，违者以侮辱政府论处。

原来是这么回事，赵宏伟想。忽然，他的额上沁出了汗来。坏了，秀珍要是被征走了，今天的行动就完了。他猛跑了起来。

他着急地敲着秀珍家的门，他喊人，里面没人应。过了一会儿，门才被打开。开门的是小菊。小菊的脸上，是惊魂未定。

小菊，怎么了，你娘呢？

刚才来了几个日本人，把娘带走了，说是要她去洗衣服。宏伟伯伯，我怕。

不怕，小菊。

赵宏伟说着，抱起了小菊。他的脸上，乌云密布。

赵宏伟把小菊安顿在自己家里，然后冷静了一下，就去了镇政府。这会儿路上安静了许多，也没见着拉人的日本人，也没见着闲扯淡的老太婆。但是鸟叫得很喧嚣，知了也聒噪，让人倍感心神不宁。

进了镇政府，遇上了两位汉奸同僚。他们跟他打招呼，他也懒得理他们。走过了一会儿，他突然后悔了起来，就又回转身追上了他们。寒暄了几句，就问起了今天日本人征洗衣工的事情。他们一脸茫然，说，我们不知道哇。他们来得早，还没看见街上的告示。其中一个说，不过今天日本人那边的院子里是很吵闹，像有事。但是你知道的，我们不能随便去他们那边瞎转悠。

是的，镇政府机关大院分成两个部分，除了赵驹和赵宏伟，一般人是不能随意进入日本人的院子里的。重要的部门都在日本人那边，汉奸院里的人，做的都是狗干的事情，可有可无。

赵宏伟去了日本人那边，过院门的时候，看门的日本兵犹豫了一下，最后还是放了他进去。这个犹豫，让赵宏伟心里越发沉重了起来。

走到院子里面的一片空场上，果然看见场子里站着许多大姑娘和小姑娘，个个都是一脸的迷茫与害怕。他看见了秀珍，秀珍想喊他，他赶紧做手势，要她别喊。

他知道秀珍比其他人都要更着急，而他比秀珍更急。游击队做好安排不容易，错过了今晚，路上的形势就会有变，而夜长梦多，再要走，就不知难不难了。

渡边悄无声息地从背后走了出来，拍了赵宏伟的肩膀一下，吓了赵宏伟一跳。

赵镇长，今天怎么有空来这边？

哦，没什么，一时有空，想过来看望看望太君，顺便向您汇报一下我准备的六月初一讲课方案。

好，这个讲课的事情，本来我也想再跟你谈一谈，这样，下午来我办公室，我约了两个记者，你跟他们吹吹牛，讲讲竹内的好话，也讲讲我的好话。哈哈哈。

好，好，没问题。

渡边笑着，两手合拢，拄着军刀，志得意满地望着场子里的那些女人们。

“太君，今天我看见告示，说，皇军要征洗衣工？”

“嗯，是的，你不是看见了吗，就是她们。”

“以前，我们不是从来没有……”

赵宏伟没有把话说完，渡边也没有接话，只是笑眯眯地看着那些女人。他转动着拄在地上的军刀，终于说：赵镇长，大日本皇军的命令，是不需要解释的。

是，是，是。赵宏伟诚惶诚恐。

渡边手一挥，一队日本兵，端着一盆又一盆的脏衣服来到了场地上。女人们开始洗衣服。天依旧阴得可怕。赵宏伟看了秀珍一眼，秀珍求助地望着

赵宏伟。

赵宏伟忽然发现，渡边的目光，指向的也是秀珍那个方向。秀珍正卖力地洗着衣服，鬓边几缕头发垂下，一动一动地，像春风里柔软的柳。

下午，送走了记者，趁着渡边高兴，赵宏伟向他提了个请求：他有位亲戚，此刻正在义无反顾地为皇军洗衣服，忠诚地为大东亚共荣尽绵薄之力，但是她的孩子今天病了，正在家里发烧，能不能请皇军开恩，让她回去照顾一两天孩子？或者哪怕只是在天黑前让她回去看一眼孩子也行。

渡边略一沉吟，说，这样吧，天黑前我们会让一批洗衣工回家，你的那个亲戚，要是运气好的话，就可以不用再来了。

初一听，赵宏伟感觉这话很鼓舞人心，但再一想，不对。事情很糟糕，渡边完全没有一点要特事特办的意思，他甚至连赵宏伟所说的那个亲戚是谁都不问。但是渡边又好像已经给了他赵宏伟很大面子似的。在渡边这只老狐狸面前，赵宏伟能时刻感到自己的无知与无能。

“太君，那请你待会儿一定先让我那亲戚回家，她叫王秀珍，叫王秀珍，她的孩子还在家里等她。”赵宏伟斗胆又补充道。

渡边不耐烦了，手一挥，说，你出去吧。

赵宏伟出去的时候，那些女人还在洗衣服。下午又新征来了几个小姑娘。女人们的场子周围站着日本兵，五步一岗，荷枪实弹。赵宏伟总觉得这里面有些不对。他的心跳得厉害，头也有些痛。他想去场子里看看秀珍，但一想，那样太招摇了，还是别节外生枝了。他在日本兵的后面站着，望着秀珍，秀珍也望了一眼他。两个人的眼神交流里，全是焦急，焦急。

赵宏伟走出了镇政府，看到有一些人围在镇政府外面。他问了问一位同僚，才知道都是那些洗衣女工的家人，他们是来问讯的。赵宏伟看了一眼，虽然天色已暗，但是那些围站人众的眼睛里却都像是喷着火，亮得吓人。他们就像是一群受到了威胁的羊，眼里虽然喷着狼一样的怒火，怒火的后面，却还是羊一样的恐惧和哀求。赵宏伟并不害怕他们，却很可怜他们，就像可怜他自己一样。这种可怜让他此刻的心情异常复杂，以致让他忽略了隐蔽自己，忽略了羊的怒火也是火这一基本事实。

有人认出了赵宏伟。人们开始要求他出来对话。赵宏伟起初还有些犹豫。要不是外面有日本兵拦着，赵宏伟就要被几个情绪激动的小伙子给拎出来了。赵宏伟万分后悔，他本不该在这里多作停留的，他还有更要紧的事。

他向后面的台阶上退了几步，以取得一种对人群的居高临下的姿态。然后他清了清嗓子，就将渡边刚才对他说的话的意思又向大伙讲了一遍。下面有人问：一批人先出来，那剩下的人呢？她们几时出来？

赵宏伟想，我也想知道哇。

他不再作回答。返回身，又进了镇政府，从后门溜了出去。他知道大家此刻一定在用最仇恨的心情咒骂他，但是他哪还有心情管这些。他得赶紧去找方远梦。

半路上他就碰见了方远梦。方远梦已知道事情生了变。两人找了一个僻静的角落说话。方远梦说，来接应的小秦已在镇子外面候着了，就等我们出去了，可是看样子这事怕是要耽搁了。方远梦还说，小秦说，今天很奇怪，不光是赵家镇的日军在征洗衣女工，江庆县下面的其他几个镇子里也在征，真是太奇怪了。

但是两个人也没有太多的时间去细细揣摩这件奇怪的事情。两人临时决定，方远梦先回去，做行动万一延后的准备，而赵宏伟则是回镇政府里去，想办法让秀珍早些出来，准时离开赵家镇。

分别时，方远梦对赵宏伟说，你也别光想着秀珍，你要想办法探探清楚，这次日本人葫芦里到底卖的是什么药，都是同胞姐妹，我们不能只想着自己。

赵宏伟说“唉”。

回镇政府的路上，赵宏伟感到了惭愧。方远梦是不想真的批评他，他明白。其实方远梦最后一句的意思就是：你不能只想着自己。是啊，他光想着要让秀珍出来，不就是只想着他自己吗？大家都是同胞姐妹呀！

天黑了下来，赵宏伟闻到，空气里到处都像是有死尸的气味。这死尸可以是一片树叶，也可以是一只知了，更可以是一只鸟，一首歌。

他跑了起来。

镇政府前面的人群并未散去。镇政府里还亮着灯。可能是聚集的百姓并没有做出什么过激的行动，所以日本兵也并没有对他们做强硬的驱散。有两

个百姓手里还提着两个灯笼，他们的嘴紧闭着，脸色像石板一样难看，眼睛直直地望着镇政府大门口，那在高高台阶之上的大门口。他们令赵宏伟想到了雕像，那翘首等待着妻子或女儿归家的表情，仿佛比死亡来得更深刻。现场并没有爆发什么冲突，双方都在沉默的僵持里等待。等待什么？就像是在等待一场冲突。

赵宏伟正准备溜去后门，忽然，镇政府的大门开了。出来了一些白天征进去的女工。人群骚动了起来。赵宏伟一兴奋，忘了自己的身份，就也冲进了人群里去。他焦急地寻找着秀珍。没有人管赵宏伟，认出了他来也没人在乎他。大家都在混乱里找着自己的亲人或爱人。没有秀珍，没有秀珍。在哪？在哪？

还有一些人也没找到自己要找的人。刚和谐了一点的场面，又开始骚乱了起来。

另一个汉奸从镇政府里面走了出来。他示意大家安静，然后对大家说：大家不要多担心，皇军就是需要有人帮他们洗一下衣服，你们不要以为有多大事似的，今天这些先放出来的，是衣服洗得不太好的，你们瞧，就是这些洗得不好的，她们手里不还是每人拿了一块大洋？剩下那些洗得好的，皇军会多留几天，管吃管喝，完了还会有赏钱。所以说嘛，你们瞎折腾个屁，聚在这里干啥？快回吧，快回吧。往后几天也都别来了，等衣被都洗完了，皇军自然就会让她们都回家了。散了吧，都散了吧。

那些被放出来的女工也向周围的人证实：是的，是这样的，你们瞧，我一块肉都没有少。一个胖姑娘还说，早知道真没事，还有钱拿，我白天就该好好洗，真想再多洗两天，多赚一些。一个脸长得比较难看的姑娘说，我洗得挺好的呀，怎么就不要我了，我隔壁那个狐狸精洗得一塌糊涂，怎么就没淘汰她。站在这姑娘旁边的一个老头就说，哎哟，我的傻闺女，你不知道爹在这里等得多急，心都要焦了，你倒好，还嫉妒上待在里面的了。周围有些人就笑了。又有人说，还是大洋好，法币跌得那么快，纸票哪有银圆来得实在。

气氛松了，大家也都开始散了。那些不需要再来洗衣服的姑娘，走得都很兴高采烈。那些没领到人的，心里虽然还有些担心，但是看着那些拿到了钱的兴高采烈的姑娘们，又觉得不需要太担心。大家终于还是很和谐地散了，并且相互表示，就听话吧，明天不要来这里等了，免得给待在里面的姑娘惹事，把好事弄成了坏事。

只有赵宏伟依然很呆愣地待在原地。焦急已在他心里偃旗息鼓。此刻秀珍还没能出来，那今晚逃跑的计划是铁定不会成功了，焦急在此刻已是个无用之物。此时此境，他赵宏伟已不允许自己的脑袋里还装着什么无用之物。此刻，只有一片强韧而密实的恐惧，在他的心里和脑里飘来飘去。黑色的忧惧像猛兽的脚步在他四周铿锵徘徊，他寒栗四起，颤抖不已。千百种猜测和担心在他的眼前游来游去，一个就在刚才被他发现了的事实却在变得越来越清晰：那些被放出来的女工，不是长得有些胖，就是长得有些丑。这个镇上的人他大半认识，所以这样一个归类式的判断，在他的心里来得并不费力，只是来得非常之巧。这个发现有些隐秘，就像是一堆乱麻之中隐藏着的一根红线。而这个线头不小心就被他赵宏伟给捡了起来。他既不敢确定这根线是不是答案之底，又不敢随意与人讨论这一带有恐怖意味的危险话题，一切只能靠他自己去细细咀嚼。夜的风就像是张着血盆大口，他就像是在一头巨兽面前思考。这思考既毫无用处，又只能给他徒增更深的忧惧。他希望能在事件里找出一些令人宽慰的线索来，但结果却只是证明：他的发现，是一个黑色的暗示。

赵宏伟往台阶上走，夏夜的风此刻令他感到十分憋闷。他刚要推开镇政府的大门，大门就被人从里面打了开来。是刚才对群众讲话的那个汉奸。“哟，赵镇长，是您哪。”

赵宏伟点点头。怎么，你去哪？他问。

我回家，这不刚忙完，日本人让我走了。

刚才我就在下面。今天的洗衣工究竟是怎么回事？刚才你对老百姓说的那些话，都是真的？

唉，赵镇长，连你都不知道的事情，我哪里会知道？今天大家都觉得很奇怪，但谁敢去问日本人呢？都是日本人让我对老百姓那么说的，谁晓得那是真话假话。

嗯。

那赵镇长我回去了，儿子还等我回去给他煎药呢。

行，那你走吧。

赵宏伟走了两步，忽然转回身，想再问他两句，想想还是算了。

到了里面，白天女工们洗衣的那个地方已经空空如也。他问站岗的日本兵，人呢，人都去哪儿了？日本兵说，天晚了，长官安排她们去仓库里睡了。赵宏伟就跑去了仓库。仓库没有窗，只有一扇很大很大的门，门外站着两个哨兵。从外面看不出仓库里是否亮着灯，他侧耳细听，也听不出仓库里有什么明显的声音。夜色里，只有镇政府里的一点微弱的灯光照在这座仓库的前边一面墙上，仓库黑得就像是躲在夜里的一头巨大的猫。微显神秘，也微显可怖。夏夜的闷热依旧，天上没有一颗星。赵宏伟走上前去，向哨兵表明了身份，然后问，这里面是不是住着白天的那些洗衣女工？哨兵说，是。赵宏伟提出要进去看一看，哨兵不许。哨兵生硬地说，这是渡边大队长亲自下的命令。赵宏伟问，什么命令？哨兵说，不准那边院子里的中国人进去。赵宏伟大声说，我是镇长，你们渡边大队长的朋友！哨兵说，命令里没有说你可以例外。赵宏伟大骂“混蛋”，俩哨兵无动于衷，完全不在乎。赵宏伟开始大喊：秀珍，秀珍，你在不在里面？在不在里面？你出来！你出来呀！

声嘶力竭的叫喊惊动了一片夜。两个日本兵听不懂汉语，见赵宏伟乱喊乱叫，就朝赵宏伟端起了枪。从日本人的院子里还跑出了几个看热闹的来。日本人的三八大盖是真长，插上了刺刀，比他自己的人还要长。这种武器设计也不知是不是源于日本人对冷兵器和肉搏战的热爱。赵宏伟看着那长长的枪和尖尖的刀，还想喊，张大了嘴，却发不出声。发不出声，心里难受得就像要爆炸了似的。

这时，仓库的门低沉笨重的“吱呀”了一声，开了一条缝出来。

“宏伟哥——”

“秀珍！”

一个哨兵转回身，用原来指着赵宏伟的枪指着秀珍，用日语大喊：回去，回去！

但是秀珍听不懂日语。赵宏伟要哨兵不要乱来，他和她说几句话就好。秀珍不敢出来，赵宏伟不敢上前，两人就那么隔着一片黑影站着。远处映过来的灯光实在太暗，仓库里也没开灯，赵宏伟虽然离秀珍很近，却也不能看清她细细的模样。此刻她看他，想必也是这样。赵宏伟的内心忽然很忧伤，这样的距离，这样的模糊，多像两人这么多年来比邻而居的一个缩影。

秀珍，你现在怎么样？

我没事，大家都在睡觉。

没事？

没事，日本人说，过两天衣服都洗完了，就放我们回去。

哦。

宏伟哥，帮我照顾小菊。

你放心。

秀珍还想再说，哨兵已开始轰她，要她回去。秀珍被哨兵推得摔了一跤。

“你放心，秀珍，我一定会救你出去的！”

哨兵关门前，赵宏伟突然喊了这么一句。喊完了，他才觉得自己这话有些莫名其妙。干吗要说“救”呢？自己真是想太多了。

赵宏伟去了一趟渡边的办公室那里，想跟渡边求求情，先放了秀珍。但是办公室的门紧锁着，从窗口望进去，里面黑漆漆的，甚至还透着股阴冷。赵宏伟想，自己真是犯糊涂了。渡边这大晚上的又怎会在镇政府里。他一定是在他的私邸里。但是，一直以来，赵宏伟都从没关心过渡边的私邸在哪里。他从未想过要去给渡边送礼拍马屁。真是关系门路大如天，一到用时方恨浅。

离开了镇政府，赵宏伟在没有灯的黑乎乎的路上走。他先回了一次自己的家，给小菊做了晚饭。小菊饿坏了，吃得狼吞虎咽。她的眼里满含着疑惑与忧惧，问赵宏伟，赵宏伟也只能拿些谎话来骗她。小菊睡下以后，他就又出了门。

他要去找方远梦，跟他讲一讲现在的情况，问问他的想法。赵宏伟的心底里，不相信日本人的话。但是日本人究竟是不是在说谎呢？他也不知道。他当然是希望日本人没有说谎，一切只是他在杞人忧天。但他的聪明程度又不允许他这么糊弄自己。人活着就是这么矛盾。

到了方远梦那里，赵宏伟将事情一说，方远梦也有些半信半疑。最后只能决定，静观其变。方远梦说，他明天一早就想办法去和小秦会面，看能不能知道一些周围镇子上的情况。

赵宏伟回到了家，躺在了床上，心里却越觉忐忑不安。为什么放出来的女人都是长得不好看的呢？而他所知道的一些镇上的漂亮姑娘都还在仓库里。这难道仅仅是一种巧合吗？真的只是他自己想太多了？他又没看见仓库里到底有哪些人，也许仓库里也还有一些丑姑娘呢，是不是？这样的话，他赵宏伟的推理和担心不就不成立了吗？对。就是这样的，赵宏伟想。

可是，这赵家镇上，又哪来那么多的丑姑娘呢？自古江南多美女呀，天杀的！他不禁又沮丧地想。

他辗转反侧。他觉得自己该去找找渡边，可是已经是大半夜了，有些事，就怕弄巧成拙。

小菊忽然哭了起来。

他赶紧开了灯，去看小菊。小菊哭着说，宏伟伯伯，我想娘了。

赵宏伟说，小菊乖，你娘去给你找好吃的了，找到了，就会回来了。

小菊说，我不要好吃的了，我要娘。

赵宏伟说，那好，小菊乖，明天我就帮你把娘找回来。

小菊说，宏伟伯伯你一定要对我娘好，我娘很喜欢你的，她做梦的时候经常会喊你的名字的，我娘不让我说。

赵宏伟的眼泪忽然就下来了。他说，我知道的，我知道的，我一定会对你娘和你好的。

天快要亮了。

赵宏伟一夜未眠。

他一直惆怅地看着窗外那又远又黑的天。没有心音来入梦的一夜，他发现自己的心里脑里装的全是秀珍。人生有时就是这样一件奇怪的事情，梦里的你和现实中的你未必是同一个你。而此时的赵宏伟又究竟是哪一个赵宏伟，赵宏伟自己也不是十分清楚。昨天下午和记者会面的时候，赵宏伟听到了一个新闻：上海军统站副站长叛变的消息一传到重庆，戴笠震怒，就把这位副站长留在重庆的独子给抓了起来，亲自执行了枪决。枪决完毕之后，戴笠还在内部为牺牲了的上海军统人员举办了一场隆重的追悼会。而据说，被枪毙的这位独子，其实只是一个很老实的孩子。昨天听这条新闻的时候，赵宏伟并没往自己身上想，可是经过这彻夜未眠的思虑，他忽然从这条新闻里看出了一丝切身的可怕来。政治是如此复杂而残酷，他身为军统暗杀名单中的一员，将秀珍和小菊送往重庆，岂不是没事找事，送羊入虎口？他后悔自己的考虑不周，责怪自己在政治上幼稚。想着想着，忽然又觉得，秀珍错过了这次出逃的机会，也许并不是件坏事。起码，她还没去重庆，他可以重新考虑出逃的目的地。

赵宏伟在这不眠的一夜里，想秀珍想得很深。这种深，几乎令他自己有些措手不及。就像有一个什么东西，深深地把根长在了他的心里。拨开浮尘，他才发现她的气息，缠绕在他的肉里和骨里。他蓦然发现，自己可能也没自己想的那么不爱她。不然，他对她的想念，在今夜又怎会这般如火如荼？就算只想到她的一个侧影，他也会思念得发抖。更何况，她现在的侧影，还在日本人的仓库里。突然清晰的痴迷和不能解决的困境纠缠在一起，将赵宏伟软弱的心灵折磨得死去活来。他忽然又开始后悔没有好好珍惜以前和秀珍在一起的日子，他忽然又开始后悔自己这一生做出的一个又一个错误的选择。前天最后一次和秀珍在一起吃饭，他居然还是带着满满的欺骗和虚伪的真情，这不是对人生的糟蹋又是什么？这不是对自我的侮辱又是什么？他明明忍不住要喜欢她，他明明忍不住想拥有她，但是他却一直在用另一个自己面对她，这都是什么道理！他想她想得都已不敢再想她，再多想一点点，他就会崩溃。她的美令他撕心裂肺，因为他根本没有能力保护她一点点。痴迷、无能、自省、懊悔、矛盾，共同将赵宏伟煎熬着，令他肝肠寸断，痛不欲生。他在自己灵魂的旋涡里面对着秀珍这个女人，他仿佛越爱越深，越深越痴。而心音一次也没有出现。究竟哪个是梦，哪个是真？他已无力再辨，只有哀凉满胸臆。

天亮了，赵宏伟给小菊准备了早饭。吃完了早饭，赵宏伟要小菊乖乖待在屋里，不要乱跑，然后，他就出了门。

一路上，赵宏伟还在盘算着他的各种救人计划。他深信自己一夜的考虑是不会白费的。但是，很快他就会知道，思考，是这个世上最可笑的事情。

临近镇政府时，他看见门外的哨兵在换岗。这让他暗暗有些奇怪：这个时候，原本是不会换岗的呀。但是日本兵的确在换岗，而且看样子还换得挺兴高采烈。换岗时日本兵之间还眉飞色舞地在说着些什么，赵宏伟站得太远了没有听清楚。换下来的日本兵又跑回了镇政府里去，仿佛还透着些喜笑颜

开，真是莫名其妙。

赵宏伟心事重重地进了镇政府，径直去往日本人的院子里找渡边，但是到了院子的门口被拦住了。赵宏伟怒不可遏，斥问日本兵，日本兵说：大队长下的命令，这几天，中国人一律不许上这边来。赵宏伟说，我不是中国人，我是皇军的朋友。日本兵说，你仍然是中国人。

赵宏伟不敢真的硬闯，而且那样也不利于问题的解决。他相信这两个看门的日本兵一定是新来的，或者是没有正确理解渡边的命令，或者是不了解他赵宏伟和渡边的关系。他赵宏伟是谁呀？是可以自由进出日本人院子的赵镇长啊，是赵家镇的头号大汉奸哪！

赵宏伟忍气吞声地离开了日本人的院子。他想，欲速则不达，还是忍一时风平浪静，退一步海阔天空吧。

他也没有去汉奸院，就在日本院外面不远处的一个地方坐了下来。他要等渡边。渡边总是要在这里进出的，等等总能等到的。他想好了，今天一定要想办法求渡边先把秀珍给放了。再怎么说他也是个镇长，是个汉奸的楷模，真要死缠烂打，渡边一定会给他这个面子的。他想。

等了很久，没半个人经过。天空安静得发闷。阴云在空旷的天上层层堆积，像看不到边际的烂泥，令人莫名压抑。还是没半个人经过，今天日本人的院子外面，异乎寻常地空空荡荡。赵宏伟在这空荡里，甚至能感到一股只有冬天才会有的寒意。寒意令一切都分外肃静。肃静里，赵宏伟甚至有些窒息。窒息中，赵宏伟却又像是有些幻觉，仿佛能听到，在那阴暗而遥远的天空中，有人在痛苦地呻吟和惨叫。而他的面前，依旧是只有空荡和肃静。他能感到的，依旧只有寒意与窒息。但他必须还要等，他要耐心耐心再耐心，只要功夫深，铁杵磨成针。真是太难受了，他觉得。他难受得几乎要吐了。他开始强迫自己进行深呼吸。他真怕自己的神经一松，就会跌进崩溃中，成为一个在肃静与幻觉里发疯的鬼魅。

终于有一阵嘈杂的声音传来了，是从日本院那边过来的。声音很多很杂很乱，有脚步声、笑声、说话声、枪掉地上的声。赵宏伟看见了，从日本院那边出来了一队日本兵。令人惊奇的是，他们个个都吊儿郎当的，衣衫不整，嬉皮笑脸。

“我挑的那个女人可真白，身体像蒸熟的馒头一样又热又软。”

“哈哈，你差点被她咬到！”

“没什么，只要刺刀在你的手里，你就是她们的皇帝。”

“等会儿我要再去玩一次那个穿旗袍的！”

“快去撒尿吧！哈哈哈！”

赵宏伟像被雷劈了一样地呆坐着。他的脑子里“嗡嗡”直响，以至于他在几秒钟里，眼前是漆黑的，耳朵里是聋的，心跳是停的，像是心肌梗塞，像是灵魂突然地出窍，像是头脑突然地碎掉死了一样。

这队日本兵大摇大摆地从赵宏伟面前经过，津津有味地谈论着某几个女人的大腿和胸部，完全不在乎赵宏伟的存在。赵宏伟突然站了起来，像疯了的野狗一样追上了那队日本兵，死死地拖住了一个，声泪俱下地问：“你们在说的，是不是昨天进来的那些洗衣女工？是不是？是不是！”

日本兵厌恶地甩开了他，说：“当然，不是她们还能是谁。难道你不知道？真奇怪！”

两个袒胸露肚的日本兵哈哈笑了起来。然后，他们走了。

赵宏伟眼睛血红地冲到了日本院的门口，要往里硬闯。哨兵将他推倒在地。他爬起来，又闯。哨兵对他举起了枪。他粗壮地吼道：“你们试试看，要是敢开枪，我看竹内联队长会不会要了你们的脑袋！我死了，谁还敢来给日本人卖命！”

哨兵放下了枪，但死抱着赵宏伟，就是不让他进去。赵宏伟和一个哨兵厮打翻滚在地上，赵宏伟痛哭流涕。“我操你祖宗！”赵宏伟一记重拳，终于砸倒了这个哨兵，爬了起来。没等另一个哨兵来抓住他，他已是冲进了日本院。他发了疯似的狂奔。

走廊里没人，空场上没人，办公区里没人。在哪儿？在哪儿！赵宏伟转身了再转身，头晕目眩，不见一人。他仰望苍天，撕心裂肺，终于长啸：“秀珍——”泪流满面间，他忽然恢复了一点思考的能力，他想到了：她们一定在仓库。

他踉踉跄跄、头重脚轻地跑着，朝仓库那里跑着。他感到有血在自己的喉咙里涌，他感到自己的两只脚和两只手就像不是自己的，他感到自己的整个身体都被一种毁灭捣了个稀烂，他感到自己的整个灵魂都被一个魔攥在了手心里。秀珍的影子在他眼前被撕碎，他连一片也保不住。

还没看见仓库，连绵的惨叫已侵入了赵宏伟的耳。原来那静坐时隐约听到的不是幻觉，而是真相！仓库出现在了赵宏伟的眼前。仓库的门一半敞开着，可以看到仓库里灯火通明。一队只穿着裤子的日本兵零零散散地坐在仓库门外，他们一边说笑，一边抚摸着手里的枪和刺刀。跑得更近了，日本兵都发现了他。他听到了震耳欲聋的女人们的惨叫声和哭泣声。在那凄惨的哭叫海洋里，还航行着此起彼伏的男人们的怒吼声和喘息声。男人们的声音不高，却都强大得可怕。赵宏伟的胸膛，又被几条枪给顶住了。

“滚开！你们都给我滚开！”赵宏伟玩命地大喊，眼睛红得就像是要喷出血来了。

没人听他的。

“我叫你们滚开——”赵宏伟声嘶力竭地怒喊，一下子就拉坏了声带，他痛得吐出了一口血。

还是没人听他的。

“是竹内联队长要我来视察，耽误了正事你们就等着被枪毙吧！”赵宏伟沙哑地撂下一句谎话兼狠话，不管不顾地，避开了枪头，直接就往仓库里冲。几个原先拦着他的日本兵就愣在原地，不知该怎么做才对。

到了仓库里，赵宏伟惊得跌倒在了地上。他简直不敢睁开自己的眼睛。一个惨绝人寰的屠宰场，一只只不停被宰的羔羊，几十条排成长龙的刺刀队，铺天盖地的血腥味。侵略者的天堂里，奴隶们只是非人的肉体。不，赵宏伟是真的闻到了血腥味。他转头一看，一个很幼小的小姑娘，正在一个日本兵的身下流血，血流个不停。

“畜生！”

赵宏伟爬起来，就将那个猝不及防的日本兵揍倒在地。小姑娘从床板上滚了下来，赵宏伟去扶她，才发现她已气若游丝，神志不清。赵宏伟举目四望，海一样的裸体，海一样的波澜起伏，海一样的罪恶，海一样的窒息。

赵宏伟被揍倒。他的手在地上沾到了一摊白糊。他恶心得要哭了。而他的背后，是另一个正在兽性大发的日本兵。那个女人的光脚，就在他赵宏伟的耳朵旁痛苦地蜷曲着，再蜷曲着。

赵宏伟爬起来，拉过自己身后的那个日本兵，就用自己那只被弄脏了的手，狠狠地扇了他一记耳光。赵宏伟看见，那个女人，一只奶头已经不见了，上面还在不断渗出着新鲜的血。

终于，赵宏伟大口地呕吐了起来。

“畜生！你们这群畜生！我、我操你们祖宗十八代——”

赵宏伟吼声未绝，后脑一痛，就晕了过去。

他被人砸了一枪托。

醒来时，仓库里的集体兽行仍在继续。刺耳的哭叫与喘息依旧像海一样无边无际。旁边的一个女人被折磨到失禁，地上的尿流着，流到了还坐在地上的赵宏伟的长衫上。赵宏伟想爬起来，却一点也使不出力，使不出力。女人们痛苦的叫喊，男人们肮脏的排泄，就像吸光了赵宏伟四周全部的空气，让他透不过气来，透不过气来。他痛恨自己不是瞎子，他痛恨自己不是聋子。在这个原始动物的森林里，他找不到人类存在的证据。而那一张张床板前面排着的队伍依旧很长，有些从前面下来了的日本兵，坐在地上歇了一歇后，又会站到另一个队伍的后面去排队。他们不知疲倦，每个女人胯前的长队，都没有因为时间的推移而缩短一点点。赵宏伟的脑袋都像要被箍碎了。他哭了，不是为秀珍，也不是为自己。

他的痛苦没有改变任何东西，该继续的都还在继续。没有一个日本兵在乎他，只要他不捣乱。他张开嘴，喊了几声“秀珍”，但是声音哑得连他自己都几乎听不见，更何况仓库里满是苦惨的声浪。他的喉咙痛得火辣，他知道是嗓子坏了。他看见，仓库顶角墙上的大挂钟，时针已指向十二点。他看见，一个已是浑身瘀青的女人，两条腿被掰成了残忍的形状，然后，突然“咔嚓”一声，断掉的白骨就从她的皮肉里血淋淋地戳了出来。

赵宏伟闭上了眼睛。

他狠狠地睁开眼，猛地站了起来。几个还在排队的空闲的日本兵去捡起了枪，以为他又要闹事。他抱歉地摇摇手，说，不打扰你们，你们继续，继续。日本兵将信将疑地看着他。他擦去眼泪，笑笑，又笑笑。

他开始恬不知耻地去各张床板边视察。一个女人，又一个女人，不是秀珍，还不是秀珍。每走一步，他的腿都像有千斤重；每看一眼，他的眼睛就刀割一样地痛。有些女人被绳子捆得结结实实，身体局部已开始发紫发黑，但是日本人仍然不管不顾；有个女人的两只手被砍掉了，血流了一地，赵宏伟发觉她已没有呼吸，但是她的胯前还排着五六个日本兵。赵宏伟把自己的

嘴唇都咬碎了，多少个刹那里，他想要去拿起一条枪来，但是，他不停地对自己说着：不关我事，不关我事，自保就好，自保就好。

几十张女人的脸都被他细细地看了一遍，但是没有一个是秀珍。他想喊，却不敢再在日本兵的面前喊。他想问，又实在是没脸去问那些躺在床板上的女人。他又找了一遍，真的没有。一个日本兵向他招招手，对他说：来，你也可以排队。赵宏伟突然仰天喷出了一腔热血。

他倒在了地上。

再次醒来时，他看到的是灰白色的天花板，周围很安静，安静得几乎能听见钟的嘀嗒声。他一转头，看见窗外的天是阴的，墙上的钟指针指向一点半。他再一转头，才发现这里是自己的办公室，而自己正躺在办公室里的木沙发上。

他的头依然昏得厉害，周围依旧很安静，甚至连外面的走廊里都没有人的脚步声。突然而来的寂静令他不禁产生了一丝惶惑：难道刚才的一切都只是一个噩梦？

但是他的手和衣服分明都还是脏的，他的嘴里还满是血腥味。他站了起来，跌跌撞撞地跑出了办公室。他找了几间办公室，都没人。仿佛无边的静止和非常奇异的陌生包裹着他，一种难以捉摸的惶恐像一只看不见的拳头，不停击透着他的胸膛，那力量是那么密，那么实。他能清晰地听到自己的呼吸声，粗重而虚弱，连绵而欲绝。空旷里的某种东西似乎正在压碎他，他感到了一阵天旋地转。他就像突然被抛进了另一个世界里，一切都是那么熟悉而正常，一切又都那么陌生而怪异。就像他经常做的那些有心音在其中的梦，一切都是真的，一切又都仅存在于不存在中。迷乱的惶惑搅拌着他，他甚至已无法找到一个自己真实存在的证据。眼前的空静是假的，仓库里的事情是假的，秀珍是假的，心音是假的，这个可怕的想法让他的心跳都快要停掉。他怀疑自己是不是跌进了一个醒不过来的噩梦里，而自己已在这噩梦里度过了半生。他疑心自己落入了一个不认识的世界里，他怕得只想快逃，快逃。恶魔就像在他的四周舞蹈，他觉得自己快要疯了，疯了。存在与不存在，这是一个多么疯狂的问题！

“赵镇长——”

赵宏伟的背后突然响起一个喊声。赵宏伟一转身，就是昨天那个在镇政府门外向群众喊话的汉奸。

“你是谁！”赵宏伟就像是个疯子一样，沙哑地问。

那人愣了愣，“赵镇长，你咋了？我是曾林哪，日本人把你打坏了？”

“曾林，曾林。”

“对，曾林。赵镇长你咋了，咋不认识我了？奶奶的小日本，居然对自己人也下手！”

“曾林，曾林。”

叫曾林的汉奸扶着瘫软的赵宏伟，开始朝外边大喊：“快来人哪，快来人哪，日本人把赵镇长打疯了，赵镇长被打疯了！”

三四个汉奸跑了进来。走廊上又热闹了起来。

赵宏伟被猛烈地摇晃着，他开始清醒了过来。“曾林你别喊，我没疯，我没疯。”

“赵镇长你怎么了，你被日本人扔过来的时候脸上和胸前的衣服上都是血，人也昏迷着，这都是咋了？他妈的日本人是不是要跟我们翻脸？上次出去大扫荡，我们没有冲在前面，他们一定是恨上我们了，他奶奶的！”

“不是，不是，曾林你别嚷，别嚷。”赵宏伟爬了起来，“今天是几号？”

“五月初七呀。”

五月初五，五月初六，五月初七。赵宏伟的头脑开始彻底清醒，他开始清醒地明白：没有一件事情是假的，没有一个噩梦是不存在的。一切都只是他在自欺欺人。

“是我和福宝把你弄干净了放在沙发上的，福宝去请医生了，现在还没回来呢。”曾林说。

“怎么办公室里都没人？”赵宏伟问。

“唉，都被拉去站岗了。那些站岗的日本兵都要去仓库里快活，不肯再站，就拉了我们上去。倒霉呀，外面的老百姓要是知道这里在发生这种事，还不冲进来先宰了我们这些站岗的！”

“那群畜生是什么时候进的仓库？”

“据说是昨天半夜，突然袭击。日本人白天让她们洗衣服，一是真的有衣服要她们洗，二是好糊弄外面的百姓，三，其实就是要选一下美。”

“仓库里的女人一个都没跑出去吗？”

“能跑哪儿去？日本人还拿着两挺机枪在仓库外面吓唬她们呢，能不乖乖听话吗？不听话也没用，日本人有绳子呢。狗日的！”

“不对，仓库里少了一个女人，仓库里少了一个女人！”

“哦，你说这个呀，不是少了一个，是少了五个。昨天晚上，一开始就有三个女人为了不想给日本人糟蹋而自杀，后来又有两个女人因为咬伤了日本人而被杀。”

“什么！”

“真的，尸体就丢在日本人牢房后面的垃圾场里，现在还没拉走。”

赵宏伟“腾”地就冲了出去。

垃圾场在日本人的院子后面，和汉奸院之间用一道高高的铁栅栏隔开。平时这边的汉奸往那边丢垃圾很容易，只要从铁栅栏的格子中间或顶上面丢过去就行了，但是现在赵宏伟想要去那边找人却很麻烦。他去了日本院的门口，看门的已不是日本人，而是两个汉奸。他要往里闯，他们死命地拦着他，比原来的那两个日本哨兵还要尽职尽责。他们相互厮打、谩骂了一番，最后一个汉奸哭着跪下来求他，说：赵镇长，您不是外人，何苦要为难兄弟们呢，日本兵拦不住您，那也就拦不住了，我们拦不住您，那先不说您会不会有事，我们可都是要被任杀任剐的呀！给兄弟们一条活路吧！

急红了眼的赵宏伟站着，心急得都要从喉咙里跳出来了，可是他看着那个跪下来的汉奸，眼睛却不禁一酸。汉奸何苦为难汉奸，他想。他一跺脚，立即转身往院子后面的铁栅栏那边跑了去。

经过那些牢房外面的时候，赵宏伟发现大部分看守牢房的日本兵都没有换下来，只有一小部分汉奸上了岗。而且，到了垃圾场的外面以后，赵宏伟发现，就在靠近垃圾场的最后一排牢房的中间一间牢房的周围，有些异乎寻常地集结了几十个日本兵，个个状态严肃，在分开着来回走动巡逻。队伍里没有一个汉奸。气氛有些森严。

赵宏伟收敛了一下自己的脚步和气息。垃圾场里的垃圾堆积如山，妨碍着那些日本兵的视线，没什么人发现他，偶尔有个别日本兵看见了他，也只当他是过来丢垃圾的，没有特别注意。

赵宏伟看到了远处一堆垃圾里有两条光光的人腿，像是女人。他的心顿时紧得像被捏成了一团，连吸气都有些疼痛。他看着那高高的铁栅栏，眉毛都拧成了锁。早知今日，幼年时真该去习武，他再次想。

他走到了一个日本人肯定看不到的角落，憋足了劲，开始爬栅栏。一切都比他想象的困难得多。他摔下来三次，手上弄出了血。第四次终于爬上了栅栏顶，却没想到那栅栏顶上的铁尖都锋利得跟刀尖一样，赵宏伟的两腿和臀部立马都被扎出了血，一条腿上还被扎得挺深。他从栅栏顶上摔了下来。摔在了厚实的垃圾堆里。他的头闷撞了什么硬物一下，眼前短暂地黑了一黑，但马上醒了过来。他爬了起来，发现只有一只脚崴了，没事，没有惊动日本兵。整个过程里，他都坚持着没让喉咙里发出声音。此刻此举，没什么比隐蔽更重要了。

他爬到了那双光腿旁边，一看，果真是个女人。女人全身赤裸着，死状很惨，看不出是自杀还是被杀，下身狼藉不堪。她不是秀珍。

他很快又找到了另外四具女尸。她们一样都是全身赤裸，下身狼藉不堪。看来，那三个自杀的女子，在死后也没能逃脱魔鬼的蹂躏，其中一个姑娘看起来还是个孩子，最多也就十三四岁的样子，她的头顶上全是血，头盖骨摸上去是碎的，也许是日本人嫌不方便，她的下体被割成了一个大口子；一个女人的牙齿被全部敲碎，她的嘴里，塞着一大块血淋淋的肉，赵宏伟发现，这块肉，就是这个女人自己的屁股肉。还有一个女人，肚子是被剖开的，头上套着一个非常奇怪的血淋淋的套子，赵宏伟为了要看脸，所以就给她剥掉了那个套子，可是，到最后他才突然发现，原来那个套子，竟是这个女人自己的子宫！

“呃——”一声，赵宏伟不顾一切地大口呕吐了起来。他翻江倒海，吐得自己的五脏六腑几乎全滚了出来。他的眼前漆黑一片，脑子里直冒金星，像是要昏过去。五具死尸里没有秀珍，可是他觉得比看到了五个死去的秀珍还要更难受，还要更令人生不如死！

狗娘养的小日本！

赵宏伟从垃圾堆里站了起来，痛哭着大吼。

日本兵发现了他。子弹迅速上膛，大量日本兵向末排中间那间牢房处收拢，举枪向外，是誓死要守住那间牢房的意思。五六个日本兵大喊着“不许动”，举枪向赵宏伟走来。

这一刻，赵宏伟前所未有地痛恨汉奸，他痛恨自己竟然是个汉奸！

他不想活了地，奔跑着，朝一个日本兵扑了上去。日本兵一刺刀，就刺中了他的大腿。他摔倒在地。

“打倒日本帝国主义！”赵宏伟发了疯似的大喊。

“打倒日本帝国主义！”

从日本人死守着的那间牢房里，蓦然传出了一个虚弱但仍极有力的声音，呼应着赵宏伟的怒喊。那是一个男人的声音，那呼号，铁血而慷慨，悲愤而激越。

“中国万岁！”

牢里的那个男声，再次呼喊。

“中国万岁！”赵宏伟也跟着喊。刚喊完，他就又被日本人一枪托给砸晕了过去。

醒来时，赵宏伟发现自己已被吊在了刑架上。他的脑壳外面和脑壳里面都在隐隐作痛。经过刚才的乱叫乱喊，他的喉咙也痛得更厉害了。他开始恢复理智，他开始认识到自己闯了大祸。他摇了摇手，他的手被绳子绑得很结实。他的腿上还在流血。一个日本小军官走进了审讯室，他看见赵宏伟醒了，就去拿鞭子。鞭子拿了起来，他想了想，又放了下去。

赵宏伟看见他去烧烙铁了。

“别别别，误会、误会！”赵宏伟赶紧主动开口求饶，他的声音已嘶哑不堪，但他还是努力要把话讲清楚。

小军官放下了烙铁，开始和他对话。日本人主要是怀疑，赵宏伟是不是对牢房里的犯人有什么企图。赵宏伟百般解释，说自己只是想要找亲戚，找一个女亲戚，这事渡边太君也知道的。至于他今天做的那些疯事和说的那些疯话，都是一时糊涂，是一时犯了疯病。他说，他对皇军的忠心，天地可鉴。他求日本人饶了他，放了他。

小军官对赵宏伟的话半信半疑，他说，他要去向渡边大队长请示。然后，他就离开了审讯室。

赵宏伟的腿上还在流血，他想，是不是可以先求日本人给他包扎一下伤口？

蓦然间他觉得自己十分可笑，也十分可恨。

他发现自己今天做了太多的蠢事，他竟然忘记了自己是一个汉奸。汉奸是什么意思？就是要和日本人同声同气，乐其所乐，忧其所忧。而他今天的所作所为，分明已不再是一条忠诚的狗，他已在日本人的面前，肆无忌惮地表露了他的不忠。想到这里，赵宏伟的后背上就冒出了冷汗。怎么办？怎么办？如果日本人关注的焦点仅仅只是他翻墙而入的真实目的，那他倒是不会有大麻烦，因为他真的对牢房里关的犯人没有兴趣。但他最后喊了两句反日的口号，虽然喊的是汉语，但那些日本兵未必就不懂，毕竟他们也听多了。更何况他今天骂日本人又不是只骂了那两句。他这辈子从来不用粗话骂人，可今天全破了戒，真是千年道行毁于一旦，一失足成千古恨。

那个日本军官还没回来，也没人来看他，审讯室里阴森森的，气味也很恶心，赵宏伟越来越感到害怕。他今天做的第二件蠢事，就是今天第一次闯进日本院里去的时候，竟然没有去渡边的办公室里找一找渡边，他当时真是急疯了，也急傻了，结果就把一切都搞砸了。如果他当时直接就去找渡边，那一切问题也许就都能用文明的方式来解决了，他就可以通过正常而权威的渠道将秀珍救出来了。其他女人关他什么事呢？又不是他亲戚。他现在都后悔死了，觉得自己真是败坏了圣人三思而后行的圣训，以至于现在把自己害成了这样。

话说回来，那么，秀珍究竟在哪儿呢？不在仓库里，也不在五具死尸中。究竟在哪儿呢？难道死尸不止有五具？赵宏伟蓦然又开始后悔自己当初的冲动，他当时就不该从垃圾堆里站起来去骂人，他应该再在垃圾堆里多翻找一会儿的，兴许还会发现第六具女尸。不，不，呸，呸，不会有第六具女尸的，不会有的，秀珍一定还活着，一定还活着。

归根结底，还是应该要去问渡边的。他当初就该去找渡边的，而不该去什么仓库。真是匹夫之勇害死人哪！况且，听刚才那个小军官所说，他要去向渡边请示，那么就是说，今天渡边是在办公室里的。妈的！

但是，今天的哨兵为什么会不让他堂堂的赵镇长自由进出日本院呢？仅仅是哨兵不懂事吗？还是渡边不让他进去？——为什么不让他进去呢？是怕他受不了那种刺激，还是怕他义愤填膺？如果真是这样，渡边的预计倒是没错，他的确是愤怒得炸了膛。但是，事情不会如此简单。赵宏伟的直觉告诉

他，阴暗的事情，深度往往不会只有那么浅。

那么，难道是渡边已经放了秀珍？两人仅仅只是在路上错过了，没有碰到？也许就在赵宏伟早上到达镇政府的时候，秀珍也已是回到了家？很可能就是这样！

各种猜测、担忧、焦虑、冲动围绕着赵宏伟，他恨不得现在就冲出去，验证一下自己的各种假设，尝试一下自己的各个行动计划。但是他现在还在刑架上，腿上还在流血。他想起小菊一直还没吃饭，也不知现在是什么时候了，审讯室里没有窗，看不见外面的天色，他答应过秀珍，他要照顾好小菊的，可他竟然让小菊饿肚子了。

那个日本小军官回来了。赵宏伟正忐忑不安，想为自己继续辩解一番，小军官就已是去拿起了鞭子，将鞭子沾了水，走到了赵宏伟的面前来。

“太君，我真的是一时糊涂，我根本就没想过要去打扰那些守卫牢房的太君……”

赵宏伟话还没说完，军官手里的鞭子已是招呼到了他赵宏伟的身上。这是完全出乎赵宏伟意料的。

“啪、啪、啪”，赵宏伟第一次知道，原来挨鞭子的感觉是这样的。衣服破了之后就是皮开，皮开之后就是肉绽，血珠有时还会往外飞溅。鞭在身上的每一下都是那么沉着有力，就像是用棍子打的一样，根本就想不到那么一根柔软的东西竟然能有这样的威力。伤口里很辣，火辣辣的痛。结结实实的一鞭又一鞭，赵宏伟硬憋着气顶着，每一次松气去呼吸，那皮肉里的痛就会直往他的五脏六腑和骨头里钻。他痛得眼冒金星。结实而威猛的疼痛让他的头脑里一片空白，他都忘了自己原来还想说些什么。巧舌如簧真是一项最无用的技能。

还好没打脸，他想。狂暴的又一鞭，他差点痛晕了过去。

终于，军官打累了，他放下了鞭子。他问赵宏伟：你去后面真的就是为了找亲戚吗？

真的，真的，如有半句虚言，任凭太君处置。

嗯，看在你是我们大日本皇军朋友的分上，就相信你这一次。希望你能明白，若果真与我们皇军作对，最终会有怎样的下场。

明白，明白，绝对不敢，绝对不敢。

刚才给你这一顿鞭子，是因为你今天对我们皇军的勇士做出了许多无礼的举动，还说了很多不该说的话。本来，我是还要往你的伤口上撒盐的。瞧瞧，就是这盆盐，你试想一下，当它们大把大把地钻进你的伤口，进入你的血液，你会得到怎样的战果。——但是，考虑到下周县里还有一场我们皇军举办的记者招待会需要你参加，我们不希望你看上去太憔悴，所以这次，就饶了你。

谢谢，谢谢，皇军万岁，大日本帝国万岁。

记住，在我们日本人的脚下，没有什么县长和镇长，有的只是一群狗，一群只有对我们忠心才会被允许活着的狗。

知道，知道，汪汪，汪汪。

哈哈哈哈。

军官走了出去。

一会儿，进来了两个日本兵，解开了绑着赵宏伟的绳子。赵宏伟一下子就瘫倒在地上，费了好大劲才又爬起来。一走路，他的左脚脚踝处痛得厉害，他才想起来，自己的一只脚崴了。也真奇怪，他从垃圾堆里朝日本人冲过去的时候，竟然并没感到脚踝处有多痛，可是现在一走动，却痛得让人发抖。可能就是跑坏了筋吧，他想。不过话又得说回来，他现在全身又有哪里不痛呢？吊在刑架上时有一口气撑着，他倒也不觉得这里那里有多痛，现在放了他下来，他心里一松，气一缓，全身就都要死要活地痛了起来。真是人凭一口气呀，他想。

日本兵催他快走，赵宏伟一瘸一拐地就赶紧瘸出了审讯室。他想，你还以为我乐意多待呀。

日本兵押着赵宏伟出了日本院，他们对他说：别再惹事了。

太阳还没落山，赵宏伟庆幸时间还不是太晚。他现在还不能就这样回去，那会吓坏小菊的，况且他的腿上还在流血，虽然血流量好像不是很大，但毕竟已流了这么久。赵宏伟到现在才发现，原来自己的身体也是很结实很硬朗的，可惜了，年轻时居然没有去参军。百无一用是书生，真没错。他想。

曾林和福宝给赵宏伟包扎了腿上的刺刀伤口。曾林说，这一刀是幸亏没刺着大动脉，不然真完了。福宝说，赵镇长，您今天这是干吗呢？怎么弄成

这样了？

赵宏伟也不说话。释放的喜悦散去，深思的痛苦重来。他想，那个审讯室的小军官第一次进来时也没敢动他赵宏伟，就是装模作样地吓唬了他一下而已，可是他去请示完了渡边之后，第二次进审讯室，二话不说就拿鞭子招呼起了他赵宏伟，这一定是渡边的意思。那个军官只是个小角色，怎么可能自作主张对堂堂的一镇之长下狠手？北川是竹内的亲信，见了他赵宏伟也是有礼貌地微笑，一个小小的负责审讯的又怎么会真敢打他赵宏伟？所以，真正想教训他赵宏伟的，其实是渡边。这顿鞭子和那顿训斥，都是渡边的要求，赵宏伟确定。

赵宏伟身上的鞭伤和被铁栅栏弄伤的伤口，也都简单处理了一下。扭伤的脚踝处也抹了些跌打酒。他跟曾林借了身衣服，把自己身上的破衣服给换了下来。然后他去洗脸洗手。他狠狠地洗着自己的手，恨不得能洗脱一层皮才好。

水流的冲击渐渐让赵宏伟恢复到了冷静之中。身上的痛还是在痛，没解决的事情依旧没有解决，但是他已不能再犯错。不知是不是昨晚一夜没睡的缘故，他觉得自己今天的脑子非常不好使。很多错误已犯下，再后悔也没用。从现在起，他要步步为营。

洗完了脸和手，他去问曾林和福宝，赵驹在哪？两人一齐摇头，说，今天谁都没看到他。福宝说，听人说，赵驹今天一整天都在靶场。

曾林说，赵镇长，你要想见渡边，何不先给他办公室里打个电话？

赵宏伟摇摇头。事情发展到这个地步，这个电话已经不太好打了。如果今天早上曾林就能给他提这么个醒，那么恐怕事情也不会发展到这个地步。但是哪能重新再来呢？圣人曰，三思而后行，他怎么就是给忘了呢！冲动个屁呀！

赵宏伟买了十个热包子，匆匆回家。因为脚疼得厉害，他只得雇了一辆黄包车。车夫跑得很卖力，车子很颠簸。一路上，他一直在幻想一幅很美的图景：他还未进门，秀珍和小菊已在屋里等他。这幅图景刺激着他内心许多复杂的情感，忧伤伴随着追悔，留恋缠绕着沮丧。而有一个字，似乎正在他纷乱的内心中央急速膨胀，开疆拓土，这就是：爱。怜爱也罢，情爱也罢，他已来不及再去细细思量。此爱火热，烫得人白发顿生。他蓦然做了一个决定，见到了秀珍，他立马就带她和小菊走。不是让她们自己走，是他和她们一起走。他不要骗秀珍，他不要骗她。他要实现他对她说的每一句话，他要真的让她知道，他爱她！他爱她爱得发狂！管他这个那个呢，天下这么大，总有日本人到不了的地方，总有军统看不见的地方，他赵宏伟只要隐姓埋名，改个发型，换身打扮，总能在某个偏僻而安宁的地方和秀珍母女一起生活下去的。谁说不是呢？

到了家门口，赵宏伟蹦下了黄包车，他的脚脖子一阵剧痛。他给了车夫钱，赶紧去开自家的门。进了门，没看见什么人，他一瘸一瘸地去各个房间找，什么人也没有。他才想起来大喊："秀珍！小菊！你们在哪儿？你们在哪儿！"

小菊从厨房里跑了出来，"宏伟伯伯，我在这儿。"

"你娘呢？小菊，你娘呢？她在哪儿？她有没有来找你？她有没有来找你？她在哪儿？"

"没有，我娘没来找我，我不知道她在哪儿。"

对了，对了，她一定是在隔壁的家里。赵宏伟发了疯似的自言自语说着，一瘸一瘸地又跑了出去。

他来到了隔壁秀珍家的门前，用力地拍着门，大喊："秀珍，秀珍，快开门，是我，赵宏伟，小菊在我这里，小菊在我这里呀，你快开门哪！"

赵宏伟用力地拍着门，大喊着"秀珍"。

小菊跑了过来，举起手，将一把钥匙晃了晃，说："宏伟伯伯，你干吗不用这个？"

对，对，忘了，小菊有门前大锁上的钥匙，抱她出来的时候，还是他让她拿好的钥匙。他猛拍了两下自己的头。顺便，他也想起了，他的手里还拿着一纸袋的包子。

他蹲下来，将已经只剩微温了的一纸袋包子交给了小菊，说："小菊乖，今天一定饿坏了，快吃包子吧。"

赵宏伟开了门，奔进各间屋子里寻找，一边大喊着秀珍的名字。但是，半个人也没有。他又找了一遍，真的没有。他不喊了，一屁股坐在地上，像傻了一样。

暮色深沉，屋里很安静，街上只偶尔有些平常的人声。直到听到了低低的啜泣声，赵宏伟才惊醒。他一回头，看见小菊就站在他的身后，怀里抱着一大袋的包子，在低低地哭泣。

宏伟伯伯，我娘是不是出事了？小菊哭着问。

不是，不是。赵宏伟赶紧起身，蹲着抱住了小菊，说，不是的，小菊，你娘没事，没事。

那我娘呢，她在哪儿？小菊问。

赵宏伟哑口无言。他到现在才意识到，自己的失态是直接向小菊暗示了一些糟糕的事情。他后悔不已，又无力圆谎。他想起自己最后答应秀珍的事情是要照顾好小菊，他的心里又愧疚不已。他的心底像被火烧穿了一个洞。

是这样的，小菊，伯伯暂时不知道你娘去了哪儿，但是伯伯一直在找，一定能找到的。赵宏伟说。

小菊哭得更厉害了，哭声里还起了一丝儿童的绝望，赵宏伟顿时手足无措。他从未真的带过小菊，更不懂得如何哄孩子，他真后悔自己又说错了话。小菊哭着说，“我要娘回来，我要娘回来”，又哭又说的，都咳嗽了起来。赵宏伟赶紧给小菊拍背，他说，小菊，你不要哭，不要哭。

小菊哭着说，我一定再也不惹娘生气了，我再也不调皮了，我要娘回来，我要娘回来呀。

赵宏伟自己的眼圈也红了，他说，小菊，你不要哭，不要哭，伯伯一定会把你娘找回来的，一定会的。

小菊“呃呃”地哭。赵宏伟也抹着泪。他到今天，才真正知道，国家羸弱，百姓会有什么样的下场。国破家亡的悲愤在他心里激荡，最终却还是都化作了不争气的眼泪。

赵宏伟和小菊一起抱头痛哭着。他知道此刻自己是不该掉眼泪的，可是他的心里就是酸痛得像是打翻了药水，他情不自禁。

等两个人都哭累了，天也黑了。赵宏伟还是用一些阳光灿烂的话语骗过了小菊，让她以为她的哭泣是不必要的，而他的心里，黑暗却是更深重了几层。

他在秀珍家里的桌上留了字条，然后便带着小菊又回了自己的家。他蒸热了包子，又弄了两碗蛋花汤，跟小菊一起吃晚饭。他什么都吃不下，但还是强迫自己吃了两个包子。小菊也吃了两个包子。吃完了包子，赵宏伟再次嘱咐小菊，这几天不管他在不在家，她都要好好地待在家里，不要乱跑，不要出门。小菊说好。赵宏伟已隐约预感到了一场风暴的来临，他想，不管怎么说，在这里，镇长的家总是要比其他地方更安全些。但是，他隐隐地又觉得自己的这个想法并不十分可靠。镇长的头衔在一般情况下是能唬住一些一般的人，但是动乱若起，又哪里还有什么一般情况。毕竟，他的门前没有卫兵。他是可以要求日本人给他两个卫兵的，但是他以前没要。现在他也还是不能要。不然，秀珍若回来，岂不是又要羊入虎口？绝对不行。

各种想法在他的头脑里纠缠，他开始意识到自己昨晚一夜没睡是个重大的失误，也是一个残酷的讽刺。他想，就是在他东想西想，做着最无用的各种打算的时候，日本人雄气冲天地闯进了仓库里。而他什么也没有做，知道了也什么都做不了。秀珍又不知所踪。他该怎么办？

安排小菊睡下后，赵宏伟就又出了门。今天的夜色特别黑，但他还是决定不打灯笼。自从日本人来了以后，别说老百姓晚上不敢出门，就算实在是要出门，也很少有人敢打灯笼。赵宏伟本来是不怕打灯笼的，但是他现在是要去找方远梦，所以他不想没事惹事。渡边已经对他这样了，谁知道他今晚走夜路时背后会不会有人盯着？该死的日本人。

由于一直要小心背后是否有人跟踪，赵宏伟走得很慢。路上又是黑灯瞎火，他摔了两跤。他的心情越发沮丧了起来。他觉得今晚其实并没有什么人在跟踪自己，但是他又实在不敢自信，不敢走得快一些。

终于到了方远梦的家门前，他敲门。他不确定今晚方远梦是否会在家。敲门的声音是有着特别的节奏的，方远梦一听就会知道是他。门开了，方远梦说，进来。

进了屋，赵宏伟看见了一个年轻人，隐约觉得有些眼熟，仔细一想，才想起来，这就是他在玉山上被打晕后醒来时第一个见到的那个游击队里的年轻人。方远梦介绍说，他就是小秦。

赵宏伟伸出手去，和小秦握手，说，你好，你好。小秦和他握手握得有些勉强，只“嗯”了一声。

方远梦对赵宏伟说，你来得正好，不然再晚一会儿我也要去找你了，我们吃了败仗，从赵家镇通往大后方的几条道路预计明早就要重新被日军封锁

住了，秀珍出来了没有，过了今晚就真的没办法出去了。

赵宏伟一阵急火攻心，他疲软地坐了下来，摇了摇头，说，没有。他的脸在昏暗的灯光里像是苍老了好几十岁。

方远梦觉得不太对，问，你今天是怎么了，喉咙怎么这么哑？刚才我看你走路还一瘸一瘸的，是不是出了什么事？

赵宏伟不知该怎么说，或者说，是不知该说些什么才好。他脑袋一痛，无力地说，秀珍不见了。

方远梦很诧异，问，不见了？什么意思？怎么回事？

渡边再次累得睡了过去。他就那么直接睡在秀珍全裸的身子上，他都懒得从她的身上滚下来。秀珍的手和脚分别被牢牢地绑定在床头和床尾，呈渡边最爱的“大”字形。秀珍的屁股下面被垫上了一块厚厚的大砧板，她的身上满是牙印和瘀痕。她的嘴里被严严实实地塞着一大团布，所有的惨呼与痛哭，都只能在她的胸腔和喉咙里翻滚，来回翻滚，变成血一样的微弱呜咽。她的眼角流着淡红色的泪。睡着了的渡边，手里还紧攥着她的两缕长发。

渡边梦到了骑马。那还是在他少年的时候，他从马上摔了下来，所有的人都笑他，连他暗地里一直很仰慕的一个女孩子都笑他。半夜里，他就拿着刀，去割断了那匹马的喉咙。马血喷出来的那一刻，他感到了一种很特别的快感。他梦见自己策马奔腾在广袤的土地上，周围的每一个人，都在向他屈膝下跪、谄媚地笑。他感到了自己的身体在极舒服地膨胀。他模模糊糊地醒来，还以为自己是在日本的家乡。

他揪着秀珍的头发和皮肉，再一次狂野地动了起来。他听着身下这个娇弱的中国女人想喊却喊不出来的呜咽，觉得，这真是世上最美妙的音乐。

“畜生！”

小秦一拳砸在桌子上，震得茶杯都打翻了。

方远梦的眉头锁成了一个铁疙瘩，在屋子里来回地走。

赵宏伟讲完了他今天在镇政府里看到的真相，就像是重新又走了一遍地狱。他已经没有了愤怒，只剩下满腔的悲哀，冰冷的悲哀，甚至可以说是绝望，一种对于明天的绝望。不管是对于他个人，还是对于其他人。这是一种强大的黑暗，它能让你觉得，你做再多的挣扎，别人做再多的挣扎，都是白费力气，甚至对于寻找秀珍，他也感到，希望是那么的渺茫。他内心的一切焦虑和担忧，在此时此刻，很奇怪地都是以一种极冰冷的触感出现的，他觉得，他已真的是太累了。

他又跟方远梦说了一遍，他没有找到秀珍的事情。小秦一下子就火了，说，你在这个时候，居然还只想着自己的相好！

赵宏伟一下子就像被人打了一记耳光，他的心里冒起了一点火苗，但这火苗很快就又被一种极慵懒的东西给浇灭了。他不言不语，没有回应。他想，他骂得对，但是我又能怎么样呢？

“中国就是因为有太多你这种自私自利的人，所以才会贫弱到这个地步！”小秦继续义愤填膺地说，“你这种人，心里时刻都只想着自己的利益，只关心自己的喜怒哀乐，就算国家亡了，民族灭了，只要你自己还衣食无忧，你就不会有一点儿伤心！”

“好了，小秦，你说什么呢！”方远梦制止小秦。

“你别拦我，我就要说。方远梦同志，你知道吗，现在队里对你的意见很大，都说你是在和汉奸交朋友，敌我不分，犯了严重的政治错误！你这样是会给我们带来危险的，万一赵宏伟他是个奸细呢？万一他有一天出卖我们呢？”

“他不会的。”方远梦说。

“我不会的。”赵宏伟说。

“你不会？谁知道你会不会！你这种软骨头，只要拿死来吓唬你，你还有什么是不能出卖的！不然你怎么会当汉奸？人有什么理由非要当汉奸不可？说破了天，日本人最多也就只能拿死来吓唬你，你要是不怕死，日本人还能像变戏法一样把你变成汉奸不成？软骨头！”

“我没有做什么对不起中国人的事。”赵宏伟说。

“我呸，你还有脸说！你三天两头在报上发表一些鼓吹大东亚共荣的文章，还教中国的孩子说日文，让孩子们喜欢日本，你居然还有脸说你没有做对不起中国人的事情！我真想一枪毙了你！”

“好了！小秦！”方远梦喝道。

“方远梦同志，你以前一直是爱憎分明的，现在怎么会变成这样！你太

让我失望了！你知道吗，队里根本就没人愿意来执行这一次的任务，让我们冒着生命危险，送一个汉奸的相好去重庆，这是一件多么荒谬的事情！要不是政委跟我好说歹说，说我们共产党人要有恩必报，我根本就不愿意来！”

“小秦同志，你可以恨我，但秀珍只是一个老百姓，她和我完全不一样，真的，她只是想要逃离有日本人的地方。”赵宏伟说。

“哪一个中国的老百姓不想逃离有日本人的地方？我们如果都这样一个一个地特地去送，我们部队里的战士早就死光了，还怎么去打日本人？我是真恨你们这些汉奸，日本人为什么打中国能打得那么厉害，占中国能占得那么快？还不都是因为有你们这些卖国贼在帮着他们！他们的武器再厉害，军事素质再过硬，可是来到中国，人生地不熟，语言又不通，如果没有你们给他们引路、翻译、提供情报，他们能在中国节节胜利、势如破竹吗？要是中国人个个都不怕死，不当汉奸，齐心抗敌，日本人又岂能占我们国土一寸！现在，你的相好被日本人抓走了，这完全是你的报应！你给老虎带路，老虎来了却吃掉了你的女人，活该！”

“小秦，你怎么能说这种话，秀珍只是一个百姓，老百姓是无辜的！”方远梦训斥小秦，“你再这样，我回去要告诉政委了！”

小秦不说话了。他生气地捶了凳子一拳。

赵宏伟站了起来。小秦同志，你骂得对，是我对不起国家，对不起百姓，我无地自容。

赵宏伟说完，便向方远梦告辞。方远梦说，小秦还年轻，一些气话你别放在心上。赵宏伟说，小秦同志说的都是真话，也都是对的话，中国若有一万个这样的我，就真完了。

赵宏伟说完，便径自出了门。方远梦也没再挽留。

走在回家的路上，赵宏伟觉得自己的脸上凉凉的，一摸，全是泪。他想，我真的有罪呀！

“秀珍，你在哪儿——”他哭着，对黑暗说。

赵宏伟死死地睡了一夜。吃完早饭，他便去了镇政府。

到了办公室里，他先给渡边打了一个电话。他等了一会儿，电话一直没人接，他以为渡边不在。就在他要挂断电话时，渡边接了电话。渡边的声音听上去有些疲惫不堪。他点头哈腰地刚说了两句“太君好”，渡边听出来是他，就不耐烦地打断了他：混蛋，谁允许你给我办公室里打电话的？这几天不准来烦我，你好好反省反省自己做错的那些事，你若再敢对我们皇军不敬，我一定将你军法处置！

说完，渡边就挂了电话。

点头哈腰的笑还没有从赵宏伟的脸上退下来，赵宏伟的脸像是有些僵硬。他放下了电话，咬了咬牙，想骂一句什么，却没骂出来。

他心事重重地在办公室里来回走。走完了又去外头日本院的外面来回走，但他已不敢再往日本院里闯了，说什么也不敢了，而且那么做很蠢。

他问了两个出来撒尿的日本兵，得知他们还在继续做昨天的事情，并且仓库里又新死了三个女人。他礼貌地祝他们生活愉快，然后便回转身，去汉奸院里找起了赵驹。曾林说，赵驹还在靶场。

赵宏伟去了靶场。

赵宏伟想过了，要是赵驹也没有办法帮他找到秀珍的人或尸，那么他就什么都不管了，他一定要在靶场里偷一把枪，然后去日本院里，痛痛快快地杀几个日本鬼子，那样的话，无论秀珍是在活着受辱还是已去了黄泉，他也都算是给她报了仇了。但是，一会儿之后他又想，我死了，小菊怎么办？

坐在黄包车上，一路上他看见老百姓的生活依旧还像几天前一样。他想，洗衣工的谎言败露的那一天，就将是赵家镇血流成河的那一天。不，血流成河的，将不仅仅只有赵家镇一个镇。老秀才当年看轻江南的男人，那只是气话，日本人却真以为江南无好汉。赵宏伟必须要赶在大动乱发生以前，找到秀珍的下落。

昨天晚上他又给自己的脚上抹了一些跌打酒，还吃了一些伤口消炎的药，今天感觉好多了，嗓子也不疼了。他想，身体发肤受之父母，是该要好好珍惜才是。

赵宏伟最后是在靶场的一个角落里找到的赵驹，赵驹正在就着花生米喝白酒。他看见了赵宏伟，顿时就忽逢知己似的笑了起来，说，来来来，正愁没人陪我喝酒，喝一杯。

赵宏伟走了上去，也不坐，也不喝酒。他想，今天我好不容易神志清楚一些，岂能再喝酒误事？

赵宏伟问，赵驹，这两天镇政府里发生了什么事你知道吗？

赵驹问，哟，你声音怎么了？

赵宏伟说，没啥，嗓子不小心弄坏了。

赵驹说，不要紧，洪亮依旧。

赵宏伟说，是，吃了药，好得挺快。赵驹，这两天镇政府里发生了什么事你知道吗？

赵驹问，你吃的是中药还是西药？清咽利嗓，还是中药好。

赵驹，我在问你事呢！赵宏伟“噌”一下就火了。

唉，你急什么急。赵驹懒洋洋地又喝了一杯酒，然后说，我有什么不知道的？我连你这嗓子是怎么坏的都知道！前天夜里，就是我去仓库里给日本人当的翻译。我说，姑娘们，你们向皇军效忠的机会来了，从今晚开始，你们就将成为大东亚共荣事业中伟大的一分子，帝国的圣战需要你们，帝国的勇士们需要你们，都乖乖听话，脱光了衣服，去床板上躺好，让天皇的勇士们来宠幸你们吧。

说完，赵驹仰脖又干了一杯酒。他不再说话，往嘴里丢了一粒花生米，闭上眼，细细地咀嚼着。

赵宏伟脸色铁青，他说，赵驹，你杀人也就罢了，居然还帮着日本人做这种事情！

赵驹的眼睛依旧没有睁开，他往自己的嘴里又丢了一粒花生米，丢得还挺准。他说，你这话真可笑，日本人睡女人这种事情，需要我帮忙吗？我只是一个翻译而已。

日本人就是因为有了中国人做翻译，才会在中国事事精通、横行无忌！赵宏伟激愤之下，说起了小秦的话来。

日本人又不是光用中国人做翻译，他们自己也有中国通。再说了，你自己就不是翻译？别自命清高。我不翻译，那行啊，你去。赵驹说完，用鼻子冷冷地“哼”了一声。

赵宏伟觉得自己把话题引到了岔路上，心中略感后悔。他不能忘了自己此行的主要目的。他又换上了一副笑脸，甚至略微还带了一点儿谄媚，说：赵兄莫要生气，小弟一时失言，您海涵。

赵驹睁开了眼来，笑着说，哎哟，你今天是怎么了，怎么突然对我这么客气了？

赵宏伟实在是站得腿酸了，况且他本来就腿脚上都有伤。他就一屁股坐了下来。他讨好地给赵驹斟起了酒，赵驹忙说不敢不敢。赵宏伟说，不瞒兄台，小弟今日此番前来，实在是有一事相求。

什么事，只管说，同僚一场，你又难得开口，我能帮一定帮。

刚才听你说，前晚日本人初入仓库之时，你也在场，那真是太好太巧了。小弟想要向你打听一个人的下落。

什么人？

赵宏伟从衣袋里拿出了一张他今天一大早就准备好了的照片。照片上是秀珍。

赵驹接过了照片，一看，又还给了赵宏伟。

原来是住在你隔壁的那个小寡妇。

正是正是，她叫秀珍，王秀珍。

没想到哇，看来你是真的对这小寡妇有情。我原来还想，昨天你吃了那么多苦头，今天总不会再到处找她了，你总不会为了一个女人而真的跟日本人一直闹下去，看来是我想错了。我高估了你。

赵兄真是手眼通天！你人在靶场，院子里的事情却知道得一清二楚！望赵兄成全！请赵兄告知我秀珍的下落！求赵兄了！

赵宏伟激动万分，就差给赵驹跪下了。

你真想知道王秀珍在哪儿？

当然！

你知道了也没用。

什么意思？

要是没什么太大的变化的话，你的那个秀珍，现在还被绑在渡边办公室后面的卧室里的那张床上。

什么！

前天晚上，渡边是和那群日本兵一起进的仓库，他首先就让两个兵把王秀珍给捆了起来，塞住了嘴，抬去了他办公室后面的卧室里。他说他要单独享用这个女人。

怎么会这样？怎么会这样？

赵宏伟脸色煞白，喃喃自语，仿佛痴呆。

现在你知道了，但是你又能怎么样？赵驹问。他悠悠地喝着酒，仿佛这一切都只是一些很平常的小事。

我能怎么样？是啊，我能怎么样？赵宏伟喃喃自语。

你该庆幸，起码她还活着，你要祈祷，王秀珍她不会做出什么过于激烈的反抗动作来，不然，惹怒了渡边，她一定会死得很惨。赵驹冷漠地说。

赵宏伟拳头捏得“咯咯”响。他牙关紧咬，却又不知该如何是好。

我倒是奇怪了，你既然这么在乎这个王秀珍，干吗不一早娶了她呢？赵驹问。

赵宏伟说不出话来。

你想想看，你要是一早就娶了她，那么她现在就是镇长夫人，日本人再怎么横行无忌，总不至于会拉个镇长夫人去做洗衣女工吧？王秀珍只要不去给日本人做洗衣工，那么后面的事情，自然也就落不到她的头上了，是不是？

赵宏伟落下了泪来。

赵驹，你帮我，求求你帮我救救秀珍，帮我救救秀珍！

赵驹推开了赵宏伟。不是我不帮你，你自己想想看，我能怎么帮你？去叫渡边那老王八蛋从床上滚下来，放王秀珍走？你还不如拿了一挺机枪去劫人呢。

赵宏伟一抹泪，起身真的去拿了一把枪，一把驳壳枪。

赵驹也站了起来，跑过去，朝赵宏伟手肘的穴道上一捏，赵宏伟手里的枪就掉了下来。

赵驹捡起了枪，拿在了自己手里，说，你别不识好歹了，送死也不是这么送的，你连把枪都拿不住。

赵宏伟蹲在地上就号啕大哭了起来。赵驹不理他，自己去打起了靶。“砰、砰、砰”不断的枪响，赵宏伟渐渐止住了哭泣。

他擦干净了自己的脸，然后去喝光了赵驹留下来的酒。他也去打起了靶。他狠狠地开着枪，虽然都没打中，但他依旧打得眼红了又红。

赵宏伟平静中仍略带着颤抖，他问，日本人这次为什么这么做，他们的目的是什么？

赵驹说，东北那边过来的慰安团，被国民党的飞机给炸了个稀巴烂，这个团原来是从上海借调去东北的，里面的货色非常好，还有四个极漂亮的荷兰洋妞，本来的计划是，她们慰问完江庆县的日本兵之后，就要回上海的慰安所去了，物归原主。但是谁能想到，她们却是在来江庆县的路上全成了灰。竹内自然难辞其咎。他必须要赔给上海一个慰安团，人数不能少，货色不能差。竹内最近正发愁，上哪里去找金发碧眼的洋妞来赔给上海的慰安所。下个月，他就要去南京担任旅团参谋长了，他可不想在这种破事上遭人诟病。

所以，这些被抓起来的女人，最终都会被送去上海的慰安所？赵宏伟问。

是的。赵驹回答。

那么，如果我一定要救秀珍出来，我该怎么做？

我劝你不要有这种幼稚的想法。渡边现在玩得正起劲，你若惹恼了他，小心王秀珍人头落地。

我要去找竹内！

你觉得竹内和你很熟吗？他会为了你这么个小角色，让渡边满脸尴尬地从一个中国女人的身上滚下来吗？而渡边一旦知道了你拿竹内来压他，恐怕你还没从竹内的办公室里出来，王秀珍就已是被剁成了肉泥。

那难道我们就只能眼睁睁地看着日本人为所欲为而什么都做不了吗？

事实就是这样，国军败了，白姓又能干什么？人为刀俎，我为鱼肉。赵驹冷冷地说。说完，又开了几枪。

赵宏伟哆嗦着，脸无血色。他绝望地坐到了地上，看着旷远的天，眼里空无一物。

你再耐心等等吧，只要王秀珍能保得住命，也许就还有出来的可能。赵驹说。

赵宏伟一骨碌从地上爬了起来。他激动地说，请赵兄明言，小弟感激不尽！

渡边也许很快就会把王秀珍玩腻，等他玩腻了王秀珍，自然就会把她像丢垃圾一样地丢出来了。到时，你也许就有救她出来的可能了。

这让我怎么等！要是渡边一直不放她出来怎么办？也许明天早上的太阳

还没出来，竹内就要送她们去上海了！

竹内在找齐四个漂亮洋妞以前，是不会把这些女人送到上海去的。另外，渡边是不会占有王秀珍太久的，不管他愿不愿意，最多也就还有个把礼拜。

为什么？

下个礼拜县里的那场记者招待会结束之后，渡边就要变成中佐了，他将会离开赵家镇，正式来县城里担任副联队长一职。而北川大尉则会离开县城，去赵家镇日军大队任大队长。你说渡边他再怎么喜欢王秀珍，总不可能带着她来县城的联队总部里上任吧？这点羞耻心他渡边总还是有的。

但是北川素来与我有些不睦。

这个不重要，重要的是，北川他痛恨日本人的慰安妇制度。

哦？

这一次，江庆县下面的几个镇子里都征了女工，却唯独只有县城里没有征，你知道是为什么吗？是北川用他左手的小手指换来的。本来，竹内也是要在县城里征一批女人的，县城里的日本兵嚷着要女人都已经嚷了很久了，但是北川以死相谏，断指明志，拒不执行竹内要他在县城里征女人的命令。最后，竹内倒也是给了北川一个面子，县城里的女人，他就不征了。但是下面的镇子里，照征不误。竹内其实也并不是真的给北川面子，他是突然想明白了一个道理，他若在县城里征了女人，他日一旦激起民变，他所直接管辖的县城，局面就将会变得非常糟糕，万一失控，那他的前途也就完了。但是这慰安团又一定是要赔给上海的。他仅仅在下面的各个镇子里征，那么，有了功劳，就是他竹内的，一旦发生了骚乱，出了差错，那责任，也只是下面的各个队长的。

北川杀人如麻，想不到，他会这样做。

若不是他曾经为竹内挡过三颗子弹，他这样顶撞竹内，早就要被命令剖腹自尽了。你知道北川为什么不愿意执行强征慰安妇的命令吗？因为北川的妹妹，就是一个慰安妇。北川的父母死得早，从小就只有他和他妹妹两个人相依为命。后来，北川参军来到了中国，上了战场，就只剩下他妹妹一个人在日本。他妹妹因为想念哥哥，就参加了日本的女子挺身队，也来到了中国。参加挺身队的日本姑娘们都以为所谓的女子挺身队就是护士队、后勤队，她们还以为她们来到中国，是为日本的勇士们洗衣、做饭、包扎伤口的。但其实那些勇士们，需要的只是她们的肉体。随时随地为那些日本兵打开她们的双腿，这才是她们真正的工作。不过当然，洗衣做饭包伤口那些事，她们有时也是要做的。挺身队的姑娘，平均每天都要接待十几个日本兵，就算是被弄大了肚子，也不能休息。最后，北川的妹妹，在第三次流产之后，剖腹自尽。她到最后也没看见她的哥哥，她不知道，其实只要再过两天，她所在的这支女子挺身队，就会来到北川所在的大队了。

赵宏伟不禁怆然，说，日本的军国主义会有报应的，他们的天皇，最终会害所有日本人下地狱的。

赵驹又开始举枪射击。他说，你知道你为什么总是打不中靶吗？

为什么？

因为你不知道，你究竟该恨谁。你只有真正懂得了恨，你才会百发百中。

“那你恨不恨渡边？”赵宏伟突然问。

赵驹又打了一枪。“你错了，我恨的不是渡边。”

“那是谁？”

“蒋介石。”

赵宏伟艰难地咽着饭粒。他给小菊做了午饭，他不能再重复昨天的错误了，他要照顾好小菊。小菊吃饭很乖，也没有再问起她娘的事情。赵宏伟也不知道自己的谎言究竟还能蒙小菊多久。在一团黑暗的残酷世界里，要怎样才能保护好孩子心中的一点光明，赵宏伟以前从未学习过，对此也一无所知。他感到自己很对不起多年的校长称谓，他除了会教孩子们背背书以外，还会教孩子们什么呢？他其实根本就不配当孩子们的老师。

赵宏伟每吃一口饭，都觉得胃里在泛恶心，就好像他的食道里完全是满的，而他却还是在往食道里硬塞食物一样。虽然他的食道里和胃里其实是空着的。但他实在是无法再咽下一口饭了，再吃，他就要吐了。他对小菊说，他要出去一下，然后，他就丢下了饭碗，跑去了茅房里。到了茅房里，他才开始流出了眼泪。眼泪一流出来，他整个人开始慢慢崩溃。

此刻秀珍也许还在渡边的房间里，而他赵宏伟却什么也做不了，只能

躲在臭烘烘的茅房里黯然流泪。他什么也不敢想，只能祈祷，秀珍千万不能自寻短见。他忽然想起了赵驹曾经对那个女人说过的话：活着就好，活着就好。他感到，对活着的渴望，在这个残酷的年代，似乎已成了一个流着脓的梦想，或者是一个恶毒的许诺。

外面的街上一阵嘈杂，赵宏伟听到有日本人在喊“集合”。他赶紧擦干了泪，走出去，只见有几队日军正在匆匆跑步。他想找个人问问发生了什么事，但中国人都不理他。日本兵也都跑远了。最后还是听一个老太婆跟另一个老太婆说，是游击队和日本人在镇子的两个出入口处打了起来。一个老太婆说，游击队怎么可能打得过日本人呢，他们的装备那么差，要是国民党的枪炮都给了游击队就好了。另一个老太婆说，不管他们，只要子弹不打到我们老百姓头上就好。

赵宏伟回去跟小菊说了一声，然后就出了门。他要用最快的速度去镇政府。

他想，如果老太婆说的都是真的，那么赵家镇的日军大队，此刻大部分肯定都已离开了镇政府，若要救人，此时不去，更待何时。

但是到了镇政府门前，赵宏伟的心里就凉了一大截。给镇政府看门的不仅依旧是日本兵，而且，日本兵在镇政府的门前还架起了一挺重机枪。赵宏伟不禁在心里嘲笑自己在军事上的幼稚，枪战来临，日军的老巢里又怎会没有守备？想要从这里救一个人出去，无异于虎口拔牙。

进了镇政府，赵宏伟心乱如麻。一切并没有像他想象的那样发生，镇政府并没有陷入混乱，大门口也并没有放松警戒。想想也是，日本人打了那么多仗，对付这种事情还不是熟门熟路、小菜一碟？他觉得会乱，只是因为他自己没经历过打仗而已。希望落空的沮丧一下子又将他整个人变得冰凉，而他现在又是站在这个令他觉得万分罪恶与肮脏的镇政府里，他感到心里憋得慌。他想，军队和老百姓到底是不一样的，军队事事都训练有素，而老百姓却什么都不懂。

他不知自己该往哪里去，想马上离开这里，又很不甘心，毕竟，秀珍现在就在镇政府里。就在离他咫尺之近的地方。他不能走，他要救人，必须要赶在事情进一步变得不可挽回之前行动起来。

赵宏伟发现镇政府里又空又静。他在几条主要的走道里走过，居然都没碰见半个人。既没有日本人，也没有汉奸。这与镇政府大门外的严阵以待形成了鲜明的对比。赵宏伟停了下来。他开始谨慎地思考。他想，如果日军出动的部队的确是赵家镇大队而不是别的部队，那么，镇政府里此刻的这一份空静就是真实的。而如果这一份空静是真实的，那么，他的希望就还在。渡边的大队人数本来就不多，一旦出去作战，剩下来的兵不会有多少。虽然大门被日军守住了，但救人的方法多得是，他可以带着秀珍翻墙而出，也可以把秀珍化装成男人从大门正常走出去。看门的日本人现在都在提心吊胆地防着游击队，哪里还会有心思管他？太好了，他想。

他来到了日本院的门口，发现只有曾林一个人在守门。他上去和曾林搭话，问他日本人都上哪去了，是不是还都泡在仓库里。曾林说哪儿啊，全他妈的出去了，游击队炸掉了镇子西边一个出入口处的鬼子炮楼，看样子像是要大规模进攻，日本兵大都被派出去拦击了，只剩下少数鬼子守着镇政府的大门口和后面的粮仓、牢房、弹药库。他奶奶的，他们玩了那么久女人，居然还有力气打仗，我咒他们个个脚软眼花打不准！

赵宏伟问，那我们的人呢，也都派出去了？

派出去了一小部分，他妈的又是打先锋，我好不容易才留了下来看门。其余的兄弟都在里面看守那些仓库里的女人。曾林说。

那么渡边呢，是不是也走了？

当然，他不带队谁带队。

太好了，赵宏伟大喜过望。他说，你就当没看见过我。说完，他就要往日本院里走。

别别，曾林赶紧拦住了赵宏伟。赵镇长您想干吗？

我要进去，找个人。很要紧的人。

男人女人？

女人。

不行不行，您不能进去。

怎么，日本人都不在了，你还要拦我？

赵驹把事情都跟我说了，我不能放你进去，那样你和我都会完蛋的。

赵驹？

是的，赵驹中午前从靶场回来了。出发前，他见是我留下来看日本院

的门，就特意嘱咐我，你若是来了，无论如何不能让你进去。他说，你喜欢的一个女人，这两天正躺在渡边办公室后面的那间卧室里的床上，你若要进去，定是劫人。赵镇长，我没想到你竟然真会这么糊涂！这里是谁在做皇帝？是日本人在做皇帝！他们看上了的东西，你也敢往回要？一个女人而已，哪里值得让人往枪口上去撞！况且，这两天下来，再好的女人也一定是成了残花败柳了，不要也罢，不要也罢。

你走开。

赵镇长，你不会是真的要这么做吧？

你走开！

曾林死死地就抱住了赵宏伟。赵镇长，我不能让你进去，不能让你进去！你好好想一想，你和日本人抢女人，不是找死是什么？不光是你死，我放了你进去，我也会死的呀！求求你了，赵镇长，我家里还有一个生病的儿子，没了我，你叫我儿子怎么办哪！

赵宏伟憋着一股气，顿时软了下来。他呆愣地在地上坐了坐，一咬嘴唇，忽然跪在曾林的面前。曾林，你就当没看见我，就当没看见我，或者，你干脆让我把你打晕，让我把你打晕，这样日本人就不会怪你了，一定不会！

曾林也给赵宏伟跪了下来。赵镇长，日本人哪有这么傻呀！他们要是这么好骗，中国就不会弄成今天这个样子了。求你了，赵镇长，别为难我了，我留下来看门，是想求条活路，不是要寻死啊！

曾林泪流满面。赵宏伟也流起了泪来。秀珍就在里面，就在里面哪！机不可失，时不再来呀！再晚几天，她们兴许就要被送去上海了呀！

赵镇长，您进去了也没用，渡边临走前，在他的办公室外面派了四个守卫，您进去了又能怎么样啊！

赵宏伟狠狠一拳砸在地上。他拼命地砸着地，砸得手背上都有了血。日本鬼子，你们为什么非要把人逼到绝路上！

赵宏伟擦干了眼泪，站起了身来。曾林也站了起来。对不起，赵宏伟突然说。说完，他就猛地一拳，打倒了猝不及防的曾林。曾林被打晕了过去。

赵宏伟拿了曾林的枪，潜入了日本院。他迅速地往渡边办公室的方向跑，还没跑到，远远地，他就已是看见了站在渡边办公室外面的日本哨兵。

是四个，曾林没有说谎。赵宏伟知道，那间卧室没有后门也没有窗，要进去，只能从渡边的办公室里进。但是这间办公室的门外，此刻正站着四个荷枪实弹的日本兵。

赵宏伟在一个较隐蔽的墙角处蹲了下来。想来想去，他都觉得，想从那四个日本兵的眼前把秀珍带走，是一个很大的笑话，而他也没能力打死那四个鬼子。再说了，枪一响，他还能往哪儿逃？

深重的沮丧击垮了赵宏伟。枪在他垂着的手里一晃一晃，像个没用的玩具。他从未如此绝望地感到过自己的无能。曾林说得不错，他现在已经进来了，但是又能怎样？秀珍就在他能看得见的那间屋子里，他在这里喊一声，秀珍一定听得见，但是他敢喊吗？枪里的弹匣也是满的，但是他又能用这把枪做什么？赵驹说得对，要是惹恼了渡边，那秀珍就真是死路一条了。他也不敢去想，秀珍现在怎么样了，稍微一想，他的心就会被刀绞碎。他痛不欲生。他只祈求，秀珍能活着就好。

他把枪藏在了衣服里，离开了这个令他痛苦的地方。他要去叫一个汉奸，和他一起把曾林抬到医务室去。趁着日本人还没回来。

他去了仓库那里，因为他听曾林说，他们都在看守那些女人，但是远远的，他在仓库外面并没有看见一个人影。

他在仓库里看到了更加令他不能接受的一幕。他的那些汉奸弟兄们，此刻正一个一个无一例外地全都趴在那些可怜的中国女人身上。他们在做着和那些日本畜生一模一样的事情。而最令他目瞪口呆的，是十九岁的福宝。瘦小的福宝正在一个高大而美丽的女人身上动得飞快，他闭着眼睛，嘴里流泻着狼一样的声音。女人们的表情，大都像死了一样。不，比死了更绝望。一切，都比死了更残酷。

一切，都变得好陌生。赵宏伟觉得，他的眼前，就像是有无数只又黑又大的苍蝇，正在吸食一具具尸体的血。他快要吐了。他一把就将福宝从那个活死人一样的女人身上拉了下来。

“全他妈的给我滚下来！”赵宏伟大吼。

众人皆惊，才发现赵镇长已大驾光临。一些人依依不舍地从那些女人的身上滚了下来，而还有一些人，则没听见似的继续在动。赵宏伟大声地又吼了一遍，他们只是动得更快了一些。赵宏伟一把拔出了枪。他走上前去，一

个一个地，用枪顶在他们的脑门上，逼他们下来。众人只得听命。只有最后的一个已是六十多岁的老年汉奸天不怕地不怕，枪顶在他的脑门上，他仍照动不误。赵宏伟怒不可遏，脸色血红，直想一拳打翻这个老畜生，看着他满头的白发，却又下不去手。赵宏伟再次大声命令了一遍，但老头还是不理他。后面就有汉奸哄笑了起来。赵宏伟拿枪的手在微微发抖。

赵宏伟脑子里正金星乱冒、“嗡嗡”直响，这个老头终于结束了。他从女人的身上爬了下来，心满意足地长出了一口气，然后嘲笑地看了赵宏伟一眼。“赵镇长，你拿枪对着我们干什么？”老头说，“赵镇长，你是不是真的把自己当成了日本人哪？”

“她们、她们可都是我们的同胞姐妹呀！”赵宏伟颤抖着说。

“放心，我们都验过了，这里的女人，没一个是我们的姐妹。”老头挑衅似的笑着说。

又有几个汉奸笑了起来。

“砰”一枪，老头的脑袋开了花。血全溅在肮脏的墙上，浓浓厚厚一大片，像一个腐烂的伤疤。

尸体横在地上。仓库里肃静一片。

赵宏伟不敢相信，自己杀了人。

渡边击败了游击队后，就直接领兵回了镇政府。而此时，赵宏伟已是被留守的日本兵给五花大绑地浸在了水牢里。

渡边提审了赵宏伟。曾林给赵宏伟作证，说，赵宏伟是想去视察仓库那边的保卫情况，结果没想到就出了事。枪是他借给赵宏伟的，因为怕有女人会突然造反，伤害到手无寸铁的赵宏伟。

赵宏伟在渡边面前痛哭流涕。他说，他是因为实在无法忍受那群肮脏的中国人竟敢那样肆无忌惮地玷污皇军神圣的慰安妇，所以才一时失手，杀了人。请皇军开恩，千万开恩。

最后，赵驹在渡边的耳旁说了几句话，渡边点了点头。赵宏伟被释放。而那些监守自盗的汉奸，则被随便抽出了几个人来，拉出去执行了枪决。福宝也被枪毙了。渡边拍拍赵宏伟的肩膀，笑着说，你做得好，你对皇军，非常忠心。

等到一切都结束，赵宏伟回到家时，已是第二天的清晨。

赵宏伟担心小菊昨天没吃晚饭，会不会饿坏肚子，小菊说她昨天晚饭吃了，吃的昨天中午剩下来的那些饭菜，很饱。赵宏伟就略感欣慰，庆幸自己昨天做了午饭。

赵宏伟累得睡着了。在梦里，他无缘无故地呕吐着，吐得肠子都流了出来。他看见了漫山遍野的血，而他的两只手，都插在荒凉的坟墓里。

醒来时，小菊手里端着一碗水，正站在他的床旁边。

“宏伟伯伯，你是不是生病了？”小菊问。

“没有哇，伯伯好得很。”

“我看见你睡着了一直在发抖。”小菊将水碗一放，小手往赵宏伟的额头上一摸。“宏伟伯伯你额头好烫，你是不是发烧了？”

赵宏伟自己一摸额头，却感觉不出烫不烫，因为他的手心里也是烫的。“没事，小菊放心，伯伯没事。”

赵宏伟看了看时间，是该做午饭的时候了。他只做了小菊一个人的份，他实在是什么也吃不下。看小菊吃完了午饭，他收拾了一下碗筷，然后又出去买了一大盒的油酥饼回来。他对小菊说，小菊乖，以后要是伯伯不能准时回来给你做饭，你就先吃这个饼填填肚子。伯伯不会经常这样不回来的。小菊就很听话地点点头。

赵宏伟觉得自己整个人都昏昏沉沉的，一动也不想动，但他还是不能躺下。他知道自己还有太多的事没有做完，虽然他并不知道自己到底该怎样去做才对。

他出了门，不知道该往哪儿走。路就在他眼前，却又好像根本就没有路。他用力地开动脑筋，想要反省一下自己这两天的所作所为，筹谋一下下一步的行动方向，却感到脑子里是满满的一罐糨糊。他觉得自己该去买一些药了，他觉得自己从头到脚都十分难受。可能真是病了，他想。他感到全身都很冷，就像流干了血一样。他再次想起了从那个老头的脑袋里流出来的脑浆。他觉得自己像是快要死了。

走到半路上，赵宏伟看了一眼灰蒙蒙的天，想，为什么天总是这么暗。然后，他就突然失去了知觉。

他倒在了马路上。

昏迷中，赵宏伟觉得小秦还在骂他是狗汉奸。他感到自己到哪里都无法逃脱这一片骂。他想睁开眼，又睁不开。他觉得自己像是到了一个油锅里，在被阎罗王炸。

终于睁开了眼来，赵宏伟见到了很多白色的东西。白的床，白的墙，白的桌，白的屏风。他感到十分诧异。他动了动，才发现自己的手背上还扎着针，是正在挂药水。

从屏风后面走出了一个人来，赵宏伟仔细一看，不是方远梦是谁。

“你醒啦。”

“方兄……”

“快躺下，你病得可不轻。”

一个爽朗的声音从屏风后面传了出来:“没事，他只要醒了就好。”接着，一个人从屏风后面走了出来，是赵宏伟上次带进赵家镇来给方远梦治病的医生。

“是老周在路上看见了你晕倒，把你背回诊所的。”方远梦说。

“谢谢你，谢谢你。”赵宏伟对医生老周说。

三个人说了一会儿话。老周告诉赵宏伟，是他腿上最深的那条伤口发了炎，所以引起的高烧。老周指了指，就是赵宏伟腿上被日本兵的刺刀扎的那个地方。老周说，这么深的伤口，简单包扎是不行的，必须要缝起来，刚才我已都给你弄好了，现在你没事了。赵宏伟说，谢谢，谢谢。老周笑了笑，说，你可真是遍体鳞伤。赵宏伟尴尬地笑笑。

赵宏伟将自己在赵驹那里打听到的新消息都告诉了方远梦，方远梦愁眉不展。赵宏伟问，昨天是不是玉山上的游击队在攻打赵家镇的日军？方远梦点点头，皱着眉说，可惜失败了。老周说，政委不该听小秦的，我们最近弹药这么紧，怎么可能打得过渡边的大队？还好竹内没派援兵给渡边，不然同志们就都回不去了！政委太冲动了！方远梦说，也不能怪谁，那些姐妹们多在日本人的手里待一分钟，就多受一分钟的苦，我们岂能见死不救？只是我们的力量实在是太小了。赵宏伟说，昨天渡边的大队都出去了，镇政府里只有一点点日本兵，要是那时候有一支武装冲进镇政府里去，肯定都能把人救出来！老周说，唉，哪有人呢，当初要是江庆县的锄奸队不走，我们兴许还能联合他们一起来个调虎离山，救出人来，可是现在镇子上和县城里，哪还有抗日的武装？我们从外往里攻，那就是小刀捅石头，你说能捅得动吗？

三个人都觉得很沉重。方远梦说，现在抗日的形势很严峻，但我们不能失去希望。方远梦对老周说，老周，今后我在这里没有做好做到的事情，希望你能做好做到。赵兄刚才给我们提了个醒，我们不能光把尖刀插在鬼子的大门外，我们应该要把我们的武装建立到鬼子的屋里来，那样才能在今后的斗争中争取到主动！不能害怕一时的危险与牺牲，不然今后的危险只会更大，牺牲只会更多！

老周说，放心，我会努力去做的。

赵宏伟不禁问，怎么，方兄，难道你要离开赵家镇了？

方远梦点点头，说，是的，我要去上海开展新的工作了。现在上海的形势很严峻，我党在上海的地下工作站遭到了日本宪兵队的破坏，几位重要的同志已牺牲，而上海军统站在不久前也被日本宪兵队给摧毁了，根据最新情报，被活捉的那些军统人员，现在已经集体叛变，全部投靠了李士群。叛徒们正在帮着日本人抓捕潜伏在上海的抗日分子。现在的上海，可以说是一片黑暗。

赵宏伟闻言，心中五味翻滚。他既觉得形势太残酷，又不禁有些无地自容，毕竟，他自己正是一个叛徒们的楷模。

方远梦说，组织上是从一个月前开始安排老周进来的，老周在这里开了一家诊所，目前看来，一切尚好。我要到下个月才走。你的情况老周也都知道，以后我不在，你要是有什么需要帮助的，可以跟老周说。

赵宏伟说，谢谢。

老周对赵宏伟说，你休息吧。然后，就跟方远梦一起走了出去。

赵宏伟却无法闭上眼。只要一闭上眼，他就会看见许多脑浆和血，还有那飘飘然的花白头发。他确信，从某个他不甚清楚的时刻开始，这个世界正在向他展露他觉得十分陌生的一面。这种陌生是他无法理解的，也是令他感到恐怖的。比如，一个老人怎会如此无耻，他觉得简直是天方夜谭。再比如，福宝怎么竟能发出那样的狼一样的声音来，他觉得这根本就是自己的错觉。太多的人和事，忽然让他感到陌生，就像是有一只残忍的手，将他放到了一面镜子的反面。而他最不能相信的，是自己居然已经杀过了人。他还是

他自己？他已不是他自己？他懵懂无知。

但他无疑又感到了一种隐秘的快感。老头死去的那一刻，他心中的郁怒刹那全消。他，就像是狠狠地击碎了自己的某一片仇恨。这种感觉很快活。这种快活，令他陷入了对自我的一片恐惧中。他开始认识到，他并不十分认识自己。

天暗下来的时候，赵宏伟要求老周给他拔掉针头。他要回去给小菊做晚饭了。他不能让小菊吃饼充饥。他既然救不出秀珍来，那么起码就该照顾好小菊。

离开诊所的时候，赵宏伟随口问了一句，方兄去了哪里。老周却并不愿意告诉他。赵宏伟也不介意。只是在回去的路上，赵宏伟莫名感到了一种伤心的孤单。方远梦走了，以后在这个镇子上，他也就再没有朋友了。万一碰上困难，他也没有了可以求助的对象。虽然方远梦说他有事可以去向老周求助，但是他知道，老周和方远梦毕竟是不一样的。老周会像方远梦一样拿他赵宏伟当自己人吗？老周会像方远梦那样肝胆相照地信任他赵宏伟吗？赵宏伟觉得答案都是否定的。赵宏伟还想，说不定方远梦此次的调离，就是因为他赵宏伟的关系。毕竟他赵宏伟是个汉奸，方远梦一直和他走得如此近，方远梦的组织上难保不会有一些必要的担心。这样对方远梦也好，赵宏伟想。赵宏伟有一些伤心。他想，也许这就是孤家寡人的滋味吧。

吃晚饭的时候，小菊怯怯地问：宏伟伯伯，你是不是去找我娘了？找到我娘了吗？

赵宏伟兴高采烈地说，正要告诉你呢，找到你娘了，你娘在隔壁镇子上的一间客栈里，她一切都好，就是脚崴了，暂时不能走动，还不能回来，过段时间，等伯伯医好了你娘的脚，你就能看到你娘了。

小菊疑惑地问：那我娘干吗不坐黄包车回来呢？

赵宏伟想了想，就说，因为黄包车夫们最近都在罢工，所以雇不到黄包车。

小菊问：什么是罢工？

赵宏伟说，就是不愿意干活。

小菊就说：哦。

吃完了饭，赵宏伟做贼似的赶紧去洗碗。他待在厨房里，都不想出去。他无法面对小菊。他在拿一些愚蠢透了的谎言欺骗小菊，他在欺骗一个什么都不懂的孩子。他都不知道自己究竟在干什么。

他感到自己已经陷入了一个绝境。秀珍的事情令他如坐针毡，但他又毫无解困之道，只能是眼巴巴地等完了天亮等天黑，等完了天黑等天亮，而唯一能指望的方远梦，也行将离去，况且，事实已摆在眼前，游击队打不过日本人。难道真的是只能像赵驹说的那样，等、等、等？到底该怎么办？他已经在短短的两天时间里，连续两次进了日本人的大牢，他是真的不能再犯错了。

晚上，他睡在床上，想一些事情，却什么也想不出来。最终还是睡着了，睡得很沉。直到天亮时，他才是被一个噩梦吓醒。梦里，又是子弹与血。

他起了床，又开始做早饭。他吃不下，他只做了小菊的份。小菊已经有很多日子没有去上学了。开始时是因为就要出逃了，所以赵宏伟就跟秀珍说，不用再送小菊去他那学校里上学了。而接下来糟糕的事情发生得接连不断，赵宏伟自然也就没有心思再去想小菊上学的事情。偶尔想到，他也一把推开。他是早就不想让小菊再去他那所学校里上课了，只是碍于日本人的政策摆在那里，没有办法。而小菊因为常被同学欺负，所以对赵家镇小学也并无半分留恋。赵宏伟想，还是想个办法帮小菊退学吧，毕竟我是校长，这点权力还是会有的。他想，我完全可以自己来教小菊。他把一本《三字经》给了小菊，要她自己慢慢看，然后他就出了门。

赵宏伟先去了老周那里，又挂了半天药水。经过慎重的思考，他觉得还是要先把身体给医好，身体强壮了才能披荆斩棘开山裂石。其次，他也实在是暂时无处可去。待在家里怕小菊要问他事情，去镇政府更是令他不能接受。能去哪里呢？还是先在老周的诊所里治病吧。

老周过来说，接下来，几个镇子上怕是都要大乱了。赵宏伟明知故问，为什么？老周说，女人们一直待在镇政府里不回家，那些男人们难道就不会起疑？一旦发生冲突，老百姓只能是白白送死啊！只怕死的人会堆成小山！

赵宏伟说，那就要看日本人能瞒多久了。

老周长叹了一声。他问，你们这些人里面，对日本人不满的多不多？

赵宏伟知道老周所说的“你们这些人”是指汉奸。他回答，哪里会有人对日本人感到满意，日本人从来不拿我们当人看的。

老周就说，那你们为什么不起义？你们要拿到枪很容易，你们一起义，镇政府岂不是就会不攻自破？

赵宏伟苦笑了笑，说，他们要是会起义，当初就不会选择当汉奸了。

老周眉头一皱，看了看赵宏伟，就说，也是。

赵宏伟的脸上像是被人给刺了一刺。

外面下起了雨来。起初雨很小，后来雨越下越大。窗外的天色，雾蒙蒙一片。

赵宏伟陷入了一种疲软的焦虑和疲软的悲哀中。他仍在时时刻刻地担心秀珍，为她难过，为她焦急，但是，这担心、难过、焦急，都像是被雨打湿了的柴，怎么样也再燃不起干脆的猛火来了。他的满腔悲哀也同样是如此，又湿，又软。他整个人，就像是一块被雨泡湿而生了厚厚的锈的废铁。

在不知道秀珍被渡边占有以前，他还考虑过要用金条去贿赂渡边。在知道了事情的真相以后，他只想用枪解决问题，但事实用枪给自己惹来了更大的麻烦。而当渡边审问他的时候，他只会像一条狗一样地摇尾乞怜。他原本一直以为，他再见到渡边，是一定会阉了他的。想象与现实的差距如此之大，他以前从未想到过。

而他只要一闭上眼，那个下流老头的该死的脑浆还会在他的眼前不断盘旋。他真恨不得剁了自己那只开枪的手。他想好好静一静。

他终于还是睡着了。

醒来的时候，已过了中午。他想起自己没有回去给小菊做午饭，但是转念又一想，没关系，小菊还有油酥饼。可一想就又觉得很对不起秀珍，他居然让小菊以饼充饥。他感到真累。

药水挂完了。赵宏伟将诊费和药费都付给了老周。老周收了钱，说，还要再挂两天药水。赵宏伟说，不用了，就给我配一些吃的药吧。老周就给他配了一些药。赵宏伟说了谢谢，然后就跟老周借了一把伞，离开了诊所。

赵宏伟要回去给小菊做午饭。他想雇辆黄包车，但是路上竟然真的没有黄包车。天上打起了雷，轰隆隆，轰隆隆。赵宏伟想，小菊一个人在家，一定会害怕的。他快步走着。

赵宏伟伞撑得很低，一般人不容易看出他的脸。他觉得这样走路很有安全感。一路上，他先后碰到了两拨人，他们都在急匆匆地往镇政府赶，嘴里还都在说着，日本人给的大洋可真新，我们坚决不要纸币。赵宏伟开始没在意，自顾自地赶路。可走着走着，心里却还是犯起了嘀咕：又出了什么事？日本人难道是在发钱给老百姓？

赵宏伟又走了一会儿。他终于还是停了下来，决定先去镇政府看看。他想，别又出了什么事情。他转回身，往镇政府赶去。

镇政府的大门外，又聚集了很多人。雨下得很大，大家都撑着伞，看上去黑压压的一大片。雨下得很密，水珠乱溅，天和地都像是泡在一团水雾里。赵宏伟站在人群的最后，也不敢往前挤，更不敢吭声。

听了一会儿前面两个老太婆的议论，赵宏伟才开始明白从昨天到今天发生了一些事情。镇子上有几个年轻女人，肚子里本来都已是有了两个月或三个月的身孕，按照征工启事的规定，她们原是可以不用参加这次洗衣的劳役的。但是不知为什么，她们还是照样被日本兵给征走了。她们的男人，在初六那天的大集合中，本来是想要跟日本人要人的，毕竟日本人的白纸黑字写得那么清楚，他们要人也算是要得有理有据、合法合情。但是后来看见洗衣服有大洋可以拿，他们就又都动摇了。毕竟大洋也是很重要的。后来集合的人都散了，他们也就随波逐流地都各自回家了。但是昨天下午终于还是有两个男人，来镇政府向日本人提出了要人的请求，他们说，他们的女人是孕妇，有医生的诊断可作证明。最后的结果是，日本人说她们既然已经来参加劳动了，那么如果现在中途退出，就一定会影响皇军正常的工作安排。日本人要他们再耐心等几天，不要给皇军添麻烦，同时也请他们放心，她们在皇军的庇护下一切都很好，身体健康，心情愉快。日本人说，你们让你们怀有身孕的妻子来为大日本皇军服务，皇军十分感动，放心，我们皇军不会亏待对我们忠心耿耿的奴仆。日本人赏了那两个男人每人三块大洋，并且说，等衣服都洗完了，你们的妻子会得到双倍的工钱。

本来，这件事情会就这样以双方都十分满意的结局收场。谁知树欲静而风不止，孕妇女工的优厚待遇很快就从一个男人的嘴里溜了出去，瞬间飘满了全镇。其他几个孕妇家的男人就也都去了镇政府里要赏钱。而那些不是孕

妇的普通女工的家人，则愤愤不平：凭什么，一样是洗衣服，凭什么孕妇就能拿双倍的工钱？又没有流产！

于是，日本人就给自己惹来了一场麻烦。而中间还出现了日本人不再给大洋只肯给纸币的传言，人心和局面就更乱了。

赵宏伟听着前面的人议论来议论去，抱怨这抱怨那，不禁悲哀地摇头。他的心里填充着满满的冷，满满的难以言说的哀伤。就像那不停的雨，冷得那么彻骨，而又让人望不到尽头。他很想结束这场可笑的悲剧，告诉在场的所有人，不要再去计较钱多钱少了，人都已经完了。但是，他知道，他一说，他们就都会死在这雨中。

曾林出现在了镇政府大门前的小走廊上。他开始大声地向雨中的人们讲话。赵宏伟并没认真去听他的讲话，他知道，曾林是一定有办法解决这种问题的。赵宏伟转身走了。转身的一刹那，他觉得曾林看了他一眼。他觉得有些冷。

他忽然想到，他害死了福宝，害死了那么多同僚，今后，他将如何自处？

农历五月十一日。

雨一直没有停，时而淅淅沥沥，时而倾盆滂沱。昨晚打了一夜的雷，小菊吓得紧蜷着身子，像一只受伤的小兔子。

赵宏伟在雷声轰鸣中一夜未眠。过多的黑暗与苦闷郁积在他的心头，他也真希望那刺眼的闪电可以劈进他的胸膛，让他得到一片痛快的光明。湿闷的夜是那么沉重，在一次又一次的闪电之间，夜的漆黑分外耀眼，就仿佛那光并不是为了击碎黑暗而来，而只是为了让你更明白地看清夜的深广、厚重与无敌才存在。雨把天地浸得湿漉漉，就仿佛是为了要掩盖人的泪水，遮蔽无边的悲伤。赵宏伟觉得一切都太压抑了，而他还必须要在这压抑里走下去。

天亮以后雨小了很多，雷也停了。赵宏伟又去了镇政府，他要想办法见一见渡边。无论如何他都想试一试，他想给渡边两根金条，请他高抬贵手，放了秀珍，不知他会不会答应。他不断地告诫自己，见了渡边，一定要和颜悦色，点头哈腰，就好像什么也没有发生一样。

到了镇政府，赵宏伟察觉到了一丝发生在他周围的异样的变化。没有汉奸再来主动和他打招呼，说赵镇长早上好。汉奸们见了他，都默默而自觉地绕行。有些汉奸看他的眼神里带着恶毒的恨，有些则充满了彻底的鄙夷。他感到了一种孤立，这种孤立让他觉得有些害怕。

曾林在走廊里看见了他，也没有叫他，只是向他微微地点了一下头，算是打了个招呼，然后便与他擦肩而过。赵宏伟转身想叫曾林，但是想想还是住了口。一种被孤立的难受在他心里左冲右突。他听见了几句微小的议论：看见没有，这才是真正的狗，给日本人看尿壶都看得那么尽忠职守！听说他自己的女人也正在被日本人当尿壶使，活该！不会是他自己主动把自己的女人送给日本人的吧？真不要脸！

赵宏伟关上了自己办公室的门，他突然莫名有了一种想哭的冲动。日本人不拿他当人，中国人不拿他当人，现在好了，连同样是汉奸的汉奸都不拿他当人了！他还可以去哪里证明自己是一个人？

他给赵驹的办公室里打了一个电话，他并没指望这电话真会通，因为大家都知道赵驹很少待在他自己的办公室里。但是赵宏伟准备死马当活马医，如果赵驹不在这里，那么他也要去其他地方找到赵驹。他今天是一定要把贿赂渡边这件事情给办好的。一定要。千错万错送钱不会错，这也是没办法的办法了，他只希望能钱到路开。

赵驹接了电话，赵宏伟大喜过望。他卑躬屈膝地问，你现在有没有时间，我想找你说点事。赵驹说，你上来吧。

赵宏伟去了楼上赵驹的办公室。在楼梯上碰到了两个从上面走下来的汉奸，看赵宏伟的眼光都是冷冷的，甚至还都有些避之唯恐不及的意思。赵宏伟的心被刺了一下，就好像他是一个比汉奸更令人不齿的东西。他觉得在这个世上似乎已失去了同类。这种感觉很难受也很怪。

赵宏伟给了赵驹一根金条，赵驹笑纳了。赵驹笑着说，这黄鱼可不好拿，说吧，有什么事？赵宏伟说，有两件事，第一，我想知道，秀珍现在是不是还好好地活着。赵驹说，我只能跟你说，在今天早上新拉出去的那堆女尸里，仍然没有你的王秀珍。这一点我可以确定。赵宏伟就欣慰地点了点头，然后说，第二，我今天一定要见到渡边。赵驹问，你要见他干什么？赵宏伟说，我要给他送金条。赵驹说，大后天，渡边参加完县里的记者招待会

之后，就不会再回到赵家镇上来了，你何不耐心再多等两天呢？赵宏伟说，我一分一秒都等不下去了！谁知道秀珍此刻是否还活着！

赵驹笑笑，就给渡边打了一个电话。电话通了，赵驹点头哈腰地问渡边此刻忙不忙，今天有没有时间。最后，赵驹说，是这样的，赵宏伟他有一些礼物要当面送给您，不知您今天是否能抽空见他一面？电话那头说了一些什么，赵驹感激涕零地不停说谢谢。

电话挂了。赵驹说：渡边说，他现在正在上厕所，没空见你，不过今天傍晚时你可以去他办公室见他。

赵宏伟焦躁地坐了下来，说，又要等一天！他哪里是在上厕所，厕所里哪来的电话！

赵驹笑笑，说，他肯见你，已是皇恩浩荡了。

赵宏伟在桌上捶了一拳，愤怒地说，他们倒真是来中国做起皇帝了！他沉默了一会儿，然后出神地自言自语说：也不知秀珍现在怎么样了。

赵驹说：你没听明白吗？渡边说，他现在正在上厕所。

赵宏伟以为外面的雨已经停了，其实没有。淅淅沥沥的雨一直细细密密地下着，他从未感到过江南的雨是如此令人厌。连天也不肯多给这世间一点点的光明，要用云来遮去晴朗，他想。

他给小菊梳着头，他对小菊说，你娘现在一切都很好，很好，她的脚就快要好了，好了就能回来了。小菊听后很高兴。小菊说，等我娘回来了，我要天天给她捶腿。赵宏伟说，小菊真乖。

赵宏伟在心里说，菩萨保佑，让我钱到路开，财去人安乐。

赵宏伟焦急地等待着时间的流逝，他要快点等到傍晚，那时，他就可以见到渡边了。不是以一个犯人的身份，而是以一个体面的镇长的身份。

他的金条，是从他上次给秀珍的那盒财产里拿的。不然他手头上根本就没有金条可用。他在秀珍的屋里找了好久才找到那盒财产，秀珍保管得很仔细，盒子上面还盖了一块漂亮的鸳鸯手帕。赵宏伟看着那手帕，心里就很酸。秀珍一直以为，他是真的要和她们一起去开始新的生活了。她是那么天真。她以为他会娶她。可他其实就是个骗子。

他想，放心吧，秀珍，我不会再骗你了。他想，这次，一旦救出秀珍，他就真的是要和秀珍母女一起远走高飞了。不管是会去哪里，只要在一起就好。

他也曾想过，要给渡边三根金条，但是又一想，觉得还是留一点储备的好。渡边是一头让人猜不透的狼，不能把赌注全押在他一个人身上。

他不断地祈祷着，秀珍只要活着就好。活着就好，这是一个多么卑微的恳求，又是一个多么奢侈的愿望，更凝结了无尽的提心吊胆与痛不欲生在其中。他发誓，秀珍要是死了，他一定会把渡边炸个稀巴烂。

而幸亏赵驹还一直是对他留有仁慈。不然，他真可谓已是死路一条。赵驹曾经对他说，我并不是想要帮你，我只是十分好奇，像你这样的一个人，最终会不会成为我的一个同类。从我第一次带着渡边去你家的那天开始，我就看到了一场戏的开幕。也许有一天，当你走到戏的结尾，你会由衷地感到，当年那个高高在上的赵宏伟，真是可笑。

赵宏伟说，不，我永远不会有那样的一天。

可是，赵宏伟在心里感到，自己已经走到了戏的结尾，或许赵驹也已看到了他想看到的。当年那个有足够的资格看不起赵驹的赵宏伟，已重新投胎转世了好几次。孤家寡人的赵宏伟，在赵家镇上只剩下了赵驹这根救命稻草。赵驹当年叫人砍了赵宝贵的一只手，而他赵宏伟今日却巴不得能和赵驹称兄道弟，这不是汉奸是什么？他又有多少资格可以看不起赵驹？他已默念了那么多次“活着就好”这句话，他离赵驹的那条路又真的还有多远？他也已杀了人，他的手还干不干净？他有时也会想：如果能忘了自己是一个中国人，那么也许就不会再痛得这么辛苦。他的明天，谁说又不会是一个恶魔的咏叹？

赵宏伟说，不，我永远不会有那样的一天。但是，他的人生，他说了不算。

赵宏伟敲了敲渡边办公室的门。他心里怦怦直跳，胸前甚至在不停地出汗。他不停地告诉自己要镇定，他都已经教育了自己一个下午，但是他的手还是抖了起来。

渡边开了门，说，进来吧。

赵宏伟满脸堆笑，走进了渡边的办公室。办公室里没有其他任何人。办

公室里的一扇小黑门紧闭着。赵宏伟知道，这扇小黑门的后面，是一条只有两三步短的过道，而这条过道的尽头，就是那间专供渡边休息用的卧室。

赵宏伟太阳穴上的青筋跳了两跳。他镇定了再镇定，努力让自己笑得更无邪。

你来找我有什么事？渡边问。

哦，太君好，冒昧打扰，实在是有事相求。

有事相求？赵驹不是说，你有一些礼物要当面送给我吗？礼物呢？

哦，是，是。太君，这两条黄鱼，是我孝敬给您的一点心意，请不要嫌弃，还望笑纳，笑纳。

哦哈哈哈，宏伟君怎么这么客气，大家都是朋友嘛。好，那我就恭敬不如从命啦，哈哈哈。

谢谢太君，谢谢太君，太君不嫌弃这一点点心意，就是我赵某人前世修来的福气了。

哈哈哈，宏伟君，我真是越来越喜欢你了。你放心，你想要什么，我很清楚，既然你这么慷慨，那么请放心，我一定会让你如愿以偿的。大家都是朋友嘛。哈哈哈哈。

谢谢太君，谢谢太君，谢谢太君！

好了，那么你先回去吧，你的要求这几天内我暂时还无法满足你，你也懂的，我权力有限。但是等我去了县里的联队总部，我一定会尽快给你办，一定办好，你放心，好不好？

好，好，谢谢太君，谢谢太君！

慢走！

请留步！

办公室的门临关上的时候，赵宏伟好像听见从办公室里小黑门后面的最深处，传出来了一些响动。是秀珍吗？是她弄出来的声音吗？是她在挣扎吗？是她想叫他吗？虽然他和渡边说的是日语，秀珍听不懂，但是他的声音，她总还是能听出来的。秀珍哪秀珍，真是令他情何以堪。

办公室的门关上了，赵宏伟脸上谄媚的笑还僵着，褪不下去。走廊里的日本哨兵还以为赵宏伟是在对着他笑，就也对着赵宏伟笑了笑。

赵宏伟离开了渡边的办公室，心里流动着喜悦的希望。渡边已经都答应了，等他去了联队总部，就会请求竹内放人。竹内一定会同意的，赵宏伟想，毕竟只是放一个女人而已。他还想，还剩两根金条，到时还可以贿赂竹内。

但是，他心里又隐隐有些不踏实。事情比他预计的要容易得多，没有尴尬，没有周旋，没有阻碍，没有危险，甚至他还没有把话尴尬地挑明，渡边便已爽快地应允了一切。一切似乎都太顺利了。但是，顺利一些不好吗？赵宏伟自问。毕竟有金条开道，一切难题迎刃而解那是理所当然的。而且，渡边那么聪明，难道他会等着你无限尴尬地对他说，请你把你床上的女人给放下来？

赵宏伟决定不再多想。事实已证明，多思无益。他现在要做的，只是祈祷与等待。

雨还在下。

赵宏伟又梦见了心音。一会儿，心音在梦里流着泪问他，宏伟君，你是不是变心了？赵宏伟慌忙地说，没有，没有，怎么会呢。一会儿，心音又兴高采烈地告诉他，宏伟君，我参加了女子挺身队，就要和你一起去中国了，我们可以永远在一起了。

赵宏伟惊得醒了过来。一种长久沉淀着的痛苦，在他心里如雾一样弥漫。他想，是啊，心音若没死，又会不会被骗去女子挺身队呢？心音的父亲，就是因为参加了日军侵略台湾的战争，所以在噩梦中度过了一生。心音一家当年若都没死，而今战事又起，他们的命运又会变成什么样呢？会不会又是另一场悲剧？战争啊战争，你到底是怎样的一个恶魔！

赵宏伟没想到自己会在这种时候又梦见心音。梦真是一种令人无法摆脱的东西。这么多年了，心音在他的梦里一直都还是栩栩如生，她在他的眼前是那么清晰，他甚至能看清楚她的每一根发丝，而他却似乎从未真正看清过自己。爱，也许就是活着的一场病，到死也未必会痊愈。

而赵宏伟又觉得自己分外对不起秀珍。赵驹说得对，他要是一早就娶了秀珍，让她成了镇长夫人，她又怎会被日本人征去当女工。他这一生，做错了多少事！

他想，也许他是既爱心音，又爱秀珍吧。人生中，也许本来就没多少可以真正分辨得很清楚的事情。他想，心音早已死了，他又怎能再失去秀珍？

农历五月十二日。雨。

赵宏伟很久没去学校了，他去了一次学校。本来他根本就不想再去管那学校的事，但是现在既然秀珍释放有望，那么他就不能在工作上让渡边和竹内失望。万一渡边和竹内生了气，那么秀珍的事就又会节外生枝。他要认真工作，办好奴化教育，准备好公开课的相关事宜，让渡边放心，让竹内满意。只要秀珍一放出来，什么狗屁校长、狗屁镇长，就全见鬼去吧！

赵宏伟也已经是在地图上找好了几个地方，都是些没有战略价值的小乡或小镇。他准备将来就带着秀珍和小菊去这几个地方中的某一个地方生活，安安乐乐的，无忧无虑。当然，这安乐和无忧，只是他的一个憧憬。他连自己将来改叫什么名字都想好了，就叫赵安乐。这姓是不能改的，不然会对不起祖宗。最后还剩两根金条，能不送出去就不送出去了，以后重新开始生活也是需要本钱的。法币他固然也有，但是法币不断在贬值，万一以后成了废纸就完了。能做一点小生意就做一点小生意，做不了小生意也没关系，他赵宏伟学富五车，出去给人写个大字、算个卦，那也一样是能赚钱的。这些都好办。

至于将来究竟是要去哪个地方落脚，赵宏伟觉得这无所谓，脚长在人的身上，爱去哪里去哪里，能在哪里待下来就在哪里待下来，这些都不是问题。只要能离开日本人的势力范围，离开有他赵宏伟汉奸阴影的地方。一个全新的赵安乐，会有全新的生活。

要怎样才能离开沦陷区？赵宏伟打算到时还是要去麻烦一下方远梦或老周的。无所谓了，脸皮厚一下就厚一下，反正当初游击队也是答应了要帮他送人出去的，这不是暂时没帮成吗，那承诺应该是仍然有效的。

而那些仓库里的女人，赵宏伟觉得就不关他什么事了。他能做什么呢？能自保就不错了。一个国家的军队都败了，他连枪都拿不稳，又能去救谁？还是别狗拿耗子多管闲事了。救民于水火，那是蒋委员长才应该考虑的事情。草民赵宏伟，只求能苟安于乱世，莫问天下兴亡。

但是他又想起了那个老头该死的脑浆，他的手上仿佛还拿着枪。他问自己：我这辈子，又真的还能安乐吗？他想，其实小秦骂得一点儿不错，他赵宏伟，就是个只关心自己利益的人。自己是民族的败类。

下午，他又在镇政府里待了一会儿。没有汉奸理他，他就去和两个日本兵聊了一会儿家常。他了解到，渡边今天也去了仓库里，与大伙儿同乐。渡边还发明了一种比赛，就是看谁能在女人的体内动更久。每赢一次，可以得到两罐牛肉罐头。渡边一上午赢了两次。

赵宏伟想，看来渡边是真的放过秀珍了，他不再折磨她了，这样很好。金条果然是最有用的东西。

两个日本兵还说，明天，就要给这些女人们文上号码。她们每个人都将得到一个编号，文在肩头上，这样，想逃也逃不了，一查就能查到。多么聪明的办法。

还是有女人在死掉。大多是自杀，少部分是因为伤害了我们皇军而被杀。有两个倒霉的家伙，居然被女人咬断了生殖器。真是太可怕了。渡边大队长对大家提出了要求，说，不能再让女人死去了，不然人数就要不够了，刚开始时有四五十个女人，现在只剩下了二十几个，绝对不能再死了。当然，我们皇军的士兵也要注意，不要被这些女人伤害到，不要低估她们的反抗意识。

日本兵撒完了尿，跟赵宏伟道了个别，就又都走了。赵宏伟待在走廊里，无处可去，站在原地。

走廊外的雨淅淅沥沥，赵宏伟的心里有些难受。说不出的难受。他还记得那天在仓库里看到的一些惨不忍睹的女人的鲜血和眼泪。难道她们就将一直如此，直到死去吗？还将有多少中国人会成为日本人的奴隶？我们这一代是完了，那么我们的下一代呢？小菊长大了以后呢？中国的明天呢？难道我们要世世代代做日本人的牛、羊和狗？他们日本人可以一直想怎么样就怎么样？国军在哪里？武器在哪里？

赵宏伟胸闷无比。他想，中国要是完了，我和秀珍、小菊又真的可以逃去哪里？覆巢之下，岂有完卵。

回到家里，小菊在很乖地看书。小菊说她想学《论语》。赵宏伟说，小菊乖，明天开始，伯伯教你《武经七书》，等你长大了，要学穆桂英、花木兰，做女中豪杰，行岳飞之事，驱除倭寇，恢复中华。说完，赵宏伟自己的

眼眶却是红了。

但使龙城飞将在，不教胡马度阴山。赵宏伟咏道。

小菊发现了那坛用报纸裹着的状元红，觉得很好奇。赵宏伟撕掉了报纸，将酒坛给小菊看。小菊嗅了嗅，说，真香。赵宏伟说，这里面是酒，上好的酒，等你娘回来了，我们就一起喝掉它，给你也喝一碗，好不好？小菊小手一拍，高兴地说，好。

第二天，赵宏伟既没去学校，也没去镇政府。他就待在家里，教小菊《武经七书》。赵宏伟说，小菊呀，伯伯小时候，就是因为学孔子学得太多，学孙子学得太少，所以才遇上了很多伤心事，你长大了，千万别跟伯伯一样，你要有一颗坚强的心。

赵宏伟说，小菊呀，再过几天，你娘就要回来了，到时候，我们可能就要不住在这里了。伯伯会带你娘和你去另外的一个地方生活，那里没有日本人，没有刺刀和炮弹，有花花草草，有青山绿水，鸡犬相闻，落英缤纷。我们在一起，一定会生活得很好的。

小菊一直很乖地点头。

小菊背书的时候，赵宏伟就去后院的屋檐下站了一会儿。雨水在屋檐前织成了一道雨帘，亮晶晶，冷飕飕。院里的那棵桂花树还是那么硬朗，风过雨过，都只是将它锻炼得更挺拔、冲洗得更清亮。只是，赵宏伟觉得自己好像已经是忘记了它开花时的香味。那悠悠的桂花香，他再怎么想，也想不起来了。他的鼻子和记忆里，都像是被满满的血腥味与火药味给堵住了，那香，仿佛只是一个幻觉，但那分明不是幻觉。他很想再闻到它的香味，那样也许他就能想起以前的自己究竟是个什么样的自己。但是他想，今年，自己怕是看不到它开花了。他就要离开了。它像个观众一样观看了他父母的一生和他的一生，它用一年一度的花香给这个院子里带来了很多欣喜与安慰，而现在，他就要跟它告别了。是该结束了。

赵宏伟给小菊买了一大包云片糕。小菊吃了一片，说真好吃，然后就把云片糕又重新包了起来。赵宏伟问，怎么不吃了？小菊说，我娘最爱吃云片糕了，我要等娘回来，和娘一起吃。

下午的时候，雨猛然又大了起来，而且还打起了雷。赵宏伟觉得这老天爷也真是不开眼，人间已是一片愁云惨雾，你还来凑什么热闹，这该死的雨，一下就是好几天。难不成是要发大水了？

雷打得越来越频，轰隆轰隆不间断，雨也有了倾盆之势，哗哗的雨声大得吓人。小菊很害怕，蜷在赵宏伟怀里。赵宏伟说，不用怕，不用怕，这是雷公和电母在吵架呢，吵完了就好了。

到了傍晚，天被云遮得严严实实，整个人间都像是陷入了黑夜。赵宏伟没有点灯，所以看不清小菊的脸。雷像连环炮一样不停地打，雨下得像决了堤的洪水。轰隆隆和哗啦啦的声音混合在一起，宛如万马奔腾，群虎齐啸。赵宏伟甚至听到有疯婆子在街上大喊：天要塌啦！

“轰隆隆！轰隆隆！”两声惊雷，天空几乎成了漆黑。雨势狂骤。赵宏伟心惊胆战。疯婆子在街上大喊：天狗要吃太阳啦！要吃掉太阳啦！

小菊紧闭着双眼。赵宏伟捂着她的耳朵。

天狗没有吃掉太阳。只是，暴雨冲开了旷野中的两个死人坑。坑上原本堆得厚厚的石块和土都被雨冲了个一干二净，坑旁的两棵遮云蔽日的大树都被雷劈成了焦黑的碎片。坑里，埋的正是从镇政府里拉出去的那些女尸。

夜色漆黑。外面已没有雷，也没有雨。只有不停的骚乱，骚乱。

锣鼓声、怒吼声、悲恸声，不停地从外面的街上流过，层层叠叠，声势浩大。赵宏伟缩在家里，不用出去，也知道外面肯定又是出了什么事。出了什么事呢？他想出去看看，又觉得，多一事不如少一事。

明天就要去参加在县政府里举行的记者招待会了，他要让自己看起来精神奕奕。他也要准备好各种措辞，以防在记者面前说错话。万一说错了话，那么渡边和竹内就会不高兴，他们一不高兴，那么释放秀珍这事情就会有麻烦。虽然赵宏伟早已见过许多许多次记者，对于记者提问这种事情早已不当一回事，但是这一次的情况却是有些不一样的。这是竹内在江庆县召开的最后一次记者招待会，也是规格最高的一次。受邀来参加的，不仅有日本的记者和亲日派的中国记者，还有德国记者和意大利记者。可谓具有国际阵容。一个小小的县城，被竹内搞出了这么大的花样，南京的日军总部也已经对竹内发生了兴趣。竹内准备在记者会上畅谈大东亚共荣的美好未来，然后，他就将抱着满满一筐的写满了溢美之词的报纸，去南京的旅团里走马上任。

大佐只要再往上升一级，就是少将了，竹内离他的将军梦，也就只有一步之遥了。

而赵宏伟明天要做的，就是口吐莲花，尽全力为竹内的功德添砖加瓦。比如，中国的孩子经过教育，已经充分认识到了大日本帝国的伟大和大东亚共荣的美好，他们对腐朽落后的中国痛恨不已，不仅万分欢迎皇军的到来，而且十分渴望长大后能为大日本帝国的神圣事业鞠躬尽瘁，死而后已，等等。诸如此类的言论，赵宏伟装了满满一肚子。早在一个半月以前，渡边就已给了他厚厚一摞书面材料，让他务必将里面的内容全部背熟。材料里，有一些是赵宏伟自己写的汉奸文章，有一些，是其他沦陷区的知名汉奸写的文章，还有一些，则是竹内自己写的政治要点。只是当时赵宏伟并不知道渡边要他背这些东西来做什么。后来知道了，是要他去给竹内吹牛。其实赵宏伟也看得出来，在一系列事关竹内前途的重大事件上，渡边的态度都是非常矛盾而痛苦的。他既不希望竹内成功，又不希望竹内的事情是毁在他的手里。因此，赵宏伟曾经也很彷徨，究竟要怎样拍马屁，才能同时让渡边和竹内的心里都舒舒服服？最后，他从中国几千年的太监史中得出了一个明智的结论：不要去管这些事情，不管主子之间怎么斗来斗去，奴才只要做好奴才的本分就好。总之主子让做什么，奴才就做什么。

此刻，赵宏伟在心中又重新温习了一遍那些早已被他背得滚瓜烂熟的狗屁材料，他想，明天一定要好好表现。他想，这些材料倒挺有用，到上公开课的那天，或许我也该背一段。转念又马上醒悟：不对，那时我早已和秀珍、小菊跑了，又哪里还来的什么公开课？赵宏伟微微一笑，想，到时候，谁愿意接我的班就让谁接去。老子不伺候了。

外面突然又有一阵号啕大哭经过，赵宏伟心中疑窦丛生。他对小菊说，你好好待在家里，不管外面发生什么事，哪里也不要去。然后，他就偷偷溜出了门去。

黑乎乎的夜，路上的几盏灯都坏了。剩下没坏的两三盏路灯，昏暗地亮着，像疲倦的眼睛，像暂时还没找到坟的鬼。借着微弱的光，赵宏伟看见路面上撒着许多纸钱。是谁家在夜里出丧？排场怎么这么大？细细一想，却又不像。那喧闹，那嘈杂，分明就是一场可怕的骚乱。可是怎么会有纸钱？赵宏伟悄悄地在黑暗的四周走了一圈，想看看能不能碰到爱说闲话的老太婆，听听究竟是怎么回事，但是家家户户都门窗紧闭。也许闲话早已说过了？应该早点出来看看的，不该缩在屋里。

夜空是那么黑，路上的光又是那么暗，赵宏伟在黑与暗中徘徊，听到风吹的声音，莫名有些毛骨悚然。路上没有半个人，空静得可怕。真是难以想象，刚才还闹得那么厉害，赵宏伟想。一扇门“吱呀”了一下，赵宏伟以为有人出来了，可是看了又看，哪都没人。

忽然，“啪啪啪”，远处像是有人在放鞭炮。赵宏伟以为自己听错了。夜是那么静，那么黑，那么空，谁会在半夜里放鞭炮？

可是，又一阵“啪啪啪”。声音是从很远的地方传来，夜很静，声音很明确。赵宏伟没有听错。

又一阵“啪啪啪”。赵宏伟突然醒了。那是镇政府方向，那不是鞭炮声，而是机枪声！

赵宏伟跑了起来。

“冲啊！跟小日本拼了！”

“还我女儿！还我女儿！”

“你们这群畜生！我老婆肚子里还怀着孩子啊！我跟你们拼了！”

“啪啪啪”“啪啪啪”“啪啪啪”。

十几个男人又一起倒在了血泊中。

镇政府的前后门和围墙四周，亮如白昼。日本人开满了探照灯和一切可以开的灯。白花花的灯光里，血气沸腾。

镇政府的每一面围墙，都有一条街那么长。现在，四条街上已躺满了死尸。镇政府的前后门外，尸体更是堆积如小山。

许多死去的男人手里，都拿着斧头、锤子、菜刀之类的铁器，但是看样子，他们连日本人的头发丝也没碰上。鲜血在街面上淌成了河。有些男人的胸膛被打成了马蜂窝，有些男人的脸已烂得根本看不清。日本人的脚下，掉满了子弹壳。

那些死在围墙边的，看样子原本都是想要翻墙而入。但是很明显，他们只要在围墙的上边一露头，日本人的子弹就会命中他们的额头。然后，他们就会像一只只没有生命的麻袋一样，从围墙上重重地摔下来，躺在街

上，一动不动地任凭自己的血流干。血汇聚在街面上，像打翻了一桶又一桶的红漆。

镇政府的前后门外，都架着日本人的机枪。对于那些一次次发起冲锋的老百姓，日本人感到不可理喻：你们有枪吗？没有枪还往机枪前撞，不是找死是什么？

也有些男人，拿了些石头、砖块往机枪手身上扔。刚开始时，是伤到了一个日本人，但是很快，日本人就拿出了铁制盾牌来，保护住了机枪手。原始的飞矢不再有用，手中无枪的人们只能是一样地迈入死亡。

一个少年血红着双眼，拿着一根耀眼的红缨枪，风一样冲向日军的机枪手，大喊：把姐姐还给我！最后一个字还没喊完，少年的喉咙已被一串子弹贯穿。他跪在地上，脸朝下地倒下，手里的红缨枪，像一条死去了的龙。

赵宏伟躲在一条阴暗的小巷里，看着镇政府大门前发生的一切，泪流满面。他紧抿着自己的嘴，不让自己哭出声来。他的眼睛很痛，真的很痛，就像有针在扎，就像有铁在烫。他的喉咙里就像有一个烧红的秤砣在滚动。他全身的血都在往头顶上涌。怎么会这样？怎么会这样！他欲狂呼，却开口无声。他痛哭流涕，痛哭流涕。

又一群人涌向了镇政府。他们的手里都举着火把。他们到了围墙外，一齐将火把往围墙里扔。

镇政府的里面骚动了起来。但是驻守在镇政府外面的日军，依旧冷酷而镇定，如一条钢铁防线。

丢火把的人们，也都倒在了血泊中。镇政府里的火被扑灭了。日军将丢火把的人的尸首拖到了一起，然后，用他们的火把，点燃了他们的尸首。

火光熊熊。

机枪手后面的两面盾牌拿开的时候，赵宏伟看到了坐在机枪手正后方的指挥官，北川。北川端坐在一张椅子上，他的双手交叠着，拄着一把长长的军刀。他的左手手掌上缠着厚厚的白纱布，没有戴手套，四根手指露在外面。他一动不动地看着眼前的一切，没有什么表情。有那么一瞬间，赵宏伟觉得北川是已经看见了藏在阴暗处的自己，但是北川还是没有说什么也没有做什么。

火熄了，丢火把的人们都已成了焦炭。北川依旧一动不动地坐着，机枪手也依旧时刻准备着。

街上的血腥味，浓得让人想吐。

突然，“砰”的一枪，机枪手的脑袋开了花，倒在了地上。日军大惊，举枪乱指。拿盾牌的日本兵赶紧护住了北川，但是北川推开了他们。

“砰”的一声，又一个日本兵倒在了地上。

北川站了起来。

新机枪手上位。一个日本兵正要用盾牌去保护新机枪手，“砰”的一枪，这个拿盾牌的日本兵又倒在了地上。

北川丢开军刀，干净利落地从身旁的一个日本兵的手中拿过了一条步枪。他端起枪，往他对面斜上方的某个位置一瞄准，“砰”的一枪，一个人就从屋顶上摔了下来。

赵宏伟探出脑袋看了看，原来，是镇上的一个老猎户。老猎户早已不打猎了，想不到今天会重出江湖。老猎户的头被日本兵割了下来。

北川丢开枪，捡起军刀，走进了镇政府大门里去。他一直没有再出来。

新机枪手一直待在他该待的位置上。

赵宏伟溜了回去。

天快亮了，小菊睡得很熟。

赵宏伟无声地流着泪。他也不知道自己为什么要哭，但就是忍不住。他想起了老秀才临死前写的那两句诗，“中国不可欺，南北多豪杰”，不禁想，豪杰的下场，就是死。他很难过。

小菊醒来，看见赵宏伟在流泪，就问，宏伟伯伯，你怎么哭了？

赵宏伟赶紧擦掉了眼泪，笑了笑，说，没什么，伯伯昨天看见一些老朋友死了，所以有些难过。

哦，宏伟伯伯不要难过，人都是要死的，长生不老是骗人的。

呵呵，小菊真聪明。伯伯不该怕死。

嗯，小菊就不怕死。

呵呵，小菊真勇敢。

小菊长大了要当花木兰，花木兰是不会怕死的。

嗯，小菊真乖。

天亮了，赵宏伟去煮了十个鸡蛋。小菊吃了两个。赵宏伟将剩下的鸡蛋放在桌上，对小菊说，伯伯今天有事，可能中午不能回来给你做饭吃，你要是饿了，就吃这桌上的鸡蛋。小菊点点头。

赵宏伟推开窗，探出脑袋，想看看外面的动静。巷子里一片肃静，没有人影。偶尔有风吹过，带着些阴惨的味道。赵宏伟心中黯然。他想起，日本人昨夜拿的那几块盾牌里，有两块还是他当初帮渡边拿去铁匠铺里特地补好的。日本人的坚不可摧里，也有着他赵宏伟出过的力。他是助纣为虐了。赵宏伟心中哀恻。那些铁盾牌，据渡边说，是因为有一次他的部队在中国的一个村庄里遭到了一支弓箭队的袭击，所以才置备的。虽然那支弓箭队最终被渡边剿灭了，但是渡边的队伍里也死了几个人。这件事给了渡边一个启示：对付某些还处在冷兵器时代的暴徒，还是需要某些冷兵器时代的工具的。渡边承认，强劲的箭，是有着和子弹相似的神韵，但是，推动两者前进的年代毕竟不同。箭遇盾即落，而子弹，是见佛杀佛。

令赵宏伟感到悲哀的是，赵家镇百姓投向日军的，甚至还不是箭，而只是一些石块和砖头。枪炮与刀剑的战争注定不能成为战争，而只能成为屠杀。赵宏伟想起自己在日本的所学。一个国家要怎样才能拥有火力威猛的枪与炮？那必须要有雄厚的工业力量作基础。可怜哪，他赵宏伟，当年在日本学的就是机械，想的就是要振兴中国工业。可是到最后，他却只是当了个毫无意义的教书匠，满脑子的投机钻营名利梦。他从未想到过，人生的此岸与彼岸，相距竟会是如此遥远。今天的他和昨天的他，就像是两个互不相识的陌生人。世路何其艰。

“咚”，一块石子砸在赵宏伟的头顶上。赵宏伟痛得眼冒金星。他按着自己的头顶，伸脖子朝巷子里望，看见有两个人影一闪而过。

他看看自己刚才摸过了头皮的手，确认没有血。但他的头顶还是痛得厉害。也许会肿起来的，他想。

他关了窗，坐了下来。他看了看怀表，再过一个多小时，他就要去镇政府了。按照原计划，他将和渡边乘坐同一辆小汽车去县政府参会。但是他想起昨夜镇政府外面的激战，对今天的行程又不禁起了疑。出了这么大的事，还会召开什么狗屁记者招待会吗？

赵宏伟去看看小菊，小菊正在很用功地读书，赵宏伟感觉很欣慰。他想，以后要不要教小菊读《列女传》呢？想想还是算了。不要再让下一代的脑子里，装上些坟墓里的言论了。

赵宏伟打开大门的时候，才是吓了一跳。他家的大门上，插着一把匕首。匕首上带着一张纸条。纸条上写着：狗汉奸不得好死。

赵宏伟拔下了匕首，撕掉了纸条，关上了大门。他背靠着大门，拿着匕首，心里寒意丛生。匕首的刃和尖都是那么亮光逼人，就像在等着喝血。赵宏伟的手一哆嗦，匕首掉在了地上。

他感到四周的肃静里，含着一片未知的可怕，就像是待在一片荒凉的夜里，远处有几双狼的眼睛正在盯着你。他似乎又听到了一些枪声，但再仔细一听，又都像是幻觉。他的心很乱。

街上和巷子里都没有骚乱。至少在他赵宏伟目前所能感知到的范围内是如此。也是，昨晚都死了那么多人了，哪里还会有什么骚乱的人呢？老百姓是怎么知道女工事件的真相的呢？也许一切都只是必然吧，世上哪有不透风的墙？日本人早该料到会有这一天。只是，遭殃的还是老百姓，他们以卵击石，死得没有半分价值。

而老百姓的矛头好像在转移。丢在赵宏伟脑袋上的石子和插在他家大门上的匕首已经说明了一切。虽然赵家镇的百姓一直以来也没有对赵宏伟做出过什么过激的举动，但是现在日本人都已经是在赵家镇上大开杀戒了，作为日本人走狗的他，赵宏伟，又还有什么理由可以要求镇上的父老乡亲们对他网开一面、手下留情呢？他完了。

他感到了一股彻心的悲凉。中国人也恨他，汉奸也恨他，还有哪个族群是可以容纳他的？他现在就是左边众叛亲离，右边举目无亲。他也不知自己怎么就会一步一步地走到了今天这个地步。也许，从他在渡边面前服软的那一刻起，一切的破灭就已成了注定，他想。他感到了绝望。

他捡起了掉在地上的那把匕首。匕首寒光闪闪，令他心惊胆战。他将手心里的那团碎纸丢在了前院的垃圾桶里，然后，找了个杂乱的墙角，将那把匕首给藏了起来。一直以来，除了菜刀，他还没有拥有过什么兵器，这下好

了，他有一把匕首了，能用来防身了。他暗想。

他很明确，自己的人身安全现在已经受到了威胁。一旦百姓的怒潮决了堤，那他赵宏伟就有可能会成为日本人的替罪羊，被众人五马分尸。这里面没有道理可讲，就好比两军对垒，死在对方手里的人，手上未必已沾有对方的血，一切只是阵营不同使然，这便是战争。赵宏伟现在不仅很担心自己，也很担心小菊。他当然知道，百姓是不会伤害一个小女孩的，但是这世上谁还没有个万一呢？小菊一贯与他亲近，现在又生活在他家里，祸难若来临，谁能保证不会殃及池鱼？刀剑无眼，若不小心伤着小菊怎么办？就算没伤着小菊，吓着她总是难免的。难道要让她看着她的宏伟伯伯突然由一个大活人变成一个血淋淋的死人？不行，绝对不行。赵宏伟想，自己出事是小，绝对不能让小菊受到一丝伤害。时代已动乱如此，难道就连小孩子的眼前也不能再保留住一片清净？

赵宏伟觉得自己应该要申请日本人的保护了。让日本人给他家门前派几个荷枪实弹的哨兵。赵宏伟知道这件事是很容易办到的，北川以前就要给他派哨兵，是他自己不要。现在或许是该去日本人的树下躲躲了？

但是转念一想，还是不行。秀珍就要出来了，他很快就要带着秀珍和小菊出逃了，若是几个日本哨兵往他的大门外后门内一站，他的出逃计划哪还有成功的可能？他的一举一动都将暴露在日本人的眼皮底下。别刚跑出了几米远，就被日本人像抓小鸡似的给抓了回来。到那时，他和秀珍，就恐怕要真的完蛋了。日本人或许可以容忍你的冲撞，但是绝对不会容忍你的背叛。

赵宏伟忽然想到，可以暂时将小菊交给方远梦或老周照顾，待风波平定，再接回小菊。当然，这样是一定会给方远梦或老周造成很多不方便，但是不管了，他赵宏伟已经是再没有其他的办法了。他就是想要保护一个无辜的小孩，不要让她受到自己的牵连，相信方远梦和老周是一定能理解他的苦衷的。只要共产党能帮他，他愿意拿共产党当佛来拜。他赵宏伟是不能预测未来，但他相信，得民心者，必能得天下。

打定主意，赵宏伟决定立马出门。先去找方远梦。

大门一打开，他刚迈出门，一辆小汽车却刚好是开了过来，就在他的面前停了下来。

赵宏伟认出，是镇政府的车。

北川从车上下来，右手里还握着一把手枪。他径直走到赵宏伟面前，说，赵镇长请上车，今天将由我亲自护送您去县政府。

为什么？渡边中佐呢？时间不是还早吗？赵宏伟问。

中佐已经出发，请先上车，路上我再跟您慢慢解释。北川说。

北川话音刚落，抬手就朝右边开了一枪。赵宏伟顺着枪指的方向看去，一个老汉倒在地上，他的手里拿着一块砖。赵宏伟大骇。

“你稍等，我一会儿就来。”

赵宏伟说完，马上转身跑回了家里去。他往屋里跑，小菊正在往屋外走，他拉着小菊又回到了屋里去。小菊问他外面是什么声音，他说刚刚有人放了一个炮仗。

赵宏伟跟小菊说，小菊乖，伯伯现在要出去了，今天可能会晚些回来。你要记住，今天不管外面发生什么事，你都不可以走出这个屋子，你就好好待在这屋子里，鸡蛋和水都在这桌上，除了我和你娘，谁敲门喊人你都不要应声，要是有人闯进来，你就躲到床底下去，要是有人把你抓了起来，你就说，你恨赵宏伟。记住没有？

为什么？宏伟伯伯，我不恨你。

小菊乖，这就是个游戏，像捉迷藏一样，你被人抓到了，你就会输掉。而你只要对抓到你的那个人说一句，你恨赵宏伟，那个人就会放了你，你就还没有输。这是游戏规则，懂了吗，小菊？

哦，我懂了。放心吧，宏伟伯伯，我都记住了。我捉迷藏可厉害了，一定不会被人抓到的。

好，好，小菊真乖。刚才那个炮仗响，就是告诉大家，游戏开始了。小菊你好好看书，伯伯走了。

伯伯再见。

赵宏伟在上车前，对北川说，请你派两个哨兵来守卫我的家。北川点点头，就让司机下车，对司机说，快去镇政府，传我命令，派几个哨兵过来，保卫赵镇长的宅邸。赵宏伟对司机说，麻烦你对哨兵说，就在前门和后门外守着就好，不要到屋里去，屋里有孩子，别吓着孩子。司机望望北川，北川点点头，说，不要吓着小孩。

司机跑步走了。赵宏伟上了车，北川收了枪，坐上了驾驶位。

出发了。

车子经过镇政府外面的时候，赵宏伟看见有很多日本兵正在拎着水桶冲水洗地。地上血水横流，车轮胎的滚动不时激起血花朵朵。镇政府的围墙外面有几个地方一片焦黑，透着狼狈。各条街上几乎没有人，寂静里饱含着阴森。

北川告诉赵宏伟，昨夜江庆县下面的几个镇子上都发生了暴动，原因都是老百姓发现了皇军征洗衣女工的真相。老百姓都想救出自己的妻女，而一些已经确认妻女死亡了的百姓，则完全只是想要和皇军拼命。事情真相的败露，说来也很蹊跷。据说，就是在昨天的天黑以前，各个镇子上埋着死去了的慰安妇的坟，统统都被暴雨给冲了开来。雷电纷纷劈在那些坟的周围，照亮着尸体，吸引了老百姓的注意。连我们皇军的一些士兵也感到了恐惧，他们说，是不是神灵在发怒。

今天早上，镇政府又遭到了一批百姓的袭击。他们将装着汽油的玻璃瓶纷纷丢进镇政府的围墙内，然后，再将火把往围墙内扔，这样，他们就等于是往镇政府里投掷了燃烧弹。虽然他们很快就都死了，但是我们皇军也有了伤亡。我早就劝告过竹内大佐，不要低估中国人的愤怒，愤怒有时可以将人推向进步。

你的几个部下今天早上在来镇政府的途中遭到了暗杀。看样子，不是专业的军事人员干的，应该是赵家镇百姓的仇杀。他们身上的枪被拿走了。所以渡边中佐要我亲自来接你。渡边中佐由赵驹护送，他们早出发，现在可能已到了县政府。你说谁？哦，曾林，他没事，没有被杀。

“赵家镇上不会再有太平了。”赵宏伟说。

“军人就不是为了太平而生的。”北川说。

进了县城，赵宏伟略微感到了一些祥和。县城里没有发生暴动，这里面多少也有北川的一些功劳。但是据说竹内早已对北川感到了厌倦。北川是个有原则的人，这是竹内难以接受的。总是会有一些事情，被北川办得令竹内不甚舒服。也许归根到底，竹内也就是拿北川当一条狗。一条不能百分之百听话的狗，就算再怎么能力超群，也无法让主人喜欢太久。既已生厌，多留身边又有何益？竹内就是个老奸巨猾又无情无义的野心家，赵宏伟觉得。他看看正在默默开车的北川，蓦然就生出了一些同是天涯沦落人的感慨。

“以后我们就要在一起共事了，希望合作愉快。”赵宏伟说。

“合作愉快。”北川说。

到了县政府的外面，赵宏伟感到了一片宛如幻觉的喜气洋洋。地上铺着红地毯，围墙外居然还挂了一圈红灯笼！听说待会儿还会放鞭炮。赵宏伟无语以对。他若不是本地人，此刻远道而来，初见此景，也定是会以为此处实乃人间歌舞升平之所。但他赵宏伟不是外地人，他刚从暴动的余悸中走来，北川所开的车子的轮胎上，也定残留着暗淡的血水，从彼境突兀落入此境，实在叫人情何以堪！赵宏伟摇头不已。

车子停在县政府的大门外，北川陪赵宏伟下了车。停在北川车子前面的另一辆车子的旁边，有几个洋鬼子正在交头接耳，谈论不休。经过他们身边的时候，赵宏伟侧耳听了听，是德语。德国以前出了那么多伟大的文艺家和哲学家，而现在却和小日本站在一起，这实在是令赵宏伟感到万分的悲哀。

走进了县政府，赵宏伟更是有些目瞪口呆。县政府的前院里，居然摆满了漂亮的花卉！竹内这个老王八蛋，赵宏伟暗骂。他感到了一种很难受的愤怒，但他又说不出究竟是难受在哪儿，愤怒在哪儿。他捏了捏拳头，又感到自己的这个动作很傻。

北川要告辞了，今天的记者会，他并没有被邀请。他跟赵宏伟说，要是回去的时候还要用车，可以给他打个电话，就是以前渡边办公室里的那个电话，那个办公室现在是他的了。赵宏伟问，办公室后面的那个卧室里，现在还有人吗？北川觉得这个问题很奇怪，说，没人哪，我和渡边中佐现在都在外面，那卧室里现在怎么会有人呢。今天离开办公室前，我还亲自将那间卧室打扫了一遍。难道你是说贼？

赵宏伟忙笑着说，不是，不是。

赵宏伟就和北川道了别。然后，赵宏伟就去了县政府的大厅。

大厅富丽堂皇。里面摆上了很多长条桌，桌上铺着精美的桌布，上面放着水果、点心、酒杯等东西，宴会的派头十足。天花板上的几盏旧吊灯也不知是在何时被换成了新的，新灯金光闪闪，气势非凡。一些人物已在大厅里徜徉，赵宏伟不愿惹人注意，便找了个角落站定。站定以后，细细端详，才发现自己的衣着打扮，分外寒酸。一个脖子上挂着照相机的洋鬼子过来对他

说了几句话，发现他听不懂，便十分鄙夷地离去。赵宏伟想，洋瘪三只要一来中国，就能尝到当老爷的滋味，你说他们怎么能不喜欢侵略的感觉？

不断有人从外面走进来，大厅里的人陆陆续续地多了起来。赵宏伟的心情有些忐忑，很复杂的忐忑。他不知今天外面的形势又会发生多大的变化，这变化又会不会波及他自身的安危或利益。待在这金碧辉煌的大厅里，只能让人坐立不安，不停地生闷气。眼前这一片热乎乎的安定与繁荣，只能让人感到臭烘烘的无聊与恶心。他不知赵家镇上此刻是否仍在死人，他不知百姓究竟已恨他到何种地步，他不知北川的哨兵是否已守住了他家的前后门。太多的担心和忧虑，让他恨不得能立刻离开这可憎的大厅，回赵家镇上去办自己的事。但是日本人的命令就是铁条一样的纪律，你要走，你也挣不开那铁条。

不知镇上的暴动究竟会发展到何种程度？不，更准确地讲，只能说是不知镇上的百姓还会死去多少。对日本人不能构成伤害的暴动简直就不能称之为暴动，只能说是送死。老秀才若还在世，恐怕也不会支持百姓的这种英勇，而百姓若伤不了日本人，又会把气撒在哪儿？这是个令人不寒而栗的问题。今早死去的那几个汉奸无疑就是对这个问题的最好说明。而他赵宏伟今早却为什么只是受到了威胁而并没有被暗杀？这是个值得推敲的问题。是他家的院墙不好翻吗？肯定不是。是他们不敢杀镇长吗？也肯定不是。那么，赵宏伟唯一能得出的结论，就是赵家镇的百姓，对他赵宏伟还有一些感情。是啊，他赵宏伟，曾经是老秀才的得意门生，是赵家镇上公认的最聪明的孩子，在省城念过中学，在东洋念过大学，当了小学校长以后，又教出了不少好学生，免去过不少穷人家孩子的学杂费，对工作一丝不苟，对街坊和蔼热情，这样一个曾经让赵家镇人津津乐道、敬佩有加的赵宏伟，你说他们怎么能突然下得了杀手呢？这个结论令赵宏伟的心中颇感欣慰与惭愧，他想，我当汉奸，真是侮辱了我自己。

但是人的忍耐与手下留情，也总是会有个限度的，就怕有个万一。现在他让日本哨兵守着他的房子，这事有好也有坏。好的一面，就是他家有了日本人的保卫，而坏的一面，就是他无疑是在提醒赵家镇上的百姓，他跟日本人是一伙的。他的心里就像是有火苗在滚来滚去，却也实在无可奈何。他只希望，小菊能平安无事，不要被他连累。

而现在最让赵宏伟牵肠挂肚的，依旧是秀珍的安危。虽然从北川的话里已可知，秀珍已没有再被囚禁于那间卧室之中，但是这又有什么可值得庆贺的呢？万一秀珍又被丢回了那间仓库里呢？真是不敢想象。但是再想想，渡边总不至于会那么混蛋吧？毕竟他已收了他的金条，在秀珍被释放之前，他总该保证秀珍不会再遭受太多或太大的伤害吧？赵宏伟觉得自己大可不必如此担心。他应该要相信渡边的诚意和信誉。

赵宏伟在来时的路上已想好了，接下来要抓紧做的一件事情，就是要租好一处房子。他在那紧急而无奈的情况下，将日本兵请到了自己的家门口去做门神，这已是无法挽回的事实。接下来会有一些什么麻烦他心里有数，比如请神容易送神难，比如被保护的同时也要被监视，等等。所以，秀珍一旦获释，他不能接她去他家，那样会逃不掉的。她也不能回她的家，因为她家就在他家隔壁，同样在日本人的视线范围之内。他必须要将秀珍和小菊安顿在第三个地方，静待时机，然后在突然的某一天，他们三个人一起从日本人的视线里消失。赵宏伟觉得，自己的计谋还是很多很不错的。

一些洋鬼子在大口地吃着各种点心，喝着各种酒。赵宏伟听见两个日本人在说，这些德国人真是没有教养，现在还是上午，已经吃成了这样。赵宏伟就觉得有些悲哀，日本人拿中国人的东西去招待德国人，德国人吃完了会帮助日本人欺负中国人，这叫什么事。

一直没看见渡边和赵驹，赵宏伟心里有些焦躁不安。他纷乱地想着各种事情，担忧着各种担忧，越发觉得待在这大厅里难受。他想去给北川打个电话，问问他，那几个奉命保护他家的日本哨兵是否已到位，他想再次叮嘱北川，不要让他们吓着屋里的孩子。他想再去找渡边谈一谈，能否尽快放秀珍出来，不管要用什么办法，他赵宏伟都会尽力去做。但是那该死的记者会却还没有开始，大家都在谈笑。

一个汉奸在对一个日本记者说，今天晚上，这里会有盛大的歌舞表演，相信那些德国人和意大利人也是会喜欢的。日本记者嗤之以鼻，说，他们喜欢的，是瓷器和金币。

赵宏伟去撒尿。在厕所里，他偷听到了两个日本兵的谈话。甲兵说：知道吗，我们很快就能有女人玩了，下面八个镇上的慰安妇，马上就要被送到县里来了。乙兵说：是吗，太好了，他们都已经玩了那么久了，我们却还一

直饿着，知道吗，井上那小子，临死前还在念叨着，他这辈子还从没碰过女人，真是太可怜了。甲兵说：都怪北川那个家伙，他根本就不知道我们这些小卒子的痛苦，打起仗来，我们都是死得最快的人，要是都像井上那样，一生还没碰过女人就死了，那我们活着还有什么意思。乙兵说：真想离开这场战争，回到家乡去，正正经经娶个老婆，生几个儿子，过自己的生活。

两个日本兵走了，赵宏伟的心又乱了。镇上的慰安妇马上要被送到县城里来了？怎么办？

事态的发展再一次超出了赵宏伟的料想。他感到自己的心弦在一次又一次地被人拉到极限，他总是在自以为诸事妥当的时候，感受到人算不如天算的痛苦。他的美好计划总在不停地被事实打乱，他在寻求解决问题的过程中总是会遇上更多的问题。他感到自己就像是一叶逆水前行的小舟，多少次已累得想要放弃，但是总不能放弃。他努力抛却着自己之前一切纷乱的思考，想要重新寻找出一条现在该走的路来，但是他的头脑里乱哄哄的，就像一个垃圾场。他都快要把自己辛苦背下来的那些发言材料给忘了。

赵宏伟出了厕所，没回大厅里去。他想要去找找看渡边或者赵驹，他必须要尽快把秀珍给救出来，时局这么乱，夜长梦多。万一竹内真把人送去了上海，那他可就是回天无力了。他想去楼上的会场里看看，但是哨兵说，记者会还没有开始，没有联队长的命令谁都不准上去。赵宏伟怏怏离开，在外面转了一圈后，换了一个楼道口，对另一个哨兵说，我是赵家镇的镇长，有重要的情况必须马上向竹内联队长报告，请放行。这个哨兵要他出示证件，他出示了。然后这个哨兵就放了他上去。他故意走得不慌不忙，他暗自庆幸：在这样的一个时代，没有一颗大胆的心和一张会说谎的嘴，真是很难混下去呀。

出了哨兵的视线，他跑得像贼一样飞快。他估计今天的记者会开始之后，他是没什么机会能和渡边单独聊聊了，所以他现在必须要抓紧时间，找渡边谈一谈。当然，渡边也许会怪他擅入大楼之罪，但是他估计渡边看在那两根金条的面子上，不会真的跟他计较这种小节。重要的是正事，关于秀珍的正事。也许他应该再给渡边一根金条？金条哇金条，真是用到你时方恨少，哪里有你哪里好。

经过会场的时候，他听到了咆哮声。他偷偷溜到门边，发现门虚掩着，没关实。他往门缝里一看，里面一排并站着渡边、赵驹和各镇的负责军官。听那咆哮的声音，正是竹内。

“是雷电和大雨通知了百姓真相？你们当我是傻子啊！给我查，查出来消息是从哪个部队里泄漏出去的，我重罚！”竹内大吼。

“中佐，哦不，大佐请息怒，我们镇上的暴动，已被我镇压下去了。”一位军官说。

“我们也是。”“我们也是。”众军官纷纷说。

“只怕是野火烧不尽，春风吹又生。”渡边说。

一个军官居然笑了出来。竹内大怒，说：“有什么可笑的，你听不出来这是诗吗！”竹内问渡边：“那你有什么办法？”

渡边说：“很简单，颁布一个暂行法令，一人造反，全家斩首，看谁还敢袭击我们大日本皇军。”

竹内沉吟片刻，说：“不行，这样只会越杀越多，我们要占领的是活的城市，不是死的城市，渡边君，你太野蛮了。”

渡边很尴尬。这时赵驹开口了，他说：“两位太君的话都有道理，我们不如来个折中的法子。那就是先不要累及全家，但是要把暴动者的头全砍下来，挂满各镇的大街小巷，以儆效尤，震慑暴民。先看效果，再酌情制定新的方案。”

众人片刻沉默。然后渡边说“不错”，竹内就说“好”。

竹内说：“另外，你们记住，明天中午以前，务必要把那些女人全部安全地送到县城里来，不得有误！”他长叹一声，缓和了语气，又说：“你说你们怎么办的事，让你们征女人，给你们玩女人，你们却弄死了那么多的女人，你们难道是吃人的老虎不成？天皇的脸，真是让你们给丢尽了。”

竹内让渡边留下，其他的人都出去。赵宏伟赶紧躲到了一个隐蔽的角落里。待人走清之后，他又回去偷听。还好，门依然是虚掩着的。

“怎么样，那个姚志招了吗？游击队在玉山上的布防情况，他到底说不说？”竹内问。

“他还是不招，不肯告诉我们半个字。”渡边说。

“英雄啊，都这么长时间了，他居然还挺得住。真可惜，他不是我们大日本帝国的军人，不然，他是一定会受到天皇的嘉奖的。”竹内惋惜地说，

“怎么样，他真的就没有一点弱点吗？”

“恐怕真的是没有。金钱美女与高官厚禄，他都视如粪土；皮肉之痛与濒死之苦，他都不屑一顾。他的生命，就像是全部用忠诚与信仰打造而成的，除此之外别无他物。这样的人，我这一生，也很少见过。”渡边说，“我们割他的皮肉、剁他的脚趾，他连哼都不哼一声；我们每隔一个月就会将他全身的骨头重新打断一遍，可是他连泪水都没有掉过一滴；最残忍的那一次，是我们割去了他的生殖器，当他醒来的时候，我们让他看着狼狗在他的面前吃掉了他的生殖器，但是他的脸上却仍然没有一丝恐惧。这样的人，的确是真正的勇士。”

“那他有没有什么亲人？”

“没有，他是一个孤儿。”

“那他有没有爱的女人？”

“应该也没有。根据情报，他从十六岁起开始参加战斗，一直都在不停地打仗，跟土匪打，跟军阀打，跟国民党打，跟我们大日本皇军打，像一匹不会停下的战马一样。他的人生中，似乎还从未有过女人。”

竹内沉默良久。他说：“这样的人，是不可征服的。这样吧，再拷问他几天，到我离开江庆县的前一天，如果他还没有招供，就杀了他吧。记住，要让他死得痛快一些。”

渡边一声“哈依”。然后，渡边低声问：“您的意思，是不让田中中佐得到他？”

竹内笑笑，反问：“难道你想给田中一个立功的机会吗？”

两人一齐笑。竹内说：“田中盘踞在青梅县，一直野心勃勃，若不是因为我的阻挠，去年这江庆县就也会变成他田中嘴里的肥肉。他若一人得了几个县城，那还了得？岂不是要直奔将军之位而去了？更何况他还有他的叔叔给他撑腰。他一向对你我不敬，我和你又怎能让他称心如意？”

“大佐您现在已不用顾忌他，他这次得罪了北野少将，上面命令他来江庆县接替您的位置担任联队长，明看着像是一般调动，不升不降，其实就是让他离开他的老部下，到这里来，领导起一支素来与他彼此厌恶的部队，做一只伸不开翅膀的孤鹰的。”

“嗯，话虽如此，但仍不可大意，毕竟他还有一个当中将的叔叔，要翻身也是很容易的。只是委屈了你，我原本的计划，是想让你接任联队长一职的，以后一有机会，再让你来南京，继续当我的左膀右臂，但是现在只能暂时委屈你了。”

“大佐心意，令属下感激不尽！大佐放心，我在江庆县，一定会想尽办法扳倒田中！到那时，少将大人一定会对大佐您刮目相看！”

“好，好。”竹内满意地大笑。

赵宏伟还想继续听他们说些什么，忽然，一只手在他肩上一搭。他大惊，回头一看，是赵驹。

赵驹竖起一根手指放在嘴巴前。赵宏伟噤声。赵驹笑得有些冷。

竹内在主席台上滔滔不绝地讲着话，他每讲一段，德语翻译和意大利语翻译就要分别翻译一段。时间过得特别漫长。赵宏伟坐在下面，感到心里憋得慌。

他没有机会和赵驹说上话，赵驹去了赵家镇，向北川面授竹内的某些指令。而渡边更是没有工夫理他赵宏伟。一切都必须要等到今天的记者会结束。而记者会进行得又是如此慢条斯理。赵宏伟心里有种恼怒在膨胀。

明天中午以前，那些女人就都会被运进县城里来了。里面当然也会包括秀珍。事情似乎正在往糟糕的一面发展。而他赵宏伟只能被牵着鼻子走。他似乎永远都无法跑到事情的前面去，去改变一些什么。他就是这样的无能。

赵宏伟掏手绢的时候，忽然发现塞在他口袋里的字条。字条上写着：别太相信渡边，就算是对最忠顺的狗，他也不会网开一面。

赵宏伟握紧了字条，赶紧往四周一看，并没有他的什么熟人。那么是谁在什么时候给了他这张字条呢？赵宏伟又重新看了两遍这张字条，像是赵驹的笔迹。

没错，应该就是他。因为不方便说话，所以才用了字条。但是这话是什么意思呢？难道赵驹说的，是秀珍的事情？

赵宏伟额头上的汗就下来了。趁人不注意，他把字条吃了下去。他觉得自己的屁股后面像是着了火，再也坐不住了。

但是他又不敢站起来。一切胜利的自信和美好的打算都在刹那间化为了泡影。如果赵驹的确是在提醒赵宏伟，不要相信渡边释放秀珍的承诺，那么

一切就完了。赵宏伟没有备用方案，也许赵驹以为他有，所以才会给他提个醒，但是事实上他比赵驹想象的更无能。没有备用方案，就等于是死路一条。

赵宏伟冷静了再冷静，想，也许这只是一个恶作剧。受人钱财替人消灾是黑白两道通用的职业道德，难道渡边他堂堂的一个日本军官会连这点起码的道德标准都没有？不可能。那也太贬低渡边了。这一定就是个恶作剧。赵驹归根到底就是看不得他赵宏伟顺风顺水万事如意，他一定要能在他赵宏伟面前摆出一副居高临下冷嘲热讽的姿态才会觉得舒服。不能自乱阵脚，坏了大事。赵宏伟自我告诫。

轮到赵宏伟上台发言了。他整了整衣衫，活动了一下嘴脸，抖擞了一下精神，然后潇洒登台。是到了展现他那一口纯正流利的日语的时候了，他一定要好好表现，让竹内和渡边共同满意。赵宏伟挤出了满脸的笑容，清了清嗓子，正准备开讲，却突然打了一个响亮的饱嗝，都是刚才那张字条给闹的。

照相机的闪光灯不时亮起，赵宏伟被人拍了很多照。在发言中，他不时以天皇的子民自称，他注意到了竹内和渡边满意的笑。他吹牛说，这里的孩子们都以能看到天皇的照片为毕生最大的荣幸，他们是多希望能亲吻一口日本的土地呀。他动情的发言简直都有了一些诗朗诵的韵味，他看到了台下那些日本记者微仰而敬佩的眼光。他的内心有些激动，在某些瞬间，他甚至还以为自己说的都是真的。他想，电影演员站在台上，可能也就是这么个感觉吧。我小时候真该去唱戏。

赵宏伟的发言暂时告一段落，大家要去吃午饭了。赵宏伟觉得自己应该要回去看看小菊，要是时间允许的话，起码得给孩子煎两个葱油饼充当一下午餐。但是转念又一想，不知午餐时，能否和渡边说上话？

大家在大厅里吃饭。原本放在长条桌上的烛台和鲜花之类的摆设都被拿了下去，换上了一盘盘可口的菜肴，又新添了几张长条桌，人都坐得满满的。

为了照顾不同民族不同的口味，大家都是按国籍入座。德国人和德国人一桌，日本人和日本人一桌，依此类推。所以赵宏伟没能和渡边坐在一桌上。赵宏伟深感懊悔，想走，却已不合适再走。

每个民族一套菜。洋鬼子的桌上有牛排，日本人的桌上有寿司，中国人的桌上有豆腐。赵宏伟吃了一口豆腐，觉得有点馊味，就不再下筷。

中国人都吃得默默无声，大家也并不聊天。不像那些洋鬼子和日本人，一会儿干杯，一会儿干杯。一个中国人说，操，吃的都是中国的东西。另一个中国人就用手肘撞了撞他。中国人就又都陷入了沉默里。

竹内带着几个心腹去各桌上敬酒。最后到了赵宏伟这一桌上，竹内敬大家酒，大家都受宠若惊。喝完坐下后，皆面有喜色。

赵宏伟觉得有点胃痛，也不知是不是吃了纸的关系。微小的痛苦让他的脑子又稍稍清醒了一些。这欢乐的宴会只是一朵浮云，那抒情的发言也只是一朵浮云，而他体内的那一丝丝痛，才是他脚下实实在在的大地。他居然忘了，他只是日本人的一个小工具。还喝什么酒？呸。

他又琢磨起了肚子里字条上的那句话。赵驹像是在恶作剧吗？他像是在耍他玩吗？真不像。赵驹哪有那么无聊。那么他到底该怎么办才好呢？赵宏伟看看不远处的渡边，渡边此刻正红光满面，满嘴流油。渡边的目光从不瞟向赵宏伟这里。赵宏伟又感到了一阵胃痛。

“嗨，你们知道吗，日本人在各个镇子上都以征洗衣女工的名义征了不少慰安妇，老百姓们发现了，起来反抗，都被杀死了。”一个中国记者低声说。

“嘘——”另一个中国人提醒他，“你要死啊，在这里说这个！这事谁不知道，可是你敢写吗？你今天写了，明天日本人就诛你九族！”

“可是刚才，我听见有两个德国记者也在谈论这件事，我懂德语的。”中国记者说。

“别傻了，难道你还指望德国佬会来给中国人伸张正义？说句老实话，今天坐在这里吃饭的，有哪一个是好东西？那些洋鬼子记者，可都是拿了竹内钱的！”那个中国人说。

赵宏伟放下筷子，喝了一小口酒。他不再去听中国人之间的谈话。他默默地坐着，感到很难过。是啊，今天这里在座的，又有哪个不是日本人的帮凶？自己弄到今天这个地步，从某种角度来说，难道不正是自己的报应？

赵宏伟想，要尽快将姚志的事情告诉方远梦。姚志还没死，还没叛变，这是个好消息，可是他再不叛变就要去死了，这又是个坏消息。方远梦知道

了这件事情，一定又会寝食难安吧。说不定又会发生死伤惨重的枪战。这个世界真是已经到了一个很荒谬的地步，没有枪战和死伤就根本不能解决问题，打输了死掉了还只能算是白白牺牲。孔子总说不要讲武力，而事实上却是有了武力才能讲道理。孔子真是害死了中国人。

那么，姚志现在究竟是被关在什么地方呢？以前，游击队的几次营救行动，都是针对县监狱展开的，日本人会仍将姚志关在原处吗？据赵宏伟所知，游击队一直没有得到关于此问题的新情报。而从竹内与渡边的谈话内容来看，审讯姚志的工作应该是一直由渡边负责，那么，为了方便省事，渡边会不会将姚志转移至赵家镇镇政府的牢房里？这个也不能断定。毕竟，渡边和赵驹在镇政府工作时，也是要三天两头往县城里跑的，办公地点不能说明任何问题。而游击队以前安插在鬼子内部的那个内应，显然在日本人的机关里级别不高，没能给游击队提供更多的信息。没有准确的信息就无法进行正确的判断与推理，没有判断与推理，就无法行动。赵宏伟忽然就有些头痛，他想，这些都是方远梦应该要考虑的问题，我瞎操什么心。

赵宏伟又一次按捺下了一阵胃痛。他忽然自问：我若是做了共产党的间谍，在危急时刻，又是否能铁骨铮铮？

他自嘲地一笑，想，恐怕是不能的。是条汉子的，又怎么会当汉奸？这个道理，是个明眼人，恐怕都能看明白。

赵宏伟喝下了一杯酒，酒滴从他的嘴角淌下，他拿手一抹，心里冷冰冰的。

下午，记者会再次开始。记者开始提问，日本人开始回答。双方交流得十分愉快。一切都像演戏一样。有时候问答双方都假得简直让人有些恶心。

赵宏伟也上台回答了一些记者提问。他把话都说得十分漂亮，简直有些汪精卫的风范。各种投降理论都已被他背了个滚瓜烂熟，所以他只要一开口，就是一个杰出的傀儡政治家。什么抵抗亡国、和平兴邦，什么经济无国界、文化非政治，一套又一套，大珠小珠落玉盘。竹内眉开眼笑，有人掩嘴偷笑。

终于，有个德国记者向赵宏伟提出了问题：“听说赵家镇上的百姓，因为某些原因和日本士兵发生了严重的冲突，有不少人员伤亡，您作为赵家镇的镇长，是否知道此事？对此有何解释？”

赵宏伟惊讶地望了望德语翻译，德语翻译对他耸了耸肩。他又转头看了看竹内，竹内的脸色有些难看。意大利语翻译刚要翻译这个问题，竹内说，不许翻译。

赵宏伟尴尬地站着，台下的人都望着他，什么表情都有。他转头又看了看渡边，渡边竟然也正在看着他。他发现渡边的脸上是微含着笑意的。这个笑意的含义是什么？他已来不及思考。台上台下一片寂静。这些寂静的重量现在全压在赵宏伟的身上。赵宏伟知道，这片寂静是能毁了这场记者会的，而这场记者会要是被这片寂静给毁了，那么，他赵宏伟就完了，秀珍也完了。

赵宏伟清了清嗓子，潇洒地用手一抹头发，满面春风地说：“这位德国朋友怕是误会了，赵家镇上，这几天是发生了流血事件，但是，与皇军发生冲突的，不是老百姓，而是玉山上的土匪。”赵宏伟又清了清嗓子，“众所周知，玉山匪患，由来已久，祸害一方，自从皇军到来以后，百姓才得以喘息，恢复耕读。然匪性凶顽，几日前再度下山，抢劫百姓，残害无辜，所幸皇军及时出兵，与匪交战，百姓才是逃脱了又一次的虎狼之灾。皇军英勇，此次滋事之匪，至今日已基本全歼。大日本皇军万岁！”

除了翻译的声音，全场依旧寂静无声。那个意大利语翻译不敢开口，竹内对他说，如实翻译。译完，竹内带头站起来，热烈鼓掌。全场都鼓起了掌。掌声雷动。赵宏伟鞠躬致意。

赵宏伟坐回了台下自己的座位上。他听到有个中国记者在说，见过不要脸的，没见过这么不要脸的。赵宏伟假装没听见。

熬着熬着，记者会终于要结束了。渡边向大家宣布了一下晚上活动的内容，然后便请大家去大厅里自由活动。

夕阳晚照，大厅里的留声机里放着舒缓的音乐。走到大厅外，望向日落的地方，会感到十分刺眼。傍晚的天空没有云，干净地透着蓝。赵宏伟忧伤地觉得，这个世界真漂亮。淡淡的音乐声从大厅里飘出来，夹杂着一些人的嘈杂，让人不想说话。

赵宏伟觉得自己今天是立了一个功。凭着这个功，他想，应该就能交换出秀珍了。他在县政府的院子里踱着步，脸色晦暗，神形萧索。

他在走廊里急切地走着，呼吸乱了节奏，每一步都战战兢兢。

他敲了敲渡边新办公室的门，直到门被打开，他还没有想好，接下来该怎么办。

开门的是渡边。赵宏伟谦卑地笑着。“太君好，太君好。”

“哦，原来是赵镇长，请进，请进。”

“谢谢，谢谢。”

办公室里只有渡边一个人。

“一会儿就要开始晚宴了，赵镇长怎么不在大厅里玩？”

“哦，都是外国人，语言不通，难以交流。”

“不喜欢那些德国人吧？我也是。自以为了不起的家伙。”

“是，是，不喜欢。”

“坐呀，大家都是朋友，不要客气。”

“好，好，谢谢太君。”

赵宏伟笑着，搓着手，心里七上八下，如履薄冰。

“太君，其实今天我来，是有事相求。”

“哦？赵镇长是遇上了什么麻烦吗？”

“不是不是，就是上次，我跟您说的那个事……”

“哎，赵镇长，你也太心急了嘛，我这才刚刚上任，你就来催了。”

“不敢，不敢，小的哪敢催太君。只是……只是听说那些女人明天就都要被送到县城里来了，我想、我想能不能尽快先将我的秀珍给放出来，我……我实在是很想念她。请太君谅解，望太君成全！”

“女人？什么女人？你的事情和女人有什么关系？”

“……太君，上次我去找您，还给了您礼物，您可是答应我的，会帮我放我的秀珍出来。”

“秀珍？什么秀珍？你上次来找我，不是为了想要当副县长的事情吗？我已经答应你了，会尽快向上面提议，一定把这事办成。怎么你突然在说一些莫名其妙的事情？”

“……这、这……不是，太君，怪我上次没说清楚，我想求您的事，就是想要请您帮忙，把赵家镇上的那些慰安妇里面的一个人，一个叫王秀珍的女人，给放出来，放她回家，不要让她当慰安妇。她是我没过门的媳妇，是我的妻子。请太君帮忙，求太君开恩！”

“王秀珍？谁是王秀珍？我不认识。”

“……就是……就是太君您曾经请她去过您办公室后面的卧室里的那一位。”

“混蛋！我什么时候让女人去过我的那间卧室！”

“太君息怒、太君息怒，她没有去过您的卧室，没有去过！是我胡说，是我胡说，我自己掌嘴！——太君，这样，我拿一张她的照片来，给您认识一下，请您放了她，求您放了她！我给您磕头了！太君万岁！”

“照片？——哈哈哈！可爱的宏伟君，我哪里需要什么照片呢？你的那个王秀珍，她身上又还有哪个地方，是我不认识的呢？只是我要纠正你的一个错误，她不是我请去的，而是我绑去的。”

“好，好，太君绑得好。只要太君高兴，怎么样都行。太君，您看，我是这么想的，竹内大佐就要把那些慰安妇都送到上海去了，您要是喜欢王秀珍，那她去了上海之后，您就再也见不着她了，但是您只要肯放了她，我可以向您保证，只要您需要，我可以随时随地将她送到您的面前，您说好不好？求太君开恩，求太君开恩！”

“宏伟君，你比我想象的更无耻。看着你现在像一条狗一样地跪在我面前求我，善良的我，倒还真是有些心软了。但是怎么办呢？你的建议倒是不错，只可惜，我对你的那个王秀珍，已经是一点兴趣也没有了。本来，我倒也是考虑过，玩完了她，就放了她，再怎么说，她也是你的心上人。可是，胆大包天的她，却居然咬了我！她咬了我两次！哦，那张可怜的小嘴，怎么会有那么大的力量？呵——我发誓，一定要让她这辈子，生不如死！”

“不！不！太君开恩，请您将她的罪，都算在我的头上，一切由我来承担！只要您肯放了她，叫我做什么都可以！让我死也行！”

“如果我让你去吃屎，你吃不吃？”

“吃！”

“真是可惜啊，王秀珍她要是能像你这么听话，那她现在早就自由了。你应该一早就教教她的，你该让她知道，皇军的命令，是绝对不能违抗的，皇军就是上帝，躺在了皇军的床上，她就应该要比一个最谄媚的妓女更温柔百倍。”

“是，是，我会教她的，求太君开恩！”

“晚了，现在说什么都晚了。今天我怎么看着你也有些讨厌？哦，对了，谁让你帮竹内撒谎的？你不知道吗，今天那个德国记者只要能将竹内中日共荣的谎言当众戳穿，竹内就会变成一个弄巧成拙的蠢货、小丑，这场记者会就会变成打在我们大日本皇军脸上的一记耳光，上面一定会大发雷霆，把竹内踢进垃圾堆里。到那时，竹内的如意算盘和美妙前途，都只是一个笑话了。他会成为一个屁。可是你，却为他编造了一个那么完美的谎言，令他险中得胜。你还真是足智多谋哇！”

“我错了，我错了！我现在就去告诉那个德国记者真相！”

“现在去？你是想让我成为竹内公开的敌人吗！”

“不是、不是——这样，您说要我怎么做，我就怎么做！”

“晚了，能在那样公开而重要的场合令竹内狠狠摔上一跤的机会已经溜走了，机不可失，时不再来。那个王秀珍也一样，我不是没给过她特别的机会，假如她当初选择的不是用她那坚硬的牙齿来咬我，而是用她那温柔的舌头来舔我，那么我恐怕早已对她网开一面。但是很可惜，人生没有回头路，现在，机会不存在了。”

“不，太君，求您大发慈悲！求您大发慈悲！我替她向您道歉！她不舔，我来舔！我来舔！”

赵宏伟像条疯狗一样舔着渡边的鞋。他的脸上，鼻涕眼泪一塌糊涂。

“滚开！你这个下贱的中国人！”渡边一脚踢开了赵宏伟。赵宏伟的嘴角流出了血。

“太君，只要你肯放了秀珍，你要我做什么事都可以，我愿意做你最忠诚的狗，求求你放了秀珍！求求你放了秀珍！太君——”

赵宏伟涕泗纵横地给渡边磕着头。

“你本来就是我们皇军的一条狗，如果不是，那你就得死。这有什么可说的？你又有什么能为我做的？你是能出去打死一支国民党部队，还是能出去给我抓回几个地下党来？你说你能为我做什么？我凭什么就要放了你的那个王秀珍？”

赵宏伟的嘴唇苍白，哆嗦着。

“告诉你，我要让我们皇军的每一个士兵，都好好尝一尝那个王秀珍的漂亮肉体，我要让王秀珍知道，一个奴隶，如果胆敢反抗她的主人，会有什么样的后果。懂了吗，宏伟君？”渡边拍了两下赵宏伟的脸，像打耳光一样。

“不，不，太君，不要这样！求求你不要这样！”赵宏伟跪在地上，泪也都流干了。他哆嗦着嘴唇，说：“如果你肯放了秀珍，我可以……我可以……”他想说，我可以带你去捉地下党。但是，他哆嗦了好久，终于还是没有说出来。

“你可以什么？”

“我可以……再给您两根金条。”

“这样吧，明天你把那两根金条交出来，不然，我派人抄你的家。”

赵宏伟像个雕像一样跪在地上，没有声音，一动不动。

“宏伟君，其实我还是非常同情你的，你说你贵为赵家镇的一镇之长，却为了一个已经沦为了我们皇军士兵的公用尿壶的女人，跪在我的面前，又是哭泣又是磕头，你说你可怜不可怜？——说真的，其实你对我们皇军来说，也没什么实际用处，但是怎么说呢，我们想要演大东亚共荣的戏，那台上总得有几个精致的木偶吧？你是赵家镇上有名的聪明人、文化人，用你们中国人的古话来说，你是个状元之才，所以，我们才选择了你。我们需要木偶，是你还活着的唯一原因。成为一个木偶，是你继续活下去的唯一途径。所以，你不要再奢求什么了，操纵木偶的人，有时也是会扔掉几个令他厌烦了的木偶的。”

赵宏伟依旧像个雕像似的跪着。

“忘记那个尿壶一样的女人，想想你的明天吧。要是你听话，副县长、县长，这些职位，你都可以有。你这个木偶，原本就是我创造出来的，只是一直被竹内霸占了去，去给他演了戏。现在竹内就要走了，你很快就会重新回到我的手上，为我的明天而演戏。宏伟君，我是需要你的！我也愿意让你成为副县长、县长。想想看，你若成了一个杰出的县长，人人都会知道，我渡边才是真正在为大东亚共荣做贡献的！到那时，就连将军也会对我刮目相看！清醒吧，宏伟君。这才是男人的事业，女人，只是一种糕点。——这样吧，宏伟君，我也不是一个无情的人，既然你这么喜欢那个王秀珍，我就给你一个特权：在王秀珍离开江庆县之前，你可以像我们联队的士兵一样，随

时去享用王秀珍的身体。我想，这才是一个男人最想得到的东西吧？这已经是我对一个中国人做出的最大的让步了，宏伟君，就这样吧。”

赵宏伟面无表情地站了起来，他说：“我不会接受这种侮辱。中国有句古话，头顶三尺有神明。人做什么事，天上的神灵都会看得见。”

渡边背转身，说：“我从不相信这个世上有神。”

赵宏伟说：“我也不信神，但是我相信，有一种扬善惩恶的规则，始终凌驾在我们每一个人的灵魂之上，任何人都不可违逆它，否则，这个人便会被规则给撕碎。”

“混蛋！”

赵宏伟开始向门外走去。

“赵宏伟，我警告你，你要是敢去竹内那里诬陷我，或者胆敢用竹内来与我作对，我一定会让你看见，王秀珍是怎样被自己的肠子给勒死的！”

“——你放心，我是不会蠢到那种地步的。”

赵宏伟擦干净了自己的脸，走出了竹内的办公室。

天色已昏暗。没有一丝风，闷热仿佛能将人的血液凝固。几只鸟从天上飞过，孤单得没有一丝生气。

赵宏伟坐在路边上，失魂落魄，像个乞丐。他远远地看到，县政府那边，正在放烟火。烟火那么美，简直像在过春节。他想起了自己曾经的许多美好岁月，他想起了秀珍小时候，欢天喜地地看他放烟火的情景。那时的她还只是个爱吃糖的孩子，谁能想到她有一天会长大成人呢？一切都像是上辈子的事情。那些没有战争没有匪寇没有仇恨的岁月，是多么的美好！小小的安宁与平静，真是这世上最可宝贵的东西。但是生逢乱世，谁又真能主宰得了什么呢？赵家镇也不是桃花源，哪能逃得过这乱世的洗礼呢？那些安宁的岁月片断，更像是一场时代浩劫开始之前的饯行酒，饮完唱罢，大家便须去刀山火海之中再见了，没得选择。

县政府里的烟火还在放，有许多县城的百姓在驻足观赏。赵宏伟忽然就很荒唐地笑了，笑得像个丑八怪。他想，我该怎么办？

什么都完了。

什么都完了？

不。

我还有两根金条，赵宏伟想。

他咬了咬牙，站了起来。他想，我命不休，此事不休。就是追到上海，我也要把秀珍给救出来！

赵宏伟叫了一辆黄包车，说，去赵家镇！

白昼的最后一丝光亮，在垂死挣扎中，被黑夜吞进了肚子里。

路灯是那么的昏暗。

赵家镇的街上没有一个人，死气沉沉，阴森可怖。

黄包车夫一到赵家镇的街上，就把赵宏伟给丢了下来，不肯再拉。因为，赵家镇的街上，到处都挂着血淋淋的人头。人头在黑暗里随风晃动，忽隐忽现，令人毛骨悚然。浓烈的血腥味像是在闷热的天气里经过了发酵，让人恶心得翻江倒海。县城里的黄包车夫哪里知道这镇子上发生了什么事，吓得腿都软了，还以为是走错了路，来到了鬼城。

赵宏伟给了车夫钱，车夫逃命似的拉着车就跑了。赵宏伟一个人在路上走着，有路灯的地方是昏暗，没路灯的地方是黑暗。在一个昏暗的地方，赵宏伟认出了一颗人头，那是卖油条的老张。老张的嘴里还在滴着血，血一滴一滴地滴在灰暗的路上。赵宏伟想起，自己以前，最喜欢吃老张炸的油条了，老张炸的油条，总是最香最脆。赵宏伟曾经一直以为，只要与世无争，小日子总是能过得很滋润的。

赵宏伟莫名落下了两滴泪来。他快步地走了起来。他的脚步里带着一股恨。是谁，是谁毁了我们的生活？是侵略者，是战争！操他妈的日本鬼子！

不止一条街上挂着人头，各条街上都挂着人头。赵宏伟想，其他镇上，应该也是如此吧。王八蛋赵驹，都是你想出来的好主意！

赵宏伟在恐怖的街上走着，心里充斥着破碎的悲哀。面对着这样的现实，人会连号啕大哭的力气也没有。只有满满的像碎玻璃一样的悲哀。死亡的味道是这么真实，断头就像吃饭一样平常。

赵宏伟不知自己会不会有一天也变成他们这样，头是无身头，身是无头身。跟日本人作对，下场就是这样。

一路上真的没看见半个人，连猫猫狗狗都没有。人们是都躲在家里吗？他们真的都投降了吗？赵家镇上还会有暴动吗？人们的愤怒会在压抑中死去吗？到处阴风惨惨。

快要到家了。远远地，赵宏伟已看见站在自己家门口的两个日本兵。他的头皮一下子就有些发麻。自己从一个满是日本人的地方跑出来，到最后，却还是回到了一个有日本人的地方。人生就是这么滑稽。

赵宏伟问了问看门的一个日本兵，日本兵告诉他，今天白天因为人手不够，所以暂时只给他家里派了四个守卫，前门两个，后门两个，不过北川说了，晚上只要一空，就会马上增派人手过来，一定保证镇长家的安全。

赵宏伟问，今天白天有没有人来找麻烦？

日本兵说，没有。

赵宏伟就说，告诉你们北川大队长，不用再派人过来了，他的好意我心领了。

赵宏伟开了门，进了家。

家里静悄悄的，黑咕隆咚，也没有灯光。赵宏伟走到屋子前，轻轻地喊了一声“小菊”，没人应，又喊了一声“小菊”，屋门才“吱呀”一声开了出来。

“宏伟伯伯，你回来啦——”

小菊高兴地说着，就扑到了赵宏伟的怀里。

“小菊乖，小菊乖。”赵宏伟心里蓦然也很高兴，就好像没发生任何悲剧一样。

到了屋里，赵宏伟开了灯。昏黄的灯光虽然很暗，赵宏伟却莫名感到有些温馨。在这个混乱而残酷的年代，已经没有多少东西可以让人感到暖意了，而他赵宏伟却还有这么个家，还有小菊，他已经很幸运了。

赵宏伟看到桌上还剩三个鸡蛋，就问小菊饿不饿。小菊说不饿。赵宏伟说，伯伯给你做一碗炒面吧，很好吃的。

赵宏伟很认真地做着炒面，炒着炒着，心里忽然就很酸。小菊告诉他，今天她一直待在屋里，没有出去，外面也没有人进来，但是她听见了外面有日本人的声音。赵宏伟就告诉她，不用怕，外面的那些日本人，是来给中国人扫地的，今天外面太脏了，大家都没办法出门。

小菊吃炒面的时候，赵宏伟就去拿了两根金条。他把这最后的两根金条放在了身上。他准备去贿赂北川，县官不如现管，现在赵家镇上北川最大，只要他肯放人，秀珍就还有一线生机。是成是败，就全在今晚了。

他也不做什么慢吞吞的打算了。秀珍今晚只要一出来，他就会将她暂时先安置在方远梦或者老周那里，然后，他就马上回来接小菊，去和秀珍会合。他必须不露声色。最后，他、秀珍、小菊就会在共产党的掩护下，安全地离开这个恶魔之城。

一切都会顺利的，他想。

赵宏伟给小菊冲了一碗热热的白糖水。小菊喝了一口，快乐地说，真甜。赵宏伟说，伯伯没有照顾好你，让你喝了一天冷水。

赵宏伟说，小菊呀，伯伯今晚要出去做一些事，这些事情若是做成了，你就能见着你娘了。如果伯伯办完事情回来，带着你往外走，那就是要带你去见你娘了，到时候你什么都不要问，也不要说话，只要跟着伯伯走。在路上，你会看到一些像人头一样的东西，但是你不要怕，那些都是日本人用木头和猪皮做出来的玩具，是他们日本人玩的皮球。总之，你要不说话，走得快，这样才能跟着伯伯去见你娘，懂了吗？

“嗯。”小菊点点头。

很好。赵宏伟说。

小菊“噔噔噔”跑去抱了一大包东西过来。赵宏伟一看，就是他昨天给小菊买的云片糕。小菊问：“我可以带着这个走吗？我要带着它去给我娘吃，我娘最爱吃云片糕了。”

赵宏伟心里一酸，说，可以，可以，小菊真乖。

小菊问：“那么那个捉迷藏的游戏结束了吗？”

赵宏伟一愣，旋即想起自己今天早上对孩子说过的那些话。孩子都是天真的，大人说什么他们都会信。大人不该骗孩子。但是活在这样一个令人作呕令人恐惧的年代，除了撒谎，大人又还有什么办法可以保护孩子幼小的心？难道要告诉她，外面路上挂着的都是真人头？难道要让她明白，她的宏伟伯伯是侵略者的帮凶，愤怒的百姓随时会找他来报仇？那样会毁了孩子的明天的。

赵宏伟蹲下来，摸摸小菊的头，说，不，游戏还没有结束。在伯伯回来

之前，不管外面发生什么事，你都不要走出这个屋子，谁叫谁喊你都不要应声。万一有人闯了进来，你就躲到床底下去，要是有人把你抓了起来，你就对他说，你恨赵宏伟。不然，你就会输，我和你娘也会输，明白了吗？

小菊点头，说：“明白。”

赵宏伟又摸了摸孩子的头，然后，站了起来。他关了灯，说，不要开灯，等伯伯回来。

“嗯。”

赵宏伟走出了屋子。

赵宏伟迈出家里大门的时候，一小队日本兵就跑了过来。有十多个人。他们向赵宏伟报告，是北川大尉派他们来的。他们准备五步一岗，包围着守住赵宏伟的宅子，以保万无一失。

赵宏伟想，不行，太招摇了，而且，很容易被软禁。

赵宏伟说，不要不要，你们回去，我这里有四个人就足够了，你们去帮北川大尉做些别的事情吧。

又说了几次，那些兵才表示，要回去向北川大尉请示一下才行。赵宏伟问，北川大尉现在是在什么地方？日本兵告诉他，就在镇政府里，还在处理事情。赵宏伟说，很好，那你们先走，去告诉北川大尉，晚一会儿我会去拜访他，有事相商。

那十多个日本兵走了。只剩下了四个日本兵，前后门各两个。赵宏伟给前门上好了锁，又去后门看了看。后门是他在里面闩好的，他用力推了推后门，后门纹丝不动。非常好，他想。他对看后门的两个日本兵说，辛苦了。

他想先去找一下方远梦，向共产党提出协助逃难的请求。虽然他也知道自己这么做是有些不要脸，并且会给共产党添不少麻烦，但是他已走投无路，只能厚着脸皮做事了。他相信方远梦是一定会帮他的。老周就不一定了，毕竟老周和他赵宏伟不熟，不太可能会为了一个汉奸而两肋插刀。

赵宏伟不会让游击队白辛苦的，他想好了，作为回报，他会将姚志的新情况告诉方远梦，这样，他也就不算欠游击队太多了。有了方远梦的友情和姚志的新情况这两样东西，赵宏伟相信，游击队是一定会帮他和秀珍、小菊逃出这个恶魔之城的。

走了半条街，赵宏伟忽然又想：先去找方远梦太浪费时间了。既然已料定方远梦会帮自己，那么现在就不该再在这件事上花时间。现在最重要的是什么？是要先把秀珍从日本人的手里给救出来。万一就在他和方远梦说话的时候，北川把那些女人都送去了县城，那可就是竹篮打水一场空了。

他马上转身，奔镇政府的方向而去。他想叫一辆黄包车，但是路上一个人也没有。他的一颗心被紧紧地吊了起来，因为他突然发现了自己的一个失误。今天白天，在赵驹走后，他又偷听了两个来自其他镇上的负责军官的谈话。他听他们说，他们各个镇上的负责人都已经商量好了，明天早上再将那些慰安妇送到县城里来。因为没有一个镇上的士兵会愿意提前告别那些女人，他们可不想挨手下士兵的骂。而竹内，就让他再被他的兵多骂一个晚上吧。他们说得挺高兴。而赵宏伟也就在心里确定了秀珍被送离赵家镇的时间是在明天早上。但是赵宏伟现在脑子里却忽然是打了个激灵：他们说的“他们”，里面又是否包括北川？毕竟，北川今天没有参加记者会，也没有参加竹内的训话会。北川被竹内排斥已是个半公开的事情，那么，北川和那些暗地里想要看竹内跌倒的人又是否能站到一起？好像也不能。因为据说，北川是个愚忠的人。这样，赵家镇上的慰安妇被送离赵家镇的时间，就有了模糊性。北川究竟是会听从哪一方的规则？赵驹又是否会向北川传达什么讯息？一件事情，思考之后总比思考之前来得更复杂。赵宏伟现在很担心，也许秀珍此刻已经是被送去了县城。

赵宏伟快跑了起来。虽然他的腿上和脚上还有些痛，但是这些痛在现在又还能算得了什么呢。一股气在他体内左冲右撞，就像是要让他爆炸一样。

进了镇政府，赵宏伟直奔日本院而去。日本院的门口依然有哨兵，但是哨兵不再阻挡赵宏伟。赵宏伟朝那个仓库跑去。远远地，他看见仓库外站着八个哨兵。仓库的门紧闭着。赵宏伟心乱如麻，疑惑一团。

他走到仓库前，向哨兵请求，要进去看看。哨兵不许，说里面有重要物资，闲人不得入内。赵宏伟说，物你祖宗，不就是藏的女人！我要找人！一个哨兵说，真的是物资，是今天新到的药品。另一个哨兵就将一扇仓库门打开了一半，进去开了灯，让赵宏伟站在门口看。真的都是药品。赵宏伟感到了一阵天旋地转。

开门的那个哨兵就又关了灯，然后出来关了仓库门。他告诉赵宏伟，这些药品，一半是要运到青梅县里去的。

赵宏伟失魂落魄地问：那些女人呢？那些被征来的女人呢？

哨兵回答他：她们都被安置到了牢房里，北川大尉一来，就下了命令，不许大家再玩女人。现在就等明天，将她们装车运到县城里去了。

赵宏伟差点欢呼起来。他激动地大声问：北川大尉现在在哪儿？在哪儿？

众哨兵像看怪物似的看着他。

赵宏伟深吸了两口气。他敲了敲北川办公室的门。“咚咚”的敲门声里，仿佛按捺着一股狂躁。静夜的静，是那么让人难以忍受。

“谁？”“太君，是我，赵宏伟。”

赵宏伟的声音平和谦逊，彬彬有礼。

北川开了门。他很有礼貌地请进了赵宏伟。赵宏伟心中的狂跳安宁了许多，面对着北川，他莫名感到自己的一只脚还是踩在希望之船上的。只是他必须要小心、用力，波浪那么大，希望随时会被卷进汪洋大海里。

“请坐。”

“谢谢太君。”

赵宏伟等北川坐下后，自己再坐下。他看着北川那只还缠着纱布的手，心中的忐忑莫名又激烈翻滚了起来。

“我听回来的士兵说了，你不想要那么多的士兵围着你的家，这个我可以理解。那么，如果你有需要，我再派人吧。”

“谢谢太君。”

“那么，你今晚特地来找我，是有什么事呢？”

赵宏伟站了起来，心跳得厉害。他不明白，在这种重要的时刻，自己的身心怎么会如此不听指挥，就好像他的身心在此刻并不属于他，而是属于一匹狂躁的马。赵宏伟克制着自己的热，用衣袖擦了一把额上的汗。他摸出了那两根金条来。他毕恭毕敬地用双手捧着那两根金条。“太君，这是我的一点小小心意，请您笑纳！”

“赵镇长，这是怎么回事？你有事说事，不要用这种方式。”

赵宏伟咽了口唾沫。他看了看北川，北川十分严肃。他就先将金条放在了北川面前的茶几上。北川站了起来。

“太君，我的未婚妻，被征来做了慰安妇。”赵宏伟心中原有百句话，到头来，却只说出了这么一句来。他想再多说一些，但无奈唇舌都像被挂上了秤砣，重得无力多动。他的胸中更像是被一座山塞着，连喘气都很费劲。

北川没有说话。他顿了一会儿，问：“就在这镇政府里？”

“是的。”

“当初是她自己来应征做洗衣工的，还是皇军的士兵拉她来的？”

“是士兵硬拉她来的。”

“那她当时有没有告诉士兵，她是你赵镇长的未婚妻？”

“……我……我一直还没有告诉她，我想娶她。”

陷入了长久的沉默。赵宏伟心里突然剧烈地一痛，旋即，他心中的巨山就像是化为了千万把锋利的刀。他的心仿佛都被刀捅烂了。他哭了出来。

他面向着北川跪了下来，他流着泪说：“求太君放了她！求太君放了她！求您了！”

他给北川磕着头。

北川长长地叹了一口气，空气中像有很多凝固的东西，瞬间重得能把人压垮。他说：“我都明白了，你快起来吧。”

赵宏伟没有动。剧烈颤抖的紧张缠绕着难以言喻的痛苦，他赵宏伟就像是一根即将要被拉断了的麻绳。他既不知自己此刻该怎样做，也不知自己接下来会做什么。只有冰冷的泪，依旧在他脸上麻木地流。他的心中还有千万句恳求，可是都像是堵在了喉咙里，怎么冲也冲不出来。他忽然才发现，对于心而言，口舌是那样地苍白而无能。他无声地颤抖着，只恨不得能将自己的心挖出来，直接用心来向北川乞求。

北川无言地沉默着。他去扶赵宏伟。他硬是将软塌塌的赵宏伟给扶了起来。他背对了赵宏伟，说：“你的心情，我十分理解。但是，我不能放人。”

赵宏伟的一半神经被拉断了，他的头脑里像闪过了一个霹雳，他的意识一片空白。没有太意外的惊愕，只有加倍痛苦的绝望和撕心一样的疼痛。他感到自己的血液都像是沸腾了起来。他有一种清晰了起来的痛恨自己的悲怆。

“就在昨天，那些女人们的肩上都被文上了编号，有了编号，她们就是正式的慰安妇了。她们都被登记在册，除非是死了，否则不会被注销。”北

川说。

“……求求您，帮我证明她死了。我可以保证，她在她的余生中，一定会像从这世上消失了一样地活着，你们的人，绝对不会再看见她一眼。”

“难道，你要我向我的国家撒谎？难道，你要我背叛大佐的命令？就为了一个中国女人？真是太可笑了。”

“太君，中国女人也和日本女人一样，有兄弟、丈夫和孩子。如果一个哥哥，知道自己的妹妹是做了慰安妇，他会有怎样的痛苦？这种痛苦，是没有国界的，也没有种族之分。”

北川背对着赵宏伟，长久地不说话。夜之静，像死亡一样永恒又沉闷。赵宏伟看见，北川那只裹着纱布的手，在微微地发抖。

北川用手擦了擦眼睛。

“对于一个军人来说，他首先是一个军人，其次才是一个哥哥。没有国家的胜利，也不会有个人的幸福。而我是一个军人，服从命令，是我的天职。对不起，宏伟君。”

北川深吸了一口气。他顿了顿，转回了身来，拿起放在茶几上的那两根金条，将它们塞回到了赵宏伟的手中。他说：“你拿着这个，去找竹内大佐吧，不管是在政府里还是在军队里，真正能决定一个人的生死与去留的，都只是长官。而江庆县现在的最高长官，就是竹内大佐。只要他肯下令放人，我一定马上放。你不要在我这里浪费时间了。”

赵宏伟手里拿着沉甸甸的金条，喉咙里只感到有一股血腥味。怎么办？北川说得也不错，征人本来就是竹内下的命令，放人的权力，自然也是在竹内那里。偷着放不如真的放。但是，如果他去找竹内，无疑就是与渡边公然为敌。与渡边为敌，他和秀珍会有什么样的下场？可是，就算不与渡边为敌，他赵宏伟的下场又能好到哪里去？秀珍会被渡边踩成烂泥！伸头一刀，缩头一刀，干脆和渡边拼了，来他个鱼死网破！赌一把！

“谢谢太君，我明白了。离开之前，我有一个小小的请求，希望您能答应。”

“请讲。”

“我想见一见我的未婚妻。”

“可以。她叫什么名字？”

“王秀珍。”

“你等着，我去提人。”

“多谢太君。”

赵宏伟将金条放回了身上。他用衣袖擦干净了自己的脸，又用手抹了抹自己的头发，尽量使自己看起来还是那么仪表堂堂，没有一点落魄相。

夜之静，还是像死亡一样永恒又沉闷。赵宏伟听着自己的呼吸，自己的呼吸是那么杂乱而无力。时间在未知中延伸，前路在未知中展开，而自己，似乎正在未知中窒息。

赵宏伟听到了脚步声，渐渐由远及近。

门开了，北川领着一个女人走了进来。这个女人一头蓬乱，形销骨立。她穿着破烂的囚衣囚裤，两只脚光着，脚上还结着一些血痂。

她抬起头来，看到赵宏伟的那一刹那，目光碎成了血花。她后退了半步，却再也不能挪动，就像一座雕像般死木。北川问赵宏伟，是不是她？赵宏伟忍着心酸，点点头，说，是。

北川说，你们慢慢聊。说完，北川便走了出去。

赵宏伟关了门。他去拉她的手，他一碰到她，她却就像触电了似的弹了开去。她缩到了墙角里，蹲在了地上。赵宏伟哽咽着说：“秀珍，是我呀，赵宏伟。”

她却掩面哭了起来。她哭的声音不大，却凄厉得肝肠寸断。赵宏伟的泪也掉了下来。他说：“是我呀，秀珍。”

他把自己的鞋脱了，蹲下来，轻轻托起了秀珍的一只脚，要给她穿鞋。她却惊慌万分地推开了他。她哭着说：“你别碰我，我脏。”

赵宏伟不顾一切地就抱住了她，她再怎么推他，他也不松手。“秀珍，我不许你这么说，不许你这么说！”他用力地吻着她的脸，哭着说。

她推着他，推着他，力气越来越小。终于，她死死地抱住了他，在他的怀里，号啕大哭了起来。

大哭了起来。

“秀珍，我很快就能救你出去了，很快！我只是想告诉你一件事，你一定要记住，千万记住：接下来，不管还会发生什么事，你都要千方百计地活

下去，一定要活下去，只要活着就好，只要活着就好！你明白了吗？你一定要记住，只要活着就好。不管是到天涯海角，只要你还活着，我就一定会救你出去！出去之后，我就娶你。这么多年了，我一直没告诉你，其实我有多么爱你！你比我的生命还重要，你能让我发疯发狂，我愿意为了你去做任何事，你是这个世上最美丽的神！秀珍，我爱你！我爱你，你记住了吗。我要娶你，秀珍，你是我的妻子。你是我的妻子，小菊就是我的女儿。小菊一直住在我那里，她过得很好，你不用担心。她很乖，很孝顺，她天天都在想念你，等你回去。秀珍，你一定要好好活着，等我救你出去！”

秀珍流着泪，不停点着头。赵宏伟深深地吻住了秀珍的嘴唇。

“宏伟哥，我爱你——”秀珍哭着说。

秀珍，我没有骗你。赵宏伟在心里说。他吻着秀珍的泪。

赵宏伟亲自送秀珍回了牢房。走的时候，他没有再回头多看秀珍一眼。他怕，自己一看，就不能再走了。

而他必须要走。为了未知的明天。

赵宏伟把鞋给了秀珍穿，北川看赵宏伟没了鞋，就给了赵宏伟一双日本军靴。赵宏伟谢了谢北川，穿上了靴子。赵宏伟知道北川对他已是很关照了，因为他看到在牢房里，有很多慰安妇并没有衣服穿。他再次谢了谢北川，然后就告辞了。

赵宏伟再次踏上了他的救亡之旅。他唯一的筹码，就是他的乞求和他仅存的两根金条。他都没有发现，他是多么的可怜，多么的可笑。

赵宏伟打算先将小菊送去方远梦那里。

他一个人在深夜无人的大街上奔跑。见过了秀珍，他感到自己浑身又充满了力量。一种誓不罢休的力量。只是，街上挂着的人头，还是那么血腥恐怖。

渐渐接近他的家了。远远地，他觉得有些不对。那个方向的天空，怎么泛着金与红的光，就像是有朝霞，正在漆黑的夜里展开。静夜中，有些东西倒塌的声音。

转过了那个街角，终于看见了他的家。他的家，正在冲天的大火中燃烧。烈焰熊熊，火光映红着漆黑的天空。

赵宏伟惨叫了一声，疯狂地冲向火场。火焰像海水一样淹没着他的家。他看到，看守他家大门的日本兵，脖子全被割开了，倒在血泊中。赤艳的火舌正在从大门的门缝里往外蹿。赵宏伟声嘶力竭地狂喊："小菊！小菊！"

他跑去了后门，一看，守门的日本兵也是死了。脖子被割开，倒在血泊中。他拼命地撞门，撞门。门被撞开的一刹那，一团火就从里面涌了出来。

赵宏伟看到，自己的整座屋子，都已被大火含住。大火正在猛烈地嚼，猛烈地嚼。他想冲进去，但冲不进去。

"小菊——小菊——"他撕心裂肺地喊，但是没有人回应他。

"快来人哪——救火呀——"他哭泣着喊，但是没有一个人来帮他。

火光冲天，烈焰撕夜。"轰隆"一声，他家的屋顶塌了。他的家，被火嚼烂了。

"苍天哪——"赵宏伟仰天长啸，喷出了一口血，晕了过去。

而火还在烧。

安静地烧。

最后，是北川将赵宏伟从火里救了出来。

大火被日本兵扑灭了。一切都成了废墟。

赵宏伟醒来时，东方已现鱼肚白。

赵宏伟发了疯似的去废墟里翻找。终于，他在一张烧塌了的床下，找到了一个烧焦了的小人儿。小人儿的怀里，还死死地抱着一团东西。赵宏伟仔细一分辨，这团东西，就是他给这个小人儿买的，云片糕。

"我要带着它去给我娘吃，我娘最爱吃云片糕了。"小菊说。

赵宏伟号啕大哭。他抱着小菊焦黑的尸体，号啕大哭。

他疯狂地扇着自己耳光。是他，都是他！是他叫小菊不要走出这个屋子，是他叫小菊躲到床底下去！都是他害的！

他哭得魂飞魄散。

"老天爷——"赵宏伟仰天狂号。

赵家镇再次戒严。北川挨家挨户搜查杀害日本兵的凶手。

纵火的方式已查明，是汽油瓶加火把，和老百姓袭击镇政府的方式一模一样。

赵宏伟的家被烧毁了。隔壁秀珍的家也被连累到，烧坏了，但这些已都不重要了。

那棵桂花树也烧焦了。赵宏伟还记得，它昨夜熊熊燃烧的样子，像极了一束从地里喷出来的血光。那种姿态，居然是那么美好。

而堪称奇迹的是，他家的那坛状元红，居然在烈火中幸存，完好无损。他想起，他曾对小菊说过，等她娘回来了，三个人要一起喝掉这坛酒。而当时，小菊还小手一拍，高兴地说，好。

一转眼，已物是人非。

赵宏伟很后悔，当初是他赶走了那些北川增派过来守卫他家的日本兵。如果守卫他家的日本兵能多一些，那么，这场惨案也许根本就不会发生。

赵宏伟在废墟里又找到了那把匕首。就是那把原本是被百姓拿来吓唬他的匕首。它居然也是完好无损。它寒光闪闪，他用手指碰了碰它的刃，它的刃上立马就沾了血。

整片废墟里，幸存下来的，就是一坛酒和一把匕首。赵宏伟觉得真有意思。他一手抱着酒坛，一手拿着匕首，身上穿着文质彬彬的中国长衫，脚上穿着威风凛凛的日本军靴。这军靴的靴底上，说不定还沾着不少中国人的血。赵宏伟觉得这幅图画真是好笑至极。

他都笑出了眼泪来。

他坐在废墟里，一场笑，一场哭，一场哭，又一场笑，就像一个疯子。哭完了，也笑完了，他就将酒放到了地上。他双手握着匕首，将匕首的尖对准了自己的肚子。说实话，这么多年过去了，他对于藤田武当年的剖腹自尽，始终有些不能理解。但是今天，他理解了。

各个镇上的慰安妇都被塞住了嘴，捆住了手脚，装进了麻袋里。这些麻袋都被装到了卡车上。各个镇上的运人卡车，都开始往县城里开。

赵家镇上的卡车是最晚出发的。直到中午前，北川仍然没有接到竹内的放人命令，于是，北川命令卡车出发。

各镇的慰安妇，都被运到了县城里。总计有两百多人。县城的日本兵欢呼雀跃。竹内感叹，中国的江南，真是美女如云。

赵宏伟蜷缩在一个无人知道的角落里。

他的肚子上流着血，但是流得并不多。他并没有完成他的剖腹自尽。就在刀尖刚划开他肚子皮肤的那一刻，他感到了巨大的恐惧，排山倒海一样的恐惧。他想，我死了，秀珍怎么办？

软弱无力的他，中止了自己英勇果断的自尽。当时的时间，还没到中午。他知道自己还没有去找竹内，他知道自己此刻的沉沦正在使自己离营救成功的希望越来越远，但他就是站不起来，也走不动。更何况，他肚子上的皮肤，正在流血。于是，他就在地上爬。他爬离了这片废墟，爬离了他的家，爬到了一个没有人会看见他的角落里。他感受着痛苦的折磨，感受着绝望的摧残，感受着慢慢地流血。他看着天上的太阳，骄阳似火，烈日当空。

他想，小菊死了，我该如何面对秀珍？

又一个日本兵，残暴地打开了秀珍的双腿。

秀珍的下身在流血。她紧咬着牙关，拼命忍受着。她闭上眼睛，仿佛又看见，赵宏伟、她、小菊，正围坐在一起，在一起吃饭、唱歌。小菊正在唱：长亭外，古道边，芳草碧连天。

三个人在一起，快乐地生活着。

日本兵又是一口狠狠地咬下去，秀珍痛得惨叫了起来。

她的胸前在流血，那血，仿佛是从心里流出来的。

傍晚了。夕阳像个血窟窿一样，在天边恶心着这个人间。

赵宏伟站在长风中，给小菊撒着纸钱。纸钱飘飘洒洒，像雪，像叶，像泪，满地，满眼。每一片纸钱在夕阳余晖中飞舞，像是一场无声的恸哭。

赵宏伟用一个下午的时间，好好地安葬了小菊。现在，站在这个孩子的坟前，他觉得自己的心都已经痛得麻木了。是的，麻木了。就好像，心里的血都流干了。这个残酷的时代，连一个孩子也不能放过，究竟又还有什么痛苦，能让这个时代感动？麻木，也许才是活着的唯一解脱。

长风中，赵宏伟泪水干涸。他说，小菊，伯伯下辈子，再给你烧好

吃的。

那双日本军靴，被赵宏伟丢到了垃圾堆里。

他赤足行走在夜里，坎坷的路面，不时割破他的脚底。疼痛让他觉得很满足。路的两旁依旧是那些人头，但他已不觉得恐怖。

就在刚才，他去找了竹内。但是他还没开口，竹内就将他劈头盖脸地骂了一顿。原来是渡边早已先他一步，在竹内的耳旁进了谗言。渡边跟竹内说，赵宏伟垂涎于某慰安妇的美色，企图将她从军中赎出，占为已有，为了这事，赵宏伟已不惜与皇军中的多位军官发生了口角，并伴有行贿的事实。渡边说，赵宏伟这种无耻又可恨的行为，实在是对我们大日本皇军的极大挑衅与侮辱。

竹内正怒不可遏，赵宏伟却轻轻一笑，说：太君，您误会了，区区一个女人，我早已不再留恋，今天我来，只是想要为您再写一篇文章，我想问问您，希望我写什么。竹内龙颜大悦。

离开了县政府，回到了镇上，赵宏伟就开始赤足行走。疼痛让他有一种清醒，清醒的爱与清醒的恨。他开始认识到，跟日本人谈放人，无异于与虎谋皮。

路是那么的冷，那么的硬，那么的尖突不平，而他还要走下去。现在，也只有痛还能让他再走下去了。一步路，一步血。也许，只有在痛与血中，人生才能真正地走向强韧与不屈？他懂得还太少。他是多么渴望自己能拥有磐石般坚硬的勇气与胆量，在狂风暴雨般的痛苦冲刷中，仍然能无畏地走向明天未知的洗礼。但他似乎生来就被敏感与脆弱占据了灵魂。这敏感与脆弱，给了他善知善辨的聪慧，却也剥夺了他长出一副铁骨来的可能。活在这样一个充满了生死纠缠的年代，要怎样才能真心不死地活到明天？他真的不懂。

走到了方远梦的家门前。他敲起了门。方远梦开了门。

进了门，他就无力地跌坐在了地上。他掏出了那两根金条来，说，给，你们拿去，买枪买炮买炸药，帮我杀光这里的日本人。把日本人都赶出中国去！

方远梦问，你怎么了？

赵宏伟一张嘴，眼泪就流了下来。他说不出话，发不出声，只有泪，像水一样地流。

听赵宏伟说完了所有的事情，方远梦微微地叹了一口气。他也没有发表意见，也没有安慰赵宏伟。他重新帮赵宏伟包扎了一下他肚子上的那条可耻的伤口，又帮赵宏伟处理了一下他脚上的那些新伤口。他给了赵宏伟一双他的鞋。他说，试试看，合不合适。赵宏伟一试，刚巧合适。他就说，你穿着吧，别光脚走路了，你的脚哪有路硬。

方远梦说，你不要再去求日本人了，求来求去，事情反而会越来越难办。你放心，我们组织上已经决定了，这些女人，我们一定会去营救的。

方远梦将金条还给了赵宏伟，说，我们是缺钱，但你现在也是一无所有了，你要重新开始生活，没有钱怎么行。

赵宏伟沮丧地说，我哪里还会有什么生活。

方远梦问，你想不想有一天，可以带着你的秀珍，在一个和平而自立的中国无忧无虑地生活？

赵宏伟沮丧地说，当然想。

方远梦说，如果连你自己都不能真的相信会有这一天，这一天又怎么会真的来到你面前？

方远梦告诫赵宏伟，绝对不要再在竹内和渡边的面前表露出想要救出秀珍的愿望，事情已经发展到这个地步了，他若再真情流露，只会将秀珍推向更不利的境地。现今之计，唯有暂时以静制动。

另外，渡边说了，要向他讨要另外两根金条。不管渡边当时说的是不是一时的气话，他都要做好上交金条的准备。当然，他现在房子被烧了，家没了，他若自己花掉了半根或一根金条来重新置业起家，想来渡边也是不会过分追究的。要追究他也师出无名。但是这金条绝不能随便送人。不然渡边万一问起来怎么办？这也是方远梦不收这两根金条的一个原因。

方远梦说，你一定要好好生活下去。

赵宏伟说，我知道的。

方远梦说，不，你知道得还不够。如果你破罐子破摔，弄得自己狼狈不

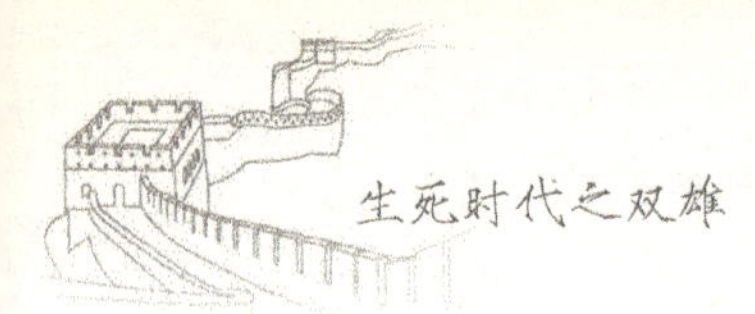

堪，那么，日本人很快就会将你弃如敝屣。而你如果被日本人弃用，那么，你想救秀珍的愿望，就可能会成为一个天方夜谭。

赵宏伟问，你们打算怎么救那些女人？

方远梦说，竹内要将她们运到上海去，我们就在路上下手，把人救下来。

赵宏伟问，有什么是我可以做的？

方远梦说，我们需要知道他们出发的时间、路线，还有随行护送的日军数量。

赵宏伟说，好。

方远梦说，另外，如果可以，希望你能为我们打听一下，姚志他现在究竟被关押在什么地方，我们不能眼睁睁地等着他被鬼子处死。

赵宏伟说，你放心，我一定会尽我所能。

方远梦说，谢谢。

方远梦考虑了一下，又说，最后，有一件事情，我觉得应该要告诉你。六月初一那天，竹内要去听你讲课，你讲课结束之后，千万记住，不要与竹内一起离开学校。因为我们计划，要在竹内返回的路上，将他刺杀。

天又亮了。

赵宏伟好好地洗了一把脸，告别了方远梦。

赵宏伟走在路上，脚上穿着方远梦的鞋，心里被一股澎湃的热情鼓舞着。小日本，最后的时刻就要到了，我们会送你们下十八层地狱！

赵宏伟在心里对自己说：赵宏伟，你一定要做一回有用之人！当一次英雄！

将近镇政府时，赵宏伟远远地看见，镇政府的大门外，有些混乱。

赵宏伟跑近了前去，才看到是日本人抓的一些百姓，大概有十多个人，都五花大绑着，其中一个人和赵宏伟很熟，就是曾卖臭油条给赵宏伟吃的老李。

一个日本兵告诉赵宏伟，这些人都是今天早上刚抓起来的，他们，就是纵火烧了你家的罪犯。

老李朝赵宏伟狠狠地吐了一口唾沫，大骂：“狗汉奸！老天无眼哪，居然没有烧死你！你卖国求荣，助纣为虐，死后阎王爷一定会让你下油锅！你个不要脸的狗汉奸，我呸！让雷劈死你！”

老李他们都被日本兵押进了镇政府里去。混乱一时又成了寂静。只剩赵宏伟，呆呆地站着，脸上还挂着老李的唾沫。

无云的早晨，天晴得那么刺眼。

不知是什么原因，渡边一直都没有真的跟赵宏伟要那两根剩下的金条。赵宏伟想，渡边可能也是不想逼人太甚，以防他赵宏伟狗急跳墙。他以前跟渡边讨论过穷寇勿追的道理，看来渡边是真领会了。毕竟，渡边对竹内的不忠，是见不得光的，万一吵得众人皆知了，无论事情是真是假，对谁都不好。

赵宏伟拿出一根金条来，兑换成了现大洋。方远梦说得对，他还是要用钱来重新开始生活的。他租了一处房子，买了一些日用品，就又开始了他的生活。北川给他派了八个哨兵，他觉得已无必要，想拒绝，却又懒得再去费这番口舌。随便吧，他想。

有时，他还是会去那片废墟前看看。这里是他生活了大半辈子的地方，如今却只剩下了断壁残垣。一场火，像是将他的人生也烧了个精光。隔壁秀珍家的房子也被烧坏了，焦的焦，断的断。赵宏伟想起了年轻时在秀珍家里度过的很多美好时光，那时候，谁能想到今天的图景。眼前的遗迹，真像是他人生惨况的一个绝妙譬喻。

赵宏伟闭上了眼睛，仿佛还能看到自己当年教秀珍写大字时的情景。秀珍总是学得很认真，她写字的时候，安静得就像一汪雪山的水。她是那么爱笑，笑起来就像天边漂亮的彩虹。那时，窗外总会有鸟叽叽喳喳地叫；那时，写完了字，她总是会去倒一碗糖水给他喝；那时，他从未觉得，时光是那么美好，人生是那么精妙。

而现在，小菊也死了。从时光的那一头到时光的这一头，中间隔着的，又岂止是千山万水。一场梦，从死去到怀念，中间隔着的，又岂止是撕心裂肺。

睁大着双眼，此刻的眼前，只有无尽的焦黑。灰飞烟灭里，像是写满了曲终人散。

赵宏伟开始致力于跟日本人和汉奸搞好关系。比如，经常请一些日本军官吃吃饭喝喝酒，经常拍拍一些汉奸头目的马屁。这些事情，都是赵宏伟以前不屑去做的。他对别人说，我这次是大难不死，老天既然没让我被火烧死，我就要好好重新做人。什么女人孩子，都是浮云。觥筹交错间，赵宏伟红光满面。

在赵宏伟的帮助下，老周的特别行动队成功混进了赵家镇，潜伏了下来。他们，就是来执行刺杀竹内的任务的。赵宏伟甚至还帮他们搞到了一把狙击枪。

那些一直悬挂着的死人头，在腐烂发臭之后，就都被日本人取了下来丢到火里烧掉了。日本人也怕不卫生，怕烂人头会弄出瘟疫来。

赵家镇上一直没有再发生什么暴力冲突。据说其他镇上也是这样。日本人的恐怖政策收到了预期的效果。

竹内收获了极高的声誉。德、意、日、中四国的多家媒体都在主要版面刊登了表扬竹内的文章。他们都称赞竹内是在构建大东亚共荣乐土的伟大事业上做出了一个光辉的表率。竹内乐得嘴都合不拢。

北川决定枪毙老李他们。赵宏伟找到北川，说，我不想追究这件事了，你把他们打一顿，然后就放了他们吧，别再杀人了。北川说，赵镇长，你弄错了，我们之所以要枪毙他们，不是因为他们烧了你的房子，而是因为他们杀了我们的四个士兵。

老李他们，是被押到赵家镇的大广场上执行的枪决。临刑前，老李想对赵宏伟说几句话。老李哭着对赵宏伟说：对不起，我们都不知道你家里有孩子，我们只是想杀了你，没想到会烧死孩子。请代我们去孩子的坟上，向她道个歉。对不起！

“砰、砰、砰”一串枪响，老李和他的同伴们的脑袋都开了花。血在广场上四溅。无人围观。

老李他们的尸体将被吊在大广场上暴晒三天，以儆效尤。看着被吊起的尸体，赵宏伟难受地闭上了眼睛。他默默地说：一路走好。

竹内已最终确定，将在六月初一这一天的上午，赴赵家镇小学听课。早前定下的来回路线，也不再做任何更改。竹内已尝到了被舆论追捧的甜头，于是，他又临时决定，此次听课，要多请几个记者同行。相应地，随行的保卫部队人数也就有了增加，由原来的三十多人增加到了五十多人，足足一个小队的规模。

而老周的行动队，只有十几个人。纵然他们个个本领高强，也难敌日本兵人多势众。而行动队的人数也已很难再增加，毕竟，短时间内若有太多的陌生面孔进入到城里或镇上来，会很容易引起别人怀疑的。潜伏进来了十几个人，已经不少了。

而在日军中还混杂了记者，这就给行动队的攻击造成了障碍。老周和方远梦都觉得那些记者是无辜的，刺杀行动绝对不能伤害到无辜。赵宏伟却提出了异议，他说，那些记者无辜个屁，你们想想看，肯给竹内写吹捧文章的记者能是什么好东西？他们就是侵略者的帮凶！一起炸死他们！

老周无言地看看赵宏伟，赵宏伟一时就觉得，自己好像是在骂自己。赵宏伟就有些无地自容。

方远梦十分感谢赵宏伟给行动队提供的各种帮助，特别是赵宏伟打听到的那些情报，对这次行动都十分重要。赵宏伟说，没什么，应该的，只是求你们以后一定要帮我救出秀珍！

各种细节问题都考虑妥当之后，方远梦最后做出了决定：六月初一，行动队就埋伏在竹内从赵家镇回县城的路上，行动务求速战速决，只要击毙竹内，不要把子弹浪费在小兵身上，打完就撤。如果实在杀不了竹内，也撤。尽量不要有牺牲。

赵宏伟激动地说：你们一定要杀了竹内，如果不是他，赵家镇上根本就不会征什么慰安妇，老百姓也不会死掉那么多！他就是个罪魁祸首！

赵宏伟将他五月初六那天交给方远梦的那封信要了回来。当时，赵宏伟是嘱咐方远梦，要他在秀珍和小菊到达重庆之后，将此信交给秀珍。这封信里写的是赵宏伟当时想对秀珍说的一些话。他说，对不起，秀珍，其实我并不爱你，也从未真的想过，将来要和你生活在一起，我之所以骗你，只是

想要给你一个逃出赵家镇的理由，好让你能在一个安全的地方好好地生活下去，希望你能理解我的一片苦心。你我今生的缘分已尽，将来恐怕不会再有相见之期，你一定要好好保重，好好生活下去。今世负你太深，已不求你能原谅，只望来生若能再见，倾我一世还你一生。

赵宏伟将这封信丢到了自己新住处的角落里。此一时彼一时，这些日子里发生了这么多事，他的情感和想法早已和写信之前截然不同。之前他一直不想和秀珍一起走，主要原因一是他心中梦里有心音，二是他怕自己的汉奸身份会连累秀珍。但是现在他心中的激流早已改变了奔腾的方向。人生本已苦且短，旦夕难料祸与福，又何必要将那大好的时光虚掷在无谓的徘徊与忧惧上呢？追念固然不可敌，但故人已远，眼前玉人不珍惜，弹指也会成云烟。更何况，他对秀珍的爱，也许从来就没他想的那么淡。人到去时方悔迟，情到断时才恨晚，也许儿女之情自古便是如此。他又怎么会再让秀珍独自上路？生死天涯，必当同行。至于他的汉奸身份，他想，总是有办法可洗脱的。古人治军尚有将功赎罪之法，他不信自己此生就无回头路可走。要是共产党能宽宏大量原谅他，他愿意跟着共产党走。良禽择木而栖，贤臣择主而事，这本是圣人之训。退几步讲，就算红尘里已再容不下他，他去学那陶渊明，采菊东篱下，想来总是可以的。总之他是一定要和她在一起的，两个人，能在一起多待一天，就多待一天，不求年年月月长久，只求分分秒秒厮守。已没有什么事情，能再令他退缩。在爱面前，一切忧惧都是渺小的。他要用自己的无畏与火热，来补偿她对他半生的痴情。爱她，将是他余生中唯一的信仰。

从赵驹的口中得知，秀珍一直还活着，赵宏伟内心略感欣慰。那天在北川的办公室里，他对她说了那么多的话，其实无非就是想将四个字刻进她的心里：活着就好。他要她明白，不管怎样，她还有他，她还有小菊。他是想用他和小菊对她的爱与牵挂，来给她一个必须要活下去的理由。他是真怕，她会撑不到被解救的那一天。但是幸好，她仍然还活着。活着，是一件多么困难而艰难的事。

不过，当然，她还并不知道，小菊已经不在了。

赵宏伟也并不知道，将来若见到秀珍，他该怎样告诉她小菊的死。也许他该以死谢罪，但是他若死了，她就连他也没有了。叫她还怎么活下去？

活着，永远是一个太难解答的问题。

赵宏伟又去坟场看望了两次小菊。他给她烧了一些纸做的衣服、纸做的点心。他还告诉了她，老李他们，已经向她说了对不起。他说，小菊，其实真正对不起你的，是伯伯我。他说，小菊，等你娘出来了，我就带她来看你。

坟场旁有一条小河，江南的小河永远都是那么清澈而宁静。一些金色的光在河面上活泼地跳跃着，就像孩子欢乐的嬉闹。河水不停地东去，阳光却一直在原处闪耀。赵宏伟泪眼蒙眬，他对小菊说，小菊，投胎的时候要记住了，去一个好的时代，不要有金戈铁马，不要有颠沛流离。

坟场里，没有声音。

青梅县的田中中佐，将在六月初二那天来江庆县，正式接任竹内的职位。江庆县的日本军官对此都颇有怨言，不喜欢田中的到来。

而如果没什么意外的话，六月初一，就是枪毙姚志的日子。

但是，赵宏伟到现在为止，仍没有打听到关于姚志的新消息。他估计姚志是被关在县监狱里，但是具体在哪个牢房，他却无法知道。他在县里认识的人本来就不多，监狱方面更是什么人都不认识。他的人际关系有些捉襟见肘。

至于慰安妇事件方面，他只知道，竹内到现在为止，仍然没有抓到半个金发碧眼的西洋女人。在中国的西洋女人本来就不多，就算有，大半也都有外交背景，是不能乱抓的，更不要说是抓了去做日本军妓，简直是开国际玩笑。竹内对此头痛至极。赵宏伟再次深切感受到了国家强大的重要性，一个国家强大了，这个国家的女人他们都不敢随便碰。中国女人之悲哀，正是中国之悲哀。

赵宏伟又给渡边送了两次礼，都是托北川送去的。北川带话给赵宏伟，渡边说，过去的事，既往不咎。

赵宏伟又请赵驹喝了一顿酒。

酒楼上，没什么热闹，很是冷清。坐在靠窗的位子，从窗户里望出去，下面的街上也甚是寂寥。各镇的屠杀结束之后，整个江庆县就像是陷入了一个黏稠的泥潭里，活气全无，有如坟墓。并没有什么明显的不对劲，也没有值得警惕的异常，老百姓们不再暴动，日本人也希望一切都能恢复正常。但整个江庆县就像是在泥潭里越陷越深。每一寸的下陷都是缓慢的，但每一寸的下陷都是令人绝望的。这片土地，还有这片土地上的人，都像是正在被一个来自地狱里的魔鬼给慢慢地吞进肚子里。那种窒息是恐怖的，那种恐怖是无法言说的。死亡的气息看不见摸不着，但是却笼罩在每一个活人的脸上。活人见了活人，就像死人见了死人。这里的百姓，已都是行尸走肉。

而从窗户里望出去，上面的天空依旧高而清。

赵宏伟又给赵驹倒了一杯酒。

赵驹告诉赵宏伟，竹内已经和上海的慰安所那边达成了协议，他们不要竹内赔洋妞了，只要竹内能尽快把这里的两百多个慰安妇全部安全地送到上海那边，竹内就可以功成身退了。竹内原本还一直担心洋妞的问题，但是从上海的慰安所那边来的负责人，去现场一看，立马就决定，不再在洋妞的问题上浪费时间了。为什么？江南的女人，不是一般的漂亮啊。况且，是足足两百多人，两百多人哪！只有傻子才会算不清这笔账。竹内决定了，六月初一，装运慰安妇的车队在中午以前全部集结至县城的东城门内，十二点整，准时出发去上海，两百多人全部运走。由一个中队来护送。

“什么，一个中队？”赵宏伟不禁问。

“是的，一个中队。”赵驹说。

赵驹自斟自饮。赵宏伟吃了一片牛肉，味同嚼蜡。

赵宏伟装作不经意地问，以前日本人抓的那个游击队队员，后来死了吗？

赵驹说，在我眼里，他从被抓住的那天起，就已经是个死人了。

赵宏伟问，他就没说一点有价值的东西出来？

赵驹说，真想要让他开口，总是有办法的。

赵宏伟说，共产党的嘴是很难撬开的。

赵驹说，是个人，总会有所爱，只要能找到这个人的所爱，就等于是找到了这个人的死穴。

赵宏伟问，那你们找到这个人的死穴了吗？

赵驹说，渡边说，为什么要找到呢？真撬开了这个人的嘴，消灭了玉山上的游击队，只会再给竹内添上大功一件。

赵宏伟说，原来这就是日本人的政治。

赵驹笑笑，喝了杯酒，问，那天，你偷听到的事情应该已经不少了，何必还要来问我呢？

赵宏伟说，年纪大了，耳朵不太好使了，很多事情，看得见，听不清。

赵驹说，小心，耳朵长得太长，会被人当草割下来。

赵宏伟说，耳朵倒是不怕割，命我还不想丢。

赵驹说，命丢不丢，决定权并不在自己的手里。你好自为之。

赵宏伟说，谢谢。

赵驹说，不用谢，只求大家太平，我也省心。

赵宏伟说，谢谢你那天给我的字条。

赵驹说，什么字条，我不明白。

赵宏伟笑了笑，就不再说什么。两个人默默喝了一会儿酒。

赵驹问，那个王秀珍，你真不救了？

赵宏伟说，真不救了，一个女人而已，我不要了。

赵驹说，我不信。

赵宏伟说，信不信由你。我现在想要的，只是荣华富贵。

顿了顿，赵宏伟倾向赵驹，笑着问，你想要的，是什么？

赵驹也倾向了赵宏伟，笑着说，和你一样。

赵宏伟说，我不信，你会真的不恨渡边。

赵驹说，最想杀了渡边的人，应该是你吧。

两个人面对面地相视着，像两个僵硬的塑像。阴冷、残酷、凝重，构成了两张男人的脸。赵宏伟说，我们可以一起想办法，杀了渡边。

赵驹说，谁杀了渡边，谁就是死路一条。

赵宏伟问，你怕死？

赵驹说，不怕死，又怎么会当汉奸。

赵宏伟说，我们是男人。

赵驹忽然哈哈笑了起来。他坐正了身子，转开了头去，重新又喝起了酒，他笑着说，从我们当汉奸的那一天起，我们就已经不是男人了。

赵驹说，今天，就当我们什么都没有说过。来，喝酒。

赵宏伟和赵驹喝着酒。窗外的天还是那么远，楼下的街还是那么静。鸟

在无助地飞。这一天，赵宏伟和赵驹谁也没有掉眼泪，只是，赵驹最后喝醉了。赵宏伟听见赵驹在梦里说，丽云，对不起。

赵宏伟还是要求北川把那些守卫他新住处的哨兵给撤了。说不出理由，他就是觉得这样让人很难受。那些日本兵就像是在时刻提醒他，他是个汉奸。而正因为他是个汉奸，所以小菊才会枉死。自己就是自己一切悲剧的罪魁祸首，这是一个令人伤心欲绝的困境。

说了几次，北川终于同意了撤人，而一直也没有老百姓来攻击他赵宏伟。天气一直都是那么好，好得让人莫名感到很空旷，空旷得让人有些想哭。

赵宏伟又通过其他渠道打听了一下，确认了赵驹说的运送慰安妇的那件事情是真的。他还打听到了一些新情况。那就是，六月初一那天，运送慰安妇的车队在出城之后，会顺道先将车上装的一批药品送去青梅县，然后再去上海。就是赵宏伟在仓库里见过的那些药品。而护送那些慰安妇的日军，的确是一支一百六十多人的中队。

铜墙铁壁一般的押送。

另外，竹内那天的听课行程中，将不会出现渡边的身影。这件事情有些令人意外。竹内听课的这件事，一直都是渡边在积极做准备，而且，赵家镇的奴化教育计划，渡边可说得上是始作俑者。现在竹内要走了，带着记者来留个纪念，于情于理，那纪念的照片上也是该有渡边的一席之地的。但是竹内已确定了，不要渡边同行，北川陪同即可。赵宏伟估计，竹内一定是已经听到了一些什么，渡边要开始失宠了。活该，赵宏伟想。

赵宏伟将他打听到的新情况告诉了方远梦和老周。方远梦和老周都陷入了深深的苦思中。

老周说，一个中队的鬼子，怎么打？就算我们出动整支游击队，打掉鬼子的一个中队也需要不少时间。枪炮声一起，县城里的鬼子一定会派增援出来，我们和那一个中队的仗还没打完，鬼子的援军就肯定已经到了。我们不是找死吗？而且，有两百多个女人在鬼子的部队里，我们不能乱打乱炸。怎么办？

方远梦眉头紧锁，不说话。

赵宏伟心里一时就很焦急，说，我们不能看着鬼子把那些女人送去上海。

老周说，那我们也要救得了她们才行啊。

方远梦做了个手势，要他们别吵。方远梦沉吟了一会儿，说，人是一定要救的，现在的问题是，怎么救。

赵宏伟和老周都说不出话来。是啊，怎么救？赵宏伟想。

方远梦和老周一直讨论到了晚上。最后，方远梦拿出了一个方案来。

运送药品和慰安妇的日军车队，如果是在六月初一那天的中午十二点准时从东城门出发，那么，按照计算，在十二点一刻左右，日军的车队会从狮丘山的一条山路上通过。这条山路的两旁，就是设下埋伏的最好地方。要想尽快地消灭日军的一个中队，至少需要出动大半支游击队，我方的人数越多越好。当然，玉山上也要留好防守力量，不能让玉山成为一个空巢。而为了牵制日军的增援部队，另外还需要做两件事：一、是六月初一中午的十二点一刻以后，需要有人在县城里制造爆炸，吸引日军的注意，要是人手够的话，甚至可以对县政府发起佯攻；二、是最重要的，那就是刺杀竹内的行动队，也许要成为敢死队。原来的刺杀计划是，能杀则杀，杀不了就撤。现在必须改成：不惜一切代价，杀死竹内。只有这样，才能最大程度地将日军的增援部队吸引到这边来。日军车队通往上海的那条路是在江庆县城的东边，而竹内由赵家镇返回江庆县城的那条路，则是在江庆县城的西边。只要竹内身陷险境，日军的增援部队肯定会优先往西边的这条路上来。如果竹内被击毙了，日军更是一定会将全部力量集中到西边来，剿灭行动队。他们不可能为了留住一批慰安妇，而让一支刺杀了他们大佐的行动队在刺杀成功之后扬长而去。需要说明的是，行动队在成功刺杀竹内之后，也不可以马上撤离，而必须要与日军的增援部队作战，尽一切力量吸引日军、拖住日军。这样，西路和中路的战斗，就能为东路的营救争取到更多的时间。最后，东路的营救成功之后，要马上打出信号弹，来通知其他两路的同志撤退。由于一颗信号弹的通知范围有限，所以从东到西还要暗设几个通信员，这边信号弹起，那边的通信员看见了，就也发一颗，依此类推，传递信号。要确保能将撤退的信息及时通知到所有同志。

老周问：要怎样才能保证，竹内通过我们行动队埋伏点的时间，刚好是

在东路的战斗打响之后呢？万一早了，岂不是竹篮打水一场空？

方远梦面向了赵宏伟，说，这就要靠你了，希望你能拖延讲课时间，让竹内在刚好的时间，通过我们的埋伏点。

赵宏伟说，你放心，我虽无能，这点本事还是有的。

老周有些颓然地坐了下来。他说，我答应过我的队员，今年秋天，要带他们去看红色的枫叶。那个最小的同志，今年才十七岁。

方远梦就有些沉默。他说，革命，解放，就是要用我们今天的血，给百姓带来明天的光。

方远梦连夜回了一次玉山，向队长和政委汇报情况。

方远梦的计划得到了队长和政委的同意。队长将亲自率领三百人去东路伏击日军的车队。政委带人留守玉山。另外，要尽快再往江庆县内增派潜伏队员。

在赵宏伟的帮助下，三十名佯攻县政府的游击队员被送进了县城里，藏在县城的一座废弃仓库中。而老周的行动队，也再增加了五个人。赵宏伟又去黑市上买了一些炸药，交给了负责佯攻的游击队员。

赵宏伟感到北川对自己已经有了一些怀疑。他想，管他呢，只要再过几天，行动成功了，我就要远走高飞了。

方远梦已确定会参加东路的战斗。而老周，将率领他的那支二十三人的行动队，在西路刺杀竹内。

而赵宏伟，要做的就是带好一块怀表，练好他的三寸不烂之舌。

胜利的希望似乎已不遥远，但是赵宏伟却忐忑得睡不着。天气一直很闷热，黑夜一直很压抑。

东路的游击队大部队会打胜仗吗？我方的人数固然是比日军的中队多了一倍，但是日军的武器那么好，东路的营救行动又是否真的能做到速战速决？这场战斗的关键就在于必须要速胜，如果不能速胜，战斗一旦陷入胶着，那后果是不堪设想的。狮丘山不比玉山，无险可守，易攻难守，万一日军的增援部队及时赶到，对游击队进行反包围，那三百个游击队员，恐怕都将埋骨青山。

竹内外出之后，渡边就是江庆县日军联队的最高指挥官。也就是说，这一场仗，日军的成败在很大程度上取决于渡边的调派。渡边会将竹内的生死放到首位来考虑吗？恐怕渡边也是非常希望竹内死的。但是，在渡边指挥期间，竹内若死了，渡边恐怕也是要吃不了兜着走的。这是一件很矛盾的事情。到时，渡边究竟会做什么样的选择呢？

赵宏伟一直非常希望，此次陪同竹内去听课的人会是渡边。这样一来，渡边就极有可能会和竹内一样遇刺身亡。赵宏伟花大力气给老周的行动队搞来了一把狙击枪，其实是希望渡边能死在这把枪下。而他最不希望，此次竹内的身边会有北川或赵驹。因为北川和赵驹，都是神枪手，且都心狠手辣。但是，事实上的结果却是，竹内指定了要北川陪同，而不要渡边。

中路和西路的那两支行动队，力量都很薄弱。虽然游击队已将他们最好的武器装备给了这两支行动队，但是，这两支行动队所要面对的，可能会是十倍于自己的敌人，甚至更多。他们又是否真的能拖住日军的大部队？就算拖住了，又能拖多久？如果东路的营救战不能速胜，那么，这两支行动队，都会被日军绞成肉泥。而日军只要消灭了这两支行动队，东路的游击队也就陷入了危机。

又或者，日军只要识破了中路和西路的这两支行动队在人数上的劣势，行动队想要拖住日军大部队的计划就会落空。被困在狮丘山上的那支日军车队里，不光有上海日军要的两百多个慰安妇，而且还有青梅县日军要的大量药品，江庆县的日军主力又怎么会不拼命去支援？而中路和西路的行动队，在人数上已到了极限。他们的行动，是需要将队员提前安排到江庆县城里或赵家镇上来潜伏下来的，人多了易暴露，北川像是已经闻到了一点味道。而且，人多了也不容易迅速撤退。

想来想去，问题确实很多。忐忑搅得赵宏伟心烦意乱，头脑微痛。他在黑夜里来回踱着步，胸口里闷得难受。

他忽然想：赵驹告诉我的会不会是假情报？我打听到的那些消息，会不会都不可靠？这件事，会不会从头到尾就是日本人设的一个圈套？

换一个角度来想，如果想要消灭玉山上的游击队，那么，最好的办法，就是引蛇出洞，调虎离山。如果能将游击队的主力消灭在狮丘山上，那么，玉山上剩下的那一百几十个人，就算有天险可守，也绝对敌不过日军大部队的围剿。游击队只要决定了去救人，那么，他们的被剿就成了定局。

赵宏伟的心一下子颤抖了起来。他冒出了冷汗。

他跌坐在了床上。

怎么办？怎么办？自己是不是想太多了？赵驹难道真的会帮着日本人来骗自己？他难道真的是死心塌地地要给日本人做狗？自己难道真的如此无能，连一条准确的情报都打探不到？自己难道真的会成为日本人消灭游击队的帮凶，为日本人立下大功？

难道真的要把自己的这些顾虑去告诉游击队？那万一自己的这些顾虑是多余的呢？这可是救出秀珍、救出那些女人的最后一次机会，自己要是弄错了，让游击队取消了行动，那就等于是自己亲手将秀珍、将那些女人推进了魔窟里去呀！秀珍会死的！

怎么办？到底该怎么办！

赵宏伟垂着头，十指深深地陷在头发里。他用手挤压着自己的脑袋，脸痛苦得都变了形。

夜，压抑得令人窒息。

赵宏伟蜷缩在床上，痛苦地颤抖着。

他决定不说。

每一场战争都充满了未知的变化，情报、谋略、行动，没有任何一个环节的成功可以向战争的结局承诺胜利。海呼浪啸的冲突中，多的是意外与懵懂的水珠。风云奇变的激流里，谁又真能主宰明天的阴晴？

人生，就是一场赌局。时代，创造着未知。

赌一把。赵宏伟想。天若怜百姓，定会诛妖除魔。

赵宏伟腿上的那条被日本兵刺伤的伤口长好了。老周给他拆了线。

方远梦也在，三个人都没说话。

赵宏伟默默地看着诊所里的一切，蓦然觉得有些感恩。人活着真好。白色的桌子，白色的椅子，白色的屏风，白色的床单。桌子上有一盆绿色的仙人掌，窗外晴朗的光照在仙人掌上，那绿色像是有了蓬勃的活力。洁白的诊所，真是人间一个美好的所在。能活着真好。

老周终于开口了，他对方远梦说，这两个月，你不能去上海了。

方远梦沮丧地说，是的，小夕被抓了。

老周捏了捏拳头，说，戴笠真不是个东西，把我们的情报交给日本人，让日本人把金条还给他，要钱不要脸的东西！

方远梦说，在蒋介石的眼里，我们共产党和日本人一样，都是他的敌人，甚至，他觉得我们比日本人更该死。

老周一拍桌子，说，中国就是坏在蒋介石的手里！他这个阴谋家、独裁者！

方远梦低着头，不说话。

老周沉默了一会儿，说，你放心，我们的同志一定会想办法把小夕给救出来的。

方远梦很难过地说，那一年，小夕说，想要和我拍一张合影，可是我却说，我们不可以在一起拍照。我真怕，有一天我会再也看不见小夕的样子。

老周行动队里那个年纪最小的少年，赵宏伟见过。剃着一个光头，像个小和尚似的，特别爱笑，走起路来像一阵风。他爱吃桃子，说吃了桃子能像孙悟空。他的外号就叫孙悟空，是老周队里最年轻的狙击手。孙悟空的父亲和哥哥，都是被国民党活生生地挖掉了心脏而死的。孙悟空告诉赵宏伟，他哥哥活着的时候，最爱看《西游记》，老说，玉皇大帝是个坏东西。

赵宏伟心里觉得很惭愧。在这样一个战火纷飞的年代，每个人似乎都在为了一些值得去坚守的东西而经历着血雨腥风，经历着家破人亡，但是他赵宏伟呢，是否追求过什么，坚守过什么？似乎什么都没有。他没有坚守过民族气节，没有捍卫过生命尊严，没有信仰过胜利与明天，没有追求过豪迈与慷慨。他对秀珍的爱，从来不是清清楚楚又一心一意的；在乞求渡边放过秀珍的时候，他还有过出卖方远梦的念头。他是怎样的一个不忠不仁、寡情背信的垃圾！他一直只想着自保，从来只懂得苟安，除了会摇头晃脑地念念书、讲讲学，又真的还会做什么！国家危难之时，他在伤春悲秋；民族存亡之际，他在蝇营狗苟。呸，一个可耻的赵宏伟！

赵宏伟感到很伤心。

他想，方远梦和老周，是不会不知道这次营救行动的危险性的。游击队的队长和政委，都是从大风大浪里出来的人，那些连他赵宏伟都能想到的麻烦问题，他们难道会想不到吗？这不可能。

也许，他们也是在赌。他们是在用自己的性命，来赌那些可怜女人们的明天。

他们比他伟大。他是在用别人的性命赌自己的幸福，而他们，是在用自己的性命赌别人的幸福。那个孙悟空，今年才十七岁。

赵宏伟不能容忍，自己这样的无耻。他不能容忍，别人在这次行动中抛头颅洒热血，而他却只需要在课堂上动动嘴皮子。如果他可以容忍，那么他已不配为人！不，绝不！

他想，不管他得到的那些情报里，究竟有多少消息是真的，最起码，竹内听课这件事，一定是真的。竹内的身边有了北川陪同，老周行动队的刺杀，一定不会那么容易成功。一定需要一个人，贴身刺杀竹内！

而这个人，可以是他赵宏伟。

这次的行动如果可以成功，那么那些原本要被运往青梅县的药品，都将会被送去根据地。根据地缺药缺钱，这些药品到了根据地，可以救活一大批抗日的英雄。而如果到了日本人的手中，只会让更多的恶魔复活。

那些女人如果能成功获救，游击队会根据她们的意愿，安排她们去大后方或根据地。有亲戚的可以投奔亲戚，没亲戚的共产党也会给她们安排一个落脚处。但是江庆县下面的各个镇子上，她们是回不去了。也许要到抗战胜利的那一天，她们才可以真正地回家。

而赵宏伟，并不打算把自己的参战计划告诉方远梦或老周。如果告诉他们，他们是一定不会同意的。无谓的争论只会浪费大家的时间，到最后肯定还是谁也不能说服谁。没错，他赵宏伟是没练过打打杀杀，他想去刺杀，那的确有点像笑话。但是，他想证明给所有的人看，他不是一个真正的卖国贼，这一点，比他的生命还要重要。也许这很冲动，但是，他要这个冲动。

他不打算带枪，枪在他手里就是个摆设，他根本打不准什么东西。他打算，就用那把匕首。就是那把老百姓原本用来吓他的匕首。他是没用刀捅过人，但是他用刀宰过鸡、切过肉，想来手法应该都是差不多的。他要证明给老百姓看，他外表虽然是一个汉奸，但内心仍然是一个中国人。

他把匕首磨得霍霍响。看着锋利雪亮的匕首，赵宏伟呵呵一笑。他忽然想，我去了，会不会碍事？

我只会成事，不会碍事。他又想。

中西两路的行动队，都有全员牺牲的准备。毕竟，这将是一场恶仗。老周也做好了牺牲的准备，他对他的队员们说，如果你们死光了，我也不会独活，大家要走一起走，人多了黄泉路上也热闹！

在那以后，赵宏伟心里对老周就有了一份尊敬。一个人是不是真英雄，也许，真的是只有到了鬼门关前，才能知道。

赵宏伟看见方远梦陪老周喝了一顿酒。赵宏伟听见老周说，我不怕死，可是我就怕，这次行动，我和我的队员们都死了，竹内也没死，那你说我们死得还有什么意义？

方远梦又向赵宏伟问起了两次姚志的事。赵宏伟最后一次说了“不知道”以后，方远梦深深地叹了一口气。赵宏伟知道，大家只能是在心里，默默地送姚志上路了。

后天就是六月初一了，一切都仿佛很平静。赵宏伟总觉得还像有什么事情没有做完。他出着神，在镇政府里行走。走着走着，一阵臭味扑鼻。他惊醒过来，原来不知不觉，是已走到了汉奸院的尽头，大垃圾场的铁栅栏外。

看着眼前的场所，他又想起自己那天爬铁栏进去翻尸体的情景。一切就像在昨天一样。可是从昨天到今天，人生的皱纹又深了几层。

悲愁之余，赵宏伟忽然发现，在垃圾场前的最后一排牢房的中间那一间牢房的周围，依旧是站着比其他的地方要密集得多的日本兵。他们个个荷枪实弹，表情严肃，在那间牢房外，构成了两层保护圈。

赵宏伟忽然想起了，那一天，那个高亢男声的呼号。

他的脑袋里“嗡”地响了一下。难道，这里面关的就是姚志？

赵宏伟从日本院那边过去，试图接近那间牢房。但是他刚一靠近，守卫的日本兵就警惕地要他止了步。他想编几句谎话，北川却刚好出现。北川问他要做什么，他说是刚丢了垃圾，随便走走，正要返回。北川问他丢的什么垃圾，他说，西瓜皮，西瓜皮。北川说，丢完了就快走吧，别在这里待着了，这里不是你该来的地方，以后要丢西瓜皮，就在铁栅栏外面丢。

哈依，哈依，太君，告辞。

赵宏伟转身就走，差点给了自己一记耳光。

大事将近，切勿节外生枝。他在心里告诫自己。

赵宏伟还有什么事情没做完呢？

遗书。

既然已决定了要去刺杀竹内，那么，死，当然是他必须要考虑的事情。风萧萧兮易水寒，荆轲的下场他是十分清楚的。专诸的结局他也是了然于胸的。总之，无论他的刺杀会不会成功，只要他真的出了手，他就会有死的可能。而且这可能的概率，还真的不低。他确实很害怕，但冲动让他无法退缩。人生自古谁无死，留取丹心照汗青，也的确是到了他用行动来向先贤们致敬的时候了。他已没有太多的考虑。冲动是不需要考虑的，甚至也不需要理解。

但是遗书是必须要写的，最好是能留下一首一唱三叹、催人泪下的七律。或者能留下几行名句也好，像谭嗣同的“我自横刀向天笑，去留肝胆两昆仑”就颇有壮士之风。不过据说，这两句并非谭公的原句，而是被活下来的梁启超修改后的改句。这总让赵宏伟莫名有些遗憾。他不喜欢修改历史，也不喜欢被历史修改。

赵宏伟挥毫泼墨，在灯下笔走龙蛇。他写了又撕，撕了又写，总觉得诗句了无生气，有画虎不成反类犬之嫌。他将笔一搁，颓然一坐，想，我真是个腐儒。

他想，我死了，秀珍一定会很伤心吧。

他闭上眼睛，感受着夜的寂静和孤独，心里忽然就有些酸痛。他很少会让自己去感受孤独，但是在这一刻，孤独却侵占了他的全身心，而他的脑海里，全是秀珍的影子。

孤独是给活着的人品尝的苦果，死了，就感觉不到了，他想。

莫名的忧伤像藤蔓一样生长了起来，时间与空间相缠，他的秀珍在藤蔓里美若女神。而忧伤浸透了所有的美丽与回忆，一切都在昏黄下摇曳。心酸像洇开的墨迹，时间也许会让它变干变淡，你却永远别想将它洗去。人的心思总是那么神奇，一缕情思倏忽而来，令人肝肠寸断，你却永远别想追根溯源，将它干干净净地掐断。思念或者忧伤，有时就像一幅油画，你想到的，看到的，也许都只是对真实的一份临摹，但就是这份临摹，比真实更撕心裂肺。因为让你难过的，不是在世界中的那个她，而是，在你心里的那个她。也许，一个人只要敞开心扉，就无法拒绝悲伤在某些时刻的突然降临；一个人只要不是没心没肺，心里就总会有些不能排遣的烙印。平时这些悲伤或忧郁都会隐姓埋名，可是只要夜幕来临，你的心，就会开始放映一部令你神往又神伤的电影。这便是爱情，这便是人生，这便是不能忘怀的记忆，这便是时间与空间给人织下的一张网。网里，有你永远伸手够不到的东西。这东西，似酒，如醉，昏黄，明丽，静止，生动，连诗也无法捉住它的一缕。它太美，美在你的生命里。

说不出的难受，像一条挣不开的绳索，像在悬崖的边上抓着一个人的手。突然翻涌起的渴望像是要扑进梦里去的鱼，可是梦里的水都是干涸了的幻觉。从此岸到彼岸的遥不可及，宛如从前生到来世的素不相识。最美的就在眼前，一伸手却是永别。距离将爱恋撕成雪片，雪片将呼唤冻成幻觉。没有什么能将真与假合成一体，海市蜃楼便是红尘最后的譬喻。就算是诗，也无法为你摘下一颗真实的星星。

缠绕的难过令赵宏伟难以喘息，一阵锥心的疼痛将他刺醒，某个声音逼迫着他睁开了眼睛。这个声音对他说：你死了，秀珍会绝望的。

是啊，她一定会受不了的。怎么办？

小菊已经不在了，他要是再死了，叫秀珍如何承受？

怎么办？

他一定不能死，但是他的生与死，他自己说了不算。那么就退出这次刺杀吧？绝对不行。如果他和她的幸福，是纯粹用别人的鲜血与生命换来的，那他宁愿丢弃这种幸福。想想看，要是那个小孙悟空在这次行动中牺牲了，而他赵宏伟却没有在这次行动中付出一滴血，那么他还有什么理由可以把自己当成是一个男人？他都不是男人了，还怎么去面对秀珍？儿女情事小，生死义事大。这点绝不能糊涂。

那么，就让上天来决定吧。要是行动失败了，那么他就会人头落地，而秀珍会被送去上海。要是行动成功了，他没死，秀珍也被救了出来，那么，他和她就会远走高飞，一起去开始新的生活。

要是秀珍被救了出来，而他却死了，那么，秀珍就需要一个谎言。他要

留下一个谎言给秀珍。这个谎言，必须要能让秀珍相信，他还活着，只是，今生她已不会再看到他。

他相信，只有这样，才能不至于让秀珍万念俱灰、绝望到底。

那么，这该是怎样的一个谎言呢？他该怎么编？

赵宏伟想起了那封被他丢到了角落里的信。就是那封，他原本想叫方远梦转交给秀珍的绝情信。

赵宏伟手里拿着这封信，眼泪忽然簌簌地掉了下来。他真的不知道，这样做到底对不对。

如果他也死了，那么，有什么理由可以让秀珍一直见不到他和小菊，但是却还能以为他们一直仍活着？——就说，他送小菊去南洋读书了？那么万一她想跟他和小菊通信呢？就说，他和小菊失踪了？难道要她费尽周折地满世界去找他们？就说，他和小菊被困在江庆县，出不去？那要是抗战胜利了呢？先骗一会儿是一会儿？到真相大白的那一天，她会不会崩溃呢？他已不在了，到时还有谁会安慰她？等等。

赵宏伟心乱如麻。

他想，小菊的死，是一定瞒不久的。但是，他的死，兴许瞒得住。只要给她这封信，让她知道，他并不是真的爱她，并不是真的想和她生活在一起，那么，他从她的世界中的消失，就有了完整而可信的理由。

只是，她会不会伤心欲绝？这伤心欲绝，会不会同样让她走向彻底崩溃？

赵宏伟真的不知道。

要么，让她知道，他爱她，但是他已死了；要么，让她知道，他还活着，只是并不爱她。

这无疑是一场赌博。他在赌，她可以失去什么。

最后，他还是选择了后者。

他想，只要她知道我还活着，也许，就还会有一丝爱的希望。只要有希望，人生就不会灭亡。

这是一场赌局中的赌局，他已在其中，押上了他所拥有的一切。他不知道最后的结果会是什么，他只知道，在这样的一个生死时代面前，他别无选择。

明天就是六月初一了。

赵宏伟将这封信交给了方远梦，说，时局动荡，大家都是朝不保夕，如果有一天我死了，请你为我做一件事，那就是千万不要把我的死讯告诉秀珍，另外，一定要将这封信交给她。

方远梦说，你怎么会死，真是胡说。

赵宏伟说，大战在即，意外难免，我只是未雨绸缪罢了。

方远梦说，明天，我还不知道自己会不会活下来。

赵宏伟说，我们都不会死的，我们都会活下来。明天的战斗，我们一定会胜利！

农历六月初一。

昨天，赵宏伟又去了一次小菊的坟前，看望小菊。他不知道该和小菊说些什么，他只是很想再来看看她。他感到很内疚，小菊是被他连累而死的，他到死也不会原谅自己。那么小的一个生命，连这个世界有多大还不知道，就已经被战争和仇恨的火焰烧成了惨不忍睹的尸体，这是谁的错？这都是大人的错。时代的每一次扭曲，都是人类千万个错误的合力。在战争面前，不抵抗者的不抵抗和侵略者的侵略，犯有等同的罪。侵略者杀戮无辜，不抵抗者放任侵略者的杀戮。所以，不光小菊的死里有赵宏伟的错，外面更多的人的死里，也有赵宏伟的错。从他投降、屈服的那一天起，他就已经是个罪人。

他在小菊的坟前站了很久，想了很多，心里难受，默默无言。最后，他说，小菊，伯伯要去杀鬼子了，伯伯不是汉奸。

赵宏伟没有将他怀疑姚志就被关在赵家镇镇政府的那间牢房里的事情告诉方远梦。因为，他毕竟只是怀疑，没有真的探查过。那怀疑，也只是电光石火一样突然袭来的一种感觉，他并没有什么确凿的证明或推理。他以前就一直没在意那间牢房的不同寻常。不过，也许他那突然而来的直觉也的确是错的。那里面也许是关着其他的重要犯人呢？军统特务，抗日分子，甚至是获罪的日本军官，都有可能。这种机要的事情，日本人又不会告诉他们汉

奸。所以，赵宏伟还是觉得，不要节外生枝的好。

另外，赵宏伟觉得，就算那间牢房里关着的真的是姚志，这个消息，对游击队来说，也已是没有了意义。因为，无论如何，他们都已是不可能再来得及去救姚志了。竹内当时给渡边下的命令是，到他离开江庆县的前一天，如果姚志还没有招供，就杀了姚志。竹内离开江庆县的前一天，那不就是六月初一吗？时间已迫在眉睫，什么都来不及了。

昨天，赵宏伟已嘱咐了方远梦，秀珍救出来以后，小菊的死，要暂时向她保密。她刚从那种环境里出来，暂时不能再受什么刺激了。方远梦说，我懂的，你放心。方远梦告诉赵宏伟，那些女人获救以后，游击队会先带她们上玉山落脚，等过一段时间以后，再分批将她们送去安全的地方。方远梦要赵宏伟也准备好，等大战结束之后，尽快从赵家镇上脱身，去玉山上与秀珍会合。游击队会安排他和秀珍两个人远走高飞，去一个安全的地方。方远梦说，你不用担心我会不会牺牲，就算我死了，我们的其他同志也会像我一样帮助你，我们共产党人不打诳语。

赵宏伟真的十分感动。如果有一天，中国的老百姓真的能够拥有选择执政党的权利，那么，他愿意选择共产党。

赵驹曾经说过，他赵宏伟还不知道自己究竟该恨谁，所以才发不出狠，打不中靶。赵宏伟觉得他说得不对。仇恨的子弹只能带来无尽的毁灭，一个人，只有有了爱，才能真正地一往无前。打枪不一定要狠，勇一样能让子弹直飞靶心。

火红的太阳从地平线上升了起来。今天的天空很明净。

赵宏伟想，很好，要是天上下了雨，那些埋伏在狮丘山上的同志就要受苦了，老天还是有眼的。

赵宏伟洗漱完毕，吃完早饭，穿戴整齐，便端坐了下来。

他小心地将那把匕首藏在了身上。很安全，很隐蔽。他有些激动。今天就是救出秀珍的日子，而他，也要在今天的行动中献出一份力。

他希望，今天正义的一方能赢得胜利，就算这是一场赌局，老天也不该把注押在罪恶的一边。

赵宏伟喝了一口水，然后站起来，走向了门外。

门外长风清朗，天空万里无云。

竹内刚迈进赵家镇小学的大门，两排长长的学生队伍就开始用日语集体欢呼：天皇万岁！大日本皇军万岁！竹内大人长命百岁！

赵宏伟仪表堂堂地站在学校操场的正中央，亲自点燃了六串鞭炮。鞭炮“噼里啪啦”地长响，鲜红的纸屑满地飞舞。学生们开始热烈鼓掌，大喊“欢迎”。

竹内身后的记者们，开始殷勤地拍照。竹内红光满面，笑得嘴都合不拢。

竹内向前走着，一边拍手，一边向站在两旁欢呼的学生微笑致意。赵宏伟迎到了竹内的面前，竹内十分高兴地和赵宏伟握了握手，说，赵镇长，辛苦了。

赵宏伟一个鞠躬，说，能为皇军效劳，是我最大的荣幸！

竹内哈哈笑了起来，连连拍手，说，好，好。

赵宏伟看见，陪着竹内的，果然是北川，而北川的身旁，是曾林。

赵宏伟领着竹内一行人去学校里的各处参观。他一边走，一边向众人讲述着这间学校的历史，着重赞扬了日本人到来以后，这间学校发生的可喜变化。学校走廊里的墙上，挂满了日本名人的画像或照片，在一间小礼堂里，甚至还供奉着一尊日本天皇的塑像。竹内对这尊塑像很感兴趣，赵宏伟介绍说，中国是一个喜欢崇拜神灵的民族，中国人崇拜什么神，就会把这个神塑成像，供奉起来，毫无疑问，大日本天皇，就是这些孩子们现在以及将来的神。竹内鼓掌，说，好，好。

竹内一行人在小礼堂里坐了下来，小憩了一会儿。赵宏伟为众人奉上了准备好的茶点。然后，就让一群孩子进来，表演起了准备好的节目。孩子们站得整齐，大声朗诵起了日本的一些诗歌，朗诵完了，又合唱了两首日本的民歌。记者们不停地拍照，竹内眉开眼笑。竹内对赵宏伟说，宏伟君，没想到这些孩子的日语已说得这么好，还会唱我们日本的歌，你劳苦功高，我十分喜欢你，你是我们帝国的有功之臣。

赵宏伟说，功劳不敢当，为天皇尽忠，是我分内之事。

竹内满意地大笑。他招呼了几个孩子过来，分给了他们一些糖，问，小孩，我们皇军好不好？

几个小孩异口同声地说，好。

竹内又问，等你们长大了，来当我们皇军的士兵，为天皇打仗，好不好？

小孩们又异口同声地说，好。

竹内真是高兴到了骨子里。他给了面前的每个小孩一把糖，然后又搂着两个小孩，让记者拍照。拍完了，他又让所有的孩子都围拢到了他身边来，让记者拍大合照。记者们拍完了一卷胶卷，赶紧又换上一卷新的胶卷。闪光灯亮个不停。

竹内忙着拍照的时候，曾林和赵宏伟站在礼堂门口。

曾林说，你还真是有本事，把这些孩子教成了这样。

赵宏伟说，没什么，我只是告诉这些孩子，他们将要和大人们做一场游戏，这场游戏的名字叫作，说假话不脸红。

曾林说，我就知道，你是个阳奉阴违的伪君子。

赵宏伟说，其实我们两个人没必要变成这样。

曾林说，是你害死了福宝，你忘了他平时是怎么对你的了？你从来就没有把我们当成是你的兄弟，你是个没有良心的人。

赵宏伟不再说话。曾林去了另一边抽烟。

赵宏伟看了看怀表，时间消磨得刚刚好。他一直以为自己今天会害怕的，结果，他冷静得出奇。

竹内和孩子们拍完了照，赵宏伟就又带着孩子们集体参拜了一下天皇的塑像。赵宏伟领着孩子们，在日本天皇的塑像面前，行了三跪九叩之礼。竹内感动得都无语了。

礼毕之后，竹内拍了拍赵宏伟的肩膀，说，宏伟君，你放心，我一定会举荐你做江庆县的县长的。你若不做，我问心有愧。

赵宏伟说，太君知遇之恩，宏伟没齿不忘。

众人出了小礼堂，赵宏伟便带他们去了大教室。

学生纷纷落座。竹内等人，坐在教室里的最后一排。记者们又开始换胶卷了。

竹内的原定计划是，中午十一点左右离开学校回县城，十一点半与众人在县政府的食堂里会餐，会餐之后，竹内便要准备临别事宜了。据悉，竹内下午还会召集联队里的主要军官和县政府里的汉奸头目，作一番临别演讲。可谓节目丰富。而赵宏伟必须要完成的任务是，确保竹内会在中午十二点左右离开学校回县城。因为只有这样，才能保证，在东路的营救战开始之时，竹内的队伍刚好是进入西路行动队的伏击圈。赵宏伟必须要让竹内在学校里多待一个小时。

赵宏伟将一幅大大的日本地图，贴在了教室里的黑板上。贴好以后，他还十分爱惜似的用手在地图上慢慢地抚摸了两下。然后，他用日语对学生们说，大家记住了，这，就是日本。

赵宏伟开始了今天的讲课，他今天讲的内容，主要是日本的名胜风光和历史文化。他一会儿讲中文，一会儿说日语，在两种语言和文化之间自由穿梭，游刃有余。中国人听得明白，日本人听得高兴。孩子们都是赵宏伟事先选择好并且训练好的，他们与赵宏伟配合默契，该笑时笑，该问时问，该鼓掌时鼓掌，该回答时回答。课堂上的气氛活泼又和谐，自由又紧凑。赵宏伟的话语时疾时徐，声音富有弹力而充满磁性，叙述张弛有度、收放自如，所讲内容生动别致，引人入胜。从富士山到北海道，从日本佛教到日本剑道，赵宏伟侃侃而谈。他引经据典，风趣幽默，口若悬河，滔滔不绝。站在讲台上的赵宏伟，就像是一个纵横天下而驰骋自由的骑士，他刀枪不入，锐不可当，意气风发，光彩照人。这是一种由内而外无法言说的魅力，这是一种学识与自信结合之后生成的权威吸引力。赵宏伟已经很久没有认认真真地讲过课了，以至于在今天以前，他还一直在担心自己是否宝刀未老。但是今日一课，犹如背水一战，他若折戟沉沙，后果不堪设想。于是他只得拼命，一拼命，没想到就至了化境，由无畏而至无敌的化境。

竹内也忍不住在下面露出了入神的笑容。他已完全陶醉在了赵宏伟的言语世界中，赵宏伟动听的讲述，就像是一匹奔驰的骏马，驮着他竹内在一个由想象与回忆交织而成的天地里自由地飞奔、散漫地流浪，他感到了难言的惬意与舒畅。赵宏伟用日语说了一个世外桃源的故事，竹内觉得这就是说给他听的，这个故事真的是太美妙了。竹内忽然开始十分向往没有战争的生活，他忽然发现了那种生活的美妙，他很想可以坐在自己家乡的花园里，喝喝清酒，吃吃寿司。为什么要出来打仗，为什么要向往权力，这些真的是对人生之美莫大的践踏。他觉得，赵宏伟真是一个古代田园里的诗人。

时光在愉悦的氛围里慢慢流逝，快要到中午十一点了。气温像是在渐渐升高，赵宏伟感到了一片燥热。他的心危险地晃动了起来，忐忑不安的火团在他的胸膛里上蹿下跳，隐秘的战栗越来越猛烈。他头脑里的神经绷得越来越紧，但他还是努力保持着镇静，挥洒着才情。他不小心掐断了一支粉笔，他的手差点抖了起来。是啊，他固然已做好了充分的准备，但世事并不总是在按照着人们的计划或预料行进，老天总是为万事准备了许多的意外。万一今天中午他不能将竹内拖到十二点钟离开，那么，今天的整场营救行动可能就会遭遇惨败。如果不能让竹内身陷险境，江庆县的日军主力就会无所顾忌地去围歼狮丘山上的游击队。到那时，他赵宏伟，就是千古罪人。搞不好，人家还会以为，是他勾结了日本人，出卖了游击队。

一切，都只能乞求老天的垂怜。

赵宏伟正在用中日双语讲述唐朝时日本与中国的交流关系。他说到了一段野史：当年，杨贵妃在兵变中被赐死，但是她其实并没有死，而是逃去了日本。

正说到扣人心弦的精彩处，下课铃刚巧响了。一切都和赵宏伟预先设计的一模一样。他微笑着停止了讲述。他对学生们说：同学们，今天就讲到这里吧，下课了。

学生们却都闹起了别扭，他们不肯下课，要听赵宏伟继续讲下去。赵宏伟假装为难地挠了挠头，又挠了挠头。他征询地望着竹内。竹内一时倒也是有些犹豫。

这时，两个和竹内贴身合过影的大孩子站了起来。他们欢快地跑到了竹内的面前，其中一个用流利的日语对竹内说：“竹内大人，我们都十分喜欢听赵老师讲的日本文化课，特别是今天有您在场，我们都觉得上课有了非常神圣的意义呢！今天赵老师讲的故事很有趣，里面不仅有日本的武士，还有中国的贵妃，我们真的很想听下去，就请竹内大人再多陪我们上一堂课吧！我们真的很喜欢您陪着我们一起上课，请求您了！”

另一个孩子也说：“是啊，竹内大人，就请您再多陪我们上一堂课吧，我们真的非常喜欢您！”说完，他又对一个拿着照相机的记者说：“我们真的非常喜欢竹内大人陪着我们一起上课，这种感觉真亲切！”

竹内看着面前的两个孩子，一时竟有些不知所措了起来。这时，北川对竹内说："大佐，我们必须要回去了。学生们喜欢听赵镇长讲课，那就让赵镇长留在这里继续给他们讲课，但是我们必须要回去了！"

一个稍小些的孩子就跑了过来，撒娇似的拉住了竹内的手，用流利的日语说："竹内大人，您是这么的慈祥，这么的可亲，我们今天见了您，才知道皇军的长官原来是这样容易亲近！我们都觉得您就像是我们的父亲一样，真的。父亲不是应该要和孩子一起听故事的吗？孩子如果没有父亲的陪伴，那么就算故事再精彩，听着又有什么意思呢？竹内大人，就请您陪我们一起听完这个故事吧，好不好？我们是真的好喜欢您哪，我们今天真高兴！就请您留下来吧，不要让您的孩子失望。"

学生们都喊了起来："请留下来吧，请留下来吧！"

北川对竹内说："大佐，我们必须要回去了，您下午还安排了许多事情！"

站在竹内面前的三个孩子一起恳求竹内："就请您再陪我们多听一堂课吧，亲爱的竹内大人，我们像爱父亲一样地爱您！"

学生们又一起喊："我们爱您，请留下来吧！请留下来吧，父亲！"

竹内激动得热泪盈眶。他握住了两个孩子的手，说："好，好，我留下来，陪你们一起听故事，一起上课，好不好？多可爱的孩子！"

北川又要劝谏，竹内做了一个手势，制止了北川说话。竹内陶醉地说："你听见了吗，这些孩子把我当成了他们的什么人？他们把我当成了他们的父亲！是父亲！真是多么美妙的赞美，多么美妙的赞美！"他对那些记者说："把这些孩子说的话统统都记下来，一个字都不许漏。特别是他们说我像他们的父亲的那些话，一定要在报纸上多印几遍，多印几遍！"

竹内大声地对所有学生说："亲爱的孩子们，我也真的是非常喜欢你们，喜欢和你们在一起呀！我们就一起来继续听赵老师给我们讲课，好不好？"

"好！"学生们都欢呼雀跃了起来。

赵宏伟擦了一把额上的汗。孩子们成功了，这是他最奢望而又最不敢奢望的事情，但是，孩子们居然成功了。用孩子的话语来留下竹内，本是赵宏伟心中最完美的方案，但是他对这个方案却始终没有多少成功的信心。虽然他已经训练了他们一段时间，但是他们毕竟还都是孩子，在这一刻以前，他从来也没敢在他们身上真正地放心。在他的心里，原本还预备着两个不太完

美的方案，但是，他最终还是选择了让孩子们上阵。因为，不完美的方案，就算成功了，后患也是无穷。他宁愿赌一把。所幸，他赌赢了。孩子们用他们出色的表演，帮助赵宏伟飞过了最难飞越的峡谷。他们已经为他留下了竹内，而到底能否将竹内拖到中午十二点，就要看他的了。

赵宏伟抖擞精神，披挂上阵。他不允许自己再有太多的思虑，因为思虑只会给他带来太多防不胜防的恐惧。他不允许自己再有一点点恐惧，因为恐惧只会令他丧失掉他眼前拥有的一切能力。他必须不去想那可能存在的许多意外，因为意外本是上帝的领地。人类能做的，只有尽力而已。

赵宏伟侃侃而谈，妙语如珠。他毕生的学识与才情，都像是为了今天而准备的。叙述的吸引力，在这里已远远超出了叙述本身的意义。谈古论今、挥洒才情，在这里已经成为一场生死搏斗的重要组成部分。赵宏伟的内心，有些滚热的激动与感恩。他这一生，都在百无一用是书生的哀叹中前行，生逢乱世，他一生的所学与才华，他精通的诸子百家，都只像是无用的屠龙之技，除了让他的头脑变得臃肿繁复、负重难行以外，没有为他的生命增添过一丝的光明与璀璨。站在轰轰烈烈、炮火纷飞的生死时代面前，他一直只是个无能为力、气若游丝的病人。但是今天，命运却给了他一个洗雪前耻、精忠报国的机会。不用他上马，不用他提枪，只要他站在课堂上，用他的才华作刀枪，跟敌人打一场没有硝烟的仗。他终于可以以一个书生的身份，去做一个战士才能做的事情，这是多么的不易。这场仗，他一定要打得漂亮。不图青史名，只为英雄气。今天，或许便是他那一身的才华，最有意义的一次绽放。

赵宏伟旁征博引，纵横古今，硬是将一段小小的贵妃野史拉成了一部大大的长篇传奇。叙述有声有色，论证有根有据。中国的历史文化与日本的历史文化被他搅成了一锅，却又丝毫没有胡扯之感。故事情节跌宕起伏，人物命运扣人心弦。无论是日本人还是汉奸，都不由自主地深深坠入了赵宏伟的叙述魔洞之中。赵宏伟为了更强更牢地吸引住竹内，干脆放弃了中文解说，采用全日语叙述。

时间在不知不觉中一分一秒地过去，赵宏伟一丝一毫不松懈地牢牢抓紧着竹内的注意力，他甚至不敢偷偷地看一眼自己的怀表，他怕自己任何的一个不寻常的小动作，都会引起难以想象的后果。他的头脑被绷得紧紧的。他感到，自己就像是在和时间进行一场拔河比赛。这场比赛，生死攸关。

赵宏伟瞥见了曾林轻蔑的目光，那目光冷冷的，饱含着厌恶。赵宏伟隐隐地有些难过，莫名感到很孤独。曾林一定以为，他这么费尽心机挥汗如雨地大拍竹内的马屁，是想要升官发财吧？他想。他觉得很孤独，因为他不属于任何一个群落。

竹内忽然发现，自己已经很久没有这样惬意过了。无所事事，听听故事，这是一种多么悠闲而自在的生存状态。他想起了自己年轻时在家乡的生活，那时的自己，还不爱权力，不爱地位，更不爱杀戮。那时，博学的父亲，也总是会在傍晚时的菜地里，讲故事给他听。那些岁月是多么美好。但是，时代却将每一个人的命运冲进了不一样的激流里。听着杨贵妃的故事，他还想起了自己年轻时热烈追求过的那个少女凉子。当年，如果不是军部派他去上海做间谍，那么，凉子也不会转而喜欢上那个叫藤田武的青年。凉子如果没有喜欢上藤田武，那么后来，凉子也就不会为了藤田武而自杀。他到现在还记得凉子临死前对他说过的那句话:“我不喜欢双手沾满了鲜血的男人。”是啊，像凉子那样美丽纯洁的少女，又怎么会真的爱上他这么一个以杀人为天职的军人呢？他觉得十分伤心。也许，从他将自己的人生和命运献给天皇的那一天起，他就已经和生命中的所有美好与幸福割断了联系。对于凉子死后的他来说，除了追求将军之位，又真的还有什么能让他感到一丝快乐呢？没有了，没有了。在漫长的杀戮生涯里，他甚至已很少再能想起凉子。凉子，那个清纯如茉莉的少女。但是今天，回忆与感伤却莫名如潮而至，令他隐痛不已。父亲在世时，曾告诉过他，一个人只有在临死前，才会想起自己生命中最重要的东西和最惋惜的事情。他一直是打算，要到自己年老时再去怀念凉子的，但是今天，赵宏伟却让他又情不自禁地想起了凉子，想起了那个太过美丽的凉子。赵宏伟在上面说些什么，对他来说其实并不重要，但他是真的希望自己能在这里再多坐一会儿，再多坐一会儿，他是真的希望，赵宏伟能再多说一会儿，再多说一会儿。忘记战争的感觉真好，忘记将军之梦的感觉真好。他真想能在今晚的梦里，再见一眼凉子。他真想回到初见凉子的那一刻。那一刻，凉子还不认识藤田武；那一刻，他的双手，还没有沾上鲜血。他，感谢今天赵宏伟漫长的讲述。他，感谢今天神明赐予他的追忆。而明天，他将依旧踏上追求将军之梦的道路。明天，他会依

旧踩着无数死者的头骨，去朝拜那权力与欲望的信仰。人生，永远没有重来的机会。

在十一点以后增加出来的上课时间里，不再有下课铃的提醒。而赵宏伟又不敢偷偷看表，怕会引起日本人对于时间的注意。因此，赵宏伟就只能靠看钉在教室窗台上的一根钉子的影子的位置来判断时间的进程。他嘴里说个不停，一颗心却始终都吊在嗓子眼里。他就怕突然又有人提醒竹内，是时候该离开了。

所幸，什么意外都没有发生。赵宏伟的演讲与叙述，连北川都听得入了迷。

终于，赵宏伟想：时间差不多了。他偷偷地看了一眼怀表，刚好是十一点五十分。

赵宏伟用了三四分钟的时间，圆满地结束了自己今天所讲的一切。赵宏伟对学生们说：同学们，下课了，老师要和你们说再见了。

学生们都站了起来，齐声说：老师再见！赵宏伟就笑了。他忽然有些舍不得这些孩子，有些伤感。他想，希望将来有一天，这些孩子，能受到真正良好的教育，长大了，做中国的栋梁之材。

竹内也站起来，和孩子们道了别。孩子们欢送了竹内。

赵宏伟会随竹内一行人一起去县政府里吃午饭。本来按照方远梦的要求，赵宏伟应该要推托掉这顿午饭，但是，赵宏伟并没有照方远梦说的做。赵宏伟知道今天这条回城的路通向的当然不是县政府里的餐桌，而是血肉横飞的鬼门关，他本该回避，但他无法退缩。想想那些幼小的孩子，长大了也许会做日本人的奴隶，他这个当老师的，是不是应该要为孩子们留下一个英雄的背影？至少要让那些孩子们长大了能知道，他们的老师，不是一个真汉奸。

赵宏伟要曾林留下来为他整理办公室，曾林不愿意。赵宏伟说，你就在学校里随便吃一点吧。曾林愤怒地说：你欺人太甚！

曾林还是上了车。

赵宏伟打开怀表一看，正是十二点零三分。

竹内邀请赵宏伟和他坐同一辆车，赵宏伟欣然应允。赵宏伟上了车。车子发动了。

车队浩浩荡荡奔县城而去。只有赵宏伟知道，这是一趟死亡之旅。

竹内感慨良多地对赵宏伟说，你讲课讲得真好，故事也说得好听，你把日本说得很美，让我想起了我的家乡。

赵宏伟说，谢谢大佐夸奖。

竹内说，等战争结束了，你可以去做一个诗人，一个能让别人想起家乡的人，必是这个世上最优秀的诗人。

赵宏伟说，到战争结束的时候，必是有很多人，已回不到自己的家乡了。

竹内说，是啊，是啊，我们有太多的士兵，已死在了中国的战场上，今天中午，我一定要敬那些死去的士兵一杯酒。

赵宏伟说，今天中午，我也想给那些再也回不到家乡去了的人敬一杯酒，我们要一醉方休。

竹内说，好，好，我们一起喝个痛快，喝个痛快！

车子在路上颠簸，车窗外的风景逝如流水。赵宏伟一直以为，到了这个时候，自己会陷入难以自拔的恐惧，但是，他没有。未知的死亡，似乎并没有散发出什么黑色的魔力，令他望而生畏，神志崩溃。今天最令他感到恐惧的就是他不知自己能不能成功地拖住竹内，但是现在，这一关已过去了。一切都在按照计划进行，胜利就在不远的前方等候，他又还有什么可害怕的呢？他以前从不知道，原来，自己并没有自己想象的那么怕死。

但是，他很忧伤。看着窗外流逝的风景，等待着战斗的临近，他的内心莫名卷起了一股忧伤的风暴。这令他十分意外。在一场生死攸关的战斗到来之前，他没有感到害怕但是却感到了忧伤，这是他没有料到并且也无法理解的。这股忧伤是那么滚烫，而波澜壮阔。他想起了自己人生中那许许多多最终落空了的美好愿望，他想起了自己人生中那许许多多再也见不到的熟悉面孔，他想起了自己人生中那许许多多无法再重温的灿烂情怀，他的内心泪流不止。人活着是为了什么呢？如果只是为了活着而活着，活着又真的有什么意思呢？白天若只有无尽的阴云，那么白天又有什么比黑夜更值得去珍惜的呢？活着如果只有绵绵的沮丧与不绝的痛苦，那倒还真的不如轰轰烈烈地去

死。当人生已碎得无法收拾，心中的千疮百孔已不可能再痊愈，用自己的生命来赌一场明天的日出，未必不是一个最美的选择。只是，自己还能看到那美丽的日出吗？日出之后，自己又能得到美丽的重生吗？一切都没有答案。只有对于自己人生中的那些病痛的忧伤是真的。它们强烈得足以令人去赴汤蹈火而不知畏惧不觉痛楚。赵宏伟忽然开始有些懂得了革命。大概，革命就是为了让活着能真正拥有活着的意义。一个人的痛苦积聚到了无法承受的地步，就会想要去拼命；一个国家、民族的人民痛苦积聚到了无法承受的地步，自然就会爆发革命。道理彼此相通。那些前赴后继的革命者，谁的背后又没有一片生命的眼泪？想此念此，赵宏伟死志愈坚。

竹内正在座位上闭目养神。此刻，这辆车内只有司机、竹内和赵宏伟三个人，赵宏伟若要杀竹内，此时此刻无疑是最佳时机。但是，不能忘记，杀竹内不是西路行动队此次战斗的最终目的，西路战斗的真正目的，是要吸引住县城日军的大量兵力，迫使县城的日军无暇去增援东路的押送部队。杀竹内，只是用来吸引日军兵力的一个手段。此刻竹内的卫队还没有进入老周行动队的伏击圈，双方还没有打起来，赵宏伟若在此刻就杀了竹内，只会让整个西路行动计划彻底泡汤。

赵宏伟摸了摸藏在自己身上的匕首。他有些开心。没有一个日本人，想到他赵宏伟今天身上带了匕首。日本人再狡诈，终究也还是人。人会犯的错，日本人都会犯。所以，日本人不是不可战胜的。日本军队也不是打不垮的。只要坚持打下去，抗战定会胜利，他想。

赵宏伟看了看怀表，已是十二点一刻。东路的战斗应该已经打响，可惜在这里并不能听见那么远的地方的枪炮声。赵宏伟将头探出车窗，看了看外面的情形。马上就要进入老周行动队的伏击圈了。

赵宏伟看见，天空晴得真美。

竹内的车队，快要接近江庆县城的西城门了。

“嘭”的一声巨响，竹内车队的第一辆车，被炸成了一团熊熊燃烧的火球。

整个车队的行进戛然而止。有那么一两秒钟的时间，整个世界都仿佛是寂静的。然后，便是像洪水决堤了一样的骚乱。北川将头探出车窗外，大喊:“倒车！倒车！”

“嘭”的又一声巨响，竹内车队的最末一辆车，也被炸成了一团火球。烈焰张牙舞爪，火光红艳冲天。前后两团烈火织成了两道峭壁，整个竹内车队都像是被困在了危急的峡谷中。

北川跳下车，拔出军刀，大喊:“保护大佐！准备战斗！”

站在两辆卡车上的五十多个日本兵，全部跳下了卡车，围绕着竹内所坐的汽车，形成了两层保护圈。几个汉奸也都下了车，自觉地站在了保护圈的最外围，充当日本人的盾牌。那些记者，则是都下了车，自顾自地逃命去了，也没人管他们。

一刹那，从大路左边的废旧城墙后与大路右边的树林里，同时射出了密集的子弹来。日本人也开了火。一瞬间，枪火乱流，子弹如雨，鲜血四溅。

竹内蜷缩在车厢里，赵宏伟也蜷缩着。赵宏伟从未经历过这种阵势，他有些目瞪口呆，头脑空白。外面的枪声震耳欲聋，惊心动魄。赵宏伟的心像筛糠一样发着抖。他壮起胆子伸头往车窗外一望，只见就在这辆车子的不远处，日军的机枪手正在用机枪向树林里猛射。“嗒嗒嗒”的机枪声像最恐怖的惊雷，连绵不断地响个不停。子弹如暴雨的雨点般密集，树林里木屑横飞，枝折叶碎。赵宏伟看见一名行动队的队员，脑袋被子弹打了个稀烂。

赵宏伟缩下了脖子，他还从未见过人的脑袋被打得稀烂的样子，但是现在他看到了，他的眼睛里就像是被钉进了两根钉子。他痛得想哭，又怕得想哭。他发现，自己的脚软了，手也软了。自己今天仿佛一直拥有着的一副钢筋铁骨，像是突然被人给抽走了。自己今天一直满满地鼓在胸腔里的一团气，也像是都被外面的子弹给震碎了。他不是蜷在车厢里，而根本就是软塌塌地瘫在了车厢里。

软弱不期而至，抵抗无能为力。对自己的失望在一瞬间就占领了赵宏伟的全身心。这失望让人钻心地痛，这痛里还晃荡着几分绝望。难道自己的勇敢只是暂时的？难道自己终究只是个胆小鬼？一种痛彻心扉的沮丧令他的心跳冷若冰霜。他打起了寒战，而他的心越冷，气越软。但是一个微弱的声音却又同时在他的心里不断地回荡着：一定要救出秀珍，一定要救出秀珍。这声音就像一把钢锥，每刺他一下，他就痛得几乎想要跳一跳。灰暗而纠缠的痛苦在他的软弱与不甘间来回冲撞，伴着外面激烈的枪声，将他折磨得有气

无力，意志消沉。但是那个声音却还在不停地响：一定要救出秀珍！

赵宏伟深吸了一口气，又深吸了一口气。他像默默念咒一样地要求自己：英勇，英勇！

一颗子弹从北川的肩膀处擦过，北川的皮被蹭破了。火辣辣的疼痛让北川不得不重新估计一下眼前的形势。对方是谁？对方究竟有多少人？对方的目的是什么？这些暂时都还很难判断。对方的火力不如自己这边，这点现在已可确定。但是，对方是在左右夹击自己的部队，他们有城墙和树林做屏障，而自己这边，只有一排排成长蛇形的汽车，士兵们无论是躲在汽车的哪一边，都暴露在对方的枪口之下，毫无遮挡。若不是有两挺机枪压阵，对方露头很难，自己这边的伤亡恐怕会更大。怎么办？

北川看着自己这边已倒下了十几个人，而对方，似乎才死了三四个人，不禁眉头紧皱。他离开了士兵围成的保护圈，孤身一人飞快地奔向那辆停在后面的大卡车。子弹从他身旁“嗖嗖”地飞过，他毫无惧色。终于跑到了那辆大卡车的驾驶室旁，“啪”，一颗子弹，击中了他的左臂，血流如注。北川看都不看自己的伤口一眼，右手打开了驾驶室的门，一下子就跃进了驾驶室里。

北川将这辆卡车开到了与另一辆卡车平行的位置，两辆卡车之间，留出了一段宽阔的地带。这条地带里，子弹基本飞不进来。北川跳出了驾驶室，往竹内所坐的那辆小汽车旁跑了过去。

竹内蜷缩在车厢里，正在愤怒地空骂着北川，抱怨他为什么还没有把袭击者解决掉，突然，“咣当”一声，又一扇车窗玻璃被子弹给打碎了。紧接着，又一颗子弹飞进来，刚巧就把这辆车里的司机给打死了。这个司机本来是趴在竹内身上保护竹内的，现在他中弹死了，血流了竹内一身。竹内也不敢将这个死人推开，毕竟他还是需要用他来挡子弹的。竹内开始大喊北川，要北川过来。

赵宏伟不知道那些逃跑的记者是否已将竹内遇袭的消息报告给了县城的日军。对于传递竹内遇袭消息的这一个环节，方远梦他们是做了三种准备。第一，就是那些逃跑的记者会去向县城的日军报告；第二，就是北川会派兵去向县城的日军报告；第三，就是游击队的人，会装成老百姓，去向县城的日军报告。相应地，老周的行动队事先也做好了安排：一不杀逃跑的记者，二不杀单独突围的日本兵。但是，在赵宏伟心底，始终是不相信那些记者的素质的。汉奸记者都是些胆小怕事好大喜功恬不知耻的东西，他们在逃跑之后，不一定会马上去向县城里的日军报告竹内遇袭的情况。他们要是先去酒馆里喝压惊酒怎么办？他们要是先回家去舞文弄墨怎么办？他们又不是军人。

“大佐，我们的人看样子是顶不住了，要快让北川大尉派人去县城里叫援军才是。”赵宏伟说。

“对，对，要快去叫援军！”

“万一对方是共产党的大部队，那他们的目标恐怕就是您了。一定要叫渡边中佐派大部队过来增援，这样才有救您出去的希望。我们不怕玉碎，但您不同，您绝对不能出事。”

“是的，是的，我是绝对不能出事的！”竹内将车门打开了一条缝，往外大喊：“北川！北川你个混蛋！快过来！”

北川刚巧跑到了竹内的小汽车旁边，他拉开了小车的前后车门，气喘吁吁地对竹内和赵宏伟说，快，快出来，这里不安全，我带你们去那边。

北川的话音刚落，又有两颗子弹，打在了这辆小车的车头上。竹内赶紧爬出了车厢。赵宏伟提了一口气，抖擞精神，也爬出了车厢。

赵宏伟一出车厢，城墙后跟树林里的射击忽然就都停止了。北川没有留意，趁着空，赶紧护送着竹内和赵宏伟跑去了那两辆卡车中间的安全地带。然后，他便是又叫那些战斗着的日本兵，也都躲进了那条安全地带里。两个机枪手向北川报告，今天大家带出来的子弹都不多，不能再一直用机枪了，不然子弹很快就会被用光。北川用右手捂了捂自己的左臂，嘴唇一咬，没有说话。

行动队没有开火，日本兵也停了火。世界一下子又变得很安静。安静得仿佛只留下了人的喘息。竹内惊魂未定地东张西望着，摸了摸自己那把漂亮的军刀，想要拔，犹豫了一下，改成了拔出别在腰里的手枪。北川从自己的衣服上撕下了一根布条，布条的一端用牙咬着，自己给自己包扎了左臂上的伤口。赵宏伟则一动也不敢动地蹲着，连呼吸也小心翼翼，就仿佛他只要稍微用力地呼吸一下，这个世界的和平就会被他给碰碎。安静是那么的可贵，还是没有人开火。

竹内要北川马上派人去县城里叫部队来增援，北川说好。另外，北川还想多派一个人，去叫赵家镇上的部队也过来增援。竹内说好。竹内说增援的人越多越好。

赵宏伟并不担心赵家镇上的日军会过来碍事。因为他和方远梦他们早就算计好了，设下伏击圈的这个地方，离县城里的县政府和兵营都十分地近，而离赵家镇的镇政府却是相当远，竹内和北川若是调援兵，第一选择只能是去调县城里的兵。远水救不了近火，这点日本人不会不明白。而基于对竹内身份的考虑，从县城里派出的援兵，数量肯定不会少。当然，要想让县城里调出大部队来，还必须要让竹内和北川相信，他们面对的不是一小股军事力量。而现在北川提出了也要调赵家镇上的部队过来，就说明他已经是陷入了不自信的判断里。他起码已不能断定，双方战斗力量的确切比例。而只要一切进行得顺利，等到赵家镇上的日军增援赶到这里时，东路的营救行动恐怕已是进行了大半。到了那时，就算这里的县城日军要回撤过去增援东路受困的日军，再也来不及了。所谓的围魏救赵，声东击西，恐怕就是这么个意思。

北川叮嘱去县城报信的那个兵，一定要让县城里多派些人出来，不然真的会顶不住。竹内对那个兵大吼，告诉渡边那个混蛋，给我调一个大队过来，一个大队！带迫击炮！

北川大喊，跟我一起掩护他们出去！

除了竹内和赵宏伟，所有人都冲出了那条安全地带。他们分成了东西两拨人，一拨掩护那个去县城报信的兵，一拨掩护那个去赵家镇报信的兵。一时枪声大作，吼声四起。

但是，行动队只是稍稍回应了几枪。

两个报信的日本兵都跑了出去。掩护他们的日本兵都迅速回撤到了安全地带。

赵宏伟想，其实那个去赵家镇报信的兵，应该要打死他才对。

但是一直都没有再响枪。

日本兵都靠在卡车上喘气。他们开始起了疑惑：是不是对方撤了？

只有赵宏伟肚子里明白是怎么一回事。老周他们一定是突然看到了他，才停手的。他的参加事先没有通知任何人，老周他们现在一定是疑惑重重。

赵宏伟的心里一紧。他绝不能给行动队帮倒忙。他抬眼四望，看见这里的汉奸已经只剩下了三个人，其中一个是曾林。他们都背靠在卡车上，正在给枪里装子弹。赵宏伟深吸了一口气，站了起来，走到了曾林的面前，曾林很意外地看着他。他真诚地握住了曾林的手，轻声地说，以前的事希望你能原谅我，不管你相不相信，我都想告诉你，我一直真的拿你当我的兄弟。

说完，赵宏伟就向另外的那两个汉奸一抱拳，胸一挺，用汉语十分大声地说："兄弟们，今天就是我们同生共死的日子，能和你们一起走过这段路，我荣幸之至！今天，就让我们一起，送敌人去见阎王爷！"

说完，他又向三个汉奸深深地作了一个揖。三个汉奸都被感动了。"赵镇长，我曾林糊涂，说过的那些混账话，你别放在心上。"曾林激动地说。

三个汉奸的手，都和赵宏伟紧紧地握在了一起。

赵宏伟激动地伸起了一个拳头，用汉语用力地大喊："兄弟们，一会儿都给我狠狠地打！狠狠地打！"

话音一落，行动队枪声大作，子弹又都像雨点一般往日本人这边飞了过来。

汉奸们都吓得蹲了下去。赵宏伟也抱头蹲了下去。

北川锋利地看着赵宏伟，问，你刚才喊了些什么？

赵宏伟还没开口，曾林就抢先替他回答了北川的问话。他告诉北川，赵镇长是在鼓舞他们的士气，说要和他们同生共死，共抗敌军。竹内听了点点头，赞许地说，很好，很好，赵镇长是个勇敢的人。北川就不再说什么了。

两辆大卡车并排地停着，无论是从树林里还是城墙后射出来的子弹，都没有办法打到两辆卡车隔出来的中间地带里去。而在这两辆卡车的左右两边，就是大路的两旁，地势都有些起伏，行动队的人没有办法往卡车底下打子弹。行动队倒是还有手榴弹，但这是要用来对付日军的增援部队的，再说了，赵宏伟现在也躲在两辆卡车中间，不能炸。

日本人都躲在两辆卡车隔出来的安全地带里，只要不随便露头露身，就不会有事。行动队的子弹在卡车的铁皮上叮叮当当地响了一阵，就也不响了。行动队又停火了。

赵宏伟大着胆子探出半个身子去张望，看不见行动队员的人影子。他们隐蔽得很好，这让他觉得很欣慰。但是他们现在打不着日本人，战斗僵持

着，该怎么办呢？赵宏伟心沉沉地，将身子缩回了安全地带里。他看见，竹内的神态，已经开始变得冷静了起来。

四周很安静。

北川用右手对两个日本兵做了几个手势，日本兵点点头。然后，北川就丢掉了手枪，端起了一条步枪。

赵宏伟心里一颤。随便哪条步枪到了北川的手里，就是一把狙击枪。他要干什么？

两个日本兵大喊大叫着，跑出安全地带，朝着树林里猛开了几枪，然后，又迅速地跑回了安全地带里。就在日本兵回到安全地带的那一瞬，北川就蹿了出去。

北川从容地对着树林里开了一枪，然后，就又躲了回来。

两个日本兵又大叫着跑出去，对着城墙那边乱开了几枪，然后一下子跑了回来。北川紧接着就跳出去，对着城墙那边迅速开了一枪，然后再次躲了回来。

一片死寂。

赵宏伟心底一团疑惑。他把心一横，探出头去再次张望。只见，在树林那边和城墙那边，各新死了一名行动队员。他们的尸首躺在地上，脑袋上流着血。

曾林一把将赵宏伟拉了回来，“你不要命啦！”曾林关切地说。

赵宏伟明白了。北川是先让小兵出去乱打，然后引行动队员出来打小兵，而就在行动队员露头出来要打小兵的时候，他北川，就刚好可以打爆行动队员的头。露头的行动队员，甚至还没能来得及开上一枪，就已死在了北川的枪下。

北川这个魔鬼。

北川又故技重演了一次，但是这一次，行动队并没有再上当。

战斗再一次陷入了僵持，一片死寂。

太阳火辣辣的，天晴得有些苍白。阳光很耀眼，认真去看，眼睛会觉得有些痛。在两辆卡车隔出来的中间地带里，躺着三具日本兵的尸体。他们是战斗一开始就死了的，死相各异，其中一个日本兵的两条腿，还被压在一个卡车轮胎下。是北川将这辆卡车开过来作屏障时轧到的。这个轮胎就这样停在这两条腿上面，就像一个秤砣压在两根面条上。被压住的腿的部分明显变得很扁，跟没被压住的腿的部分形成了鲜明的对照。可以想象得出，那里的骨头一定已是粉碎，就像一只口袋里被砸碎的瓷器。被轧处鲜血淋漓。血的红，在没有阳光照到的地方散发着幽暗的冷，这冷，宛如生锈的金属。赵宏伟想，说不定，这个兵也曾糟蹋过秀珍。

死亡的气息是这样实在。此时此地，死亡已不再只是一种揣测，选择里也已无法再容纳更多的迟疑或考虑。每分每秒的流逝都快得像闪电，又慢得像龟爬。一切的发生都蕴含在饱胀的战栗之中。恐惧在这里已不再让你意识到它是恐惧，它满满地不断膨胀而无法外溢，只能浓缩成饱含重量的压抑。赵宏伟的脸皮发烫，脑子里却冰凉。一串子弹将人的脑袋打得稀烂的画面，在他的脑海里像发了疯似的不停旋转，不停旋转着，夹杂着恶心、怜悯、痛苦、恐怖的复杂感情，就像一瓶看不见的药水，将他今天一直仰仗着的那股英气概全部泡成了软泥巴。他以前从不知道，人是可以在头碎了以后，再倒下去的。

从恐惧在他心中重生的那一刻起，他就又开始了与自己的斗争。很奇怪，他这一生，似乎总是在与自己斗争，与自己的七情六欲斗，与自己的思想考虑斗，与自己的软弱无能斗。他这一生，似乎就是光活在一场永无止境的心灵战役里了。他很疲惫，也很无助。他的心灵斗争，从来没有给他带来过功成名就，也从来没有给他带来过一帆风顺，相反，不如意事倒是常有常新。三思而后行，似乎就是对他人生的一个诅咒。他自问这一生事事都对得起儒、道、佛三家的精神和智慧，但是他的人生路却莫名一日比一日更难走。英雄每多屠狗辈，走到了人生的后半段，他却分明开始向往无知无畏。他的心中充满了不可调和的矛盾。

日本兵踩踏着日本兵的尸体。在这样一个生死交错的时刻，已经没有人还会注意到要尊重尸体。奔跑时踩到了哪具尸体的肚子，嫌碍事将哪具尸体踢开了一些，这些事情在这一刻都获得了理所当然的意义。如果你在这一秒钟里因为要顾念感情而不踩着尸体前进，费事去多绕两步路，那么在下一秒钟里，你就很有可能会成为一具新的尸体。一些日本兵就站在日本兵的血泊里，而他们丝毫也没有感到恶心或罪恶，这就是战争，这就是现实。

而这个现实却让赵宏伟难受得快要吐了。一个死了的日本兵流出的肠子

上，停了好几只苍蝇。一个日本兵脑袋上的枪眼里，钻进去了一条黑虫子。赵宏伟觉得这条虫子就像是钻到了他的嘴里。赵宏伟觉得很恶心。他想闭上眼睛，但眼前的一切却又仿佛具有某种力量，迫使他无法闭上眼睛。他无法回避现实。而事实上，他这一生，也没能躲过任何现实。眼前的这个战场，仿佛就是他这一生中那无数细碎而无际的心灵斗争的一个缩影。他从来都不是很清楚，自己在一场斗争里，究竟能为自己做些什么。或者说，他从来都不知道，能令自己前进的勇气在哪里。勇者无惧，什么是勇？在这场战斗真正开始以前，他还以为自己今天已经做到了英勇，但是，看来是江山易改，本性难移。他感到了来自灵魂深处的沮丧。这沮丧，哀入肺腑，浸透骨髓。

他想，不知道秀珍现在怎么样了？想起了秀珍的脸，他的心里碾过了一片重重的难过。他差点掉下泪来。他赶紧深吸了一口气，又深吸了一口气。一定要救出秀珍来，他又想。

天空凝固着，没有流动的云或飞翔的鸟。太阳的光带着连绵的热，只要伸手摸一摸那光里的温度，就像是摸到了天公的心窝。天空离人从来都不是那么遥远。阳光缠绕在人的手上、脸上，人就像是天空之树上的一片叶子。赵宏伟想，此刻的秀珍，不知是否也已看到了这美妙的阳光？如果看到了，那么，他和她，就已是被上帝之手紧紧地连在了一起。自然是多么美好，人与人之间的相连，又是多么奇妙。如果秀珍愿意，他愿意陪她看一辈子的阳光。只愿人生不再有一丝阴霾。想念是那么浓重，以至于让人都无法再想起想念的理由。时光若可倒流，只愿时针能永远停留在那心不想离开的地方。穿过重重的沮丧与失望，虚无缥缈的思恋，还是像太阳一样炽热耀眼。

竹内车队的首尾两头，两道火屏依旧在张牙舞爪。火焰熊熊燃烧，废车阻塞于道，车队进退无路。在大路左右两边的泥地上，紧靠着那两道火屏的地方，又刚好是各有着一大片又宽又长的乱石地带。那些石块或石条大小不一，高高低低，有棱有角，汽车的轮胎根本就不可能过得去。竹内的车队被困死在一个接近于八边形的包围圈内，更何况，不远处还有许多的子弹和炸药都在等待着出击。日军焦头烂额。

但是，同在这一困境中的赵宏伟心里却是很清楚，日本人的这一困境只是暂时的。真正的困境属于老周的行动队。只要日军的增援一到，老周的行动队就会陷入覆没的绝境。死神就躲在时间的背后，张开着血盆大口，等待着行动队往它的嘴里行进。行动队的队员，已经不到二十个了。安静地去听，你几乎能听到每一个明亮的生命在死神的嘴里被嚼碎的声音。就像落叶窸窸窣窣的低语。行动队的赴死之路不可更改，他们唯一能做的，也是必须要做的，只是将这条路拉得更长，把激战的时间拖得更久。这就是他们今天的任务。赵宏伟不知道，今天过后，他们之中是否还会有人幸存。赵宏伟不知道，在视死如归之前，他们的心中，是否也曾有过恐惧和软弱。赵宏伟不知道，在他们之后，还会有多少人走上他们的道路，后来人的脸上，是否也会有着和他们一样的义无反顾。赵宏伟只知道，今天，他和他们在一起。

在行动之前，大家最担心一个问题，那就是竹内会不会被日军的增援部队给活着救走。毕竟，没有人能保证，一定可以杀死竹内。赵宏伟之所以参战，就是想要为刺杀行动的成功多创造一个机会。但是，事情的发展却总是和事先的想象不太一样。日本人都挤在安全地带里，众目睽睽之下，他赵宏伟根本就不可能拔出匕首来刺杀竹内，拿枪也没机会。而且，他和日本人在一起，反而还妨碍了行动队，让他们没办法直接扔手榴弹。真是诸事不顺。

赵宏伟偷偷看了一眼竹内，竹内已经褪尽了慌乱的神态。他就那么蹲在地上，在默默地把玩着他的那把手枪。他的脸上结着一层冷酷的冰，安静得毫无表情。这样的一个竹内，让赵宏伟的心里起了一丝寒意。

从远远的西城门方向，传来了隐隐的爆炸声。北川和那些日本兵都起了一丝慌张，他们面面相觑，不知道究竟是发生了什么事。

赵宏伟估计，是中路行动队在佯攻县政府了。

这时，突然，一个站在安全地带里的日本兵中了枪，倒了下来。又一个站在安全地带里的日本兵中了枪，倒了下来。日本兵们大惊。惊骇中，又一个兵中了枪。子弹都来自安全地带的西边，一个看上去根本就没有任何人在的方向。日本兵们纷纷都举起了枪，向着西边胡乱地射击了一通。子弹都飞入了茫然的空旷中，就像瞎了眼的鸟。没人知道自己究竟是在打什么。一眼望出去，依旧是空旷的大路和空旷的土地。哪里有什么敌人？恐惧就像空旷一样庞大。

又一个日本兵中枪身亡。

北川这时举起了枪，跑到了这条安全地带西边的边缘处，向外连开了几枪。同时，他要求所有人都挤到安全地带的东南角里去，挤得越紧越好。

北川看到了敌人。敌人是一名狙击手。就在这条安全地带的西南方向，距离安全地带极远的一个地方，有着一座小小的民房。这座民房那么小，那么远，从日本兵所在的这里望过去，它简直就像是一只已经死了很久的昆虫。它灰黑肮脏，破败不堪，死气沉沉，而微若尘埃。但是就是从它的屋顶上，射出了令人无法躲避的子弹。待在这座民房的屋顶上，刚巧可以从侧斜面看见将近半条安全地带里的事物。而凡是狙击手的目光所能到达的地方，狙击手的子弹也同样可以到达。日本兵们无处躲藏。

只有安全地带里的东南角，是狙击手的目光所难以到达的。因为狙击手所在角度的关系，现在的这条安全地带里，还有一块三角形的区域是子弹无法触及的。但是这块三角形区域里，最多只能容纳十几个人。竹内和赵宏伟本来就在这块三角区域里，倒也无事。小兵们不敢太挤着竹内。小兵们都想挤进这块三角区域里来。但是这是不可能的。于是，在安全地带东边的边缘处，就不断地有小兵被挤出去。而无论是哪个日本兵，只要他被挤出了安全地带，迎接他的，就只有从城墙后和树林里射出的子弹。日本兵此刻全都成了热锅上的蚂蚁，他们都想求生，但是在混乱中，又只是在不断地送死。

北川的连续射击，一时压制住了远处的狙击手。狙击手无法抬头。但是北川身上的子弹已所剩无几了。况且，他也已意识到了背后正在发生的混乱和伤亡。他的心一时也乱了。他又一次装填子弹的时候，居然忘了后退至三角区域隐蔽。

似乎是天意，一直都没有再抬头的狙击手，在此刻，重新又抬起了头来。

“啪”一枪，北川的左肩中了弹。北川的步枪一下子就掉在了地上。

竹内一下子就站了起来。他对拥挤着的士兵大吼：全部给我滚到北川那边去！向着狙击手隐蔽的地方射击！保护你们的长官！

日本兵们全都涌到了北川的身旁。不管打得准打不准，他们开始集体向狙击手所在的方向开枪。

又一个日本兵倒下了。

竹内大声地问：北川，你还能不能战斗？

北川用一只右手捡起了枪，大声地回答：能！

竹内说：好，那我们就准备突围吧！

赵宏伟一下子就急了。他赶紧说：大佐，你不能冒险！

北川犹豫了一下，也说：是啊，大佐，我们应该等待援军，贸然突围，您会很危险的。

竹内对北川说：你没看到我们的士兵已经死了多少了吗？再在这里待下去，所有人都活不了！

北川说：我再去开一辆汽车过来，只要有汽车挡着，我们就能坚持下去。

竹内说：被动防守，守得再久也只能是坐以待毙！渡边那个王八蛋，到现在还没派援兵过来，我怀疑他就是想看着我死！

赵宏伟说：大佐三思！三思！敌人众多，我们冲不出去的！您的生命宝贵，我们绝不可以冒险！

竹内说：包围我们的，最多只是一支小股部队。你们没发现吗，在炸完汽车之后，他们连一枚手榴弹都没扔过。他们要是还有手榴弹或其他炸药，我们早就都被炸死了。大部队有这么穷的吗？

赵宏伟无言以对。

竹内命令：北川大尉，立刻率领所有人，保护我向西城门方向突围！不惜一切代价，送我进县城！

北川下令，全体人员不惜一切代价护送竹内大佐突围。突围的方法很简单，就是从火屏与树林之间的那片乱石地带中间跑出去，跑上大路，跑向西城门。不计较伤亡，只要护得严，只要跑得快，竹内完全可以安然无恙地冲出这个伏击圈。

又一个日本兵中了狙击手的子弹。

北川大喊了一声“大日本帝国万岁”，然后便是率领着众人，保护着竹内，从安全地带里冲了出去。

行动队的子弹密集地飞向了日本人。赵宏伟故意和日本人拉开了一些距离，以免妨碍到行动队的射击。曾林和另外两个汉奸一起保护着赵宏伟。

日本兵层层围裹着竹内，充当着竹内的人体盾牌。北川的左袖已完全被鲜血浸透，血不断地往地上滴，但他依然还在保护着竹内。他单手持着步枪，还在不停地射击、射击。他的牙齿紧紧地咬合在一起，双唇绷得僵硬，两颊的肌肉像扭曲的铁块一样隆起着。痛苦在他的脸上凝固着，像敲

不碎的石板。一支枪里的子弹打完了，他就丢掉这支枪，重新又在地上捡起一支来。

日本人一边在乱石地带里飞跑，一边与左右两边的行动队员激战。保护着竹内的日本兵，一个又一个地倒下。一个又一个地死去。不时还有人被地上的石块或石条给绊倒。有的日本兵一不小心跌倒时，脑袋刚好磕在石条的尖角上，直接就给磕死了。乱石地里，血液横流。

日本人终于穿过了乱石地，跑上了大路。老周他们苦心设计的伏击圈，被日本人甩到了身后。赵宏伟一边跟着日本人跑，一边心急如焚。完了，完了，居然被竹内给逃出来了！

情况紧急。行动队的队员们不得不抛弃了废城墙与树林的掩护，纷纷也都跑上了大路，追击竹内。这样一来，行动队的真实人数就完全暴露在了日本人的眼前。而且，此刻在大路上，谁也没有任何掩护物。战斗的形势发生了剧变。赵宏伟猛烈地感到，死神一下子就追近了整支行动队。行动队边追边打，日本人边跑边还击，双方是短兵相接，狭路相逢，各有伤亡。这时，北川忽然就停了下来，他大喊了一声：机枪手，准备！

赵宏伟赶紧用汉语大喊：日本人上机枪啦！喊完，他就是拉着曾林，拼了命地往大路旁边的泥地上跑，另外两个汉奸也紧紧跟随着。赵宏伟边跑边跟汉奸们解释说，子弹不长眼，我们要离日本人远一点。

曾林激昂地高喊："保护赵镇长！"

两名日本机枪手逆向而行，脱离了逃跑的队伍。两挺机枪黑洞洞的枪口瞬间就已对准了追上来的行动队。说时迟那时快，小孙悟空抬手一枪，就打中了其中一名机枪手的肩膀。另一挺机枪开了火。行动队员纷纷滚向泥地，借地势躲避。老周丢出了一枚手榴弹。"嘭"的一声，两名日本机枪手就都被炸成了血人。

行动队重新冲上大路，追击竹内。竹内大骇："他们有手榴弹！"北川一边开枪，一边命令两个兵，回去捡回那两挺机枪。

一名行动队员又拉开了一枚手榴弹，正要往竹内的方向丢，突然，北川一枪，正中了这名队员的额头。手榴弹从这名队员的手中滑落，滚向了行动队。电光石火的一刹那，老周冲上前去，奋力一踢，便是重新又将这枚手榴弹踢向了日本人的方向。"嘭"的一声，手榴弹在空中爆炸。

一颗子弹从老周的腰部蹭过，血一下子就渗了出来。

竹内向北川大吼：不要恋战！

又一枚手榴弹飞向了日本人。日本人全体卧倒。“嘭”的一声。

赵宏伟从泥地里爬起来，看看自己和三个汉奸都没事。再一看，竹内也没事。日本人再次和行动队展开了枪战。

离开了伏击圈一段距离之后，地势慢慢发生了变化。越往东边的西城门方向跑去，大路两边的地面越低。低下的地面与高起的路面之间就形成了高低起伏的陡坡。越往东，坡面越大。于是，战斗的形势渐渐地就又发生了一些变化。面对面的枪战又渐变成了堑壕战。双方的死伤速度都缓了下来。但是，一种绝境的窒息感却莫名越来越浓。双方都对同一件事暗暗地产生了疑惑：怎么县城的日军援兵，还没到来？

行动队打上了大路，日本人就滚下坡面；行动队追到了坡面，日本人就又跑上大路。双方边跑边打，来回战斗，纠缠消耗。为了节省弹药，老周不许行动队员再扔手榴弹。日本人将两挺机枪捡了回去，但是很快就被行动队员抢到了自己的手里。那个在伏击圈战斗僵持时跑去民房屋顶上射击的狙击手，一路奔跑着，此时终于也追上了行动队，参与到了追击竹内的战斗里。这个狙击手所持的，正是赵宏伟搞来的那一把狙击枪。这把枪的质量很不错。但是，此刻边追边打的形势，对狙击手作用的发挥却并不利。好几次，日本人乱枪的子弹都差点打中了狙击手。日本兵的射击水平并不低。

由于被行动队紧咬着，竹内的逃跑速度没法加快。眼看着身边的士兵一个又一个地倒下，竹内开始气急败坏。北川左半边的衣服都已经被鲜血浸透了，被血浸湿了的衣服上又都沾满了泥。血和泥混在一起，散发着一股地狱的湿冷气味。北川侧躺在坡面的下方，还在艰难地给步枪里装填子弹。他的脸色苍白，嘴唇在微微地发着抖，全身在不停地冒着冷汗。他觉得冷极了，又难受极了，就像是在雪地里发着烧，或是在冰河里忍受着窒息。而天上的太阳是那么刺眼，仿佛整个夏天的热量都已聚集在了今天的日光中。他感到很疲惫，就像是一匹已经跑了太久太远的马，他很想睡，却又清醒地知道自己不能睡。他想起了自己这一生跑过的枪林弹雨，忽然却开始疑惑，自己的奔跑是否真的有意义。生命原本是那么美丽，如果这场战争并不崇高，那么自己在子弹的罗网里飞舞的一生，又究竟有什么价值？他惊讶于自己此刻这

个想法的荒唐，内心却又情不自禁地泪水模糊。他一阵眩晕，仿佛看到了自己的妹妹，仿佛看到了自己曾经的家。

北川，你怎么了，还能不能战斗？竹内大声地问。

能，大佐。北川虚弱地说。大佐，我一定会保护你，保护你回县城去的。

渡边你个王八蛋，为什么援军还不来？你是不是想害死我！竹内仰天狂呼。

北川说，大佐，像现在这样，我们被敌人纠缠着，跑不快。这样，我带几个人留下来断后，拖住敌人，您带着其他人只管跑。这里离西城门已经没多少路了，只要进了县城，您就安全了。

好，好，竹内连忙说。

日本兵一共还剩十八个，北川留了八个，其余十个给了竹内。再加上曾林他们三个汉奸，一共还有十三个兵可以用来保护竹内。北川对这十三个兵说：记住，用生命保护大佐。

“是！”日本兵异口同声地答应。

北川大喊了一声“大日本帝国万岁”，然后便领兵冲上了大路。

其他的人，则保护着竹内，继续往东逃跑。

两颗子弹同时穿过了北川的脑袋，北川血流满面地倒在了地上。竹内回首，看见了北川的倒地，他大喊了一声：“北川！”然后，愣了愣。他就像是忽然忘记了时间，忽然忘记了很多的事情，陷入了一片难言的痴呆。

赵宏伟继续跟着竹内奔跑。赵宏伟的心里火烧火燎地焦急。县城就在前面了，已经能够远远地看见西城门了，怎么办？怎么办？

绝不能让竹内回到县城，必须要让他死在这里！

赵宏伟再也顾不得许多，他一边加快速度，跑近竹内，一边就是伸手，去摸自己藏在身上的匕首。

突然，“轰”的一声，清清楚楚地，从县城里传出了巨大的爆炸声。竹内猛地停住了脚步。赵宏伟准备拿匕首的手赶紧停了下来。

“县城里究竟发生了什么事？”竹内既像自言自语，又像是在问着谁。

可是，没有任何人回答他。

太阳还是那么宁静地照耀着大地，淡黄色的光成片地落下来，在空旷中将人的身影抹得分外模糊。阳光仿佛过滤了噪音，遮蔽了喘息，只给人留下了一个空荡荡的天地。在这个天地里，人的躯壳支离破碎，人的目光遁入深暗，人的灵魂孤孤单单。压抑与沉闷，就像是藏在阳光背后的两只手掌，在将阳光下感到孤单的每一个灵魂按扁、碾碎。生命是那么的深邃，而又空洞。竹内深深地感到孤独，就像旷野中失群的一匹狼。阳光简直就像是一个嘲笑，或是引人掉入深渊的幻梦。没有什么能止住灵魂深处的抽搐，竹内感到很难受。

“大佐，县城里不知发生了什么事，您绝不能再往前走了。万一县城里此刻也有敌军，那您进了县城，岂不就是凶险万分？”赵宏伟赶紧说。

“那你说怎么办？”竹内问。

赵宏伟一只手指向了不远处泥地里的一排破旧民房，说：“不如我们先去那里暂避，只要援军一到，我们必能反败为胜。”

竹内一咬牙，说：“我们不能一直等待！”竹内下令：清点弹药！

“我还有三颗子弹。”“我还有两颗。”“我还有四颗。”

每个兵身上都没几颗子弹了。但是十三个兵加起来，还是有四十多颗子弹的。竹内说：“这些子弹够了！我就不信，县城里有皇军的大半个联队，有什么人能把这座县城给打下来！我们就靠这四十几颗子弹冲进县城，只要能和大部队汇合在一起，我们就都安全了！”

竹内拿着手枪的手一挥，正要冲，赵宏伟拼命地就死死拉住了竹内。竹内勃然大怒：“混蛋！干什么！”

赵宏伟激动地说：“太君，实话告诉您吧，我怀疑，今天的一切，根本就是渡边的阴谋！”

“你说什么？”竹内讶然。

“不瞒太君，其实渡边副联队长在背后早已恨您入骨了，他曾多次跟我说，若不是您一直在窃取他的功劳，他早就已经可以坐上联队长的位子了。您仔细想想看，您今天出来和回去的路线与时间，当初还不都是渡边给定下的？除了我们内部的人，外面的人又怎么会知道这些详细情况？他们又怎么能够设下如此精心的一个埋伏？而且，他们的武器也不差，又有手榴弹，又有狙击枪，我怀疑他们根本就是渡边的人。渡边就是要他们化装成土匪或者共产党，在路上把您给杀了。另外，渡边又在县城里故意制造混乱，自己打自己，一方面就是为不派援兵创造理由，另一方面，就是为了以防万一。

万一路上的杀手没能杀得了您，让您逃回了县城，他还可以在县城里趁乱杀了您。事后他只要随便将罪名往共产党或土匪的身上一推，便可全身而退，万事大吉。太君，您一定要三思啊！”

“混蛋！渡边你个混蛋！我要杀了你！”竹内狂吼。

“太君，县城里的部队此刻都在渡边的掌握之中，要他们来增援看来是不可能的了，但是好在北川大尉还派了人去赵家镇上要援兵。渡边虽有阴谋，但是皇军的部队毕竟不是他口袋里的玩物，赵家镇的部队要来救您，别说他事先未必能想到，就算想到了，他也未必能阻止得了。算算时间，赵家镇派出的援军可能很快就要到了，太君，我们还是先去那些破房子里躲一躲，然后再静观其变吧！”赵宏伟苦口婆心地劝说。

“是啊，太君，赵镇长说得有道理，”曾林也开了口，“我们还是先去破房子那里躲一躲吧，待会儿万一打起来，弟兄们也好有个避子弹的屏障啊！”曾林用日语向竹内表达了他的意思。

竹内还没来得及做出决定，身后便又响起了枪声。行动队追上来了。竹内拔腿就往破房子那里跑了去。众人紧紧跟随。

赵宏伟已经累得快要没有力气了，如果不是因为竹内还没有被杀死，他是真想马上倒下去装死。他从来没有这样长时间地拼命奔跑过。从开始突围到现在，一路上他都不能跑得比竹内慢，他必须也要像逃命一样地跑，不然，万一行动队追了上来，却又不打他，那么他是内奸的这件事情马上就会暴露，日本人肯定立马就会毙了他，所以他只能拼了命地跑，跑得喘不过气了也还要继续跑，绝不能被行动队的人给追上。一种疲劳到了麻胀的感觉在他的胸口里充塞，他觉得自己的肺就像随时都会炸掉一样。他的双腿沉重到了无骨般地发软，每多跑一步，他都觉得像被打了一顿般的痛苦。酸痛在他的每条筋脉里窜动，但是事情还没有结束，他的任务还没有完成。他为自己软弱无能的身体感到羞耻。他咬紧了牙，不让自己输给自己。

竹内冲进了一处破院子里，院子里没有一个人。院子里有一间屋子，竹内冲进了这间屋子里，屋子里也是空无一人。屋内尘埃遍布，肮脏凌乱。看来此处早已被废置了多年。赵宏伟暗暗庆幸。他当时是为了让竹内停止逃跑，情急之下才胡乱指向了这边的这排民居。现在竹内闯进了这间屋子里来，这间屋子里倘若有人，日本兵多半会伤及无辜，那样他赵宏伟的过失可就大了。不过现在看来还好，此地的这排民居，各院各屋全都像是已被废置了很久的样子，相信这些房屋里应该都不会有人。赵宏伟莫名感到，今天，老天爷一定不会让他赵宏伟失败。

竹内带着赵宏伟一起躲在这间屋子里，屋外留了两个日本兵守卫。其余的人，则都待在了这处院子大门外边的一道矮墙后，借着墙体作掩护，与行动队激烈对战着。

枪声交织，生死激烈。

赵宏伟觉得没有比现在更好的机会了，再不动手，恐怕真的就要功亏一篑了。可是竹内一直在快速地走来走去，手里还握着一把手枪，赵宏伟总是刚一走到他的背后，他就又烦躁地转回了身来。赵宏伟连拔出匕首来的机会都没有。赵宏伟又不敢迎面而上地刺杀，竹内毕竟是个军人，手里又有枪，他赵宏伟若硬来，恐怕匕首还没拔出一半，脑袋已被竹内的子弹击穿。赵宏伟心火急烧，眉头锁成了一个铁疙瘩。

每一秒都过得像一年那么慢，赵宏伟心里就像是煮沸了一锅开水。他全身是汗，手心湿得滑腻无比。他脑子里又急又乱，思想就像是在一间没有门窗的黑屋子里乱闯乱撞，疼痛无比。竹内每多走一步，他的背上就像是多压上了一座山。他的呼吸越来越急促，几乎要不由自主地发出不正常的声响了。他把手心贴在衣服上，擦了又擦，他要自己冷静，他要自己再想一想秀珍，他要自己再想一想自己英勇的决心，他要自己做个有勇有谋的人。

忽然，外面的枪声停了。竹内很诧异。赵宏伟一时也很疑惑。突然，竹内的脸，白得像一个死人。

竹内绝望地喃喃道："完了，我们的子弹打光了……"

竹内疯了似的猛冲到了屋子的门口，对守卫在屋外的两个日本兵大吼："快出去，叫他们上刺刀！和敌人拼了！到了你们为天皇效忠的最后一刻了！"

两个日本兵向竹内敬了个礼，然后便是飞跑出了屋外。

竹内的嘴唇紧闭着，苍白得像抹了烟灰。他的眼神，像看到了坟墓一样地绝望而哀伤。他闭了闭眼睛，深吸了一口气，然后又睁开了眼睛来，正了正自己的衣冠，整理了一下自己的装束。

赵宏伟已快步走到了竹内的背后。他正要拔出匕首时，竹内忽然转回

了身来。赵宏伟大惊失色。竹内看着赵宏伟奇怪的样子，不禁问：“你干什么？”赵宏伟慌乱极了地说：“没什么，没什么，我只是想看一看外面。”

竹内狐疑地看了赵宏伟一眼，正要说什么，忽然，外面响起了连绵的爆炸声。一声又一声，那么猛，那么近。紧接着，又是一片规模颇大的喊声和吼声。如果赵宏伟没有听错，那应该是日本人的喊杀声。可是不对，外面的日本兵最多剩十个，他们又怎能发出如此浩荡的喊杀声？

这时，曾林兴高采烈地从外面跑了进来，他激动地向竹内报告：“报告大佐，我们的援军到了，终于到了！他们还带了迫击炮！我们有救了！”

竹内几乎不敢相信自己的耳朵。他瞪大了双眼，眼神里泛着死而复生的光。他问：“他们是从哪里来的援军？大概有多少人？”

“我看到他们是从县城那边过来的，估计是渡边中佐的部队。具体来了多少人我不知道，但看上去起码有两三百人，稍后也许还会有更多的部队赶来。”曾林说。

“太好了！”竹内精神大振。他命令曾林：“快去叫一个小队过来！保护我！保护我！”

“是！”曾林转身便跑了出去。

“太好了！”竹内快活地说着，转身往屋里走去，“赵镇长，是你误会渡边君了。渡边对我有所不满，我早有耳闻，但是，我们毕竟都是帝国的军人，同为天皇的子民，他是不会害我的。”

“是，是，是小的误会了渡边中佐，小的该死！小的该死！”赵宏伟一边说，一边扇着自己耳光。

竹内呵呵地笑，他伸了一个大懒腰。

曾林通知了一名日军中队长，要他马上派一个小队去院子里保护竹内。通知完，曾林就又往竹内所在的那处院子里跑了去。他要去做一个忠心耿耿率先保护竹内的样子，不然，回去了日本人又会怪罪他们贪生怕死，不为皇军出力。

竹内站在屋子里的西窗边。阳光从窗外洒进来，洒在竹内的身上，竹内微笑着。他已很疲惫，但忽然发现活着是多么可贵。不是热，也不是冷，而是一种暖洋洋，充斥在活着的主体意义里。这种领悟和这份感觉是那样的令人怡悦与陶醉，竹内蓦然觉得自己的一生都过得太苍白了。竹内的微笑有些苦涩。他忽然有一种强烈地想要抓住时间、让时间停下来的感觉。这种感觉又让他想起了凉子。时间与爱情，都是想爱想留不能留的东西。也许这便是命运的魔力，竹内想。他感到了来自命运深处的忧伤。这忧伤像血一样流淌。

“大佐你看！窗外的那不是北川大尉吗！”赵宏伟突然惊呼，一手指向了西窗外。

竹内大惊，赶紧转身面向了窗，往外张望。

说时迟那时快，赵宏伟一个箭步飞冲上前。

冰凉如雪的匕首，从背后，深深地插入了竹内的腰部。

赵宏伟拔出了匕首。竹内血如泉涌。赵宏伟后退了两步。

竹内转回了身来，向着赵宏伟举起了枪。赵宏伟走上前去，抱着竹内，又捅了他两刀。竹内手里的枪掉在了地上。

“……为什么……”竹内问。

“我求你们放人，你们不肯，我就只好自己动手了。”

“……你在课堂上讲的故事……真好听……”

“我讲的故事，都是假的。”

赵宏伟拔出了匕首，松开了竹内。竹内倒在了地上。

赵宏伟转回身，却发现，曾林就站在屋子里的东墙那边。

“原来、原来你是内奸！”曾林恐惧地说。

赵宏伟丢掉了匕首。曾林转身就要往东墙右边的屋门口跑。赵宏伟飞快地捡起了竹内掉在地上的那把手枪。

“砰”的一枪。

有如神助。赵宏伟竟然在这么远的距离，一枪就打中了曾林的后心窝。

曾林倒在了屋子的门口，像一棵倒下的枯树。

赵宏伟略一思索，将枪塞在了死去的竹内手里，然后，又去将匕首塞在了曾林的手里。

赵宏伟听见了许多日本兵跑进这处院子里来的声音。他一咬牙，拼尽全力，将头撞向了墙壁。

赵宏伟倒在了地上。他的头，鲜血横流。

战斗依然在继续。

剩下来的行动队员，依靠着一处院子外面的矮墙作掩护，继续与日军激战着。

赵家镇的日军也已赶到。但是，因为行动队此时所在的那处院子，就在竹内死去的那处院子的旁边，所以，日军的指挥官下令，不准再使用迫击炮和手榴弹，要保护竹内大佐的死亡现场，要保护竹内大佐的遗体。

密密麻麻的日军，包围着老周的行动队。

时间一分一秒地艰难过去。老周的行动队，依然在用生命拖延着时间。

鲜血四溅，血肉横飞。

但是，信号弹仍然还没有升起。

一个行动队员死去了，又一个行动队员死去了。阳光，热血，火热，闪耀。

行动队只剩下老周、小孙悟空、狙击手三个人了。

老周和小孙悟空的身上流着血，继续在用机枪向日军扫射。狙击手的腹部，也已中了弹。

终于，三个人到了弹尽粮绝的时刻，最后只剩下三枚手榴弹了。

双方停了火，顿时一片宁静。

宁静中，世界仿佛初生一般美好。

老周丢掉了枪，说：“对不起，我不能带你们去看秋天的红叶了。”

狙击手说：“马革裹尸，此生无憾。”

小孙悟空说：“去了阎王殿上，我再多吃他几个桃子！”

三人哈哈大笑，一人拿了一枚手榴弹。

老周笑着对小孙悟空和狙击手说：“走吧，我们一起去黄泉路上，与同志们相聚！”

三人拉开了手榴弹，一起跑入了日军阵中。

“嘭”“嘭”“嘭”三声巨响。

西路行动队成员，全体阵亡。

阳光抚摸着大地，鲜血凝望着苍天。

苍老的中国，像是也发出了微微的呻吟。

终于，在县城西边的上空，升起了一颗信号弹。

信号弹的光，璀璨夺目，绚烂万丈。

战争永远比想象的更残酷，也永远比预料的更复杂。

渡边派兵围剿了玉山。

事情的经过是这样的：在六月初一中午十二点一刻左右的时候，渡边所在的江庆县县政府首先遭到了一股不明武装力量的袭击。日军与敌方在县政府的正门外展开了战斗。不久，又有一名记者与一个农民同时来向县城的日军报告，说是竹内的车队在西城门外的大路上遭遇了袭击。渡边正要派兵去救援竹内，从东边又来了一个报信的，说是押送慰安妇与药品的车队在途经狮丘山时遭到了一支大部队的伏击，形势危急。渡边正疑窦丛生之时，从西边又来了一个日本兵，该兵再次向渡边报告了竹内遇袭之事，并向渡边传达了竹内的命令。

渡边迅速做出了判断：江庆县的日军，同时在东、中、西三路遭到了敌人的突然袭击，这绝对不是一串偶然事件，而必定是一场敌人有预谋的战役。而细数江庆县周边的抗日力量，唯一有胆量并且有实力这么做的，只有玉山上的那一支共产党的游击大队。不，事情也许比这还要糟糕。驻守江庆县全境的日军足足有一个联队，游击队敢发动一场如此大规模的全面攻击，他们必定已是联合了其他的抗日武装。而这三路敌军到底有多少人，情况暂时还没有摸清。怎么办？

渡边马上做出了安排：从县城里现有的日军兵力中，调出三分之一来，即刻奔赴玉山，剿灭游击队的老巢。另外再派三分之一的兵力，去东路支援遇袭的日军，保住慰安妇，保住药品。最后剩下的三分之一兵力，则留在县城，由渡边亲自指挥，保卫县政府，守卫县城。渡边暂时没有派兵去救竹内。他命令那个竹内派来的报信的兵，先去下面等着。

渡边谙熟中国的三十六计。玉山游击队这次对江庆县的日军发动了这样大规模的一场攻击，他们的队员，想必已是倾巢而出。此时不去直取他们的老巢，更待何时？只要拿下了玉山，游击队无家可归，人心一乱，自然就会溃不成军。兵不厌诈，是中国人教给全世界的一条道理。而根据陆陆续续送来的新情报，已可确认此次和日军战斗的敌人的确就是玉山游击队，这样就更没有什么好顾虑的了。既然判断没有出错，那么，局势尽在自己的掌握之

中了，渡边确信。

渡边准备以兵力不够的理由，尽量拖延给竹内派救兵的时间。他是真希望那些抗日武装能帮帮他的忙，早点送竹内去见可爱的上帝。这次竹内去赵家镇小学听课，故意不带他渡边，分明就是在给他难堪，给他警告。这个举动里面包含的多重意味以及这次事件之后所能带来的连锁反应，对渡边来说都是非常不利的。日军内部的派系斗争幽暗而激烈，从军部传出的争吵声经常会像幽灵一样到处飘舞，最终成为不少下层军官茶余饭后的谈资与笑料。田中所属的一派与竹内所属的一派已经势成水火，许多人已经到了不得不选择一个阵营加入的时候了。渡边已经跟了竹内许多年了，但是如今，他忽然很想换一个阵营。竹内对他的不满已经明朗化，而田中又即将要成为他的顶头上司，他又何苦还要为了竹内而与田中不睦呢？田中本人是没什么权力，但是在田中的背后，却是站着好几个权力人物。如果能博得田中的好感，那么，他渡边的明天是否会更加美丽一些？

但是，就在渡边苦苦盘算着自己的进退的时候，他却忽然接到了一个电话。接完这个电话，他不寒而栗，呆若木鸡。这是一条最新消息：就在一个小时前，青梅县的田中中佐在喝水时不慎中毒，暴毙于办公室内。日军对外宣称这是共产党所为，其实内部有信息传来，田中是死在自己人手里。

渡边的额头冒了一阵冷汗。眼前突然发生了太多太多的事，一波未平，一波又起，一战未捷，一战又至。世事瞬息万变，人算不如天算。渡边立刻下令：前去支援东路被困日军的部队马上撤回来，改去西路救援竹内。要快、快、快。

渡边暗使了一个小计策：先前，他是盼着竹内死，所以他必须要去保住那些慰安妇和药品，不然竹内死了，丢失慰安妇和药品的罪责就会由他渡边来承担；但是，现在他要救出竹内，他已不必再去保住那些慰安妇和药品，因为只要竹内回来了，丢失慰安妇和药品的罪责最终自然会由他竹内来承担。能让竹内多摔一跤也是好的。

政委带领着一百五十多人留守玉山。到了行动开始的时间，政委坐立不安。他思来想去，总觉得中、西两路行动队在此次战斗行动中必是凶多吉少。最终，他决定，留下五十余人守山，由他亲自带领一百人出山，兵分两路，去支援中、西两路行动队。

政委带着一百名战士出了玉山，走了不多久，正要分成两路，各奔战场，突然，遇到了急行而来意图剿灭游击队玉山大本营的日军部队。日军大概有六七百人。双方狭路相逢，激烈交火。政委的部队，寡不敌众，只能边打边撤。政委带领众人退回了玉山，据险而守。日军开始猛烈攻山。

双方血战良久。日军正逐渐占据上风。这时，东路行动队却突然出现在了攻山日军的后方。东路行动队在狮丘山一战中大获全胜，人员伤亡极小，且又缴获了大量日军的精良装备，此刻士气正锐。而攻山的日军却是突然后背受敌，被打了个措手不及，阵脚大乱。东路行动队用上了刚刚缴获来的迫击炮和重机枪。日军受到了游击队的前后夹击。

战斗一直持续到了傍晚。双方血战，形势不相上下。游击队开始担心，县城里的日军若在此刻派来援兵，那么后果将不堪设想。东路行动队此时正在玉山之外，若被日军前后合围，则恐有覆灭之势。而攻山的日军则开始忧虑，天色一黑，己方对地势不熟，怕是会遭受更大的损失。黑灯瞎火的，被全歼也不是没有可能。

双方都在忐忑里继续激战着。

天色暗了下来。这时，游击队的队长下令，集中兵力于三面，给日军空出一条逃走的路来。于是，游击队原本紧密的包围圈，开始空出了一条大口子来。日军见状大喜。他们一边打，一边纷纷往口子外面逃。游击队又放了几声炮，日本兵丢盔弃甲，抱头鼠窜。

攻山的日军很快就逃了个干干净净。游击队也松了一口气。

战斗终于结束了。

中路行动队炸掉了江庆县城里的三个军火库。他们与县城的日军苦苦战斗了三个多小时，有效牵制了日军的注意力。

中路行动队成员，最后全体阵亡。

直到傍晚时分，沮丧至极的渡边才收到了攻山部队的求救讯息。从县城里赶去增援的日军，跑到半路就遇上了正在集体往回逃的攻山部队。于是，这一次围剿玉山游击队大本营的行动，也就不了了之。

今日之整场战斗，游击队共伤亡一百余人，日军共伤亡六百余人。运往上海之慰安妇，全部得救，无一损伤。大量药品被游击队运往了我党之抗日根据地。

江南日军，为之震动。田中中将亲自向青梅县与江庆县的日军下令，要求两县之部队，务必在今年入秋之前，合力歼灭玉山游击队，玉山之上，寸草不留。

风萧萧，马长嘶。

六月初四，下午。县医院。

西斜的阳光从窗户里照进来，照在赵宏伟的脸上。赵宏伟的眼皮动了两下，终于，他苏醒了过来。

模模糊糊地睁开眼，他觉得什么好刺眼。亮亮堂堂的，金红一片，还似乎带着些火的温度。恍恍惚惚中，他终于明白了过来，这是阳光。自己还活着。

他辨认出了，这里是医院，自己正躺在病床上。他动了动身子，想要坐起来，忽然一阵头痛欲裂。他用手一摸，才发现自己的头上缠满了纱布。

又一阵钻心的头痛袭来，赵宏伟的意识彻底清醒了过来。他从床上坐了起来。

他想起了自己最后做过的那些事。一瞬间，许许多多要命的问题就一下子全挤进了他的脑子里。竹内和曾林当时真的都死彻底了吗？今天是几号？老周他们怎么样了？游击队的营救行动成功没有？秀珍有没有被救出来？日本人有没有发现自己的诡计？

整间病房里除了赵宏伟以外，空无一人。他忽然感到了害怕。一种觉得自己渺小而又无依无靠的感觉，让他的心里直发毛。他现在几乎都不敢相信，竹内是自己杀的。他现在甚至已经能感觉到，一种即将要被凌迟处死的恐怖。他好想去撒尿。

他在昏迷之前的最后那一刻，急中生智，以头撞墙，本意不是求死，而是求生。虽然，他当时也完全不能肯定，这一撞，他究竟是会生，还是会死。毕竟，撞头不是闹着玩的。他是希望，进来收拾残局的日军能产生一个错觉：曾林杀了竹内，竹内杀了曾林，而他赵宏伟和竹内一样，都是受害者。

就是不知道，渡边到底会不会上当。

赵宏伟下了床，还没迈步，一阵头晕卷来，他摔倒在了地上。一个护士开门走了进来。这个护士用汉语向门外大喊：他醒了！他醒了！

山本信玄，日本陆军大尉，一直等候在赵宏伟病房外面的走廊里。听到护士的喊叫，他风一般迅疾地冲进了病房里去。可惜，赵宏伟又昏了过去，就像一条死鱼一样。山本踹了赵宏伟一脚，赵宏伟也还是躺在地上，无知无觉。山本抬起头来，捏了捏这个护士的脸蛋，然后猛地给了她一耳光。山本用汉语说：“我已经没有耐心了，不管用什么方法，马上让他醒过来！不然，我送你去当慰安妇！”

这个护士往赵宏伟的头上猛浇了三盆冷水。赵宏伟迷迷糊糊地就又醒了过来。

赵宏伟抹掉了自己脸上的水，湿淋淋地从地上爬了起来。他看看陌生的山本和护士，又看看莫名其妙湿透了的自己，不禁木讷地问：“怎么回事？”

山本利索地转过身，凶狠地打了这个护士四记耳光，用汉语大骂：“臭婊子，你怎么能这样粗暴地对待赵镇长！给我滚！”骂完，他便用力地一脚将这名护士踢翻在地。护士连滚带爬地逃了出去。

山本转回身来，笑呵呵地微微伸了伸脖子，向赵宏伟虚敬了一个礼。他皮笑肉不笑地说：“赵镇长，你终于醒过来了，真是可喜可贺。我叫山本信玄，是新任的赵家镇大队大队长，今后，我们就是在一起工作的朋友了。”

赵宏伟莫名觉得眼前的这个人十分令人恶心，比北川差多了，但他还是抱拳向山本行了个礼，说：“幸会，幸会，今后还请山本太君多多关照小人才是。”

又一阵头晕袭来，赵宏伟躺回了病床上。

“山本太君，你汉语说得好流利呀。”

“家父很早就预料到了，中国会成为天皇陛下的猎物，所以让我从小就学习汉语，以便有一技之长。”

“哦，令尊真是有远见。对了，今天是几号了？”

“按中国人的农历来讲，今天是六月初四。赵镇长，你已经昏迷了三天三夜。”

赵宏伟点了点头。

赵宏伟通过上面的几句故意的闲聊，心里面基本已经确定，自己还没有

暴露。自己杀竹内的事，日本人还不知道。不然日本人不会依然对自己这么客气。不过日本人诡计多端，也不可掉以轻心。现在外面的情况究竟如何，游击队战斗的结局到底是怎样，自己都是一无所知，因此必须要处处小心。

“赵镇长，请你跟我说一说，六月初一那天，竹内大佐在路上遇袭的情况。还有，你是怎么受伤昏迷的？这些你应该都还记得吧？”

“记得，记得。”赵宏伟不作犹豫地回答。山本的语调虽温柔，但赵宏伟看到了山本眼里的狡黠。此时的回答若不紧凑而主动，山本必然起疑。

赵宏伟原原本本不增不减地将竹内当天在路上遇袭的情况说给了山本听。因为他说的都是实情，所以他说得无懈可击。最后，他说到了自己的昏迷一事。他说，他当时正面壁而立，在内心感谢上苍终于给竹内大佐派来了援军，突然，他听到身后传来了一串急促的脚步声，还没等他回头呢，有一个人从后面猛抓住了他的头，这个人又快又狠地将他的头往墙上猛撞了过去，然后，他就眼前一黑，什么都不知道了。

“你没看清楚这个人是谁吗？”

“没有。”

“你就真的一点也没看到些什么吗？哪怕这个人身上的一片衣角？”

“这个……好像……”

“好像什么？”山本紧盯着赵宏伟的眼睛。

“这个人，好像是曾林。”赵宏伟看着山本的眼睛说。

山本走了，说还会再来。他要赵宏伟好好休息，暂时不许离开医院。

那个挨踢的护士领了一个医生进来，医生将赵宏伟头上的湿纱布都取了下来，换了新的上去。赵宏伟问医生，自己这头怎么样了。医生说，头盖骨没碎，不过可能是裂了，但是没关系，过段时间它自己会长好，另外，脑袋里还可能有瘀血，会不会有后遗症这不知道，但是也没关系，现在醒了就好。没办法，这里的医疗水平就这样，谁让你伤在脑袋上呢，要是想做更深入的检查和更彻底的治疗，那你得去上海的大医院。

赵宏伟感到这个医生对自己这么个汉奸不是很友好，就也不再多问什么了。而他现在也的确是没心思多关心自己的伤势。这颗脑袋，是不是真的能保得住还不知道呢，伤不伤的又有什么关系。医生说得不错，现在醒了就好。只要醒着，自己就可以想办法。

赵宏伟现在已经弄清楚了，这里是江庆县大医院。而那个挨踢的护士，医生叫她小燕。赵宏伟问小燕，知不知道他当时是怎么来的医院。小燕说，是一个叫赵驹的人背他来的。当时医院里挤满了日本伤员，是赵驹用枪逼着医生先抢救的他。

医生和护士都走了出去。病房里又只剩下了赵宏伟一个人。一阵头痛袭来，赵宏伟心烦意乱。

赵宏伟走到了窗边，茫然地看着窗外。夕阳已沉，日光在天边收拢，暮色渐浓，冷风乍起。

这里是四楼，也就是县医院主体大楼的顶楼。从这个高度望出去，可以看得很远。傍晚时的县城，显得有些静谧。那黑瓦白墙的民房，那袅袅婷婷的炊烟，那蜿蜒多致的小巷，多像一幅美好的中国水墨画。静中有微动，朦胧又细腻，今韵点缀着古意，多么诗意的江南晚景。只可惜，站在这里，还能看到县政府里高高飘扬的那一面日本旗。旗在风中猎猎舞动，色彩鲜艳，图案分明，它就像是在提醒所有的中国文人：你看到的不是一幅画，一首诗，而只是一片废墟，一座地狱。

赵宏伟想起了文天祥，不禁潸然泪下。自古以来，中国圣贤豪杰辈出，而今，巨龙却为何只似一个慰安妇。我自横刀向天笑，去留肝胆两昆仑，中国若人人有谭公气度，只求死，不贪生，只为国，不为己，倭寇又岂能横行于我中华大地？悲也！愤哉！想想杨家将，想想岳家军，真是感时花溅泪，恨别鸟惊心。赵宏伟抹了抹眼泪。

赵宏伟还没有想好接下来到底该怎么办。他也还有很多的事情没有探明，但是山本又不许他离开医院，这到底该如何是好？

他想起了小燕说过的日本伤兵。目前住院的日本伤兵应该会有不少，也许他可以去伤兵们那里打听打听情况？

他又想起了山本，总觉得山本这个姓有些熟。但是究竟熟在哪里，又说不上来。想想还是算了，可能是自己过于敏感了，一个姓而已，跟赵钱孙李一样，有什么熟不熟的。

赵宏伟振奋精神，走出了病房，去找日本伤兵。

大战之后，江庆县的日军就像是成了一条瘸了腿的狼。士兵的士气低迷，而作为当时整场战斗的最高指挥官，渡边，也是被弄得焦头烂额。上司的责问，同行的嘲笑，令他颜面无存。而青梅县的日军还要向他要药品，上海的慰安所又还要向他要女人。渡边夜不成寐，每天一睁眼，就觉得自己快要疯了。

但是，渡边并不是沮丧得一塌糊涂。他还是有一些高兴的事情的。或者，也可以这么说，如果没有那些糟透了的军务上的残局要他来收拾，那么，他还是十分感谢游击队的这次袭击行动的。因为，他现在已经暂时是江庆县日军联队的联队长了。没有“副”字。而这“暂时”，恐怕也一定会是暂时的。只要他能将功补过，就一定能被任命为正式的联队长。

战斗结束之后，败绩上报，北野少将亲自给渡边打来了电话。北野在电话里将渡边骂了个狗血淋头，直吓得渡边差点想要卷款潜逃。但是，骂到后来，北野却又转变了语气，开始安慰起了渡边，告诫他不要试图剖腹谢罪，而要努力争取戴罪立功，搞得渡边简直有些丈二和尚摸不着头脑。直到最后，北野说，我会让你暂时担任竹内的联队长一职的。这时，渡边才算是恍然大悟：自己的运气来了。一个新的时代，就要开始了。

很快，渡边就接到了正式的通知，上面要他暂时担任江庆县日军联队的联队长一职，掌管江庆县一切军政要务。而北野已经向渡边暗示过了，只要他能将功补过，“暂时”就一定会变成“正式”。

渡边很快就理解了自己的因祸得福。有消息传来，说是北野派人毒死了田中中佐，但是北野显然不会承认。而田中中佐的叔叔田中中将，暂时也不能拿北野怎么样，因为北野在军部的靠山十分强硬，他的势力不容小觑。田中中佐一殁，田中中将即刻让他的心腹松尾去了青梅县，接任了青梅县日军联队的联队长一职。田中中将还想染指江庆县，意欲派一名站在他的政治阵营中的老军官前往江庆县，去接任联队长一职。这名老军官曾经在江庆县的这支联队里待过，担任过副联队长，人缘很好，因此不会被这支联队排斥。北野当然不想看到这件事情顺利地发生发展，可是，他的阵营中一时又实在调派不出合适的人来。于是，渡边的好运就来了。据北野所知，渡边一向是竹内的心腹，其政治立场也向来是与自己这方同路。那么，扶植渡边上台，代替死去的竹内，无疑也是个不错的选择。

渡边请记者写了一篇《帝国名将陨落中国江南战场》，该文的内容配合了渡边向上面所做的报告。渡边相当小心地隐瞒了自己故意拖延救援竹内的事实，而将责任推给了共产党，说都是因为当时城中的共产党部队阻击得太猛烈，所以导致城中的救援部队无法及时脱身前去救援竹内，最后只能是调回了派往东路的援军来解燃眉之急。渡边向上面承认了自己指挥失当的错误。另外，渡边又成功地将上面的注意力转到了竹内的具体死因上。已有充足的证据表明，竹内是死在内奸的手上。而既然竹内是死于内奸之手，那么，其实竹内的死，和救援部队的是否及时赶到，关系也就不大了。最后，上面要求渡边尽快彻查内奸一事，而对于渡边的指挥失误问题，上面决定不再细究。

渡边老谋深算，过关斩将，在经历了这样的一场大败仗之后，居然没有受到上面的什么处罚，反而还升了官，这不能不说，也实在是他的一种本事。但是，上面的处罚他是逃过了，一场败仗过后所留下来的许多麻烦，他是逃不过的。本来他也没料到竹内真的会死，所以就想留下一个烂摊子等竹内回来收拾，但是没想到竹内真的死了，而他自己又成了暂时的联队长，于是，这个烂摊子就成了他自己送给自己的一个难题。青梅县的松尾紧咬着渡边，向他要药品；上海的慰安所紧催着渡边，问他要女人；田中中将又下了死命令，要他们在今年入秋以前，剿灭玉山游击队。他渡边的官运看似来得容易，其实，艰险深藏。过得去，这运才是运，过不去，这运只是祸。渡边又怎么能睡得着呢？他天天如履薄冰。

药品的事情比较好解决，渡边打算在江庆县的百姓头上再刮一笔钱，用这笔钱去买药品，买好了就赶紧给松尾送过去。但是慰安妇的问题就很难解决了。已没有办法再在江庆县全境内征一次女人了。第一次强征慰安妇的成功，是依靠了先欺骗后镇压的办法，但是现在，这办法已无法再用第二次。欺骗，老百姓哪里会再上当；镇压，恐怕江庆县会被老百姓鱼死网破地烧成一片火海。毕竟，要想当统治者，就不能把老百姓全往死路上逼。狗急了跳墙，民急了造反，渡边记得以前赵宏伟跟他讲过水浒的道理。而且，第一次的强征，基本上已是将江庆县境内的上等美女给一网打尽了。再征，除了第一次强征时没动过的县城里可能还会有一些漏网的上等货以外，下面的几个镇子上，恐怕最多也只能再出一批中等货了。而如果这批慰安妇的质量不

高，那么，上海那边一定会要他渡边赔出四个金发碧眼的洋妞来。那他可就真的是要吃不了兜着走了。

所以，思来想去，渡边觉得，最好的办法，还是把被游击队救走的那批女人给重新抢回来。而只要能够剿灭了游击队，那批女人，自然就会重新回到皇军的手中。所以，剿游击队和交慰安妇这两个问题，其实是一个问题。

只能多费些唇舌，让上海那边再等一等了，渡边想。

另外，绝对不能让青梅县的部队捷足先登，单独地成功剿灭玉山游击队。如果他们单独完成了剿灭游击队的任务，且又得到了那批慰安妇，那么，他渡边就会只剩下过，而没有丝毫的功。到时，恐怕不仅北野会觉得他没用，将他弃如敝屣，而且，上面还会来个老账新账一起算，治他一系列的罪。真是错不得半步。

那么，要怎样才能让这剿灭游击队的功劳，单独地完全落入自己的囊中呢？渡边并非全无胜算。玉山游击队与江庆县日军联队相比，在人数和装备上都不占任何优势，游击队唯一所倚仗的，就是玉山的地利。只要这地利一破，游击队自会全军覆没。那么，要怎样才能破这玉山的地利呢？渡边的手中还有姚志。

姚志没有死。原本，渡边是要在六月初一那天的下午枪毙姚志的。但是六月初一那天突然发生了那么多事，渡边就把姚志的事给忘了个一干二净。之后，竹内和中佐田中全死了，姚志就完全没有了被枪毙的必要。渡边成了江庆县日军的最高指挥官，姚志这张活地图，他当然要好好保存。一旦撬开了姚志的嘴，他渡边自然就会走向一段锦绣前程。那么，姚志的嘴究竟撬不撬得开呢？渡边相信，自己绝对有这个能力。以前是为竹内办事，所以，他对自己的手段还有所保留。而现在，他是为自己办事，所以，他绝对会使尽浑身解数。正如赵驹所说，只要是个人，就会有所爱，只要有所爱，就会有死穴。姚志的所爱是什么？既不是钱与权，也不是女人与自己。他爱的，是国家，是百姓，是明天。那么，这些，就是他的死穴。

至于内奸一事，由于证据有限，渡边暂时还只能认定，曾林就是内奸。当时，竹内毙命的现场并没有被保护好。这件事情要怪赵驹。增援竹内的日军在第一时间就将竹内毙命的消息传给了渡边，渡边在得知消息后，即刻就派赵驹前往现场去处理一切事宜。可是赵驹一到现场就犯了错。他怕那破屋子受到了炮火的震动会塌，居然让人把竹内、曾林和赵宏伟都搬到了屋子外头去。而曾林手里的匕首和竹内手里的手枪，因为在尸体搬动的过程中掉在了地上，所以莫名其妙地就又经过了好几个人的手。这对整桩案件的侦破来讲是最致命的。本来，只要将这两样东西送去上海日军特高课那边做一下指纹鉴定，一切真相便会水落石出，但是现在，匕首和手枪上都已沾满了乱七八糟的人的指纹，指纹鉴定对破案的意义已经不大了。不过渡边还是将这两样东西送去了上海日军特高课，希望最终的鉴定结果多少能为破案提供一些蛛丝马迹。

现在除了赵宏伟以外，已没有人能说清整场西路战斗的情况。那些随行的记者，都是在战斗的一开始，就自顾自地逃命去了。而后来从战斗队伍里派出去的那两个报信的日本兵，也只是参加了开始时的一小段战斗。参加了全程战斗的竹内卫队士兵和共产党的行动队员已经全都死光了，现在，也只有赵宏伟，才能说出整场西路战斗的来龙去脉了。渡边固然不太信任赵宏伟，但是眼下这个情况，也只能是听他的一面之词了。

根据赵宏伟提供的情况，渡边与山本推演出了竹内遇刺的情形：是曾林先将赵宏伟撞晕，然后用匕首刺了竹内，而竹内当时并没有立刻断气，于是就在曾林逃跑时向曾林开了枪，杀死了曾林。

那么，曾林为什么不用枪呢？渡边和山本的答案是：当时竹内的卫队已经弹尽粮绝，曾林的身上已没有子弹，而且，既然是刺杀，当然无声最好。而对于曾林为什么没有杀死赵宏伟这个问题，渡边的看法是，因为曾林跟赵宏伟有交情，所以他手下留情了。但是山本的看法是，曾林应该是想要撞死赵宏伟的，只不过赵宏伟运气好，没有死罢了。

许多问题，似乎都可以找到合情合理的解释，可仍然有诸多无法回答的疑问。比如，曾林为什么要杀竹内？他是军统特工或者地下党吗？他若要刺杀竹内，何不在战斗刚开始的时候就动手，却偏偏要等到最后？等等。某些问题，渡边和山本若不刻意去为它们寻找解释，它们看起来根本就不合逻辑。

在渡边的心中，当然还存在着另外一种可能，那就是赵宏伟也许是在说谎。而赵宏伟如果是在说谎，那么赵宏伟就极有可能是真正的杀人凶手。但是，这一假设也同样是存在着许多令人费解的地方。凭赵宏伟的本事，他杀得了竹内吗？曾林可是被人一枪毙命，赵宏伟有那个枪法吗？赵宏伟为什

么要杀人？事情的真相到底是怎样的一个故事？这些统统都没有答案。又或者，真凶另有其人，赵宏伟是在帮人掩饰真相？什么都有可能。一切又都没有证据，不成逻辑。渡边心烦意乱。虽然根据山本的判断，赵宏伟说的都不是假话。但是，渡边还是决定，改天要亲自审一审赵宏伟。内奸不除，后患无穷。

北川死后，渡边即调山本去赵家镇上接任了大队长一职。山本是一个半月以前才调来江庆县的，与联队里的人都不熟，按理说是会坐一段时间的冷板凳的，但是渡边在听说了山本在军界的一些关系以后，就开始努力拉拢起了山本，尽量对他委以重任。其实赵宏伟的直觉一点也没有错，这个山本，他听着是该有些耳熟。他，就是当年那个满日本追杀赵驹的黑帮头子老山本的儿子。老山本并非如赵驹和赵宏伟当年所想象的那样，仅仅是个地头蛇而已。老山本的黑帮，在日本的军政两界都颇有些影响，日军中有几位高级将领，当年甚至还是老山本的手下。这样的一个老山本的儿子小山本，渡边又怎么会不尽力去笼络呢？

世事，有时就是这么巧妙。当你走到了尽头，才会发现，其实有些噩梦，你从来都没有甩掉过。

赵宏伟输完了液，吃了药，躺在病床上，不能入睡。窗外漆黑的夜，像一个令人惊恐的世界。

这两天，通过不断地与楼下那些日本伤兵聊天，赵宏伟已经大致了解清楚了在自己昏迷以后所继续发生的诸种事情，包括玉山之战和渡边的升官等等。赵宏伟没有想到，战事和政事的复杂程度与变化发展都远远地超过了他原来的预计。也许，这才是战争的本来面目吧。不过幸好，日本人败了。在这一场天地赌局中，老天让正义的一方获得了胜利。赵宏伟一方面固然为游击队的大捷暗暗感到高兴，另一方面，内心却也忐忑不安。战斗那样激烈而复杂，方远梦是否安好？秀珍是否安好？这两件事情，他都无处去打听。

另外，赵宏伟的心里还有一层深深的恐惧。刚从昏迷中醒来时，他莫名不敢确定，自己当时是否真的彻底地杀死了竹内与曾林。毕竟，当时一切发生得都很突然，他杀完了人也都没再验一验他们的鼻息与脉搏。后来，他从山本的嘴里验证了竹内与曾林的死，心里着实是松了一口气。但是现在，他发现在这件事情上，还留有两个大麻烦。第一，是指纹。他是在与日本伤兵聊天的过程中才知道的，有时在一些难以侦破的案件中，特高课的指纹鉴定会帮上大忙。这是赵宏伟的一个大疏忽。他很早以前就已知道了指纹技术在西方警界的成功运用，但是他忘记了，特高课怎么会没有指纹鉴定！那把匕首和那把手枪上，可都有他赵宏伟清清楚楚的指纹；第二，是他的长衫不见了。本来，他一直以为，是医院里的护士给他换了衣服，可是后来他去一问，护士却告诉他，他进来的时候，身上根本就没穿什么长衫！而他记得，自己的长衫上，还溅有竹内的血迹！

赵宏伟惶恐不堪。恐惧像一副尖利的牙齿，在他的全身不停乱咬。他觉得自己在日本人面前已是破绽百出。他感到自己的那些小聪明，尽是一些大笑话。他觉得自己已经黔驴技穷。他想从医院里面逃出去，可是医院的外面守卫森严，连一只老鼠都溜不出去。他只能继续在煎熬里待下去。

山本走后，一直没有再来，赵宏伟觉得这不是一个好兆头。说不定山本下次再来，就会给他送来一件囚服和一副手铐，他想。他的头好痛，一阵阵的剧痛，就像是有人在拿凿子凿他的脑壳一样。而又没有人能告诉他，这毛病到底好不好得了。他觉得自己就像是掉在了一片流沙里，他越挣扎，沉得越快。恐怖带着滚烫的温度，将他慢慢吞噬。

他沉到了死一样的噩梦里。

第二部

赵驹的孤独回忆

月黑风高。夜深人静。

赵驹家中的院子里，一盆火在熊熊燃烧。

赵驹寂寥地站在火盆的旁边，低头看着铁盆里左右猛晃的火焰，面无表情。飘忽的火光在黑暗的院子里显得有些刺眼，不似旁边昏黄的屋里稳稳的灯光柔和。但那柔和也如这黑暗一样长久地寂静着，显出了与这黑暗同质的孤冷。没有什么人在那灯光里等候着什么。除了这一盆火，屋里屋外，也并没有什么温暖存在。赵驹的黑影像一个鬼魂般萧索，他也像一个鬼魂般萧索。火照亮着他的脸，却照不亮他的眼。他偌大的一个家里，除了他以外，已再没有一个人存在。他沉默着，犹豫着，最终还是将手里的那件衣服，丢进了火盆里。火星四溅，火焰被压了一压，然后猛地就又蹿了起来，随风狂舞，热烈熊熊。

这，就是赵宏伟的那件溅有竹内血迹的长衫。

战斗发生的那天，当赵驹赶到竹内毙命的现场时，有日本兵向他报告，说是竹内、赵宏伟和曾林三人都已经死了。不知道为什么，在听到赵宏伟死讯的那一刻，赵驹竟莫名有些哀伤。很意外的哀伤。他一个人走进了竹内毙命的那间屋子里，果然看见了仰面倒在地上的赵宏伟。赵宏伟的头上全是血，那血从他的头上流到地上，在地上积成了一摊血泊。那摊血泊的样子，很像一幅中国地图。赵驹没有想到，赵宏伟最后的死相竟然会是这样。赵驹一一验过了三人的鼻息和脉搏，确认他们的确是都已经死了。然后，赵驹就又在屋子里看了一圈。突然，赵驹愣了一愣。他马上走出了屋子，问外面看守现场的几个日本兵：这里面的三具尸体，有没有被人动过？大家都说没有。两个日本兵告诉他，当时原本准备进来保护竹内的那些士兵，在发现竹内出事之后便立即都退到了屋外，并没有移动过那三具尸体。而战场指挥官桥本在得知竹内出事之后，也是要求部队在战斗过程中尽量以保护竹内的遗体为念，不要乱打乱炸，并且要阻止敌人接近竹内遗体所在的那间屋子。在此地的战斗结束之后，桥本也只是带人进屋里去验了一下三人的死活，并没有移动过三人的位置。所以，至少到目前为止，屋里的三具尸体，应该仍然是保持着最初时的样子。

赵驹回到屋里去又勘察了一段时间，最后，便是出来向看守屋子的日本兵下了令：从此时起，除我之外，任何人都不得再踏进这间屋子半步，违者一律按内奸嫌疑犯论处，交送渡边副联队长发落。

赵驹下完了令，就重新又返回了屋子里。他想关上屋门，可是曾林的尸体就躺在屋门口那里，门关不上。众目睽睽之下，他也不能搬动尸体。他一时情急，就只好是以勘察现场为由，又下令，要站在这处院子里的士兵全都站到院子外面去。士兵们都不理解，但赵驹是渡边派来全权处理此事的负责人，所以士兵们还是都服从了命令，跑到了院子外面去。

赵驹假装盛气凌人地骂了几句粗话，然后生气地粗暴地就将院子的门给关了起来。院门一关，赵驹忙擦了一把汗。事不宜迟，他小声地迅速地跑回了屋门口那里。他戴上白手套，蹲了下来，取下了曾林手里的那把匕首。他用自己的手帕仔细地擦拭着匕首的手把。他一边擦，一边竖着耳朵，小心地听着周围的动静。

没错，赵驹已经识破了这个被伪装过的现场。这是一个表面看起来合情合理，实则留有多处破绽的假凶案现场。从表面上看，这个现场无疑是在告诉人们一个故事：曾林刺杀了竹内，竹内击毙了曾林。但是，若仔细观察，就不难发现，如果子弹真的是从竹内所在的那个位置射出来的，那么，这颗子弹根本就不会以这样的一个角度进入曾林的身体。当然，也可以怀疑，曾林刚中弹时并不是在现在的这个位置。但是，这颗子弹进入的是曾林的后心窝，曾林是被一枪毙命，且地上也并没有留下任何曾林倒地后爬动的痕迹。而且，日本兵们也都说了，在事发后，并没有任何人移动过尸体。这三具尸体，基本上都保持着事发时的原样。

那么，整桩事情就变得十分可疑了。有人在制造假象。究竟是怎么一回事呢？最终，还是赵宏伟长衫上的血迹，向赵驹暗示了事情的真相。在赵宏伟长衫的腹部，有一片血迹，但是在赵宏伟本人的腹部，却并没有任何伤口存在。而竹内腹部的伤口，倒是与赵宏伟长衫上那片血迹的位置差不多等高。如果竹内和赵宏伟能面对面地站着，那么，那个伤口和那片血迹刚好就是差不多相对应。真相似乎已初露端倪。当然，现在暂时也还不能确定，这片血迹就是竹内留下的。不过究竟是不是，日本人很容易就能验出来。而万一被日本人验出了是，那就什么都晚了。

现场的脚印虽然已十分破碎杂乱，但是因为这是一间久无人居的旧屋，地上的灰尘甚厚，所以新留下的痕迹还都算是不难分辨。赵驹循着各种迹象前行，一条又一条的线索在他的脑海里越织越密。一切都很顺利，就像是有一股神奇的力量，在不断地为他指点迷津。最终，一个真实的故事在他的眼前栩栩如生了起来：赵宏伟刺杀了竹内，然后转回身来，发现了曾林，曾林逃跑，赵宏伟就拿起了竹内的枪，追上去一枪打死了曾林，接着，赵宏伟便伪造了现场，最后，他撞墙自尽。这个故事，令赵驹震惊不已。

但是，赵驹还不能相信自己看到的这个故事。他还需要寻找一点证据。最终，他在曾林的弹匣里，找到了最后一颗子弹。既然曾林还有子弹，那么，他又为什么要用匕首来刺杀竹内？答案全都清楚了。

当时，就站在屋门外的日本兵并没有太在意赵驹验枪的这个动作。但是赵驹自己却被吓出了一身冷汗。就在他冷静地将曾林的枪放回到曾林身上的那一刻，他做出了一个决定：他要帮赵宏伟将这场戏做好。如果被日本人查出来赵宏伟就是内奸，那么赵宏伟的尸首一定会被大卸八块。赵宏伟的头，一定会被高悬于城门之上，在日光里发臭，于暗夜中生蛆。他不想看到赵宏伟有如此惨的下场。于是，他就走出了屋门，下了不许任何人进屋的命令，好方便自己行事。

赵驹将匕首手把上的指纹擦了个干净，然后，便将匕首重新又塞回到了曾林的手中。匕首的刀身上满是鲜血，不用擦，也不能擦。赵驹又将曾林握着匕首的手用力地握了握，使曾林的指纹确定无误地重新又回到了匕首的手把上。接着，他又取出了曾林的手枪。他擦掉了自己刚才验枪时在枪上留下的指纹，并且取走了枪里的那颗子弹。然后，他又仔细地搜了一遍曾林的身，确认曾林的身上已再无子弹。

赵驹又处理干净了竹内手中的那把枪。然后，他便是将地扫了一遍。地上的脚印痕迹被毁了个彻底。屋内的其他一些蛛丝马迹也都被他破坏了一通。总之，刚才他是如何找出真相的，他就将那些引他走向真相之门的线索都毁得干干净净。最后，只剩下了两个棘手的问题，那就是曾林的位置和赵宏伟身上的长衫。赵驹不能亲自去移动尸体，那样做太招人怀疑了。而赵宏伟身上的长衫也不好脱，总得有个像样的理由才行。这时，赵驹就注意到了，在屋外这处院子的一角，地上有不少新鲜的鸟屎。他有了主意。

赵驹故意捅掉了屋顶上的几片瓦，然后在自己的头顶上弄了一些灰。他动静很大地骂骂咧咧地去打开了院子的门。他对院子外面的日本兵说，他妈的，那间破屋子看样子是快要塌了，快去把里面的三具尸体都搬出来，快。

日本兵们连忙都冲了进去搬尸体。赵驹的心里七上八下。他的手心里甚至都已经出了冷汗。他忽然才发现自己还没有脱手套，于是赶紧就把手套给脱了。他觉得自己今天太冲动了。冲动得一切都找不到理由。而自己现在所做的一切手脚，也实在是太过危险，如果桥本在场，自己恐怕早已被揭穿。赵驹的心绪一时纷乱而纠缠，太多矛盾与忧惧像一根套在他脖子上的绳，勒得他难以呼吸。

在搬动尸体的过程中，曾林手里的匕首和竹内手里的枪都掉在了地上。日本兵们又是捡又是递的，所以这两样东西就又经过了好几个人的手。赵驹暗暗叫好。不错，这样就更能掩饰真相了。

赵宏伟的尸体也被搬了出来，放在了院子里的水井边。这个地方离那片拉有鸟屎的角落较远，不行。赵驹必须要把赵宏伟的尸体滚到鸟屎上去，那样，他才可以有说得过去的理由，帮赵宏伟把他的长衫给脱下来。

赵驹紧皱着眉头，走到了赵宏伟的尸体旁。赵驹刚要开口说话，忽然，桥本从院子外面走了进来。“怎么样了？”桥本问大家。

赵驹心里咯噔一下，完了。桥本不是小兵，就算有渡边做后台，他赵驹也是万万不敢在桥本面前狐假虎威的。要穿帮了。赵驹悔恨死了自己今天所做的一切。

突然，一个日本兵惊呼了起来。他指着赵宏伟的尸体，惊恐万状地说：“他、他、他在动！”

赵驹忙回转身一看。没有哇，哪里动了？

忽然，赵宏伟的手指，又是动了一下。赵驹连忙蹲下身去，一探鼻息，一摸脉搏，奇了！赵宏伟又活了！

赵驹二话不说，背起赵宏伟就往外跑。他一边跑，一边对身后的桥本喊了一句：“我送他去医院！”

赵驹背着赵宏伟猛跑。他没有用日本人的汽车。在这样的情况下，他并没有激动得失去理智。该做的事还没有做完，如果将赵宏伟放到了日本人的汽车上，日本人一定会亲自送赵宏伟去医院，而要是那样的话，那么赵宏伟的这件长衫恐怕就不会再有机会被销毁了。只有趁着乱，在乱中取胜。在混乱中做的一切事情，都是容易找着免责的理由的。

有日本人在后面喊赵驹，赵驹理也不理，只管背着人猛跑。赵驹一边跑，一边对赵宏伟说：“赵宏伟，你个王八蛋，你挺住了，我送你去医院。”

赵宏伟头上的血，一滴滴地滴落在赵驹的额头上。赵宏伟的血和赵驹的汗混在了一块，混浊不堪，咸苦刺眼，血腥扑鼻，像一个时代最无奈的泪水。

渡边命令桥本在战斗结束之后驻守在西城门外的西路战场上，严防敌军再次袭扰，所以从西路战场直到西城门口，一路上都是或疏或密地聚集着桥本部队的士兵，赵驹根本就没有机会把赵宏伟放下来给他脱衣服。没有办法，只能是进了县城再说了。

赵驹背着赵宏伟冲进了县城。

当时，县城里的战斗还没有结束。枪炮声似乎比赵驹出城时更猛烈了。赵驹先找到了一个无人的角落，将赵宏伟放了下来，给他脱掉了那件长衫。长衫的肩颈部已经新染上了不少赵宏伟自己的血，是赵驹将赵宏伟背起来以后从赵宏伟的头上流下来的。赵驹又仔细检查了一下赵宏伟的内衣内裤和鞋袜，很好，除了内衣的颈部有一些新鲜的血渍，估计都是这会儿从他赵宏伟自己的头上流下来的，赵宏伟此刻身上穿着的衣物上已再没有半点其他的血迹。这样就可以安心了。赵驹将赵宏伟的长衫塞进了一个墙洞里，然后，就又背起了赵宏伟，拼命地往县医院的方向跑去。

从赵驹此刻所在的这个位置来说，去县医院一共有两条路可走，一条是近路，一条是远路。若走近路，则必须要穿过县政府旁边的一条街，而县政府周围，此时正战斗激烈；若走远路，固然无枪炮之危险，但必须要绕过半条河，路程曲折。而赵宏伟头上流下的血，都已将赵驹的衣服弄湿。赵驹一咬牙，选择了走近路。

赵驹背着人一路狂奔，离县政府越来越近。血战正酣的恐怖巨响与焦煳味道，正将他围得越来越紧，压得越来越重。他咬了咬牙，又咬了咬牙。赵驹背着赵宏伟，骂了一句粗话，然后，就直冲进了县政府旁边那条炮火正猛烈的街。日军正与敌人激战，机枪声、爆炸声此起彼伏，震耳欲聋的枪炮声宛如咆哮的海浪，一遍又一遍地冲击着天与地，像要把天地都击碎。硝烟弥漫里血肉横飞，人间不是地狱，却比地狱更令人胆战心惊。火蛇四舞，子弹横飞。

一颗日军迫击炮的炮弹在赵驹身旁的不远处爆炸，赵驹被掀翻在地。赵驹爬起来，赶紧看看赵宏伟，赵宏伟还是老样子。赵驹用日语向日军大喊："你们不长眼哪！是自己人！是自己人！"

赵驹重新背起赵宏伟，继续往前冲。赵宏伟的血混合着赵驹的汗滴在地上，一滴一滴，触目惊心。每往前走一步，赵驹都不知道自己会不会迎来一颗子弹；每往前冲一段，赵驹都不知道两人会不会掉入死亡的坟墓。勇敢在这里只是一种求生的本能，活着在这里只是一种上天赐予的运气。赵驹感到不能把握的世界是那样强大，人在沧海横流中只是一只微不足道的小蚂蚁。他的两耳中充满了死亡之音，他的双眼中映满了战火纷飞，而这也许便是乱世的本质。他的头脑里除了冲冲冲，已无法再思考更多的事情。而这也许便是活着的最后生机。

一颗子弹从赵驹的腿边擦过。赵驹愣了一愣，没有跌倒。他双眼血红，大吼一声，向着枪声与炮火最猛烈的街尾直冲了过去。火焰在他的脚边奔窜，子弹在他的耳旁飞过，而他除了往前猛冲，什么都不管，什么也不顾。他怒睁着双眼，看着子弹在自己的面前交织成雨，而他什么也不想。在死神的眼皮底下求生，想得越多，怕得越厉害，怕得越厉害，死得越快。要想不被子弹打中，只有比子弹跑得更快。

奇迹般地，赵驹跑出了那片枪林弹雨。而他背上的赵宏伟，也没有被一颗子弹伤到。离县医院不远了。赵驹正要再次发力猛跑，忽然，一把枪，顶到了他的太阳穴上。

赵驹一呆。完了，他背着人，拔枪不方便。再说了，也来不及了。真是大意了。

“你是汉奸？”拿枪的人问他。

赵驹一看，自己今天，穿的是一条日本军裤。

赵驹不说话。

忽然，拿枪的人看了看赵宏伟的脸。看完了赵宏伟的脸，那人居然放下了枪。他问：“你背着他要去哪里？”赵驹说：“我要送他去医院，再晚怕要来不及了。”那人说：“那你走吧，快。”

赵驹不敢停留，拔腿就跑。枪声炮声，在他身后越来越远。

跑着跑着，赵驹忽然笑了起来。他说，赵宏伟，想不到你还真是和他们一伙的，算我没有帮错你。他笑着，都不知道自己为什么要笑。

事后，赵驹又小心地去墙洞那里拿回了长衫。在得知赵宏伟已无大碍之后，他独自去酒楼喝了一顿闷酒。很多时候，他都不知道，自己所做的，究竟是对是错。

此刻，看着火盆里的长衫渐渐变成焦黑的一团，赵驹长长地叹了一口气。直到现在，他都仍然不能理解自己，自己为什么要救赵宏伟。他分明是一直盼望赵宏伟走霉运的。他想，也许帮了赵宏伟，对自己也是有利的，因为当初毕竟是他撺掇渡边去拉赵宏伟来做汉奸的，万一赵宏伟被查出来是内奸，那他赵驹也一定不会有好果子吃。但是这一层利害关系是他事后才想到的，当初为赵宏伟消灭罪证时，他的脑子里并没有这样一个合情合理的动机，这让他对自己感到很失望。他觉得，自己是输给了那个自己不想成为的自己。自己是日本人的鹰犬，但是自己却救了日本人的敌人，自己不是疯子是什么？赵宏伟身在曹营心在汉，这本来跟自己没什么关系，可是自己帮他消灭了罪证，自己就成了他实实在在的同伙，自己不是自找死路是什么？真是一失足成千古恨，再回首已百年身。

另外一方面，赵驹也并不能确定，自己是否真的已经将事情做到了尽善尽美。内奸一案，赵宏伟是否还留有什么破绽？自己当天行事匆忙，考虑多有不周，诸多举动，若有人仔细推敲，实在疑点多多。桥本当天也曾入现场验人死活，他是否也发现了什么？渡边会不会认真详查当天诸事的细节？太多的问题，赵驹都无法给自己一个确定而自信的答案。各种担忧如蜘蛛一样，在他的心里结着纤细的网，他依然保持着往日的冷静，但这冷静里，已不可回避地有了难言的忐忑。毕竟，这次，他是真的背叛了日本人。

赵驹将自己的手套和手帕也扔进了火盆里。火势很旺。等到盆里的东西都成了灰烬，赵驹就往火盆里浇了一盆水。火灭了，火盆和火盆里的灰烬一下子全跌进了冷冷的黑暗里。黑暗的灰烬在黑暗的水里浮沉。等到火盆冷却，赵驹就将盆里的水和灰烬全部倒进了两只装有屎尿的马桶里。最后的证据也已成了夜香，希望万事会大吉。

赵驹坐在正屋里，屋里灯光明亮。夜已那么深，可他还是不想睡。坐到了深夜，才会懂得，夏的夜，也会那样凉，凉薄的凉。赵驹看着屋里的一切，眼里也是觉得凉。一只蚊子停在他的手背上，他也只是凉薄地笑了一笑。

赵驹仔仔细细地擦拭着一块牌匾。在这样一个心微乱、灯还亮的深夜里，这块老旧不堪的匾，竟硬是被赵驹擦得发出了几分微弱的光，就仿佛是不管岁月再怎么侵蚀，也还未能完全吞噬掉它往日的辉煌。这是一块红底金字的大横匾，匾上的四个大字，正是“威远镖局”。

赵驹已经记不清，这块匾究竟是哪一年被取下来的了。也许是父亲被官府抓起来的那一年？或者更早？又或者，其实从父亲投靠玉山帮的那一天起，这块匾，就已经是没有挂着的意义了。很多时候，不想起往事，人都不会觉得，时间过得真快。

赵驹还记得，自己小时候坐在院子的角落里看父亲和镖师们打拳的样子。那时的天总是那么蓝，空气里也仿佛总带着青草的香，蟋蟀们总是那样热闹，毛毛虫总是又讨厌又可爱。父亲打拳的样子总是很漂亮、很威武。父亲舞起大刀来，刀风更是呼呼作响。那时候，镖局里的师傅们都以父亲为傲，说，整个江南武林之中，能与赵总镖头匹敌的，没有几人。那时候，自己一直觉得，父亲是个了不起的大英雄。

但是，父亲却从来不肯教自己习武。或者，也可以说，是父亲压根儿就没有想过要教自己练武。父亲总是对自己说，驹儿啊，祖上传下来的江湖饭，到你爹我这一辈，怕是要吃到头了，爹不想再教你走练武的这条路了，爹想要你读书，自古以来一直都是文贵武贱，武夫功夫练得再好，也不过就是个市井强人，你要是能把书读好了，将来中个秀才举人什么的，那可是比

大刀王五还要强上千倍百倍呀，到那时，你不仅是为咱们赵家争了光，而且，你和你的子子孙孙，还会有享不尽的荣华富贵，你说，这可不是要比刀光剑影地行走江湖好上千倍万倍。

当然，自己那时并不十分明白，为什么父亲要说，武夫不如文人。自己还是喜欢看父亲和镖师们练武，那些苍劲洒脱的招式里，总像是藏着谜一样的美丽与奥秘，它们像仙境一样吸引着自己。而私塾先生要自己读的四书五经，干巴巴的，令自己感到厌恶与恐惧。自己依旧尚武轻文，那分明的好恶，就像是奔腾在体内的血液一样有力而鲜活。直到最后，自己被父亲痛打了一顿。记忆中，父亲从未那样愤怒过。父亲的脸，像渗血的树皮一样可怕。父亲的眼，像碎了的太阳。从那以后，父亲练武时，再不许自己在旁观看。那是一道铁铮铮的命令。自己总觉得，正是这道命令，将自己的童年剖成了两半，黑白分明。

自己是在长大以后，才从父亲的口中大概地知道了母亲的故事。母亲曾经很爱父亲，那爱像天上的太阳一样光明无比又温暖无尽，但是一个书生的出现却改变了一切。那个书生有着满腹的诗书与满嘴的绚烂，天下的凡夫俗子在他面前几乎都会自惭形秽，知耻知贱。而正是这个书生，将父亲的人生送进了黑夜。在一个秋意浓郁的夜晚，书生带着母亲去了遥远的北方，从此再无音讯。而那时，自己尚在襁褓之中。母亲走后，父亲每天都会抱着自己，去赵家镇北面的路口处张望。直到自己长大，父亲也没能盼到母亲的一丝身影。书生当年对父亲说过一句话：一介武夫，纵然打遍天下无敌手，于国于家又有何益处。

父亲不许自己观武之后，自己真的就走上了读书人的道路。读书之后，自己才知道，自从子不语怪力乱神之后，武不如文便成了中国两千多年来的历史传统。你再不服气，又怎能拗得过一个观念几千年的根深蒂固。万般皆下品，唯有读书高；书中自有黄金屋，书中自有颜如玉。这不仅是一个书面的理论，更是一个历史的现实。自己不得不承认，父亲教训得对。父亲是个聪明人，他懂得，与其在自尊中被历史抛弃，不如在改变中重塑金身。放弃对武的热爱，是自己人生中的第一次投降。

晚清动荡，科举制度最终还是走向了灭亡，但是父亲并没有因为科举的取消而改让自己去习武。父亲说，洋人会造洋枪洋炮，就是因为他们读了洋书，读书到底是比练武强，而且，读洋书更比读中国书强。于是，父亲就送自己去了洋学堂里念书。父亲的希望是，待自己长大了，也可以像洋人一样，会造洋枪洋炮。父亲终究是个争强好胜的人。

自己是在辛亥革命发生的那一年，目睹到了父亲的失败。自己还记得，那是一个秋高气爽的日子，天空清澈得像一块洗干净了的玻璃。父亲带着八个镖师押镖外出已有十余天，算算日子，应该再有几天就能回来了。自己正在俯身捡拾院子里的落叶，忽然，就响起了低沉的拍门声。家仆们去开门，一开门，却见到了披头散发、满脸瘀青的父亲。自己惊呼了一声，奔向父亲，父亲却是一把将自己推开，要自己回房里去看书。自己转脸看去，跟在父亲身后的众镖师，也全是一副狼狈的模样，自己不知究竟发生了什么事。留在家里的几位镖师闻讯也都跑了出来，他们见父亲走路有些瘸，就都忙去搀扶他，却都被父亲拒绝了。父亲走到院子中央时，一片落叶飞到了父亲的头上，父亲突然就吐出了一口血来。父亲倒在了地上。

事后，自己才知道，父亲这一次，是失了镖。记忆中，这似乎是父亲的第一次失镖。父亲这一次，押运的是两箱金银珠宝，据说价值不菲。父亲和众镖师一路上千小心万小心，最终还是遇上了一群土匪。这群土匪的手里，有十条枪。父亲对这群土匪说尽了好话，报尽了江湖上一些朋友的名号，却毫不奏效。土匪们就是要抢这两箱金银珠宝。土匪头子说，不是我故意要跟你赵总镖头过不去，谁让这两箱珠宝的主人是那个死老太监呢，有仇不报非君子，只好得罪了。父亲就准备要和土匪们动手。谁知，一个练少林派功夫的镖师刚出手，手还没碰到土匪的身上，他的脑袋就被土匪的子弹给打穿了。父亲赶紧示意众镖师停手。土匪头子哈哈大笑，说，任你们拳脚功夫再厉害，在这洋枪面前，你们就是一群等死的猪，识相的就快跑吧。他话音刚落，父亲就飞跃了出去。父亲是想要擒贼先擒王，一举抓住那个土匪头子。父亲的动作疾如闪电，谁知，子弹却更快。就在父亲的手快要抓住土匪头子的脖子时，一颗子弹打中了父亲的手臂。父亲被土匪打倒在地上。四条枪一齐指住了他。

土匪头子并不想多害人命，就让众土匪把父亲围起来打了一顿。包括父亲在内，没有人再敢反抗拿着枪的土匪。土匪头子临走前，割了父亲的辫子，说，我们要去投靠革命党了，这两箱财宝，你们就当是孝敬给了反清事

业吧。土匪们哈哈笑着，扬长而去。

记忆中，那一年的秋天，世道乱得厉害，就连一向太平的赵家镇，也到处充斥着恐慌与不安。当然，那时，谁也没想到，大清朝真的会完。也根本就没有人会相信，不久之后，中国会再没有皇帝。一个有着几千年帝王史的中国，怎么会突然就不再有皇帝呢？赵家镇上的人，都不相信革命，就连最懂革命的老秀才，也说中国不会没有皇帝。但是，事实上，中国的历史走向了惊心动魄的大转折。

那时，自己始终不能接受父亲被打败的这个事实。那几天，自己一直想去病床前问问父亲，他们说的这些事情是不是真的。但是，自己每次一走近病床，就会失去开口的勇气。病床上的父亲总是在咳嗽。一听到父亲的咳嗽，自己就想逃。太可怕了，太可怕了，但究竟是什么可怕呢？自己又不知道。自己只知道，父亲手臂上的那处枪伤，的确是真的。

父亲出钱厚葬了那位死去的镖师。以前大家都知道这位镖师的硬气功厉害，他能用喉头顶断红缨枪。但是，他终究没硬过子弹。在肉体面前，子弹是无敌的。

那位丢了财宝的老太监，并没有来向镖局索赔。在听到镖局失镖的消息之后，老太监便上了吊。上吊前，老太监留下了一封血书。县衙里看过这封血书的几个人无不三缄其口，绝不肯对外透露出血书中的半点内容，其战战兢兢，犹如惹上了什么要命的官司。老太监死后的第三天，这封血书就被人从衙门里盗走了。血书被盗走的第二天，衙门就将老太监一案匆匆了结，再无下文。由于老太监没有半个亲人，所以，镖局自然也就不用再赔给老太监什么钱了。镖局里的人无不庆幸，都说，幸亏老太监死了，要不然，就算把这镖局给卖了，怕也是赔不起那笔钱的。

不过，在溥仪退位之后，一个关于老太监的故事，还是在赵家镇上悄悄地流传开来。三十八年前，一个雷电交加的夏夜，当时还很年轻的老太监奉了旨，要秘密处死一个宫女。这个宫女当时已怀有七个月的身孕。她苦苦地哀求老太监，说，她死可以，但是请他一定要留下这个孩子，孩子已七个月，拿了出来，兴许能活。老太监不允。她就说，你知道这个孩子姓什么吗？他说，我不想知道。她说，这个孩子，姓爱新觉罗。

宫女死后，老太监剖开了她的肚子，取出了孩子。他瞒天过海，将这个孩子送出了紫禁城，交给了一户姓姚的山野人家喂养。这个孩子活了下来。那户人家给他取名叫姚凡。老太监一直躲在暗处留心着这个孩子的成长。寒来暑往，这个孩子终于长大了，而这个太监也真的成了老太监。本以为日子会一直就这样平静地流淌，但是终于有一天，姚凡还是察觉到了自己身世的不对劲。于是，老太监只能寻求逃避。老太监在一个恰当的时候，打断了自己的一条腿，让自己成了一个瘸子，然后，他便向宫里提出了告老还乡的请求。老太监躲到了江南，躲到了赵家镇，就是为了不让姚凡找到他。

但是，姚凡的养父母在临死前还是告诉了姚凡老太监的下落。姚凡不远千里赶来江南，就是为了要弄清自己的身世。但是老太监却怎么样也不肯告诉他真相。姚凡情急，问，莫非我父母的死与你有关？老太监犹豫了一下，说，是。姚凡大笑，说，不管你说的是不是真的，从今日起，我就且当你是我的仇人了，我不杀你，但定要你不得安宁，除非你有一天肯把事情的来龙去脉都给我说清楚。

后来的姚凡，便成了土匪头子。老太监的家里，三天两头失窃。就算不失窃，也会碰上其他的一些不大不小的麻烦，但老太监从不声张，所以，赵家镇上的人以前根本就不知道，三天两头有土匪光顾这个镇。终于，老太监忍受不了了，就想要逃去云南。但是，他托威远镖局先行运去云南的财物，还是被姚凡给劫了。他知道，姚凡就是在逼他开口。

老太监的血书，其实是写给姚凡的一封信。他知道，他留下的血书，姚凡必会来盗。他在信中说出了全部的秘密。他说，我一死，纵有惊天的波澜掀起，我也不用再怕了。他说，其实你娘一直来我的梦里向我索命，但她哪里知道，当年最不想她死的那个人，是我。

据说姚凡看过血书之后，在老太监的坟前跪了七天七夜。然后，便带着兄弟们加入了推翻清朝的革命大军。从此再无音讯。策马离开赵家镇前，姚凡说的最后一句话是：帝制吃人，天下人的生与死，不该再由一个人来决定。

父亲的身体慢慢地还是好了起来。虽然老太监的死使镖局免去了一场赔偿之灾，但是，父亲还是对老太监的死充满了内疚。毕竟，如果不是父亲输给了姚凡，老太监就不会自尽。后来，当老太监的故事在镇上暗暗地流传开来以后，父亲虽然不全信，却也觉得自己有愧于忠勇二字。未能以死护

雇主之财，是为不忠；未能舍生死与匪斗，是为不勇。不忠不勇，愧对武人武魂。父亲说，他当初看到老太监的那两箱财宝时，便已知老太监当年定曾荣宠一时，只是一直很疑惑，老太监既有如此多的财产，又为何还要在这镇上自甘清贫冷落，一不置产二不娶妻。现在才知，原来老太监求的便是一“隐”字。父亲说，老太监定是有三怕：一怕姚凡知晓身世之后会报杀母之仇；二怕朝廷知晓其当年瞒天过海之事后会将其追捕猎杀；三怕姚凡的身份一旦为世人所知，天下必会风起云涌。姚凡不需要真正的天子血统，只要有人相信他是皇子，自然会有曹操出来挟天子以令诸侯。这才是真正折磨了老太监一生的大恐惧。但是，老太监想错了。中国几千年的帝制已经走到了尽头，有些悲剧，已再也不会有重演的舞台。天下大势，浩浩汤汤，顺之者昌，逆之者亡。自己那时虽然年幼，却也已相信革命。

父亲的精神始终未见好转。虽然，拳脚败给子弹并不是一件十分可耻的事，但是，对于一个武林高手来说，这终究也是个不小的耻辱。更何况，有人死了，父亲却还活着，难免就有些不好听的闲言碎语在父亲的背后打转。那一年的冬天，辛亥革命成功了，但是自己的父亲，却走进了一条死胡同。

直到现在，自己还记得父亲那时站在院子里叹气的模样。冬天，院子里的树掉光了树叶，弯曲的树枝很像跳着舞的鬼怪。父亲就那样颓唐地站在树下，独自发呆，时而叹一口气。自己并不知道父亲在想些什么，也不敢问。自己很想过去陪陪父亲，又怕父亲会赶自己走。现在想来，其实，那时的父亲是真孤独。那时的父亲还没有变坏，那时的父亲心中还思念着远走他乡的母亲。自己是在长大之后才理解父亲那时的悲哀。在最心爱的女人面前，父亲败给了书生；而当武功成为父亲最后的骄傲与自尊时，武功又败给了进步着的时代。就在土匪们殴打父亲的那一刻，父亲成了个一无所有的人。这种孤苦，无药可医。父亲是那样的可怜。

而父亲的厄运还在后面。原本，江湖上的人都知道父亲的八极拳是打遍江南无敌手，所以凡是威远镖局押的镖，一般没人敢打歪主意。但是自从父亲败给了姚凡、败给了洋枪之后，阿猫阿狗们的胆子全都壮了起来。虽然一般的角色很容易被父亲给踢走，但是再硬的墙，也是禁不住众人齐砸的。终于，父亲又失了两次镖，而且是连失。一次是因为一种西洋迷药，一次，还是因为洋枪。父亲的声誉跌入了谷底，威远镖局的生意开始惨淡。陆陆续续地，开始有镖师离开威远镖局。父亲敢接的和接到的生意都越来越小。想当初，总有天价的财宝需要父亲来押运，父亲也敢接这种生意。但是如今，不仅不再有这种大生意来找父亲，而且就算有，父亲也已不敢接。丢失的财物越贵，赔给雇主的钱也就越多，父亲始终都不敢忘记一件事，那就是当年若不是老太监自寻短见，威远镖局恐怕早已不复存在。父亲成了一个畏首畏尾的人。镖局的生意越来越惨淡。好运抛弃了父亲，时代抛弃了父亲。

其实，自从父亲败给了姚凡的洋枪之后，自己就已经真的懂得，父亲为自己选择的读书路是正确的。做父亲的，总是想要让儿子有一个锦绣前程的。识时务者为俊杰，父亲不是个庸人。自己以前读书，是迫于父命，但在父亲被打败之后，读书便成了自己的自愿。自己无法忘记那个披头散发、满脸瘀青的父亲，永远都无法忘记。那张脸上，没有一丝丝的自豪，甚至没有半点点的自尊，除了痛苦，只有痛苦。那是一张自己永远难忘的脸，父亲失败的脸。父亲的那种痛苦，令自己感到恐惧。而这种恐惧，又是否有解药？

除非，儿子可以用自己将来的荣光，来抚平父亲的创伤。尊严，有时候就是一种令人深深疼痛的东西，有时候，就是一份债。从那时起，读书就成了自己孤注一掷的寄托。姚凡毁掉了父亲和自己生命中的太多东西，这些东西无形而珍贵，游离于生存之外而又缠结于命运之内，它们的生灭足以使一个人的人生从此不同。而姚凡没想过这些。自己深深地恨着姚凡，那是自己第一次懂得一种恨。

小时候，私塾先生总夸自己聪明，别的小孩学个《论语》都很费劲，但是自己却居然连《尚书》都能背出来，这在赵家镇上甚至是江庆县内都是罕有的。那时候，父亲只要听到私塾先生对自己的夸赞，脸上就会浮起快乐的微笑。那种微笑在父亲的脸上是少有的，那种快乐是从父亲的心里涌出来的。就算在父亲比武胜利之时，自己也未曾见过父亲有这样的快乐。在奉命读书的那些年里，正是父亲的这份快乐，支撑着年幼的自己对读书的努力。而在赵宏伟这个名字出现之前，自己用读书来给予父亲的快乐，始终是满满的。

科举取消之后，自己与赵宏伟同在县里的新式小学堂里念书，同校不同班，其实是同学。但是在开始的两年里，自己的确是从不知这世上还有赵宏伟这么个人。直到赵宏伟所作的《怀古八首》在学堂里流传开来以后，自己才知晓，原来在赵家镇上，还有一个神童存在。而且，人家赵宏伟的启蒙老师，是赵家镇上有名的老秀才。自己后来不禁暗暗感慨，父亲终究是个江湖中人，北方武林有什么风吹草动他都能马上知晓，而对于赵家镇上如此重要的文人文事，他多年来竟一直闻所未闻。

自己在打听到了赵宏伟的诸多事迹之后，不禁便有些惺惺相惜之意。传说赵宏伟七岁便能作诗，八岁即可赋词，古风格律皆通，观其《怀古八首》，所言当真不虚。那一年，自己主动去认识了赵宏伟。自己当初是真希望，能和他成为好朋友。

但是，赵宏伟对自己却似乎并无英雄惜英雄之意，自己在他的眼里，似乎就是个泛泛之交与泛泛之辈。他连比赛弹弓都不会叫上自己一起去。有一次，自己问他：你会背《尚书》吗？他却不屑地说：背《尚书》有什么用，就算你会背，老百姓也根本就听不懂。

赵宏伟的骄傲既是一种吸引力，也是一种锐气，所以两个同样骄傲的人在一起，是永远也无法成为好朋友的。一山难容二虎，纵然这两只虎还都只是幼虎。自己和赵宏伟的友情后来慢慢地也就淡了，以至于到最后，两个人就算在学堂里偶然碰到了，彼此也都懒得打一声招呼。说实话，自己对此感到有些悲哀。自己很孤独，自己没有朋友，那些不如自己的人，自己根本就瞧不上，而自己欣赏的人，却又瞧不上自己，这也许就是人生中难以妥协的尴尬。

赵宏伟在学堂里是首屈一指的优秀学生，自己当然也优秀，但是自己永远在赵宏伟之后。父亲后来终于也知道了赵宏伟这个名人，但却是以一种相当尴尬的方式。老师对父亲说，要是你们家的孩子，也能像赵宏伟一样聪明就好了。

自己记得，当时父亲的眼神里，有一丝瑟缩。这丝瑟缩，自己至今记忆犹新。父亲以前一直很自豪地以为，他的儿子是全县第一，但是现在，却突然有人告诉他，他的儿子不够格。他的儿子应该要向另一个人的儿子学习，而那个人，只是一个文不能文、武不能武的裁缝。没有什么能比儿子的不优秀更令父亲丢脸。没有什么，能比被一个自己素来瞧不起的人超越更令人感到羞耻。没有什么快乐，能敌过别人眼里的比较。没有什么自信，能抵挡如潮的人言。父亲还是一直很为他的儿子感到自豪，只是这自豪，不再有以前那样真正的快乐，满满的快乐。被庸俗的大众拿来与别人作庸俗的比较，是一个人一生最不幸的事，但也是每个人都无法逃脱的事。无知的比较毁掉了人心的自足，而我们却都无计可施。

好像是命运故意要与自己作对。从那以后，“赵宏伟”三个字，便不时会出现在自己和父亲的生活中。有时，人们在父亲的面前夸赞自己，完了也会说一句：赵家镇上那个叫赵宏伟的孩子，最近又写诗了，他可真聪明。父亲便会应和着说：是啊，那个孩子我也听说了，是个很聪明的孩子。自己以前其实并不讨厌赵宏伟，可是，众人却为什么偏偏都要拿自己来和他作比较！有什么可比的！

自己为读书付出的全部努力，已很难再换来父亲发自肺腑的欢笑。自己有时也想写两首伤春悲秋的诗，却总会把平仄给弄错。而自己会背的《尚书》，又的确是一点用也没有。世人当真是只懂风月，不知圣贤。一切都糟透了。

小时候，自己只是因为想要让父亲高兴，所以才会去努力读书。自己曾经也的确是做到了，用自己的聪颖与出众，来抚慰父亲饱经沧桑的心。父亲在江湖中是个英雄，所以并没有人会懂得父亲的脆弱。父亲今生唯一想要战胜而又永远也无法战胜的敌人，其实就是那个带走了母亲的书生。怎样在一个空空荡荡的擂台上打败一个虚无缥缈的人，成了父亲一生的痛苦与噩梦。而自己在文才上的出众，却给了父亲由衷的解脱。没有什么，比儿子的胜利更能证明父亲的强大。如果儿子是个状元，那么父亲就算只是个低贱的武夫那也没什么可耻的。这就是人生的逻辑，百姓的道理。父亲就是这样，在自己的身上盼望着人生的光荣与梦想。回过头来想想，其实，父亲是那样可怜。

本来一切都很好，但是，既生瑜，何生亮。世人并不懂得文无第一的道理，在世人的眼里，莫名其妙地，赵宏伟就是比自己聪明。且不说究竟是谁比谁更聪明，其实自己也根本就不想和赵宏伟作比较。聪明有什么可比的？文才有什么可比的？这些东西根本就是没法拿来比的。但是，在世人的眼里，万事万物皆分三六九等，各行各业皆有第一第二。你固然可以清者自清，不落俗套，不合众议，但众人皆怎样说，你在众人的眼里便只能是怎样

的一个人。这是人世的大悲哀。人生之立身立影，并不在于本我之心，而只在于众人之口；人生之高低分等，并不在于自己怎样做，而只在于众人怎样看。这是一个世俗的桎梏。在父亲的心里，他的儿子当然是无人可比的，做父亲的，当然也总想为儿子感到由衷的高兴，但是，若总是不停地有人提醒他，“你的儿子不如人家裁缝的儿子”，你说让一个父亲怎么还高兴得起来？那个纷扰无尽而又无聊至极的舆论擂台，就算你自己不想上去，众人也会硬推你上去。而父亲，在擂台上，是从来不曾输过的。他又怎能看着儿子的输，还笑得出来。所以，回过头来想想，其实真正夺走了自己和父亲之间那种简单又纯粹的快乐的，是世俗的舆论，庸俗而无知的舆论。这不关赵宏伟什么事。可惜，自己年幼时，哪懂这些，只知凭着感觉去做人做事。

若不是父亲败给了姚凡，让自己真切地看到了武人之哀，自己那时恐怕已放弃了读书。因为自己本不爱读书，而庸众的瑜亮之比，又残忍地剥夺了父亲为自己由衷地感到自豪与快乐的权利，所以，自己那时实在觉得，读书对自己来说，已毫无意义。但是父亲在洋枪面前的失败，却狠狠地砸碎了自己转身的念头。开弓已无回头箭，男儿笑里多藏泪。那时，自己想，就拿人生当成是一场老天开的赌局吧，在这条路上继续走下去，看看自己最后会不会赢，自己输赢不悔。

那些年，世道也真是乱，袁世凯称帝、张勋复辟，一桩桩一件件，阴晴不定，弄得百姓是胆战心惊，无所适从。大清的县衙变成了民国的县政府，但是坐在里面的县长，却还是以前的县老爷。革命革命，革了个有头无尾、乱象丛生、四分五裂。

和那世道一样乱的，是父亲和自己的人生。随着镖局生意的败落，父亲的人生也开始变得一蹶不振。在姚凡事件之后，父亲首先迷恋上的便是酒。以前父亲也喝酒，而且是大碗大碗地喝，但那时的父亲，喝的是英雄酒，喝出来的是一股天下无敌的豪气。而现在，父亲喝的却是颓唐酒，喝出来的只是一股不省人事的死气。开始时，大家都以为，父亲只是一时想不开，需要借酒消愁，过段时间他自然会好起来。但是，谁能想到，父亲的失败会接踵而至，不幸会连连登门。父亲，再也没能从颓废里爬起来。

有时候，自己看父亲喝得烂醉，便会上去拉拉他，说，爹，你不要再喝了。但是父亲却只会赶自己走，要自己回去读书。有一回，自己哭着求父亲，要他不要再喝了，但是，他仍然只是要自己回去读书。那一刻，自己哭得稀里哗啦。那哭，不是为父亲，也不是为自己，而是为了谁也阻止不了的崩塌、为了谁也逃脱不了的桎梏。那哭，痛彻心扉。

其实，现在想想，父亲也确是时运不济。在民国乱世之中，有不少八极拳名家，仍然创出了一番作为。有入军中教拳杀敌的，有伴大帅左右护其周全的。东北闻名的霍殿阁，更是凭着独步天下的八极拳，得以追随在溥仪身旁。而父亲，虽贵为江南武林翘楚，却终生止步于这镖局的祖业之中。曾经也有人劝父亲外出闯荡，父亲却婉言谢绝。父亲不搏于天下，天下自然也就不会借运于他。父亲是舍不得这镖局的祖业，还是舍不得这个家？自己当时不得而知。

堕落是个无底洞，有了开始，就不会轻易有结束。继酗酒之后，父亲又迷上了赌博。十赌九输，赌博加速了家业的衰败。那时，谁都已经看出了父亲的大势已去，镖局里的镖师，已寥寥无几。自己那时，是怎么样也想不明白，一生素来俭朴自律的父亲，怎么就像换了一个人似的，会堕落至此。那时，自己经常暗自垂泪。自己一生崇拜父亲，但自己崇拜的，是那个英雄一样的父亲，而不是这个如一摊烂泥似的父亲。可是父亲又始终是父亲，不管是那个还是这个，都只是同一个父亲。自己能做的，只有接受英雄的堕落。命运，又逼着自己投降了一次。

嫖赌不分家，继赌博之后，父亲又开始嫖妓。父亲曾说过，他今生不会再找第二个女人，但是，他现在却开始了嫖妓。人生之错愕缭乱，莫过于此。自己曾在偎翠楼的门口死死地拉住过父亲，但是结果，却招来了父亲的两记耳光。自己还记得妓女们在那一刻哄堂大笑的样子。那一刻的自己，恨父亲。

那时候，自己常常会一个人站在镖局的大门外，望着那块镖局的牌子黯然发呆。金灿灿的“威远镖局”四个大字，那时还是那样光鲜。只可惜，门庭冷，落叶满，暮气生。以前父亲常说，江湖残酷，其实，这个世界比江湖更残酷。

一直跟随父亲到最后的镖师，只有于叔一个人。于叔练的是梅花螳螂拳。父亲曾经说过，螳螂拳是一门好功夫，只可惜于叔用心不专，练得不深。于叔有些孩子心性，所以自己孤独时，总喜欢和于叔待在一起。自己很

少能从父亲的口中听到关于武林的事，相反，于叔却总是愿意滔滔不绝地跟自己讲述各种江湖传奇。什么南少林与天地会，杨露禅与董海川，于叔说起时总是如数家珍。但是于叔并不敢教自己武功，连一招半式都不可以，因为父亲在这方面早已下过了令，在镖局里，没有人敢违抗父亲的命令。自己以前总是觉得很奇怪，同样是武林中人，为什么于叔对江湖的感情是那样热，而父亲对江湖的感情是那样冷。后来，于叔告诉自己，他对江湖的感情热，是因为他还从来没有得到过江湖的桂冠，而父亲对江湖的感情冷，是因为父亲早已饱尝了高处不胜寒。

父亲堕落之初，于叔也曾劝过父亲，但父亲痴醉如旧。几次之后，于叔就也不再劝了。自己要于叔再去劝父亲，于叔就说，没用的，你爹心里的难受，治不好的。自己不明白，于叔就又说，是洋枪夺走了你爹头上的桂冠，而你爹又没办法打败洋枪，你说你爹他能怎么办？

这是一座无法翻越的山峰，这座山峰挡在了父亲的面前，就连自己，也为父亲感到了绝望。是啊，父亲他又还能怎么办？是这个时代，要淘汰父亲这一辈武人。谁也战胜不了时代。于叔只是替父亲感到惋惜，说，当年北洋军派人来请你爹去军中教拳，你爹若答应了，现在也不会落魄至此。

自己却只是哭，为了无原因的原因哭。父亲是最憎恶男儿流泪的，可是，自己仍是这样不争气，总是要哭。于叔安慰自己，说，没事的，你爹只要不抽鸦片，就还是条汉子。赌坊妓院有哪个男人不爱？只不过是有些男人没钱去而已，或者就是有老婆管着，不让去。男人只要一进了赌坊和妓院，天大的烦恼也会烟消云散。你爹遭遇了无法翻身的失败，如果让他一直在冷冷的痛苦里死待着，他恐怕会被他自己给逼疯。现在这样也好，银圆、女人，输输赢赢、热热闹闹，只要能让你爹忘记了战胜他的洋枪，就好。这个世界本来就很肮脏与无常，而男人活在这个世上，如果只认干净和恒常的理，那么早晚会被撞得头破血流。不嫖不赌，不是男人，会嫖会赌，还是活人。

自己记得，于叔当时说完后，就沉默了。仿佛揭露了什么连他自己也觉得意外的真相，他的神情分外沮丧。红尘是那样的大，大得可以让人永远也找不到某样分明存在着的东西；红尘又是那样的小，小得可以让人连一个躲起来给自己舔伤口的地方都寻不着。人生就是这般荒谬。从那以后，于叔就很少再和自己说话，也很少再和父亲说话。就好像，大家的世界，忽然都换了一片天空。

自己是在十六岁那年，跨进赌坊的。那一次，自己赢了不少钱。赌徒们都说，第一次进赌坊的人，都会赢钱。赢钱之后，自己去了妓院。那个取走了自己第一次的年轻女子，长着一双水汪汪的漂亮眼睛。大人们说得真的不错，色子解烦困，女子最销魂。自己第一次尝过了赌和嫖，那滋味就再也忘不了。当自己从妓院里走出来的时候，自己想的是，爹，我恨你。

自己染上嫖赌的事，终于还是被父亲发现了。那一天，父亲的脸上涨满了永远也无法形容出来的暴怒与苦痛。响亮的耳光一记又一记地打在自己的脸上，铁硬的拳头一次又一次地砸在自己的身上，自己被打得晕头转向，痛苦不堪。父亲怒吼着“我没有你这么个不争气的儿子”，一掌便拍断了院子里一棵胳膊粗的小树。自己始终沉默着，没有喊痛，也没有落泪。自己相信，那一刻的父亲，是想要打死自己这个不争气的东西的。小树倒在地上，风吹过时，落叶依然簌簌。自己在那一刻，忽然开了口，对父亲说：你有什么资格打我。

父亲再次被激怒了。他正要再次痛打自己，于叔死死地将他抱住了。于叔求他：总镖头，你饶了少爷吧，你饶了少爷吧！说完，于叔便放开了父亲，拦在父亲面前，给父亲跪了下来。“总镖头，是我不好，是我说了不该说的话，教坏了少爷，你要打打我吧，你要打打我吧！”于叔说完，便是狠狠地自己打自己耳光，几下就打得他自己满嘴是血。

“不该说的话？你教了他什么？”

“我……我对少爷说，不嫖不赌，不是男人，会嫖会赌，还是活人。”

“你疯了！于三你个王八蛋，你竟敢这样教坏我儿子！你为什么要这样害我！我宰了你！”父亲像头发了疯的雄狮，一脚飞起，便将于叔踢出了两丈远。于叔倒在地上，接连吐出了几大口的鲜血。

父亲还要打于叔，自己就扑到了于叔的身上，挡住了父亲的拳头。自己转过身去，对父亲说，于叔为什么要对我说那样的话，你自己难道想不明白吗！

父亲愣在原地。

“我不配做你的儿子，你也不配做我的父亲！”自己对父亲说。

父亲一声怒吼，双眼血红地将自己拎起来，甩了出去。“咔嚓”一声，自己的胳膊脱臼了。

一场吵闹，就这么结束了。一切似乎又都平静了下来。但是，只有时间才知道，痛苦之后的平静永远不会是平静，沉默背后的安宁，其实是深渊。

后来，于叔告诉自己，父亲在那一天晚上，哭了。于叔说，他生平还是第一次见到总镖头哭。那天晚上，于叔咳着血，跪在自己面前，求自己不要再去赌钱嫖妓。他说，他说的那些都是胡话，怎么可以当真呢，要是自己拿他的那些话当了真，那他的罪，可就是万死难赎了。自己答应了他，不会再去赌钱嫖妓。于叔很高兴，站了起来，说，你要早这么说，那总镖头怎么会舍得打你呢。

但是，自己其实是在骗于叔。正如于叔此时说他那天说的话全是胡话一样，他也是在骗自己。人生有时的确是需要相互欺骗的，因为真相太可怕。有时甚至会可怕得让人再难活下去。而什么才是人生的真相？于叔在那一天所说的，才是真相。红尘的本质是灰暗，人生的本质是困难，谁能离开了肮脏的大地飞翔于蓝天白云之间？色子能给人刺激，妓女能给人快活，谁可抛弃近在咫尺的欢乐而自愿沉陷于牢不可破的痛苦之中？爱上了色子，爱上了妓女，自己的人生，就不可能再回到原来的路上了。

但是，从那以后，父亲却再没去过赌坊妓院。他只是加倍地在家里喝闷酒，从天亮喝到天黑，从天黑喝到天亮。他喝下去的，就好像不是一坛一坛的酒，而是一片一片的海。苦涩而深邃的海。现在回想起来，父亲真是可怜。一个人要有多少沉重无解的痛苦，才会想要把自己融化到酒缸里？一个人的现实要有多么可怕，才能让他宁愿醉死也不要清醒？一个人要有多少哭不出的眼泪，才能喝下那一片又一片辽阔的酒海？与其这样，还真不如让他天天去赌钱嫖妓，那样，起码还能如回光返照一般，活一天，高兴一天。可惜，自己那时，又懂什么。

父亲喝醉了，嘴里就经常会喊“雪兰、雪兰”。雪兰是自己母亲的名。父亲的喊声总是那样的微弱，而又带着一丝小心翼翼，仿佛摇曳的烛火，仿佛远风的低呜。也许就连在父亲的幻觉中，母亲也只是一个无法靠近的幻影，所以他才会呼唤得那样虚弱、那样无力，就仿佛只要喊得稍微用力一些，那个幻影就会被震碎。哀伤总是如风中四处飘零的落叶。有一天，父亲在醉中，流着泪对自己说：“你知道爹当年为什么不愿意去投靠北洋军吗？爹是怕，我们一走，万一有一天你娘回来了，就再也找不到我们了……”父亲说得涕泗纵横。

可悲的是，父亲虽然一生都留在了赵家镇上，但是，他却至死也没能再见到母亲。

人永远也无法知道，自己明天还会遇到什么痛苦，这份痛苦会有多重，会不会嵌入自己的生命中。这就是人生。开始时，给予了父亲深重痛苦的，只有那个书生。但是后来，洋枪又给了父亲沉重的打击。到最后，父亲没想到，连他自己的儿子，也会变成他的痛楚。这些悲苦，无一不是害人性命的毒药，拌在一个人的人生里，会令人肉烂骨断，撕心裂肺。而在活着的折磨里，父亲既没有解药，也无法自拔。的确，父亲除了喝酒，又真的还能为他自己做些什么呢？

父亲的痛苦，令自己更加痛苦。而自己又不想恨自己，就只能加倍地迷恋色子和妓女。那色子摇滚时发出的声音，仿佛是人间最美妙的天籁；而妓女那销魂的肉体，简直是男人生命里的止痛药。那时的自己，是真不知道，要是离开了赌和嫖，自己还能怎样活下去。可是，赌过嫖过后，自己又常常会感到一种沮丧的空虚。就好像，自己所做的一切，都只是在逃避一个流泪的自己，而那个流泪的自己只要还活着，自己的心底就会永远有一个洞。有了那个洞，自己所能得到的一切快乐，都只是海市蜃楼。

而为了忘记这种空虚，自己必须更兴奋地去赌，更投入地去嫖。纸醉金迷，花天酒地，对酒当歌，人生几何？

那时，自己已经对读书感到了厌倦。自己既不想再为了父亲而读书，也不想再为了自己而读书。读书有什么意思？这本来就不是自己喜欢做的事情。而所谓的前途与争气，又更只像是一个可悲的笑话。在初小和高小念书的那些岁月里，自己的存在，仿佛始终都只是为了被别人拿来与赵宏伟作比较。自己的聪明不凡，似乎只是为了被别人拿来衬托赵宏伟的更胜一筹。自己有多么优秀，赵宏伟就有多么更优秀；赵宏伟有多么更优秀，自己就有多么不值得人们一提。这是一种很奇怪的逻辑，但是事实上这奇怪的逻辑就是舆论的真理。这是一种比受到侮辱更令人感到难堪的感觉，但是那些平庸的蠢货们却永远也不懂，不，是不屑于去懂。自己是被逼迫着，深深地理解了

周瑜的痛苦。只要有诸葛亮在，人们就会觉得周瑜是那么可笑，那么可悲，那么可怜，甚至，人们会说，周瑜真是个蠢货。但是事实上周瑜不蠢，他比所有的蠢货都高明百倍。但这就是比较本身所带的毒，在比较中，有优必有劣。而在平常百姓的舆论中，这劣，会被失去了节制地无限放大，直至最后成为一个被扭曲的公论。而这公论，就会像个烙印一样，永远地刻在那个劣者的脸上。时间久了，甚至连那个劣者自己都会觉得，自己真的是一摊不值得一提的烂泥。这便是舆论的暴力。人活至此，情何以堪。

所幸的是，到上中学时，自己终于不再和赵宏伟是同学了。自己和他虽然同在省城念中学，但是两人并不在同一所学校里。在省城里，终于不再有人会拿自己去跟赵宏伟做比较了，自己终于解脱了。但是，这一解脱却已经来得太晚。经过了那么多年无故被人贬低的折磨，那时，自己对读书这件事已经感到万般厌恶。自己对读书的憎恨，已经变成了一种生命的本能。自己已经回不了头。世事有时就是这样弄人。本来，自己虽然一直被舆论置于赵宏伟之下，饱受或明或暗的贬低或轻视，但是，看在父亲被洋枪败得那样惨的分上，自己曾经还是真心想要读好书、争口气的。谁知，后来父亲堕落成了那样，自己哪里还能好好读书？在外得不到赞扬，在家得不到鼓励，这书读着还有什么意思？而且，很多事情还形成了恶的互助。因为父亲的堕落，自己在外倍受讥笑；因为倍受讥笑，自己厌学愈深；因为厌学愈深，父亲之责怪频至；因为责怪频至，自己厌学更深。父亲心情越差，去赌坊妓院寻欢的次数就越多；而父亲越堕落，自己也越绝望。自己越绝望，对赌坊妓院里的快乐也就越好奇，直至最后发生了后面的一切。命运真是一团可怕的乱麻，更是一部严丝合缝的推进机器，你以为一切都是偶然，其实全是必然。到了省城里，没人再拿自己去和赵宏伟做比较了，但这还有什么屁用？自己的心和人生，早已被踩成了烂泥。一个已经堕落了的人，哪里还能重新站起来？

省城的赌坊比县城的赌坊要繁荣得多，里面的玩法更新鲜；省城的妓院也比县城的妓院漂亮得多，里面的妓女更勾魂。自己泡在省城的赌坊妓院里，有时也会想起自己那可怜的父亲。父亲因为儿子的痛苦而放弃了嫖和赌的麻醉与欢愉，可是儿子却因为父亲的痛苦而再不愿从嫖和赌的麻醉与欢愉中挣脱出来。人生就是这样荒唐与滑稽。

家里的家业，败落得极快。镖局本就没有什么生意，再加上以前父亲的嫖和赌与现今自己的嫖和赌，家中的钱财已快被挥霍殆尽。有时候，自己为了摆阔，还会给妓女买贵重的首饰和衣服。好好的一个镖局，好好的一个家，就这样，像着了魔似的，在一个绝望而疼痛的泥潭里，越陷越深，越陷越深。有时候，自己在梦里，也会看到镖局那块曾经金碧辉煌的牌子，而醒来，自己才会清醒地想起，“威远镖局”四个大字，早已是尘垢满面。

自己在省城嫖赌成性的事情被父亲知道了以后，父亲又将自己痛打了好几回。可是，自己却像是着了魔似的，再不愿学好。真的，色子只要一滚起来，自己的人生就好像充满了意义；妓女只要一解扣子，自己的灵魂便仿佛脱离了苦海。人活一世与天赌，红尘极乐在花酒；不痴不癫何其苦，不如污浊学风流。于叔又跪下来求了自己好几次，自己却只是告诉他：不关你的事。

父亲不给自己钱，自己就在外面赊账，让债主们亲自去问父亲要钱。父亲无法，便只好又给自己钱，供自己在省城里花天酒地。于叔再看见自己，便会远远地躲开，就好像是看到了什么可怕的鬼一样。自己、父亲和于叔，都像是变了一个人。没有人能理清这变化的开始，也没有人能预见这变化的结局。自己还恨父亲吗？也许早已不恨了。父亲还有痛苦吗？也许早已麻木了。于叔仍感到愧疚吗？也许他已只剩下了悲哀与无奈。人生就是这样奇怪。

中学毕业那一年，父亲卖掉了家里的田产，将自己送去日本读书了。也许父亲以为，他的儿子，去了日本就能改过自新了吧？但他不知道，其实日本和中国是差不多的。不，应该说，其实这世界上的每个地方都是差不多的。只要有人痛苦，就会有供人买乐买笑的酒池肉林。只要一个人自己讨厌白天，黑夜就会永远做他的天空。自己只是一摊烂泥，自己喜欢做一摊烂泥。

到了日本，自己先去了一所日语学校里学日语。那时候，自己还无法料到，赵宏伟会在第二年也来到日本，并最终和自己进了同一所大学。平心而论，其实自己还是很佩服赵宏伟的，他比自己晚到日本大半年，但是他日语就是学得比自己快，说得比自己好。还是那句话，自己对赵宏伟，其实一向有英雄惜英雄之心，只不过，是他一直看不上自己罢了。至于纠缠了自己许

多年的嫉妒之情，那就是被众人一起作恶，给硬逼出来的。自己其实是多想有机会能和赵宏伟一起坐下来，青梅煮酒，谈笑风生。

父亲送自己到日本去学的是机械。也许父亲还一直记得，他以前对儿子的期望：长大了要像洋人一样，会造洋枪洋炮。想想，以前的父亲真好，以前的自己，也好。可惜，一切都回不去了。

父亲入伙匪帮的事情，自己是后来才知道的。匪帮的头领，大当家的，叫金顺。这伙匪帮并没有什么正式的称号，因长期盘踞在玉山，所以俗称玉山帮。玉山帮里有将近一半的人，以前是姚凡的部下。当年，姚凡离开赵家镇之后，便隐瞒身世，率领着手下的弟兄投奔了蔡锷。最终，在讨伐袁世凯的护国战争中，姚凡壮烈殉国。据说，姚凡在临死前，仍然在怒喊："打倒帝制！革命万岁！"其呼喊之声摧肝裂胆，令敌不敢上前。而姚凡死后，其手下的弟兄即分裂成了两拨。一拨愿意追随姚凡之志，誓死效忠革命，投身共和伟业。而另一拨，则以金顺为首，只想退出部队，落草为寇，饮酒狎妓，逍遥自在。而这个金顺，就是当年开枪打死那位少林派镖师的土匪。

金顺带着一帮没出息的手下离开了姚凡为他们选择的正义大道。他们在这个乱世里四处流窜，劫财劫色，过着食民而肥的匪帮生活。直到最后，他们来到了玉山，发现了玉山简直就是一座天然的堡垒，于是，他们就在玉山上安定下来，占山为王，建起了匪寨。他们以玉山为大本营，外出四处侵扰，不愁饱暖与淫欲，因为，这里是江南。江南有的是钱粮，有的是美女。不得不说，这正是江南之悲哀。

父亲被金顺想起，完全是一个意外。金顺在玉山上闲来无事，追忆往昔，深觉他此生所遇之人多为鼠辈。而他最为敬佩的只有两人，一个就是他曾经的老大姚凡，另一个，就是曾经败在他手中洋枪之下的赵总镖头。与姚凡的爱枪靠枪不同，金顺崇拜中国传统武术，他自己也会几下咏春，只可惜练得不深。父亲当年虽然一出手就败给了子弹，但是其迅猛的动作还是技惊众人，给金顺留下了极深刻的印象，更何况，父亲曾经在江南武林中也有着赫赫的威名，其江湖地位非寻常武人所能撼。因此，金顺从很久以前起，就对父亲充满了仰慕之情。满怀感慨之际，金顺就下令，派探子下山去打听父亲的近况。

当时，父亲已是个被人打了也懒得还手的酒鬼，烂酒鬼。匪帮的探子寻到父亲之时，父亲正像个乞丐一样地坐在街边的地上喝酒。父亲满脸污浊，浑身酒气，那个探子踢了父亲两脚，父亲也只是笑笑。这让探子大为疑惑，实在是不敢将眼前的这个酒鬼与大当家的口中的英雄等同起来。这个探子又经过了几番周折，最后才真正地确定了父亲的身份。探子回到了山上，向金顺禀报了情况，金顺竟潸然泪下。他说：一代英雄，沦落至此，可悲可叹！

那时，仍然追随在父亲身边的，已只剩于叔一人。家中的家仆已散尽，镖局的买卖名存实亡。于叔开始上街卖艺，表演胸口碎大石。父亲花着于叔的钱，每天除了喝酒之外，就是思念远在日本的儿子。其实父亲当时还有不少卖田产所得的钱，这些钱足以让他和于叔过得体体面面，但是，这些钱，都是父亲要留着寄给远在日本的好儿子的，所以，他只能花于叔的钱。父亲也曾动过要上街卖艺的念头，但是被于叔死死地劝了下来。于叔说，您堂堂一个总镖头，江南武林的一面旗，若上街卖起了艺，我还有什么脸面活？少爷还有什么脸面活？

其实现在回想起来，自己当年真的不是个东西。父亲含辛茹苦地养自己这么大，父亲心中的苦，自己可曾真正体谅过？父亲一心想培养自己成才，可是到头来，自己竟然一头扎进了欲海，再也游不出来。自己哪里有一点点的孝心？还记得，自己临去日本前，父亲破天荒地两天没有喝酒，可是自己给予父亲的，却只是冷冷的一句：“哟，您今天怎么不喝了？”自己实在是个不孝之人。父爱如山，只可惜，为什么做儿子的，总是懂得太晚。人活一世，为什么总是要有那么多欲哭无泪的后悔。自己对不起父亲。

金顺登门时，父亲和于叔正在吃咸菜面。于叔一眼就认出了金顺是当年杀镖师的那个枪手，以为来者不善，一个冲动，喊了一声“当年就是你杀的老崔”，然后二话不说就上去和金顺打了起来。但是于叔天天在表演胸口碎大口，筋骨伤得厉害，而金顺的力气又大，所以几招下来，于叔便落了下风。眼看于叔就要吃亏，父亲腾地便从饭桌旁跃起，落在了金顺和于叔中间的空隙里，父亲只简单的一招，便将金顺弹出了两丈远。金顺从地上爬起，哈哈大笑，说，好，好，赵总镖头果然是宝刀未老，好！

父亲也不搭理他，继续回去吃咸菜面。父亲要于叔也坐回去吃面。父亲一边吃，一边就问：“你真的就是当年杀我们镖师的那个人？”

金顺说：“不错，正是在下。刚才这位兄弟功夫不行，眼睛却厉害。想

不到这么多年过去了，这位兄弟还记得我的样子。”

于叔当时就怒了，拍案而起，说：“老崔死了这么多年，你知不知道人家家里的孩子有多苦！今天你自己送上门来了，不要走，跟我一起去见官！”

金顺哈哈大笑，笑个不停。他说：“跟你去见官？真是要笑死我了！你以为我今天来这里就是为了要来投案自首的？你真是长了个猪脑子！”

于叔发怒，丢了碗。父亲喝令于叔坐下。父亲吃完了最后一口面，问：“不知兄台今日前来，有何贵干？”

金顺哈哈一笑，坐了下来，说：“还是和赵总镖头说话有意思。其实当年杀了贵镖局的镖师，罪不在我，都是我当年的老大姚凡挑起的事端，不过姚凡他现在早已不在人世，有什么血债，他也都算是还清了。今日在下前来，其实是求贤若渴，想效法当年刘备三顾茅庐之举，诚心来邀赵总镖头出山，助我金某人披荆斩棘、无往不利。”

“不知阁下尊姓大名？在何处高就？”父亲不冷不热地问。

“好说，在下姓金名顺，正是近日来令周边官府闻风丧胆的玉山山大王！”

“啊？原来你就是那个土匪头子！”于叔惊诧之后，转身便去拿来了一把大刀，紧握在手中，“你就是那个劫了财还要灭人家门的玉山匪帮的头子？”

“不错，就是我。你想怎么样？”

“我今天就要为民除害！”于叔说着，就要动手。

“于三！坐下！”父亲大喝一声。

金顺冷冷一笑。他用手指了指于叔，这一指，阴冷得可怕。

“金大当家的，我们井水不犯河水，今天，我就当你没来过。你走吧。”父亲说。

“赵总镖头，我冒着被官府捉拿的危险，今日亲自登门来请，实在是因为对您的一身功夫佩服得紧。我邀您入伙，并不是要您跟着我们去打家劫舍，只是希望您能上山，教教我们八极拳，做我们的总教头。如今世道混乱，虎豹横行，人若不食他人，则必为他人所食，我不觉得我们做土匪的有什么可耻。想当年，禁军教头林冲开始时不也是一个正派人物吗，可到后来，还不是做了土匪？他们还造了皇帝的反呢。我有他们过分吗？赵总镖头，我也不是非要请人教我的弟兄们武功，你知道的，我们都有洋枪。我们只是久仰您的大名，真的不想看着您和您的一身功夫，就这样埋没于泥淖。您的八极拳独步江南武林，可是您现在却只能坐在家里吃吃咸菜面，您说您甘心吗？我和我的弟兄们，是诚心佩服您，想跟您学八极拳。当然，您若不愿意，我们也不勉强。”金顺说完，从口袋里掏出了一沓庄票，放在了父亲面前的桌上，“这些，是我和我的弟兄们孝敬您的，没什么，就是一份真心的仰慕。”

于叔抓起庄票就扔在了金顺的脸上，说：“别用你的赃银，侮辱了我们总镖头！”

金顺将庄票捡起来，重新放回到父亲面前的桌上，然后他笑了笑，一抱拳，说了句后会有期，就离开了。

两天后，于叔在街上表演胸口碎大石的时候，忽然来了一群起哄的壮汉。他们先出四个人将于叔仰面按在地上，然后剩下的八个人就去抬来了一块巨石，将巨石压在了于叔的身上，接着，他们再一起抡锤猛砸巨石。等到父亲闻讯赶到时，壮汉们早已杳无踪迹，巨石下，只有全身骨碎、血流满地的于叔。父亲一人搬掉了那块巨石，但是于叔早已气绝身亡。于叔死状其惨。父亲怒啸一声，一掌拍在那块血淋淋的巨石上，巨石应声裂开。父亲泪流满面。

金顺第二次登门时，父亲与其人战了一场。金顺虽然早有准备，在身上穿了护甲，藏了暗器，但他终究不可能是父亲的对手。父亲将其擒住后，他说：你越厉害，我越喜欢，听说你儿子在日本读书，一定要花不少钱吧？接下来你打算怎么办？卖房子吗？卖完了房子以后呢？你还能卖什么？

父亲松开了金顺。这一次，金顺又给父亲留下了一沓庄票。

父亲去街上卖了一次艺，围观之人尽皆讥笑，无一掷钱。最后，众人起哄：“威远镖局的赵总镖头在卖艺啦，大家快来看哪！”父亲落荒而逃。

金顺第三次登门，父亲向金顺俯首称臣，说，愿为其效犬马之劳。

三顾茅庐请出英雄来做土匪，成了金顺一生的得意之事。每当他志得意满之际，便喜欢拿出这段故事来说给别人听，不管父亲在不在场。金顺曾经还拿这段故事来教训过自己，他对自己说：你爹就是为了你才豁了出去，才

跟我做了贼，可是你呢，在日本都干了些什么？废物！

自己不得不承认，金顺骂得对。

关于姚凡的故事，还有一个尾声。一次，父亲在听金顺讲述了姚凡从军殉国的故事之后，不禁问：那么，姚凡可有子嗣留于人间？金顺摇了摇头，说，老大只在年轻的时候有过一个女人，那个女人后来被甘肃的七星帮劫了去，再无下落。老大没有子嗣留世。这兴许是天意。

自己在得知父亲从匪的消息之后，曾从日本赶回过家乡一次。自己当时还不知道事情的原委，也还没有听金顺得意扬扬地讲过他那“三顾茅庐”的故事。自己当时站在轮船的甲板上，望着海里无垠的波浪，根本就无法相信自己从那个中国同乡嘴里听到的消息。父亲怎么可能当土匪呢？一定是以讹传讹。可是，自己拍给父亲的电报，父亲为什么迟迟不回？

最终，自己只能是承认了现实的残酷性。在父亲点头承认事实的那一刹那，自己觉得，整个天都塌了。真实的命运永远在人的想象之外，真实的人生永远不在人的预料之中。自己知道父亲会在痛苦的泥潭里不停下沉，自己知道父亲的堕落早已不可救药，但是，自己是怎么样也不会想到，父亲会加入匪帮！

一切，都让人情何以堪。

父亲年轻时，收徒谨慎，想来学艺者众多；婚姻失败后，父亲决心不再授人以武，但是想来拜师者依旧不少；直到落魄了，父亲想要重开山门，授艺赚钱，但是人们都已知道时代变了，武艺不如枪械，与其辛苦练武，不如持枪防身，没有人再愿意给父亲这个挣钱捡自尊的机会。父亲之一生，与武艺相恋相虐，可谓是成于武艺，败于武艺。但是，父亲以前从未想到，有一天，他会被迫收徒，他更没有想到，他这一生，会收一群无恶不作的土匪为徒。人生最惨痛之事，莫过于向命运举手投降；人生最惭愧之事，莫过于背叛自我之信仰。父亲后来曾亲口对自己说，他这一生，爱武，更恨武。

世人皆不甘平庸，但是，只有真正爬上过顶峰的人才会懂得，文也好，武也好，平庸最好。这是渡边在手臂受伤之后对自己说过的一句话，这句话令自己无法平静。当然，这些，都已是自己后来在东北的辛酸往事。

父亲只负责教匪徒们习武打拳，并不参与打家劫舍的行动。但是，他有时也会向匪帮报告一些周边富户的情况。总之，他与匪帮匪事，已再脱不了干系。父亲说他没有亲自去做伤天害理的事情，那只是自欺欺人之语，若不这么说，他难以自处，这点所有人都心知肚明。不过，父亲也做了一件好事，金顺答应他，只要他还在做兄弟们的教头，兄弟们就不会去打赵家镇的主意。父亲的罪孽感因此减轻了不少。其实父亲的罪孽，越来越深。匪徒们的功夫越来越好，胆子就越来越大。他们的胆子越大，做下的坏事就越多、越恶。烧杀抢掠，奸淫掳劫，玉山帮无恶不作。而父亲所挣到的财物里，满满的都是眼睛看不见心却看得见的血。父亲只能不停地说，他没有亲自去做伤天害理的事情。父亲从没想到，他自己竟是如此懦弱的一个人。

向父亲印证了事实的当天，自己在家里哭了一夜。父亲并没有向自己做任何解释，于叔的死，自己当时也还不知道。所有事情的原委与真相，自己都是在几年后，被山本耕作那个老王八蛋给逼回了国内以后，才开始逐步明了的。父亲向自己承认从匪事实的那一天，自己生平头一次抓住了父亲的衣领。自己大逆不道地双手紧抓着父亲的衣领，向他怒吼："为什么？为什么！"可是，直到自己的怒吼变成了哀求，父亲也仍然没有回答自己一个字。自己只是看到了父亲眼中的绝望与淡红，那种神情与颜色，自己终生难忘。

哭过一夜之后，自己要父亲退出匪帮，父亲却只是摇头。自己又开始怒吼，问他为什么。但是这次自己没有再抓父亲的衣领。父亲说，开弓没有回头箭。自己一把抓起茶杯怒掷在地上，杯子碎了一地。自己说：我没有你这个父亲！父亲不说话。自己就歇斯底里地又说了一遍。父亲还是没有说话。只是，他的脸上流下了泪来。

父亲是最憎恶男儿流泪的。但是，恐怕没人不懂流泪的滋味。现在想来，自己真的好后悔，自己这一生，愧对父亲。纵然天下人皆视父亲为败类，但是在自己的心中，自己的父亲永远是英雄。

最后，自己又登上了返回日本的轮船。那一次临行前，自己冷冷地对父亲说：我知道你为什么要加入匪帮，你就是为了钱，我知道你没出息，可我没想到你会没出息到这个地步！

说完，自己就准备接受父亲的耳光，可是，父亲却并没有打自己。他木然得就像是一块木头。自己心酸得像是心口里被人撒了毒药。

在轮船上，自己醉得一塌糊涂。在醉中，自己忽然问自己：自己和父亲

又有什么不一样？失败、买醉、痛苦、流泪、赌钱、嫖妓，还有明天未知的更堕落。自己和父亲又有什么不一样？

实在是太可笑。

回到日本后，自己比以前更加放浪形骸。自己拿钞票点烟抽，用书页擦屁股，在妓女的嘴里喝酒，在赌场的地上睡觉。自己是真想把自己从这个世界上抹掉。自己知道自己花的每一块钱都是赃款，自己知道自己的每一次挥霍都是耻辱，但是自己就是要将这堕落进行到底！自己就是要在堕落中找回自己失去的一切东西！

其实现在想想，年轻真是一个幼稚的好归宿。年轻，也真是一团狂乱的火。自己没有想过要不辜负父亲为自己所做的一切，却一心只想着要报复这个肮脏混乱的世界。自己没有珍惜自己大好的青春年华，青春年华也没有珍惜自己。在黑与白的厮杀中，自己的灵魂弱不禁风，失去了方向，碎成了残渣。西风凋碧树，乌云满苍穹。

好在那个知道赵总镖头入匪帮的中国同乡只在日本待了大半个月，就回到了国内去，再没来过日本。所以此事在日本的华人圈里并没有传扬开来。听说过镖头入匪帮这一趣闻的几个人，既不知此事的真假，更不知其实自己就是那个镖头的儿子；而知道自己的父亲是赵总镖头的几个人，又完全没听说过镖头入匪帮这一趣闻。所以，自己在日本并没有被人揭开过伤疤。

在东京念大学的时候，赵宏伟曾经和自己走近过一段时间。毕竟，在异国他乡能遇上一个老家的旧相识不容易，这是一种极其难得的缘分。自己能看得出来，开始时，赵宏伟也是真心想要和自己做朋友。这曾一度令自己感到很兴奋。能和赵宏伟做朋友，不，做好朋友，是自己许多年以来的愿望。虽然以前在家乡的小学堂里，自己也算是和赵宏伟有过友情，但是那友情，在赵宏伟的眼里，也许根本就算不上是友情，只是泛泛之交的礼貌相处而已。人生有时候就是这样，一份情，在你看来是情，在他看来也许根本算不上是情。而现在在日本，赵宏伟是真心想要和自己做朋友，这怎能不让人高兴。

但是，赵宏伟在心底里，终究是瞧不上自己的。就算他是因为在异国感觉孤单而想要交一个朋友，可是自己在他的心里，终究还是无法与其平起平坐。他不会将自己视作他的心灵伙伴，也许永远也不会。这真是一种灰色的无奈。曹操想与刘备结盟，刘备只是视曹操为贼子。道不同终究不相为谋。赵宏伟与自己最终还是渐行渐远，谁也没能打破小时候隔在两人中间的那道樊篱。都说爱情不能强求，其实友情也是。有些人，从一开始就注定了永远不会成为朋友，不管你再怎么努力。青梅煮酒论英雄的结局，其实就是拔剑相对、血洗天下。

为了求得一种心理平衡，自己在被赵宏伟疏远之后，也就开始在心里鄙视他。赵宏伟就是个穷鬼，书读得再好有个屁用，自己常对自己说。这么一说，自己的心灵就会舒服很多。当然，这种时候，自己是不可以去想自己所用的钱是否都干净的问题的。那时候，自己的人生是真混乱。自己的心，像瞎了一样，是多么渴望光明，渴望被治愈。但是，并没有人来救自己。自己告诉自己，友情并不重要，与赵宏伟的彼此厌恶，就像与一个陌生人的彼此厌恶一样，对自己的人生根本无足轻重。

自己对赵宏伟的感情，永远都是那样复杂与矛盾。不，自己这一生，就像是活在复杂与矛盾纠缠的命运里。

在那些灰暗而浑浑噩噩的日子里，廉价的妓女给了自己不少甜美的夜晚。但是妓女毕竟是妓女，这一刻，她对你百般温柔，下一刻，她又会在另一个男人的怀里撒娇。一切都是假的，都只是拿钱买来的乐子，花钱看的戏。人生就是这样空空如也，可悲可怜。

最终，自己因为喝醉了酒，在一家高级妓院里撒野，而触怒了日本的一个黑帮头子，山本耕作。自己那时并不知道，这个黑帮在日本的势力是那样庞大，地位是那样显赫。自己是不小心摸了老虎屁股。山本下了追杀令，自己开始了逃亡的生涯。其实自己罪不至死，自己只不过就是打了他们的妓女几个耳光，就因为自己是个中国人，所以，山本觉得，帮会的尊严被玷污，而且是被一个中国人玷污。所以，自己必须要死。

自己在日本亡命天涯的时候，没有一个人来帮助自己。饿了，自己就去偷东西吃；累了，自己也不敢睡着。杀手纷至沓来，自己一不会武二没有枪，若不是天生身手敏捷，恐怕早在第一次被杀手寻到时就已经身首异处了。黑帮派出的杀手满日本地追杀自己，自己逃过了这一个的刀子又会迎来下一个的枪，那是一段怎样恐怖的岁月！自己就像一只老鼠一样，东躲西藏，白天无法见光，晚上不能开灯，不仅人生地不熟，更无一人来帮忙。那

段时间，自己甚至起过自杀的念头。但是自己还是告诉自己，只要活着就好。自己被逼至那样一个残酷惨烈的死亡绝境，原因却仅仅就是惹山本生了气！仅仅就因为是一个中国人惹他生了气！这真是一个多么微不足道的理由！这是一个多么荒唐的逻辑！在日本人的眼里，中国人就那样不配活着吗？

最危险的那一次，刀尖已经抵住了自己的喉咙。在那一刻，自己是真的以为自己就要死了，自己想起了父亲。自己在那一刻，忽然很懊悔，懊悔自己还没有向父亲道歉。自己是带着对父亲的辱骂离开的家，自己还没有告诉父亲，其实自己不恨他。最后，自己捡到了地上的那把枪，一枪就打中了那个杀手的腹部。杀手倒在了地上。自己并不知道那个杀手后来究竟有没有死，但是在记忆中，自己总觉得，这，就是自己第一次杀人。

最后，自己终于逃回了国内。所幸，日本的杀手并没有追到中国来。也许，老山本也是觉得，再追下去就太不合算了吧。毕竟，跨洋追杀是要花费成本的，若只是为了出胸中的一股恶气，不值得。再说了，到了中国，这地盘就不再是老山本的了。他若是派人去中国的江湖中打听打听，人家一定会告诉他：嗬，赵三牛的儿子你也敢动，吃了豹子胆了？

父亲，始终是自己的骄傲。

回了国，自己并没有向父亲道歉。也许，人临死前的想法和还活着时的想法终究是有些不同的吧。自己也没有告诉父亲自己在日本的遭遇。为什么不说？直到现在也还是不太明白。但是，自己就是不想说。也许，自己是怕给父亲一个责骂自己的理由吧。或者，自己是怕给父亲一个保护自己的理由。自己不想让父亲知道，自己比他更堕落。自己不想将自己的不争气与没出息，再在父亲的面前放大一百倍。人就是这样奇怪。有时候，你最想亲近的人，就是你最不想让他亲近的人。

自己在日本的学业未成，半途而废，令父亲感到十分伤心，但是他既没深究，也没责骂自己。也许，他是以为，自己是因为不堪忍受他入了匪帮的事实，所以才中断了学业。自己能感觉到父亲的愧疚，这几乎令自己无地自容。儿子的没出息令父亲感到了失望与伤心，但是，父亲却以为这一切都是做父亲犯下的错，儿子只是一个受害者。这种复杂的痛苦令父亲面容憔悴，令自己难以承受。可是，自己还是宁愿在这种折磨里沉沦，也不愿告诉父亲，自己是因为被追杀所以才离开的日本。可能，归根结底，自己还是怨父亲。自己想看到他愧疚地面对自己，而不想看到自己愧疚地面对他。自己大不孝。可是，只有这大不孝，才能冲淡自己的怨。现在想来，自己那时，除了自私、怯弱，还懂什么？

有时候，自己还是会在噩梦中被惊醒。梦中，自己仍在东京夜晚的街道上奔跑，没命地奔跑。街上空无一人，鸦雀无声，星光暗淡，路灯残损。自己的喘息声与跑步踏地声交叠在一起，震耳欲聋，幽深似鬼。身后，始终有一个看不清脸的杀手在紧紧地追赶自己，他越追越近，越追越近。自己拼尽了全力也没办法再跑快一点点。终于，杀手追了上来。黑暗中，他的刀尖抵住了自己的喉头。自己拼命地抗拒着。但是，那寒气如霜的刀尖，还是在一点一点地深入自己的喉咙，很痛，很冷。忽然，街上一道光掠过，自己看清了他的脸。他竟然就是自己。他怒吼一声，用力将刀一插。自己就吓得醒了过来。

每次惊醒后，自己总是大汗淋漓。而窗外夜凉如水，静谧如水。一切都只是个梦，自己知道。但自己就是感到恐惧，感到极度的恐怖。自己想去找父亲，和父亲说说话，有几次，自己都已经走到了父亲的房门外。但是，自己没有一次能迈出最后一步。那是一个恐怖而奇异的梦，那是一个自己杀自己的梦，那里面包含着某个灵魂之谜。但是，自己不懂，父亲也不会懂。从那时起，自己忽然渐渐开始明白，父亲，已保护不了他的儿子。因为，每个人一生最致命的敌人，都只是自己的灵魂。

自己也曾去玉山上的匪窝里吃过年夜饭。说实在的，金顺过得也真是不比什么大帅差。钱粮满库，刀枪林立，兄弟成群，女人一堆。山上的匪徒们一起欢呼起来时，玉山好像都会发抖。金顺说，能做一日土皇帝，胜做十年大将军。不得不承认，当年，玉山帮真是威风八面。

自己每次上山和下山，都是被蒙了眼抬着走的。金顺为了安全起见，从不让帮外的人知道山上的路。凡是知道山上地形的帮外人，不是被拉进了匪帮，就是被送去见了阎王。所以，父亲对于儿子的一无所知感到很放心。父亲确认了金顺并没有要拉他赵三牛的儿子下水的意思。父亲本人对山上的地形自然也是一直守口如瓶。那时，自己已经是在县政府里当差。当然，那官职，是父亲用赃款买来的。

其实，父亲一直想将儿子划于匪帮之外的努力是幼稚的。在父亲看来，儿子只要没入匪帮，在事实上就是与匪帮没有关系的。但是，在百姓看来，只要父亲是匪帮中人，其儿子在事实上又怎么可能会和匪帮没有关系？这真是一对挺可笑的矛盾。但是，是也好，非也好，自己也都不在乎了。金顺有句话说得很好：不要看不起土匪，其实有些朝廷大官，手上沾的无辜人命比土匪多多了。

金顺害死了于叔，这个仇自己一直记着。自己相信父亲也记着。但是自己没有想过要报仇。因为那是谁也做不到的事情。要怪，就只能怪于叔自己命不好吧。或者想得更光明一些，那就是善恶到头终有报，不是不报，时辰未到。也许有一天，不用自己和父亲动手，金顺就会死在谁的枪下，到那时，就是天给于叔报了仇。也许这些都只是自己怯弱的自我安慰，但是，谁又能怎么样呢？杀了金顺，父亲和自己，都会从这个世上消失。

不知从什么时候起，自己也不再那么厌恶匪帮了。毕竟，是匪帮让父亲和自己又重新捡起了昨日的富贵。至于人命，在这个炮火纷飞的乱世里，哪天又没有无辜的生命逝去？人不为己，天诛地灭。有钱总是好的。有了钱，就能买官做；做了官，就有了权；既有了钱又有了权，这世上还有什么事是做不到的？山珍海味吃不尽，豪赌千金似平常，花魁绝色嫖不完，富贵荣华是真经。堕落，有堕落的极乐。或者，这个世界，本来就该以堕落命名？

误以为人间清澈者，是何等的痴妄。

自己在那欲望的海洋里沉醉着，身心舒坦，就连每一个汗毛孔里，都像是流淌着愉快的汁液。每天早晨，都会有美人将自己吻醒；每天中午，自己都可以和县长在一起吃饭；每天晚上，自己都会在赌桌上一掷千金。人间还有比这更快乐的生活吗？权钱美色，也许便是上天赐给人间的福寿膏。吸上一口，就可飘飘欲仙，忘忧忘愁。天堂在哪里？或许就在欲海的最深处。自己甚至开始感谢玉山帮，感谢他们给了自己和父亲重新做人的机会。可是，每当深夜来临，自己又会不禁自问：难道自己，已真的将父亲当成了土匪？难道自己，已真的将自己当成了土匪的儿子？

别人再怎么说是，也不如自己说是，来得是。有时，自己离开了妓女，独站于月下，会不禁问天：当年的那个赵总镖头去了哪里？当年的哪个镖局少爷，去了哪里？

答案总是无尽的冷寂。也许，他们都已永远地消失在了往日。

后来，赵宝贵举报了父亲，但是自己又容易地就将父亲救了出来。其实这甚至都算不上是什么“救”，因为从一开始，自己就知道父亲不会有事。从抓到放，这一切，都只不过是官场上的一些小游戏。而其中之奥妙与规则，未涉过官场的小老百姓，是怎样也不会明白的。

金顺要派人去杀了赵宝贵，以儆效尤。但是父亲说不要。父亲说，还是派人去烧了赵宝贵的裁缝铺吧，让他尝尝活着受穷的滋味，那远比让他死了难受。金顺摇头，说，太便宜他了。自己就添了一句话，说，那就再剁了赵宝贵的右手，让他生不如死。金顺一拍大腿，说，好！

自己知道，其实父亲是不想害死赵宝贵。但是父亲不明白，无论他做了什么力避杀生的事情，人们最终仍会把仇恨都记在他的头上。因为，损人一千与损人八百的差别在本质上并不大，人们永远只会记住自己已经失去的，而不会留意自己依旧拥有的。这就是人之常情，这就是世间许多仇怨的根基。与父亲不同，自己说要剁了赵宝贵的手的时候，自己的心中，的确是带了对赵宝贵与赵宏伟的恨。这恨当然是不应该有的，但是这也是人之常情。举报之仇，鄙视之恨，两怨相加，自己要他赵宏伟父亲的一只手，名正言顺。自己就是个坏蛋。

自己曾经很愚蠢地以为，这种很舒坦的日子，会一直延续下去，直到改朝换代。但是，命运的发展永远在人的预料之外。既没改朝换代，也没天翻地覆，自己和父亲的人生，就都走到了悬崖边上。

事情的起因，是金顺在青梅县里掳到了一个漂亮的年轻女人。金顺将这个女人留在了匪窝里，娶她做了他的小老婆。而她，名叫雪兰。她与自己的母亲同名，不同姓。

父亲爱上了这个女人。他爱得热烈，爱得痴迷，仿佛初恋。开始时，自己并不知道这件事。自己只是觉得很奇怪，父亲怎么突然就活得兴高采烈了起来，好像一下子年轻了几十岁。从自己记事起，就从未见到过父亲焕发出如此青春的光彩。直到后来，自己知道了这件事，顿时就被吓出了一身冷汗来，可是父亲，却仍然沉陷在他的爱情里，不能自拔。

父亲说，那个女人也爱他。自己对父亲说：她是金顺的女人，你这么做，我们都会死的！父亲却拉住了自己的手，对自己说：我们逃吧，我带着

雪兰和你，我们一起去北方，重新开始我们的生活！自己甩开了父亲的手，对他大吼了一声：你疯了！

自己永远都记得，那一刻，父亲的眼神里，竟有着孩子般的不知所措。

其实，现在想来，那段爱情，就是父亲人生路上的最后一段幸福。有时，自己甚至会觉得，其实人间发生了什么，上天都看在眼里。也许，上天是因为怜悯父亲，所以才在父亲的末路上，给了父亲最后的一个美梦，虽然，这梦只是一场海市蜃楼。美丽的幻影在最后虽然还是破碎了，但是，父亲已经得到了他最后的幸福，最后的美梦。自己相信，父亲无怨无悔。

事情败露的那一天，非常不巧，自己竟然也在山上。金顺要自己多给他们介绍一些武器贩子，他们要多买一些枪。自己当时还在暗自庆幸，金顺什么都不知道。谁知，就是在那一天，有人在雪兰的房里发现了父亲的贴身玉坠。面对金顺的询问，父亲竟然说出了一句语惊四座的话：我爱雪兰。

这件事情，糟就糟在父亲没有狡辩。如果父亲狡辩了，金顺就算识破了真相，兴许也仍会装个糊涂，放父亲一马。毕竟，只是一个女人的问题，没什么大不了的。但是，父亲却是在众目睽睽之下，说了，他爱雪兰。这样，金顺的脸就没了。大家装一次糊涂的路，就断了。

自己和父亲，当晚就被五花大绑地关进了山上的铁牢里。自己直到那一刻，还在责怪父亲。自己气急败坏地对父亲吼道：你快去向金顺道歉，求他饶了我们！他还要我给他买枪，只要你去跟他道歉，他一定会饶了我们的！你快去求他！快呀！

不！我不会去求金顺的！父亲大声说。

为什么！自己大声问。

雪兰是他抢来的，本来就不是他的！凭什么要我去求他！父亲愤怒地说。

“爹！我不想死，我还不想死啊！”

“孩子，你明不明白，你明不明白，我等了雪兰一辈子了！我等了雪兰一辈子了！我不能再失去她第二次了！绝不能了！”

“爹，你疯了！她不是我娘！她不是我娘啊！”

“不！我没疯，我没疯！她就是我等了一辈子的雪兰！她就是我的雪兰！你们不会明白的，你们不会明白的！疯的是你们，疯的是这世上所有的人！”

“爹——你醒一醒，你醒一醒啊！为什么会这样！苍天哪！”

“孩子，你不要怕，爹没有疯，爹没有疯！我们都不会死，都不会死的！这小小的一座牢，根本就困不住我赵三牛！”

父亲怒喝了一声，捆在他身上的绳索，立时寸断。父亲一招八极铁山靠，“轰”地就将牢门给撞了开来。

那是父亲人生中的最后一次辉煌。一代武林英雄，尽显铁血本色。他没有愧对武术，没有愧对祖先。他练了一辈子武，仿佛就是为了迎接最后到来的这一场大厮杀。父亲拳影乱人眼，铁腿断虎骨，刀光溅敌血，剑影封龙窟。一杆长枪在手，枪尖雪花飞点，杆身龙腾虎跃，喋血金刚罗汉，横扫千军万马；空手擒拿格斗，铁掌碎石裂金，钢身金钟气罩，一击马头迸碎，三步尸首成堆，甚至，父亲还躲过了子弹，躲过了那疾如流星、恶如魔鬼的子弹。一颗又一颗的子弹飞向了父亲，但是，父亲却像是变成了雄鹰、变成了流星，没有人能看清他飞闪的身影。枪手一个接一个地倒下，父亲在敌人的血泊中不断前行。

父亲在他人生的最后一程中，奇迹般地战胜了子弹，战胜了他一生畏惧的洋枪，这是一个武林神话。这个神话太神奇，太令人难以置信，以至于在许多年以后，很多武林小辈已不再相信赵三牛的存在。但是，只有自己，才知道这个神话一点也不稀奇。因为，那一天，父亲要保护的，不是别人家的财宝，而是他自己的儿子，还有他自己的爱情。

自己拉着雪兰，一直跟在父亲的身后。自己可以感觉到，这个女人一直在瑟瑟发抖。自己对她说，你不要怕，爹一定会带我们出去的。但是，她的脸上，却只有恐惧，近乎绝望的恐惧。自己仔细看了看她的脸，拿她的脸和家里画像上母亲年轻时的脸作比较，发现，其实，她长得一点也不像母亲。

终于，父亲遭遇了金顺。金顺站在聚义厅的正中央，一动不动，像一尊铁塔。金顺脸色发黑，面无表情。整个匪窝的空气里，都像是飘着可怕的血腥味。火把熊熊，火光艳丽得仿佛死神的舞衣。父亲继续往前走，自己拉着雪兰，也想跟着父亲继续走，可是，雪兰却突然甩开了自己的手。自己一惊，猛回头去看雪兰，只见，她摇摇头，脸上竟是一副求饶的表情。那一刻，自己心中一暗。自己知道，父亲完了。

父亲没有看见在他背后发生的这一幕。自己攥了攥拳头，硬是重新又去拉住了雪兰的手，自己恶狠狠地瞪了她一眼。整个聚义厅里，灯火通明，鸦雀无声。

金顺没有与父亲交手，他笑了笑，抬手直接就是对着雪兰开了一枪。这一枪，既出人意料，又至关重要。

子弹直奔雪兰的心口而去。说时迟，那时快，雪兰还来不及惊呼，父亲已侧跃横飞，以身作盾，替雪兰挡住了这颗子弹。子弹正中父亲的右侧锁骨。父亲一个趔趄，没有摔倒。金顺嘿嘿一笑，抬手又一枪，子弹打在了父亲的左大腿上。父亲，终于还是倒下了。

残余的匪徒们蜂拥而上，围住了父亲。金顺挥挥手，叫所有人散开。父亲重新又站了起来。父亲的鲜血，染红了他的衣裤。

雪兰使劲挣开了自己的手，后退了好几步。她瘫倒在了地上，面如死灰，惧如见鬼，魂魄崩溃。自己看看父亲，又看看雪兰，头皮发麻，大脑空白，如哑如瞎。

金顺走到了父亲的面前，笑呵呵地问他：你说，你爱雪兰？

是的！父亲说。

那么，你知道雪兰她爱你吗？

当然！

好，那既然是这样，我不如就帮你问问雪兰，如果她真的爱你，我就放你们一家三口走。

金顺狠狠地将雪兰拽到了父亲的面前。他问她：你爱赵三牛吗？

大当家的饶命，大当家的饶命！雪兰跪地求饶，痛哭流涕。我错了，我知道我错了！求求你饶我一命！求求你饶我一命！雪兰涕泗长流，磕头不止。

我在问你，你到底爱不爱赵三牛！回答我！回答这里所有的弟兄！金顺怒吼。

不、不爱。

你说什么！说大声一点！金顺咆哮。

我不爱赵三牛！我不爱赵三牛！我只是逗他玩的，谁知道他这么认真！雪兰哭着大声说。

父亲愕然地看着雪兰。“雪兰，你不用怕，只要你说实话，金顺是会放我们走的。”父亲痴痴地对雪兰说。

“你这个疯子！傻子！哪个女人不会对男人说几句假话？你还当真了，闯出了这么大的祸来！实话告诉你，我就是玩玩你而已，想看看你拜倒在我裙下的可怜模样罢了。我怎么会爱你！怎么会爱你！”雪兰声嘶力竭、气急败坏地说。

“不，不……”父亲喃喃自语。

“你说的这些，我也不信，”金顺慢条斯理地对雪兰说着，拔出了一把匕首，递到了她的面前，“除非，你能证明给所有人看。”

雪兰愣住了。

“快，证明给所有人看。”金顺温柔地说。

时间仿佛凝固住了。

雪兰哆嗦着，接过了匕首。

她紧咬着嘴唇。她闭上了眼睛。

终于，深深的一刀，捅进了父亲的腹中。

“爹！”自己失声惨叫。“你这个臭婊子，我宰了你！”自己捡起了一把刀，不顾一切地就朝那个女人冲了过去。三个匪徒将自己摁倒在地。

匕首一寸一寸地，又从父亲的腹中拉了出来。

父亲的血，流了一地。

雪兰瘫跪在了金顺的面前，厉哭着求他：大当家的，饶了我吧！饶了我吧！

金顺一脚，将雪兰踢到了一旁。

金顺走到了父亲的面前，问：后悔了吧？

父亲不说话。他沉默着，像一块石头。他沉默着，像一具死尸。时间与空气仿佛都定住了。定得那么安静，定得那么慈悲。一切，都像是要窒息。一切，都像是要破碎。世界滑入了深渊中，存在落进了荒谬里。黑夜与白天，一齐失去了颜色。爱，或者恨，什么都不存在。生，或者死，全部只是荒谬。

父亲的眼中，流下了两行泪。那泪，不痛不恸，清亮清静。

可惜，你后悔也晚了，你杀了我这么多弟兄，就算我想饶你，也不能饶

你了。金顺说。

父亲缓缓地，在金顺面前跪了下来。父亲说：我死不足惜，只求你放了我儿子，他的手上没有沾过半滴弟兄的血，他是无辜的。

金顺点了点头，说，好，我不杀你儿子。

父亲就笑了。他笑得很灿烂，仿佛看到了蓝天，仿佛触到了云边。他笑得很坦然，仿佛见到了永恒，仿佛融入了彩虹。那笑，无牵无挂，大慈大悲。

金顺问：你知道规矩吧？父亲笑着说：三刀六洞，五马分尸。

“不！爹——”自己哀号。

金顺叹了口气，正准备叫人行刑，父亲却向金顺提出了最后的一个请求：他想在这聚义厅里，最后再打一次拳。

金顺的外甥提醒金顺：小心有诈。父亲笑着问那外甥：我都已经这样了，难道你还怕我吗？

金顺手一挥，说，好，你打吧。

父亲站了起来。父亲站在那里，望着自己，对自己说：“儿子，爹对不起你，爹从小就不肯教你武艺，还逼着你去念书，爹知道你活得不开心，是爹错了。今天，爹就把我们赵家的八极拳打给你看，爹只能打一遍，你能记多少是多少。今日之后，你一定要远走他乡，永不回来，忘记恩仇，一生平安。若能如此，爹在泉下也便安心了。”

“爹——”

“儿子，看好了！”

父亲大喊一声，然后便奋力地打起了拳。他一边打，一边大声地念着八极拳的口诀。父亲龙形虎步，啸声震天，拳破南山，脚碎北海。疾时赛雄鹰，徐时如磐石。掌开梅花千万朵，腿似铁桩地根生。进则如狮扑，退则似山固。追风降龙九天中，摧金伏虎地狱里。万马奔腾劲，千钧一发力。吞吐山河英雄气，横扫雷霆将军意。四书安天下，八极定神州。开天辟地豪杰情，沧海横流壮烈心。

父亲血流如注，衣裤红透里外；自己泪眼蒙眬，所见惨不忍睹。这一刻，整个聚义厅中，竟都蒙着一层肃穆。众匪屏气凝神，鸦雀无声。这一刻，自己撕心裂肺，生不如死。

拳打完了，父亲问自己，你都记住了吗？

自己说，记住了。

父亲说：记住了，要忘记恩仇，一生平安。

自己哭着说：记住了！

父亲欣慰地笑了笑。

父亲蹒跚地走到了雪兰的面前。他俯首，在她的耳边说了一句什么。她，突然泪如雨下。父亲仰面倒在了地上，面带惨笑。地上，满是父亲的血。

鲜血沾湿了父亲的白发。

三把长长的尖刀，穿透了父亲的胸膛。最后，五马分尸。血漫天地，惨绝人寰。

五马开奔的那一刻，自己闭上了眼睛。自己忽然想起了，自己，还一直没有对父亲说一句对不起。自己，还一直没有，向父亲道歉。

但是，父亲已经不在了，永远不在了。

“爹……”

自己最后的呼喊，细如蚊吟。

出乎了所有人意料的，是雪兰。雪兰失魂落魄地闯进了刑场，她抱着父亲血淋淋的头颅，淡淡地说了一句，三牛，我错了，你等我。然后，她便是用那把金顺给的匕首，割开了她自己的喉咙。雪兰和父亲死在了一起。

众匪目瞪口呆。

父亲最后对雪兰说的那一句话，成了一个谜。没有人知道，究竟是什么话语，可以具有这样大的魔力，能让无情转眼变痴情，能让偷生转瞬成殉情。有人说，父亲只是说了一句简单的“我爱你”；有人说，父亲只是说了一句痴傻的“我不后悔”；也有人说，其实父亲什么也没有说。也许，这个谜已永远不会有答案。也许，爱情本身就是一个谜。也许，在爱情中，永远也不会有什么对与错、真与假、醒与醉，有的，只是相信，或者不相信。

父亲在牢里对自己所说的那些疯话，自己在雪兰死后，懂得了一些。或许，父亲是说，他已经等了爱情一辈子了。或许，父亲是说，他终于懂得了爱情。

爱情是什么？或许，就是生死相随。

也许，每个人都在一生中等待过一场爱情。只不过，有些人，等到了，

有些人，没等到。

父亲死后，金顺的外甥要金顺斩草除根，免留后患。金顺给了他外甥一个耳光。金顺走到了自己面前，问：你会来找我报仇吗？自己说：家父遗言未冷，忘记恩仇四字，我绝不敢忘。金顺说，好，希望你不要辜负了你爹的一片苦心。

金顺下令，将赵教头的碎尸抛到赵家镇的大街上。雪兰的尸体，则剁碎了拿去喂狗。

自己，被匪徒打晕之后，运下了山。

自己给父亲收了尸，安葬了父亲。跪在父亲孤零零的坟前，自己的悲痛，无法控制。自己的整个人、整条命，都像是化作了酸辣的泪水，连活着的感觉都不复存在。无尽的悲痛像洪水一样在自己的体内翻搅、膨胀，自己的眼睛根本就止不住可恨的泪。自己的眼前，仿佛仍是那些血淋淋的场景；那些惨不忍睹的画面，就像一把把铁钳一样，死咬着自己的心不放。自己像摊烂泥一样，根本就站不起来。自己对父亲说了无数遍对不起，可是，坟场里，只有乱草纷披，黄花迷离。自己想告诉父亲，其实他在儿子的心中，一直都是个英雄。可是，父亲再不能听见。生命，就是这样残酷，永远无法重来；命运，就是这样无情，谁都无能为力。

自己没有听从父亲的遗言，忘记恩仇，远走他乡。自己没有离开赵家镇。杀父之仇，不共戴天，自己发誓，一定要血洗玉山帮。

自己用半箱黄金，暗雇了七星帮的杀手营，要他们去取金顺的首级。另外，自己又撺掇当时的县长，要他去借兵来剿玉山帮。自己对县长说，眼下的局势，是北伐军节节胜利，北洋军一溃千里，孙传芳新败，国民党刚来，在这个节骨眼上，您若想维持自己的前途，那光改换阵营是不够的，还必须防旧小人、找新靠山。听说那严司令刚来这边，就跟人问起过玉山匪患的事，您想过没有，他是怎么知道玉山帮的事的？怕是早有谗言在耳。为今之计，您必须先声夺人，尽快主动去找严司令，向他借兵去剿玉山帮，以明您壮勇之志，否则，日子长了，万一有人给您编出些不干不净的谣言来，那可就不好办了。总之，匪患一日不除，您就有把柄在政敌之手，而您若铲除了玉山帮，不仅自己可以得到一半的功劳，为您将来的仕途锦上添花，您那送给严司令的另一半功劳，更是可以让您和严司令结下交情，以备将来不时之需，此事两全其美，何乐而不为。县长拍手一笑，说，好，妙，我这就去严司令那里借兵，调他半个团过来，不信灭不了那玉山帮！

当时，自己真的以为，自己很聪明。

但是，这一天的傍晚，小得财却来敲响了自己家的门。小得财是自己安排在县政府里的一个心腹，每有要事来报，自己总会赏他不少钱财。这一次的敲门声急促而慌乱，自己门还未开，心中已然有些紧张。果然，门一开，就听小得财上气不接下气地说，大事不好了。

县长收到了一封举报信，信中详述了自己和父亲与玉山帮勾结多年的事实，并且随信还附了一张自己亲手写给金顺的收据。自己替玉山帮买军火时，若要先从帮里领出应付款项去，总要先亲手给金顺写下一张收据，收据上还要写清各项明细条目。这是金顺立下的规矩。据小得财说，县长已经验过了笔迹，那张收据上的字，的确和自己平时写的字一模一样。而县长在大发雷霆之际，又有小人趁机进言，向县长添油加醋地讲述了自己以前行贿前任县长、为父脱罪的事情。县长拍案大骂：可恨，可恨！

小得财说，后面的话他没再顾得上偷听，就赶紧跑来报信了。小得财说，这件事情看来已经不可收拾了，说不定县长马上就会派人来抓你了，你快逃吧！

事情发生得太突然，自己一下子就懵了。这时，忽然沉闷的一声，有一大袋沉甸甸的东西，被人从围墙外扔了进来。自己赶紧开门去看，像扔了东西的两个人，已跑远。关了门，自己和小得财去看袋子，但是刚走近，一股血腥恶臭就扑鼻而来。暮色中，只见袋子上血迹斑斑。自己打开了这个袋子，袋子里，竟是许多个血淋淋的人头！

小得财惊呼了一声。自己赶紧要他别出声。自己迅速镇定了心情，仔细地察看了一下袋子里的那些人头。人头一共有十二个，他们全是七星帮杀手营里的杀手。其中一个，竟然还是杀手营的首领——铁豹。自己跌坐在了地上。

袋子里还有一张字条。字条上清楚醒目地写着两行字：天堂有路你不走，地狱无门你闯进来。

自己认得，这是金顺的笔迹。

是了，一定是金顺写的举报信。知道自己通匪的人固然有很多，但是从

来就没人有什么真凭实据。只有金顺，才有那些收据；只有他，才了解所有事情的真相与细节。

自己还是太嫩了，一败涂地。

自己正要去给小得财拿钱，准备让他再回县政府里去打探打探消息，忽然，自家的宅子外面就是响起了一行杂乱而密集的脚步声。这种脚步声自己平日里很熟悉。他们不是军队就是警察。

自己还没来得及祈祷，猛烈的拍门声已经响起。“开门！快开门！”凶狠的叫门声。

小得财吓傻了，自己也傻了，一切都比自己预料的来得更猛、更快。

外面的人，像是在用枪托砸门了。

“快，跟我去后面，我们翻墙走！”自己说着，便领了小得财往后院跑。

自己和小得财刚翻出墙，就被守在后门旁的两个警察给发现了。自己和小得财拼命地跑，警察在后面拼命地追。警察开始开枪。暮色中，枪声惊心动魄。

那一刻，自己感到，像是又回到了在日本亡命天涯的日子里。风在耳旁呼啸，路在前方迷茫，子弹在身后追击。你永远也不会知道，你的下一步，会不会就是你人生里的最后一步。人与死亡的赛跑，总是充满了欲哭无泪的绝望。

还好，这民国政府里的警察，大多是混日子过的流氓。他们追了一阵，大概是嫌累，就都不再追了。自己和小得财，逃进了树林里。

天黑了下来。自己在喘息中平静了下来，心中苍白一片。树影幽黑错列，天地孤冷萧索，风吹枝丫鬼叫，四顾绝境纵横。自己完全无法接受眼前的事实，自己根本不能理解命运的奇怪。自己不仅仇没报成，还反而是将自己推向了鬼门关，这算是恶有恶报吗？老天爷简直是疯了！

那时，自己还不知道，县长已经是下了要就地枪决自己的命令。自己只是惧怕金顺，怕金顺会将自己五马分尸。小得财更害怕，他原本只是想来讨个赏，结果赏没讨到，还被一起卷进了这场风波里。自己安慰他，说，等事情过去了，我给你三根金条。

夜风黑冷，自己和小得财在树林里过了一夜。那一夜，自己被困在无尽的惊惧与绝望中，一夜没有睡着。自己真的又像是回到了那些在日本亡命天涯的日子中。不，应该说，是比那些日子更可怕、更绝望。在日本，自己还有希望，自己的希望是回国、回家、回到父亲的身边。但是现在，自己又还能有什么希望呢？父亲已经没了，在这个世上，自己已失去了最可靠的保护神，失去了最后的避难所，自己已是个孤家寡人，自己还能怎样逃脱死神的追杀？自己欲哭无泪，只有天风凄冷长空。

那一天，是一九二七年四月十二日。后来，自己才知道，这也是中国历史发生重要转折的一天。在此之前，在国共两党的团结战斗下，长江以南地区已完全为北伐军控制，北洋军节节败退，形势原本大好。但是，蒋介石为了自己的政治利益，在上海纠合了包括青洪帮在内的多股势力，发动了“四·一二”政变，开始大规模屠杀共产党人。不久之后，与蒋介石势不两立的汪精卫，也开始了血腥的分共清共行动。北伐黯然搁浅，国共血腥分裂。宋庆龄宣布退出国民党中央执行委员会。南昌起义爆发。最终，在一致反共的基础上，宁汉合流。可以说，蒋介石和汪精卫这两个诡计多端又厚颜无耻的野心家，携起手来，一起在中国的头上拉了一堆屎，这就是政治。多数老百姓都以为政治只是政治家们的事，其实，大家都活在政治里。政事，只是天下事的一个浓缩。

天亮以后，自己要小得财回去看看情况，小得财死活不愿意，说，那不是去送死吗。自己说，又没人知道你是我的人，也没人知道你给我报了信，虽然我们都被警察追了一段路，但那时天已暗，他们未必就看清了你的样子，而且警察局里的人应该也都不认识你。小得财想了想，觉得有道理。但他只答应去街上看看，不愿意去县政府里刺探消息。自己说，你若是突然不去上班，和我一起失踪，那样才会惹人怀疑！小得财还要扭捏，自己火了，说：好了好了，事成之后，我给你十根金条，快去！

小得财一下子就蹿了出去。

自己当时就觉得既悲哀又可笑。危难之际，仍和你站在一起的人，也可以不是你的忠诚朋友，而只是一个仍然拿你当摇钱树来看的贪心蠢货。人生就是这么灰暗。其实自己骗了小得财，当时，自己家里一共也就剩六根金条，而且还全是小金条。而自己此刻的身上，更是分文没有。自己有些戏谑地想，不知道小得财知道了，会不会觉得很失望。

快到中午的时候，小得财气喘吁吁地跑回树林。小得财焦急地说，不好

了，县长已经定了你的罪，说要枪毙你。他们正在县城和各镇的每个出入口上设卡，要全城搜捕你，县长还说了，如有反抗，可就地枪决。另外他们还要在全县贴出抓你的悬赏通缉令，谁能抓到你，不论你是死是活，都赏黄金一两。你说现在该怎么办？

自己忙问，那赵家镇上的出入口，现在设卡了没有？小得财一脸茫然，然后懊悔地说，这个没想到，没去看。

自己恐惧与烦乱满腔，不禁便自嘲地说了一句：想不到，我赵驹的命，竟然只值一两黄金。

是啊，怎么这么便宜。小得财也愤愤不平地说了一句。

自己心里顿时更不舒服，但也没心思去骂小得财了。形势已经如此紧迫，自己在天亮前还在幻想的以全部家产去收买县长的计划，看来已完全不可能实施，因为自己现在只要一露面，说不定就会被哪个只贪一两黄金的蠢货给杀死，况且，现在在县城里和赵家镇上，应该都已埋伏下了金顺派出的杀手。为今之计，只能是逃为上策了，自己想。自己到了这一刻，才是真正懂得了父亲最后那几句遗言里所饱含的阅世沧桑与爱子心切。如果自己一早就忘记恩仇，远走他乡，何至于弄到今天这性命岌岌可危的地步！

自己问小得财：有人怀疑你了吗？

没有。小得财说。

那一路上有人跟踪你吗？

也没有。

你都确定？

那还用说，我又不是第一次干这种事。小得财得意地说。

那就好。自己说。忽然，自己看着小得财，问他：那你为什么不杀了我，去拿那一两黄金的悬赏呢？

小得财顿时就急了，说，你把我小得财看成是什么人了？我贪财不假，可我从不出卖雇主，别说悬赏只是给一两黄金，就算悬赏是给一百两黄金，我小得财也绝不会做出卖主求荣这种缺德事来！

小得财的话，说得情真意切，那时倒也的确让自己有了三分感动。于是自己不再怀疑和担心什么。小得财问自己，接下来该怎么办，自己就告诉他，自己在奉天市有一个远房表叔，以前父亲还经常和他通信，就是这几年才没了联系，现在，自己只能是去投靠这个远房表叔了。小得财说，这样也好，就是不知道你能不能逃出这个赵家镇去。自己说，不用担心，我自有办法。

至于小得财本人，自己建议他留守原地，一如既往，静观其变，以俟将来。因为他并没有暴露，所以没必要自乱阵脚，跟着自己仓皇出逃。小得财说，心有灵犀一点通，他也是这么想的。

自己要小得财把他身上带着的钱全拿出来。小得财问，干什么？自己说，别废话，给我看看。小得财就把他身上带着的钱全掏了出来。自己数了数，这些钱够自己去奉天市的路费了。

自己说，看不出来你还挺富。然后就把他掏出来的钱全拿了过来。小得财就有些急。自己笑着跟他说，你别急，我暂时跟你借一下这些钱，我现在身上分文没有，钱全在家里，但是我家周围现在肯定都待满了盯梢的人，我和你都不能去取钱，所以我就只能是跟你借一些路费了，还好你身上有这么些钱，不然我还得麻烦你回一趟你家里去取钱来。

小得财就问：那你说好了给我的金条呢？自己说，你别急，我告诉你，等这风头过去了，监视我家的那些人全都撤了，你就去我家里拿金条。金条就放在我床底下的一个暗格里，你自己去摸。记住，进去时钻窗，别撬坏了我家的锁。总有一天我还要回来的，相信时间不会太长。到时我们重聚首，我再重重地谢你。

小得财千恩万谢，说，就知道你不会亏待我小得财的。自己笑笑，转过身去，将小得财的钱全装进了自己的衣袋里，然后，刚要开口和小得财说再见，忽然，一个又冷又硬的东西，顶住了自己的后脑勺。

没有悬念，那就是枪。

那一刻，自己真的是惊讶的。自己惊讶的，是自己怎么会在这生死危难的一刻，竟然那么轻易地就相信了人性。

自己说，你别乱来，我和你是一根绳上的蚂蚱。

小得财阴冷地一笑，说，你死了，就永远没人知道我是你的兵了。

自己问，刚才怎么不动手？

小得财说，因为刚才，我还不知道你家的金条究竟放在哪里。

自己说，你就不怕我会杀了你吗？

小得财说，你根本就没那个本事。

自己说，我忘了告诉你，我爹在临死前，已经传了我八极拳。

自己感到，顶在自己脑后的枪，顿时一哆嗦。说时迟，那时快，自己头一偏，后退一步，直接就扳住了小得财拿枪的那只手，用尽全力狠狠往下一折。“咔嚓”一声，小得财的那条手臂就骨折了。

枪掉在了地上。自己飞快地捡起了枪，指住了小得财的脑袋。小得财跪地痛哭，乞求饶命。他说，他只是一时糊涂，财迷心窍，不是真的想杀人。自己说，你太贪了，我已经答应了给你金条，你却还想要拿那区区一两的赏金。小得财把头都磕破了，求自己看在他多年为自己潜伏探听、跑腿报信的分上饶他一命，还说，他真的没想杀人。自己捡起了一块大石块，说，可是，我想杀人。说完，自己就将石块往他脑袋上一砸。

自己没有开枪，因为枪声会引来追兵。自己用石块狠狠地砸着小得财的脑袋，一下，一下，又一下。自己冷酷而残酷。生在这样一个黑暗的年代，礼崩乐坏，仁破义碎，不让自己变得冷酷一些，自己只会被野兽撕碎；活在这样一个绝望的世界，人为财死，鸟为食亡，不让自己变得残酷一些，自己只会被万箭穿心。生不逢时，或者活不明白，都是可悲中的可悲。

小得财的血溅在自己的脸上，自己麻木地笑了。小得财没了呼吸。

自己逃出了树林，偷偷回到了镇上，果然看见了通缉令。上了大路，又看见了关卡。看来小得财在消息上并没有骗自己。自己又潜回了镖局宅子的附近，果然发现了不少监视者。最终，自己劫了一条船，乔装打扮，在水路上骗过了搜捕的警察，逃出了赵家镇，逃出了江庆县。

自己是在跟随渡边打回了赵家镇以后，才知道了当年自己出逃后，江庆县上接下来发生的一些事情。小得财并没有被自己砸死。小得财被人救起后，送进了县医院，他醒来后，被一个警察认出了样子，说他就是和逃犯赵驹一起逃命的那个人。县长亲自审问，小得财就交代了一切，还说出了自己准备逃往奉天市远房表叔家的事情。当然，小得财当时在交代的过程中，究竟有没有全部如实回答，或者究竟有没有刻意隐瞒、编造些什么，现在就没人能说得清了。只是，县长后来并没有深究小得财的罪。而且，听人说，小得财一出院，就将他的大半家财都捧出来献给了县长。后来，小得财还带县长去查抄了威远镖局。据当时参加行动的人说，县长从地下的暗格里抄出金条后，笑得眼镜都掉了。不过，小得财终究也还是没能多活太长时间。一九二八年的夏天，就在皇姑屯事件发生不久后的一天，小得财在偎翠楼里嫖妓时，突然口鼻血崩，血涌不止。等到妓女们请来医生时，小得财已气绝身亡。都说，是他当初脑袋里被砸坏的地方没长好，被妓女玩得太激动，血就一下子全喷了出来。据说，后来偎翠楼的生意不但没有因此而变得萧条，反而还特别红火了一阵，因为，有不少男人都很想去尝一尝，那能噬人性命的无上销魂餐，究竟是个什么滋味。这就是男人的本性，也是欲望的本性。

而县长，后来真的从严司令那里借来了剿匪的部队。这支部队装备精良，声势威武，听他们自己说，他们可是蒋介石的王牌部队。可是这支部队大张旗鼓、火力全开地连续剿了玉山帮好几次，竟然都没能伤到玉山帮的筋骨，反倒是他们自己，损兵折将，伤亡惨重。严司令大发雷霆，怒不可遏，要县长赔偿一切损失。县长叫苦不迭，后悔莫及。县长是又赔金条又送女人，可是严司令并不肯善罢甘休。严司令一方面不肯撤走部队，要部队继续全力剿匪，另一方面，又不断地以部队损失为由，敲诈勒索县长。县长是欲哭无泪。他曾长叹：我这哪里是请来了什么剿匪部队，我是请来了活阎王啊！而县长因此也是更恨这件事的始作俑者，赵驹。恨之入骨。所幸，后来很快便爆发了南昌起义，国民党将严司令和严司令的部队，全部都调到了剿共的第一线去。玉山帮重整旗鼓，再度威武；县长如获重生，激动落泪，谢天谢地谢祖宗。一•二八事变发生的那一年，严司令死于一场军队哗变之中，而这个县长，则去了李宗仁的身边高就。江庆县的百姓都说，这江庆县的县长是换了一任又一任，可是这一任又一任，全都只像是一个人。江庆县从孙传芳的地盘变成了蒋介石的地盘，可是这变来变去，只不过就是将旧军阀换成了新军阀。

金顺最后是死在他亲外甥的手里。国军无法剿灭玉山帮，便想招安玉山帮。但是金顺不是宋江。金顺和他的那帮老兄弟，当年原本就是脱离了蔡锷的部队去当的土匪，现在哪里还肯重新再被部队收回去。这就与玉山帮中的少壮派发生了矛盾。金顺的外甥劝金顺，现在的国军和以前的蔡锷部队不一样，国军是吃喝嫖赌、百无禁忌，且做什么都是名正言顺、无人敢骂，只要打仗的时候别冲在前面送死，那平时就和做土匪没什么两样，换皮不换肉，何乐而不为。何必要戴着个土匪的帽子惹人来打？但是金顺就是不同意。金

顺认为年轻人看问题太简单。军政斗争，复杂程度远非一般人可以想象，一旦进了部队，那生死和自由，就全听不得你自己的了，别以为耍点小聪明就能逍遥自在、水火不沾，还是占山为王来得开心痛快。玉山帮中的这两派，哪派也说服不了哪派。于是，最终，金顺的外甥便决定夺权篡位。一天，金顺聊发少年狂，带了人下山去抢那个叫王秀珍的女人，金顺的外甥便趁机杀了守山的二当家的，控制住了山寨，然后，带了一群亲信，扑下山去，杀死了金顺。金顺死后，玉山帮便入了国军，离开了玉山。据说，金顺的外甥最后在华北的抗日战场上当了逃兵，最后被长官一枪毙命。

生死时代，乱世浮沉，善恶纷争，终有了结。

自己逃出江庆县后，先去了上海，想从上海乘火车去东北。但是，自己到了上海，才知道上海发生了四·一二政变。军队、警察、帮会流氓都在到处捕杀工人领袖和共产党人。满街血雨，千里腥风。全上海到处都是罢工、集会、游行与暗杀、追杀、屠杀。血流成河，满城鬼哭。军警和流氓都遵循着“宁可错杀三千、不可放过一个”的原则，在上海各处滥捕乱杀。尸首漂满黄浦江，丧音响彻上海滩。自己亲眼看见，几个国民党的士兵将一个正怀着孕的女共产党员吊在教堂的门前，活生生地肢解。血肉模糊的胎儿被踩烂在地上，像一颗被剁烂了的巨大心脏。场面惨不忍睹，当场呕吐的不下十余人。都说，蒋介石手段之残忍，比起阎罗王来，真是有过之而无不及。自己当时是真后悔来了上海这个是非之地。后来，自己也被杜月笙的几个手下当成了共产党，一路疯狂追杀。幸亏自己身上是带着那把小得财的手枪，才大难不死地又逃过了一劫。最终，自己总算是离开了上海，登上了开往东北的火车。

睡在火车车厢里的小床上，听着嘈杂的声音，自己忍不住无声哭泣。是什么让自己的人生黑暗如此？至亲尽失，一贫如洗，命悬人手。是什么让自己的生命绝望至斯？十面埋伏，四面楚歌，走投无路。是自己一次又一次地做了不该做的事，还是自己一次又一次地活在了不该存在的时代？是自己在不停地糟蹋着命运，还是命运在不停地糟蹋着自己？自己从一个自命清高的读书郎，变成了一个自甘堕落的下三滥；自己从一个光鲜亮丽的少爷，变成了一个政府通缉的罪犯；自己从一个干干净净的普通人，变成了一个双手染上了人血、双脚踩踏过尸体的亡命徒。这一切，究竟是谁的错，是谁将自己推进了人生的黑洞，是什么扭曲了自己命运的轨道？这个被欲望、无序和灭亡充斥着的世界，到底还要吞噬掉多少纯洁而新鲜的灵魂才能走向安宁？这个被野心、动乱与战火控制着的时代，究竟还需要多少清白而无辜的人生为其殉葬？明天是否还会变得更糟，明天究竟还能糟到什么程度？从个人到国家，从眼前到历史，一切都像是上帝编排的悲剧。人，到底还能为自己做些什么？自己真想一了百了。

父亲最后教给自己的八极拳，其实自己并没有学会多少。自己骗小得财自己已经学会了八极拳，那是为了吓唬他，让他分神。在父亲那如烟花盛开般绚烂而短暂的最后演示中，自己泪眼蒙胧，痛心疾首，又怎么还有可能会去真的用心记住那些招式和口诀。自己所能记住的，最多只是一些片断而已。而江南赵家的八极拳，世代的流传都只依靠口传身授心悟，家中并无什么拳谱。这也是传统武人保护自身价值、防止恶人窃技的一种方式。父亲生前曾告诉过自己，其实他教给土匪们的，都是一些看似厉害、实则有致命破绽的假功夫，一旦遇上武林高手，土匪们自会命送敌手。父亲当时说，他什么都出卖了，但他没有真的出卖八极拳，他什么都背叛了，但他没有真的背叛一个武人最后的良心。可是，当时的父亲，恐怕怎么样也不会想到，他最后的这一片自我安慰与自我坚守，在他生命的最后一刻里，也会无奈地崩坍成了废墟、破碎成了瓦砾。父亲在临死前，想要将八极拳的真功夫传给他最宝贵的儿子，可是，这传，又只可能是在众匪的注视之下传。教了儿子，也就等于教了众匪。人生有时就是这样的无奈。自己不知道父亲在那最后的时刻里，有没有看见来生的海市蜃楼，但是自己相信，父亲在他最后一次的授艺中，已经看破了人生的一切桎梏。也许，让土匪们看见了八极拳的真经，即意味着父亲人生防线的最后失守，但是，只要能让儿子继承到这门功夫的精髓，又何尝不是父亲生命意义重新建立之希望？也许，让儿子继承八极拳的衣钵，即意味着父亲望子成状元心愿的最终破灭，但是，只要能让儿子去做他真心最喜欢做的事，又岂不是一个父亲在临走之前所能给予儿子的最大最好的爱？功夫本身就是一条修行的路，高手走到了最后，自会看见涅槃的光。只是，父亲不知，自己早已不是他心中的那个儿时的自己了。自己已不再会全心全意地喜欢什么，也不再会彻头彻尾地讨厌什么。自己那天生的聪慧与善记，也早就已经成为昨日的一场美丽云烟。自己只不过是一把已经生

了锈的刀，被锈腐蚀透了的刀。人生有时就是这样让人欲哭无泪。命运的残酷，有时就是在人的想象范围之外。而这个世界的逻辑，永远在人的理解能力之上。最终，自己只学会了八极拳的一点皮毛。而土匪们，看起来功夫倒是进步得很快，不然，驰名江湖的金牌杀手铁豹，又怎么会就这样轻易地命丧江南，人头落地。这真是又一个悲剧。

卸下小得财手枪的那一招，是自己急中生智，从父亲的招式里临时化用出来的。从下山到出逃的那段时间里，自己每晚都会在暗黑的夜色中独自练拳。自己练着自己还记得的那些招式，默背着还记得的那些口诀，常常泪流满面。自己是那么喜欢那样暗黑的夜，因为在那清冷如霜而又浓稠似漆的黑暗里，没有人能看见你的一滴眼泪，没有人能看见你可笑而笨拙的半个动作。自己不想听到有人说，赵三牛的儿子连他爹的一个动作都学不会。自己不想给父亲一生的武林英名续上一条可耻的狗尾。有时候，自己哭着哭着，就会以为，父亲仍然活在自己的身旁，他在看着自己练拳，他在听着自己背口诀，他虽不言不语，却慈爱深长。可是，只要天一亮，自己就会清醒地知道，还活着的父亲，只是自己的幻想。这个世上，既没有能让亲人再看一眼的鬼魂，也没有死而复生的温暖。这个世界是多么无情而冰冷。不孤独与不悲伤，对孤独与悲伤的人来说永远只是个神话。天亮和清醒，对一无所有的人来说，永远只意味着最后的残酷与掠夺。

有时候，自己会祈望，能在某一个神奇的梦中，回想起父亲最后所教功夫的全部，但是这世上又哪里会有什么神奇。有时候，自己又会试图钻进自己记忆的深远处，去寻找自己儿时曾看到过的父亲练拳时的详细画面，可是那些画面全都已经被岁月腐蚀得模糊不清、残缺不全。自己绞尽脑汁，仍然无能为力。也许，这就是命运吧。唯有夜，还是那么黑，那么暗，包裹着自己的一切伤痛，包容着自己的所有悲伤。只有站在夜的黑暗里，一个人才可以拒绝知道，他已永远失去了什么，他已永远不再是谁。只有站在风的凛冽中，一个人才可能真正明白，活着有多重要，活着就有多惨烈。

火车上的自己，是脆弱与窘迫的。自己的手枪，已经在与杜月笙手下的最后一战中被自己遗落在了火海里，当时自己只顾着逃命，也没想到要再去捡一把枪。自己已筋疲力尽，如果在火车上再遇上一个想要自己命的人，恐怕已不会再有什么能力反抗。而自己的口袋里，只剩下了三块大洋，自己也不知道，这三块大洋，能不能撑到自己寻到表叔。只能是走一步算一步了。真是屋漏偏遭连夜雨，船迟又遇顶头风。

那时，自己并不知道，金顺会不会像当年的山本一样，派人满世界地追杀自己，誓不罢休。自己也不知道，江庆县那捉拿自己的通缉令，会不会进一步地发向全国，广布罗网。自己是同时在黑白两条路上走进了绝境，鬼门关在自己面前洞开，自己的绝望与惊惶，远胜当年在日本逃命时。其实自己早该想到会有这一天的，从自己也与土匪沆瀣一气的时候开始，就应该要想到的，但是自己没想到。

走不尽的天涯路，闯不完的生死关。要活着，就必须受罪。

不过，自己也并非毫无生机。一切，就要看自己能不能顺利地进入东三省了。张作霖在一九二六年的一月，为了收拾郭松龄倒戈留下的乱局、防备外敌，已经宣布了东三省独立。也就是说，江庆县的通缉令就算会发向全国，也发不进北洋政府的地盘，更发不进东三省，自己只要真的到了东三省，就不再是一个通缉犯了。北伐只要一日没有成功，南方政府的号令就一日到不了张作霖的地盘上。乱世的乱就是如此玄妙，它既可将好人逼上绝路，也会给恶棍留一条活路。无理无法，千变万化；生死成败，各凭造化。

因为自己小时候常为父亲寄信取信，所以这远房表叔家的地址自己一直都还大致记得。当然，那具体的街道和门牌号自己都已是记不太清了，不过这不是什么大问题，东北人豪爽，到了奉天市，只要多跟人打听打听，路自然就会清晰起来。

但是，乐观总是虚妄的，总有些令人意外的沮丧甚至是绝望，会出现在你祈求一帆风顺的道路上。到了奉天市后，三块大洋支撑了自己没多久，便全化为了乌有。自己在饿了两天以后，终于打听到了表叔家确切的地址。但是，自己还没来得及高兴，就又听人家继续告诉自己：你的这门亲戚，在几年前，就已经全家死光啦。自己顿时傻了，还以为这个好心人是在说笑。

自己惊惶失措地找到了表叔的家，果然，只见一片断垣残壁。那一刻，自己觉得，整个人都好像是虚脱了。自己又跟周围的几户人家打听了一遍，确认了，这真的就是自己那个远房表叔的家。而这个家里的人，也的确是都已经死光了。几年前，张作霖的军队征兵，拉壮丁拉到了这里，表叔的小儿子要被征去当兵，表叔和小儿子、小儿媳死活都不同意。表叔的大儿子已经

死在了军阀混战的战场上，这个小儿子，已是家里唯一的一条男根，哪能再让他去战场上为了军阀们的利益白白送死？于是，几个虎背熊腰的大兵，就去了表叔家里硬拉人。小儿子藏了起来，大兵们就在表叔家里四处乱闯找人。两个大兵强闯进了小儿媳的房间，恰逢小儿媳在给她刚满月的女儿喂奶，雪白袒露。大兵们邪念顿生，恶扑而上。表叔拼了命地和大兵们搏斗了起来，小儿子闻声，也从藏身的后院那边跑了过来，拼死地和大兵们厮打了起来。最后，表叔和小儿子都死在了大兵的枪下，而小儿媳在惨遭大兵们轮奸之后，也被击毙。至于那个刚满月的小女孩，则是被某兵摔死在了地上。大兵们将表叔家里的财物洗劫一空，临走时，还在表叔家里放了一把火。大火烧了两天一夜，火光冲天，却无人敢救。后来，军队向外宣称，表叔家的惨案，是飞贼所为。再后来，军队在这里的征兵，就出奇顺利，征谁谁到，无人不从。只是，人们都说，在夜深人静的时候，仿佛仍能听到被灭了门的表叔家的那几个冤魂的惨叫，鬼哭狼嚎，昏天黑地。

看着那片又经过了几载风雨洗礼的废墟，自己呆若木鸡。父亲生前常以为，表叔一直不再写信给他，是因为知道了他入匪帮的事，却没想到，其实表叔全家，在那时已是被灭了门。这个世界的荒谬出奇，简直令人无法面对。修桥铺路无尸骸，杀人放火金腰带。在乱世中，军队与匪帮的差别，真的又有多大呢？那已长满了苔藓的残断墙根，那有老鼠乱爬的乌黑瓦砾堆，那积着发绿发臭的雨水的半截破水缸，就像是上帝给这个黑暗年代作的一首诗。诗里有小孩的啼哭、女人的惨叫、老人的哀号、青年的悲恸，诗里有没烧碎的白骨，诗里有烧焦了的皮肉。人的脂油定然已是浸入了这片废墟中，所以废墟已永远不能洗去尸体的气味；人的眼珠可能就掉在瓦砾间某堆苦涩的土里，还在寂寥地看着这个世界的日出日落。灵魂和鲜血，都已成了这个时代献给地狱的礼物，活着，是怎样的残酷。

自己在废墟前，一直呆呆地站到了天黑。直到复苏的强大饥饿将自己唤回。自己顿时有了想死的心。自己所期望的投奔，已经明白无误地成了废墟，自己已山穷水尽，仿佛已经走到了世界的边缘。如若不死，自己又该怎样活下去？还能怎样活下去？

自己想伸出手去跟人讨些食物，却怎么也开不了口。自己想去偷些吃的，可这一时半刻又能上哪里去偷？饥饿，这种人类最原始的痛苦，像个强大而无敌的魔鬼一样，紧紧地包裹着自己，简直要令自己窒息、瘪碎。自己在暗夜的街头流浪，像一条无家可归的狗，像一头两眼发绿的狼。饥饿的滋味是那样难受，没有饿过的人永远也不会懂得。而难受又不仅仅只是难受，要知道，在许多真正的饥饿背后，往往还绽放着一个死神的笑容。因为一个得不到食物的人如果真的一直不能得到食物，那么，等待他的只可能是死亡。这种恐惧，是那些衣食无忧的人们永远也无法理解的。易子而食，只是饥饿把人逼疯的小小一例。大自然将野兽变成了人，却又在人的身上留下了许多危险的机关，有时只要轻轻一触，人就会变回野兽。

最终，自己在一盏明晃晃的路灯下，看见了一条正在吃饭的狗。那是一条大狼狗，它面前的食盆里，不仅有饭，而且还有肉，好像是红烧肉。自己慢慢地靠近它，不看它的眼睛，争取不引起它的警惕。自己以迅雷不及掩耳之势，飞快地从它的食盆里抓了一把饭出来，塞进了自己的嘴里。自己狼吞虎咽地嚼着，脑子里空白一片。自己又抓了一把饭，还抓了两块肉，那条狗居然没有叫，只是呆呆地看着自己。自己简直有了感激这条狗的心情。自己看看四周没有人，干脆就趴了下来，像条狗一样地和这条狗一起吃起了食盆里的饭和肉。自己不敢抢走食盆独享，因为自己猜，它也许可以接受分享，但是一定不会接受被抢。还是不要节外生枝的好。狗的口水流在饭里，使有些饭有些黏糊，但是自己毫不在意。恶心与廉耻那一刻都已在自己的身上消失，自己的灵魂是不存在的。那一刻，自己的体内只有一个巨大的空缺，致命的空缺，需要自己以食物去填补，如果补不上，自己的生命就会流失殆尽。这个世上，没有比求生更本能的欲望了。自己吃掉了食盆里的最后一块肉，狼狗突然对自己瞪圆了眼，露出了牙。自己本能地一慌，站起来撒腿就跑。自己听到了狼狗在后面猛追着狂吠的声音。静夜里，狼狗的猛吠声，显得那样狰狞。

自己摆脱了狼狗的追逐，在一个街角停了下来。饥饿与恐惧暂时地消除了，恶心与廉耻就又跑了回来。一想到自己居然吃下了狗的口腔分泌物，自己就忍不住想吐，猛烈地想吐，本能地想吐。但是自己又知道自己不能吐，一吐，就等于白吃了。最终，自己没有吐，只是哭了，哭得没有理由，哭得没有躯壳，哭得没有下一刻。夜，是那么黑，那么狰狞。

时光逼仄，容不下太多的悲伤与退缩。要是不想死，就必须马上找到脱

离绝境的办法。当务之急，是自己必须要想办法谋生。于是，天一亮，自己就开始四处去找活干。只要是能给口人饭吃，自己什么活都愿意干。但是，世事总有出人意料的地方。不少小老板都把自己当成了乞丐，逐之唯恐不及。看看也是，自己经过了这一段时间的逃亡，衣衫已是褴褛，满面肮脏的污垢，头发如鸟窝般蓬乱，身上由于长时间没洗澡而臭不可闻，自己不像个乞丐又像什么？可是，自己现在如一条丧家之犬，身无分文，举目无亲，食无可食，居无可居，又怎么样才能不像个乞丐！

一个好心的包子铺老板施舍给了自己几个肉包子，自己千恩万谢。蹲在街角狼吞虎咽地吃着包子，自己忧心如焚。接下来该怎么办？下一次的饥饿，又会在何时强势来袭？自己现在已无路可去，只能在这里就地生根，但是，自己要怎样才能在这里扎下根来？难道下一次饥饿来袭的时候，自己要厚着脸皮再去那个包子铺前转悠吗？自己又不是真的乞丐。而在这一时半刻间，自己又真的可以去哪儿找到活干？自己连件装门面的像样衣服都没有！到底该怎么办？此时此地，最简单的吃饭，成了自己最险峻的难题。生存，就这样简单粗暴地袒露着它最原始的残酷与血腥，炫耀着它最强大的恐怖与黑暗，而自己在它的面前，弱小而绝望。

当晚，不甘心坐以待毙的自己，入室行窃，偷了四个馒头和一套半新的男人衣裤。月黑风高，无人发现自己。记得当初自己回国时，曾暗暗发誓，今生再不偷盗，哪怕偷盗的只是一片面包。可是命运就是这样出人意料。第二天清早，自己又去偷了一桶水。自己就着那桶水，将自己从上到下地彻底清洗了一遍。然后，自己换上了那套偷来的衣裤，重新开始四处去找活干。

没人再拿自己当乞丐看了。可是，潜在的困难又开始一一呈现。自己原本就没奢望自己能找到什么体面的活干，自己只是去了一些不起眼的小馆子和小店铺里碰运气，希望人家老板能雇自己做个杂役什么的。可是，就连这些小地方，都死死地不肯赏个活给自己干。人家要么就是不雇人，要么就是不雇外地人。自己也想冒充本地人，可是自己一开口，就没有那股东北味。也有老板起了疑：你好好的一个南方人，到这苦寒军争的东北来干什么？还只想当个小杂役，别是在南边犯了什么事逃过来的吧？

整整四天过去了，自己一无所获。在这四天里，自己又去偷了一次食物。没办法，自己不偷财物，也算是对得起失主家了。最后，自己又去了车行和码头找活干，心想，做个苦力总没那么难了吧？谁知，还是不行。奉天市的车行和码头都由奉天市本地的两个大黑帮控制着，自己不敢在黑帮的手底下干活。江湖的脉络总是比你所能看到的要更复杂，金顺闯荡江湖一生，难保就不认识这东北的黑帮。万一有一天，他的人顺藤摸瓜地找了过来，那自己岂不是死路一条？绝对不行。更何况，要进车行里去拉车，还得先交押金，自己哪有什么钱！

那时候，自己是真觉得要死了。人到绝路是什么感觉？就是你明明还活着，却已知道，自己没办法再活下去了。再多活一天，也只是受罪。自己想哭，却一滴眼泪也流不出来。自己看看天，天上只有乱云横流。自己想骂人，想杀人，却一句话也喊不出来，一步路也迈不开腿。上苍叫人活着，究竟是为了什么？

一个叫花子从自己身边走过，自己恶狠狠地叫住了他。他傻愣愣地看着自己。他缺着一颗门牙。自己用命令的口气，叫他把他手里的那半个馒头给自己。他真给了。自己突然笑了，笑得死去活来。自己把那半个馒头丢到了天上，然后，疯了似的，奔跑了起来。

自己做了一个真正偷钱的贼，不再偷那可怜的食物，而专偷令人憎恨的钱财。自己的堕落，不需要解释。偷一次钱，自己可以大吃大喝很长一段日子。只要不被人抓住，这样的生活，有什么不好？

可是，自己毕竟没练过那手指夹肥皂的童子功。终于有一天，自己还是被人给抓住了，被打得吐了血，两根手指也差点被剁掉。他们打完了自己，还要送自己去警察局。自己死死地咬住了那个胖子的耳朵，胖子的姨太太叫得像被杀的猪。最终，自己趁乱逃了出来。

自己在大雨里奔跑，雨水浇痛了自己的眼睛，淹没了自己的呼吸，自己还得奔跑。因为自己只要一停下来，那些该死的为富不仁的小丑，就会举着刀枪从后面追上来，把自己剁碎、剁烂。自己的胸口在痛，自己的后背在痛，自己的全身都在痛，自己的心脏像是被打碎了，自己的肚子里像是有火在烧，自己痛苦得快要流泪，喉咙里满是血腥味，可是自己还要不停地跑。真是庆幸他们没有打断自己的腿。自己每跑一步，脊梁骨都像被锤子砸了一样痛。自己的脑壳里，不断地“嗡嗡”作响。自己又他妈的笑了，笑得肆无忌惮。自己吐出了一口血来，摔倒在了街上。雨水兜头盖脸地泼来，自己失

去了知觉。

醒来时，自己看到的是一张颠倒的、灰黄的脸。因为颠倒，所以陌生得特别奇异。自己微微一慌。那张脸笑了，露出了一个缺着门牙的小黑洞。

“你醒了？”他说。他好像很高兴。他换了一个方向看自己，这时，自己才认出来，他就是被自己无缘无故抢了馒头的那个乞丐。

自己想要坐起来，一用力，肋骨处却一阵剧烈的痛。自己咬牙撑了撑，实在撑不住，还是躺了下去。他说：“你发烧了。”

自己发烧了吗？可能是吧。自己全身说不出的难受，脑袋里似昏似胀，嘴里发着苦。自己伸手摸了摸自己的额头，自己的手很冰，头很烫。寒与热在自己的体内顿时打起了架。自己倒霉得想哭，但是这些都并不重要，重要的是，自己多半还肋骨骨折了。

“放心，这里是破庙，除了我们，没有人能找得到你。”

“是你救了我吗？”

“不是我一个人，是我们四兄弟一起救的你。他们三个给你去抓药了，一会儿回来。我叫孔仁，你叫什么？”

“我叫赵驹。那天抢了你的馒头，对不起。”

“没事，都是出来混的，谁还没个想不开的时候。第一次做乞丐前，我还用头撞过墙，现在不一样还是活得好好的。”

劲风从破庙的大门外吹进来，杂草乱飞。孔仁去关门。自己看了看四周，蛛网四结，凌乱肮脏，破败不堪，而且，这庙里居然破得连个神像都没有。在原本应该放神像的地方，乱七八糟地堆放着锅碗瓢盆等日常生活用品。庙里一共搭了四张床，说是床，其实就是在每块门板的四角各垫上了两三块砖头，使门板不着地而已。床低低的，躺在床上，能听到床底下老鼠的窸窣声。一条脏兮兮的毯子盖在自己的身上，散发着臭烘烘的气味。但是自己的心里微微有了些暖意。

自己身上穿的，已经不是原来的那套衣服了。也是，那身衣服在雨中已经湿透了。一身干燥的破烂衣服，穿在自己的身上。应该是他们在自己昏迷时给自己换的。自己正在戏谑地想，不知这身衣服上的虱子可多时，另外的三个人回来了。

另外的三个人，分别叫孟义、朱理、黄道。他们看见自己醒了，都说，醒了便不会有事了。孔仁去取水煎药。孟义跟自己打招呼，说，不好意思，你原来的那身衣服没了，你烧得太厉害，我们又没钱，你身上也没钱，我们就只好拿你的那身衣服去药铺里跟人家换了药。自己说，没关系，谢谢你们。朱理说，老板太抠，只肯给四帖药。黄道说，没事，先吃着，四天后可能病早好了。自己说，没错。大家就都笑了起来。

自己还是挣扎着坐了起来，肋骨处钻心的痛，但自己忍着。没事，就算是骨头断了，长着长着自然也就会长好了。更何况，也不一定就是断了。可是又一阵剧痛袭来，自己实在撑不住，就只好又躺了下来。他妈的，那胖子的手可真够黑的。有钱人就是这样，不拿下三滥的人的命当命。

孟义他们问自己怎么了，自己说没事，只是有些头晕。他们说，头晕那你就躺着吧。

孟义、朱理和黄道拿着饭碗和竹棍又都出去了。孔仁说，他们还得去找晚饭。孔仁说，以前要饭还容易些，现在时局越来越乱，要个饭也越来越难了。

煎药时，孔仁说了一些他们四兄弟的事。他们本不是亲兄弟，只是因为都在奉天市要饭，相互结识之后，便一齐结拜成了兄弟。大家都有一笔伤心事。孔仁的全家，是被地主恶霸给逼死的；孟义的新婚妻子，是被英国人拐卖到了南洋做妓女；朱理的一条胳膊，是在军阀互斗的战场上被炮弹给炸飞的；黄道那才一岁的儿子，是被青帮的人给剁成了肉泥。大家虽然都来自五湖四海，但脸上流的是一样的泪。地主、洋人、军阀、黑帮，他们的身上负了多少中国人的血债？可是又有谁能去向他们要回一个公道？只能忍受，无尽地忍受。

问起这座庙时，孔仁说，这原本是一座关帝庙，外面有匾额。可是他们从发现这座破庙起，就没见过这座庙里的塑像。当年，他们四兄弟结拜时，也就是对着庙里那关老爷的空位拜的。孔仁开玩笑说，兴许是这天下太乱，连关老爷都坐不住了，要赶紧出去投个胎，再生成人，好辅佐明主，匡扶社稷。

自己笑笑，说，关老爷就算再生成人，怕是也已对付不了今天的洋枪洋炮。

喝药时，孟义他们回来了。孟义兴高采烈，他双手拿着两口碗，每口碗

里都装着几个山芋。朱理则是一只手替他们拿着两根竹棒。最后一个进来的是黄道，他双手横拎着一块旧门板，高兴地对孔仁说：大哥，你今晚又有床睡了。

自己的烧很快就退了下去。第二天早晨醒来，全身的难受已好了大半。只是肋骨处依然非常痛，身体难以大动。但是自己还是从门板床上爬了起来。这年月，身上断根骨头多个窟窿都是很正常的事，没必要躺着不动让人同情。又没再吐血，东西也吃得下，不会有什么大问题。孔仁看自己有些出冷汗，就问自己要不要紧，自己说，没什么，都好了。

看自己好手好脚的，不需要再让人照顾，孔仁他们就一起出去要饭去了。临走前，孔仁还嘱咐自己，一会儿别忘了自己煎药给自己喝，一天一帖，一帖两煎。自己说，知道了，谢谢。他们嘻嘻哈哈地走远了以后，自己便重新又去门板床上躺了下来。

一只老鼠在破庙里钻来钻去。看了一会儿，自己才发现，应该是有两只。自己莫名就想起了以前那些干干净净的日子，那样的日子可真好。但是自己并不想伤感。接下来该怎么办？这依旧是个难题。在这里白吃白住吗？不可能。重新回去做小偷吗？自己仍然心有余悸。再说，肋骨的伤也还没好，哪能做得了贼呢。要不，干脆跟他们一起去要饭？开玩笑，自己还要不要这张堂堂赵三牛的儿子的脸了！再怎么丢人，也不能丢到这个份上。

自己心烦意乱，只好不去想这些事情。想也是白想，不会有答案。躺了一会儿，自己去煎药，煎好了药，自己又喝药。中午时，孔仁特地回来了一次，给了自己一个大饼。自己很过意不去，说，以后我会还你们的。孔仁就有些不高兴了，说，什么话，大家都是穷苦兄弟，难道这一个饼还要记账不成？

孔仁又出去要饭了。自己吃完了饼，又在床上躺了一会儿，觉得有些百无聊赖，更兼前路迷茫。自己看看自己的手，心中不禁悲伤。父亲希望他儿子的手是一双拿笔的手，是一双能托起天下兴亡的状元之手，可是结果呢，这双手却成了一双贼手，成了一双可耻的鸡鸣狗盗之徒的手。荒谬的人生，就是这么让人欲哭无泪。

下午自己又喝了一次药。喝完了药，自己想离开这里。可是走到了庙门口，自己又没法再走。能去哪里呢？能去哪里呢？天下虽大，但是自己又能去哪里呢？留在这里，好歹也还有口东西吃，一旦离开这里，自己去哪里找吃的？难道要马上再去偷？自己看看自己的手，这是一双没练过贼功夫的手，再偷，又有谁能保证一定会成功？

自己又去门板床上躺了下来。肋骨处一阵剧痛。

晚上，和四兄弟一起吃的野果。吃完了，五个人躺在五块门板上，聊聊天。夜深远地充盈着幽暗，像看不见的水，像摸不到的时间。在夜之下，各种孤独像风，像絮，像永远不会碰面的两棵树。老鼠与人和谐相处，没有憎恨，没有杀戮，没有怀念，也没有忧伤。他们想听听自己的故事，自己就告诉他们，是土匪杀了自己的父亲，自己报仇不成，反被县长陷害，成了通缉犯。孔仁他们没有怀疑自己的故事，他们对自己表示了同情。黄道说，同是天涯沦落人，相逢何必曾相识。

其实，在这样一个既没有饥饿也没有寒冷的美好夜晚，自己真的不想回忆过往，更不想撒谎。但是，为了不让人觉得自己是个罪有应得的坏人，为了这个夜晚的美好不要轻易碎掉，自己只好撒谎，说自己从来没有通过匪。自己发现自己撒谎的本领很高。但是，话又说回来了，天下那么多的故事，谁又真能知道，其中哪些是真相，哪些是谎言？真正的历史，总在隐隐约约的迷雾里。夜那么黑，能睡着是一件多么幸福的事。

待在破庙的第三天，趁他们都出去要饭的时候，自己帮他们打扫了一下破庙。自己白吃白住在这里，总该要为他们做些什么才好。虽然肋骨的疼痛使自己无法做什么大的动作，但是打扫打扫卫生总还是没有问题的。庙里的老鼠一时都被自己赶到了庙外去，可是不一会儿，它们就又都跑了回来。自己便又赶。如此反复了几回，自己就也不赶了。它们要待在这里，就让它们待着吧。自己笑了。自己想，只能待在这破庙里的人，其实又和老鼠有多大的差别呢？

孔仁他们回来，看见破庙里变干净了，都很欣喜。他们感谢了自己，自己挺高兴。晚上一起吃了几个馒头，还吃了点花生。吹熄了蜡烛后，大家又都躺下聊起了天。沉沉的幽暗，浮在淡淡的安宁之上，混合着时光散漫地流淌，竟让人生出了几分忘怀的惬意。自从逃亡以来，自己要么日夜胆战心惊，要么时刻忧饥怕寒，未曾有过片刻身心的坦然，结果却没想到，在这破庙里、乞丐堆中，自己倒反而是莫名重获了温饱与安心。就连这里的臭与

脏，自己都感到了亲切。这是不是命运的某种暗示？又或者，这一切仅仅只是一个落难之人的苟延残喘？

孔仁他们说起了白天的见闻，说起了雄心勃勃的张作霖，说起了嚣张跋扈的日本浪人。自己跟他们一起空骂了一会儿日本浪人，忽然觉得很好笑。挺无聊的，但很快乐。也许，这就是一无所有者的喜乐吧。自己不再说话，自己在思忖自己的明天。明天还有最后一帖药，喝完了这帖药，自己就该离开这里了。离开了这里，自己该去哪儿？要不要再去城东偷一回？

像是听到了自己内心的讨论，孔仁忽然问："赵驹，你以后有什么打算？"

大家都静了下来。自己的心里挺乱，不知该怎样回答。也不确定，他们的意思是不是要赶自己走了。自己支吾了两声，终究也没说成什么话。

"要不你留下来吧，跟我们一起当乞丐，我们欢迎你。"孔仁说。

自己一时感到了意外，却也毫无准备。当乞丐？像他们一样？怎么可能？

自己依旧像个傻子一样无知而沉默。人生有时就是这么尴尬，当一个重要的抉择即将来临时，你还根本不知道，自己该怎样选择，所以这世上才会有那么多的懊悔和遗憾。

"我知道，你也许是大户人家出身，根本就看不上我们这些乞丐。可是你想过没有，你做贼，不一样是在辱没祖宗？"孔仁说。

自己的心像被重重一击，是啊，做贼，又是什么光彩的事呢？自己在黑暗中勉强笑了笑，说："我从来不偷穷人，我只偷富人，我这不是偷，是损有余而补不足，替天行道。"

"说得再好听也没用，人家抓到了你，会说你不是贼吗？其实做贼还不如做乞丐，你想想，我们乞丐虽然又脏又臭又被人看不起，但起码光明正大。你做贼，万一被人抓到，不是被打个半死，就是被送去警察局，去了警察局，还得坐牢。你天天都得在刀口上行走，是不是？"孔仁说。

自己没吭声，长久地默然着。这时，孟义就有些生气地对孔仁说："大哥，你跟他说这些干什么？他根本就看不起我们！"

"不，我不是这个意思！"自己赶紧说。

"我们又不是傻子，听不懂人话。我们也没别的意思，就是好心好意想留你，你不愿意就算了！”孟义气呼呼地说。

自己也接不上什么话了。其实孟义说得不错，自己就是看不起叫花子。自己又何必要骗他们呢？可是孔仁说得也不错，贼难道就比叫花子高贵吗？做贼还充满了生命危险，被人打死了也得不到一眼同情。自己到底该怎么办？

一直无人再说话。时间久了，大家都打起了呼噜，他们都睡着，而自己是装睡，自己觉得，现在还睡在他们的床上，真是够不要脸的。

第二天天还没亮，趁他们还睡着，自己就离开了破庙。既然已经说穿了不入伙，那也就没脸再去占人家的便宜了。人家要点饭也不容易，自己凭什么去吃人家的？太没道德了。还是去偷有钱人的钱吧。

可是自己转悠了一天，也没得手一次。自己身上穿的是叫花子的衣服，有钱人一看见叫花子就躲得老远，哪里还有机会给你偷？自己真是沮丧到了极点。自己肚子又饿，肋骨又痛，真是觉得要活不下去了。自己蹲在墙角，一个有钱人牵着一条狗走过，竟然丢给了自己一块大洋！

是一块大洋！

自己就差对着那人磕头谢恩了。自己大喊了十几声谢谢，那人牵着狗走远了。那一刻，自己忽然开了窍。如果被人同情，可以让自己活下去，那么，这又有什么不可以？自己活得这么惨，难道不该被人同情吗？被人同情与施舍固然是没有尊严的，可是，尊严能当饭吃吗？这个世界上，有多少人在丢掉了尊严换饭吃？再说了，做贼就很有尊严吗？

自己又想起了那次与狗同吃狗饭的情景。一股由衷的恶心再次从胃里泛了起来。不，自己绝不要再落到那种境地！绝不！做乞丐固然也会常常挨饿，可是，人多饭缘广，和孔仁他们在一起，大家有饭同吃，有水同喝，总不会那么容易就饿死啊！

主意打定，自己兴冲冲地就拿着一块大洋去了酒楼里，买了一只烧鸡和二十个肉包子。自己抱着这些食物，又回到了破庙里。那时已是傍晚，他们还没回来。自己看见，在小桌上，有一碗已经煎好了的药早已冰凉了的。

自己登时就感到了一股心热。这个世上，什么朋友最真？穷苦朋友最真。就为了这股情谊，自己也愿意留下。

孔仁他们回来了，看见了自己很惊讶。看见了烧鸡和包子更惊讶。孟义

以为这些是偷的，自己说，不，是我要饭要的，那个有钱人居然给了我一块大洋，一块大洋啊！

大家面面相觑，呆愣无语，旋即，便都笑了起来。孟义问，你今天出去要饭了？自己骗他们说，嗯。孟义哈哈笑，说，你挺有本事的，居然要到了一块大洋，了不起！

自己说，以后让我跟着你们吧，好不好？

孔仁说，那你不做贼了？

自己说，不做了。

大家就都高兴地笑了起来。孔仁说，好，那我们以后就都是一家人了，大家有饭同吃，有饿同挨，哈哈，好！来，吃！

大家一起吃起了烧鸡和包子。那晚的情景，很令人快乐。直到多年后，自己仍然对这一幕感到不解和怀念。自己不解的，是为什么在决定了向现实妥协以后，自己反而会如释重负？是反抗太累，还是妥协太迷人？是死亡太可怕，还是活着太诱人？也许都是，也许都不是。而自己怀念的，则是这帮已永远不会再醒来了的好兄弟。

一个多月以后，自己的肋骨已不再大痛，想来伤口已在愈合。而自己也与孔仁他们在破庙里结拜成了兄弟。五个人，就是一起对着那关公的空位磕的头、盟的誓。自己排行老三，孔仁是大哥，孟义是二哥，朱理成了四弟，黄道成了五弟。五个人一起出去要饭，或结伴而乞，或分散行动，很少有个个空手而归的时候。虽然不能天天吃饱，但是总没有饿死的危险。人多力量大，人多饭缘广，穷苦的人们，的确是只有抱成了团，才能在这恶劣的世上活得下去。听说共产党有一句口号，是全世界无产者联合起来，这的确是一句真理。

肋骨的疼痛好了以后，自己又重新开始练习八极拳。虽然自己记得的招式不多，但是能练多少就练多少。除了套路的招式以外，自己还特别着重地练习了扎马步，天天练。因为父亲在最后的教授中说过，这是武术的基本功，练拳不练功，到老一场空。自己记得，这扎马步样子最好学，真练起来却最难。小时候天天看见父亲和镖局师傅们像一根根木桩似的站在院子里扎马步，还以为他们是在偷懒，现在才知道，扎马步比练招式累多了。自己总是扎不了多久，就累得腰酸腿痛，不想再练。但是自己又知道这是一项必须要着重苦练的技能，不然，父亲那时和镖局师傅们天天扎马步干吗？又不是闹着玩。

看见自己会练武，孔仁他们兴奋了起来，就想跟自己学。自己也不吝啬，会多少，就教他们多少。自己心里其实也明白，这赵家的八极拳，到了自己手上，八成是要失传了，还不如趁着有机会，多教给别人一些，以后好歹也能在这世上留下赵家八极拳的一招半式，不致湮灭无闻。再说了，孔仁他们都是好人，总胜过了那些该死的土匪。一想到这个就来气。

后来，在这破庙里就经常会出现很滑稽的一幕：五个叫花子，在一起练着一套残缺不全的拳术。孔仁他们坚持不了天天扎马步的练习，自己就也不勉强他们了。毕竟大家都是叫花子，谁也没想变成武林宗师，他们练拳的主要目的，就是想在受人欺负的关键时刻，能亮出个威风凛凛的招式来，好震慑敌胆，趁机开溜。但是自己依旧练自己的，不为别的，只是因为，自己很想念父亲。

很快便到了冬天，这一年就要过去了。一九二七年，中国发生了许多惊天动地的事情。政变、分裂、斗争、失败，整个国家，都在血雨腥风之中欲哭无泪。而自己，也改换了自己的人生。自己从一个江南阔少，变成了一个东北乞丐，有时想想，也真是可笑。人生有时就是这么奇怪，活着活着，竟能活出可笑的味道。真是让人情何以堪。

而天下太平，还只是一个很遥远的幻梦。这一年的六月，张作霖在北京就任安国军政府陆海军大元帅，统领北洋势力，雄视南方。八月，蒋介石在汪精卫等多股军政势力的逼迫下，被迫下野，暗斗激烈。十二月一日，蒋介石与宋美龄在上海举行婚礼，全国瞩目。而在不久之后的一九二八年一月，蒋介石即东山再起，重掌大权。军阀、党棍之间的斗争，激烈而无尽。另外还有日本人对中国东北的虎视眈眈。天下四分五裂，江山风雨飘摇。处在这样的一个时代，谁又能知道自己的明天究竟会怎样？傲骨凛然与得过且过，到底哪个才适合做活着的原则？时代仿佛充满了迷雾，世界好像结满了冰霜。除了无尽的迷茫与不断地跌倒，天地之间仿佛已不再存在其他的感觉。人活着，是多么的痛苦。自己活着，是多么的狼狈。快乐的乞丐，说到底，都只是悲惨的可怜虫。

而就是在这一个冬天，自己邂逅了自己人生中唯一的一场爱情。是的，

自己称它为唯一。虽然直到最后，自己还是没能将“我爱你”这句话对她说出口，依然不敢去相信，其实自己可以和她在一起。毕竟，自己只是一个叫花子。一个真实的叫花子，且满手血腥，仇家成群。但是，自己知道，自己唯一地爱过。它不是一个空幻的梦，就像父亲最后的那场爱情一样，绝不是虚缈的入魔。

她叫庄丽云。她年轻、漂亮，美得如一朵云，美得如云做的水。她纯澈、娇娆，仿佛天使的投影，仿佛自己心灵最无瑕处的一个祈祷。在她之前，自己从未有过心灵的爱情；在她之后，自己再不会有爱情。在她之前，自己看到的天就是天；在她之后，自己看到的天全是血。那些血，用一生的泪来洗，也不可能洗得淡。

第一次，她路过看见自己，给了自己十个铜板。自己头磕在地上，连声说谢谢，这是行规。可她却有些受宠若惊，惊慌失措了起来。她甚至还不嫌脏地来扶了自己一把。她挺难为情地跟自己说，不用谢，不用谢。她走了，自己不禁就觉得有些好笑。这年月居然还有人会这么认真地对待一个乞丐的道谢，她真是太好骗了。想完，自己又轻轻打了自己一个嘴巴。好人难得，自己怎么能当人家傻。

第二次，她路过看见自己，犹豫了一下，便给了自己两角小洋。小洋虽比不上大洋，但仍然是乞讨中难得要到之物。自己正又要磕头致谢，她赶紧摇手，推住自己，说，不要行这么大的礼，不要，就一点点钱而已。说完，她冲自己一笑，然后就跑走了。那一刻，自己忽然就有些愣神。像是觉得好笑，像是觉得莫名地快乐，自己居然傻笑了起来。这姑娘一定是没见过什么乞丐吧，真是太可爱了。自己不禁想，想完，自己又打了自己一个嘴巴。

第三次，自己背着孔仁他们，在一条街上用欺骗的方式乞讨。自己在一张大纸上用毛笔写了一些子虚乌有的催人泪下的惨痛经历，然后将这张纸铺在自己跟前的地上，假装落泪，吸引人们来围观。果然，围观者甚众，但并没有人掷钱，直到她再次出现。也不知道是不是自己的文采太好，她看完了自己写的东西以后，竟隐隐有落泪之状。她居然一下子就给了三块大洋。自己震惊之余，正在犹豫要不要向她磕头致谢之时，她已迅速地消失在了人群里。既然有人做了表率，一些好心人就也纷纷慷慨解囊。但是没有人能再给出三块大洋这么高的数额来。自己一边不停地向人们磕头致谢，一边注意着街上或停或走的人们，希望能再看到她的身影。但是这一天，直到夜晚，她都没有再出现。

当晚，回到破庙，自己的心情很沮丧。按理说不应该，自己一天要到了这么多的钱，简直该好好庆祝才对。可是自己却深深地沮丧。孔仁他们问，怎么会有这么多的钱？自己就骗他们，说，一对有钱的夫妻吵架，那个男人一生气，就把身上的钱全给了我。孔仁他们相信了。孔仁是不同意行骗的，他常说，乞丐也要有乞丐的道德，不能骗不能抢，得靠真可怜要饭。兄弟们都听他的。孔仁是个老实人，他说的道理，其实自己在心底里也很欣赏。但是，自己不是个老实的人，也不是个干净的人。自己很现实，一现实，就难免会在老实人的面前阳奉阴违。自己的心，是有些坏的。

但是这一晚，自己却也真的是对自己今天的行骗感到了懊悔，甚至有些说不清的恼怒。就好像，自己是在菩萨面前杀了鸡，做了一桩对神明大不敬的事。自己辗转反侧，难以入眠。

除了那个女人给的三块大洋，其余的钱自己都拿出来和兄弟们分了。也说不清原因，从她消失在人群中的那一刻起，自己就有了要把这三块大洋还给她的想法，这个想法还异常坚定。自己内心的各种质疑嘈杂纷乱，但那股还钱的冲动就是坚不可摧。

可是后来，自己在骗钱的那条街上等了好几天，却再也没见到她的身影。这让自己怅然若失。想想也是，和一个陌生女人在三个不同的地方偶遇了三次，这本身已十分偶然了，哪里还会有第四次呢？只可惜，自己和她的偶遇，却居然是以一个欺骗收场，这多少总会让人感到有些遗憾，甚至是残忍。

自己就一直藏着那三块大洋。在大家都一无所获而不得不饿肚子的时候，自己也没有拿出那三块大洋来。这是一种在当时令自己也很难理解的坚持。似乎在冥冥之中，自己仍相信会与她有第四次的相遇。不，甚至还会有更多的交集。饿肚子可以忍忍，钱没了，拿什么还她？

自己还从来没有在精神上思念过一个女人，但是，自己思念起了她。这是一件十分荒唐的事，自己当时甚至都还不知道她叫什么，甚至，自己都还不能十分清楚地想起她的容貌。自己只是记得，她对自己笑过。那个笑，纯洁无瑕，美丽无比。这种思念很纯净，自己以前从不知道，像自己这样的一

个惯以嫖妓为乐的腌臜货，心里居然还会有对一个女人的纯净的思念。自己感到很意外。

在东北，冬天能看到鹅毛大雪，江南见不到的鹅毛大雪。雪可以积到几寸厚，河面能完全结成冰。要是换成小时候，自己一定会为这些奇异的冰雪景色欢呼。可惜，时移事易，冬天，只是一个会让乞丐的日子更难过些的季节罢了。待在雪地里乞讨，一天下来，整个人都几乎会被冻成冰棍。脸是麻木的，鼻唇间结满了霜屑，手指根本无法弯曲，就算讨到了食物，手也没法抓东西吃。很多时候，等不及双手回暖，只能是像狗一样地将嘴凑到碗里去啃。但这些还都不是什么要命的事。最糟的，是冬天人们减少了外出，要到饭的机会越来越少，而野果也不可能再有，若讨不到东西，便只能挨饿。最惨的那次，是五个人一起饿了三天。那时，自己蜷缩在门板床上，听着兄弟们的哀怨，心里愧疚得渗血。因为，自己的身上还有三块大洋。但是自己翻来覆去地纠结，最后还是没把钱拿出来。后来，自己提议，要不大家捉老鼠吃吧？大家沉默了一阵，就都同意了。烤老鼠的时候，自己不敢看兄弟们的脸，他们的脸上都是饿，可自己的心里，却在想一个陌生的女人。自己是个太自私的人。

自己一直没再用欺骗的方式乞讨，所以像上次那样大丰收的景况就再也没出现过。孔仁他们不明就里，还一直以为自己是个福将，便专门挑繁华的路段让自己去蹲，而他们则各自去其他路段上乞讨。可自己乞讨的本事并不高，常常会浪费不少机会。自己好几次想向他们说明一下情况，可又不知该从何开口。对他们的愧疚，在自己心里越积越多。自己也越来越喜欢他们，他们是真的拿自己当成了家人，而自己，又可以拿什么来爱他们？

春节前，自己弄到了许多旧报纸和一罐糨糊，破庙的四壁都透风，自己准备修葺一下。自己将四壁的裂缝和窗户都用旧报纸糊了起来，一层不够就糊两层，直到外面的风再也没办法吹进来。自己又去砍拾了不少的柴火，堆满了破庙的一角，想着，这样，过春节时大家就不用再去找柴火了。孔仁他们要饭回来，看见这些都特别开心，说自己想得周到。他们一开心，自己就也觉得很欣慰。一家人，不就应该是这样互帮互助的吗？虽然自己骗过他们，但自己是爱他们的。虽然自己想念那个女人，但自己不会不爱兄弟。

自己仍然天天练习扎马步，黄道曾打趣说，你天天练这个练得满头大汗，这个一动也不动的招式到底有什么用啊？自己就老实说，有什么用还真说不上来，但这是基本功，总会有用的。他们就笑，说，你呀，要是会些惹人爱看的功夫就好了，比如胸口碎大石、霸王枪什么的，那样咱们就能去卖武艺了，组个赵家班，不愁吃和穿。自己就也笑，说，你是看人挑担不吃力，卖武艺的一天下来骨痛筋麻，挣的还不一定有我们多，咱们做了叫花子，就该知足。孔仁就笑，说，最后这句是我的话，我爱听。大家都哈哈笑。

天寒地冻，白雪茫茫。在奉天市做了叫花子，虽然至低至贱，但起码性命无虞，糊口不忧。那时候，自己也没想过什么以后，叫花子会有什么以后呢？只求天天能要到饭，不被人赶，不被人打，不要生病，这样就很好了。但是，就连这最低微的安宁，自己也不知道究竟可以拥有多久。毕竟，天下还是这么乱。在一个大时代的乱流里，你一个小小的叫花子却在祈望一片安宁，这本身不就是一个不切实际的笑话吗？自己不知道，金顺有没有派人追杀自己；或者，金顺派出的人，何时会找到自己。自己也不知道，北伐会不会继续，国民革命军最终会不会胜利。如果北洋军垮了，奉军败了，那么，张作霖会不会服从蒋介石？东三省一旦纳入国民政府的管辖范围，那么，那张江庆县发出的通缉恶贯满盈的赵驹的通缉令，会不会发到奉天市？如果真的有那么一天，那么，自己恐怕就真的是天网恢恢、死路一条了。当然，希望这一切，都只是自己的杞人忧天。

在要饭的苦寒与烤火的欢乐中，这一个冬天慢慢地过去了。那个陌生女人的嫣然一笑，在自己的心里似乎也已越来越淡。但是自己仍然对她有一种莫名的不能忘怀。不能忘怀之余，甚至有一些伤感。淡淡的说不清的遗憾。那三块大洋一直还在自己身上，就像一个恐怕永远也送不出去了的道歉。自己惆怅万端。

终于，在春暖花开的一个白天，自己又见到了她。她走得很急，没有看见自己，自己想喊她，但又觉得不太合适。况且，这一天自己是和朱理一起结伴在乞讨，自己不想让朱理知道自己骗钱和藏钱的事。于是，自己就向朱理撒了个谎，说，我要去上茅房。然后，便起身去远远地跟上了她。

直到走进了另一条街，超出了朱理的视线范围，自己才开始快步直追。恰好，她在一座大宅子前停了下来，然后，便是要进去的样子。自己一边赶

紧喊“小姐请留步”，一边为防唐突，将快步重又改成了慢步。她转回了身来，不确定地左右看了一下。自己又喊了一声。她看见了自己。

自己尽量端庄地走到了她的面前，一时却走得有些太近，闻到了她身上淡淡的茉莉花香。自己心里顿时一乱，赶紧就又后退了一步。出乎自己的意料，她并没有忘记自己。她向自己莞尔一笑，一边问“你女儿的病好些了吗”，一边就是伸手去手提包里又拿出了几块大洋来，要给自己。自己顿时无地自容，慌忙推辞，说，不，不。

慌乱无措的自己，将原先准备好的许多话，都忘了个一干二净。自己从身上掏出了那三块已藏了许久的大洋，还到了她的手上。“我并没有什么生病的女儿，我那天是在骗钱，对不起。”说完，自己扭头撒腿就跑。

她喊了一声：“喂——”

自己转回身，倒退着走。她依旧站在原地，看上去是那样亭亭玉立。她看着自己，却又没再说什么。距离在变远，变远，自己看不清她的眼神，不知她此刻正在如何看自己。自己忽然有些自嘲，又有些酸楚。自己看了一眼这座大宅子大门上方的匾额，上书两个大字：庄府。自己再次背转了身，快跑了起来。她没有再喊。

跑回了朱理蹲着的地方，自己拉起了朱理，要他跟自己一起换个地方去乞讨。他觉得莫名其妙，自己就硬拉了他走。这里离庄府太近，自己不想再看见她。不，是不想再被她看见。这些想法有些没来由，但就是这样强烈。自己本不是个多愁善感的人，可是这一刻，各种纤细的甚至是脆弱得令人讨厌的感觉，都在向自己猛烈涌来。自己是怎么了？

好几天，自己都没再去庄府附近的几条街上乞讨。自己是个外乡人，不知庄府究竟是什么人家，但是看那宅子的派头，就知必是大户。自己也没拿这事去问孔仁他们，怕被他们看出可疑来。一个衣不蔽体的叫花子，居然对一个衣着上流的阔小姐起了思念，这不是丢人的笑话是什么？简直是烧坏了脑子的疯癫！

那些绵绵不绝的愁丝忧绪，令自己感到了可怕。是的，可怕。而今想来，不知为什么，当真正的爱情向自己走来时，自己的第一个反应却竟然是觉得可怕。自己害怕爱情。可是，自己又真的是爱上了她。她是谁？庄府的小姐？老爷的姨太太？新进门的少奶奶？还是少爷的亲戚、小姐的同学？

自己什么都不知道。这是一件多么糟糕的事情。癞蛤蟆要是真的迷上了白天鹅，最后惨死的只可能是癞蛤蟆。不，不要，自己不要爱！

自己用一颗警觉的心，命令自己不要再去想起她。和自己耳鬓厮磨过的美人不知道有多少，自己才和这个女人见过几面，难道就会被她的影子给缠住？不可能的事。

但是，她的嫣然一笑，她的茉莉香味，却又钻入了自己的梦中。梦醒时分，自己不得不惊惶失措地自问：难道，自己真的是遇上了命定的爱情？

自己开始偷偷去庄府的附近看她。可以肯定，她就住在庄府里。她有时步行，有时乘车。每次只要远远地看见了她，自己就会在心底里感到高兴，仿佛收获了什么奇异的果实一样，既兴奋，又珍贵。自己知道自己的这种心情很幼稚，但是，这种幼稚，自己却无力抗拒。这段时间，自己会常常想起父亲，想起父亲那痴迷不悟的一生的爱情，自己开始有些理解父亲了。无情之人看有情，男女痴傻皆可悲；有情之人看无情，愚顽如石真可怜。也许，自己是在变成又一个着魔的疯子？也许，自己是在变成又一个爱情的受难者？命运不可预测。而自己，爱得卑微，爱得可笑。

一九二八年四月，蒋介石联合了冯玉祥、阎锡山、李宗仁，组织了四个集团军，开始了第二次北伐。张作霖的军队和蒋介石的军队陷入了血战。一直垂涎东北的日本人也开始了蠢蠢欲动，奉天市的日侨不断横生事端，弄得各处鸡犬不宁。自己嗅到了一股动乱逼近的气息，内心开始重新翻涌起了流亡的恐惧，害怕就连现在这样的乞丐生活也会失去，害怕自己会变得比一无所有更悲惨。可是恐惧又有什么用呢？时代的洪流谁也无法掌控，活在这狂乱奔腾而又去向难测的激流里，只能走一步算一步。

这一天，早上起来，孔仁兴奋地跟大家说，今天有一家新的百货公司开业，大家一起去那里要饭，运气好的话说不定还有红包拿。大家听了都很振奋。自己和弟兄们已经有两个月没吃上过一口肉了，大家都馋坏了。

走在四月暖洋洋的天气里，心情有时会莫名变好。饥饿只要不来捣乱，生活就像花一样美好。人只要能学会逃避烦恼，就能让日子好过许多。不可以当一个理想主义者，因为理想主义者永远也学不会自我麻痹。自己走着走着，甚至高兴得挥舞起了手里的打狗棒，孔仁他们和自己欢笑着嬉闹，就像一群无聊的无赖，就像一群灿烂的少年。时光是那样芬芳。

终于看到了那家崭新的百货公司，可是自己却愣住了，一时停了步。原来，这家百货公司的全称是“奉天市庄氏大百货公司”。庄氏？和那个女人有没有关系？自己一时惶恐而疑惑了起来。公司大门外已经围了一大圈人，熙熙攘攘的，煞是热闹。孔仁他们已经走到了人群外靠近人群的地方，正招呼自己过去。自己犹豫了一下，也走了过去。

叫花子是不可以往人群里挤的，挤到了人，是要被人打的。遇上蛮横的，会被打个半死。所以只能是站在和人群有一些距离的地方，这样不会惹人嫌弃，特别是在这样的好日子，礼仪做得周到，说不定讨到的钱也能多一些。平时出来要饭，都是觉得人家施主给得多了，才会给人家磕一个头，要是给得不多，就只需喊声谢谢，但是今天孔仁吩咐了，人家就算给得少，咱也得踏踏实实地给人家磕头，因为毕竟人多，且大多是有头有脸的人，万一人家一高兴，说不定还会重新再给。总之，今天这要钱的机会，是一定多。

开业典礼还没开始，已经有人给了朱理几个铜板。朱理乐得笑开了花。自己却无心要钱，心里莫名忐忑。这个庄氏会不会就是那个庄府人家？要是被她看见自己怎么办？要不还是走吧，自己想。

可是自己的脚步却与想法相反，自己走近了人群。还好自己不是很臭，并没有人回过身来赶自己。自己也并不跟人家要钱，自己只是想看清楚一些百货公司大门前的情况。莫名冲动地，自己想能在这里再见到她。在庄府外面，自己已经有很久没能好好看看她了。她最近进出总是乘车，所以自己只能看见她几个瞬间。自己是真想再好好看看她。

很意外地，自己听到了人群里两个男人的谈话。他们在谈论的，是一个叫庄丽云的女人。她是庄家的独生女，原本日子过得很美好，在四年前二十岁时嫁给了奉军中的一位颇有权势的团长，但是可惜，两人结婚才没多久，张作霖和吴佩孚就又打了起来。第二次直奉战争爆发，她的丈夫带部队开拔前线，最后在九门口争夺战中被一颗子弹打中了脑袋，立时毙命。她的公婆就说，她是扫把星，他们的儿子征战多年，一直福大命大，连一点皮外伤都从来没受过，谁知一娶了她，就见了阎王。她的公婆将她赶回了娘家。她就只好在家服侍她那个天生眼瞎的娘。但是屋漏偏遭连夜雨，去年庄老爷一下子就病倒了，至今还没能从病床上起来，庄家那么大的产业，就只好全由这个独生女来支撑经营。可是她这么一个年纪轻轻的女子，又哪里能做得成什么事呢？庄老爷只要一断气，庄家的产业立刻就会被人瓜分。所以说，庄家现在最要紧的，不是新公司开业，而是要给这独生女再找一个靠得住的好男人。庄家只要有了男人，那些贪婪之辈，就不敢轻举妄动。

他们的谈论，被一阵猛烈而喜庆的鞭炮声给打断了。阵阵惊响，飞红碎舞，喜气洋洋。几个年轻人拥挤着，挡住了自己原先的视线。只听他们热烈地说，快看，庄丽云出来了。

自己赶紧换了一个位置，又找到了一个可容视线通过的空隙。自己踮起了脚，使劲地往前看。果然，一个身着粉色旗袍的妙龄女子，正在几个像是职员的人的簇拥下，走向百货公司大楼旁搭起的一个主席台上。她袅袅婷婷，明艳动人。上了台，略显羞涩，又落落大方。不是她又是谁？原来她叫庄丽云。

她在话筒前说了一些感谢和庆祝的话，然后，就又请政商界的几位嘉宾上去讲了一会儿话。自己就站在那个不起眼的角落里，远远地看着她，从低处仰望着她。她的笑是那样灿烂，灿烂里还含了天真，简直就像一幅不该落在俗世的画。在这热闹而又广阔的空间里，她的美，甚至让人感到了纤弱和易碎，仿佛风浪只要再大一些，她就会被生生摧毁。她没有看见自己，自己不知道她会不会看见自己。也许这个距离、这个角度，正是对自己和她的关系的绝好譬喻。她的人生，注定在自己的世界之外；自己的迷恋，注定只是痴人痴梦。如果自己还是当年的那个少爷，或许还有资格向她一诉衷肠；可是自己如今食不果腹、衣不蔽体，恐怕就连走近她，都是对她的一种亵渎。人不该轻易去爱上一个人，因为在太多的时候，爱只能给人带来折磨。求不得，爱难割。无法走近的爱恋，何尝不可称其为自虐？人真的很可笑。自己忽然想到，如今在她的眼里，自己会不会只是一个令人讨厌的骗子呢？如果她再看见自己，眼神里会不会只剩下不屑一顾？自己顿时瑟缩了起来。想要逃走，又踌躇不定。

忽然，人群后边两个男人的谈话像风一样钻进了自己的耳朵里。自己一个激灵。这是多么遥远而又熟悉的一种语言：日语。那两个男人西装革履，头发锃亮，正在旁若无人地谈笑。也许，他们以为，这里根本就没人能听懂他们的语言。

自己看清了其中一张男人的脸。这张脸，自己永远也不会忘。他，就是

后来改变了自己一生的渡边。

渡边说，这个女人的腿真美，让人一看见，就会生出想要征服这个国家的欲望。

另一人说，不错，对于我们大日本帝国来说，中国，只是一个在等待被征服的女人，美丽而又下贱的女人。

渡边说，相信不需要再等太久了，很快，我们就会成为这片土地的主人。中国已经打了这么多年的内战，就像一个已经病入膏肓的病人，我们只要随便出一拳，就能把这个病人打得断气。

另一人说，张作霖看来不会这么容易就答应我们的要求，我们是否要重新再提交一份方案上去？

渡边说，不要这么紧张，你没看战报吗，蒋介石的军队志在必得，他会帮我们好好教训张作霖的。中国有句古话，叫鹬蚌相争，渔翁得利，你该好好学习一下中国古人的智慧。

另一人说，是。

渡边说，樱花会社的社长已经在指责我们无能了，为什么还没有搞垮庄氏的企业，你要加紧行动，别让我为难。

另一人说，是。

自己怒不可遏，顿时就想举起打狗棒来打他们，但是忍了又忍，咬咬牙还是忍了下来。日本人不好惹，况且今天是庄氏百货开业的好日子，自己不能闹事。一旦当场把事说破，别说自己会出事，恐怕连庄家，都会立马遭殃。圣人曰三思而后行，忍一时风平浪静。

渡边和他的同伴离开了，自己向着渡边的背影，狠狠地吐了一口口水，骂了两句脏话。

剪彩结束了，又放了一阵喜气洋洋的鞭炮。人群散了开来，孔仁他们开始正式去向那些看起来挺富贵的人们乞讨。自己怕人群稀了以后自己会被庄丽云看见，就跟孔仁他们说了一声肚子痛，然后便离开了开业典礼的现场。

孔仁他们兴高采烈地回到破庙的时候，每人手里都拿着一个红包。每个红包里是两块大洋。孟义说，除了红包，另外他们还从那些宾客们的手里要到了不少零碎的钱，这真是一场大丰收。朱理说，要不是后来又来了两批别处的叫花子，他们本来还可以讨到更多的。孔仁说，别贪心，要知足。

孔仁和孟义每人拿出了一块大洋来，给了自己。自己愧不敢收。孔仁说，当初结拜时怎么说的？有福同享，有难同当。做哥哥的有富余，要先周济给弟弟。自己听罢羞愧万分，觉得好像又欺骗了他们。他们一直诚心诚意待自己，自己却总是大谎小谎不断。自己对不起兄弟。

晚上，自己辗转难眠。那两个日本人，很可能就是黑龙会或者特高课的特务，他们究竟想要做什么坏事？他们究竟想对庄家做什么？庄丽云她斗不斗得过日本人？不对，自己想错了，她怎么可能斗得过日本人呢？自己翻来覆去，心乱如麻。

后来，自己向庄府里投了一封信，要他们小心日本人和樱花会社。但是过后，又觉得自己有些狗拿耗子多管闲事。别人家的商业纷争，关自己什么事？要是让人知道这封信是一个乞丐写的，庄府一定会被人笑死。但是，自己又着实是担心庄丽云，担心得要死。那种牵肠挂肚，百转千回，不能自解。有时蹲在角落里，远远地看到她回家，是真想走过去和她说两句话。但是自己知道，那样一定会吓着她，或者会自取其辱，还是不要发疯的好。兴许，爱情这种事情，就像患上了一场感冒一样，过了一段时间之后便会自愈。一旦自愈，便不留痕迹，哪里需要担心什么一生一世。仿佛海市蜃楼，来时美丽，去时干净。但自己仍然很矛盾，愁绪万千的矛盾。烦闷至极时，无酒解忧，自己便打拳散心。拳风起处，寂寞生凉。

五月，遇上了一件事情。一天，自己走在一条僻静的街上，突然，却发现与一个胖子擦肩而过。自己一愣，胖子也一愣。自己忽然反应了过来：他就是把自己打得吐血的那个胖子！自己立马想逃走，岂料胖子动作更快，已是拦腰抱住了自己。他大喊：你个贼，看你还往哪里逃！

喊罢，他就用腿来绊自己。这胖子像是练过摔跤，他的腿十分壮实，上次自己就是这样被他绊倒的。情急之下，自己不自觉地就往腿上灌了劲，希望摔下去的时候能撑着些，不要磕着膝盖。这胖子的劲狠，上次自己摔下去，就差点磕碎了膝盖骨。但是这一次却奇怪了起来，他的绊腿没起丝毫的作用。他奇怪了，自己也奇怪了。他使劲地绊，到最后他甚至放开了自己的腰，腾出手来专门抱自己的腿，想要将自己摔倒。但是自己，却竟然就像落地生根了一样，纹丝不动。

胖子傻了眼了。

自己却刹那开了窍，兴奋得几乎想要跳起来：自己天天练马步，难道是已经练出了千斤坠？

自己干脆狠狠一运劲，踹了胖子一脚。胖子滚出了三尺远。

胖子像头大象一样，扑上来与自己搏斗。自己用上了套路里的招式，没两下，居然就把胖子按在了地上。

没想到，真的没想到！

原来武功的练成，是在不知不觉中！

胖子大声地求饶，自己笑得欢天喜地。见自己笑得这么莫名其妙，胖子吓得发抖，以为自己要折磨他。胖子掏出了他身上所有的钱，哭着喊着要给自己。自己把他的钱全丢在他的脸上，大声对他说：不许再叫我贼，不要让我再看见你，否则见一次就打一次！

胖子捡起钱，屁滚尿流地逃走了。

当晚，自己就和孔仁他们说了自己的变化。孔仁他们的兴致一下子就高了起来，纷纷表示愿意继续跟着自己练马步。于是，从此以后，在这座没有神像的破庙里，就有了五个真正的武丐。每每回首往事，忆念至此，自己都会心痛不已。是自己教会了他们真正的武功，却也等于是自己改变了他们人生最后的结局。他们带着一身的武功，昂首于敌寇之前，惨死于乱枪之下。直到那一天，自己才真正地明白了，为什么有一种爱，叫作不教人武功。

蒋介石的军队势如破竹，奉军节节败退。明眼人都看得出，张作霖败局已定。这国家元首之位，已非蒋介石莫属。天下权柄，已握至蒋介石一人手中。自己也没别的奢望，只希望张作霖一旦败退关外，至少总还可以守住这东北的老巢。要不然，自己可真就是死路一条了。自己在上海还杀过杜月笙的手下，要是在当时的最后一战中，有流氓没被炸死，回去做了报告，那自己就惨了。杜月笙的势力会随着蒋介石势力的扩张而扩张，政客与黑帮头子沆瀣一气，万一将来国民党统一了中国，拿自己当共产党来通缉，那自己就算是有一百条命也不够丢。

又遇见她的那一天，早上下了一场濛濛细雨。雨丝轻凉，点落红尘，淅沥有声。雨停后，大家分配了一下今天各自的乞讨区域，然后，便一起离开了破庙。自己向兄弟们夸口，说今天晚上一定带十个肉包子回来。他们笑着说不信。

走在湿漉漉的道路上，自己微微感到很轻快。自己原先的那双鞋已经被穿烂了，朱理就特地留了心去找，终于在昨天捡回了一双半新的布鞋来。自己一试，大小还刚刚好。别提有多高兴了。想当年，自己的皮鞋只要不小心踩上了一点点鸟屎，自己就会将这双皮鞋当垃圾丢了，而今，却真是恍如隔世。有时候，自己甚至会有一种错觉：今天自己讨到的宝贝，其实全是自己昨天丢掉的垃圾。这种感觉，让人很纠缠。

这一天，自己的运气很好。自己想出了一些新的吉祥话，跟人一说，人们都很高兴，也乐于慷慨解囊。到下午时，自己已要到了一角小洋和三十个铜板，兜里鼓鼓的，特别满足。自己得意地想：哈哈，黄道哇黄道，你们不相信我晚上能带肉包子回来，我今天就一定要给你们一个惊喜！

早上雨停之后，到下午一直没再下过雨。中午时还放了一会儿晴。天虽然大部分时候是阴着的，但空气十分清新，树梢上鸟声啁啾，莫名地怡人。中午自己没吃东西，想着到了晚上再好好吃，但到了下午，这饿劲忽然就猛烈了起来，让人有些招架不住。

那时大约是下午三四点钟吧，乞丐没有钟表，看时间只能靠天色。虽然不想先于兄弟们独享美食，但自己实在是太饿了，于是便决定先去包子铺里买两个肉包子吃。自己正匆匆赶路，路过一家非常高级的名为“Memory”的西饼店时，却命中注定似的停了下来，往店里看了一眼。就是这一眼，让自己又见到了她。

她正坐在西饼店里靠窗的一个座位上，在优雅地喝着一杯咖啡。一个秃头的中年男人坐在她的对面，正在不吃也不喝地向她说话。她今天打扮得特别漂亮，唇红齿白，美发及腰。她时而浅浅说笑，时而抿嘴嫣然，眼波流转，婀娜多姿，宛如桃花落流水、杨柳拂春风。那一刻，自己忘记了饥饿。

那一刻，世界的嘈杂仿佛都从自己的生命里退了场。那些令人抽搐的肉体痛苦，那些逼人崩溃的精神困境，此时全都化成了不真实的冷涩飞烟，让位给了唯一的灵魂剧痛：那火辣辣的爱恋与求不得的绝望相决裂而拉出的万丈深渊。自己站在道路的正中央，车水马龙将自己紧紧围裹，天与地都像在褪色，人与物都像在成空，唯有那苦涩的爱恋在突兀地生长，唯有她，鲜艳得炫目。

自己想走，却迈不开步；想再好好看看她，又怕她看见自己。自己真想

打自己两个耳光，让自己好好清醒清醒，可是，自己又怕，这梦真的会醒。

秃头站了起来，向店的里面走去，可能是去上厕所吧。他一走，她就转头向窗外看了过来。自己一个激灵，立即背转过身，蹲了下来。那一刻，自己是真恨不得眼前有一个地洞，能让自己马上钻进去。

自己正困窘不已，不料还因挡了人家的道，被人踢了两脚，骂了几声。自己又窘又羞，手足无措，一边向人家连连道歉，一边竟退向了西饼店的大窗旁！

那个凶狠的人走了，自己蓦然才醒悟过来：完了，她现在就在自己的背后了！

黔驴技穷，自己只得马上又蹲了下来，缩往墙根，让自己的人形尽快从玻璃窗前消失。不知为什么，紧缩在墙根的那一刻，自己真的有一种想流泪的冲动。自己不仅没有办法去爱自己所爱的女人，还要在她的面前，在大庭广众之下，被人当成一条狗一样地踢踹与辱骂，自己还有什么尊严可言？自己还怎么以一个男人的身份活在这个世上？这一切到底是为什么！

自己正抱头难受，准备迅速逃离，忽然，有人拍了拍自己的肩膀。自己抬头一看，是一名侍者。他右手托着一只大盘子，正淡淡地看着自己。自己疑惑地站了起来，只见盘子里盛着一大块完整的奶油蛋糕。蛋糕色泽雪白，花纹精美，简直像一件艺术品。

自己不明所以，呆若木鸡。侍者左手一指西饼店的大玻璃窗，说：“喏，是这位小姐给你的。”自己惊讶地转回了身，只见，她微笑着，隔着清澈的窗玻璃，向自己招了招手。她的笑，冰清玉洁，灿若彩蝶。

侍者将蛋糕倒在自己要饭的碗里，然后便拎着盘子回到了店里去。自己蹲到了西饼店对面不远处的一个墙角里，开始狼吞虎咽地吃蛋糕。秃头回到了座位上，她又开始喝起了咖啡。

自己伸出舌头，将碗底也舔了个干净。这个动作很不雅，但是自己已经做了这么久的乞丐，饥饿已经将这个动作深深地烙入了自己的生命里，仿佛自己一出生就带着的某颗黑痣一样。吃完了蛋糕舔完了碗，自己又看了一眼坐在秃头对面的她。她也向这边转了转头，但是目光还没碰到自己，就又转了回去。自己此刻并没有再想逃走，相反，自己在思忖，不知今天有没有机会走近她一次，在她单独时。不为别的，自己就是想郑重地向她道个谢。刚才隔着玻璃，街上又吵，自己说的“谢谢”声音又低，也不知她听到了没有。若是没有听到，总是不太好。她给的蛋糕是全新的，不是吃剩的，这是令自己深深感动的一件事情。况且这里的蛋糕全都价格不菲，照规矩，自己怎么也得给她磕了个头再走是不是？

自己忽然又沮丧地想：也许，什么都是借口。自己只是一个懦夫。

天空白花花、灰蒙蒙的，自己不喜欢这样的一个天。云层背后的天空，本应是阳光灿烂、生机勃勃的，可是云层却就是那样顽固地存在着，你触不到它半点，更拨不开它分毫。它可以让你认命，可以让你屈服，可以让你随波逐流，就是从不给你一点主动。

秃头走了，离开了西饼店。她还在那个座位上坐着，在静静地喝着咖啡。这幅画面忽然让自己觉得很美，仿佛夏天热绽的花，仿佛秋天冷落的叶。而她，就是画里那一滴不小心掉落的眼泪。

她从店里走了出来，自己走了上去。出乎意料，自己居然没有跪下来给她磕头，自己只是万分诚恳地对她说了一句：“谢谢！”她扑哧一笑，说，你已经说过了。

天上却忽然下起了雨。自己和她，赶紧躲到了西饼店的屋檐下。雨珠带着些沉甸甸的重量从阴沉沉的云层里落下，将街上本就已不多了的行人哄了个四散，行人们或避雨或快跑，热闹得湿漉漉。唯有那些黑壳子的小汽车，依旧在雨里不紧不慢地往来着。风卷着雨湿，在空旷里冷飕飕地舞动。

“以前……那次我骗了你的钱，真是对不起。”自己低着头说。

“没事，知错能改，还是好人。”她笑笑说，“其实，你也不算是在行骗。一个人都只能是出来乞讨为生了，那他的背后必定是有一个很不幸的故事，而这个故事究竟是什么样的，又有什么重要呢？”她淡淡地说。

自己莫名有些颤抖。隔了许久，才说：“谢谢。”

“有什么可谢的？”她微微俏皮地说，“对了，你骗人用的那张大纸上的毛笔字，是谁写的？”

“我写的。”

“那整篇文章呢，是谁想出来的？”

“也是我。”

她就故意看着自己，抿嘴，肯定地点了点头，然后笑着转头看向了雨

中，说：“你还我钱的那一天，我就猜，你绝对不会是个普通的乞丐。能写出那么好的文章和那么好的大字，你的故事一定不简单。”

说完，她又是很快乐地笑。她是那么天真。

自己嗫嚅着，说：“没什么，我只是念过两年私塾而已。”

“你知道吗，我看见了你吃蛋糕时的样子。这家店里的蛋糕，是全市最高级的，而你看见了这样子的一块蛋糕，除了最简单的饥饿和最真诚的感谢以外，竟然没有表现出半点新鲜与好奇，所以我猜，你以前一定是吃惯各种西饼的。”她很认真地说。

自己忽然就被她的认真样给逗笑了，到底还是年轻的小姑娘。自己笑着说：“你是想学福尔摩斯啊？”

她不禁得意地一拍手，笑着一指自己，说：“看，你还知道福尔摩斯！”

自己忽然就觉得有些像在玩火了。自己赶紧冷静了一下，也不敢再看她，只好看着哗哗的大雨，说：“我都是听别人说的。”

她也就不再说什么了。雨势愈来愈大，清凉的雨流从屋檐上泻下，不停不断，如练如柱，屋檐下像是挂了一张水帘。下雨的时刻，街上总是安宁得出奇，仿佛雨水可以令所有的嘈杂安眠。又一辆湿淋淋的小汽车在街上驶过，可以看到滚动的车轮在街面上溅起的一层水花。气息清凉。西饼店的屋檐下只站着她和自己两个人。她没有重新回到店里去，自己也没想离开她。这样，就构成了一幅挺可笑的图景。自己觉得，似乎该站得离她远一些才好，这样才不至于令她惹人笑话。可是，她又似乎毫不介意，或者完全就没想到别人的眼光。她刚才还和自己说笑来着，自己要是走开了，她会不高兴吗？

她伸出手，调皮地拨弄了一下屋檐上流下的雨帘。清亮的雨水弄湿了她美丽的手指，晶莹的雨丝在她纤纤的指尖上绕了个弯，重新又落流向地。她笑了，眼里跳动着像水一样清澈的光，跳动着像雨一样活泼的火。她收回了手，像是自言自语地说：“我是一个喜欢好奇的人，可是现实中能令人感到好奇的事情好像并不多。有时我会很想去过一种无拘无束的生活，就像小说里都爱写的那样，可以自由地去冒险，可以自在地去浪漫，说不定，还能遇到一个武功盖世的英雄，可以和他一起去惩奸除恶，助人为乐。”她笑了起来，笑得捂起了嘴。笑完了，她痴痴地看着雨，像是在问雨：“这些想法都挺可笑的，是吗？”

雨下得哗哗响。

“等天下太平了，每个人就都可以去自由地追寻自己想要的生活了。”自己说。

“可是，真的会有那一天吗？”

“天下大势，合久必分，分久必合。再乱的世道，乱到最后，也必会有一个真正的王者出来，荡平群雄，一统四海，收拾山河，安抚天下。会有那一天的。”

她就笑了。她面向了自己，说：“我姓庄，叫庄丽云，一朵美丽的云，你呢？”

“我姓赵，叫赵驹，一匹奔跑的马驹。”

自己和她都忍不住乐了。

“上一次，在百货公司那里，我看见你了，可是你后来为什么跑了？”

“哦，我肚子痛，去找茅房了。”

“那次你来还我钱时，看见的那座宅子就是我的家。以后你要是饿了，就来我家敲门，我给你好吃的。”

“谢谢。你真是个好人，我给你磕头。”

“不要，我不要你磕头。你要是愿意，以后只要告诉我你的故事就行了。我很好奇。”

“好吧，那以后再说。”

“一言为定。”

“一言为定。”

雨势越发滂沱了起来。街面上的积水越来越厚，雨点密集而沉重地落下来，涟漪处处，水花晶亮。本已是傍晚，天色越来越暗。阴郁一望无际，日没即将来临。西饼店里亮起了电灯，明晃晃的一片，从窗外看，都仍然会觉得耀眼。

她的腕上戴着一块精致的手表。她看了看表，又看了看雨，然后，转身便走进了西饼店里去。

自己在窗外看见，她和一个店员说了几句什么，然后就走到了店的里间去。

等了一会儿，她出来了。她的脸上隐隐有了些不安和焦虑。

“怎么了？”

“本想打电话回去，请司机谭叔开车来接我一下，可是家里的电话却一直没人接，平常家里应该一直都是有人的呀。”

“那这店里有没有伞？你借一把。”

“问了，刚好昨天被人拿走了。”

说完，她又看起了雨。但她此时的看，已是一种焦虑。

“——我有办法，你在这里等我。”

说完，自己就以碗遮头，冲进了大雨里。

“喂，你干什么去呀——”她在后面大声问。

雨声喧哗。大雨直浇得人睁不开眼、张不开嘴。自己没有回答她。自己用最快的速度奔跑了起来。

街上的积水，被自己踏得啪啪响。雨珠不断地砸进自己的眼睛里，还真痛。无遮无挡地处在雨中，感觉雨声大得吓人，就像整个天都在怒吼，要压下来把人埋葬一样。

跑过了两条街，终于看到了那家雨伞店。幸好，还没打烊。店里亮起了昏黄的灯。

老板一看见自己进店，就抄起了扫帚要赶人。自己忙说，我是来买伞的。

到了店里，自己忽然才后悔，没跟她要几块钱。一腔的热情，光想着要帮她，却忘了想一想，自己到底有多少能力。店里的雨伞都很精致，价格也都不便宜。自己看中了一把很漂亮的，问多少钱，老板说，两块大洋。自己又看中了一把比较漂亮的，问多少钱，老板说，一块大洋。自己顿时就悲哀、懊恼了起来。

最后，自己只能挑了一把最普通的伞来问价格，答案是五角小洋。自己燃起了一丝希望，掏出了身上全部的钱，就是那一角小洋和三十个铜板，对老板说：老板，您行行好，我身上就只有这么多了，请您把这把伞卖给我吧！

老板不同意。老板指着放在店里墙角处的一把破伞，说：你买这把吧，这把只要一角小洋。

就是死，自己也不会拿这种破东西去给她用的。想着，自己就给老板跪了下来，求他把那把最普通的伞卖给自己。但老板说：五角小洋，最便宜了。自己就给老板磕头，磕得咚咚响。老板不耐烦了，说：我还真是奇怪了，你一个臭要饭的，浑身都已经湿透了，还要买什么伞？

自己还是求他。老板烦了，就说：五角小洋已经是我这店里的最低价格了，你只有一角小洋和三十个铜板，我是无论如何也不会卖给你的，除非你能再加上一角小洋或者十个铜板，那样，我也就勉强可以算你是出了五角小洋。要是没有，那你就快走吧。

自己把脚上那双半新的鞋脱了下来，和碗、竹棒一起，放到了老板的面前，问：那您看这几样东西加在一起，值不值十个铜板？

老板火了，开始骂人、赶人。自己不走，他干脆重新抄起扫帚，开始了打人。自己任他打，一边继续求他：这鞋是半新的，真的半新的！求您行行好吧！就把这把伞卖给我，您多子多孙，长命百岁！

老板打累了。他拿起那只自己要饭的碗，狠狠地往地上一摔。“啪唧”一声，饭碗四碎，碎片一地。老板收了自己的钱和物，将伞丢给了自己。他说：滚吧，别让我再看见你，否则见一次打一次！

谢谢！谢谢！

自己抱了伞，转身就往外跑，忽然，脚底狠狠地一痛。原来，自己是踩上了碎碗的尖渣。

自己光着脚在雨中飞奔，就像一个疯子或者傻子。雨打在自己的眼睛里，真的觉得好痛。自己的视线不时模糊，还好，是因为下着雨。这样，就没有人能分得清，一个人脸上在流着的，到底是泪还是雨。

“——这伞是我跟一个朋友借的，你快拿着，回家去吧。”

“你……你衣服全湿了……呀，你的两只脚怎么都在流血！你的鞋呢？”

“没事，我路上不小心摔了一跤而已。你快回家吧。”

“你跟我一起走，我带你去看医生。”

“不用不用。我走啦，你快回家去吧。路上小心，再见！”

“赵驹！赵驹——”

自己义无反顾地逃远了。她的呼喊，远远地，消失在了雨的喧哗里，自己甚至没敢再回头多看她一眼。

爱情，是一件多么让人痴傻的事。

晚上，雨停后，兄弟们陆续都回到了破庙。大家看到了自己的倒霉模样，都很惊奇。自己只好撒谎，说是今天要到的钱太多，引起了一个日本浪人的注意，被他给打了劫。大家都不相信，说是赵驹你不是会武功吗，怎么能被人给打劫呢。自己只好硬着头皮继续编，说，那个日本人会唐手，很厉害，一脚就能踢翻好几个人。这样，大家才算是相信了。这一天，兄弟们都没要到任何东西，只能忍饥挨饿。孔仁找来布条，给自己包了包两只脚上的伤口。他问，怎么弄成这样？这次自己没骗他，说：我的鞋没了，然后碗又碎了，我不小心踩在了碎片上，后来在路上跑，又跑过了一段碎石子铺成的路，脚就被割成了这样。孔仁问：痛吗？自己答：当时还好，过后越来越痛。

大家都把湿衣服脱了下来，放在火上烤了烤。孟义开玩笑说，要是这烤的是羊肉，那该多好。大家就都很沮丧。

自己一晚上没睡，心里愧疚得难受。原本，今天是大丰收的，自己可以给兄弟们买回好多肉包子来，大家能够美美地吃一顿。可是，结果却是自己不仅没有带回来一个铜板，而且还丢了鞋、碗、棒，弄了两脚伤。那双鞋，可还是朱理特地去给自己找来的呀！但是，一切却全被自己出卖了，就为了一个女人。而且，自己其实是已经吃过了蛋糕，事实上，今天自己并没有和弟兄们一起饿肚子。自己觉得很惭愧，没有对得起结义时的盟誓。自己已经不是第一次这样对不起兄弟们了。自己是敬重义薄云天的关老爷的，自己不想做个不忠不义的人。

想起她，自己一时又有些不放心。今天她打给家里的电话为什么会没人接？像她说的，一般不会这样。是日本人做了什么吗？应该不会吧，毕竟现在这里还是张作霖的地盘。但是想想那天那两个日本特务的谈话，自己又不寒而栗。不行，明天得去庄府外面看看。

但是半夜里，自己却忽冷忽热了起来。冷得如缩冰窟，热得身似火烧。最终，这冷和热终于汇聚成了同一股力，将自己推进了昏厥的深渊里。

自己发起了高烧。据孔仁说，是自己脚上的伤口里都进了泥水，发了炎，外加淋了雨，所以才引起的。兄弟们又费尽心机地去给自己弄来了药，孔仁给自己敷药、煎药。看着弟兄们同情的目光，自己真想打自己两个耳光。赵驹呀赵驹，你到底都做了些什么？为了一个根本就不可能亲近的女人，你不仅把自己弄得失魂落魄，还重重地拖累了兄弟们，你到底都做了些什么！

可是，自己就算在昏昏沉沉的迷睡里，也仍然在止不住地想她。那场倒霉的雨，那片灰暗的天，在自己清晰的记忆里，竟然都充满了美好的感觉，洋溢着醉人的浪漫，就连那条只有光了脚才能体会到它究竟有多锋利的碎石子路，自己都感到铺满了诗情画意。自己是疯了，还是被烧糊涂了？

连续两天，孔仁都没让自己离开破庙。自己心里担心庄府，却又没办法去看，只好旁敲侧击地向兄弟们打探。自己问，今天外面有发生什么事吗？回答都是没有，没有什么特别重大的事。除了张作霖的兵败。

黄道捡到了一双半新的草鞋，送给了自己。自己十分感谢。终于又可以穿鞋了。朱理给了自己一根竹棒，孟义给了自己一只大碗。自己要饭的家伙就又齐全了。

烧退了以后，孔仁就不再看着自己了。自己赶紧先去了一次庄府附近。经过观察，觉得庄家上下一切照旧，就也放了心。远远地又看见了她几次，心里莫名就有些伤感。这伤感绵绵密密，忧愁纤细，叫人魂不守舍，不堪一击。就像鱼追寻着鸟的踪迹，迷恋里闪耀着哀伤，痴情里躲闪着绝望。身上被扫帚打出来的伤痕还在隐隐作痛，自己贪恋地远望着她，忽然感到有些疲惫。

一九二八年的六月，中国再次发生了惊天动地的巨变。张作霖输给了蒋介石，宣布退兵出关。就在张作霖所乘坐的专列经过京奉铁路和南满铁路交叉处的三洞桥时，日本关东军引爆了预埋的炸药。张作霖重伤，回奉天市后，不治身亡。为防日军乘机动兵，奉天当局暂时秘不发丧。直至张学良秘密潜回奉天市，接掌了其父之军政大权后，才对外正式宣布了张作霖的死讯。举国哗然。

时局的突变，令自己彻夜难眠。自己似乎已嗅到了一丝厄运来临的味道。国民党的军队胜利了，那么，自己在南方欠下的那些生死债，又何时会追到东北来？

夏天不好过，蚊子特别多。待在太阳底下，一会儿就一身汗。汗出多了就臭，臭了就惹人讨厌，惹人讨厌了就要不到钱。日子不好熬。有时看着天

上红彤彤的太阳，心里就会很怅惘。太阳千年不变地东升西落，从来不会因为人的乞愿而变得冬暖夏凉一些，这多像躲在人们命运背后的某个主宰。人在无助或者失落时，总想求助于某个神明，希望神明能看到自己的情有可原或楚楚可怜，但是这世上又哪来的什么神明。于是人就成了一种无根无源、无助无能的漂泊动物，在许多的大风大浪前都显得那么不堪一击、无能为力。这或许是生命的悲哀，也可能是时代的罪责，但是就算再经过一万次轮回，又有多少生命可以变得真正坚韧牢固、无惧无求？顿悟从来都是空妄的许诺，活着本身便是磨难碾碎智慧。一个没有神的世界，漂泊与彷徨就是根本的信仰。

庄氏百货以经营国货著称，华商会和学联号召抵制日货的时候，庄氏百货就成了主角，被推上了最光彩的舞台。看到爱国报纸上对庄氏百货的赞誉，自己心里很是高兴，可是担忧也分外沉重。她是那样的善良纯洁、美丽无邪，甚至有些童真未泯、稚气未脱，宛如一块无瑕而生脆的白玉、一朵纯净而娇嫩的莲花，于雅室观之甚好，于花园赏之甚好，可是，一旦被抛入这生死时代的激烈旋涡之中，一旦被推进那残酷无情的明争暗斗里面，她又能否不受伤害、不被摔碎、不染尘埃？答案是现实的，只是自己不敢面对，更不想面对。

她要自己饿了就去她家里要吃的，但是自己很显然不可能会去这样做。可以将这理解成是一个男人的可怜的虚荣心，也可以将这理解成是一个男人的可悲的自尊心。反正这两者之间也并无什么悬殊的差别。说到底，都只是一个单相思病人的自怨自艾与无地自容。自己依然习惯躲在那个隐蔽的角落里，像眺望星星或海岸一样地远看着她。自己有多么想靠近她，就有多么害怕靠近她。像自己这样的一个叫花子，不要说爱，就是和她在一起站久了，都会令她的声誉蒙羞。这是一件多么令人痛彻心扉的事实。这是一种多么令自己死去活来的折磨。地位、身份，永远是人与人之间不可跨越的鸿沟。共产党说阶级，这真的是一个很生动的譬喻。只要人类还有阶级存在，人类就不可能有什么真正的自由。乞丐爱上千金，这就是一个活生生的例子。

在报纸上看到秃头和她订婚的消息的那一天，自己找了个没人看得见的角落，在那里哭了很久。泪水安静而汹涌地流淌，滑过脸颊，滚进嘴角。嘴唇痛苦地一咧，就能尝到满口的苦涩，像海水一样的苦涩。有时想想，造物主是真的神奇，把眼泪做成了与海水相似的味道。也许，上帝就是想告诉人类，全世界有多少海水，人活着就可以流多少的泪水。海水不干，痛苦不尽。

秃头的名字叫潘兆。报纸上说，他是奉天市华商会的会长，德高望重，实力雄厚。自己懂得，这场结合对她来说无疑是有益的，是恰逢其时且恰到好处的。值此内忧外患、暗流汹涌之际，她最需要的，就是一把可以真正为她遮风挡雨的大伞。而在奉天市的商界，还有比华商会的会长更强大的保护伞吗？你那把五角小洋的小伞，算个屁。

秋天的风，凉得萧瑟无语。万物都在凋零，黄叶安静得孤单。在一些无人的角落，风的呼呼仿佛人的呜咽。天气一天冷过一天，总是阴多晴少。落寞的自己，有时总会误以为，自己就是那风里的碎叶，一片片，一片片，没有方向，没有呼吸，除了飘零，唯有成泥。

这一天，在一条热闹的街上，自己却偶然地又遇到了她。这偶然来得太突然，让自己避无可避。

她一个人，见到了自己，倒是喜出望外的样子。“赵驹，好久不见。不是叫你饿了就来找我的吗，怎么从来不来？”

“因为我每天都吃得很饱哇。”

“你骗人。”

“不骗你。”

“真的？”

“真的。”

“对了，那天……你脚上的伤好了吗？”

“早好了。”

“谢谢你，也谢谢你朋友，改天你来找我，我把伞还给你。”

“好。对了，那天你回去，家里都还好吗？”

“那天下午，是樱花会社的社长去了我家，把我爸爸气得吐了血，后来家里人就一起送爸爸去了医院，所以才会没人接电话。”

“令尊现在怎么样了？”

“还好，就是肺病一直治不好。”

“日本人很危险的，你要多小心。当年霍元甲就是烂肺而死的。”

“我会小心的，谢谢。那我走了，记得来找我。这个给你——”

“不要不要——”

“哈哈，再见！”

她硬给了自己三块大洋，然后笑着向自己挥了挥手，转身就跑。她笑得那样天真，仿佛孩童与玩伴道别。一阵轻柔的风拂过，似有淡淡的茉莉花香飘来，又有几片鲜艳的秋叶掉落。

东北局势紧张。坊间有传言，说土肥原贤二怂恿张学良独立称帝，被张学良严词拒绝。张学良愿意与国民政府和解，促成中国统一大业。但是日本人却需要东北独立，需要东北有一个可以任由他们主宰的傀儡政府。奉军与日军，剑拔弩张。日本人千方百计破坏东北地方政府与南京国民政府的和谈，用尽手段阻挠中国统一大业的完成。张学良对日本人恨之入骨，不光是因为杀父之仇，更是因为国家民族之仇。东北就如一颗随时会被引爆的炸弹，没有人知道表面的和平究竟还能维持多久，没有人知道在它爆炸以后，中国究竟会何去何从。

这是一个危险的时代，这是一个残酷的时代。这个时代充满了可悲的生死谜题，这个时代充满了可怜的命运哭泣。自己究竟是应该希望东北归顺蒋介石，还是应该希望东北归顺日本人？如果东北归顺了蒋介石，那么自己很可能会变成一个死刑犯；如果东北归顺了日本人，那么自己马上就会变成一个亡国奴。自己真的不想死，没有人会想当死刑犯的；自己也不想当亡国奴，看着东北变成日本人的殖民地。可是，这两种愿望又是不可能并存的。要是不想看着东北落入日本人的囊中，那就必须做好被国民政府枪毙的准备；要是不想被推上国民政府的断头台，那就必须希望日本人控制东北。而自己如果有了要日本人控制东北的希望，那么，自己就是一个卖国贼。不折不扣的汉奸。自己该怎么办？怎么办？时代似乎已在复杂的局势中将自己逼进了道义的死角，活着在荒唐的逻辑里已不知不觉地站到了正义的反面。死，是那样不甘与无奈；生，又是那样可耻与悲哀。在这个充满血泪与挣扎的年代，天亮仿佛只是为了让人看见更多的死尸与苦难；在这个写满无奈与痛苦的世界，眼泪仿佛只是无能、可笑之人给自己准备的海葬。这个世界到底是怎么了？这个时代到底是怎么了？为什么一个时代生了病，为其殉葬的是千千万万无辜的生命？为什么一个世界出了错，为其赴难的是无数人原本好好的命运？生逢乱世，自己究竟该何去何从？

又一个冬天到了，雪花纷飞，寒意凛人。很奇怪，从出逃到现在，自己心里一直没再惦记过赌钱和嫖妓。固然，作为一个乞丐，你就算是想要去赌和嫖，你也没那个条件。但是，自己是不想。那些以往痴迷成依赖的刺激和快乐，再想起来，竟都如白水一样寡淡、云烟一样飞散。是丧父之痛令自己后悔莫及、一改前非？是流离之苦叫自己自惭形秽、不敢他想，还是自己的确放下了欲望，立地成佛？又或者，那一切的一切，只是因为，自己爱上了庄丽云？自己不知道。自己现在，甚至连多看一眼赌坊和妓院的兴趣都没有。深深喜欢了那么多年的一些东西，会在突然之间，因为某些连你自己也弄不清楚的原因，完全对你失去了意义与吸引力，那么，是不是也就暗示着，人生在任何阶段对任何事物的迷恋，都不可能拥有真正的永恒？昨天你以赌博消忧愁，今天你以练武忘烦忧，昨天你迷雪肤红唇，今天你恋心灵爱情，那么，明天呢？明天的你，是会又爱上赌与嫖，还是接着做一个伏虎罗汉与单相思病人？什么都是未知与不可把握的。自己只感到，越来越无法相信自己曾经拥有的一切，也越来越不能肯定自己还可以得到什么。时代的动荡，生活的漂流，往昔的幻灭，眼前的无奈，都将自己的灵魂深深地囚禁了起来。灵魂累了，也开始懒了。懒得去想，懒得去挣扎。这就是生活。

洁白的冷从天飘落，积成厚厚的柔，将山、路、屋、树都妆成了美丽的纯。破庙里的柴火总是贮存得不够多，呼啸的寒风总是比预计的更刺骨。有时候，柴火没了，火堆熄了，自己和弟兄们便只好打拳取暖。那套残破的八极拳，大家都已练得很熟，因为毕竟是残破的，所以威力有限。很多地方，大家都练得糊里糊涂。不过，所幸自己马步记得很清楚、学得很正确。自从自己击败胖子以后，孔仁他们也跟着自己坚持练起了马步，但是，他们所能坚持的时间，还是不能和自己一样长。其实，自己经常扎很长很长时间的马步，不是为了想要真的把自己练成什么高手，自己只不过是想要得到一种精疲力竭的疲惫，最好是能累得一躺下就睡着。这样，一个人的心就不会受到什么煎熬了。在一个你无论怎样做都不会有任何改变的困境里，让灵魂睡觉，无疑是一个用来对抗痛苦的最聪明的办法。只是，人睡着了还会做梦。在梦里，自己始终泪流满面。

已经到了十二月下旬，一九二八年很快就要过去了。已经有一段时间没

去庄府附近看她了。自从看见了几次潘兆傍晚送她回家时的情景以后，自己便命令自己，不要再沉溺在这样的不切实际的单相思里了。事实上，自己和她之间，什么都没有发生过。自己不是在空无地爱着一场什么也不存在的空无吗？一切都只是自己虚幻的憧憬、脆弱的迷恋、自我的欺骗。自己只是在一个显而易见的泥潭里越陷越深，在一点一点地沉进那最后的心梦俱碎、一夕崩溃里。既没有醍醐灌顶，也没有大彻大悟，自己到底该怎样从痴愚中解脱？在自我说服与自我放逐之间，自己究竟该用哪一种灭亡，来延续自己苍白无力的存在？

十二月二十七日那一天，自己在不知不觉中，又走到了庄府附近。人烟有些冷清，夕阳已经低垂。自己走到了惯常待着的那个无人的角落，像要躲避什么似的，蹲了下来。几只蚂蚁在地上没有方向地乱爬，一洼积水脏得像尿。太阳的温度几乎感觉不到，天空越来越暗，像要死去的梦。自己轻拈起了一只蚂蚁。它在自己的手上爬动，从指尖到手心，又从手心到手背。整个手掌都很不舒服，像痒，又像痛。这种不舒服毫无征兆地从这里游向那里，又从那里游向这里，既快，又意外，带了一些陌生而难测的恐惧。这恐惧是那样渺小，而微不足道。

直到夜晚降临，路灯亮起，也没看到她的身影。她也许是还没回来，也许是并未出门，还可能，是根本已经不住在这里了。别忘了，她已是潘兆的未婚妻。一想到这个，自己便心如刀割。自己狠狠扇了自己两个耳光。冷冷清清的寂静里，耳光声特别响亮。

该走了，痛都是自己给自己的。该走了，与爱情无关的生活还是那样漫长。走在坚硬而冰冷的夜的道路上，自己神思恍惚。走在淡淡而惆怅的路灯光下，自己黯然神伤。影子像深渊一样可怕，夜空像深海一样光滑。空旷包围着瑟缩，黑暗陡峭了痛涩。自虐不能带来清醒，清醒只是另一种自虐。

忽然，远远地，自己听到了女人的呼救声。夹杂在呼救声里的，还有日语的笑骂声。自己猛然一个激灵：这女人的声音，好像是她……

（未完待续）

生死时代之双雄

（下册）

高 淳 著

三个日本浪人，正将她逼在墙角，在笑骂着对她动手动脚。昏黄的灯光下，她的脸上充满了极度的恐惧、极度的愤怒，还有极度的绝望。直到看见了自己，她脸上那一层仿佛将死一样的厚厚冰霜，才刹那迸裂。“赵驹，救我——”她呼喊着，眼里火热地奔燃着的，是得救的光。那光里闪耀着一种无理由的信任，这信任比宝石更璀璨，比天长地久更震撼。

路上空空荡荡的。有远远地转身就跑的，没有闻声来见义勇为的。这世道。

那是自己第一次与真正会武功的人交手，而且竟然一上来就是一对三。跟他们打和跟胖子打，简直是有天壤之别。自己完全不知深浅，不识对方的武功路数，只能是拼了命地去打。当时的自己，还是只闻过唐手之名，所以并不知道，自己正在面对着的，就是著名的日本武功唐手。日本人出手毒辣，只要被打中一次，就会痛入肺腑。自己所练出的千斤坠，在他们面前完全就是个屁。自己被他们摔倒了四次。自己嗅到了死亡的气息。他们不是在赶人似的打，而是在杀人似的打。他们是想要打死自己。自己心底的一股狠劲被逼了出来。自己憋上了全身的力量，使出了八极铁山靠。三个日本人，全部被自己撞出了几丈远。他们爬了起来，面面相觑，呆若木鸡。而自己，腰部似已扭伤。腰部自损，是铁山靠的唯一弱点。他们又一起冲了过来。没办法，自己只能杀人了。自己折断了一个人的手臂，正要去拧断另一个人的脖子，腰部却是猛然一痛，劲没运上来。自己只好赶紧变招，将其踢翻了事。剩下一个还要扑上来，自己赶紧用日语大喝了一声：住手，混蛋！

他们全都愣住了。她也愣住了。

自己强装镇定，忍着发抖，向三个日本人大喝：你们胆敢和黑龙会的人动手，是不是不想活了！

才说完，自己就后悔了。完了，好久没说日语，口音全走样了，这是要命啊！

但是，他们好像也很紧张，竟然一点也没注意到这口音的问题。也许，自己的奇怪口音，是正巧和他们日本的哪个乡村的口音相似吧。他们不敢确信地、小心翼翼地问：难道，你是黑龙会的人？

废话！你们见过有哪个中国的乞丐会格斗的？会格斗的还用得着在这里当乞丐？我这是乔装，我正在执行任务，你们懂不懂？混蛋，现在全被你们破坏了！

他们愣了一会儿。忽然，一个日本人用手指着她，问：那你为什么要帮这个中国女人？你不是应该要为我们日本人的利益服务才对吗？

自己指了指她，讥讽而凶恶地对他们说：你们以为她是普通的中国女人吗？她是黑龙会的内田良平首领与头山满顾问吩咐要特别保护的人！保护她就是我的任务！谁知道我才去撒了一泡尿，回来就看到了你们！你们还真是活腻了呀，居然敢对她不敬！混蛋！

那个发问的日本人又继续问：那你们黑龙会为什么要保护她？为什么要保护一个中国女人？

自己发怒地大吼了起来：难道我们黑龙会做事还需要向你来汇报吗？你是个什么东西！今天我和你对话，已经是你此生莫大的光荣！帝国在满蒙的利益已岌岌可危，你们却还只知道喝酒玩女人，你们简直是帝国之耻！我一定要把今天的事情禀告给首领和顾问，让他们去好好质问一下军部的人，为什么要让你们这种垃圾和寄生虫跑到满洲来！你们叫什么名字，全都报上来！

三个日本人，终于落荒而逃。

看到他们跑远了，自己差点就瘫倒在了地上。心还在可怕地急跳，冷汗仍在不停往外冒。真是差点就死了。

自己去捡起了落在地上的她的外套。自己给她披上了外套。她问，你怎么会说日语？自己说，我在日本念过书。她问，你和他们说什么了，他们那样害怕？自己说，我骗他们，说你是黑龙会要保护的人，而我就是黑龙会派给你的保镖。她说，谢谢你。自己说，不用谢，我送你回家吧。她掏出手绢，给自己擦了擦额上的汗。一阵淡淡的茉莉花香。自己说，把你手绢弄脏了。她说，你一点也不脏。

风大了，呼呼地响。自己替她裹紧了外套。

自己没有去捡破碗和竹棒。那一刻，自己仿佛与这两样东西素不相识。那一刻，自己跌进了一个迷人而痴浓的错觉里，就仿佛自己真的从来不是一个乞丐，而只是她的一个最忠诚的保镖。这错觉纯粹而深浓，美如繁花，又勾魂摄魄，真实得像风，真实得像雪，自己甚至害怕再去多看那破碗和竹棒一眼，就好像只要再多看一眼，那美好的海市蜃楼就会被戳破，散成黄沙，飘成飞絮。不，自己不要醒。

路上，她告诉自己，今晚她是在朋友那里吃了晚饭，所以才回来得晚。本来是坐的谭叔的车，可是快到家时，车子却坏了。她看路已不远了，就决定步行回家，而谭叔则去修车。谁知，走着走着，便突然遇到了日本人。她说，还好有你，谢谢你，赵驹。

风越来越大了。冬夜的风，像冰结成的刀，一片一片，全都可以锋利地侵浸到人的骨头里去。怕是又要下雪了。她有些瑟缩。自己有心想要脱件衣服下来给她披上，可是想想，若将乞丐的衣服披到她的身上，那成何体统。有好多话想跟她说，可是，却一句也说不出来。

她说，真没想到，你还会武功。

自己就告诉她，自己的父亲，是镖局的总镖头，除了洋枪，他一生从未败给过任何人。父亲从不肯教自己练武，他一心只希望自己可以做个读书人。可是他在临终前，却还是将他的一身武艺传给了自己。只可惜，自己只学会了十分之一都不到。

她问，那后来呢？

自己就笑了笑，说，昨天的后来，不就是今天的现在吗。

她就也笑了笑，不再问什么了。她和自己一起走着，大风不时将她的头发吹乱。自己真的很想替她挡一挡风，却又不敢再有丝毫举动。风吹得人眼睛都痛了。她走得离自己又近了一些。还是有好多的话在自己心里翻滚，这些话，在空无一人的时候，自己已对着想象中的她说了许多遍，可是，现在，自己却一句也说不出来。今夜的风，就像一个调皮的小孩，特别喜欢和大人过不去。轻轻地问她，冷吗？她轻轻地说，还好。自己就和她在风中继续默默地走着。

自己一直保持着警惕，就怕那三个日本人会突然脑子开窍，恍然大悟，然后跑回来滋事行恶。自己的腰已扭伤，要是他们再来，那自己肯定只有被

打被杀的分了。不过还好，一路平安无事。

到了庄府的大门前。

奉天的局势越来越乱了，你以后出门要多加小心，每次尽量和朋友一起走，千万不要再一个人走夜路了。自己嘱咐她说。

谢谢你，我知道了。她说。

自己看着她，还想再说两句关心的话，但觉得不适合了，就也不说了。想着要说再见了，心里有些难言的伤惘。

她却突然说：天气这么冷，进来喝杯热茶吧。

自己略顿了一下，还是说：不了，我还有事，再见吧。

可是，忽然，自己的肚子却是饿得咕咕叫了起来。这叫声又响亮又明白。在这样的一个时刻，这种声音，简直让自己尴尬得无地自容。

她却轻轻地笑了。她问：你还没吃饭？

自己恨不得找条地缝钻下去。不，我吃过了。低头说完，自己转身便想走，但是，她却拉住了自己的手。她说：你没拿我当朋友。

怎么会？

上次说好的，你要是肚子饿了，就来找我，我给你好吃的。可你为什么从来不来？

自己无言以对，忽然有些脸红。

她放开了自己的手，说，你救了我，我请你吃顿饭，不应该吗？

自己不知该说什么才好。她就好看地笑了。她说，滴水之恩，涌泉相报，难道你想要我对你愧疚一辈子啊？

她敲了门。一个叫蔡嫂的女佣人来开的门。

看见自己进门，蔡嫂一脸惊愕。她很淡然地对蔡嫂说：他是我的一个朋友，他今天刚演完戏，身上穿的是戏服。

庄家的宅子很大，起码比威远镖局的宅子大三倍，但是宅子里却十分冷清，空空荡荡的，荒无人烟。走廊里挂着的灯笼全是摆设，统统暗着，没一盏是点亮的。只有少数几间屋里才亮着煤油灯或电灯，其他的屋子里全是黑的。在有电灯光亮的地方看那些走廊里的红灯笼，红灯笼都已破旧不堪。风一来，灯笼全都摇摇欲坠，晃得人心生萧瑟。

她带自己走进了一间有电灯的屋子里，说，你先坐，我去换一下衣服，就来。她走了出去，蔡嫂端了一杯热茶进来。先生请慢用，蔡嫂说。谢谢，自己答。蔡嫂忍不住又好好看了自己两眼。自己强忍着笑。蔡嫂还是没忍住，问，先生，你是演文明戏的吗？自己说，哦，不，文明戏早过时了，我是演电影的，上个月刚从上海那边过来，阿拉是上海人。

蔡嫂走了，自己快要笑死了。她来了，换了一身新的衣服。她见自己在笑，就很好奇，问自己在笑什么。自己就告诉了她。她忍不住也捂嘴笑了起来。她笑说，你真坏，骗人骗得比我还顺溜。自己便说，我这不是在帮你圆谎吗。她就很认真地问，你会不会怪我骗人家说你是演员？自己说，怎么会呢，大户人家嘛，最怕的就是两件事，厉害的贼，佣人的嘴，你那么说是对的。她问，那你以前应该是少镖头喽？自己说，不，我从未做过镖头，除了今天，我这辈子，还从未押过一次镖。她一时不明白地问：今天？但是转瞬，她就又明白了。她笑得特别开心。她抿着嘴，想忍住笑。

蔡嫂端来了一只烧鸡、一盘牛肉、一碗饭和一壶热酒。蔡嫂说，今天太晚了，厨房里就只剩下这些了。自己说，真是麻烦你们了，太不好意思了，今天片场收工太晚，真是来打扰了。自己又向蔡嫂道了好多声谢。蔡嫂走了。自己便吃了起来。

她问自己，刚才在打斗时有没有受伤？自己说没有。她说，可是我看你那两跤摔得挺厉害的，真的不要紧吗？自己说，要是我受伤了，那现在哪还能坐在这里大吃大喝呀，是不是？她就笑了，又说了一句“谢谢你”。自己说，别说谢了，再说我就要不好意思吃下去了。她笑着，就去一旁的一张椅子上坐了下来。

她说，听说东北就要易帜了，要是中国统一了，那日本人兴许就不敢再欺负中国人了。

是啊。自己心口不一地说。

她说，真希望奉天这里可以安定下来，政府可以把日本人全部赶走，那样，大家就都可以安居乐业了。

自己往嘴里塞了一大块鸡肉，点点头，只“嗯”了一声，心里不禁有些悲伤。她对时局的看法是如此天真，对生活的希望又是那样光明，而这个黑暗不堪的年代，最终又能否不让她伤心欲绝？党棍军阀们在地图前斗得你死我活，最受苦的，却全是底下的普通老百姓。被践踏与踩烂的，全是一朵朵

像花儿一样美好的鲜活生命。

她跟自己讲了一些她的故事。这些故事里，有些是自己已经听说的，有些是自己没有想到的。她说，其实庄家的生意早就已经外强中干了，原先的三家面粉厂和两家纱厂，都已濒临倒闭。她说，日本的樱花会社想要在奉天市里开纱厂、办商行，华商会的人心里都不同意，但是又没人敢出来公开反对日本人，结果，父亲出来领了头，和日商作对，最后落了个一病不起。她说，华商会的人其实还没华工会的人有良心，父亲病倒后，华商会的人树倒猢狲散，连看望都不来看望父亲，反倒是那些以前闹过罢工的工会代表，因为敬重父亲与日商斗争，都来看望过父亲好几次。庄家的生意之所以到现在还没倒塌，很大程度上，都是那些工人们在撑着。

自己说，工会基本上都是受共产党领导的，蒋介石反共，你要小心。

她说，党派的事我不懂，我只知道，好人会给我们雪中送炭，坏人会给我们雪上加霜。

她说，她的母亲天生就什么也看不见，可是，她的父亲，却还是爱了她的母亲一辈子。母亲一辈子就只生下了她这么一个女儿，有多少人劝过父亲要纳妾，就连母亲自己都劝过父亲再娶，可是父亲却一生都没再娶过第二个老婆。父亲常说，谁说女儿不如男，看那穆桂英、花木兰，都是巾帼不让须眉的英雄。

她说，她一直都很羡慕像她的父亲和母亲那样终生不渝的爱情。曾经她以为，她已经找到了这样的一份爱情。她的丈夫对她很好，平时，甚至都舍不得让她绣一个荷包，就怕她会扎疼手。丈夫牺牲消息传来的那一刻，她昏倒在了地上。醒来后，她哭了三天三夜。她以为，她的整个世界都已经被毁灭了。她甚至准备好了要上吊，去陪她那孤孤单单的丈夫一起。可是，就在她丈夫死后的第四天，却有两个浓妆艳抹的女人找到了她夫家的门上来。她们一个挺着大肚子，一个手里牵着一个小男孩。她们说，这一个已经生下来了的和那一个还没生下来的，都是这个已经死了的色鬼的种。那一刻，她的公公和婆婆，喜上眉梢。那一刻，她觉得，她真是这个世上最滑稽的小丑，最可怜的笑话。她说，本来，她还以为，是战争夺走了她的爱情和幸福，但是其实，她根本从来就没有被爱情和幸福眷顾过。她说，这真是可笑哇，可笑。她笑着，眼里甚至都有了些红红的泪光。

自己说，爱情只是一种运气，有些人遇到了，很好，有些人遇不到，天命。不要伤心，不要难过，因为，也许明天一转身，你就会遇到你的运气。

她就笑了，擦去了泪光，说，你父亲是对的，你应该做一个文人。

自己说，我如果做了文人，今天哪里还能坐在这里，吃上这一顿饱饭呢。

她笑了笑，就不说话了。过了一会儿，她才像是自言自语地说，不会了，再也不会遇上了。

自己的心里，忽然就感到很酸痛。一种热辣辣的苦痛，像藤蔓一样，瞬间就缠满了自己的全身。自己嘴里还在嚼着鸡肉，却已完全失去了味觉，只感到自己仿佛是在咀嚼满口的泪水。痛苦得难以下咽。用力去咽，却难受得想吐。只感到，喉咙里有一股满满酸楚的热。想问她，爱潘兆吗。可是，只有一股更强更热的酸楚，堵在自己的喉咙口。自己再也不能咽下任何东西了，那强大得让自己误以为会无穷无尽肆虐下去的饥饿，在这一刻，凭空消失得无影无踪。而自己，其实才吃了以前在家时的饭量的一半。她就坐在那里，离自己很近。自己甚至能看清她睫毛的每一次扑闪。但是，自己又知道，她就像是坐在天之涯，而自己，就像是坐在海之角。淡淡的灯光下，她美得像画里的人一样，而画，永远都在另一个世界里。

自己喝起了酒。她说，酒凉了，我去给你温一下。自己说，不用，我就爱喝凉的。她说，酒冷伤肝，这你都不懂。自己说，真不用。她的目光不小心就和自己的目光撞在了一起，莫名有些胶滞。她像是忽然有了些不知所措。她就又坐了回去，不再看自己，也不再说温酒的事。她默默地低头坐着。

自己大喝了几口，然后说，你太容易相信别人了，在这个世道里，你会吃亏的。

她没有抬起头来，只轻轻地“哦”了一声。

自己说，比如，你怎么就能肯定，我不是一个坏人呢？

她就有些乐了，抬起了头来，说，哪有人这么说自己的。

自己说，真的，你以后千万不要再这样轻信人了，不然，你会受到伤害的。

她双手放在并拢着的膝盖上，脸上甜甜地笑了笑，低了低头，然后又抬

起了头来，看着自己，说，其实我想过的，你要是坏人，那哪里还会沦落到做乞丐的地步呢，好歹你也可以在帮会里做个小喽啰呀。

自己就忍不住笑了起来，说，你还真是很会推理呀。

她就笑了，笑得天真而灿烂。看着她纯净的笑，自己心里不禁又是狠狠一痛。只好又是闷头喝酒。

她说，你还一直没有告诉我，你是怎么变成今天这样的呢。

自己放下了酒壶，顿了顿，就告诉她，自己的父亲是被土匪杀死的，自己想给父亲报仇，结果仇没报成，反倒惹来了土匪的追杀，于是，就只好是从江南，逃来了东北。

她听完了，点点头，"哦"了一声，忽然就像是愧疚了起来。她像个做错了事的孩子似的，说，对不起，我总是想知道你的故事，却害你又提起了伤心的事，我不好。

自己一笑，说，没事，故事本来就是要用来说和听的，否则，一个没有故事流传的世界，该有多寂寞。

她笑了笑，就又低下了头去，没有再说什么。

自己看着她，微微有些痴怔。那一刻，自己是真希望时间能永远停下来。停在这一刻，再也不要往前走。这一刻，既没有往昔的疼痛，也没有来日的恐惧，只有眼前的美好与曼妙。自己没有醉，却恍若醺醺然。那些人生中永不能愈合的伤口仿佛再也与自己无关，好像，只有此刻的浪漫，才会在以后的日子里，陪伴自己到天荒地老。自己像个傻子一样，感到幸福。

她轻轻说，今天没能给你什么好吃的，下次你再来，我好好招待你。

她抬起了头来，自己赶紧移开了注视着她的目光。她站了起来，说，我给你去换一壶热酒。

自己说，不用，不用了。自己用衣袖一抹嘴，然后就站了起来。

"我吃饱了，该走了。今天谢谢你，我已经有很久没吃过肉、没喝过酒了。以后，我们有缘再见。"

"赵驹——"她却是叫住了自己。

自己转回了身来。

她嘴唇动了动，却又是无言。

自己就笑了，说："放心，我不会让你愧疚的，下次我来，给我准备一头烤全羊，小心我把你家吃穷啊。”

她扑哧一下子，就笑了出来。笑得那不知从何而来的忧伤，一时又都藏到了大家想让它们藏起来的地方。

“赵驹，来我们公司上班吧，好吗？”她突然说。

“什么？”

“我们公司需要一个日语翻译，你来吧，好吗？”她凝眸看着自己，说。

她的眼睛，漂亮得像两汪最澄澈的桃花潭水。自己痴然失语。那淡淡的茉莉花香，像是一下子就将自己推到了酒醉的最深处，自己毫无抵抗，不想抵抗。海市蜃楼一样的浓重痴醉，将自己重重包围。除了发怔，自己别无他想。除了她，自己像是再看不见任何东西。她的美，无法形容。自己，愿意为她去死。

“好，我来。”自己醺然地说。

她高兴得双手合了起来，说，太好啦。她天真地欢笑着，像一个在许愿的小女孩。自己清醒了一些，才忽然是想到，还应该要说一声谢谢。

她又说了好些话。她话多的时候，真是挺可爱的，像个会唠叨的小孩，让人挺想笑。自己笑着笑着，忽然就挺想流泪。这样快乐的时光是多好哇，开心多好，可是，这些，都会是命运突然给自己的恩赐吗？自己爱上了她，这会是一个美丽的故事吗？真的挺想流泪，不为什么。也许，真的只是太开心了。

她说，我们有员工宿舍，还有员工食堂，这样，你就吃住都不愁了。她说，我一定要帮你好好打扮一下，让你真的像个电影演员一样，这样，公司里的人才不会问东问西。她说，再过几天就是元旦了，你就在元旦那天正式来上班，我们一起辞旧迎新，你再也不用当乞丐了。她说，你不要以为我是在报恩，我又不是白娘子，你呀，要是翻译得不好，害我出丑，那我就得扣光你的工资。

她看自己老是在笑，就也忍不住和自己一起笑了。她说，有什么可笑的，我说得很滑稽吗？自己说，不是啊。自己说完又笑，她就也不问了，只是和自己一起笑。她笑说，你真像个傻子，只有傻子才会莫名其妙一直笑。自己笑说，你不也是。她笑得都哈哈了起来。那一天，那一段时光，真是莫名地开心。人生有时就是这样，有些快乐，简直就不需要理由。又或者，那

些快乐，还是有理由的，只不过，理由，都被我们深埋了起来。难忘的开心，开心得难忘，她和自己一起笑，她像自己一样犯傻。一切，都快乐得像个无尘的童话，像个无边的美梦。自己幸福得忘乎所以，甚至都忘记了一条真理：命运又怎会对人如此宽容、如此友善？

半夜了，自己真的该走了。她要送送自己。谁知一打开屋门，就看见了外面正在下雪。鹅毛大雪。屋子里的灯光薄薄地撒在院子里，院子里的地上，一片雪白。雪花飘飘洒洒，随风轻舞，悠扬孤零，纠缠旋转。照在地上的灯光里，映着两条被拉长了的人影。人影铺在雪地上，雪花又撒在人影里，让人影仿佛分外萧瑟了起来。夜是这样安静，雪也是这样安静，唯有远处几声狗吠，唯有寒风偶尔呜呜。一阵风劲，雪花扑面而来。自己不自觉地抬了抬手，想给她挡一挡扑脸的风雪，但寒冷毕竟还是可以让人清醒的，自己将刚抬起的手，又放了下来。雪花粘在自己的脸上，冷冷的，像醒酒药。

她没有说话。自己向她挥了挥手告别，然后便想走进雪里去。她却说，雪太大了，你留下来吧，反正我家里闲置着的客房也多。

雪花不停扑打在自己的脸上。自己还是又向雪里跨了一步。她说，雪这样大。

自己站住了。风雪冷得坚硬，令人发抖。没有声音。

自己回头，看见，她痴惘地伸出一只手，一片晶莹的雪花，在她的手心里冰凉。她看着手心，又看着飞雪，无语凝默。

蔡嫂领自己去了一间客房。自己等蔡嫂走后，在地上睡了下来。毕竟，自己太脏了，不能弄脏人家好好的炕。

这一夜，自己没怎么睡着。喜悦、忐忑、猜想、自卑、不安、伤怀。自己的心，像是生病了。病得很重，重得快乐，快乐得痛苦。她的模样，一遍又一遍地在自己的心里滚烫；她的笑貌，一次又一次地将自己淹没。自己像是发了烧，又像是溺了水，心乱如麻，又欲罢不能。真是宁愿在这种感觉里窒息，也不要一丝清醒的呼吸。爱情真的是个魔鬼。

第二天的清早，雪停了。打开窗户，望出去，是一片洁白而美丽的世界。自己深吸了几口新鲜空气，觉得这世界真是美好。

一大早，蔡嫂就给自己端来了一顿丰盛的早餐。因为骗过蔡嫂，自己觉得特别过意不去，对蔡嫂也就格外客气。也不知这好心情是不是也会传染，蔡嫂今天看起来也特别高兴。蔡嫂笑吟吟地说，赵先生一会儿吃完了，跟我走，我们小姐吩咐了，要我今早带你去理个发，理完了发，再带你回来洗个澡。

自己有些意外，原本以为，这一顿是最后的早餐，却没想到，故事还没完。

自己含糊地应答了几句。

蔡嫂看自己尴尬，就笑了。蔡嫂说，赵先生，其实我看出来了，你不是演员，演叫花子，哪里用得着真把头发留这么长？

自己噎住了。

蔡嫂说，我知道，你和小姐合起伙来骗我，是怕我会说闲话，但是，我蔡嫂哪里会是这样不知好歹的人？从你的谈吐，我就猜出来了，你以前一定是小姐的同学，或者什么好朋友，你是南方人，因为南方打仗，所以才逃到了这边来，是不是？

自己不置可否，只能笑笑。

蔡嫂接着说，其实，我们这府里，没人喜欢那个潘会长，那王八蛋，除了有钱有势，什么好地方都没有。你知道吗，那杀千刀的，有时候连我们这些老妈子的便宜都要占，你说我们恨不恨！

自己有些愣了。

蔡嫂说，所以，你和小姐放心好了，你们的事，我半个字也不会往外乱说的。你从昨天进来起，就一直谦恭有礼，看得出你是个有教养的人。你要是真能把那个潘兆给挤走，那我们这府里的下人，全都感谢你。

自己赶紧说，您想多了，真想多了，我就是临时不方便，过来暂住一晚的。

蔡嫂就笑了，说，我这一大把年纪了，要是连你们年轻人的这点小花样都看不懂，那岂不是白活了？小姐要对你没意思，能留你一个大男人在我们庄府过夜？

那是因为昨晚要走时，外面突然下起了雪。自己辩解。

下雪？下雪你不会撑一把伞走哇？蔡嫂说。

自己说不出话来了。是的，昨夜，自己为何不撑一把伞离开？是真的自己没想到，还是自己其实不想走？旁观者的话太犀利，自己不愿再自问。再

自问，自己只会陷进无尽的纠缠里。

自己埋头吃包子。

蔡嫂不再问了。她沉默了一会儿，只是叹了一口气，说，我也不是真想要问你什么，你们年轻人都喜欢有小秘密，这我懂。我只是想要告诉你，你和小姐若真有意思，那就请你一定要认真对她，好好待她，切莫只将这一切当作是电影里的游戏。我们家小姐命苦，从小上学时，就一直被人家取笑，说她娘是个瞎子，她以后生下来的孩子，也必定会是个瞎子。后来好不容易以为是嫁了个如意郎君，却谁知道那男人竟是个伪君子，成天在窑子和赌场里混，还在我们家小姐面前装孔子门生。小姐回娘家以后，那夫家的公婆在外面造了许多难听的谣言，为的就是要掩盖他们儿子的不是，让人家觉得都是我们家小姐活该。小姐她也从来没有去向人家澄清过一句。再后来，老爷病倒了，庄家没有男人，小姐就只好站出来，勉强维持庄家生意上的正常运转。可是，那些官场和生意场上的老狐狸们，又岂会真的看得起一个黄毛小丫头？他们能暂时不动什么歪脑筋，就已经是看在老爷还没死的分上了。日本人又一直虎视眈眈，想要吞掉庄家的产业。你说我们小姐，从小只习诗画女红，哪里能有什么本事去对付那些豺狼虎豹？无奈之下，她才只好是去抱上了潘兆这棵大树，希望潘兆能庇护我们庄家。可是，潘兆的儿子都已经快要二十了呀！你说我们小姐有多委屈。更何况那潘兆根本就不是什么好东西！太太只是天天哭。而老爷还根本就不知道这事。老爷最疼小姐了，要是知道小姐马上要嫁给那个秃头老男人了，还不得立刻气死！唉，其实要我们说，庄家怕是气数已尽了。在庄家的产业和小姐的幸福之间，大家只可以选择一样。太太要小姐幸福，小姐要庄家不倒，老爷则人事不济。谁又能怎么办呢？唉，都怪这倒霉的年月，统统把人往绝路上逼。我说赵先生，我们家小姐既然能喜欢上你，那你就肯定不会是个普通人，我听你的谈吐，也不像是没见过世面的小户子弟，你要是真的既能给我们小姐幸福，又能重振我们庄家的威风，那你可就是我们庄家的大恩人啦！

自己呛咳了起来，慌忙摇头又摇手，说，您想太多了，真的想太多了，我就是一个借宿的。吃完我就要走了，我和你们家小姐是清白的，我吃完就会走的。

自己有些语无伦次。

蔡嫂瞪大了眼睛说：难道你也是嫌贫爱富、胆小怕事之人？莫非你之前勾引我们家小姐只是为了图她的富贵，而今听我说了庄家气数已尽，你便打起了退堂鼓？

这都哪儿跟哪儿啊，我又不是没见过钞票的人，哪里会图你们庄家的什么钱财。自己忽然就有些生气了。

蔡嫂却笑了。自己忽然才发觉，好像是踏入了蔡嫂所设下的一个话语圈套里。自己顿时有些发窘。蔡嫂停了笑，正色说：知道吗，我一直很担心，小姐她会遇上骗子，还好，你不是。

自己低头不语。

蔡嫂见自己不说话，便说：你刚才不是说要走吗，那好，去剃个头，把自己洗洗干净，然后再去和我们家小姐正式道个别。

自己点点头，说，好。

断发落下，看着镜中肮脏不堪的自己，自己忽然有流泪的冲动。多久没照过镜子了？还认识自己吗？镜子里的那个乞丐是谁？对自己，自己充满了怨恨与厌恶，但是在这恨与厌里，又分明飘满了凄风苦雨。从良心上来说，很多事情，其实自己都是罪有应得。但是，自己又真的，从来没想过要做一个坏人。很多事情就是这样矛盾与纠缠。回想人生路，自己从未真的要去误入歧途，但是，莫名，却已走到了流亡天涯的那一步；自己也从未真的要去伤天害理，但是，莫名，却已背满了血腥难当的生死债。人活着，好像就是越活越奇怪了起来，越活越觉得荒诞不经。而这奇怪与荒诞又是那样残酷不堪，它们会告诉你一个令人战栗的真相：只要你今天在路上被人撞偏了一点点，那么，你脚下的那条路，就已不会再是原来的那条路，纵然它们在此刻看起来仍然只是同一条路。一个新的世界取代一个旧的世界，总是在倏忽之间；一个黑暗的归宿取代一个光明的归宿，总是在知觉之外。明天，自己还会迎来什么？真的不知道。总不会比乞丐更差了吧？也许是的。自己看了一眼日历，这一天，是一九二八年的十二月二十八日。

去洗澡前，蔡嫂拿来了一整套崭新的衣物，从内衣到外套，从皮带到皮鞋，一应俱全。自己很诧异。蔡嫂说，这有什么好奇怪的，难不成你剃完了头、洗完了澡，还要穿回你身上那套又臭又脏的乞丐衣服？那你还洗什么？蔡嫂说，别辜负了小姐的一番心意，这些都是她一大早，在你吃饭的时候，

特地去店里给你买的，就是衣物的尺码全是猜的，你先将就一下吧，不合适的以后再说。

洗完了澡，自己开始穿上这些新衣服。很奇怪，她的眼光很准，除了内衣太小太紧了以外，其余的衣物的尺码，大小都刚刚好。这算不算是一种冥冥之中的神奇呢？难道，这就是佛说的缘分？

自己又一次站在了镜子前，镜子中的自己，衣裤笔挺，皮鞋锃亮。自己抹了一下自己的头发。那个以前的赵驹，好像又回来了。

看见了新的自己，她愣了一小会儿。那样子有些好笑，她就像是突然看见了一件什么很稀奇的东西一样。自己都笑了，说，喂，你发什么呆。她就笑了，跑过来，说，哇，我真把你打扮成了电影演员哪。她笑得可高兴了，像是做成了一件什么很重要的事一样。自己说，你笑什么呀，大小都不合适。她说，哪件不合适？我给你去换。自己就笑了，忍都忍不住，说，算了，老板给的，再不合适都是福利。她说，你这么快就叫我老板啦？自己说，那叫你什么，难道是老板娘？她笑得背都弯了，自己也忍俊不禁。其实有什么好笑的呢？但就是从心底里想笑，想用整个生命来欢乐地尽情地大笑。想和她在一起，永远无拘无束地笑下去。就仿佛和她在一起，实在是有挥霍不尽的快乐，怎么笑，都笑不够。那一刻，自己和她，又像是都成了傻子。太傻了，傻得都让人想笑。

她说，快跟我来，我要带你去见我娘。

什么？

哎呀，我娘知道你救了我，想要当面谢谢你。快来呀。

哦。

见到了庄家的太太，是个很慈祥的妇人。只可惜她什么也看不见，双眼很分明地灰暗着。但是那灰暗又不是一种死气，在那眸子的盲瞎里，始终还跳跃着一份灿烂的笑意。很多明眼人，睁着眼睛，也未必能让人感到这一份灿烂。

庄太太千恩万谢，自己愧不敢受。丽云向她娘介绍，说，她已聘了自己做公司的日语翻译。庄太太颇喜。问及来由，自己即述说了一番在日本留学的经历。庄太太拊掌微笑，说，赵先生那可真是人中龙凤、文武全才了。自己说，哪里，哪里，时局艰难，读书无用，落魄至此，真正赧颜于祖先。

庄太太问及丽云与自己的渊源，丽云说，我们是好朋友。庄太太就笑了，说，朋友好，朋友好。庄太太转而又问自己，将来可有何打算？自己说，家已被贼匪所毁，此身于这洪流乱世之中，漂泊难依，现既已于东北暂定，南归之志便也渐息。

三人又笑谈了一番，自己便拟起身告辞。庄太太吩咐丽云，一定要留自己在府里多住几日，好生款待。庄太太又向自己说，你救了丽云，就是救了我们全家，你是我们庄家一辈子的恩人。自己忙说，不敢，不敢，朋友之谊，举手之劳而已。

经过庄老爷的屋子时，丽云站在窗外看了看，但是并没有进去。她小声说，父亲肺病难愈，晚间咳累了，白天便睡，一日瘦过一日。自己放轻了脚步。她看着窗里屋中昏暗暗的一片，隐隐悲然。自己想安慰她两句，又觉得自己实在是不配在此多言。

离开了庄老爷的屋子，丽云说，你这几天，就住在我家里吧，等上了班，给你分配了员工宿舍，你再去宿舍里住，好吗？自己说，好。默然走了几步，她又说，今天去得匆忙，你身上这些衣物的尺码，都是我估摸着瞎猜的，一定会有不合适的，你告诉我哪些尺码不对，我去给你换。自己说，不用，都合适。她说，刚才你还说不合适的。自己说，那是逗你玩呢。她就笑了，说，你现在才是逗我玩呢，我瞎猜着给你买的，哪能都合适？不合适的穿着不舒服，你别和我客气，你救了我，我就是给你买屋买地都是应该的。自己说，真的，你信吗，你给我买的衣服、皮带、鞋子，没有一样是不合适的，就好像，我们真的是早已熟识了好多好多年。她就不说话了，微垂下了头，像是有些想笑，又像是有些娇羞。自己就笑了起来。她说，你笑什么。自己说，不知道。然后，就大笑着跑了起来。她就笑着追。两个人，开心得就像要过年的孩子一样。雪地里，一行行欢快的、洁白的脚印。那些笑，自己一辈子也忘不了。

中午，自己拎了三只烧鸡，回了一趟破庙。自己从心底里感到非常对不起兄弟。对兄弟们来说，从昨夜开始，自己就已经下落不明了。他们肯定都急坏了，却绝不会想到，其实自己正在一个人吃香的喝辣的。这种愧疚让自己十分不安。在自己最困难的时候，是兄弟们救了自己帮了自己，而今，自己却已脱下了乞丐的衣服，准备独自走向另一条道路，一条至少是能吃穿不

愁的道路。当初结拜时说好的，有福同享有难同当，现在自己这样，算不算是背弃了盟誓？自己的心里很乱。很奇怪，自己总是会因为她，而做出一些对兄弟不讲义气的事情。是自己真的太爱她，还是自己在骨子里，就不是一个义薄云天、赤胆忠心的英雄好汉？自己无心无力去想。

街上，一些店铺和学校的门前，都还插着北洋政府的五色旗。五色分明，五色鲜艳，五色飘扬。在雪白的背景里，这些五色旗，鲜艳得萧瑟，飘扬得凛冽，醒目得分外刺眼。北伐结束，北洋已经成为历史。大中国的蒋介石时代已经来临。除了东北，中国的大地上，已经飘满了青天白日满地红的旗帜。而这五色旗，究竟还能在这东北飘扬多久？传闻蒋介石早已与张学良谈妥了东北易帜的事宜，只是由于日本人的多番极力阻挠，张学良才迟迟未能行事。自己究竟是该为此喜还是为此悲？国家贫弱不堪，事事受西洋人和东洋人的控制，作为一个中国人，实在是感到屈辱不堪、悲愤莫名；但是，作为一个被国民党的地方政府所通缉的要犯，自己又实在是很希望，这不受南京国民政府管辖的东北，可以是自己最后的避难所。忠私两难，自己无可选择，不想也罢。

孔仁他们见到自己的第一刻，全都目瞪口呆。他们四人，昨晚一夜没睡，四处去寻找自己，就怕自己遇到了什么不测。看着他们身上被雪洇湿了的衣服，自己简直羞于启齿自己所遇到的命运转机。

自己告诉他们，昨晚，自己在一个很偶然的机会下，很偶然地救了那个庄家的庄小姐一命。然后，自己就想去她家里，跟她多要一些烧鸡或大洋回来。谁知，到了庄家后，她的家里人对自己是千恩万谢，好不热情。庄老爷和庄太太不仅要留自己在庄府里多住几日，而且，在听说了自己曾经辉煌的经历之后，还立刻就聘请了自己，要自己做庄氏企业的日语翻译，新年元旦那天就可上班。自己对孔仁他们说，我想，这可是一个千载难逢的好机会呀，只要我在公司里站稳了脚跟，那到时，把你们也从这里带出去，还不就是小事一桩，我们兄弟五个的苦日子啊，可算是要熬到头了。

孔仁他们，激动不已。他们激动得连烧鸡也顾不上吃了。黄道一个劲儿地问，是不是真的，是不是真的。朱理说他，当然是真的，看你乐得跟个傻子似的。孟义则拉着自己的衣服看了又看，赞不绝口。孔仁则在一旁坐着，喜悦地笑。朱理说，要是真能成的话，那就太好了，我们可以再也不用当乞丐了。孟义说，只要能让我当个看门的，我就心满意足了。孔仁说，是我们的赵驹兄弟有福气，我们都是沾了兄弟的光。黄道说，还是念书好，还是念书好，念好了书，就算一时当乞丐，翻起身来还是易如反掌。大家都哈哈地笑。大家七嘴八舌地又说又笑，自己也不自觉地从隐秘的愧疚中挣脱了出来，开始与他们一起欢笑。自己虽然将自己与丽云的真实故事隐瞒了起来，告诉了他们一个似是而非的假故事，但是，在这个假故事里，自己有一个心愿是真的，那就是待自己稍有基础之后，自己一定会将孔仁他们四个，从乞丐堆里拉出来。

自己将自己在丽云那里预支的十块大洋薪水拿了出来，给了兄弟们。黄道高兴地都要抱着自己亲一口了，孟义笑着拉开了他，说，你脏死了，也不看看，兄弟他现在穿的是啥衣服，亲一口可以，别弄脏了这么好的衣服才是。大家大笑。自己也畅快地大笑。那些笑里，都充满了希望和阳光的味道，有露珠在青草上滚动的美妙。那一刻，自己是真的以为，命运要仁慈地给予自己一个崭新的黎明了。临走时，自己还答应了兄弟们，过几天，会再送一些钱和食物过来。他们高兴得都跳起了舞来，跳得磕磕绊绊，摔倒了还停不住笑。

晚上，是和丽云、庄太太一起吃的晚饭。自己特意留心地又看了看丽云的手。当初，在潘兆和丽云订婚的报纸新闻里，有一张照片，拍的是潘兆给丽云戴上了一枚漂亮而昂贵的订婚戒指，但是，很奇怪的是，自己好像从没见丽云的手上戴过这东西。是的，反正自己是没见过。在她订婚之后与自己的那次街边偶遇中，自己就没见她手上戴那枚耀眼的戒指。难道真的如自己所想和蔡嫂所说的那样，她根本就不爱潘兆的？甚至讨厌得连戒指也不愿戴？自己莫名有些开心。这开心，有些痴妄。丽云给自己夹菜，自己快乐得哑然失笑。她在桌子下面轻轻踢了自己一下。自己忙忍住了笑，专心吃饭。抬眼去看她，却见她在粲然偷笑。

晚上，睡在了客房里暖暖的炕上，心里快乐得想大呼小叫。才和她在院子里分别了没多久，又满满地想念起了她。就好像，看不见她的时间每多增加一分钟，在自己的生命里想念她的时间便会延长好几天。这种感觉美妙而深浓，美得像春江花月，深得似碧海青天。如发烧，如疯癫，患病似的受折磨，又痴迷不悟地要追求；被淹没，被窒息，清楚地看到自己沉到了酒醉的

最深处，却只希望这酒醉可以来得更猛烈一些。这即是相思病，春蚕到死丝方尽的相思病，蜡炬成灰泪始干的相思病。这就是爱情，问世间情为何物的爱情，直教人生死相许的爱情。这一晚，自己在心里，反复地感谢了命运，感谢了命运之神终于呈现出来的慈悲为怀；自己忏悔了曾经，忏悔了自己曾经千百次地恶毒辱骂命运之神的可悲可恨行为。这一晚，自己在感激涕零的祈望与真诚无比的忏悔中，感到了热烈而澎湃的幸福。这种幸福的感觉，无比实在，无比火热，无比永恒。那一晚，自己是真的以为，自己的人生，要重新开始了。自己是真的以为，自己的爱情、自己的幸福，真的来了。那种感觉，是那样纯洁，那样光明，那样崇高。

然而，自己忘了，这是一个生死时代，无情年代。

东北的冬天，总是分外寒冷，冷到极致。

一九二八年十二月二十九日，张学良发表全国通电，正式宣布东北易帜。东北地方政府正式接受南京国民政府管辖，奉军被统一改编为国民革命军东北边防军。五色旗降下，青天白日满地红旗升起。北洋政府彻底而正式地退出了历史舞台，中国在形式上完成了统一。

一梦醒来，天已大亮。只闻街上鞭炮齐鸣，锣鼓喧天。自己笑吟吟的，还以为，是哪户大户人家，在一大早迎娶新娘。

洗漱完毕，穿戴整齐，自己走到了院子里。庄家的大门敞开着，丽云、蔡嫂等人都站在大门外，东张西望。看样子，像是发生了什么特别值得关注的事。

又一阵锣鼓喧天，鞭炮齐鸣，自己也往大门外走了去。丽云回头看见自己，激动地飞跑到了自己的身边，她兴奋而喜悦地说：“赵驹，东北易帜啦！东北易帜啦！中国终于统一啦！”

什么？

什么！

五雷轰顶。

自己呆若木鸡。一刹那，只觉天旋地转，天崩地裂。丽云又说了一些什么，自己完全没有听清。只有满脑子的“嗡嗡”“嗡嗡”。自己像是失去了听觉，失去了视觉，失去了触觉，自己像是成了一根木头，一个死人，一把碎冰。生命、阳光，全都在自己的体内碎成了仿佛从未存在过的云烟；喜悦、向往，全都在脆弱的眼前被摧毁成了任风吹走的灰烬。失血的冷，濒死的痛，将自己碎尸万段。原来，昨晚，自己真的只是做了一个梦。而这个梦，竟然真的，只有一晚这么短。命运之神，嗜好的，终究还是残忍的血腥、痛苦的泪花。

丽云兴高采烈地拉着自己走到了大街上。只见，机关、学校、商店的门前，都已悬挂起或插上了青天白日满地红旗，还有一队队的士兵，手里举着旗，在各条街上游弋、宣传。整个奉天城里，都飘扬着那刺眼的青、白、红三色，那青似鬼、白似丧、红似血。不断地有鞭炮声响起。人们在欢呼“中国统一，赶走倭寇”。自己的双眼酸楚难当，忽然，就流下了眼泪来。

“咦，赵驹，你怎么了？”丽云天真地问。

“我高兴，太高兴了。”自己忍着哭泣说。

“以后，日本人再也不敢随便欺负我们啦。”丽云欢快地说。

自己拉着丽云的手，走入了欢呼的人群里，和他们一起振臂高呼：“中国统一！赶走倭寇！中国统一！赶走倭寇！”自己喊得热血澎湃，泪流满面。

这个该死的时代！

老百姓们也领到了青天白日满地红旗。自己陪着丽云，也去领了一面。各户人家的大门外，陆续都飘扬起了这青、白、红三色的国旗。自己帮丽云把这旗挂在了庄家的大门外，旗帜随风飘扬，煞是好看。丽云欢天喜地，美若桃花。自己站在青天白日满地红的国旗下，仰望着蓝天，让泪不要再从眼眶里奔出来。天是那样清澈，风是那样柔和，人们是那样欢乐，只有自己，是迎来了末日。自己微笑着，轻声对天空说了一句：到头来，还是你赢了。

空旷无穷无尽。

飞鸟孤单地划过天际。

自己躲在屋子里，不敢再出门。想要离开庄家，又举棋不定。走到院子里，看见蔡嫂从外面买菜回来，心里也怕得要命。那张要命的通缉令，会发到东北来吗？会不发来吗？什么时候会来呢？会永远不来吗？也许，江庆县政府里的那群蠢货，早就已经把这事给忘了呢？时局这么乱，天天要死那么多人，谁又会当真来专门记住你赵驹呢？像金顺，不是也并没真的派人来追杀吗？不对，这只是自己一厢情愿的猜测。也许，金顺是派出了人来追杀

的，只不过自己运气好，一时还没被杀到而已。这事不一定的。现在，东北被统一了，南边要派杀手过来，太容易了。另外，还有自己在那该死的上海闯下的祸，自己千不该万不该，就是不该杀了杜月笙的人。要不怎么说人倒霉起来连喝口凉水都会塞牙呢，谁能想到，自己只是想去上海乘个火车而已，却会碰上蒋介石政变这种倒霉的破事。蒋介石自己躲得远远的，却叫白崇禧和杜月笙在上海大开杀戒，乱捕滥杀，像自己这样莫名其妙遭受池鱼之殃的人，还不知道有多少呢。现在可好了，蒋介石权倾朝野，白崇禧和杜月笙之流全成了国家功臣，那杜月笙还不是只要一句话，就能把你赵驹放到油锅里去炸个十八回？完蛋了，自己这次真是要死到临头了。

午饭自己也没吃，丽云和自己说话，自己也心不在焉。她问自己怎么了，自己也只好含糊其辞。怎么办？接下来自己该怎么办？

也许，还是要往好的方面去想。也许正如自己所希望的那样，万事都会有侥幸存在。时局这么乱，江庆县的县政府里，天知道是已经又换了几朝天子几朝臣，谁还会有心思来和你赵驹计较当初的那一点点小破事？而金顺，对身为一代武林英雄的父亲，多少还是有些感情的，他当初可能就只是想吓唬吓唬想报仇的自己而已，并不会真的让赵三牛断子绝孙。江湖也是有江湖的舆论的，要有威望，凡事就不能做太绝。至于杜月笙，他一天到晚要烦那么多事，哪里会真在乎他手下几个虾兵蟹将的死活？也许在那最后一战中，那些流氓真的已经全被炸死了，那么，杜月笙就根本不可能知道，这世上还有一个叫赵驹的人存在。这样就太好了。而且，大家都知道，虽然东北已易帜，但实际上，东北仍是少帅张学良的天下，蒋介石和南京政府，对东北没有实际的控制力。也许，东北易帜，除了换一面国旗以外，什么也不会发生变化，一切仍会照旧。这样，就真的是太好了。

自己就像是得了寒热病，一会儿恐惧一会儿侥幸地不停思虑。自己既想要离开庄府，又实在是不甘心。好不容易终于盼来了命运的一丝转机，难道只好就此放弃？不，也许，真的只是自己在杞人忧天罢了。一切事情，都还没有变坏。庄府上下，依旧待自己如上宾；丽云，依旧兴高采烈得像过节。自己为什么要为了那还没来临甚至是根本就不会来临的厄运而自乱阵脚、未赌先输？自己现在与丽云这样亲近、这样开心，自己这一生还从未有过像现在这样的甜蜜幸福，自己为什么要无缘无故地仓皇出逃？不，绝不。人生就是一场赌局，自己与老天爷的赌博还没有结束，老天爷还没有亮出他最后的底牌，所以，自己还没有输。还没有真正地输，却误以为自己已经输了而选择认输的蠢货，才是真正的失败者。因为，很可能，老天爷的手里，根本就没有什么狗屁的底牌。人输给谁都可以，就是不可以输给自己的恐惧。因为，很有可能，这恐惧，只是一场子虚乌有的闹剧。

到吃晚饭时，自己乱七八糟的心情才算是重新又被自己理出了一个头绪来。还是依然当作无事发生吧，或者只是发生了一些与己无关的事。原来该怎样继续，就还是怎样继续。走一步看一步吧。就算明天自己会被关进监狱，今天，也还是先让自己饱尝了幸福再说。古人怎么说的？今朝有酒今朝醉，明日愁来明日愁。

晚饭后，自己心情已定，便与丽云一起出去散了一会儿步。自己跟丽云说了一会儿唐诗宋词、文人命运后，心情愈发明朗了起来。看那暮色渐浓，余晖绰约，自己甚至还朗诵了一首自己年轻时所写的婉约词。丽云倾慕，自己倍觉快乐。只是，街上那一面面的青天白日满地红旗，在暮光之中显得有些阴瘆瘆。每当自己谈至兴浓之时，心中便会蹦出一截模棱两可的心惊肉跳来，使自己的欢畅不能真正彻底地欢畅。现在想来，自己还真是有做小丑的天赋。

直到一个人睡至炕上，那短暂的快乐才褪去了它虚妄的外衣，露出了内里的悸动不堪来。怎么办，依然是自己不能摆脱的问题。自己被这个问题折磨得疲惫不堪。昏昏然，又心碎难医。

半夜里，自己又觉得愧对丽云。丽云以前的那个丈夫，是个伪装成正人君子的嫖客、赌棍，其实，自己又何尝不是这样的一个可恨无耻的人呢？自己也是个嫖客、赌棍，而且还是个通过匪的通缉犯，却一直在她的面前装成是一个文武双全的留学生，这，不是比她以前的那个丈夫还要可恶与可恨吗？自己不是个混蛋是什么？自己不是个杀千刀的是什么？自己从炕上坐了起来。自己是在骗丽云吗？自己是个混蛋吗？这样下去，结局会是什么？真相对于丽云来说，会意味着什么呢？自己到底该怎么办？

太多的纷扰、纠缠都聚集在了一起，让这个夜变得沉重黏稠。不断的恐惧与忧虑重叠在一起，让自己头痛欲裂，更有那愧疚与爱恋在搏斗，让自己不知该何去何从。黑夜是那样深沉而广阔，似乎可以将一切彻底吞没、销

蚀。而这被吞没、销蚀的痛苦滋味，又只是专为那些在夜里不能成寐的人们所特地准备。被黑暗吞到了肚子里，整个人也就像是成了这夜与黑的一部分。自己可以在这黑暗里游泳，可以在这痛苦里呼吸，却绝不可能逃出这绝望的牢笼去。只能等着被那黑暗的汁液所浸透、再浸透，直到看见自己皮腐肉蚀，露出死亡的白骨，却还只能是在这销人性命的痛苦里无助地摸索，或麻木地大笑，甚至连那带着些体温的眼泪，都只是一种奢侈。自己不想做坏人，却已经是个坏人；自己爱丽云，却不能告诉她，自己其实，真的不是一个好人。这就是欲哭无泪的感觉，这就是被黑暗嚼烂的感觉。夜，却还是那样深浓、凛冽。而眼泪，除了可以暖一暖哭泣者自己冰凉的脸，从来，就不能改变任何事情。当黑夜结束，黎明升起，所有的痛苦、绝望，只会走向更激烈的纠缠，而并没有消融，更没有消失。一切美好的事物，都只是空幻的想象。这想象，可怜，又可悲，无助，也无益。一切浪漫的希望，都只是徒劳的挣扎。这挣扎，温暖，又冰凉，欢笑，又悲泣。这便是哀伤的人生，人生的哀伤。

活着真好，却又叫人怎样才能好好地活下去？

天又亮了，人生还在继续。

洗漱完毕，穿戴整齐，自己在临窗的光亮里坐了一会儿。那阳光真好，美得似梦，美得似幻。也许，在上帝面前扮演着小丑角色的，不光是只有自己一个人。每一个对命运有着苦苦乞求的人，都只是上帝看台上的一个木偶。上帝看得高兴了，就会赏你一块糖，不高兴了，就会抽你一鞭子。人们可以拿起武器，推翻皇帝，可是人们又可以用什么，来推翻那操纵命运的上帝？不可能，不可能。一个人到底要怎样，才能将自己的命运掌握在自己手中？一个人到底要怎样，才能不用活得那么荒诞、那么可笑？一个人到底要怎样，才能拥有自己想要的幸福？这世上的许多幸福，其实就和这阳光一样，看起来近在咫尺，看清了，才发现远在天涯。最痴心的是夸父，追着那永不可能追到的太阳，一直追到了死。命运哪命运，你到底是怎样的一个恶魔？你凭什么可以对人随意生杀予夺？你凭什么可以将人玩弄于股掌之间？你到底是什么？

你到底是什么。

自己闭上眼，让阳光吸干了自己眼角的泪湿。自己站起身，走出了屋子。

上午，丽云去了公司，办妥了新聘日语翻译的各项事务。中午，丽云回来，很高兴地告诉自己，说，大家都同意，要给翻译高一些的工资，他们都说了，要给翻译多一些钱，这样翻译才不会胳膊肘往外拐，去当汉奸。说完，她不禁哈哈大笑。自己也笑了，笑完，自己说，我背叛谁都可以，但一定不会背叛你。她忍住笑，问，真的？自己看着她，说，如果有一天，人们看见我当了汉奸，那么，我也一定是想要为了替你做什么事，才去当的假汉奸。她就说，不要，你替我去做什么都可以，就是不要替我去做汉奸，假的也不可以，不然，我开除你。说完，她又笑了。自己就也忍不住笑。自己说，好，我答应你，这辈子，死也不会当汉奸。她和自己，一起忍俊不禁地大笑了起来。

下午，阳光很温暖。丽云没有再去公司。天蓝得鲜艳，没有风。蔡嫂从地窖里拿出了一些苹果来。明亮而橙黄的日光洒在院子里，洒在屋顶上，从窗口和门口照进屋子里。自己和丽云坐在屋子里，时而闲谈，时而静笑。时钟的指针虽然依旧在走，但是，时间仿佛已不再往前流淌。静静的欢乐在凝滞中沉淀，默默的幸福在不语中浓烈。这真是一种很奇妙很美妙的感觉。谁也没有诉说过或者暗示过爱情，可是，爱情，却仿佛就站在这里，右手牵着她，左手牵着自己。

昨天下午，丽云去给自己买了一些要换洗的衣物回来，但是自己昨天心里一直很乱，就也没有多在意这些事情。当时，甚至连谢谢都说得很马虎。今天想想，心中十分愧疚。自己没有珍惜好丽云付给自己的每一分热情，自己觉得很对不起她，就好像，自己并没有做到某种爱的承诺一样。这种感觉有些揪心。这种感觉，不痴不傻的人不能明白。自己很想重新跟她说声谢谢，可是那样又太婆婆妈妈，非男子汉大丈夫所为。于是，自己一时心血来潮，干脆就拿起了桌上的一只苹果，说，我给你削一只苹果吧。

她说，不用，我自己来，可自己还是削了起来，削得很认真，也削得很精妙。小小的水果刀在自己的手里，就像是长在自己手掌上的一根手指那样灵活。削下来的苹果皮又细又长，连绵不断，整只苹果都削完了，这条苹果皮也没断过一次，就像一根长长的绳子。丽云简直惊叹了。

自己将削好的苹果放到了她的手里。

“你削苹果的手法真好，我就不行。”

“多练练就行了。”

“嘿嘿，我在家里一直不动手的。”

“看来你是女中君子。”

“君子不器嘛。”

两个人就都吃吃地笑了，笑得很有默契，就好像这默契本身也很值得让人笑一样，快乐有些无边无际。“谢谢！”她说。“不用谢。”自己说。她就笑着，吃起了苹果，她说：“真甜。”她说：“你以后，也要教我削苹果，让我像你一样厉害。”自己就说，好，以后我教你。她开心地吃着苹果，脸也像苹果一样，微微地红红着。

她和自己说了一些她小时候的事情。她说，她小时候养过一只小兔子，那只小兔子特别可爱，雪白雪白的，叫它也能听懂，吃起东西来特别好玩。她找不到小朋友一起玩时，就会和它相伴在一起，和它说话，和它游戏。可是，后来它却生了病，怎么治也治不好，它再吃不进东西，最后，还是死掉了。它死的那一天，她哭了整整一天，只觉得，她最好的朋友不在了。以后再只剩下她一个人的时候，她就真的只能是孤独地一个人待着了。她将它安葬在了一片小树林里，孤独时，便会去它的坟前待一会儿，就好像它还没有离开她一样。可是后来，这个坟，又被什么野兽给刨掉了。这只可怜的小兔子，最后落了个尸骨无存。发现小兔子的坟被刨掉的那一天，她在小树林里大喊、大哭、奔跑，像疯了一样。那天，她在树林里许愿，下辈子，一定也要做一只小兔子，这样，就可以永远和它在一起开心地玩耍了。说完，她笑了笑，看着空荡处，像是自言自语地说，我是不是很傻。

其实，人长大了，就是要和孤独做朋友的。自己说。

可是，我却总希望，在我孤独时，可以有一个好朋友，能够替我赶走孤独。她痴痴地说。

这就说明，你还没有长大呢。自己说。

她就笑了。笑了一会儿，她就安静地沉默了。

自己看着空荡处，说，以后，你孤独时，我会陪着你的。

静静的，从窗外照进来的阳光很温柔，很温暖。清澈的金色，像微燃的火焰，像丰收的玉米；纯净的光华，像宁静的溪流，像睡着的时间。空气中仿佛氤氲着一股芬芳，带着淡淡的茉莉花香。纤细的忧伤，仿佛暂时都站到了远处，只留下一些空灵的回响，在空荡处脆弱而美丽地跳动，宛如有看不见的天使在舞。没有风，没有冷，静静的两个人，静静地相视而笑。那笑里，都满含着没有忧伤的天真，没有风雪的温暖。那笑，是那样永远，又那样短暂。窗外晴朗的阳光里，还有鸟啼声声，那叽叽喳喳里，似乎也饱含了蓬勃的喜悦。一切，都是那样美好、满足、快乐。

夜晚又一次来临。睡在炕上，自己忽然又有了忧虑，那潘兆的事情怎么办？

她还从未真的和自己说起过她和潘兆的事情，为什么？是她不想，不敢，还是不知究竟该怎样去说？就像自己不想、不敢、更不知究竟该怎样去问一样？她爱潘兆吗？她爱赵驹吗？如果她不爱潘兆，那么，接下来，她还会继续和潘兆走向婚姻殿堂吗？那么，自己算什么？自己接下来，又到底该和她何去何从？人生就像是一个充满谜题的无边丛林，千辛万苦地走过了这一片，却还有更让人头痛欲裂的另一片。忧虑和忧伤从来就不会轻易放过可怜的人类。似乎在上帝看来，只有让人类永远沉陷在痛苦、无尽而又可笑的思索中，这个世界才会不那么萧索和寂寞。在本该安睡的夜晚，却又突然想起了这些令人不愉快的问题，自己真是感到十分懊恼。时间还有很多，也许，以后的事情，应该以后再想才对，自己对自己说。

十二月三十一日，一九二八年的最后一天。上午，丽云带自己去店里，给自己买了一块男式手表。这块手表很精美，但也很昂贵。自己深感惶恐，不敢接受。可是丽云却说，你救了我，我买一块手表给你，这有什么过分的，难道我的命还没这块手表值钱？自己一时无言以对，她就笑着，给自己戴上了这块手表。戴好后，她调皮地将她戴表的那只手举起来，和自己戴表的这只手并排放在一起，开心地说：看，多配！说完，她哈哈大笑。自己也笑了，觉得，心里很幸福。

兴高采烈地和她一起到处玩了一会儿。明天就是元旦了，新的一年就要到来了，人们似乎都笑得特别灿烂。生活仿佛充满了希望。有孩子在玩爆竹，嘭的一声，将自己和她吓了一跳。之后，自己和她笑得更无拘无束了。真的是好像有许许多多的快乐，挥霍不尽的开心。生命，真的好像是怒放的花朵一样。喜悦无边无际，无穷无尽，就好像，只要和她在一起，快乐，就

是全世界，甚至，就连那满大街上猎猎飘扬着的青天白日满地红旗，都已再不能损伤自己分毫的喜悦。狗屁的国旗，狗屁的统一，只要可以和她在一起，管他三七二十一！什么恐惧，什么忧虑，只要能看见她的笑，自己天不怕地不怕！

自己快乐得在街上奔跑了起来。停下来，回转身，看着已在远处的她，她美得宛如旷野中的一枝玫瑰。她欢笑着向自己挥手，自己就又向她奔跑了过去。那，真是自己人生中最难忘的欢乐记忆。这记忆，像锋刃一样不可触碰。

中午，回到庄府时，蔡嫂已将府里的那些破旧红灯笼全部换了下来，换了崭新的上去。红艳艳的一片又一片，喜气洋洋，亮亮堂堂。整个庄府，都仿佛焕然一新了。

午后，天气却渐渐阴沉了起来。天空的蔚蓝在慢慢退却，一层粗糙灰白的阴暗，已爬上了原本光滑如镜的穹顶。橙黄的阳光在悄悄消隐，原本在地上黑得分外显明的人影，已渐渐黯淡地模糊了与周边无影处的界限。起风了，热烈的温暖正在被渐起的阴冷取代。灰蒙蒙的风呼，又在张扬冬的冷郁。蔡嫂说，怕是又要下雪了。

因为是这一年的最后一天了，所以午饭后，丽云给府里的每个下人发了十块大洋的赏钱。下人们都乐坏了，丽云也高兴。昨天丽云已经吩咐了厨房，今天晚上要做一只烤全羊，这会儿，她又吩咐下去，要厨房好好多准备些菜，今天晚上开两桌，庄府上下，不分主仆，都在一起吃。大家都快乐极了。蔡嫂高兴地说，小姐已经有好多年没这样开心过了。

丽云安排完了家里的事情，又拉着自己出去，买了好多爆竹回来。她兴高采烈地说，晚上我和你一起放爆竹玩，我们一起看烟花！

自己快乐得只是笑，幸福得只是笑，却没注意到，那广袤的天空中，已经布满了严严实实的乌云，泛满了灰黑茫茫的阴冷。风呼啸得紧，满大街的青天白日满地红旗，在迎风招展。

谭叔匆匆地跑了过来，告诉丽云，有电话找她。于是，她就去堂屋里接电话了。自己站在原处等她，可是等了好久，她却还是没有回来。自己便有了些疑惑。她和自己正在说的话还没有说完，按理说，她接完了电话以后，还会回到自己的身边来的，可是，她却一直没来。难道，那通电话讲了这么长时间还没讲完？她是怎么了？

自己又在原处等了一段时间。那些喜气洋洋的崭新红灯笼，在风中，飘摇而晃荡。

自己去了堂屋，堂屋里空无一人。电话机也是安稳地放着。自己伸手去摸了摸电话机话筒的把手，把手冰凉冰凉的。自己皱起了眉头。

恰好蔡嫂走过，自己就问了问蔡嫂。蔡嫂说，小姐接完电话后，就一个人回到了她住的屋子里去，看样子，是闷闷不乐的。

自己走到了丽云的屋门前，屋门是紧闭的。自己抬起手，想敲门，犹豫了一下，又垂下了手。自己是什么身份呢？有什么理由去问人家的事情？自己和她是什么关系呢？有什么理由可以去关心她？在这些问题都得到正确解答之前，自己又有什么理由可以去敲她的屋门？

时间无限沉闷，空间无尽压抑。冬天的风，又冷又硬。

她却开了门。蓦然相对，都很意外。隐秘的慌乱里，自己正想找些话出来说，却在无意间，瞥见了，丽云的手上，戴上了一枚戒指。自己呆呆地，看清楚了，这，正是潘兆送给她的那一枚订婚戒指。

她登时有些尴尬地，将手藏到了背后。

“正想去找你……你……进来坐一会儿吧。”她勉强地笑着，说。

“哦，我……是……”自己想编个恰好路过的谎，却竟然，一时语塞了。素来巧舌如簧的自己，竟然死死地语塞了。自己心乱如麻地看了她一眼，发现她也在看自己，自己莫名其妙地，就脸红了起来。

“进来坐吧。”她又说。

直到坐下来，两个人还一时都是无话。这种感觉很奇怪，就好像两个原本最亲密的人，忽然又变成了刚刚相识的陌生人。是什么在作祟呢？是那个奇怪的电话，还是这枚耀眼的戒指？是自己在贪求什么，还是她在害怕什么？

她给自己倒了一杯水，放下茶杯，她就又忙将手缩了回去。自己眼睛故意看向别处，装作没在意那枚光芒晶闪的戒指。自己不知如何是好地喝了一口水，却又被水呛得咳嗽了起来。自己预感到，自己又要开始走霉运了。

没了金黄的阳光，屋里的光线有些暗，光亮惨白惨白的，灰蒙蒙，像飘扬着尘埃，像沉浸在傍晚。安静是依旧的安静，那些一直都在的快乐，

却已杳无踪迹，仿佛从未来过。细碎的纷乱在心上不断碾过，淡淡的无措于没有表情中膨胀。尴尬像一杯被打翻了的水，大家都看着它，却也对它无可奈何。

“我……看你一直没有过来，所以……就想来看看你。”

“哦……我本来……也要去找你了。”

“哦……”

“……”

“……他……对你好吗？”

“……你……都知道了？”

“……在报纸上，我看到过这枚戒指。”

“……报纸……呵……是啊……报纸上都有的。”

“……在西饼店外，我看到过他的。”

“嗯……是啊……呵……”

“……”

“……知道吗，原本……我以为……我们可以一直不用提到他的。可是……呵……他就是我的未婚夫。这一点，谁也改变不了……我骗了你，赵驹……”

“不，你没骗我，我什么都知道……”

“……”

“……既然……你不喜欢这枚戒指，今天……为什么又要戴上它？”

“……刚才那个电话，是他打来的。他要我今晚陪他参加迎新舞会。”

“哦……”

“……”

“……你从一开始，就不该选择他。”

“……他追求我很久了，本来，我一直不想接受他……直到有一天，我在家里前面的院子里，捡到了一封好心人丢进来的信。信上说，日本人和樱花会社，想要吞掉我们庄家的产业，好心人要我们千万小心。——日本人的企图，我们又怎么会不知道呢，可是，我真的是没有本事，没有本事……我什么都不会，好多事情根本就做不好，而那些看着我长大的叔叔伯伯们，也根本就不肯帮我……我是一个没用的人，我对不起父亲……后来，潘兆对我说，只要我嫁进了潘家，那么，往后庄家的事就是潘家的事，而潘家的事，就是整个奉天华商会的事。潘兆说，日本人可以吞掉庄家，但是，日本人可以吞掉整个奉天华商会吗？……于是，我就答应了潘兆。我这一辈子，从来没有为家里做过什么有用的事，可是，我绝不能看着我们庄家几代人的心血，就这样毁在我的手里……赵驹，你能明白吗……啊……”

“……丽云……你不要哭……”

“……”

“……”

“……你……叫我什么？”

“……我……我……”

“……你以后……就这样叫我……”

“……”

“……要是……要是我不嫁给潘兆……那你……你可以保护我们吗？”

“……”

“……告诉我……”

“……我……我不知道……”

“……”

“……不知道——”

哽咽着，自己的泪水，几乎夺眶而出。到这一刻，自己才突然是痛彻灵魂地懂得了父亲一生的疼痛与彻悟：一介武夫，纵然打遍天下无敌手，在这大时代的狂风恶浪面前，又真的可以保护得了谁？在这个世上，唯一能战胜枪和子弹的，只有权与势！而要得到权与势，只有成为状元之才、人中龙凤！那一刻，自己痛不欲生。那一刻，自己是真想跪在父亲的面前，让父亲狠狠地打上一百个耳光。可是，再不可能了，再不可能了。时光已逝，自己没有好好读书，没有珍惜年轻时上进的机会，现在，自己会武功了，会自己儿时梦寐以求的武功了，可是有个屁用！自己能保护丽云吗？自己能保护庄家吗？别做梦了，日本人有枪！自己要是一早听了父亲的话，好好念书，好好做官，现在在蒋介石的身边捞了个一官半职，带上了几班党政军警的亲信，看他狗屁的樱花会社敢对你怎么样！看他狗屁的日本人敢不敢对着你举起枪！看还有谁敢伤害丽云、伤害庄家！可是，现在，这些已经全都是屁话

了。全都是屁话了！

武夫无用！武夫无用！

可惜，丽云却还不明白。

而最荒唐的，就是自己写了那封该死的告诫信。原来，是那封信，将丽云往火坑里推了一把。原来，是自己，将丽云推到了潘兆的怀里。命运，是多么的奇妙，是多么他妈的奇妙！除了欲哭无泪，自己又还能做什么？

而丽云还什么都不知道。

天是那样暗沉，暗沉是那样辽阔。在这一个残酷的生死时代，芸芸众生的悲喜与血泪，对老天来说又算得了什么呢？这个世上，最无情的便是天与地。不，天与地，原本便是无情物，只是有太多的痴人，一直在以为，头顶三尺有神明，神明心中存怜悯。而这个世上，其实根本就没有什么神。是时代在主宰着众生，而又是军阀和党棍，在主宰着这个时代。若中国自强，自己和丽云，又怎会被局势逼到这个地步？可恨，可恨！这一个黑暗的大时代，究竟要肆虐到何时才能结束！

灰灰暗暗的屋子里，只有丽云的泪和那枚订婚戒指，在晶莹地闪亮。

“……晚上……几点钟回来？”

“……不知道……可能会很晚吧……”

“……其实……你想过没有，也许在你父母的心中，只有你的幸福，才是最重要的……”

“……呵……如果庄家倒了，日本人会放过我们一家吗……”

“……”

“……其实，我想过的，以你的才学和本事，只要给你一个起点，假以时日，你是一定能做出一番大事业来的，到那时，你就可以保护我了……你说……是这样吗……”

“……丽云……”

“……”

“……”

“……好啦，我们为什么要这样子呢……我只是去参加一个舞会呀，呵呵……新年了，我们都要高高兴兴的……以后的事，就以后再说吧……呵……”

“嗯。”

“晚上，等我回来了，你还要陪我一起去放爆竹、看烟花——”

“好。”

“明天一早，我们一起去上班。”

“嗯。”

“呵呵，这就对啦，今天我不该掉眼泪的，是我把开心的事情忘掉啦……我相信，只要诚心诚意地去向老天许愿，老天是一定会让人的心愿成真的。”

“你许什么心愿啦？”

“不告诉你——”

丽云擦去了眼泪，重新又高兴了起来。真好。她就像是一个还没长大的孩子，如果生活在一个美好的年代，她该会有多幸福。天空是那样辽阔，苍白也是那样辽阔，如果老天有情，希望老天也能听到这人间的天真与美好。

时光默默流走，安静地伴坐相守，只渴望天长地久。细语轻轻漂流，没有彼岸的此在，只仿佛海枯石烂。世界从世界中隐退，浪漫于浪漫中宝贵。天涯海角太远，能够和她在一起的地方，就是最美好的世外桃源。屋里亮起了灯，灯光橙黄清亮，分外可人。

而窗外天光渐暮，苍白愈加暗淡。

“赵驹，江南漂亮吗？”

“人人尽说江南好，游人只合江南老。春水碧于天，画船听雨眠。垆边人似月，皓腕凝霜雪。未老莫还乡，还乡须断肠。”

“以后要是有机会，你带我去江南玩。”

“好哇。”

“一言为定。”

“一言为定。”

“呵呵——”

风声呜呜，如泣如诉。

丽云上了车，走了。

晚上，大家聚在一起吃了一顿饭，都觉得挺高兴。只是，庄老爷依旧卧病在床，而丽云又不在，大家再怎么自娱自乐，也赶不走那暗涌着的一股

忧郁，笼罩在庄府上空的一股忧郁。庄太太虽然看上去也挺喜气，但终究掩不住脸上落寞哀伤的神情。旧的一年就要过去了，新的一年就要来临了，明年，庄家又会走上一条什么样的道路？

庄府里挂着的红灯笼，全部被点亮了。这些灯笼全是新的，红得那么清澈，红得那么干净。看着那一盏盏被点亮的红灯笼，甚至能闻到一阵扑鼻而来的新年味道，新的气味。风虽然没停，凛冽得紧，但，终究能感到，这里有一片暖意。

酒过三巡，歌唱三遍，大家最后都尽兴而散了。那只烤全羊，自己心里知道，是丽云特地为自己准备的，就因为自己当时跟她说了那一句玩笑话。可是，到头来，自己却一口也没能吃得下。晚宴上，自己只喝了两壶酒，其他的什么也没能吃得下。自己的脸虽然一直是笑着的，自己的嘴里虽然一直都是在说着些快乐的话，但是自己的胸口里，始终酸痛得难受。这种难受是实在的，不是譬喻，不是抽象，而真的就是心如刀绞，但没有眼泪。真的好难受，结结实实的酸痛。席间越热闹，心里越难受。只要一想到丽云，就像是有人在往自己心口捅刀子，而坐在庄府里，又到处是丽云的幻影。丽云，丽云。

丽云不在的时间里，不，应该说，丽云在潘兆那里的时间里，自己失魂落魄，心碎如渣。而这种痛苦越猛烈，自己越需要装得兴高采烈。不然，难道要叫所有人来看笑话？一个叫花子，已经一朝翻身成为公司职员、小姐亲信，难道，还真的要癞蛤蟆想吃天鹅肉不成？只可惜，酒不够烈。酒若真能如火烈，怕也烧不尽心中凛冽。

自己一个人坐在屋门口外的台阶上。院子里已经静悄悄了。天上没有星星，也没有月亮，只有刺骨的风在吹鼓。已经十点多了，而丽云还没有回来。临走时，谭叔说好这次汽车不会再坏了，所以，自己其实根本就不用担心，但是，自己还是如坐针毡，而转念想想，迎新舞会，不就是应该要过了十二点才结束的吗？

吃屎的潘兆！

一股深深的醋意在自己心里翻搅，让自己原本就很乱的心更乱更难受了几倍。自己没有办法再去想什么事情，只能站起了又坐下，坐下了又站起。远望着安静的大门口，希望能听到外面敲大门的声音。

然而，夜是这样安静，静得沉闷。

只有风，像个爱捣蛋的孩子似的，又在呼呼猛吹。自己看看戴在手腕上的手表，不禁又想起了她可爱的样子。“看，多配！”她开心的模样，真是这世上最美的烟火。人人尽说江南好，其实，最爱的人在哪里，故乡才在哪里。

不得其解的矛盾在自己心里上下浮沉。丽云的意思，是要帮助自己涉足奉天华商界，要自己尽可能迅速地成为一个强大的人物，这样，她就可以不用再依赖潘兆的保护了。她想要自己保护她。她想要的，是一个叫赵驹的男人给她的保护。她说，我相信你一定行的。可是，她想得会不会太简单了呢？自己究竟有多少能力，自己也不敢保证，她现在觉得自己那么好，全是因为自己在她面前吹了不少牛。其实自己在日本根本就没有毕业，其实自己以前一直就是个只会吃喝玩乐的花花公子。她现在把自己看得这样好，自己会不会是在害她？别人欺负她涉世不深也就算了，自己怎么也可以这样糊弄她呢？这不是在害她吗！

可是，自己又真的是想变成一棵可以让她放心依赖的大树。自己想为她遮风挡雨，阻隔刀剑，给她一片纯净而无忧的小天地，让她可以永远天真地在里面自由玩耍，不改童心，不改纯洁。要是可以，自己甚至愿意用自己的生命来保护她，保护她和她的家人。如果可以跟上天要一个恩赐，自己只想恳求，让自己能够保护她一生一世，保护她生生世世。所以，无论如何，自己都是不想放过这次她给自己的机会。谁说自己就一定不行呢？好歹，以前在赵家镇上，除了赵宏伟以外，没有谁的脑子可以和自己相提并论；好歹，自己也算是在黑白两道都混过；好歹，自己也杀过人。谁说，自己就一定不可能在奉天闯出一番天地来呢？为了丽云，也为了自己，自己一定要取代潘兆的位置。对，一定行！

风冷得像冰，站在静夜里，自己的脸冻得有些僵硬，但自己就是不想回屋。她还没有回来，自己在屋里哪能待得住。她还在和潘兆跳舞吗？自己的心，越发烦躁。潘兆会留她过夜吗？自己的心，颤抖不已。空黑而寂冷的时间越是往前延续，自己在往前延续的每一秒钟里，就越是焦躁、痛苦得无边、无底。但对于一切，自己又都无能为力。毕竟，丽云是潘兆的未婚妻，而自己，才刚刚离开叫花子这个行当。这是一种多么刺眼刺心的对比。

丽云说过，今晚，要回来和自己一起放爆竹、看烟花的。自己在心里说。这么一说，自己的心，便好像又温暖了许多。

红亮亮的灯笼在风里飘摇而晃荡。自己看了看表，快十二点了。自己打开了庄府的大门，走到了门外去。

远处有好看的烟花升起。断断续续地，又有一些爆竹声传来。想来，定是也有那不知时代苦闷的孩子，正在欢快地辞旧迎新。辞旧迎新好，毕竟，再过一会儿，就可以告别这烽烟不断的一九二八年了，新的一年来到，希望可以天下太平，国泰民安。

路灯黄黄亮亮。午夜深旷深寒。自己正对丽云牵肠挂肚、担心不已之时，忽然注意到了，这条街上，好像发生了一点小变化。在这条街两边的两排民宅的墙面上，歪歪扭扭而零零散散地贴着许多苍白乌黯的布告，而自己分明记得，傍晚送丽云出门时，那些墙面上，还没有这些膏药。是才贴上去不久吗？是什么紧急重要的告示，需要让人连夜开工张贴？

自己走近了那些布告。路灯的光亮下，布告上的字和画都很清楚。一张张、一张张、一张张，竟然全都是通缉令！全都是南京国民政府发出来的全国通缉令！

天地崩溃。

自己发了疯似的，满大街跑、满大街找。通缉令上通缉的，全是政治犯，有共产党，有国民党左派，还有北洋政府的一些顽固的遗老孤臣，而命运果然没有宽恕自己，果然没有宽恕自己！自己居然也在政治犯之列！

通缉令上说，赵驹，通匪、通共，勾结玉山匪帮，烧杀抢掠，无恶不作，又于北伐革命之时，勾结上海工人纠察队，勾结共产党，在上海残忍杀害了十几名国民党骨干党员，纵火焚烧军需仓库，罪大恶极，人人可得而诛之。悬赏一千块大洋捉拿，死活皆可。

通缉令上，还惟妙惟肖地画了一个自己的头像。他妈的惟妙惟肖！他妈的通匪通共！自己什么时候烧杀抢掠了？自己什么时候勾结工人纠察队和共产党了？那些青帮的臭流氓什么时候成国民党骨干党员了？这个南京国民政府还讲不讲青红皂白了？这个天下到底还讲不讲道理了？自己是通匪了，可从来没跟着土匪去做过一桩恶事；自己是杀人了，可杀的全是死有余辜的青帮流氓！自己早料到会有一些莫须有的罪名要加到自己的头上，可是没想到会加得这样离谱！这样的一个新政府，和以前的旧政府又有什么区别！

不过，捉自己的赏金，倒是提高了许多倍。另外，这通缉令不是江庆县政府发的，而是南京国民政府发的。这两个小小的出乎意料的抬举，是不是说明，在第二次北伐之后，自己这个对党对国来说本来是微不足道的小人物，已经变得越来越值钱、越来越受到国民政府的重视了？

夜的深黑与路灯的亮黄缠绕在一起，冷酷而迷离，孤绝而彷徨。站在光亮里，看着黑的无边，听着风的厉呼，感觉黑夜即将把自己吞没。那既没星星更没月亮的铁硬天空中，像是布满了细细而尖利的牙齿，恐怖而鲜血淋漓。站在黑暗中，触摸那路灯光照到的地方，像是暖暖的，其实冰冷冰硬。风鬼哭狼嚎地吹，有光有暖的地方，像是一个永远也驶达不了的苍茫彼岸。在暗与亮的交错里、在黑与光的模糊中，青天白日满地红旗，依旧在冰冷刺骨的风中猎猎张扬。国旗下，黑与白的寒冬里，是一张又一张的通缉令。杀无赦的通缉令，政治清算的通缉令，血流成河的通缉令。

“嘭——嘭——嘭——”

远方深沉无尽的天空中，绽放出了瑰丽的烟花朵朵。缤纷得眼花缭乱，绚烂得如梦似幻。火花红艳，光焰璀璨。自己看了一眼手表，正好，刚过十二点钟。是新年了。终于是到新的一年了。

终于，是到新的一年了。

滚烫的泪水，在自己脸上恣肆地奔流。痛彻心扉的灭亡，将自己全身的血液冰固。当痛热与死冷缠住，自己的心脏，宛如停止了跳动。绝望的血泪一起从心底喷出，自己悲恸得跪倒在了地上。

“嘭、嘭——”新年的烟火，依然在喜悦地绽放。

一张，又一张，自己发了疯似的，撕剥着墙上的通缉令。自己彻底疯狂地，撕剥撕毁着墙上的全部通缉令！

狗屁的通缉令！

狗屁的蒋介石！

狗屁的国民政府！

狗屁的疯狂年代！

自己的指甲缝里，已经滴出了血来，但是自己一点也没感觉到痛。自己只想撕，只想撕！撕光这些魔鬼的快乐，撕光这些地狱的歌唱！自己疯狂地

在墙上撕剥，撕剥，再撕剥！自己要让所有的荒诞、所有的不合理，统统去见鬼！见鬼！让这个腐烂的时代和这个腐烂的政府，一起去灭亡！灭亡！

自己指尖的血，划满了墙壁，划满了通缉令。夜，黑得像墨；光，那么刺眼；冷，坚如磐石。自己还在撕，还在剥。贴得可真他妈的牢。

可是，撕完了这条街上的通缉令，还要去撕下一条街吗？撕完了下一条街，还要去撕再下一条街吗？能撕光这全奉天市的通缉令吗？能撕光那发到全中国去的通缉令吗？不可能，不可能，不可能！

从国民政府为自己定罪开始，自己就已无路可逃。从蒋介石天下无敌的那一刻起，自己就已迈进了死亡。从自己踏上逃亡之路的那一天起，自己就不该再心存希望。

结束了，一切，全结束了。

只是，今天是元旦。本来，今天，该是自己第一天正式去丽云的公司里上班的日子。

现在，全结束了。

苍天，从来不会有情。命运，从来不懂怜悯。

自己将满怀的碎纸抛上了天。被撕碎了的通缉令，漫天飞舞，纷纷扬扬，像下雪，像飘絮，像有人在哭。

而远方，依旧有烟火在灿烂，美如山花开遍，美如浪漫笑靥。

屋子里，亮光浅浅，暖意融融。

自己已经脱下了丽云买给自己的全部衣物，将它们整整齐齐地放在了这间屋子里的炕上。自己重新又穿上了那身原本就应该是与自己相般配的叫花子衣服，自己重新又穿上了破破烂烂的草鞋。站在镜子前一看，就是头发太短了一些。想想真是可笑，几天前，自己才在镜子面前找回那个光鲜的自己，现在，自己在镜子面前又变回了这个不堪的自己，人生真是充满了可怕的玩笑，镜子真是一种可悲的道具。从王子变成青蛙，是坚不可摧的现实；而从青蛙变成王子，却只是一戳即破的泡影。命运就是这样，坏的事情永远无法改变，好的事情却永远只是昙花一现。自己这几天却居然还这么蠢，以为自己是迎来了上帝的宽恕，受到了命运的馈赠。原来，给你一个梦，只是为了让你醒来更痛。

庄府外面的那条街上，捉拿自己的通缉令一共贴了五张，自己剥了一张完整的下来，是想留给丽云。自己不想欺骗丽云，也不想她从别人嘴里知道自己离去的原因。自己希望自己的不辞而别，能以这张自己留下来的通缉令，作为一个清楚明白的结束。也许，只有这样，才会对她更好。也许，也许吧。

自己端端正正地，将这张通缉令放在了自己叠好的衣服上，然后，便想转身离开了。可是，自己还没转身，背后就传来了她惊讶的一声呼唤："赵驹——"

蓦然回首，只见，不知何时，她已是站在了这间屋子的门口。

无声无息，空空落落。敞开的门口处，虚廓的灯影与迷离的黑夜相浸透，纠缠出一片碎乱而凝固的萧索。她就站在那萧索里，惊讶得目瞪口呆地看着自己。"你这是做什么？"她不知所措地问。

她跑到了自己的面前，不知所措地问："你这是做什么？"

看着近在眼前的她，自己忽然才发现，她左边的脸有些红。不，不对，不是红。这，分明是一个巴掌印！

自己顿时急火攻心，忘记了其他一切地，连忙问她："你脸怎么了？"

她一愣神，忽然才反应了过来，像是意识到了什么。她赶紧一手捂住了她的左脸，急忙转开了身去，支支吾吾地说，是在路上不小心摔了一跤。

就是在路上不小心摔了一跤，真的。她面对着墙壁，哆哆嗦嗦地说。

她的样子，痛苦而恐惧，无助而脆弱。自己的心尖，像被人狠狠剜了两刀。

自己伸出手，轻轻地，想将她扳转过来，让她面对着自己。可是，却猛然重新看见并惊醒：自己身上穿着的，已是乞丐衣服。

已是乞丐衣服。

自己的手，像迅速枯死的树枝一样，僵住了。那些冲动的想要给予，全都化作了清醒的想要逃走。在还没有真的触碰到她的肩膀之前，自己，缩回了手，放下了手。她，似乎什么也没有察觉。似乎。

她不看着自己，自己也不看着她。两个人都一动不动，也不说话。屋里静悄悄的，默然如死。自己想要开口，却如鲠在喉，不能出声。她和自己的影子，在浅浅的灯光下，黑得像夜一样深沉无底。仿佛两条可以将夜吞没的深渊。这两条深渊，看似全都岿然不动着，可是，又全都像在剧烈颤抖着。

颤抖得夜都像在摇晃，颤抖得泪全像在瓢泼。

“你……你为什么要穿成这个样子？”

“……我……要走了。”

“什么？”

“……我要走了……离开这里了……我……辜负了你的好意……对不起。”

她面对着自己，惊愕得瞪大了眼睛。“为什么？究竟发生了什么？”

自己畏惧地避开了她的目光，心头火辣辣的，无法回答。时间像在往地心里沉沦，黑夜像在往心口里贯穿。

她看见了自己身后叠放着的那摞衣服，还有，最重要的，放在衣服上的那张折起的大纸。“这张是什么？”她疑惑地指了指，问。

自己无颜回答。

她走到了炕前，自己的身边，拿起了那张就在自己身后炕上的大纸。她的长发擦过了自己的肩膀，自己刹那心酸得无以复加。自己故意走开了两步，站得离她远了一些。她讶然而困惑地转头看着自己，眼神痛苦而凄怨地瑟缩了一下。

自己闭上了眼睛。

自己听见了她打开大纸的声音。安静是那么恐怖，无声是那样紧绷。自己垂着头，还是不敢睁开眼睛，就怕一睁开眼，眼泪会掉出来。

灭亡着等待，等待着灭亡。

睁开眼时，看到的，只是泪流满面的她。

“这……这……这上面说的……说的……是不是真的——”

“……有些是真的，有些是假的……”

“……哪些是真的？哪些是假的？”

“我帮土匪买过军火，卖过珠宝，但是我从来没有做过烧杀抢掠的事。我在上海杀过人，可我杀的全是青帮流氓，不是国民党党员。另外，我也根本就不认识什么共产党。就是这样。”

“……你……你以前为什么从来没有告诉过我这些……”

“……我不是一个好人……对不起……”

“……我……我还可不可以相信你……”

“……是我欺骗了你……真的对不起……”

“……怎么会这样……怎么会这样……”

“……对不起……真的对不起……”

“……为什么……”

她绝望而颤抖地哭泣着，跌坐在了椅子上。冷酷而血腥的通缉令从她手中黯然飘落，落在地上，白得像雪，轻得像泪。她低头垂泪，自己无言以对。

“……我……不会连累你们庄家的……我马上就走——”

“不——你别走——”

“……”

“……你别走……我去想想办法，看能不能找人，帮忙撤销你的通缉令——”

“不，你不要做傻事，我现在不是普通的杀人犯，而是政治犯，你若帮我，只会惹祸上身。”

“不，我一定要救你！”

“不要，你听我说，听我说——他们现在给我定的罪是通匪通共，通匪通共，重点就在这通共上！蒋介石和汪精卫早就表示过，对待共产党，是宁可错杀三千、不可放过一个，谁要是有了通共的嫌疑，那就是必死的罪！你现在若去给我求情，岂不是也会惹上通共的嫌疑？那些想害你们庄家的人，正好可以落井下石。——所以，你不可以做这种傻事，绝不可以！”

“可是，政府总要讲道理，只要你没做过，总应该能把事情和他们讲清楚，难道只能任他们冤枉——”

“你太天真了，这本来就不是一个可以讲道理的时代。蒋介石靠什么得的权？就是廖仲恺被刺事件和中山舰事件。廖仲恺有什么罪？就是坚持联俄联共。中山舰事件的核心是什么？就是栽赃冤枉。这样一个以耍阴谋为能事的蒋介石所组织起来的以他为首脑的政府，能和老百姓讲什么道理？青帮的几个老大，全是蒋介石的亲信，我杀了青帮流氓，可不就等于是杀了他的国民党党员吗？你说这道理能怎么讲。这个年代，就是杀人犯好救，政治犯难赦，流氓可登天，英雄最低贱。”

她默默地流着泪，瘦弱的影子投在地上，在不停地瑟瑟发抖。一切都像

是凝固着的，除了泪水。自己觉得是时候该走了，趁着心里的意志还坚定，趁着那被压抑的脆弱还没有起来反抗。是时候该走了。

“……你别走——”她却幽幽地，只是哭着说了一句。

自己笑了笑，又笑了笑，只能猛地背转过了身，不能再面对着她。

心里的酸痛全在上冲，眼睛里再控制不住湿润。何曾想走？何曾想走？只是这个时代，这个黑白颠倒的生死时代，不让自己留下！

泪水奔涌而出，自己用衣袖抹着泪水。自己已经穿上了乞丐的衣服，已经是穿上了乞丐的衣服哇！

“我……我不会被他们抓到的……你放心，我不会被他们抓到的……我会躲好的，你放心……”

“不要走——”她哭说着，站起来跑到了自己的背后。她一下子，紧紧地就抱住了自己。

她哭泣着、颤抖着。自己的心，全都碎了。

“……我可以去求潘兆，他一定可以帮得上你。他认识南京政府的人。”

“不，不要，我不允许你这么做。”

“我一定要救你！”

“我不要！”

“潘兆一定可以救你！只要我求他！”

“我不许你求他！不许！”

“我不要你死！”

自己哭得泪雨滂沱。整个人，都碎成了雪片。纷纷扬扬的雪片。

“……今天，是不是潘兆打了你？”

“……不是，就是我摔跤摔的。”

“摔跤能摔出一个巴掌的形状来吗？”

“……”

“妈的，果然是他！”

“……”

“他为什么打你！”

“……不为什么。”

“他个王八蛋！”

自己分开了丽云从后面抱着自己的两只手，转回了身来，看着她，看着她的脸。她捂着脸，流着泪，转开了身去。自己想抱住她，但是，自己身上的乞丐衣服，再次制止了自己。

时间在空茫的痛苦中流走，泪水滚烫了冰凉，冰凉了又滚烫。循环无尽，悲凉叠加。心口已被千刀洞穿，躯壳只是在哀痛地苟活。真想不再这样悲伤，不再这样痛苦，一死了之，可是，一死，便不能再见到她。人世为何要这样叫人悲欢离合聚散转瞬，红尘为何要给人千般柔情万般爱恋？如果从来没有爱过，又怎会这样撕心裂肺，如果从来没有牵手，又怎会这样百转千回？人间为什么总比地狱更苦，命运为什么总比阎王更可怖？这无尽苍茫的痛呼，又有什么神能听见，那比血还浓的泪水，又有什么主能怜悯？

只有无语相凝噎。

夜，漆黑如墨，深浓如胶。寒冰似铁。

“……丽云，以后……不要再和潘兆在一起了……要保护庄家，总有其他办法的……不要委屈自己……”

“我的办法就是你，可你现在就要走了——”

“我不是你的办法，我就是一个骗子——”

“不，你不是骗子！——你救过我——”

“……其实……我真的没你想得那么好……我不是一个好人——”

“我从来没有把你想成一个圣人，在这个乱世之中，谁的身上又能干干净净的没有一丝污点？我只是真的……真的……真的需要你这个朋友……好朋友……”她转回身来，啜泣着看着自己，“——你要我不要和潘兆在一起，那你还说要走？”

自己忍不住又哭了，哭得很凶。“不是我想走，是我实在不可以留。我若留下，别人就可以诬陷你们庄家是窝藏了通共分子。窝藏通共分子，严重的可以满门抄斩！”

“我不怕！”

“我怕！”

“潘兆他一定有办法帮你洗脱罪名的！”

“你不要去求他！”

“为什么不要！”

“这个世上没有免费的午餐！”

“他不可能要你什么的！”

“他会要你！”

“我愿意！”

“你说什么？”

“只要能救你，我做什么都愿意！”

“……我不愿意……我不愿意！”

“……为什么不愿意？”

“……因为，你是我最好的朋友，最好的朋友。”

自己擦去了自己的眼泪，也擦去了她的眼泪。自己笑了笑，她也笑了笑。都笑得比哭还难看。她说，你是不是觉得我太幼稚？

自己说，不，你是个好人。

她就笑了，带着泪光，笑得挺灿烂。她说，你说过的，以后，我孤独时，你会陪着我的。

自己笑了笑，说，我还答应过你，以后要是有机会，会带你去江南玩。

她痴痴地问，这些话，还都算数吗？

自己忍着哽咽说，算数，等这天下太平了，我来找你。

她“嗯”了一声，点点头，还是撕心裂肺地哭了起来。

自己却还是没有抱她。

自己笑了笑，说，我走了，要不然，等到天亮了，我就真的无处可逃了。

自己走到了屋外，才发现，外面不知从何时起，已是下起了鹅毛大雪。这雪，和自己来庄家的那天晚上下的雪，一模一样。光亮映照着雪花，雪花冰冷着光亮。时间仿佛从未流走，一切，都只是停留在开始的那一刻。时间仿佛从未再走，一切，都只不过是做了一个转瞬即逝的梦。蓦然回首，只是玉人笑靥不见，空留泪痕遍野。

雪，纷纷扬扬，飘飘洒洒。冰冷彻天地，寒风诉凄凉。

自己没有说再见，也没有再看她一眼。自己走入了漫天的风雪之中。风雪迎面扑来，寒彻肌骨，自己却只渴求，让风雪可以来得更猛烈一些，好将自己埋葬，埋葬。

走出了庄家大门，走到了街上，她却追了上来。

“雪这样大——这个，给你——”她含着泪，将一把伞打开，塞到了自己的手里。

正是那把自己在雨中买给她的伞。

大雪在风中狂舞，大风在雪中狂啸。伞下，她泪眼看着自己。

她伸出一只手，指了指远处的一个角落。她含着泪，笑着说，知道吗，你是个笨蛋，其实你每次站在那里看我，等我，我都知道。

说完，她潸然泪下。说完，她便转身，跑入了茫茫的风雪之中。

最后，她又回头看了自己一眼。

她消失在了大门之后。庄府的大门关上了。一切，似乎又都恢复了平静。一切，似乎都从未发生。

只有撑着伞的自己是实在的。只有撑着伞站在风雪之中的自己是实在的。只有撑着伞站在风雪之中悲哭不尽的自己是实在的。只有孤独是实在的，只有绝望是实在的。只有黑暗与悲伤，是永恒的。

天地茫茫，风雪漫漫，血泪斑斑，唯有前面的不平路，还是那样无穷无尽。

自己恨这个时代。

这是一个应该被送进坟墓的时代，这是一个应该被摧毁的时代。

如果有朝一日，共产党能打败蒋介石，自己只希望，蒋介石死无葬身之地。

雪，吹进了自己的眼睛。

回到破庙的时候，天还没有亮。以为弟兄们都熟睡着，自己便轻手轻脚地走路，怕吵醒了他们。沉寂的黑暗里，孔仁却忽然开了口，说，你回来了。自己一怔，还以为他在说梦话。

孔仁起来，点亮了蜡烛。孟义和朱理也都从床上坐了起来。只有黄道是真的在熟睡，结果被孟义给叫醒了。自己看见，在桌上的蜡烛旁边，铺开放着一张破损的大纸。这，正是捉拿自己的通缉令。

一股深刻的疲倦从自己的心底涌了上来，回荡着些许被封抑着的痛苦，自己无力地，吐了一口气，在一张凳子上坐了下来。不想说话，今晚，自己真的不想再说话。

昨天朱理晚上回来得晚，结果，就看见在街上，有警察在贴这个。孔仁说。

没错，这是抓我的通缉令，你们要是把我交出去，就可以领到一千块大洋了，一千块，够你们做点小生意了。自己不冷不热地说。

孟义是个急性子，一下子就火了，一巴掌就拍在了桌子上，说，你不要话里带刺！我们要是真想出卖你，你现在早被警察和特务给抓了！我们就是想知道，通缉令上说你烧杀抢掠、滥杀无辜，这些是不是真的？要是真的，那我们就当是瞎了眼，错认了你这个兄弟！我们和你割袍断义，今后大家分道扬镳、各不相干！

我从没干过烧杀抢掠、滥杀无辜的事，通缉令上说的，全是屁话。

那政府为什么要冤枉你？

我杀过青帮流氓，蒋介石和杜月笙是穿一条裤子的，所以，政府当然要帮青帮缉拿我。

黄道问，你杀过青帮流氓？

是的，我以前告诉过你们，我是因为替父报仇不成，反被县长通缉，所以才逃离的家乡，但是离开家乡后，我又惹上了更大的祸，我在上海被青帮的人当成了工人领袖汪寿华的同党，他们拼了命地追杀我，没办法，我才杀的他们。

孔仁说，这些事，你以前为什么从来不说？

都是伤心事，有什么可说的。

朱理说，你要我们怎么相信你？

我没办法让你们相信我，你们爱信不信。你们要是不信，我可以现在就走，绝不会连累你们半分！

黄道却突然扑通给自己跪下了。大家都愣住了。“兄弟，我信你！你若真杀了青帮流氓，那你便是我黄道这辈子的恩人！”黄道哭了起来，“青帮十恶不赦！他们的人都该下十八层地狱！当年，我只不过就是因为救了一个被他们侮辱的卖花姑娘，打了他们，结果他们就把我的儿子……就把我的儿子给剁成了肉泥……我老婆死得更惨……这群畜生，他们就是死上一百遍都死有余辜！他们的罪，就是用整条黄浦江的水来洗都洗不干净！兄弟，你这不是在杀人，你是在杀鬼！杀掉欺负老百姓的恶鬼！政府不替我们申冤，兄弟，你却替我们报了仇！”

黄道悲痛哭泣地说着，便是要给自己磕头，自己忙上前去扶住了他。“好兄弟，使不得、使不得，你快起来，起来。我没你说的那么好，我当初，也就是为了想要逃命，才迫不得已杀的人，我也不想得罪青帮的人，可是，是他们逼得我要杀人见血。兄弟，你快起来——”

黄道站了起来，擦掉了眼泪，转身对孔仁他们说：“兄弟们，我们沦落到今天这个要饭的地步，有谁不是被这个世道给害的？有谁不是被那些个昏庸的政府给害的？大家想想看，赵驹兄弟和我们在一起这么久了，我们可曾见他做过什么伤天害理的事情没有？他有一身武功，若真是那烧杀抢掠、狼心狗肺之人，又岂能真的和我们一起受这乞讨要饭的苦？他大可以去帮会里做个打手，威风八面，吃香喝辣，哪里还会跟我们来称兄道弟？而那蒋介石，本身就是青帮老大黄金荣的徒弟，那他弄出来的那个什么南京国民政府，又会跟黑帮的总舵有什么太大的区别？这个政府发出来的通缉令，又有什么可相信的？这就是一个黑白颠倒的社会，这就是一个好人受苦的世道！我们的兄弟遇上了危难，我们没有好好地想办法来帮助他，反而还一起怀疑他，我们怎么对得起这庙里的关老爷！”

一片小小的沉默。

黄道拿来了一碗水。“以前，一直没好好地称呼过你三哥，今日起，我和三哥你，真正血脉相连。”说完，黄道用碎碗片在腕上一划，将血滴入了水碗中。

“好，五弟，今日起，我们血脉相连。”自己拿过碎碗片，慷慨一声，也在腕上一划，将血滴入了水碗中。

“三弟，今日是我们不对，我们不该怀疑你，请你切莫放在心上，不要怪罪。”孔仁说完，拿过碎碗片，也在他的腕上一划，然后，将血滴入了水碗中。

“三弟，我脾气躁，你别怪我。”“三哥，刚才的事，对不起了。”孟义和朱理说着，也相继在水碗里滴了血。

一碗鲜红的水里，混合着五个人的血。

“好，那我们就前事不计，一口义气。从今日起，我们五个人，真正血脉相连！”孔仁说完，便是首先端起水碗，喝了一大口血水。“今日一碗红，

明日生死同！”

孟义接过碗，“今日一碗红，明日生死同！”说完，也豪饮了一口血水。

接下来，是自己。然后，是朱理。最后，是黄道。喝完后，黄道将空碗往地上一摔，五个人痛快得一起哈哈大笑。

孔仁说，三弟你放心，我们一定保你周全。

谢谢大哥，谢谢兄弟们。自己说。

天亮时，自己才昏然入睡。睡梦中，自己的头脑里仿佛仍在隐隐作痛，就像一只被摔裂了的西瓜，就算一动不动地安静睡着，冷冷的血还是会往外渗漏。那一觉，自己究竟是宛若梦魇的真的睡着了，还是好似天昏地暗地其实醒着，自己也已弄不清楚。只不过，痛得没有尽头，倦得精疲力竭。好想让自己躲到时间的背后，从这个世上凭空消失。

醒来时，是下午，是元旦这一天的下午。兄弟们都不在破庙里。桌上放着两个馒头和一碗白水。自己吃了一口馒头，觉得不饿，就又把馒头放回了桌上，只喝了一碗水。喝完了水，才觉得自己好像是醒了。醒了。

走出破庙，看见天气很好。雪不知在什么时候停的，西边的太阳鲜艳澄亮，皑皑的白雪覆盖着大地。阳光斜斜而宽阔地映照在雪地上，温暖与洁白相重叠，光明与纯净交辉映，原本是一幅多么美好而圣洁的图景。只可惜，一个罪人站在这幅图景的边境，一段悲伤，在无声处呻吟。真的好煞风景。

自己在雪地里慢慢行走，一步一步地走。穿着草鞋的脚，和雪粒雪水相粘相浸在一起，冷得叫人哆嗦，冷得让人清醒。虚无的空气中，既洋溢着阳光的芳香，也满盈着寒冬的刺鼻。看，那一团一团呼出的热气，像飘扬的白马，像下雨的天堂。惆怅与泪水，完全模糊不清。自己走到了一处阳光很浓积雪很厚的地方，懒懒的躺了下来，仰面朝天地躺着，那种感觉真好。蔚蓝无际的天空近在眼前，铺盖着自己的全身，自己就像是贴在天上的一张纸。而身下的那片雪地，就像是一个根本就不存在着的世界，就像是一个空虚到了极致的泡影，就好像，雪只要轻轻一化，自己就会以这样的一个姿势，立刻掉进传说中万丈地狱。自己的身体在渐渐冰冷，自己的脸庞在渐渐麻木，但是这样真好，自己的心口里烫得难受，只有这样，才能让自己继续苟延残喘下去。自己不想流泪，真的不想流泪，可是就算把脸埋进了雪里，眼睛还是烫得发痛。阳光是那样美好，白雪是那样漂亮，可是在这苍茫无垠的冰天雪地里，却好像独独只剩下了自己这一个疯子。一个不知为何会流泪，也不知该怎样停止悲伤的疯子。只有那无尽的雪野，依旧在用它美丽的姿态，嘲笑着天地间一切丑陋的哭泣。在纯净的冰雪之上，自己就像一堆屎一样肮脏。

而这一天是元旦，自己原本应该在这一天，正式成为丽云的翻译。现在，往事俱成飞烟。

夕阳西下时，光像血一样滚烫。

自己藏身在破庙里，不能再出去要饭，全靠兄弟们养活。兄弟们每天外出，除了要饭，就是偷偷地撕通缉令。虽然撕通缉令本身并不能使通缉这件事情从本质上消失，但是按照孔仁的话来说，就是撕一张少一张，少一张好一分。外面的形势很严峻，从弟兄们的谈话中得知，这一次的大通缉，还真不是虚张声势。每天都有人被抓，每天都有人被拉到广场上去公开枪毙。这不是一场普通的捉拿漏网罪犯的大通缉，而是一场为了巩固国民党右派政权而进行的大清洗，是一场以巩固北伐胜利果实为名而发动的大屠杀。不断地有工人领袖被杀，不断地有共产党嫌疑犯被杀，不断地有窝藏共产党的老百姓被杀。东北一归顺，蒋介石便开始伸张他的权力欲望。

对于自己的安全，孔仁很有信心。孔仁开玩笑说，乞丐窝里两样宝，老鼠和跳蚤，警察见了跑，特务远远绕，再要加上传染病，谁还管他通缉令。大家都哈哈大笑，但是，不言自明的现实恐惧，还是让每个人都无法躲避。

自己感到很对不起兄弟们。对待兄弟们，自己从来都没有彻头彻尾地坦诚过。自己没有告诉他们，其实自己真的帮土匪做过事。自己对他们说的真话，还远没有对丽云说的多。自己就是个天生的骗子。自己不仅没能如梦想的那样带他们一起脱离乞讨的苦海，反而还连累了他们，要他们陪自己一同泡在惨白的死亡恐怖里，自己真是愧对关老爷。

那晚歃血盟誓之后，兄弟们彼此之间便不再呼名道姓，而皆以排行相称，宛若亲生手足。这份愈来愈真诚而坚固了的兄弟情义，既令自己感到分外温暖，又令自己倍感负罪。温暖的是，和他们在一起，自己根本不用像提防小得财那样提防任何人，自己完全不用担心会被背叛或者出卖；而负罪的是，自己害怕会连累丽云，却忍心连累兄弟，这一界限分明的心底事实，令

自己难逃不义不悌的自我谴责。也许，自己当时就不该逃回破庙来，不该让兄弟们沾上窝藏共产党嫌疑犯的罪名，可是，除了这儿，自己又还能去哪儿呢？天下虽大，可是又有什么地方，可以允许自己的存在？

条条是绝路，处处是绝境。

一九二九年，开幕便是生死泪水。

东北易帜之后，中国在形式上完成了南北统一，但在实质上，依旧是群雄逐鹿，王者未出。日本关东军兵强马壮，雄踞一隅，对张学良麾下的东北军是虎视眈眈，剑欲出鞘。而在第二次北伐时曾短暂团结起来的蒋、冯、阎、李等几派大军阀，在北伐成功之后，便立即又陷入了纷纭复杂的利益之争里，明争暗斗，战云阴集。汪精卫，则仍然是想要取代蒋介石，想要成为继孙中山之后的新一代领袖。国民党内部，可谓是春秋战国，血腥不休。而另一方面，在南昌起义之后，国民党又疯狂派兵，追杀工农红军，誓要将共产党斩尽杀绝。井冈山根据地建立之后，蒋介石又组织了多次大规模的进剿、会剿，欲将根据地夷为平地。炮火连天，千军百战。右派战争狂人野心勃勃，中正大独裁者一手遮天。国民党内反蒋阵营蠢蠢欲动，各大军阀合纵连横计谋百出。自己对丽云说过，这天下早晚会太平的，可是，这天下，到底要到何时才能太平？在自己的有生之年里，自己是否真的还能看到这一天？在自己的有生之年里，自己是否真的还可以，在天下太平之后，去找她？

这个世上，为什么要有战争？那能荡平天下群雄、一统江山的真正王者，到底要到何时才会出现？

自己，究竟还有没有机会，能看到那一天？

冬天，还是那样无边无际。

风雪漫漫，万物肃杀。

日日夜夜，自己都在悄无声息而又漫无边际的心痛里挣扎与彷徨。丽云的身影就像是一幅幅已经刻在了自己脑子里的图景，无论自己怎样用力去抹，都抹不淡她的一丝丝轮廓，抹不掉对她的一点点想念。她一直就像是坐在玻璃窗后的椅子上，自己既无法穿过那层玻璃，也无法移开眼睛。而从她到自己的距离，就包含了这世上一切折磨与煎熬的譬喻。爱的无力，反而成了爱的无法舍弃；她的不在，反而成了她的无处不在。始料未及的绵绵相思如浪潮一般日夜冲刷着自己的心岸，难以承受的断情之痛如藤蔓一般时刻箍缠着自己的每一根神经。自己沉没在绝望之海的海底，看着海面上漂浮的她的影子，可望而不可即。只有撕心裂肺的苦咸，在将自己慢慢锈蚀，在让自己渐渐腐烂。也许只有当相思成了白骨，那肝肠寸断的痛苦才会烟消云散，也许只有当风雪凋尽了沧桑，那如痴如醉的爱恋才会被人遗忘。可是，自己不想忘，就算沧海变成了桑田，疼痛将自己剔成了白骨，自己也不想忘记丽云，不想忘。可是，如果不忘，又叫自己怎样继续活下去？红粉荒冢，一念执着，一念看破，可是殊不知，念念之间，皆生生世世。只要爱了，就不会再有什么解脱。

自己要兄弟们每天捡些旧报纸回来给自己看。自己一直很担心，自己在庄家住过的那几天，会不会给庄家带来什么麻烦。但是还好，庄家的一切都还好。庄氏大百货公司的生意一直不错，而庄氏的那几家原本已都半死不活了的纱厂和面粉厂，因为得到了潘氏企业在各方面的支持，又都重新积极运转了起来，开始扭亏为盈。报纸上还登了一张丽云和潘兆的合影。合影中，丽云笑靥如花。很好，这样，就很好。只要潘兆能好好地做庄家的保护伞，为丽云遮风挡雨，那么，自己就可以放心了，真的。

但是，那天，丽云脸上的那个巴掌印到底是怎么回事？究竟是发生了什么事？在表面的锦绣风光之下，到底还隐藏着什么黑暗或者辛酸的故事？而这故事，又会不会与自己有关？一切都不得而知。自己夜不成寐，寝食难安。

一九二九年二月五日，奉天省改名为辽宁省。旧的时代已经在血雨腥风之中真实地消逝在了历史的背影里，而新的时代还在风雨飘摇地病痛呻吟、流血不止。明天在哪里？出路在哪里？谁能知道。

白天一个人的时候，自己便打拳练武。自己练得很猛烈，每一招，都憋足了全身的劲去发力，像狮子搏兔，像疯子撒泼。拳风呼呼作响，筋骨格格有声，大汗淋漓中，自己直练得筋疲力尽、手脚发软，也仍然不肯停。自己喜欢这种感觉，自己需要这种被彻底掏空、被彻底耗尽的感觉。只有让自己的体力完全枯竭，才能使自己的灵魂昏昏欲睡；只有让自己的灵魂沉睡不醒，才能使丽云的身影不再那么频繁地出现于自己虚渺的回忆。自己和丽云的故事，就像一朵注定会被命运消解于沧海的浪花，美丽得太绝望，绝望得

太痛惘，自己承受不起这样的失去，自己不愿再想起有过的哭泣。自己最怕的不是死，而是在彻底的无能为力里流泪，在永恒的失去面前撕心裂肺。无论是拥有过还是已失去，只要一想起，便不可抗拒。不可抗拒，就会痛得死无葬身之地。爱情是一种魔力，当这种魔力被命运嚼碎，碎掉的，是人的一生悲喜。自己不信四大皆空，又无钱买酒自醉，除了把自己累成一摊无力再思考的烂泥，自己又还可以用什么办法，让自己不要再痛得那样无休无止深入骨髓？自己要让自己的脑子里，只剩下对于练武的渴望；自己要让自己的心肝脾肺肾里，不再有残余的一点点回忆。

自己在练，只是在徒劳地练；自己在忘，只是在徒劳地忘。

时光如水。

春节过后，天气渐渐暖和了一些。自己被剪短的头发又重新长长了，自己又重新拥有了一副乞丐的仪容。外面的风声依旧很紧，但是自己一直躲在这间无人问津的破庙里，倒也很是安全。兄弟们每天早出晚归，用他们要到的食物来养活自己，自己心中甚是过意不去，却也无能为力。自己只能在破庙里给他们生生火、烧烧水、打扫打扫卫生，他们也挺高兴的。但是，其实大家都能感觉到，那团隐蔽的害怕被捕的恐惧的阴云，从未在这个破庙里散去。有时候外面乱得慌，兄弟们甚至都不敢出去要饭。他们既怕自己会被捕，也怕他们自己会被抓。断头司空见惯，世道人心惶惶。

东北受辖于南京政府之后，日本人在东北或明或暗的活动都明显收敛了许多，所以，自己在心底里，还是乐见这东北易帜的。对于庄家来说，对于丽云来说，日本人才是真正的威胁，要是这东北不及早投入南京国民政府的怀抱，任由日本人垂涎蚕食，那，自己就算天天守护在丽云的身边，也绝护不了她的周全。所以，不管自己现在已是落到了怎样的地步，自己对于这东北易帜本身，绝无怨恨。想想那天丽云遭遇三个日本流氓的情形吧，多么令人后怕无穷。好在，东北如今已弃日投蒋，统一于中国；好在，丽云现在还有潘兆，他总不会让别人欺负他的老婆。至于自己，烂命一条，贱人一个，通缉就通缉了，有什么了不起？脑袋掉了，不过碗大一个疤。或许，死了还能舒服些。

那套残缺不全的八极拳，已被自己练到了行云流水的地步，只是因为有很多衔接处和空白处的招式都是自己瞎猜着摸索出来的，所以，这套残拳就算被自己练到了极致，威力也很有限。在那许多个或者清醒或者睡梦的时刻里，自己都曾希望，可以重新再想起父亲传给自己的全套武艺。但是，再也想不起来了。想不起来了。人有时候就是会这样痴心妄想，一样东西，明明在很早以前就已失去了，却还误以为，能在未来重新找得回来。这便是痴妄。兄弟们看见自己拼命练武，都以为自己是想练好了武功以便对抗警察和特务，自己笑着说，当然了，练好了武功的确是可以在逃跑的时候派上很大的用场，只要他们不开枪。自己哈哈大笑。

从春节期间开始，孔仁便像是忽然交上了什么好运，不仅每次出去乞讨都不会空手而归，而且还三天两头地能带回一些鸡鸭鱼肉来，大家常常都能吃得满嘴流油。自己也曾感到有些疑惑，便问他，怎么大哥你最近经常有大丰收？他就说，城里新来了几户富人家，好心，看见我，便总会多给些好食物，没什么。自己不是很相信，但也不便表示怀疑。毕竟，都歃血盟誓过了。反正，自己只要相信，他们不会出卖自己就行了。其他的，都无所谓。

元宵节过后，兄弟们以前经常去要饭的几个地方，都成了两个来路不明的恶霸的地盘。他们自称是七星帮的长老，却又从没亮出过七星帮的狮符。说他们是冒牌的，他们又的确是甘肃口音，武功高强。他们专收穷苦人和小商贩们的保护费，连乞丐都不放过，这他妈的哪像长老干的事？但没有人能反抗他们，谁不服从，就会被他们打得鼻青脸肿。按理说，孔仁他们四个人，也都是有武艺在身的，虽然单个功夫都不强，但四人合力起来也不弱，在恶霸面前不至于逆来顺受。但是，孔仁说了，谁都不许反抗，谁都不许惹事。弟兄们也纷纷表示同意。其实，自己也明白弟兄们的难言苦衷和良苦用心。弟兄们无非就是怕，万一惹了什么事，会拔出萝卜带出泥，节外生枝，把自己这个隐藏的通缉犯给暴露了。毕竟，要钱的恶霸并不是最可怕的，要命的警察和特务才是最恐怖的。自己一方面觉得愤愤不平与愧对弟兄，另一方面，却也不禁更加疑惑：既然外面的情况这样恶劣，那，孔仁又哪来的大鱼大肉？

难道，孔仁或者孔仁和弟兄们，真的是有什么事情瞒着自己？

三月，乍暖还寒，阴晴不定。自己依旧一直躲在破庙里，无计可施，也无可奈何。冥思苦想中，既看不到活着的出路，也拉不住活着的留恋。思潮起伏里，生存的欲望变得越来越寡淡，想死的念头却像盛开的罂粟。就连

练武这种本应是威风昂扬的事情，对于自己来说，都只不过是颓废的加浓药剂。这条泥泞不堪的人生路，不是自己不想再走下去，而是这老天，到底还让不让自己走下去？

还有多少自己不能承受的痛苦，会在前面的路上，等着自己去承受？

无声听雨，默然沉寂。

这一天，孔仁兴高采烈地拎回了一盒蛋糕来。他说，今天运气好，要到了两块大洋，就买了一个蛋糕回来，让弟兄们都尝尝，乐一乐。自己躺在床板上，不想吃也不想喝，孔仁却执意说，来，三弟，你先吃。自己是真的什么东西也不想吃，但孔仁还是很热情地执意说，来，三弟，你先吃。

走到了桌前，才发现这个蛋糕做得精美绝伦，宛如一件艺术品。自己心底的那团疑惑不禁又升腾了起来，于是，就去看了看那已是被丢在了一边的蛋糕盒盖。盒盖上很飘逸地印着一个美丽的英文单词：Memory。自己心里忽然一个激灵。忐忑跳跃不停。Memory？这不就是那家能做出全奉天市最高级的蛋糕来的西饼店吗？这，不就是那家让自己和丽云得以在雨中相伴聊天的西饼店吗？

“大哥，这个蛋糕，你是在什么店里买的？”

“哦……这个……是在昌和蛋糕店里买的。”

“大哥，你知道吗，盒盖上的这个英文，就是店的名称。”

“噢，原来昌和的英文是这么写的呀。哈哈哈——”

“不，大哥，这个英文词的意思，不是昌和。——为什么要说谎，大哥？”

顿时，鸦雀无声。

孔仁呆若木鸡，无言以对。

“难道，大哥你是在这蛋糕里下了毒，想拿我的尸体去换一千块大洋？”

“三哥，你说什么呢，大哥不是这种人！”黄道着急地说。

“大哥，这到底是怎么回事？”孟义问。

“三弟，你觉得我会给你下毒吗？”孔仁说。

“我觉得不会，可是，有些事，大哥你要是瞒着我，那可就是比给我下毒还要让我难受了。”自己说。

“其实，我也想问，为什么从春节开始，大哥你总是能有大鱼大肉拿回来？我们不是怀疑大哥你什么，只是，我们大家既然是兄弟，彼此间就应该无话不谈，坦诚相待，不要有什么秘密。”朱理说。

孔仁叹了一口气，坐了下来。他对孟义、朱理和黄道说，这件事，和你们三个没关系，别掺和。然后，他看着自己，说，既然你都点破了，那我也就不瞒你了。这蛋糕，是庄家的庄小姐给的，今天是她生日，她想让你也吃一份蛋糕。春节前，是庄小姐来找到了我，给了我许多大洋，要我好好照顾你。那些大鱼大肉，就是我用这些大洋买的。庄小姐还说，只要我们能保住你三个月，她就一定有办法救你。她说，她已经托了人帮忙，希望政府能撤销对你的通缉，要是不能撤销，她就会送你去香港，总之，她一定会救你。

话音掷落，自己跌坐在床板上，眼前一片灰白。

“想不到庄小姐对三哥这么好。”黄道自言自语地说。

“你们三个出去。”孔仁说。

孟义、朱理和黄道就都很识趣地走了出去。破庙里，一时就只剩下了孔仁和自己两个人。

“庄小姐要我什么都别告诉你，一定要瞒着你。可是，从我第三次买肉回来起，我就在你和四弟的眼睛里看到了怀疑。虽然你们一直都没说什么，但是，我知道，总有一天你会先开口。因为，这本来就是一个因你才起的秘密。人对一桩围绕着自己而生的事情，总是会有一种特殊的敏感。如果你感觉不到，那，庄小姐倒是痴心白付了。”孔仁说着，微微一笑。

自己沉默难言。孔仁叹了口气，说：“其实，你本来就不是一个叫花子。”

自己一笑，说：“没有谁，天生就是叫花子。只不过，我们都只能做今天的我们。”

“那你，以后有没有什么打算？”

“做一天和尚撞一天钟，得过且过。”

“你知道我问的不是这个。”

“关于以后，谁也不会有回答的把握，还不是只能得过且过吗？”自己笑着说。孔仁就也笑了笑。都笑得挺苦涩。

“大哥，庄小姐给的钱，还剩多少？”

“今天又给了十块大洋，一共还有十五块。”

“帮我还了吧。我只是一个乞丐，欠人家的太多，我怕会一辈子还不清。”

“好，大哥帮你还。”

“谢谢大哥。”

孔仁站了起来，走过来，拍了拍自己的肩膀，然后，便往外走去。走了两步，他又停了下来。他说：“其实，我们都听见过你在梦里的哭。那哭，就像一只垂死挣扎的哑巴野兽。在梦里，你喊过庄小姐的名字。”

孔仁离开了破庙。没有人进来。残破的夕阳余晖洒在庙里的地上，像一堆碎了的金子，像一片无际的落叶。

自己站了起来，走到了桌前，吃了一口蛋糕。甜甜的，像幸福的味道。自己说了一句“生日快乐”，空旷中，泪珠滚滚而落。

以为自己已经可以忘怀，其实她却从来没有离开。

一九二九年四月二日，奉天市改名为沈阳市。春暖花开的四月，一切都仿佛欣欣向荣。

四月十日中午，兄弟们欢呼雀跃地拿回了一张告示和一份报纸来。告示是当天新贴的，报纸是当天新发行的，上面都有一个同样的消息，那就是：嫌犯赵驹，经查无罪，撤销通缉，不再追捕。

兄弟们纷纷击掌庆贺，自己手拿着告示和报纸，笑得却有些心事重重。丽云最后说过的那些话，又一次像烧红的炭一样滚落在自己的肺腑心间。一些致命的问题在像钢针一样不停地刺痛着自己的神经。政府果真撤销了自己的通缉令，为什么？如果真的是丽云帮的忙，那么，她又到底是怎样做到的？从视共产党为死敌的南京国民政府手里救出一个有通匪通共之罪甚至是有共产党嫌疑犯之罪的人的性命来，可绝不是一件轻而易举普普通通的事，以丽云自己的能力，是根本不可能办到的。那么，故事的真相又究竟是什么？自己没办法再向自己继续提问，因为，自己怕自己会越来越接近真正的答案。很多时候，人的自我思辨，其实只是在自欺欺人，只是在充满侥幸心地想要将自己明知的一种答案换成另一种答案，就好像只要自己的思辨在逻辑上能够成立，事实上的结果或真相也就可以被置换了似的。这是多么徒劳的一种悲剧。可是，在不能面对的许多事实面前，又有多少人不是在重复着这一自我欺骗的游戏？自己只是众多可怜的悲剧囚徒中的一个而已。自己装作若无其事地，挺高兴地，将告示和报纸揉成了一团。

自己走出了破庙，想去街上逛逛。天空是湛蓝的，花草树木都带着几分许久不见的新鲜，无风无雨的春天，温和得让人忘记季节。在庙里躲了太久，眼睛还无法在骤然间面对太阳直射的光，眼前的一切，都像是披着一层刺眼的闪亮。这些闪亮仿佛在吸引着自己，不停地往前走。要走到哪里去？不知道。也许是阳光不再那样刺眼的一个地方，也许，往前走的目的仅仅只是不想停下。闭上眼，面对着太阳，眼前红亮得像一团火，像一个天堂。那感觉十分美妙，美妙得让人不想再看这个世界。心里的悲哀也并不结实，涣散着，像游离的蜉蝣，像抓不住的风，任它们自由自在，与它们相伴相安。能这样地站在阳光里，真好。真的好。人生，又为什么还要有其他的纷扰与痛苦？

到了大街上，自己在偶然间看到了一份昨天的报纸，四月九日的报纸。报纸的头版上，印着一条重要新闻：四月八日，沈阳市华商会会长潘兆与庄府千金庄丽云正式结婚。报纸上还登了一张潘兆亲吻丽云脸颊的照片。照片中，丽云依旧笑靥如花。

自己仰起头，认真地看着那轮血红的太阳。笔直而强劲的光芒，像柔韧而锋利的箭一样，完全地穿透着自己的双眼，自己的眼前，除了火热的红色与无尽的金光之外，再也看不见任何东西。没有疼痛，也没有泪水，只有无边无际的失去，仿佛从高山坠入深海的长久，仿佛从完整散成粉碎的空无，感觉不到什么了，那轮太阳还是滚烫得像一颗不灭的火球。流泪有什么用？答案早已全部注定。

逃到天涯海角，也逃不出如影随形的宿命。

时光，没有悲喜而无声无息地往前走。很快，就到了五月。

自从要求孔仁不可以再拿丽云给的钱以后，大家的日子艰难了许多。那两个什么狗屁长老的严苛盘剥，实在是压得兄弟们快要喘不过气来了。而平时哪几帮乞丐可以在哪几个区域内要饭，也是有规矩划分的，兄弟们不好随便去别的地盘上分其他苦兄弟的粥吃。大家都感到了进退无路的窘迫。自己一早就想要动手，想去打跑那两个王八蛋，但是孔仁却制止了自己，他说，三弟，你不知道，有一次，我亲眼看见那两个长老在街角和几个警察分钱，他们多半是一伙的，你才刚刚被赦罪，千万不要再惹祸上身了。其他三个弟

兄也都点头说是。于是，大家便只能是无奈地忍耐着，也没有什么办法。孔仁自嘲地说，这世道，我们穷苦人，不就是只能事事忍着吗，难不成还可以起来造反。

但是，这一天，却发生了意外。中午，自己要到了四个大馒头，便兴冲冲地赶回了破庙去，想看看兄弟们回没回来，要是回来的话，就一起吃馒头。谁知，还没进破庙呢，就听见里面传出了痛苦的呻吟声来。自己赶紧跑进去，一看，兄弟们四个全在，但是，孔仁和朱理，都是血淋淋地躺在床板上，在痛苦地不住呻吟。

自己忙问怎么回事。黄道说，大哥今天好不容易要到了一大碗蛋炒饭，谁知却被那两个该死的长老看见了，他们就走过来，问我们要保护费，我们说没钱，他们就往我们刚要到的蛋炒饭里吐痰，二哥一下子就怒了，和他们动起了手来，我们也忍无可忍了，于是就想干脆四个一起上，不信打不过他们。谁知，他俩只出了一个人，就打倒了我们四个。打倒我们后，他们两个又一起上来，把我们往死里打了一顿。大哥护着我们，伤得最重，一条腿被打断了。四哥一直在吐血，也不知道究竟是伤在了哪儿。

“那你们两个还待在这里干什么？还不快去请医生！”自己大吼。

孟义突然就落下了泪来，说：“请了，可医生不肯来，人家一听是断骨和吐血，光出诊费就要收三块大洋，我们哪有钱！就算请得起医生也买不起药！只能白白等死——这就是我们穷光蛋的命！”

“他妈的！”自己骂着，转身就往外走。

“三弟——”孔仁却是虚弱地叫住了自己。自己停了步。“你不要去惹事，千万不要——你才刚刚留住这条命——”孔仁吃力地说着，说完，又是痛得呻吟了起来。

“大哥放心，我不是去打架，我去请医生——你们等我回来。”自己头也不回地说完，便是跑出了破庙去。

风在耳边呼啸，自己太阳穴里的筋在跳。一种对于这个世界的愤怒在自己的血液里燃烧，一种对于这个时代的痛恨在自己的全身暴动。自己恨不能一把摧毁这个疮痍满目的世道，自己恨不能一击粉碎那所有加在穷苦人身上的厄运。为什么安分守己的人只能被人欺负？为什么没钱的人受了伤就只能白白等死？这是一个没有公义的世道！这是一个没有人道的世界！这是一个应该被摧毁的时代！万恶的时代！

自己拼了命地奔跑，像一颗燃烧的子弹。现实已容不得自己再作任何考虑，自己现在必须要马上去做的，就是找丽云借钱。自己当然一直很渴望能够再见到丽云，但是，自己绝想不到的是，再见，居然就是去借钱。自己心里不舒服得只想钻到地洞里去，但是，现实已经紧迫逼仄得叫人没有空间和时间去难受。兄弟们在流血，医生晚一刻到，就多一分悲哀。

离潘公馆越来越近，自己的心揪得越来越紧。那是一幢漂亮的白色的小洋楼，与庄府大宅的风格迥然不同。丽云结婚后，就住在这里。为她的嫁人而伤心时，自己曾来公馆外面看过一次，但是那次并没有看见丽云，后来自己也没敢多停留就走了，因为，又有谁能保证，那一刻，她没有刚好站在公馆楼上的某条窗帘后面看着自己呢？同样的错误，自己从来不想犯第二次。

到了公馆的大门外，透过精美的铁栅栏，可以看到小洋楼前的花园里空无一人。热烈的花开仿佛泡在一坛冷寂里，多少有些让人意外地寥落。自己的手在门铃前踌躇。自己急切地想按门铃，但是，又缩回了手来。丽云现在在不在公馆里呢？万一来开门的是潘兆呢？自己是要立马跪下来向他乞讨吗？自己的贸然出现，会不会给丽云带来意外的麻烦？不，自己绝不能节外生枝，绝不能给丽云惹出额外的是非来。这门铃，自己不可以按。

自己退到了远处的一个角落里，蹲了下来假装要饭。旁边的一家商店里，墙上刚好挂着一只钟。自己决定了，要是在一小时之内，没能恰好而适当地遇见丽云，自己就直接去医生那里，先礼后兵，医生若肯不要钱地给乞丐看病便罢，若不肯，自己便揍他到肯为止。只能是这样了。

时间在一分一秒地过去，自己焦躁得像热锅上的蚂蚁一样。自己可以想象得到，此时，孔仁和朱理正在承受着怎样剧烈而残酷的痛苦，甚至，他们会撑不住，而因此正在逐步向那地狱里的死神靠近。自己冲动了好几次，想要去主动按响那门铃，但是都被自己压抑住了。如果是潘兆或者潘兆的仆人来开的门，自己该如何应对？装作陌生乞丐乞讨，说自己有朋友快要死了，急需几块大洋救命？他们会信吗？他们会给吗？不然，难道可以告诉他们，自己是丽云的朋友吗？这简直就是开玩笑。难道自己想把丽云变成一个小丑或者潘兆的羞耻符号吗？这狗日的阶级社会！

自己绝不会做任何有损于丽云的事情，哪怕这损害仅仅只是可能，哪

怕这损害只有一丝一毫。没有任何困境可以逼迫自己越过这条底线，没有任何情感可以要求自己放弃这份坚持。哪怕，自己明知兄弟已危在旦夕。自己宁愿做关老爷殿前的罪人，也绝不愿给丽云带去一丝麻烦。自己在等待中煎熬，自己在等待中负罪。时间已过去了半个多小时，而潘公馆的大门内外，依旧还没出现过半个人影。

自己觉得不能再等了，还是直接去揍医生来得比较干脆。至于医生将来会不会报警，那就等将来再说吧。

自己起身，最后又到潘公馆的大门外面站了一会儿。虽然明知此刻不宜多愁善感，但内心的酸涩依旧如溃堤般涌来，令自己无法自持，脚步如滞。以前在庄府的许多情景在心里重演，而眼前，分明已物换星移。人面不知何处去，桃花春风两依稀。

自己给了自己一个耳光。抹了抹眼睛，自己便想转身离去。但是，就在此时，透过铁栅栏，自己看见一个人从小洋楼里跑了出来。不是丽云是谁？

蔡嫂紧跟在丽云后面，也跑了出来。

自己激动地一下子将身体紧贴在了公馆的大门上，双手不禁紧握住了大门上半部分镂花铁栅栏上的铁条，将脸死死地紧贴在了铁条之间的空隙里，就好像自己能将自己整个人从这窄窄的空隙里塞过去一样。自己的心口发烫、发颤，想要大喊一声“丽云”，火热的声音却只是在喉咙里原地打转，压抑着被紧缩。

丽云跑到了自己的面前，“我在楼上看见你了，你怎么来了？”她一边匆匆地问着，一边急忙地开着门上的锁。

蔡嫂却是追了上来，一把就拉开了丽云。“小姐你怎么就是不听劝呢？这个骗子已经把你害到了这步田地，你为什么还要理他？要是让好事的人看见了，告诉了潘老爷，你又要吃不了兜着走——”

“你不要再说了——就放我这一次，算我求你——”丽云哀求着，挣脱了蔡嫂的阻拦，又跑来开门。

“我看你等了很久，很着急的样子，知道你一定是有事找我，快说吧，是怎么了？”丽云强颜欢笑地一边问，一边开了门。

自己惊愕而一无所知地，不知该怎样开口。“……我兄弟被恶人打了，受了重伤，危在旦夕，但是我们又没钱看病，所以……所以我想跟你借几块大洋。”

蔡嫂劈头盖脸地就打了过来，“你这个骗子！不要脸的东西！一见面就是跟我们家小姐要钱！你知不知道，我们家小姐为了救你这个通缉犯，毁了一辈子！毁了一辈子！你为什么不去死——”

“蔡嫂！你不要再说了好不好——你不要再说了——”丽云突然哭了出来，“求求你让我安静一会儿行不行——就一会儿——”

“小姐——”

“你快去，帮我拿五十块大洋出来。”

“小姐！”

“是不是现在连你也不再听我的话了？你是不是和谭叔他们一样，都不再帮我了？”

“小姐你别这样、别这样——我去拿，我去拿。”

蔡嫂摇头叹气地去了小洋楼。丽云背转身，擦着眼泪。自己就站在那里，被一种复杂的痛苦折磨着，眼前模模糊糊，默然心如刀割。

“你是怎么救的我？”

“不是我救的，是潘兆救的。”

“潘兆他为什么会救我？”

“……不为什么。”

“到底发生了什么事？”自己心痛得无以复加，失去了理智地，用力抓住了她的双臂。她却不禁低嘤了一声，顿时痛得哆嗦了起来。自己一怔，赶紧松开了双手。她全身往后一缩，后退了半步。自己震惊地瞪大了眼，不由分说地就是拉过了她的一只手来，捋起了她的衣袖。只见，她的手臂上，青一块，紫一块，瘀痕累累。在肩膀处，还有被点烫过的痕迹，像是用烟头干的。她使劲地挣脱了自己的手，蜷缩发抖地连退了两步。泪珠无声地从她眼里纷纷滚落，满面晶莹的悲恸。

“啊——”自己撕心裂肺地怒吼着，发狂地一拳砸在了公馆花园里的石狮子头上，“这究竟是怎么一回事！”

“什么事都没有——什么事都没有——”

“告诉我，谁干的！谁干的！我宰了他！宰了他！”

“不——不——不——”

“是潘兆！是潘兆对不对！他为什么要这样对你！为什么！”

“你不要再问了——你不要再问了——”

“我要杀了他！我要杀了他！杀他一千次！一千次！”

“不！不要！杀了他，你就会被国民政府枪毙！那我做的一切，就全都白费了！全都白费了！你明不明白——明不明白！”

“啊！”自己摧肝裂胆地悲吼着，用尽生命的力量，又一拳砸在了石狮子的头上。自己的拳头上，鲜血淋漓，却一点也没有痛。没有痛！

“为什么——为什么！”自己痛哭流涕。

“忘了我吧——从此以后，忘了我吧——”她摇着头，哭着说，“就当我们从来没有认识过——从来没有认识过——”

“不——不——”自己悲哀而无力地喃喃。喃喃。

她只是哀泣长哭。

啼血一样的长哭。

而自己，除了无语泪流，再说不出一句话，再说不出一句话。

蔡嫂从小洋楼里出来，给了自己钱，然后，就将自己赶出了公馆。丽云消失在了自己模糊的视线里。自己转身走出了很远，才听到了背后轰隆的一声。回头去看，原来，是那头石狮子的头，突然碎裂了。自己看着自己的拳头，血淋淋的拳头，哈哈大笑，然后号啕大哭，就像一个疯子一样，就像一个疯子一样。自己转身狂奔，跑得比子弹还快，就好像，一个人，只要能跑得足够快，就可以逃出他自己的灵魂，逃出他自己的身体。

自己这样活着，究竟有什么意义？

唯有狂风长啸，苍天永寂。

有了五十块大洋，自己与兄弟们将孔仁和朱理送去了正规的西医院里救治。朱理的血止住了，孔仁的腿接好了，医生说，只要安心静养，不会再有大碍。春天就要过去，夏天就要来临，佛祖说，一花一世界，三藐三菩提。

白天变得越来越长，黑夜变得越来越短。应该忘记的痛苦无法安息，不能释怀的绝望漫天飞舞，闭上眼，总见山花烂漫，空谷岑寂。朝阳还是那样鲜艳，夕阳还是那样刺眼。无处安放的眼泪层叠成海，无力呼喊的心痛沧桑几度，睁开眼，只有孤鸿悲飞，长天云碎。孔仁告诉自己，丽云曾经说过，希望自己在被赦罪后，可以好好找一份工作，不用再过吃了上顿没下顿的生活。自己笑笑，说，此身已非昨日身，明日何须再明日。

这一天，自己正在一条僻静的小巷里走，忽然，听到背后有一个陌生的声音喊了一声“赵驹”。自己停了脚步，回转身去看。一个头发长长的，遮住了半边眼睛的男人，站在小巷的中间，一动不动。“赵驹？”他问。他的眼睛里，射出鹰一样冷锐的光，那光，像刀片一样闪亮。

自己蓦地有些不寒而栗。仿佛出于本能似的，自己嗅到了一股危险的味道。自己没有动，也没有应答。

他从衣袋里，掏出了一张折好的纸。纸打开后，很大。自己认了出来，这，是自己的通缉令。他看了看纸上的画像，又认真看了看自己的脸。然后，他笑了笑，半是自言自语地说，头发长长了。他将通缉令面向了自己，抖了两抖，轻蔑地问：“这上面画的，就是你吧？赵驹。”

“这上面画的，的确是我。但是，这张通缉令已经失效。因为，国民政府已经赦免了我的罪。不信，你可以去警察局或政府里问，报纸上也有。”自己一边说，脚下已暗暗运起了劲。

“不用了。”他说着，笑笑，便将手里的通缉令丢到了一边。“政府已经赦免了你，但是，我们青帮没有。”话音未落，他右手从腰间一擦，一件什么兵器已是雪光飞舞地闪耀在了他的手里。他的速度如电光石火般迅疾，除了父亲之外，自己生平还从未见过这么快的身手。还没等自己反应过来，他已是如猎豹一般敏捷而凶猛地冲到了自己的面前。他的右手飞舞着雪光，在自己喉咙前飞快地一划。自己纵然已及时后仰，喉咙处的皮肤，也已是渗出了血来。三招过后，自己连退十步。

自己抹了一把喉咙前的血。他兴奋地放慢了全身的速度，停在原处，将手里的兵器炫耀似的、慢慢地一甩、一甩。自己这时才看清楚，原来他手里的东西，是一把蝴蝶刀。自己全身的汗毛都顿时竖了起来。自己曾听父亲说过，蝴蝶刀，是南洋最狠辣的杀手使用的武器，如果你无法看清这把刀飞舞的痕迹，那么你的命就只能任由敌人来取。而自己，在一开始，居然连这东西是把刀都没看清！

“兄弟好功夫，不知高姓大名？”自己一边后退一边问。

他一边进逼一边回答：“青帮第一快刀手徐冷，便是在下。你也不赖，今日的江湖上，能躲过我一刀破喉的，已没几个人。怪不得我们杜老板要我

亲自出马，你果然不是泛泛之辈。”

“如今我已只是一介乞丐，蝇营狗苟、聊度残生而已。青帮为何定要苦苦相逼，非置我于死地不可？”

“一介乞丐？我看非也。听杜老板说，你是送了一个名媛给国民政府的高官，让这个女人陪人家睡了七天，才换来了你的那张赦免令。你说，像你这么有能力的一个仇家，我们青帮又怎么会允许你继续活在这个世上呢？”

“你说什么？我的赦免令是怎么来的？”

“不和你废话了，今天，我的刀要喝饱血。”徐冷说着，全身的动作便重新又快了起来，他手中的蝴蝶刀，再次变成了一团耀眼的雪光。

他如一头饿极的疯狼般扑向了自己。自己连接十招，胸腹前的衣衫尽被划破，几处皮肤已被刀割开。鲜血淋漓。他冷笑着，越打越快，越打越快。自己快要招架不住。蝴蝶刀在他的手中，似乎已不是一件兵器，而是一件任由他意念驱使的神物，是他灵魂的一部分，是他全身动作的先锋官。他的刀法，出神入化，无懈可击。他的功夫，凶残毒辣，招招致命。一刀，又一刀，自己的双眼，差点被割瞎。

自己腿上中了一刀，终于被他扑倒在了地上。他的刀，迅猛如龙地冲向了自己的心脏。自己仰面朝天，用双手拼命地握紧着他拿刀的右手，向上推挡。他冷冷一笑，将他紧压在刀把上的左手稍微转了一转，然后，突然一股更凶猛的力从他的手上迸发了出来。自己拼尽了全身的力来抵挡，但是刀尖，依然在越来越近地逼向自己的心口。刀尖刺入了自己的衣服，刀尖穿透了自己的皮肤。自己感到，死亡来了。

“知道吗，四·一二的时候，我一个人就杀了三百多个共产党，你要是在那时候就碰上了我，那你根本就活不到今天。”

“……你刚才说……我的赦免令是怎么来的……你再说一遍……”

“一个马上就要死了的人，为什么还要装出一副无辜的样子来呢？怎么，难道是想在去见上帝之前，让自己显得纯洁和无罪一点，好骗过那些终将要来对你进行死后审判的各路神仙？”

“……告诉我……”

“是你，叫一个漂亮女人去陪南京政府的高官睡了七天，才换来了那张赦免令！你的这条贱命，是靠女人卖肉换来的！你听清楚了吗？你个没用的乌龟！”

“啊！啊——”

肝肠寸断的狂悲中，自己全身的每一根血管都像要爆炸。一瞬间，自己也不知是从哪来的力量，猛地一下子，便将徐冷弹了出去。自己站了起来，徐冷半蹲在地上，一手撑地，惊讶极了地望着自己。

自己不要命地冲向了徐冷。在蝴蝶刀重新飞舞起来之前，自己已一把抓住了蝴蝶刀的刀刃。刀刃锋利得出奇，就在自己握住它的那一刹那，它已几乎无痛地深深切开了自己整个掌心的皮肉。自己几乎是在用赤裸裸的手掌骨头，来握住这把如蝴蝶一样美丽绚烂的快刀。

徐冷与自己开始了单手对打。十招之后，徐冷终于将刀从自己的掌中抽出。自己掌心的碎肉飞了出来。自己将涌出的鲜血洒向了徐冷的眼睛。徐冷一闪。就在那一闪的停顿里，自己得到了使出八极铁山靠的机会。没有偏差，没有失误，徐冷被自己撞得飞了起来，然后，重重地摔在了地上。

徐冷爬了起来，吐出了一口血。自己和他，又对冲在了一起。他一刀刺向自己。自己将左肩迎上，让他深深地将刀插入了自己的左肩之中。然后，自己猛力扭转身体，用肩膀的力量，与徐冷硬扳那把蝴蝶刀。徐冷想将蝴蝶刀从自己肩膀上拔出来，就在他使力的那一停顿间，自己双手扳住了他的右手臂。自己怒吼一声，徐冷一声哀号，右手臂已是被自己生生折断。徐冷左手疾出，从自己肩上拔下了蝴蝶刀。自己鲜血狂喷。

徐冷的左手功夫与他的右手一样出色。那把美丽的蝴蝶刀，又一次幻化成了一团夺命的雪光，扑向了自己。那雪光，绚烂得近乎纯净，漂亮得宛如梨花。只是上面沾满了血，仿佛被火烧焦了的春江花月夜，仿佛生错了时代的人面桃花相映红。泪水模糊中，自己好像终于看清了这把蝴蝶刀飞舞的痕迹与规律。不，不是好像，就是真的。一招，又一招，二十招之后，自己终于重重的一脚，踢在了徐冷的太阳穴上。

自己又折断了徐冷的左臂。

徐冷满脸是血地躺在地上，笑了一笑，又笑了一笑，说，如果不是这个乱世，我们也许都不会成为有罪的人。

自己闭上眼，一用力，折断了徐冷的脖子。自己对着徐冷的尸体说，可惜，我们都已没有回头路可走。

自己撕下了几块布条，绑住了自己身上几处严重的出血口。然后，自己捡起了徐冷的蝴蝶刀，便往那两个混蛋长老的住处走了去。

那两个长老各自的武功，都不及徐冷的三分之一。一场大战之后，他们两人，都死在了徐冷的蝴蝶刀下。自己将他们两人的尸体和徐冷的尸体放在了一起，然后，将徐冷的蝴蝶刀，插在了一个长老的胸口上。

自己感到，这个世界，终于又清静了。看着自己双手上满满的鲜血，自己仰天狂笑。笑声在寂静里，分外狰狞。

一切，都像被风卷走的黄沙。

六月，多雨伴随着炎热一齐涌来，天空经常暗得可怕，雨声大得像河流在喧哗。而天地间，总是灰蒙蒙湿漉漉的，就好像这晦暗与阴湿，才是红尘幻象后的本色。听着那雨的喧嚷与人的寂寞，有时候，自己会感到连呼吸也很压抑。

除了孔仁心知肚明地知道自己又杀了人以外，没有人知道，自己的手上又沾了新的血腥。其他三兄弟都信了自己的谎，以为自己的一身伤是被日本浪人打出来的。而从报纸上看，警察局是将徐冷和那两个长老的死，判断成了青帮与七星帮的互斗，因而并没予以太多关注。对于帮会之间的打打杀杀，警察局一向都是敬而远之视而不见的，所以，这个结果十分符合自己当初的安排设计。只有孔仁，洞穿了一切，又缄默不语。他只是摇头叹气。

血腥这种事情，看来这辈子都不会从自己的命运之中被剥离出去了，自己心里十分清楚。谁知道明天会不会又有什么你死我活的事情在等着自己呢？自己和这个世界已经结下了太多的仇怨，自己的双手已经沾上了太多由生至死的鲜血，自己的内心已经填进了太多麻木不仁的冷酷，这样的一个自己，又哪里还会有什么重新开始的机会？一切，都只能是破罐子破摔而已。就连生死，对于自己来说，也仿佛早已没什么可值得在意的了。有时候，自己甚至特别期望，能一了百了地告别这个世界。

唯一叫自己死了也放不下的，是丽云的事情。为了救自己，丽云到底做了些什么事情？徐冷的话究竟是不是真的？从头到尾，那到底是一个什么样的故事？潘兆为什么要打丽云耳光？潘兆和丽云正式结婚的日子，为什么和自己被赦免的日子那样接近？婚后，丽云到底又经历了些什么变故？潘兆为何要那样残暴地虐待丽云？而在杜月笙告诉徐冷的那一个故事里，那一个漂亮的名媛，到底是谁？是丽云吗？是丽云吗？一切，全都是一个谜团。没有答案的谜团。令自己不敢去触碰的谜团。难道可以去找丽云，一件一件事情地向她问清楚吗？难道可以去找潘兆，用拳头威胁他，叫他不要再伤害丽云吗？难道可以去找蔡嫂，让她帮忙约丽云出来见一面吗？不要再傻了，不要再蠢了。毫无疑问，像自己这种人，多接触丽云一分，就会给她多带来十分的麻烦。怎么，难道自己还嫌连累得她不够多不够惨吗？怎么，难道自己还想让所有撕心裂肺的痛苦没完没了地在她和自己之间继续吗？怎么，难道自己还真以为有人能告诉自己在丽云的身上及周围到底都发生了些什么事吗？不要再傻了，不要再蠢了。也许只有让自己从丽云的世界及内心里彻底滚蛋彻底消失，才能将自己给她带来的连累和伤害降到最小最低。也许只有让自己像个无情的人那样绝不再想起和丽云有关的半点事情，自己才不至于又会给丽云带来什么意料不到的悲哀和执迷不悟的痛楚。让谜团永远成为谜团，谁也不要再去触碰；让过去永远成为过去，谁也不要再带着一点留恋。或许，这样才是能让人继续活下去的好方法。不然，又还能怎样呢？

只是，徐冷的话，依旧令自己彻夜难眠。闭上眼，自己就能看见丽云的眼泪和伤痕，闭上眼，自己就有克制不住的想哭的冲动。自己到底该怎么办？怎么办？

丽云还给自己的那把伞，是自己唯一仍可实在拥有的想念。只是，在时间的浸泡与悲酸的腐蚀里，就连这份最后的想念，也正在变得越来越破碎和越来越不可捉摸。而在那破碎与不可捉摸里，又膨胀着越来越强烈的无法面对。当眼泪流干，直接而凶猛地出现在自己心里的，是对于丽云之谜的所有疑问，还有自己命运中对于丽云的所有爱与愧疚。而这所有的所有糅合在一起，又结成了无法面对自己对丽云最刻骨铭心的想念。自己就像是掉进了一个永远轮回无法超脱的痛苦地狱里，而这个地狱的名字，就叫作求不得、爱别离。

也许，于人而言，情爱本身，便是一种无法参透的折磨。

七月，炎热流淌，树叶碧绿而滚烫。庄老爷因病去世了。看到报纸上的消息时，事情已经过去了一周。自己无法去想象丽云的痛苦，因为，她的痛苦，自己已根本无法面对。就连轻轻地碰一碰，自己都会战栗不已。更何况，时至今日，丽云的故事，恐怕早已经是另一个故事的延续。而自己对那

个故事的内容，毫不知情。这是一种十分悲哀的感觉，就好像，在她的世界里，自己已经早就重新退回到了陌生人的位置。不，这不是真的。

或许，只是自己太懦弱。是自己没有勇气再去面对她，是自己没有能力去拯救她。但是，自己真的可以在假设中确定，自己在她面前的再一次出现，会是好事而不是坏事吗？自己可以给她什么？可以帮她什么？什么都没有，自己一无所有。就算脱下了这身乞丐的衣服，自己也不过就是一个只比乞丐略好了一些的无产者而已。自己连潘兆的一根毛都比不上。自己又可以凭什么，去重新走进丽云的世界？

更何况，连自己都不知道，在自己前面的路上，还会有多少纠缠不清或没完没了的江湖仇杀在一脸阴笑地等着自己。

九月，初秋微凉，树叶开始三三两两地落下。庄太太因病去世了。见到这则消息的那一刹那，自己几乎不敢相信这张报纸的真实性。自己偷偷去了一次庄府的附近，看到，庄府果然又在办丧事。那一刻，自己颓唐地跌坐在了地上。这是怎么了？命运，到底想要干什么？为什么要这样对待丽云？

为什么！

庄太太出殡的那一天，自己远远地躲在一个角落里，向着经过的庄太太的灵柩鞠了一个躬。可惜，一个很慈祥很善良的人，就这么走了。风裹卷着凉意在地上奔窜，几片凋落的树叶在风里凌乱地滑动。自己看见了披麻戴孝的丽云，她的脸上惨白地淌满了悲戚。她就像是一张在风中发抖的纸，只要风再来得更猛烈一些，她就会被活活撕碎。她的背影在簌簌颤抖，她低下头，在擦着眼泪。自己忽然潸然泪下。从此以后，在这个世上，还有谁，会真的疼爱她？

出殡的队伍看不见了，那些悲哀的声音，也都已消失在灵魂远去的方向。而自己眼里的泪仍在不停落下。她的脸和样子，就像是一幅令自己无法不悲恸无法不痴悲的魔画，哭泣的烈火越焚烧，画上的一切越鲜活。鲜活得让人肝肠寸断。而一片落叶掉在自己的头上，就像是上帝对自己的嘲笑。

十一月，冬风很凛冽。潘兆唯一的儿子，在一场车祸意外中惨死。据说，开车撞死潘兆儿子的，是一个日本人。坊间开始有了传言，说，其实庄老爷和庄太太，都不是正常死亡。而撞死潘兆儿子的那个日本人，其实身上的酒气是洒上去的。一些与日本阴谋有关的潘家故事，开始在市井间流传。

自己开始变得寝食难安。传言未必可信，但是，细想想，自己当初见到庄太太时，庄太太的身体仍十分健朗，怎么会才过了大半年就因病去世了呢？况且庄家有钱，就算庄太太真生了什么病，只要请来了名医，人怎么样也不会走得那么快。事情确实是有些蹊跷。自己开始深深地恐惧了起来。也许，那个什么狗屁的樱花会社，想要吞灭沈阳商界的野心从未消失。而如果日本人真的是在实施什么阴谋的话，那么，下一个受害者会是谁？

自己一定要保护丽云。

一九二九年很快就要过去了。统一以后的中国与易帜以后的东北，都并没有如人们当初所期望的那样，走进和平，迎来光明。一九二九年五月，张学良派兵于苏联驻哈尔滨领事馆内逮捕了三十九名苏联共产党。七月，发生中东路事件。苏联于七月十七日宣布对华绝交。二十一日，蒋介石即发表声明，号召全国将士一致对俄。八月，发生边境冲突。十月，苏军与东北军激战，东北军连败。而与此同时，日军乘机向长春增兵，并举行实弹演习，向东北张开了血盆大口。至十二月，中苏方停战议和。而在这一年里，国民党内部新军阀之间的争斗，也从未停止。在全国统一之后，蒋系、桂系、冯系、阎系四派大军阀在地盘分配与军队编遣问题上发生了严重的分歧与冲突。谈判桌上无法解决矛盾，于是，军阀们便以武力说话。神州大地战火重起，先后爆发了蒋桂、蒋冯、粤桂、蒋唐战争，各战均以蒋系势力的胜利告终。蒋介石的军事实力，已无人能敌。唯有百姓，苦难流离，惨不堪言。

已是到了一九三〇年。

离开丽云以后，一直没再想过要去偷偷地守望她。是既怕她再看见自己，也怕自己再看见她。那种只要能够远远地看上她一眼便可欢欣鼓舞的痴迷与简单，在发生了这么多的事情以后，已被分割得支离破碎，包裹得铁茧重重。一方面，她后来的故事已离自己越来越远，而在那个未知的故事里，自己究竟欠了她多少，自己完全无法预料，也不敢去想。另一方面，自己对她的爱，在长久的痛苦侵蚀里，已变得越来越清醒与自卑：自己到底是个乞丐，是个比无产阶级还要低下的臭叫花子，自己对丽云的爱，除了可以给头脑正常的人带来一些不可思议的惊讶与耻笑、狂笑的快乐以外，又还有什么存在的意义呢？难道一个乞丐配爱上一个富家小姐吗？难道乞丐的爱也配称得上爱吗？不，绝不。自己被人耻笑就可以了，绝不能玷污丽云的身份。要

是让人知道有个乞丐喜欢她，她会被人笑死。不，绝不可以。这就是阶级的现实性和残酷性。自己配去担心丽云吗？不配。更何况，丽云早已经是潘太太。他依旧会虐待她吗？就算会，自己又能做什么？自己又能为她做什么！自己只是一个无用的乞丐，自己只是一个无意义的存在！自己所拥有的爱或被爱，只是自己一生的煎熬与情债！

逃遁，从这个纷纭繁华的红尘世界里无影无踪地消失，或许才是自己最稳妥而淡泊的去处。让时间来逼迫自己告别过去，让永不再见来斩断自己给她造成的一切困扰与忧愁，这便是自己可笑而明智地参悟出的最好出路。但是，随着潘兆儿子的意外去世，那件被自己强硬披在自己身上的忘情外衣，迅速便化成了粉末。丽云的父母在那么短的时间里相继去世，紧接着，潘兆的儿子又无缘无故地被一个醉醺醺的日本人给开车撞死了，这一切会是巧合吗？别说市井小民们爱瞎想，不相信，就连自己，也觉得这些事情都发生得太巧。东北易帜之后，老百姓根本就没有等来渴盼已久的安宁与和平，反而只是迎来了血腥的清党与边境战争，那么，又有什么理由可以相信，日本樱花会社的野心已经收起或者泯灭？一切，只是盲目的乐观，只是国人对于和平的一厢情愿。自己绝不能袖手旁观，自己绝不能允许日本人伤害丽云一丝一毫。

自己开始暗中跟随、保护丽云。看她去公司，看她回公馆。除非她是坐上了汽车，否则，一般情况下，自己是能一直跟住她的。自己估计，日本人如果想要对丽云动手，在庄氏大百货公司外面下手的可能性是很大的。因为，第一，这里平常车水马龙、熙熙攘攘的，别说根本就看不出什么人的形迹可疑，就算在这里有亡命的车祸发生，也没什么可大惊小怪的。第二，庄氏百货一向被沈阳的华商界推为抵制日货的标杆，日本人如果真是想杀一儆百，无疑，在这里下手，会是一个很好的选择。自己在庄氏百货的附近找到了一个适合藏身的角落，当丽云走进了公司大楼以后，自己便会蹲在角落里，注意着楼前那条大街上的来来往往。

一直没有什么事情发生，一切都平常得像平常一样。仅就那段时间自己的观察结果而言，自己当时的确是怀疑自己是否在杞人忧天。但是，自己又明白，自己对她的跟踪保护，其实是很不完全的，比如，她在公司里或公馆里时，自己就不可能跟着她，而她要是坐进了汽车里，自己根本就跟不上她。自己只能是在一些有限的大庭广众的地方远远地守望着她。所以说，自己对她的这种跟踪保护，其实又是十分虚弱与苍白的。她完全有可能会在公司里或公馆里出事，也完全有可能会在汽车里出事，但是，对于这种令人不寒而栗的可能，自己又能做什么呢？

她一直没有发现自己的跟随和存在，至少在自己看来是如此。这对大家来说都是一件好事。自己不想打扰她，也不想被她看到自己对她的念念不忘。因为，自己对她的这份感情，能够给她带来的只有可耻，而能给自己带来的，只有可笑，就好比是一只癞蛤蟆爱上了一只白天鹅，这种故事除了最终会沦为市井小民嘴边的滑稽笑谈以外，一点值得存在的理由也没有。自己不想变成一个荒唐的小丑，更不想因为自己而令丽云的声誉蒙羞。一点点都不可以。自己可以被人嘲笑，但是，自己绝不允许这嘲笑，沾到丽云一点点。要是有人讥讽丽云，说她居然会爱上一个叫花子，那，自己一定会杀了他，有一个杀一个。就算要与天下为敌，自己也毫不在乎。只要能不让丽云受到一点伤害。不然，叫自己怎么活？

不知不觉中，自己又沦陷在了对丽云的深浓感情里。明明想要逃避，却莫名其妙地又回到了爱与矛盾的原点。也许，从自己决定要跟踪保护丽云的那一刻起，自己就已经是在糊里糊涂中，又踏进了自己给自己设下的感情陷阱里。自己应该想到，自己是不能再见到丽云的，哪怕只是远远地、警惕地看到。只要再看到，自己的爱，又哪会不死灰复燃？只要再看到，自己的眼，又哪会不痴醉成梦？已经明知自己保护不了她什么，却还依旧在紧紧跟随着她，自己究竟是想多保护她一点还是多看她一眼？已经明知这样的贪恋只会给自己带来吞毒的痛苦，却还乐此不疲、执迷不悟，自己究竟是爱她太深还是愚顽太真？一切的自问，都从来没有确切的答案。而自己，也只能是依旧听凭着心的操纵，跟随着她，守望着她，躲避着她。危险也许只是子虚乌有的推断与讹传，但是，自己还是想尽自己所能地保护她。自己只恨不能将她捧进自己的胸腔里，让自己分分秒秒地用命来爱她、护她。

深冬在严寒里泼洒着冰雪，沈阳的冬天总是洁白晶莹，而又刺人肌骨。兴许是自己一直跟她保持着很远的距离的缘故，兴许是自己还是在很多的时间里不能望到她的缘故，总之，自己是没再见到过一次她开心的样子。没有笑颜，没有活泼，她整个人，都像是沉浸在深深的悲哀之中。一丝丝的开心

都没有。当然，也可能是自己没看见，或没看清。但是，看到她的每一眼，自己的心，总像是能感觉到她的心在悲伤地哭。她的脸上虽然始终都很平静，也并没有在大庭广众之下流泪，但是她那一举一动，自己看得出来，是她的心在痛苦地哭泣。这种感觉总让自己莫名的悲伤和深重的痛苦。自己总希望自己的感觉是多余的，判断是错误的，但是，那种只有相爱过的人才能感受到的心有灵犀，却是怎么样也无法躲避与自我否认的。自己想去安慰她，想去分担她的一切悲哀与痛苦，但是很显然，这些都只是痴人说梦。自己永远只能远远地望着她，看着她像一只受了伤的孤独的小兔子一样，在雪地里瑟瑟发抖，绝望痛楚，而自己只能待在原地，无能为力，枉悲空痛。

她如今总是会在公司里待很长时间。有时，甚至会到晚上八点多才下班。而谭叔的汽车总是会在楼下静静地等她，像一只在表面上依旧温顺的蜗牛。冬天的夜晚总是冷而黑暗，纵然有路灯照明，那微弱的光亮，也丝毫无法削弱一点点夜的压抑和冬的苦闷。覆盖在大地上的冰雪，寒气弥漫着四际，在黑夜里望去，只是一片无光也无色的荒寂。有时候，看着那茫茫的夜和漫漫的雪，只是觉得人生的寂寞还是个活着的生命。而这个生命，在这无尽的冰天雪地里，却也只是在白白地盲目地受着折磨，不停地原地打转，不能跑，也不能跳，就连喊，也是无声地压抑。夜晚的街道总是很空旷，和白天的熙熙攘攘迥然不同。大概是时局使然吧。在这动乱的年代里，许多炫目的繁华只是一件虚伪的外衣，到了夜晚，舞台一暗，这个貌似喧哗的城市便只剩下了一具干裂破碎肌肉塌陷的尸体。大家在尸体的余温中入睡，都梦想着等明日天一亮，舞台重新开场。日复一日地在死亡的实质上舞蹈着生的悲喜剧。这个年代和这个城市，都在冰雪的掩盖下，散发着令人恐惧的尸臭味。而重生的梦想，又始终仅仅只是个梦想。谭叔的汽车一般开得都不快，所以以自己的功夫，有时也还能一路随行，要是实在跟不上，那也就只好是不跟了。在丽云回公馆以后，自己便也会回到破庙。自己会像其他的人一样，在这个外强中干的城市的朽烂气息中沉沉睡着，只是，在自己的梦里，并没有对明天白天的渴望。

从春节前的一段时间起，每天傍晚，在百货大楼楼下大门外的不远处，总会摆开一个小小的馄饨摊来。这个馄饨摊，傍晚时生意最好，入夜后食客渐稀。但是就算没什么客人了，这个馄饨摊也会一直摆到晚上九点多钟才收工。馄饨摊上的蒜香味总是飘得很远，让蹲在角落里的自己，不由得更加饥肠辘辘。馄饨摊上总是热气氤氲，在寒冷的冬夜里，分外拥有天堂一般的诱惑力。有时候冷得厉害饿得厉害了，是真想过去好好地吃上一大碗又热又鲜香的馄饨，但是，自己没有钱。有时想去向摊主乞讨，想想又算了。馄饨摊的摊主是个哑巴，卖几碗馄饨和收几个铜板，都是用手势来向别人表示，想来挣点钱也不容易。何必要再去分掉他的钱呢？损不足而补不足，是违逆天之道的。于是，在那些个等待丽云下班出来的夜晚里，自己凭空的守候总算是有了一些慰藉的理由：看，人家哑巴都还活得这么认认真真，作为一个没有生理缺陷的人，自己实在是不好自暴自弃。但是，自己又总会旋即便哑然失笑，感到自己的所有思想活动尽是一出没完没了的滑稽透顶的讽刺剧。你个臭叫花子，混得还不如人家一个卖馄饨的哑巴呢！你活着有个屁用！就是这样。

春节过后，冰雪又厚重了许多。这两个月，因为自己根本没有好好乞讨，所以，自己基本上是在吃兄弟们的。自己有些过意不去。自己开始犹豫，是不是仍有必要继续跟踪保护丽云？也许，根本就没有什么所谓的危险存在，一切，只是自己在疑神疑鬼。或者，自己只是在借着保护之名，故意接近丽云？以欺骗自己之手段，满足心与眼之不舍贪恋？自己难以抉择。在许多个或者困倦疲惫或者难以入睡的夜晚，自己仍会清晰地想起徐冷那时说过的那些话，那些话，一直像钢针一样扎在自己的心坎里，不动还好，一动，心血淋漓。自己当初到底是怎样被赦罪的？丽云究竟做了些什么？徐冷说的那些事，是不是真的？时光的流逝，丝毫没有减损掉这些问题在自己心中的重量，反而帮助它们生长出了密密实实的藤蔓，这些藤蔓像不能说话的债主，日日夜夜地缠紧着自己灵魂里的每一条神经。自己时常会被压抑得喘不过气来。

潘公馆的花园里，依旧立着一头威猛的石狮子。它完好无损，栩栩如生，只是模样和以前的那头稍微有了一些不同。应该是他们在去年换的吧。也不知去年自己打坏了狮头以后，丽云是怎样向潘兆做的交代。一想到这些，自己便又懊悔万分，自责得无法面对。丽云苍白的模样就像无数片树叶一样在自己的心周围飞扬，自己不敢透过树叶再去想象一点点丽云可能的凄惨模样。一阵阵的抽搐和酸楚在自己心里起伏，自己除了逃避、自责、

再逃避，一无他想。痛苦，就像无影无踪又无处不在的风，没有人能从风中逃脱。

元宵节后的一天晚上，自己回破庙时，居然在一个破败不堪的荒凉角落里，发现了醉得不省人事的潘兆。一开始自己还不能相信自己的眼睛，但是走近一看，却真的是他。他躺在地上，浑身酒气，双目紧闭，嘴里犹在无声地喃喃自语。他的西装皱成了一团，上面布满了像是呕吐物的污秽，一只空酒瓶在他的屁股旁安静地躺着，他的裤子上还有两只虫子在爬。此刻的他，真是比叫花子还要脏，还要臭。若不是那一身的西装革履，谁又能想到，他竟是富甲沈阳的潘兆。

自己拍拍他脸，又叫了他几声，想弄醒他，可是他却连无声的呓语都停止了。他一动不动地，就像一具死尸一样。自己赶紧探了探他的鼻息，又摸了摸他的脉搏，还好，他只是睡着了。

自己轻轻踢了他两脚。他没有什么反应。想要用力再踢一下，想想还是算了。自己弄掉了他身上的虫子，然后，便将他背了起来。

自己背着他，转身重新往潘公馆的方向走。或明或暗的路灯照亮着一段又一段不同的路，或松或紧的寒风拂乱着自己飘忽不定的心。自己背着一个自己不知道该用什么态度来对待的人，自己走向着一个自己不知道该不该去的地方。除了低头看路，自己无甚可想。夜如黑水，潮声在哑默里澎湃回响，迷茫摇荡，空虚在无尽的海平面下浮动。

潘兆又开始了喃喃自语。他的嘴巴就在自己的耳朵边，自己听到了他微弱的、像游魂一样悲哀而酸戚的梦呓：“儿子……你回来啦……儿子……你终于回来啦……”一会儿，他又说：“丽云……为什么你不爱我……丽云……为什么你还是不爱我……”声音都是一样的哀酸难禁，薄如蝉翼，仿佛只要轻轻一撕，拥有的便会失去，失去的便会消失。自己无疑应该恨潘兆，但是，至少在这一刻，自己恨不起来。自己甚至觉得，从某种意义上来说，自己与他，同是天涯沦落人。

到了潘公馆的大门外，自己犹豫了一下，还是按响了门铃。蔡嫂来开的门。蔡嫂很讶异。自己向蔡嫂说明了情况。蔡嫂明显是背不动潘兆的，于是她就叫自己将潘兆背进了公馆里去。走过了光线幽暗的公馆花园，到了小洋楼前。蔡嫂按响了小洋楼门外的门铃，是丽云开的门。

蔡嫂让自己先将潘兆背到了一间客房里放下，她得先把潘兆的脏衣服除去，把他弄干净。一个丫头又打了一盆给潘兆洗脸用的热水进来。自己自觉多余，便离开了客房。

到了客厅里，只有丽云一个人站在那儿。她倒了一杯茶给自己，说，你坐。但是自己看着那干净而豪华的沙发，没敢坐。茶也没喝。自己闻到自己身上有股秽臭味，自己心知是潘兆身上的呕吐物沾在了自己的衣服上才造成的，但是，这臭味分明就像是叫花子身上本来便会有的气味一样。自己十分局促不安，尽量站得离丽云远一些。丽云又要自己坐，自己还是没坐，她就笑笑，不再说什么。

“谢谢你把他背回来。”

“没什么，刚好碰巧。”

“……你现在……过得怎么样？”

“呵，你看，老样子。”

“……我以为……你会重新找一份工作。”

“呵呵，朽木不可雕也，我就是烂人烂命，已经烂到骨子里了。”

“我不是这个意思……”

“我知道。”

“……”

“……你呢，现在过得还好吗？”

“好，挺好的。”

“真的？”

“如果不是真的，那又能怎么样呢？”

“……”

自己说不出任何话来，她颓废地笑了笑，也不再说任何话，只是一个人喝起了水，喝了又喝。

“我……我走了……”

“我送送你。”

丽云送着自己，走到了花园里。无华的枝叶在暗淡的光里了无生气，天空依稀还闪亮着几颗纯洁的星星，只可惜，它们的亮太远。丽云的脸在幽暗的光线里特别楚楚可怜，虽然她并无任何明显悲伤的表情。也许，不

快乐，本身就是一种没有表情的悲伤，就好像星光熄灭的夜，熄灭即意味着黑暗密布。

她走得很慢，自己也走得很慢。

“……丽云……”

“……还是叫我潘太太吧……”

“……潘太太……”

“……”

“……我有一件事情，想问你……”

“什么事？”

“……去年……我究竟是怎么被赦罪的？”

丽云的脚步，一下子就停了下来。

“……我、我不知道——”

“你是不是去过南京？”

“没有。”

“你是不是去找过南京政府的上层？”

“没有，没有！”

她几乎是惨痛地，后退了两步。她惊恐的表情，就算是在灰暗里，都显露得那么清清楚楚。

“……我只是想知道真相——”

“没有，没有真相，没有——”

她痛苦地瑟缩着，眼里刹那布满了泪光。她的泪光是那么晶莹浓烈，她是脆弱得那样再经不起一丝丝伤害。自己想要再问，却终究无法开口再问。自己向她走近了一步，她颤抖着，又后退了两步。她垂头拭泪，自己肝肠寸断。她就像是一只受了伤的小兔子，而自己，无法为她抹去一点血迹，更不用说将她治愈。自己心中一酸，气息欲绝。

“你不要怕，我不会再问了……什么都不会再问了……你不要怕……”自己说着，却掉下了泪来。

她擦去了眼泪，抬起了头来，却是激动地突然对自己说：“赵驹，你不要再自作多情了，我和你之间，根本就从来没有发生过任何事，所以，就算你……就算你死了，我也绝不会为你掉一滴眼泪。我真心爱的人是潘兆，没错，只有他。以前我对你好，只是想要故意气气他，仅此而已。至于我说过的要救你的那些话，也只是在骗你，我就是喜欢看你被我欺骗的样子。没错，我是去过南京，我是去求过南京的某些混蛋办事，但是，我做这一切，都只是为了潘兆的利益，与你无关，和你没有半点点的关系。我知道外面有些什么样的传言，以至于让我每每想起这些都恨不能一死了之，但是我是为了我爱的人才去做的这一切，我无怨无悔心甘情愿，而这个我爱的人就是潘兆，是富甲沈阳如日中天的潘兆！不是你，不是你赵驹！所以，请你无论如何都不要再在未来的日子里又想起我，无论如何都不要再去相信那些曾经有过或不曾有过的虚假的一切，更不要错误地以为在你我之间还存在着什么子虚乌有的给予或亏欠，因为你和我甚至连最基本的朋友都算不上！也请你不要再来打扰我，不要再让我为了对你的欺骗而忐忑不安心有惭愧，不要再让我好不容易才忘记的一切再一次地重新回到我的眼前！你走，你走！”

她泣不成声，泪雨滂沱。

自己在她面前跪了下来，然后，磕了三个响头。

自己头也不回地跑出了潘公馆。一路上，自己腾空跳跃、翻转飞奔，跑得要多疯狂有多疯狂。踏碎了几户人家的瓦，踩破了几辆汽车的窗玻璃，夜深人静里，自己酣畅高歌，宛如疯癫，宛如撒泼。兴致极高时，忽然天降大雨。大雨里，自己终于跪地长哭。“为什么——”自己仰天长啸，却唯有冷雨倾盆。抬望眼，前路凄恻；再回首，一路血歌。

春寒料峭。季节的轮回仿佛一个奇妙的圆圈，大同小异的寒暑可以在这圆圈里不停地周而复始，但是人，却不能从这个冬天的终点，迈入上一个春天的起点。人如流水，每一分钟里的这滴水，都不会再是上一分钟里的那滴水。季节永不疲倦地重复，所带走的只是人的过去和回不去，而生在时间的洪流之中，不可逆流才是真正的命运。当沧海桑田不再只是一首诗歌，切肤之痛便成了这首诗歌最好的棺木。在那个没有感情的季节圆圈里，死去的只有人的悲欢，不可摆脱的，只是无尽的迷离与怅惘。

很多很多天，自己都没有再跟踪保护丽云。其实自己早该清醒，不该等到丽云把话给说出来。一个癞蛤蟆似的臭叫花子，本就不该对一个白天鹅似的公主用情。如果用了，那便是自作多情。每多爱一分，便是对自己多一分嘲讽；每多看一眼，便是对她多一分贬损。她说得一点儿都不错。自己，实质上就仅仅是个可笑的存在而已。自己就应该有多远滚多远，从她的世界里彻底消失。

三月初的一天，自己在报纸上看到了一条消息：潘氏的两家水泥厂和庄氏的一家纱厂已于日前正式被日资企业吞并。另外，报纸上还有报道说，日方在中国东北境内的走私活动日益猖獗，除走私一般商品外，甚至还以武装力量来走私鸦片、吗啡和海洛因，一遇我方缉查，即开火激战。各界有识之士在报上联合呼吁，要东北政府严防日本之经济侵略，且应坚决严惩日方走私毒品之罪犯。

放下报纸，自己忧心忡忡。一种十分不祥的预感在自己心里横冲直撞，搅得自己坐立不安。不，那甚至都说不上是什么预感，而根本就是显而易见的推断。日本人已经吃掉了潘家和庄家的一部分产业了，而很明显，日本人是不可能适可而止就此罢手的。先是庄老爷和庄太太，再是潘兆的儿子，接下来是水泥厂和纱厂，然后呢？然后又会是什么？自己居然会在这几天里开始相信，潘兆的儿子的确是意外死亡；自己居然会在这几天里开始相信，丽云并不可能遭遇什么危险！自己真是越活越糊涂！还是自己在一开始时的想法，最正确和最清醒！日本人就是在用阴谋来对付潘家和庄家！

可是，自己真的还应该去暗中跟随着丽云吗？自己真的能确定，自己为她所做的一切，对她来说都是有意义的吗？如果是无意义的，那就真的是太荒唐和太滑稽了。

正在踌躇不前犹豫不决之时，自己忽然又想到了一件很奇怪的事情。一般来讲，聋和哑这两种残缺，总是相连在一起的。耳聋是原因，喉哑是结果。哑巴一般都是因为耳朵聋了，所以才不能讲话。可是，在庄氏百货底楼附近摆摊卖馄饨的那个哑巴，却是可以正常听到别人的讲话！难道他会读唇语？另外，有很多个夜晚，明明已满街无人，不可能再有什么食客，但是他却依旧不收摊，就在那儿慢悠悠地继续裹馄饨。现在重新仔细想一想，其实他每一天的收摊时间，都必是在丽云晚上下班之后！也就是说，他极有可能，只是在等丽云去吃他的馄饨！

我操！

自己立即冲出了破庙，奔向了庄氏百货公司。

到达百货公司前面的大街上时，夕阳正分外红艳浓烈。人流尚熙攘，喧哗未安宁。自己看到谭叔的汽车就停在百货公司底楼的外面，便知道丽云今天应该还是在公司里。那个卖馄饨的哑巴还没出现，只有自己一个人在人流里发呆伫立。一个贵妇人从自己身边绕过，不屑地说了句，呸，脏。

自己又躲回了自己惯常躲着的那个角落里，远远地注视着百货大楼外面的人来车往。一种本能的嗅觉在告诉自己，自己最初的那些判断都是正确的。但是又有一个清醒的声音在不断对自己说，你只是在杞人忧天。而丽云那天对自己说的那些绝情话，又再度在自己身边响起。她说她爱潘兆，她说她和自己连朋友都算不上是，她要自己不要再自作多情。她说的都是真的吗？自己真的是在自作多情吗？自己的心，酸楚而惶惑，纷乱而狼藉。

那个哑巴出现了。他照常开始摆摊。诱人的蒜香味又在空气里四处漂流。傍晚，正是他生意最好的时候。有些食客看来已经与他相熟，他们会笑着对他说些话，而他，则会回应他们一些简单易懂的手势。气氛是平常而活泼的。这个哑巴，看起来的确只是个憨厚而勤快的可怜人。难道真的是自己太过敏感了？

夜幕很快便降临了。华灯亮起，人流渐稀。霓虹敞亮的夜晚，对于这个时代的这个城市来说，只是一些纷争与罪恶的乐园。帮会火并与权贵谈判，在许多灯红酒绿的掩盖之下明目张胆地喧哗着动乱。腐尸的气味里，灯火血腥而美丽。无法无天的辉煌里，灯火绚烂的地方比一片漆黑的角落更充满了死寂。这样的一种夜晚并不属于普通百姓，因为普通百姓爱不上这种冒险的乐趣。谁会愿意在一个与己无关的夜里邂逅一场莫名其妙的帮会厮杀或军政变动？所以，沈阳的夜，总是萧瑟如死。除了那些专为上流人物准备的销金窟，入夜后的沈阳，各处都寂静得荒凉。普通百姓都门户紧闭，唯恐会看到什么不该看到的，听到什么不该听到的，引来无妄之灾。但是，那个哑巴，却仍旧倔强地在夜色中卖着他的馄饨。纵然此刻的夜与此刻的街，已经空旷得一目了然，寂静得孤独不堪。

自己忽然想，不知自己没来的这些日子里，丽云有没有吃过他的馄饨？

夜愈深。

无人时，哑巴会将双手放在背后，双腿微微分开地站着。这种站姿颇为挺拔，全无卑躬屈膝之相。往日里自己倒也没觉得这有什么异样，可是此

刻，自己却想：君子慎独尚且不易，一个素来卑微受贱之人，为何于无人时却反而能显出一番轩昂气象？难道他原本就不是一个卑贱之人？

自己的想法是在越来越偏离正轨，还是在越来越接近真相？自己心乱如麻，无从推断。也许，一切都只是自己错钻了牛角尖。

时间已经很晚了，从远处的钟楼方向，传来了九声钟响。夜气寒凉，天幕无星。

谭叔在馄饨摊上吃了一碗热馄饨。吃完后，他没有给钱，也没有离开，而是继续坐在桌子旁，像要再吃一碗似的。但是他并没有再吃。他只是那么安静地坐着，像一根木雕，眼睛凝滞地望着某个地方，表情空洞，又像是心事重重。哑巴也没问他要钱，也没赶他走，只是继续在一旁慢悠悠地裹着馄饨。案板上的生馄饨显然已经多到了多余的程度。

而锅里的热气犹在空空地沸腾。

丽云从大楼里走了出来。

谭叔站了起来，向她招了招手。丽云走到了谭叔的面前，两人说了几句话。然后，丽云便像是要了一碗馄饨。哑巴点头哈腰手脚麻利地将一盘生馄饨倒进了锅里。锅上热气蒸腾，锅下火苗四溅。

哑巴往桌上新摆了一副碗筷。丽云转过身去继续和谭叔说话。然而，就在这时，自己却看见，哑巴在丽云的背后，往锅里丢入了一粒什么东西。他的动作，疾如闪电。是茴香吗？太远了，看不清楚。可是，放茴香动作干吗要那么快？太不正常了。但是，自己现在在这个狗屁的角落里，又怎么能肯定那不是一粒茴香呢？万一是一粒很正常的花椒呢？

太多的怀疑和自我怀疑，都已没有了思考的余地。因为，哑巴已经开始在盛馄饨了。丽云在桌边坐了下来。哑巴将盛好的那碗馄饨，放在了丽云的面前。谭叔笑了笑，将一把小勺子，递给了丽云。

不得不承认，其实很多时候，冲动才是人生真正的主人。

自己冲向了馄饨摊。

丽云舀起了一只馄饨。

“等一下，潘太太！”

丽云愕然地抬起了头来。

哑巴和谭叔，也都十分惊讶地看着这个突然不知从哪儿来的自己。

“这种路边摊太脏了，你还是不要吃了，我快饿死了，你就把这馄饨给我吃吧！”自己一边说，一边就抢过了丽云面前的那碗馄饨和她手里的勺子。

哑巴向自己连连摆手，示意自己将馄饨放下。他的嘴里发出“呜呜呃呃”的声音，好像很生气的样子。

“你是说，你这里的馄饨很干净，给谁吃都不要紧？”自己特别问哑巴。

哑巴点点头，继续做手势，要自己把馄饨还给丽云。

“那你重新下一碗给我吃好不好？我给你钱。”自己继续和哑巴说话。

哑巴拼命点头，一边仍然在做手势，要自己马上把手里的那碗馄饨还给丽云。

“好，那我把这碗馄饨还给她，你快去给我下一碗新的吧。”

哑巴点点头，喜悦地笑着，向自己竖了竖大拇指，正要往锅台方向转身，突然，他呆住了。

而事实上，丽云和谭叔也一齐呆住了。因为，自己说的最后那一整句，是日语。而他，居然听懂了。

一股森然的战栗，刹那弥漫了自己的全身。

点头哈腰的姿态从他身上褪下，一丝阴寒的冷笑从他嘴角泛起。“好聪明的中国人。”他用日语说了一句。

丢开手里的馄饨，自己向丽云大喊：“快上汽车！”

他纵身一跃，猛然将铁锅踢飞。铁锅带着沸水与火星，直往丽云扑去。说时迟那时快，自己一把抱住丽云拼力侧跃，才勉强护住了丽云，未受沸水浇淋。火星在地上熄灭，铁锅在地上咣咣作响。自己放开了惊魂失色的丽云。才转身，哑巴的双爪已于无声中直扑自己的面门。

迅猛得几乎难以招架的鬼爪。疾如风，快如电，无声无息，幽冥凌厉。有两次，自己的眼皮已被他的指甲触到。他的假动作很多，出招让人防不胜防。越是防守，越趋被动。在幽暗的路灯光下，哑巴就像是一个矫健而猛厉的鬼影，击于左而闪于右，飞于前而隐于后，铁爪无影，快步无踪。自己对各门派的武功都没什么了解，但看他出招阴毒幽厉的样子，便猜，这也许就是日本伊贺或甲贺的忍术。哗啦一声，自己左臂的衣袖被整只撕去。自己后跃了一大步，没想到却刚好落在了丽云的旁边。哑巴等于是摆脱了自己的缠

斗。他直接扑丽云而来。

自己不再防御，直接硬开硬打。自己虽有受伤，但哑巴也中了自己几招。自己一边打，一边连喊了谭叔好几次，要他快送丽云走，但谭叔就像吓傻了似的，待在原地一点反应也没有。自己心下又慌又急，而哑巴，似乎也已对这种难分胜负的缠斗感到了厌烦。哑巴飞跃后退，自己正要进击，突然，哑巴双手一扬，一枚手里剑，直奔丽云而去。

自己抱住了丽云。锋利的手里剑，刺入了自己的肩胛处。自己将丽云推向了谭叔，自己向谭叔大吼："你愣着干什么呢！快送小姐走哇！"话音刚落，自己感到背后掌风。已来不及回身，自己被哑巴击倒在地。

哑巴奔丽云而去。自己从地上爬起，顾不上拔去肩胛处所中的手里剑，便是从哑巴背后狂追而上，一跃将他扑倒。自己拼尽了全力将哑巴绞缠在地。自己向丽云大喊："丽云，快上车！"

这时，被自己锁缠在地的哑巴，却突然是用他那半生不熟的汉语也喊了一句："你还在等什么！"

真是莫名其妙，自己都不明白他喊这句话是什么意思。这时，他却是双腿一夹，反过来，将自己缠按在了地上。

这时，令自己震惊而恐慌的一幕出现了。谭叔拔出了一把刀，走向了丽云。丽云吓得连连后退。谭叔说，对不起，小姐，我的老婆和孩子，都在黑龙会的手里。

那一刻，自己真的想哭。

哑巴死死地缠按着自己。自己的双手，扣扼着哑巴的鬼爪。谭叔抓住了丽云，丽云哭了起来。自己猛地放开了双手，让哑巴的鬼爪，生生嵌入了自己胸前的皮肉里。鬼爪挖向着自己的肋骨。自己忍着剧痛，用腾出来的手，拔下了自己肩胛处的手里剑。自己用一只空手，拼命按紧了哑巴深陷在自己胸前血肉里的鬼爪。哑巴一惊间，自己已将另一只手里的手里剑的锋刃，划过了他的喉咙。

哑巴倒下了。谭叔大惊，不再犹豫地猛然举刀，刺向丽云的心口。但是，谭叔是不可能比自己快的。自己击倒了谭叔。谭叔倒在地上，吐了一口鲜血，然后，嘲讽地笑了一笑。

突然，"砰"的一声，一道亮丽而刺目的红光，冲向了漆黑无际的夜空。

是躺在血泊里的哑巴，垂死挣扎地发射了一枚信号弹。

自己打开了车门，对丽云说：“我送你去安全的地方。”

天上下起了雨。

雨势迅急，雨点密密麻麻地不停砸在车窗上。雨刮器不停地摆动，挡风玻璃上水痕朦胧。自己一直死劲地踩着油门，就恨不能让这辆车像鸟一样飞起来。信号弹已出，很显然，日本人今夜不会轻易罢手。必将有更残酷的凶险在未知的下一刻到来。而自己所能做的，就是尽快地在尚且安全的这一刻里，将丽云送至警察局。在这个显然会被日本人的武力所撕碎的夜晚里，唯一有能力保护丽云的，不是潘兆，也不是自己，而是荷枪实弹的兵营，或者警察局。在赤裸裸的武力面前，只有赤裸裸的武力，才是唯一的保护伞。

自己的胸前还在不停地淌着血。丽云哭泣着，撕下了她的衣服，给自己捂着伤口。但是，血还是怎么捂也捂不住。她哭得梨花带雨，凄恻凝噎。她说，去医院，快去医院。自己说，好，这就去，这就去。

他妈的这车子就没法开得再快一点了！

离警察局还有一段路。突然，前面横着开出了一辆汽车，停下来挡住了自己和丽云的去路。自己暗叫不好，慌忙倒车，退了没几米，后面又横出来了一辆汽车，挡住了自己和丽云的退路。左右是墙，前后是车，丽云的这辆车子，被困住了。透过雨痕朦胧的车窗玻璃，自己看到，有许许多多个拿着日本刀的日本武士，正从四面八方，围拢过来。

丽云吓傻了。

自己预感到了死亡的来临。自己握住了丽云捂在自己胸前伤口处的手，想最后告诉她一句，我爱你，但是，却说不出口。自己只是对她笑了笑，说，你趴下，在车里躲好，闭上眼睛，什么事都不会有。

然后，自己便打开了车门，下了车。

雨水滂沱，淋得人几乎睁不开眼睛。那一刻，自己想起了那天为丽云买伞时的情景，那一天，也是下着和今夜此刻一样大的雨。

日本刀纷纷出鞘，滑亮的弯刃，在雨水里清晰地映着路灯昏黄的光。自己忽然好想再回到和丽云一起站在屋檐下躲雨的那一天，那一天的美好，真希望可以被拉长到永恒。

雨声喧哗得仿佛一片海。那一刻，自己忽然想：也好，今天，可以和丽

云死在一起了。冷雨滂沱里，自己感到了一丝温暖。

自己怒吼一声，便冲向了那些日本武士。

刀光剑影，冷雨飘零。一个，又一个，一拳，又一拳。血水在雨水里飞溅，生死在转瞬间烟灭。锋刃一次次擦颈而过，恐惧在恐惧中麻木残酷。一刀，又一刀，劈砍在自己的四肢和身体，疼痛伴随着鲜血涌出，英勇仿佛只是为了更清醒地承受。自己的身上全是自己的血和日本人的血，大雨冲得再猛烈，都无法为自己洗去一点点杀人的罪孽和被杀的恐怖。雨点在刀刃上散开，血水在脚下肆意地流，冷酷的搏杀像不能停止的大雨滂沱，生与死的此起彼伏像海一样浩瀚无际。又一刀狠狠地砍在了自己的后背，自己跪倒在地。抬起头来，自己看到，丽云正在车窗后面，痛哭流涕地看着自己。

自己狠狠地砸碎了一个日本人的脑袋。自己捡起了他的刀。刀刃与刀刃的碰撞溅出了激烈的火花，钢铁与钢铁的厮杀划拉出了刺耳的摩擦。劈砍，劈砍，再劈砍。在雨水无情的浇淋里，生死的搏斗已无招式的讲究，你砍我一刀，我砍你一刀，谁的血先流尽，谁就是一个死鬼。自己的身体似乎已经感觉不到血液的热度，不断在流失的，仿佛只是大雨的冷冰冰和痛苦。自己的眼前，只有一片又一片的鲜红，满天满地的血，无边无际的死亡飘忽。多少次，日本人企图冲向丽云所坐的汽车，但是，结果都是被自己劈了脑袋。自己不想让丽云见到这些恶心的一切，真的不想，但是，她却始终大睁着眼睛，痛苦而绝望，恐惧而悲惨，美丽而哀伤。自己只能用自己还有的生命来做尽可能的挣扎，能多保护她一秒钟，就再多保护她一秒钟。只要自己还没倒下，自己就绝不允许丽云受到一点点的伤害。

终于，自己的肚子，被一刀刺穿。冰冷的刀身在自己的腹内搅动，很奇怪，自己居然没感到多大的疼痛。自己又一刀，劈碎了对方的脑袋。自己看着自己的血，从自己的肚子里，喷薄而出。这一刻，自己听到了丽云撕心裂肺的哭喊：“赵驹——”自己回头看了一眼，想再看一眼丽云的脸。但是，车窗的玻璃上满满的都是混合了雨水的日本人的血水，自己已看不清丽云哭泣或悲伤的模样。自己感到自己的生命已经到了最后，自己想对丽云说一次，我爱你，但是，自己却已虚弱得说不出一点点声音。还有最后三个日本人。自己，再一次举起了刀。

一刀，刺穿了自己的右胸。自己觉得，自己已经没有了呼吸。还剩最后一个日本人了，他就在自己的背后。自己向丽云笑了一笑，不知她有没有看到。最后的这个日本人，从背后，勒住了自己的脖子。自己举起刀，对着自己的肚子，狠狠一刺。刀身从自己的腹部穿过，刺入了背后那个日本人的肚子里。

“赵驹——”丽云撕心裂肺到极致的哭喊。

远处响起了激烈的枪声。丽云奔下了汽车。自己想对她喊“回去”，喉咙却已完全失声。自己想要再撑，但是，真的不行了。

不行了。

丽云痛哭着抱住了自己。自己拼尽了剩余的所有力气，对她说了一句“快跑”，然后，便是眼前一黑，失去了知觉。

什么都消失了。

像是进入了漫长的死亡。

无尽的空白。

重新睁开眼时，眼前看到的是干净而宽敞的病房。自己的身上，缠满了绷带，几乎不能动弹。滚烫的疼痛不时从全身各处泛起，火烧火燎的难受。医生是洋人，金发碧眼的老头。三个佣人站在自己的病床旁，她们说，自己已经昏迷了五天六夜。

佣人是潘兆请的，她们说，潘兆要医院不惜代价救活自己。自己不停地向她们追问丽云后来的情况，她们说，别的她们真的什么都不知道，但是，潘太太现在很好，很安全，这是真的。

自己问得她们烦了，后来，她们干脆就给自己看了一张报纸。报纸上说，潘太太夜间归家途中，遇上流窜作案的强盗，司机谭叔拼死护主，不幸遇害，不过所幸案发地离警察局甚近，警察局在接到报警之后，迅速武装出动，全歼了这伙强盗，潘太太安然无恙。

安然无恙。想来，这一点，报纸总是不会说谎的。只要丽云真的没事，自己就安心了。

孔仁换了一身像样些的衣服，代表兄弟们来医院里看望了自己几次。孔仁说，是一个叫蔡嫂的，去破庙里告诉了他们兄弟出事的事和这医院的地址。孔仁说，庄小姐的确是没出什么事，现在很安全，不用担心。孔仁说，听蔡嫂说，后来是有一伙拿枪的日本人，正要奔你们出事的那地方去，结果

在路上不知怎么的就遇上了警察，双方交上了火，打了没多久后，日本人就撤了，也许日本人是怕会把事情闹大吧，毕竟，武装交火是有外交风险的。孔仁说，潘兆现在请了一支全副武装的保安队，整天整夜地守在潘公馆外面，除了待在潘公馆里，潘兆哪也不许庄小姐去，庄小姐现在应该很安全。

时间在疼痛里流走，火焰像在伤口里燃烧。一片片火辣辣的肉体之苦在自己的全身内外安营扎寨，胸闷、腹痛如一刻不停的蒸汽机令自己昼夜不得安宁。睁开眼，医院洁白的天花板总会令自己想到，自己现在是在花着潘兆的钱；闭上眼，丽云的笑靥泣颜，又会难以阻挡地纷至沓来，像一个个难以磨灭的幻梦。酸涩、苦楚、爱恋，像一条裹卷着碎石的激流，不停地在自己身上冲刷而过，自己疼痛难忍而又渴饮不已，无所适从而又无能躲避。和有药剂正在治疗着的身体伤痛相比，无药可医而又无影无形的灵魂挣扎似乎才是自己最难承受的折磨。躺在病床上，有时，真的好想丽云可以来看一看自己，但是，自己又知道，这是不可能的。而丽云她现在还好吗？自己不知道。只希望，她可以平平安安，安然无恙。只希望，潘兆不要对她不好。而自己，其实是不应该再在丽云的世界里出现的一个泡影。惋惜只有在惋惜中才不会伤悲，遗憾只有在遗憾里才不会流泪。清醒的克制与应该的忘怀，自己都明白，只是，自己还是不能自已地想念丽云，想念她的一切。哪怕想念会让自己走向毁灭，自己还是想用毁灭来交换想念。

漫长的一个多月之后，自己的身体基本上已恢复了健康。洋医生要自己继续治疗，但自己已不想再在这里待下去。一个佣人给自己拿来了一张五千块大洋的庄票，说，这是潘老板给你的，算是谢谢你对潘太太的救命之恩，潘老板希望你拿了这笔钱后，可以离开沈阳，离开东北，要是钱不够，潘老板可以再给。

自己笑了笑，把庄票放在了病床上，然后，就穿着医院里的病人衣服，离开了医院，回到了破庙。

除了那一身的伤疤，一切，都像是没有发生过。

站在逆流的春风里，有时会觉得心神疲倦。天黑了，坐在路边，有时会想要就这样坐到天亮。无可排遣的孤寂和无望，令自己只想泡在无望的孤寂里去遗忘。没有路人经过，不需要乞讨的时候，自己总会被一种残酷而憋闷的现实感给撕开。隐藏在自己生命里的许多美梦，都会从这个被现实撕开的口子里经受阳光的暴晒和风雨的侵蚀，然后，一一凋零，逐个破碎。很多自己以前虽然有所觉悟但仍执迷不悟的事情，在自己的眼前和心里，都被剥去了虚幻的企盼，而只剩下了风化后绝望的本质与暗淡的图景。零零碎碎，摇摇欲坠。比如，自己开始认识到，孤独必将会成为自己此生的宿命。没有原因，也不需要佐证，命运就像是在自己的眼前，用某种类似于直觉而又超越于直觉的方式，向自己敞开了这一个可怜又可悲的秘密。而自己以前并不是这么玲珑剔透地认识自己的人生与将来的。以前，自己固然知道自己很惨很孤独，但是，还真是没想过，自己会有孤独至死的命运。可是，自己现在看到自己的命运了。自己会爱丽云至死，但是，自己不可能和丽云在一起一秒钟，这就是现在及将来最明白无误且不可改变的事实。孤独，将成为自己的生命。而这个生命，你不可去设计，也不可去摧毁。只有漫长的忍受，是上帝给你的存在礼物。

有时，还是会走过“Memory”，走过庄家老宅。“Memory”的生意依旧不错，而庄家老宅，早已门庭冷落人空去。繁华与绚丽，总像是红尘中一个短暂的梦，而只有冷清与孤寂，仿佛才是世界不变的本质，人生终了的结局。站在“Memory”敞开的店门外，不时会闻到烤面包或咖啡的香味，或浓或淡，都奔涌着生活热烈的美妙，低奏着尘世烟火的旋律。而站在早已人去宅空的庄府前，又会不得不顿悟，一切有为法，如梦幻泡影，如露亦如电。但是，再玄妙的顿悟，都不可能解开半分人生实在的悲哀，只不过，会让你的悲哀更加惆怅而已。千花香浓竞眼过，一夜西风凋残落。浓得化不开的悲哀与怅惘，才是人活在这世上最想逃躲却又偏偏最无法逃躲的真理。而，真理如果不死，悲剧就是这宇宙的永恒。回忆总是美好在悲哀开始之前的山花烂漫里，美好总是永恒在回忆消亡之前的海市蜃楼中。而这些不实在的一切，便都是人生最实在的痛苦。只有看不见的拥有和失去，才是最清楚明白的欢笑和恸哭。有时候，自己还是会想起丽云在那一天说过的那些绝情的话，自己分不清什么是真，什么是假。自己只是真的好想知道，她是否也曾像自己铭心刻骨地爱她那样，铭心刻骨地爱过自己？自己，想要明明白白地知道。

潘公馆的确是由一支全副武装的保安队保护着，不管是白天还是黑夜，都有荷枪实弹的保镖在公馆的内外站岗巡逻。这让自己很放心。枪战交火的影响是很大的，尤其是在如今中日关系的敏感期，现在这里有了这么多条枪

在守卫，谅他日本人也不敢再有什么过火的举动。所以说，潘兆的财与势，终究还是比匹夫的武功要有用得多。有时，自己还是会禁不住内心的枯寂与冲动，又跑去潘公馆的外面，像个傻子一样地凝望，期盼能再看见她一眼。这种凝望无望而漫长，可笑而悲凉，就像是独自站在一望无际的大草原上，等待着一颗不可能出现的星星。而这颗星星就算出现了，也与守望者没有半分关系。后来，自己看见她在小洋楼上的窗口中出现了一次，但是，她好像并没有看见自己。她消失了，就像没出现一样。但自己没有怅惘。自己只是想看一眼，她是否真的还好，现在看到了，她的确还好，那自己又还有什么可失望的呢？儿女情长皆是虚妄，长相厮守本是奢求。只要她平安无事，安然无恙，自己诸心可放，多情可抛。潇潇洒洒，好不快活。只不过，唯一有些遗憾的是，自己还从来没有真正地告诉过她，自己爱她。但是，算了，就这样吧。天地广大，人各飘零，本是造化。

一九三〇年五月中，中原大战正式爆发。冯玉祥、阎锡山、李宗仁等实力派军阀与汪精卫等在国民党内具有相当政治影响力的政客联合了起来，组成了一个反蒋大联合，要求蒋介石结束独裁，立即下台。蒋介石调集大军，与冯、阎、李之讨蒋联军决战于中原。战火纵横祸结兵连，硝烟漫天炮火连月，百姓流离失所，家国千疮百孔。战争开始时，蒋军屡战屡败，反蒋声浪震撼全国。而张学良在反蒋派与蒋介石的分别拉拢下，决定先按兵不动，保持中立，静观其变。

六月，沈阳又到了夏天。这一天，自己正在破庙里烧水，忽然听到外面由远及近地传来了一片脚步声。一开始，自己还以为是孔仁他们回来了，但很快，就发觉声音不对。一回头，只见三个日本浪人，已是站在了破庙的门口。

自己站了起来，神经不禁暗暗紧绷。可是，看着这三个日本人，自己忽然莫名觉得有些眼熟。他们注视着自己，脸上忽然也有了几丝困惑的表情，像在努力回忆着什么。自己想起来了，他们，就是前年在路上调戏丽云的那三个日本人。他们一刹那恍然大悟了似的，交头接耳了起来。

中间那个瘦子往前走了一步，微微笑着，用日语说："喂，中国乞丐，我们认识，你还记得我们吗？"

自己心知，以自己今时今日之武功，他们三人已远非自己对手，便有些有恃无恐。自己用日语嘲讽地说："当然记得，你们是我手下败将嘛。"

"你是一个狡猾的骗子，我们是在加入黑龙会以后，才知道你当初跟我们说的那些话全是谎言，你可真会演戏。"瘦子微愠地说。

"是你们太蠢了而已。"自己说。

"混蛋！"瘦子右边的那个长头发发了怒，要走上前来，被瘦子一把拦住。

瘦子左边的白皮肤对瘦子耳语了两句话。瘦子点点头，然后，用眼睛环视了一圈破庙内的一切，最后，将目光定在自己这个乞丐的身上。

"你，是不是叫赵驹？"瘦子问。

"是。"自己干脆地回答。

长头发轻蔑地一笑，然后转头对瘦子和白皮肤说："他武功不错，应该就是他了。这次，我们三人终于可以独享一份功劳了。"

白皮肤向长头发摇了摇手，长头发闭了嘴。瘦子继续向自己追问："前段时间，有个胆大包天的中国人，在一夜之间杀了我们黑龙会四十名武士，这个中国人，是不是你？"

自己仰天大笑，说："没错，就是我干的。不过你不说我还真是不知道，原来那晚被我宰掉的废物有四十个那么多，看来，你们黑龙会也不过就是一个废物窝呀。哈哈哈哈——"

长头发勃然大怒，"混蛋！今天就是你的死期！"

自己正色道："你们黑龙会四十个人都打不过我一个，今天光凭你们三个，难道还想取我的命？"自己冷冷一笑，"今天，还是让我送你们上西天吧。"说完，自己便摆开了架势。

他们三个相互看了看，突然都肆无忌惮地笑了起来。笑完后，一起轻蔑极了地看着摆好了架势的自己。白皮肤说："真是愚蠢的中国人。"说完，他们三个，一起从衣服里拔出了枪来。

三把枪，一齐对准着自己的脑袋。自己目瞪口呆，头脑空白。那一刻，还摆着武功架势的自己，分明是这个世上最可被嘲笑的白痴。

是自己忘记了父亲在壮年时所受的屈辱。是自己忘记了，威震武林的父亲，一生，正是被枪所败。

苍天！自己的愚蠢，丢尽了祖宗的脸！

纵然你武功天下第一，面对洋枪和子弹，还不是毫无招架之力！

这分明是自己在少年时便懂得的道理！

是自己丢弃了自己曾经的聪明！

人之一生，难道真的只是一场可笑而可怕的轮回？

“跪下！”瘦子笑盈盈地命令道。

自己一动不动。

“砰”，瘦子开了一枪，子弹打在自己脚尖前的地上。

“跪下。”瘦子冷冷地，又说了一遍。

自己跪了下来。

长头发狂笑了起来。白皮肤对瘦子说：“我早劝过车田君那个傻瓜，叫他不要再迷恋冷兵器时代的武士神话，但是他和这个中国人一样愚蠢，害得我们白白损失了四十名勇士。其实，这根本就是只需一颗子弹就能解决的小事。”

瘦子笑着，回答白皮肤：“没错，中国的武功再厉害，能厉害得过我们手中的枪吗？哈哈哈哈——”

长头发得意地将枪口晃了两晃，狂妄地命令自己：“你，赵驹，在地上爬两圈，学狗叫。”

自己一动不动。

长头发朝空地上开了一枪。

自己还是一动不动。

“混蛋！”长头发怒吼了起来，“我命令你，像猪一样在地上爬！学狗叫！”

白皮肤二话不说，直接开了一枪。子弹，穿透了自己的小腿。

凌厉的疼痛，像蛇一样，直接从自己的小腿，奔向了心脏。一阵发自心底的胆寒，惊恐不堪地蹿入了自己的头脑。

自己，拖着奔涌的鲜血，在地上爬了起来，像猪狗一样。

三个日本人，欢快地大笑了起来。

“学狗叫！学狗叫！”他们一起喊。

两滴眼泪，不争气地从自己的眼里掉了出来。

自己的头脑嗡嗡作响，像是没了意识，没了血流。那一刻，自己的心里既没有对于死亡的判断，也没有关于生存的信念，而只有弥漫到天涯海角的无力与失败、软弱与怯懦。这种怯懦，像是被冰封在自己记忆深处与本能深处的一个恶魔，而这一刻，这个恶魔，终于被日本人的子弹给唤醒了！只有无尽的破碎在自己周身涌荡，只有无际的寒冰在自己血管里流淌。自己一直以为自己很英勇，其实，自己像父亲一样，怕枪！从自己见到父亲因枪失败的模样的那一天起，自己就怕！这就是可怕的命运，可怕的命运！

“三弟！”“三哥！”

两声惊诧的呼喊，令自己回过了神来。自己忙起腰转头，一看，孔仁他们，已是跳进了破庙里来。

“三哥，你快起来！”黄道大喊一声。

孔仁、孟义、朱理、黄道已与三个日本人厮打在了一起。

“砰、砰、砰”三声枪响，孟义腿上中了一枪。一颗子弹从朱理腰间擦过，朱理单手便夺下了白皮肤手里的枪，然后，回身一枪就打在了白皮肤的额头上。

一番激斗后，瘦子和长头发，被兄弟们制伏在了地上。而自己，还依旧痴呆地跪在原地。

朱理将枪递给了自己，然后，扶自己从地上起来。

自己拖着伤腿，走到了两个日本人的面前。他们被按在地上，极力地仰着头，愤怒地瞪着自己。

自己将枪口顶在长头发的头顶上，说：“我们中国人，不是中国猪。”

长头发哈哈大笑，然后，瞪着血红的双眼，恶狠狠地说：“大日本帝国万岁！中国人，你们连做猪做狗都不配！”

“砰”一声，自己开枪打穿了长头发的脑袋。

自己将枪口指向了瘦子，“说，你们黑龙会和樱花会社是什么关系？除了杀我，你们接下来还有什么计划和行动？”

瘦子阴冷地笑了笑，咬牙切齿地说：“真想回到那一个夜晚，把你的脑袋给剁下来，让你的脑袋滚在地上，看着我们怎样残酷地折磨那个下贱的中国女人。”

“回答我的问题！”

“其实你是个无能的失败者，那天晚上，你根本打不过我们，只能依靠

卑劣的欺骗来逃过一劫。今天，你毫无反抗地就跪倒在了我们的枪口下，若不是突然有人来救，你现在已经是具尸体了。你是一个真正怯懦的东亚病夫！”

“我要你回答我的问题！”自己怒吼。

瘦子不再开口。自己痛恨至极地，丢掉枪，用拳头，砸碎了他的脑袋。

污浊的血，沾满了自己的拳头。兄弟们说了几句什么，自己没有听清。自己的耳边，依然还回荡着瘦子的声音：你是一个真正怯懦的东亚病夫！

天昏地暗的眩晕。

从三个日本人的身上搜出来不少钱，自己和孟义就用这些钱去治了枪伤。兄弟们将三个日本人的尸体绑上了石头扔进了河里。那三把枪，孔仁问自己怎么处置，自己心里知道这枪是好东西，但却还是对孔仁说：“扔了吧，不然万一被警察发现，我们就完了。”

于是，这三把枪也就一起被扔进了河里。兄弟们都不知道日本人说了些什么，但是，自己知道，瘦子最后说的那几句话，没有错。自己不敢面对那三把枪。对于自己来说，它们揭开的，不是一个伤疤，而是一个黑洞。它们是给自己带来软弱与耻辱的祸根，掩耳盗铃也罢，自欺欺人也罢，总之，自己是不想再看一眼这凶残的武器。

为了防止日本人再次找上门来，自己和兄弟们不得不选择搬家。大家费了一番周折后，才终于找到了一间废祠堂，可以作为新的住处。将废祠堂清理干净以后，大家便把家搬了过来，安顿了下来。自己对兄弟们很感愧疚，兄弟们却并不介意。孟义说，做兄弟的，就应该有福同享有难同当，生死一条心。朱理说，去年要不是庄小姐给了我们五十块大洋救命，我和大哥哪里还能活到今天，那帮杀千刀的畜生，居然敢动庄小姐，真是死有余辜。孔仁说，日本人欺我中国太甚，竟然在我们的土地上要杀便杀要打便打，简直无法无天，狂妄至极，三弟现在和日本人对着干，我们誓死支持！

兄弟们豪情满怀，无所畏惧，自己心中的惭愧却越发浓烈。因为他们不知道，自己的心，其实已被恐惧打得瑟瑟发抖。从那三个日本人一起用枪指着自己的脑袋的那一刻起，自己，已是被撕去了英勇的外衣。无敌的武功只是夜郎可笑的自大，无畏的英勇只是自我虚假的梦幻。灰暗的少年记忆才是自己对这个世界最深刻的认识，失败的无可奈何才是这个世界给予自己的最本质人生态度。自己懂得悲剧的清醒，只不过，是在一直逃避清醒的悲剧。而日本人的枪，打碎了自己的迷醉。“日本人有枪！日本人有枪！”只剩下那颗脆弱而失去了外壳的心，在自己胸膛里不停絮语。这絮语，令人清醒非常，丢盔弃甲，软弱无力。

七月，坊间有传言说，潘兆染上了海洛因的毒瘾，住了医院也没治好。

八月，一张潘兆在赌场里一掷千金的照片被登在了报纸上，照片里的潘兆，形容枯槁，像极了一个鸦片鬼。

而中原大战激战正酣。枪炮无情，死伤无数。七八月时，战争形势发生了逆转，蒋介石的军队由被动转为主动，反蒋联军开始败退。而汪精卫，正在积极准备重新组织政府。

九月，潘氏在外地的两家棉纱厂相继破产倒闭。有传言说，潘兆与樱花会社的社长赤木赌了一局，结果，潘兆一局就输掉了五万大洋。

反蒋联军败势已定，于是，张学良于九月十八日发表拥蒋通电，东北军入关助蒋作战。反蒋联军一溃千里，全线崩溃。

十月，庄氏百货公司遭受炸弹袭击，炸伤顾客十三名，职员五名。警察局立案调查。

同月，冯玉祥、阎锡山均战败下野。汪精卫等国民党内的反蒋政客也只得作鸟兽散。蒋介石依靠英美势力与江浙财阀的支持，利用反蒋联军内部的不团结，使用金钱美女收买的手段，取得了这次战争的绝对胜利。中原大战之后，冯、阎、桂三系损兵折将、土崩瓦解，从此再也没有了问鼎中原、与蒋争雄的形势与实力。

十一月，传说赤木再开赌局，与潘兆赌了三场。第一场，潘兆就输了五十万块大洋，第二场，潘兆便输掉了庄氏的两家面粉厂。第三场，潘兆赢了，他赢到了半斤海洛因。

十二月，沈阳的天空中，又飘满了冰凉的雪花。雪在风中飞舞着落下，像不愿坠落的精灵，像被撕碎的白云。雪落在脸上，清凉刺骨，融化后，会像泪一样流下。漫天的雪若太密，站在空旷的悲伤里，会有被埋葬的叹息。孩子们会堆出可爱的雪人，雪人的快乐总是永恒。若是喝黄酒，需要在炉子上将酒热一热，然后，才不会喝出雪冷的感觉来。一脚踩在厚厚的雪地上，都不能将地上的积雪给踩透，只有无尽的绵冷会从脚底升起，直达心扉。在

东北，在沈阳，已度过了一个又一个冬天，而未来的冬天也许还有更多。从地上抓一把雪，看着雪是那么洁白，心里说不出的难受。站在风卷白雪的严寒中，看不见人生的下一个春天。也许，春天本身就只是一个幻想。而幻想本身，就跟这雪一样，若握在手心，就会化为乌有，烟消云散，空空如也。

半年了，一直再没有什么日本人来找麻烦。也许是自己和兄弟们隐蔽得好，也许，是日本人早已转移了视线和目标。再想想，那天那个日本长头发说过三人想要独享功劳之类的话，也许，自己的行踪和姓名，原本就只是被他们三个日本人给查到了，而他们一死，黑龙会里根本就没人知道自己的情况。各种可能都是存在的，但是自己也懒得再去仔细推敲，反正眼下太平就好。能活一天活一天，得过且过。反正已经活到了这样一塌糊涂的地步了，生死与安危，已都是不需要再认真去对待的事情了。活着，是烂泥做成，苦海无边，真要是死了，怕也坏不到哪儿去。

据说，潘氏与庄氏的产业已折损过半。而在这半年里，樱花会社的势力在沈阳及东北发展迅速。日本人开矿办厂，打击华商，倾销日货，走私违禁，像幽灵一样蚕食着东北乃至华北的经济命脉。在经济金融这片没有硝烟的战场上，日本人已经单刀直入，势如破竹。一个大时代的崩塌，已近在眼前。

而自己唯一还关心的是丽云的安危。丽云一直还在潘公馆里，受着保安队的保护，偶尔出门，身旁也有佩枪的保镖跟着，护卫得很是周全。从这一点上说，自己其实很感激潘兆。时代乱流激荡，倭寇阴险狡诈，潘兆给予丽云的保护，是自己想给予而不可能有能力给予的。只是，如果真的如传言所说，潘兆已染上了海洛因，那么，他又到底还能坚持多久？他是否能抵挡住堕落恶魔的拖拽，力挽狂澜，不至于掉进毁灭的深渊？而一旦潘兆毁灭，丽云又将落入怎样的境地？

怎么办。

担心和挂念，在很多时候，其实只是一种空虚的思恋。这空虚的程度很深，深得令人望而生畏。就算你思恋得呕心沥血，对方也无法知晓或懂得你的分毫。因为思恋或爱，是空虚的，而距离与遥远，是实在的。她的身影和面容在你的心里和梦里也许都像烙印一样深刻，深刻得也许会让你痛，痛得嗷嗷叫。但是这种深刻又有什么意义呢？除了让你在孤独里继续孤独，在疼痛里延续疼痛，对于坚固的现实，它完全没有半分改变的能力。爱一个人，必会想要和一个人在一起，但是，爱和在一起，又完全是两件相距太遥远的事情。爱来自灵魂火热而不羁的颤动，而在一起，则需要乞求命运宽大的怜悯和现实恰好的交叉。陷在无法自拔的深爱里，却没办法牵一牵她的手，甚至无法多看上她一眼，这样的爱，与单纯的折磨又有什么不一样的定义？但是，爱又终究是割舍不了的爱，折磨只能是自己甘愿承受的折磨。从爱上她的那一刻起，不，从她出现的那一刻起，苦痛，也许便已注定。折磨，也许只是对爱的另一种证明。而爱，又只会在折磨里越酿越浓。这便是人生的不归路，命运的苦中甘。

只是，自己还从未真的告诉过丽云，自己爱她。也许，适合说这话的时刻，早已在很久之前便过去了。而一过去，再想说，就显得很不合适了。时光总是无情得让人想哭，总以为前面的路还长着呢，其实，一迈出，就是沧海桑田。这个世上最悲哀的事，就是在可以拥有的时候无法拥有，在无法拥有的时候想要拥有。而什么是遗憾？就是在一无所有的时候，会突然想起，其实曾经可以拥有。

而丽云说，你不要再自作多情了。也许，她是对的。也许，自己根本就从未拥有过任何东西，只不过是自己一厢情愿地在以为，那个梦是一个梦。说来好笑，梦，其实不就是一场空吗？自我的肯定原本就只是一个否定，执迷本身便只意味着海市蜃楼。在执着的道路上，越是用尽全力，越是会坠进空无痛苦的深渊。你拥有过什么呢？在铭心刻骨的深爱中，你一无所有，不能拥有。只有泪和血，孤独与痛苦，充斥着你的日日夜夜。丽云爱过赵驹吗？这个问题是多么的没有意义。她爱你，又怎样？不爱你，又怎样？你能做什么？你能创造什么？你能改变什么？在现实这位伟大的舵手面前，再撕心裂肺的爱情，也只是一朵小小的微不足道的浪花，完全可以不屑一顾。只有哭是你的自由，只有痛是你的礼物，你哭死了痛死了，现实也不会过来给你献上一朵同情的鲜花。所以，已没有必要再去追问远去的究竟，也不必再沉溺于消失的曾经。就让梦依旧依靠梦活着，让真相，在谜一样的现实世界里自由地徘徊。也许，有一天，真相会独自走到你的灵魂面前，轻松而肯定地告诉你：嗨，你个蠢货，你知道她有多爱你吗？

有时候，自己也会怀念家乡，会想起江庆县，想起赵家镇。江南的山山

水水，是自己人生中不可推倒的一个大背景，是自己头脑中无法抹去的根本印记。家乡虽然还装载着自己满满的疼痛，但是，那里毕竟是自己出生长大的地方，与自己血脉相连。自己的性格，从骨子里来讲，也还是被水乡养育出来的江南男人性格。偶尔，在梦里看见自己，那个梦里的自己，也仍是站在家乡小河里的乌篷船上。江南是锦绣而典雅的，不过，这些年炮火依旧不断，仗越打越多、越打越大，想来，家乡也必已是生灵涂炭、一片狼藉。再好的繁华，也挨不住金戈铁马三天两头的光顾。有时候，自己也会想起赵宏伟，那个素来自命清高而又实际软弱可怜的家伙。说起来，他也算是深刻地影响过自己曾经的一段人生。是他，夺走了自己儿时视若珍宝的聪明第一的荣光；是他，令自己被迫地懂得了自卑、妒忌与面对庸众的无奈。阔别经年，在这个分崩离析而又视人命如草芥的烽火年代里，他，可还保留着他的性命？若是死了，想想也可惜，自己未必不会感到有些寂寞。若是没死，不知他现在又混得怎样。但是想想，以他的性格，若还活着，是总不至于会像自己这样，沦落到做乞丐的地步的。在他赵宏伟的心里，儒者的尊严是高于一切的。他就是这么个死书呆子。所以，他终究还是比自己强，自己不得不承认。

而自己并不想要回到家乡。且不说家乡如今对自己来说，已无可留恋，纵然有朝一日，这沈阳会变成一片刀山火海，自己也不愿离开这里半步。不是因为自己喜欢东北，不是因为自己已将他乡认作故乡，只是因为，自己爱丽云，而丽云在这里。何为家乡？何为故里？最心爱的人在哪里，哪里才是真正的故乡。自己曾答应过丽云，以后有机会要带她去江南玩，而今想来，方知是痴人痴梦痴语，不痴的，唯有那满襟之长泪血啼。

已是到了一九三一年。

二月，庄氏大百货公司被樱花会社吞并，沈阳华商界的一面旗倒下了。新公司被命名为“大东亚共荣百货公司”，大楼里，到处都挂上了日本国旗。

三月，外界传闻，潘兆的负债金额已高达四百万大洋，每天都有从外地各省赶来的债主，不依不饶地要催着潘兆还钱。而据说和潘兆相熟的几位南京政府的高官，因为在中原大战期间曾有过同情反蒋联军的言论，所以在战争结束之后便被蒋介石秋后算账，统统给关进了大牢里，生死不明。

四月，风雨如晦。春暖无花。赤木和潘兆最后赌了一局。在这场最后的赌局中，潘兆输光了潘、庄两家全部的财产，包括庄家老宅和潘公馆。赤木最后丢给了潘兆一包海洛因，但是潘兆没有再拿。潘兆上吊自杀了。据看见过潘兆尸体的人说，那时的潘兆，已瘦得只剩下皮包骨头，就算还活着，也已和干尸没什么两样了。

令自己莫名感慨的是，潘兆在临自杀前，还特地多付了保安队一个月的工钱。他要求他们，不管发生什么事，都要再多保护丽云一个月。然后，潘兆就走了。

那么，一个月之后呢？也许，他是知道，还有一个依旧留在沈阳的自己吧。

在沈阳各界的舆论压力之下，日本人没能立马收走潘公馆。中国人说死者为大，日本人只好同意了丽云要在公馆里为潘兆办完了丧事再走的要求。潘兆出殡的那一天，送葬者寥寥无几，阴雨连绵。

从得知潘兆自杀消息的那一天起，自己就又回到了潘公馆的附近。自己就像一个愤怒的幽灵，躲在无人可见到的地方，充满戾气地日夜关注着潘公馆外面的风吹草动。潘兆这样响当当的一个人物，都被日本人玩到了自杀的地步，日本人若想要进一步再加害丽云，可叫丽云如何是好？莫名的如火燎一样的愤怒在自己心里细密地流窜燃烧，而更有一种阴森可怖得令人颤抖的恐惧在自己的骨头里打磨。潘、庄两家联姻之后所形成的商业王国是那样强大，可是，在日本人种种手段的攻击下，却瓦解得那么迅速而彻底，并且，潘兆还死得那样没有尊严。日本人可怕不可怕？

如果日本人真的还想要再加害丽云，自己又是否真的能保护得了她？自己的内心第一次对此感到了动摇。这种动摇，细微入骨，又强烈非凡，令自己恐惧不已。夜深人静时，看着那些已是在各自打瞌睡的保镖们，自己的胸腔里填满了绝望。完了，已经完了，真正可以给予丽云周全保护的潘兆已经死了，而自己，只是一个除了拳脚以外什么都没有的无用武夫！不，呸，自己连武夫都算不上，自己只是一个臭乞丐！

自己看见了一只时代车轮的滚滚而来。这只车轮巨大无比，带着雷霆万钧，滚到哪里，哪里的天和地、人和事都会被碾得粉碎，被压得血肉横飞。庄老爷、庄太太、潘兆的儿子、潘兆都已经死了，潘、庄两家的商业王国都已变成了日本人的财产，沈阳的华商界已经彻底败给了日本的樱花会社，下

一秒，又还会发生些什么？没人知道。

日本人遣散了潘公馆的保安队。在趾高气扬的日本人面前，那些膀大腰圆的保镖们都卑微得像一条狗。日本人将丽云的行李箱丢到了潘公馆的大门外。丽云和蔡嫂，都被赶出了潘公馆。潘公馆的大门关上了，以后，这里将再不属于中国人。

往昔繁华惨淡过，支离破碎几春秋。烟云桃花犹在眼，一场沉睡一场空。日本人放狗出来咬丽云，自己赶紧跑了出去，装疯卖傻，吓跑了狗，弄烦了日本人。日本人厌恶地踢了自己几脚，然后，便得意地回到了潘公馆里去。

蔡嫂和丽云抱头痛哭。蔡嫂说："小姐，以后我不能陪着你了，我要回老家去了。"

"蔡嫂，你也要离开我了，你不要走。"丽云哭着说。

蔡嫂哭着说："小姐，没办法，我也要吃饭的。"

蔡嫂推开了丽云，抹掉了眼泪，从身上掏出了一个布包，塞给了丽云，说："小姐，这是我攒的私房钱，三十块大洋，只有这么多了，你拿着，多少能挨一段日子，以后的路，就要靠你自己走了。"

蔡嫂转身看向了自己，像有很愤怒的话要冲自己吼，但是终究没吼。她最后只是摇了几下头，像哀叹一样地，对自己说了一句："你以后，不要再来烦我们家小姐了。"

蔡嫂走了，越来越远，最终，背影消失在了暮色中。

孤零零地，只剩下了丽云一个人。

自己想到，往后，丽云是真的只有一个人了，一股莫名的辛辣的难过便从眼里奔了出来。这种既孤独又令人害怕的感觉，融合在暮色无际的迷茫中，令自己永生难忘。远处有炊烟袅袅，丽云却只是哭得更加悲切。

帮她拎着摔坏了的行李箱，和她一起走在一条破旧的无人的巷子里，夕阳没有再给天地间留下一点光芒，只有满目步入昏暗的悲凉。她擦干了眼泪，告诉了自己一些这一年多来发生的事情。这些事情，有的和传言一样，有的和传言不一样。她说，她的母亲，是被谭叔下药害死的，而谭叔死后，日本人便杀了谭叔全家。她说，潘兆儿子的死，的确不是意外，而是樱花会社社长赤木的安排，潘兆想要报仇，却反而被日本人将计就计，拖进了圈套。她说，潘兆在外面有一个情妇，叫云曼，云曼给潘兆吃了一种会胃痛的药，痛起来没完没了，潘兆去看医生，结果医生给他开了一种立马就能止痛的德国药，谁知，这药就是海洛因。她说，日本人用海洛因控制了潘兆，但是潘兆并没有恨云曼，就在去年冬天，云曼割腕自杀了。丽云说，云曼死后，她见到了她的照片，那是一个看起来十分纯洁朴素的女孩。

自己对丽云说，你要小心，日本人狡诈得可怕。

丽云一笑，说，不用再担心了，日本人想要得到的产业，已经全部都得到了，我现在已经一无所有，对他们来说已再没有任何值得算计的价值了。

她笑了笑，泪水突然又奔涌而出。她哭着说，父亲知道我嫁给潘兆的时候，气得吐了血，我跪在父亲的病床前向他发誓，说一定会保住庄家的一切，可是，到头来，我不仅没保住庄家的一砖一瓦，还害得潘兆落到了如此下场，我真的是个扫把星，我真的是个扫把星！

丽云痛哭流涕，自己心如刀绞，想安慰她，但看看自己一身的破烂，便没有向她走近半步，只是空空地对她说，你不要这么想，不要这么想。

令人疼痛的泪水在她脸上肆意地流淌，而天空，看起来愈发像一块在阴暗里生锈的铁皮，就是这块铁皮，将人间弄得乌烟瘴气，惨惨戚戚，像极了一座炼狱。身后是瓦砾满地、繁华尽成废墟，前路是一片荒芜、迷茫不知何处，此时此地此境，真是怎样不叫人绝望、恐惧。令人愁肠哀转的伤感还在纷纷徘徊，激厉突变的恐怖犹在暗处作祟，往后生存的困难重重又已是以一种居高临下的姿态来到了眼前。自己问她，往后你有什么打算？她却只是垂泪摇头。那种心疼到极致而又无能为力到极致的难受，简直像要把自己五马分尸。但是，自己又能为她做什么呢？

丽云暂且在一家旅店里安顿了下来。自己没有送她到旅店外面，因为自己的身份实在不合适。自己看着她，在华灯初上的夜色里，艰难地拖着行李箱，敲开了旅店的大门。临分别时，她说，再见，自己也说，再见。但是自己知道，自己不会就此离开。

自己开始痛恨，为什么自己是一个乞丐。但是，不做乞丐，自己又能做什么？自己已杀了那么多的人，得罪了那么多的恶势力，玉山帮、青帮、黑龙会，如果正正经经地去露脸做事，会不会又招来防不胜防的杀身之祸和没完没了的江湖麻烦？如果不像一只老鼠一样地躲在这个社会的最暗角落里，

自己又是否还有活下去的机会？自己的人生，似乎早已没有自主的选择，只能任凭命运摆布。若与命运对抗，结局很可能只是两败俱伤，鱼死网破。而自己要是死了，往后，还有谁能保护丽云？

自己依旧潜伏在旅店的附近，观察着旅店周围的动静。自己总是不放心。虽然说，丽云的确已没什么值得日本人再去算计的了，但是，天知道日本人会不会翻旧账，暗算到底。自己不敢大意。这群日本人的狡诈令人感到害怕，这种害怕，深入自己的心扉，几乎能令自己丧失对人间一切安全感与依赖感的信任。所以，自己必须要守着丽云。潘兆都能做到对她守护到底，自己难道还会做不到。

几天以后的一个上午，自己看见丽云拿着一个首饰盒，去了当铺。从当铺回到旅店以后，中午的时候，她就拖着她的行李箱，从旅店里走了出来。看样子，她是要离开旅店了。她走了一段路，到了僻静处，自己便追了上去，帮她拎起了行李箱。

她很惊讶，问，你怎么在这儿？自己说，刚好路过。她就笑了，说，正好，帮我拎箱子。自己也笑。问她，你不住旅店了？她说，旅店太贵了，我另外租了一处民居，便宜，实惠。

自己看见，她身上原来一直戴着的那些首饰，都没有了。耳环、项链、手镯、戒指、手表，全没有了。自己想对她说些安慰的话，却又感到，安慰是这个世上最苍白的东西。自己的心里堵得很难受。

到了她租的地方，是一个十分偏僻的所在。房子很小，又破又旧，房子四周砌着一圈土墙，算是围出了前院和后院。推开两扇院门，“咣啷”一声，一扇院门就从门框里掉了出来，摔在地上。

帮她修好了院门，然后，又和她一起将房子的里里外外都打扫了一遍。她看上去挺高兴的，一直微微笑着，但是自己的心，却像在被一根手指戳来戳去。

她去井里打水，打好了水以后开始烧水。烧水的时候，她就坐在灶台旁边的一张小矮凳上。西斜的阳光从歪扭着的小窗口里照进来，照在她的身上，她还是像从前一样美丽。只不过，她的鞋上已经沾满了烂泥。自己想起了她以前坐在庄家大宅里时的样子，心中不禁萧瑟一酸，像被什么车轮碾过。

和她说了几句话，然后，便去帮她打好了两桶水，接着，自己就告辞了。她像是还有什么话要说，但是，还是只说了再见。她一直微笑着。

当然，自己其实并没有走远。虽然看起来，日本人的确是已没有必要再加害丽云，节外生枝，但是，不怕一万就怕万一，而且，丽云现在落到了这步田地，就算没有日本人来害她，也难保会没有阿猫阿狗来欺负她。总之，她现在的这个样子，自己是一万个不放心。

房子里只剩下了丽云一个人以后，自己听见了丽云嘤嘤的哭声。这哭声，令自己肝肠寸断。是啊，她哪里会真的高兴呢？而今的她，已是家破人亡，无依无靠，孤苦伶仃，衣食堪忧，这种从拥有到一无所有的突变远比生存的艰难严峻更令人悲痛欲绝、无所适从。她又怎么能不哭泣？

而自己，又能真的为她做什么？

傍晚时分，她去了点心铺。自己看见，她想买肉包子，但数了数钱以后，她却只买了两个白馒头。当她把馒头塞进嘴里的时候，自己的心塌了。自己给了自己两个耳光。

我要挣钱，我要挣钱！

自己的心，在大喊大叫。

可是，自己却只是一个比她更一无所有的乞丐，臭乞丐。

六月，炎热而多雨。道路泡在时断时续的雨水里，烂糟糟，滑腻腻，泥泞不堪。将树叶踩在路上肮脏的水洼里，会感到，整个人都好像被这难受的夏季给碾成了烂泥。

庄家的大宅，已经变成了樱花会社的办公场所。每次经过，都能看见有日本人在里面进进出出。曾经在这里度过的几天美好时光，依旧历历在目，眼前，却已物是人非。那些铭心刻骨的珍贵过去，只能唯一地保存在记忆的仓库里，缥缈、空灵、游荡，而眼前真实的旧迹，却只能任由着敌人的占有与践踏。丽云曾经想要保护的一切，都被日本人给毁了。她曾那样天真地以为，只要她付出了她的全部，牺牲了她的幸福，她就可以保住庄家的一切，保住她的父辈、祖辈们所辛辛苦苦留下来的一切，但是，看呐，日本人正在她家的院子里吐痰，两条日本狗，正在庄宅的大门外哼唱着得意的日本小调。丽云失去了她的父亲，失去了她的母亲，失去了她想要用生命来守卫的庄家的尊严，失去了她想要死死地保护住的所有一切。她在乎的、不在乎

的，都已被残忍地毁灭；属于她的、不属于她的，都已被敌人占有。一无所有的她，唯一还拥有的，只是一望无际的痛苦和绝望。在形销骨立、满目疮痍之外，再无半分生的痕迹与光的暖意。而这一切，都是拜侵略者所赐。当实在的美好只剩下缥缈的回忆，当曾经的拥有只余下被剥夺的痕迹，明天，我们又会再失去些什么？在日寇猖獗的铁蹄面前，明天，我们是会又失去一个所爱，还是再失去一份拥有？当我们被逼退到最后，背后会是一个怎样壁立千仞的悬崖？

而自己，又能为丽云做些什么？

沈阳的帮会分子，经营着一家地下格斗场，供人赌博。自己换了衣服，戴了面具，去做了格斗场的拳手，每晚打两三场黑市拳。每赢一场，可得五块大洋。碰上打假拳，若假得漂亮，可得十块大洋。

不管是真赢还是假输，自己每晚都能稳赚十到十五块大洋，极少有真输的时候。每次打完拳出来，都已是凌晨两三点钟，空旷清凉，月朗星稀。漆黑的夜就像一个永远不会醒的梦，在天空弥漫沉睡。走在这样的夜里，自己的心情是雀跃的，毕竟，每晚能挣这么多钱，是自己以前从没想到过的。也只有在这样的时候，自己才会在内心里觉得武功还是有用的。打黑市拳，远比卖艺和乞讨要挣得多，多得令人惊喜。而且，自己打的还不是生死局，如果打生死局，输了是死，赢了，收入是普通格斗的十倍、二十倍甚至更多。

每晚，自己都会在黎明的太阳升起之前，去一次丽云的住处那里，将自己挣到的那些大洋，从粗陋的门缝里塞进去。一盏破旧的路灯竖立在这座破旧的小院子旁，每当有风猛烈地吹过，路灯的铁皮灯罩便会哐哐作响，像是有鸟在顽皮地踩踏，像是灯泡随时会从灯柱上掉下来。它的灯光乌油昏暗，有时还会莫名其妙地灭断。丽云的小院子，在夜里，在这样的微弱光亮里，就像一只随时会摔进黑暗里去的生鸡蛋，就像一艘随时会被黑色的海洋吞没的破船，就像一幅随时会被黑夜浸湿然后蚀烂的油画。一种安静的美莫名与这小破院子结合着，使得自己在黑夜里，在昏暗中，如本能般地只向往这个地方。当身体隐隐作痛，关节酸肿，只要自己还能守护着这座小院子，自己就会莫名感到幸福。只要自己知道，丽云在这里，在这里的她还一切安好，这里，便是自己的圣地。自己绝对不能，看着她连一只肉包子都吃不起。

每过五天，自己便会攒下三块大洋来给兄弟们。他们都劝自己不要再去打黑市拳，说那些打黑市拳的有哪一个最后不是非死即残，但自己总是笑笑，说，在沈阳，能把我打残的人还没出生。说多了，他们也就不说了。只是在很多时候代替了自己去远远地保护丽云，好让自己多睡睡觉，储存体力。孔仁说，你好好休息，要保护庄小姐，我们也行，你放心。自己也不知还该对他们说些什么，自己的事，他们也许都明白，但他们也没笑话自己，也没怨恨自己，这让自己又分外觉得对不住他们。但孔仁说，没事，庄小姐也是我们的恩人，我的腿要不是治得及时，早废了。自己当时就想，总有一天，自己一定要好好报答这些好兄弟。

但是，自己从来没有兑现过对兄弟们许下的任何承诺，不管这承诺，是说出来过，还是没说出来过。

刚开始打黑市拳的那段时间里，自己对付各路拳手都稳操胜券。但是，随着身上各种伤痛的增加，每一晚的格斗，都开始变得越发艰难了起来。而与其他拳手的搏斗越是变得艰难起来，自己身上的伤痛，也就增添得越快越多。这是一个互为因果不断促进的恶性循环，一旦跌入了这个循环里，那就无异于是陷进了一片要命的沼泽中。自己出拳的速度变得越来越慢，有时甚至还会眼花、耳鸣，而自己的两只膝盖，也都已在之前的格斗中受了伤。有两次，自己甚至差点被当场打掉了脸上的面具。观众和赌客开始对自己的表现感到失望，他们由以前对自己的助威，开始变成了向自己的对手大喊："打死他！打死他！狗屁的八极拳王！"

而，自己的身体越是疼痛，内心越是恐惧和悲哀，就越是渴望能够在比赛结束之后，可以去丽云的小院子外面多待一会儿。靠在那不高的、破旧的院墙上，看着那黑的夜、暗的光，自己能感到，好像是丽云就站在自己的身边一样。而自己，又的确是离她这样近，只不过她在屋里、自己在院外而已。这是一件多么幸福的事情。只要能和她这样近地在一起，那一点点的伤痛，又能算得了什么。自己要挣钱，要挣更多更多的钱。

一次又一次地重新投入赛场，一次又一次看着别人流血或自己流血，疼痛在胜负面前已经变得微不足道。自己不能输，因为输了就没有钱拿，输了自己就没有钱给丽云。听着对手骨头断裂的声音，看着赛场的天花板在眼前天旋地转，有时候，真觉得自己是已经掉进了一个疯狂的世界里。不管是

谁倒下，总会有胜利的赌客起来欢呼；不管有谁痛哭流涕，总有失望的观众起来大声诅咒。这真的是一个疯狂的世界。只要是走上了擂台的拳手，就不再是一个人，而只是一头被用来娱乐的野兽。自己和对手的鲜血与呻吟，是老板用来赚钱的道具；两个无冤无仇的生命的以死相拼，是观众和赌客们的最大乐趣。而自己又甘当一头将生死给人娱乐的野兽，只因自己没有钱，没有保护一个自己所深爱的人的能力。自己想让丽云重新过上好的生活，但是自己只是一个被社会仇恨的人，自己只是一个被社会鄙弃的人。除了将生命和尊严一起献给她，自己已实在是没有任何可以拿得出手的东西。只要是为她，杀人也好，被人杀也好，自己都在所不辞。自己的灵魂和肉体，都一钱不值，只要能对她有一点点的用处，便是自己最大的荣幸，自己愿意不惜代价去付出和争取。这，也许便是乞丐的爱情。

这一晚，自己打了两场，输了两场，一块钱也没有挣到。脱臼后又复位的胳膊，在出击时已明显力不从心，被人扭住后，自己也不敢再用力反转，只能处于劣势。混浊而深沉的挫败感像海水一样包围着自己，既令自己感到恐惧，又令自己的心腌臜难受。武功是自己最后的自信，但是现在，就连这最后的自信，也在被一点点击垮。自己真的感到了一无是处的痛苦，那种对自己的失望，比对命运的绝望还要让人无法忍受。就好像，自己的一切困顿与痛楚，都只是自己的过错，与天无关。伤处还在火辣辣的疼痛，但是比这肉体之苦更痛的，是自己对自己的失望、怀疑与自己对前路的绝望、迷惘、惆怅。

出了格斗场，自己摘下了面具，换回了乞丐的衣服。自己已精疲力竭，但又痛得不想睡眠。今晚，自己没有钱可以给丽云，但是，却又比以往任何时候都更渴望可以见上丽云一面。虽然，自己也知道，这是不可能的。夏的夜，星空是分外高远而辽旷的，带着热度的风，就像是从星辰之外更远的空间里吹来，辽远而陌生，孤单而无人，看不见来路，更没有去处，只有永恒的徘徊与回荡。

还是去了她的小院子外。似乎只有那迷离的路灯光，破旧的土院墙，才能暂时地将自己从现实存在的痛苦与困厄中解救出来，给予自己一片和真实无关的安宁，赐予自己一抹和存在隔绝的温柔。身体的伤痛和心灵的沮丧在这样令人慰藉的幻梦里，只不过就像是一只蚂蚁的悲愁，渺小得微不足道。

而有时候在这幻梦的边缘，自己又能触摸到这安宁与温柔本身暗涌的一股悲酸：梦外的她是一只飞鸟，梦里的自己是一条海鱼，鱼深爱着鸟，梦本身也就只能是一片苦海。但这样的领悟也还不至于让自己落泪，只要她还安好，自己的爱并不重要。

抚摸着粗粝的院门，有怅然若失的细小哀愁，好像在从院门的皱纹里渗入自己的指尖，融进自己的血液，游向自己的心田。夜，越是靠近黎明，越是沉潜至冰凉深静的潭底。这潭水，都能冷得让人心尖发颤。细密的怅惘，扯着自己的心思，像是让自己的灵魂离开着自己的躯壳。又一阵空旷而辽远的风吹来，吹得很猛烈，路灯的灯罩都发出了剧烈而战栗的声响，自己才算是回过了神来。不禁深深叹了口气，自己正准备离去，忽然，院门却打开了。丽云，就站在打开的院门口。

幽寂而昏昧的路灯光洒在丽云的身上，照亮着她瘦而苍白的脸庞。她就像是一只忽然飞近了海平面的小鸟，扑棱着翅膀，却无处停靠。至少，在那一刹那，自己是这样以为。但是，她却伸出了一只拿着小布袋的手，对自己说："给，这是你的钱，拿回去。"

自己傻站着。

她两只手捧着那只小布袋，走到了自己的面前，将布袋往自己怀里一塞，说："还给你，屋里还有一大袋，我拿不动，你自己去拿。"

自己一摸布袋，里面全是大洋，便赶紧装糊涂，说："丽云你说什么呀，这怎么可能会是我的呢。"

"你以为我有那么傻吗，我会相信天上掉大洋到我院子里来？"她说。

自己说不出话来。

她默然了一小会儿，便说："其实，你第二次送钱来的时候，我就知道是你了。那晚我没睡，我就蹲在一张凳子上，等到快天亮时，听到动静了，我就从凳子上站起来，趴在墙上往外看，结果，就看到了你。"她笑了笑，像是笑，又像是很忧伤，"我还怕你看见我，但是，你看起来很累的样子，竟然都没发现我在看你，塞完钱后，你就匆匆忙忙地走了。"

自己无所适从，不知该怎么向她解释。忽然怕她误会这钱是自己乞讨得来的，便又忙向她澄清，这钱绝对干净，不是要饭要来的。

她转了个身，笑了笑，说："这个我知道，你要饭，一天又哪能要到十

块十五块大洋？更何况，是天天这么多。所以，我也就觉得奇怪了，你怎么会突然有了这么多的钱？”她后退了一步，笑容里浮着一层说不清道不明的忧伤，“我一直想找你谈谈，问问你，这些钱是哪来的，你为什么要这样做，可是……每次想要开门时，又忽然很怕问你这些，呵……我也说不清……后来，我想，你是总不至于会去做伤天害理的事情来赚钱的，对不对？”

“这钱是干净的。”自己说着，眼睛却莫名不敢看她。

“知道吗，我从来没有觉得你不干净，你要饭要到的钱，也不是什么脏钱，可是，反倒是你自己，好像还一直是站在以前少爷的位置上，在看不起你今天的自己。我说得对吗？”

自己苦笑了起来，想告诉她，这和站在什么位置看无关，乞丐的肮脏和低贱是一个无人可以改变的社会事实，但是，看到她眼中闪烁着的像星光一样的忧伤，自己又不想在这个时候，去和她争辩些什么。而且，她说乞丐不脏，这又有什么可争辩的。

“今天，我看见了孔仁，是他告诉我，这些钱，是你打黑市拳挣来的。我问他，什么是黑市拳，他说，就是像罗马斗兽场一样，奴隶在下面斗个死去活来，贵族在台上取乐赌钱。”

“你别听他胡说，你看我，好好的，一根汗毛都没伤到。有谁能打得过我。”

“那你今天也打赢了吗？”

“当然，有谁能打倒我。”

“那钱呢？”

“什么钱？”

“你赢了不是会有钱吗？你赢到的钱呢，拿出来给我看。”

自己拿不出来。自己低下了头。

她，忽然哭了出来。“……你会被人打死的……”她哭着说。

自己的心忽然塌软得没有了一点点防御力，心酸无比。“……傻话，我怎么会被打死呢。”

“……你会被人打死的……”她只是啜泣着说。

“不会的，绝对不会。偶尔输一两次，总有的。”自己说。

“我不要你的钱，我不要你可怜我，我不要你拿命去挣了钱来可怜我……”她哭着说。

“我没有可怜你，我不是可怜你，我……我……”自己想说，我是因为爱你，但是，这话却终究还是无法说出口，“我只是在还我欠你的钱，你还记得吗，以前我花了你那么多的钱，却从来没有还过你半个铜板，我现在只是在还我欠你的债。”

“你没有欠我——”

“不，欠的，欠很多，所以我要慢慢还，都还给你。”

“那照你这么说，我的这条命也是你的了。因为是你救的我，我欠你一条命。”

“不，你的命是你的，你不欠我。”

“你以为我都忘了吗，在那个雨夜，我躲在汽车中，你独自和一群日本人厮杀。当日本人的武士刀劈中你的时候，你却还给了我一个微笑，你以为我已经忘记了这些吗？”

“我为你做什么都是应该的，你不要觉得欠了我，不要。”

“可事实上，我欠你的。”

她擦去了眼泪，眼里的哀愁像融化了的雪，形状已匿，凉意沁地。这种哀愁莫名让自己的心弦绷得难受，就好像自己和她同陷在一个迷宫里，她已看到了什么绝望或悲哀，而自己还在翘首以待，不明所以。难以言说的情感已经像藤蔓一样缠住了她和自己的交谈，使自己和她在一个看不见的泥潭里沉陷。这种沉陷，剪不断，理还乱。

“说救命，如果没有你，我赵驹哪里还能活到今天，我心里都知道。”自己心意凝结地，不禁说。

她沉默着，转过了身。她的眼里噙起了泪花。自己忽然又后悔自己说错了话。自己真的好想抱住她，叫她不要再流泪，但是，自己却只是像一截木头一样地站着。她双手搂了搂肩，说，以后不要再说这些了。她自嘲地笑了笑，说，我们这样算来算去，怕是到天亮也算不完的。

自己只是傻站着。风有些大，她好像有些冷。自己却只是傻站着。

她看着自己，幽幽地说：“答应我，不要再去打拳了，好吗？”

她的眼里闪烁着破碎的光，光在残余的泪水里分外晶莹。她的眼睛看着自己，自己在刹那间却不能面对她。就好像，鸟儿想带鱼儿去天上飞翔，鱼

儿能选择的，却只有逃避。

她走到了自己的跟前，自己又闻到了她身上淡淡的茉莉花香。她热烈地看着自己，说："答应我，好吗？"

自己真的好想紧紧抱住她，告诉她，以后不要再哭了。但是，自己却只是将钱袋塞回到了她的手中，说："我答应你，以后再不去打黑市拳了，但是这些钱，请你一定要收下。"自己看着她晶莹漂亮的眼睛，说："我只是希望你能过得好。"

说完，自己后退了一步，对她笑了笑，然后，便转身跑走了。她在后面喊了两声"赵驹"，但是，自己没有回头。风在身旁逆向吹过，只有她的香和泪，依旧在自己心尖停留。

八月，酷暑像一把无法灭绝的烈火，在天地万物的毛孔里奔窜。自己没有再去打黑市拳，也不敢再去看丽云。不敢再去看丽云，却又还是放心不下她。于是，就还是依旧叫兄弟们帮忙保护着她。

这一天，孔仁却是拿回了一大袋银圆来。自己诧异，问他，他就说，庄小姐还给你的。孔仁说，是他们不小心，被庄小姐发现了跟踪，庄小姐问得紧，没办法，于是他们便只好是把受委托跟踪保护她的事给全说了出来。孔仁说，庄小姐说，不用再保护她了，日本人根本已经不需要再对付她了。孔仁又说，庄小姐说，她现在已经在皮货店里找到了一份工作，可以自食其力了。

孔仁说："庄小姐还要我问你，你以前说过的话，是不是还算数？"

自己还以为，丽云是想提醒自己，别忘了自己说过的不再打黑市拳的那些话。可是，晚上，看着从废祠堂的窗外透进来的一片月光，自己却忽然想起了很久很久以前，她和自己说过的一些话。

"……你说过的，以后，我孤独时，你会陪着我的。"

"……我还答应过你，以后要是有机会，会带你去江南玩。"

"……这些话，还都算数吗？"

"……算数，等这天下太平了，我来找你。"

难道，她说的是这个？

又或者，是自己又在一厢情愿？

只有无尽的忧伤，伴着月光，倾泻在自己的心里。那些一直感觉近在眼前恍如昨天的过往，细数数，其实早已几经风雨多番变迁，还没敢伸出手去重新触摸，早已于千里之外遥不可及。人生有时就是这样充满了错莫的疼痛和失去的不可逆。而我们又根本无能为力。只有从现在到过去的断裂距离，还在丈量着我们的心酸生长的年龄。那些说过的话、想过的事，在一轮又一轮命运的折磨里，似乎只是一些忧伤的种子、遗憾的梦境。美好的一切，在擦肩而过或失之交臂以后，便永远只是结束在了过去的故事。结局无法重写。生活，人生，命运，一步步只是在将我们往未知的前路上推，偶尔站定，被回忆包裹，只有欲哭无泪的难受。我们又能怎样去怨恨自己的人生、诅咒自己的命运？唯有遗憾，仿佛在为我们证明着生命的确实存在和悲剧的永不消逝。默默承受，看着花落，或许才是面对遗憾、存在、悲剧的最好顿悟。只是，丽云，你要我怎样才能平静而不哀伤地想起你？

那袋银圆，自己全部分给了弟兄。自己把挣来的钱全拿去给女人而不给弟兄，这事，说起来真的是很不地道，也不义气。自己没有办法心安理得地面对与自己朝夕相处患难与共的兄弟。现在，既然她已把钱还给了自己，而弟兄们也都看见了，那么，自己也就不好再将钱留着，只能是都分给大家了。也好，这样，多少也能让自己减轻一些对兄弟们的愧疚。但是，她以后怎么办呢？且不说她是否真的已找到了工作，就算她现在有了工作，世道这么乱，她的工作又能长久吗？她的钱够用吗？她万一碰上个头疼脑热、沟沟坎坎，要花钱怎么办？她现在已经是个平民了，要是再缺了钱，岂不是会落到和自己当初刚到东北时一样的境地？不，不行。自己不放心，也不能允许这种厄运的发生。

格斗场的老板又找到了自己。自己决定打生死局。每场的酬金是两百块大洋。但是当然，这钱，得赢了才能有命拿。

生死格斗比自己想象的要艰险一千倍，残酷一千倍。对于金钱的急切渴望和对于自己身手的过度自信，使自己一时忽略了一个十分简单易懂的道理：敢打生死局的，必定都不是身手平庸之辈。上了生死局的擂台，双方在争的，其实已不是大洋，而是一个唯一的活下去的机会。开赛的铜锣敲响的那一刹那，就已命定，站在擂台上的两个人，一定要有一个死去。

自己感到了恐惧。

第一天第一场，和自己对战的是一名朝鲜人。他的两条腿，简直像两柄

疯狂挥舞的斧头，招式变化莫测，出招凌厉致命。上场才一会儿，自己已被他从背后踢倒，一脚踩在地上。观众嘘声四起。自己赶紧脱身爬起。看着擂台四周拉紧的铁丝网，看着擂台上方耀眼的灯光，自己忽然感到了一种步入死境的绝望。是的，这就是一个死境，要么你杀了别人，要么别人杀了你，虽然你们素不相识、无冤无仇，但只要上了这个擂台，你们就必须脱去人的外衣，变成两头狭路相逢必须你死我活的凶残野兽。流血、倒下、爬起，再流血、倒下、爬起，终于，在观众沸腾的欢呼声和诅咒声中，自己将这个朝鲜人的两只膝盖全部打碎。在自己拧断他的脖子前，他对自己说了一句朝鲜话，但是，自己没听懂。

第二天第二场，和自己对战的是一名苏联人。他的身材非常魁梧，身上的肌肉像一块块大石头那样鼓着，整个人看起来简直就像是一头熊，威猛无比的野熊。打他，他几乎都不会疼，但是被他打到，就像是被石狮子砸了一样。由于自己第一天已被朝鲜人打伤了筋骨，所以，在这个野熊一样的苏联人面前，自己十分被动。原本自己应该休息几天再打，但是老板不同意。自己知道，在自己杀死朝鲜人之后，押自己胜的人一定会增多，所以，其实老板是不希望自己再胜第二场的。这就是生意人的本质，只有利润才是最重要的，你的死活，关他屁事。而且，这本就是生死赌博，总要有一个人死。死哪个才能让他赚更多的钱，这才是他需要考虑的问题。这就是他妈的资本主义。最后，自己像打石狮子一样，一拳打碎了这个苏联人的脑袋，全场爆发出了震耳欲聋的欢呼声。

老板让自己休息了五天。五天后，自己迎来了第三场生死格斗。临开赛前，自己才知道，这一次自己的对手，竟然是东北黑拳界的新一代拳王，暹罗人巴占。巴占已打了三十多场生死局，他的泰拳，无人可敌。自己想去和老板说理，却被老板的手下给拿枪逼着，走上了擂台。擂台四周的铁丝网，又升了起来，拉得紧紧的。在擂台上决出生死之前，铁丝网不会撤下，擂台上的拳手，想跑也跑不掉。

观众没有欢呼，全场都像在屏气凝神。自己看着巴占，看着他那传说能断铜裂铁的双肘和双膝，真是有想要跪下来求饶的冲动。但是，自己知道，这里是没有求饶的。今晚，在自己和巴占之间，必须要死一个。巴占冲了上来，他一肘撞来，自己挥臂去挡，一挡之间，自己就已知道，今晚自己输定了。

痛苦的搏斗，残酷的拼命。巴占的全身，都像是铜墙铁壁。自己和他拳对拳，腿对腿，硬碰硬之间，自己感到自己的全身都像要散架。他一腿扫来，自己被他扫翻在地。他的膝盖直往自己的脑壳扑来，自己全力一翻，才勉强躲过。观众见了血，开始兴奋，有人在大喊“泰拳、泰拳”，有人在大喊“八极、八极”，还有人在尖声骂人。整个格斗场里，血味弥漫，人性黑暗。

自己被巴占丢到了铁丝网上，自己又从铁丝网上摔到了地上。自己的一条腿，已经扭伤了。巴占又连攻数招，自己根本招架不住。自己瞅准一个空当，抬腿往他腰间踢去，却反被他一膝盖，差点折断了腿。

从骨头与内脏的深处，涌来了连绵不绝的痛楚，痛得想哭。自己感到了死期的到来。是的，今晚，自己怕是要死在这擂台上了。巴占就像是个铁人，就凭自己的那套八极残拳，根本就不可能打赢他。除非父亲在世，否则，这巴占简直是天下无敌！

自己的脑袋，被巴占一拳击中。自己的面具，掉了下来。自己，昏天黑地地，倒在了台上。昏黑中，自己像是听见丽云在哭着说：“……你会被人打死的……你会被人打死的……”自己一阵心酸，剧烈的心酸。这心酸，几乎都盖住了自己全身的伤痛。

自己被巴占举了起来，狠狠摔在了台上。自己的左胳膊脱臼了。从额上流下的血，迷住了自己的眼睛，自己的眼睛痛得睁不开。自己的脑子里，天旋地转。

“不是我想走，是我实在不可以留。我若留下，别人就可以诬陷你们庄家是窝藏了通共分子。窝藏通共分子，严重的可以满门抄斩！”

“我不怕！”

“我怕！”

“潘兆他一定有办法帮你洗脱罪名的！”

“你不要去求他！”

“为什么不要！”

“这个世上没有免费的午餐！”

“他不可能要你什么的！”

“他会要你！”

“我愿意！”

“你说什么？”

“只要能救你，我做什么都愿意！”

“……我不愿意……我不愿意！”

澎湃的泪水，从自己眼中肆无忌惮地奔出。肆无忌惮地奔出！

“我死了，丽云怎么办？我死了，丽云怎么办！”

泪水，为自己冲去了眼里的血。

巴占又向自己冲了过来。

“啊——”

自己怒吼着，也冲向了巴占。

自己与巴占紧抱在了一起。自己狠狠一口，咬住了巴占的耳朵。巴占惨叫，全场沸腾。自己死死地紧抱着巴占，撕咬下了他的一只耳朵！又撕咬下了他的一只耳朵！

巴占往死里挥着拳。自己的脑袋，中了他一拳，又中了他一拳。

“我不能死——”自己大喊着，哭着，用手指，生生挖出了巴占的双眼。

自己痛哭流涕。“啊——”自己惨呼着，巴占也惨呼着。

自己的右胳膊被巴占扭住，也脱了臼。自己大哭着，对天空中的死神说：“我不能死！我不能死！！”

“啊——”自己的双腿绞住了巴占的脖子。自己脱臼的胳膊，被巴占死死地紧拉着。自己和他，都在血泊里哭泣。

哭泣。

“丽云、丽云，你等我、你等我……”自己哭泣着，喃喃自语。

喃喃自语。

终于，巴占断了气。

全场鼎沸的欢呼，鼎沸的咒骂。

铁丝网撤下。

自己挣扎着，站了起来。

“拳王！拳王！拳王！拳王！”

在全场疯狂沸腾的欢呼声中，自己吐血倒地，失去了知觉。

灯光耀眼，黑暗一片。

最后的这场比赛，老板给了自己三百块大洋，加上前面的那两场，自己一共挣到了七百块大洋。自己把钱埋在了一个秘密的地方，没有告诉兄弟们。兄弟们也并不知道自己打生死局的事，只以为自己是又打了普通场的黑市拳，还输了。自己固然知道这样欺瞒兄弟是很不义气的行为，而且，藏钱的事，万一被他们知道了，一定会令他们很伤心，但是，在自己的心里，又的确是没有什么事情可以比丽云的事情来得更重要。自己要给丽云存钱，就算她现在不要这钱。与其让兄弟们知道自己有一笔想送又送不出去的钱，还不如别让他们知道，免得生出许多尴尬，空生嫌隙。自己想隐瞒自己的单相思和可笑，也想隐瞒自己对义气二字的亏欠。

格斗场的老板说，现在，你已经是东北黑拳界的新一代拳王了。他说，你先好好养伤，养好了伤，以后，我会让你挣更多的钱。自己说，我不想再打了。老板说，你已经是拳王了，打或者不打，已经由不得你自己来决定了。自己知道老板的人都有枪，自己无法与他们对抗。当时，自己还很悲伤很绝望地想：看来，自己余下的人生，只能是去重走巴占最后的那段路了。但是，后来很快便发生了九一八事变，日本人占领了沈阳，占领了东北，没有人再有闲情逸致去看赌拳，帮会也不敢再搞什么地下格斗，怕被日本人冠上“宣扬暴力、豢养武士”的罪名。自己好歹算是捡回了一条命，不用像巴占那样，在早晚必死的路上挣扎到最后。后来，有时候，自己也会很自嘲地想：日本人，算不算是救了自己一命？

养伤期间，孔仁他们又都苦口婆心地劝自己，不要再打黑市拳了。自己有苦说不出，只能说，好，好。他们也就相信了。兄弟们给予自己的情义和信任，总是多于自己对他们的忠诚和亲近，这时常会使自己的良心感到不安，而且，这种遗憾，也已永远不能弥补和偿还。那是自己和他们最后相处的一段时光。那时，自己还以为，能和他们一起走的路，还有很长。人生有时就是这样，总会在不自觉中将某些暂时的存在或拥有误以为是永恒的停留或不会逝去，结果，这世上就有了如烟波般浩渺的遗憾与懊悔。自己唯一还可自我安慰的，是孔仁他们在最后的那段时光里，过得很开心。因为有了自己分给他们的那袋银圆，他们吃上了人生中最丰盛的一顿大餐，且每天有鱼有肉，不必再为了填饱肚子而四处奔波。他们还添置了很多新的生活用品，

那口烧饭用的破铁锅，也被换成了崭新的。他们是真的拿大家一起住着的地方——不管是破庙还是废祠堂——当成是一个家的。每每想起这些，总是最令自己心酸难禁。

九月，天朗气清，阳光绚烂。上旬的时候，自己还去看过一次丽云。她在皮货店里上班，她看见了自己，自己没有躲。她笑得很灿烂。她跑出店来，问自己："你有没有再去打黑市拳？"自己说："当然没有，你说的话，我怎么会不认真遵守呢？"她就笑了起来，笑容还像以前一样纯真而灿烂。自己问她："那你呢，现在过得还好吗？"她说："还好哇，不开心的事情都过去了，我要好好活着，才对得起父母。"自己说："你能这么说，我就放心了。"她就笑了，说："你有什么可不放心我的，我才不放心你呢，怕你被人打成缺胳膊少腿的。"自己也笑了，说："我还要保护你呢，哪能那么容易就变成残废。"她咯咯笑着。老板叫她了。她说了句"下次见"，就跑回了店里去。她的背影活泼而动人。她还是像只小白兔一样，单纯，美丽，善良。让人心疼得可以抛弃全世界。

一个黑暗的时代，终于还是来临了。

一九三一年九月十八日晚，日本关东军派兵炸毁了柳条湖附近南满铁路上的一段路轨，诬称是中国军队所为，并以此为借口，炮轰东北军驻地沈阳北大营。东北军部队接受蒋介石及张学良不准抵抗的训令，除小部分军人自发英勇抵抗外，大部分皆不战而退，将国土拱手让给了日本人。十九日上午，沈阳全城沦陷。四个多月后，东北全境沦陷。

十八日当晚十点多，自己和兄弟们在废祠堂里正准备睡觉，却突然听到外面远远地传来了一声惊天动地的"嘭砰"巨响。开始时，孟义还以为，是不是哪户富人家放了个大爆竹。但是，很快，事情便明朗了起来。令人胆战心惊的轰鸣声、"嗒嗒"声此起彼伏、持续不断。很显然，这是炮声和枪声。一定是附近的什么地方，突然在打仗了。

所有人都不知所措。孔仁说，声音像是从北大营那边传来的。黄道说，他们在和什么人打？朱理犹豫了一下，说，会不会是日本关东军？

枪炮声不断，夜的安宁被炸得粉碎。自己坐立不安。自己对孔仁说，我要出去一趟。孔仁问，去哪里？自己说，我想去庄小姐那里看看。孔仁说，好，你自己多小心。自己就和兄弟们道了个别，然后，便匆匆跑出了废祠堂。

赤裸的夜空下，枪炮激战的声音分外刺人耳膜。炙热的战火，一阵阵地擦亮着漆黑的天幕。惊心动魄的炮声火光里，天地都像在恐惧地战栗。城中的街道上，要么一片混乱、嘈杂不堪，要么四周门窗紧闭、死寂如坟。有的百姓紧紧地躲在家里，连灯也不敢开；有的百姓只敢将头探出窗外，畏惧地短暂一望；有的百姓像热锅上的蚂蚁，在街上或者乱跑，或者兜圈，逢人就问，又问不出任何名堂。有零零散散的部队在城中奔跑，据说是撤退逃跑的，也有说是去布置城防的。有抬着担架的士兵在夜色下匆忙地跑过，嘴里在不停地骂骂咧咧。有两个赤手空拳慌忙奔跑的士兵在街角处撞到了一起，短暂地谈了一会儿话。

“你们团也撤了？”

“废话，你们不也撤了！”

“那谁还在打？”

“是王团长的部队，他撤退的命令接得晚，现在怕是被日本人给包围住了！”

“他妈的，要不是上面下了死命令，不准抵抗，要我们把枪械全缴到库房里去，我们哪里会逃得这么惨！”

“我们窝囊啊，日本人武器再好，也就几百人，我们有上万人，难道还会打不过他们！不战而降，奇耻大辱哇！”

“你快跑吧，晚了怕跟不上大部队。我还想去和小柔道个别，今日一走，以后也不知还有没有命能和她相见了。”

“好，那你赶快，和她说完了就赶紧追上来。”

慌乱的人流，死寂的民众，被战火撕碎的夜空。

到了丽云的住处，四周一片静默。那盏破路灯一暗一亮的，闪闪烁烁，像是即将也要跟随着这个摇摇欲坠的时代一起跌进黑暗里去了。那灯光明明灭灭的，也真像是在发抖。

自己使劲地敲了两下门，用力而低声地喊了两声“丽云”。门一下子开了，她惶恐而惊喜地站在那里，说：“你来啦——外面究竟发生了什么事？我一直没敢出去看——是打仗了吗？”

“是日本人和东北军打起来了。不过你不要怕，我会一直在这里陪着你

的。”

走进了院子，自己仔细地关好了院门。又是长长的一阵猛烈的火炮轰鸣声。自己的左手臂一下子被丽云的双手紧紧地抓住了。她离自己是那样近，自己都能听到她因害怕而变得压抑了起来的呼吸声。自己故作轻松地说：“没事，我在路上都问了，日本人才几百个，而驻扎北大营的东北军有上万，你说日本人不是找死吗？哈哈。”

她慢慢地松开了手。炮火声依旧在轰鸣。自己离她远了一些，才终于敢转回身来看她。路灯光又开始不稳定地明明灭灭，照得人忽然像是存在，又忽然像是不存在。

“谢谢你。”她说。

自己笑笑，说：“有什么好谢的，我是要饭来了，哈哈。”

“刚才我一个人的时候，就想，只要我还在这里，你就一定是会来的。”她说。

自己默然了一小会儿，说：“有我在，你什么都不用怕。”

路灯闪闪烁烁，她的容颜和身影不时被黑暗吞没。短暂的明亮，似乎只是为了让人更加厌恶失去和恐惧黑暗。而重复的黑暗，只是让人无限神伤与怀念光亮。

自己端了一条长凳，在前院的正中间坐了下来，面对着紧闭的院门。自己要丽云只管回屋去睡觉，什么也不要怕，什么也不要想。丽云想在自己旁边也坐下来，自己说，我一个人就行了。丽云顿了顿。自己又补充说，你休息好了，我才放心，万一要跑，你也能有体力。她就笑了笑。该死的路灯光终于停止了闪烁，又暂时地恢复了正常。

丽云回屋去了。自己喝着她倒的一杯水，却还恍惚觉得她依旧那么近地就在自己身边。又一阵令人惊恐的炮声传来，自己的心才从儿女情长中抽身而出。

纷乱的思绪在自己头脑里纠结。外面的仗打得怎么样了？日本兵真的只有几百个吗？东北军真的在不战而撤吗？政府为什么要不抵抗？如果东北军真的全撤了，那么，这座沈阳城是不是就会被日军占领？日军一旦占领了沈阳，之后又会怎样？根本不敢再想。或者，只是自己听错了？或者，是自己的预想太悲观？也许，政府很快就会发起反击呢。也许，军队只是在佯败诈敌呢。毕竟，面对敌人的侵犯，我们又有什么理由要不抵抗？

炮火声稀疏了下来。外面的情形究竟已是什么样，自己心中一片忐忑。而这场战事的来龙去脉到底是怎么样，当时的自己也和所有老百姓一样，心里一团糊涂。虽然大家都知道，关东军和东北军怕是早晚都要打起来的，但是谁也没想到，真的就是打起来了，而更让所有老百姓想不到的是，后来，东北会那么轻易地全境沦陷。百姓总是在渴望安定与和平，而时代却总是嗜血。乱流激荡里，被摧毁的，总是微小者的人生和普通人的愿望。

路灯又开始明明灭灭了起来。虚幻而沉闷的灯影倏然而来，又倏然而去，每一次的闪烁，都像是在往人的心里泼进一片忧伤，或一段压抑。那忧伤从空灵里来，往消失处去，经过的地方，只有一片芳草寂静、黯然神伤。而那压抑，分明是躲在黑暗处的战栗，它就像是有无数条触须，谁被这触须刺穿，谁就能透过那忧伤，看到无论是个人还是时代都难以逃脱的悲剧命运。因为悲剧，从来只是某些显而易见的真理。自己将水杯放在了身旁空着的半截长凳上，心底一阵惆怅。自己是多想和丽云紧挨着坐在一起呀，可是，自己莫名又害怕离她太近。想要靠近又只能拒绝，是一个自己也无法解释又不能抗拒的痛苦死结。这死结，不打开是命运，打开了，就是悲剧。而这个时代的明天又是否像这死结一样让人进退两难、来去白费？不打，是国土沦丧；打，只是再多死些人罢了。而结局，从来都不会有什么改变。

路灯暗了，没再亮起来。自己依旧紧盯着黑暗中紧闭着的院门，仔细聆听着外面各种可能会有的动静。沉陷在这样一个深重而动乱的黑夜里，自己别无所求，只希望可以竭尽全力为丽云守住一方小小的安宁，不要令她担惊受怕。只祈求外面纵然再乱，也不要乱到这一个小小的破院子里来。一旦和平被击碎，兵匪横行，自己只希望，自己还有能力可以保护丽云不受伤害。自己已经只是个除了一点武功以外什么也不会什么也没有的人，如果战乱真的要不可抗拒地袭来，自己只祈求，还能为她看好这扇家门，还能为她守好这个小院，好歹可以让她睡个安稳觉，若能如此愿便足矣。

秋夜凉心。

将近黎明时，令人担忧的枪炮声再度密集而猛烈了起来。并且，这一次的炮火声，像是逼近了许多。有些爆炸声，震耳欲聋，似乎就从极近的地方传来。而各种枪声，更是已从远远的隐约中，来到了真切清晰的耳边。

很显然，如果没有猜错，日军已经攻入了沈阳城。

自己的心，一下子就提到了嗓子眼里。自己站了起来。背后有灯光亮起，转回身，看见丽云已是站在了屋门口。

“你一夜没睡了，我屋里刚好有张小木榻，刚才我收拾了一下，你进去睡一会儿吧。”她说。

“哦，没事，不用。”自己忙说。说完，没理由地转过了身不看她，只往院门口走了两步。

她似乎想再说些什么，却只是沉默着。自己转回身，看着她，笑了笑。光影里，她像一个绚烂得虚幻的梦。

忽然，一队急促而有力的脚步声从外面“嚓嚓”奔过。有日本指挥官的声音在喊：“快！快！不惜代价，占领兵工厂！”

自己猛地跑进了堂屋，一下子关掉了电灯。黑暗在一瞬间，如海水般淹没了一切。丽云吓得一下子就钻到了自己的怀里来。自己赶紧搂住了她，低声说，不要怕，不要怕。

日军的脚步声跑远了。附近响起了狂风暴雨般猛烈的机枪声。又有连续不断的爆炸声从远处传来。黎明即将到来，战火却已在黎明未来的脸上涂满了血光。

丽云在自己怀里瑟瑟发抖，自己捂着她的耳朵，说，不用怕，不用怕。黑暗中，敌军已至的绝望像冰一样寒冷，只有和所爱的人相拥的温暖，仿佛还能给人一丝希望的幻象。

激烈的枪炮声暂时又安宁了下来，天边已露出了一丝曙光。自己轻轻地推开了丽云，说：“我去外面看看情况，你简单收拾一下东西，如果日本人真的占领了沈阳的话，我带你离开沈阳。”

“你要小心——”

“放心。”

自己没有开门，直接从土墙上跃了出去。

天色越来越亮了。沈阳城中，已是一片狼藉。依然有枪炮激战的声音，断断续续地从城中的不同地方响起。有的地方死尸成堆，血流满地。死的有老百姓，有东北军，很少有日本兵。有一个中国士兵，是和日本兵抱着死在一起，他的脑袋，被削去了一半。有一堆中国百姓的尸体聚在一起，是两个老人、一男一女两个年轻人、三个稚子，他们的身上都布满了弹孔，其中那名年轻男子的腿还断在一边。这怕是一个家庭。到处是暗红的血，到处是被毁坏的景象，火药的味和死尸的味混在一起，令人恐怖而恶心想吐。有些人家的门窗依旧紧闭，有些人家的大门已完全敞开，敞开的院里或屋里，却又毫无人气。街上有奔跑的士兵，也有奔跑的百姓。那些跑着的士兵，不知是去参战还是在撤退；那些奔跑的百姓，不知是在逃离还是在回家。天越来越亮，激战的声音越来越弱。自己看见，又有大批日军开进了沈阳城。沈阳的防卫，已经完全崩溃。一个街角，有一位老人在哭泣，他哭着喊：东北军全跑了，东北军全跑了，不肯跑的全死了，不肯跑的全死了！路过的日本兵嫌他吵，一枪打爆了老人的头。自己看见，一辆日军的卡车上，装着十几名五花大绑的中国战俘，押送他们的日本兵用枪托一个个地砸着他们的脑袋，一边放肆地笑骂：猪，猪！有中国士兵痛哭流涕。自己听见，有日本兵在击掌欢庆，他们说：这场仗真是打得太漂亮了，我们才伤亡了二十多人，就拿下了整座城市，中国人根本就不配做我们的对手！自己又看见，有拖家带口想要往城外逃出去的百姓，统统死在了日军机枪的扫射下。有会说汉语的日本人站在高处大喊：服从皇军，保你平安，妄图外逃，格杀勿论！有没听见和听不清的百姓，依旧在往外逃。也可能，他们是听见了也听清了，但他们还是依旧选择要逃。于是，机枪又开始扫射。天已大亮，城中还有激战的枪炮声响起，还有零星的中国守军在战斗。但是，自己已知道，他们的战斗是徒劳的，大局已定，沈阳已沦陷，再反抗，只是再往死尸堆里多添几个中国人而已。死神似乎正站在有战火燃烧着的每个地方，张开着他的血盆大口，等待着失败的人献出生命来做他嘴里的咀嚼物。胜者活败者死，战争就是这么简单而残酷。自己像个幽灵一样在阴暗的角落里飞奔或潜行，瞪大着眼睛，竖起着耳朵，想要找出一条可以和丽云安全逃出去的路，却怎么样也找不着，不想看到那些触目惊心的恐怖或残酷的景象却无处不在，如潮水般灌入自己的眼中。血流遍了沈阳的土地，百姓或战士的生命就这样被侵略者夺去，那些死掉的无辜的生命，有的甚至还没来得及看到今天即将到来的天明。他们在黑暗里死去，现在太阳升起了，却只能照亮他们的尸体。他们的死，还满带着失败与被征服的屈辱。这不是一个公平的世界，更不是一个充满了善意与怜悯的世界，也不是一个乐于给人以尊严的世界。这只是一个供

强者奴役与消遣的世界，失败者与懦夫，只是强者娱乐的牺牲品。面对敌军的侵略，撤者生，战者亡，这是一个多么可悲而又真实的情况！难道说，其实退缩才是求生的最佳方案，而勇进只是送死的代名词而已？难道说，秦桧才是真正的有功之臣，而岳飞只是一介愚蠢莽汉？中华上下五千年，为何可悲的历史总在不断重演！

出来的时间久了，怕丽云一个人有事，于是便顾不上再找线路，只好赶紧回了丽云的小院。丽云看见自己回来了，赶紧跑了上来，抓住了自己的右手臂，说："你可回来了。——外面怎么样了？"

自己不知该怎么和她说，只能强装笑颜，说："东北军暂时败了，不过，兴许还会打回来。"

"那我们要不要走？"

自己无能为力得不敢看着她，只好说："暂时怕是不能逃出去了，外面乱得很，子弹不长眼，遇上了就麻烦了。"

丽云"哦"了一声，便不再问了。

自己宽慰地对她笑了笑，说："没事的。"她也笑了，说："我知道。"她说："你去睡一会儿吧，我去做早饭。日子该怎样过，还得怎样过，不是吗？"

"我给你生火。"自己笑着说。

灶膛里火光跳动，鲜艳活泼。自己又往灶膛里塞了两根柴。丽云在做早饭，她笑吟吟的，似乎真的已不再害怕。而自己的内心，却纷乱而惧怕。别说暂时无法逃出去，就算逃出了沈阳去，自己又该带着丽云去哪儿落脚呢？丽云已经满门覆灭，而自己，也早已举目无亲。两个孤家寡人，在这乱世之中，又该去哪儿安身立命呢？而日军在攻下沈阳之后，又还会有进一步的军事行动吗？这惨烈的战火，究竟还会烧到哪些地方？到底会烧到何时为止？

外面已不再有一丝一毫的枪声或炮声。很显然，那些不肯撤退而留下来抵抗的守军，已经全军覆没了。好好的一座城，就这么沦陷了。

自己和丽云一起吃了顿早饭。丽云问，东北军很快就会打回来吗？自己说，应该会的，我们的军队可能只是在诱敌深入。丽云说，嗯。自己说，没事的，日本人在这里逞不了几天强，等东北军打回来，打得他们满地找牙。说完，自己还刻意笑了两声。丽云吃了两口粥，低着头说，有你在，我不害怕。

吃完了早饭，自己又出去了一次。和自己想的一模一样，沈阳已全城沦陷，再无一丝半点的抵抗力量存在。一些日本兵正在清理尸体。一些死掉的中国士兵的尸体，还要再被清理尸体的日本兵再扎上几刀。日本兵一边扎还一边笑。满地的血。老百姓们已不再乱逃乱跑，绝大多数已躲回了家里。没来得及躲起来的，若是碰上了日本兵，多半也就是死路一条。自己在路上看见了一个死去的婴儿，赤身裸体，浑身是血。不知是怎么死的，也不知为什么会死。这个婴儿的家人呢？也许，这就是战争的绞肉本质。问为什么，是可笑的。沈阳全城已戒严，日军开始对内清除可能的残余抵抗势力，对外采取防御措施，转攻为守。一些普通人家的大门被踢开，日军开始挨家挨户地搜查。

自己回到了丽云的身边，不敢再离开她半步。自己对她说，一会儿日本人可能会来搜查抵抗分子，你不要怕，他们要搜就让他们搜，只要顺从，就不会有事。她点点头。她和自己坐在一起，自己没有再逃避。自己抓紧着她的一只手，她的手冰凉冰凉的。自己用很小的声音，给她讲各种各样的笑话。开始她不笑，后来她终于笑了。自己还是握着她的手。

很幸运地，日本兵没有闯进丽云的院子里来搜查。也许，是有什么更重要的事情吸引了他们的注意力吧。这一天很难熬地就这样过去了，除了胆战心惊，自己实在无法形容这一整天里自己的各种心情。自己的战栗与恐惧，不是因为自己，而是因为丽云。自己只是个乞丐，又没抗日，且懂日语，就算碰上了日本兵，也不会有什么太大的问题。但是，丽云不同，且不说，她与日本人有许多沸沸扬扬的旧仇，光凭她是一个漂亮的年轻女人这一点，足以让人生出一层深深的不能说的忧虑来。怎么办？怎么办？最好还是逃。可是，日军已全城戒严。逃就是死。

傍晚时，因为怕那盏破路灯到了晚上又会一闪一闪的，引来日本人的注意，自己干脆就去弄坏了它，让它再也亮不起来。也许，在黑暗中，最好的隐蔽方法就是黑暗。古人说“木秀于林，风必摧之”，真是大智慧。在这样一个动辄见血要命的年代里，卑微得让人看不到或视而不见，或许才是一种真正的福气。自己当时还不知道格斗场的老板已再也不会来找自己，所以心里总还隐隐忧虑着这件破事。自己想，自己若身手平平，也便不会被逼上生

死格斗的绝路，而丽云，当初若无万贯家财，也便不会与日本人结下仇怨，而在这如狼似虎的凶恶乱世里，一个女人若姿色平平，即是她最大的平安稳定。只可惜，世事都错乱了安排。

吃过了晚饭，自己要丽云早些去休息。自己说，你放心，只管安心睡，我会给你看好家，守好夜。她说，不行，你也要睡觉的。说完，她和自己一时都觉得有些尴尬。自己说，我可以几天不睡，我来这里就是为了给你看家护院的，你不用担心我。她说，你帮我把那张小木榻抬到堂屋里来好不好？自己一笑，拿两张长凳往前院里一放一拼，然后往上一躺，说，你看，这多简单，我睡这里就行了。她还想说什么，却又好像不好意思再说。自己笑说，你知道吗，我睡长凳，可以练睡梦罗汉功，一举两得。她脸微微一红，说，你就胡说吧，不管你了。

丽云去她睡的屋里，关了门，不再出来了。自己帮她把堂屋里的灯关了。然后，自己坐回到了院子里的长凳上。

黑咕隆咚，万籁俱寂。毕竟是秋天了，夜气像流动的泉水一样清凉。就算在黑暗里，自己也仿佛能看到秋叶落黄满地的模样。只不过，这一个秋天，落满沈阳土地的，恐怕就不是黄叶，而是鲜血了吧。想起白天见到的种种惨象，自己的心尖不由得还是缩紧、发痛，一种不知厄运何时就会来到跟前的恐惧，怎么样都擦抹不掉。那浓烈的血腥气，就像时刻萦绕在自己的脑海里，只要一想到，味就飘出来，令人作呕，令人打战。自己今天没让丽云看一眼外面的世界，也没把心中真正的判断告诉她，只是连哄带骗地跟她说了很多宽慰的话，让她以为这沈阳的沦陷只是一时半会儿的事情，且情况并不严重。当然，这或者也是自己心底的一种期望。虽然，在自己的心底，对眼下的时局还有着十分悲观的看法。但是自己很显然不想在时局进一步恶化之前就先将那些悲观的判断传递给丽云。她只是一个单纯、善良而柔弱的女子，战争真实的可怕，她又怎能承受。如果自己待在她的身边，不能为她挡去这些可怕，不能护住她的纯洁和乐观，那么，自己陪在她的身边又有什么意义？自己还有什么用？

自己开始后悔，没在昨夜就和丽云一起外逃。自己的反应，终究还是迟滞了。昨夜枪炮声一起，自己就该带着丽云逃出沈阳城去的，而不该对东北军的守城态度与守城能力心存什么希望。

既然暂时已逃不出去，就得想办法和丽云在这里安全地继续生活下去。自己一定要好好保护好丽云，一定要。但是，自己又真的有这个能力吗？自己固然已是黑拳界的新拳王，但是，日本人用的是枪。侵略者若要欺负你，不会文明得放下枪支，与你空手对空手。而枪，无疑是自己一生的死穴。只要一想起那些死尸身上的弹孔，一想到子弹会以比风快千倍的速度向人袭去，自己就会不寒而栗，从心底里直到每个神经末梢都渗出苍白的冷汗。就好像，自己在枪面前，根本就是个手无缚鸡之力的婴孩一样。自己也用过枪，也用枪杀过人，但是，这种对枪的恐惧，是你用枪去杀再多的人也治疗不了的。而且，最奇怪的是，自己的武功越是精进，自己骨子里对枪的那种恐惧便越是浓烈，越是清晰。就像是从自己的骨头里散发出来的一股腐朽的药味，令人提神醒脑，而又沮丧痛苦。自己怎么样也不会忘记，武功再怎么高强的父亲，最后终究是因为中了枪，而踏上了逃不脱的死路。这似乎就是一种命运的表示。父亲怕了一辈子枪，在他生命中的最后一战里，他甚至还短暂地战胜过枪，但是他最终还是被枪打败，被送上了死路。无论他的武功有多么出神入化、超凡脱俗，无论他想保护他所爱的人的勇气和决心有多么排山倒海、坚不可摧，枪就是枪，子弹就是子弹，枪一响，子弹一飞，结局就是那么无情而残酷。拳脚在枪炮面前，就是稀泥一团；武功在热兵器的时代里，只是复古的陶瓷摆设。父亲的武功冠绝江南，尚不能与枪为敌，自己的武功且不及父亲的十分之一，自己又有什么理由可以自信，自己能于日寇之枪口前，护得丽云之周全？自己只想打自己耳光。自己现在很后悔，当初就不该让孔仁他们把那三把日本人的枪给扔掉。要是现在手里有枪，那该多好。自己总是因为害怕而拒绝，却又总是会在拒绝之后感到后悔。也许这就是命运的玩笑与人性的谜团吧。

自己摸黑去了厨房里，找到了一把菜刀。紧紧地握着菜刀，自己又坐回了院子里。外面静悄悄的，偶尔有人跑过。自己很害怕，会有日本兵突然来踹门。白天没轮到，晚上未必就轮不到。要是有抗日分子，最好也别往这边跑，要打，去别处打。外面并没有枪炮声，可是自己的耳朵里，却老是炮火轰鸣。菜刀被自己紧紧地握着，自己一点也没觉得好笑。要是真有日本人欺负上来，自己可以砍他们吗？如果只有几个日本人，或几十个日本人，自己倒不怕大开杀戒，只要杀光了，就不怕有后患。可是现在，全沈阳都是日

本人的天下，日本人要欺负上来，上来的也不是日本帮会日本流氓，而是日本军队日本野兽，你杀了他们，日本军队会放过你吗？就算你不怕枪，杀了一百个日本兵，可是，全沈阳城的日本兵都会来杀你，你有可能带着丽云逃得掉吗？更何况，你根本就不可能不怕枪，根本就不可能赢得了枪。那么，还是只能祈求平安无事吧。或者，应该做个顺从的良民。只要听日本人的话，他们也许就不会要自己和丽云的命吧？毕竟，侵略也是为了统治，只要什么都听他们的，他们应该就不会为难老百姓吧？不然，还能怎么办？

天上地下一片黑暗，自己头脑中思绪纷乱。只是想到丽云此刻兴许已安睡，心中才稍觉释然。如果没有战争，没有侵略，这样的一个夜，本该是多么美好哇。丽云在安睡，她的梦或许可以很美，自己守护着她，可以看看她甜美的笑颜，而无忧无虑。这是多么甜美而幸福的一个图景。但是，现实却似乎从不容许美梦成真，再浓烈的对幸福的渴望，再微小的对美梦的追求，在现实的面前，总是一堆毫无意义的稚子痴话。自己是真的好想，可以在一个平安稳定的年代，和丽云静静厮守，陪伴欢喜，男耕女织，一生无求。但是，命运并不允许。

自己不知是在何时睡去，睡得很深很沉，无梦也无喜。于寒凉中模糊半醒时，感觉有人在往自己身上盖东西，睁开眼，天还黑着，堂屋里的灯却已亮。丽云就站在长凳旁边，自己的身上盖着一条暖和的毯子。自己赶紧坐了起来。

“对不起，把你弄醒了。”

“没有，我本来就没睡着。谢谢你。”

“天气这么凉，你快去屋里的木榻上睡吧。”

“不，我不困，我要守夜。”

“傻话，守什么夜呀，日本人又不会来。再说了，日本兵若真要往家里闯，你难道还真准备去拦住他们吗？我可不许你做这种傻事。”

“现在这么乱，就算没有日本人，贼呀偷的也多，不能不防。”

“有你在，我难道还会怕那些小毛贼和小流氓？你看你，居然还拿了一把菜刀。”

她忍不住笑了，自己一时就也不禁觉得有些好笑。自己笑着，放下了紧握着的菜刀，将毯子还给了她，说：“谢谢你，不过这几天晚上我确实睡不着，还是等天亮了我再睡一会儿吧。你回屋去，只要你能睡得安心，我就高兴。”

她接过了毯子，也没走。她看着自己，说：“我已经不是以前的庄丽云了，我没那么娇贵。”

自己说：“可是，你始终是我最珍贵的朋友。无论沧海桑田，这珍贵也不会有一点点改变。”

她看着自己，自己也看着她。她就笑了，抱着毯子，说：“好吧，傻瓜，你要做我的保镖，就做吧，我可不管你了。”说完，她乐得直笑。

她回了睡屋。自己又去给她关了堂屋的灯。一丝丝的甜蜜从自己心里流过。要是没有日本人，这一切该有多美好，自己想。

坐回长凳上，自己又拿起了菜刀。自己很伤怀地想：她不知道，其实真正在感到害怕的，是我，是我赵驹。“赵驹只是个懦夫，而她，却错把赵驹当成了一个英雄。”自己很痛苦地想。菜刀，在自己手里瑟瑟发抖。秋夜，凉冷如水。

吃过早饭后，为了履行诺言，自己真就在长凳上睡了一觉。外面不时有纷乱的声音奔过，她却一丝不怕。自己隐隐又有些觉得对不起她，明明是很糟很危险的情况，自己却让她以为并不要紧，自己这样做，会不会害了她？

一觉醒来时，刚过中午。和她一起吃过了午饭，自己决定再出去看看情形。

沈阳城里已不再有一丝半点的武装抵抗力量存在，但是，流血依旧不断。总有各种各样的原因不小心被日军杀死的百姓，总有各种各样的原因无辜被日军欺侮或抢掠的人群。城里挂满了日本旗，秋风一阵一阵地紧，凉意在心而不在身。落叶掉在未干的血泊里，枯黄的颜色被暗红所浸透，像地狱里的装饰，像小鬼才喜欢的祭奠。听见几个日本兵在唱歌庆祝，好像是又打了什么胜仗，自己心生疑惑。这样不行，困在城中，不知外面的局势，就犹如瞎了眼在生活，无法判断是逃是留是顺从还是反抗才好。于是，自己就潜入了一户门户大开又无人在内的富人家，偷了一台收音机出来。

回到了丽云那里，丽云倒也没责怪自己不问自取。毕竟，现在是非常时期。最多，以后再赔偿人家吧。自己打开了收音机，丽云调低了音量，然后，她开始调台。终于，收听到了关于东北时局的消息。不听还好，一听，

晴天霹雳。

原来，日本关东军不止袭击了北大营和占领了沈阳，他们是全面出击，至九月十九日中午为止，已先后攻占了沈阳、四平、营口、凤凰城、安东等南满铁路、安奉铁路沿线的十八座城镇，而且，就在昨夜，长春沦陷。东北军受不准抵抗的命令之约束，全线撤退。有不肯撤退的，则战死沙场，败于敌手。日本关东军势如破竹，乘胜挺进，东北危急。

关上收音机，自己和丽云面面相觑，压抑难言。事实比自己原有的悲观猜想更糟糕，自己还以为就沈阳沦陷了，或者最多再搭上周边的个把城镇，却没想到，日军的侵略规模是这样巨大。自己对于军事政治的看法，终究还是太幼稚。而中国军队的不抵抗姿态与屡战屡败的战斗力，实在是让人不能接受，又无可奈何。丽云呆呆的，突然无声地落下了泪来。自己心一惊，想说些什么安慰的话，又觉得，此刻什么话都是苍白的。她啜泣着说：父亲与日本人斗，庄家最后家破人亡，却没想到，政府竟将我们沈阳的百姓，全送给了日本人！

自己刹那也险些落泪。自己想说，我们爱国，但政府不爱我们。想想，却终究没说。蒋介石只想安内，不想攘外，普通百姓再恨再怨，又能拿他如何？自己看着丽云压抑得掩面而泣，心中悲酸，却又不知该如何是好。自己只能将手放在丽云的肩膀上，说，会过去的。丽云止住了哭声，泪却落得更多。她问：以后怎么办？

自己原来还幻想，东北军的撤退，只是佯败；自己原来还希望，就算不是佯败，中国军队也应该很快就会来收复沈阳。但是现在看来，幻想已成笑话，希望也十分渺茫。自己该对丽云说什么？说什么都是无力的。日军的旗帜已在沈阳全城飘扬，这里的中国人，已是亡国奴。

丽云靠在自己肩上，只是流泪，也不说话。自己心中的思绪，也是纷乱而没有着落。兴许是她的悲伤也浸湿了自己，自己的眼里也止不住地一阵阵模糊着。好好的一个庄家，全部毁在了日本人的手里，日本人不仅夺走了庄家辛苦积累起来的所有产业，还夺走了丽云双亲的生命。而丽云为了守护庄家而付出的全部代价与努力，也都在日本人的摧残之下化为了瓦砾与泡影。当丽云所珍视和拥有的一切全部被侵略者野蛮地夺去，伤痕累累的她，只能站在孤独无助中与曾经的人生悲伤告别。除了失败与痛苦，她还要忍受嘲讽与贫穷。而现在，日本人居然还真真实实地占领了整个沈阳！实在是让人情何以堪！而自己最担忧的，还有丽云和自己的安全问题。毕竟，丽云和樱花会社有旧仇。而自己，也杀过黑龙会的人。现在沈阳成了日本人的天下，自己和丽云，又将会面对什么样的麻烦？

丽云擦去了眼泪，痴痴地看着自己，问，以后怎么办？

自己心疼得又用手绢给她擦了擦眼泪，只能是笑了笑，说：我们的军队，会打回来的。

她说，我害怕，当年清兵进了关，就做了两百多年主子。

自己无言以对，只能说：我们改变不了这个时代，但是，我会尽我所能，不让你受到伤害。

她低下了头，没再掉眼泪。

下午四点时，有汉奸来踢门，说，皇军要收钱收粮。丽云说没有，汉奸就要打人。自己忙和汉奸说好话，然后，给钱给粮。汉奸临走时，很奇怪地说，你有毛病吗，干吗穿得像个叫花子似的，是不是想装穷骗人？

好说歹说，送走了汉奸。

关紧了院门，丽云眉头紧锁。她没说，但自己心里明白，这家里的钱和粮都被拿走了大半，日子往下可怎么过？丽云不知皮货店有没有开门，自己告诉她，关着呢。米铺、油店、果摊、酱园，全歇业了。

傍晚时，自己告诉丽云，自己要回废祠堂去看看兄弟，出来两天了，得回去和他们说一声。

丽云有些害怕，却还是点点头，说，好。

自己说，你放心，我就回来。日本人收了一次钱粮了，不会马上又来。

她点点头。

没吃晚饭，自己就离开了小院。自己不想再吃掉丽云的粮食了，自己要去拿钱来给丽云。多亏自己当初未雨绸缪，还存了七百块大洋，现在能救命了。

沈阳正全城戒严，越到晚上，日本兵巡逻得越密。许多道路全被封了起来。自己一路躲避着日本兵，万一被他们碰上了，可就麻烦了。终于潜回了废祠堂，这时天已黑，祠堂里也是一片漆黑。自己喊了两声，没人应。于是，自己就摸黑点亮了蜡烛。

兄弟们都不在。起初，自己还以为，是他们都还没回来。但稍微坐了坐，便发觉不对。这两天什么情况，难道他们还会出去要饭不成？不可能啊。那么，他们是去哪儿了？

自己又发现，废祠堂里烧水用的水壶，还放在前天自己离开时所放的地方。上前去一摸，水壶是冰凉的，上面已蒙了薄薄的一层尘。揭开壶盖，看到壶里还有一些凉水，不过，这些凉水的水量，怎么看，都好像和自己前天最后一次喝水时在这壶里看到的水量差不多。难道，他们这两天都没喝水烧水？

自己心里忐忑了起来。又不敢往坏处想。想想，现在虽然是战乱，但以他们四人现在的身手，逃命保命总应该是没问题的。或者，自己的忐忑是多余的？

又坐了一会儿，他们还是没回来。自己心里乱糟糟的。他们现在手里又不是没钱，有必要这两天还出去乞讨吗？哦，会不会是因为有钱也买不到吃的，所以只好又出去乞讨？这都什么乱七八糟的呀。自己的脑子里一片紧张而毫无头绪。自己去翻了翻他们的布袋，他们的钱，又各自都在。莫名的不祥的预感，伴着摇曳的烛火，在自己心上晃荡了起来。

看看外面黑漆漆的天，算算自己已出来许久了。丽云一人在家，可会害怕？日本兵或汉奸，会不会又去踢门？自己实在放心不下，归心似箭。在废祠堂里自己又踱了一会儿步，想想还是算了，就留张字条给兄弟们吧。还是赶快回到丽云身边要紧。自己还要去取那藏起来的七百块大洋，从这里到藏钱的地方再到丽云的小院，一路上躲来躲去的，可还要费不少时间，不能让丽云等太久。

主意打定，自己便在废祠堂里留了字条，然后，吹灭了蜡烛，离开了祠堂。

去取钱的路上，自己躲来躲去，躲过了几拨巡逻的日本兵。瞅准了一个空当，正要加速跑时，背后却突然轻轻的一声“嗨”。

自己转头一看，昏暗的路灯光下，是猫着腰的一个旧相识。他是格斗场老板的一个手下，叫短毛，往日和自己还算有几分交情。

自己的脑袋一下子就大了。这都什么时候了，难道老板还在开格斗场？难道他还要找自己去打拳？真是要钱不要命啦！

“干什么？”自己一边问，一边准备逃走。

“你怎么躲在这里？想杀日本鬼子吗？”短毛问。

“神经病！别胡说。我就是出来办点事，日本兵不停巡逻，我走不出去，所以才在这儿暂时躲一下。”

“操，还以为你也是个不怕死的好汉呢。”

“开玩笑，谁不怕死。告诉你，那该死的格斗场我是再不会去了，再说了，现在是什么情况，日本人来了，你们老板要是再搞武力格斗，他和你们，还有那些拳手，都会被日本人抓起来的！日本人现在最忌讳的就是中国人还有武力！”

“放心，我们老板哪有那么傻，格斗场这几天都关着呢。今天老板派我出来，就是要我把我们的那些枪支弹药全藏起来，不然，万一被日本鬼子给搜到了，就全玩完啦。这不刚办完事，正要回去交差呢。”

“哦，好。”原来短毛不是来叫自己去打拳的，自己真是松了口气。

“那我先走了，你多小心。千万别惹日本鬼子，能活着就好，我也和你一样死了兄弟，但这种仇，是只能吞进肚子里烂掉的，不然只会白白送死。”

“——什么叫和我一样死了兄弟？”

“——你干吗？”

“你说我兄弟死了？！”

“不就是你的那四个叫花子兄弟吗？你怎么了？”

“你说什么？！”

“干什么——怎么，你居然不知道？！——好多人看见的，我还以为后来是你给他们收的尸！”

“你说什么！”

“嘘！日本鬼子又来了，我们换个地方说话！”

短毛拉着自己躲到了一处暂时没有日本鬼子经过的角落里。黑暗中，自己的手脚冰凉发麻，心脏像要扑出胸腔，脑子里成片的眩晕纠缠在一起。怎么回事？怎么回事？这一切究竟是怎么回事！

黑暗中，短毛轻声地向自己述说了孔仁他们最后的故事。九月十九日上午，日军部队大规模开进沈阳。百姓四散逃避。一个四五岁大的孩子摔倒在地上，日军步兵直接就给了这孩子一刺刀。孩子的母亲哭喊着上去抱尸体，

日军的军用卡车已是开了上来。日本鬼子眼都不眨一下地，直接就将卡车从这位母亲的身上开了过去。卡车的车轮将这位母亲的身体和那个孩子的脑袋给碾了个稀巴烂，地上一片血肉模糊。这辆卡车开过去了，后面紧接着又是第二辆卡车。日本鬼子一丝停顿也没有，弯都懒得拐一下，直接就是又将铁山般沉重的卡车从尸体上开了过去。那位母亲和那个孩子的尸体，被碾得惨不忍睹。周围有百姓哭了起来。日军步兵朝天开枪。这时，孔仁他们四个，就跑了出来。他们不惧也不怕地，就去收那两具可怜的尸体。日本鬼子就对着他们喊话，叽里咕噜的，也没人能听得懂。孔仁他们没有理那个喊话的鬼子，只管收尸，于是，两个鬼子就向孔仁他们举起了枪。孔仁大声说："我们在中国的土地上，为中国人收尸，有什么不可以！你们这群倭寇，简直丧尽天良！"估计鬼子也没听懂中国话。一个鬼子直接便将刺刀向孔仁扎了过去。但是，孔仁竟然很轻易地就躲开了。于是，日本鬼子就愣了。一个拿指挥刀的鬼子喊了一句什么，五六个鬼子便一齐举枪包围住了孔仁四人。孔仁激昂悲愤地大声说："国民党和东北军怕你们，我们叫花子不怕！兄弟们，今天就和这群畜生拼了！最多，我们来生再聚！"其余三人也慷慨悲愤地一齐大喊了一声"来生再聚"，然后，他们便一起冲向了日本人。日本人乱枪齐发。孔仁四人，共赴黄泉。

自己泪流满面，泣不成声。短毛叹了口气，说，他们是真正的英雄好汉，我短毛以前一直瞧不起他们，可现在我知道，我不如他们。

自己哭着问，他们的尸首在哪里？

短毛说，不知道，昨天下午我经过那里的时候，尸首已经不见了，我以为是你收的尸。既然不是，那么，也许他们的尸首是被鬼子拖走了吧。这两天死的中国人，鬼子都拖去了圣母医院后面的荒地里，听说过几天会集中焚烧。你要不可以去那里找找。

自己说，谢谢。

短毛问：他们出事的时候，你在哪里？

自己没脸告诉短毛，兄弟们死的时候，自己正在全心全意地保护一个女人！

自己失魂落魄地，跑去了圣母医院后面的荒地里，果然，那里尸首成堆，血腥扑鼻。借着医院周围的路灯光，能看清小半片荒地里的惨景。死尸堆叠在死尸上，血色深红在血色中。尸臭的气味如看不见的一片湖，凝结在无形中，浓稠胜血，恨愤可触，血与死的味道在此处之蓄积，其可怖与作呕的程度远胜过了猪牛嚎叫的屠宰场。嗜血的苍蝇成群结队地在荒地里飞舞，嗡嗡声如疾风暴雨之密，它们对死尸叮咬之贪婪，毫不逊色于残暴之杀人犯。荒地的土壤已被血染成暗红，不，黑红。整个荒地，就像是一块巨大的触目惊心的血痂。脚踩在荒地上，整个活着的自己都感到了发抖。就好像那些早已干透的血，还活生生地连着那些死者未死的心脉一样。死尸里有中国士兵，有中国百姓，大部分是百姓。百姓里有男女老幼，还有婴儿、孕妇。一个血淋淋的婴儿孤零零地趴在荒地里，像一条不小心死去的小狗，他的脑袋很大，头发还没长出来，他死了，就好像是睡着了一般。但愿，他能睡得香甜。尸堆里还有一名全身赤裸的孕妇，死状惨绝人寰。大多数的人身上都布满了枪眼，一个又一个的血窟窿，成了苍蝇们聚集的营地。有一名青年男子的腹腔被完全剖开，肠子流了一地，在那血淋淋的肠子上，有黑色的虫子在蠕动咬食。自己忍着恶心，呼吸着浓稠的血腥气，拼了命地在死尸堆里翻找，翻找着孔仁他们的尸体。一种忽冷忽热的痛苦在自己全身奔腾，奔腾得让人心血麻木，恶心不堪，悲酸难抑，又哭不出来喊不出来。自己拼了命地翻找着，不顾一切，也不怕会不会引来巡逻的日本人。日本人来了才好，和他们拼了！拼了！

但是，并没有日本人过来，连中国人也没有。整座圣母医院，也像是死了一般，虽然灯火通明，整栋楼，却只像是住满了看不见的鬼。寂静，无尽的寂静，在死气中阴森压抑到极致的寂静。就好像，自己只要狂暴地怒吼一声，眼前的这片人间地狱，就会变成一片茫茫的火海，烧到天上，烧到地下，焚尽一切黑暗不堪的现实。但是，自己一点点声音也吼不出来。

终于找到了黄道的尸体，接着是朱理、孟义、孔仁。他们浑身是血，眼睛都还没有合上。抱着他们冰凉的尸体，自己仿佛窒息般透不过气来。心血仿佛都在往喉头上涌，自己咬紧了牙关，泪水止不住地流。自己吸气，拼命地大口吸气，告诉自己不能崩溃，告诉自己不可以崩溃。血腥和死亡的味道被自己大口大口吸入体内，感到自己好像也已成了这片荒地里的一个鬼魂，一个怒恨不已而又无能为力的幽冥鬼魂。合上了兄弟们的双眼，自己狠狠地打了自己四记耳光。清亮的疼痛不能减轻或麻痹自己心中一丝丝的愧

疚和罪孽，只能让自己更加清楚地看见这愧疚和罪孽的无底深沉和无边深远。泪水在自己眼中疼痛地收干，因为自己感到，自己都没有资格在兄弟们的面前哭。还记得当年和兄弟们在破庙里结拜，说好的同生共死，患难与共，而今，却只剩下了自己一人还好好地活着，还好好地活着！这算什么！恨只恨，自己从未对兄弟们尽忠尽义。他们出事的时候，自己要是和他们在一起，那就一定会阻拦他们，就算拦不住，他们和日本人起了冲突，自己起码也还能当个翻译，避免矛盾恶化。可是，当时自己在哪儿？当时自己在哪儿？一切全是屁话！什么都晚了！

黑夜静谧无声，无声中，却又能听见日本兵巡逻经过的声音。这静谧不是安宁，而是恐怖的压抑。没有人敢大哭大喊，因为一哭一喊，都有可能导致丧命。无边的黑像张牙舞爪的猛兽，猛兽集合着猛兽，像要一起来把这里的活人生吃。又经过了一队日本兵，自己不敢再放任悲酸奔流，只得赶紧想办法，去找了一辆板车过来。自己将兄弟们的尸体放上了板车，然后，推着板车便匆匆离开了这片荒地。医院里有好几个人都看见了自己收尸体，但他们在看见后都躲开了。像人间地狱一样幽冥可怕的荒地，在身后越来越远，但它那浓极的血腥气与森然的威慑力，却像一根冰寒的铁锥，在自己心里越刺越深，走得越远，记得越深，恐怖不已，又挥之不去。自己推着板车在黑夜里冰冷地前行，既要压抑着悲酸，不让自己难过，又要时时刻刻提防着日本人，自己感到，这个世界真像是被揉成了一团碎屑，我们每一个人，只是被困在碎屑里的虫蚁。生和死，从极其重要沦为极其渺小；伤和悲，从个别角落走向时时处处。人间地狱，避无可避。路上遇到了两次日军的盘查，自己仗着会说日语，好歹都混了过去。自己推着板车，往废祠堂方向走，自己要带兄弟们回家。

回到了废祠堂，自己将兄弟们的尸体从板车上抱了下来。板车放在废祠堂外太惹眼，自己就又将板车推到了不远处的一个角落。回到祠堂里，看到兄弟们浑身枪眼的尸体，自己的眼泪一下子就又都涌了上来。谁能想到，前日一别，竟是永诀。当时，自己满心只想着要去保护丽云，连对兄弟们最后说的那声“再见”，都说得那样心不在焉。现在，自己已无法再和他们说上半句话，愧疚之言也罢，情义之诉也罢，他们再也听不到。想想，从自己落难逃至东北开始，便一直是在依附于兄弟们而活。饿了，大家一起找东西吃，冷了，大家一起生火取暖，有肉一起吃，有酒一起喝，有苦一起受，有难一起挨。大家互帮互助，同甘共苦，就像一个大家庭一样。拿孔仁的话来说，就是一根筷子好折断，五根筷子难折断。在这样一个激流动荡的乱世中，在自己命运的诡谲凶险里，若没有兄弟们的全力帮助与尽心爱护，自己不知已是几番沉陷几番溺毙！若没有这个苦中作乐虽贫却暖的大家庭，自己不知已是在阎王殿上做鬼几时！可是现在，他们都死了，都已经死了。兄弟们都不在了，这个大家庭，也刹那烟消云散了。自己那时还不曾领悟，人生之聚散只如青烟一缕，此时不着意，彼时空叹息，留待回首处，无言说孤独。自己深深懊悔，兄弟们在世时，没真心想过报答与尽忠尽义，总以为路还长，以后有的是时间重新去爱兄弟、修情义。可是，结束，说来就来了。也许，这本也只是命运之一种。面对命运，我们又能说什么呢？自己也后悔自己当初教了兄弟们武功，如果他们一点拳脚也不会，恐怕也不会如此冲动托大，以至于在日本人的枪口前白白丧了性命。但是，他们不会武功就不敢和日本人拼命了吗？假设都是空留遗憾的，自己不愿再想。也许，已发生的，就是一切如果的结局，所以，在结局之外，不存在任何如果。这就是宿命。

种种思绪仍在心中纷乱悲伤，自己却也不能再空空落泪。自己知道自己还有很多事要做。自己潜入了一家成衣铺，偷了四套新衣服，放了八块大洋在柜台上，算是买。然后，自己想去买棺材，但想想现在这情形，棺材那么大，实在是不方便偷或买，于是，就只好去偷了四张新席子，也将钱照价放在了那店内的柜台上，算是买。最后，自己回到了废祠堂。自己打了些水，替兄弟们擦净了脸，擦净了身子，给他们换上了新的衣服。然后，每人，用一张新席子包了起来。自己拿了一把铁锨，去了祠堂后的泥地上，挖起了坑。

依稀的光亮里，泥土纷纷扬扬。自己使劲地挖着土，就好像和自己有仇的是这泥土，而不是日本人。人有时候就是这样，要等到永远不会再见到某个人了，才会蓦然发现自己心中有深深感情的存在。这么多年了，自己虽然始终对女人好多过对兄弟好，但是，毫无疑问，自己在心底，是默默将兄弟们视作终生的依靠和陪伴的，自己是真拿他们当成了亲兄弟的。可是，日本人突然就把他们给杀了！全杀了！自己又成了个一无所有的人！铁锨被自己

挥舞得呼呼有风，自己真恨不得，那狠狠的每一铲，都能铲在日本人的脑袋上！让那些双手沾满鲜血的畜生去死！可是，短毛说得对，这种仇，只能吞进肚子里烂掉，不然只会白白送死，白白送死！日本人有枪，有炮，连东北军都闻风丧胆，自己一个老百姓，又能做什么！没错，自己是拳王，但拳王有个屁用！子弹永远比拳头硬！

牙齿咬得咯咯响，泪水在自己眼眶里不停地打转，但自己拼命忍着不再让泪落下来。因为自己是没有资格在兄弟们面前哭的。抬头看看那黑暗而辽远的天幕，自己不知道时间，但估计可能早已是过了半夜了吧。自己又想起了丽云。临走时，和她说好，很快就会回到她身边，可自己这一走，便是整夜未归，她该急坏了吧？她不会有事吧？可惜丽云那里也没电话，不然好歹也要和她说一声才好。自己给了自己一个耳光，这是兄弟们的最后一程了，无论如何，自己都不该再在此时，想起女人。自己要尽忠尽义地，送好兄弟们这最后的一段路。不然，自己将终生不安。

在一棵树的前后左右，自己挖出了四个大坑。自己将兄弟们的尸体，小心仔细地分别放入了这四个大坑中。自己对着每具尸体，分别郑重其事地道了一次别，然后，又重新拿起铁锹，往坑里回填泥土。一铲铲的泥土落到包着席子的尸体上，自己知道，永别了。时间会将这些曾经活生生的生命，最终也变成一撮撮的泥土。他们的肉体最终会和大自然融为一体，就像他们从来没有来到过这个世界上一样。这就是生命和人生在本质上的空无，存在从不存在中来，又回到不存在中去，于是，存在本身也就成了一个传说。四个坟包堆了起来，在依稀的光亮里，像四座荒芜了千年的远山。自己还是又哭了起来，这一次的哭泣里，没有怒，没有恨，甚至也没有太多悲伤，只是空无，空无得让人无法承受、痛不欲生。一切纷乱而复杂的痛苦情感，在这种空无感的包裹里，都显得太渺小，而这空无感，本身就成了最巨大的哀伤。这哀伤，难以形容。像站在生的尽头讨论死，像睡在死的梦里怀念生，失去本身成为一座囚笼，在一无所有中，死亡是永远等不到解脱的禁锢。

找不到木牌等任何可以充当墓碑的东西，天渐渐亮了起来。自己拿刀，在四座坟包中间的那棵树的树干上，分别刻上了孔仁他们四人的名字，每人的名字，向着每人坟包的方向。刻完了字，自己割开了手指，将血涂在了那些字的刻痕中。自己的血没让自己感到一点痛。只有愧疚，绵绵不断的愧疚。而这愧疚，此生都再不会有机会被减轻与被赎救。

自己去弄了些纸钱，在四人坟前烧了。烧完了纸钱，自己跪在他们的坟前，说："来生若能再见，我再不会离兄弟而去。"

擦净了泪，吹熄了蜡烛，自己坐在光线已澄亮的废祠堂中。祠堂里的物件还依旧如几天前，一些兄弟们新买的东西，还崭新得像刚买时一样。自己感到了孤独，这种孤独，彻头彻尾，完全彻底。祠堂空了，兄弟死了，又只剩下自己一个人了。不会再有热热闹闹的嬉笑，不会再有患难与共的帮扶，从此以后，在这里，能够陪伴着自己的将只有无尽的空荡与失落，长啸一声，能听到的也只是孤零零的飘荡回声。自己的冷暖饥饱，将只是自己一个人的生存经历；自己的生与死，将只是自己孤独世界里一个人的悲喜。这种感觉真是很可怕，这种举目四望空无一人的感觉真是令人不寒而栗。孤独，再无亲人朋友的孤独，就像一座冷绝的冰窖，谁待在里面，谁就能看见一种比死更可怕地活着。就好像一个人漂浮在大海上，如果注定只能一个人漂浮到死，那还真不如尽早死了的好。

自己忽然又想起了丽云。丽云她，不也早已是举目无亲孑然一身？想来，她所经受的痛苦和彷徨，也不是几句话就能说清的。自己一直觉得丽云是柔弱的，但是细想想，其实她比自己所能想象的要坚强得多。人活着，最难的就是活着去承受，承受所拥有的失去，承受所坚信的陨落，承受所追求的破灭，承受自己所亲所爱的人一一先自己而去，承受自己面对悲剧与宿命时的无能为力，承受一切大悲大喜幻灭之后的孤独至极。而丽云，又是什么力量在支撑着她，使她在经历过了如此多的变故之后，依旧那样清纯、灿烂、美丽？

天上下起了雨。自己应该收拾起心情，回到丽云的身边去了。已经让她等待、担心得太久了。既然对兄弟的亏欠已不可挽回，那就不应该再损伤自己给她的承诺。说好了要保护她的，自己不在，她还好吗？

自己将兄弟们留下的钱装了一袋，准备连同自己藏起的七百块大洋，一起拿去给丽云。雨越下越大，自己拿了钱，撑了伞，就准备去取那七百块大洋。然后，便可以回到丽云那里去了。

走在去取钱的路上，看到偶尔有人从窗户里投来异样的眼光。自己蓦然才发现不妥。一个叫花子打扮的人，撑了一把伞，感觉是很异样的。另外，

自己身上带了钱，很多钱，万一碰上日本兵搜身，这怎么解释？叫花子哪来的这么多钱？

自己看见，昨晚去偷过的那家成衣铺，依旧没有开张，于是，便又潜了进去，偷了一套新衣服。自己换上了新衣服，又顺便洗了个脸，剪了剪头发，然后，站在镜子前照了照，忽然，感觉又好像是回到了曾经的某一天。似曾相识，不愿想起。自己看了看手中那把湿淋淋的雨伞，这正是当年，自己在雨中送给丽云的那把伞。难道，命运真的只是一遍又一遍的轮回？

外面乱哄哄的一阵骚动。听见有日本人大喊大叫着跑过。自己一阵紧张，忙放下了伞和钱袋，空身跑出去看。

只见，倾盆大雨里，一名姿容艳丽的女子，正被一群日本兵围困着。女子身上的衣服已被撕得破破烂烂，滂沱的雨水中，她衣不蔽体，惊惶失措，逃无可逃，除了哭，她什么也不会喊，连“救命”也没喊。日本兵有的已赤裸了上身，有的在拿步枪上的刺刀向她一指一指。他们已牢牢地围困住了她，却又似乎并不急于捉住她。他们这个上去撕掉她一片衣服，那个上去摸她一把，戏耍她，恐吓她。她越恐惧害怕，他们越兴奋快乐。她的每一次惊呼与痛泣，都只会引起他们快活的哄堂大笑。她就像是一只已注定逃不掉的猎物，而他们，正在享受吃掉猎物前的那种戏弄的快乐与控制的快感。他们说了不少话，别人也许听不懂，但自己全听懂了。污言秽语，不堪入耳。终于，一个年轻的日本兵撕光了这名女子的衣服，将她扑倒在了地上。他们快乐地大呼小叫。而她，直到此时，才惨不忍闻地喊出了一声：“救命啊——”

一个日本兵会说中国话，他对她说：“花姑娘，你只要乖乖享受就好。”他把这话翻译给了他的同伴听，他们又是一阵哄堂大笑。附近也有一些中国人在看，但是，大家都只是在畏缩地看。有人看不下去，就跑了，连敢哼一声的人也没有。除了日本人围起的那个喧闹的圈子，周围都是一片死寂。寂静得连雨声都有了让人疼痛的感觉。哗哗哗，雨那么大，冲不淡这世界的一点点肮脏。

一个日本人从地上爬了起来，另一个又扑了上去。许多远看的中国人都走了，自己松开了拳头，也正准备躲回店铺里去。突然，惊天动地地响起了热烈的枪声。“砰、砰、砰”，一个日本兵中了枪，又一个日本兵中了枪！

一个男人，双手持着两把枪，正疾奔而来！

“小柔！”男人大哭着，疯了似的向日本兵开枪。

日本兵有枪的全转入了战斗状态。

双方激战了起来。

这个男人让自己感到有些眼熟。自己想了起来。他，就是十八日当晚，自己看见的那个说是要去和女人道别的东北军士兵！

“阿台哥！”女子哭着喊了一声。

战斗很快就结束了。结局很显然，那个叫阿台的男人，身中数枪，倒在了血泊中。雨水冲刷着血水，血水在雨水中，像恣肆的汪洋大海。

女子爬到了奄奄一息的男人身边，哭着抚摸他的脸庞，问他：“你不是走了吗？”

男人说：“你在这，我哪儿也不想去。”

“砰”一声。第一个强奸这名女子的日本兵，往这个叫阿台的男人头上开了一枪。阿台死了。女子号啕惨哭，哭声撕心裂肺，惊天动地。雨下得凄厉，也凄厉不过这人间的惨剧。

日本兵又欢笑着向女子围了过去。女子大哭着，突然捡起了枪。“砰”一声，她打中了一个日本兵的肩膀，再扣扳机，却已没有子弹。

中弹的日本兵大怒，向女子连开了两枪。女子倒在了血泊中，不再动弹。她全身赤裸着，像这雨里最美艳的一束花朵，像这天地间最悲惨的一滴眼泪。

那个会说中国话的日本兵，走到了女子的身旁，他蹲下去，又摸了摸她的脸庞。他用中文说：“你这么漂亮，要是不反抗，我们根本就不会杀了你。真可惜。”

已没有中国人再在远远地看，天地间，除了这场悲惨的大雨，仿佛已空无一物。自己也天旋地转地躲回了成衣铺里。激烈的血流仍在自己冰冷的脑壳里不停地冲击、凝结、冷却，自己头晕目眩，浑身战栗。自己的双手松软，根本握不成拳头。闭上了眼，自己真想把刚才所见的一切从头脑中抠掉，抠掉！耳中仿佛又隐约听到了日本兵的欢笑，自己跌坐在了地上。雨声更猛了。自己听见的，却只像是汩汩的流血声。自己知道，自己怕是无法忘掉这阿台和小柔的故事了。因为，这个故事不仅打了上帝一个耳光，更像是摧毁了所有软弱者心中最后的勇气。包括自己在内，没有一个中国人上去帮

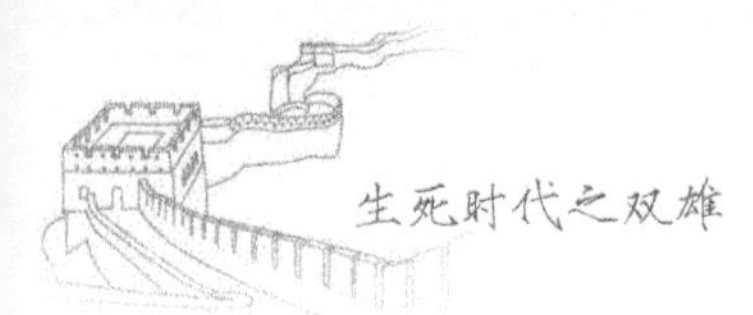

助过阿台和小柔，为什么？因为，谁上去，谁就会白白送死。这就是理由。这是理由吗？

冷汗在自己的脑门上流。深深的恐怖，不，比恐怖更绝望而悲惨的一种情绪，在自己的血管里奔流。就好像天狗永恒地吞掉了太阳一般。睁眼所见的一切，仿佛都泡在血泊中，而面对四处横行的畜生，自己却又只像个手无缚鸡之力的侏儒！可自己明明是拳王啊！自己甚至开始自责地想：刚才，自己若能出手帮那个阿台一把，说不定他能带着小柔离开！自己是拳王啊！可是，这不是很可笑吗？那么多日本兵，那么多条枪，你帮一个不可能胜利的人与一群不可能失败的人作对？你不是找死是什么！这就是现实，而现实，也许本来就是要让人忍受和承受的。

自己拿了伞和钱，蹿上了房顶，在日本人看不到的地方奔跑。离开成衣铺时，街上的那群日本兵依旧在侮辱小柔的尸体。

取出了自己藏的七百块大洋，终于回到了丽云的小院那里。可是，院门开着，院里和屋里空无一人！

自己的脑海里划过了一道晴天霹雳！

自己丢下了伞和钱，疯了似的跑出了小院。丽云，丽云，你在哪里？你在哪里！

大雨发了疯似的猛落，雨水浇得自己睁不开眼。自己在雨中到处狂奔。丽云，丽云！

小柔倒在血泊中的样子又一次从自己的脑海里划过。自己恐惧极了地，像是在血泊里看到了丽云的样子。“啊——”自己在雨中仰天长啸。泪水奔了出来。“丽云——你在哪儿——你在哪儿——”

天地苍茫，乱世空旷。

“赵驹——”

自己急忙转身，只见丽云全身湿透地站在大雨里。“丽云——”自己疯了似的，狂奔上前，再不顾一切一把紧紧抱住了丽云，死死地、紧紧地。自己说不出话来，只是不停地流泪。大雨那么冰凉，泪热得疯狂。

“你一晚上没回来，我以为你出事了，所以出来找你，可是到处找也找不到——我害怕、我害怕再也找不着你了——”丽云啜泣了起来。

“不会的，不会的——我再也不会离开你了，再也不会了——”自己喃喃地说着，紧紧地抱着丽云，狂热地抱着丽云，就好像只要稍微一松手，她就会从这世上消失不见。

雨势小了许多。丽云不哭了。她紧紧依偎在自己胸前，像一只怕冷的小猫。天边仿佛露出了一道金黄的阳光。阳光很温暖。

日本关东军司令官本庄繁将沈阳的名称又改回了奉天，同时，任命日本大特务头子土肥原贤二为奉天市市长。土肥原组织了一班全部以日本人为骨干的行政人马，迅速地全面接管了沈阳城的各项市政管理事务。并且，土肥原还迅速而牢固地拉拢起了一批在张作霖、张学良时期于东北地盘上颇有些权势与威望的中国人，成立了辽宁省地方维持会，欲以其暂代省政府职能。维持会中设众多日本顾问，会中大权皆由日本顾问掌控。军警宪特遍布沈阳的大街小巷，荷枪实弹，日夜巡逻，凡遇有抗日嫌疑者，就地击毙，格杀勿论。有八个小孩只是因为趴在铁轨上想听听远方火车的声音，即被日军判定为敌军情报员，当场刺杀。日军还将这八个小孩的头都割了下来，高悬示众。冰冷的秋风裹卷着浓稠的血腥味，在这样一个萧瑟不堪的秋天，吹遍了沈阳这座沦陷之城的每个角落。白天如黑夜，黑夜如地狱。锋利的惶恐撩拨着阴森的恐怖，让人日不能宁，夜不能寐。

每天晚上，自己都会关好了院门、屋门，将那张木榻搬到堂屋里，睡在木榻上面。苍白的月光有时会从破旧的窗户外照进来，推开一片漆黑的拥堵，让人触摸着天空微弱的澄明，而自己在每一个夜里，都似睡而半醒，难以真正入眠。说不清的恐惧总在耳边和心头不停盘绕，自己醒着是害怕，睡着了也是做噩梦。梦里，自己能清醒地听见日本人说话，能清醒地看见兄弟们被杀，能清醒地记起阿台和小柔的悲惨故事。悲伤和恐怖总会像石块一样压在自己的胸口，令自己痛不可忍，又无法逃躲，直到自己从梦魇中惊醒，这样的难受才会渐渐消停。而自己睡在木榻上，抚摸着丽云给自己铺的毯子，心口又有一堵解不开、冲不破的忧伤之墙。自己想做丽云的保护神，但是，自己是神吗？

每日从收音机里传出的消息都只能令人更加忧惧、沮丧。日本人依旧在不断地打胜仗，东北的各城各镇都在陆续地沦陷。而面对日军如狼似虎般的攻势，国军却奉行不抵抗政策，不是撤退、逃跑，就是突围失败后投降、变节，百姓无人庇护，生灵涂炭。只有共产党的武装力量和小股不服从撤退命

令的东北军士兵仍在坚持与关东军作战，民间自发组织起的武装抵抗斗争也此起彼伏，但这一切也都只是螳臂当车，抵抗军人数少、装备差、无粮草、无支援，打得越英勇，只是牺牲得越多。而具备抵抗能力的国军正规部队，却又只知退避三舍、一撤再撤。日军的战焰如洪水般四处奔流，战锋锐不可当，大有迅速攻陷全东北之势。不，简直可以说，是大有侵吞全中国之势！如今沈阳全陷，城中百姓朝不保夕，人人自危，谁都不知道该怎样在敌军的统治之下继续生活下去。自己思来想去，都想要带丽云离开沈阳这座沦陷之城，但是，沈阳周围及外面的各路各处，也都已是烧满了日军的战火，谁又能保证，带着丽云出逃，一路上能安然无事？而且，自己带着丽云，又能逃去哪儿呢？东北会不会全陷？中国会不会全陷？未来的时局，究竟会怎样发展？如果全中国都会被这群丧心病狂的日本畜生给占领，那么毫无疑问，逃出沈阳是没有任何意义的。除非自己能带着丽云逃去国外，逃去欧美，因为显而易见，日本再猖狂，也是绝不可能敢对欧美动武的，但是，自己又怎么可能有能力将丽云送到国外去？若是换成以前，庄、潘两家未倒之时，丽云要出国是一件十分容易的事，可是现在，人事皆非，树倒猢狲散，又哪里还有什么办法和门路可以让她去国外躲避战祸？若还有人能帮她，当日，她又哪里用得着去变卖珠宝首饰，哪里用得着住到这种破小院里来？现在，她的身边已只剩下自己这个叫花子了，而一个叫花子，又能帮得了她什么呢？除了依旧和她待在这座沦陷之城，除了依旧和她躲在这处破小院里，除了依旧和她每日提心吊胆地生活在日寇的鼻息之下，自己又可以为她做些什么事呢？自己想要守护她，可是，在这沈阳城里，又哪里还有什么中国人的安全？自己想要带她出逃，又实在是无处可去，无路可逃，无可求助，无法冒险。这就是一个绝境！

自己能听懂日本人说话，而他们毫无防备。自己听见日本兵说：以日本的军事实力，只要不惜代价全面对中国开战，几个月内便定可占领整个中国。他们还说：原以为这次战争，皇军的勇士会大有损伤，谁知道，中国的军队逃得比兔子还快，真是天佑日本。自己绝望至极，而又悲愤莫名。自己从不将这些话告诉丽云半句。自己总是告诉丽云：倭寇不过一时得志，日本弹丸小岛，人少物稀，如老鼠而已，老鼠再强，焉有咬死大象之理？丽云说，对。而自己的心里却总是在问：中国，还是一头大象吗？

孔仁他们不在了，对他们的悼念和复杂的哀伤，就像一根时光凝成的刺，深深地扎在自己的心脏上，与自己的心跳融合在一起。只要安静下来，那痛便会跟着心跳，一起变得清晰而有力起来。那淡淡而深深的哀伤，一下一下地搏动，让你难受得很，却又并不会因此而流泪。因为一切都是不可改变的事实，是已然发生的命运，那哀悼的眼泪，滚热了几次，便都已被无奈、无能为力的苦涩给冰冻住。而这冰冻让人深深恐惧现实的冷，这冷，是一种庞大的迷茫；这冷，是一种无处不在的坚硬，像四面紧紧压迫着你的铜墙铁壁。失去和命运，是人永远无法面对的两个魔鬼。而当你背对着魔鬼，面向自我之时，一个叫孤独的黑洞又会赫然而巨大地暴露在你面前。的确，在失去了你所拥有的东西和被命运残酷地玩弄之后，在你隐蔽而沉沦的灵魂之中，除了孤独这么个要人命的黑洞，你又还能有什么呢？每当自己在夜深人静中感到这种孤独时，便会分外想要抱紧这个夜。就好像，在这样的夜里，还有着什么能拯救自己的火光。而自己又知道，这火光，未必能真的被自己拥进自己的生命里。因为，自己知道，在拥抱之外，自己还有着太多的卑微不堪。

有时候，丽云看见自己一个人默然地坐着，知道自己是又在悼念兄弟了，便会过来陪自己坐一会儿，和自己说说话。她不是很会安慰人，也不善于说什么解忧的话，于是很多时候，她也就干脆什么都不说了，只是那样默默地和自己坐在一起，陪伴着自己。一切都很安静，也很温暖。有时候，月亮很清晰很明亮，其实自己想告诉她，只要她在自己的身边，自己的心里便填满了阳光。这阳光像火一样热烈，像信仰一样令人追求。她总是会努力说一些开心的事、开心的话，想要让自己和她都能忘记一些悲伤，多拥有一些快乐，其实她不知道，她这样有多让自己心疼，多让自己感到无地自容。其实自己想告诉她，现在，你已经是我在这个世上唯一最亲近的人了，除了你，我的灵魂已再无可停泊之处。其实，自己想牵她的手，每当她靠近自己，自己便想紧紧地拥抱她，永远不放开。但是，自己什么都没说，也什么都没做。自己只是很珍惜和丽云坐在一起的每一个片刻，不管自己当时的内心有着何种原因的悲伤或者何种结果的向往，也不管丽云的心在沉默或者期望。这世上总有太多的事情或者因果，是让人无法去仔细辨析和追寻的，或者就算辨析清了和追寻到了，也只是一场令人欲哭无泪的悲剧，或一个让人

无法突围的绝境。所以，有时候，的确是只有发生在眼前的，才是真正已经获得了永恒的。这种永恒很美好，只是很多时候，我们也许都不知道。有时候，自己甚至会默默对上天说，只要能将我和丽云的此刻延长成一生，我愿死后永远在地狱被折磨。爱情就是会让人像个傻瓜。

丽云刚看到自己拿来的那些大洋的时候，十分惊讶。她不知道自己曾打过生死局，所以，她不明白自己为什么会有这么多的银圆。自己肚子里预先早就编好了一个谎，于是骗她：格斗场老板一直生不出儿子，算命的要他多积点德，所以他便订出了一条规矩，凡是决意要金盆洗手退出黑拳界的拳手，他概不强留，且一律奉送七百大洋安家费。丽云不相信似的小嘴一嘟，问："真的？"自己心虚而极认真地说："当然是真的，难道我还会骗你？"她就掩嘴笑了起来，然后，自己的脸就被她轻轻地拧了一下，她调皮地说："就知道你不敢骗我。"那些日子，只要和自己在一起，她就总是开心得像个孩子。这份开心真实得像呼吸，简单得像心跳，美丽得像蜜糖，而又脆弱得像花朵。丽云死后，自己每每再想起这些，便会碎尽肝肠，痛哭整夜。

丽云一眼就认出了当年那把的雨伞。她擦净了伞上的雨迹，摩挲着它，自言自语地说，想不到，它还在。自己说，你看，还没有坏。她笑了笑，打开了伞，痴痴地说，以前的日子，真好像一场大雨。自己说，雨总会停，雨过后，天就晴了。她说，就算雨不停，只要伞还没坏，又有什么可怕的。

沈阳城中还是会有零星的枪战发生，毕竟仍然有人在反抗。土肥原精于算计，手段毒辣，日军和伪警察终日在城里城外搜捕、开战、屠杀，血雨腥风不断。城中百业停歇，民生凋敝，百姓生活步履维艰。大街小巷里都布有日军岗哨，百姓凡经过，必遭搜身、洗劫。若稍有不从，即脑袋开花。汉奸们则狐假虎威，为虎作伥。除了这些，还有日军与汉奸们随时随地的闯宅搜查、入室抢掠，百姓就算是躲在家里也一样担惊受怕，不得安宁。若有漂亮女人被日军发现，女人自然又是一番灾难。日军滥杀无辜，不分男女老幼，全凭一时心情；他们砍人头颅，不论从逆顺背，只仗一时喜好。他们比老虎更可怕，因为老虎还有吃饱的时候，而人，永远吃不饱。

家里的粮食快没了，自己带了钱，想去米铺看看，想照着当初偷衣服的法子，偷些米，然后将钱照价放在柜台上，当是买。但是，自己还是把事情想得过于美好了。米铺里还有狗屁的米，早就都让日本人给抢光了！连柜台也被砸了个稀巴烂。墙上还有两排弹孔。有日本巡逻兵经过，自己赶紧躲到了屋顶上。

躲在屋顶上，自己愁思缠结。对于自己和丽云来说，其他的困难和危险，暂时还没到严重的地步，但是，这缺粮的问题若拖下去，则会变成一个大麻烦。难道要让丽云饿肚子？一挨饿，要挨多久？在这种战乱的环境里，饿死人也不是什么稀奇的事情。不行！必须要想办法。难道去偷老百姓家里的粮吗？那真是造孽了。而今，沈阳城中，粮食最多的，就是日本人，不偷他们，偷谁？

但是，偷日本人的粮，这不是找死吗？

深夜，当自己背着两袋粮食跳回小院里的时候，丽云还没睡。屋里昏暗地亮着灯，丽云着急地跑了出来，她的眼中莫名像是隐隐泛着泪光。她问："你去哪儿啦？早上说去买米，怎么现在才回来？"

"哦，米铺关着，我后来找到了米铺老板的家，才跟他买到了米，所以弄得这么晚。"

"你没事就好。我去热热晚饭——呀，你肩膀后面怎么破了，流了这么多血？！"

"噢……我路上跑得太急，不小心摔了一跤，被钉子划开了一点儿皮，没事，小事情——"

"还说没事——快进来，我给你看看，先消毒包扎一下。"

"哎，好。"

说完，远处突然就响起了凌厉的枪声。深夜的低沉里，这枪声格外刺耳。丽云惊恐地顿了顿。她看了看自己的脸，自己笑了笑，说，别怕，不关我们的事。话音刚落，自己被日军枪托砸中的膝盖就又猛地一痛，自己差点跪了下来。

其实有时候，自己并不知道，要怎样做，才是真正对丽云好。自己为她存储了银圆，但是，她若知道，这些钱是自己用对手的死亡换来的，她该会有多么恐惧、难受、恶心？自己为她取来了粮食，但是，她若知道，这些米是自己戴了面具穿了寿衣去日本人那里偷来的，她该会有多么着急、害怕、担心？而为了不想让她恐惧和担心，自己对她撒了一个又一个的谎，她若知道了这些，又该会有多么难过、痛苦、伤心？世间的事往往就是如此自相矛

盾，让人难以分辨更难以抉择。想要对她好，又只能去做一些会伤害到她的事情。这个悖论，自己永远无法理清。或许，这个世界本就充满了悖论，让人无可奈何。

有时候，丽云也会一个人坐着发呆。远远地望着她，自己莫名会隐隐心痛。萧瑟的夕阳斜照中，自己甚至能清晰地洞见她兀立的孤独。而这种孤独，自己十分懂得，就好像一个灵魂在镜子里看到了另一个灵魂一样。她只有看见了自己，她的孤独才会烟消云散。而这，却让自己更加心疼。她一直那样傻傻地相信着自己，痴痴地留恋着和自己在一起的一切，如果，有一天自己再次离开了她，她该怎么办？

但是，自己又为什么要去想再次离开她呢？这一次，自己能不能，真的和她厮守一生？

自己的偷粮行为，没给日本人留下什么线索或把柄，而且，就在自己偷粮的当晚，日军在沈阳占领的兵工厂遭到了武装袭击。日本人根本就没空去管偷米那种小事。自己侥幸全身而退。为了应付日军和汉奸时不时的闯宅搜查与入室抢掠，自己在柴房的地板下面挖了一个不小的暗格出来，将最要紧的银圆和粮食藏了进去。自己又去成衣铺里“买”了两套新衣服，以作自己平日里换洗之用。另外还买了双新鞋。那件被刺刀划破且染了血的衣服，丽云拿去洗了，衣服晾干后，她仔细地进行了缝补。补好后，衣服看起来就像新的一样。自己夸她手艺好，她乐得咯咯笑，笑靥如花。想着她低头咬线的模样和天真快乐的笑容，自己那时忽然痴痴而出神地想：今生若能娶她为妻，该是何等幸福之事。

而这痴痴的一个念头，就像一个甜蜜的魔咒，令自己牵肠挂肚，魂不守舍，甚至，有时都会忘了，自己和她，正活于日寇之铁蹄下。而悲剧，在一开始的时候，总是会让人误以为，幸福是一件可以去盼望和幻想的事情。

面对漆黑的夜，自己内心隐藏着的恐惧仍然蠢蠢欲动。有时候，这恐惧甚至会像一头张牙舞爪的怪兽，挣脱了自己理智的控制，拖拽着自己的灵魂奔向一片幽冥而极寒之地。那里除了满目的荒凉、绝望和悲哀，一无所有。那种恐怖，像火焰填满了世间、冰雪充塞着天地，烫得人成灰，冻得人粉碎。没有人知道，偷米那晚，当自己面对着日本兵枪口的时候，内心有着怎样的悸动与颤抖。死亡的可怕、枪械的冷酷、命运的残忍织缠在一起，像一个上帝的命令，命令着自己投降、放弃、任凭处置。这命令不能反抗地绝对，绝对地不能反抗，就像一个生生不息的噩梦，从自己心中的宗庙流出，又像一个铜墙铁壁的绝境，已被自己的人生反复证明了没有出路。当时，自己几乎便要放下手中的米。可是，就在那短短的一刹那，自己又想起了丽云。如果没有粮食，丽云就会挨饿，甚至饿死；如果自己死了，就不能再保护丽云、照顾丽云。所以，那个日本兵的脑袋，就被自己打成了烂西瓜。自己害怕死亡和枪械，害怕命运和轮回，但是，自己最害怕的，是丽云有事。只有她，才是自己灵魂的最深主宰。

在迷惘而半醒的睡梦里，自己还是会经常想起阿台和小柔的故事。那个日本畜生最后对小柔尸体所说的话，一直在自己耳边嗡嗡作响："你这么漂亮，要是不反抗，我们根本就不会杀了你。真可惜。"总有一股愤怒与无能相织而成的冰流，会被这句话深深地推进自己的心窝，令自己疼痛无比，又无能为力。当日，阿台如果不出现，那他现在兴许还活着；那时，小柔如果不反抗，那她或许真的不会死。就像国民党的撤军一样，只要不抵抗，部队就不会有太大的伤亡。但是，如果小柔面对强暴不作任何反抗，人的生命还有何尊严可言？如果阿台看着小柔受辱而不挺身拼命，人的存活又还有何意义可说？就像这国土的沦丧，若是整个国家都亡了，那部队实力的保存又有什么价值？——可是，人若死了，又哪里还能谈什么尊严和意义呢？阿台和小柔都死了，尊严和意义，对他们来说，又还有什么价值？就像收音机里说的，国军若贸然与日军交火，只会死伤惨重，而国军若亡了，又哪里还能指望国土之收复？这一切的一切，都是让人难以抉择的纠缠，不可分辨的矛盾。在反抗而惨死与忍辱而苟活之间，人，究竟该作何选择？是活着重要，还是尊严重要？人之生命，真正的意义究竟是什么？又或者，其实不管你做出的是什么选择，在命运的强横欺凌面前，所有的一切都只会归于灰飞烟灭？就好像，其实不管小柔是死是活、是抵抗了还是没抵抗，从她被日本畜生看上的那一刻起，她就已被注定了逃不过受辱的命运。或许，所谓的选择，本就只是人给自我的一份美好欺骗？在命运残酷的玩弄面前，你又真的有权选择吗？在上帝给予的绝境里面，谁又真的有反抗的希望？

绝望、迷惘、恐惧，总会在那一个又一个的夜里，深深地折磨着自己。零星的枪响、凌乱的奔跑，总会莫名令自己心惊肉跳。自己怕死、怕枪、怕

命运，但是为了丽云，自己可以什么都不怕。可是，就算自己什么也不怕，也仍然还是保护不了丽云，那自己该怎么办？——有时，自己甚至会突然可怕极了地想：如果我是阿台，究竟要怎样才能救下小柔？没有答案。

自己开始握着菜刀睡觉，这总会惹来丽云的嘻嘻笑。她说，你要是睡着了把口水流在上面，叫我怎么切菜呀？她的笑，是欢快的。在她心中，她眼前的这个男人，是个勇士，是个英雄。这个男人要手中握着一把菜刀才能睡着，在她的眼中，也许也只是他傻得可爱。但是，她不知道，其实，这个男人，只是个懦夫，只是个软蛋，只是个小丑，只是个乞丐。而他之所以非要在睡着时握上一把菜刀，不只是因为他太爱她，怕能力不够保护不了她，更是因为，他深深地绝望、迷惘、恐惧、哀伤。她根本就不该信赖他。

因为兵工厂遇袭的事，日军又在挨家挨户搜查、抓人。日本兵和汉奸又闯到了小院里来两次，所幸自己会说日本话，他们又走得急，所以并没有发生什么节外生枝的事。九月的最后一天，自己给丽云梳了一次头。她的头发乌黑细滑，宛若温柔的瀑布，宛若阳光里的雨丝，美丽，清澈，又娇弱。自己梳得极小心，生怕会弄坏它一点点。丽云坐在梳妆台前，大概是在镜子里看见了自己小心翼翼的模样，就忍俊不禁了起来，笑着说，你真傻，头发又不是纸，弄不坏的。自己依旧小心地梳着，说，我怕弄痛了你的头发，到了晚上，它们会在你耳边说我的坏话。她捂嘴痴痴笑了起来。她说，那你多陪我说说话儿啊，这样，我就没空理它们啦。自己笑了笑，说，傻孩子。她也就笑笑，娇柔地低着头，没再说什么。

给她梳好了头，自己放下了梳子，然后，踌躇了一下，便对她说："丽云，把这长发剪了吧。"

她很惊讶，还以为自己是在开玩笑。自己说："我说真的，你听我的。"

她就有些委屈，痴痴地问："你不喜欢我留长发吗？是不是这样子不漂亮？"

"不是的，我喜欢你留长发，你这样子非常漂亮，真的。"自己看着她，轻轻爱抚了一下她的长发，说："但是，你这样子就是太漂亮了，知道吗？这样很危险，我会担心你，不知道要怎样才能保护你，我很害怕，你能懂得我的意思吗？"

她抿嘴想了想，然后便点了点头。"好吧。"她灿烂地笑了笑，说："那你帮我剪。”

刀刃如流水般光洁，青丝乌亮胜雪。宛若溪水流经雪野，轻轻一剪，芳华散断，馨香碎乱。丝丝缕缕，都像落英缤纷，花瓣凋残。手握着丽云柔润如雨的断发，自己的心头疼痛似剐，复杂的疼惜和忧伤在心湖里此起彼伏，却又只能归于无法叹息的无奈和沉入湖底的沉默。

橘黄而浅淡的阳光飘洒在屋子里，飘洒在断发上。丽云看着长长的断发，不禁有些伤感，轻轻说：“知道吗，头发是不会腐朽的，就算有一天，我死了，尸骨烂成了污泥，这些头发，也还是会像我活着时一样又黑又亮。”

“傻话，说什么死啊活的，你要长命百岁，等到这些头发都烂了你还在我身边，这样我才会一辈子高兴。”

她就吃吃地笑了，然后，也不说话，一双秀美的妙目痴痴地望着空荡处，静静默默。

自己的心，莫名就有些乱。想要多看看丽云，又不敢再看。阳光浓烈了起来，让人的心发烫。空气中像有千百朵玫瑰在盛开，看不见的蝴蝶，比海市蜃楼更绚丽多彩。真的好想吻她。

“这些头发丢了可惜，送给我吧，好吗？”

“好哇。”

她粲然一笑，像个孩子似的开心。自己是真的好想，能永远看见她的笑。而上帝，又是否真能听见人的祈愿？

傍晚时，自己拿了钱，去向老百姓买了一些陈旧而难看的农妇衣裳回来。真的是买，不是偷。丽云不太情愿地去屋里换上了这些衣服。从屋里出来后，她伸开双臂，在自己面前转了一圈，笑问：“怎么样，我难看吗？”

“还是很漂亮。”

“真的？”

“真的。”

“好吧，我就当你说的是真话。”

说完，她哈哈笑了起来。自己也笑了。其实，她没明白，自己真的说的是真话。她只要一笑，那份美丽，便怎样也遮盖不住。这是一种刻在骨子里的漂亮，是一份上帝只赐给了少数女人的诱惑力，这本来也许是一种幸运——但是——但是，谁又能肯定，当上帝摘下面具时，那个至高无上的

神，不是万魔之王？

十月，秋叶飘零，枯黄满地。萧瑟的风凌厉地吹拂着灰暗的城，苍茫的压抑无边无际，飞鸟的孤影，像飘零的纸屑般无声无息。

十月二日这天，自己一大早便离开了小院，想要去找找陆屠夫，看能不能私下向他买些肉食。丽云已经很久没吃过荤菜了，自己感觉很心疼。丽云生来就是一个千金小姐，有锦衣玉食的生活，而今却只能每日以咸菜下饭，自己看在眼里，心疼难已。她不是一个男人，可以被反复打磨和糟蹋——就好像自己这样，做过了叫花子，就算吃屎都不会感到太委屈——她只是一个女人，是一个需要被认真呵护和好好心疼的小女人，自己现在每日在她身边，若不能想方设法让她过得好一点，那么，自己的存在又有什么价值？爱，除了痴迷地厮守，更是真切的生活。

就在去陆屠夫家的路上，又响起了该死的枪声。而且这枪声显然就来自隔壁的那条街。枪声连响，突兀而惊人。自己正恼怨交加地不知该往哪儿跑，一个蒙面人没头没脑地就从对面冲了过来，一下子便和自己撞在了一起。

他的手上握着一把血淋淋的短刀。他的面罩滑开了一半。

“短毛？！——怎么是你！”自己认了出来，这个蒙面人竟然是短毛！

短毛赶紧一把扯好了面罩。“操，赵驹，你怎么穿得人模人样的？你不当叫花子啦——”

“你杀人了？”

“快跑！不许出卖我！”

短毛一把推开了自己，继续往他的方向逃跑。追兵的声音临近，自己不想和短毛往一个方向跑，又急又怨，没办法，急中生智，只好蹿上了这条巷子旁边的一片屋顶。

一队日本兵在下面跑过，领头的边跑边喊：“快、快！抓住刺杀岩崎少尉的凶手！”

子弹空虚地打在斑驳的墙上，墙皮飞溅，一片片，像草叶迸碎。

君子不立危墙之下，自己迅速逃离了这片区域，也没办法去关心短毛的安危，只能祈望他福大命大。天上下了几点零星小雨，徒然为这世间增添了几分阴郁。潮湿的风阵阵徘徊，令人胸臆不畅。走在路上，处处可见迎风招展的日本旗，那旗上鲜红的旭日，就像一个阴森的血窟窿，令人不寒而栗。又看见，有一队日本兵在驱赶着一群老百姓，像是要将他们赶到哪里去的样子。要赶他们到哪里去呢？运气好的话，也许是叫他们去唱歌跳舞，庆祝日军在东北又打了胜仗；运气差一点的话，也许是叫他们去工地上和矿上，做长期免费的苦力；倒霉的话，也许便是拿他们当成了抗日嫌疑分子，要送他们上断头台了。总之，日本人逮着谁，谁也就离阎王殿不远了。在沈阳，哪里还有什么基本的法律和道理可言？老百姓，有的只是做奴隶做猪狗的命运。自己经过了上次去偷收音机的那户富人家，只听见房子里满满的都是日本人和女人的嬉笑声，还有靡靡的日本音乐声。原本，丽云还在打算，要自己什么时候把收音机还回来，或者来这里给人家留下一笔偷盗赔偿金，但是，现在看来，这些都已经是没有必要了。这栋宅子，已经是属于日本人了。而至于这栋宅子里原本的那些人，他们现在是否还好，是否都还活着，也成了一些会令人徒增伤感、白白扼腕的问题。这是一个没有黑白对错的年代，人在这个年代里，能够活着已是幸运，又哪里还能去关怀现实之凄怆、悲叹人世之沧桑？一切，都只求蝇营狗苟罢了。若要打抱不平、奋力抗争，结果，只会是白白化作枪下鬼。自己莫名就又想起了短毛，真是想不到，他居然敢去刺杀日本人，往日里，还真是小瞧了他。自己帮不上他什么忙，只希望，他能平安脱险，好歹别落在日本人手里。

买好了肉，回到小院时，看见丽云正在洗衣裳。自己怕她累，要帮她洗，她说不用。她说，这些本就是女人做的事情，你去里面坐着吧。她问，你哪来的肉？自己说：碰上陆屠夫，他说他家有多余的肉，问我买不买，我说，我早馋坏了。她就哈哈笑了，说，一会儿我去烧，保证好吃。她的一绺头发垂在腮边，明媚动人，娇柔万分。自己是真希望，小院外的那个世界，可以永远和小院里的这个世界无关。就算外面爆发世界大战，只要丽云安好，自己便别无所求。可是，这可能吗？覆巢之下，焉有完卵。

十月三日上午，日军再次挨家挨户入室搜查，要捉拿抗日分子。这次领队的少尉很不好说话，在丽云的屋里发现了收音机，他暴跳如雷。汉奸不停地进行着翻译，丽云生气地便要上前去理论，自己赶紧一把挡住了丽云，然后，给日本人跪了下来。自己一边不停地用日语向日本人辩解、拍马屁、吹牛、套近乎，一边不停地自扇耳光，最后，自己又亲手将收音机摔了个粉

碎，并且，将被少尉看见了的放在屋里的二十多块大洋全部送给了他，这才平息了日本人狂暴的怒气。自己送走了日本人，丽云哭泣了起来。她哭着说：“你为什么要给日本人下跪？”自己说：“没什么，我以前要饭，天天给人下跪，说好话就跟放屁一样。”她哭着说：“可你现在不是乞丐！”她哭着跑回了她睡觉的屋子里去，紧紧地关上了房门，不再出来。

自己的心有些酸，想要去叩她的门，却又终究没有挪动脚步。自己扫去了地上的收音机碎片，又将被日本人翻搅得凌乱不堪的堂屋收拾整理了一遍，然后，便在木榻上坐了下来。时间像凝结成团的蜘蛛网，让人感觉灰暗而沉闷无比。

向着仇敌奴颜谄媚，为了活命卑躬屈膝，以自辱保太平，扮猪狗求苟全，这些在自己的眼中，都是生逢乱世理应必备的生存伎俩，但是，在丽云的眼中，这些事情，却都已是跌破了为人的底线，践踏了生命最基本的尊严。没错，活着是很重要，但是，没有底线没有尊严地活着，又有什么意义？自己能懂得并且理解丽云的想法，毕竟，自己不是笨蛋。可是，懂得和理解，不等于选择和实践，在危急关头，委曲求全仍是自己的本能反应。而反过来讲，自己的委曲求全，丽云她真的不理解吗？她那么冰雪聪明，会真的不理解，自己为什么要在日本人面前低三下四、自轻自贱？她，应该是懂的。只不过，自己说过了，懂得和理解，不等于选择和实践。也许，是她突然太意外地看到了一个懦夫式的赵驹，一时还不能接受；也许，是自己突然动摇了她心中某些习以为常的理想和信念，令她不知所措。总之，自己是突然看见了，在自己和她之间，存在着的一条深深鸿沟。在鸿沟的那一边，是她和阳春白雪；在鸿沟的这一边，是自己和藏污纳垢，这便是天意。

也许从一开始，自己就不应忘记，癞蛤蟆和白天鹅之间，原本有着怎样遥远的距离。且不说自己做乞丐时，是怎样的污秽不堪、低贱非凡，就算将时光推回到自己那表面光鲜亮丽的少爷时代，自己又真的是一个好东西吗？自己整日醉卧于妓女之怀抱，在青楼里做尽了肮脏之事；自己成天浸泡于赌博之刺激，在赌桌上掷光了父亲的血汗钱；自己有书不好好念，用那大好的年华，来毁尽了父亲的良苦用心和毕生希望。自己，是什么好东西吗？这些藏污纳垢、腐烂不堪的过去，丽云她全然不知。自己和她的第一任丈夫——那个表面正人君子内里男盗女娼的感情骗子——又有什么区别？如果丽云知道了这些事情，自己还会是她心目中的那个英雄吗？很多事，其实从一开始就有天意，只不过，人会被海市蜃楼给蒙蔽。

细细的秋雨又下了起来，像令人惆怅的喃喃痴语，绵绵密密。天色是那么阴郁，仿佛忧伤的仙女，用手帕擦去了太阳，天空不再有一丝光芒。时光走走停停，忧伤无边无际。

晚上，丽云像个做错事的孩子似的，站在自己的面前，说：对不起，我白天不该那样说你，我知道你都是为了我好，你受了罪，我还那么对你，都是我不对，真的对不起。

她微垂着头，尴尬地道着歉，昏黄的灯光下，她就像一朵含羞的娇美百合花。自己一把就抱住了她，冲动得想将她压倒在木榻上。自己感觉到她并没有要抗拒的意思。可是，一股恐惧却紧紧卷住了自己：“不，难道我还是以前的那个赵驹？”

自己放开了她，转身便往外跑。她喊：“赵驹，你别走！”自己还是头也没回。

清冷的长风在荒凉的天地间盘旋呼啸，风声萧索而苍老。自己狠狠打了自己许多记耳光，仰望夜空，心如刀割。对于命运的灰暗预感，令自己疯狂地害怕，自己最终会失去丽云；对于失去的恐惧，令自己疯狂地想要得到丽云，但是，这种得到又分明只是一个懦夫对于爱情的亵渎。不，不，自己绝不可以这样对待丽云！自己是真的想要好好呵护她一辈子的呀！

可是，自己又真的可以娶她为妻、与她厮守一生吗？闻闻自己的双手，上面是穿透了肌肉浸没了骨头的血腥味和死亡味。这是一双杀人无数的手，这是一双累积下了许多生死恩怨的手。这样的一双手，也配去触碰她冰清玉洁的肌肤吗？这样的一双手，如果牵着她的手，那么，会不会给她带来意料不到的灾祸？而且，自己身无养家之技，将来若和丽云在一起，靠什么来给她很好的生活？在那储存的几百块大洋用完之后，自己难道要再去打拳挣钱？自己的现实出路是这样逼仄，自己凭什么来好好地呵护、照顾丽云？而像丽云这样的好女人，完全可以嫁一个有钱有势又爱她的男人；就算不是有钱有势的，起码也可以是一个干净无罪的。总好过像自己这样既罪孽深重又一无所有的一个脏东西。自己的爱，只能给她带来不幸福，妨碍她的人生路，让她在一片除了幻景以外什么都没有的沙漠里白白浪费青春和美丽。自己忽然想起了，那个带走了母亲的书生当年对父亲说的那句话:“一介武夫，纵然打遍天下无敌手，于国于家又有何益处。”自己欲哭无泪。是自己太蠢，所以，才没能逃出这命运的轮回。

夜太黑，像一片深沉寂寞的海洋，自己在海洋里漫无目的地漂流，失魂落魄。风在夜里不停地发出幽幽的声响，这声响既凄怆，又孤苦，还渺茫。自己每走一步，都觉得离丽云越来越远，每多走一步，都撕心裂肺地痛。茫然无措、不知不觉中，自己竟走到了日军的岗哨处。

自己差点被一枪打死。好不容易逃脱，自己慌不择路之下，就跑到了庄家大宅旁边的那条路上。日本兵无心缉捕，没再多作追逐。自己无处可去，就在一个阴暗无人的角落里蹲了下来，依旧仿佛一个乞丐。远远地，望着那依旧灯火通明的已成了樱花会社总部的庄家大宅，自己内心一片凄惶。凄惶，就像几根被剪断了的琴弦，余音犹在，佳梦难续，爱断情伤。

忽然，看见一个黑影蹿上了庄宅的屋顶。心下虽一阵疑惑，却又判定自己并未老眼昏花。起初不想去理会，免得蹚浑水，但这庄宅对自己而言终究是有着不一样的意义，自己无法对那个黑影的出现坐视不理。于是，自己避开了路灯光，在黑暗里，也向庄宅奔了过去。

从背后轻轻搭上了那人的肩膀，他惊慌得立即回身一拳，自己一闪躲开。昏暗的光亮里，他停了手，自己也停了手。

“怎么又是你？”他低声抱怨了一句。他揭开了一下面罩，晃了晃脸，然后又戴好了面罩。

“短毛？”自己惊讶而很想骂人，“你半夜来这干吗？”

大院里走过了几个腰间佩着刀的日本浪人，短毛赶紧做了个噤声的手势。等浪人们走过了，他低声说:“我本来也正想找你，走，我们换个地方说话。”

短毛和自己先后从墙上跃下，一起去了庄宅外面的一个黑暗角落里。

“我以为你昨天难逃一劫。”自己说。

“我福大命大。”

“你不是说，千万别惹日本鬼子，能活着就好吗？”

“是你的那四个乞丐兄弟，让我懂得了什么是英雄。”

“用以卵击石的牺牲，换取一个英雄的定义，你觉得值得吗？”

“以前我觉得不值得。”

“那现在为什么变了？”

“因为我喜欢的女人死了。”

黑暗，沉默。

“报了仇，就走吧。”自己说。

“我的仇人，是侵略者，我能往哪走？”

“你一个人，能杀多少？”

“还有很多和我一样的人，都和我站在一起。”

“你们能杀光整支关东军吗？”

“不能。但是，我们要存在。否则，我们只是奴隶。”

“日本人用的是枪，还有飞机、坦克。”

“我把老板要我藏起来的那批枪支弹药，都偷了出来。”

“你觉得老板会放过你吗？”

“他现在还什么都不知道，等他知道了，大不了他杀我，我杀他，看谁命大。”

“活着不易，何必意气用事。”

“赵驹，你加入我们吧。”

“你说什么？”

“我说了，我本来也正想找你。和我们站到一起吧。”

“要是你们有了一个师的兵力，我会考虑的。”

“你是拳王，难道还会怕死？”

“就是因为不想死，所以，我才成了拳王。”

“你看见没有，每天都有无辜的中国人在被日本畜生欺辱、杀戮！今天是我，明天就可能是他，后天就可能是你！覆巢之下无完卵，只要一天没把侵略者赶出去，我们就谁也逃不过任人宰割的命运！”

“短毛，我有喜欢的女人了。她在这世上孤零零的，除了我，已再没有人可以依靠。”

沉默，黑暗。

长久的沉默。黑暗里，自己听见短毛哽咽地苦笑了两声。他说：“要是我们没有活在这个时代，该有多好。”

自己说："命运选择了我们，我们却无权选择命运。"

黑暗的夜空，像磐石般坚硬。

"你今晚来这干什么？"自己问。

"樱花会社的赤木，在东北做尽了坏事，还贩卖鸦片和海洛因给我们中国人，他最近就住在这座大宅子里，我要想办法杀了他。"

"你杀不了他。你没看见那里面有多少日本武士吗？更何况，赤木还有黑龙会撑腰。"

"黑龙会已经和樱花会社分道扬镳了。樱花会社的目标仅仅只是钱，而黑龙会想要的却是在日本军政两界的地位，他们终究是道不同不相为谋。况且，黑龙会现在正在忙改组为大日本生产党的事，哪里有闲心和工夫来管赤木的死活。"

"那你打算怎么干？"

"先看看能不能远程狙击或近身刺杀，要是实在不行的话，我们会干脆就把这座宅子给炸了，让赤木碎尸万段。"

自己猛地一把摁倒了短毛，在黑暗里紧紧地掐住了他的脖子。

"你干什么！"短毛低声惊呼。

"你给我听清楚了，你和你的那帮人，要是敢弄坏这座宅子里的一砖一瓦，我赵驹，会一个一个要了你们的命，我发誓！"

"你帮日本人？！"

"去你妈的！我巴不得你有本事杀了赤木那个王八蛋！可是，我绝不允许你们弄坏这座宅子！"

"为什么？"

"不关你事！"

"痛死我了，你先放开我，先放开我——"

自己松了手。

"那你帮我们去杀了赤木，我们只是想要杀赤木，不是想要炸宅子。"

"你们想过没有，杀赤木有什么意义？一个赤木死了，樱花会社自然会选一个新的赤木出来做社长，他们会依旧贩毒，依旧作恶。除非你们能把整个樱花会社给灭了，否则，杀一两个人能起什么作用？"

"那你的意思是无为而治了？只要什么都不做，一切自然也会变好？"

“我没说无为了就可一切变好。”

“那你说，杀赤木究竟有意义没意义？”

自己无言以对，哑然沉默。不做，是纵恶；做，只是徒劳。这个时代所能给人的选择就是这样逼仄而充满了颓废。

“杀不杀赤木，是你们的选择，我不想去参与这种思考和行动。我只是想求你们，千万不要弄坏这座宅子，好吗？就算是我赵驹求你们，行吗？我求求你们了——”

一阵沉闷的嘈杂声传来，打断了自己和短毛的低声争执。一片亮光由远及近地推过来。自己伸头去看，那是车灯照出的光。

一辆小汽车，正不急不慢地向庄宅这边驶来。小汽车的后面，还跟着一小队日本兵。

自己和短毛，赶紧换了个地方躲起来。寂然不敢再出声。

小汽车在庄宅的大门外停了下来。一个身穿日本军装的军官，从车里钻了出来。看门的武士进去通报。不一会儿，一个肥头大耳的日本人，就从庄宅的大门里走了出来，亲自迎接这名日本军官。

这两个人的脸，在灯光里，都被照得十分清楚。这名日本军官，让自己思绪翻涌，忍不住回溯过去。他的脸，可真让人感觉熟悉！

自己想了起来，他，不就是庄氏大百货公司开业那天，在人群后边用日语和他的下属谈论阴谋的那个日本人吗！

短毛低声说：“看见没有，那个胖子，就是赤木，别看他笑得像个弥勒，其实为人心狠手辣，做事斩尽杀绝，是一只笑面虎。而那个日本军官，名叫渡边次郎，听说以前是个间谍，现在被调到了宪兵队，军衔是大尉。他最近和赤木走得很近。”

渡边和赤木谈笑风生地走进了庄宅里。日本兵在宅子外站岗。自己怕在这里再待下去，会节外生枝，便准备要走了。自己再次要求短毛，千万不要炸庄宅。短毛则要自己再好好考虑一下帮忙杀赤木的事情。他说，我们就在城西的废木料场里，你要是想通了，来找我。

自己一阵奔窜，离开了短毛，离开了是非之地。

黑夜依旧深沉无声。包围着自己的黑暗就像可以被吸入身体的空气，自己在一呼一吸间，仿佛被黑暗吞没、溶解，生命感觉只是一种飘浮，人生似

乎不复存在。整个人，都像是一粒看不见又微不足道的尘埃。

自己不知道该往哪里去。风在寂寥中发出清晰的声响，显得这世界是多么空旷，仿佛群鸟都可自由地翱翔。而这种自由对于没有翅膀的人类来说，又只是一种多么美妙而荒诞的幻想，这种幻想除了让人感到人如灰尘般微不足道并且只能随波逐流以外，一无是处。这种一无是处，让人无比彷徨。

自己不知道该往哪里去。彷徨在天际下的冰凉中，周遭的事物仿佛皆是幻影。这些幻影无边无际，又皆如磐石般坚硬。一切在不可触摸的同时又不可抗拒，正像一个大时代的轨迹，正像命运所谓的天意。存在于磐石和磐石构成的夹缝里，人又真的可以做多少自己想做的事情？追求着那些明明存在却又如梦幻泡影的东西，究竟又有多少人可以心愿成真？这些疑问，让人无比深邃地哀伤。

自己不知道该往哪里去。哀伤像一首只有自己才能听到的歌，你并不愿去想起它，它却总会在你最茫然的时候再给你一点绝望的泪水。脆弱和孤独总是深藏在某些你最不注意的地方，等你经过时，便突然将你抓住。被抓住时，你才会幡然醒悟：原来在我的世界里，被抓的只是我一个人。这种醒悟，让人无比孤独。

自己不知道该往哪里去。孤独像一头对夜嚎叫的狼，既苍茫凛冽，又血腥可怕。真正被孤独咬伤的人，心里会永远流着凄怆的血。这血，有原始的腥味，有狼牙的惊畏。不管是站在苍茫的时代洪流里，还是跪在自我世界的对话中，孤独总是每个人逃不掉的宿命。而在这宿命里，几乎每个人，都在祈求救赎。这种救赎，超越生死，甚至超越宿命。这种祈求，是无比深邃的对爱的渴望。

自己不知道该往哪里去。对爱的渴望是一道无法自愈的伤，是上帝埋藏在人血液里的怅惘和忧伤。当痴迷之树开出最绚丽的花，最痛的悲伤会化成海洋。这海洋是不悟又愚钝的蜜糖，是远在天边的孟婆汤。从未等到过花开的人生是枯梦一场，等到了花开的人又逃不过花谢的必然命运。奢望永恒只是一个永恒的奢望。而在那春去秋来花开花谢的命运里，饱含的是泪水对这片红尘最美的眷恋。这泪水，清澈如泉，又混浊似海。这眷恋，是自己不能割舍的对丽云的深爱。

自己不知道该往哪里去。对丽云的深爱是一场撕心裂肺的悲哀，是一片没有彼岸又风浪滔天的深海。情动是天意的注定，而悲欢是命运的捉弄。爱到了天荒地老的痴心处，才见千山万水的隔绝路；走到了长相厮守的祈求中，方知沧海桑田的血泪红。于广袤天地间邂逅一片令自己情有独钟的雪花，是多么的幸运，而这幸运又终将在自己眼前融化，无影无踪于手心和天际，这是怎样一种残酷？

自己不知道该往哪里去。

自己想念丽云，才离开她一点点时间，自己心中的相思和牵挂已如蛛网般缠结。但是，自己已不知该怎样面对丽云，是该告诉她，我爱你，我想永远和你在一起？还是应该告诉她，对不起，我配不上你，你和我在一起，不会有幸福？懦弱像一条毒蛇，自己的灵魂被它缠得铁一般紧。或许，自己真的只是一个懦夫，是个既没勇气给出承诺又不舍得放手的混蛋，是个会因为害怕失去而竟想要马上得到对方的流氓。或许，自己的确是从来不敢去相信，自己可以和她在一起。

风依旧在黑夜里来回地吹，秋凉似水。自己紧抱着自己的头，瑟缩，而害怕再去思考任何的问题。自己就那样蜷缩在一个无人的街角，既不想去哪儿，也不想等待天明。只希望让一切停顿，让一切空白。

可是，时间不会停顿，世界不会空白。

隐约地，远处又响起了零星的枪声。自己在泪眼蒙眬里，又好担心丽云。自己走了，她一个人怎么办？她要是又傻傻地出来到处找人，那怎么办？

难道，为了逃避爱情的折磨，自己就要不再保护她了吗？

不，不可以。

就算这不可以，也许只是自己逃避矛盾的又一个借口。就算这不可以，也许只是自己逃避失去的又一个理由。

自己要回到丽云那里。是的。

风依旧在黑夜里来回地吹。自己不知时间已是几点。

丽云就那么孤零零地站在小院中央，脸上淌着晶莹的泪，啜泣而颤抖。

“……对不起……”

“……你说过你再也不会离开我了——”她喃喃地哭着说。

“对不起……”

“你说过你再也不会离开我了——”

她哭泣着大声说。

自己愣在那里。

她一头扑进了自己的怀里，像一头受伤的小兽。她紧紧地抱着自己，在自己胸前痛苦哭泣。她无言、战栗。自己心如刀绞，又欲哭无泪，想从这里消失，又后悔几小时前为什么要从这里逃跑。她的泪水洇湿了自己的心口，自己想抱抱她，却终究还是一动未动。夜，像一条冰凉的河流，河水淌过，每个人，都只能被这冰凉静静地淹没。

“丽云，其实我爱你。”自己在心里说。

夜，静谧得像一首凄凉的歌。

面对日军肆无忌惮的侵略，国民政府寄希望于国际调停。九一八事变发生以后，国民政府驻国际联盟的全权代表就向国联报告了该次事件，提出了申诉，请求国联出面主持公道。由英美控制的国际联盟出于对他们自身在华利益的考虑，在舆论上要求日本撤军，但日本对无武力的舆论置若罔闻。日本向国际社会辩称，关东军在东北的所作所为完全都是出于自卫，他们是在保护日本侨民，保卫日本的正当利益。国民政府请求国际联盟派出代表，亲赴东北调查事件真相。

土肥原开始着力恢复沈阳的表面秩序，营造社会共荣的假象。日本人在报纸上刊登了大量美化侵略、颠倒黑白的文章，宣扬东北独立，鼓吹满洲自治。商店老板和大小摊贩纷纷被逼着重新出来开张做买卖，稍有不从，一命呜呼。而另外一方面，日本人更加紧了对残余抗日分子的围捕和剿杀。往往是商店空开着门，路上只有死人。沈阳城中，一片惨淡景象。

自己的心很乱。

丽云的话少了很多，她寂然独坐时，经常默默垂着头。自己还是住在丽云的堂屋里，但是，自己越来越感觉这样很不妥当：孤男寡女长住在同一屋檐下，你这不是在毁了丽云的清白吗？皮货店的老板死掉了，皮货店的门只是日夜空空地敞开着。未来对丽云来说，只是更灰暗更无望了一层。当然，她并没说什么。自己万分心疼她，却又刻意保持着距离，希望这样可以让彼此都少受一点伤害。但是，这样却又似乎只是在让彼此心如刀绞。自己又感到再这样住下去真是不好，想要搬走，但是一来无处可去，二来，这无疑又是一种对丽云的伤害。自己的心很乱，不知究竟该怎样做，不知究竟该怎样想。似乎有些选择正在等待着自己，而自己只是在莫名退缩。自己又想起了短毛的那些事情，自己不知他们会不会真的去炸了庄宅，要是庄宅被炸了，丽云的心里不知更会多出多少难过来。她已经是个一无所有的人了，要是连那些曾经的美好岁月所在的那个家都没了的话，叫她在这个世上还怎样有所回忆地活下去？自己是真觉得短毛他们是群王八蛋。但是，正是赤木这个恶魔将丽云一家毁灭的，正是这个万恶的侵略者，让丽云落到了今天这个凄惨而一无所有的境地，无论怎么说，自己都应该要为丽云手刃赤木才对。所以，其实这样说来，自己反倒还不如短毛他们了。事实就是如此，可是，又正像自己对短毛所说的那样，杀一个赤木，有什么用？自己要是现在去杀了赤木，除了会引来无穷无尽的追杀以外，又还会有什么？而日本人若蜂拥而来，自己还说什么保护丽云？事情就是这样矛盾。但是，现在的这种平静又挺让人觉得不解，如果真像短毛说的那样，赤木是一只喜欢斩尽杀绝的笑面虎，那么，他又怎么会给丽云留一条生路？是丽云真的已不值得他一顾？还是他一时疏忽？又或者短毛完全是在扯淡？自己既理不出头绪，也推理不出结论，因为自己对太多事无知，因为命运给人的意外已多得让人不敢再去揣测天意。自己只能祈祷，丽云平安无事就好。如果有事，起码还有自己这个保镖在，起码自己还能为她最后挡一挡。所以，自己又怎么可以离开丽云呢？自己的心太乱，一切问题永远只是在原地打转。丽云是个太让自己心疼的女人，而自己的存在，究竟是在保护她，还是在伤害她？自己的心，太乱太乱。

丽云还是会坐在自己身边，和自己淡淡地聊天，就好像那天晚上的哭泣根本就没发生过一样。但是，她的孤戚，还是显然而浓烈的，让人知道发生过的伤心是不会隐遁无形的。而有时回想，自己甚至都会记忆模糊地不明白，那晚，自己到底是在害怕面对，还是在害怕逃避？而这种提问又总是徒劳的。自己将丽云的断发收藏在一只首饰盒里，平时装作不在意，她睡觉时，自己却会看着那只盒子发呆。这是一种情不自禁的伤怀。隐约中，自己总感觉丽云断发那天说的话有些不吉利，就好像，她真的有一天，会先于这些头发而去到另一个世界。这真是一种可怕的悲伤，更是一种莫名悲惨的预感。这预感让自己觉得：你真是疯了。

在不敢去爱丽云的同时，自己爱她爱得已近发疯。这种矛盾这种感觉，没有人能懂得。就好像一只癞蛤蟆，对天鹅的仰望。癞蛤蟆只要多往前走一步，就会害得天鹅和他一起掉进地狱。事情就是这么简单，而进退维谷。只有爱情，在两个人的天空越变越浓，越哭越红。

在凉冷的夜里，自己有时又会想起那些似乎已逝却又并未真正了断的恩怨。金顺现在怎样了？他真的没有派人出来追杀吗？这是个不确定的事情。青帮已忘了赵驹这个王八蛋了吗？他们真的会将徐冷的死，算在七星帮的头上吗？自己的确是聪明过人，还是只不过在自作聪明？这又是个不确定的事情。还有，自己可是杀了黑龙会整整四十个武士啊！难道真像丽云说的，黑龙会一直以为是潘兆的手下杀的人，所以潘兆一死，他们便觉得仇已报，不再费神去详细追究了？难道真的是只有那三个想要独享功劳的日本蠢货，查清了自己的确切身份？那三人一死，赵驹对黑龙会来说，就成了一个谜？会有人来解这个谜吗？不知道，不确定。或者，是因为黑龙会现在和樱花会社决裂了，所以，黑龙会里那些因为以前帮樱花会社做事而死掉的成员，就都成了不需要被记住的弃子，并且，他们也都已不值得黑龙会再去为他们报仇？或者，黑龙会真的只是因为最近太忙了，所以才暂时没人没空去翻那些陈年旧账？不确定，不知道。什么都有可能，而这些可能，又都由不得自己做主。也许，那些纷纭的血海深仇，真的会从此与自己再无半分瓜葛；也许，有一天，自己会被仇人们一起剁成肉酱。毕竟，一个双手早已沾满了人命和仇怨的人，又怎么能去奢望和往日的一刀两断呢？所以，自己再爱丽云，又怎么敢去相信，其实自己可以和她在一起。

自己的心，狼藉、纷乱、萧瑟。

十月六日，清晨下了一阵细雨。天空中蒙着一层薄薄的灰，沉闷而压抑。风挺大，裹挟着一股湿冷的迷离。

每逢刮风下雨，自己身上的旧伤都会隐隐作痛，好像风湿病一样。痉挛般的痛楚总会在皮肉深处长久地翻滚扭动，像刀割，像拉锯，位置忽左忽右，痛感时轻时重，搅得人难以忍受，无所适从。有时候，当这些疼痛袭来，自己又会想起曾经的那些受伤时的情景。这些情景都很可怕，每一次，自己都在生死边缘，每一次，自己都是满手鲜血。全是恐怖的噩梦。有时候，痛得厉害了，自己会感到，自己的身体里，好像又被捅进了一把日本武士刀。

曾经脱臼过的关节，在天气变换时最是痛得彻心彻肺。这种痛，像钉子一样深钻在骨头里，让人咬牙切齿，却又无可奈何，只能听凭天气处置。每当这种时候，自己总会想起孔仁曾对自己说过的话：“打黑市拳的，有哪一个最后不是非死即残？”自己没有死，也没有残，但，落下了一身难忍的痛。这或许就是代价，你再要强，也逃不过。

不管是被日本人砍烂过的皮肉还是被拳手们打伤过的骨头，它们的旧痛难愈，都一样地在不断地提醒着自己杀戮的恐怖和恐怖的难以摆脱。就好像有无数双血淋淋的手，总在将你往一片未知的沼泽地里拖。每当想起那些被自己亲手杀死的人，自己的心中总会莫名涌起巨大而强烈的罪恶感。当然，自己可以说：他们都是些该死或可死的人，如果我不杀他们，他们就会杀了我。但是，这种理论上的道义辩护和自我安慰，对于自己灵魂中的罪恶感的阵痛，丝毫没有治疗的作用。杀人不像杀鸡宰鱼，当自己将敌人的脑袋劈开或将对手的脖子拧断时，那种只存在于杀人者和被杀者之间的极致战栗，只有真正杀过人的人才能明白。而自己害怕这种战栗，它就像一个会把人吸进去嚼碎的黑洞，就算自己是那个活着的胜利者，这种害怕，也并不减色。自己厌恶这种杀人的血腥，它就像一堆会把人咬成千疮百孔的毒虫，就算自己会被誉为正义的英雄，这种恶心，也不会减轻。所以，不管自己杀的是好人还是坏人，那种令人不安令人作呕令人感觉自己肮脏不堪的罪恶感，始终都会在自己的灵魂中悸动。或许，自己真的就是个懦夫吧。似乎正是那种潜藏在自己的骨子里的懦弱，在千方百计地阻止自己向丽云靠近，这是一种说不清道不明的困境。这种阻止，究竟是对，还是错，自己也不知道。

上午，灰蒙蒙的天上没有再落下雨滴。丽云打了些井水，准备在院子里洗衣，自己看见了，就要帮她洗，但她不要。自己坚持不要她动手。自己笑说：“你看我游手好闲的，要是再不让我帮你洗洗衣服做做饭什么的，我就真成了一个摆设了。你就让我活动活动筋骨吧。”她就笑了笑，没有说什么，也没再坚持。

自己捋起了衣袖，坐到矮凳上，开始了洗衣。丽云去了堂屋里。小院里除了哗哗的洗衣搅水声，悄然无声。几滴水珠溅在自己的额头上，凉凉的，像从静默里蹦出的雨。自己莫名想回头看看丽云，想和她说两句亲近的话，

最终却还是既没回头也没开口。水滴从额上流下，带了些温度，经过眼角、鼻梁，最后流到了自己嘴唇上。自己抿了抿嘴，尝到了水滴里有些咸苦的滋味。这滋味，忽然让自己的心里干涩得很难受。

自己用力而专注地洗衣，试图将有用无用的思想都抛弃在时间的乱流里，轻装前行。然而，自己又莫名感到越来越空旷和揪心，仿佛某根琴弦的崩断，自己洗衣的动作一下子停了下来。这停止，突兀而没有缘由，就好像自己突然掉下某个悬崖，就好像自己突然掰断了一段时间。

意外地，丽云拎了把小凳，在自己旁边坐了下来。自己回过了神来，莫名一阵心慌意乱。自己低头继续洗衣。怕把脏水溅到她的身上，自己洗得小心翼翼。

一只捋起的衣袖松脱了下来，袖口滑至了自己的手腕处。自己双手都湿着，不方便去重新捋，就只好用另一只手的手臂去将这只衣袖往上蹭，以达到捋的效果。但没两下，这只衣袖便又滑落了下来。自己有些窘，丽云轻轻笑出了声。她凑过来，将这只衣袖一层一层往上卷，卷至了手肘上方。她说："好啦，这样就不会掉下来了。"说完，她就又将尚未开始下滑的另一只衣袖也依样卷了一下。

自己说："谢谢。"

她说："干吗这么客气。"

自己无言地笑了笑。

她静静地坐着，忽然用手指了指自己裸露着的左前臂上的两条蜈蚣似的疤痕，轻轻问："这些伤，还痛吗？"

自己说："不痛。"

她痴惘地凝滞着，说："像蜈蚣一样。"

自己开玩笑，说："还有像蛇一样的呢，你没看见，看见了吓死你。"

她却没笑。她痴痴地看着自己，问："是从肩上到腰里的那一刀吗？"

自己顿住了。放下了手里的衣服，自己默然难语。

她的指尖轻抚着那两条蜈蚣，她痴痴地说："你为我受过多少伤，日本人的每一刀砍在你什么地方，我都记得清清楚楚，永远不会忘。"

自己缩回了被她指尖轻抚着的手臂，自己低声说："记这些干什么，都忘了吧。"

她说："我忘不了。"

自己笑了笑，说："不关你的事。我爱国，就算不是为了你，我也会和日本人拼命。你不要把这些都记在心里。"

自己看见，丽云的眼里噙起了泪花。她转过了头去，幽咽着说："那时，我想来医院看你，恨不能分分秒秒守着你，可是，潘兆捆住了我，把我锁在了房里，我根本就逃不出去。"

一滴眼泪，从自己的眼里掉了出来，掉进了洗衣的水里。自己赶紧闭了闭眼睛。自己说："都过去了，还提这些干什么。"

自己又开始了洗衣服。哗哗的搅水声响着。丽云说："我去做饭。"然后，她便离开了自己。

自己一心一意地洗着衣服，不想有任何思想或情绪。可是，心酸就像千万匹流着血的野马，在辽阔的草原上嘶吼狂奔。自己，魂不守舍地悲伤。

下午，自己在院子里劈了些柴。因无法面对而想要逃避的冲动不时在心尖跳跃，但是，自己又想：我走了，难道让丽云劈柴？一种对自我的深刻嘲讽让自己感觉很痛，自己想：因为爱而不敢去爱，究竟是对彼此的保护，还是对彼此的伤害？这种深刻的嘲讽，让自己心乱如麻。

劈完了柴，自己回到了堂屋，坐在了丽云的对面。丽云正在缝一件破了的农妇衣裳。自己看着那亮亮的针尖，不禁说："小心，别扎着手。"丽云顿了顿，没有抬头，只"嗯"了一声。

线不够了，丽云想去拿线，自己就要帮她去拿。她说，就在睡屋书桌左边的第二个抽屉里。自己去了她的睡屋，打开了书桌左边的第二个抽屉，拿到了线。自己刚关上这个抽屉，忽然，左边第一个抽屉上的铜拉手，一下子掉了下来，"嗒啷"落在地上。

自己捡起了铜拉手，想先将它放在左边的第一个抽屉里，改天再修。但，拉开这只抽屉后，自己呆住了。

这只抽屉里，除了一块手表，空荡荡的一无所有。像被一股电流击中，这块表，瞬间便勾起了自己别样清晰的记忆。自己拿起了这块表，看到，在底盖上，还有一个独一无二的产品序号：0214。这，正是自己当年临走前，一起留下还给庄家的那块表。这，正是丽云在一九二八年的最后一天，特地买了送给自己的那块表！

自己的眼前一片滚热的模糊。丽云当掉了她的表，当掉了她全部的珠宝首饰，却唯独还留着它！

却唯独还留着它！

自己心如刀绞，只想给自己两记耳光。

“线找到了吗，是白色的——”丽云一边问，一边走到了睡屋门口。

她呆住了。

自己克制着眼泪，将手表轻轻放回了抽屉里，然后，轻轻关上了抽屉。

时间似玻璃碎落一地，心酸比沧海无边无际。静默如连绵的雪或雨，落叶听不见天空被撕裂的哭泣。

“……其实，离开庄府的那个雪夜，我本以为，此生已隔千山万水。”自己喉咙发烫地说。

“……其实，那晚回来，我本想告诉你，我已经和潘兆说了分手。”

“……所以，他打红了你的脸？”

“……嗯……”

自己潸然泪下。丽云，忽然泪流满面。

“赵驹……你现在，是不是……是不是……是不是嫌我不干净？”

“——你说什么？”

丽云低着头，只是痛苦极了，却不说话。

自己一头雾水。

“你以前问过我……问我是不是去过南京……那时我就知道，你已经什么都知道了……我想忘记这些，假装一切只是流言……可是，我只是在自欺欺人——”

“你说什么呢？！”

自己突然醒悟：一定是自己那天对她鲁莽之后的突然逃跑，在她的心里产生了另一种意义！

丽云掩面痛哭着，逃了出去。

自己给了自己两个大耳光，然后，狂追了出去。

自己一把拉住了丽云，抱住了她，不让她再跑。她哭着挣扎，悲伤欲绝。自己肝肠寸断。

“丽云，我不许你再这样说你自己！不许你再这样想你自己！我从来就没有想过那些，从来没有！你在我心里，就像上帝的天使一样纯洁，是我自惭形秽！你明白吗！”

她哭着挣扎。

自己抱紧了她，一下子，深深吻住了她的唇。

自己不管她的抗拒，不管她的哭泣，只是深深地吻着她。忘记了一切地，热烈无比地，吻着她。

两个人的泪水，混在了一起。这个世界，仿佛只剩下了她和自己。

这个吻，是那样长久，那样滚烫，那样唯一，那样永恒。

丽云也紧紧地抱住了自己。

那一刻，自己只想把她的泪，都吻成快乐的笑，就像她以前开心时的甜蜜。

直到遥远的地方又响起了一声惊人的爆炸，自己的吻，才离开了她的唇。

她依偎着自己。自己说:“丽云，我不会再让你流眼泪了。”

她点点头。

远处又有了枪战的声音。

自己想：上帝，如果我的逃避是一种错，那么，请让我爱她到天荒地老。

天上下起了雨，像一场没有结束的哭泣。

秋叶如飞花零落，水色千大际暗沉。痴爱比彩虹更绚烂，永恒，是否像天晴般可期盼？

微风摇曳，命运飘舞。

除了那一个至深至热的吻，自己没有再多碰丽云一点。自己火热得直想将她装进自己的身体里，恨不能分分秒秒抱着她、深吻她、占有她，却又害怕会烫着她、窒息她、亵渎她。这种最真最深又最纯粹的灵魂之爱，自己这辈子，只对丽云一人有过。自己爱她，就像爱一件世上最珍贵最漂亮最洁白而又最纤薄的瓷器那样小心翼翼，唯恐一不小心，便会伤害了她。这种爱，烫得像岩浆，痴迷进了骨髓，却又清淡得像风，如果对方的耳朵不贴着你的胸口，对方甚至都会不知道，其实，你早已爱得发了疯、生了狂。这种爱，一生只要有过一次，只要有过一瞬，你便会觉得，死而无憾。

而那些因为自己对爱情的刻意躲避所以使丽云承受过的冰凉伤心，令自己感到十分愧疚与懊悔不已。那种因为爱所以害怕爱的逻辑，究竟是从爱的极深处绽放出来的无私光芒，还是理性的恶魔用悖论设下的一个陷阱？如果自己对丽云的疏远只能换来她痛苦的泪水，那么，自己配不配得上她与将来会不会拖累她之类的问题，又是否还有存在的意义？当自己面对着丽云瑟瑟发抖的痛苦的时候，自己真觉得，自己是这个世上最最愚蠢的一个人。爱是那么简单而纯真的一个东西，自己又为何要用各种形而上学的问题与尚未到来的将来去给爱情上刑？那样，既苦了自己，又苦了丽云。何必要让彼此的牵肠挂肚变成共同的肝肠寸断。不错，自己以前是个嫖客，是个赌棍，但自己早已洗心革面，浪子回头。是的，自己是做过肮脏的乞丐，是沾满过杀戮的鲜血，但丽云从来都没有过嫌弃的意思。至于以后，自己有手有脚，难道还怕真的会让丽云饿死不成。形而上学的思虑与彷徨，再怎么必然和必要，始终是站在明日彼岸的幻影，而刻骨铭心的爱情，再怎么短暂和脆弱，终究是近在眼前的实在拥抱。站在彼岸与此在的坚硬夹缝里，面对着命运汹涌的急流，自己忽然很想牵着丽云的手，勇敢地闯一次。谁说自己和丽云的爱情一定会夭亡？谁说自己和丽云在一起一定不会有美好的明天？说不定，那些自己对爱情有过的顾虑和担心，统统只是杞人忧天的愚蠢执念。凡事何必要想得太远，只要今天能看见丽云灿烂的笑颜，今天便是最重要的永远。

丽云又恢复了刚开始时的开心，这开心很安静，很饱满，就像一朵鲜花在风中倔强地开放，香气四溢，如诗如画。那些自己令她流泪的短暂伤心时光，只如一个飘然逝去了的坏梦，好像并没有在新的生活里咬坏什么重要的东西。自己和丽云，对彼此爱情的依赖，仿佛又浓烈了许多。自己只要离开她一小会儿，她就会望眼欲穿，而自己则归心似箭。自己不知道，在这浓烈里，是否包含着某种对于昙花一现的恐惧。如果是，则自己终究还是在丽云心里留下了伤。

站在安宁的小院里，自己有时会幻想，这小院是一艘诺亚方舟，会载着丽云和自己，安然渡过这个洪水横流的年代。丽云在窗户上贴了一些剪纸，这些剪纸在金红色的夕阳光里，漂亮得就像秋天燃烧的枫叶。坐在丽云的身旁，看着她剪刀灵巧地微动，自己是真想呵护她全部的憧憬和希望。纸屑细细地落下，她那入神的微笑，娴静得像成熟的麦田，欢悦得像跳跃的喜鹊。

只要和她在一起，她的眼中总含着甜甜的明媚，仿佛蝴蝶无忧的飞旋；而对自己来说，她，就是点亮整个世界的一把火。如果幸福是个美梦，自己真想把这片红尘灌醉。只要她还活着，自己愿意用全部的生命与热血来守护她的天真和欢笑。没有什么，能夺走自己对她的爱。

但是，自己忽然发现，自己依旧没有告诉过她，我爱你。自己是否真的已准备好了，要紧紧牵着她的手，穿过命运的急流与世事的泥泞，和她一起奔向那如梦境般甜美的彼岸？自己是否已足够勇敢？

十月九日，清晨的天空如玻璃般透彻，秋风湿润，安宁无雨。

丽云小屋顶上的几片瓦坏了，若是下雨，屋里会漏。自己想修葺一下屋子，但又无砖瓦等材料。欲求助于房东，房东又早已难觅踪迹，甚至不知是死是活。看看外面太平无事，甚至还经过了一个挑担的货郎，自己便想揣了钱去街上转转，看能不能买到些砖瓦。丽云说，小心些。自己说，知道了。

街上有些商店已在正常营业，摊贩们也出来了一些，在有商业活动展开的区域，日本军宪的分布密度也稀疏了很多。市场在一定程度上有了复苏。这一方面是日本人营造共荣景象的要求，另一方面，也确实是百姓继续生活之必需。不管那天要怎么变，人只要还在地上活着，就得照常吃喝拉撒睡，衣食住行缺一不可。市场上的买卖要是真的全停了，那不光想卖东西挣钱的人得困死，那想买东西生活下去的人也得困死。所以，这市场还真是复苏了的好，要不然，高高在上的日本人不会死，低低在下的老百姓，全得缺菜少粮而亡。人就是这样一种脆弱而又坚韧的生物，苦心建造的家国天下不堪一击地就那么破碎了，想要生存下去的接近本能的意志却还能卑贱而倔强地燃烧着。自己买了四个肉包子，想带回去给丽云尝尝。

走了几条街，也没找到卖瓦片的商家。途经了几户早已是人去屋空的人家，本欲到这些屋顶上去揭些瓦下来给自己用，但转念一想，还是罢了。毕竟，那些背井离乡逃了出去的人，说不定哪天还是要回来的，而这里，就是他们的家。不要拆了同胞的屋子去补自己的屋。有老鼠在这些空屋子敞开着的门窗中窜进窜出，乌七八糟的一片，令人既恻然，又胆怯。

在“Memory”的附近，找到了卖瓦片的小贩。将买好的瓦装进了麻袋里，自己一手拎着麻袋，忍不住走去“Memory”那里，想看一看。而映入眼帘的只是一片惨淡景象。原本装饰精美的门面已面目全非，整洁的墙上布满

了弹孔，一块墙面已脱落，露出了里面已碎裂的几排砖块。残破的窗玻璃像一排犬牙，突兀嶙峋地反射着尖锐的太阳光，让人感到可怕。而灰蒙蒙又空荡荡的店里，已再没有了烤面包和咖啡的香味，那精致得如艺术品一般的甜美蛋糕，也只有在回忆中才能再见到。走到了“Memory”的店门口，只见，店里的地上，是大片大片已干透了的殷红血迹。自己惊得倒退了两步。阳光照在自己脸上，暖暖的，自己心中寒意丛生，沮丧莫名。又后退了两步，好像不能面对似的，自己闭上了眼睛。一闭上眼睛，自己就仿佛又看到了以前的“Memory”——那家总是会让自己莫名有种幸福感的甜蜜的西饼店。

而现在，一切已不复存在。侵略和杀戮，像无情的机器，铲平了人类花园里所有娇嫩的美好与绚丽的奇妙。唯有死一样的寂静和肃杀，在长久地随风呼啸，不停不息。

自己忽然无限想念丽云，想念她的过去和现在，想念她的点点滴滴。她不在自己身边的此刻，就像一个蓦然陷入了停顿的时间空洞，让人心虚得发慌。人的存在是那样脆弱，就算近在眼前的鲜活，也会刹那化为乌有；这个世界是那样不可信任，就算今天你还拥有什么，那也不能确信，明天你仍会继续拥有。站在时间伤感的缝隙里，对失去的恐惧和对恋人的爱念，像呼吸一样不可抗拒。对往昔的负疚和对未来的踌躇，都只是对时光空枉的辜负，珍惜眼前所拥抱的存在，才是这个世界留给人类的唯一真理。睁开眼，重新看着面前疮痍满目的建筑物，自己突然想：我要娶丽云。

回去时，经过庄宅，看着挂在庄宅大门外的日本国旗和樱花会旗，心中隐隐恻然。大门外除了站着几个日本武士，还站着几个日本兵，大概是又有什么日本军官来拜访赤木了吧。想起上次短毛跟自己说的那些话，自己心里既忐忑不安，又起伏不定。庄宅的大门紧闭着，看不见里面的情形，自己怀念庄府，一时冲动，就去了庄宅的后院外面，爬上了墙。

远远看去，屋子一间间还是以前的模样，但除了屋子以外，一切都已莫名显得陌生。花草树木全变了样，院子里摆满了樱花造型的盆景。日本国旗和樱花会旗在大宅内的四角猎猎飘扬，在屋里和院里走来走去的，全是穿着黑色浪人服装的日本武士，还有日本音乐从一间屋内悠扬地传出。自己暗暗骂了句粗话，却也仅此而已，无可奈何，就连悲伤，也像是一件很陌生了的事情。

以前庄老爷住的那间屋子的门，打了开来。渡边从里面走了出来，赤木从里面走了出来。渡边转身客气地对赤木说："社长请留步，不必相送。您待我如知己，不以我为卑贱，我真是三生有幸，若有机会，我定当为社长效犬马之劳。您放心，您和荣仓大佐之间的小小误会，我定当全力帮忙消除，请放心！"

赤木拊掌微笑，说："很好，很好，荣仓大佐若能与我一聚，席间我定当为你多多美言。"

"谢谢！"

"另外，下一批鸦片和海洛因即将秘密运抵奉天，护送队员的名单你是否已经确定？"

"已经确定，您放心，他们都是陆军中的精英，枪法精准，身手过人，而且，最重要的是，他们的嘴都很紧。"

"嗯，很好。中国的蒋介石，通过上海的青帮，秘密贩卖毒品，以贩毒所得维持其军费开支，以便他继续剿灭中国共产党，这对我们大日本帝国来说，原本是一件好事。但是，蒋介石若垄断了毒品市场，那对我们生意人来说，可就是一件大大的坏事喽。"

"的确，帝国的利益有时与我们的利益并不一致。不过您大可放心，依我看，凭着您和军方的合作关系，军方会始终照顾您的利益的。"

"但愿如此，做生意嘛，就是要互惠互利。你可以去告诉荣仓大佐，我会继续为军方提供活体试验者，中国人这么多，抓掉一片都不会有人在乎。这种小事，你们根本就不需要去麻烦黑龙会的人。要知道，黑龙会可没我这么单纯，荣仓他若与蛇为伍，小心有朝一日被蛇反咬一口。"

"明白，社长的意思，在下十分清楚，我会劝告大佐。总之，不管局面怎样变化，我都会始终站在社长您这一边，听凭差遣。"

"好，好，你下次来，我让美子陪你。"

"社长真是慷慨。"

"女人而已，你想要，我多的是。"

"哈哈，做个自由的武士果然是要比当个军人快乐呀，我可真是厌烦透了那些空谈而已的所谓军法，那些条文，只不过是长官用来排挤下属的工具罢了。"

“哈哈。上次我们说起的那个女人，你已经得到她了吗？”

“社长见笑。近来实在是公务繁忙，我还无心念此。”

“哈哈，那你可真是辜负了我的一番美意呀，要不是你说念她已久，我早已将她喂狗。听说，你折磨女人的手段可是一流。”

“诋毁之言，诋毁之言。”

“哈哈哈——”

几个武士，向自己所在的方向走来。虽然有树的枝叶在墙头挡着，但日本人毕竟不是瞎子，自己怕被他们发现，转身便往围墙外一跃。落地，摔坏了麻袋里的两片瓦。自己没来得及多想，迈步就跑。

其实并没有日本人追来，他们可能甚至都没发现墙头有人。

跑过了两条街，自己才停了下来。才确定根本没有追兵。自己在一个街角蹲了下来。

自己心里乱糟糟的，心神不宁，忐忑莫名。听到了那些本不该自己听到的事情，就像突然吞下了一些令人恶心而惊悚的生物。贩毒、内战、走私、勾结、女人、收买、派系、斗争，这世上的事情，永远比表面呈现的复杂。简直让人难以消化。一张长满了利齿的大嘴像在自己面前张开：什么是活体试验者？日本人在搞什么？赤木想把哪个女人喂狗？怎么回事？——疑惑有时远比明确更具杀伤力，自己越困惑不解，越胡思乱想，越胡思乱想，越胆战心惊。怪兽张开的大嘴是那样恐怖，自己整个人，都像已被利齿穿透。望着街对面某些已空空如也的房屋，自己忽然毛骨悚然地想：谁说他们一定逃走了呢，说不定，是被日本人抓了去。刚才，真该再多听一会儿那两个日本畜生的谈话！他们要去折磨的那个女人，究竟是谁？！

自己握紧了拳头，却又只是空空地握紧着拳头。恐惧令自己胸中寒意丛生，疼痛阵阵。自己看着自己的拳头，欲哭无泪。这双拳头，其实是世上最无用的东西。自己有想保护的爱人，有想保护的家园，有想保护的忠义，有想保护的尊严，但是，在强大的侵略者面前，自己除了担惊受怕、苟且偷生，又做过什么有用的事情？自己又何曾相信过，自己能真的保护什么？黑暗的时代将生死碾成了粉末，而自己，只是在这些粉末中四处逃躲的一只跳蚤罢了。

松开了无用的拳头，自己突然想：也许，我该加入短毛的队伍？如果是担心赤木早晚会报复丽云，那么，何不先下手为强，干脆宰了赤木这个罪魁祸首？短毛他们手里有军火，大家一起上，自己应该能杀了赤木。

街上的商贩又多了一些。市面颇有了些热闹的味道，纵然这热闹里还包裹着一片阴惨的调子。想想也是，风再狂，雨再大，天再黑，人只要还没死，不就得拼了命地活下去吗？

自己收敛起了满腔的纷扰和沮丧，准备以一副开心的模样回到丽云那里。看到街上有卖水果的，自己还买了四个苹果，准备回去给丽云吃。这样笑着笑着，自己的心情居然还真的明朗了起来。

只是，回去的路上，看到了早上那个挑担货郎的尸体。一把狭长而锋利的日本刀，穿透了货郎的腹腔，血还在刀刃上滴滴答答。没有人知道是谁杀了货郎，为什么要杀他。也许，只是货郎今天的运气不好吧。地上大片的血液早已冷透，在这个民命如草芥的年代，死一个老百姓，比死一只蚂蚁还平常。又何必长吁短叹？

中午，自己下厨，给丽云做了顿饭。做得不太好吃，但丽云还是吃得很高兴。蒸热的肉包子每人吃了一个，还有两个留着晚上吃。吃完了饭，自己去洗碗。自己打算以后都不再让丽云碰洗衣做饭洗碗之类的粗活了，她本来就是个千金小姐，不该做这种下人干的活儿。而且，人有旦夕祸福，自己就应该要趁来得及，多对丽云好一点。

洗完了碗，自己上房去换瓦。丽云在下面扶着梯子，自己说，不用，你回屋歇着。她不敢松手，仰着头，说，你小心。自己就笑了，说，我哪用得着小心，你忘了，我会轻功。她就“哦”了一声，想了想，然后就松了手。自己忍不住笑了起来。她问，你笑什么？自己说，你傻得很可爱。她反应了过来，一扭身，娇嗔道，好心就是会被坏蛋欺负，懒得理你。自己哈哈大笑，她跑回了屋里去。

阳光暖暖地照在身上，自己看着湛蓝的天，听着静静的鸟叫，忽然觉得这样的生活真美好。这一刻，耳旁没有枪声和炮声，眼前也没有刺刀和死尸，真是让人觉得身心惬意。要是这个小院，能一直与世隔绝该多好。太阳就像一个鲜红的咸蛋黄，高高地晃荡在天上，让人充满了对柴米油盐的普通生活的向往。这种向往，也许，就叫作热爱吧。

不错。只要有丽云在，自己是多么热爱生活，热爱活着。

一片云，以奔马的形状在天上飘动，一行鸟，在这片云下的低空不停盘旋，云行鸟行，云止鸟止。自己觉得这个景观很奇特，忙唤丽云出来看。阳光镀着云边，云朵绯红，鸟羽载着金黄，美丽非常。丽云仰望着天，也看得痴了。

过了许久，云才散开，鸟才飞走。自己回首下望，只见丽云依旧凝然望着蓝天，眼神澄澈如秋水。丽云的这个样子，在自己心中久久不能被磨灭，每次想到，自己都会有种错觉，会以为，她的归宿，就应该在某个不食人间烟火的远方，某片最纯澈的云的故乡，谁都不配拥有她。

换好了瓦，着了地，丽云端来了一碗水。喝着清甜的白开水，有那么一刻，自己都忘了，外面的战争正进行得如火如荼。水的清澈像镜面，镜面里甚至能见到天之蓝。自己喝水喝得欢，一下子，就像把满满的空旷的蓝，给灌进了自己的胸腔里。丽云问：外面的情况怎么样了？自己说：好。丽云问：好？自己说：商店在营业了，日本人不怎么杀人了，可不就是好吗。

自己又要去劈柴，丽云笑说，你就像是要把几天的活儿都一下子干完似的。自己忽然就想到了那个死去的货郎，他还没来得及把他担子里的东西卖掉，就那么突然死了，这人生，还真是譬如朝露，存在没有任何硬度，消失始终尾随在时间背后。自己丢开了木柴，自嘲地笑了笑，说：是啊，日子还长。

太阳红扑扑的，像少女害羞的脸庞。空气中飘来了一阵不知是谁家的饭菜香，自己和丽云相视而笑。这种感觉真好，不是血腥味，不是火药味，而是菜香味。时代好像在这恍惚的一刻里，卸下了沾满鲜血的铠甲，换上了整洁的家常布衣。自己高兴地对丽云说，我给你削个苹果吧。丽云笑着说，好哇。

细长的苹果皮在自己的指缝间不停滑动，像条绳子一样连绵不断地下垂、盘曲，淡淡的果香荡漾了开来，像沁人心脾的某种晴朗。丽云饶有兴趣地看着，还抿嘴笑，于是自己索性就增加了一些表演的成分，在成功地将苹果皮一次未断地削下后，自己又快速地在圆溜溜的光苹果上刻了一个楷体的“云”字。丽云开心地拍起了手，哈哈直笑。

丽云将苹果捧在手心里，说：真像艺术品，不舍得吃了。自己说：吃吧，不吃就黄了，艺术家在这里呢，你想看艺术品，有的是机会。她笑得前仰后合。自己也不禁笑了。倏然间，自己又想起了以前在庄府中和她一起度过的时光，那些令自己魂牵梦绕的美好欢笑，现在，分明就又真真切切地来到了眼前。只要伸开双臂，自己就能抱住这份美好，再不让它溜走。这分明是上帝慈悲的恩赐。曾经那相思入骨的悲彻，不就是为了祈求今日这相伴而笑的厮守？自己真是何其愚钝。

丽云将苹果一切为二，递了一半过来。自己接了苹果，顿了顿，说，那年，我答应过你，要教你削苹果不断皮的方法。

她就笑了，说，你还记得呀。

自己笑笑，点点头，说，趁着今天有苹果，待会儿，我就教你。

丽云咬了一口苹果，调皮地一笑，说，不要，我不学。

自己问，为什么？

她说，我不学会，就可以一辈子叫你削苹果给我吃了呀，嘿嘿。

她调皮而天真地笑，自己的心，顿时像水一样柔软。橙黄的阳光洒在屋内，像飘着白云的美，像散着青草的香。其实自己想告诉她：丽云，我爱你，我会一辈子和你在一起。可是，那明亮的天光，又像在自己的耳边悄悄追问：你配吗？

丽云吃着苹果，腮帮子鼓鼓的，脸蛋就像一个可爱的红苹果。看着她，自己心里既喜欢得想笑，又酸楚得生痛。自己愣愣的，她说：你吃啊。自己大口大口地嚼着苹果。她说，这苹果真甜。自己说，嗯，真甜，下次我再买。

丢掉了苹果核，丽云坐在屋门口，静静而淡淡地和自己说着话。秋风微微在动，清亮的光，将她的影子长长地拖在地上，那淡暗的影，像一泓美艳的秋水，像一道裂开的伤口。自己想坐到她身旁，却只是走近了她的影。自己凝视着她的影，就像飞鸟美丽地追逐着云。真的很想吻她。

她说，其实这世上有很多事情，走了一圈，又会回到原点。小时候，同学们笑我娘眼睛看不见，都不肯和我玩，我觉得很孤独。后来我拿了钱，买了许多好吃的分给他们，他们才愿意和我一起玩游戏。可是，有一天，我忽然想，要是我没有了买糖的钱，他们还会愿意和我一起玩捉迷藏吗？那一刻，我莫名其妙地很害怕。后来，他们来找我，我却不愿意再和他们一起玩。我还是觉得很孤独，就像开始时一样，就好像，他们从来也没和我一起

玩过。

自己说，有时候，人总要飞过了沧海桑田，才会想起以前。小时候，我很讨厌家里那幅母亲的画像，因为我总以为，这幅画就是让父亲流泪的原因。我做什么都是为了让父亲高兴，而父亲最希望见到的，就是我不会成为一个和他一样落魄的人。我的人生，似乎从小时候起，就充满了各种让我难以理解的矛盾。而年轻时的我并不明白，懵懂无知就是一种幸运。当我在某个瞬间蓦然回首，发现往事中那些曾令我困惑的矛盾都是那样容易理解时，我已成为了一个落魄至极的人，我已懂得了，一个男人，为什么会对着一个女人的画像哭。疼痛就是一本三字经，不读，不会识字，识字了，就再不会忘记疼痛。

她说，以前，我特别喜欢五代词和南宋词，国家不幸诗家幸，话到沧桑语始工。十五岁时，为了买到一本陆游的诗词集，我跑了七家书店，买到后，高兴得整晚没睡着。那时候，我还不明白，一个人的眼泪，就算美得像花，终究是一个伤疤，只不过，我们隔着时间的纱，摸不到伤疤表面的粗糙，触不到眼泪里面的温度。父亲病倒后，有一次，我又翻到了那本陆游的诗词集，书的纸页都已蜡黄，想起少时天天读它爱不释手的情景，想再看看书里的诗和词，却又莫名不愿再看，害怕看。后来，蔡嫂烧掉了这本书，我只留下了当年我给这本书买的一张书签。书签上画着一个古代美女，沉鱼落雁，我一直以为，这就是唐琬。

自己说，其实我经常做噩梦，这些梦的内容大体相同，日子久了，它们有时就会伪装成人生经历，混进我的回忆，让我惆怅莫名。在家乡时，我经常会做一个梦，梦里，我考上了文状元，金榜题名，风光无限，而就在我骑着高头大马准备衣锦还乡时，我却会突然想起：我还没有交考卷。这个梦总会让我在恐怖与惶惑中惊醒，它一直折磨了我很多年。而来到东北之后，我只做过一种噩梦，这个梦的内容每次都相同，梦里，这个天下终于太平了，我去庄府找你，敲了很久很久的门，都没人来开，我喊着你的名字，丽云，丽云。天上下起了雪，我忽然才发现，我的胡子和头发都是白的，我的手上满是皱纹，我忽然才想起，原来，我已经七十五岁。

丽云落下了两行泪来。

她靠在了自己的怀里，说：“傻瓜，我就在这里。”

自己轻轻抱着她，说："是啊，你就在这里。"

她痴痴地说："要是有下辈子，我愿意投生在江南来找你，而不要你受苦流浪来东北。"

自己说："你在哪里，我的家乡便在哪里。"

"我们生生世世不分离。"

"嗯，生生世世不分离。"

城上斜阳画角哀，沈园非复旧池台。伤心桥下春波绿，曾是惊鸿照影来。梦断香销四十年，沈园柳老不吹绵。此身行作稽山土，犹吊遗踪一泫然。

十月十日。

昨晚想了一夜，最后还是决定今天要去找短毛。只要一想起赤木和渡边的那番谈话，自己就感到毛骨悚然、寝食难安。什么活体试验，什么女人，不行，自己绝不能再让丽云留在沈阳，绝不能。要逃，必须要逃。但是，那时，自己作为一个普通百姓，对战局的走向和发展还很无知。当时，外面烽火连绵，战况正紧，日军攻得疯狂，国军败得凄惨，自己在很大程度上是以为，这一次，中日将全面开战，侵略与反侵略的搏杀，将在全国遍地开花。自己并没有想到，在东北沦陷变成满洲国后，日军的兵锋会在华北滞塞了许多年，而日本的全面侵华与中国的全民抗战，要迟至一九三七年才爆发。而正是由于对时局的难以判断，所以导致了自己在生存决策上的举棋不定。自己不知道，究竟该带着丽云往哪儿逃，怎么逃。总不能带着她乱闯乱跑，或者往火坑里跳。时代就像一道谜题，你若猜不透它的谜底，你就会被厄运吞噬。所以，思来想去，自己觉得，还是只能求助于短毛了。好歹，人家是抗日武装，知道的情况和拥有的门路，总要比普通百姓多。

当然，自己也有顾虑。短毛他们若真的肯帮忙，那么，他们多半会要求自己去刺杀赤木。不是自己不想杀赤木，只是赤木真的不是一个小人物。没错，自己是杀过青帮的人，杀过黑龙会的人，甚至还杀过守粮的日本兵，但是，细想想，自己所杀的那些人，不都只是些鹰爪走狗小喽啰吗？而赤木，是日本樱花会社的社长！青帮、黑龙会跟自己的旧账还未必已真的了结，自己若再杀了赤木，岂不是这辈子都别想再从血海追杀中爬出来了！自己若真的惹上了樱花会社的追杀，那么，自己带着丽云的出逃，还有意义吗？自己

只能求个侥幸，希望短毛他们，可以无条件帮忙，或者，他们开出其他条件也行。

自己准备傍晚去找短毛，因为城西的废木料场周围，傍晚时没有巡逻兵。白天下了一点小雨，地上有些浅浅的水洼。落叶掉在水洼里，像搁浅的船，只能等着被风吹干。丽云找到了一些剩余的茶叶，泡了两杯茶。茶香氤氲中，她的微笑依旧如烟火般美丽。自己想：我和她，要是能生活在世外桃源，那该多好。一片茶叶漂进了自己嘴里，停在舌头上，微苦，芳香，甘甜。自己想：要是真的可以逃，逃跑前，我一定要正式娶她。

清甜而美好的时光，就像细薄的苹果皮一样滑溜，很快就到了傍晚。自己跟丽云说了一声要出去买东西，然后便离开了小院。离开前，自己将手里耍练着的菜刀交给了丽云，开玩笑说：记住，我走了，要是有坏蛋来欺负你，你就像剁馅一样剁他。丽云说：有比你更坏的坏蛋吗？你是想提醒我别忘了做晚饭吧？自己说：其实菜刀是个好东西，哪朝政府禁兵器，也都没禁到菜刀头上，而且它比榔头斧头什么的都要轻便好使，等我哪天发明出了一套菜刀刀法，一定要好好卖个大价钱。丽云说：是啊是啊，你就使劲琢磨，以后用力去坑厨子们的钱吧。自己哈哈大笑，丽云忍俊不禁，哭笑不得。

跑在去废木料场的路上，自己心中的快乐还久久没有散去。这快乐很坚韧，像被海浪尽情拍打而无所变易的礁石；这快乐很盲目，像孩子般毫无目的又无所顾忌的游戏。夕阳的光迎面扑来，像大自然原本应有的美好那样。自己都忘了，这个时代有多么的不堪。

在一个十字路口，自己触目惊心地看到了一具吊挂着的尸体。那是一个女人，全身布满枪眼，血肉模糊。听人说，这是一个共产党，因为炸过日本汽车，今天被日本人捉住，乱枪打死了。这个女人的血在地上汇成了一片血泊，夕阳下，血泊亮光如雪。没有人敢走近。一个男人讽刺地说，在防共反共上，日本人倒是和蒋介石齐心协力，同心同德。一个老人说，可怜哪，都没人给这孩子收尸。

自己失魂落魄地继续往废木料场跑去。一种难以言喻的恶心在胃里左右翻滚，扑鼻的血腥味仿佛依旧在面孔周围缭绕，令人窒息。渐渐落下地平线的夕阳，残余的光比血还鲜红，既炽亮又尖锐，让人无法直视，仿佛只要一直视，人的双眼就会被凶狠地灼瞎。自己像被一张看不见的网勒得生痛。

到了废木料场，大门虚掩着。自己走了进去，里面一片荒芜景象。自己也不敢乱喊，只得先四处看看再说。看到里面有一间棚屋，自己便走了过去。这时，一个道士打扮的人，恰巧也从棚屋里走了出来。

“您好，请问短毛在这里吗？我想找他。”自己很有礼貌地问这个道士。

“短毛？”道士一脸讶异，像是听不明白。

“哦，短毛是他外号，他叫曹英。”自己补充道。

“这里没有这个人，你一定是弄错了，请你离开。”道士冷冷地说。

自己纳闷地走到了空旷而破败的大门口，想想觉得不对，就又折了回去。道士见自己又走了回去，眉毛立即皱了起来。

“是短毛要我来这里找他的，他还告诉过我，你们要刺杀樱花会社的社长赤木，对不对？”

“你是谁？”

“在下赵驹。”

“你就是那个打死了巴占的新拳王，赵驹？”

“巴占是我打死的，但拳王不敢当。”

“可是曹哥说过，赵驹不会来。”

“凡事都有个意外。”

“在下武当龚汉江，久仰东北新拳王赵驹之名，想要切磋一二。你若真是赵驹，今日过招乃我生平之幸；你若不是，冒名顶替之贼今日休想再走！请！”

龚汉江话音刚落，双掌气劲已出。自己本不想节外生枝、招惹是非，无奈掌风已扑面而至，自己只得接招。别看这道士性格粗糙，武功却着实不弱。武当天下闻名的绵密内劲，被他用凌厉的气势使了出来，纵然他的修行还远未到家，他功夫的威力却也真的厉害。五六招下来，自己居然还没有制服他。自己暗想：打得久了，他怕是真的会拿我当假的。于是，自己出了狠劲，一下子，将他摁倒在了地上。怕是已扭伤了他的筋。

自己松开了他。他爬了起来，痛得咧了几下嘴。他揉着肩，欢快地笑了起来。“太好了，太好了，赵大哥你来了太好了——刚才真的不好意思，快请屋里去坐——”

自己向他抱拳行了个礼，以示歉意。

太阳已落下地平线，天色昏暗灰沉。龚汉江说，曹哥今天去见枪贩子了，我们想买一箱手榴弹，估计天黑前他就能回来。他说，曹哥经常跟我提起你，说你怎么怎么厉害，今日一见，果然名不虚传。自己说，你武功也很好，而且你是从武当出来的，有正式的师父教，以后比我厉害。他说，我师父早死了，门派内乱，我是带着三个师弟，逃到东北。自己一时感触，说，结果没想到，日本人会打东北，对不对？他笑笑，点点头，叹了口气，说，离开了武当，我才知道，练武无用，在这个子弹横飞的年代，武功，是既防不了身，也救不了人。说完，他自嘲地摇摇头，笑笑。

棚屋里比外面暗，几近黑暗。龚汉江去角落里摸出了一根蜡烛来，点上。烛光摇曳着亮起，微弱地照亮着棚屋里的一切。看得出，这里的条件十分艰苦。他说，原本有一盏煤油灯的，前天打坏了，就只能用蜡烛将就了，别介意。他倒了一碗水，放在桌子上，说，赵大哥，你喝水。自己说，谢谢。

龚汉江说，曹哥跟我讲了几次，说你不会加入我们，没想到你今天却来了，真的太好了，我们现在虽然才十几个人，但是一定会慢慢壮大起来的。他乐呵呵地笑着。自己却觉得尴尬了起来。好在棚屋里光线暗，自己的表情，龚汉江也看不清。自己岔开了话题，说，我来的时候，在十字路口那里，看到了一具女尸，听人说，她是个共产党。龚汉江咬咬牙，恨恨地说，她是不是共产党我不知道，但是，她杀过日本畜生，就是个巾帼英雄，明天，等兄弟们到齐了，我们一定要去把她的尸体救下来。他说，这个女人很有本事，我曾亲眼见她干净利落地杀死过五个日本兵，据说，赤木的特务侄子，于前年死在她的枪下。这一次，她是中了赤木老贼的圈套，才这样惨的就死了。自己问：你和她认识吗？他摇摇头，惨然一笑，说：我想认识她，但可惜，已永远来不及了。

外面的天，完全暗了下来。橘黄色的烛光，轻微地摇晃着，在完全的黑暗里，却显出了格外的明亮。自己和龚汉江的影子凝固在墙上，像两个既近似又迥然不同的雕像。屋里寂静无声。自己喝了一口水，还是不知该说什么才好。只能茫然地等待着短毛的归来。在从昨夜至今天的反复思考中，自己已基本上确定了一个主张：要和丽云逃，就得往南方逃，越往南越好。首先，日军的攻势是由北向南，就算即将爆发全国范围的大战混战，想来，南方之战也应该会晚于北方之战；其次，一旦到了南方，去香港或者下南洋就会方便很多，总比待在沈阳要便利。所以，自己今天就是想来问问短毛：你们有没有一条通道，可以让人安全地离开沦陷区，去往南方？如果有，要怎样，才能借此路于我一用？但是龚汉江在一开始，就误解了自己的来意，这真是让人万分尴尬。自己只能默默喝水。

自己问，你们做道士的，怎么也会来干这个？

他说，本来，我们也不想做道士了，只是现在，还没脱下这身衣服。这些年，我们师兄弟几个，多少也攒了些钱，本来，是打算以后不做道士了，脱下这身衣服，经营一点小生意，往后各自娶妻生子，在这烟火人间里，做个凡夫俗子，美好地生活下去。哪知道，战争会说来就来。

自己说，你们可以选择不参加这场战争，你们是道士，若要远离世间的纷争，没有人会怪罪。

他说，日军进城那天，我和三个师弟就躲在一间仓库里。我们在窗户里看见，手无寸铁的中国兵，被日军砍去了双臂和双腿，丢在路上慢慢等死……我的小师弟和三师弟，几次三番要往外冲，最后，都被我打昏在了仓库里。他们醒来后，哭着问我，我们活了下来，又有什么用？我说，有，我们可以给惨死的人们报仇。

自己沉吟不语，无言以对。

短毛回来了。

短毛见到自己，又惊又喜。“你想通啦？太好了，真让我意外——”短毛兴奋地说。龚汉江说：“赵大哥来了好一会儿了，一直在等你，我们正在聊天呢。”短毛高兴地笑。自己只能支吾了两声。

龚汉江问短毛：“怎么样，兄弟们明天几时到？”

短毛说：“人不够。有兄弟不愿意，说那个女人是共产党的人，我们要是帮了共产党，以后国军收复了东北，我们会不仅没有功，反而还有罪。”

龚汉江立马火冒三丈，说：“什么屁话！我们现在是在反抗日本人，又不是在替蒋介石卖命，哪用得着去管他什么党派斗争！”

短毛说：“你别急，明天一早我再去说说，兄弟们一定都会来的。”

“不来拉倒，我倒不信了，我们四个武当兄弟，难道连从日本人手里救一具尸体出来的本事都没有！”说罢，龚汉江拂袖而去。

“龚兄弟你别乱来——”自己想去拉回龚汉江，短毛拦住了自己。短毛说，别担心，他是一时说气话，他不会要他的师弟们拿性命去冒险的。

自己和短毛聊了一会儿，很快，谈话便切入了正题。自己直截了当地向短毛说明了真实的来意，短毛无限失望地坐了下来。自己和短毛都沉默了一会儿。烛光飘摇，像坠落的轻纱。

短毛叹了一口气，说：“我就知道，要你改变，没那么容易。”

“这与改变无关，只是我们每个人所能看到的道理不同而已。”

“争辩无益，我和你还是说主题。我们自己并没有什么外逃的门路，但是，今天和我谈生意的枪贩子们，可以带人去广东。”

“太好了！”

“先别高兴，世上没有免费的午餐，走一个人，要一千块大洋，而且，现在东北的战况日趋激烈，情况日益糟糕，他们说不定还会任意加价。”

“——太贵了。”

“兄弟，他们是卖军火的，又不是善男信女。不过话说回来，这价钱其实也不贵。东北现在就是个死人窟，只要能逃出东北，命就算是保住了。一条命，一千大洋，你说贵吗？”

“的确不贵。可是，我的钱，只够走一个人。”

“那么，你想要谁走？”

“我当然想要我女人走，但是，我不能让她一个人跟着那群枪贩子走。”

“的确不能。可是，你的钱又不够。”

一切又都陷入了沉默。

在一个短短的片刻里，烛火纹丝不动地僵硬着。静止着的燃烧，简直不像燃烧。火焰终于又抖动了起来。

短毛沉吟之后，欲言又止。他说：“我有一个主意，你不妨听听。”

“愿闻其详。”

“我们这里，现在还有一千六百多块大洋，都是我和兄弟们凑的，准备用来添置弹药，但是，这笔钱我一个人做不了主，只有兄弟们都同意了，才能借给你。”

“不行，我不拿抗日的钱。”

“你只要能帮我们杀了赤木，你就不算白拿了抗日的钱。赤木如果真的死在了你手上，那么，兄弟们必定愿意把钱送你。”

“我要是杀了赤木，这辈子都得亡命天涯！”

“凶手的罪名，可以由我们来担。”

“日本人没那么蠢的！”

“不试试怎么知道？”

“这种事可以试吗！”

短毛不再言语，低头沉默。自己一下子站了起来，心中憋闷得像要爆炸，整个心膛却又坚硬得根本炸不开。只有说不出的无穷难受，像火一样在心里膨胀、再膨胀。自己整个人面向着棚屋黑暗的墙，双手无力地按在墙上。自己叹不出气，更难以呼吸，整个脑袋里，都是令人窒息的沮丧，还有绝望。

“短毛，你不明白，我除了有双拳头，什么本事也没有，而光凭一双拳头，在这样的一个时代里，又真的能做得了什么呢？再怎么天下无敌的武功，在子弹的面前，也只不过就是一只纸糊的老虎。赤木身边保镖如云，你以为他们身上真的只带着武士刀？如果没有枪林弹雨的掩护，我根本不可能贴近赤木。你不是要我去杀人，你是叫我去送死啊——”

“对不起……我以后，都不会再说这个了。”短毛说。他的声音，莫名也有几分悲伤。

谁也没有再说什么，沉默像一摊坚固的血迹，既不流动，也不消失。唯有微弱而黄亮的烛光，依旧在轻盈而朦胧地摇曳。

道了声别，自己离开了棚屋。杂乱而空寂的废木料场，在黑暗的夜空下，苍凉得宛若一个坟场。秋风萧瑟地游荡，没有枪声的夜晚，比杀戮更压抑。借着微弱的路灯光，自己看到，龚汉江在一个邋遢的角落里独自喝闷酒。他背靠着一堆木料，就那么坐在地上，大口大口地吞着酒。他没有看见自己，自己也就没有过去和他道别。酒精，莫名让这夜空下的一切，看起来更像一片绝望的废墟。自己跑出了废木料场。

重新经过了十字路口。女尸依旧吊挂着，负责看守的日本兵大概有十来个，个个荷枪实弹。也许，短毛那些不愿来救尸的兄弟的选择是对的，日本人这么曝尸，分明不只是在杀鸡儆猴，更是在守株待兔。况且，她还可能是个共产党。灿亮的灯光照射着尸体和血，夜幕像一幅巨大的背景，将死亡和

静止托举在时间流动的冲刷中，她像一具雕像，用没有生命的永恒，让人怀念着各种活着的短暂。她的血像已流干，风将她吹得晃动了起来。她那沾满血污的长发飘散了开来，自己看清了她的脸，她还是个十分年轻的女人，十分美丽。血腥的味道在空气里扬洒，一种比惋惜更深沉的悲哀，莫名在自己胸中洇开。自己像是又听到了，龚汉江惨然一笑地说："我想认识她，但可惜，已永远来不及了。"

夜，没有感情地黑暗着。自己忽然觉得很难过。

自己一咬牙，做出了一个冲动的决定：救下这具尸体。

行动的过程并不复杂，需要的只是一连串的侥幸。自己在离十字路口不远的地方，放了一把火。然后，将一条被自己打死了的日军狼狗，远远地丢到了女尸的脚下。女尸晃荡了起来，负责看守的日本兵，全都乱了阵脚。他们中的大半人，立马全奔去了火灾现场，然后，又有几个人，不知跑去了哪里——可能是去叫援兵吧——只留下了两个人，如旧地看守着女尸。自己作了一声鬼叫，然后，从黑暗中扑出，迅速地拧断了这两个日本兵的脖子。自己用刺刀割断了绳子，解下了女尸。自己抱着女尸疾步快跑，背后响起了凌乱的枪声。

摆脱了日军的追捕，自己抱着女尸，去了废木料场。短毛和龚汉江，惊讶不已。自己将女尸交到了龚汉江的怀里，龚汉江刹那落下了泪来。他说："谢谢！"自己说："先将她好好安葬，然后，尽快派人联系共产党。——另外，请记住，这件事是你们做的，与我无关。告辞！"

不等他们再说什么，自己已转身，飞奔离开。

轻轻一跃，落回小院之中。丽云闻声，跑了出来。她吓得"啊"了一声。自己一看，原来，是自己衣服上沾满了女尸的血迹。自己不知如何是好，忙编了个谎，说：路上遇到个摔得浑身是血的人，就帮忙救了人，抱人家去了医院。丽云将信将疑，又不再多问。她要拿血衣去洗，自己拉住了她，说，这种粗活，还是我来。

夜晚，睡在榻上，自己心事重重。冒险给人收尸这事，令自己后怕不已。冲动是魔鬼，做完了善事之后，自己收获的只有无尽的恐惧。这恐惧令自己毛骨悚然。睡不着，自己坐了起来。又想起了赤木和渡边的那番对话，自己如坐针毡。赤木想要渡边去折磨的那个女人是谁？会不会就是今天这个死了的女共产党？照龚汉江所说，正是这个女共产党，枪杀了赤木的特务侄子，那么，赤木恨得想要将她喂狗，也是一件合情合理的事情。应该就是这样——应该就是这样。但是，赤木真的已经忘记丽云了吗？

自己站了起来。夜黑得像间地狱。钱不够，钱不够！现在这种时局，上哪里去才能一下子弄到一千块大洋？又不能让丽云一个人走，她一个弱女子，若独自跟着那群如狼似虎的枪贩子上路，天知道会发生什么。但是又不应该继续留在此地，万一赤木想着要报复丽云呢？只有短毛他们，现在手里正好有钱！也许自己杀得了赤木，也许日本人会把账都算在短毛他们的头上。今天，自己不就成功逃过了日军的追捕吗？何不趁着好运未散，再冒险一次，做一票大的？只要大洋到手，自己就能带着丽云去广东了！到了广东，哪里还用怕什么日本人！

自己激动得握紧了拳头。但是，自己真杀得了赤木吗？杀完了赤木，日本人真的会把账算在短毛他们的头上，而不来追杀自己这个真凶吗？要是刺杀失败，自己死了，剩下丽云一人怎么办？要是自己刺杀成功了，满世界地被樱花会社的人追杀，可叫丽云怎么办？难道要她跟着自己亡命天涯？这不是把她往火坑里推吗。怎么办。

怎么办。

自己头痛欲裂。黑暗像涌动的潮水，将人淹没在绝望里，却又不让人因窒息而死去。命运给了人选择的机会，却又在每一个机会的背后设下了一个陷阱，让人心甘情愿又怨不得谁地跌入万丈深渊，万劫不复。现实就是一个没有出口的迷宫，每一次充满希望地搜寻，其实只是为了收获碰壁。碰到头破血流，也没法找到出口。

黑暗中，自己不小心碰到了那只收藏着丽云断发的首饰盒。抚摸着盒子，自己忽然痛心疾首。难道真的什么也做不了吗？只能人为刀俎、我为鱼肉？不是说好了要守护她的吗？不是想好了要和她在一起美好地生活吗？叫她剪发换装扮丑，这算什么守护？和她一起厮守于危墙之下，她又哪里会有什么美好的生活？当时代用迷雾和陷阱遮蔽了人生的方向和希望时，人，是否真的无计可施？丽云那样痴情一片，自己是否真的什么也不能为她做？不，人生，就该赌一回。不赌，怎知输赢。

天蒙蒙亮了。自己在小院里，无声地练起了武。自己已经有很久没再

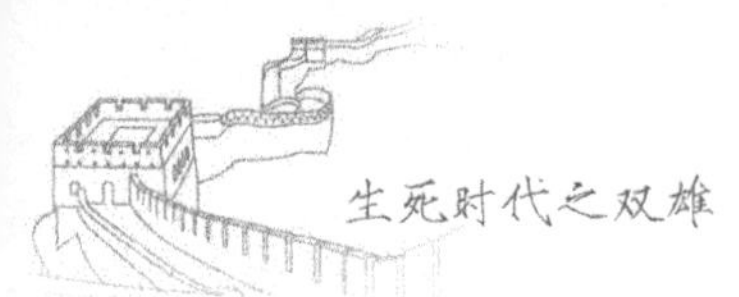

练过这套父亲留下的残拳了，此刻，自己是多想能从这套拳中获得一种更强大的力量，强大到足以让自己穿透重重警卫直接击杀赤木的力量。但是，残拳依旧是那套残拳，自己并没能想起什么新的父亲留下的招式，而在旧的招式里，自己也并无新的领悟。一阵苦涩涌上心头，自己拳路缭乱。父亲哪父亲，您若在天有灵，请告诉我，我要怎样才能带着我爱的女人，离开这片沦陷之地？

天亮了起来，秋叶在朝阳的光辉里零落，美若破碎的彩虹。不知何时，丽云已站在了小屋的门口。自己忙停止了练武。四目相对，她的眼神莫名含着忧伤。

“我还是第一次看到你练拳。”她说。

“吵醒你了，不好意思。”自己说。

“你没有声音，是我本来就一直没睡着。”

“一直没睡着？”

“我听见，你昨晚也一直没睡。”

“哦……嗯，这——我……”

“你知道吗，我很害怕。”

“害怕什么？”

“害怕你有事瞒着我，害怕你骗我。”

“我怎么会骗你——”自己说着，却又不敢看她雾蒙蒙的双眼。

“我害怕，有一天，你又会从我的世界里消失，一声告辞，离我而去。”她悲伤地说着，眼里泛起了泪光。

“不会的，我……”自己不知该说什么才好。

“男人们总是以为，要把令人担心的事情瞒着女人，才是对女人好，却不知，这样只会让女人更担心、更害怕。”

自己无言以对。

她走到了自己的面前，抱住了自己。她的头靠在自己的心口，像一个暖融融的太阳。她痴痴地说：“我不是笨蛋，所以，答应我，以后不管发生什么事，都不要瞒着我，不然，我只会胡思乱想，更加担心你。我什么都不怕，除了，不能了解你的世界。”

自己心中一阵滚烫，不禁抱紧了她。

“丽云，你恨不恨赤木？”

“恨。”

说完，她却呆住了。她推开了自己，望着自己，问：“为什么问这个？”

“我想带你离开沦陷区，现在有一个机会，可以让我和你安全地去广东，但是这事有一个前提条件，就是我必须要去刺杀赤木。只要杀了赤木，我们就能一起远走高飞。”

“不，不可以！绝对不可以！”她脸色刹那惨白，拼命摇头。

“没事的，会有十几个人掩护我，他们武器充足，还有手榴弹呢。杀了赤木，他们会把罪名担下来，我们只管去广东——”

“你会死的，你会死的！不要，求求你不要这么干！”她哭了起来，拼命地抱住了自己，“我哪儿也不想去，只要待在这里，只要待在这里……”

“沈阳已经沦陷了，天知道国军什么时候才能打回来！你在这里危险！”

“我不怕，能有什么危险，只要你在我身边，我什么危险也不怕！”

“可是我怕！”自己推开了她。

丽云悲恸不已，哽咽失声。“赤木不是一般的日本人，他要是容易杀，潘兆早就派人杀了他了！可是结果呢，想要对付赤木的人，最后全死了，最后全死了！就剩我一个了——”丽云哀哭欲绝，“我在这个世上，已经再没有半个亲人了，只剩下你了，只剩下你了……我不要你去送死，不要……求求你不要去呀——”

丽云哭得战栗不已。“你若不在了，我活着还有什么意思——”她撕心裂肺地说。

自己潸然泪下。怎么办？怎么办？怎么办！

自己紧紧地抱住了丽云，抚着她的头，不停地说：“对不起，对不起，对不起……”

“答应我，不要去——”她死死地紧抱着自己，把头深深地埋在自己胸口，悲泣着哀求。

“……不去，我不去……我答应你。”自己紧抱着丽云，喃喃地对她说。

天地就像一座监牢，无论你做什么选择，其实，你都在困境里。冒险，也许会死，也许不会死；不冒险，也是也许会死，也许不会死。谁能看到未来的答案？也许，人活着，只要有选择，就是在赌博。就算不选择，也是赌

注下在了不选择上，还是赌博，而赌局的结果呢？全凭老天爷做主。自己放弃了冒险，不是选择了不选择，而是根本就不知该如何选择。也许，丽云是对的吧。自己又为什么要为了一件连自己都不知道结果的事情，而让丽云悲痛欲绝、伤心流泪呢？天若有情，就请天，可怜可怜自己和丽云吧。不要再让命运的迷宫，把人折磨得血肉模糊。

丽云亲手又将那块男表戴到了自己的手上。她对自己说："你要一直戴着它，看到它，就想起我，不管做什么事，都千万不要拿性命去冒险，为了我，为了我们，好不好？"自己点头。

对丽云的愧疚，自己无法用语言来形容。自己没给过她什么开心，却一直在让她流泪。她一直在温暖着自己，自己却总是让她陷入冰凉。自己只奢望，能用余生的时间，尽心疼爱她。但是，思想在现实的面前，似乎总是个小丑。

这一天过得很快。为了让丽云忘记担心，为了让自己忘记她的眼泪，自己一直在哄她开心。而她只要笑了，自己就觉得，生活很幸福。要是自己和她的世界，能够真的简单得只剩下爱情和欢笑，那该多美好。要是憧憬从来不会碰上意外，那这人间，简直就是天堂。

傍晚时，汉奸来敲了门。汉奸通知：明天家家户户所有人都要上街，逛逛，走走，买买东西，营造出欢乐热闹的气氛，日本人请了记者，要拍照，向国际社会报道奉天的中日共荣情况。

残阳如血。黄叶，无知无觉地飘落。落叶旋转着的圆圈，切割着光线照射的轨迹。风，令人怅惘地吹动着树枝。树枝，似乎在簌簌低泣。

十月十二日。

天气凉了。清晨的寒意很浓，空气里像结着冷冷的露珠。丽云煮了半锅热粥。喝粥时，自己问，家里米还有吗？她说，还有。自己说，日本人让人重新做生意了，米铺或许会重开，到时我看看，再多买些粮食回来。她点点头，说，嗯。她说，要是外面的秩序真的恢复了，我得重新去找份工作，皮货店没了，我也不知道还能干什么。自己说，这个不急，外面毕竟还是日本人的天下，乱糟糟的，你暂时还是待在家里安全，我也放心，挣钱这种事情，我来做好了。她点点头，看着自己，欲言又止。自己笑了，说，放心，我不会再去靠打拳什么的挣钱了，我会好好地找一份正经工作，和你一起安心地把日子过下去。她灿烂地笑了，说，嗯。她有些害羞地低着头，只管喝粥。

粥是温暖的，丽云是美好的，自己对她说的都是真的，自己是真的想，和她一起安心地生活下去。待在这里就待在这里吧，又不是只有几户老百姓没走，留在沈阳城里的中国人，成千上万，自己又何必要去节外生枝？别真的是自己把赤木给杀了，结果引来了无尽追杀，那自己可就坑苦了丽云。还是维持现状就好，只求无灾无祸平安便好。有时候，能够拥有一点仅存的幸福就已经很不容易了，想要更好或更长久，结果却反而会令眼前仅存的东西灰飞烟灭。命运就是这么个让人无法计划无法掌握的魔鬼东西，经历过的无常太多，自然便会谨小慎微地懂得珍惜眼前。尽管这种懂得，对谁来说都可能意味着无奈，意味着向命运必然的屈服。但是，人生在世，又何必要对各种选择和道理追根究底？你不明白，困境在那里；你明白了，困境还在那里。

丽云没有问关于那件血衣的事，她没有再问任何自己不想说的事，她是个很乖顺的女人。而她的乖顺，有时候，会让自己特别愧疚。自己明白她那彻夜难眠的担心和害怕，不了解是这世上最可怕的猛兽，它能将人悬置于无所依凭的半空中，然后突如其来地开始撕咬人的血肉。就像那一年，那张突如其来的通缉令，给她造成的伤害和痛苦一样。她祈望能和自己一起回到那时的温甜相伴，当然也就会恐惧那种结局的卷土重来。血衣，谁见到了不会害怕？但是，她只说了她害怕，她只要求了今后的坦诚，她没有问。自己通晓一切，却知而不言。是她眼里的幽惶让自己无法诉说，还是自己依旧无法向她真正打开自己世界的大门？似乎是，似乎都不是。或许，两个灵魂再相爱，沟通依旧是一场充满了恐惧与退缩的艰难旅程。撇除距离的等待，信任就像树顶的阳光，要有勇气离开地面才能沐浴蔚蓝。

自己的害怕是一场模糊不清的拉锯战。丽云或许懂得，或许无法懂得。但是自己对她毫无保留的爱，她是拥抱着的。就像自己洞彻且拥有着她毫无保留的爱一样。虽然在很多时候，自己越爱，却越是在她面前无法言语，但是，这或许正是爱在灵魂的证据。这种赤热，就像黑夜里，看不见光明的天际之外，太阳火球仍在熊熊燃烧着一样。或许，有些话的确不用都说出来，纯粹的爱若经过了语言的编排，味道未必就会纯如一体。就好像，她那小心翼翼的不再多问，其实，也是一种无法言喻的对恋人的宽容之爱。珍惜，是一件不能用退缩来解释的神圣美好之事。或许，在不可捉摸的愧疚里，自己更应捧出的，是一杯与她共饮的憧憬之美酒。俱往矣，长路在长期，今后，好好牵着她的手，一步步走下去，才是美好的真理、有益的思量。不论安定或动荡，都不要再让她伤心或害怕，这才是爱的表达。

“丽云……”

“嗯？”

“昨天你说的，我都会记住的。”

“我知道的。”

“……”

她扑哧一笑，“你多吃点。”

“唉。”

自己快乐豁然。她笑得清纯灿烂。秋天，就像一个金黄而丰收的起点。

集合上街的时间还没到，自己想先带着丽云去街上走走，散散心。像今天这种招呼记者的日子，日本人想来应该是不会对老百姓怎么样的。出门前，自己还在丽云脸上抹了些灰，丽云嘻嘻笑。自己说，跟着我，别走丢。她说，好的。自己问，一直让你躲在家里，是不是要闷坏了？她说，不会，你都说了，这里是家嘛，是家我就喜欢待在里面。自己笑笑，不再说什么。

偏僻的街道上还好，没什么日本人的氛围，若不是偶尔会在墙上看到弹孔，气息倒也真称得上宁静。但是到了宽阔的大街上，映入眼帘的就是密布的日本旗了。各家各户各商铺，门前窗旁都挂着飘扬的日本旗。旗帜迎风猎猎，人声嘈杂而低沉。站在这样的氛围里，自会色彩鲜明地感悟到，小街道里的那种宁静不是宁静，而是死气。当然，这里大街上的热烈也不是热烈，而是攒动的苟活。一队日本宪兵在人群里嚷嚷着跑过。丽云有些害怕，她抓紧了自己的胳膊。自己拍拍她的手，说，别怕，今天会是日本人对老百姓最客气的一天，你看，那里居然还有红气球。

商店看样子都已开始正式营业，但生意好像都很冷清。大街上的人越来越多，几条大街上都是如此。中国人多了，仿佛潜伏在大街上的恐惧气息也淡薄了许多。有人开始说笑了。汉奸开始给人签到，每家每户要在纸上按手印，以示出席。有人轻声地拿话骂汉奸，汉奸听到了，但是因为在场的中国人多，也不好发作，只能瞪瞪眼。这样一来，在场的中国人就都莫名高兴起来。一人说，恶棍也怕人多。另一人说，要是沈阳的百姓都有枪，日本畜生哪能占得了沈阳。这人说完，大家又都不敢说话了。

趁着日本人还没正式来，自己拉着丽云逛了几家店。丽云由害怕慢慢变得高兴了一些。在一家珠宝店里，丽云凝伫了片刻。自己知道，她是看到了和她以前用过的首饰一样的东西。她的眼里有隐隐的伤怀。这让自己的心里有些疼。过去属于她的一切，她都不再拥有了，还有什么能抚慰她的回忆？自己看着自己手上的那块表，想，这是她唯一不舍得忘却的。几缕幽惘缠住了自己的心。

丽云看着一枚漂亮的宝石戒指，眼里露出了喜欢的神情。老板问：喜欢吗？丽云摇头，说：不喜欢，就看看。老板说：两百块大洋，有钱就是你的。丽云转身便想走。自己拉着丽云的手，回头对老板说：东西留着，过两天，我来买。老板只冷冷地哼了一声。

经过了一间米铺，自己进去看了看。铺子里的东西品种和数量都不多，且只有杂粮和小米，没有大米。自己问伙计，伙计说：大米全让日本人拿走了，而且听说，以后日本人就要不许中国人吃大米了。自己看了看价格，说：明天你们铺子还开吗，我来买些小米。伙计说：开，当然开，我们也要挣钱吃饭活下去的呀。

日本人给老百姓发了宣传手册和问答集，要老百姓以后对外谈起东北之事，全得按照问答集上的标准回答来讲，不得乱说。汉奸在主席台上大声讲话，记者们在角落里数钞票，中国人在台下骂骂咧咧过嘴瘾，日本兵在到处叽里呱啦地恐吓人。现场乱糟糟的，就像老鼠开大会，就像村夫演话剧，想想，也挺可笑。台上的人可笑，台下的人也可笑。有种悲剧，就叫大家一起演戏。

日本人要拉一群中国人去和手捧鲜花的日本人合影，丽云不巧也被拉了过去。分手时，她很害怕，自己说，没事，我就在远处看着你。

自己远远地看着台上人群里的丽云，丽云也看到了自己，她安心地笑了。自己笑了笑，眼角的余光，却似乎在台下瞥见了一张认识的日本脸孔。自己转头去搜索，没错，是站在宪兵队里的渡边。他的目光，直直地远视着丽云。而丽云，此刻站在阳光里，安心地微笑着，恰如一枝素洁海棠。一股

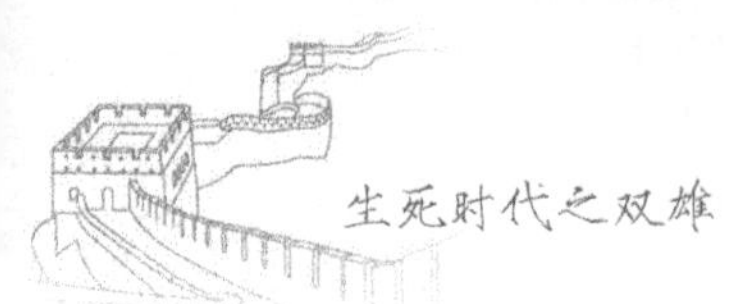

莫名的战栗从自己心头蹿过，顷刻隐入了幽深的黑暗里。自己去看丽云，她正望着自己。自己又去看渡边，渡边却已不知所踪。

自己再次想起了赤木和渡边关于女人的那番对话。他们当时所说的那个女人，真的会就是那个已经死了的漂亮女共产党吗？

一股强烈的不祥的预感，从自己心底升腾了起来。

十月十三日。

去买米时，在米铺的外面看见了一张招工启事，是米铺要招搬运的伙计。自己大喜过望。自己问卖米的伙计：你们招不招外地人？伙计谑笑着说：日本人都来了，我们还会不要外地人吗，今时不同往日啰。自己说：那太好了，你们招我吧，我有的是力气。说完，自己一手拎起了两大袋米，提起又放下了两次，面不红气不喘，像提小鸡似的。卖米的伙计不禁喝了声彩。他说：我看行，今天老板不在，你后天来，他肯定会要你，你一个人能顶两个人的活儿。自己说：好咧，多谢！

自己拎着买的一袋小米，兴奋地离开了米铺。走在宽阔的大街上，喜悦在心里左右晃荡。橙黄的阳光迎面照来，自己好像看见了好运的大门已微微敞开。晴朗的天空仿佛蕴含着无限的善意，只要你努力呼吸，一帆风顺便会从天堂中降落进你的身体，不需犹豫，不需担心。在这样一个烽烟四起的乱世里，不管是静居一隅还是颠沛流离，挣钱吃饭总是活下去的必需。现在自己找到了一个正经工作的机会，若真能被用，自己和丽云今后的生活定会稳妥许多。日本人侵略了中国，他们若真想坐江山，就应该会给老百姓留下生存的空间和道路。另外，说不定国军很快就会收复失地打回沈阳呢？希望总是有的。

昨天密布在大街上的日本旗，还在迎风飘扬。看着这满街旗帜的景象，自己总会想起那年东北易帜的时光。那一次，自己和丽云是走向了生离，这一次，自己和她最终又会走向何方？似乎东北的每一次大变局，都与自己的心愿背道而驰，那些满街飘扬的旗帜，总像是命运得胜后张牙舞爪的嘲弄。世界动荡不安，时代冷漠无情，流泪的祈祷与切肤的疼痛，都只像风中的飞沙一样缥缈和渺小。看着那些胜利的旗帜丑恶地飘扬，自己又突然不敢对上帝的垂怜抱太大的希望。惶惑是那么幽暗而隐蔽。这一次，自己是真的想和丽云白头到老，不管命运的海洋上还将掀起什么惊涛骇浪，自己都不想再离开丽云半步。自己爱她，想娶她，想全心全意地守护她，疼爱她一辈子，但是，命运这次真的会对自己网开一面吗？

“砰、砰、砰——”

枪声骤起，波澜翻涌。两个持枪的中国人，边战边跑进了这条大街。一队日本兵在后面紧追不舍。乒乒乓乓，枪战激烈，玻璃迸碎，人群尖叫，四散乱跑。刚才还一片安宁的街，顿时就乱成了一锅粥。自己紧紧地拎着米袋，混在人群里，随流奔逃。一个拿枪的中国人脑袋开了花，他倒下时，满街的日本旗随风狂舞。这个景象，莫名令自己毛骨悚然。

逃离了那条街，逃离了人群，跑进了一条小巷里。自己按捺着起伏的心跳，靠在墙上喘气，忽然，听到了一阵轻微的痛苦呻吟。循声找了两步，在一间敞开的破屋里，短毛坐在地上，一条腿鲜血淋漓。

短毛听见响动，立即举枪指向门口，看清了是自己，他才放松下来。

“我右腿中弹了。”他有气无力地说。

自己放下了米，走进去，从他的上衣上撕下了布条，紧紧地绑住了他的伤口，以控制出血。

“有个姓荣仓的日军大佐，今天要给樱花会社一批军火，我们想去劫了那辆车，结果却失败了。”

“你们的事，我不想知道。”自己说，“你必须要去医院，否则这样会死的。”

短毛笑笑，说：“去了医院才会死呢，枪伤，医院会报告日本人。龚汉江会治外伤，我只要回了废木料场，就会没事。”

“你这样怎么回去？”

“我还有两个兄弟，他们过一会儿应该会来这里找我。”

“他们是不是都穿着蓝上衣黑裤子？”

“是的。你怎么知道？”

“我看见他们中的一个已经死了，还有一个，估计现在也已经死了。”

“什么？！”

“你们以卵击石，这不是必然的结果吗？”

自己话音刚落，小巷口便传来了杂乱的日军声音。自己赶紧将米袋拎进了破屋，然后，关上了破屋的大门。屋里顿时一片昏暗，像浸入了泥潭

的囚笼。屋里很静，能听到短毛颤抖的喘息声。从窗缝里挤进来的光线照在短毛汗津津的脸上，他的脸因为疼痛而不断扭曲。像有一只看不见的手，在不停给他上刑。看着他，自己也害怕了起来，就好像这个昏暗的空间会把人绞碎。

日军开始在小巷里挨家挨户地砸门、搜查了。短毛拿出了一枚手榴弹，低声说:“你快跑吧，别被我连累。”

“你要干什么？”

“等这帮畜生一来，我就和他们同归于尽！”

“你疯了！”

“其实我早他妈的生无可恋了，要不也不会出来玩命，我早就等着上路的这一天了。”

“阎罗王今天不会收你。”自己说着，抢走了他的手榴弹和手枪，“你在这躲着，等我回来送你走。”自己一边说，一边用块抹布蒙了脸。说完，自己带着手榴弹和枪，便从破屋后面的一扇木窗里钻了出去。

自己绕到了小巷里的这队日军的后面，朝天放了一枪，然后，玩命地往另一条街上跑。每跑一段路，自己便会朝天放一枪，以告知日军位置。他妈的这是自己最不可理喻的一刻疯狂！自己应该不管短毛的！

日军在后面哇哇狂追，子弹在自己身后乱飞。那一刻，自己的头皮是完全发麻的，灵魂仿佛飞在身体之外。天知道，自己是怎样逃过了那片子弹雨！

自己跃上了屋顶，在屋顶上飞跑。屋檐上的瓦片被日军的子弹打得乒乓乱飞。尘土激扬，黄叶洒落。自己在一处高高的屋顶上趴了下来。日军的子弹在墙面上叭叭击响。自己拿出了手榴弹，准备拉开后丢向日军，但是，自己看到了自己手腕上的那块表，自己想起了丽云担惊受怕的眼神。自己的头脑一下子清醒了过来，灵魂仿佛飞回了身体。

自己将手榴弹丢在了日军队伍前面的空地上。日军看到手榴弹，一下子全吓得趴在了地上。自己就趁着这个空隙，往后撤退，爬下了屋顶，跳进了另一条巷子里。“嘭”的一声爆炸，自己跑得飞一样快。

回到了破屋里，自己迅速地用短毛的上衣将他的伤腿裹了个严严实实，这样一来可以防止路上流血，二来可以防止自己的衣服上又沾红。自己把枪往短毛手里一塞，然后，背起他就往外跑。

离开了昏暗如囚笼的破屋，跑上了去废木料场的道路。短毛在自己背上哽咽了起来，他说："我一直觉得你是个王八蛋，没想到你会舍命救我，这辈子，你是我恩人。"

"去你妈的，以后别再让我看见你，见你一次我倒霉一次。"自己笑骂。

"唉，好，以后我一定躲着你。"短毛吸吸鼻涕说。

将短毛送回了废木料场，自己告诉了他和龚汉江，上次自己听到的赤木和日军联合秘密运毒以及抓活体试验者的事情。短毛则告诉自己，昨天，有八个穿着黑衣服的上海人，去了已关闭的地下格斗场，说是要找小赤佬赵驹。

"上海人？"自己不禁纳闷。

"是的。他们的面相都挺凶，而且身手彪悍，我看着不像是什么好人，怕是你的仇家，就骗他们说，你去了湖南当共产党。"短毛说。

自己一笑，说："亏你想得出来，谢谢。"

龚汉江去给短毛做手术了。

自己洗了把脸，洗去了脸上抹布留下的异味，然后，又仔细看了看身上的衣裤，还好，都没有血迹。自己跟龚汉江道了声别，就走了。自己去破屋拿回了米袋，离开了小巷。

走在回小院的路上，自己的心，忽然隐隐作痛。青帮的人，终究还是来了，自己绝望地想。自己只祈望，他们能相信短毛的谎言，相信，小赤佬赵驹，已经去了湖南当共产党。

烈日血红，光芒灼心。

十月十四日。

外面下着大雨，雨水哗哗地响。天幕阴暗沉重，秋气凉寒入骨。自己站在小屋的门口，看着院中如帘的雨丝，心中纷扰纠缠。丽云走到了自己身边，伸手接了接外面的雨，说：再过不久，又要到冬天了。

自己握住了她被雨淋湿的手指，看着她的脸，想说，丽云，我们结婚吧，却又莫名说不出来。她的脸还是那么清纯而妩媚，她只要一笑，就会自然地流露出一种用泥灰也遮盖不住的美艳，只要不是个蠢男人，便都能看得到她这种生在骨子里的漂亮。而渡边，显然不是一个蠢男人。自己现在很后

悔，前天带丽云上了街。

丽云看自己呆呆地看着她，笑了。她说：看什么呢，我脸上有字吗？

自己说：有哇，你脸上写着，我是天下第一大美人。

她不禁失笑，看着自己，用拳头轻轻地打了自己两下，说：你好不要脸。

自己轻抓着她的小拳头，认真地说：不管你会变成什么样，在我心里，你都永远是这世上最纯洁、最美丽的天使，从认识你的开始，到我生命的结束，永远也不会改变，不会改变。

她紧紧地将头靠在了自己的胸膛前，自己搂着她，心怦怦直跳。自己想说：丽云，我爱你，永远爱你，却又莫名不敢承诺。总仿佛有隐蔽着的恐惧，在将自己从她身边拉开。纵然此刻她紧紧地依偎在自己怀里，也不敢真的相信，自己可以拥有她。因为，自己是个太危险的人。

为了救短毛而去引开日军并被日军死死追击的场景，昨晚整夜地在自己头脑里轰鸣，每一幕都像一块旋转的刀片，在自己的脑壳里令人恐怖地飞舞。起初想想，觉得是自己不走运、太冲动，深思一下，这又何尝不是自己人生状况的一个绝妙隐喻呢？致命的危机，总带着自己甩不掉的厄运，一桩接一桩地追击着自己，这么多年以来，自己似乎总是在不停地逃命、逃命、逃命。自己真的太累了，也太怕了。累得几乎不敢再去奢望幸福，怕得甚至不敢对深爱的女人说一句“我爱你”。假如这种不停被追杀的厄运是命运的一个诅咒，自己又能否逃出这诅咒的戏弄？

大雨依旧下个不停。

而丽云什么都不知道，她在自己眼里就像一张珍贵的白纸，自己不想在纸上画上一点点黑暗的色调，或血腥的味道。自己觉得，这就是男人爱女人的方式。哪怕这种爱，会包含着欺骗，包含着拒绝，会让她离理解她爱的男人的世界越来越远，自己也不后悔这样的选择。男人爱女人爱到至深的时候，就会把她当成一个孩子，除了想要给她呵护，给她疼爱，给她一个纯净而美好的世界，其他的什么都不会想要。自己爱丽云，自己只希望她能在两个人的爱情世界里，只看到阳光白云、蓝天暖意。

然而，外面的大雨，依旧下个不停。

下午，日本人忽然在外面猛烈地拍门，自己吓得心惊胆战。自己匆忙地在丽云脸上抹了把灰，然后，伞也顾不上打，就急忙跑去了院里开门。

四个日本人，带着两个汉奸，穿着雨衣，闯了进来。在汉奸的解释下，自己知道了，日本人因为昨天遇袭，所以今天要挨家挨户地搜查，看有没有伤员藏匿。不光是因为自己做贼心虚，更是因为这次带队的日本人，是十月三日那天来过的那个凶暴少尉，所以，自己在言语和行动上，更是多加了几倍的小心。

好不容易伺候到他们将要离开，这时，一个汉奸，为了拍马屁，拿起了屋里的一把伞，要去给少尉撑上。而这把伞，正是自己当年买给丽云的留情之物。

丽云忍了忍，还是一言不发地上去拦住了汉奸，拿回了这把伞。

汉奸愣了愣。少尉转回了身来。

“啪”，少尉响亮地打了丽云一个耳光。丽云被扇倒在了地上。自己的脑门“嗡”一下就热胀了起来。

“你在干什么！”少尉用日语向丽云大吼。汉奸赶紧翻译。

“这是我们的东西。”丽云捂着脸，怒目而视着日本人，安静而坚决地说。

不等汉奸翻译，自己赶紧扑上去护住了丽云。“误会！误会！”自己急忙用日语说。自己拿过了丽云手里的伞，跪在地上，毕恭毕敬地将伞捧送向了日本人。“对不起！对不起！她是一时没弄明白怎么回事，这只是一个小小的误会！太君息怒！”自己又慌又急地用日语说。

少尉一脚将伞踢飞。他怒瞪着眼睛，歇斯底里地向丽云大吼：“你，下贱的中国人，打你自己耳光！向我们道歉！”

汉奸连忙翻译。

自己忙“咚咚咚”地向日本人磕头，哀求：“太君息怒！太君息怒！”

少尉暴跳如雷，一把揪住了丽云的头发，将她拖到了大雨里。雨水寒凉如冰，滂沱如倾。丽云在汪洋恣肆的大雨里，像一艘即将被摧毁的纸船。自己冲进了大雨中，抱住了丽云。一股狂暴的怒火，在自己胸中爆炸。

“说，你是低贱的中国猪！”少尉吼叫着，一把又要抓向丽云的头发。自己一伸手，牢牢地抓住了少尉的手腕。

少尉一愣，挣扎了一下，没挣脱，又挣扎了一下，还是没挣脱。

“混蛋！”少尉怒吼了起来。

日本兵刷一下，全部举起了枪。三条步枪的枪口，指着自己的脑袋；一个汉奸的枪口，指着丽云的脑袋。

这是一场不可能胜利的反抗。自己的武功，快不过枪。

大雨如泣如诉，倾盆而落。

“太君，我们是低贱的猪，求您宽宏大量，不要和我们这种猪狗不如的东西计较。”自己放开了少尉的手腕，再次哀求。

少尉怒吼一声，拿过一条步枪，抡起枪托，就狠狠地朝自己的太阳穴上砸了过来。自己的脑袋像被猛地砸裂了开来，眼前一黑，便不禁松开了丽云，倒在了地上。

短暂的晕痛过去，眼前重新恢复清醒时，只见，丽云正用她娇弱的身躯护盖着自己，在为自己承受日本人残暴的殴打。粗暴的鞋跟、铁硬的枪托，此起彼伏地不停砸在丽云的身上，凌厉而凶悍，像铁锤击打着小鸟。丽云紧紧地抱着自己，保护着自己，不让日本人砸到自己一次，她哭泣着，在自己耳边说：对不起，对不起。

日本人拖开了丽云，少尉拔出了手枪。自己跪在地上，太阳穴上，顶着少尉的枪口。大雨冰冷而无情，瓢泼般无尽，日本人穿着雨衣站在雨里，像看不清脸的魔鬼，像没有心的屠夫。丽云惨哭着，在日本人面前跪了下来，用力地自扇着耳光。“啪、啪、啪”，耳光声像霹雳一样响亮而惊恐。“不许打，不许打！”自己青筋暴突地向丽云大声说。雨声哗哗，在雨线织成的模糊里，看不清哪里是泪，哪里是雨。丽云依旧在自扇耳光，整场大雨，就像一场哭泣。

自己冲过去，紧紧地抱住了丽云，不让她再伤害她自己一点点。日本人又围拢了过来。他们又开始了殴打。自己用身体死死地护盖着丽云，不让日本人再伤害她一点点。少尉的脚，踩在自己的后脑勺上。自己用双手将丽云的脑袋搂护着。自己笑着，在她耳边说：对不起，丽云，我让你失望了。

枪托疯狂地砸向自己的后背和脑袋。丽云，在自己怀里，颤抖地哭泣。

雨下得疯狂。

最后，少尉注意到了自己手腕上的那块表，才算是停止了取乐般的殴打。他将自己手腕上那块丽云送的表取了去，自己没有反抗，丽云也没有反抗。汉奸给少尉撑起了那把伞，他们哈哈笑着，扬长而去。

落叶在雨水里飘荡，雨珠砸在叶子上，叶子像没有生命的甲板，左右摇晃。

自己将丽云抱回了堂屋里。擦去了丽云额上的血珠，自己攥着毛巾，难过得不敢看她的眼睛。她却伸出手来，摸了摸自己脖子上的伤口，难过地说：对不起，我不该去拦着他们，真的对不起。自己的心一下子像被撕得更痛。自己伸出手，想触摸一下她被打得红通通的脸，手却僵在半空，无法再靠近她。自己低下头，说：该说对不起的是我，丽云，我是个窝囊废，真的、真的对不起。她却握住了自己的手，将自己的手贴在了她冰凉的脸颊上。自己摸到了她滚烫滑落的泪珠。她说：我们说这些干什么呢，我们现在，不还是好好地在一起吗，这样就足够啦。她尽量开心地笑笑。自己不能面对她。

雨势小了许多，但仍淅淅沥沥地冰凉着天地。各自换了衣服，又抹了些跌打酒，时间就在无言而沉闷的悲哀里走了过去。天黑了下来，像一片无边无际的浮动的海，雨丝从海水里掉落。苦涩的味道，咸痛的心绪，像在空旷的空气里蔓延。如藤蔓的生长，看不见的绝望和沮丧，几乎填满了自己的整个胸腔。对丽云的巨大的愧疚，压得自己喘不过气来。自己想宰了那个日本少尉。

自己将丽云抱放在木榻上，然后要去做晚饭。丽云笑着说，我脚又没崴，不用你抱来抱去的。自己低着头，说，让我服侍你吧，这样，我心里好受些。丽云愣了愣，说，你说什么呢，你又没做错什么。自己狠狠给了自己一耳光，说，我就是个窝囊废，我说过要保护你，结果却只是个窝囊废！我对不起你！

丽云紧紧拉住了自己的手，她摇着头，看着自己，说：你不要这样说自己，不要这样，我知道你忍让是对的，我们不该为了一点小事激怒日本人，要不然我们现在可能都已经死了，我懂的，我不许你这样骂自己，你不是窝囊废，不是。

丽云的眼里含起了痛苦的泪光。

愧疚却更剧烈而深刻地在自己胸中翻腾了起来，看着她痴痴而深爱的眼神，自己心如刀割。自己吻了吻她的手，然后转身去了厨房。

微小的火星在灶膛里四散飞起，又转瞬即灭。自己的思想也在明暗之间闪烁不停。自己想给丽云一些安慰，实际上却是连自己也安慰不了。除了自责和愧疚，自己没有什么可以捧出来给丽云看。而那些自责和愧疚，又只会令丽云感觉难过。自己真的是个窝囊废。

菜刀黯淡无光地躺在案板上，自己莫名不敢触目那条锋利的刀刃。对于压迫和欺凌，自己从未这样绝望地感觉到无能为力。面对侵略者的暴力，自己反抗，只会危及丽云，不反抗，又只能看着丽云挨打，这个两难的谜题究竟该怎样解？丽云只是想保护一把她很珍惜的伞，就遭此欺凌，日本人这样无法无天，往后在沈阳的日子可怎么往下过？一桩桩一件件，都是让自己无可选择又无可奈何的难题。

而丽云的情深义重，又令自己悲从中来。自己不仅什么也给不了她，而且，竟然还没有能力保护她，自己这么个废物，哪里还配被她爱？自己真的很难受。想起丽云护盖着自己被日本人暴打的场面，想起丽云强装笑颜要自己别沮丧别自责的模样，自己的心里就会流血。自己要怎样才能配得上丽云的爱？自己应该要怎样来好好爱她？对于爱，自己真的懂得太少。

吃晚饭时，自己不再去触碰白天的事情。自己怕，自己知道她也怕。自己讲笑话，逗她开心。丽云看上去很快乐。

晚上，自己给丽云洗了一次脚。丽云开始不愿意，但自己还是去打了热水来，表示想给她洗一次脚，她想了想，最后点了点头。

自己轻轻地给她洗着脚，就怕用力了会弄疼她。把她的脚焐在热水里时，自己还是忍不住，又跟她说了一句：丽云，真的对不起。

她顿了顿，轻声问：是不是因为这样，你才要给我洗脚？

自己顿了顿，说：要是那帮畜生真的开枪，我一定会和他们拼命的，真的。

她明媚地笑了笑，说：我知道的，你是不会真让他们欺负我的。

自己说：我只是想，我们只要还活着，就好，没到生死关头，不可鱼死网破。

她点点头，说：嗯，我知道的。

自己就笑笑，没再说什么，也不敢看她。

气氛静静的。

她说：其实人生，最美好的就是活着，只有活着，才能看见阳光和鲜花，只有活着，才能记住并想念那些自己爱的人和事，也只有活着，才能和自己喜欢的人在一起，朝朝暮暮，永不分离。

自己说：丽云，谢谢你，这辈子对我这样好。

她倩笑着说：我也要谢谢你呀，还给我洗脚呢。

自己忍俊不禁，说：你要是愿意，我可以给你洗一辈子啊。

丽云的脚小小的，皮肤雪白，趾甲像透明的贝壳般整洁又可爱。轻轻擦拭着她圆润的脚跟，自己忽然心慌意乱了起来。丽云羞涩地将脚缩了回去。

自己的脑袋里突然响了一下。自己真是被赎罪的念头给一时蒙住了，竟然忘记了，在中国传统里，女人的脚，是男人的禁区。

十月十五日。

天气晴朗，阳光普照。

风静无声，树叶缓慢地降落。秋日的太阳像低语的天神，用微笑的光芒俯瞰着万丈红尘。

去了一趟米铺，经老板面试，自己被录用了。老板说，你后天开始来干活吧。自己激动得向老板鞠了一躬。

走在街上，听老百姓说，国联可能很快就要派调查团来东北了，调查团只要查清了事变的真相和东北的真实现状，国联应该很快就会迫使日本从东北撤军。

经过了那家珠宝店，自己走了进去，一看，丽云喜欢的那枚宝石戒指还在。自己掏出了十块大洋，放在店里的柜台上，对老板说：这戒指我订下了，明天就来付钱，你不许给别人。老板说：要两百块大洋！自己说：我知道。老板立即满脸堆笑，赶紧收下了那十块大洋，说：好，好，这戒指明天我就给您包装好，欢迎老板您有空常来。

回了小院，丽云一脸喜悦，她告诉自己，皮货店原来那个老板的表姐裘姨，刚刚来过了。裘姨接下了皮货店，准备要重新开张，她来问丽云，还愿不愿意回去上班，丽云答应了，说好了过几天便去。自己也告诉了丽云自己已找到工作的事，还告诉了她老百姓说的国联调查团的事。自己和她都觉得特别开心。两个人的工作一下子就都有了着落，而国际社会也可能要来收拾日本人了，好事真是接二连三。当然，自己还没有告诉丽云，自己准备，明

天向她求婚。

自己真的有种临近了幸福的感觉。

生活仿佛一下子就让人看到了芬芳的曙光。火热的憧憬和希望，像怒放的花朵，姹紫嫣红，鲜艳满园。

傍晚，自己带丽云去了一座废弃的水泥高楼的楼顶，坐在这个楼顶上，能看到最美的日落。这里没有日本人，没有战争，远离地面，高拔空旷，除了金红色无边无际的夕阳，就是清新而自由自在的空气。丽云依偎在自己的肩膀上，伸手在光亮里捕捉太阳，像个顽皮的孩子。她快乐地微笑着。自己握住了她的手，在心里说：丽云，我爱你。

夕阳娇美无限，长风清凉安谧。

这一刻，是永恒。

十月十六日。

趁着丽云不注意，自己去柴房的暗格里取了两百块大洋出来，然后，远远地跟丽云说了一声“我出去一下，很快回来”，就揣着钱跑出了小院去。待会儿，自己想给她一个惊喜。

珠宝店老板没有食言，果然留着戒指，且已包装得非常精美。自己验完货，将戒指放回了包装盒里，然后，便将余下的一百九十块大洋付给了老板。老板没有加价。自己谢了谢老板，然后，欢天喜地地离开了珠宝店。

晴空万里。摸着放在衣兜里的戒指盒子，自己幸福地想：今生有了丽云，我死而无憾了。

自己还从来没有真的对丽云说过“我爱你”这三个字呢，待会儿，自己一定要大声地对她说：丽云，我爱你，嫁给我吧！

自己欢天喜地地走着，一路傻笑。

阳光明媚。

到了一条偏僻的巷子里。

几个黑衣人，拦住了自己的去路。回头一看，自己的退路，也被几个黑衣人阻住了。细细一数，前后两路黑衣人，加起来刚好是八个。

自己的脑袋，嗡一下，炸了。

如果没猜错，他们，就是青帮的杀手。

一个光头黑衣人，掏出了那张多年前的通缉令。他很利索地将手中的通缉令抖了两下，然后，阴森地笑了笑，问："赵驹，你还认得这张通缉令吗？"

"抱歉，几位大爷，你们一定是认错人了，我叫王恭，只是米铺里的一个小伙计。"

光头冷冷一笑，"真是出人意料，没想到你是这么幽默的人。"光头温柔地将通缉令撕成了两条长片，然后一松手，让它们慢悠悠地轻轻飘落在了地上。他阴森森地咧嘴一笑，说："那要不这样吧，为了避免误会，我们一起去见一见那个和你住在一起的女人，问问她，你到底叫什么。"

"一人做事一人当，你们不要伤害她！"

光头笑笑，说："真遗憾，你要是能死撑到底，说不定，我们还真的是会被你给骗过去的哦。"光头冷笑着调侃道。一阵肃杀的秋风卷着落叶扫过，地上的通缉令缩成了一团。光头在风中收起了阴森的笑，双手从腰间拔出了两把雪亮的匕首，摆出了架势，正色道："青帮八头鹰，奉杜老板之命，来报帮中兄弟徐冷被杀之仇。"话音一落，其余的黑衣人，也都纷纷拔出了匕首。一人两把，八人，十六把。匕首在阳光下熠熠生辉，锋刃，在冷风中凛若冰霜。

"沈阳现在是日本人的地盘，你们竟敢在这里恣意杀人、炫耀武力，看日本人到时会怎样追捕你们！"

"放心，我们不会惊动日本人，你没发现吗，我们特意没用枪。你会死得无声无息的，就像一片落下的叶子那样。"光头冷笑着说。

"关东军侵略中国，你们既然这样厉害，为什么不去对付日本人，而偏偏要咬着我这个中国人不放！"

"蒋介石和张学良都不打日本人，保家卫国关我们屁事。我们是帮会，只管杀人放火，要钱，要女人。"

"民族败类！"

"你真的很幽默，要不是待会儿还得赶时间去杀你的女人，我倒真想坐下来，再看你多演一会儿喜剧。"

"我说了不要伤害她！！她是无辜的！！"

"哦，你忘了吗——"光头扭了扭脖子，然后，哈哈大笑，"我们，是青帮！"

话音落，刀光起。光头飞扑而来。其余黑衣人，也一起蜂拥而上。

青帮八头鹰，八人十六刀，四攻则四守，两袭上盘两袭下盘，一人伤而一人补，刀锋如织，密密匝匝，变化多端，防不胜防，八人一体，宛如死亡的铜墙铁壁。

自己全身的皮肤都已被划伤流血，而他们还未被自己伤到一根毫毛。火辣辣的疼痛在自己身体的表面乱窜，看着眼前身后的雪光乱舞，自己感到了死神掌心的温度。一把匕首向自己的衣兜处刺去，那里有自己买给丽云的戒指。自己慌忙用手一挡，“刷”一下，自己的手被割伤，血流不止。

自己奋力跳出了八人围成的圈子。想要逃跑，一想不行，跑得了和尚跑不了庙，若现在回去带丽云一起跑，只会将杀手们引向小院，若现在自己单独往别处跑，则杀手们也可能会直接去抓丽云。最好的办法，只能是在这里就地解决这场厮杀，而且，自己必须不能死。

一户人家的围墙上，平搭着一根晾衣服的竹竿。八名杀手挥舞着匕首，再次扑来。自己一跃身，从围墙上，抽下了那根竹竿来。这根竹竿，不短不长，刚好能在巷子里用。

自己和八头鹰，又厮杀在了一起。

刀光飞舞，竿影飘忽。精短锋利的匕首，在这八名杀手的手中被使用得异常灵活，正握和反握的转换有时快得根本无法用眼睛来辨认。往往是，匕首的刀尖从这个方向往那个方向划过，自己才闪开，刀尖却已在杀手手中掉转了方向，又回马枪似的刺来，让人避无可避。自己用快用猛，他们更快更猛，且人多势众。自己只能用竹竿，被动地抵挡着进攻。

“当当啷啷”，竹竿和匕首不停地激烈碰撞着，自己有时也能打到他们的脑袋，但这毫无用处。竹竿毕竟温柔，伤得了人，却杀不死人，而眼下，自己最需要的，却是对手的尽快死亡。这不是一场比武游戏，而是生死杀戮。自己以一对八，时间拖得越久，自己的体力消耗就越大，形势对自己就越不利。八头鹰又像一个铁圈一样，收紧了起来。自己被压迫得快要喘不过气来了。

光头正面跃起，凶猛地一刀劈下，“咔嚓”，自己手中的竹竿，被砍成了两段。自己被狠狠踹倒在地。光头暂时停了手，其他人也停了下来。

光头干笑了两声，吐了口唾沫，说：“唉，看来徐冷那小子，也是只纸扎的老虎，还以为他是死在多厉害的人手上，原来不过如此。”众杀手也纷纷露笑。

自己又被光头狠狠踢了两脚。光头笑呵呵地说：“喂，小赤佬，听说你是东北拳王，这名号是你自己吹出来的吧？你就是用这名号，在东北混吃混喝混女人的吧？你还真是浪得虚名，够不要脸的。”光头笑得尽兴，“不过话说回来，你的女人倒是长得真漂亮，你要是现在给我磕磕头求求我，我说不定会大发慈悲，在杀了你以后，不杀她。——我们八兄弟可以把她卖到上海百乐门去，让她当舞女，然后，让她天天给你这死鬼戴一摞绿帽，你说好不好？哈哈哈哈——”光头狂笑。众杀手也大笑不已。

自己抹掉了额头和眉毛上的血，说：“其实，你们八个人，每个人的武功都不如徐冷，跟徐冷比，你们的速度，简直慢得像蜗牛。”

光头的笑戛然而止。

自己笑了笑，说：“你猜怎么着，虽然我现在看起来全身血糊糊的，但是，你们统统都只是割伤了我的皮肤而已，没有一刀是入肉的。”

众杀手默然。光头后退了一步。

自己继续说：“也就是说，其实我和你们的格斗，现在才刚刚开始而已。另外，你个光头王八，我要谢谢你，帮我把竹竿砍出了尖角来。”

自己话音未落，便已是将自己手中的一截断竹，猛地飞投向了离自己最近的一个杀手的喉咙。尖锐的断竹，瞬间穿透了这个杀手的喉咙，鲜血喷涌而出。自己就地打滚上前，一下子，就拿到了这个杀手手中的两把匕首。

光头如梦初醒，勃然大怒。“把他剁成肉酱！”光头怒吼着命令道。

自己再次杀入包围之中。“当当咣咣”，铁器与铁器的摩擦和碰撞，迸出了刺耳的尖叫与绚烂的火花。秋风呼呼地响动，黄叶在空中凌乱地飘舞。血花四溅，天地的温度在滚热和冰冷间模糊，生死的感觉在杀人与被杀间凝固。自己拼命地杀，拼命地杀，忘记了害怕，忘记了留恋，只求可以在自己死之前，先杀光这群魔鬼。不然，剩下丽云一人怎么办？

又一个杀手，被自己割断了喉咙。地上掉落的匕首，越来越多。自己以匕首代替拳头，以拳法使用匕首，获得了出人意料的好效果。自己身上虽也多处中刀，透肉及骨，但都非即刻危及性命之伤。八头鹰的阵形，已残破不堪。

只剩下四个杀手了，光头的眼睛血红着。四人再次扑来，自己飞奔迎上。一刀从自己眼前割过，自己的双眼差点被划瞎。自己的大腿忽然被一把匕首深深刺中，痛入骨髓，自己一咬牙，回手一刀，砍下了这名杀手的手掌。又一名杀手跃身扑来，自己直接将手中的一把匕首掷出，正中其心口。自己拔下了自己大腿上的匕首，回身又一刀，刺在了又一名杀手的后心窝。血光猩红，刀光惨白，秋天的太阳是那么鲜艳，照得人都睁不开眼。金黄的叶子掉落在暗红的血泊里，像被染了色，像被加了重，不再清洁，不再轻盈，只像搁浅后迅速被铁锈吞噬的船。浅蓝的天空下，你死我活的杀戮，像一场永恒的隐喻。空荡荡的风，呜呜地响动。

只剩下光头一人了。光头阴惨惨地笑笑，说："赵驹，你以为杀了我们，你的厄运就结束了吗？你还记得吗，你还杀了七星帮的两个长老！连我们都能查明徐冷之死的真相，你以为七星帮的人会放过你吗？！你必死无疑！"

"杀过了几个仙，也就不在乎再多杀一个佛了。"自己冷冷地说。

光头手中的两把匕首，化成了两团锐利而雪亮的光，这光像滴着血的火球，滚滚而来。自己举刀相迎。

一番恶战之后，终于，自己的两把匕首，都刺入了光头的胸口。光头倒在血泊中，咳嗽了一声，说："是我太自信，刚才，我们应该先去捉你的女人。"

"我说过了，不要伤害她，她是无辜的。"

"她是无辜的，但是，谁让她是你的女人呢。生在这个时代，手段比道理重要。"光头又咳嗽了一声，然后，吐出了两大口血来。他笑了笑，断了气。

自己又检查了一遍，八个杀手，的确都已彻底地死了。一阵虚脱般的晕眩袭来，自己差点也倒在了地上。自己摸了摸自己的衣兜，那枚戒指还在。自己捡起了那两片被撕开了的通缉令，自己的眼里，突然奔出了热泪。

"老天爷，你终究还是没有放过我。"自己哭着，笑着，说。

去了废木料场，自己请龚汉江为自己处理了一下全身的伤口。龚汉江问，谁干的？自己说，老仇家。龚汉江说，你伤得不轻。自己说，请帮我包得隐蔽一点，我要穿上衣服以后，让人看不出来我受了伤。龚汉江点点头。

用温酒服下了白药。龚汉江为自己包扎好了全身的伤口。他打来了一盆水，又拿来了一套干净的衣服，然后，走了出去。

自己将全身的血迹擦洗干净后，换上了新的干净衣裤。自己将血衣兜里的十块大洋和戒指盒子都取了出来。戒指盒子的表面也染上了一些血迹，自己拿湿毛巾仔细地擦拭，小心地清洁。弄了一会儿，才终于将戒指盒子的表面清理干净了，恢复成了崭新时的模样。轻轻打开盒子，戒指，就安静地躺在盒子里，漂亮得没有一丝瑕疵，璀璨得让人充满美妙遐想。这一切，原本是多美好哇。而现在，都结束了。自己合上了盒子。

自己洗干净了大洋，放在了棚屋里的桌子上。然后，自己又擦洗干净了自己鞋底的血迹。自己又漱了漱口，因为刚才用酒服过了白药，若嘴里酒味太浓，会被丽云察觉异样。自己照了照镜子，自己的脸上和手上有瞒不掉的伤口，但是，自己觉得，这种程度的小谎，是不难撒的。

自己握着戒指盒子，心里又一阵剧痛。自己将盒子放进了新的衣兜里。十块大洋自己打算留给龚汉江，毕竟，又治伤又拿衣服的，麻烦人家了。

走出棚屋，阳光有些刺眼。又一阵晕眩袭来，自己几乎跌倒，但自己没有跌倒。龚汉江拿来了火柴，自己烧掉了那两片撕开的通缉令。淡淡的火光里，陈旧的通缉令，萎缩着变成了灰烬，像一个假死后又随时会复活的噩梦，像一个遁入了无形又依旧无处不在的魔怪。形体的消亡总和存在一样空幻，厄运的不灭就像灵魂一样永恒。龚汉江什么也没有问。

自己向龚汉江，道了谢，道了告辞。

走在回小院的路上，天旋地转的眩晕不停袭来，像一群群来回飞舞的乌鸦，像一把把来回拉动的锯子。阳光照在眼睛里，让人感觉很恶心。自己难受得想要跪下来，却又十分明白，这种难受并非来自于肉体的失血和痛楚，所以，一切身体的动作都无法减轻灵魂的痛苦。自己只能走，不停地走，不哭也不笑，任内心的崩溃将自己活着的意识吞噬。那眩晕，简直像刀割似的让人疼痛难抑。自己在往哪儿走？接下来该怎么办？谁能给自己一个答案。也许，自己真的会拖累丽云，也许，自己应该要离开丽云。自己心如刀割，想哭却哭不出来，胸口里像在被蛇咬。

回到小院时，已是下午一点多。丽云一直在焦急地等待着自己，连饭也没吃，而自己给予她的，却是又一个谎言。自己说，我碰上了几个喝醉的日本兵，莫名其妙要抢我身上的衣服，我脸上挨了几拳，手也不小心割开了，

最后就把衣服裤子都给了他们，之后，我去旧衣店重新买了这一身穿的，所以，回来晚了。丽云可能不太会相信这个故事，但是，她应该更不会相信，那个她爱的赵驹，会真的一次又一次地骗她。虽然，很多时候，自己对她的欺骗，都是为了保护她，但是，后来，自己才明白，这终究是一种怯懦，是对爱和现实的怯懦。自己不敢将纸船放进河里，是因为，自己将太多的东西，看成了纸船。

丽云问：你真的没事吗？

自己说：真的，我没事。

她问得犹豫不决，自己答得斩钉截铁。这里面是否包含着一种残酷，自己不敢认真去触摸。一触摸，怕就会提前崩溃。青帮的再次出现，真的是个必然。自己不以为这是命运突然的捉弄，自己只认为，这是从来就黑暗的命运，在重新让它的奴隶认识它的坚如磐石和威力无穷。帮会仇杀，一旦沾上，就不该再有金盆洗手的美梦。而丽云，只要在自己的身边，毫无疑问，就会有遭遇危险的可能。只要敌人们把她当成了赵驹的女人，她，就会成为一件无辜的牺牲品。仇杀的牺牲品，爱情的牺牲品。亡命天涯应该是自己的命运，而不是她的命运，自己爱她，就不应该连累她。自己要她好好地活着，就应该将她推出自己的世界。自己爱她，就应该不要再被她爱。

丽云小口小口地吃着饭，眼里沉默的忐忑，像泪珠一样晶亮。刺痛的惶惑在自己内心层峦叠嶂，人生的矛盾在选择面前迷雾重重。自己想让丽云拥有快乐和幸福，结果却只是在让她品尝不安和委屈，这种愿望和现实的天壤之别，是否正说明了自己和她的爱情如梦幻泡影？自己不告诉她今天发生的事情，是怕她会不肯和自己分开；自己想要和她分开，是怕她会因为自己而受到伤害。然而，自己这样做，究竟是在保护她还是在伤害她？目的和结果之间的距离，往往是一场肝肠寸断的悲泣。自己迷失在了抉择的迷宫里。

自己笑着说：明天我就要去米铺干活了，以后，我们缺什么也不会缺米了。这话一落定，自己内心蓦然霜花满地。自己的本意是想安抚丽云，然而，此时此境，这安抚多像是脱口而出的嘲讽。自己还没想好，要用什么借口，才能好好地离开丽云；自己又实在不忍心看着丽云此刻郁郁寡欢地担忧。自己想让丽云依旧开开心心的。可是，这不是一件自相矛盾又绝望不堪的事情吗？自己都已经要准备和丽云分开了，哄她这一时的开心，又有什么用？——又或者，其实，是自己的决定，连自己都还不能接受。自己还无法接受，那些好不容易才被自己和丽云拥抱住的幸福与希望，都还没来得及一一实现，便即将要被命运推向结束的悬崖。也许，自己是真的仍在憧憬：明天我就要去米铺干活了，以后，我们缺什么也不会缺米了。一切已经全都不同，而自己还在假装依旧。蔚蓝的天空已在自己心中沾满了血，且四分五裂，自己却还错误地在回首凝望昨天，以为今天的一切全是错觉。——自己企图要欺骗的，分明不只是丽云，还有自己。自己真的想哭。

自己又哄了一会儿丽云，让她放下了她的聪明和直觉，放下了真实的担忧和不安。她说：那我明天早上也去皮货店看看，看有没有什么能帮上忙的。自己说：行，那明天早上我送你去。她说：嗯。

她笑了笑，像昨天一样好看。

时间过得很快，很快就到了傍晚。自己离开丽云，独自站在小院的角落里悲哀发呆。夕阳的光暖融融的，照在人的身上，就像天父的手在抚摸你的伤口。如果不够清醒，便会以为自己身上的伤口真的在神奇般愈合，便会以为这个世界真的像有神般仁慈而美好。而所谓的清醒，又只不过是几把看不见的刀，锋利，且充满血腥。人生或许本就如此，要么在幻梦里跌落悬崖，要么在清醒中忍受痛苦。摸着兜里的戒指盒子，自己的手僵硬而尴尬。表面上看起来，这枚求婚戒指是握在自己的手里，要不要把它拿出来，全由自己决定。然而实际上，人做每一个决定，都必须要考虑这个决定所带来的结果，人实际上是在被预料中的结果操纵着每一个开始时的决定。自己都已经知道了丽云以后和自己在一起会有危险，自己又怎么还能把这枚戒指拿出来求婚？所以，归根到底，命运的选择权，不在人自己的手里。那些看不见的逻辑，摸不着的牵绊，就是命运的实体。人，只是环境中一个无奈的存在。人生总是充满了失之交臂的惋惜与错愕，其实这一次，自己真的只差一步，就能走上幸福的道路。但是可惜，上天没有祝福自己。跟东北易帜那年一样，就在自己和丽云的幸福即将要瓜熟蒂落的时刻，命运露出了它青面獠牙的本相。痴爱再浓，也敌不过命运紧追不舍的通缉；厮守一生，是一个多么单纯而永远无法抵达的彼岸。也许，都是自己的错；也许，是乱世的捉弄；也许，这就叫宿命。

“我们生生世世不分离。”

“嗯，生生世世不分离。”

撕心裂肺的痛，像海潮般将自己淹没。

天与地，都冷得像冰。

十月十七日。

风萧索而寒硬，呜呜的声音，像有看不见的石块在空气中摩擦、碎开。黄叶泛着红，在风里旋转、飘零，地上的叶片，像秋的坟墓。这坟墓微小而美丽，哀凉又醒目。

早上，自己和丽云就要一起出门了。自己想：以后，怕是没有机会再一起回来了。自己忍不住就紧紧抱住了丽云，抱得深浓而沉默。丽云觉得异样，轻声问：“怎么了？”自己抱着她，在她额上吻了吻，说：“丽云，你要记住，你只有过得平平安安、开开心心的，我才有勇气在这肮脏的世上活下去。”她温柔地说：“我也是。”自己最后紧紧地抱了抱她，忍住了泪水，然后，放开了她。自己笑着，说：“走吧，我送你去皮货店。要是店还没开，我就先带你去逛会儿街，然后我再去米铺。”她开心地点头，说：“嗯，好。”

皮货店开了，自己没能和丽云最后再逛一次街。一名中年妇女正在店里忙活，丽云说，这就是裘姨。自己便放开了丽云的手，微笑着对她说：“那你去吧，小心别累着。照顾好自己。”她说：“知道啦。”她背向着皮货店，一边倒退着走，一边灿烂地笑着说：“我中午回家去做饭，等你回来吃。”自己说：“好。”她挥挥手，开心地说：“中午见。”自己也挥挥手，说：“丽云，再见。”

自己也倒退着走，直到看着丽云走进了皮货店。自己泪眼模糊，蓦然哽咽。

转过身，自己迎风狂奔。风将沙吹进了自己的眼，自己泪如雨下。天和地大得无边无际，而这世间，却再不会有自己的一个家。此生最爱，就此人各天涯。苍天，你为何对人如此无情！

唯有风，依旧在呜呜作响。秋，凋谢了万丈红尘。

自己擦干了眼泪，回了趟小院，给丽云劈好了许多许多的柴。然后，又打好了几桶水。接着，将这段时间里一直放在堂屋中的木榻搬回了丽云的睡屋里。最后，把屋里院里的每个角落都打扫收拾了一遍。做完这一切后，自己躯壳里空荡荡的，像失落了整个生命。说不出哭不出的难受，在自己全身的血管里膨胀。自己想：以后，就再没机会为丽云做什么了。屋里院里静得只剩风声，这种静，像消亡了一切的空寂，像将灵魂剥离了世界的哀泣。这是临别的哀悼，这哀悼，令人痛不欲生。

自己又看了看那盒丽云的断发，黑亮柔滑，就像刚剪断时一样。自己想带着丽云的断发离开，好歹以后能让自己有个念想，可是，自己又知道不能这样做。自己不能让丽云明白，自己心里爱着她。因为那样，只会害了她。自己关上了盒盖，泪珠，猛然掉下。

自己抹去了眼泪，怆然一笑，转身，便要走了。

可是，突然，院门响了一下。

丽云回来了。

她开了门。

四目相对，她有些惊讶。

“咦，你怎么不在米铺，这么早就回来啦？”

“丽云……我要走了。”

“什么？”

“我……要离开了。”

“——你说什么？”

丽云惊讶得瞪大了眼睛。

“当初，我就是想要保护你，所以才来的这里，现在，外面也安定下来了，我想……我也是时候该离开这里了。”

一阵沉默。丽云的眼圈红了，她的嘴唇哆嗦了起来。

她跑到了自己的面前。自己的手臂，被她紧紧地抓住着。“到底发生了什么？到底发生了什么！”她惨白地悲问。

自己轻轻推开了她。“没发生什么。就是……我该走了。”自己也说不出话来，不能面对她。

她啜泣了起来。“你这段时间，和我在一起，就只是为了保护我？”

“是的。”自己强制着平静地说。

她哭着，摇着头，问：“那你为什么要保护我？”

“因为，你以前施舍过我，我要报恩。”

“难道从开始到现在，你为我所做的一切，都仅仅只是因为我施舍过你，

你要报恩？”

“是的。”

“不！你骗人！你究竟为什么要这样？为什么要这样！！”

丽云失声痛哭。

她悲泣着，紧紧抱住了自己。自己想再次推开她，眼泪却差点掉了出来。

万箭穿心的痛。

她可怜地颤抖着，“你说过再也不会离开我的，你说过再也不会离开我的呀！！为什么突然就变成了这样，为什么呀？！赵驹，我爱你，真的好爱好爱你，我想一辈子和你在一起，你为什么要这样啊——”

自己眼前的世界，变得破碎而血红。

“丽云，我配不上你，真的，配不上你。从我们相遇的第一天起，命运就已经决定了我和你之间的距离，你是一个千金大小姐，而我，只是一个卑贱的臭乞丐——”

她拼命地摇着头，哭着说：“我早就不是什么大小姐了，你也已经不是乞丐，你难道不明白吗，是命运在眷顾我们，才最终让我们一步一步相聚在了这个地方，这个普通老百姓生存的小院子里。我们之间再没有阶级的差别，我们是平等的男女。失去一切我都不觉得绝望，富贵荣华对我而言无半分可喜，只要能和你在一起，就算让我去行乞，我也觉得幸福无比。求求你，不要这样对我——”

萧萧风鸣，呜呼哀哭。

自己还是推开了丽云。

“丽云，其实，我没你想得那么好。我少年时，就是个浪荡子，不学无术，吃喝嫖赌。我曾连续一个月住在妓院里，每日与不同的妓女厮混狎戏，我的灵魂和身体里，都烙满了洗不掉的污渍；我曾把父亲辛苦供我上学的钱，一次全掷在赌桌上，与狐朋狗友赌得昏天黑地，我是个只顾自己享乐却不念及亲人难受的不孝之子；我杀过许多许多的人，我的双手沾满了血腥，这种血腥浸在我的骨头里，我就算洗一辈子，也洗不淡半分身上的恐怖。我不仅是个卑贱的乞丐，更是一个肮脏的嫖客、无耻的赌徒、可怕的杀人犯。我的灵魂和人生是如此劣迹斑斑又污浊不堪，一切的一切，都是我欺骗了你，你错信了我——对不起——”

“我不在乎，我不在乎——你说的这一切，我都不在乎！！我不在乎你以前有过多少女人，我不在乎你曾经品行有多坏，我不在乎你究竟杀过多少人，我不在乎你到底有没有骗我！！我爱你，没有条件没有要求，只想和你在一起，一辈子能看见你，和你风餐露宿也好，亡命天涯也好，我都不在乎！！假如没有你，我的生命将失去一切意义——因为我爱你——”

丽云泪雨滂沱。

撕心裂肺的沉默。

“……可是，那些，我都在乎。我在乎，我配不上你。丽云，对不起——”自己，轻轻地说。

丽云哭得眼睛鲜红鲜红。

“……忘了我吧……以后，要照顾好自己。一切，都是我对不起你。”

说完，自己绕过丽云，走出了屋子，走出了小院。

自己没有回头。

自己听到，身后，传来了丽云肝肠寸断的一声哀号。

天地苍茫，秋风无情。

自己的泪，奔涌而出。

自己，淡淡地问了天一句：你，为什么要这样折磨人？

秋叶带着血红在光里纷飞，碎裂的枯萎，锐利地切割着这个没有生命的世界。

自己回到了废祠堂里，穿回了乞丐的衣服。

坐在冰冷的地上，自己渴望变成一座冰冷的雕像。自己憎恶自己的生命，憎恨自己的活着，因为自己的有感觉的生命，除了会连绵不断地给自己的灵魂带来生不如死的悲痛以外，几乎一无所善。怨天尤人固然全是枉然，奋力抗争却也尽属徒劳。人在命运的魔掌中，只能眼看着厄运的肆虐，静等着痛苦将自己活着的感觉吞灭。滚烫的泪水依旧在自己脸上汪洋恣肆，但是，自己知道这毫无意义。哭能改变什么？哭连减轻哭本身的痛都做不到！可是，不哭也同样毫无意义。是的，自己的活着，真的已经毫无意义。不管自己做什么、想什么，悲痛，都已是注定的宿命。哭也好，笑也好，一切只是悲剧散场后的疯癫。对如今的自己而言，就连生与死的差别，也都已失去

了全部的界限。一切，都已空空荡荡。灵魂、感觉、生命，仿佛都在眼泪里，被风带去了幽冥中。自己想死，一了百了。

灰白色的蜘蛛网，从屋顶垂下，在半空里缠结、晃荡，像一个残破的躯壳，像一个死了的灵魂。它安静得没有半点声音，像死亡从坟墓里伸出的手爪。

自己握着那枚戒指，号啕大哭，就好像，自己是个死人，正在哀悼自己曾经的一生。

夜深了，自己陪在孔仁他们的坟墓旁。他们的尸体就在土地里，自己不知道，他们的灵魂是否已重新生根发芽。黑夜像一张无边的网，所有难以言说的哀伤，都不可能在夜里飞向不可捕捉的渺茫。越是想要忘却的东西，在黑夜里，越是会被大网聚拢在一起，凝结成幻影，让你要么在痛苦里清醒，要么在睡梦里想起。呼吸着秋夜的凉意，自己重新触摸到一种割心的孤寂。自己仿佛看到了，自己的世界，已只是一片无垠的沙漠。而自己那么向往那么珍惜的爱情，那唯一可救自己的爱情，又已被自己亲手无情地埋葬。自己的痛苦，是自己选择的结果。而这选择，又是谁的过错？

秋夜，萧索而寂静，天地仿佛一座无形又无情的囚笼。人活着，就是在服刑。

十月十八日。

秋风凄厉，秋雨淅沥。

丽云淋着雨，出现在了废祠堂的门口。自己愕然而不知所措。

她走了进来。雨水从她的头发上往衣领里滴，她的脸上全是水，也分不清是泪还是雨。自己的心里一阵抽搐，怕她会着凉，但又说不出口。她失魂落魄的悲伤样子，令人心如刀割。

自己沉默地看着她，她痴痴而悲伤地望着自己。她说：“想不到，你真的在这里。”

自己硬是笑了笑，说：“这里是我的老窝呀。”

她眼眶里掉出了两滴清泪，轻轻问：“你为什么要又穿回乞丐的衣服？你为什么要这样自暴自弃，又作践你自己？”

“没什么，我只是回到了原形而已。”

“你不是回到了原形，你只是又想躲起来了。”丽云苍白地笑了笑，“你难道没发现吗，这两天发生的一切，都和东北易帜那年的情形如出一辙？”

自己强装着笑脸，说：“你胡思乱想了，其实，我只是想做一个自由自在的乞丐。”

“知道吗，昨天晚上我突然发现，暗格里少了两百块大洋。我原来还以为，你应该会用这些钱，先在旅馆里住一段时间。我甚至还想，要是你说的都是真心话，我就把钱都送到旅馆里去还你。可是，我找哇找，找哇找，没想到，你却真的只是在这里。”丽云哽咽了起来，“究竟是发生了什么事，要让你变成现在的样子？你为什么不愿意告诉我？”

看着她的哭泣，自己比死更难受。自己说：“前几天，我遇到了以前的一个相好，她来了沈阳，正好缺钱，我就偷了暗格里的两百块大洋给她。”

丽云凄恻而嘲讽地笑了笑，说：“来沈阳？谁会在这种时候往一座沦陷之城里跑？”

自己一时语塞，心乱如麻。

丽云流着泪，说：“你带我去看看你的相好，看到了，我就相信。”

“丽云，你别这样。”

“那你要我怎样？”她伤心欲绝地哀哭了起来，“那你要我怎样——”她哀恸着。

她捂着脸，泪水成行成串地从指缝里流出来。她的痛苦像一张网，把周围的一切全绞了起来，绞出了黄连一样的苦味。自己感觉快要崩溃了。她的泪水晶莹而冰凉，像在不断地消解着她可怜的生命。她痛哭得不住战栗着，像站在一个冰窟窿里，像站在一道绝望的悬崖边。

她悲泣着，说：“我真的不明白，你为什么要这样。我们好不容易才能在一起，你却为什么又要这样离去。我一直以为我们早已是最亲密的人，可以彼此袒露心扉、无话不说、生死相随，可是你现在为什么要这样对我，对我冷若冰霜、情爱两绝。我知道这一切都不是真的，不是真的。求求你告诉我到底是发生了什么事——求求你告诉我到底是为什么——”

丽云嘶哑地哭泣着，哀求着。

自己后退了一步，又后退了一步。天旋地转。自己真的不想再活着了。真的。

“丽云，我不爱你，我不想骗你。”自己语调平静地说。

“我不信！”丽云哭着说。

“真的。”

“你看着我的眼睛，再说一遍！！”

“……我，不爱你。”

“我不信！！！”丽云号啕大哭着喊。

自己，眼睛里看到的东西忽然都变成了血红色。斑驳的破墙是血红的，残缺的门窗是血红的，窗外的天空是血红的，吹着的风下着的雨是血红的。在撕心裂肺地痛哭的丽云是血红的。然而又并没有什么在流血。那一刻，自己的心，分明是麻木的。

“……为什么……为什么……”丽云喃喃地痴问着。“这到底是为什么呀……”丽云哭得蜷缩成了一团。

自己无言以对。冷冰冰的空气，冷冰冰的无情。残酷的人生，残酷的活着。

“丽云，你走吧。”

丽云没有走。她又哭了很久很久。自己也一直没再说话。她哭着，她身上淋湿着的雨，最后，都像是被她给哭干了。整个废祠堂里，都是她眼泪的味道。这味道，是一片海。自己知道，这片海，将淹没自己一辈子。痛苦，已无法再用语言说明。

天黑了，雨下大了。

丽云说，我不会相信你的，因为我爱你。

说完，她便踉踉跄跄地走出了废祠堂，走入了大雨里。她在雨中隐约的背影，像一片飘摇的落叶。

自己，瘫坐在了地上。

谁也不能告诉自己，明天，该怎样活下去。

唯有风声雨声，交相缠织，凄凉伤人。

从九月十八日算起，自己和丽云，整整相聚了一个月。

时代的车轮，依旧在无情地向前滚动。

为了应对国联调查团的可能来访，日本人对占领区内的各项部署都做了表面上的调整。奉天市地方维持会会长赵欣伯替代土肥原，做了奉天市的市长。市政公所里的各科科长，也都相应地由日本人换成了中国人。关东军大部队陆续撤出了沈阳城，驻守在南满铁路沿线，城内的防务等诸事都交给了日本宪兵和中国警察接管。表面上，中国人又拥有了一定的自治权，实际上换汤不换药。

天气一日比一日更寒冷了。金黄而绚丽的秋天在急速地褪色，灰蒙蒙又单调的霜冷，在慢吞吞地从地底下爬出来。阳光阴晦，风雨凄凄。干枯的树枝像没有生命的骨头，在风中瘦弱地抖落着死气。灰暗的雨湿冷着天与地，空气里满满都是咸苦的气息。

自己依旧还活着，像具行尸走肉。自己重新做回了乞丐，每天蹲在路边要饭。自己觉得这样挺好，像自己这种人渣，就该受尽世间的惩罚与折磨，才能稍微赎清一点点自己身上的罪孽。有时候，自己特别想去招惹个把日本宪兵，好让他们过来把自己捅个稀巴烂。自己觉得，自己只有被捅了个稀巴烂，才能稍微赎清一点点自己对丽云犯下的罪。自己给丽云的伤害，已经不是用眼泪可以表达的痛苦。自己每天想哭，又觉得自己的哭是不要脸的，是丑恶的。自己对丽云的对不起，是百死难赎的。自己像活在丽云的眼泪里，自己每天痛得睡不着。

然而，自己和丽云的故事，还没有走到结束。

丽云很快就又出现在了自己的面前。她穿得娇艳动人，打扮得特别漂亮。自己一见，大惊失色，不禁焦虑地对她说:“现在沈阳是什么环境，你怎么能打扮得这么漂亮？”

她就笑了，故意问:“我漂亮吗？”说完，她伸开手，在自己面前漂亮地转了一圈。

她走近了一步，笑着说:“告诉你，刚才路上有好多男人看我呢，里面还有日本宪兵。”

“你这是干吗呢？”自己着急了。

她哈哈笑了，说:“你害怕了吗？你是在担心我吗？”

自己无言以对。

“你要是担心我，就回来保护我呀。”丽云天真地说。

“丽云，你不要这样，你这是在拿你自己的安全来开玩笑！”

“我就是要这样，告诉你，我以后天天都要打扮得这么漂亮，我要让那些大街上的男人都盯着我看，对我动坏脑筋！”

“你这是干什么？！”

“我要你回来保护我！我知道你是爱我的！！”

“我不爱你！”

“这不是真的！”

“这就是真的！”

自己和她，都沉默着。她落下了泪来。她一边哭，一边笑，说：“既然你不爱我，那就不用担心我会不会被人欺负了。”

她说完，就走了。

但是第二天，自己在路边要饭的时候，便又看到了她。她还是那么漂亮，像一朵娇艳欲滴的海棠花。她是特地找到这里来的。她的手里拎着一盒精致的点心。她走到了自己的面前。自己故意不看她。她将手里的盒子递过来，说：“给。”自己也不理她。

丽云顿了一会儿，就将点心盒子放在了地上。自己看到，忽然有两滴水珠，掉在了点心盒子的盖子上。自己心一紧，不禁抬头看丽云。丽云真的又在掉泪。

自己一咬牙，狠狠心，说：“你不用可怜我，我不想被你施舍。”

她哑哑地说：“我没有可怜你，我只是害怕，你会要不到吃的，会饿着，我怕你会饿肚子。”她无声地落着泪。

自己咬咬牙，想再说些什么狠话，却莫名怎样也想不出什么话来说。除了剜心剜肺的难受，自己的脑里心里，空空如也。

丽云哽咽着说：“我真的不明白，你为什么会突然像变了一个人。你一直都对我那么好，我们在一起一直都好好的，你为什么突然非要和我分开，突然对我这样无情？一定是发生了什么事，你为什么不肯告诉我——”

“其实没什么，我只是突然看清了我自己的内心，我的心不想和你在一起，所以，我就回到了现在的这副真面目。”自己玩世不恭地说，“对你造成的伤害，我感到很抱歉。谢谢你以前对我的照顾，以后，还是不要再见了。”

丽云悲凄地笑了。她说：“你突然看清了你的内心？难道这么多年来，你对我出生入死的好，都不是爱？”

“我只是想滴水之恩、涌泉相报罢了。今天你给了我点心，他日你有难，我还是会救你。”

“我不会相信的，我会每天来找你，缠着你，直到你告诉我真正的原因。”

丽云走了。

自己觉得，生不如死。

丽云真的说到做到，不管自己躲到了哪条街上，大多数时候，她总能找到自己。就算有时候，她白天没能在街上找到自己，到了晚上，她也一定会来废祠堂里找人。她每天都会送来一盒点心，自己每天都要面对一次爱情，她每天都会伤心欲绝地哭一场。才短短的一段时间，丽云，就像已哭尽了一生的悲哀。自己，是有罪的。

自己不再东躲西藏，因为那样，只会害得丽云东奔西跑，还会害她走危险的夜路来废祠堂。反正自己是躲不掉的，还不如就待在一个固定的地方，让丽云好找一些。丽云每天送来一盒精致的点心，自己怕她这样会花掉太多的积蓄，就又故意拿话伤害她，嫌东西不好吃，要她改成了每天只拿来两个白馒头。丽云哭得情意皆碎。自己觉得，自己真的是个人渣、恶魔。

自己并不想和丽云这样似断非断、藕断丝连。因为丽云只要还和自己有半点关系，自己就无法达到让她置身事外的目的，而如果不能让她置身于仇杀追杀之外，自己和她的分手，就毫无意义。如果不能达到保护她的目的，那么，自己故意对她造成的情感伤害，就完全是多余的造孽。自己不想这样，但丽云毫不放弃，痴心不悔。自己想干脆离开沈阳，一走了之，但是，万一丽云天涯海角地去找自己，怎么办？

而且自己也根本做不到真的离开。

丽云故意每天打扮得花枝招展、娇艳欲滴，这让自己如坐针毡，寝食难安。要不是有国联调查团即将访华的消息在约束着沈阳城内的日军宪兵，自己就算有十条命，也来不及救丽云。但丽云她还是这么傻，这么痴，什么也不管，什么也不顾，只想用这种激将法，让自己放弃谎言，回到她的身边。她真的是个天真的孩子，一个傻孩子。自己知道，她的爱有多深，有多不要命。但是这种知道，除了叫自己彻夜痛哭，一无所用。自己真的，不知道该怎么办。

自己，还是经常会偷偷地回到小院附近，去悄悄地看看丽云。时逢乱世，自己不可能真的不担心她。而且，对她说过了那么多冷冰冰的绝情话

后，自己是更加寝食难安，就怕她会有事。这真的是一道矛盾重重的难题。自己是为了保护丽云不受伤害，所以才离开的丽云，但是自己离开后，只剩下了丽云一个人，万一发生什么意外，谁来及时保护她？另外，青帮暂时还没继续派杀手前来，但是丽云的心，却已被自己伤害得千疮百孔，自己这样做到底对不对？可是，自己若不离开丽云，万一明天杀手就来了呢？怎么办？自己真的想不出答案。几乎每次站在小院的围墙外，自己都能听到从屋子里传出的丽云的抽泣声。她真的是天天在哭，以泪洗面。自己是真怕她这样下去，会把眼睛给哭坏。她的每一滴眼泪、每一声哭泣，都像火辣辣的鞭子，直往自己的心坎里抽。抽打得猛烈，抽打得凶狠。自己痛得要命，但是，又能做什么呢？丽云被破碎的爱情折磨得痴悲难已，自己深深地感到，自己是对她犯下了难以宽恕的罪。另外，自己也深深地明白，自己和她，再也回不到从前了。是真的回不去了。

自己一直固定地在一个比较僻静的角落里要饭，这样，丽云有时就能和自己说上很久的话。丽云还是一直在无比执着地追问着真相，她始终坚定地相信着她和自己的爱情，相信得斩钉截铁，相信得生死不渝。而自己，依旧在编造着各种分手的理由，依旧在对她说着各种冷冰冰的绝情话。自己真的很害怕和她每天如此的相见，这种彼此折磨的见面，既让她肝肠寸断，也让自己痛不欲生。可是，如果自己逃走，就会害她天涯海角去找。而扪心自问，如果真的一天看不见她，自己恐怕也活不下去。这真的是一个剪不断、理还乱的矛盾。事情和自己原先设想的完全不同。她爱得海枯石烂，而自己，根本也放不下她。自己在拼命地割断着爱情，却没想到，爱情是这样强韧而粗壮，除了割出了满手满地的血，自己，什么目的也没能达到。怎么办？

丽云每天送来两个馒头，馒头是她亲手做的，做得特别大，一个能抵两三个。自己明白她的心意，她就是怕自己会要不到饭，会饿肚子。每次想到这些，自己都难禁哀泣。每次吃着这些馒头，自己都是在吞着眼泪吃。丽云的情意，丽云的好，自己怎会不懂，可是，懂又能怎样？又能怎样？自己说了那么多条分手的理由，其实，有一条真的没说错，那就是，自己配不上她。真的，配不上她。自己，就是个彻头彻尾的混蛋！

而让自己最感到深深悲哀的，是丽云和自己的原本好好的爱情，已被自己切割得伤痕累累、血迹斑斑。就算明天青帮覆灭了，自己和丽云，也再回不到从前的爱情里去了。真的，回不去了。将一杯淡水倒入海水里容易，但是，永远也没有人，可以从海水里重新再取回这杯淡水。人生的沧海桑田，就是如此简单的道理。走出了第一步，就不会再有回头路。

半夜，在寒风鼓噪的废祠堂里，自己可以抛弃伪装，肆无忌惮地悲伤流泪，而不必担心会被丽云突然撞破、洞察真相。空荡荡又黑乎乎的环境中，自己哭声的回音，像极了鬼魅的幽咽。自己心底里觉得很可笑很滑稽：可不是吗，自己不就是活得人不像人鬼不像鬼吗？黑夜里的回音，真像自己困境的提醒。自己是多想可以活得像个人，站在阳光下劳动，站在自由里呼吸，坐在安宁中吃饭，坐在爱人身边细语。但是，这个时代，却似乎总在逼迫着自己，要自己做鬼。自己不可以被人发现行迹，自己不可以自由地拥抱阳光，自己不可以安心地睡觉，自己不可以真心地向爱人表白。自己必须要披着一张鬼皮，才能在这世上苟延残喘地活下去。活着，对自己究竟还有什么意义？

在黑暗的夜色里，自己总会不禁想起曾经有丽云的一幕又一幕。相聚的，分离的，欢乐的，忧伤的。丽云说得一点也不错，自己和她，是多么不容易才走到了一起呀！为什么要就这样把一切毁掉？为什么！她为了帮自己撤销通缉令，不惜毁掉了她自己一生的清白；自己为了救她，也可以不要命。两个人明明已经爱得生死不渝，为什么还要如此生离死别？命运哪，你究竟想要做什么？

自己除了以泪洗面，真的想不出一点点办法。如果自己为了爱情，和丽云在一起，那么，万一下一次杀手们又来，丽云也许真的会死的。也许真的会死的。自己是打不赢那无穷无尽的生死搏杀的。一个男人若真心爱一个女人，又怎会舍得连累她受罪？爱她，第一要紧的，就是要能让她好好地活着呀！

自己，只能坚持和她分手。

到了十一月了。

风凛冽地刮了起来，冷得像刀。空气很粗糙，像被石头打磨过。有太阳的时候，天也灰沉沉的。下雨时，连绵的云都像在哭。

树皮上的凹凸，像被利刃割出来的皱纹。雨后的水珠在皱纹里爬行，像

岁月在生命表面的老泪纵横。被风折断的树枝泡在水洼里，宛如奄奄一息的伤兵。整座沈阳城，在这个秋冬之交的季节里，都散发着一股浓郁的死气。

自己身上的伤口都结了痂。很奇怪，从受伤开始到现在，自己都没怎么感到过这些伤口的痛。有时候，自己甚至都会完全忘了它们的存在。倒是那些以前留下的旧伤，在这天气变冷了的季节里，频频隐痛，令人难忍难忘。自己在想，不久的将来，当自己身上的这些新伤也变成了旧伤，它们，会不会也时常在阴寒的季节里，痛得让人不能忘怀？看得见的血淋淋的伤口，总是比较容易长好的。人真正不能摆脱的，是那些从表面钻进了血肉深处、刻到了骨头缝里的伤痛。这种伤痛，只要人还活着，就不可能治愈，似乎这种伤痛本身就是活着的证明一样。而细数曾经，自己的每一处疼痛里，都深深浅浅地烙着丽云的影子。烙着自己没能对她表白的爱。自己是真的愿意为了爱她而去死，可是现在，命运要让自己做的，却是活着说不爱她。什么叫生不如死？体会过的人才懂得。

丽云还是每天会过来，送给自己两个她亲手做的大馒头。她还是满怀着热烈的爱情，满怀着这爱情给她带来的剧烈的悲伤。而自己，则依旧每天坚定不移又愁肠百结地冷漠对待着她。这冷漠，总让自己的头脑里又冷又胀，仿佛在被毒虫叮咬，可是，自己又无可奈何，既不能不这样对待丽云，也无法让自己不感到痛苦。矛盾像沙漠一样让人垂死，又没有解救。渐渐地，丽云不再那么执着地追根究底了，她不再问“这到底是为什么”了。她只是伤心地恳求着自己，要自己回去，回到她的身边，重新和她生活在一起，不要离开她。自己知道，丽云是已经有些相信了自己的那些绝情话。从坚定不移地追问分手的真相，到伤心欲绝地只求挽留爱情的不要离去，自己知道，丽云内心的纯洁堡垒正在坍塌，她灵魂中最用心守护着的那座美好的爱情花园，正在百花凋残。她的眼泪，每天都像断了线的珠子一样，纷纷往下掉；她秀丽的容颜，一天比一天憔悴。自己真的受不了了，真的受不了了。自己的无情折磨着她，她的痛苦折磨着自己。而自己和她，原本就是真心相爱着的呀！为什么会变成这样？为什么会变成这样！

丽云啜泣着说：“我们以前一起说过的，要生生世世不分离，你都忘了吗？”

自己压抑着悲伤，无情地说：“以前，是我想错了，真的对不起。”

丽云梨花带雨，哭得蜷成了一团。她说：“你回来吧，我们还和以前一样，好不好？求你了——”

“我们……回不去了。”自己差点哭出来。

丽云肝肠寸断，泪如雨下。“知道吗，你不要我了，我在这个世上，就真的再没半个亲人了。”

“……我希望，你以后一个人，可以好好地活下去。”自己不知道，该怎样才能告诉她，自己说这句话的真正含义。或许，这已经不重要了。因为，在无法改变的结果和冷酷无情的现实面前，动机，真的只是一个百无一用的跳梁小丑。

丽云悲凉地笑了笑，继而泪雨滂沱。她摇了摇头，凄苦而乞求地说：“我知道的，你一定是有苦衷。我知道，你是这个世上最最爱我的人，对不对？”

自己被她紧紧地抱住了。她的哭泣，滚烫得像火，寒冷得像冰。她整个人都在剧烈地战栗。战栗得像碎去的玻璃，像濒死的小动物。

自己还是残忍地推开了她。“不是的，我并不爱你，丽云，真的对不起。”

丽云惨白地后退着，后退着。她苍凉地笑笑，哭着说：“我一直以为，你是这个世上最最爱我的人。”

丽云说：“我爱你，到死也不会变。”

她痛苦地走了。

风雨晦暗，寒空碎如沙粒。

丽云悲伤哀泣的模样，就像一个铁箍似的箍在自己头上，只要一想起来，自己就痛得无处可逃。自己回小院附近的次数越来越多，每次待的时间越来越长。自己明知这样不对，却还是控制不住自己。无尽的矛盾，像重叠缠绕的锁链，让人挣扎不已，又逃脱不得。自己深爱着丽云，却要假装绝情将她抛弃；自己要她断情忘爱，却又忍不住一次次想要回到她的身边。有时候，自己甚至感到，只有悄悄地站在小院围墙的外面，自己才能让被压抑的呼吸重新活动起来。只有靠近了丽云，自己才能活得下去。可是，自己又并不能让她知道这些，自己要和她彻底分手。这真的是一个循环往复的悖论。以前，自己一心追求的就是爱丽云，想要和她一辈子在一起，可是总有外在

的或内在的各种原因，在阻碍着自己和她把爱情修成正果；现在，自己全力以赴地想要割断那根坚韧的爱情之绳，祈望丽云可以尽快死心、离开，但是，她痴心不悔的爱，自己难以割舍的恋，总在阻碍着自己和她的真正分离。而，如果不能和她真正分离，她就可能会迎来死亡的阴影。造化弄人，把纯美的爱，由真心的追求变成了夺命的阻碍；命运无情，要人因为爱所以放弃爱，要人因为珍爱所以选择伤害，要人因为相爱所以彼此虐待，要人因为海枯石烂，所以走进生离死别。自己，最终没能紧紧牵着她的手，穿过命运的急流与世事的泥泞，和她一起奔向那如梦境般甜美的彼岸。自己甚至，连那一句“我爱你”都没来得及对她说过。

天意无情，人间无佛。

那座自己和丽云最后去过的水泥高楼的楼顶，自己又登上去过几次。入冬的风，在高处吹得很刚猛，刮得人脸庞生痛。手心摩挲着粗糙的水泥颗粒，一种空荡荡的疼痛会弥漫全身，就像风带着冰凌在整个身体躯壳内穿梭。丽云依偎着自己的情景还历历在目，甜蜜的温柔已被时间送入了消逝的河流，永难回头。自己藏在心里的情话还没来得及向丽云诉说，一切已经沧海桑田，爱情被时间的改变塞进了命运的牙缝。每次重新站在楼顶上的夕阳光中，自己都会有种想要跳下去的冲动。人生已经破碎得彻底，最美好的已注定不属于自己，依恋成了绝望，伤害无法救赎，曾经的拥有在时间空幻的长度里变成了一碰就痛的回忆，如今的失去在再没有了阳光的未来里只会将人生变成一片绝望的深海，这样的活着，到底是惩罚还是奖励？高楼望断，夕阳依旧，人面不再；笑靥犹存，星移斗转，爱断情伤。何不就那样被风裹挟着，冲向地狱，一了百了？

十一月八日，发生了天津事变。

十一月初，土肥原从沈阳秘密潜入天津，策划事变，准备挟持溥仪出津。驻天津日军招募了两千多个中国打手，向他们分发了枪支弹药，安排了具体作战任务。十一月八日晚，日本军警宪特及中国汉奸打手倾巢而出，分数路强攻天津的中国政府机构。省、市政府危难，中国军警奋起反击，全力抗敌。枪炮激烈，搏杀反复，中日双方激战不已，百姓死伤无数、流离失所。而就在中日双方交火激战之时，按照土肥原的计划，日军趁乱将装甲车开到了溥仪的天津居所静园的门口，将其挟持上车，离开了天津。后几经辗转，溥仪被秘密挟至旅顺。而婉容皇后，也被女间谍诱骗到了长春。日军开始实施建立满洲国的计划。

时代风雨飘摇。

寒冷越来越浓。

丽云还是每天会送两个馒头过来，但是她的话语越来越少了。她不再追问什么，也不再乞求什么，她那满满的热烈的爱情和剧烈的悲伤，似乎都已化成了满怀的哀凉的绝望。这绝望，不是空荡荡又干瘪了的死亡，而是在不断激烈回响又膨胀着的挣扎。这挣扎，紧密地缠绕在她欲言又止、徘徊不前的默然里，晶莹地闪亮在她每天依旧难以控制的落泪中。在这种情况下，自己却反而会经常想要主动对她说些什么。可是，可以说什么呢？是可以柔声细语地安慰她吗？还是可以再接再厉地拒绝她？人生是多么的荒诞，而没有出路。只有沉默不语，才是自己唯一的可做。自己的沉默黏合着她的沉默，她和自己每天的相见，都像一场无言的悲剧。自己知道她在无声地追问和乞求，她也知道自己在沉默地躲避和拒绝，自己和她既在不言不语中心有灵犀，又在心有灵犀中彼此折磨。相爱相虐，苦海无边。她的绝望和挣扎铺天盖地、饱满浓烈，自己的挣扎和绝望，也漫山遍野、重峦叠嶂。

丽云噙着泪，说：“知道吗，女人是为了爱而活着的。”

自己说：“可是男人，却是为了活着而爱的。”

丽云哭泣着，说：“可是没有了你，我活不下去。”

自己说：“只有离开了我，你才能好好地活。”

无法言喻的悲伤和鸿沟，将自己和她无情地分隔在了两个不同的世界。这种分隔，透明柔软得像薄纱，坚硬牢固得像钢铁。人，只是笼中的困兽。

自己会一个人呆呆地看着那枚戒指，看很久。戒指的光芒在孤独的寂静中像月牙般皎洁，绵长的哀伤在无声的回忆里如流水般清冽。丽云在小院里的嘤嘤哭泣，总会像一只在幻影里不停生灭的漂亮蝴蝶，在自己的脑海中不停地盘旋、飞舞、变幻。这是一种令人心思破碎的灵魂回首，这是一片叫人不能回避的感情轰鸣。——丽云说，你若不在了，我活着还有什么意思。丽云说，假如没有你，我的生命将失去一切意义。丽云说，知道吗，你不要我了，我在这个世上，就真的再没半个亲人了。丽云说，女人，是为了爱而活着的。——矛盾的旋涡，将自己卷得喘不过气来。自己爱丽云，所以要她

好好地活着，而要让她好好地活着，自己就必须要离开她，因为只有离开了她，才能让她远离杀身之祸，而为了达到和她彻底分开的目的，自己又必须要将自己和她的爱情真的打碎，打得粉碎。但是，失去了爱情的丽云，被自己这样残忍抛弃后的丽云，又真的可以好好地活着吗？丽云说，可是没有了你，我活不下去。这，是一个根本就解不开的悖论。自己，究竟该何去何从？自己的爱，是要丽云好好地活；而丽云的爱，是要生死在一起。自己，究竟该如何选择？如果自己的离去，只能给丽云带来一辈子生不如死的痛苦，那么，自己故意的离去又有什么意义？自己现在不就是已经在每天承受着生不如死的痛苦了吗？更何况丽云呢？爱情和生命，究竟哪个更要紧？自己无从选择。只有戒指，依旧在泪光中璀璨、在悲伤中绚烂。自己一直记得，本来，那一天，自己是想要大声地对丽云说：丽云，我爱你，嫁给我吧。然而，命运没有允许，时代没有答应。若问人间离愁有几许，千江血泪千山泣。

我爱你，丽云。自己只能在黑夜里，独自哭泣着说，不停地说。

但是，回答自己的，只有暗淡的空旷的回音。这回音，像垂死的乌鸦，从悬崖坠落。

快要到十一月下旬了。

寒风陡峭，冰雨锐利。时间没有感觉地不紧不慢地走着，生活就像一具行尸走肉。天空总是阴惨惨的颜色，就连日出，都灰蒙蒙的，毫无生机。地上结着冰霜，枯死的树干兀立在地表之上，像从地狱里伸出来的一只手。人间没有热气，火堆提供的暖意，在苍凉中是那么的破碎和渺小。活着真像是坐牢。

深沉的绝望缠绕着自己，自己开始无时无刻地担心，会再也看不见丽云。自己开始出乎意料而又不可遏制地担心，自己会真的永远失去丽云。丽云每天送馒头来的那一小段时间，成了自己最渴望留住的时光。自己的内心深处，只渴望她能每天在自己的面前停留得长久一些、更长久一些。有几次，站在小院围墙外的自己，甚至都会忘了，自己是为什么要离开这里。真的是太想她了，太想了。这种想念，深入骨髓，绵延至星光的亮处，无论白天还是黑夜，都像火一样炽烈，比墨色更浓郁不可见底。对于失去爱情的恐惧，超越了自己的理智和想象地占据了自己的全部身心。对丽云的爱，从过去开始到现在，仿佛全部聚集了起来，堆积在了自己的胸口里，分分秒秒让人难以呼吸、掉进回忆，在回忆中不停窒息。自己就像是站在一个濒临毁灭的边缘，时间只要再往前多走一步，填充在自己整个生命中的整场与丽云相恋的爱情，就会被地狱之火焚成灰烬，化为乌有，再难寻觅，烟消云散得宛如从未存在过一样。这种感觉比生命的死亡更可怖，就好像要被活着装进坟墓，就好像要把灵魂永远关进暗无天日的地牢。不死，比死更恐怖。自己疯狂地想要拖住时间的后腿，就怕时间再往前走一步，爱情真的就要不在了，丽云真的就要不来了。可是，从一开始，自己想要的，不就是彻底的分手吗？自己，到底该怎么办。真的好爱丽云，好爱好爱她，没了她，自己也活不下去。没了她，自己真的想去自杀。可是，自己又不能放任自己的爱，自己必须要活着不爱她。听明白了吗？是要活着，并且不爱她。这样才能保全她。

自己真受不了了。受不了了！该怎么办！

没有答案。

自己也想过，要来个痛快的。那就是干脆自己去上海，在青帮众人的面前谢罪自杀。这样反而痛快。可是，青帮毕竟是黑帮，谁能保证，自己自杀以后，青帮就不会株连九族地去欺负丽云？要是自己不在了，万一丽云有难，怎么办？而且，对丽云和自己有威胁的也不只青帮一家，还有黑龙会、樱花会社、日本兵，各式各样。在这样一个黑白颠倒、龙蛇混杂的乱世，谁能预料到下一刻的危险究竟是从哪个方向袭来？所以，自己不能就这样把命交给青帮。好歹，自己苟活着，总还能在暗处保护着丽云，就像以前一样。而且，其实自己并不欠青帮任何东西，一个为非作歹无法无天的流氓黑帮，自己就算杀了他们的人，那又怎么样，自己是替天锄恶，凭什么要叫自己去谢罪自杀？自己这条命，要死，也只会为丽云而死。绝不能明珠暗投。护花殉情，自己死得愿意、死得真心；屈从黑帮，自己死得愚蠢、死得耻辱。

可是，自己现在这样子活着，又只是在折磨丽云、折磨自己。只是在让丽云和自己一起饱尝生不如死的煎熬与悲苦。这样子活着，又是否比愚蠢、耻辱的死亡更有意义、更有价值？自己只有无尽的怀疑与悲痛的追问，却没有一丝一毫解答的能力与思索的强硬。一切的逻辑和疑问，都只是环环相扣的矛盾。这些矛盾首尾相衔、旁逸斜出，形成一个巨大的悖论旋涡。困在这

个旋涡里，自己无力逃脱，只有随波逐流，听天由命，沉沦，沉沦。

风萧萧，雨飘飘。鸿雁浩渺出天际，马踏冰霜道别离。相思千番却无语，哭到泪干此生虚。人影灭，夕阳血，情意绝，烟花碎。

丽云哭着问："你是不是真的不爱我了？"

自己说："是的。"

丽云泪如雨下地说："你为什么要这样对我？"

自己说："真的对不起。"

丽云撕心裂肺地问："你不爱我了，这是不是真的？"

自己说："是的，真的。"

丽云肝肠寸断地说："我始终不相信，可是，却偏偏就是真的。"

丽云绝望得像一只掉下了悬崖的小兔子。自己忽然想起，以前对她说过：以后，你孤独时，我会陪着你的。自己心如刀绞。丽云哭得瑟瑟发抖，就像一朵从空中熄灭后陨落的烟花。自己知道，她心中的爱情，已经碎成了一地的纸屑。

自己说："以后，我们还是不要再见面了，你也不用再过来给我送吃的了。"

丽云伤心地哭着，说："我是怕你会饿着。"

自己说："不会饿着的。以后，你还是不要再来了。"

丽云伤心欲绝，问："你真的这么讨厌我吗？"

自己说不出口。

长久地沉默着。

"你真的……这样不想看到我吗？"

丽云泣不成声。

长久的沉默。

沉默。

自己说不出口。

时间痛苦地流淌。

丽云自嘲地笑了笑，然后，抹去了眼泪，说："我知道了。以后，我不会再来找你了。不会了。真的。"她一边抹着眼泪，眼泪一边从她的指缝间源源不断地滚落出来。凄恻断肠，哀凉如霜。

自己说："对不起。"

自己说："以后，不要再打扮得这么漂亮。以后，自己千万照顾好自己。"

她说："知道了，我会的。"

她说："谢谢。谢谢你以前为我做过的一切，谢谢你以前给过我的一切。"

自己说："再见。"

她说："再见。"

她走了。

走了。

一切，都灭亡了。

自己在旷野中仰天长哭。冰凉而沉重的雨从天而降，落在脸上，眼睛里像火烧一样的痛。旷野无边无际，自己站在大雨里，疯狂地喊叫，大喊大叫。像有千百条毒蛇在往自己的心口里钻。痛得受不了了，真的受不了了。自己疯狂地击打着一切自己可以击打的物体，树木、石块、土地，自己捶胸顿足地哭喊。可是没用，自己的心，还是在被千刀万剐、蛇咬虫钻。原来，这个世上，有一些心痛，是你哭也好、叫也好、打也好、喊也好，都减轻不了一点点的。自己的心，就像是被人给掏空了，这辈子也长不好了。只剩下心被撕碎的伤口，在汩汩地流着血。自己知道，自己的生命里，只是被拉走了一个叫庄丽云的女人。而这个女人，就是自己生命的全部。

昏天黑地的世界，行尸走肉的人生，生不如死地活着。

站在夕阳照耀下的高楼楼顶，自己闭上眼睛，想要一跃而下，听着风在耳边呼啸的声音，冲入告别世界的地狱，一了百了，痛痛快快。可是，自己又总是怕死。自己真的是个懦夫，是个窝囊废。是个既没勇气生也没勇气死的胆小鬼。是个一味耽于思虑而又毫无能力改变实际的灵魂侏儒。自己是多么可笑、多么痛苦。夕阳的余晖金黄而鲜红，像飞散的血，像飘零的落叶，像摸不着的风筝线。风在暗地里尖叫，嘲讽着绝望，渴望着死亡，撩拨着哀伤。自己没有再哭泣，因为一哭，自己就觉得自己活像个荒诞又滑稽的小丑。表演者叫痛苦，观看者叫伤口，台上台下，血肉模糊。

站在楼顶的边沿，朝下望去，空间深邃而陡峭，悬崖般的绝望，由下往上摇晃着爬动。孤独地仰望那辽阔的天空，无边无际的天幕就像一堵密不透风的墙，低垂着压迫在眼前，令人无法呼吸。天与地，就像要合起来把人嚼

碎一样。黑暗的痛苦像个无底洞，自己在痛苦中，永远也落不到尽头。风凌厉地呼啸着，自己头痛欲裂地兀立着。灰茫茫的眼前，灰茫茫的一切。自己觉得自己就要疯了。忽然，自己想：我为什么不可以和丽云在一起呢？就算会和丽云一起被人杀死，也总好过像现在这样两个人一起生不如死啊！

这个念头，就像一根针，划破了自己铜墙铁壁的思虑。自己感到了一阵头晕。

连续三天，丽云真的没有再出现。自己心绪难宁，坐卧不安，望眼欲穿。本妄想用那一句“再见”，割舍今生这场进退两难的至深爱恋，却想不到，再大的决心、再决绝的抛弃，也都只是一如既往的自欺欺人。自己爱丽云，想见丽云，揪心揪肺地想，一日不见，如隔三秋。可是，自己又知道，这一次，恐怕是真的不会再见了。那根坚韧的爱情之绳，是终于被自己割断了。断口处，满满的都是丽云和自己的血，心血。自己割断的分明不是一根绳，而是两颗原本紧紧相连相依在一起的心，真心。事到如今，覆水难收；爱到分别，沧海桑田。自己好想念丽云，真的好想念，想得欲哭无泪。可是，自己又明白，现在这样，就是最好的结果。这么长一段时间以来，自己一直在拼命追求的，不就是和丽云一刀两断、再无牵连吗？在这样一段漫长煎熬的日子里，自己每天那么残忍无情地去伤害丽云，为的不就是要她彻底地离开自己吗？现在好了，目的达到了。可是，为什么，自己觉得不值得？自己觉得，不值得。

自己没有再悄悄回到小院的附近去看丽云。丽云是好不容易才死了心，若是万一被她发现自己对她余情未了，事情又将难以收拾。自己不想再在拖泥带水的分手中反复地伤害她了，这简直就是造孽。现在既然已经断了，那就干干脆脆地断了吧，千万别再藕断丝连。这样，也挺好。

这样，也挺好。自己不停地对自己说。

然而，语言的伪装，根本平息不了自己胸中撕心裂肺的悲苦。自己觉得不值得，真的，越来越觉得自己这么做不值得。自己为什么一定要和丽云这样肝肠寸断地分离？相爱着一起死和分离着各自活，究竟哪个更值得人去追求？爱一个女人，究竟是守护她的生命重要，还是守护她的爱情重要？自己不得而知，更难以抉择。自己想要丽云好好地活着。自己爱她，就这么一个希望她好好活着的简单愿望，可是，命运和环境，却将事情变得无尽复杂，宛如一座人性的迷宫。自己真的不知道，应该怎么办。

那时，自己是无论如何也不会想到，今生今世，自己已只剩下了两次再见到丽云的机会。那时，自己总想着，若实在相思难熬，自己总还是可以回小院那里去偷偷看望看望丽云的。那时，自己一直以为，可恶的命运，是要让丽云和自己饱尝相爱却生离的痛苦，可是，却没想到，命运这个魔鬼，这一次，真正为丽云和自己准备的，是永远的死别。上穷碧落下黄泉，两处茫茫皆不见。天长地久有时尽，此恨绵绵无绝期。

到了第四天的晚上，自己正在昏黄的废祠堂里黯然独坐，忽然，外面传来了一阵哧啦啦的声音，是有沉重的东西在粗糙的地上拖过的动静。声音由远及近，断断续续。自己头脑昏沉沉的，也无意去关心。然而，自己又恍如错觉般地，好像听到了丽云迟疑的脚步声。

声音到了大门边，忽然一下子全停住了，像一潭死水的静默。

当听到了脚步声的离去，自己弹跳了起来，一个箭步冲出了废祠堂。

“丽云！”自己忍不住喊了一声。

她停住了。真的是她。漆黑的夜色中，昏黄的光亮里，她迟疑着转回了身来。自己看到，她又穿回了那些难看的农妇衣服，脸上和头发上也没有再打扮，就和那一个月的相聚时光中的旧样子一样。一阵心酸从自己心口猛烈地漾开。那些朝夕相处的旧时光，自己无法平静地触及。

废祠堂大门外边的地上，躺着一只丽云的行李箱。丽云说，我不是来找你的，我只是想来把这个还给你。说完，丽云蹲下，将沉甸甸的行李箱拖了过来，打开。自己一看，箱子里，就是那一大袋原本藏在暗格里的银圆。丽云将袋子打了开来，银圆在昏黄的光线里泛着乌黑的光。她说，这些钱都是你的，我还给你。说完，她站了起来。

自己心如刀割，以往的人生，就好像忽然在眼前清晰地被割成了两半。那种怅然若失又无力回天的疼痛，真的比死还难受。

自己和她就那样在暗淡的亮光中面对面地站着，周围一片死寂。寒冷的风在静默地吹，缠结的痛在破碎地飞。相爱如初，悲凉入骨，真情至深，只可辜负。

自己弯下腰，合上了行李箱的盖子。自己一只手拎起了箱子，对丽云说：“没了这箱钱，你一个女人，往后的日子怎么保障？走，我帮你拎回去。”

“你为什么还要关心我的以后？”

“我说过的，你给我的恩太深，不管怎样，这辈子我都会报答你。”

“那你还冒死救过我的命呢，这个怎么算？”

“是你有恩于我在先，我应该为你赴汤蹈火、在所不辞。”

“我和你之间，什么时候就变成了知恩图报的关系了？我真的不明白，到死都不明白！”

自己难受无言。

丽云小小的脸痛苦地哆嗦着，像一只垂死的小鸟。晶莹的泪花在她的眼眶里满满地打转，却一直没有掉下来。她紧咬着嘴唇，紧绞着小手，像一个可怜的小孩子，像一只痛不欲生的小兔子。

“你还在乎我，对不对？”

她战栗地问。

自己不可能回答。

她痛苦地等待着。

风像魔鬼一样缠绕，冰冷的思绪像把生命冻成了地狱。

“我把钱给你送回去。”自己只是低声说。

“可是我在乎你！”她说着，终于还是哭了出来。“可是我还是在乎你！”

她扑到了自己的怀里，紧紧地抱住了自己。紧紧的，就像生死相依的藤蔓，就像难以割开的石块。

“我后悔和你说再见！我不想和你说再见！！”

丽云嘤嘤哭泣着说。她整个身体都在剧烈地颤抖，像发烧，像着魔。她像一个滚烫的火球，流淌着火一样的眼泪，哭泣着血一样猩红的悲苦。凄恻的爱情，悲凉的绝望，让漆黑的夜，布满了难以掩盖的伤痕。伤痕累累，疮痍满目。

“知道吗，我每天都做了好多的馒头，好多好多的馒头，想给你送来。我怕你饿着，又怕你赶我走。我怕你饿着，又怕你赶我走——为什么要这样对我——”

丽云痛不欲生地悲啼着。

“还记得吗，你抱着我，吻着我，然后对我说，你不会再让我流眼泪了。那一刻，我真觉得自己是这世上最幸福的女人。我真觉得自己是这世上最幸福的女人！——我真想死在那一刻里！早知有今日，我真想死在那一刻里！！”

她撕心裂肺地诉说着。

她，悲痛欲绝地诉说着。

“我爱你，赵驹！我爱你，赵驹！！我爱你，赵驹！！！——你为什么不要我——”

她，肝肠寸断地悲恸着。哭尽了年华，哭碎了悲伤。

哭殒了星辰，哭灭了人生。

钱箱，从自己手中，重重地落下，落在地上。

自己又何尝不记得，在那一刻里，自己曾向天许愿：上帝，如果我的逃避是一种错，那么，请让我爱她到天荒地老。

自己，潸然泪下。

天地冰凉，人间无情。

自己的眼泪，落在了丽云的脸上。

丽云抬起了头来。她疑惑的双眸里，猛然亮起了希望的星光。

“你是爱我的，你是爱我的，对不对？——我就知道，你说的那些都是谎话，你是爱我的——赵驹，请你告诉我真话，不要让我这样难过——我知道你是爱我的——”

丽云痛苦地乞求着，哭诉着。

自己泪如雨下，不能自已。

自己的心，在疯狂地吼叫，疯狂地吼叫！

丽云悲凄欲绝地说：“假如老天有眼，我庄丽云愿意用一生阳寿，换你说一句你爱我。只要你是爱我的，就算老天现在便让我去死，我也死得心甘情愿、幸福美满——”

丽云声如泪水，痴心温柔。

“不要再说了，不要再说了——”自己痛苦地流着泪，还是用力地推开了丽云。

整片夜都像是塌陷了下来，在往自己的脑壳里冰冷地钻。自己痛苦得天旋地转，彷徨得无地自容。绝望，迷茫，混乱，自己的心，在胸膛里失去了节奏地乱跳。自己的眼前，是求婚的戒指，是杀手的尸体。天上像是滴着泪，地上像是淌着血。

“我不爱你，我真的不爱你，我从来就没有爱过你——”自己擦着眼泪，说。

丽云呆呆地站在那里。

“你从来就没有爱过我？”丽云痴悲地问。

“是的。”自己残酷地说。

“你真的从来就没有爱过我？”丽云痴悲至极地问。

“真的。”自己泪流不止地说。

“你在哭，我不信。”丽云痴爱、痛哭地说。

“我只是被沙子弄痛了眼睛。”自己使劲地揉着自己的眼睛，眼睛痛得就像要瞎了。泪水流满了自己的双手，从手掌上直往手肘上淌。自己的脸，烫得发麻。烫麻里，冷热交替，像濒死的错觉。

“你难道，就真的一点都没有爱过我？”丽云痴哀凄凉地问，“你难道，就真的一点也没有爱过我吗？——哪怕，只是爱过一秒钟——”

“真的，一秒钟也没爱过。对不起。”自己痛哭着说。

丽云，瘫软地跪倒在了地上。她哭泣着，痴痴地说：“你明明在哭，我听见你的心里在说，你爱我。我听见了。——你明明在哭——”

她说：“我真的听见了。”

她说：“我活不成了。”

她傻笑了起来。她哈哈笑着，大声说：“我听见了你的心里在说，你爱我，你这辈子最爱的人，就是我。哈哈哈——我真的听见了——我再也活不成啦——”她像疯了一样地大笑着，“赵驹，我要是死了，你要记得，我爱你，我这辈子最爱的人，就是你。你一定要记得。我真的很开心，我们是相爱的，我们是真心相爱的。只是命运不让我们在一起。我知足啦，有你真心地爱着我，我这辈子就是幸福的。哈哈哈哈——只是命运不让我们在一起——有你爱我，我就是这世上最幸福的女人——”

风激烈地旋转，夜像被绞成了碎片。黑夜无尽深沉，光阴像一首悠长的挽歌。

雪，落了下来。

雪，飞舞着，落了下来。

自己哭泣着，把丽云抱了起来，放到了废祠堂里的小火堆旁。

“丽云，你别这样。这辈子，是我辜负了你，真的对不起。真的对不起。我要走了，要离开沈阳了，我以后，再也不会回来了——你忘了我吧，就当这是一场梦——再见了，丽云——”

自己说完，一抹眼泪，转身就逃。背后，传来了丽云悲极的哭声，哭声尖利得像一把刀。自己没有回头。

大雪纷飞，白色的悲伤像无尽的海洋。自己在雪中无尽地奔跑，不知想要跑向何方，只求可以逃出悲伤。雪片细细长长，像从天上掉下的碎玻璃，落在人的身上，仿佛只要一融化，就能冰冷地扎进人的心脏。自己身上落满了雪片，自己感觉不到一点寒冷，自己像个死人。

夜，依旧广大而漫长，没有痛的感觉。

自己脸上的泪，都像是结成了冰。悲苦、疼痛，火辣辣的在自己的灵魂里燃烧、张扬。自己，真的想离开这里了。也许，只有这样，才能真的让丽云忘记过去，忘记一切。

可是，一个鞭子一样的声音，又不停在心中拷问着自己：为什么一定要她忘记呢，为什么呢，你和她，明明是真心相爱的呀！

自己头痛欲裂。周围的一切都像是隐没在了破碎的风影里，碎片四散远逝，世界是那么孤独而安静，只有雪花在瑟瑟地落下，宛如冻结的哭泣，宛如洁白的悲伤。

自己失魂落魄地彷徨着，心如死灰地行走着，面前是绝望，背后是哀凉。雪片用揪心的冰凉无尽地切割着这个世界，世界被尖利地划成了无数条碎片，碎片清晰地在虚空中飘摇，飘摇得仿佛无数张落叶。落叶陨灭，世上的一切都像在化为乌有；陨灭成灰，天地间从来空旷得无限。而在这无限里，自己又只是一只被活着的逻辑摧毁了心灵的微小蝼蚁。似乎，风只要再吹得猛烈一些，自己就能被送入星空之外，坠进永恒的隔绝之中，与生命的窒息为伴。渺渺茫茫，恍恍惚惚。冷得透骨。

寒风，雪夜，昏黑，凛冽。自己感到自己整个人，都在忍不住地蜷缩起来，不是因为冷，而是因为一种比雪更冷更纷纷扬扬的害怕。自己害怕，丽云会出事；自己害怕，自己是真的做错了。这种害怕让自己的双腿越来越沉重，越来越走不动，自己整个人都像在变成石块。悔恨、懊恼、内疚、自责

缠绕着自己的内心，但是自己又茫然无措地不知究竟该怎么办才好，只能任由时间向前延伸，任凭难过和恐惧在心中翻腾。自己一动不动地在雪中呆立着，不知道，自己到底是应该离开沈阳好，还是应该回去找丽云好。直到夜的深处又零星响起了几片枪声，自己才从混乱纠缠的思绪里惊醒，赶紧找了个角落躲了起来。

离开沈阳，搁置如流水般不绝的思念，丽云就可以再也见不到自己了；回到丽云身边，向她说清真相，恳请她的原谅，自己和她就可以生死在一起了。人永远是在选择中决定着命运，而命运永远是在选择之外限制着决定。进退两难的痛苦中，丽云的崩溃，又令自己担忧不已。自己除了给自己几记耳光，什么也做不了，什么也做不到。

夜是那么漫长，雪是那么纷扬。枪声不再奏响，整片夜，像死一样沉寂。雪片悄无声息地落下，寒冷仿佛在发出巨大的声响。自己似乎听到了一种世间万物都在被碾碎的声音，这声音，既静悄悄，又轰隆隆。难过和恐惧就像一座山似的压在自己心上。丢失了爱情，伤透了丽云，困惑于自我的决定，这些痛苦的灵魂煎熬，远比眼前的夜和雪更加黑暗与悲凉。自己无比憎恶自己，由衷地憎恶。

自己开始透彻地悔恨，透彻地懊恼。自己开始透彻地感到自己做错了，自己做得不值。其实有什么呢？不就是黑帮的一个死亡威胁吗？自己干什么要去那样无中生有地伤害丽云呢？丽云的爱是那样纯洁、热烈、毫无保留、不顾一切，她就像一个孩子般天真地信仰着爱情，自己为什么要去摧毁她的信仰呢？就是为了要让她好好地活着吗？可是，她都已经被爱情的破灭伤害到了生不如死的地步了，她还怎么能好好地活着呢？也许，是自己从一开始就错了。自己忘记了，灵魂之生，高于肉体之生。与其和丽云这样痛苦地共同接受爱情毁灭的折磨，还不如就和她朝夕厮守在一起，共同去面对生死难卜的未来，祸福与共，生死相依，不离不弃。花开堪折直须折，莫待无花空折枝。何必要为了一个还没到来的灾难，而提前去将自己和最爱的人推进生离死别的旋涡？大好人生，珍贵爱情，尽被白白辜负。与其未雨绸缪，趋生避死，还不如今朝相爱今朝欢，明日祸来明日完。

痛彻心扉的后悔，在自己体内翻腾、发酵。滚烫的悔恨交织着冰冷的无奈，像一头伤痕累累的笼中困兽，在不停地咆哮、抓挠、挣扎。自己明确地感到，自己胸中那只用坚固的生存逻辑铸成的钢铁心笼，正在不停地动摇、变形、松裂。一种瞬间膨胀的疲惫席卷了自己，自己的灵魂变成了空白一片，思绪成了自由的流水。爱情碎灭的痛苦和悲伤在这流水中火花迸溅，权衡利弊的理智一败涂地、沉入水底。自己真的不想再这样空枉无益地折磨爱情、折磨丽云和自己了，自己真的不想再去考虑除了爱以外的任何事情了，自己只想回到丽云的身边，向她说明真相，请求她的原谅，和她重新好好地在一起。重新好好地在一起。

可是，已经被残忍割断了的爱情绳索，还能重新接合起来吗？

不知现在，丽云是否还在废祠堂里？

雪还在纷纷扬扬地下，自己身上的白色，覆盖了一层又一层。自己就那样一直蹲在角落里，自己害怕动弹，就好像只要自己一动弹，未知的命运，便又会来捉弄自己。自己真的渴望时间和空间能够静止下来，让自己可以在不会越来越后悔的情况下，再好好想一想，再好好想一想。到底该怎么办。

天色在缓慢地变化，自己凝滞地仰望着天空。天空慢慢亮了起来，雪也停了。饥饿与口渴袭来，自己抓了一把雪，放在嘴里吃着。生命的感觉是停顿着的，只有一种对爱和温暖的渴望，在自己干涸的灵魂里热烈地奔流。雪的味道是那样冰冷寡淡，而自己的内心，五味杂陈。自己不知道丽云现在是否已回到了小院，又或者，她仍在废祠堂里？如果她现在还在废祠堂里，那么，自己眼下该不该回去？回去以后，怎么面对她？该说什么？要是不回去，自己又能往哪儿去？离开沈阳，是不可能实现的想法。爱了丽云这么久，所谓的离开，真的只是一句自欺欺人的鬼话。

阳光穿过了厚重的云层，普照在大地之上。光线微黄而柔和，像带着醺意。自己还是想回去了。希望丽云还在废祠堂里。自己想要和她说明一切。自己想要和丽云好好在一起。该想的都想过了，会错的也都错过了，自己不想再在痛苦的泥潭里悲伤沉陷了。命运想怎样就怎样吧，自己要和丽云在一起；明天要变坏就变坏吧，自己要和丽云好好相爱。如果自己会把丽云给害死，那么，自己也一定会和她一起去死。不管是生还是死，一切，都不要再来阻隔自己和她的爱恋了。人，不是为了活着才活着的。

自己转身踏上了回废祠堂的路，胸中充满了诚挚的勇气和决心。虽然，

还有一些隐蔽的说不清的颤抖会时不时地让自己陷入迟疑和慌乱，但是，没什么比丽云的崩溃更让自己不能承受了。自己一定要救回爱情，救回丽云的心。至于死亡和明天，听天由命吧。要是丽云不在废祠堂，自己就去小院找她。回家，多好。自己这么想着，就跑了起来。

太阳，晴朗地照耀着大地。

然而，就是在回去的途中，自己看见了日军的行刑队。阳光尖利地照耀在日军的刺刀上，刺刀反射着惨白的光。在一辆日军的卡车上，装满了五花大绑的浑身是伤的犯人。老百姓们簇拥着，自己听见一个大汉低声说：看哪，日本人现在就要把这些人送到广场上去枪毙啦。一个犯人在卡车上抬起了头来，自己看到，他竟是短毛。于是，自己愕然停了步。

跟随着卡车，自己一直跑到了行刑的广场。犯人们的嘴都被塞着，说不了话。短毛在卡车上时便已看到了自己，看到了自己的跟随。他一直在摇头，一直在微笑。他说不了话。他的身上都是血污，一条腿上还在不停地滴着鲜血。他的笑是豁达而晴朗的，充满了回家的感觉。他的摇头，自己明白，他是想说：你千万不要动手。

荷枪实弹的日本兵有几十个，就算再来十个赵驹，也伤不了日军一根汗毛。自己怎会不懂。可是，就看着短毛去死吗？

广场旁，聚集着一些老百姓，听他们说，这二十多个抗日义士，就是因为劫了樱花会社运毒品的车辆，所以才被一网打尽的。一个壮汉说：日本人太聪明，设了圈套让这些人钻，可惜了。

短毛他们，一个个地都被绑到了广场上的柱子上。一个日本中尉，站到了广场的中央，开始用半生不熟的汉语大声讲话。自己的脑子里紧绷绷的，嗡嗡直响。事情来得太突然、太凌厉，让人不知所措。自己应该要救短毛，但是，很显然，自己上去只会送死，连日本兵的一根汗毛都伤不了。枪弹，是拳脚的天敌。

自己紧握着拳头，像根木桩，站在原地一动不动。自己热泪盈眶。上一次，自己还跟短毛开玩笑，说，去你妈的，以后别再让我看见你，见你一次我倒霉一次。没想到，今天再见到，竟然是即将永别！这个朝生暮死的乱世啊！

短毛始终保持着微笑，那种感觉，像皈依，像回家，从容，而并不凄凉。自己记得，短毛以前说过，他喜欢的女人已经死了。也许，此刻对短毛来说，正是要启程回到最爱的女人身边去了吧？但愿慈悲的佛陀没有欺骗世人，但愿这宇宙中真有六道轮回存在，那样，恶魔便终会下地狱，而念念不忘的人，终能在死后重新相见。那样，死亡便真的只是一场重生的启程，一场圆满的归宿。

短毛一直在对自己摇头。自己知道，他是怕自己会去救他。但他不知道，其实自己的内心充满了怯懦。对枪和子弹的畏惧，是深烙在自己人生记忆中的洪水猛兽，就算自己偶尔能够克服这种畏惧，那也必须是在有取胜把握的前提之下。而眼前，几十个荷枪实弹的日本兵，自己该怎么办？恐惧在自己的骨子里翻滚。对自我的失望和责怪在隐蔽地流窜，自己感到了阵阵头皮发麻。自己甚至不敢远远地正视短毛的眼睛，就怕他会看懂自己的软弱。自己甚至需要假装出一种怒发冲冠的冲动，好让短毛有所欣慰。短毛就要死了，自己不想让他在这个时候发现：其实赵驹是个软蛋，赵驹根本就没有上刑场救人的勇气。如果被短毛看穿了这一点，那么，不管对谁来说，都是残忍的。自己只希望能让短毛感觉到：赵驹是真的想要救人的。

自己是真的想要救人的，只不过，日本兵太强，自己不敢送死。是理智，折断了自己的勇气。

日本军官的讲话结束了。自己突然又流下了泪来，轻轻说了句：兄弟，你要走好。短毛听不到，但他又似乎听到了。他冲自己笑笑，点点头，眼睛闭了闭。自己明白，这就是告别了。自己想对短毛挥挥手，但是又怕被日本人发现自己与短毛相识，就没敢举手挥别。

日本军官下了令：“预备——”

自己背转了身。

“嘭嘭砰砰——”乱枪响起。广场边上没有转身的一些百姓，纷纷惊呼、惨叫了起来。

人群四散。

自己没有回头地，逃离了广场。自己知道这时不能回头看，因为一看，自己就会忘不了：自己没有救短毛。

泪水无声在脸上滑落，自己说不清哭的原因。是哭这个世道太他妈的黑暗？是哭自己太软弱的可悲？是哭朋友突然的永别？是哭命运残酷的安排？

自己不知道。唯有心冷如霜。

短毛临终前的微笑，一直刻在自己的脑海里。自己真希望，自己在临死的时候，也可以绽放出这样一份视死如归的情怀。短毛他们，是真正的英雄。

而赵驹，只是个懦夫。自己痛苦地想。

自己忽然想道：咦，龚汉江呢？刑场上，分明没看到龚汉江的人影。如果这批抗日义士是被日本人一网打尽的，那么，龚汉江去哪儿了？他是侥幸逃脱了吗？又或者，难道是他做了叛徒？不，龚汉江不可能投敌。自己想。

回到了废祠堂，废祠堂里空无一人。只有一个已熄灭的火堆和那只装着大洋的行李箱。丽云不在了。废祠堂外的雪地里，有丽云离开时的脚印。她是在雪下了很久以后才离开的，或者是在雪停了以后才离开的，否则，外面留不下清晰的脚印。她一定是在这里等了很久，她在等自己回来。她一定是那样痴心而悲伤地等待着，长久地期盼着，期盼着自己这个负心汉的回心转意。可是，她最后一定还是失望了，绝望了，她还是什么也没等到。又或者，丽云，真的已经死心了。

也许，她，真的已经死心了。

她的崩溃，依旧历历在目，揪人心肺。

自己的心很乱。自己不知道该怎么办。自己想等天黑了以后去给短毛他们收尸，自己要找到龚汉江，问清事情的原委。等这些事情都做完了，自己才可以去找丽云，和她好好谈一谈自己的真心。

可是，这些事情的结果到底会怎样，自己又都毫无把握。只有隐约的悲哀和矛盾，仍在心底躁动不已。

枪毙短毛他们的枪声，仿佛仍在自己耳后隐隐作响，像一种隐蔽的跟随，像一种不懈的追击。自己真诚地感到，对于他们的死，自己并没有袖手旁观。自己的本能是想营救他们的，要不然自己也不会一路跟随着行刑队，只不过，客观上的无从下手最后掐灭了主观上的营救愿望。自己是这么想的。这个想法是真实的，也是正确的，但是，这个想法，这个逻辑，就是让自己浑身难受、心里憋屈。就仿佛，自己是真的做错了什么事；仿佛自己应该和他们一起死了才痛快。但是，自己为什么要死呢，自己和他们本来就不是一伙的。

自己的怯弱是不可回避的一个黑洞。这个黑洞生长在自己灵魂的深处，既无法掩盖，也难以治愈。它始终在以岁月的力量来释放着绝望的情怀。自己可以忘记它的存在，但不可能真的以为它不在。恐惧在某些时候是理智的基石，但理智在更多的时候只是怯懦的遮羞布。当人面对着客观上的生死绝境时，究竟该做出何种选择？勇敢一搏，可能会死无全尸；退缩求饶，也许可苟延残喘。是要选择勇敢，还是选择退缩？是要选择死亡，还是选择活着？当价值意义与生死本性发生悖逆，当情感追求与生存逻辑反向而行，人，究竟该何去何从？而，如果没有了生命存在，情感价值又可依附于何物？肉体的生与灵魂的活，从来是相互依附、缺一不可。而，思维与存在的矛盾，终究是个难解的悖论。

自己尽量忘却着枪声，忘却着死亡。淡淡的负疚隐隐膨胀，而自己也无可奈何。

夜幕降临，自己悄悄潜去了广场，想要给短毛他们收尸。但是，等自己到达时，广场上早已空空如也。日本人并没有在广场上曝尸。是日军将尸体都运走处理了，还是已经有人早一步来给这些义士收了尸？自己希望是后一种情况。自己希望，短毛他们可以早日入土为安。尸体不在了，自己也并没打算再去多作追寻。毕竟，人死不能复生，还是不要节外生枝的好。自己的心意和无奈，短毛若泉下有知，也应该会明白的。空荡荡的广场上寒风凄冷，血腥味浓重得层层叠叠。在路灯的照耀下，广场上大片大片的血迹，都泛着热且亮的光芒，宛如活物。阴气惨烈，血味悲凉。自己跪下来，对着广场上的血迹磕了几个头，轻声说：兄弟们，一路走好。

离开了广场，自己转道去了废木料场。自己想要找到龚汉江，问清楚整件事情的来龙去脉。另外，自己也想确认，龚汉江究竟是不是叛徒。如果是，自己定会为短毛清理门户。

谁知，自己还未走到废木料场那里，远远地就看到了一片熊熊的大火。是废木料场被烧了，整个被烧了。火势巨大，火焰静静焚毁着一切。火舌伸向着苍茫的夜空，黑夜被橘黄的火光照亮。一队日本兵从远处向火场奔去，步伐整齐有力。自己忙抽身离去，以免遭池鱼之殃。深夜里，枪声零星地响起。自己的内心，莫名充满了恐惧。自己就好像是看到了一幅奇异的景象：眼前的黑夜，是一条张开着血盆大口的怪鱼，自己和自己身边的一切都在往鱼嘴里流去，水势湍急。而自己，就是这洪流里的一颗微粒，连虾米都算不上。毁灭，是一种不可抗拒的力量。毁灭，只在时间的尽头静候。这是一个恐怖的时代。

回到了废祠堂里，自己莫名像被抽空了力气。一种釜底抽薪般的疲倦在脑壳里铺天盖地。自己倒在了破床板上，不受控制地，沉沉地睡着了。

梦境，是一个隐藏的地狱。自己在梦里活得异常清醒，清醒得不知疲倦。自己看见，父亲的身体被金顺的子弹穿透，鲜血像泉水一样潺潺不止。一把武士刀从眼前掠过，三个日本浪人的枪口，又在自己脑门前耀武扬威。自己肝胆俱裂，而无处可逃。烽火将天空烧出了一个大窟窿，自己从窟窿里爬了出去，却看到阿台和小柔的尸体静躺在鲜艳的血泊里。禽兽似的日本兵们正在轮奸女尸。自己义愤填膺，怒发冲冠，却又冷汗直冒，不敢出声。自己转身要溜走，背后却响起了大片的枪声，枪声中，短毛在后面大声喊："赵驹，你快跑！"自己慌不择路地跑了几步，却又羞愧难当地停了下来。整个世界，都像被突然泡进了一场无休无止的大雨里。雨是那么凄凉，世界是那么寂静，莫名的悲哀，缠绵而苦涩。自己转回身去，却只看到，大雨中，一条步枪的枪口，紧顶着丽云的太阳穴。丽云在雨中嘤嘤地哭泣着，撕心裂肺地说："可是没有了你，我活不下去。"热泪模糊了自己的视线。枪声惊悚地崩响。自己疯狂地扑上前去。惊醒。

醒来时，天已大亮。

惊恐和痛苦，依旧从梦里延伸出来，在自己现实的清醒意识中沉重地爬行。眼前所见到的一切，都只像是一面面梦的镜子。忧惧和悲哀，从四面八方聚拢过来，把人包围，仿佛一种嘲弄。阳光和着寒风在白昼里舞动，自己很想推开眼前的一切，但一切都纹丝不动。思维与时光一样难以倒流，昨天和眼前一样客观存在。饥饿与口渴笼罩了自己，自己望着空虚，感到生命就在空虚里悸动和战栗。走了两步，看着窗外苍白的光亮，内心里莫名又充满了对自我的厌恶。打开了丽云的行李箱，里面是满满的结实的大洋。自己拿了一个，想去买东西吃，一股辛酸却从喉咙里泛起。自己失去了食欲。饥饿与口渴，很奇怪地从自己身上退却，就像两只突然被箭射死的奔跑的小鹿。冷冰冰的银圆，就像是孤零零的囚徒。尖锐的疼痛，在自己心口里扩张。自己躺回了床板上，不想吃喝，不想睡觉，不想动弹，不想呼吸。自己对这个世界，充满了绝望和厌倦。

自己再次想起短毛的死，他的死是那么突然又那么迅速，让人难以接受又难以挽救。也许，人生的本质就是难以预测和难以把握的无常？也许，生命的真谛只在于眼前此瞬的实际拥有？或许，命运的长河其实是个幻象，人真正活着的时间，只有现在的一刹那。昨天与明天，只是坟墓和幻想。而回忆与希望，只是无用的思想和考量。今天才是开在掌心的鲜花，握住才是真正现实的活过。如果死亡根本就是一种不能预料的厄运，那么，躲避又有什么意义？如果躲避根本没有意义，那么，自己和丽云的分手，就只是一场无价值的悲剧。愚钝的思维用逻辑的方式完成了对存在的糟蹋，虚妄的幻象以警惕的名义完成了对现实的毁灭。自己的幸福被未来的恐惧所破碎，自己的世界被文明的欺骗所埋葬。人，就是活在一座看似富丽堂皇实则荒冢遍地的迷宫里。迷宫的出口，只是一切不存在的事与物的消失。而剩下来的，便是你的世界本来应该有的那个美好样子。

自己的世界里，本来应该有的，是与丽云在一起的美好爱情。自己想。

自己真的想要救回爱情，但是，又莫名对自己不信任。你真的已经坚定信念不再动摇了吗？要是你以后还会这样犹豫不决摇摆不定，那就仍然会像如今这样再次伤害丽云。你真的可以保证不会再让丽云流一滴眼泪了吗？要是你的醍醐灌顶如梦初醒只是一时激情而已，那么你的愚不可及冥顽不灵就依然会在某个命运的转弯口戕害爱情。你真的可以相信自己吗？你真的可以做好吗？你的爱如烈火誓不屈服是真正的勇敢无畏吗？你的归心似箭愧疚无限是真正的大彻大悟吗？要是你做不到，做不好，就不要让丽云重新陪着你，再等待一回命运的捉弄。最美好的爱情，只有真正勇敢的人才配拥有。如果你是个懦夫，那么，让丽云离开了你，也好。

自己无力地睡在床板上，无法回答自己的质问。

整个世界，像是堕进了一个永恒的空洞里。

两天两夜，自己没吃没喝。一丝丝的灵魂，都像在从脑壳里往外游离，缥缈无迹。空荡荡的，自己觉得身体很轻，呼吸宛如一种漂浮。对丽云的想念，一种单纯又浓烈的想念，是唯一将自己联结在大地上的绳索。自己想和丽云永远在一起。就是这份舍不得，在阻止着自己去往死亡。自己想好好地活着，因为只有活着，自己才能爱丽云。

到了第三天，自己的灵魂和生命，才像是完全复苏了过来。饥饿与口渴，以排山倒海的力量，冲击着自己的四肢百骸。自己简直要饿疯了。自己需要好好地吃一顿，然后，向丽云表白。自己拿起了一枚银圆，想去买东西吃，但是想想，又放下了。自己笑了，自己想：还是去跟丽云要两个馒头吃吧。自己洗了把脸，漱了漱口，然后，将戒指盒子揣进了兜里，就踏上了回小院的路。

一切，都过去了。一切，都会重新开始的。自己迎着阳光，充满朝气地想。

自己想：我一定要乞求丽云的原谅，告诉她，我爱她。

寒风，吹拂着冰冷的大地。命运，高深莫测，残暴血腥。

到了小院外，小院的门没有关。屋门也没关。屋里传来丽云的哀号与呼救声。自己冲进了屋里，看到，渡边竟然带了三个鬼子，正在侮辱丽云。

"赵驹，救我——"

两个鬼子端起了枪。枪口直指着自己的脑袋。

自己呆住了。

自己用日语说："冷静，冷静，我只是来要饭的，我只是来要饭的。"

屋里的桌上，放着一盘大馒头，馒头上还冒着热气。自己知道，这是丽云亲手做的。

"赵驹，救我——"

自己抓起了桌上的两个馒头，就去角落里大吃了起来。

鬼子放下了枪。

丽云拼命地反抗着、呼救着。而自己，就像是没看见，没听见。

菜刀就在不远处的地上，而自己并不敢去捡。一共四个日本人，有两个手里拿着枪。

丽云放弃了挣扎，不再呼喊，只有悲惨的哭泣。

是比悲惨更绝望的哭啼，是比绝望更可怕的死寂。

菜刀，就在不远处的地上。而总有两个日本人，手里拿着枪。

日本人糟蹋着丽云。渡边一边大声笑说："赤木给我的这份礼物真是太好啦！哈哈哈——"

时间过得像死了一样慢。

渡边最后又糟蹋了丽云一次。他穿好了裤子，正要把手枪掏出来，自己就冲了上去，跪在他的面前，用日语说:“把这个女人留给我吧，就像赏赐一个乞丐，就当是可怜一条狗。”

说完，自己还去舔了渡边的鞋。渡边高兴地哈哈大笑，就收起了枪，一挥手，对其他人说，走。

渡边他们出了门。

自己正赶紧想去给丽云穿衣服，一回身，却只听到，丽云哀泣着，轻轻说了句：这一次，我们真的要说再见了，再见了，赵驹。

自己刚明白丽云的意思，丽云已经捡起了地上的那把菜刀。她冲出了屋去。

她，是想求死。

自己疯了似的追出去，死死抱住了她，拼命地对她说，活着就好，活着就好。

自己，苦苦哀求地说。

可是，丽云摇了摇头，摇了摇头。

她冲着日本人，大喊了起来。

渡边回过了头来。

自己紧紧捂住了丽云的嘴。

自己的手臂，被丽云狠狠地咬了一口。她的泪水，像河一样流淌。

流淌得滚烫。

滚烫得绝望。

“砰、砰——”渡边开了枪。

丽云，血流满身的倒在了自己的怀里。她颤抖地捏着自己的手，微笑着说：赵驹，我以为，你会救我的。

她的微笑，就像以前两个人在一起时那样美丽。她的微笑，淌满了泪珠的血红。

她说：知道吗，爱过你，我这辈子不后悔。

丽云的手掌无声滑落。她，永远地闭上了眼睛。

而自己，却再也没脸对她说：我爱你，丽云。

天地萧萧，沧海寂寥。

自己浑身战栗，咬碎了一颗牙。

那一刻，自己唯一恨的，是自己。因为只有自己知道，真正害死了丽云的，是什么。

是自己，害死了自己最爱的女人！

唯一的女人。

苍天，为什么要这样？！

为什么。

风冷如刀。

渡边问，她说了什么？

自己说，她说，我恨日本人。

渡边问，你怎么会在这里要饭？

自己痛哭流涕，说，千仇万恨，一言难尽。

自己脱下了衣服，包裹住了丽云的尸体。自己抱着丽云，逃离了这个地方。

天地苍茫，云碎天涯。

天上下起了雪，无边无际的大雪。

“我是一个喜欢好奇的人，可是现实中能令人感到好奇的事情好像并不多。有时我会很想去过一种无拘无束的生活，就像小说里都爱写的那样，可以自由地去冒险，可以自在地去浪漫，说不定，还能遇到一个武功盖世的英雄，可以和他一起去惩奸除恶，助人为乐。——这些想法都挺可笑的，是吗？”

“等天下太平了，每个人就都可以去自由地追寻自己想要的生活了。”

“可是，真的会有那一天吗？”

“天下大势，合久必分，分久必合。再乱的世道，乱到最后，也必会有一个真正的王者出来，荡平群雄，一统四海，收拾山河，安抚天下。会有那一天的。”

“我姓庄，叫庄丽云，一朵美丽的云，你呢？”

“我姓赵，叫赵驹，一匹奔跑的马驹。”

雪花纷飞，舞动如泪。

自己和丽云，终究是没等到天下太平的那一天。

万物死寂，冰冷成泣。

雪白，覆盖了大地。

自己将所有的银圆拿出来，为丽云买了最好的棺材、衣服、首饰。丽云生前爱美，自己一定要帮她穿戴得富丽堂皇，打扮得漂漂亮亮。

自己将丽云抱入了棺材。自己想最后吻她一次，却又觉得，自己不配。自己，只是个不配被她爱的懦夫。

自己将那枚求婚戒指从盒子里拿了出来，放在了丽云的手心里。自己没给她戴在手指上，因为，自己知道，自己根本不配。

看着丽云最后的容颜，自己流着泪说："其实，我爱你。"

"你是我一生最爱的女人。丽云，我爱你。"

"我想一辈子和你在一起，白头到老，不离不弃。"

"你是我唯一想娶为妻子的女人，丽云，我爱你。"

自己泪如雨下，痴说痴话。可是，丽云却再也听不到了。

听不到了。

盖上了棺盖。

自己将丽云，安葬在了她父母墓穴的旁边。

自己在丽云的墓前，跪了三天三夜。

"丽云，你放心，我一定会为你和你们庄家报仇，等报完了仇，我就来黄泉路上找你。你等着我。"自己在丽云的墓前哭着发誓。

自己离开了墓地。

自己在丽云的小屋里找到了那盒断发。青丝依旧黑亮如新，人面却已香消玉殒。时光仿佛还在曾经，丽云似乎就在隔壁。然而，错觉改变不了现实，失去的终都已经失去。

自己将这盒青丝抱在胸前，就像丽云还活在自己怀里一样。自己知道，在这辈子剩下来的时间里，自己都只能靠幻觉活着了。

看着厨房里剩下的大馒头，自己撕心裂肺地痛。丽云，其实还是每天在相信着爱情，每天在担心着她爱的赵驹。说不定，那天，她做了这些馒头，正是为了再来找自己。她也许，还是想知道，自己到底为什么要离开她。

自己流泪，而自嘲。一切，都已成空。烟消云散，不再有。

自己带走了那盒青丝，将小院和小院里的一切，付之一炬。

烈火熊熊。曾经有过的美好，最后经历的悲惨，都在鲜艳的大火中，化为了炙热的灰烬、湮灭的废墟。时光入土，一切埋葬。好的坏的，从此往后，只在心间永存。

再见，过去。再见，美好。

站在大火前，自己知道，自己剩下来的生命，将只为复仇而活。不管要经历多少时间，不管要付出多少代价，自己，一定要为丽云和庄家报仇。在大仇得报之前，自己，必须要铜皮铁骨地坚硬活下去。

而待将来做完一切之后，自己只想，可以死在丽云的墓前。人活着，和恋人再相爱，也总逃不过生离死别，而只有死亡，才可以成全两个人永恒的厮守。自己，向往着那最后的死亡。

自己的灵魂，追随着丽云的爱情入了土。从此以后，时光只是虚设，活着只是躯壳。丽云不在了，还在活着继续的一切，都已不值得自己再去记忆。一天又一天，自己和丽云的幻影厮守着；一天又一天，自己全力计划着复仇。这，便是自己的余生。而，对自己来说，最幸福的家，只是丽云所在的墓地。

除了渡边以外，另外三个畜生鬼子的脸，自己也都记得很清楚，自己发誓一定会找到他们，让他们一个一个受尽折磨而死。另外，自己不会忘记渡边说的，丽云是赤木送给他的礼物。庄家的一切灾难都是赤木老贼设计的，还有潘兆和短毛，也都是被赤木给害死的。新仇旧账，自己要一起算。自己不会让赤木舒舒服服地死，自己要让他亲眼看到，他苦心经营的樱花会社，是怎样灰飞烟灭。

而要做到这一切，光凭自己一个人的力量，是不可能完成的。在沈阳，只有日本人的力量，才足以消灭日本人。而要怎样才能得到日本人的力量？答案只有一个：加入日本人。

这，必须是一个潜伏计划。

自己，得到了龚汉江四兄弟的帮助。

自己是在买纸钱的时候，看到的龚汉江。自己以为他是叛徒，和他打了一架。他最后掏出了手枪，说：我如果真的是叛徒，根本不用和你打，我早就对你开枪了。

龚汉江带自己去见了他的三个师弟。龚汉江讲述了短毛最后的那场战斗。他说，是格斗场老板和那群广东枪贩子联合起来，帮日本人害死了曹哥。曹哥得到的樱花会社运送毒品的路线图，是假的。那一天，我们整支队伍的所有人都参加了行动，却没想到，日本人早有准备，还安排了迫击炮。我们带了两箱手榴弹，本以为可以安全突围，却没想到，那两箱手榴弹，竟然全是哑弹！兄弟们牺牲的牺牲、受伤的受伤，日本人包围上来，要抓活的。曹哥提议，要剩下的所有人，一起掩护我们四个道士逃走。我们不肯，曹哥说：我们这支队伍，好不容易发展到四十多个人，要是死光了，多可惜，总得留下几颗种子，将来好给我们报仇雪恨，而且，你们是道士，其实，本来就不该死于战争。最后，只有我们四个师兄弟，逃了出来。曹哥和兄弟们被枪毙之后，是我们去收的尸，就埋在小坟岗。

自己去小坟岗上祭奠了一次短毛。纸钱飘飘，灰屑袅袅。自己对着短毛的坟头说：兄弟，你的仇，我会一起给你报。

自己和龚汉江他们，一起去杀了格斗场老板。然后，五个人又一起去闯了枪贩子的地下巢穴。那天，二十个枪贩子刚好都在，一个不落。枪贩子们个个都有枪，且腰圆膀阔，但是，自己和龚汉江他们却都没有怕。双方搏杀在一起。昏暗而肮脏的地下室里，子弹乱飞，有两颗子弹甚至是擦着自己的头皮飞过去的，但是，自己却竟然丝毫不惧。不仅不惧，自己甚至是希望自己可以被子弹打中的。自己，是有求死之心的。可是，有了求死之心的自己，横冲直撞，反而丝毫也没被子弹伤到。自己手握着一柄钢刀，就像一个发了疯的刽子手，手起刀落，一刀一颗头。自己杀人时抱着一股莫名的仇恨，就像是在恨他们为什么不把枪打得准一些，好把我给杀了。踏着湿漉漉的血泊，自己就像是要杀自己一样地杀着敌人。对自己有多恨，自己杀得就有多狠。

枪贩子们死光了。自己和龚汉江他们，竟然毫发无伤。只是，自己从头到脚都溅满了敌人的血。龚汉江的小师弟说：赵大哥果然神勇。自己听了这话，却只想痛哭。

自己知道，自己已经只是个疯子。从丽云死去的那一刻起，自己就已经疯了。自己之所以还恬不知耻苟延残喘地活着，只是为了报仇。在仇人死光之前，自己必须铜皮铁骨地活着。

漫漫大雪，漫漫征途。

龚汉江说：你的刀，只攻不守，是玉石俱焚的砍法。

自己说：够狠，够快，就行了。

龚汉江说：我们现在，都是亡命之徒了。

自己说：是啊。

龚汉江说：男人，总是要在最爱的女人死了以后，才会变得不怕死。

自己说：道士不是更应该容易看破红尘吗？

龚汉江说：尝过了爱的撕心裂肺，才会知道看破红尘只是一个永恒的谎言。

冬雪飘飘，北风呼啸。

到了一九三二年。

自己向龚汉江阐述了全盘计划。自己告诉他，要想彻底消灭樱花会社，依靠目前周围的那点抗日力量是不可能做到的，现在唯一可行的办法，只有以夷制夷，借日本人的刀，砍日本人的头。自己说，有利益的地方，就会有争端，日本人也不是铁板一块，他们也有内讧，荣仓偏爱黑龙会，与赤木素有嫌隙，赤木恃势傲物，有时连军队也不放在眼里，只要有人能够从中使诈，让日军和赤木的关系恶化，让黑龙会和樱花会社的矛盾激化，那么，樱花会社的覆灭，也就是必然的了。

龚汉江说，你的意思是，离间之计？

自己说，渡边对我会说日语这件事感兴趣，只要有人能把我送到渡边的面前，我就有把握可以让他留下我来，叫我做他的狗，而只要做了渡边的狗，那么，我就可以有机会接近荣仓，实施离间计划。

龚汉江说，把你送到渡边的面前这不是难事，有许多种方法，但是，问题在于，就算你能结识荣仓，他堂堂一个日军大佐，又怎会轻易听你挑唆？

自己说：因为，荣仓有一个秘密。

龚汉江问：什么？

自己说：荣仓有断袖之癖，他，尤喜肌肉强壮之男子。

龚汉江惊讶而沉默。他起身，郑重行礼，说："家国多难，血仇难报，赵大哥，你为复仇，肯为如此忍辱含垢之事，令我等汗颜！您说，有什么是我们可以做的，虽赴汤蹈火，定在所不辞！"

自己说："其实整个计划中，真正的难题是，怎样才能让渡边真正地相信，我是真心实意地愿意给日本人做狗。而这，正是我想请你们帮我做的。”

说完，自己在龚汉江面前，跪了下来。

“赵大哥这是做什么！快快请起，有话直说。”

自己谢绝了龚汉江的搀扶，依旧跪着。

“荆轲刺秦王，献上的是樊於期的首级，我想用你们四兄弟的命，来换畜生渡边的信任！”

沉默如血。

龚汉江将自己扶了起来。他平静地说：“好，能够为赵大哥做一次死间，我们死得其所。您放心，三个师弟面前，我去说。只愿赵大哥能够马到成功，我们死而瞑目。”

自己，再拜龚汉江。自己说：“大事了结之后，我们于黄泉路上再聚！”

风萧萧，雨雪寒。

烈马长嘶，江河落日。

离间计的实施要以死间计的成功为前提，而死间计的成功，要以葬送义士的生命为代价。自己的复仇计划最后到底能不能成功？自己其实也不知道。自己只是在赌博，拿自己的命来赌，拿别人的命来赌。这很疯狂。但是，从丽云死的那一刻起，自己，就已经是个疯子了。只要能够为丽云报仇，自己可以不惜一切代价。龚汉江应该也清楚，死间计划和离间计划，是一场疯狂的赌博，可是，他还是愿意相信，复仇计划最后会成功。其实，大家都在赌。这个风云变幻的时代，本身就是一场血雨腥风的大赌局。时代里的每个人，都身不由己。

只是，龚汉江死后，自己就再没有帮手和朋友了。自己将独入虎穴。这很孤单，也很恐怖，但是，自己已经不怕。疯子赵驹，余生，只为复仇而活。

死间计划的步骤都已安排妥当。自己和龚汉江四兄弟，喝了一顿别离酒。大家开怀畅饮，仿佛明天无限灿烂。

临行前，自己又去墓地里看望了一次丽云。小雪飘飘，微风徐徐。想起曾经和丽云在一起的点点滴滴，自己泪如雨下，伤惘断肠。真想回到过去，永远活在那短暂的相聚里，和她相爱厮守到天荒地老。然而，一切只是痴想，一切只是痴惘。逝去的永远不会回来，明天只会离曾经越来越远。这个

世上，最残酷的，就是活着。

雪停了，自己给丽云烧了许多纸钱。自己笑着说：丽云，等着我，等我报完了仇，我们就再也不会分开了。

离开了丽云的坟墓，自己又依次去给孔仁和短毛他们烧了些纸钱。自己知道，在不久的将来，自己还会给龚汉江他们烧纸钱。自己的活着，就好像是专门为了送葬与哀悼而存在。自己的存在，就好像是专门为了承受失去而活着。除此之外，自己又还拥有什么？曾经烂漫的回忆，伤惘不堪的念想。

自己对孔仁他们说：放心吧，等我有了空，还是经常会来给你们烧纸钱的。

自己对短毛说：早点投胎吧，下辈子，别进帮会里混了。

灰烬一地，天地寂寥。

死间计划开启。

一切顺利。

一九三二年二月五日，日军占领哈尔滨。日本人在东北的统治得到了全面巩固，东北的局势趋于沦陷之稳定。关东军司令部召开建国幕僚会议，筹划安排建立满洲国之事宜。一九三二年二月十六日，东北各省之汉奸领袖在沈阳大和旅馆召开了东北政务会议，会议由关东军司令官本庄繁亲自主持。会议确定了各大汉奸在新政权里的相关职务和地位，并决定了要迎接溥仪担任满洲国执政。一九三二年二月十八日，东北行政委员会发表《独立宣言》。一九三二年三月九日，满洲国宣告正式成立，年号为大同。溥仪举行就职典礼。长春改名为新京，为满洲国之首都。

而所谓的国联调查团，要迟至一九三二年一月二十一日才正式成立。团长为曾任印度总督的英国爵士李顿。调查团几经辗转，于一九三二年四月二十一日抵达沈阳。调查团逗留东北期间，东北各阶层百姓冒死进谏，通过各种途径寄送给调查团的揭露日军禽兽罪行的材料证据有一千五百余份。从中国军官到中国百姓，都寄希望于国联调查团，期望国际社会能够为中国和中国百姓主持正义、讨回公道。而直到一九三二年十月，调查团才在日内瓦、南京、东京三地同时向国际社会公布了《国联调查团报告书》。报告书的大意为：日本人这么做是不对的，中国的东北应该在外国的保护下实行高度自治，以国际共管取代日本独占。

多么荒唐的结论，多么无用的调查。

而当时，自己已成功地潜伏到了渡边的身边，成为渡边最喜爱的一条狗。想起当初，自己和丽云也曾兴高采烈地盼望过国联调查团的到来，自己的心中真是悲酸难已。丽云最终没有看到调查团的到来，而自己，最终没有盼到调查团的正义。人去，事空。在这个悲酸的时代，人活着，只是为了见证希望的可笑、感受正义的荒诞。丽云若泉下有知，恐怕也会为这个时代流下绝望的泪水。而好在，从丽云逝去的那一刻起，自己就已经是个绝望的疯子。自己没有再期望过天地的公道和人间的正义，自己只相信，以杀制杀，以血还血。自己从不寄希望于世界和上帝。要想报仇，只有靠自己。

自己秘密地将龚汉江四兄弟的尸体安葬在了短毛他们的旁边。好歹，也算是让他们热闹一些吧。一有空，自己就会去小坟岗上拜祭这些义士，给他们烧些纸钱。自己对龚汉江说：好兄弟，你放心，一切都在按计划进行，我们会成功的。

短毛嬉皮笑脸的样子，有时还会浮现在自己的眼前。以前他活着时，自己也从没觉得他是个义士、是个英雄。自己老把他当个流氓。而今对着茫茫的荒冢，自己却不禁悲从中来。什么是英雄？以死抗天者，以死抗命者，就是英雄。

自己每次都要在祭奠完了小坟岗义士和孔仁四兄弟之后，才去看望丽云。因为自己每次都会在丽云的墓前待上最久的时间、说上最多的话。风冷冷，草萋萋，独对荒凉，痴语谁懂？忆往昔，看哀冢，悲泪千行，悔不当初。佳人玉殒黄泉，此去一别经年，音容笑貌犹在，人间沧海桑田。深情不忘在时光，千般相爱千般望，星移斗转天地荒，痴悲何处话凄凉？魂魄风中逝，相恋泪成霜，生死爱入骨，昼夜哀断肠。

“他们都说了，要给翻译多一些钱，这样翻译才不会胳膊肘往外拐，去当汉奸。”

“我背叛谁都可以，但一定不会背叛你。”

“真的？”

“如果有一天，人们看见我当了汉奸，那么，我也一定是想要为了替你做什么事，才去当的假汉奸。”

“不要，你替我去做什么都可以，就是不要替我去做汉奸，假的也不可以，不然，我开除你。”

“好，我答应你，这辈子，死也不会当汉奸。”

当年笑语欢颜犹在，岂知一语成谶、几番泪干。

而自己最后唯一还渴望着的，就是可以在复仇成功之后，自尽在丽云的墓前。从此往后，再不分离。自己只想和她，永远在一起。

做了渡边的狗以后，自己得到了拿枪的资格。与从前致命的恐惧截然不同，自己对枪械产生了一种近乎狂热的痴迷。自己不停地练枪，不停地开枪，白天拿着枪吃饭，晚上抱着枪睡觉，就好像，征服枪，也是自己必须要为了丽云而去做到的事一样。有时候，握着发烫的枪管，自己会感到一种自我惩罚后的轻松。自己已经不清楚自己是否还害怕枪，因为，每一次开枪后的战果，都只会令自己产生一种还要开枪的强烈欲望。就好像，深埋在自己灵魂中的对枪的恐惧，也是杀害丽云的凶手之一，自己有多想报仇，就有多想杀死自己的恐惧。疯子赵驹，每一次开枪，都无比渴望能够杀死自己。因为，自己也是害死丽云的凶手之一。

那时候，渡边的手还没有受伤，他还是日军中著名的神枪手之一。他看到了自己对枪械的近乎疯狂的征服欲，他感到了一种很奇异的乐趣。他竟然真的开始教自己正规的射击，手把手地教，以训练一个狙击手的标准教。自己大喜过望。自己疯狂地学习、练习着狙击。一条崭新的步枪，被自己日日夜夜地握在手里，枪不离人，人不离枪。练习端枪要在枪管下系上砖头一块，自己系上了三块；练习瞄准要以铜钱作为目标，自己将铜钱换成了绣花针。从严寒到酷暑，自己每天狂热地进行着枪法训练、狙击锻炼，雪中、雨中、酷热中，自己纹丝不动、坚定不移；从水里到山里，自己不停地冷酷地猎杀着各种飞禽走兽，用它们的血，冲洗着自己灵魂中的恐惧，磨炼着自己复仇的本领。自己像个疯子一样嗜杀成性，自己时刻保持着一股残酷的狠劲。因为，只有这样，才能既被日本人欣赏，又让自己具备复仇所需的能力。终于，有一天，在自己隔街打死了两个奔跑的百姓之后，渡边笑着说：你已经不需要再练习了，你已经是个和我一样出色的神枪手了。

自己穿过了一整条街，走到了那两个被自己遥远地打死的中国百姓的尸体旁，自己看到，一个人的怀里，还抱着一只买给小孩玩的布老虎。那一刻，自己的心是停顿的。

自己因为练成了百步穿杨的枪法，所以得到了荣仓更加深刻的喜爱。荣仓说：我已经很久没遇到像你这样矫健又强悍的男子了，抚摸你，就像在抚摸一把宝刀。荣仓从未在自己的眼中看出过半分叛逆的破绽，自己始终像个温顺的妓女一样全心全力地侍候着他。曾经有一个时期，自己只要不出现，荣仓就吃不下饭。而就是在这个时期里，自己为樱花会社和日本军方的反目埋下了祸根。同性交媾的污秽恶心与荣仓玩法的肮脏不堪，对自己来说根本就不算什么，只要能为丽云报仇，自己可以去做任何事。自己发过誓，一定要让每一个伤害过、欺侮过丽云的畜生，都受尽千刀万剐而死，且必须是死不瞑目。为了取悦荣仓，自己甚至还经常在荣仓的面前喝下他撒的尿。自己觉得，这一切，都是自己应该受到的惩罚。因为，自己也是害死丽云的凶手之一。

不，不是之一，而是唯一。只有自己知道，其实，真正害死了丽云的凶手，只是自己。只是自己。

从丽云逝去的那一刻起，自己就只是一部复仇的机器。而这部机器的最终任务，就是自我毁灭。

自己只渴望，无比热烈地渴望，最后，可以自尽在丽云的墓前。向她道歉，求她原谅，对她表白，与她相伴，厮守终生。这些，都是自己在她活着时，应该做而没有做的事。自己希望可以完成这些愿望。

每一个夜晚，自己都泪如雨下。而陪着自己的，只有丽云的断发和她的幻影。这样的余生，真的可以让人明白，活着，是一件最不值得让人去追求的事。

自己从未在日本人的面前显露过自己的武功。父亲被迫在匪帮授艺的遭遇自己始终刻骨铭心。自己不想有朝一日，会被日本人逼着出卖中国武学，助纣为虐。那样，既不是自己的所愿，又会给自己的复仇计划增添障碍。所以，自己一直隐藏得很好。而且，自己在练成了枪法之后，就算不用武功，也不必担心自己平常在各种环境下的攻防能力。除非是到了最后时刻，否则，自己绝不会在日本人的面前使出八极拳术。

在整个复仇计划中，渡边和荣仓，是自己准备要留到最后才杀的人。因为他们两个是自己的靠山，是自己在复仇中必须要使用的武器，一旦失去了

他们两人的青睐，自己根本无权动摇樱花会社。所以，自己必须麻痹自己。麻痹自己狂烈的恨、火暴的怒。否则，自己又怎么能和渡边朝夕相处。这种令人发疯的矛盾与忍耐，普通人根本不会明白。而那些能够明白自己的人，又都已不在这个世上。自己是那些已死去了的人们中的一员，但是自己却依然还在这个世上苟且偷生。自己，是个孤独的战士。

那三个和渡边一起糟蹋了丽云的日本畜生，被自己一个一个地先后找了出来，依次秘密杀死。自己悲哀地知道，不管自己做什么，丽云也不会再活过来了。一切都是空虚，一切都是无用。而自己，还将继续活下去，为了杀人而活。

在那三个日本畜生依次死后，自己分别做好了毁尸灭迹的工作。自己的目的，只是要让这些畜生死不瞑目。日军很快便对人员的失踪产生了警惕。为了转移开日军的怀疑视线，将杀人的嫌疑栽到抗日分子的身上，自己又用不同的手法多杀了几名鬼子，以混淆视听。那个曾经殴打过丽云的凶暴少尉，最后也死在了自己的刀下。自己还想找到当时和这个少尉一起殴打过丽云的其他几个畜生，可惜，一直都没再找到。也许，他们都已死在了侵略战争中；也许，他们都还十分逍遥地活着。时代就是这样一个无限扩大着的迷宫，每个人的命运，都只是一粒沙子在风中划过的痕迹，人们在迷宫里伸出手，能抓住的是幸运，抓不住的，就是天意。

光阴似箭，一转眼，丽云逝去已有两年多。一九三四年三月，春寒料峭。溥仪在长春南郊杏花村举行登基典礼，重新称帝。满洲国改为了满洲帝国，年号改为了康德。

自己跟随荣仓赴长春办事时，曾经远远地看见过一次溥仪和他的武术教师霍殿阁。溥仪很瘦，走起路来轻飘飘的，像个病人。霍殿阁虽然身形步法如虎如豹，但也难掩失意困顿之态。溥仪和霍殿阁边走边谈，溥仪在犹豫不决地摇头，霍殿阁在愁眉苦脸地叹气。溥仪经过之处，无人向他下跪。个别日本兵，甚至还在溥仪的背后指指戳戳，谑笑不已。溥仪回头看了看，日本兵发出了刺耳的大笑声。而溥仪和霍殿阁，只是默默地继续走路。那一刻，自己的心是揪紧的。这，就是中国曾经的皇帝，而站在皇帝身边的，就是威震神州的八极拳一代宗师、华夏武林之王。可是，他们却连一个日本小兵的无礼冒犯，都不敢呵斥教训。这是中国的耻辱，是中国人的悲哀。想起小时候，父亲总是说："等你长大了，考上了状元，就能亲眼见到皇上了，皇上是真龙天子，他只要一句话，就能改变天下所有人的命运。"自己真觉得悲哀无限。自己真的亲眼看到了皇上，可是，却早已君非君、臣非臣。所有人，都只是侵略者手中的玩物。中国，悲哀至此。

一九三四年的夏天，在关东军与黑龙会的合力围剿之下，樱花会社终于走向了彻底的灭亡。樱花会社的资产财富全部被充公，由关东军和黑龙会平分。樱花会社的成员被斩尽杀绝，少数漏网之鱼由黑龙会负责派人继续追杀。樱花会社灰飞烟灭，赤木的势力土崩瓦解。

当自己带领着一支日军小队在一片荒地里包围住赤木的时候，赤木已经孑然一身、落魄不堪。包围圈渐渐缩小，赤木呆若木鸡。他绝望地嚎叫了一声，丢掉了手里的半个包子，瘫软地跪倒在了地上。

自己一个人走了上去。

赤木面如土色，全身发抖。他惊恐而绝望地哀求："我要见本庄司令官，我要见本庄司令官！荣仓大佐的儿子不是我杀的，真的不是我杀的！我也没有给北野将军下毒，绝对没有！我怎么会有这个胆子——求你们相信我！"赤木痛哭流涕。

自己拔出了匕首。尖利的刀刃闪耀着雪亮的寒光。赤木目瞪口呆，跪在地上，不停地往后爬。自己的牙齿咬得咯咯响。丽云惨死的模样又一次浮现在了自己的眼前，自己的眼前一片滚烫的血红。

自己两步上前，抓住了赤木。赤木拼命挣扎，但他怎么可能是自己的对手。自己勒住了赤木的脖子，将匕首的尖刃顶在了他的喉咙上。他不敢再动。

自己捂住了他的嘴。

自己凑到了他的耳边，轻轻地用日语对他说："你还记得吗，以前，有一个叫庄丽云的女人，她是庄家唯一的女儿。你不仅害死了她所有的亲人，甚至在她一无所有之后，你还不肯放过她，竟然怂恿渡边那个畜生去糟蹋她！你还究竟是不是人！你根本禽兽不如！！——告诉你，庄丽云的亲人没有死光，我，就是她的爱人！荣仓的儿子是我杀的，北野的毒是我下的，我做这一切，就是为了要让你亲眼看着你的樱花会社和你的人生一起毁灭！我要亲手杀了你，给我最爱的女人报仇！！你，下地狱去吧——"

自己的刀尖，深深地割过了赤木的喉咙。从赤木的喉咙里，喷出了一股股鲜血。赤木捂着喉咙，大张着嘴，眼睛瞪得像铜铃般大。死亡的恐怖从他脸上弥漫开来，随着鲜红的血，腥膻了整片空气。他濒死地挣扎着，垂死地捂着喷血的喉咙。

自己蓦然想哭。自己忍着眼泪，再次上前。自己手起刀落，将赤木开膛剖肚，活生生地，把赤木的心挖了出来。

许多日本兵都害怕得转开了头。

自己看着一片血肉模糊的赤木的尸体，哈哈大笑，哈哈大笑。笑完，自己泪如雨下。

“丽云，我好想你呀，你回来吧——我真的受不了了——”自己痛哭流涕着，在心中悲惨地呼喊着，呼喊着。

然而，只有空气、血腥、日本兵。

没有丽云回答的声音。

自己像个疯子一样，抓着赤木血淋淋的心脏，又哭又笑，又笑又哭。

卧薪尝胆，一别经年。而今复仇即将了结，丽云却已在时光的埋葬中越走越远。自己最想要的，只是可以再好好地看丽云一眼，可是，这却已永远不可能。就算自己杀光了所有仇人，丽云也不可能起死回生。

丽云哪，丽云，你回来呀，回来呀！求求你不要离开我！

自己的心，在疯狂地惨呼，惨呼。

自己捏碎了赤木的心脏。几个日本兵呕吐了起来。

就剩下一个渡边了。自己一定会让这个畜生，死得比赤木还恶心。自己笑着想。

自己眼前一黑，昏倒在了血泊里。

经过了剿灭樱花会社这一役的大小十几次战斗，自己在日军和汉奸队伍里有了杀人魔王和疯子赵驹的绰号。渡边得意扬扬，到处跟人说：赵驹，是我饲养的狗哇。

自己不打算杀荣仓了。因为，荣仓并没有伤害过丽云，但自己却杀了他无辜的儿子。自己和他，就算是扯平了吧。说到底，从一开始，就是自己在利用他。自己所受的污秽，怪不得别人。

而要杀渡边，却不是一件容易的事。因为渡边和其他日本人之间并没有什么矛盾，最多也就是有些鸡毛蒜皮鸡零狗碎的小纠纷，对付他，不可能用以夷制夷离间灭杀的方法，只能是由自己亲自刺杀。但是渡边是个神枪手，自己要杀他，无异于是和霍殿阁比武。如果刺杀不成，自己反被活捉或枪毙，那么，复仇大计便功亏一篑。要知道，渡边，才是自己最应该第一个杀的那个畜生啊！就是他，亲手开枪杀死了丽云！！这个魔鬼，自己一定要送他下地狱！！！

自己做好了一个周详的计划，以确保能一击即中，杀死渡边。

最终的刺杀行动开始前，自己又去拜祭了一遍小坟岗义士和孔仁四兄弟。最后，自己来到了丽云的墓前。看着丽云的坟墓，自己不禁悲从中来，撕心裂肺。自己痛恨无情流逝的时间，痛恨苟延残喘的独活。光阴似箭，丽云离世已近三年，这三年，快得像最无情的闪电，又慢得像最冰凉的飘雪。自己无数次地想停留在渐行渐远的曾经，可是时间总是像无知无觉的流水一样，不停地把曾经冲远、再冲远。自己站在活着的今天，就算再怎么去抓，也抓不住时光无情的远逝。每日每夜，依旧还能陪着自己的，就只有丽云乌亮如新的断发。然而怀抱着丽云的断发，自己除了泪如雨下、对魂痴诉，又真的还能盼到什么、求到什么？芳魂已杳，红尘孤苦。从山花烂漫的春天，到白雪皑皑的冬季，一年又一年，自己只是一个在苦苦思念着已逝爱人的孤魂野鬼。思念与伤痛，彼此浓重。唯有丽云鲜活如往昔的幻影，还在一天天地支撑着自己苟且活着的生命。自己每天都热烈地盼望着黄泉路上和丽云欢聚，盼望得让人心发痛。自己有时甚至会很害怕，不知丽云是否还在黄泉路上等待。如果她已走过了奈何桥，喝下了孟婆汤，忘记了今生的所有情和爱，那么，叫自己该怎么办？每日每夜，自己都肝肠寸断。活着，是对还活着的人的最大折磨。

自己已只剩下最后一个愿望，那就是，可以早早地，在杀了渡边之后，来丽云的墓前自尽。这个愿望，就快要实现了。

自己视死如归地，开始了最后的刺杀行动。

但是，命运又一次残酷地玩弄了自己。

东北的局势已和三年前大不相同，日本人在东北建立了牢固的统治，而东北抗日武装力量的强大，也已不是三年前的小打小闹可比。早在一九三四年的二月二十一日，东北人民革命军第一军第一独立师司令部便召开了有

十七支抗日军队代表参加的会议，通过了《东北抗日联合军宣言》，成立了东北抗日联合军总指挥部。抗日名将杨靖宇，任该军总指挥。东北，进入了一个火热的战斗时代，一个全面反抗与残酷镇压血腥交织的年代。

就在自己要向渡边下手的那一天，日军和抗联之间突然爆发了一场大规模的激烈战斗，日军伤亡惨重。当时渡边早已是从宪兵队调到了陆军，在一支十分骁勇的日军中队里担任中队长。当日，渡边所在的联队奉命紧急赶往战场增援。而自己，则带领着一支满军随渡边同行。大队长竹内当时刚晋升为少佐，志得意满之态溢于言表，他向众人高呼："活捉杨靖宇！大日本天皇万岁！"

那一天，白雪纷纷扬扬，像从天上掉下的云的碎片。雪地里满是鲜血与死尸。雪水混合着血水，整片大地，就像一个敞开着的屠宰场。战斗始终处于胶着状态，双方死伤无数。枪林弹雨中，杀声震天。日本人命令满军冲锋，带去的满军几乎全军覆没。自己心中焦灼，为今天的刺杀计划的落空感到怨恨与焦虑。怎么办？今天杀不了渡边，若要再等下一次机会，天知道是何年何月！怎么办？

大雪依旧下得纷纷扬扬。子弹在雪片中穿梭，雪片在死亡里飘落。杀戮与诗意悠长交缠，残酷与美感相映生辉。这个时代是多么的令人难以理解，地狱建立在天堂之上，人间破碎在美好之中。自己想起那一年，也是在这样的大雪里，丽云含着泪，笑着说，知道吗，你是个笨蛋，其实你每次站在那里看我，等我，我都知道。

生离死别，一去多年，蓦然回首，沧海桑田。

"丽云，我想你——"

自己的心在悲呼。

日军的迫击炮弹在纷纷飞向抗联的阵地。鲜血飞溅。

自己突然想：为何今天不就在这里，取了畜生渡边的性命？

自己血液沸腾。

紧紧跟随着渡边，自己在等待他落单的机会。只要他一落单，自己就会马上动手，出其不意攻其不备，争取一击制敌。虽然渡边枪法神勇，但若论起近身格斗，毕竟自己曾是东北拳王。两相权衡，自己的胜算颇大。而且现在大家都是身处在这生死混乱的战场上，某个人究竟是怎么死的，根本就不会有人去关注。自己如果运气好的话，完全可以在杀死渡边以后，全身而退，离开战场，去奔向那自己最后向往的归宿——丽云的坟墓。这么一盘算，自己便豁然觉得，这场意外降临的战斗和这个意外身处的战场，倒也真是一个可以让自己完成最后复仇的好机会和好场所。自己甚至以为，是上天终于在帮助自己了。

只是，有许多个日本兵，始终像自己一样，在寸步不离地跟随着渡边。有他们在，自己下不了手。自己心中又反复焦躁起来。自己贴近了渡边。

渡边像是察觉到了什么，他回过头来，问：你干吗一直跟着我？

自己说：我要誓死保护太君！您对我恩重如山，请让我为您挡子弹！

渡边点点头，说：好，你很忠诚。

血战依然在继续。雪下得无边无际。

抗联那边的阵地上，出现了一名百发百中的狙击手。不断地有日本兵在被一枪穿头。一枪一个，一枪一个，日本兵脑浆四流。渡边拿过一条狙击步枪就要还击，自己赶紧把这枪给抢了过来，献殷勤地说：太君不用亲自动手，让我来，让我来。

自己三三两两地打死了抗联的几名普通士兵，但没有动对方的那名狙击手。渡边在一旁催促和咒骂，但是他也并不敢频频露头。自己对渡边旁边的那些日本兵说：你们要帮我吸引对方的火力，这样那名狙击手才能露出身来，我才好射击。

渡边对他们下令：引那名狙击手出来，让赵驹射击！

于是，那些跟随着渡边的日本兵，开始以身犯险，不停地用他们的性命来引诱那名抗联的狙击手露头露身。而自己，从未打中过那名狙击手。

渡边不停地咒骂着。

终于，跟随在渡边身边的日本兵，全死光了。

当渡边意识到在这个临时的小战壕里已只剩下他和自己两个人时，他的脸色灰白了。自己的脸上挨了渡边重重的四个耳光，他说：你是猪哇！

他夺回了狙击步枪，准备亲自动手猎杀抗联的狙击手。自己不言不语地，掏出了手枪。

最后的时刻，终于到来了。

自己在渡边的背后，举起了手枪。

渡边没发觉。他的身子晃了晃。

自己稍微挺了挺胸，将枪口对准了渡边的后脑勺。

“——畜生，下地狱去吧！！”自己咬牙切齿地，用汉语掷了一句。

扳机还未来得及扣动，自己的头顶上便爆裂似的一痛，宛如雷霆万钧穿过。血腥血红仿佛瞬间堵住了七窍，塞住了自己全部的知觉。自己的世界猛然漆黑，在电光石火中狂坠进了无底的深渊。自己一下子，彻底失去了所有的意识。

是自己的脑袋，被抗联的狙击手打中了。

自己陷入了漫长的昏睡。麻木与浑噩像用铁丝绕成的茧，将自己的意识紧紧地困住。自己时常能隐约地感到自己还活着，可是，自己又完全抓不住这种活着的感觉。自己只是在长久地睡眠，没有选择地睡眠，就像活着感受死亡一样。自己的躯壳就像一具棺材，而自己那若隐若现的意识，就像躺在棺材里的一具死尸。棺材里布满了严寒的冰霜和错乱的星辰，自己的意识在断断续续的苏醒中，只能触碰到无尽的冰凌和破碎的世界。自己什么也看不到，什么也听不到，只有半死不活的意识，在断断续续地感受着生死交替的味道。黑暗与寂静，仿佛就是生命与世界的本来面目。在昏迷里，自己无尽地游荡、游荡。

黑暗中，总有一个时而清晰时而模糊的梦境追随着自己。梦里，夜色如幻，飞雪连绵，寒风凛冽。有一个美丽的女子，站在昏黄的屋檐下，她痴惘地伸出一只手，一片晶莹的雪花，在她的手心里冰凉，她看着手心，又看着飞雪，无语凝默。自己对她有着一种非常特别的感觉，这种感觉就像一种永恒的誓言在自己的骨子里奔流涌动，但是，自己却又根本想不起来，她是谁。

她是谁？

自己没有死，可是，却失去了最宝贵的记忆。

自己是在一九三五年的春天彻底苏醒的。据看护的日本医生说，是荣仓不惜代价请到了美国最好的脑外科医生，才将自己脑壳里的子弹取了出来，抢救了自己的这条性命。这个日本医生说：你真是幸运，子弹竟然只是擦过了你的大脑皮层，而你的脑子没被打烂。他说：你已经昏睡了整整一个冬天，荣仓大佐以为你再也不会醒过来了。自己茫然地问：荣仓大佐是谁？

一个多月之后，自己的身体恢复了正常的行动能力。而自己的脑子里，却只有充满疼痛感的空空荡荡。自己所了解到的关于自己的一切，都是听日本人说的。

自己了解到，那天在战场上，就在自己中枪倒地的一刹那，渡边抓住时机，开枪击毙了抗联的那名狙击手。渡边以为，那天，自己是故意暴露身体，以此来吸引抗联的狙击手起身射击，好为他渡边的瞄准猎杀制造机会。渡边听不懂汉语，自己在渡边背后骂的那句话，被他理解成了是向抗联狙击手的挑衅。总之，自己的中枪受伤命悬一线，在渡边的解读下，成了一件向大日本皇军献身效忠的英雄事迹。日军还因此让溥仪发了一枚勇士勋章下来。荣仓亲手给自己戴上的勋章。渡边私下里对自己说：我也要谢谢你的英勇，如果那天你不吸引那个狙击手出来，我和你，最后恐怕都会死在他的枪下，他真的太厉害了。

而自己在那段时间里，也真的是以为，自己就是日本人的一条忠诚猎犬，并且还是猎犬里最出色的那一条。自己甚至以此为傲。可是，自己究竟是从哪儿来的，自己以前的人生究竟是什么样的，却没有人能告诉自己。只有一个巨大的回忆的空洞，在充满抽搐的疼痛地日夜折磨着自己。梦里，自己还是能断断续续地经常看到那个美丽的女子，可是，自己却又根本想不起来，她是谁。在自己的居所，一个暗格里，自己发现了一盒断发。这是女人的头发，而自己，为什么要把这盒女人的头发藏在暗格里？自己满腹疑惑，而又不敢声张。自己猜测，自己大概是个有故事的人。

在自己刚出院的时候，渡边就给了自己一支狙击步枪。他要求自己在最短的时间内，恢复到以前的射击水平。自己练习了一个星期，枪法就又回到了百步穿杨的水平。渡边十分高兴，他说：你天生就是一个杀手。

自己就这样，真心实意地做了日本人的猎狗。自己带领着一支骁勇善战的满军，在东北的战场上，为日本人屠杀着大批抗日义士。从湍急的河流中，到茂密的丛林里，自己紧追不舍地猎杀着每一个日军要求自己去杀的人；从辽阔的战场上，到狭窄的小巷中，自己冷酷无情地杀害着每一个铁骨铮铮的抗联将士。自己为了日本人的侵略而浴血奋战，自己的双手沾满了中国人的血。自己丝毫没有歉疚，自己觉得这是天经地义的事情。因为，渡边曾告诉自己：是日本人养活了你，是日本人教会了你过人的本领，是日本人给了你做人的尊严，而中国人看不起你，你在中国人的世界里只是一个最下

贱的乞丐，中国人还都想杀了你。

自己成了一个助纣为虐为虎作伥的血腥刽子手。服从命令就是自己的天职，到处杀戮就是自己的价值。面对宰杀没有心慈手软，面对尸体没有坐卧不安，自己冷血无情、嗜杀成性，因为，自己觉得这就是自己活着的使命。自己有时候总会在自己空荡荡的脑子里进行一些探索，想要回忆起一些东西，想要知道自己以前究竟是个什么样的人，结果，自己就能隐约而断续地想起不少血腥恶心的片断，都是自己杀人的情景。于是，自己便猜想，也许自己以前，就是一个杀人犯。而且，自己老觉得，在自己的深心里，还憋着一股要杀什么人的劲儿。这劲儿很猛，有时候半夜里都能让自己难受得睡不着。可是，自己又根本弄不明白这股想要杀人的狠劲儿到底是怎么回事。自己是想要杀谁呢？真是莫名其妙。也许，自己就是个杀人狂魔吧，自己想。要不然怎么会半夜里都想要杀了谁解恨呢？也许渡边说得不错，自己，天生就是一个杀手。

而那盒柔亮的断发，总是会莫名令自己心如刀绞。每次看到它，自己冷血无情的内心就会被瞬间翻转，心变得柔软、温和而充满莫名的疼痛。自己害怕这种感觉，自己常常对此感到惊慌失措，自己对自己感到陌生而无法理解。然而，自己又无比依恋这盒头发，就好像，它是自己心脏还在跳动的原因。没有它，自己的心会空空地痛；看着它，自己的心又很刺痛。自己无法解释这奇怪而又矛盾的事情。而且，有一次，当自己伸手触摸这些头发时，自己竟然泪流满面，心痛得像被谁狠狠地捅了一刀。失忆，令自己的人生成了一个谜。而自己总怀疑，这盒头发与自己莫名的痛苦，都必然与自己梦里的那名女子有关。她，一定与自己过去的人生有着极大的关系。可是，她到底是谁？自己，想要寻找到她。自己相信，能够反复地在自己的脑海里和梦境中出现的女子，必然不会是一个虚构的幻觉；而只要她不是一个幻觉，自己就必然能够在这世上找到她。

荣仓，没有再能和失忆后的自己说上什么话，因为，自己已经完全忘记了和他的那些事。自己只是拿荣仓当一个救命恩人来对待，而对于他不惜代价救自己的原因，自己只是理解为：日本人的惜才与慈悲。自己觉得渡边说得没错，是日本人给了自己生命，而中国人，差点杀了自己。

在一九三五年秋天的一场战斗里，荣仓身中三枪，死在了野草地里。荣仓临死前，拉着自己的手，说：要是有一天，你恢复了记忆，请相信，我不是一个坏人，我并不愿意过这样的生活，我只想在太平的岁月里，每天看到你。

荣仓吐血而亡，自己感到莫名其妙。

一九三五年的冬天，自己跟随着竹内和渡边，离开了沈阳，去了长春。离开沈阳的时候，自己莫名心酸不已、怅惘难过，就好像这里有什么自己不能失去的东西一样。可是，自己又根本想不起来，自己究竟是在留恋什么，放不下什么。自己的脑海里不断出现那个女子的样子，有她的欢笑，有她的泪眼。她似乎在对自己说着什么，可是，在模糊而破碎的回忆里，自己又根本听不见她在说什么。自己想：总有一天，我会找到你的。

自己登上了去往长春的火车。

不管到哪儿，自己要面对的，总是无尽的枪战。随着自己杀孽的增多和枪法的出名，自己也成了抗日义士们刺杀的重要对象。自己感到了疲惫。有时候看着乌黑冰冷的枪，自己既觉得厌恶甚至恐惧，又感到喜爱甚至依赖。这是一种失忆后的自己无法理解的感情。自己也不明白，当初的自己，究竟为什么要拿起枪。自己真的是因为热爱日本所以才投靠日本人的吗？

北川是日军中著名的神枪手，曾经为溥仪表演过百发百中的枪法。一次，在众人的起哄下，北川与自己比赛了一次射击。渡边示意，不可输也不可赢。于是，自己就和北川打了个平手。其实自己还是赢了。渡边十分高兴。竹内也很满意。

在长春，自己遭遇了几次针对自己的暗杀。刺客们的行动很火暴，充满了刻骨的仇恨与熊熊的怒火。他们临死前还在愤恨的咒骂：别忘了你是中国人，你对日本人来说只是一条狗！自己无情地枪毙了他们。但是枪毙完之后，自己又倍觉颓废与空虚。自己当然知道自己只是日本人的一条狗，但是，自己存在的价值，不就是要做好一条出色的狗吗？除了帮日本人杀人，自己实在是不知道，自己还有什么用；除了帮日本人杀人，自己实在是不知道，自己还能靠什么吃饭。难不成自己还能去投靠抗联，领抗联的军饷？哼，能不被他们剁成肉酱才怪。那么，要不就隐姓埋名，去做个普通老百姓，远离血雨腥风？可惜自己枪法在身，日本人是绝不会让自己退隐的。人生至此，也只能是将错就错、得过且过了。

自己感到无尽的厌倦和疲惫。

在一次保卫溥仪的战斗中，渡边为了救自己，右臂上中了一颗子弹。这令自己感觉很惊讶也很感动。这份情谊打破了自己对自己是狗的认知。渡边说：没什么，上次要是没有你，我也死了，我只是不想欠你人情。

渡边的右臂受伤后，他失去了他神妙的枪技。他的右手无法在紧张中稳定，一旦在火暴的战场中持枪，他的右手就会僵硬或者发抖。他再也不是一个神枪手了，自己真心感到内疚。但是他却说：世人皆不甘平庸，但是，只有真正爬上过顶峰的人才会懂得，文也好，武也好，平庸最好。这话莫名竟透着一股禅机，令自己久久不能平静。

失忆中的自己，并不知道自己会武功的事实。只是，有一次自己意外看到了霍殿阁练拳，莫名竟驻足偷看，看得入了迷。霍殿阁收了功，走过来，问：你喜欢八极拳吗？自己茫然地望着他。他伸手过来，在自己身上的两处穴道上按了按，问：谁教的你武功？自己疑惑地说：我不会武功。霍殿阁就没再问什么。他看看天，看看地，叹了口气，像是自言自语地说：老辈人说，文有太极安天下，武有八极定乾坤，可惜了，这一代的神州子孙。说完，霍殿阁就颓废而悲伤地走了。

自己感觉莫名其妙。

而那盒断发，始终还伴随在自己的身边。在许多个深沉死寂的夜晚，自己都会莫名抱着这盒头发入眠，因为只有这样自己才能感觉安心。恍惚的空虚总在白昼缠绕着自己，像一个挥之不去的病魔。病魔总在提醒着自己：你现在的人生是无根之木，你现在的灵魂是无源之水。水波一样荡漾着的自我怀疑，总会像刺骨的冰霜一样层层渗透进自己的血肉骨髓，令自己在无尽的彷徨和恐惧中战栗不已。而在这战栗不已里，自己又找不回半点有用的回忆。只有一些破碎的图像，在脑海里沉默而混乱地流转，也不知它们是真是幻、何因何果。只有漫长的迷惘和煎熬、矛盾的怀疑和徘徊，在折磨着自己。而只有这盒奇怪的头发和梦里的那名女子，才能唤起自己热烈的感情，虽然自己也不能确定这感情究竟为何物。但是，自己知道，这盒头发，定是某种深入自己生命的记忆。自己一定要找到她。

找到她，也许就能找到自己的人生。自己确信。

自己不想再做一个心灵无依无靠的人，不想再做一部杀人机器。自己需要回忆。

一九三六年十二月十二日，发生了震惊中外的西安事变。自东北沦陷后，日军进窥华北，步步为营，而蒋介石却依旧抱定着“攘外必先安内”的决心。蒋介石派遣张学良与杨虎城率军在西北与红军厮杀，内战不休，血流成河。东北军与西北军将士不愿同室操戈，纷纷要求北上抗日。蒋介石得到特务密报，于是亲赴西安督促剿共，张、杨苦劝其停战，无用。蒋威胁张、杨，若不全力剿共，便会将张、杨两部分别调往福建、安徽，改由中央军来占据西北、控制战局。十二月九日，西安学生举行大游行，蒋介石竟命令警察向学生开枪镇压。苦劝进谏已皆无用。最后，张学良与杨虎城发动兵谏，活捉了蒋介石，要求其停止内战，联共抗日。

很快便到了一九三七年的春天。

春寒料峭。

自己默默寻找了很久，也一直没找到那个闪烁在自己记忆碎片中的女人。她就像一朵轻盈而遥远的云，自己知道她定在这世上的某个角落里飘荡，却又完全看不见听不到抓不住云的痕迹。唯有天空广袤，蔚蓝如洗。自己甚至许多次地幻想，也许，有一天，自己会在某次不经意的蓦然回首中，准确地看到她。烟雨朦胧中，灯火阑珊里，人面桃花，久别重逢。那样，自己人生的谜底，也许就会真相大白。莫名，自己总有种不可动摇的直觉：她，必是自己最深爱的女人。这直觉锐利而坚韧，令自己对过往的谜团，有着执着破解的渴望。

然而，自己的一切相信与怀疑，都无根无据，无凭无依。这就使得自己的整个存在显得很荒唐，看起来充满了自嘲的意味。无源之水的人生，死水一潭的灵魂，奄奄一息地活着。彷徨，迷茫，费解，无望。失忆既不是遗忘，也不是死亡，它既不是主动地放弃过往，也不是被迫地接受终结，而是上天对人的一种玩弄，让你活着被剥夺最珍贵的曾经，让你不死地承受着一无所有的疼痛。人，不知从哪儿来，也就不知该往哪儿去，从而就变成了一颗飘浮的尘埃，随波逐流，在风中百般回转，也不会找到生命的归宿。所以人生需要有答案，所以活着必须有回忆。否则，存在该是一种怎样苍白的煎熬。回忆在提问，而每一个行进中的明天，都是答案的一部分。

一次，渡边向自己感慨，时光对英雄的磨灭。他说：黑龙会以前是那样凶猛的一头野兽，可是，内田良平却太痴迷于军政，想要把这头爪牙锋利的

野兽改造成一个西装革履的政客，然而他并不明白，从前的政客听命于他，正是因为他有着野兽的爪牙，一旦他把爪牙文明地卸下，又还有谁会服从于他？昭和神圣会事件之后，内田良平差点被杀，这就足以说明，成为大日本生产党后的黑龙会，已经不再能左右军部的官吏了。而如今的内田良平更是心灰意冷，只想淡出黑龙会，将位子交给头山满。真是可惜了他那么多年的呼风唤雨，苦心经营。

自己说：这都是命运的安排。

渡边说：不，没有所谓的命运，一切，只是思想的陷阱和时光的摧残，一颗再强大的英雄的心，也逃不过这两者的伏击。

一九三七年的五月，渡边兽性勃发，又强奸了一个女人。他强奸的时候，命令自己去捆绑住那个女人的丈夫，把他绑过来观看。自己开始捆绑那个丈夫，士兵们松开了原先按压着他的手。自己的心里莫名很不是滋味，一时就走了神，失了手。那个丈夫猛然挣脱了束缚，一下子就像头野熊一样跳了起来。自己被他猛地一拳，后脑勺磕在了桌角上。

一阵头痛欲裂。自己忽然听到那个刻在记忆碎片里的女人，发出了声音："赵驹，我以为，你会救我的。"

肝肠寸断，天旋地转。

"啊——"自己痛得惨叫了起来。

渡边赶紧掏出枪，几枪打死了那个狂怒的丈夫。鲜血四溅，血滴溅进了自己的眼睛里。

自己泪如雨下，撕心裂肺。

——"知道吗，爱过你，我这辈子不后悔。"

一字一句，刻骨铭心。

自己跪倒在了死人的血泊里。自己心如刀绞，泣不成声。

"啊啊——"自己哀号了起来。

渡边匆忙丢开了女人，跑了过来。"赵驹，你怎么了？"渡边问。

自己抱住了自己的脑袋。

——"知道吗，头发是不会腐朽的，就算有一天，我死了，尸骨烂成了污泥，这些头发，也还是会像我活着时一样又黑又亮。人是最短暂的。"

——"傻话，说什么死啊活的，你要长命百岁，等到这些头发都烂了你还在我身边，这样我才会一辈子高兴。”

“啊啊啊——”自己号啕大哭。

苍天哪，你为什么要这样对我！！！——自己仰天悲哭。

为什么！！！

自己，恢复了全部的记忆。

自己血红着双眼，紧握着拳头，从血泊里站了起来。

渡边和日本兵们，都诧异地望着自己。

自己收起了眼泪，怒发冲冠，准备与渡边同归于尽。

突然，自己的背后刺骨一凉。

自己回转身，看到，那个被侮辱的女人，在背后，捅了自己一刀。

日本人打死了她。

自己哀凉一笑，眼前一黑，倒在了地上。

黑暗的梦境里，自己好像又回到了和丽云在一起的日子中。那些日子，清晰得好像就发生在昨天，美好得仿佛在另一个世界。丽云笑靥如花，自己憧憬满怀。幸福，而灿烂。

自己真想永远沉睡在那个过去。

然而，醒来，是残酷的现实。岁月已逝，一去多年。

丽云长眠在一九三一年，而眼前，已是一九三七年。

时光，真的是个太残酷的东西。

自己一个人在日本人的病房里，泪流满面。

苍天真的太残忍，和丽云在一起的回忆，是自己活着的最后慰藉，可是，苍天却连这也要剥夺走！不仅剥夺走，而且，还要自己认贼作父为虎作伥，帮日本人杀了那么多的中国人！！苍天哪，你究竟是怎样的一个恶魔！！！

自己哭疯了。

自己跳下病床，拿起枪，就往医院外面跑。

自己要杀了渡边！杀了渡边！！

自己要为丽云报仇！！！

暮色昏暗。

然而，自己刚跑出医院，就在一个街角，被潜伏着的锄奸队给截住了。

逃是逃不掉了。

自己说：我知道自己罪孽深重、死有余辜，但是，求你们再让我多活一天吧。

一个大个子说：想杀你可不容易，我们又怎么会放虎归山。

自己说：我真的不想再杀人了，你们不要逼我。

大个子说：你这算是求饶，还是威胁？

自己说：我真的是在求饶。

大个子说：你这个杀人魔，不用再说废话耍花样了，想走，就从我们众兄弟的尸体上跨过去吧。只要我们还有一口气在，就誓要杀了你这个狗汉奸！

枪声骤响，血光火花。

一番厮杀。

最后，自己对倒在血泊里的大个子说：以前那些人，都是渡边要我杀的，杀人不是我的本意。

大个子冷冷一笑，虚弱地说：你比日本人还残忍，你杀的人，远比渡边多。

自己踏着血泊，欲哭无泪。

自己转身离去，身后枪响。自己的腿上，中了一弹。

倒下时，自己不禁问自己：我是谁？我究竟是一个复仇者，还是刽子手？

自己被日本兵送回了医院。渡边派兵将医院保护了起来。

自己陷入了深远的沮丧。

一种寒冷的自嘲在心头萦绕：中国人要杀我，而日本人在保护我。

这种寒冷像阴森的刺一样令自己感到恐惧。自己忽然好想回到沈阳，回到丽云的坟墓前。因为只有在丽云的身边，自己才能感到安心，感到温暖。

然而，自己如果在长春杀了渡边，就不可能再回到沈阳去了。自己忽然想，从长春到沈阳，最短也有六百里路。自己杀完了渡边以后，是不可能在这么长的几百里路上逃过日军的捕杀的。更何况，还到处有抗日队伍的锄奸刺杀。自己，要怎样才能在报完了仇后，回到沈阳丽云的墓前，去和她死在一起？

没有办法，除非，能和渡边一起回沈阳。

自己不禁悲从中来。自己离开沈阳时，竟然都没能去和丽云道个别，如此一别，也不知自己何时才能重回她墓前相见？

人生长恨水长东，天公无情弄人情。唯有漫漫的悲怆，自吞自咽。说不完的思念、哀伤、苦恨，唯有在梦中才可哭诉。

“你比日本人还残忍，你杀的人，远比渡边多。”

锄奸队员的话，依旧在耳边回响。

自己看着自己的双手，肮脏的血腥味仿佛在自己全身鼓胀。不错，这些年来，自己的这双手，用枪，打死了多少抗日的好汉？自己曾经多少次不顾性命地保护了畜生渡边？是渡边这头畜生糟蹋杀害了丽云哪！

赵驹，这些年，你都做了些什么呀！！

天意弄人。红尘中的一切悲喜，都只不过像是上帝眼里的一出闹剧。这红尘中的血泪悲欢、生离死别，是多么冰冷寒凉、坚如磐石。

渡边来医院慰问了自己。看着近在眼前的他，自己竟然没有动手。

自己只是问他：我们什么时候可以回沈阳？

渡边说：不知道，也许明天就能回，也许再也不能回，军人就是司令官手中的棋，司令官要我们去哪儿，我们就去哪儿。

无人时，自己只有独自流泪。

自己感到，已经丧失了活着的勇气，甚至就连复仇的信念，也已不能撑起自己活下去的力量。自己感到生不如死。

苟延残喘，像刀割一样的活着的疼痛。

“其实人生，最美好的就是活着，只有活着，才能看见阳光和鲜花，只有活着，才能记住并想念那些自己爱的人和事，也只有活着，才能和自己喜欢的人在一起，朝朝暮暮，永不分离。”

丽云的声音，就像从未逝去过一样，动听、温柔、清晰。

只有活着，才能记住并想念那些自己爱的人和事。自己默念着。

默念着。

夜深人静时，自己总哭得像个疯子。

自己想回沈阳，想回到丽云的身边，想和丽云死在一起。多少年了，自己最后的愿望，总还悬在半空里。自己还不能回丽云的身边去，因为大仇还

未得报。沈阳，就像一个归宿、一场皈依，在自己灵魂的原野上空不停召唤着自己。

自己一定要把渡边骗回沈阳去，杀了他，然后，自己再去丽云墓前自尽。自己打定了主意。

对沈阳的想念，是刻骨铭心的。自己对家乡——江庆县，都从未有过如此深刻的情感。就仿佛，沈阳才是自己生命中的家乡似的。试问岭南应不好，却道，此心安处是吾乡。丽云在哪里，哪里便是自己的家。自己，想要回家。人，终要回家。

一九三七年七月七日，发生卢沟桥事变。七月七日晚，日军在卢沟桥西北龙王庙附近举行夜间军事演习，深夜，日军以士兵失踪为借口，要求进入宛平县城搜查，遭到中国守城官兵拒绝。随后，日方便蓄意扩大事态，故意挑起战端，最终两军交火。日军的全面侵华就此拉开了序幕，而中国军民也进入了全面抗战的时代。神州大地硝烟弥漫、烽火连天，生死时代血肉横飞、泪水不绝。

自己跟随着竹内和渡边，踏上了南下侵华的血战征途。一路枪林弹雨，生死交错，自己满腔热泪，无处可哭。日军节节胜利，自己，离沈阳越来越远。

自己在杀人的事上表现出了过多的懒惰，终于招致了渡边的反复痛骂。他在一定程度上表现出了对自己的冷淡。自己警觉了起来。自己还没和渡边一起回沈阳呢，在此之前，自己绝不可失去渡边的青睐与欢心。于是，在侵华的战场上，自己不得不又重新表现出了英勇残暴的气质。一切，都是为了报仇。我最后反正要死的，就到那时，再偿清血债吧。自己总是一边杀人，一边这样想。

如果自己不像一个真正的汉奸，如果自己表现得与失忆时太过不同，渡边早晚会起疑心；如果渡边起了疑心，去细翻陈年旧账、查找真相，那么，自己这么多年所受的罪，就白费了。自己还没回到沈阳去，自己还没杀了渡边，自己还没和丽云死在一起，所以，自己必须继续伪装。自己时常这样提醒自己。

只不过，杀中国人杀久了，自己也感觉到了麻木。光阴似箭，在漫长的杀戮中，自己的心上已磨起了厚厚的一层老茧。很多时候，自己甚至对杀害中国人并不感到内疚。自己恐怖地感到，自己，似乎真的已变成了一个汉奸。

自己的恐惧是可笑的。你已经杀害了那么多的抗日志士和无辜国人，你不是汉奸刽子手是什么？

事实胜于苦衷。

自己欲哭无泪。

唯一还一路伴随着自己的，只有丽云的头发。自己每日每夜地怀念，痛彻心扉地想念。回忆，是自己仅有的依靠和伴侣。现实都是虚幻，只有回忆，回忆里的爱情岁月，才是自己唯一真实的乐园。

有时候，自己也会不禁自问：我，真的还能回到沈阳去吗？答案是茫然，答案是偷泣。

丽云，我想你。

丽云，我爱你。

丽云，等着我。

只有无望的呼喊，沉闷的呼喊，在日日夜夜地撞击自己颓废的灵魂。

自己，再也找不回丽云了。自己常常痛哭着想。因为，她早已不在了。

不在这个世界上了。

人生，就是这样的悲惨、荒诞、痛苦、煎熬。

活着，就是忍受折磨。

造化弄人，沧海桑田。

最后，自己跟随着日军，回到了家乡江庆县。但是，自己却只知道，自己已离家乡，有千里之遥。

自己唯一的愿望，只是想要杀渡边、回沈阳。

杀渡边，回沈阳。

人间悲，红尘苦，伤心泪，一江水。

丽云，等着我。

丽云，我爱你。

丽云，我想你。

…………

天色已亮。赵驹抹去泪水，收起回忆，抬起头来。

朝阳冉冉升起，光芒金黄而枯淡。像萎缩的箭，像割断的麦。暑气渐渐弥漫，而灰暗的图景依旧灰暗。颓废的时间混合着惨败的世界，在无意义的阳光照耀下，散发着腐朽的乌烟瘴气。这是一个活着多余的年代，这是一个眼泪无用的年代。生的目的，在这个时代里，多半不如死的放弃。蓝天广阔，明日灰淡。

上午，一个汉奸来叫醒了熟睡的赵驹，向赵驹报告说：山本大尉今日有闲，又想请你去他私宅一聚。

赵驹听了就头皮发麻。

这个山本，自从结识赵驹以来，已请赵驹去了他私宅里五六次，每次，山本都以热爱武术为名，要赵驹陪他练习空手道。然而，说是陪练，其实就是挨打。赵驹一次之后就品出了这个味儿来。而且，赵驹明显能感觉到，山本是在将他往死里打。就算有陪练护具的保护，赵驹也仍然是每次都被打得伤痕累累。赵驹武艺深藏，也不能还手，也不能躲避得太灵活。不仅如此，山本信玄这个人，还有点阴阳怪气，他打人不打脸，打完了还会向赵驹说不好意思。赵驹也就不好说什么。就算身上被打得处处瘀青，但是穿着衣服，谁也看不出来赵驹是被打了。赵驹有点哑巴吃黄连的感受。

赵驹能感到山本信玄态度中的阴险与恶意，但他一时也弄不明白原因。因为他对山本暂时还不了解。他只看出来，渡边对山本这个小小的大尉是很客气的，于是，他便猜想，这山本必是有些来头的，不好随便惹。更何况，赵驹深知，自己对日本人来说，本就只是一条狗。人要打狗，狗哪有推辞的道理。只能逆来顺受。

赵驹再次到了山本的私宅里。

又是一次陪练。

山本的空手道，招式凌厉，气劲霸道。如果没有护具的保护，普通人是万万招架不住的，而且山本生性残暴，赵驹曾亲眼看到过，山本将一个中国农民的一条腿，活生生地从身上撕下来，血腥至极，惨不忍睹。

打完之后，山本又是照例向赵驹致歉。赵驹忙点头哈腰地说：能让太君高兴，是我最大的荣幸。

山本哈哈大笑。他请赵驹喝茶，说，今天要介绍一个老朋友给你认识。

赵驹满腹狐疑。

一个日本中年大汉走了出来。山本说："赵先生，还认识他吗？"

赵驹一脸茫然，看了又看，想了又想，真不认识。

山本哈哈一笑。

大汉脱下上衣，腹部一条陈旧的伤疤赫然入目。

赵驹不知何意，讶然呆立。

大汉用日语对赵驹说："当年，在日本的出口旅馆里，你向我开了一枪，我几乎就死了。"

赵驹愕然惊悚。

赵驹认出来了，这个大汉，就是当年那个老山本派出的众多杀手中的一个。那是最危险的一次，杀手的刀尖，已顶住了赵驹的喉咙。幸亏赵驹最后拿到了枪。小半辈子过去了，赵驹一直以为，那是自己第一次杀人。

然而，现在，这个未死的亡灵，就这么活生生、阴森森地站在阳光下，站在赵驹的面前。

大汉向赵驹介绍山本信玄："这位，就是我们山本首领的儿子。"

大汉冷笑着对赵驹说："低贱的支那狗，你没想到吧，到最后，你还是没能逃出我们的手掌心。"

赵驹在山本信玄面前跪了下来。赵驹说："我现在已效忠大日本天皇，请给我个机会，留我这条命，让我为太君征战沙场，将功赎罪，效忠天皇！"

赵驹拼命磕头，磕得额头出了血。

山本信玄阴阳怪气地笑着，用汉语说："既往不咎，既往不咎，以后，记得经常来陪我练习空手道。只不过，从下一次起，你不可以再穿护具。"

说完，山本信玄和大汉都哈哈大笑了起来。

赵驹连连磕头，说："谢太君开恩！谢太君开恩！"

鲜血，从赵驹的额头上，流到了他的眼睛里。

第三部

男人的悲伤哭泣

一九三八年十二月，国民党副总裁汪精卫与周佛海等人秘密逃离重庆，潜往越南。十二月二十九日，汪精卫在河内发表“艳电”，公开投降日本。蒋介石命戴笠派出刺客，赴越南刺杀汪精卫。刺客行动失败，汪精卫迅速受到了日方力量的保护。一九三九年四月，在日本特务的保护下，汪精卫等人秘密进入上海。汪精卫与日方达成多项共识。日本人开始着手为汪精卫建立新的“中央政府”。

风云动荡，战火连天。

赵宏伟的头，还在一阵阵的痛。空荡而寂静的病房里，闷热而压抑。夏天的暑热混合着提心吊胆的恐惧，令赵宏伟身上的汗热了又冷、冷了又热。苍蝇和蚊子在他身边来回转悠，他视若无睹，不想理会。

赵宏伟醒来已有好几天，他每日忐忑不安且心急如焚，想要去医院外探听情况，但是，他始终都被困在医院里。他找了三次借口想要走出医院的大门，可是都被看守医院的日本哨兵给拦了下来。且不论他脑袋上受了这样重的伤，到底是否适合走出医院，单单就竹内疑案尚未了结这事来说，赵宏伟也是别想在短期内获得人身自由。他明白自己实质上是被软禁在医院里了。他知道这件事是必然的，但是，他必须要想办法快点出去。因为，他还不知道秀珍现在怎样了。另外，他也是担心，日军的调查一旦深入，真相必将大白，他一定要赶在日军查出他是刺客前，赶赴玉山，与秀珍会合。如果秀珍的确还活着的话。

但愿他们一切都安好，赵宏伟祈愿。

赵宏伟只能通过和医院里的日本伤兵频繁交谈，来获取各种情报。他已经知道了战斗当天西路战场上行动队的具体死亡人数，赵宏伟明白，如果自己打听到的这个数目是准确的话，那么，也就是说，包括老周本人在内的整个西路行动队，已经全体阵亡。赵宏伟不禁会想起那个小孙悟空，他还只是个孩子。赵宏伟感觉十分悲伤。在这样的一个战火年代，连孩子都已拿起了枪，为了反抗侵略而奔向战场、慷慨赴死，自己饱读诗书、自视清高，却甘做侵略者跟前的一条狗，自己简直愧为男儿、猪狗不如。赵宏伟痛心疾首，思绪翻涌。

同时，赵宏伟又万分担心方远梦的安危。当日的营救行动过程复杂而战斗激烈，赵宏伟不知方远梦是否还活着。赵宏伟觉得，要想和秀珍远走高飞，必定还有很多事情需要方远梦的帮忙。而且方远梦是唯一能够证明他赵宏伟不是真正汉奸的人。另外，方远梦也真的是赵宏伟唯一能吐露心声的知己兄弟。所以，基于以上三个原因，赵宏伟是万分希望方远梦能安然无恙。

当然，赵宏伟心里最担心最挂念的，还是秀珍。经过了这场劫难，秀珍身心俱伤，赵宏伟知道，现在除了自己，再没人能抚慰秀珍所受的伤。秀珍对他痴情了半生，而他也辜负了她半生，现在，是该需要他来好好地爱她了。不只是因为赵宏伟心中对秀珍也有深情，同时也因为，秀珍落到如此境地，除了他真心实意的爱，再也没什么灵丹妙药能治疗她心中的伤痛了。这伤痛，除了秀珍已经遭受的那些屈辱与摧残，还包括秀珍将来必须要接受的小菊已经不在了的事实。而赵宏伟深刻地明白，小菊的离世，必将给秀珍带来一次更为沉重的打击。所以，他必须要想办法尽快去到秀珍的身边，安抚她，守护她，珍爱她。

只是，住在医院的这几天，赵宏伟晚上又梦到了死去的心音。梦里的心音，依旧是当年那个天真烂漫的少女。她在如雨纷飞的樱花中欢笑、跳舞。时光越过了几个春夏秋冬，而心音，还是纯洁得像温暖的阳光，美丽得像如雨的樱花。她在赵宏伟的梦中说：我爱你，宏伟君。赵宏伟从梦中醒来，总是满腔酸楚，这种酸楚，有时甚至会浓烈得超过他对秀珍的担忧。他想：心音的尸骨还孤独地埋在日本呢，远隔着一片海，她再也看不到我，我也再

看不到她。这么一想，那些用岁月酿成的忧伤，便都填满他的胸口，使他感到，他真的不该再去爱别的女人。

人生，真的是一场悲伤的宿醉。

赵宏伟还想起一件重要的事情，那就是在营救行动开始前，他将一封致秀珍的绝情信交给了方远梦，要方远梦在他赵宏伟死后向秀珍隐瞒他的死讯，并且将那封绝情信交给秀珍。赵宏伟当时这样设计的目的，只是想要让秀珍相信，他还好好地活着，她再也见不到他，不是因为他已不在人世，而只是因为他不爱她，不想再和她相见。他当时觉得，如果自己真死了，那么，只有这样，才能将对秀珍造成的打击降到最轻。试想，如果秀珍再也见不到他赵宏伟了，那么，是要让她知道他爱着她但是他已死了好呢，还是要让她相信他还活着只是他并不爱她好呢？赵宏伟当时选择了后者，因为，他也相信，人只要活着就好，而爱情，不如生命重要。这是他当时替秀珍做的选择，也是他的赌。不过，现在看来已经暂时不用再担心这个生死与爱情孰轻孰重的问题了，因为他赵宏伟已经奇迹般地活下来了。他现在最需要考虑的，是怎样才能把他还好好活着的这个消息尽快地传送到方远梦和秀珍的耳朵里。赵宏伟很快就有了主意。他打算马上写一篇大拍渡边马屁的文章，这样的话，渡边一定会用最快的速度将这篇文章登在报纸的显眼位置上，如此一来，共产党只要能看到报纸，就能知道他赵宏伟还活着。

赵宏伟在病房里很快就完成了他的拍马屁文章。

他提出了要见渡边的请求。

事情看起来像在朝着赵宏伟希望的方向发展，但是，赵宏伟心中的恐惧又莫名越来越严重。他寝食难安，彻夜难眠。

日子很快，已经过了农历的六月十日。

山上的空气里，总透着一股青草的香。

一个女人从玉山的悬崖上跳了下去，寻了短见。

几天内，这已是第四个轻生跳崖的女子。

政委急得团团转，好不容易把这些女人从日本人的手里给救了出来，却没想到，她们还会一个个地想要自杀。政委派十几个人守在悬崖上，绝不允许再有人跳崖。另外，方远梦也组织起了游击队里仅有的几个女卫生员，让她们去做好这些被救妇女的心理疏导工作。

队长派了几个人出去，想要联络到新四军的大部队。一是因为这场大战之后，玉山游击队减员严重，虽然大捷，但部队折损了五分之一的战士，一旦日军实行围剿，游击队恐力不能敌，所以急需和大部队商量好对策；二是因为山上突然来了两百多个女人，粮食猛然吃紧，日子久了定难负担，而且日军是绝不会轻易地就此罢手，早晚还会有恶战来临，到时候恐怕再难保护好这些女人，所以必须尽快地将她们送出沦陷区。

还有一件事情，特别令队长和政委暗自忧虑。那就是，玉山的地形和暗道，现在其实已经不是秘密了。当初，在这支游击队想要进入江南地区作战的时候，是一个被游击队救起的老和尚，向游击队献上了玉山的地形暗道图。据说，这个老和尚，以前就是玉山匪帮的军师，后来，他的女儿被金顺的外甥霸占，跳崖自尽，他才幡然醒悟，去做了和尚，行善赎罪。当他听闻游击队要去江南抗击日寇，却苦无立足之地时，他便拿出了那张玉山地形暗道图来。据他介绍，这座玉山，在明朝末期曾是一座矿山，后来废弃百年，在清朝时又曾屯过兵，所以这座山上的地形被改造得十分复杂。一般人最多只能走到半山腰，再要往上去，就无路可行了。其实在玉山的腹中，有一条盘曲而上的暗道，这条暗道宽阔得可以让人跑马和开车。而围绕着这条暗道，又有许多假道，一旦走错，就会摔死。可以说，如果没有地图，陌生人想要上山，难于登天。且玉山本身外在的地形就万分险峻，只要用心布置，它就是一座天然的碉堡。游击队用了老和尚之言，按照地图，占据了玉山，以此作为战斗大本营，果然屡见奇效。日军想要剿灭游击队，简直是无从下手。可以说，地利，是玉山游击队的生存之本。而这个生存之本，又必须是以全体战士保守地理秘密为前提。原本，这不是个问题。但是，现在，这个全体战士保守地理秘密的前提，却忽然像是被撕开了一条小口子。那天，游击队营救出了这批女人，由女卫生员给她们穿戴好了衣服鞋袜后，便要蒙眼带她们上山。但是她们一下子就全惊恐地大哭大叫了起来。因为她们以为，蒙了眼，就一定又是要她们进狼窟，天下男人全一样。结果，政委最后只好决定，不蒙眼。于是，这两百多个女人，就等于是全程参观了一遍玉山的暗道秘密。这些女人是否能为玉山游击队保守这暗道的秘密，谁能知道？况且，她们很快就会被分散安置到各个地方去。无论怎么想，这玉山的地理玄

机，多半将很快不成为秘密。队长和政委，忧思重重。

方远梦从报纸上看到了日军对于这场营救战斗的描述。报纸上详细说明了三路战场上中日双方战斗人员的死亡人数。方远梦一算，便知道了老周和他的行动队员，已全部牺牲。在政委的主持下，游击队在山顶上为牺牲的战士们办了一场追悼会。大家的心情都很沉重，毕竟打胜仗也是付出了巨大的代价。唯一仍可值得欣慰的是，竹内真的死了。不过，一个日本军官死了，自然又会有一个新的日本军官上任。直到战争结束，战斗将永不停止。这就是这个时代的魔咒。

战友牺牲的忧伤在各人的心上还未淡去，大家又都心知肚明地明白，不久之后，日军必将大举来袭。每个战士，都做好着再次战斗的准备。在这样的一个烽火年代，马革裹尸对每个战士来说都只是一种必然，所以，今天自己对战友的怀念，很可能就是明天战友对自己的哀悼。这种忧伤不是悲哀，但比悲哀更沁人肺腑。

方远梦也很挂念赵宏伟，他在玉山上，暂时也不知道江庆县城里的具体情况，也不知道赵宏伟是否安好。赵宏伟曾嘱咐他一定要帮忙照顾好秀珍，但是现在这些被救出来的女人的精神状况普遍都不好，非常不好，秀珍也不例外，他实在是很担心，秀珍会不会有事。因为他知道，赵宏伟还没把小菊离世的消息告诉过秀珍。这是一个难题呀。

方远梦站在悬崖边上，看着下面空旷幽深的山谷，脸被从下而上旋转的风吹拂着，他感到很哀伤。已经有四个女人跳崖自杀了，就算将她们从日本畜生的手里救了出来，她们的人生也都已经彻底被毁了。她们的家都在江庆县城里，但是很显然，至少从目前来说，她们是回不去了，更何况，在江庆县的慰安妇事件曝光后，老百姓们发生了暴动，她们的男人，大多已死在了日军的枪下，而她们现在可能还不知道。这样的一个悲哀的残局，究竟应该如何来收拾啊？方远梦感到了一种无能为力的愤恨：就是那些欲望失控的侵略者，毁灭了无数无辜者原本安好的人生！他们摧毁的不仅是受难者的身体、受难国的土地，更是人的灵魂、生的希望！就算这场战争现在立刻结束，又有谁还能真的回到那个平静而美好的过去？不可能了，一切，都已被毁了。无数的人，就好像这些被摧残过的女人一样，再也回不到以前了，再也没有家和爱人了。一切美好而值得珍惜的东西，都已被战争摧毁了，摧毁得满目疮痍、荡然无存。这就是这个黑暗时代的真相。

方远梦紧锁着眉头，叹了口气。

小秦来找到了方远梦，向方远梦报告了一些情况。那些被救出来的女人，每人的肩头都被文了一个编号，女卫生员们想了很多办法，也洗不掉那些号码。有的女人要自己拿刀割肩上的皮肤，想割掉号码，好不容易才被卫生员拦了下来。小秦问方远梦该怎么办。方远梦焦躁地走来走去，愤怒地说：那帮日本畜生！

小秦说，其实问题还不仅在于，这种文身是耻辱，更重要的是，肩上带着这种号码，以后她们在人群里很容易被日本人重新找出来。

方远梦在一块石头上坐了下来。他思考了一会儿，说：想办法找一个文身专家来，如果实在洗不掉，那就干脆加工，用其他图案来掩盖那些号码，待会儿你让卫生员去征求一下那些女人们的意见。

小秦说好。

方远梦问小秦：秀珍她怎么样了？

小秦说：王大嫂还是那样，一声不吭，啥也不说，就到处去找脏衣服，找到了就帮人洗。

方远梦说：看好一点，防止出什么事。

小秦说：我看不要紧，能找事做，好歹不会往死路上想，过一段时间也许就能好起来。

方远梦叹了口气，说：希望时间能医好她们吧，能遗忘了就好。

小秦沉吟了一会儿，问：那个赵宏伟，现在算是我们的卧底吗？

方远梦想了一会儿，没有回答。

小秦说：他只是在和我们做买卖，他帮助我们，是希望我们能帮他和王大嫂逃出去，我觉得这样的人终究不可信。

方远梦说：小秦，你别这么说，赵宏伟给我们的帮助，还是真心诚意的，只不过，他的旧信念被摧毁了，新信念还没建立起来，所以，才会懦弱而摇摆不定。

小秦就没再说什么。

夕阳的光，照在悬崖边上，火红得像蛇，蜿蜒而鲜亮。山谷里的风，依旧在旋转，猛烈而徘徊。

方远梦望着夕阳，仿佛又看见了小夕的笑颜。

夕阳的余晖，在风里跳舞。

赵宏伟的头痛稍好了一些，但是黑夜来临，他依旧无法入眠。

杀人之后的负罪感与恐惧不是那么容易消退的，即使他杀的是鬼子和汉奸。而对于真相败露的担忧，更是像一头威风凛凛的老虎，每天在他的面前龇牙咧嘴、张牙舞爪，令人胆寒。时间缓缓往前推进，而山本信玄和渡边都没什么新的动静，这无疑让赵宏伟感觉如履薄冰。

另外，曾林之死，就像往赵宏伟心里扎了根铁刺。杀死竹内，好歹是一件为民除害的正义之事，而杀死曾林，对赵宏伟来说，却是一桩真心觉得内疚的罪。赵宏伟从没想过要杀曾林，因为曾林从没干过什么罪大恶极的事情，他做汉奸，也就是想有条活路，况且曾林家中还有一个生病的儿子，孩子事事需要曾林照顾，要靠他养活。但是赵宏伟却亲手杀了曾林，就是因为，曾林看见了他赵宏伟杀竹内。说到底，赵宏伟杀曾林，就是为了自保。这是杀人灭口。曾林是无辜的，而他赵宏伟是自私的。赵宏伟对曾林感到深切的内疚，不知道该怎么办才能减轻一点心中的罪孽感。

彷徨、迷茫。赵宏伟不知道该如何来理解自己。在这样的一个时代环境里，所有的人与事，都仿佛脱离了原有的轨道，一齐扑入了一片广大的迷雾中。在这迷雾中，人既看不清自己，也看不清别人，从事理到心理，全无半点秩序。只能在扑朔迷离里，凭着感觉前进，被未知的命运牵着鼻子走。四书五经不再管用，纲常伦理已成废墟，新的秩序，又在哪里？赵宏伟空白而无知。

赵宏伟又想起了赵驹，照护士小燕所说，自己这条命，是被赵驹给救回来的。赵驹他为什么要这么做？在赵宏伟看来，赵驹一辈子就是个流氓王八蛋，但是，赵宏伟现在又感到，他似乎从未真正认识过赵驹。他有种莫名其妙的感觉：赵驹是个谜。

赵宏伟还不知道，赵驹已经帮他处理好了指纹和血衣的事情。但是日本人迟迟没有对他赵宏伟实施抓捕，事情看起来并无什么败露的迹象。这既令赵宏伟充满了侥幸的希望，又令他加倍地忐忑不安。莫名，他有一股十分强烈的想要见一见赵驹的冲动。他幻想，要是赵驹真能帮他就好了。

赵宏伟白天越是牵挂秀珍，晚上，梦里的心音就越是栩栩如生。每次从浓郁的梦境中醒来，赵宏伟都会忧伤万分。这种忧伤，令赵宏伟感到，他的人生，真的是一场荒唐的悲剧，他也不知自己的明天究竟该何去何从。

头脑里冰凉的疼痛，一阵阵折磨着他。

渡边提拔桥本做了副联队长。

渡边和桥本谈过一次话，他向桥本详细询问了战斗当天竹内死亡现场发生的各种情况，桥本说：没什么特别的，就是赵宏伟居然能死而复生，简直太神奇了。渡边笑笑，是啊，大家都已经觉得竹内之死没什么特别的了，都觉得真相就是曾林杀了竹内，他渡边一个人还干吗要疑神疑鬼的呢？况且，上海特高课那边的鉴定已经做出来了，那把匕首和那把手枪上，什么人的指纹都有，就是没有赵宏伟的。另外，赵宏伟内衣领口上的血迹，经鉴定，也是赵宏伟本人的。

桥本并不知道，送去上海特高课化验的血迹，仅仅只是从当时还昏迷着的赵宏伟的内衣领口上取下来的一点鲜血。桥本一心沉浸在升官的快乐里，并没有专心和渡边作案情上的探讨，于是，赵宏伟的那件原本很可疑的长衫，便竟然成了一个被日本人遗漏忽略的空白。如果桥本认真地和渡边比对一下赵宏伟入院前后的情形，自然就会发现赵宏伟少了件衣服，而当时，能给赵宏伟脱长衫的，只有赵驹。

赵驹自然想到了一切，他忐忑，但并不害怕。他早已在肚子里编造好了各种情节和理由，日本人只要会问，他就能答。撒个谎，小事一桩。

而与此同时，渡边也收到了赵宏伟的见面请求。他听说，赵宏伟特地为他写了一篇极好的文章，要在报纸上发表，他不禁心花怒放。以前，竹内可是经常要求赵宏伟在报纸上写吹捧文章的，以夸大宣扬他竹内的功绩。现在可好了，竹内死了，舆论舞台上的主角，终于要换成他渡边了。这么一想，渡边就不由再次暗暗地发出了感叹：竹内死得真是好哇！

于是，虽然竹内之死依旧有许多疑点在困扰着渡边的逻辑思维，但是，渡边还是决定，应该先把这件该死的事情放一放，用充满热情的笑容去见一见赵宏伟这条才华横溢的难得之狗。

玉山上，凉风吹拂着暑热，绿树背靠着蓝空。这几天，在战士们的站岗看护下，没有女人再能从悬崖上跳下。

小秦来通知方远梦：政委让你去一趟他的办公室，小阳来了，他还从根据地带来了一支二十多人的手枪队，支援我们。

方远梦忙问：小阳有他姐姐的消息吗？

小秦支吾了一下，说：小夕姐的事，我不清楚，你去问小阳吧。

方远梦飞箭似的跑了出去。

到了政委办公室的门外，方远梦的心又一下子提了起来。他像是忽然走不动了，腿很重。他侧耳听了听办公室里是否有笑声，没有。里面鸦雀无声。方远梦的胸口里一阵莫名的冰凉和恐惧。他迈了迈腿，还是敲响了办公室的门。

政委亲自开的门。也没什么寒暄。

方远梦走进了办公室，看到了小阳，看到了小阳手臂上戴的黑纱。

方远梦宛如五雷轰顶。他怔住了。

“你姐……她……她怎么样了？”方远梦强力控制着情绪，自欺欺人地问。

小阳掉下了两行泪，哽咽着说：“我姐她……已经不在了……就在极司菲尔路七十六号里，是李士群亲手开的枪……”

方远梦一下子瘫倒在了地上。

政委忙把方远梦搀到了凳子上。

小阳从怀里掏出了一个信封，交给了方远梦，说：我姐临去上海前，说，要是这次她出了事，就让我把这信封交给你。

方远梦愣在那里，哆嗦了好久，才接过了信封。

打开了信封，里面是一张纸，纸上并排粘贴着两张照片，左边一张是方远梦，右边一张是小夕。方远梦站在党旗下，而小夕坐在花丛里。这张纸的页脚上，是小夕写下的娟秀的一行字：远梦，我永远爱你。

方远梦潸然泪下，不能自已。

他哭得撕心裂肺。

悲伤，不能控制。

小夕从来不知道，她长得很像袁荷。袁荷是当年在东北与方远梦一起并肩作战的好战友，两个人从拿起枪的那一天起就知道，他们的生命，已经只属于中国的土地。马革裹尸对于他们来说，只是一个早已明了的结局。他们一群人，一起出生入死，杀日本人，杀卖国贼，浴血奋战，从不畏缩。那时候，偶尔，方远梦甚至会以为，死神在勇者的面前，是不会出现的。

但是，袁荷最后还是牺牲了。她在沈阳，中了樱花会社赤木老贼的圈套，牺牲在了日军的乱枪之下。她牺牲后，日军还残酷地将她悬尸示众。方远梦和战友们想去救下她的尸体，但是面对防守森严的日军，势单力薄的他们一时也无计可施。最后，是一个叫龚汉江的道士，将袁荷的尸体送了回来。方远梦跪谢龚汉江，但龚汉江说，这事不是他做的，是一个不愿意留下姓名的大英雄，救下了她的尸体。

龚汉江看着袁荷的眼神是悲伤的，他问方远梦，她叫什么名字？方远梦就告诉他：她叫袁荷。龚汉江对着袁荷的尸体，自言自语地说：还好，我知道了你的名字。

方远梦并不知道自己对袁荷有没有爱情，但是，他知道，龚汉江这个道士，一定是深爱着袁荷。方远梦能理解这种无法言语的悲伤，爱还浓，人已空，红尘黄泉不相通，一别至死泪朦胧。

所以，在这样的一个年代里，方远梦不敢轻易说爱。

直到，如宿命一般，他在上海遇上了小夕。小夕长得跟袁荷是那么相像，以至于，方远梦有时候会误以为，是袁荷又回来了，她回来向他要答案了。而他，究竟该对她说什么呢？

一九三二年，方远梦奉命潜伏于江南，收集戴笠特务组织的相关情报。方远梦来到了江庆县赵家镇，做了一名普通的教书先生。每年寒暑假时，赴上海执行任务。而他的搭档，就是刘小夕。

一开始，方远梦只在有任务时，去上海，任务一结束，便回赵家镇。他害怕和小夕说话，就好像，他欠了袁荷太多东西一样。可是，小夕只要一受伤，他就会有心痛的感觉，这种感觉新鲜而明确、冲动而热烈。他想关心小夕，又不想离她太近。

日子久了，方远梦发现，小夕真的不是袁荷，她们的性格截然不同。不杀人时，小夕就是个普通的邻家女孩，温润而清新。她爱笑，爱闹，有时候

还有一点小脾气。方远梦害怕，自己的心会动摇。终于有一天，小夕问他：你为什么不爱和我说话，是讨厌我吗？那一刻，方远梦惊慌得像一个害羞的小男孩。

从那以后，方远梦的心里便住进了一个女人。他没有爱上袁荷，但真切地爱上了小夕。那种感觉，心如鹿撞。此后的每一个假期，他不管是否真的有任务需要执行，都会到上海去，在那里待上很长的一段时间，只是为了可以多看看小夕，多陪陪她。和她在一起的时候，他总会惶恐于时光的流逝，巴不得一切能够定格。因为，血雨腥风的日子早已让他有了一种本能：懂得一切都是短暂，明白美好总会结束。对小夕的爱，令他对永恒有了幻想，而这又是极不现实的奢望。于是，他唯一能做的，只是珍惜每一分钟每一秒钟的相聚。而谁也不知道，他和小夕的爱情，将会在何时戛然而止，也许，那个停止处，就是他或她牺牲的时候吧。有时候，方远梦想到这些，总会感到很难过。但他从没想过，有一天，小夕会先走一步，他一直以为，先牺牲的那个，一定会是自己。或者说，这是他的希望。而今想来，他觉得自己的以为或希望是多么的幼稚啊。小夕真实地不在了，不在了。而他，还要长久地活下去，他还好好地活着。该怎么办？这个世上再没刘小夕这个人了，就算此刻战争立即结束，她也活不过来了。让方远梦怎么办？他觉得，这比死还难受。

方远梦看着小夕的照片，哭了一整夜。

悲伤像河水一样绵长。

渡边笑逐颜开地去医院探望了一次赵宏伟。山本信玄陪同。

赵宏伟掩盖着心虚，小心翼翼地回答了渡边的各种关于竹内之死的提问，提心吊胆地应对了山本信玄的各种旁敲侧击与试探。最后，渡边向山本信玄点了一下头。赵宏伟不知道这是否意味着，自己已通过了审讯？他略微松了口气。

渡边拿走了赵宏伟的拍马屁文章，并且很满意地要求他再多写几篇。

山本信玄在医院走廊里又看见了小燕。他把她按在墙上，摸了一会儿，然后，笑着用汉语对她说：晚上，我派人来接你，不要逃走，否则，诛你九族。

赵驹又被山本信玄打了一顿。

山本信玄出招狠毒，劲力霸道，赵驹全身被打得青紫不堪。赵驹既不能戴护具，又不能用武功，只能尽量躲避。但是他躲避的次数多了，山本信玄也要生气。山本信玄猛地飞起一脚，踢在赵驹胸口上，赵驹摔倒在地，吐出了一口血来。

赵驹擦掉了血，爬起来，赔着笑脸说：太君威武，太君勇猛。

赵驹话音刚落，山本信玄猛地又是一个侧踢，将赵驹踢出了几米远。

赵驹痛得说不出话了。他喉咙里的血直往嘴里涌，那些血又硬生生地被他给咽了回去。

山本信玄十分愉悦地笑了两声。他说：怎么样，我们日本的空手道厉害吧？空手道来源于唐手，而唐手来源于中国，当初，是你们传给了我们文明的火种，而今，你们却越来越没落，我们却越来越强大，你说，这是不是一件很有寓意的事情？

赵驹趴在地上，说：大日本天皇万岁！

山本信玄皮笑肉不笑地说：唉，你只会一味挨打，我玩得好无趣呀，你应该要还手，和我对着打，就像真正的格斗一样，这样我才能真正得到胜利的愉悦。

赵驹说：我不懂武术，不会格斗，只是个手无寸铁的普通人，求太君不要再开我的玩笑，望太君手下留情。

山本信玄冷冷一笑，说：手无寸铁的普通人？大家可都知道，你是著名的神枪手哇。

赵驹说：全靠皇军栽培！我只有这微末的一技之长，我愿为皇军肝脑涂地、鞠躬尽瘁、死而后已！大日本皇军万岁！

山本信玄哈哈大笑，说：真是个不折不扣的东亚病夫哇，看来，你们这些中国猪，真是活该要被我们屠宰。

赵驹点头哈腰，说：是，是。

山本信玄说：你，要好好用你那点微末的枪技，要知道，你若不是还有这点用，我早就一拳要了你的性命了。

赵驹说：是，是，谢太君开恩！

山本信玄说：以后，你每次被我打倒在地时，都要高喊一声“我是东亚病夫”，你明白吗？

赵驹说：明白，明白，我是东亚病夫，我是东亚病夫。

山本信玄愉悦地大笑。

这时，一个小兵来向山本信玄报告：那个护士被带来了。

山本信玄嘴角一笑，命令小兵：把她洗干净，然后，绑到我的床上去。

小兵得令，转身跑出。

山本信玄向赵驹挥了挥手，说：好了，你回去吧。

赵驹感恩戴德地说：谢谢太君！谢谢太君！

赵驹疼痛不堪地离开了山本信玄的私宅。离开时，他听到一个女子在哭泣着问日本小兵：我的爸爸在哪儿？山本太君把我爸爸怎么了？求求你们放了他！

夜色深沉。赵驹双眼冰凉。

小秦愤怒地将一张报纸拍在桌上，他对方远梦和政委说：你们看看，这是今天新出的报纸，头版头条就是赵宏伟的文章，他居然在报纸上号召我们快点投降，这个狗杂种！

方远梦皱着眉，拿起报纸，看了一会儿。方远梦的眉头慢慢舒展了开来。他把报纸交还给小秦，说：第一段第一个字，第二段第二个字，第三段第三个字，依此类推，你把这些字连起来读一遍。

小秦困惑不解。

“我安然无恙，你们是否都好？盼会合。”

政委微笑了起来，说：赵宏伟是个人才呀，他不懂密码，却照样能在日本人的眼皮底下传送情报，好。

方远梦拿了报纸，说，我去看一下秀珍，把赵宏伟安好的消息告诉她，让她有点希望。

政委说，好，去吧，注意多说些宽心的话。

秀珍一个人坐在窗前，沉默不语。

身体的伤痛已在渐渐恢复，而心灵的折磨仍在延续。那些地狱般恐怖痛苦的日子，还是会以噩梦的方式在人的脑海里反复呈现，让女人感觉生不如死。秀珍不想哭，可眼泪还是忍不住往下掉。

秀珍手里拿着方远梦给的报纸，又默念了一遍赵宏伟在文章中藏下的那句话。她默念得执着而入神，就像紧攥着一根救命的绳。她将赵宏伟的名字看了又看，看得认真而痴迷，终于，才一时淡却了心中的阴霾。

“……出去之后，我就娶你。这么多年了，我一直没告诉你，其实我有多么爱你！你比我的生命还重要，你能让我发疯发狂，我愿意为了你去做任何事，你是这个世上最美丽的神！秀珍，我爱你！我爱你，你记住了吗。我要娶你，秀珍，你是我的妻子。你是我的妻子，小菊就是我的女儿。小菊一直住在我那里，她过得很好，你不用担心。她很乖，很孝顺，她天天都在想念你，等你回去。秀珍，你一定要好好活着，等我救你出去！”

赵宏伟的话，一遍遍在她心头回响。每回响一次，似乎都能增加一点她活下去的勇气。她想：是啊，我还有宏伟哥呢，他在爱着我，还有小菊也在等着我，他们就是我的家人。

这么想着，想着，秀珍就觉得，只要活着就好，人只要还活着，就会有希望。

渡边也找赵驹谈了两次话，向他询问了战斗当天他的所见所闻和所作所为，赵驹当然对答如流。

赵驹借机向渡边进言：关于竹内之死，上头虽然现在将注意力集中在内奸之事上，没有追究我们救援不力的责任，但是，政治风云变幻莫测，万一北野少将失势，有人想要整治您，自然就又会将竹内之死的重点，拨到太君您指挥不当的问题上来，到时候，我们这些参加过当天之事的人，恐怕都逃不了干系。您还不如趁现在主动权在您手里时，尽早盖棺定论，让竹内之死以一个完结的姿态早早退出将军们的视线，让他们早早遗忘此事。

渡边宛如醍醐灌顶，茅塞顿开。他觉得赵驹真是言之有理，简直是一语惊醒梦中人哪。竹内之死若一直这么查下去，必定夜长梦多。就算北野不失势，田中中将阵营里的人，也说不定哪天会用这件事来找碴。军政两界明争暗斗，防不胜防，能不小心谨慎吗？竹内遇难当天，他渡边可是故意按兵不动，拖延了救援，他那天可是真心实意地希望竹内早早去死。而这些要是被上头的有心之人查了个一清二楚的话，那他渡边也就要去阴曹地府和竹内团聚了。所以，现在来想，查清杀死竹内的真正凶手还重要吗？重要个屁！潜伏在日军内部的中方间谍成百上千，多一个少一个关他渡边屁事。最重要的是：不能再让人想起他渡边在竹内遇难那天指挥失误、救援不力的事情来！渡边感觉大彻大悟。就应该趁着现在这个战败之后狼藉一片的乱局，浑水摸鱼地把竹内遇刺这案子给结了，顺理成章地将此事束之高阁，让上头的人渐渐淡忘这件事，不再提起，不再节外生枝。

主意打定，渡边就喊来了桥本，要他起草结案报告。竹内被杀的真相就是：曾林是军统特工，他蓄谋已久，意欲刺杀竹内大佐，战斗当天，竹内大佐在遇刺之后，于临死前奋勇拔枪，击毙了逃跑中的曾林，两人玉石俱焚，皇军之英雄气概可歌可泣。

赵驹微微一笑。

赵家镇镇政府内。

阴森恐怖的牢房里。

姚志被牢牢地绑在刑架上。

山本信玄手里拿着鞭子，拎了一张凳子，走了过来。他将凳子放在姚志的面前，坐了下来。他笑了笑，将手里的鞭子轻轻一甩，用汉语说：姚先生您好，渡边联队长派我来审讯您，我奉命行事，百般无奈，多有得罪，请多配合。

姚志笑笑，说：你汉语说得真好。

山本信玄说：渡边联队长将这间牢房改造得很不像话，您放心，我回头就让人来改善一下这里的居住环境，首先就把这刑架给撤了，再给您弄一张极舒适的床。

姚志哈哈大笑了起来，说：还真的是第一次听见有人这么一本正经地跟我说笑话。

山本信玄正色道：肺腑之言，真心实意。

姚志说：不用了，就这样挺好，我腿被打断了多次，走不了路，老让你们拖着我去刑讯室受审多不好意思，还是渡边想得周到，直接在这里给我立个刑架。

山本信玄说：以前对您所做的那些极不人道的事，都是竹内那个昏君暴君吩咐的，他是一头残暴的猪，而渡边联队长和我，从内心深处，都十分尊敬像您这样坚不可摧的军人，现在好了，竹内被人杀了，以后，不会再有人对您做那些粗暴不堪的事了。

山本信玄说着，就将手里的鞭子丢在了地上。

姚志哈哈一笑，说：竹内死了？哎哟，这可真是我今天听到的最好的消息。

山本信玄说：没错，竹内那个王八蛋死了，我们也很高兴。

姚志笑得喘不过气来了。姚志说：你们还真是精诚团结呀，真希望你们也能早点追随着竹内的步伐而去。

山本信玄笑笑，说：人固有一死，无论荣辱得失，都是殊途同归，人活着与活着之间的差别，只在于，有些人活得活色生香，有些人活得生不如死，同样的一场旅途，有些人旅行在天堂，有些人旅行在地狱。

姚志笑笑，说：还真没看出来，你是个哲学家。

山本信玄说：所以，你这样又是何苦呢，中国即将被我们全面征服，所有的反抗军都将被我们杀戮，你的坚守，在你们排山倒海一样的失败面前微不足道、毫无意义，你又何必要为了一件已然毫无意义的事情，把你自己的人生铸成地狱、把你自己的活着变作煎熬？只要你开口，说出玉山全部的机关暗道，我们皇军保证，会给你足够多的金钱和足够多的美女，让你这辈子都过得足够舒服、足够快活。人生只有一次，何必要往地狱里走？就应该要过着那天堂般的舒服日子，才不糟蹋这一生一次的“活着”二字。

姚志笑笑，说：“原以为你是个聪明人，想不到也一样是个庸俗的说客。你汉语学得这么好，听说过‘我不入地狱谁入地狱’这句话吗？想要创造出一个真正美好得像天堂一样的世界，没有人出来流血流汗是不可能成功的，我们也许是会把自己的这辈子糟蹋成一个地狱，但是，我们流血流汗了、受折磨死了，我们所爱的人和我们的下一代就可以不用再受这种罪了，幸福终有一天会来临，这就是共产主义的信仰。如果每个黑暗时代的人们全都只懂得自私自利、苟安自保，那么，他们的爱人和孩子，也只能像他们一样活在黑暗的时代中，永无光明之日，这就是革命者必须要革命的原因。这世上还有什么事情，能比看到爱人和孩子的灿烂欢笑更美好呢？这就是人生最大的

幸福。所以，我们共产主义者，为了革命，为了信仰，愿意一辈子活在地狱里。——你能听懂我说的吗？”

山本信玄竟无言以对。

山本信玄笑笑，站了起来。他向前一步，直逼到了姚志的面前。姚志坦然一笑。山本信玄卸下假笑，面露狰狞。他阴阳怪气地笑了笑，然后，脱下了姚志的裤子。姚志被割去生殖器的地方，伤口还没愈合。

山本信玄观赏着那个伤口，尖利地狂笑。他嘲讽地说：爱人，孩子，那些都是对男人而言的，但是，你现在只是个太监。哈哈哈哈！

姚志淡然地笑了笑，说：所以，除了革命和信仰，我们反抗到底的原因还有一个，那就是仇恨！你们这群畜生！呸！

姚志狠狠地将一口唾沫，吐在了山本信玄的脸上。

山本信玄拿起了鞭子，疯狂地鞭打起了姚志。

姚志被打得浑身血肉模糊。

山本信玄也累极了。他停了下来，愁眉紧锁。他还不能打死姚志，要不然，渡边一定会发疯。

山本信玄准备去给渡边打个电话，商量一下对策。他愤怒而恼恨地围绕着血淋淋的姚志走了两圈，对着姚志的脸上吐了两次口水。

忽然，山本信玄于不经意间瞥见，在姚志的屁股上，有一个淡青色的图案，不像胎记，像文身。他一时好奇，凑近了去看，原来，是一个小型的北斗七星图案。山本信玄顿时就感到有些奇怪：姚志为什么要在屁股上文一个北斗七星？

这时，姚志放了一个响屁。

山本信玄一跃而起，掩鼻跳开。他又气又恼，又无计可施，只能转身离去。

山本信玄拨通了渡边的电话。

“渡边大人，实在没办法，姚志是个软硬不吃、冥顽不灵的家伙，我尽力了。要不还是尽快将他转移到您县城的监狱里去吧。过几天，不是就会有一台新电椅要运到县监狱的刑讯室里去了吗？就让那台电椅去对付姚志吧。

您觉得怎么样？”

“……好，就照你说的办，注意，要秘密押运。”

“是，请渡边大人放心！”

夜色凉冷，枯寂黑暗。

姚志就那样一直被固定在刑架上，他赤身裸体，浑身皮开肉绽。鲜血从他的伤口里，慢慢地、不停地往外流着。

姚志昏沉而疲累地闭着眼，他想好好地睡一觉，可是浑身的疼痛又总像许多条蛇一样，在不停地咬他的骨头，让他痛得睡不着。他迷迷糊糊的，半梦半醒。他想起了儿时的许多事，也想起了忧伤与怅惘。

姚志在甘肃一户普通农民家中长大，养父养母对他都很好，视如己出。姚志听养父说过他的来历，那是一个风雨交加的夜晚，姚志的养母听到门外有婴儿的啼哭声，便开门去看，结果，就在草丛里的树根旁，发现了襁褓中的姚志。襁褓里放了一袋钱和一张纸，纸上只写着一个大大的“姚”字。养父当时就估计，这姚字，应该是这个弃婴的姓氏。养父养母等了几日，也没见弃婴的父母回来寻孩子，于是，他们便收养了这个弃婴，给他取名为姚志。姚志身上并无什么胎记，只是很奇怪，从捡到姚志的那天起，姚志的屁股上，就有一个北斗七星的文身。

姚志的身世，是一个谜。

只是，在姚志三岁的时候，有一名剑客，来到过姚志养父养母的家中。他给了姚志的养父养母不少钱，然后，嘱咐他们，务必要让小姚志吃素一个月。养父问剑客原因，剑客说：因为这个小孩的生母，已于昨日上吊自尽。养父还要追问，剑客却已飘然远去。

这些，就是与姚志身世有关的全部信息，除了这些以外，姚志对自己的来历一无所知。小时候，他还会对此耿耿于怀，但是进入少年后，他便觉得，无所谓了，既然他的亲生父母都已在当初选择了抛弃他，他又何必还要一直记挂着他们呢？忘记便好。

在十六岁之前，姚志一直过着平静安乐的日子，他那时还以为，他会像他的养父养母一样，一辈子做个老实本分的农民。他觉得这样也挺好的，因为他感到人生中最珍贵的便是平静与安乐。他还想等长大了以后娶了隔壁的

小紫晴，和她平静安乐地一起过一辈子，这样就很幸福了。

但是，在他十六岁那年，一伙土匪闯进了村子里。姚志的养父养母被杀死，小紫晴被轮奸，土匪们在糟蹋完小紫晴后，还在她肚子上插了一刀。等到姚志赶到时，小紫晴已奄奄一息。小紫晴临死前，问姚志：哥哥，人死后是不是真的能去天堂？天堂里是不是真的有吃不完的糖果？

姚志还没回答，小紫晴便在血泊中断了气。

姚志仰天长啸。

当晚，姚志便带了双刀，独闯匪巢。他不要命地闯，不要命地杀，他不怕枪，也不怕死。他就是抱着同归于尽的信念来的。一个又一个畜生，死在姚志的刀下，血流遍地。但是姚志毕竟寡不敌众，最后，他还是被土匪们包围了起来。

千钧一发之际，那名剑客，从天而降。剑客拼尽全力，救出了姚志，但是，剑客的身上中了三枪。

两人逃到旷野中时，剑客终于支持不住，倒下了。姚志问他：你是谁？为什么要救我？剑客说：夫人有恩于我，今生今世，我无以为报。

剑客还想说什么，但是，终究没能说出来。剑客死了。

姚志埋好了养父养母和小紫晴，也埋好了剑客。从此，便走上了另一条人生道路。血雨腥风之路，追寻天堂之路。

姚志一生都在追杀那帮禽兽不如的土匪。乱世风云激荡，时代斗转星移，那帮畜生，后来有的加入了军阀部队，有的加入了国民党，有的做了汉奸。姚志曾发誓，此生必将这些恶人赶尽杀绝，让他们血债血偿。姚志坚信，只要能够建立起一个新中国，那么，不管这些当年的畜生如今是在什么地方，他们都必将被军队或人民抓捕，清算罪行，送入监狱，依法枪毙。也只有建立起了新中国，才能让那些禽兽不如的东西再没好日子过，再不能欺凌百姓。必须要结束这个黑暗的时代，那些凄惨不堪的悲剧，才不会反复重演。所以，姚志愿意为了建立一个全新的中国，慷慨赴死。

“哥哥，人死后是不是真的能去天堂？天堂里是不是真的有吃不完的糖果？”

只是，在那漫长的戎马生涯中，姚志依然会常常想起当年的小紫晴。记忆中，小紫晴仍然还是那样灿烂可爱。他会教她唱歌，她会给他绣鸳鸯。姚志的一生，都在回忆中垂泪。

他一直想告诉小紫晴一句话：你在哪里，我的天堂就在哪里。

姚志仿佛又看到了小紫晴欢笑的模样。

姚志微笑了起来。

山本信玄回到了姚志的牢房里。

山本信玄惊愕万分地看到，姚志满口是血！

山本信玄慌忙跑上前去察看，只见，姚志脚尖前的地上，是一截血糊糊的舌头！

——姚志咬舌自尽了！！

山本信玄惊惶失措地大叫了起来：快来人！来人！抢救！抢救！！

赵宏伟睡在病床上，被外面走廊里闹哄哄的声音给吵醒了。

他听出来，是山本信玄在叫嚷的声音：

“再从赵家镇调一支小队过来！把这层楼面全部保护起来！每个出入口架上一挺机枪！

“医生我警告你，要是救不活他，你和你的全家，就一起去死！

“你怎么听命令的？告诉你不许再让陌生人上来，滚！

“把最好的医生全部叫来！打电话去他们家里，把他们一个个叫醒，告诉他们，十五分钟内不到，全部枪毙！

“什么？渡边联队长来了，在楼下？他妈的你不早说！”

山本信玄骂骂咧咧的声音渐行渐远。赵宏伟打开了病房门，探头出去看。只见，走廊里站满了荷枪实弹的日本兵，而医生和护士，都在很忙碌地从一间病房的门口跑进跑出。

一个日本兵向赵宏伟做了个手势，要赵宏伟把头缩回去。赵宏伟就缩了回去。

赵宏伟不禁满腹狐疑：这里是住进来了什么重要病人呢？

夜色漆黑。

玉山上。

天朗气清，阳光明亮。

秀珍一个人坐在木屋外，出神地看着远处空旷的蓝天，心思飘忽，茫然不定。往事如云烟般涌来，她对赵宏伟的那么多年的爱，都像碎片一样堵塞在她的心口。这是一份以前从未让她有过希望的爱，她一直爱得痴心，又爱得无望。她知道在赵宏伟的心里一直有一个女人，因为她曾经在赵宏伟喝醉时，听他痛苦地呼唤过一个女人的名字，她叫心音。秀珍从不知道心音是谁，她也从未问过赵宏伟。因为她害怕，一旦问了，她和赵宏伟就会变成陌生人，她害怕，自己唯一的爱情会窒息死亡。她不敢面对失去，不敢面对真相，也不敢面对自己。她就一直那么痴心真心而糊里糊涂地爱着赵宏伟，她一直觉得，只要赵宏伟不说不爱她，她的爱情，就能一直是活着的。

而，赵宏伟如今向秀珍表白了爱情，秀珍心里并不确定，这会不会是一种同情。然而她当然更愿意促使自己去相信，赵宏伟说爱她，是千真万确且发自肺腑的。秀珍像突然获得了上帝的格外恩赐一样激动，她感恩，并且无比珍惜这份蓦然拥有的赵宏伟的爱情表白。他表白的一字一句，都不停地在她心头回响，给她勇气，给她暖意。但是，她又不禁深深地自惭形秽。毕竟，她已是个不干净的女人，是残花败柳，不，甚至连残花败柳都不如。赵宏伟真的能接受她吗？她恐惧，且动摇。她深深地感到，自己已再配不上赵宏伟，她莫名觉得，自己已离他有千里之遥。一想到这些，她又不寒而栗。她感到，自己的一辈子都完了。女人的肉体，既是女人的骄傲，也是女人的悲剧，更是女人的枷锁。秀珍想哭。

可是，秀珍又想到了那些赵宏伟与她、小菊在一起欢聚吃饭的场景。这些场景仿佛具有一种强大的魔力，在不断地燃起她内心的憧憬与向往的火焰。那是多么温暖而幸福的事情啊，有爱人，有孩子，一家人团聚在一起，欢乐地说着话、唱着歌。就算为了这一点希望，她也应该要好好坚强地活下去呀！这世上的一切希望，原本就都是一个个的梦，若不拼命去追求，美梦又怎会成真？更何况，赵宏伟那时已清清楚楚地许诺了，他会娶她王秀珍为妻。这是一件多么幸福的事情啊！他是真心的，她盼了这么多年，恋了这么多年，不就是为了等到他的一颗真心吗？如今终于等到了，她又为什么还要忍不住胡思乱想？对，不应该再胡思乱想。她应该要好好活下去，为了爱情，为了女儿。人生还能重新开始；未来，还有幸福在守候。人应该要学会从废墟与悲痛中重新站起，去追寻并建造一个新的美梦。而她王秀珍的美梦，就是能够拥有一个幸福温暖的家。这个家里，有赵宏伟和小菊。

“宏伟哥，我爱你。”秀珍不禁痴痴而甜甜地想。

阳光照在她的脸上，灿烂而明媚。

队长派出去的几个人回来了，他们从新四军的大部队那边，带回来了一支一百多人的队伍，用以增援玉山游击队。队长大喜过望。但是同时又有一个坏消息：这支增援部队刚过青梅县，从新四军大部队驻地通往青梅县和江庆县的那条交通要道，就被青梅县的日军给切断了。增援部队经过沿路侦察，发现日军已在青梅县和江庆县周围的许多大小道路上设置了关卡和重兵。这些军事调动看起来像是日军在增强他们所占县城的防御能力，但是实际上，他们正在切断玉山通往外界的所有道路。日军的合围部署，已初露端倪。

山雨欲来风满楼。队长愁眉紧锁。

队长没想到日军的动作会这样快。对于日军的大围剿，队长以前并不感到有多大担心，因为游击队凭着玉山的天险，有足够的能力可以和日军周旋，大不了大家可以往山肚子里的暗道中一躲，日军就算用炮轰、用火烧也没用。但是眼下的情况却大不相同了，山上有了两百多个女人，她们不仅毫无战斗能力，而且真要遇上打仗，她们还需要有人保护和照顾。另外，最重要的是，玉山上的粮食消耗，因为她们的暂住而变得巨大，日军一旦封山，存粮如果不够，那要战士们怎样和日军打持久战？断粮，将会是下一场玉山恶战最大的隐患。可是，日军现在已封锁了各处道路，游击队根本就没办法把这些女人送出沦陷区。

队长心事重重。

渡边的心情很复杂。他同时收到了一个好消息和一个坏消息。好消息是：北野已正式晋升为中将。坏消息是：松尾已开始调兵遣将，准备围剿玉山游击队。

渡边的心里五味杂陈，不知是该喜还是该悲。北野顺利晋升了，他渡边背后的靠山，按理说是越来越稳固且强大了，但是松尾却又先行一步地开始

排兵布阵了，如果真的让松尾灭了玉山游击队，那么，田中中将就等于是给了北野中将一个下马威。到那时，他渡边恐怕就真的是要剖腹谢罪了。渡边深知，在这场日本发动的规模巨大的战争中，日军在战场上每一次战斗的输赢，不仅直接地体现着那场战斗中日军底层指挥官的能力高低与决策成败，也间接地关系着日本军部高层将领们的政治荣辱与战略进退。所以，每一个日军底层指挥官的生死，不仅由战场输赢决定，也由军部的政治动向决定。渡边感到如履薄冰。

而渡边另外还感到愤愤不平。他觉得松尾真是一个无耻鼠辈。渡边好不容易才在江庆县内迅速搜刮了一笔民脂民膏，买了药品，给松尾的部队赶紧送了过去，他松尾不仅没说一声谢谢，还转眼就来动歪脑筋，想要抢渡边的差事与战功，简直可恶至极。不，他简直就是想要置渡边于死地。叫渡边怎能不又愤又恨？

渡边听桥本报告，说是在一些本应归渡边联队管辖的地区内的道路上，也已布置上了大量的松尾的重兵和关卡，松尾解释说是因为战略需要。渡边觉得松尾实在是欺人太甚，简直像在他渡边的头顶上拉屎。是可忍孰不可忍，渡边知道有这么一句中国话。他想赶走松尾的兵，但是又怕田中中将会怪罪。渡边考虑了两天，最后还是决定要给北野打个电话，向他汇报一下情况，同时探听一下他的意向。

渡边焦躁而不安。

县医院内。

四楼。

赵宏伟一个人在空荡荡的病房里来回踱着步，心情沉闷而忐忑。自从上次渡边来探望过他以后，许多天过去了，再没人来关注过赵宏伟的事情。日本人像是把他给遗忘了。只有医生和护士仍然每天来给他看看病、换换药。这种风平浪静又死气沉沉的状况大大出乎了赵宏伟的意料，令他茫然而不知所措。他想出院，但医生不许、士兵不让。他被困在了医院里，白白消耗着时间。

赵宏伟不知道竹内之死已经草草结案，也不知道渡边最近已是焦头烂额。他依然还在为自己的真凶身份感到焦灼不安，就怕哪天会东窗事发，被渡边给一枪打死。他在病房里又酝酿了两篇拍马屁文章。他坐下来，照例用中日两种语言将这两篇文章各写了一遍。日语版主要是给渡边过目的，而汉语版，才是赵宏伟用功的重点。在以前的安逸岁月里，有一段时间，赵宏伟曾专门和方远梦研究过古代藏头诗技巧的现代化运用，赵宏伟相信，方远梦对此应是记忆犹新。赵宏伟在汉语版的马屁文章里，都藏进了暗语，他相信方远梦只要能够看到报纸，就会发现蛛丝马迹。这是他目前能向方远梦传递消息的唯一方式。

当然，方远梦也许看不到报纸，也许看到了也没往深处多想一层，也可能，方远梦早已像老周一样牺牲了。赵宏伟想。什么都不一定。另外，也许日本人同样会发现他文章中的玄机，毕竟，日本人里也有中国通，就像山本信玄那样。如果被日本人发现了，那他赵宏伟就算有十条命也不够死的；如果被日本人发现了，那他们就很有可能会假借赵宏伟之名，向游击队传送假情报。要是那样的话，后果就真是不堪设想了。毕竟，什么都是有可能的。他被自己的假想吓得不寒而栗。他开始后悔自己的愚蠢行为，他把自己新写的马屁文章撕了个稀烂。他的心很乱，恐惧像条毒蛇一样向他吐着鲜红的舌头；迷茫，像雾一样包裹着他。夏季的炎热缠绕着他，他又烦又怕，浑身都是汗。他的头痛又剧烈了起来，他不知所措，像个无知无识的白痴。

他只想逃走，逃走，逃出这片恐怖的阴霾。

自从那个神秘的病人到来之后，整个四楼就一直处在日本兵的严密控制之下。四楼的病人，只有出去的，没有再进来的。而他赵宏伟一直还待在四楼，是因为他本身就是被软禁之人，本该被日本兵看守着。而正所谓池鱼之殃，因为四楼的看守严密了，所以，他赵宏伟是插翅也难逃出这里了。

四楼上再也没出现过大声喧哗的情况，所有人说话做事都是静悄悄的。赵宏伟再没法偷听到什么，也不知道山本信玄是否又来过。赵宏伟对那个神秘的病人感到了好奇。他究竟是什么重要人物？

赵宏伟对忐忑不安的等待感到了厌倦，但是他又不想再用写马屁文章的方式来吸引渡边的关注。他感到了一筹莫展，只能继续在迷茫与彷徨中等待，等待命运的宣判。

北野命令松尾将兵力撤出渡边的管辖范围，那些在渡边的管辖范围内

由松尾设下的关卡，全部由渡边派兵接管，双方井水不犯河水。松尾悻悻撤兵，渡边略解了恨。但是田中中将旋即又下了命令，要求青梅县和江庆县的日军务必全力合作，及早歼灭玉山游击队，如有贻误战机者，军法处置。

渡边感到了如履薄冰的惊恐。很显然，如果在入秋之前，他还没能独立剿灭玉山游击队，那么，不管是北野还是田中，都会要他剖腹谢罪。形势已经十分明朗，田中中将在暂且忍让着北野中将，但是，只要北野方面在政事、军事上出现了任何微小的纰漏，田中就一定会咬死不放、一击到底。而他渡边，如今不知不觉地就是站在了一个焦点的位置。他若不能按时消灭玉山游击队，那么，北野会颜面无存，田中会幸灾乐祸，北野和田中，会一起命令渡边去死。渡边真的感觉无辜又无奈。一切斗争都是一个旋涡，旋涡转哪转，莫名其妙地就会强有力地将许多旁边的人和事牵扯进去，他感到寝食难安。

而上海的慰安所又打来了电话，向渡边催要漂亮女人。渡边怒发冲冠，对着电话大骂：皇军的事业如此艰难，你们他妈的还满脑子只想要女人？漂亮女人我没有，男人这里多的是，你们要多少有多少！臭流氓！

而愤怒消退之后，渡边又很无奈地知道，一切的愤怒与郁闷都无济于事，该要完成的任务，依旧在等着他去想办法完成，如果完不成，就会下地狱。

山本信玄向渡边报告：姚志已被救活，但遗憾的是，他再也无法说话了。渡边说：没关系，他嘴巴说不了话，但手还能写字，注意，不要再给他的手指上刑，因为我们需要他写字。山本信玄说：明白。渡边说：尽快将姚志转移到县监狱，让他尝尝坐电椅的滋味。山本信玄说：是。渡边拍了拍山本信玄的肩膀，说：看在你父亲的面子上，这次姚志咬舌自尽这件事，就不追究你责任了，但是，决不能再有下一次。山本信玄一个立正，说：感谢大人栽培！

渡边又召见了桥本，和他商量了一下接下来的战争策略。

松尾部队撤下来的地方，已经都由渡边的部队补上，所以，玉山现在基本上仍然是处于被包围封锁的状态。只不过，这种包围封锁状态，是由两股不同派别的日军力量共同构成的，所以，日军包围圈的所有行动，都是僵持而不协调的。这既令渡边欣慰，又令渡边担忧。他欣慰的是，在这种状态下，松尾根本不可能独自率部队剿灭玉山游击队；他担忧的是，在这种状态下，玉山游击队也许无法被真正封锁绞杀。他和松尾的僵持状态，对他渡边来说，就像一枚硬币的两面，有利也有弊。

渡边仍然将所有的希望押在姚志这张活地图身上。因为根据渡边的判断，普通的大围剿，对玉山游击队是起不了什么作用的。以前日军又不是没这么干过，只有松尾这种蠢货，才会在失败过的方法上重新再押一次赌注。渡边不认为重新来一次和以前一样的围剿会有什么侥幸的收获。渡边猜想，在玉山的内部，一定是存在着什么密室与暗道，否则，那些游击队员，不可能在山上如此神出鬼没。所以，事情的关键，还是在于弄清楚玉山的全部地形，包括可能存在的暗道情形。只要掌握了这些，他渡边，就可以独自率领部队，对玉山发起奇袭。

而在姚志开口之前，渡边只能这样和松尾僵持着，和松尾一起半死不活地远远包围封锁着玉山，勉强控制住局面，防范游击队做出更多的军事行动。

渡边嘱咐桥本，对江庆县城以及江庆县下所辖的各个镇，目前都应采取外松内紧的策略。各路人等，均许进城，但不许出城。因为，从慰安妇被救那天三路齐发的战斗态势来看，共产党新四军很有可能在江庆县境内埋伏了特工组。在事情水落石出之前，不应再让城内人员外逃，这样才有可能在最后来个瓮中捉鳖。

桥本说好，说，我会把任务仔细布置下去的。桥本犹豫了一下，又问：要是姚志死活不交代怎么办？田中中将可是下了死命令，要我们必须在今年入秋前剿灭玉山游击队的。

渡边沉吟了一下，说：如果实在不行，我们只好请求上海方面的帮助，要皇军派两架轰炸机出来，将玉山炸为一片焦土。

桥本说：为了消灭一支小小的游击队，我们竟然要请求轰炸机出动，我们一定会被人给笑死。

渡边叹了口气，说：被人笑，总比被人用军法的名义处死要好，只要能活着，就是幸运。

桥本看着渡边愁眉紧锁的样子，一时不禁也感到了一种自危与忧伤的郁闷。他也叹了口气。他想说：还是让战争快点结束吧。但是话到嘴边，他又

咽了下去。

桥本临走时想起赵宏伟的事，便问渡边：对了，还有那个赵宏伟，要继续软禁下去吗？

渡边想了一会儿，说：要是医生说他可以出院了，就放他走，告诉他，好好为皇军效力，皇军不会亏待他。

桥本说，好。

夕阳，鲜红像血。

玉山上。

队长、政委和游击队的几名骨干一起开了个会，讨论了一下接下来的行动策略。大家都感到玉山目前的形势是比较压抑的。新四军在江南战场上的抗日斗争一直受到国民党的排挤与孤立，得不到其有效的帮助，因此，新四军的抗战十分艰难，牺牲巨大。玉山游击队在去年改编为新四军的先遣部队以后，因为可以依靠着玉山的天险而自立自足，所以一直没向新四军的大部队要求过增援。但是眼下形势紧迫，玉山游击队可能随时需要新四军大部队的增援了，从新四军大部队驻地通往玉山的交通要道却被日军用重兵给切断了。日军显然有了周详的部署，想要将玉山游击队置入弹尽粮绝又孤立无援的困境。可是，根据侦察，日军的包围圈在最近几天又出现了莫名其妙的松动，有大量的日军在无意义地换防。而且，有些原本被日军看守得很严密的小道，日军现在居然主动放弃了看守，撤兵撤防。这是什么道理？是日军要改变围困玉山的策略了吗？着实让人捉摸不透。而游击队目前在青梅县和江庆县内又毫无耳目，无法打探到日军的情报，不知日军的真实意图，不能做出准确的应对计划。

方远梦主动请缨，要求重新潜入江庆县去，收集日军情报。队长考虑了一下，同意了。刘小阳要求带领手枪队跟随方远梦一起进城，潜伏江庆县，以备武装行动时所需。方远梦反对，刘小阳坚持。队长权衡了一下，还是同意了刘小阳的请求。队长另外又临时组建了一支特工队，派其进入青梅县，长期潜伏。

会议上还分派了一些其他任务，会议结束之后，大家便各奔岗位，忙碌了起来。

晚上，方远梦来到了刘小阳的屋里，坐了一会儿。山风略微有些清凉，吹散着暑热。

“在日本人的眼皮底下活动，就像在刀尖上跳舞，有时候，说梦话说得大声了一点，也可能要送命，不像在这山上，无论生死，都可大声而坦荡地笑唱。”方远梦说。

“我知道，以前，我姐告诉过我，你睡觉时，习惯用被子捂着嘴，就是怕做噩梦时会大叫出声。做谍报工作，的确是要比明刀明枪地打仗来得艰难。”刘小阳说。

“你不会真正明白的。”方远梦顿了顿，说：“我想要你退出这次行动。我明天会去找政委谈谈。”

“为什么？！”刘小阳站了起来。

方远梦沉默了一会儿，幽幽地说：“因为，你是小夕的最后一个亲人了。”

刘小阳笑笑，说：“在抗战事业面前，你这么说，不觉得很自私吗？”

方远梦说：“就算我自私吧，我想就自私这一次，我不希望你有危险。”

刘小阳说：“我不会退出这次行动的，你找谁说都没用。”说完，他又坐了下来。

方远梦说：“你是小夕的最后一个亲人了，我想，队长和政委，是能理解我的这次自私的。你姐已经不在了，我不能再让你有事。”

刘小阳笑了笑，忽然掉下了两滴泪来。他说：“你知道我为什么一定要跟你去江庆县吗？”

“为什么？”

“因为我姐的遗愿，就是要我保护你！她对我说的最后一句话是：‘小阳，要是远梦遇上了危险，你一定要救他、保护他，因为他是我的命。’——我姐的心，你懂了吗？”刘小阳说。

长长的静默里，方远梦潸然泪下。

一种说不出的绞心的酸楚，在空气里弥漫。

还是刘小阳先擦去了泪迹，微笑了起来。他说：“我们还是一起勇往直前吧，不要为了爱护谁，而让谁畏缩不前，因为在这个黑暗的年代，所有的逃避都换不来安好，只有建立起了一个全新的时代，我们所在乎的人和我们

自己，才能获得幸福与美好。只要这个世界还是一座地狱，那么任何个人都谈不上活着。”

方远梦擦去了泪迹。他难过地低声说：“我没为你姐做过任何事，是我亏欠着她。”

刘小阳灿烂地笑笑，说：“我们都在为了明天的光明而做事，这是我们的共同目标，这是我姐和你的共同目标，有这些，就足够了。”

方远梦笑笑。他说：“等送走了那批可怜的女人，等我们的游击队度过了眼下即将来临的这场危难，我想向上级申请，离开这里。我已经在江庆县，待了太多年了，就像一棵被深深种下了的树，如果再不将自己连根拔起，挪个窝，我恐怕就要忘记，做一头猎豹是什么感觉了。”方远梦笑笑，半开玩笑地说。

刘小阳问：“独在异乡为异客，是不是终究已经厌倦了这里饭菜的味道？”

方远梦说：“此心安处是吾乡，小夕不在了，我到天涯海角再也尝不到她做的饭菜的味道了，家乡已是回想。我只想去上海，去走小夕没走完的路。我发誓，今生一定要为小夕报仇。”

刘小阳说：“有你这番心意，我姐若泉下有知，也可瞑目了。只是国仇家恨，非你一人可报。你要是申请去上海，千万记得要带上我。杀汪伪狗汉奸，怎能少了我刘小阳？”刘小阳说完，哈哈而笑。

方远梦也爽朗地笑了起来。他说：“好，我们就生死与共，杀尽那可恨的倭寇与汉奸！”

夜深空凉。每个人，都在黑暗中企盼着黎明。

县医院。

医生来给赵宏伟拆掉了头上的绷带。赵宏伟问：没事了吧？医生问：你还头痛吗？赵宏伟说：不怎么痛了。医生说：那大概就是没事了，有事的话再说吧。赵宏伟说：谢谢。医生说：不客气，一会儿到我办公室来取点药，然后你就可以出院了。赵宏伟问：我可以出院了？医生说：日本人说你可以出院了。赵宏伟激动得手足无措。赵宏伟问：那个被日本人保护着的病人是什么人呢？医生说：我级别太低，不清楚，你还是自己去问日本人吧，反正你和日本人关系不错。赵宏伟语塞，自觉羞耻。

山本信玄走了进来，医生走了出去。山本信玄满面笑容地和赵宏伟寒暄了一会儿。赵宏伟小心翼翼地问了山本信玄一些外面的情况。赵宏伟了解到，竹内之死已经结案了，案情已盖棺定论：曾林便是内奸及真凶。赵宏伟长舒了一口气，旋即又赶紧假装极惋惜地摇头叹气皱眉。

小燕过来喊赵宏伟，要赵宏伟去医生那里拿药。她看到山本信玄也在，立马转身就跑。山本信玄笑着追上去，将她拦腰抱起，抱回了赵宏伟的病房里。山本信玄将小燕丢在了病床上，扑了上去。赵宏伟吓得赶紧跑出了病房。

赵宏伟在医生那里取了药。他本想回病房里去拿点东西，但是想到山本信玄可能还在那里，就决定不拿了，打算直接离开。

山本信玄应该是嘱咐过了走廊里的日本兵，赵宏伟他今天要出院。所以赵宏伟在四楼的走廊里走来走去也没人管他。只不过他并不能靠近那个神秘病人所住的病房。

赵宏伟莫名有种冲动，想要知道那个神秘的重要病人到底是什么人。这种冲动，拖住了他出院的脚步。

走到楼梯口的时候，赵宏伟站住了。他转回了身来。他看见山本信玄从病房里出来了。山本信玄一边穿着裤子，一边吹着口哨。山本信玄走到了那个神秘病人的病房门口，用日语对里面说：开始吧。

一个被五花大绑地绑在担架上的病人，由四个日本兵从病房里抬了出来。所有的日本兵，都跟着移动了起来。他们以担架为中心，形成着一个严密的防守圈。他们朝楼梯口走来。山本信玄慢悠悠地跟在队伍的最后，嘴里哼着歌。赵宏伟看见，哭泣着的小燕从病房里一瘸一拐地走了出来，她捂着脸，哭声低咽。赵宏伟忽然莫名有些内疚，他感到，自己刚才的逃跑，分明是对恶行的包容。他感到，自己仿佛也是禽兽中的一员。

赵宏伟的思量还未平静，日本兵的队伍已到了眼前。一个日本兵向赵宏伟做了个手势，要他让开。赵宏伟回过了神来，忙一下子跳开了好远。赵宏伟有些惊惶，他看见，山本信玄鄙夷地一笑。

赵宏伟的目光，偷偷地落到了担架上的病人的脸上。他忽然有些愕然：这张脸仿佛挺熟悉！是在哪儿看到过呢？——赵宏伟想起来了，他惊诧得差

点要叫出了声：这，分明就是方远梦所拿照片上的那个姚志！

姚志还活着！

赵宏伟立马克制住了心情，假装头痛，用手捂了头，掩盖了刚才失常的表情。

山本信玄走过来，问：赵镇长，你没事吧？

赵宏伟龇牙咧嘴地说：他妈的，脑袋突然又痛了。

山本信玄说：那要不你继续在医院观察几天？

赵宏伟说：还是不要了，皇军的事业重要，我要赶紧回到工作中，去为太君效力。

山本信玄说：赵镇长忠心可嘉，实在是中日友善之楷模。

赵宏伟笑笑，然后假装不经意地指了指正往楼下去的担架，问：这是要转去别的医院治疗吗？

山本信玄一笑，说：皇军机密，赵镇长还是少知为妙。

赵宏伟忙点头哈腰，说，是，是。

山本信玄扬长而去。

走廊里又安静了下来，真正的无人的寂静。只有小燕，还在走廊尽头的一个角落里蜷缩着偷泣，哭声幽凉。

赵宏伟心中气郁，低了头，走下了楼梯。

威远镖局的老宅中。

灯光幽暗，昏黄的光亮在空荡荡的屋子里游荡，仿佛孤寂的回响，仿佛人影的消亡。赵驹独自坐着，在往身上擦跌打酒。疼痛像湿透的绳索，在他全身一阵阵地勒紧，每一阵痛，都仿佛深入骨髓的断裂。痛穿透着肌肤，到达赵驹全身骨骼与内脏的深处，令他痛得冷汗直冒、精神委靡。他又往自己身上贴了几张伤筋膏药，膏药难闻的味道刺激着赵驹痛苦的情绪，令他分外彷徨而无依。

“我是东亚病夫！我是东亚病夫！”赵驹的耳朵里，仿佛依旧充满了自己卑躬屈膝的呼号声。按照山本信玄的要求，赵驹每次被打倒在地时，都必须要高呼一声：我是东亚病夫。山本信玄以此为乐。而赵驹，只能在屈辱中不停地挨打、不停地挨打。赵驹伤痕累累，筋骨尽伤，而精神上更是到达了崩溃的边缘。有时候，山本信玄的连续攻击太猛烈太快，赵驹的呼吸都会陷入停顿，几近窒息。这令赵驹感到恐惧，他害怕自己会被山本信玄给打死。但是，赵驹又不敢还手。一旦还手，那么，赵驹就再也不可能回到沈阳去了。

是的，赵驹想回沈阳。他的故乡江庆县赵家镇就在他的眼前与脚下，但是，他却只揪心地感到，他已离故土有千里万里之遥。丽云在哪里，他的家乡便在哪里。丽云埋葬在了沈阳，他的故土，便是沈阳的那片凄凉的坟墓。他想回到丽云的身边，他想回家。可是，天不遂人愿。

渡边一直还活得逍遥自在，想要回沈阳去的欲望，一直束缚住着赵驹最后的复仇。赵驹深深地明白，杀了渡边以后，他不可能逃得太远和太久，所以，除非是能在沈阳杀了渡边，否则，他赵驹在临死前，一定是无法回到沈阳的，更不用说，可以去丽云坟前见她最后一面。可是，日军全面侵华开始之后，渡边的部队不断南下，离沈阳是越来越遥远。赵驹被长久的忍耐折磨着心志，痛苦不堪，又无计可施。赵驹好想回到记忆中以前和丽云在一起时的那个家。然而，一切都早已灰飞烟灭，岁月无情，早将最珍贵的时光埋入了永恒的消亡。

唯有那盒温柔的断发，多少年来，一直陪在赵驹的身边。赵驹看到它，仿佛就能看到丽云还活着。梦里的丽云，依旧笑靥如花，细语如珠，栩栩如生。而清醒中，只有沉痛似血。赵驹好想重新回到丽云的坟前，再和她说一会儿话，哪怕只有一小会儿也好。可是，他回不去。他想念丽云，想得要命，可是，丽云早已不在好多年了。就连她的坟，现在也已离他有千里万里之遥。他的心，哭不出的难受，生不如死的痛楚。

筋骨中的阵痛又卷住了赵驹，令他起了寒栗。他悲哀万分地想，假如丽云看到今天这个嘴里高呼着“我是东亚病夫”的赵驹，会不会难过得掩面而泣？丽云一直在心中把他当成一个英雄，可是，他，又如何配得上“英雄”二字？他只是个软弱而哀伤的懦夫。赵驹潸然泪下，悲不能已。

他右手拿起了一只酒杯，可是突然，他的右手不由自主地颤抖了起来。酒杯“当啷”一下摔在地上，摔碎了。而他的右手，还在不听使唤地发抖。

赵驹悲哀地看着自己的右手，想，再这样被山本信玄打下去，早晚会被他打成残废的，怎么办？

只有忧伤与沉寂，长久地陪伴着赵驹，挥之不去。

悲哀，就像一场无休止的雨。

赵宏伟回到了他租住的房子里。

一切都是那么的空荡和冷清。他的手碰在桌子上，桌上是一层薄薄的白色灰尘。尘埃细且密，都是时间落下的痕迹。赵宏伟叹了口气，走了几步，坐了下来。

脑袋里依旧在隐隐疼痛，赵宏伟感觉很无奈，复杂又破碎的思绪在他的头脑里堆积，他感到无所适从。只有空气里的闷热和孤冷，在矛盾地包围着他，令他莫名忧伤而不安。

赵宏伟的目光碰触到了墙角的那只酒坛，这就是那坛幸存下来的状元红。时光的沧桑与世事的沉淀，已经在酒坛上留下了灰暗的印记。而仔细辨别，空气里再也嗅不到那以前隔着坛子都能闻到的馥郁酒香了。这坛默默见证了赵宏伟一生喜怒哀乐的状元红，就像赵宏伟一样，由年轻时的锋芒毕露，走到了今日的黯然无光。本该在金榜题名或洞房花烛时畅饮的佳酿，到头来，却只成了一个无用武之地的多余之物，除了随时光继续衰老，它没有任何新的价值，却感到，这坛酒是多么好地隐喻了他荒唐悲哀的一生啊！他赵宏伟，年轻时被赋予了状元之梦栋梁之材，然而现实到后来却用铁一样的事实告诉他，他就只能做个人微言轻平凡至极的教书匠，到了如今更是荒谬绝伦了，他赵宏伟，竟然是成了汉奸，成了日本人手里的一只蚂蚁。造化真的弄人。百无一用是书生，此话真乃血泪之言。

赵宏伟想起小菊，想起秀珍。原本，他以前还幻想着，有一天，能和她们团聚着，一起喝了这坛状元红，欢欢喜喜的，也不枉费了这酒在漫长岁月里的一番存在。可是，如今，小菊已逝，秀珍就算还在，自己与她在一起时，又有谁还能露出真正的欢笑？时光与世事，不仅带走了无辜的生命，也夺走了幸存者活着的欢乐与希望。这个时代，是黑暗的，人就算活着，也看不到活着的光明。

赵宏伟找出了自己最后的那根金条。他想把这根金条，给曾林的家里送过去。毕竟，是他有愧于曾林，他不仅杀害了曾林，还利用曾林逃避了刺客的罪责，他在曾林的面前的确是个罪人。这种负罪感，是怎样也无法从内心洗刷掉的。因为，赵宏伟在心里明白：曾林不是一个坏人。但是，赵宏伟还是杀了曾林。也许，人在生死关头，就是会变成没有是非对错且又自私自利至极的禽兽吧，赵宏伟这样想。

他感到十分痛苦。这种痛苦，没有出路。

待在空冷的现在，面对未知的未来，赵宏伟又感到无限的彷徨。他像一只在迷雾中收紧了翅膀的鸟，想要展翅高飞，又完全看不清方向。他想安静地等待命运的启示，又怕命运只会给人以不怀好意的陷阱。他想趁着日本人现在放下了竹内命案不再深查的大好时机，抓紧出逃，离开江庆县，逃出日本人的手掌心，可是他又不知究竟该如何行动。而且，他也不知道秀珍现在究竟是什么情况。

赵宏伟出门，去了一次方远梦的家和老周的诊所，想看看会不会侥幸有人在。但是，门窗紧锁着，房屋里空无一人。赵宏伟倍感失落，心中越发觉得没有依靠了。他又尝试着想要出城去，但被日本兵给拦住了。他不敢再试，更不敢硬闯。

等他重新回到住处时，已是微凉的深夜。白昼的暑热散去，令人的头脑清爽了不少，而孤冷越发犀利。赵宏伟独坐着，不想吃喝，也不想睡觉。只有说不清的彷徨依旧围绕着他，让他愁眉紧锁。

他还想要把姚志的事情告诉给游击队，直觉告诉他，这件事情很重要，宜速不宜迟，但是，他又找不着方远梦。赵宏伟看见姚志的嘴里塞着一团血糊糊的纱布，姚志像是口腔里受伤了什么的。兴许是日本人打掉了姚志的牙齿，赵宏伟想。他亲眼所看到的姚志，是个血色全无、形容枯槁的半死之人，这个形象，给了他心灵一种尖锐的冲击。堂堂男儿，竟被日寇折磨得如此不人不鬼，他日若是自己落到了这步田地，那可如何是好？赵宏伟想想都觉得不寒而栗。他越发坚定了迅速出逃的欲望，只是，面对日军禁止百姓出城的严令，他又倍感黔驴技穷。他无奈又无能，只能在反复的思量与煎熬中等待天亮。

赵宏伟在无法入眠的彷徨中，非常思念秀珍的点点滴滴，许多珍贵的往昔在时间缓慢地流淌中浮向了记忆的表面。在这孤冷空虚的时刻里，他对秀珍的眷恋显得分外独一无二且弥足珍贵，秀珍对他的好，让他既感到了岁月里的温暖，也感到了对她无尽的亏欠。回首人生，他觉得自己已被命运剥夺掉了太多的美好，站在这个绚烂的红尘面前，他有时候感到自己就是一个赤条条的乞丐。这个世上，除了秀珍，还有谁会真心对他好？没有了。他很快就会老了，他的一辈子，很快就要过去了，若再不珍惜秀珍，此生，他就真的是孤单得像场从未存在过的梦了。他不愿如此空无地活着，不愿活得如此无依无靠，所以，他想和秀珍在一起。可是，秀珍现在还活着吗？她都还好吗？他不得而知。

第二天下午，赵宏伟一个人去小菊的坟前，祭奠了小菊。他烧了一些纸钱，纸钱的灰烬被风吹得纷纷扬扬的。赵宏伟很哀伤，其实，他和秀珍，怎么样也都回不到以前了，因为小菊不在了。他会永远内疚，她会永远悲痛，这内疚和悲痛，将填充在他和她爱情的每个角落里。况且，在她的心里，还必将烙有日本畜生给她留下的无尽伤疤。未来，他要怎样才能修补好两个人灵魂中的各种破碎？他要怎样才能用美好的爱情与全心的爱护来弥补他对她一生的亏欠？他迷茫而无知。他只悲哀地以为，很多时候，所谓的美好希望，都只是自欺欺人的幻觉。

坟场旁的小河安静地流淌着，仿佛人间所有的悲欢离合终将如水长逝。执着地活着或不懈地追求着，到最后，似乎也都摆脱不了化为尘土的结局。赵宏伟觉得很怅惘。他不愿再多想，他觉得越想，自己便越软弱。他不想做个懦夫。

小河安静地流淌，微弱的金光，在河面上粼粼地闪耀。

玉山上。

方远梦看着小夕给他留下来的那两张并排粘贴在一起的照片，心中的哀伤像火舌般跃动着，灼痛着他怅然若失的灵魂。小夕写下的“远梦，我永远爱你”，像拥有着一种可以将时光哭碎的魔力，令方远梦悲不能已，他在零散如雪花的回忆里后悔莫及。

时间在痛苦的泥潭里总是流淌得特别缓慢，方远梦的泪水，克制不住地流淌。他想用一些欢乐的回忆来抑制哭泣，却莫名只感到更加深切的悲伤和孤独。他，终究只是个人，会痛的人，用血肉之躯来活着的人。他感到，小夕不在了，他也就像是死了。这种感受简单而尖锐，刺穿着他所有的情感铠甲。他发誓，他一定要为小夕报仇。不管还要穿透多少困难才能向敌人刺出死亡之刃，他也一定要百折不挠地坚持到底，他要杀了害死小夕的恶魔，他要看到敌人的全部灭亡。这个意志，就像块钢铁，支撑着他的斗志。

他还想要去上海，再走一遍小夕最爱逛的那条马路；他想去小夕最喜欢的那家咖啡馆里再坐一会儿，看看小夕常坐的那个位子。他知道，当夕阳西下的时候，小夕再不能蹦蹦跳跳地在树影里走路；他知道，当他恐惧的时候，他再握不到小夕温暖的手。小夕的笑颜已如融化的雪花般消失于这个世界，他再不能在她的背后，轻轻牵住她影子里的手。她再不能笑着问，远梦，你会爱我到天荒地老吗？而他，也再不能回答。只有忧伤，会在不灭的记忆中，一生悲痛，没有拯救。

无法解脱。

男人的悲伤哭泣，是再也没有眺望的空虚，是风中飞舞的沙粒。

方远梦将那两张合并在一起的照片，小心翼翼地夹在了书页间，然后他将这本书藏在了他床边桌子的一个抽屉里。

方远梦拿出了枪，开始装子弹。明天，他就会和刘小阳他们一起下山。

小秦到了方远梦屋里来，问方远梦有没有脏了还没洗的衣服。方远梦指了指挂在椅背上的几件皱巴巴的衣裤。小秦笑了笑，抱起那几件衣服，转身就往外走。方远梦忙问：干什么去呀？小秦说：帮你洗衣服。方远梦说：你？小秦说：不是我，是王大嫂要我拿些同志们的脏衣服去，给她洗。

方远梦眉头一紧，问：她情绪低落吗？是不是又想不开了？

小秦说：不是，她挺高兴的，和以前闷头找衣服洗不一样，她是真想帮大家做点事。

方远梦松了口气，点点头，说：那好吧，这样最好，但是你也别真的给人家弄去很多衣服，别给人添麻烦。

小秦笑了起来，说：我能这么不知轻重吗？放心，我就稍微找几件衣服过去给她洗。

方远梦说，行。

小秦笑着将脏衣服交给了秀珍，说：这几件是老方同志的衣服，他一直都没洗，现在麻烦你了。

秀珍笑着接了过来，又和小秦说了一会儿话。小秦待了一会儿，有事就先走了。秀珍开开心心地去打了水，准备要给方远梦洗衣服了。

忽然，一封信从方远梦的衣袋里掉了出来。她去捡。捡到了手里，一看却愣住了。信封上，是赵宏伟亲笔写的“秀珍亲启”。秀珍意外之下，既惊喜，又疑惑。

她想了一下，便放下了衣服，微笑着，拆开了信。

……对不起，秀珍，其实我并不爱你，也从未真的想过，将来要和你生活在一起，我之所以骗你，只是想要给你一个逃出赵家镇的理由，好让你能在一个安全的地方好好地生活下去，希望你能理解我的一片苦心。你我今生的缘分已尽，将来恐怕不会再有相见之期，你一定要好好保重，好好生活下去。今世负你太深，已不求你能原谅，只望来生若能再见，倾我一世还你一生……

秀珍怀抱着这封信，悲恸着，瘫倒在了地上。她的泪，像决堤的河水。她的人生，她的希望，她的仅存的快乐，统统被打了个粉碎。她感到，自己就是个笑话。

方远梦正想去找刘小阳，说说进城后的事，忽然，小秦神色慌张地跑了进来。

“不好了，王大嫂在屋里哭成了个泪人儿！刚才她还好好的！”

方远梦问：“是发生什么事了吗？”

小秦说：“不知道，我就看她手里捏着一封信！”

信？

方远梦一拍大腿。他想起来了，赵宏伟交给他的信，就在他其中一件脏衣服的口袋里。他只顾着想念小夕，一时把这信的事给忘了。

方远梦赶紧跟着小秦往外走。方远梦一边走，一边却也不禁疑惑：赵宏伟究竟是在信里写了什么内容？

方远梦将秀珍手里的信拿了过来，赶紧看了一遍。看完以后，方远梦也是无言以对。他不知道信上的内容究竟是赵宏伟的肺腑之言，还是赵宏伟的别有深意。毕竟，这是人家两个人之间的情事，他一个外人，也弄不清情况。方远梦又仔细看了看信，想看看赵宏伟是不是在信里藏了什么暗语，结果也不是。方远梦也不知该怎么安慰秀珍了。

小秦将信拿了过去，看完后，小秦义愤填膺，说：“我早就说赵宏伟不是个好东西，你们都不听！现在你们看，他根本就是在始乱终弃，活脱脱一个西门庆！”

方远梦要小秦别说话。

方远梦详细地跟秀珍讲了一下这封信的由来，包括赵宏伟当时是在怎样的情况下交托的这封信、赵宏伟当时都交代了一些什么话。方远梦对秀珍说：依我看，赵兄当时很有可能是担心他自己会有什么三长两短，所以，才会要我在向你隐瞒死讯的同时，交给你这样的一封信，也许，他是想，这样一来，你就能以为，他还活着，只是仅仅从你的生活中消失了。

小秦插嘴，说：“这样做有什么意思呢？对一个女人来说，一个男人不爱她、离开她，和这个男人死了有什么区别？难道痛苦会减轻一点吗，我看这样只会让女人更难过！”

方远梦没理小秦。方远梦对秀珍说：别人不知道，但我清楚，赵兄为了救你，实在是舍弃了一切，我想，关于这封信，应该是有什么误会在里面，所幸赵兄他现在安然无恙，并没有什么三长两短，等赵兄出了城来，与你相会之时，你们再开诚布公地好好谈一谈，你看如何？

秀珍点点头，渐止了哭泣。

方远梦又安慰了一会儿秀珍，看她情绪真的稳定了，才和小秦离开。

回去的路上，方远梦对小秦说：我答应过赵兄，要帮他照顾好秀珍，可是没想到现在事情又突然变糟了，明天我又马上要下山去了，没办法看护好秀珍了，我是真怕秀珍会做出些想不开的事情来，所以，小秦，我下山以后，还希望你能帮忙，多费心照顾一下她，防止出事。

小秦说：这个你不用担心，我会照顾好王大嫂的，这段时间相处下来，我也看出来了，王大嫂是个好人，也是个可怜女人，我一定不会看着她做什么傻事的，但是我要说明白，我照顾王大嫂，可不是为了姓赵的那个狗

汉奸！

方远梦说：你这人脾气就是这样，听不进别人的话，但是罢了，很多道理，你以后也许慢慢会懂，不过有件事你必须要记住，千万别在秀珍面前骂赵宏伟。

小秦说：我就不明白了，姓赵的这么一个软骨头、狗东西，为什么值得你多次违反纪律地帮助他、接近他，他有表示过想要洗心革面改换阵营重新做人吗，他会真心实意地想要追随我们共产党吗，我看，那个姓赵的，将来能不出卖我们就算不错了，你向他坦露了太多的真相，无异于是在你自己胸前放了把尖刀，早晚会出事！

方远梦笑笑，摇摇头，不作口舌之争。

小秦继续说：就算他姓赵的也帮助过我们，但是很显然，他是想要和我们做交易，归根结底，他还是为了他自己的利益，他就是个彻头彻尾自私自利的人，我也真是想不明白，像王大嫂那样好的一个女人，怎么就会瞎了眼，对这个狗汉奸死心塌地，你也看到了，那个狗东西，写那样无情无义的一封信给王大嫂，把王大嫂伤成了什么样！说句心里话，我觉得，赵宏伟他根本就配不上王大嫂。

方远梦说：那是他们两个人之间的私事，我们无权妄加评论。

小秦说：可是，赵宏伟害得王大嫂的女儿被活活烧死了，你真觉得，他们两个人以后还能生活在一起吗？

方远梦停下了脚步，说：这事现在千万不能让秀珍知道！

小秦说：我知道，这事现在当然不能让王大嫂知道，不然她会真的活不了的，可是她早晚会知道的，到那时，王大嫂该怎么办？我觉得，王大嫂真该重新好好想想，她往后的日子还长，应该找个真正好的男人过日子，她可以有选择的。

方远梦说：这些话，你以后不要再说了，爱情这种事，局外人永远不懂的。

小秦忽然就很生气，说：我看，不懂的是你。

说完，小秦就独自跑开了。

赵家镇。

赵宏伟打听到了曾林的家庭住址，就怀揣了最后的那根金条，找了过去。

阴雨连绵的天气，巷子里寂静暗沉。赵宏伟撑着伞，在凉丝丝的雨水里一步步往前走着，雨滴在小水洼里溅起了涟漪，赵宏伟的鞋子湿成一片。他的心里沉甸甸的，像带着不能说的罪。每往前走一步，他都想往后逃。

到了曾林家的门前，大门十分破旧，门上满是木头年深日久之后泛出的皱纹。半张门神画像，在门上耷拉着脑袋。浓郁的破败气息，让赵宏伟有些抬不起头来。曾林的家和赵宏伟原本想象中的不太一样。这种破败，令赵宏伟心里的内疚成倍地增长。他不禁自欺欺人地想：也许这里不是曾林的家，是我弄错了。

雨水哗哗地落下。

赵宏伟敲了敲门，好一会儿之后，才由一个老太婆来开了门。门“吱呀”地响着。老太婆脸上的皱纹，和门上的木纹一样僵硬。

“请问，这里是曾林的家吗？”赵宏伟小心翼翼地问。

老太婆疑惑地看了看他，皱了皱眉，然后，点了点头，说：“这里是曾先生的家，请问，你是谁？”

赵宏伟尴尬地笑了笑，说：“我是曾林的同事，我来……我来……看望一下他的儿子。”

赵宏伟尴尬又不知所措地笑着。

老太婆“哦”了一声，说：“你也是帮日本人跑腿的呀。”

赵宏伟含糊其辞地“嗯”了一声。老太婆让赵宏伟进了屋。屋里光线昏暗，也没点灯，桌上倒着半截蜡烛，像一棵被砍倒了的树。赵宏伟收起雨伞，放在门旁，伞上的雨水汇流在地，散发出湿漉漉的霉变味道。

赵宏伟的心里荒凉一片，沉重莫名。

老太婆告诉赵宏伟，她是曾林雇的佣人，专门照顾他瘫痪在床的儿子，人家一般都叫她张阿婆。张阿婆说，前段时间也来过一个曾林的同事，告诉她，曾林出差去了，要过段时间才能回来。张阿婆对赵宏伟说：“先生啊，你知不知道曾先生他究竟什么时候能回来呀？这个月的工资我还没拿，要不是看小孩子可怜，这两天我都不想过来了。”

赵宏伟支吾地回答：“快了，就……就再过几天，曾林便回来了。”说

完，赵宏伟脸上一阵燥热。

张阿婆领赵宏伟去房间里，看望了一下曾林的儿子。一进房间，便能闻到一股中药味和屎尿味相混合着的难闻气味，差点令人呕吐。曾林的儿子就那么躺在床上，一动也不能动。张阿婆介绍说，这小孩子有骨痨，全身都是瘫痪的，吃饭和拉屎都要人伺候，没人照顾的话，这小孩子几天就会饿死。赵宏伟问：那这孩子还有其他亲人吗？张阿婆说：这孩子的亲妈早死了，至于其他的亲戚，看到这种瘫痪的孩子，还不是能躲就躲，哪里指望得上。张阿婆说：这孩子长这么大，活到如今，全靠了曾先生的辛苦，我是他去年才雇来帮忙的。

曾林的儿子弱弱地叫了赵宏伟一声“叔叔”。他有气无力地问赵宏伟：“你认识我爸爸吗？他怎么好久都没回来了？我想他——”

赵宏伟难受地说：“快了，你爸爸很快就要回来了，你放心。”

孩子气若游丝地说：“我会背《蜀道难》了，上次爸爸说，要我背给他听的。爸爸说，我会背了，就给我买糖吃。”

赵宏伟眼眶一热，受不了了。他推说要喝水，逃出了房间。

赵宏伟只想给自己几个耳光。不，只有耳光怎么够！他想：我简直是造孽呀！

他无地自容。他感到了真正的罪。是的，赵宏伟真的是有罪的！

赵宏伟把金条给了张阿婆。张阿婆惊呆了。赵宏伟说：你千万要照顾好这孩子，不要不管他，你给他多买些好吃的，以后，你每个月的工资，我来付。

赵宏伟抓起雨伞，开了门，就赶紧逃离了曾林的家。他感到，他没办法再在那里多待一秒钟，再待下去，他会疯。

杀人的血腥与罪孽，紧紧捆绑着赵宏伟的灵魂，他感到了虚弱，感到了不能承受，感到了头晕目眩。他觉得，自己是个真实的凶手。

赵宏伟走到小巷口的时候，忽然，迎面跑来了一队日本兵。他忙侧身让开。日本兵们从他身边跑过。他们穿着黑色的雨衣，浑身湿漉漉的，就像是刚从地狱里跑出来的水鬼。

天空阴森而暗沉。

赵宏伟讶异地看到，这队日本兵，跑到了曾林家的门口，停了下来。领队的小头目下了一声令，日本兵便踹开了曾林家的门。

日本兵们，蜂拥而入。

几声枪响，又是几声枪响。

赵宏伟站在小巷口，目瞪口呆。狂野的惊恐，刹那决堤汹涌。

日本兵们，抬出了张阿婆的尸体，抬出了曾林儿子的尸体。鲜血，在雨水里奔流。凄惨的雨，痛苦地洗刷着老人与孩子可怜的尸体。

小头目的手里，拿着一根金条，哈哈大笑。

伞从赵宏伟手里掉落，他像站在雨里的一具木偶。

日本兵们再次经过赵宏伟的身边时，赵宏伟像疯了一样，抓住了那个小头目的衣领，用日语战栗地问："为什么要杀他们？为什么要杀他们！"

日本兵将赵宏伟一阵毒打。等到小头目弄清楚这位就是大名鼎鼎的赵镇长以后，才客气了一些地说：曾林是内奸，是军统特工，山本大尉下令，要我们杀死他全部的家眷。

日本兵们跑远了。

赵宏伟像摊烂泥一样，泡在冰凉的雨水里。他的嘴角流着血，心里流着血。

赵宏伟哭了起来，哭得战栗不已。就好像，那个可怜的孩子，是被他亲手杀死的一样。他仰望着灰暗又压抑的天空，哭不出声音来。他感到恐惧，他感到，这片天，就是一个魔鬼。这个时代，嗜血如命。

赵宏伟的双眼，被雨滴砸得剧痛。他觉得，雨把他全撕碎了。

县监狱。

血腥味浓重的刑讯室内。

姚志坐在宽大的电椅上，大小便已完全失禁。他歪着头，看起来已有些神志不清。山本信玄手停在电流开关上，询问似的望着渡边。渡边手掩着鼻，紧皱着眉，犹豫了一下，还是挥手示意，要山本信玄加大电流。山本信玄遵命。

姚志昏厥了过去。

等候在一旁的医生和护士，忙拎了医药箱上前去，开始慌忙地抢救姚志。山本信玄吓唬医生说：救不活他，你们也得坐电椅！

山本信玄说完，便踱步走到了渡边的身旁。山本信玄轻声说：怕是不行啊，再这样来几次的话，姚志肯定就要死了。

渡边叹了口气，说：让医生和护士一直待在这里，保证姚志活着。

山本信玄说：姚志要是仍然一直不肯写供词和画地图，我们怎么办？我觉得，再给他上刑也是浪费时间。

渡边不说话，隔了好一会儿，才又叹了一口气。

姚志总算又被救醒了。

山本信玄问渡边：继续吗？

渡边不说话，过了一会儿，摇了摇头。

渡边转身离开了刑讯室。山本信玄听到了渡边在走廊里重重的一声叹息，这声叹息，响亮得简直像喊叫。

赵宏伟又回到了赵家镇的镇政府里。他感到，在目前这种无可奈何又无路可走的情况下，他还是应该要假装继续上班的好。要不然，人还没走成，先让日本人起了疑心，那就前功尽弃了。

学校都已经放了暑假，赵宏伟一个人在赵家镇小学的校园里走了一圈，心里空荡荡的，又透着迷茫。他想起自己当时在学校里为了拖住竹内而使用的各种小伎俩，心中依旧后怕不已。幸亏那天参加听课的主要人员都已死光，并且渡边又急着要给竹内之死盖棺定论，所以，才没人把怀疑的目光投向那段要命的听课时间上，否则，日本人只要好好找几个小孩盘问一下，他赵宏伟的一切阴谋都将无可隐藏。这算不算是上天在帮他赵宏伟的忙？赵宏伟不敢感恩，因为他害怕，上天放过他这一回，只是为了让他等待什么更糟的事。天意一向恐怖，他想。

不过，赵宏伟反正也没打算再在这赵家镇上久待，所以，他只是简单地祈望，在他成功出逃以前，日本人对他的态度能维持现状就好。只要他离开了江庆县，与秀珍一起远走高飞，那么，就算日本人发现了他是真凶的真相，也不能再拿他怎样。只不过，他觉得有些对不起那些配合他演戏的学生，一旦东窗事发，不知道日本人会不会拿学生撒气？他以前觉得不会，因为他完全是用蒙骗的方式利用了学生，学生们对于赵宏伟要他们做的事情完全不解其意，只是照做罢了。赵宏伟一直觉得他这样做已经保护了学生，一旦他拖延竹内时间的事情曝光，学生们都是站在被蒙骗利用的位置上，他觉得日本人应该不会去惩罚那些小朋友。但是，在目睹了曾林儿子的死之后，赵宏伟之前的这些虚弱的信念又全部倒塌了。他现在觉得，一旦学生们配合他演戏的事情被日本人发觉，日本人一定会杀很多人。这令赵宏伟倍感煎熬，他只能期望，他故意拖延竹内时间的事情，能永远埋在秘密里。在独善其身和身负内疚这两种思想感情的夹击下，赵宏伟又一次感到了深切又难解的矛盾。他不禁听到自己心里的另一个声音在斥责他：你一个人逃走了有什么用？要赶走日本人才是正理呀！

赵宏伟感到自己很无能，很渺小，很懦弱，而这些，又让他很无奈。

赵宏伟最后的金条被那个日本兵的小头目给拿走了，但是他又不敢去要回来。因为，那根金条原本就是他送给曾林家里的，如果日本人问起来，问他为何要在曾林死后给曾林家里送金条，他将十分难以回答，甚至会节外生枝引火烧身。所以，思来想去，赵宏伟还是放弃了这根金条。他想，本来这根金条就是送出去了的，不是我的了，只是白白便宜了那个鬼子。

赵宏伟在镇政府里的牢房一带认真侦察了一番。他原本非常怀疑姚志一直就被关在镇政府里那间外围看守十分严密的牢房里，但是，他现在发现，那间牢房已经空了出来，而且，在镇政府里，已经没有哪间牢房再配有那样严密的看守，各牢房都只是被稀松平常地看管着。赵宏伟由此判断：姚志肯定已经被转移走了。

而姚志最有可能的去处，无疑，就是县监狱。

赵宏伟急切地盼望着能和游击队取得联系，不管是公事还是私事，他都有许多事要说、要问。

夜色清冷，漆黑寂静。

赵宏伟的住处。

响起了轻轻的敲门声。

赵宏伟问："谁呀？"

"我。"方远梦的声音。

赵宏伟大喜过望，蹦起来就赶紧去开了门。

除了方远梦以外，门外还有一个年轻人，方远梦介绍说：这位是刘小阳

同志。刘小阳向赵宏伟点头笑笑。“都快进来吧。”赵宏伟迫不及待地说。

没有寒暄。赵宏伟马上向方远梦报告了从那天战斗开始直到今天这段时间里发生的一些主要事情，方远梦也告诉了赵宏伟一些从当日分别以后直到现在这段时间里发生的主要事情，双方迅速地交流了各自知道的一些信息。方远梦和刘小阳在得知了竹内是被赵宏伟杀死的之后，都大感震惊；当赵宏伟知道秀珍一切安好的时候，心里终于放下了一块石头。最后，赵宏伟告诉了方远梦姚志还活着的事实，方远梦告诉了赵宏伟秀珍看到了信的事情。夜色，像拧成了一个愁苦的结。

刘小阳说：我们进城以后，才发现江庆县现在是许进不许出，日本人是外松内紧，打算瓮中捉鳖呀。

赵宏伟感到一片绝望，说：那我要到何时才能与秀珍会合、一起离开呀？

方远梦说：看来，这一次日本人是非要灭了我们游击队不可了。

刘小阳笑笑，说：谁灭了谁还不一定，我这次来，还想要杀一个日军联队长呢。

赵宏伟说：但愿上天庇佑我们。

夜色漆黑。

玉山上。

阴灰的天，闷热伴随着风，像要下雨。

秀珍独自伏在桌上哭泣，双肩战栗不已，像一株濒死的植物在悬崖边发抖。她至今不敢相信自己看到的那封信，她至今不能理解信中所说的一切。现实的面目和她憧憬的道路根本是南辕北辙，他说的和他写的完全背道而驰。究竟哪个是真哪个是假？究竟哪个是虚哪个是实？困在人生痛苦的迷雾中，她既看不清方向，也看不到出路。她只明确地知道，她的爱情，碎了。

而在她的心里，还有一个她不敢面对的答案，那就是：“赵宏伟以前都不爱她，如今，她已是残花败柳，他又怎么会真心爱她？他当时那样信誓旦旦地向她表白，其实只是为了鼓励她活下去，所以，他在信中写的，都是真心话。”这个声音清楚明白又尖锐刺耳，她想好好听，可是一听，就想死。这就像是死神的蛊惑。这世上大半的真理，都仿佛只有死神才说得出口。

秀珍想到了那几个跳崖自尽的女人，她想起了她们曾经流过的那些可怜的泪水，她感到自己的泪水仿佛和她们的流在一起，她感到自己似乎听懂了她们死前的哭泣。她觉得有股冲动，在拉着她，要去走她们的路。可是，她又分明觉得还有一个小东西在牢牢地拖住着她，要她不能去死。她回头一看，恍惚就看清楚了，那个拖住她的小东西，是小菊。

是啊，她想，她还有小菊。小菊还没长大，小菊还需要她的照顾，小菊是她最后的亲人。爱情灰飞烟灭了，起码，她还有一个女儿。她想。

哪怕为了小菊，她也还是要好好活下去。她安慰自己。

下午，小秦给秀珍送来了一碗甜粥，是他特地熬的。他安慰了秀珍几句，叮嘱她记得把粥吃了，然后，他便离开了。其实他想再在她的面前多待一会儿，可是莫名又感到局促不安，心慌意乱。离开后，他却又满脑子里都是她的容颜。

他感到，她真是个太可怜的女人。

江庆县。酒楼中。

赵宏伟走到了酒楼的楼上，正欲叫一碟牛肉，一抬眼，却看到在墙角的位置坐着的赵驹。赵驹正在独自喝酒，一杯连着一杯，菜却只有一碟花生米。赵宏伟犹豫了一下，还是走了过去，在赵驹的桌旁坐了下来。

“今日幸会，不知小弟可否与你同桌一饮？”赵宏伟满脸堆笑地问。

“行，行，我正没钱吃什么硬菜，就你请客吧。”赵驹玩世不恭地说。

“小弟正有此意，实在荣幸之至。”赵宏伟谦卑地说。

很快，鸡鸭鱼肉上了一大桌，赵驹吃得很高兴。他一脸痞相地说：“吃不要钱的，味道就是香。”赵宏伟付之一笑。

赵宏伟喝了杯酒，然后，开门见山地问：“我听护士说，那天，是你救了我？”

赵驹顿了顿，然后一脸痞相地点点头，说：“没错，是我救了你，你要牢记我的大恩大德。”

赵宏伟敬了赵驹一杯酒，说：“谢谢，谢谢你。真的。”

赵驹玩世不恭地说：“没事，不用谢，你如果死了，那我多寂寞呀。你我就是诸葛亮和周瑜的关系，谁也见不得谁好，但又谁也不想真的看谁死。

这样才好玩。”

“你抬高我了，我活了大半辈子了，其实一直就是一摊烂泥，蓦然回首，一事无成，浑浑噩噩，自惭形秽。”赵宏伟自嘲地说，“所以，你根本不用和我比。”

赵驹笑笑，喝了两杯酒，说：“彼此彼此吧，你都承认你是烂泥了，我也自然不是什么好货了。人生一世，梦幻泡影，我们都白活了这一场。”

“不知从何时起，不知从何因起，原本朝气蓬勃的人生，就变成了或者荒唐或者孤独的悲剧。”赵宏伟喝了一杯酒，感慨万千地说：“也许，是我们生来就被注定了只能是微不足道的人。”

“人终究是胜不了天的，人越渴望美好的东西，就越会被命运踩得粉身碎骨。观看悲剧是上帝的乐趣。没有什么，比人与美的毁灭更能证明上帝的永恒。所以，生而为人，本来就是为了痛苦又卑微地走完这一程。”赵驹说完，又猛喝酒。

“我知天意不可违，所以很多时候，我只是想尽人事而听天命，但求无悔于回忆、无愧于良心，可是往往到最后，又会发现，所谓的尽力而为，只是南柯一梦，徒劳无功。”赵宏伟说。

赵驹笑笑，说：“像你这样多愁善感又参透了人生的人，如果去做血雨腥风且勇往直前的大事，没有不失败的道理。因为，成大事者，皆需孤注一掷，赌天赌地赌命。而你的性格，就是儒道释，自误且误人。你若去造反，我会笑死。”

赵宏伟置之一笑。两个人默默无语地干了好几杯酒，这酒却只像茶，喝不醉人。窗外风过处，绿叶悄然凋落。叶子在风中画着弧线，寂静坠向地面。

赵宏伟说：“我看，在你的心里，藏着另一个赵驹。你不是一块破铜烂铁，因为你的痛苦锋芒毕露。你是在隐藏什么，或者逃避什么？”

赵驹说：“难道你不是如此吗？我想，你一定尝试过要做一个好演员，但是蹩脚的演技，又令你自己惊慌不堪。其实人生如戏，真假与彼此，我们本就不用去分辨得太清楚，因为，从来都是戏决定着角色，而角色选择不了戏。你说是不是？”赵驹淡淡一笑。

赵宏伟叹了口气，说：“我们都是看不见的牢笼里的囚徒。”

赵驹说："人挣不脱的，都是自己选择的枷锁。"

赵宏伟说："知道吗，我以前恨你，想要剪除你，就像要为一棵家门前的树剪掉枯死腐烂的枝叶一样，以为只有这样，才能让自己的家园看起来焕然一新。"

赵驹说："不必内疚，因为我也是这样地厌恶你，这种心情早已灌注在了我们不可改变的人生回忆里，我想，我们也都无须在今天以后做出任何改变，因为，有所坚持总比无所依从更能让人活得踏踏实实。"

赵宏伟说："你真的是个谜。"

赵驹说："你能看懂你自己吗？"

赵宏伟说："不能。"

赵驹说："所以，其实我们每个人都是一个谜，只要自己不说，自己和别人就都永远不会明白。"

赵宏伟说："这或许就是人类会失去自由的原因？"

赵驹说："恰恰相反，这是人类唯一仅存的自由。"

两人举杯相碰，说："来，只管喝酒！"

酒入愁肠，风扫落叶。天地寂寥，悲苦无依。

县监狱。刑讯室门外。

渡边焦躁不安地来回踱着步。山本信玄则安静地站立在一旁。

好几天过去了，电椅的功效已让渡边失望透顶。这东西看来只能给姚志带来死亡，而并不能使他产生半分屈服的意愿。刑讯室里总是没完没了的血肉模糊的抢救，总是没完没了的姚志大小便失禁的味道，渡边站在刑讯室里的时候，简直恶心得快要吐了，但是结果呢，还是没得到半点有价值的情报。渡边火冒三丈，但又无能为力，无计可施。

山本信玄忽然冷冷地开了口，说："大人，我有一个办法，或许能让姚志放弃他所有的坚持，向我们坦白一切我们所需的情报——"

渡边眼睛一亮，急不可耐地说："什么办法？快说快说！"

山本信玄慢条斯理地说："只怕大人太过仁慈，就算我说了，大人也难以接受。"

渡边面露嘲笑，说："我？仁慈？哈哈哈哈——你这算是在讽刺我的残

忍与冷血吗？”

山本信玄说：“属下绝无此意。”

渡边不耐烦了，说：“他妈的你快说。”

山本信玄走到了渡边的身旁，附耳低语。

渡边听完，眉头渐皱。他呆立着，不发一语。

“你可真是个魔鬼呀！”渡边不禁对山本信玄说。

山本信玄冷漠地一笑，渡边后背上升起了几丝寒意。

“怎么样，要属下现在就去准备吗？”山本信玄问。

渡边犹豫不决地来回走着，他说：“要是被老百姓发觉了，闹起事来，怕是会出大乱子啊，毕竟，我们要的是统治，不是死亡。”

山本信玄说：“如果没有死亡的恐怖，又怎么会有统治的长久？”

渡边沉默着，最后还是皱着眉，微微摇了摇头，说：“还是再想想别的办法吧。”

山本信玄嗤之以鼻。渡边无奈地走开了。

威远镖局老宅内。

赵驹擦着枪，忽然，两只手同时一抖，枪掉在了地上。他想去捡，但手里一时却丝毫使不出劲，形同残废。过了好一会儿，他的双手才又恢复了正常。

赵驹捡起枪，把枪放在了桌上。他看着自己的手臂，心中惊惶而彷徨。他感到自己的身体正在逐渐脱离自己意识的控制，走向一种无形的崩溃与瓦解，就好像一栋即将坍塌的房子。山本信玄连续的殴打终于体现出了效果：赵驹很有可能会被打成一个残废。赵驹的身体，再这样被打下去，也许终将瘫痪。而这，也许才是山本信玄不杀赵驹的真正原因。毕竟，死亡折磨不了人，生不如死才是真正的折磨。

赵驹心中不寒而栗。他想，如果自己真的被打成了残废，那么，还怎么杀渡边？

也许，真的已经等待了太久，应该，是到了必须要动手的时候了。

可是，如果在江庆县杀了渡边，那么，他赵驹是无论如何也不可能再回到沈阳去了。他此生，都无法再去丽云坟前见她最后一面了。他将会死在江南，与丽云的坟，相隔千里万里。而他，最后的愿望，只是想要和丽云死在一起。这个愿望，已经在他心里种下了太多年，这个愿望，是他苟延残喘的唯一力气。

可是，似乎已到了必须要放弃这个最终愿望的时候了。因为，如果他再不对渡边动手，恐怕，他将再无机会报仇了。

丽云，丽云。赵驹痛苦地哀泣着。

他知道，他再也回不了沈阳了。他知道，他再也回不到丽云的身边了。

从多年以前开始，命运就早已为他安排了如今的结局。而他，别无选择。

丽云，丽云，我想你。赵驹痛苦地哀泣。

他只盼望，来生，还能再与丽云相见，哪怕，只是擦肩而过，蓦然回首。他将生生世世，活在对她的怀念里。

渡边约赵驹在靶场会面。

赵驹到的时候，渡边已经在靶场里练了一会儿枪了。渡边看见赵驹，十分高兴，放下枪，坐下来，倒了茶，请赵驹一起喝。

两人闲聊了一会儿。出乎赵驹的意料，今天渡边待他分外和蔼可亲，并无颐指气使的样子。有时候，渡边还会一个人坐在那里自说自话，也不计较赵驹是否真的在听。枪放在地上，就像一件被冷落了的玩具。渡边谈笑间的神情莫名有些忧伤。

渡边告诉赵驹，人生的崛起之路，是一条如履薄冰的炼狱之途，通过地狱考验的，能成为将军，通不过的，只能成为鬼魂。赵驹说，人生宛如昙花一现，功名利禄冰凉如铁，活在其中，人会被欲望杀死心中的柔软，夺走良知的温暖。渡边告诉赵驹，但这又是一条不得不走的路，因为，底层永远是被上层踩在脚下的蚂蚁。赵驹问，将军们是否又在催问剿灭玉山游击队之事？渡边苦笑，告诉赵驹，此事不提也罢，徒令人增添烦恼，所幸松尾包围之势坚固，游击队和慰安妇，都仍在如来佛的手掌心里。赵驹说，松尾倒是一面既碍事又挡风的墙。渡边说，日久见人心，还是你知我心忧。

渡边指指极远处的那些靶子，又指指他自己的右臂，告诉赵驹，这个世上，有很多东西，你原本以为会一直拥有，其实，上帝还是会用他独有的方

式来告诉你，失去才是永恒。渡边说，我曾经从未想过，我会三枪打不中一个苹果，以为技术这种东西，理所当然是一生不会丢的，但是，结果就是那么一颗小小的子弹，夺走了我一生最引以为傲的东西，那就是我的枪技。赵驹说，大人当年的救命之恩，小的没齿不忘。渡边摇摇头，说，这和忘不忘没有关系，因为，你是我的作品。渡边长叹一声，说：我的枪技在你的身上得到了延续与复活，所以，你是我真正意义上的左膀右臂。渡边说，所以，你在我手下，从来就不是一个普通的差役。赵驹说，感谢大人器重，小的定当全力效忠。渡边说，可惜啊，你我君臣一场，不能善始善终，汪精卫政府的组织日趋完备，他们的机构与编制，很快就将深入到每一块区域，你，就要被调动了，以后，你将被汪政府的人使用，而不再是属于我个人的奴仆了。渡边说，以你的身手，极有可能会被调去上海，加入七十六号特工总部。渡边说，所以，我昨天想到，我都还从没和你平等地喝过一次茶，想来真是遗憾。

赵驹很惊讶。

渡边拾起地上的枪，交给赵驹，说，来，让我再领略一次你百发百中的枪法，好让我回忆起我风光不再的曾经，以后，恐怕我不会再有这样的机会了。

渡边说着，笑容里竟开满了朴素的惆怅，宛如一田间老农。

赵驹不知所措地拿过枪，然后，瞄准了极远处的靶子。

一枪，命中。

一枪，命中。

又一枪，脱靶。

又一枪，脱靶。

赵驹的双手，抖了起来。他的枪，掉在了地上。

渡边愕然地站了起来。“你怎么了？”他看着赵驹颓丧的样子，惊讶得目瞪口呆。“你竟然脱靶了？”渡边难以置信地问。

赵驹说，抱歉，太君，我恐怕已不配被调去上海的特工总部了，因为，您最得意的作品，您那复活的枪技，已经被人给毁了。

渡边困惑不解地问：“你说什么？这是什么意思？到底怎么回事？”

赵驹脱下了上衣。只见，他的身上，伤痕累累，遍布青紫，膏药张张，伤口处处，惨不忍睹。

渡边目瞪口呆。

玉山上。

傍晚的天色灰暗朦胧，风中略带着一些清爽。

小秦又为秀珍熬了一碗甜粥，红枣独特的香气，淡淡撩拨着人的心绪。

粥还很烫，火辣的温度像藤蔓一样燃烧在碗的花纹里，让人触摸不上，一碰即痛。小秦把粥轻放在秀珍的桌上，说，凉一凉再吃吧。秀珍点点头。

小秦坐了下来，和秀珍说了一会儿话。他安慰秀珍说，过去了的糟糕的事情，都要丢到垃圾堆里，不要再回头去看，因为你一看，就会一直站在垃圾堆旁，走不开。小秦说，像我们行军打仗，有时候身上背的东西太重，跑不快，那怎么办，就得把身上背的东西取下来，丢掉，只有这样才能继续往前跑，才能比敌人更快到达目的地，掌握主动权。

秀珍说，我明白的。

小秦说，你要珍惜你如今和往后的光阴，因为人活着真的是一件非常宝贵的事情，只要人还活着，人生就有无限可能，若死了，则永远再无任何可能，你也要珍惜你自己，因为，归根到底，只有你才能对你自己的人生负责。

秀珍点点头。

小秦想了想，又说，还有，不要为男人的事伤心，这天下的好男人多了去了，不要在一棵树上吊死，你未来还可以有很多选择。

秀珍没有说话。

小秦还想再说点什么，又觉得没什么可说了。他去摸了摸粥碗，不烫了，温温的了。他就高兴地对秀珍说，不烫了，可以吃了。

秀珍说了声谢谢，就接过了碗。她低头喝起了甜粥。

粥在桌上等待变凉的时候，清甜的粥香渐渐飘散在了屋里的空气中。此刻，看着低头喝粥的秀珍，小秦却莫名有种强烈的错觉，他感到，这甜香，就仿佛是从秀珍身上生出来的一样。

他的心，开始怦怦跳。他被自己吓了一跳。他不敢再看秀珍，又忍不住想看。他觉得，秀珍低着头的样子真美。

秀珍喝完了粥，将碗还给小秦。小秦愣了愣，才幽幽地回过了神来，伸手去接碗。

碰到秀珍手背皮肤的一刹那，小秦全身酥了一下。他不禁握住了秀珍的手。秀珍猛然一惊。碗“啪啦”摔碎在了地上。小秦惊醒，忙放开了秀珍的手，去捡地上的碗的碎片。

你快走吧。秀珍惊慌失措地说。

一块碗的碎片，锋利地割开了小秦的手心，鲜血顿时流了出来。

你走！秀珍不知所措地，对小秦大喊了起来。

小秦捏着碗的碎片，赶紧逃了出去。

血滴点点在地上，空气沉闷如窒息。

秀珍感到眼前灰黑一片。

赵宏伟吃不下饭。

眼前的死气沉沉无法动弹令他忧心如焚。原本梦想中的狂野出奔却蜕变成了现在的牢笼之困，他扼腕长叹，又无计可施。

想当初，在营救慰安妇的行动开始之前，他为了解除日本人对他的防备，就到处与人酒肉往来，宣称他已完全将王秀珍弃如敝屣、视作粪土，这才换来了他从那时到现在表面上的始终宁静。没有日本人会将他这个窝囊废和火暴的武装营救联想在一起，他做到了置身事外、不受牵连。但是，他深知这种侥幸必不能长久，他只要仍然被困在江庆县，穿帮被抓是早晚的事。

赵宏伟的日子，表面上平静得像一张空白的新纸，然而在纸的下面，他的内心波澜起伏，狂潮汹涌，火花四溅，只要一个不小心，这张纸，就会被水浸烂，被火点着，然后一切全部被毁掉。战战兢兢，或矛盾徘徊，已完全无法用来形容他的心境。

他想见秀珍，在这漫长的压抑里，他对她的思念已如燎原之火。他心急如焚而迫不及待地想要向她解释那封诀别信的事情。那封狗日的诀别信！他简直后悔莫及。要是早知道自己会如此安然无恙，他又何必多此一举呢。但是，又实在是千金难买早知道。当初，他的确是抱着慷慨就义的心情加入行动的。谁知道天意弄人，他人没死，死后才有用的绝情信却是被秀珍给看到了，于是，他的良苦用心就被彻底反转为了薄情寡义，真是有嘴也难以说清了。他只焦灼地盼望，能快点到秀珍的面前，向她表白真心，解释清楚一切。

然而，一种莫名的不安又始终在他心上飘浮。这种感觉说不清，又很不祥。

在漫长、空旷又困顿的时间里，赵宏伟不禁憧憬与秀珍将来厮守的日子。这种憧憬很温暖，带着一种水一样的温柔和阳光一样的暖意，令他心里很踏实。在空虚与困顿中，仿佛只有想到秀珍，才能让他觉得自己的人生尚有意义。毕竟，细想想，如今在这个世上，除了秀珍，还有哪个女人是真心真意地爱着他呢？没有了。一个人活着，要是没人爱，那该活得多么冷冰冰啊。他害怕寂寞与冰冷，害怕那种生命无所依托的空洞，害怕在灰暗惨淡的人生尽头是一场孤独终老与不堪回首，所以，一生爱着他的秀珍，是他想要的依靠。他已不能想象，没有她的日子将是什么颜色。他要和她长相厮守，否则，他将度日如年。这是不是一种绝境求生般的爱情？他不知道，也懒得去想。人的各种渴望，都是灵魂本能，懂不懂，都一样。

只是，他会害怕，再在梦里看到心音。因为，那样，会让他感到，他是一个负心汉。心音是因他而死的，他此生，本不该再得到任何爱的温暖。他不配。与躺在冰凉坟墓中的心音相比，他已得到了太多，也快活了太久。有时候，他会有种错觉，感到只有那冰冷的坟墓，才是最适合他安心的归宿。而活着，始终只是一种隐形的折磨，一种花开凋零后的空白苦守。死亡，是个既让人恐惧又让人解脱的终点，在这个终点之后，便是人们永恒的团聚。

赵宏伟决定，要尽快找方远梦和刘小阳商量一下出城的事宜。

玉山上。

秀珍依旧沉陷在赵宏伟绝情的哀伤里，她的眼泪清亮而滚烫，流个不停。她无数次地说服自己，要自己相信这封信只是一个误会，又无数次地被自己推倒，要自己接受赵宏伟不爱她的事实。这种无声无息的折磨，令她撕心裂肺地难受。

她觉得方远梦的解释是最有可能接近赵宏伟的本意的，因为这封信就是赵宏伟让方远梦带的，她应该理解赵宏伟的一片苦心。但是，人的情感往往并不受到逻辑的控制，而现实又往往只是情感的产物。她在心中给自己树立的各种坚信，都只是沙塔，风一吹，即坍塌。她感到，现在最重要的，就是

能尽快见到赵宏伟，当面跟他把事情说清。而且，她也想念小菊，她想尽快见到她。

但是，赵宏伟和小菊，现在又都在城里面。她不知道该怎样进城去，也不知道他们该怎样出城来。谁也没有向她承诺过，她和他，到底能在何时会面。一切，都在漫长的努力和等待中。这等待，充满了变数与煎熬。她在等待中，拿着他的绝情信，自我否定，自我肯定，摇摆不定，长泪满襟。

而尤其让她无法得到爱情自信的，是她明知道，在他的心里，住着一个叫心音的女人。她曾无数次地幻想，他的关于那个女人的记忆，终将在时间的长河里死去，可是很显然，事实不会按照她的意志来变化。她根本就不知道他心里真实的想法，他的心门，一向都不对她敞开。她只能长久地在揣测与自欺中种植着那无果的爱情，独自呵护着那朵在她灵魂中盛开的痴情之花。岁月风霜洗礼，她的真心从未改变。可是这封他亲笔写的绝情信，却似乎拥有着非凡的力量，在狠心地揭开着她那长久被遮盖着的伤疤，要她看清她半生的痴心尽是水月镜花。她无法承受这种清醒的摧残，她不敢相信那可能的糟糕的结局。她不敢去想心音，她不敢去想自己不干净，她只想他爱她。他对她的爱，比她的生命要重要上一百倍。她爱他，今生，从未变过。

她的悲哀，像细雨一样缠绵冰凉。

秀珍有好几天没看见小秦了。她知道自从那天以后，小秦一直在躲着她。她觉得自己那天最后对小秦说话的语气是过分了，毕竟，是人家拼了性命，把大家从日本人的手里救了出来，而且，他也没做什么不好的事。她想起了那温暖的甜粥，心头莫名掠过几丝暖意。她想去向小秦道个歉，让他别把那事放在心上。毕竟，一个单身的大小伙子，在女人面前失态，是不应该被那样叱责的。他又不是坏人，秀珍想。她不想就此给他留下心理包袱。

秀珍打听到，小秦现在就在政委办公室里谈事。她想去等他出来。她想顺便也问问，他知不知道赵宏伟何时能出城上山来。

她向政委办公室那边走了过去。

政委办公室里。

小秦向政委报告，文身专家已经请来了，从明天开始，就可以帮女人们改造肩上的编号了，可以视情况改成各种图案。

政委点点头，问，专家来的时候，沿路情况怎么样？

小秦说，从大部队通往这里的道路，依旧被日军重兵封锁着，文身专家是好不容易被带过来的，一位负责保卫的同志差点牺牲。

政委皱着眉，说，看来日本人，这次下定了决心要用铁桶阵哪。

小秦说，其实我们也不用太过悲观，日军布置这铁桶合围的阵势，是需要安排大量的兵力驻守的，但是现在江南战场烽烟四起，抗日力量此起彼伏，日军难道还能长期让他们大量的兵力像木桩子一样定在那里一动不动吗？只要周边有什么战斗兴起，青梅县和江庆县的日军必将受到牵连，会被调动，这样一来，他们的铁桶阵自然就会松动，甚至瓦解，到那时，我们就有反击的机会了。

政委点点头，笑说，你脑子不错，是块好材料，以后有机会，应该要送你去军校深造。

小秦说，我不想学什么军事，我喜欢音乐，等战争结束了，我想去学弹钢琴。

政委笑了起来，说，好，那以后，等战争结束了，我来听你的音乐演奏会。

两人一起欢笑了起来。

政委问，对了，那些女人们最近的情况怎么样？情绪都还稳定吗？

小秦说，都还行，大多不再有轻生的念头了，就是那个可怜的王大嫂，最近一直还是在哭，真的太可怜了，我们也没什么办法帮她。

政委说，她的情况，我有些了解，赵宏伟是对我们有过帮助的人，我们能帮他的，尽量会帮他，等老方和小刘把赵宏伟送出了城来，我们就想办法帮助赵宏伟和王秀珍远走高飞，希望他们有情人终成眷属。

小秦说，但是王大嫂还有一个噩耗并不知道，她的女儿小菊，被赵宏伟藏在他家里，结果老百姓们火烧赵宏伟家的时候，意外把小菊给烧死了，王大嫂要是知道了这件事，不恨赵宏伟才怪。

小秦话音刚落，政委办公室的门，被“嘭”一声重重推开了。

秀珍脸色惨白地呆立在门口。她颤抖地问：“你们说谁被烧死了？”

小秦和政委一时不知所措。

秀珍浑身战栗地惨问："——你们说谁被烧死了？"

时间，像一具失血的尸体，死在停顿的空气里。

悲惨，没有边际地蔓延。

赵家镇。

半夜。

赵宏伟和刘小阳一齐聚在方远梦的家里，点着幽暗的蜡烛，在低声地讨论着接下来的行动步骤。

赵宏伟的身份太特殊，白天他根本不敢来找方远梦和刘小阳，怕被日本人发现以后一锅端，所以他只能在半夜里偷偷摸摸地来。但是晚上日军的巡逻也不弱，他来一次方远梦家，身上的衣服能被一路上惊吓出来的冷汗湿个透。刘小阳为此还取笑过他一次，但是赵宏伟毫不介意，因为在目前的情况下，真的是太需要有刘小阳这样什么都不怕的人来参与行动了。赵宏伟都快要被现在这种沉闷的局势给憋死了。

刘小阳对方远梦说，而今之计，只有主动出击，才会有一线生机。日军做出个铁桶阵来，就是想跟游击队拼消耗，大家僵持着，看谁先饿死渴死，如果任由日军这样静止不动地保持着阵势，被动挨打的将会是游击队。

方远梦说，我们以前有过这样的经验，日军也曾试图胶着地围困着玉山，但是，他们总坚持不了太久，周围一有风吹草动，他们就要调拨兵马另作他用。

刘小阳说，但是现在情况有了新的变化，以前这一带，日军兵力紧张，所以周边地区一有战事，青梅县和江庆县的日军立马要去增援，然而现在上海日军已向这一带增兵，就算周围有大的战事发生，也未必就会调动到青梅县和江庆县的日军兵力，所以，这一次的铁桶合围，可能会比以往来得更长久。

方远梦说，你说得不错，日军兵力的增加，的确是一个棘手的问题，我们很有可能会被长久地干耗着，这样就被动了。

刘小阳说，所以，我们现在只能主动出击，不管危险不危险，只有打破现在这个互相凝固的僵局，才能破坏日军瓮中捉鳖的企图，扰乱他们的视线，打乱他们的部署，只要他们在兵力调派或指挥策略上发生变化，我们就能有机可乘，可以乘隙进攻或者借机撤退。

方远梦说，只要日军步骤一乱，我们甚至可以引导新四军大部队向江庆县或青梅县发动大反攻，这样，我们就能化被动为主动。

刘小阳说，不错，就像下围棋一样，一小块死棋，只要能和一大块活棋连在一起，就能重新产生战略意义。

方远梦说，那你接下来打算怎么做？

刘小阳说，很简单，我们可以实施斩首行动，用炸药炸掉江庆县日军联队的指挥部，杀死他们的上层指挥官，同时破坏县监狱，放出里面的抗日人士，这样，江庆县日军联队的指挥系统必定会失灵几天，一片混乱，如果潜入青梅县的特工队能与我们保持同步行动，也在青梅县这么干，那么，毫无疑问，围困着玉山的日军部队必将在一两天的时间内陷入群龙无首的混乱状态，而我们的游击队正好可以趁着这个时机，与新四军大部队里应外合，反攻日军分散在外的合围兵力，如果周边日军救援不及时，兴许我们还有机会夺回青梅县和江庆县这两座县城，反客为主，化被动为主动。

方远梦说，这个计划不错，但是还需要仔细推敲各个细节，尤其需要派人与青梅县特工队和新四军大部队联系，做好同步的行动计划。

刘小阳说，这个我会想办法，手枪队的同志身经百战，很有经验，做这些事应该不在话下，然而我担心的是另一件事。

方远梦问，什么事？

刘小阳说，日军至今还没对游击队发动主动攻击，无疑是忌惮于玉山神秘的地形，但是，赵宏伟说了，姚志同志还活着。日本人为什么还留着姚志同志的命？很显然，他们仍想从他嘴里撬出有用的情报。抱歉，我对姚志同志并不熟悉，所以，不得不担心他叛变的可能。如果日军掌握了玉山的秘道图和地形图，那么，他们随时可以发动奇袭，以大量兵力和重武器踏平玉山。

方远梦说，姚志同志被捕已经不是一天两天了，他若要叛变，早就叛变了，对于他的意志和品质，我还是深有了解的，我坚信，姚志同志是绝对不会出卖我们的，对他而言，信仰远高于生命，他的一生都在实践“崇高”二字，所以，请你不要怀疑他。我们现在在计划军事行动的同时，还应该要迫切地考虑一个问题，就是怎样将姚志同志营救出来。他已经在敌人的折磨下

坚守了这么长的时间，我们若再不快点想办法救他出来，还有什么资格将自己视作革命的勇士？

刘小阳想了想，点头同意。

刘小阳转头问赵宏伟：你说，姚志同志是被关在县监狱？

赵宏伟说：我猜的。

寂静的夜色里，忽然，响起了急促而沉重的敲门声。

“咚、咚咚咚、咚咚——”方远梦的家门，被骤然敲响。

正在昏暗的烛光里密议的赵宏伟和刘小阳，登时顿住了。方远梦摇摇手，示意大家不要慌，他侧耳仔细一听，便急忙去开门。这敲门声的节奏是个暗号，门外是小秦。

方远梦开了门，将小秦领进了屋来。他问小秦出什么事了。小秦看见赵宏伟也在，表情就有些不自然。小秦犹豫了一下，才低声对方远梦说：王大嫂不见了。

“什么？怎么会这样！”赵宏伟不禁惊呼。

小秦愧疚万分地说：“我和政委在办公室里说事，一时说到了小菊被烧死的事情，结果，不小心被门外的王大嫂听见了。”

赵宏伟呆若木鸡。

深夜，渡边办公室。

山本信玄向渡边汇报情况，说，最近城内并无什么异动，也没发现可疑人员，就是有些乡下人进了城来，还有些青梅县的人员来了江庆县，据核实，他们都是来探望亲戚的，并无可疑，不过，我们还是看紧各个出入口，人员一旦进入，就不准再出去。

渡边点点头，表示不错。

渡边踌躇了一会儿，想要开口和山本信玄谈一谈，要他不要再为难赵驹。但是，看着山本信玄冷漠又锋利的目光，渡边却莫名不敢开口。说不上为什么，这个山本信玄，现在越来越让渡边感到不寒而栗，渡边对自己感到难以理解，一个魔鬼，居然会对另一个魔鬼产生惧意，这在渡边的人生经验里，是从未有过的。

山本信玄却又和渡边说起了姚志的事，他说，如果我们不能及时铲除玉山游击队，到时候，恐怕不光是联队长您要遭受处罚，我们这些小蚂蚁也会被牵连，遭到贬低。

渡边不禁就有些恼怒，他说，怎么，难道你的意思是说，因为我的无能，所以会连累到你？

山本信玄忙满脸堆笑地说：怎么会呢，大人您误会了，属下怎么敢有如此想法，属下只是在替大人着急。

山本信玄嘴上虽然这么说，但是，渡边分明在他的眼里看到了清晰的蔑视与嘲笑。渡边恼火了。他张了张嘴，想教训山本信玄几句，但是想到在山本信玄的背后还有一个老山本，渡边只能压抑着，闭紧了嘴。

渡边挥了挥手，让山本信玄走。

县监狱。关着姚志的牢房内。

姚志全身瘫软地蜷缩在地上，蓬头垢面，无力动弹。牢房内阴暗潮湿的气息里，像是隐藏着一头凶恶的怪兽，它血腥浓重，张牙舞爪，仿佛随时都能跳出来咬人。牢房地上新鲜的血迹下，是不知年月的久远以前的血迹，血迹重叠着血迹，阴森的痕迹宛如嶙峋的山岭，层峦叠嶂，恐怖绵长。

“吱呀”一声，牢房的门，被推开了。

山本信玄手里端着一碗食物，走进了姚志的牢房里。

山本信玄踢了一脚地上的姚志，用汉语谑笑地问，你死了没有？

姚志动了动。他身上的手铐脚镣，叮当作响。

山本信玄说，哎哟，你可不能死啊，我可是还一直在等着看好戏，想看你叛变呢。

姚志艰难地抬起头，露出了一个鲜明的冷笑。他的喉咙里发出了几声干涸的笑，模糊不清，又犀利非常。像濒死的兽，像歌唱的鬼魅，寒气逼人。笑完了，姚志往地上吐了一口血唾沫。

山本信玄也冷笑了两声，仿佛是作为对姚志的回击。山本信玄蹲了下来，将手中的那碗食物，放在了姚志面前的地上。这是一碗清烧肉丸子，碗里还带着半碗浓汤。

山本信玄说，你信吗，这是一碗有毒的肉丸子，你只要吃了它，你就会

变成一个彻底的叛徒。

姚志愣住了。

山本信玄哈哈大笑了起来，笑得前仰后合。他手指着姚志，嘲笑地说：还真以为你是一个硬汉呢，想不到，一碗肉丸子就把你给吓住了，哈哈哈，可笑的中国猪。

姚志看着山本信玄。

山本信玄把脸凑近了姚志，挑衅地说：怎么样，其实你自己心里也很害怕吧？你在害怕，说不定哪个时刻你就会熬不下去了，是不是？你怕，你最终还是会成为一个叛徒，背叛你从前所有的坚持，背叛你此生所有坚定不移的追求，所以，你会连一碗肉丸子的威胁都不敢接受，其实，你在心里早已对自己承受痛苦的能力失去了信心，我说得对不对？

山本信玄嘲弄地看着姚志的眼睛。

姚志冷冷一笑。他哆嗦着，伸出血肉模糊的手，抓起了碗里的肉丸子，塞进了自己嘴里，吃了起来。

山本信玄说，多吃一点，补充足了营养，强壮了身体，才能演好戏给我们看。

山本信玄站了起来，看着地上的姚志，阴阳怪气地笑了笑。他得意地丢下了一句“中国猪”，然后，便转身轻快地离开了牢房。

夜色，像魔鬼般恐怖。

方远梦家中。

小秦说，找遍了山上各个地方，我们都没有找到王大嫂，所以我想，王大嫂多半是回到了赵家镇上来。

方远梦气得一拍大腿，指指小秦，说不出话来。刘小阳说，这下糟了，小秦你知道吗，日本人现在明松暗紧，这城里，是进得来出不去，我们如今都被困在这里了。

赵宏伟抱着头，苦恼得说不出话来。方远梦说，事不宜迟，我们现在应该马上分头去找秀珍，看她是不是真的回到了赵家镇上来，日本人认得她，绝对不能让她重新被日本人抓回去！

赵宏伟起身，说，我去找就行了，我的身份方便，你们不能出去到处乱走，日本兵巡逻得严，你们暴露了就完了。

但小秦坚持要和赵宏伟一起出去找人，小秦说，这是我闯下的祸，我一定要负责到底。

方远梦对赵宏伟说，就带上小秦吧，小秦身手好，必要时能保护秀珍。

赵宏伟就答应了。

天色黑沉沉的，离天亮还有一段时间。

赵宏伟带着小秦，去了一次秀珍的家。因为秀珍如果回了赵家镇，多半会先回自己的家去看一看。她还不知道，在那一次的火烧事件中，她的家也受连累烧着了。她的家，也已只是一片断壁残垣。

路灯昏暗的光照里，赵宏伟看到，秀珍家的门敞开着。他不能确定这门究竟是谁推开的。他紧张万分地，和小秦一起走了进去。他轻轻呼喊着：秀珍，秀珍。微颤的声音像落叶一样飘荡在幽暗的废墟中，冷冰冰而碎乎乎。寂静的空间里除了微弱的回音没有半分响动。极远处的僻静里有狗叫声传来。

小秦忽然说，地上有脚印。

赵宏伟仔细一看，果然，地上的灰黑中，有浅浅小小又凌乱的脚印，这显然不是他和小秦的脚印。

小秦说，王大嫂一定回来过，你看，这些脚印，是在这里到处走了一遍的痕迹，王大嫂一定是想好好看一看自己的家。

赵宏伟听了小秦的话，心里就很难过。内疚与自责像刀一样割着他的心。他深知，秀珍落到今天这个地步，完全就是因为他，他对她有罪。

小秦说，你快再想想看，除了这里，王大嫂可能还会去哪儿？

赵宏伟想了想。

坟场。因为，赵家镇上死了的人，多半都会葬在那儿。

秀珍，一定会去找小菊的坟。

赵宏伟和小秦赶到坟场时，天已初亮。

远远地，就看见，在小菊的坟前，跪着一个人影。

“王大嫂！”小秦轻呼了一声，立马就飞奔了过去。

赵宏伟也跟着跑了过去。

秀珍跪在小菊的坟前，瑟瑟发抖，面色惨白，泪如雨下。她痛苦地哭泣着，却又不发出声音，那种绝望，令人撕心裂肺。

小秦看着秀珍的样子，莫名刹那竟也流下了泪来。他看着哭成了个泪人儿的秀珍，心里难过得像刀割一样。他想让她别哭了，可是喉咙里被痛堵着，说不出话来。他感到很奇怪，为什么秀珍的泪，会让他如此难过。小秦慌乱地擦去了自己的眼泪。

赵宏伟将秀珍扶了起来，然后，他在秀珍面前跪了下来。

“对不起，秀珍，是我没有照顾好小菊，是我害了她，一切都是我的错——”赵宏伟痛彻心扉地向秀珍忏悔。

秀珍却依旧只是哭，她张了张嘴，哽咽着说了一句什么，但是赵宏伟和小秦都没有听清。

秀珍泪雨滂沱，整个人都在不停发抖。晨曦洒在她的身上，像照耀着一株濒死的花树。每一道朝阳之光，都只像是在刺穿着她生命的残忍之剑。新的日出，在这坟场，只像是新的结束，新的埋葬。

赵宏伟依旧在痛苦地忏悔：“……还有那封信，不是我的真心话，我只是怕我会死，我怕我死了会让你难过，所以，才想找个借口让你忘了我——”

秀珍的眼泪落得更汹涌了。她哭着，想露出一点笑，却只是哭得更悲惨。她张了张嘴，想说什么，却哽咽着，说出来的只是“呜呜”一片的惨哭声。

赵宏伟心如刀绞，想站起来抱抱秀珍，安慰安慰她，却又感到自己有罪，不配碰她。

秀珍克制住了哭声，说：“知道吗，你说你不爱我，比杀了我还让我难受……你以为的慈悲，对我来说却是残酷……因为，你不懂，爱比活着更重要——”

赵宏伟无言以对。他说：“秀珍，我真心爱你的，我是真心爱你的——”

秀珍啜泣着，问：“那你告诉我，你的心里，现在还住着那个叫心音的女人吗？”

赵宏伟愣住了。他看着秀珍，忽然像是不认识秀珍一样。他不禁问：“你怎么知道心音的？”

秀珍凄惨地笑了起来，说："因为你喝醉时，每次都会念叨她的名字。"

赵宏伟心中一刺，不知所措，无言以对。

秀珍跪了下来，看着赵宏伟的眼睛，哭泣而乞求似的问他："你……真的爱我吗？"

赵宏伟动了一下嘴唇，却终究没有回答。他不敢看着她的目光说，我爱你。

他羞愧地低下了头。

秀珍的眼神，刹那崩碎一地。绝望的泪水无声流淌，哀凉的悲酸从她的嘴角泛起，渐渐漾满了她整张苍白的脸庞。

她笑了起来，像疯了一样，自嘲地悲哀地笑着。她哽咽着说："其实我早知道，其实我都明白，我想一辈子不问，可是，我突然觉得，要是我不问一问，这辈子我一定会死不瞑目，哈哈——哈哈……死不瞑目……"

秀珍又哭又笑着，忽然就站了起来，往一个方向猛跑了去。

赵宏伟一时没反应过来，小秦却已看懂：秀珍要跳河自尽！

"王大嫂！不要！"小秦玩命地追了上去。

赵宏伟反应了过来，立马也站了起来，疯了似的追了上去。

秀珍跳入了河中。

小秦跳入了河中。

赵宏伟跳入了河中。

河水冰凉而湍急。

秀珍挣扎着，泪流满面地，沉入了河底。

小秦猛地潜了下去。

小秦抱住了秀珍，拼命往河面上游。他脑中空白一片，只有一个最强烈的念头：不能让她死，不能让她死！

河水冰凉而浑浊，水草飘飘悠悠。河水和水草，就像舞动的死神，都想将秀珍往地狱里拉，拼命地拉。小秦不顾一切，拼了命也要救秀珍上岸！

河水流动得更湍急了。

赵宏伟深吸了口气，也潜下了河底。

赵宏伟去解开缠着秀珍的水草。两个男人一起用力，将秀珍往水面上托。

终于，赵宏伟和小秦一起将秀珍救上了岸。

秀珍吐出了一口水，终于从昏厥中苏醒了过来。

小秦掏出手枪，一下子便将枪口顶在了赵宏伟的太阳穴上。小秦对秀珍说：王大嫂，你信不信，你如果有个什么三长两短，我一定会开枪杀了这个姓赵的王八蛋！

不要！不要！秀珍慌忙说。

小秦说，好，我现在暂时不杀他，但你绝不可以再跳河，你一跳，我就开枪，我小秦说到做到！

远处，有日本人的狗吠声响起。

小秦准备先带秀珍去以前老周开的诊所里暂避，那里位置比较偏僻，不易引起日本人的注意。赵宏伟表示同意。赵宏伟身份太显眼，和秀珍的关系众人皆知，所以他不能和秀珍一起走。赵宏伟准备回方远梦那里，尽快和他们想出一个出城之策来。

小秦和赵宏伟道了个别，握了握手，赵宏伟说，拜托了。小秦说，放心。

小秦带着秀珍，前往诊所的方向。

太阳烘烤着大地。风声呜呼。

山本信玄从小燕家里出来，得意地吹着口哨，带着几个兵，在街上漫无目的地溜达。

忽然，山本信玄眼角的余光一瞥，看到在街角有两个人影晃过，他们的身上，似乎都湿漉漉的。一丝好奇浮上了山本的心头：没下雨呀，怎么他们像个落汤鸡似的？难道是我眼花？

兴致一来，山本信玄就吆喝了一声，带着士兵一起追了上去。

山本信玄带人围困住了小秦和秀珍。山本信玄不认识秀珍，但是，糟就糟在，秀珍现在身上是湿透的。山本信玄看见，这个女人的身体曲线，真是漂亮得没话说。

山本信玄问：你们两个，身上怎么都湿成了这样？

小秦忙说：太君，这位是我老婆，她刚才不小心掉在了河里，我去救她，所以才会一起弄成了这样，我们都正要回家呢。

山本信玄笑了笑，就向秀珍走了过去，他嘴里无耻地说道：大美人，你身上的衣服都湿成这样了，还是不要穿了，会着凉的，来。

秀珍大惊失色，又无路可逃。

小秦“扑通”一下，跪在了山本信玄的面前。小秦低三下四地、使尽了浑身解数地向山本信玄求饶，但是山本信玄一脚踹开了小秦。

秀珍逃躲着。山本信玄坏笑着追上去，哗啦一下，撕开了秀珍肩上的衣服。

可是，山本信玄的笑，一下子僵住了。

秀珍裸露的肩膀上，清清楚楚的，是慰安妇的编号。

山本信玄大喊了一声：“警戒！”他手还没摸到枪上，背后已响起了枪声。

小秦掏出了双枪，与敌枪战。

“砰、砰、砰——”一时枪声大作。

小秦掩护着秀珍，边撤边战。

子弹横飞，激战巷尾。血腥掠过阳光，厮杀又一次玷污了清晨的鸟语花香。

“人一个也不能放走！”山本信玄大喊。

一颗子弹飞过了秀珍的身边，又一颗子弹飞过了秀珍的身边。小秦始终舍命保护着秀珍，挡在她的前面。小秦说，王大嫂，别害怕，有我呢。

一颗子弹打在了小秦的肩膀上。小秦血流如注。小秦还是说，王大嫂，别害怕，有我呢。

秀珍的心尖上，忽然掠过了一丝被保护的温暖。她看着受伤的小秦，心里很软地一痛。

赵宏伟走在路上，远远地，仿佛听到了有枪声。他驻足听了一会儿。没错，真的是枪声！

是秀珍出事了吗？赵宏伟心急如焚地想。

还是我杞人忧天？赵宏伟不敢确信。

不会的，不会的，一定是日本鬼子又在抓人了，和秀珍无关。赵宏伟对

自己说。

秀珍有小秦保护着呢。赵宏伟想。

我还是不要多管闲事的好。赵宏伟想。

于是，他继续朝着他的方向，加快了脚步行进。

小秦的子弹打光了。

山本信玄对准秀珍打出了一颗子弹。早已浑身是血的小秦，奋力为秀珍一挡，子弹射入了小秦的后心窝。

小秦终于倒下了。

秀珍抱着他，痛哭流涕地喊："小秦！小秦！"

小秦断断续续地说："……对不起，王大嫂……我……我没能保护好你……还有……还有……那天的事我要向你道歉，我……我摸了你的手，对不起……我不是坏人……那天，我真的，只是想给你送一碗甜粥，我怕你想不开，怕你会不吃饭……我……我……对不——"小秦话还没说完，一大口血就从喉咙里涌出来，断了气。

"小秦——"秀珍抚尸哀恸。

悲风长鸣。

山本信玄手一挥，下令："把这个女人抓起来，押到县监狱！立刻通知渡边联队长，有慰安妇回城！"

日本兵奔跑了起来。

县监狱。刑讯室内。

秀珍被牢牢地绑定在刑架上。

山本信玄一边等待着渡边，一边耍弄着一把锋利的匕首。他走到秀珍的面前，用匕首的刀背，沿着秀珍的身体曲线慢慢划弄。他张开嘴，轻轻撕咬起了秀珍裸露的肌肤。

秀珍痛苦地掉下了泪来。

看到秀珍掉泪，山本信玄更加亢奋了起来。他双眼血红，邪笑着，一把丢掉了匕首，然后，他喘着粗气，尽情地亵渎起了秀珍的身体。

走廊上传来了急促而杂乱的脚步声。渡边的训话声，由远及近，如雷贯耳。刚解开裤子的山本信玄，赶紧又把裤子穿紧穿好。

刑讯室的门被“嘭”地推开。渡边带着桥本和几个兵快步走了进来。

山本信玄急忙立正，敬了个礼。

“快说，怎么回事！”渡边对山本信玄说完，便走到了秀珍的面前。

山本信玄迅速地将事情的来龙去脉向渡边陈述了一遍。渡边紧皱着眉，看着秀珍。

渡边让山本信玄做翻译，问秀珍话。

渡边问：“那个和你在一起的人是谁？你们到赵家镇上去做什么？”

秀珍不说话。

渡边拎起一根鞭子，就开始狠狠地抽打秀珍。秀珍身上立时血痕条条。

渡边问：“和你一起回来的，还有其他人吗？是不是有游击队的人，潜伏进了江庆县？”

秀珍紧咬着牙关，依旧不吭声。

渡边把鞭子丢给了山本信玄，让他继续打。鞭声带血，刷刷作响。秀珍痛得泪珠直掉，几乎昏厥，像被火烧，却依旧紧咬着牙，一个字也不说。

渡边做了个手势，让山本信玄停了下来。

渡边走到了秀珍的面前，近距离地紧紧逼视着秀珍的眼睛。渡边让山本继续翻译。渡边问：“你，既然能从玉山上下来，是不是已经见过了玉山上的神秘通道？你对玉山的地形，了解多少？”

山本信玄翻译完，秀珍狠狠一咬牙，扭过了头去，不看渡边。

渡边伸出手，用力将秀珍的头又扭了过来，硬让她面对着他。渡边更近地逼视着她的眼睛，又问了一遍：“你是不是已经看见过玉山地形的真正秘密？”

秀珍用力地啐了渡边一口带血的唾沫，然后，便是紧闭上了双眼，依旧死死地咬紧了牙关，不说话。

渡边后退了一步，哈哈笑了起来。渡边对桥本和山本信玄说：我们有救了，这个女人，知道玉山的地形和秘道。

渡边吩咐桥本：立刻打电话给赵驹，命令他重新监视赵宏伟，密切注意他的一举一动，看他是否已背叛皇军、与共军有染，一旦发现线索，务必顺藤摸瓜，将奸细与敌方人员一网打尽。

渡边又命令山本信玄：用尽所有办法，务必撬开这个女人的嘴，要她说出玉山的秘密，她，可比姚志要好对付得多。

一个士兵来通知渡边：北野中将有电话到。

渡边急匆匆地便带着桥本，离开了刑讯室。

山本信玄拎着鞭子，看着秀珍，他舔了舔自己干燥的嘴唇。

山本信玄打发走了刑讯室里的其他小兵，只剩下了他和秀珍两个人。山本信玄丢开了鞭子，又开始脱裤子。

山本信玄捏了捏秀珍的脸，说，你看我多好，都没打你脸。

他撕开了秀珍正面的衣服，但是秀珍正面的身体上已尽是凄惨的血痕，如蛇如虫，血珠滴滴，他不禁就有些厌恶。他想了一会儿，于是，便解开了捆绑着秀珍的所有绳索，将她从刑架上放了下来。

山本信玄将秀珍背面朝上地，用力压在了地上。他撕开了她后面的衣服，尽情地抚摸着她光滑的后背与臀部。她的背面身体，还如丝缎般光洁，没有被鞭刑破坏，山本信玄玩弄得如痴如醉。而秀珍，奋力挣扎，奋力挣扎，也无济于事，只是凭空给山本信玄增添了更多征服的乐趣。

这时，秀珍忽然发现，就在不远处的地上，静静地躺着一把寒光锋利的匕首。

山本信玄正要进入秀珍的身体，秀珍一个猛劲，挪动了身体，一把抓住了地上的那把匕首。山本信玄一惊，秀珍回手一刺，山本信玄松开了秀珍的身体。

秀珍挣脱开了山本信玄的控制，站了起来。她双手紧握着寒光四射的匕首，将刀尖对准着山本信玄，不让他靠近。

山本信玄坏笑了起来，说，好玩，有味道，我喜欢。

他像逗弄猎物一样，上去摸她一把，又跳开，上去摸她一把，又跳开。而秀珍，从未能真的刺中他。

山本信玄无耻地大笑着。

秀珍哭了起来，她哭得绝望无际，而惨绝人寰。她看了看自己的身体，哭得笑了起来，像疯子一样。

山本信玄一愣。

说时迟那时快，秀珍突然掉转刀尖，她向着自己的腹部，狠狠一刀扎了进去！刀子扎进去以后，她又狠狠地，将刀子往横里一拉！

秀珍剖腹了。

山本信玄目瞪口呆。

县医院。四楼走廊里。

“啪、啪”，渡边怒不可遏地，扇了山本信玄两记耳光。

“让你审讯姚志，姚志咬舌自尽，让你审讯王秀珍，王秀珍剖腹自杀！你是不会做事还是想要害我？你知不知道北野中将刚才又在打电话催促我们要尽快拿出战绩来让他扬眉吐气？你知不知道王秀珍现在已是我们的最后希望？你知不知道如果我们不能及时剿灭玉山游击队那会有什么后果？你是不是想要让我向北野中将报告，说全都是因为你的愚蠢无能所以才导致了我们在整场战局中的功亏一篑？你个成事不足败事有余的废物！！”渡边愤怒至极，接着扇了山本信玄两记耳光，“你不要以为你父亲是黑帮首领，你在这军队里就可以肆无忌惮、为所欲为！我告诉你，这是一场关乎帝国命运的宏大战争，不管你是什么人，只要在这场战争里做了有损于帝国利益的事情，天皇陛下就会要你付出代价！！”渡边咬牙切齿地骂着山本信玄。

山本信玄握着拳头，低着头，除了认罪地说“是、是”，什么也不可说。他的嘴角凝结着一丝恨意，挂着压抑的恼怒。

医生来向渡边报告，说，王秀珍已救活，暂时不会再有生命危险，但必须要好好治疗才能防止万一。

医生走后，渡边吩咐山本信玄，王秀珍绝不能再出事。山本信玄应允。最后，渡边又斩钉截铁地对山本信玄说：“还有一件事，我不管你们山本家以前和赵驹有什么恩恩怨怨，赵驹是我苦心训练出来的猎狗，他的枪法，是我用心教导出来的，他完全继承了我的枪技，你如果把他打残废了，那就等于砍掉了我的左膀右臂！所以，从今往后，我不允许你再以任何名义，动赵驹一根汗毛！他是我们皇军的出色猎犬，我绝不允许你为了个人的利益，损害皇军的财产！”

山本信玄灰头土脸地说“是”。

渡边扬长而去。山本信玄咬牙切齿地望着渡边远去的背影。他远远地啐

了渡边一口唾沫。

山本信玄派了两个日本兵，守在秀珍病房的门口。

方远梦家中。

赵宏伟昨天收到了一封匿名信，信上告诉了他秀珍目前的情况。赵宏伟大惊失色，慌乱而不知所措，只能立马拿了信来找方远梦和刘小阳。

赵宏伟痛苦难熬，急得像热锅上的蚂蚁，他想去县政府，向渡边求情。方远梦立刻制止了他这种幼稚的想法。方远梦说，渡边现在是要秀珍交代玉山秘道，你说他能放了秀珍吗？你之前好不容易假装和秀珍撇清了关系，现在你若泪汪汪地去求渡边放人，那日本人立刻就会怀疑你和营救慰安妇的事情有关。

刘小阳说，这信上已经说了，要赵兄小心自身难保。

方远梦说，这事只能我们来想办法，我们会去救秀珍。

刘小阳问，知不知道这信是谁写的？会不会有诈，是个陷阱？

赵宏伟说，这信多半是赵驹写的，他不会骗我。

方远梦问，赵驹？就是那个当初拉你做汉奸的人？他为什么帮你？

赵宏伟说，具体我说不清，但我有这个直觉，赵驹是个身上有谜团的人，他看起来对日本人唯命是从，可骨子里他不帮日本人。

刘小阳问，难道赵驹是国民党重庆方面的卧底特工？

赵宏伟说，不知道，但是我相信他，这是一种直觉。

方远梦说，这样，我们尽快派人去医院里一探虚实，究竟是怎么回事，我们很快便能知晓。

刘小阳说，好，我马上去安排。

方远梦对赵宏伟说，你要沉住气，不能自乱阵脚，你在这里伪政府中的位置特殊，长期隐蔽下去，对我们的抗日工作有极大帮助，所以，就算我暴露了，你也不能暴露，你懂吗？

赵宏伟什么都没听见地，愚钝呆立着。他的心里，满是秀珍凄惨的模样。他的心都碎了。他不争气地，掉下了两滴眼泪来。

县医院。四楼。

山本信玄估计，除了那个已死的保护王秀珍的男人，在这县城里，应该还有共产党的战斗人员潜伏着，如今玉山的秘密随时会从这个女人的嘴里抖搂出来，他们共产党，应该很快就会派人来营救王秀珍。所以，山本信玄故意只在秀珍的病房外留了两个看守，整个四楼不多安放一个日本兵。山本信玄将所有的兵力和火力都隐藏在了医院周围看不见的地方，一旦有人来医院救人，这些日军就会从四面八方收拢过来，像网一样，将来敌困死、全歼。

秀珍的神志已清醒，山本信玄在病房里文明审讯了秀珍好几天，用尽了各种心理战术，但秀珍就是像死了一样，闭着眼，不开口。山本信玄又不敢再给她动刑，怕她真死了，所以他也是无计可施。他又想起渡边那副可恶可恨的嘴脸，心里说不出的恼火。

山本信玄去找小燕。他伸手去摸她，手却被她一把打开。山本信玄一愣。小燕眼眶红红的，说，我爸爸死了。山本信玄扇了小燕一记耳光，又伸手去摸她。他的手又被她打开。她哭了起来，近乎喊叫地说：要不是你们那天打了他一夜，我爸爸根本就不会病倒！是你们杀了我爸爸！

山本信玄狠狠地又给了小燕一个耳光。他凶恶地说，一头中国猪，死就死了，还省了粮食，有什么大不了的。

小燕伸手就要给山本信玄一记耳光，但她扇出去的手掌，却被山本信玄一把就给抓住了。山本信玄咬牙切齿地说：臭婊子，你以为你是什么东西？我要不是看在你胸脯特别大的分上，早把你剁了喂狗了！

畜生！小燕羞愤地怒骂。

山本信玄把小燕拖进了一间空病房里，对她拳打脚踢。他把这些日子里积累下来的怒火一下子全发泄在了小燕的身上。他暴打着她，就像在揍渡边一样。

他把小燕打得奄奄一息，然后，他又撕开了她的上衣，贪婪地咬了上去，像狗啃肉一样。

为了能够及时和青梅县特工队、新四军大部队取得联系，同时防止日军的侦听，刘小阳启用了一套新的电台密码。他每次使用电台的时间都不长，这样能尽量避免日军情报部门对电台位置的追踪。

手枪队的同志已经侦察清楚，秀珍的确是被日军看守在县医院里。据说

秀珍已经度过了危险期。刘小阳和城外的同志联系好了，让他们想办法送一批炸药和手榴弹进来，等东西一到，刘小阳就会带人去救秀珍。

城外的同志送炸药进城的那一天，赵宏伟不遗余力、想方设法地帮他们蒙混过关。最终，炸药和手榴弹顺利地从日军眼皮底下通过，到达了手枪队同志们的手里。刘小阳和方远梦给队员们分配好了弹药，然后详细讲解了作战方案，便准备第二天动手，去医院里救出秀珍。

看着众人子弹上膛、手榴弹束到腰上，赵宏伟觉得自己真是百无一用。他那修炼了一生的文才，在这个兵荒马乱、用枪说话的年代里毫无用处，一文不值。看到自己的女人被囚禁在炼狱里，他也做不上任何事，帮不上一点忙。他对自己的无能，不仅感到羞耻，更感到痛恨。他多想像刘小阳他们一样，拿上枪和手榴弹，明天直奔医院去救人。但是很显然，手榴弹这种东西给了赵宏伟也是浪费。赵宏伟活得很无奈。他只能面朝西天，心中默念：佛祖保佑，秀珍安然无恙，同志们明天安然无恙。

没有人知道，山本信玄在医院设了埋伏。赵驹好心给赵宏伟送去的信，等于成了引鱼上钩的诱饵。

秀珍一个人躺在病房里，她的一只手，被牢牢地铐在病床的铁架子上。一晃动，金属就叮当作响。

秀珍就那么万念俱灰地躺着。活着对她来说已毫无意义，呼吸只是在延续痛苦的折磨。人生的一切都已经碎灭了，都已经不存在了，爱情、女儿、尊严，都已经灰飞烟灭了。她知道，自己已只是一个等死的人。唯一还能让她有所坚持的，就是她无论如何也不会向日本人说出玉山的秘密。共产党是救她的恩人，她死也不会做出卖恩人的缺德事。

想到共产党，秀珍不禁又想起了小秦。她想起了小秦给她熬的甜粥，其实真的很香、很甜。而她都还没有好好谢过他，而他已经不在了。她想起小秦在河里奋不顾身救她时的样子，她想起小秦在日军的包围中舍命保护她的样子，她，忽然第一次感受到了，一种被人真心在乎的感觉、一种被人全心爱护的感觉。这种感觉，和她一生的苦苦单恋完全不一样，这种感觉，让她很温暖。然而，小秦已经死了，这种感觉，也再不会复活。赵宏伟心里爱的还是别的女人，而她王秀珍，只是一个被畜生糟蹋过的女人。秀珍的心里，撕心裂肺的难受。

她看着窗外的夕阳，夕阳的光红艳无比，灼人眼球。她想，为什么没让我死成呢？难道是我受的罪还不够多？老天爷可真是个魔鬼。

秀珍对自己的一生感到了自嘲。她的绝望，像河水一样平静、绵长、永恒。

山本信玄下楼去了。秀珍的病房门口，只剩下了两个百无聊赖的日本兵。

小燕给秀珍换药时，问她，你现在能动吗？

秀珍说，能。

小燕问，你怕日本人吗？

秀珍说，以前怕，但现在不怕了。

小燕说，我现在也不怕了。

小燕问：你现在能跑吗？

秀珍说：应该能。

夕阳西下，血红灼天。

小燕给看守的两个日本兵送去了两碗绿豆汤。两个日本兵要摸小燕，小燕笑着，任他们动手猥亵。小燕喂他们喝下了绿豆汤。

两个日本兵，口吐白沫地死了。小燕从日本兵身上拿出了手铐的钥匙。

小燕解开了秀珍的手铐。秀珍十分讶异。小燕说：你跑了，渡边一定会杀了山本那个畜生，我要他死！

这时候，医院外面，突然响起了密集的枪声，还有爆炸声。

是日本人发现了原本打算悄悄进入医院的手枪队。手枪队只能执行备用的战斗计划。双方激烈枪战。埋伏着的日军倾巢而出。手枪队在战斗中向着医院大楼靠近。

小燕说，快，左边楼梯下去，那里没人，到了下面，我给你穿上护士的衣服，我带你出去。

医院外面，又是两声爆炸声。

小燕带着秀珍，匆忙跑入走廊。

两个女人，对外面突然爆发的激烈枪战感到茫然而不知所措。

小燕带着秀珍，往左边楼梯跑，刚跑到楼梯口，却突然看到，山本信玄竟然正握着手枪，在从这边楼梯的下面朝上跑来！

山本信玄一抬头，看到了小燕和秀珍居然站在上面！他惊讶得张大了嘴。

山本信玄疯了一样往上冲。

“臭婊子！我杀了你！”山本信玄怒骂着，开枪示警。

小燕拉着秀珍，赶紧往右边楼梯跑。

两个女人，拼尽力气地跑着。

山本信玄跑了上来，站到了左边楼梯的楼梯口，他看见了倒在走廊地上的那两个日本兵，他一枪，便远远地打中了小燕的后背。

小燕倒在了地上。她口吐鲜血，对秀珍说，你跑，快跑，山本不敢对你开枪！

秀珍拉着小燕的手，想扶她起来一起跑。小燕用力推开了秀珍，说，你快跑哇，你跑了，我就能报仇了，求你了，别管我，快跑！

秀珍于是丢下了小燕，拼命往右边楼梯的楼梯口跑去。

秀珍腹部的伤口已裂开，正在往外大量涌血。

山本信玄追着，经过小燕身边的时候，小燕死死地抱住了他的腿，拼了命地抱着，不让他挪动一步。大口大口的鲜血，从小燕嘴里涌出。

“放开！”山本信玄大吼着，往小燕后背又开了一枪。

小燕依旧死死抱着他的腿，不让他走。小燕含着血说：畜生，你会遭报应的。

山本信玄将枪口顶在了小燕的头顶上，开了一枪。

小燕死了。

秀珍跑下了右边的楼梯，正跑着，忽然，看到，有一群日本兵，正在从这边的楼梯下面朝上跑来。日本兵们，看到了秀珍。

秀珍往上看，山本信玄正在跑下来。

她已进退无路，上下无门。

秀珍站在三楼的楼梯间里，她的身后，是一扇破旧的玻璃窗。

血红的阳光，正从窗外照进来。

秀珍的腹部，血在不停地往外奔流。

秀珍推开了那扇窗。落日的阳光，灿烂得刺眼。

她想起了赵宏伟，想：好可惜，他终究爱的不是我。

“小菊，娘来了。”秀珍含泪说了一句，然后，爬出了窗外。

秀珍，从三楼的窗口处坠下，头部着地，脑浆四迸。

秀珍，死了。

刘小阳看到了秀珍的跳楼。

日军火力越来越猛，越靠近医院大楼，日军的火力越密集。

日军早有准备。

刘小阳下令：往外撤！赶紧往外撤！

一个队员问：人不救了？

刘小阳说：来不及了，救不了了。

他手一指，只见，医院大楼的脚下，是一具凄惨而血腥的女尸。

深夜。

凉薄的夜，狰狞似鬼魅。

渡边办公室内。

“你个废物！你是不是想要我死！”渡边怒不可遏地，拔出手枪，就对准了山本信玄的脑袋。渡边愤怒地喘着粗气，山本信玄的眼睛里，第一次有了求饶的神情。

“你知不知道王秀珍要比姚志好对付一千倍！她是我们最后的希望！现在却全被你给毁了！全被你给毁了！”

“大人息怒！息怒！”山本信玄哀求道：“我也有功劳的，我也有功劳的。我一早就向外放出了王秀珍在医院的消息，我料定那些潜伏在江庆县内的共产党必定会去医院救人，我在医院周围安排了大量兵力火力、设下了严密的埋伏圈，结果就在几个小时前，傍晚时分，果然来了一帮强闯医院的武装人员！他们的身手和装备都十分强悍，若不是王秀珍一早跳了楼，使他们及早撤退，我早已将他们一网打尽！”

“蠢猪！蠢猪！谁给你命令，要你诱捕潜伏者了？我是要你看好王秀珍！要你看好王秀珍！！你他妈的是不是听不懂人话！！”渡边气得全身发抖，“你有那么多兵力，居然只留两个人看守王秀珍，居然只留两个人看守王秀珍！你知不知道，我们现在的头等大事，不是抓潜伏者，而是要玉山地形图！要玉山地形图！！你个自作聪明的蠢猪！你不服从命令，我要你有什么用！”

渡边用枪口，用力敲击着山本信玄的额头。渡边的脸，因为极度的愤怒与绝望而一阵红一阵白，他的情绪几近失控。山本信玄害怕，渡边真的会开枪。

山本信玄跪了下来。

“大人，我错了，我真的错了！饶了我这一次吧，请饶了我这一次吧！！我和我的父亲，一定会对您感恩在心的！请给我一个将功赎罪的机会吧！！”山本信玄苦苦哀求。

渡边咬牙切齿地瞪着山本信玄。他是真想扣动手枪扳机，但是，他又不得不想到，老山本的存在。

渡边深吸了好几口气，强制地压抑着自己的愤怒和绝望。

“说，你要怎么将功赎罪？”渡边怒火难平地问。

“我有把握，能让姚志交代出玉山地形图！”山本信玄赶紧说。

“就是用你上次说的那个主意？”

“是的，大人。事实上，事情已经在顺利进行了。”

“你他妈的！又不经过我同意！你究竟有没有把我当成你的上司！！”渡边刚压下去的怒火又冲了起来。

“大人，大人！我这么做，可都是为了您！只要事情成功，功劳就全是您的呀！我是怕时间来不及，所以才提早开始了对付姚志的计划，我可都是为了大人您的利益呀！请大人三思！”山本信玄声泪俱下。

“你可真是一个虚伪透顶的恶魔呀。”渡边厌恶、愤怒又无奈地说。

“中国有句古话，叫无毒不丈夫。大人，您先让我来办这件事，办成了，是您的功劳，如果失败了，我愿剖腹自尽，向天皇谢罪！”山本信玄信誓旦旦地说。

渡边终于收起了枪。

渡边颓丧而疲惫地跌坐在椅子上，说，如果姚志不交代，用不着你剖腹自尽，因为，北野会把我们一起枪毙的，你想逃也逃不掉。

山本信玄从地上站了起来，一个敬礼，说，请大人放心，我一定会让姚志后悔他的坚持！

渡边长叹了一口气，无望地捂住了脸，累极了地说：滚。

赵宏伟住的屋子里。

赵宏伟撕心裂肺地哭了一天一夜。

痛彻心扉的悲伤像惊涛骇浪的海水一样，将他完全淹没，他在窒息中哭泣永远死去了的爱情。是的，他的爱情已永远死去，他的秀珍已永远逝去。不管他心底里究竟爱不爱秀珍，或者说，不管他心底里对秀珍的爱到底有几成，秀珍，都已永远不在了。这个世上最后一个爱着赵宏伟的女人死了。一个用一辈子的痴情来爱着赵宏伟的女人，就这样，无可挽回地，在这个世上消失了。以后，天地广袤，岁月悠悠，他赵宏伟，都只能独自冰冷地度过了。这种感觉，就像是永远进入了一座监狱，孤独的监狱。爱的开门人，已永远死去。

想起和秀珍一起拥有过的温暖时光，赵宏伟的五脏六腑都像在被时光腐蚀。他痛得在地上打滚、挣扎，而悲酸无法减轻一点点。秀珍的音容笑貌，像烙印一样滚烫又清晰，越来越清晰。他的灵魂都快要被悲伤给烧死了。他痛苦，悔恨，后悔莫及。他恨自己，为什么没有斩钉截铁而又毫不犹豫地对秀珍说上一句：我爱你，只爱你，唯你一人，唯愿天长地久。也许，他这么说了，命运就会呈现出另一番景象。可是，这世上永远没有如果。秀珍已经死——她是跳楼自尽的。他知道，是他，摧毁了她最后的活着的意志。他知道，是他，给了她绝望的一击，刻骨铭心的绝望一击。是他，粉碎了秀珍的爱情，夺走了她活下去的希望。他，对秀珍有罪。

不管爱，或者不爱，他最后的温暖依靠都已烟消云散。不管恨，或者不恨，他这破碎的一生都已再无存在的芬芳。秀珍不在了，他的活着，又还有什么意义？

蝇营狗苟，苟延残喘，破灭的人生，活着就是惩罚。痛心疾首，悲痛欲绝，回忆越宝贵，痛苦越剧烈。人间就像一座地狱，求生便是煎熬。赵宏伟，觉得自己已经活不下去了。或者说，已经再无活着的理由了。

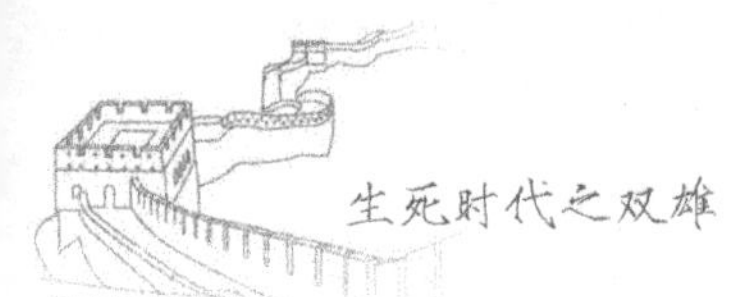

他准备报仇。他要杀了每一个欺侮过、伤害过秀珍的畜生，他要杀了渡边和山本信玄，他想在做完这一切后，就去死。

他想到了黄泉路上，再去和心音叙叙旧，和秀珍、小菊聊聊天，就像在那些无忧无虑的岁月里拥有的美好时光一样。也许，在这个悲惨的年代里，地狱反而是乐园，死去反而是快活。他感到，自己已无所畏惧。

他准备，在剩下来的时间里，全力以赴地帮助共产党，帮他们把日本畜生杀个片甲不留！以前，他一心想着逃走，现在，他终于可以死心塌地地再也不用想这件事了，因为，他已不用再求生了。当一个人死志已决的时候，他的心，是可以静如止水的。而这种静如止水的感觉，真好。人生再无希望和彷徨，只剩痛苦和仇恨。仿佛自己便是自己的敌人。

赵宏伟以泪洗面，在痛苦中咬破了自己的舌头和嘴唇。血腥味再浓，也冲不淡他心里的苦味。这苦味，漫山遍野，像从永恒的天空降下的一场没有尽头的雪。冰天雪地，孤影独行。

活着，再无温暖与希望。

阴森森的天空。

沉寂的小巷，死气沉沉的城镇，一切，都像是魔鬼口中的食物。

一位母亲，在大街小巷里到处寻找自己的孩子。

“你看见我的阿宝了吗？他刚学会走路。”

“没有哇。”

“你看见我的阿宝了吗？我去洗了洗菜，他突然就不见了。”

“没有哇，你要不再去那边问问？听说前几天，沈大哥才满周岁的女儿也被人偷走了。”

“是谁干的？”

“不知道。”

阴冷的风，无边无际地吹。

威远镖局老宅中。

赵驹喝光了一壶酒，再倒酒壶，已什么也没有。他自嘲地笑了笑，心里泛起火辣辣的难受。他感到自己喝下去的既不是甜蜜也不是痛苦，而是人在尘世中飘浮所积攒下的无奈自欺与彷徨自醉。他感到，偶尔做个醉鬼真是一种解脱。可是，他又从不敢真的让自己酩酊大醉，因为，他怕自己会说醉话，醉话会出卖一个人的内心。所以，他根本没有解脱，就连喝酒，也只是在清醒地麻醉自己。无论在真实中还是虚幻中，他从来就无法结束痛苦。

赵驹去院子里坐了一会儿。微微的风吹拂着他，让他微微有些清爽的感觉。这段时间，山本信玄没有再找他去练拳，他不知道是山本信玄最近太忙了呢，还是渡边真的帮他向山本信玄说了情。赵驹的身体在这几天里得到了休息，健康状况有所改善。但是他并不知道山本信玄什么时候又会发疯，这条疯狗，喜怒无常。所以，他觉得，还没做完的事，现在都必须要抓紧时间做了。

赵驹看着宽阔而空旷的院子，心中莫名一阵惆怅。脑海中，父亲与众镖师，仿佛依旧在这里虎虎生威地练着拳，一招招，一式式，都威风八面，力透千钧。然而穿过回忆的幻象，触摸坚硬的现实，面前只是人烟寂灭、无尽荒凉。什么都不在了，不在了许多许多年了。只有回忆，在失去中嗡嗡作响。

伤感，像陈年的酒味一样绵长。这绵长，会细细地固执地咬人心。

赵驹想到，在如今的情形下，他要杀渡边，说不定会和山本信玄交上手，这可是个大麻烦。山本信玄和普通的日本军官不一样，他那心狠手辣的空手道，实在不可小觑，而且山本信玄的枪法也不弱。一旦真正交手，他的确是个魔鬼般的对手，而赵驹暂时并没有什么能够快速制伏他的办法。赵驹仔细地回想着山本信玄用过的招式，他必须要尽快破解山本信玄的残暴空手道才行。

赵驹知道自己的时间已经不多了。

县监狱。牢房中。

一个面目阴森的狱卒，又一次端着一碗热气腾腾的肉丸子，走进了关押着姚志的那间牢房中。姚志蜷缩在地上，狱卒将碗放在了姚志面前的地上，说，吃的来了。

姚志的手脚颤抖着，手铐脚镣叮当作响。

碗里的肉丸子香喷喷的，浓汤的表面，还漂浮着青翠好看的葱花。

狱卒笑笑，说，每天一碗，吃得够吗？不够可以再要。

姚志喉咙里有声音。

狱卒走了。

姚志犹豫不决地，还是又抓起了肉丸子，吃了起来。

每天，姚志都会将一碗肉丸子吃得精光，连汤也不剩一滴。因为，自从这肉丸子在那天出现以后，狱卒就不再给姚志送除此以外的任何食物了，每天的这一碗肉丸子，是姚志唯一的饭食，如果他不吃，就会饿死。而这肉丸子说来也奇怪，它莫名令姚志感觉很好吃，越吃越好吃，虽然姚志已没有了舌头，但是，这肉丸子的美味还是仿佛能够直达姚志的脑部，令他欲罢不能。每次吃完了它，姚志都能感到身体里暖暖的，像在被一种很柔和的东西抚慰，他全身的各种伤痛，也仿佛被迅速缓解了，让他感到一种解脱般的轻松。因为这肉丸子，姚志甚至重新拥有了美好的睡眠，他感到，它就像是一种帮人止痛让人忘忧的药一样，简直令人上瘾。这真是一种神奇的厨艺。姚志对此也曾感到过困惑不解，但是，他经常将自己的这种食后舒适感理解为一种错觉，他以为，这吃饱后的飘飘欲仙感，只是他在灵魂与身体的双重痛苦中产生的自我抚慰式的幻觉，没什么特别的。毕竟，这只是一碗肉丸子，又不是鸦片，或者海洛因。

山本信玄躲在暗处，看着姚志一口一口地将肉丸子吃完，他的嘴角露出了狰狞的笑。

秀珍的血淋淋的人头，依旧被挂在旗杆上，晃晃荡荡的。恐怖的气息，笼罩着全城。街上悄无声息。

赵宏伟又一次来到了县政府，求见渡边。赵宏伟没有痛哭流涕，没有双膝下跪，他仪表堂堂，笑容可掬。

这一次，渡边接见了赵宏伟。

与渡边料想的不同，赵宏伟进了办公室，竟只字未提王秀珍的事。赵宏伟兴致勃勃地告诉渡边，他打算要为渡边写本书，歌颂他在中国战场上为大东亚共荣事业默默无闻的做出巨大贡献。渡边怀疑自己的耳朵是不是出毛病了。

赵宏伟说，真的，您没听错，许久不动笔，我已技痒，请太君给我这个机会，让我为您的事业添砖加瓦，一尽绵薄之力。

渡边心中霜雪顿消，脸上笑容灿烂。他拍拍赵宏伟肩膀，赶紧请赵宏伟坐。

赵宏伟和渡边聊起了书的内容，两人相谈甚欢。渡边告诉了赵宏伟一些他以前在中国战场上立下的功绩，赵宏伟掏出笔记本，一一做了详细的记录。渡边眉开眼笑，说，赵先生，你真有心，我相信你的文采。

赵宏伟说，太君见笑，您放心，我一定会尽我所能，在书中表达对您的钦佩和景仰之情，待将来书稿印成之时，太君您的芳名，定能传到天皇的耳朵里。

渡边掩嘴大笑，说，惭愧惭愧，哈哈哈，真是惭愧得很哪。渡边给赵宏伟泡了一杯茶，说，赵先生，你可真是我们皇军招揽到的最妙的一个人才呀，能够得到你的辅佐，真是人生幸事。

赵宏伟说，太君夸奖，小人愧不敢当，我只是想全力以赴，报答太君您对我的知遇之恩罢了。赵宏伟抱拳行礼，与渡边一起欢笑。

赵宏伟轻轻品了一口茶，滋味无穷地点了点头。然后，他不经意地问起：对了，我看到在县城中心广场的旗杆上，似乎是挂了一颗人头，怎么，难道县城又出什么暴乱了吗，要如此以儆效尤？

渡边眯起了眼，似笑非笑地看着赵宏伟，说：赵镇长，你真的不知道旗杆上的那颗人头是谁吗？

赵宏伟放下茶杯，皱起眉，一脸不解地说：不知道哇，太君此言何意？

渡边看着赵宏伟的眼睛，慢条斯理地说：那是王秀珍的人头。

赵宏伟惊得全身一震，手中茶杯落地，摔了个粉碎。

赵宏伟紧粘着渡边的眼神，问：这是怎么回事？太君，请快告诉我，这是怎么回事？

渡边眉头一皱，问：你真的一无所知？

赵宏伟急了，说：太君，您都在说什么呀，我应该知道什么呀？

渡边顿了顿，就把秀珍的事情，从头到尾告诉了赵宏伟一遍。渡边说完了，赵宏伟面有哀色。赵宏伟说：太君，您当初不该把她交给山本大尉审讯的，您应该找我来，虽然我已厌弃这个女人，连再多看她一眼都已觉得太脏，但是她并不知道我已经嫌弃她呀，我完全可以用花言巧语，来骗她说出

一切呀，现在却全完了。

渡边也不禁恼恨地一拍大腿，说：都怪山本这头猪！他刚愎自用，且目中无人！

赵宏伟淡淡地叹了口气，说：算了，现在说什么也没用了，要怪，也只能怪这个蠢女人不识好歹，不懂与皇军合作的好处，这，都是她自找的下场。

渡边说：你能这么想就好。

赵宏伟说：但是太君，有一句话我不知当讲不当讲，这在旗杆上挂了一颗女人头，实在是弄得全城人心惶惶，知道的，会说是山本大尉嗜杀成性，不知道的，还会以为是太君您残暴不仁呢，这坏名声要是传了出去，以后，再要补回来可就难了。

渡边不禁皱眉，说：其实我也不赞成山本这么做，这样悬首，除了吓人，什么用也没有。

赵宏伟说：太君，不如这样吧，我和王秀珍以前好歹也是情人一场，如今看她身首异处，说实话，我也于心不忍，我们中国有个风俗，叫入土为安，要不，您看在人之常情的分上，就让我给王秀珍收个尸吧，将她好歹安葬了，这样，您在百姓口中的名声也避免了过度受损，至于山本大尉那里，您可以将责任全推到小的身上，说是我死乞白赖要走的尸体，这样，您也可顺便测试一下山本大尉是否真的顺从于您，看他对于您已同意了的事会不会极力反对，若他果真不顾您的名声，只图他自己快活，那您以后可真得小心他。

渡边听到“山本”，不禁又捏紧了拳头。渡边想了想，就对赵宏伟说：好吧，你去给王秀珍收尸，将她好好安葬了，毕竟，这个女人也曾让我销魂过，我也不忍心看她的头被挂在那里，真的太恶心了。

赵宏伟站了起来，向渡边鞠躬，说：太君仁慈之心，令小的非常感动。

渡边笑笑，说：记得，以后也要把我做的这件仁慈之事，用优美的文字写进书里。

赵宏伟说：一定一定。

县城中心广场。

赵宏伟强忍着火烧一样的悲痛，面无表情地，从旗杆上将秀珍的人头取了下来。秀珍满头满脸都是血污，她的眼睛还没有闭上。赵宏伟将秀珍的人头装进了一个布袋子里。他一滴泪也没有掉下来。他不确定后面是否有人在监视他。

他还要去县监狱。山本信玄将秀珍的无头身丢弃在了县监狱后面的刑场旁边的垃圾堆里，没人知道她的尸身现在是否还完好、是否已被处理掉。赵宏伟要赶快去找。

赵宏伟带着渡边的手令，进入了县监狱。

县监狱，刑讯室内。

山本信玄准备好了一切，他大摇大摆地往椅子里一坐，然后，吩咐小兵：把姚志带过来。

刑场旁的垃圾堆里。

赵宏伟终于在一堆剩饭剩菜和断手断脚中找到了秀珍赤条条的尸体。赵宏伟脸色铁青地，咬碎了自己的嘴唇。他咽下了自己的血，仍然没有哭。

赵宏伟擦去了秀珍身上的菜叶和饭粒，然后，将她的无头身装入了另一个大的布袋子里。他站了起来，背上背着这个大袋子，手里拎着小袋子，开始沉重地往外走。

一步步，一步步，赵宏伟都感到莫名的眩晕，好像他身上的血在流失一样。他有种错觉，就是仿佛他每走一步，这片冰冷的土地都在吸他的血。而他如果站定下来，那种莫名的眩晕就好像会把他变成石像。他感到背上的秀珍轻飘飘的，好像一团干草一样，他不知道为什么会这样。是她的灵魂已经飞走了吗？灵魂果真是有重量的吗？还是她原本就是这么轻飘飘的，是自己从没好好抱过她，所以不知道她的重量？又或者，一切只是自己悲伤过度的错觉？他不知道。他的精神像是已到了崩溃的边缘，用仇恨与愤怒这两个简短的词，已无法形容他内心翻江倒海的悲惨。人，在这片土地上已不是人，好人成奴隶，坏人成皇帝，人的属性，只是欺侮或被欺侮、杀戮与被杀戮。个人的解救在这个时代已毫无意义，独善其身只是一个胆怯的谎言。人，在这个时代里，要么被时代吞没，要么推翻这个时代，人别无选择。

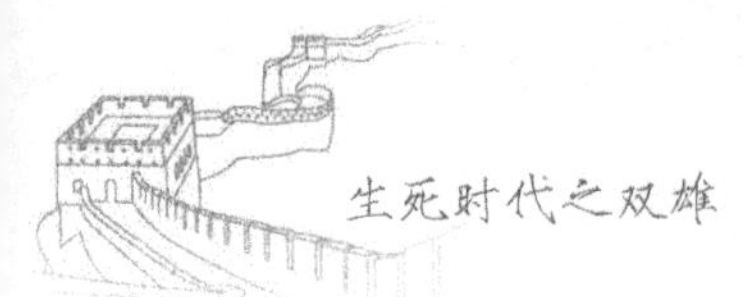

赵宏伟背着袋子里的秀珍，艰难地走着，一步一步地走着。再难过，他也不哭，因为，他在日本人的地盘上，不能再哭。他在心里，对背上的秀珍说：秀珍哪，我带你回家了。

两个日本兵拖着姚志，往刑讯室的方向走去，半道上，他们遇到了赵宏伟。赵宏伟看清了，这犯人是姚志。

原来，姚志真的就被关在这里。赵宏伟不禁想。

以前，姚志是被日本人从县监狱转移到了镇政府牢房，而今，姚志又被日本人从镇政府牢房转移回了县监狱，一个来回如同一个轮回，轮回中，总有东西在憔悴，总有东西在生长，总有东西在凋谢，总有东西在渴望。时光如流水，带走的从来不止是感慨。

县监狱刑讯室内。

姚志被绑定在刑架上。

山本信玄在姚志面前走了两圈，笑说，你气色看起来不错，最近是不是吃得挺好、睡得挺香？

姚志不置可否。

山本信玄笑笑，说，其实，你要是肯老实合作该多好，那样，我们也省心，你也过得舒服，大家何乐而不为？

姚志依旧不置可否。

山本信玄又笑笑，说，你一定正在心里嘲笑，想，这个日本鬼子是不是脑子抽筋了，今天居然用这种老生常谈来说服我，怎么可能有效。

姚志淡淡一笑。

山本信玄毫不在意，心情依旧很晴朗。他说，其实我也知道这种说服人的陈词滥调对你来说毫无用处，我本人也非常讨厌这种毫无创意的逼供，只不过，我真的是想给你最后一个机会，趁着我们大家还能心平气和好好说话的时候，看你能不能就这样把情报给招了，也省得我们多造杀孽。

姚志不屑一顾地笑笑。

山本信玄说：纸和笔就在这里，你要是肯招，就点一下头，我放你下来，你来把你知道的一切都写出来、画出来，我们想知道的很简单，就是玉山神秘的地形，如果有秘道，也请你把秘道给我们仔细地画出来，并附上详细的说明。

从姚志的喉咙里发出了咕咕的笑声，笑声沙哑而坚硬。他在嘲笑山本信玄。姚志很明确地摇了摇头。

山本信玄一笑，说，这就没办法了。

山本信玄响亮地击了两下掌。

刑讯室的门打开。一个日本兵，抱了一个大概一两岁大的小孩走了进来。

日本兵把小孩放到了山本信玄的怀里。

山本信玄逗弄起了小孩。他把孩子抱到了姚志的面前，对孩子说：来，叫叔叔，叔、叔。

山本信玄认真地教着小孩子发音。小孩子睁着明亮的眼睛，叫了姚志一声“叔、叔”，声音稚气可爱。

山本信玄逗弄着小孩，满脸欢喜地对姚志说：你看，这孩子真的好可爱，他看见了我，都没有哭，这孩子真的好乖。

姚志疑惑不已，他困惑地看着眼前发生的一切。山本信玄慈眉善目地逗弄着小孩，就像一位年轻的父亲。

小孩又叫了姚志一声“叔、叔”。

山本信玄问姚志：姚志，你知不知道，一个人，窒息多久会死？

姚志一愣。

山本信玄突然面露狰狞，一把，掐紧了怀中小孩的脖子。

“姚志，你到底写不写？”山本信玄大声问。

小孩在山本信玄的怀里拼命挣扎、拼命挣扎。小孩的脸，发青发紫。

姚志惊慌不已，居然不知所措。

山本信玄更用力地掐紧了小孩的脖子。

“快，你愿意写就点头！”山本信玄大声吼道。

姚志彻底呆住了。

姚志没有点头，也没有摇头。他在刑架上本能地挣扎，似乎以为能挣脱铁链的束缚一样。愤怒的吼叫，在姚志的喉咙里打滚，声音如闷雷，而撕心裂肺。

“你到底交不交代！”山本信玄大喊。

姚志发了疯似的挣扎。

小孩，断了气。

山本信玄叹息了一声，将怀中的小孩丢在了地上。他说：时间真的太宝贵了，才一小会儿，就死了。

山本信玄笑嘻嘻地对姚志说：记住哦，是你杀了这个孩子，因为，你原本有机会救他的。

姚志惊恐地看着山本信玄，就像看着一个真正是从地狱里爬上来的魔鬼。

空气凝固着。

姚志生不如死。

赵宏伟将秀珍的头颅和身体都擦洗得干干净净，然后，他拿起针线，将秀珍的头与脖子重新缝合在一起。缝好后，他合上了秀珍睁开着的双眼。他泪如雨下，对秀珍说：你放心，此仇不报，我赵宏伟誓不为人！

赵宏伟给秀珍穿上了崭新的漂亮的衣服，然后，他抱起她，将她轻轻放入了一口崭新的棺材里。他吻了吻她苍白的嘴唇，哽咽着说：秀珍哪，这辈子是我对不起你，欠你的，我下辈子还。

棺盖合上了。赵宏伟撕心裂肺地难受，这种难受，无边无际，没有尽头，又说不出来。

赵宏伟将秀珍葬在了小菊的旁边。凄凉的坟头，像时光深处荒凉的守候。赵宏伟感到了一种痛不欲生的孤独。真的，从此，他再也没有爱情了。

赵宏伟在秀珍的坟前跪了很久，也哭了很久，最后，他说：等报完了仇，我来陪你们。

无际的痛悲卷动着天涯的云彩，一望无际的孤独，像没有方向的哀鸿。

方远梦家中。

刘小阳已联络好了各路人马，包括青梅县特工队、玉山游击队、新四军大部队，经商议，各方确定将在十天后，共同发起大反攻，里应外合，粉碎日军的封锁，争取夺下青梅县和江庆县这两座城池。

赵宏伟拿到了县政府和县监狱的地图，还有江庆县日军的全城布防图。另外，他还弄到了一枚德国制造的定时炸弹。赵宏伟不惜代价地帮助着共产党。他对方远梦和刘小阳说，你们只要答应我一件事，那就是帮我杀了渡边次郎和山本信玄，为此，我愿意做任何事。

刘小阳经过上次的医院被围，丧失了对赵驹的信任，以为那是赵驹与山本信玄合谋设下的圈套，但是赵宏伟说：相信我，赵驹若有心害我们，我们早都被抓了，他一定是和我一样的人。

手枪队的同志都已准备就绪，只等时间临近。约好的时间一到，手枪队便会炸毁江庆县政府以及县政府内的日军联队指挥部，同时分兵闯入附近的县监狱，救出监狱里的所有抗日人士。

一场大会战，即将来临。

赵宏伟也给自己准备了一把手枪。他已决定，要在这场会战中，与敌同归于尽。

威远镖局老宅内。院子中。

赵驹一个人。

他舒展筋骨，在飞洒的落叶里，重新打起了拳。八极神威，虎虎生风。他将自己在多年前偷看到的霍殿阁的一些招式，也融入了自己的拳路中，使自己的拳法更多了一些精妙之处。但是他仍无速胜山本信玄的把握，因为他从未看到过山本信玄的全套功夫，他每次只是在山本信玄面前简单地挨打，看不到山本信玄在对战中招式的变化。另外，赵驹也担心自己的身体状况，他的手，还是会突然莫名发抖。赵驹是多希望自己能够回忆起父亲当年所教的全套八极拳，如果有父亲那样的高手在，山本信玄的空手道，简直不堪一击。

赵驹全神贯注地打着拳。树叶在风中翻滚，时间都像放慢了流速。

赵驹起伏跌宕的一生，在他自己的眼前如落叶般飘零坠地。他想起了自己儿时尚武的梦想，想起了记忆中父亲威风八面的模样，觉得往日种种，似乎犹在风中飘舞，从以前留存到将来，不会消失；他想起了自己在颠沛流离中逃命、于落魄绝境中习武，觉得这一身的武艺，也实在是命运在生命中刻下的苍凉记忆。而尤其令赵驹感到忧伤的，他都还没来得及，好好地让丽云

看他打一遍拳，看他从头到尾地、无忧无虑地、威风凛凛地打一遍拳。他还从没让她好好欣赏过他的武艺。一切，都是那么匆忙而短暂，还未得到，已永远不在。这种忧伤，比原野广阔，比日出火热，苍白的灵魂，难以承受。痛苦，像没完没了的咬嚼，把他的心在漫长岁月里化成了一具尸骨，而他的武艺，又恰是对这痛苦以及忧伤的最终凭吊。人生，就是这么荒芜又寂寥。

荒芜又寂寥。

县监狱。刑讯室内。

姚志在刑架上痛苦地挣扎着，拼命挣扎着，但是，一切都是徒劳无功。铁链哗啦啦地响，刑架纹丝不动。

小女孩叫了姚志一声“叔叔”。

山本信玄告诉小女孩：其实这个被绑起来的叔叔是个大坏蛋。

小女孩问：为什么？

山本信玄说：因为他见死不救，他明明只要点一点头，就可以救很多小朋友的命，可他就是不肯点头，你说，这个叔叔是不是个大坏蛋哪？

小女孩困惑地看着山本信玄，不知道他在说什么。

山本信玄笑了起来，对小女孩说：你听不懂吗？没关系的，你很快就懂了。

姚志的喉咙里发出了悲呼。

山本信玄拿起刀，手起刀落，就在桌上砍下了小女孩的一根手指。

小女孩呼天抢地地惨哭了起来。

山本信玄对姚志说：“今天这个游戏可以玩得久一点，十根手指，你有十次点头的机会。”

姚志悲惨地哀号着。

“啊——”又一根手指，从小女孩手掌上掉下。

小女孩晕了过去。

山本信玄用冷水将小女孩泼醒。

山本信玄对小女孩说：快求这个叔叔，只要这个叔叔肯点头，你就可以不用再被切掉手指了。

小女孩痛不欲生地惨哭着，乞求姚志：“叔叔救我！叔叔救我！求求你点头！求求你点头！！叔叔——救救我，求你了——”

“啊——”又一根小女孩的手指，被切了下来。

姚志痛哭流涕。滚烫的悲鸣声，在他的喉咙里打转。

“画出玉山的地形和秘道，我们就放了孩子！姚志，你想好了吗！”山本信玄大声吼叫着，又切下了小女孩的一根手指。

“叔叔、叔叔，救救我吧——求你救救我吧——”小女孩的乞求声已有气无力。

姚志痛苦地闭起了眼睛。

山本信玄狂笑着，又是一刀剁下。

小女孩的鲜血，已流满整个桌面。

十根手指没切完，小女孩已活活痛死。

小女孩大睁着的眼睛里，布满了痛苦的恐惧和濒死的绝望。

姚志哭得生不如死。

“哎呀呀，姚志，你真的好残忍，看着这么可爱的小朋友在你面前活活痛死，你居然见死不救，你真是个衣冠禽兽哇。”山本信玄说着，嘴里啧啧有声。

姚志狂怒地挣扎着，铁链哗啦啦地猛烈颤抖。

山本信玄拍了拍姚志的肩膀，说：“你知道吗，杀人有很多种方式，有的人用刀，有的人用沉默，你和我，在这个死去的孩子面前，都一样地，是杀人的刽子手。”

山本信玄说完，扬长而去。

姚志看着地上小孩的尸体，呆若木鸡。

赵宏伟焦灼地盼望着时光的飞逝，十天的等待，对他来说似乎太漫长了。

他总是激动地拿着枪，饥渴地盼望着大反攻的来临，他幻想着手刃仇敌的场景，似乎这是唯一能缓解他痛苦的途径。他活得分不清白昼与黑夜，活得分不清梦境与现实，巨大的痛苦，已将他的灵魂压垮。他只想快点报了仇，然后，饮弹自尽。

空旷又无际的世界里，他只感到冰天雪地。而渺无人烟的天地中，他又看不到任何火种与生机。一切都是白的黑夜，笑的哭泣。秀珍死得那样惨，他无法再对这个世界心存感激，他要攻击，攻击一切让他感觉恐惧的东西，他要毁灭，毁灭一切让他感到绝望的秩序，为了这攻击与毁灭，他要豁出命去拼一场。他觉得自己这一辈子都是白活了，活得窝窝囊囊、空空荡荡，毫无建树，又一无所得。一种从心底里膨胀起来的冰冷孤寂，像毒药一样将他泡得奄奄一息。而这世上又没有对付这种毒的解药，因为，冰冷和孤寂，是人生命中本质存在的东西。当你失去爱的时候，就会懂得这种毒药是多么可怕，且不可逃避。

赵宏伟每天都会想起以前秀珍在时的点点滴滴，大小事情，栩栩如生，皆在眼前，近得仿佛一伸手就能碰到。然而使劲清醒一下，又会发现，面前与周围其实一无所有。梦幻是那么近，而真实是那么远。他很后悔，以前没有好好爱秀珍。他想，如果以前爱得专心致志、全心全意一点，那么今天，自己会不会少一点遗憾和悔恨？答案是虚妄的。因为失去带来的永远只能是遗憾与悔恨，不管你爱不爱，不管你爱得深不深。而站在失去的时空中，忧伤是不可扑灭的大火，直到灵魂枯萎的那一天，忧伤也不会轻易退却。怀念死去的女人，怀念死去的爱情，是痛苦在绝望的折磨里生出的自我安慰，而这自我安慰，一旦清醒，又加倍地痛苦和绝望。死去的不会再复活，所以，绝望的也再得不到解救。站在灵魂的尽头，人生又还有什么可以歌颂？活着便是承受失去，承受绝望，承受不住了，却还活着，如同行尸走肉一般。这样的灵魂，这样的悲哀，又有什么神灵能够施以援手？命运从来无情，天地原本冰冷，人间的一切繁花似锦，得之是幸，不得是命。只有悲伤和哭泣，才是每个人生命里最后的留守。孤独与失去，是人永远逃不开的厄运。想念一个人，想念一份爱，是最哀伤的渴望，最绝望的歌唱。

哭泣，让赵宏伟觉得自己还是个活人。

渡边要赵宏伟把书写成汉语和日语两个版本，而且他还向赵宏伟许诺：只要你书写成了，那么江庆县空缺的副县长一职，就由你来担任了。赵宏伟冷冷一笑，想：我写你祖宗十八代！

山本信玄每天审讯姚志两三次，每天杀害小孩两三个。从第一天杀害小孩开始，山本信玄就为了防止姚志撞墙自杀，命令狱卒在牢房里也务必要将姚志捆得结结实实、不可动弹。肉丸子则每天由狱卒塞喂给姚志吃。

但是，姚志终于还是绝食了。狱卒强行塞喂也不行。

姚志的求死之心坚决而强烈，他死活都不肯再吃一口东西。然而，一件诡异的事情发生了。姚志一天没吃这肉丸子，全身的骨头中，就仿佛有蚂蚁在爬、有虫子在咬，他的脑子里，就好像有无数条毒蛇在翻绞。他的全身，从皮肤到骨头里、从神经到血液中，都又痛又痒，冷热交替，难受不堪。这种奇异的折磨，从姚志的身体深处升起、绽放，又向灵魂中心散开、深入，像冰针的游行，像火苗的撩拨，像蛆虫的蠕动。姚志感到恐惧不已。这种煎熬，连绵不断，穿心透骨，让人直感到求生不得、求死不能。仿佛只有马上再吃一碗肉丸子，才能解除身上的全部痛苦。姚志开始恍然大悟：原来这肉丸子，是被做了手脚，做成了毒品一样的东西。姚志强忍着痛苦，拼命强忍着。他要求死，死了，就都能结束了。

山本信玄对姚志的绝食给予了轻蔑一笑。他连夜赶到了刑讯室，又和姚志玩了一回游戏。

山本信玄准备了两个小孩，要这两个小孩跪在姚志的面前，求姚志吃肉丸子。十分钟到了，姚志还不肯吃，山本信玄就拉过了其中一个小孩，开始在姚志的面前虐杀孩子。

挖眼、剥皮、割喉，一系列惨无人道、令人发指的血腥行为。姚志悲鸣不已，又无能为力。

山本信玄在血污中哈哈大笑，对姚志说："你看看，你多残忍，孩子们只是想求你吃口东西，不要饿死，你却宁愿看着孩子们如此凄惨地死，也不领情。你真的是禽兽不如哇，如果老百姓们将来知道了，这些小孩子都是因为你的固执己见和自命清高而死的，他们的仇恨与愤怒，必将淹没你和你那可怜的信仰！你的党，也必将以你为耻！哈哈哈——"

姚志痛哭流涕，又无能为力。

十分钟后，山本信玄又在姚志面前虐杀了另一个小孩子。山本信玄大声吼叫："姚志，你的坚持毫无意义！你只是在害死更多无辜的孩子而已！你是罪魁祸首！你是见死不救的人间恶魔！你不是英雄，不是铁汉，你简直不配做个人！哈哈哈哈——"

刑讯室里，满地的血液。

山本信玄拍拍手，日本兵又领进来两个小孩子。这两个小孩子，一进刑讯室，看到了眼前地狱般的景象，立刻就吓得尖声大哭了起来。

山本信玄对姚志说："怎么样？还想继续绝食吗？反正我们有的是可杀的小孩，这些小孩都是从你们中国的土地上抓来的，多死几群也毫不可惜。"

姚志开始摇头。他大张着嘴，开始摇头，拼命摇头。他的喉咙里，呜呜有声。

山本信玄笑了起来。他问姚志："你是答应继续吃东西了吗？"

姚志拼命点头。

山本信玄哈哈大笑，说："这就对了嘛，你绝什么食嘛，白白害死两个可爱的小孩。"

山本信玄一挥手，那两个惊恐地大哭着的小孩被带了出去。

一个日本兵端进来了一碗肉丸子。

山本信玄嘲讽地对姚志说："其实，你自己也快忍不住了吧？没吃这肉丸子，你是不是觉得全身都像在被虫子咬？"

姚志愤怒地瞪着山本信玄。

山本信玄凑近了姚志，说："这肉丸子很昂贵的，因为每一碗，都是用大量的罂粟壳熬制出来的，你说，这东西，你吃了，能不舒服吗？哈哈哈哈——"

山本信玄狂野地大笑，笑声尖利得像鬼叫。

刑讯室里，恐怖深沉。

姚志不再挣扎地，泪流满面。

威远镖局老宅中。

赵驹怀抱着装有丽云断发的盒子，丝丝哀泣，像凉冷又沧桑的雨，浑浊地落下。被时光埋得深沉的忧伤，像天边永恒的云彩，在人心中远远地呼喊。面对沧海桑田的无能为力，像一把无形之刀，将人存在的意义切割得支离破碎。回忆的依靠，像渐渐被风吹干的眼泪，慢慢只剩下苦涩的无奈。

赵驹要杀渡边了。他知道再不杀就要来不及了。他可能就要失去矫健的身手了，他可能就要被调离了，总之，他已经预感到，能杀渡边的机会越来越少了。再不动手，他将永无机会了。而回沈阳，已经明摆着是不可能的了。或许，他真的是已经等待了太久、太久，在这漫长的痛苦的等待中，他始终被回沈阳的愿望牵绊着，从而失去了太多绝好的刺杀机会，而如今回沈阳的愿望破灭了，他刺杀的机会也不多了，这或许就是一种命运的充满恶意的捉弄。他就像是站在了一场旅程的终点线前，再往前跨一步，一切就都会结束，但是这个结束，又很显然已不是开始时所盼望的那个归宿。他深知，他已必定会死在江庆县这个他乡。而他想回的那个家——沈阳，他今生已再无法抵达。他想和丽云死在一起的愿望，今生已再无法实现。他和她，注定将一南一北，相隔万里。

而他，在现在这样严酷的战争局势中，也已不能再奢望那最后的团聚。他必须要放弃回家，以客死他乡的勇气，来全力以赴完成最后的复仇。渡边，这个亲手杀害了丽云的恶魔，必须要死在他赵驹的手上！复仇，是赵驹余生中最后的使命。不杀渡边，他死不瞑目！

只是，他再也无法去丽云坟前看上一眼了。他不知道，丽云是否会感到孤独，是否会想他。他觉得自己很没用，既没能用余生来好好陪伴丽云的魂和坟，也没能及早地彻底地为丽云报仇雪恨。回首一生，他感到悲哀莫名，惆怅难言。他的泪水，浑浊得像海水。他不知道，自己到了黄泉路上，还能不能找到丽云。他不知道，丽云是否还在千万里之外的荒冢中，痴等着他。他想她，很想她。他感到很难过。他想回家。他想再和丽云说说话。但是，一切都已不可能。只有决绝的复仇，还在等着他去完成。完成了，他就可以去黄泉路上，向丽云道歉了。他，心里很难过。这种难过，永远说不出来。只有沉默和怀念，在岁月里铭刻着泪迹。这泪迹，痴幻沧桑，百世难忘。

赵驹，做好了与渡边同归于尽的准备。

再有三天，就是发动大反攻的日子了。新四军的部队，已在外围集结完毕，只等时间一到，发起总攻。

姚志依旧没有交代出玉山的地形和秘道。

山本信玄现在每次审问姚志，起码要杀四五个孩子。一个又一个的小孩，在姚志的面前悲惨地死去，他们无一例外地，都用稚嫩的声音恳求过姚志，要姚志救他们一命。而姚志只能握紧着拳头，痛哭流涕地眼睁睁看着他们惨不忍睹地死去。他不能叛变，一旦叛变，整支玉山游击队，都会覆灭。

山本信玄丧心病狂地在姚志面前不停地虐杀着孩子，孩子们一个个惨不忍闻地乞求着姚志，一次又一次，一日复一日。山本信玄的双手沾满了小孩的鲜血，姚志的精神已被折磨得崩溃，整个人痴痴呆呆的。

刑讯室中。

又一碗肉丸子放到了姚志的面前。一个日本兵，喂姚志吃着肉丸子。姚志吃得狼吞虎咽。姚志吃了一半，那个日本兵，却再也忍不住地，呕吐了起来。

山本信玄一枪，就打死了那个日本兵。

姚志诧异地望着山本信玄，诧异地望着那个被打死了的日本兵。

山本信玄冲那个死了的日本兵骂了一句："废物。"

姚志咽下了嘴里嚼了一半的肉丸子。

山本信玄坐了下来。他问姚志："你知道他为什么吐吗？"

姚志茫然地看着山本信玄。

山本信玄说："其实，我本来想晚点再告诉你，给你一个大惊喜，但是，你实在是已经让我失去了所有耐心，所以，我想让你的灵魂，早点去地狱了。"

姚志听不明白。

山本信玄说："从第一天起，你吃到的就不是一碗简单的肉丸子，它，不仅是用罂粟壳熬制出来的毒品，更重要的是，它的原料，就是那些死去的小孩身上的肉。你每天在狼吞虎咽地吃着的，其实是人肉。"

姚志撕心裂肺地哭泣着。嘶哑的悲恸声，在他的喉咙里火热翻滚。

山本信玄说："其实，你要解脱很简单，只要你肯画出玉山的地形图和秘道图，你想怎样活或者怎样死，我都答应你。你现在所需要做的，只是点一下头，答应我们的简单要求。你看如何？"山本信玄询问地看着姚志。

姚志目光呆滞，没有反应。

山本信玄叹了口气，他响亮地拍了拍手。

日本兵从门外送进来了十个小孩子。最小的，还不会走路。

山本信玄拿起刀，抓过了一个孩子。他说："姚志，我佩服你，我喜欢和你这么玩！"话音落下，山本信玄一刀落下，孩子的一只眼睛已被捅瞎。

孩子们纷纷惨叫大哭了起来。

山本信玄又一刀捅下，这个孩子的另一只眼被扎瞎。

“姚志，你到底投不投降！”山本信玄怒吼着，一刀扎进了这个孩子的心脏。

几个大一点的懂事了的孩子，都在姚志面前跪了下来。孩子们痛哭流涕地求姚志救命。

姚志疯了似的痛哭，哭得眼睛都流了血，鲜红的血。

山本信玄杀到第六个孩子的时候，姚志疯狂地嗷嗷叫了起来。姚志在刑架上，像发了疯似的，拼命挣扎，拼命点头。

拼命点头。

山本信玄放下了手里的刀。他问姚志：“你肯交代了？”

姚志崩溃地点点头。

山本信玄说：“千万不要耍花样哦，如果我们发现你交代的情报是假的，我想你应该能想象到结局。”

姚志虚弱地点点头，表示明白。他的眼神，涣散如死人。

山本信玄放下了姚志，传令日本兵：快拿崭新的纸和笔来！

姚志哀悼地闭上眼，泪如雨下。

悲伤成烟。

天色阴冷如墨。苍凉的白昼，像没有灵魂的死夜。

还差一天，就是约好的发起大反攻的日子了。

渡边派出了最强的兵力与火力，突袭了玉山游击队大本营。有了姚志地图的指引，日军登山如履平地，玉山天险形同虚设。日军从山腹中的暗道里，直接到达了游击队的大本营。

灭顶之灾，猝不及防。枪炮轰鸣，战斗激烈。日军的炮弹如雨点般落下，游击队员在火海中冲锋反击。双方血战厮杀，杀声震天。爆炸连连，惊天动地。

玉山沉浸在了一片血与火的海洋之中。

熊熊的烈火中，游击队员一批又一批地与日军同归于尽。漫山遍野的血泊中，到处是与日寇抱在一起烧死的无名战士；连绵不断的爆炸里，到处是

游击队员们千疮百孔、支离破碎的尸体。玉山在血泊与火海中，哭着死去。

终于，最后一批游击队员，也在大爆炸中与一队日寇一起化为了灰烬。

玉山游击队，全军覆没。

日军开始抓捕躲藏在玉山上的慰安妇。女人们纷纷绝望地跑向了山上的悬崖，义无反顾地从崖边跳下。她们，就像一只只陨落的蝴蝶，在绝望与黑暗中，坠向了粉身碎骨的破灭。她们中的许多人，才刚刚欢天喜地地消除了肩膀上的编号，以为新生活即将开始。

悬崖下的山谷中，尸体满地，血肉模糊。天与地，就像一座大坟墓。

悲风血腥，哀冷葬心。

日军抓住了几十个没来得及跳下悬崖的女人，让她们就地重新做回了慰安妇。

惨哭震天，光明寂灭。

苍天无眼，神佛无情。

一切，都是这个生死时代的悲恸与哀歌。

桥本带队，在玉山上收拾残局。

桥本在游击队长的办公室里，发现了一份共产党各路兵马即将对日军发起大反攻的详细计划书，他火速派人将这份计划书送下了山去，交给渡边。

另外，桥本还在方远梦的房间里，发现了方远梦和小夕的照片。他看到了，照片上，方远梦的背后，是一面鲜艳的中国共产党党旗。

桥本想：这个人，不是赵宏伟的老朋友吗？

新四军大部队发现了事情有变，于是提前发动了总攻。

松尾率领他的联队应战。周边日军，火速增援。

新四军与江南日军，展开了艰苦卓绝的惨烈大战。

炮火轰鸣，烽火连天。

浩浩荡荡，血火交织。

战况胶着而激烈。

青梅县特工队全员牺牲，死状惨烈。

山本信玄率兵抓捕江庆县内的手枪队，但扑了个空。手枪队的人员和弹药皆不见踪影。

是赵宏伟提前一步通知了刘小阳。面对这突如其来的山崩地裂的败局，赵宏伟竭尽全力地掩护着剩下来的共产党战士，因为他知道，一旦刘小阳他们被捕，他将再无机会与能力为秀珍报仇。赵宏伟，要豁出命来保护好这支最后的特工队。

听着城外新四军与日军交战的隆隆炮声，赵宏伟欲哭无泪。因为他知道，这次大战，由于姚志的叛变，新四军已失尽了先机。后发必受制于敌，这一次，正义终于还是输给了命运。

安顿好了手枪队的同志，赵宏伟立即去找方远梦。从形势上来看，既然刘小阳他们已经暴露，那么，方远梦应该也不会安然无恙。他必须要马上去通知方远梦撤离。

而赵宏伟预感到，自己的日子也不会长了。他与方远梦过从甚密，如果方远梦出事了，那么他自己也必会受到日本人的怀疑。就算赵驹想放他一马，日本人也不会再疏忽大意。一切，都要到尽头了。

夜色苍茫，赵宏伟绝望冰凉。他不怕死，只是怕报不了仇。

方远梦正在烧毁电台的密码本。铁盆中的火焰一摇一晃，像风中摇摆的树枝。

密码本在慢慢变成灰烬。

方远梦要赵宏伟先走，赵宏伟不肯。

密码本终于全部化成了焦灰，而大门外，也已响起了日军的狼狗叫。

方远梦要赵宏伟快躲到地窖里去。

但是，来不及了。

日军已开始砸门。

赵宏伟绝望得不知所措。

方远梦淡然地笑了笑，他对赵宏伟说："赵兄，天下没有不散的宴席，谢谢你一直以来对我和我们同志的真心帮助，今生能够认识你，我很高兴。你一定要记住，不管到了什么时候，都不要绝望，只要还有人在为了胜利而努力，胜利的那一天，就一定会到来。"

赵宏伟不明所以。

方远梦掏出了手枪，说:“赵兄，得罪了。”

“砰”，方远梦向着赵宏伟的左肩开了一枪。

赵宏伟倒地的同时，方远梦的家门，被日本人砸了开来。

日本兵蜂拥而入。

是桥本一人领队，他身边还带着一个汉奸翻译。

方远梦大声向赵宏伟骂道:“你个狗汉奸，我利用了你又怎么样！你现在知道我是共产党，已经晚了！我现在就杀了你！”

方远梦骂完，就向着赵宏伟身旁的空地上又开了两枪。

赵宏伟正目瞪口呆，方远梦的手臂，已被桥本开枪击中。方远梦的枪，掉在了地上。

几十条步枪的枪口，一起对准了方远梦。

桥本慢条斯理地走到了方远梦的面前，拿出那张方远梦在党旗下拍的照片，在方远梦面前晃了晃，得意扬扬地说:“看见了吗，是你自己保存的照片，出卖了你，你真的是太蠢了。”

翻译向方远梦翻译了一遍。方远梦笑笑，什么也没说。

日本兵绑好了方远梦，将方远梦押了出去。

桥本看了一眼倒在地上血流不止的赵宏伟，问:“这大半夜的，你怎么会在这里？”

赵宏伟说:“我来借书，谁知道，看见他在烧文件。”

桥本看了一会儿赵宏伟，然后，对身边的日本兵说，快，送赵镇长去医院。

松尾的部队在战斗中损兵折将，损失惨重。虽然新四军的大反攻最终没能成功，但是也在一定程度上削弱了江南日军的战斗力，沉重打击了江南日军的嚣张气焰。

渡边的部队成功剿灭了玉山游击队，北野表示十分满意。北野向上海慰安所那边的负责人打了一声招呼，慰安所方面表示不会再向渡边纠缠慰安妇的事情了，只要渡边将现有的重新抓捕回来的那几十个慰安妇送过去就可以了，这事可以就此了结。

渡边由江庆县日军联队的临时联队长，转为了正式联队长。渡边欣喜若狂。

另外，山本信玄也由大尉升为了少佐。这不是渡边的意思，是北野下的命令。渡边听人说，是山本信玄通过熟人，擅自在北野面前报告了他亲自审讯姚志的功绩，所以，北野给了山本信玄升级的奖励。这令渡边心中愤恨不已。但是渡边又不能拿山本信玄怎么样。

桥本和渡边商讨怎样追捕手枪队的事情。渡边说，不用急，方远梦还关着，我们如果公开枪毙方远梦，手枪队的人一定会来营救，我们只要设好埋伏，到时候，一定能将他们一网打尽。

桥本说，手枪队的人不会想不到这些，他们要是不来怎么办？

渡边说，这和想得到想不到没有任何关系，因为在这个世上，有一种愚蠢是专为所谓的情意而存在的，从七十六号特工总部那边已经传来了消息，手枪队的刘小阳，是刘小夕的弟弟，而方远梦之所以会保存着那张党旗下的照片，是因为，那照片是刘小夕对他的爱情纪念，你懂了吗？

桥本笑笑，说，所以刘小阳就算知道有陷阱，也一定会去救方远梦，否则，他将永远对不起他死去的姐姐。

渡边点点头，说，只要刘小阳会去救方远梦，那么，他的队员们，就一定不会让他一个人独闯虎穴，因为，中国人相信同生共死的兄弟情义。

桥本说，大人神机妙算，属下佩服，我这就去安排。

渡边忽然想起，问：那个赵宏伟现在怎么样了？

桥本说：还在医院，我还是觉得他已不可信任，只是暂时还没查出什么眉目来。

渡边点点头，说：你安排一下，到时候，让赵宏伟在刑场上亲手枪毙方远梦。

桥本说：是，大人。

没有人，再能说出姚志后来真正的故事。有人说，玉山游击队被消灭后，山本信玄就杀死了姚志，将他的尸体喂了大狼狗。也有人说，渡边因为怨恨山本信玄，所以下令放了姚志，姚志出狱后，躺在旷野中，不吃不喝，绝食而亡，临死前，他的脸上依旧布满了痛苦与恐惧。

还有人说，其实姚志后来没有死。一位老神医在旷野中救了姚志，姚志醒来后，忘记了所有痛苦的事情。他回到了家乡，永远地守在了小紫晴的坟前。他每天在坟前喃喃自语，痴痴傻傻的，没有人能听懂他在说什么。他看到了全国解放，他活到了须发皆白。最后，他孤独地死在了小紫晴的坟前，死前，他面带笑容，泪流满面。有人说，这是姚志最好的结局，因为他和最爱的人厮守到了生命的终点。

不管哪种传说是真，姚志的故事，都像一个谜或者寓言一样，永远地消失在了历史的缝隙里。人生百年，弹指成灰，爱恨悲喜，如梦似空。

渡边下令，将在八月十五中秋节那天的下午，于江庆县城的中心广场上，公开枪毙方远梦。到时，将由县长亲自宣读审判书，候补副县长赵宏伟会亲自动手枪决罪犯。渡边、桥本、山本信玄、赵驹都将出席审判大会。

秋叶凋零，枯黄染透了整片天空。寒风乍起，悲凉穿心。

秋天，是一个告别的季节。

团圆之日，永别之时。

赵驹做了一个悲凉的梦。

梦里，他又回到了沈阳，他又来到了庄府的门前。他拍着门，呼喊着丽云的名字，可是过了好久好久，也还是没有人来开门，天地间，只有寂静一片。忽然，天上下起了鹅毛大雪，他突然才发现，自己早已是白发苍苍的老人，脸上手上都已布满了灰黑的皱纹。他老泪纵横，还在不停地呼喊："丽云，丽云，你在哪里呀——"

——"傻瓜，我就在这里。"恍如隔世般的声音，熟悉地响起。

他在梦里，想起了他和丽云曾经说过的那些话。

"是啊，你就在这里。"

"要是有下辈子，我愿意投生在江南来找你，而不要你受苦流浪来东北。"

"你在哪里，我的家乡便在哪里。"

"我们生生世世不分离。"

"嗯，生生世世不分离。"

痴痴情话犹在耳边，生死至爱，已沧海桑田。

梦里的赵驹，发了疯似的痛哭。他撕心裂肺地痛哭着，想要抓住梦境之外早已消逝了的美好曾经，却怎么可能抓得住。只有大空大幻，在悲哀入骨地飘舞。

赵驹肝肠寸断地悲吼了一声，用尽全力地推开了庄府紧闭着的苍老大门。门开之时，他的眼前，却突然一暗。等到火光亮起，他才看清，面前，已是金顺的聚义厅。父亲，正浑身是血地站在聚义厅的中央。

“儿子，爹对不起你，爹从小就不肯教你武艺，还逼着你去念书，爹知道你活得不开心，是爹错了。今天，爹就把我们赵家的八极拳打给你看，爹只能打一遍，你能记多少是多少。今日之后，你一定要远走他乡，永不回来，忘记恩仇，一生平安。若能如此，爹在泉下也便安心了。”

“爹——”

“儿子，看好了！”

父亲在血泊中威武地打起了拳。拳风阵阵，扑面而来；一招一式，清清楚楚。

父亲血流如注。而赵驹，这一次，没有再泪眼模糊。

他，在梦中，重新学会了父亲的全套八极拳！

父亲，如山一般轰然倒塌了。

赵驹，在无边无际的血海里痛哭着。他也不知道，自己究竟为什么要哭。就好像，人生来，就是为了哭才活着一样。

赵驹醒来，发现脸上真的全是泪。

他走出屋门，走入了院子中。秋风萧瑟里，赵驹，打起了真正的赵家八极拳。

虎虎生威，威风八面。拳出如蛟龙，腿起如猛虎，刚猛摧山岳，劲力碎石铁。

赵驹站在落叶中，对着天空笑了笑，说：丽云，我就要来了。

八月十五。中秋节。

中午。

赵宏伟在秀珍和小菊的坟前，放上了几个月饼。他笑着对她们说：今天

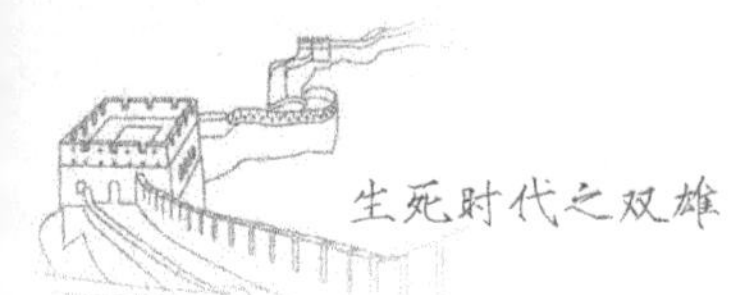

是中秋节了，是团圆的日子，本来我该来陪你们，可是方远梦说得对，我还不能绝望，只要我还能为了胜利而努力，我就不能放弃，否则，就真的只能是任由那些畜生们为非作歹了。

赵宏伟说，等那些日本畜生灰飞烟灭了，明年，我来陪你们过中秋。

赵宏伟笑得很灿烂。

赵驹，将丽云的那束断发，从盒子中取了出来，揣入了怀中的衣袋里。

他露出了团聚般的笑容。

赵驹走出了威远镖局的大门。

他回过身来，跪地，向老宅拜了三拜，说：父亲，儿子不孝，今日一别，我赵家空灭，团圆之日，诀别之时，待儿子到了黄泉路上，再来向您请罪。

黄叶飞舞，如泣如诉。

刘小阳端起酒碗，敬向众人。

“今生能与各位同行，一路烽火，出生入死，并肩作战，不曾别离，我刘小阳深感荣幸，若有来生，希望能再与各位欢聚一堂，饮酒歌唱。”刘小阳说。

“同生共死，在所不辞！”众人慷慨举碗。

碰碗。酒花四溅。

各人将酒一饮而尽。

秋风萧瑟马嘶鸣，视死如归英雄心。

县城，中心广场。

旗杆上，飘扬着刺目的日本旗，风舞猎猎。

高高的主席台上，渡边坐在正中央。渡边的左右，分别是桥本和山本信玄。赵驹领着一队卫兵，在主席台旁负责警戒，保卫渡边。

广场上，竖着一个十字刑架。刑架上，绑着方远梦。方远梦的嘴被紧塞着，他的脸上和身上，满是血痕。

赵宏伟远远地站在刑架对面，一个接近广场边缘的地方。待会儿，等那个汉奸县长演说完毕后，县长就会亲手交给赵宏伟一把枪，让赵宏伟走到方远梦的面前，爽快地将方远梦枪毙。而只要赵宏伟在枪毙过程中有任何迟疑或异动，他就会是下一个被绑上刑架的囚犯。

赵宏伟远远地看着方远梦，方远梦远远地向他笑了笑。赵宏伟在心里说了句：兄弟，一路走好。

日光金黄，秋风飒然。枯叶在地上随风行走，像没有生命的玩偶。

宽阔广场的周围，是人头攒动的围观群众。这些群众，有的是被日本人召集来的，有的是自愿前来看热闹的。他们拥挤着，东张西望，指指戳戳，像愤慨于眼前的现实，像惋惜于那失败的就义者，又像恐惧于这无边黑暗的高高在上。群众既愤愤不平恐惧不已，又喋喋不休畏缩不前，像毫无杀伤力的稻草人。

渡边端坐在主席台的正中央，他的两只手往前交叠着，拄着一把华丽的日本军刀。军刀威风凛凛，杀气腾腾。渡边用主宰一切的目光扫视着广场上及广场周围的所有事物，他的表情，威严而锋利，仿佛能砍杀一切、只手遮天。

阳光刺眼，金黄如剑。

渡边对桥本说了几句话。桥本看看广场四周，又看看表，然后示意县长：可以开始了。

县长走到了广场的正中央，开始滔滔不绝口若悬河地发表演说，他激情荡漾，但只可惜满嘴都是错字和病句。山本信玄笑着向渡边说了两句话，渡边失望地摇摇头。渡边用手指了指赵宏伟，向山本信玄说了句什么，山本信玄不以为然地一笑。

县长开始朗读宣判书，他在话筒前，大声地一一历数着方远梦莫须有的罪状。

县长读得慷慨激昂，唾沫飞溅。

突然，刺人耳膜的“砰”一声，县长中枪倒地。

鲜血从县长的胸口不停往外冒。

聚集在广场周围观看的群众立刻混乱了起来。尖叫、咒骂、哭喊，像细密的尘土般自下而上地飞扬了起来，一片片、一簇簇，洋洋洒洒，连成一体。惊恐和骚乱像波浪般荡漾开来，从东往西，又从西往东，很快，就浩

荡又汹涌地拧卷成了一股浊浪滔天的洪水。这洪水，要向四周奔流分散，逃离血腥与惊险交织的广场。但是，要逃的老百姓们却突然发现，不知从何时起，在他们此起彼伏的骚动混乱的外围，已经筑起了一圈坚不可摧的牢固堤坝。不知道是在何时从哪里突然冒出来了许许多多的日本兵，已在顷刻之间，像铁桶阵一样，将广场四周骚乱外涌的围观群众死死地堵截在了原地，使其无处可去。铁桶牢不可破，老百姓们外逃无望，只能惊惶地活在原地。

回望高高的主席台上，联队长渡边已被赵驹率领的卫队紧紧地保护了起来。而桥本和山本信玄，就像两头负责警戒的猎豹，拿着枪，站在卫队的左右两角，随时准备扑出去凶猛地撕咬。渡边坐在保护圈里，泰然自若，面露微笑。

赵驹，一动不动地站在卫队中央。他凝神静气地，拔出了手枪。

刘小阳率领着乔装成围观群众的手枪队战士，从围观的骚乱人群里冲了出来。战士们一边飞速地向广场上的刑架处冲去，一边不停地猛烈向主席台上的日本人射击。主席台上，不时有卫兵倒地、滚下主席台，但是，渡边始终被保护得严严实实，丝毫未伤。枪声与战斗的嘈杂里，渡边始终端坐着，两手交叠地拄着那把华丽的日本军刀。他的表情冷酷而坚硬，望向广场的眼神里，带着无限轻蔑的嘲笑。

从广场四周外面的各条大街小巷里，涌出来了更多全副武装的日本兵。他们个个荷枪实弹，张牙舞爪，早有准备。日本兵们纷纷穿越过了混乱不堪的围观人群，向着手枪队追击而去。奔进广场的日本兵越来越多，渐渐汇集成了一片壮观的潮水，这潮水澎湃而凶恶。日军追逐着手枪队，双方展开了血肉相对的惨烈枪战。枪战往来，生死交错。子弹擦肩而过，性命须臾定夺。包括生命在内的一切都是那么脆弱，仿佛一场茫茫人海中的赌博。激战、解救、追击、包围，血与火，在大地上不停地擦亮着乱世里的烟火。

子弹横飞的死亡海洋里，不时有群众遭受池鱼之殃，死的死，伤的伤。但是日军的铁桶合围阵依旧没有丝毫松懈，现场的所有人，都被牢固地控制在以广场为中心的一个大圆圈里。对渡边来说，今天到场的每一个围观群众，都有潜伏者的嫌疑、抗日者的嫌疑，一个手枪队已经脱颖而出了，还会不会有其他惊喜呢？渡边拭目以待。所以，现场群众死伤再多，日军也绝不会放走一个。

手枪队的战士大声呼喊着，要逃不走的老百姓们全部蹲下或者趴下。百姓们呼天抢地、鬼哭狼嚎。现场血泊片片，哀恸冲天。

赵宏伟，从开始到现在，一直站在原地，一动未动。子弹呼啸着在他耳旁飞过，他也没多眨一下眼睛，周围死伤的哀恸铺天盖地，他也没多动一下感情。他就像个没有感觉的死人一样，始终站在那个日本人要他站在的位置上，一动不动，一声不吭。死亡与痛苦像一场悲伤的雨，给予着他战争的洗礼。他懂得自己的手无寸铁与无能为力，他懂得眼前的结局注定与天意无情，所以，他选择等待和沉默。如果此刻有子弹飞向他的心脏和头颅，他也不会躲避，因为，他知道他的人生，早已不值得贪生怕死。

手枪队的战士，以广场上的一个水泥花坛为掩体，坚持着与日军的战斗。广场上的日本兵已密集如蚁群，日军用排山倒海般的凶猛火力，完全地压制住了手枪队的反击。手枪队的战士已无暇再向主席台上的日本人射击。渡边怡然自得地坐着，远远地看着广场上的枪火搏击，像观赏着一场尽在掌握的游戏。

渡边开玩笑似的对桥本说：要不，就把他们全部活捉了吧？

桥本说：玉山游击队已灭，活捉他们已无多大意义。

渡边开心得哈哈大笑，像听了一个什么笑话似的忍俊不禁。

赵驹，已在不知不觉间，靠近了渡边。

密集的日军，已如海潮般逼近了水泥花坛。

枪声短暂地停歇。

这时，手枪队的战士们，纷纷拔出了别在腰间的手榴弹。

“轰——轰——轰——”

手榴弹一颗接一颗地抛入了日军阵中，巨大的连环爆炸像澎湃的怒海，雷霆万钧而耀眼夺目地吞没着凶残的日军。风高浪急的火光直冲天际，地动山摇的轰鸣坍陷大地。

渡边所在的主席台，都颤抖了几下。

渡边的脸色难看了起来。

广场上的日军由于聚集得太密，一时被炸得损失惨重。趁着受伤的日军还没回过神来，手枪队的战士们，又奔向了刑架上的方远梦。

方远梦痛苦地向战士们摇头，他想叫他们回去、逃走，但是他的嘴，却

是被紧塞着，说不出话来。

一小队动作迅捷的日本兵，抢先一步，围护住了方远梦。手枪队的战士，包围住了这一小队日本兵。大批急忙追击了过来的日军，又团团包围住了手枪队。手枪队的战士都敞开了上衣，他们的腰间，个个别满了手榴弹。一时之间，手枪队战士和日本兵，都是互相枪对着头、头顶着枪，彼此牢牢牵制，僵持不可动弹，牵一发而动全身。

广场上顿时安静了下来。几近鸦雀无声。

渡边站了起来。

渡边让卫队散开。

他走到了主席台的前面的边沿，居高临下地看着广场上的局势。

他皱了皱眉。

渡边招了招手，让桥本和山本信玄也走到了前面来。

渡边问山本信玄：如果我们现在用子弹引爆共产党身上的手榴弹，那会是什么结果？

山本信玄说：手枪队将会全部灰飞烟灭，而我们最多只会有几十个士兵，为天皇陛下献出英勇的生命。

渡边点点头。

桥本对渡边说：大人，您还是退后吧，站在前面太危险。

渡边不屑一顾地摇了摇手。

渡边喊："赵驹！"

赵驹应声上前。

渡边问："赵驹，你的手，现在恢复到以前的战斗状态了吗？"

赵驹一笑，说："是的，依旧百发百中。"

渡边说："非常好。"

渡边用手远远地指了指刘小阳，对赵驹说："站在最前面的那个穿蓝色上衣的人，你，给我打中他腰间的手榴弹，我要他们全部被炸成碎片！"

赵驹说："好。"

赵驹抬起了拿着手枪的手。

金黄的阳光，像一抹微笑，投向着大地。

风，轻柔得像一种告别。

渡边得意扬扬而君临天下般地，看着广场上即将死去的芸芸众生。

一阵劲风袭来。说时迟那时快，赵驹突然将枪口，对准了渡边的脑袋。

没有半句废话，没有一丝犹豫，赵驹扣下了手枪扳机。

但是，就在电光石火的一刹那，山本信玄迅猛地飞起一脚，劲踢在了赵驹的侧腰上。

赵驹身子一晃。子弹从渡边的额边灼热地擦过。

渡边呆若木鸡，宛若痴呆。他的眼神，就像是突然看到了一个陌生的世界。

惊恐，像一个迅速放大的怪物，在渡边眼里跳动。

赵驹疾速又将枪口对准了渡边的脑袋，要开第二枪，但是，山本信玄已以迅雷不及掩耳之势，高高地飞起一脚，猛踢在了赵驹的太阳穴上。赵驹眼前短暂地一黑。桥本开枪。子弹从赵驹身旁穿过。

山本信玄，一脚踢飞了赵驹手里的枪。

“真没想到，原来你也是内奸！”山本信玄恶狠狠地说。

说罢，他就如一头恶虎般，残暴而疯狂地扑向了赵驹。

赵驹挥臂相迎。

拳与拳相击，腿与腿相踢。雄厚功力，对撞凌厉之劲。山本信玄目瞪口呆地发现，眼前的这个赵驹，根本就不是他所认识的那个东亚病夫！

赵驹如一头钢筋铁骨的猛虎，毫不费力地迎战着山本信玄劲霸的空手道。赵驹龙形虎步，拳脚生风，武艺之高强精妙，令山本信玄不知所措。

渡边目瞪口呆，张口结舌，看着赵驹，就像看着一个绚烂夺目的谜。

赵驹毫不恋战，摆脱了山本信玄，便立即转身扑向渡边。赵驹伸出虎爪，直奔渡边的咽喉。渡边连忙后退，惊慌失措地大叫：“卫队！卫队！”

卫队向着赵驹蜂拥而上。赵驹直奔至卫队跟前。卫队举枪。赵驹以疾风之速，飞取下了两名卫兵步枪上的刺刀，他双手各握一把，以行云流水之势，开始了干净利落的刺杀。赵驹手起刀落，一刀一命。许多卫兵都还没来得及开枪，就已被赵驹一刀穿喉。血花四溅，刀光舞动，赵驹之身形动作，如影如风。

渡边惊恐得拼命大叫，他拔出了手枪，乱开乱放。

现场所有认识赵驹的人，无不惊愕讶异。

一代拳王，终显英雄本色。

赵宏伟依旧站在原地。他远远地看着主席台上突发的变故，远远地看着赵驹英勇潇洒的身影，不禁苍凉又温暖地，笑了笑。他喃喃地说：我华夏子孙，理当如是。

桥本和山本信玄，从左右两侧，一起向赵驹开着枪。山本信玄的射击尤其疯狂猛烈，他狂暴地开着枪，就连错伤卫队士兵，也毫不可惜。密集的子弹，密密麻麻地射向赵驹。

赵驹一个跟斗，翻滚着跳下了主席台。

他落进了广场上拥挤着的日军阵中。就在他落地的一刹那，已有日本兵用步枪上的刺刀，向他狠狠地刺去。赵驹毫不迟疑地，就在地上一边翻滚，一边用刺刀割断着日本兵们的脚筋。一刀刀风驰电掣地划过，一股股暗红的鲜血喷出。赵驹滚过的地方，日本兵鬼哭狼嚎，纷纷倒地不起。

赵驹周围的日本兵，吓得肝胆俱裂地，纷纷往四周扩散逃跑。有日本兵朝赵驹开枪，但赵驹闪躲腾挪得太快，且此处日军聚集太密，所以，日本兵反而打死了自己人。一时，日本兵们都不敢再开枪，只能密集地伸出着亮晃晃的刺刀，阻止赵驹的靠近。

山本信玄则不管不顾地，往主席台下赵驹所在的地方，疯狂地开着枪。有日本兵哀号着中弹。

渡边向山本信玄大喊："给我活捉赵驹！"

渡边向广场上的日本兵们大喊："给我活捉赵驹！！"

赵驹发力，想要重新跑回主席台上去。桥本大喊："来人！保护联队长！快！！"

广场上的日本兵们，排成了紧密的人墙，奋力地堵截着赵驹。明晃晃的步枪刺刀一字排开，浩浩荡荡，在阳光下反射着惨白又灼热的光芒。赵驹一时前进不得。一队日本兵火速跑上了主席台，填补了卫队损失的兵力。日军密不透风地保护着渡边。

渡边的神情，渐渐安定了下来。

而就在赵驹那边的情势波澜起伏的同时，手枪队这边的僵持局面也发生了彻底的改变。趁着日军被主席台那边的突发状况搅得人心惶惶不知所措的时候，刘小阳率先劫持了一个日本兵，将他挡在了自己的身体前面，做防弹盾牌。其余的手枪队战士也迅速照做，很快，手枪队便在自身周围建立起了一道盾牌墙，紧逼着手枪队的日军，枪口对准着活生生的被劫持日本兵，也是无可奈何，进退不得。两名手枪队的战士，就趁着这个日军无法进逼的时机，迅速地从刑架上解救下了方远梦。

方远梦嘴里塞着的布条被拿掉了。方远梦痛苦地说:“这是一个陷阱！你们不该来！”

一名战士笑笑，说:“我们都知道这是一个陷阱，可是，我们愿意来，我们不怕。”

方远梦潸然泪下，说:“你们都被你们队长给教笨了。”

可是，方远梦的腿已经被日本人彻底打残了，他走不了了。方远梦说：你们快跑吧，不要作无谓的牺牲！快跑！

一名战士斩钉截铁地说：战友一场，我们要生一起生，要死一起死！

说完，这名战士就背起了方远梦。

刘小阳向日军阵中丢出了一颗手榴弹，爆炸升起，轰响惊天动地。日军方寸再乱。手枪队开始向外突围。

枪战激烈，爆炸轰鸣。血与火，在硝烟中绽放出意志的花朵。敌军潮起潮落，如狼似虎，突围血肉横飞，困难重重。苍白的阳光像一只失血的上帝之手，在火光与死亡里悲哀地抚摸着尘埃的宿命。敌众我寡，百战难休。意志的花瓣在燃烧中灿烂，命运的灰烬在血泊中凋零。生死重量转瞬即逝，冲锋陷阵锐意不屈。

一名手枪队战士倒下了，又一名手枪队战士倒下了。

突围依然在顽强地继续。

赵驹斩杀着拦路的日本兵，燃烧着生命中最后的信念。渡边就在主席台上，就在那咫尺之外的地方，赵驹不顾一切地冲向着渡边所在的方向。多少年的煎熬苦等，多少年的忍辱偷生，都只为了今日这最后一战。复仇的漫长征程就要在今天画上结束的句号，余生的最后追求就要在这里落下终结的帷幕，赵驹只能赢不能输。他知道这是一场仅有一次机会的刺杀，无论成功或失败，自己的结局都是死，所以，他必须要成功。他用尽了全力来搏杀，他不顾一切地冲向着渡边。他知道，丽云一直还在时光的那一头活着，而他只有杀了渡边，才能恳求上帝，带他去时光的那一头安息。他想再见一眼丽云

如花的笑靥。

日军的兵势排山倒海，一排排的刺刀犬牙交错地围攻着赵驹。日军要活捉赵驹，交给渡边发落。赵驹的刀，在险象环生的困境中，飞舞如雪光一片。刀刀相撞，火花四溅。日军杀声震天，如沸腾的海潮般围堵着赵驹。赵驹前进无路，只能后退、后退。

搏杀惨烈。

赵驹被兵势压向着广场中央，离主席台越来越远，越来越远。赵驹悲痛地怒吼着，全身爆发出了更加惊人的力量。他的速度，快到令人眼花缭乱；他的勇猛，分明是视死如归的搏命。一时之间，日军阵中再次哀叫遍野，血花满天。

与此同时，手枪队的战士们仍然在与日军殊死混战。日军人多势众，火力密集，手枪队的战士只是依靠着手榴弹的威力，才勉强支持着。然而手枪队的伤亡还是越来越惨重，有些受了伤的战士，干脆直接拉开了手榴弹，扑入敌军之中，与日寇同归于尽。爆炸轰鸣里，玉石俱焚，生命湮灭。

一部分手枪队的战士回到了水泥花坛中间的空地上，他们以花坛为掩体，持续与日军激烈交火。其余的手枪队战士，也陆续在往花坛方向撤回。日军的子弹密集地打在花坛上，水泥的碎屑激烈地飞溅。血腥味和火药味在空气中交织碰撞，浓墨重彩地勾勒着战争的惨烈。

刘小阳看到，日军的刺刀阵宛如铜墙铁壁一样重重围困着赵驹，赵驹纵然武艺高强，也绝不可能越过这千军万马之势，去取得渡边的首级。刘小阳拔出了一颗手榴弹，抛进了围困着赵驹的日军阵中。轰隆炸响，日军铁壁之势大乱，赵驹趁势突围。

高高的主席台上。

渡边已恢复了一些气定神闲的表情。他看着下面那个宽阔而浩荡的战场，甚至露出了一丝悲天悯人的神气。巨大的广场上，已经布满了灰黑的凹陷与星星点点的火焰，暗红的血泊更是在地上连接成了纵横交错的河流。像蚂蚁般细小的人，就在这片血与火的海洋里，涌来涌去，厮杀不已。渡边似乎感到了某种哲学的启迪，他哀凉地摇了摇头。广场四周那些拼命想要外逃的老百姓，正在不断地被包围着广场的日军枪杀，渡边叹了口气，说，蠢货。整个巨大的广场，整片惨烈的战场，都像是被渡边装在一个口袋里。他居高临下，运筹帷幄，泰然自若，静静观赏。

而渡边忽然发现，整个现场，除了他自己，好像还有一个人，表现出了处变不惊的气质。这个人就是赵宏伟。如果渡边没有记错，那么，从开始到现在，不管广场上的战况有多么危险激烈和千变万化，赵宏伟一直都还是站在原地，没有挪动过位置。赵宏伟是被吓死在那里了吗？渡边感到好笑。赵宏伟是在想什么呢？渡边感到好奇。

桥本告诉渡边：赵驹又在往这边闯来了。

渡边吓了一跳。

渡边皱着眉，看了看广场上血流成河的厮杀。他将手中的那把华丽的日本军刀丢给了山本信玄，说：还是你去下面结束这一切吧，完了我向北野大人上报你的功绩。

山本信玄欣喜地将刀别在了腰间。他对桥本说：那你保护好联队长。说完，他便纵身一跃，跳下了主席台，闯入了战斗中。

渡边不易察觉地微微一笑。

淡黄的阳光，带着沙漠的颜色，干枯地照亮着大地。

山本信玄端着一条步枪，疯狂地射杀着手枪队战士。他在血泊与火光中大步流星地走着，没有迟疑，没有恐惧，就像一部杀戮机器。他疯狂地开着枪，就算误打死日本兵也根本无所谓。手枪队的战士一个个地死在了山本信玄的枪下。

刘小阳向山本信玄开枪。山本信玄伸手一抓，就拉过了一个日本兵来挡子弹。山本信玄就像一个魔鬼，所向披靡，刀枪不入。

日军步步紧逼地，将赵驹和刘小阳围困在了一起。

赵驹和刘小阳背靠背地站着。

刘小阳问：“你是什么人？”

赵驹说：“一个生无可恋之人。”

刘小阳说：“大家今日殊途同归，来生若有幸，我请你喝顿酒。”

赵驹说：“你花钱，我一定奉陪。”

两人爽朗一笑。

赵驹说，送我两颗手榴弹。

刘小阳说，好，给。

赵驹丢下了刺刀，接过了手榴弹。围困着他们两人的日军，一看这情形，以为他们是想要原地引爆手榴弹自杀了，吓得赶紧纷纷转身逃窜。

但是，赵驹焦灼的目光，却是望向了极远处的主席台。

此时的他，已在离主席台极远的位置。

他紧咬着牙，憋足了全身的力气，往主席台上掷出了一颗手榴弹。

渡边看到了从赵驹手里疾飞而来的手榴弹。其速快如流星。渡边瞠目结舌，面如死灰，脑子里空白一片，根本来不及有任何反应。

桥本就地卧倒。

手榴弹已飞至眼前。

千钧一发。

然而，差之毫厘。

这颗手榴弹没能掷到主席台的上面，而是滚进了主席台下面支架的空隙里。

“嘭——”剧烈的爆炸声。

“哗啦啦——”整个主席台，彻底地倒塌了。

主席台上的所有人，都跟随着主席台猛烈的崩塌，摔落进了主席台坍塌后的废墟里。有日本兵摔死，有日本兵被断木的尖头戳穿了肚子，有日本兵被爆炸后沸腾的火焰给烧死。废墟中一片死伤的狼藉。

而渡边站了起来，庆幸自己完好无损。他正要叫桥本，看桥本是否还活着，突然，他惊恐至极地看到，又一颗手榴弹，狠狠地往这边飞了过来！

毛骨悚然的冰寒，死神来临的恐怖，瞬间填满了渡边的所有知觉。

说时迟那时快，渡边急速抓过了身边的一个日本兵，将他死死拉住并覆盖在自己身上往后仰天急倒了下去。

“嘭——”巨大的爆炸声再次响起。

火光熊熊一片。

日本兵被炸死了一大片，还有日本兵在大火中活活被烧死，他们扭曲的惨叫，像小鬼的哭闹，令这片废墟顿时布满了阴冷的地狱味道。

覆盖在渡边身上的那个日本兵被炸死了。渡边从短暂的昏厥中醒来，他仔细地感觉了一下自己身体的状况，又轻微地活动了一下自己的四肢，最后庆幸，自己只是受了一些轻伤。渡边从尸体堆里爬了起来，他惊魂未定地看着空中，害怕又有手榴弹飞来，然而并没有。他看到了被炸掉了一条左臂的桥本，桥本还活着。渡边发现自己的脸上糊满了腥重的血液。一股火焰般的恼恨在他体内和脑中奔窜。他向广场上的日军大吼：“给我杀了赵驹！把他剁成肉酱！！”

日军的杀声，在阳光下震荡。

可惜，刘小阳已再无手榴弹。

被赵驹和刘小阳劫持来作盾牌的两个日本兵，已经冰凉地死在了自己人的枪口前。赵驹和刘小阳互道了一声再见，然后便丢开了死尸，急奔向了各自的方向。

日军得到了渡边的命令，开始无所顾忌地向赵驹开枪。赵驹一边拼命狂奔，一边从地上的死人手里捡起着枪，向敌军猛烈射击。赵驹在流动的飞奔中射杀着日本兵，百发百中，枪枪夺命。一支枪的子弹打光了，他就重新再从地上的死人手里捡起一支枪，继续射击。他的奔跑迅捷如豹，他的枪法百步穿杨，他是格斗场上的一代拳王，他是日本人训练出来的杀人武器，他用尽了全力，誓要在这千军万马之势中，取下渡边的首级。不杀渡边，赵驹死不瞑目。

赵驹向着渡边所在的方向，一往无前地奋勇杀进。日本兵一个接一个地被子弹打穿着脑袋，有些日本兵还没来得及向赵驹射击，已被赵驹一枪毙命。赵驹就像一条誓要乘风破浪直捣黄龙的鱼，在风高浪急深邃无比的凶恶海洋中勇猛劈进。他不顾一切，视死如归。他要像一柄利剑一样，直刺入敌军的心脏。他必须要亲手杀了渡边。他感到，丽云今天似乎就在天上，正看着他、等着他。

枪林弹雨里，赵驹的速度快过了闪电。他锋利的身影，像飘忽的鬼魅，像闪烁的刀光，像消失的流星。日军的子弹像滚烫的毒蛇一样，成群结队地扑向他、追着他咬，却竟然怎么样也咬不上他。他本身，就像是一颗在飞速前进着的子弹一样。血肉横飞的厮杀，是他与空气摩擦产生的火花。他的心中没有丝毫的恐惧，只有最后的信念。血泊在他脚下横流，敌人在他面前颤抖。赵驹，就像他的父亲赵三牛一样，在生命里的最后一战中，完美而短暂地，战胜了枪与子弹。就像一个不灭的传说与奇迹，赵驹的神话，刻入了每个惊叹者的心里。

英雄盖世凄凉梦，红颜花落悲泪空。

沧海桑田入孤冢，天长地久寂枯荣。

没有人再敢拦着赵驹，围困着他的日军，胆战心惊而惶恐无限地，开始自我溃散。渡边心急如焚，朝天连续开枪，歇斯底里地怒喊："后退者死！逃兵军法处置！"渡边大喊着山本信玄的名字，怒吼道："你个王八蛋，快给我杀了赵驹！！"

阳光惨烈。

沙漠色的光，像一种悲悯的祈祷，给大地涂上孤独的温度。

经过连番激战，手枪队的战士们，已一共只剩下一颗手榴弹。

一名年轻战士从花坛掩体后面迅速站起，想要将这颗最后的手榴弹扔进日军阵中，但是，就在他要扔出这颗手榴弹的千钧一发之际，山本信玄一枪打穿了他的脑袋。

血花四溅，滚热的意识还未知觉到疼痛与死亡，已经被死亡疼痛地停止。

手榴弹从这名年轻战士的手中滑落。

手榴弹的拉环已被拉开。

躲在花坛掩体后面的其他手枪队战士，赶紧一齐往外跃出。

"嘭——"沉闷无比的爆炸。有手枪队战士被炸得粉身碎骨。

猎猎风中，死亡的残渣像跳动的音符一样鲜艳刺目，困境像一种失血的弹奏，绝望是死亡之河上的漂泊。

手枪队的战士，已牺牲过半。前仆后继的英勇，似江河奔流。当死亡成为一种必然，绽放宛如漂泊中的歌唱。只要这个生死时代还在继续，这种慷慨赴死的旋律就不会凋谢。血花总是孤哀，又总是灿烂。

山本信玄率领着日军，疯狂地射杀着手枪队的战士。一个战士倒下了，又一个战士倒下了。

山本信玄满脸阴冷地狞笑着，每一分钟的杀戮，都令他感到血脉畅通的舒服。他像用餐一样享受着杀戮的每一个过程，这享受，令他心满意足。他像一部嗜血的机器，对于生命没有半分敬畏与可惜，只有残酷的消灭与杀害，才能让他感觉到自身活着的美妙。他像一个战斗的魔鬼、一个不知疲倦的屠夫，追敌不休，杀人不止，毫不手软，从不怜悯。他的眼神，永远像野狼张开的血盆大口。这样的一个山本信玄，在战场上是无坚不摧的。

战斗激烈，殊死相拼。

鱼死网破，鏖战无尽。

手枪队的战士，已仅剩下了几名。

那个背着方远梦的战士，早已中弹身亡。而方远梦自己，背上也已中了枪。他无能为力地躺在血泊里，腿脚动弹不得，手里没有武器。他看着日本兵在他身边来来去去，听着同志们不停死亡的声音，他感觉到了难以承受的折磨。血液在从他身上慢慢流失，疼痛在他体内渐渐扩大，他感知到了死神的来临。他在奄奄一息中，对死亡并无恐惧，只是对人生抱着太多遗憾。还有，眼前手枪队的注定失败，令他痛心疾首。他不想让这样的惨痛继续下去，可是，对于这一切他又根本无力改变。他感到欲哭无泪。生命的寒凉包裹住了他，时代的悲哀让他喘不过气。这种折磨，仿佛命运对于想要改变命运的信仰的报复与戕害。方远梦想起了自己一生中所有狂风暴雨般的战斗，他说：可惜，我没能走到最后。

刘小阳找到了方远梦，重新背起了他。方远梦哭着说，你快跑，我已经是个死人了。刘小阳笑笑，说，你想死，我姐还不答应呢。

话音才落。山本信玄一枪，打在了刘小阳的膝盖上。

手枪队的战士，没死的都已受伤，子弹皆已打光。

山本信玄狞笑着，从别在腰间的刀鞘里，抽出了渡边给他的那把日本军刀。这把刀寒光四射，闪亮如镜，锋利非凡，杀气逼人。山本信玄爱抚了一下刀背，说，真是一把好刀，渡边用着太可惜了。

山本信玄双手紧握着这把狭长的军刀，走到了一个受重伤的手枪队战士跟前。山本信玄嘲讽地一笑，然后挥刀劈下，将这名手枪队的战士拦腰斩为了两段。站在山本信玄背后的日本兵们，都吓得一起退后了一步。

山本信玄一个个地杀着。那些受了伤还没死的手枪队战士，一个个地都成为山本信玄用来劈砍的玩具。

尸横遍野，血流漂杵。

身上中了三枪的刘小阳，就躺在方远梦的旁边。刘小阳吐着血，笑着说：今天是中秋节，看来，我们真的可以一起团圆了。

方远梦流着泪，笑说：你姐做的豆沙馅月饼，是最好吃的，一会儿，我

们一起向她讨月饼吃。

方远梦和刘小阳在血泊中，一起哈哈笑。

山本信玄握着血淋淋的军刀，来到了刘小阳的身边。

刘小阳最后笑了笑，对方远梦说：那我先走一步了。

方远梦点点头。

山本信玄一刀劈下，刘小阳的头颅，滚向了远处。

阳光鲜红，红艳似血。

赵宏伟眼中噙泪，喉中哽咽。他把目光转向了苍茫无限的天际，淡蓝色的苍穹是那么明净，简直不像这血污人间的天空。金黄中带着淡红色的阳光，柔和而均匀地布满着天空、照耀着大地，秋风肃杀里，这光似乎蕴含着悲悯的暖意。赵宏伟不知道已逝的人们，是否都已在天堂安息。如果天上有神灵，神灵们是否又会理会人间的琐事？赵宏伟觉得生命无论死活，都是这般孤独。当黑暗铺天盖地地吞没人间所有的美好时，善良的人们总是孤立无援，叫天天不应。当个人与整个丑恶的时代对抗时，个人似乎只有被恶浪撕碎的结局。彷徨，是赵宏伟一生的悲凉。

赵宏伟看到，浑身是血的方远梦，又被日本兵架着，绑回到了刑架上。

渡边正被一圈由卫兵组成的人墙保护着，往赵宏伟所在的方向转移。

赵宏伟看着死尸遍地血流漂杵的广场，哀伤无尽，却又手无缚鸡之力。手枪队的战士已经全部牺牲了，一个不剩，而且，他们中的许多人，尸体都已被山本信玄这个恶魔给劈得四分五裂，惨不忍睹。反抗或挣扎，似乎正是在以这样一种触目惊心的方式，嘲讽着寄希望于善恶有报的软弱民众。

赵宏伟想起了方远梦曾经唱过的一首歌的歌词：从来就没有什么救世主，也不靠神仙皇帝，要创造人类的幸福，全靠我们自己。

这是最后的斗争，团结起来到明天。这是最后的斗争，团结起来到明天！

赵宏伟捏紧了拳头，热泪盈眶。

整片巨大的广场上，已只剩下了赵驹一个人，还在与日军顽强地战斗。不杀渡边，赵驹誓不罢休。

广场上的日军全部集中了起来，合力捕杀赵驹。

赵驹，使尽了浑身解数，在血火辉煌的战场上，孤军奋战。

赵驹的全身已染满了敌人的血，他浑身是胆，英勇无惧，就像黑夜中最后的一颗明星，就像滔天巨浪中最后的一艘小船，就像时代洪流里最后的一个神话。

赵驹如同一柄宝刀，劈开日军的阻挠，锐不可当地冲向渡边。

渡边于重重保护之中，脸色惨白，如临末日。

保护着渡边的卫兵，一个又一个地被赵驹打穿脑袋。

渡边只能蜷缩在卫兵们的背后躲避子弹。他已面无半分血色，浑身战栗难禁。赵驹已随时有可能将他一枪毙命。死神，仿佛已紧掐住了渡边的脖子。

突然，一颗子弹追上了赵驹如电的速度，擦破了赵驹的脸皮。

又一颗子弹从赵驹胸前飞过，惊险地拦阻住了赵驹一往无前的奔进。

赵驹急忙转身一看，原来，是山本信玄正飞奔而来！是他在凶猛地射击！

一颗颗子弹，凌厉又精准地直奔赵驹的要害而来，枪枪致命，弹无虚发。赵驹闪躲腾挪，避之不及，险象环生，难以前进。山本信玄奔得越来越近，他的子弹，飞得越来越快、越来越密。赵驹被极度的危险笼罩着，困在原地，无法继续向渡边奔进。

山本信玄一边狂奔，一边亢奋地大喊："赵驹是我的！谁也不许抢！"

赵驹一边在地上打滚，一边向山本信玄开枪。

两人激烈对战。枪火缤纷。

周围的日本兵，纷遭池鱼之殃。

赵驹也向山本信玄冲了过去。

子弹来往飞奔，生死倏忽一瞬。枪火闪耀，你躲我闪，狂战进击，你死我活。

赵驹和山本信玄，在日军身躯的丛林里，猛烈地开枪，疾速地换枪，龙腾虎跃，杀意鼎沸；他们互相进击，互相躲闪，在火树银花般的死战中越来越接近。他们周围的日本兵，纷纷死伤，四散外逃。

两虎相战，生死搏杀。血光炫目，气势磅礴。

终于，两个人面对面地站在了一起。两人互相用枪紧紧地对准着对方的额头。

一片寂静。

纹丝不动。

彼此命悬一线。

渡边从卫队人墙的缝隙里观看着一切。他像是又看到了胜利的希望似的，大大地松了一口气。他站直了身子，挺了挺胸，准备不管山本信玄死活地，命令军队一起向赵驹开枪。

但是，山本信玄仿佛在一刹那察觉到了渡边冷酷的诡计似的，大声喊道：“大人，让我来杀了赵驹！”

话音未落，山本信玄已是乘势将头一偏，避开了赵驹的枪口，转身飞起一脚，踢向了赵驹手中的步枪。

就在赵驹手中的步枪被踢飞的一刹那，赵驹也已是以一套连环踢，踢飞了山本信玄手中的步枪。

山本信玄以猎豹之速，重重地向赵驹挥臂劈下。赵驹举拳相迎，双臂与山本信玄缠斗在了一起。

山本信玄和赵驹互相死死地抓住了对方。两个人，瞪着血红的双眼，紧紧地互相逼视着。

山本信玄狞笑着，说：“真没想到，你竟然是个武林高手！”

赵驹说：“我只是中国人中最差的一个！”

山本信玄说：“好，那今天就让我领教领教，看你到底是不是东亚病夫！”

说完，山本信玄猛然发力，挣脱了赵驹的控制，飞腿踹向赵驹的心口。赵驹一拳冲向山本信玄的膝盖。

两人开始激烈格斗。

铁拳相迎，力透雷霆；劲腿横扫，飞荡千斤。山本信玄使出了赵驹从未真正见过的实战空手道，霸气横扫千军；赵驹以完整无缺的赵家八极拳迎击，威力撼震山岳。骨骼与骨骼碰撞，肌肉与肌肉相抗，力量在激烈的爆发中穿透生命的极限，技巧在眼花缭乱的挥洒中绽放死亡的花朵，意志在无与伦比的坚韧中燃烧胜利的信仰。生死相抗的搏斗，将连绵的时间切成无数个死亡终点，将生死的恐惧焚为漫天飞舞的灰烬。灰烬中，拳拳到肉，击击致命。

沉闷而快速的肢体撞击声，澎湃着夺命的惊险；拳脚挥舞出的呼呼风声，激荡着死亡的斗争。格斗之外的世界仿佛万籁俱寂，对手之间的方寸空间风高浪急。分筋错骨只在须臾之间，命丧黄泉只在一招之险。连环进击犹如百兽奔吼，闪躲腾挪宛似鹰旋长空。碧浪滔天势不可当，碎石裂铁气贯长虹。山本信玄就像一个铜皮铁骨的杀人魔鬼，狰狞残暴地炫耀着嗜血的獠牙；赵驹就像一头精神抖擞的猛虎，威武顽强地粉碎着敌寇的攻杀。两人全力搏斗，拼命厮杀，紧紧相缠，险象环生，你来我往，互有损伤。赵驹越战越勇，山本信玄凶相毕露。

最终，赵驹尽全身之力，以排山倒海之势，使出了威震武林的八极铁山靠。山本信玄毫无招架之力地，被赵驹撞出了几丈远。他像一片轻飘飘又无法自主的羽毛一样在空中可笑地滑过，然后，面朝下地，重重摔在了地上。

现场一片哗然。而后，一片寂静。

山本信玄爬了起来，捂着胸口，痛苦地咳嗽了两下。然后，他又阴阳怪气地笑了起来。他的眼睛里，喷射着暴戾无比的光。这光，带着绞杀的疯狂。

山本信玄退后几步，从后面日本兵的步枪上取下了两把刺刀来，远远地丢给了赵驹。

山本信玄重新从腰间的刀鞘里抽出了那把华丽的日本军刀。

“你，中国人，还没见识过我们大日本帝国的剑道吧？来，和我比试一下兵器！”山本信玄骄傲地叫嚣道。

狭长锋利的军刀在阳光下熠熠生辉，反射着削铁如泥般的可怖光芒。这光芒里，渗透着一片刀已饮血的猩红色。

赵驹笑笑，捡起了刺刀。

秋风紧，霜意浓。寒光绚烂，血色迷蒙。

赵驹挥舞着双刀，奔向了山本信玄。

刀刃与刀刃相擦而过，发出刺耳的尖啸；刀身与刀身飞速激撞，溅出耀眼的火星。刀光剑影疾如流星，追魂夺魄接踵而至，劈砍挑刺环环相扣，穿心封喉擦肩而过，刀花炫目寒光四舞，刃冷如霜血丝冰凉，生死一瞬如履薄冰，秋意肃杀铁血惊心。金属与金属的缠斗，人与人的相杀，步步如临深渊，死神瞬息万变。山本信玄疯狂砍杀，誓要饮血方休。赵驹刀舞如雪光一片，毫不惧怕。

激烈的搏杀。

火花四溅的死亡烟火，不惧灭亡的舍身相搏。

赵宏伟望了望旗杆上的日本旗，心中千疮百孔。

赵宏伟看到，整片血流成河的广场上，已只剩下了赵驹这一个活着的刺客。日军成群结队，稳操胜券，赵驹单枪匹马，视死如归。赵宏伟知道赵驹今日已必死无疑，就像那古往今来无数取义成仁功亏一篑的悲剧英雄一样；赵宏伟也知道赵驹必然已懂得结局，就像那流芳千古的风萧萧兮易水寒的壮士传奇一般。但是赵驹依然毫不放弃地，在像猛虎一样进击，舍生忘死，拼尽全力，仿佛誓要在死前完成最后的遗愿一般。

于千军万马之阵中，取上将首级，谈何容易。赵宏伟不禁悲叹赵驹之痴顽。而赵驹究竟是什么人、到底与渡边有什么深仇大恨，赵宏伟或已永远不可得知。也许，英雄，就该是一个永恒之谜，赵宏伟哀思。

赵宏伟发现，赵驹借着与山本信玄格斗厮杀之机，仍然在渐渐地向渡边所在的方向靠近。而渡边似乎并未察觉。

赵驹和山本信玄，彼此都已身中数刀。看着赵驹在刀光剑影中血花四溅，赵宏伟热泪盈眶。

多少英雄泪，才可唤醒山河醉。赵宏伟悲心万丈。

赵宏伟向渡边所在的方向走了过去。他看到，在一个无人注意的地方，躺着一条枪。

择日不如撞日，撞日不如今日。赵宏伟慷慨激昂地想。也许，今天就该是渡边老贼的死期。赵宏伟加快了步伐。

一个士兵来向渡边报告，说桥本副联队长已经被送往医院。同时，该士兵还向渡边转达了桥本的一个请求：请务必要杀死赵驹，最好将他千刀万剐。

渡边诡诈地一笑，然后自言自语似的说：赵驹是一定会死的，但是，他现在还能帮我做最后一件事。

渡边不经意地，瞥见了赵宏伟正在往这边快步走来，渡边微微皱了皱眉。渡边又看到了，在离赵宏伟不远的一处地上，躺着一条枪。渡边猛然警觉，正要拔枪，忽然就看到了，赵宏伟在解裤子。赵宏伟向渡边点头致了一下意，然后就跑到了旁边的一处比较隐蔽的地方，开始了撒尿。看着赵宏伟的尿液在日本兵的血泊里流淌，渡边想呵斥赵宏伟，但是想想还是算了。渡边觉得赵宏伟这人真是太他妈的像小丑了。渡边挥挥手，让士兵去捡掉不远处地上的那条枪。

赵驹终于一下子压制住了山本信玄的猛攻。这时，赵驹看到，渡边不知道正在往后面看什么，他的脑袋和后背，一时都暴露在了卫兵人墙的空隙里！

说时迟那时快，赵驹用尽全力将手中的一把刺刀向着渡边的后背投了去！

千钧一发。刀似流星。

然而，山本信玄迅猛地一挥刀，便将赵驹投出去的这把刺刀打落在了地上。

天不遂人愿。沧海遗恨，珠泪空抛。

赵驹猛然发力，正要将另一把刺刀也向渡边投出，山本信玄已是挥刀又狠扑了过来。赵驹只能挥刀相迎。

两个浑身血淋淋的人，又全力厮杀在了一起。

山本信玄的厮杀纠缠，像一道铜墙铁壁，狠狠地围困着赵驹，令赵驹疲于应对。赵驹眼看着刺杀渡边的良机已白白流走，却又实在分身无术、脱身不得。只要赵驹稍微一分心，就有可能被山本信玄当场杀死。原本被多场战斗搅得散乱不堪又惊惶失措的日军，已在这样一段不短的时间里恢复了整齐有序的队形和忠君勇猛的斗志，赵驹深知，自己离刺杀成功，已越来越远。而且，赵驹已身负多处刀伤，长久的格斗，已令他筋疲力尽。就算现在没有山本信玄，他也再不能像刚才那样于枪林弹雨中来去自如、威震敌寇令敌四散溃逃了。现在，所有的日军都像墙一样围困着赵驹，只要渡边一声令下，赵驹就会被万弹穿身。一个无法挣扎的绝境，已经筑成。赵驹，已是一头被关在了铁笼子里的老虎，而渡边，正在笼子外看戏。渡边高枕无忧，安然无恙。而这该死的山本信玄，还在像个疯子一样地，向所有人证明他自己是个最棒的武士。

赵驹感到了一丝绝望。有哀凉的叹息从他心里升起。蓝天是那样纯净，阳光是那样温暖，秋风是那样柔和。而到了今天晚上，夜空中还会有一轮美丽得没有缺憾的圆月升起。可惜，他应该看不到了。赵驹透过眼前一片片的刀影和血光，忧伤地感到，丽云今天似乎就在天上看着他、等着他。她的笑容，依旧还像许多年前一样纯真灿烂，美丽无双。

而他，却还没有为她报仇。畜生渡边就在咫尺之外，而他赵驹，却已离

报仇有天涯之远。时间才过了一小段，局势已变得如此无情残酷。造化真的弄人。

山本信玄像个疯子一样，又一次挥刀狠扑了上来。赵驹怒吼一声，爆发出了一股令人恐怖的力量，他疯狂地向山本信玄砍了过去。迅猛得近乎狂暴的刀刃相砍声，以迅雷不及掩耳的速度连续迸发，没有任何人再能看清他们两人此刻的身形动作。只有碎金裂石般的响亮刀砍声，如同某种死神的乐器，在生死场内激烈地奏响，令人荡气回肠，久久不能遗忘。

终于，山本信玄满脸是血惊恐万状地，向后跳开了。他后退着，气喘吁吁惊魂难定地瞪眼看着势不可当的赵驹。赵驹双眼血红，咬牙切齿，气息粗重，就像一头即将准备鱼死网破的困兽，其威猛令人惊心动魄。山本信玄看着此刻宛如一件致命武器的赵驹，竟莫名感到了阵阵胆寒。山本信玄怯懦了起来，一时不敢上前再战。

赵驹将手中的刺刀，拼命地向渡边飞投了过去。

刀如利箭，刃射寒光，疾似闪电。

然而，渡边已有防备。这柄刺刀，只是穿透了一个卫兵的胸膛。

赵驹欲哭无泪。

渡边向山本信玄大喊：“你快上啊！还愣着干什么！”

山本信玄举刀，猛冲向了已手无寸铁的赵驹。

赵驹飞身而起，朝着山本信玄的胸口狂踢出了一套猛烈无比的连环腿。

赵驹稳稳落地。山本信玄吐出了两口鲜血。

渡边露出了满意的笑容。

没错，渡边的如意算盘，就是要让山本信玄打伤赵驹，而让赵驹，打死山本信玄。鹬蚌相争，渔人得利。

山本信玄的一只手，离开了军刀的刀把。

他以最快的速度，将手伸向了别在腰间的手枪。他要拔枪打死赵驹。

说时迟那时快，赵驹已是一个箭步冲到了山本信玄的面前。赵驹一只手紧紧地按住了山本信玄手中军刀的刀把，以防止他砍人，另一只手，则使劲地按住了山本信玄腰间的手枪，不让他拔枪。赵驹在不让山本信玄拔出枪来的同时，也试图抢到这把枪。两个人杀气腾腾地紧贴在一起，各用一只手，死死地争夺着这把生死攸关的手枪。

两人缠斗不休。

山本信玄憋足了劲，也拔不出枪来。赵驹死死地控制住了他。

山本信玄用头猛撞赵驹的头。赵驹按着山本信玄刀把的手顿时一松。山本信玄迅速抬手，将刀锋从赵驹的胸腹处割过，但是，却只是割破了赵驹胸腹处的衣衫及皮肤，并未重伤赵驹。赵驹一反手，就迅速地重新按住了山本信玄的刀把，狠狠往下一压。山本信玄的双手又被赵驹死死地控制住了，他无可动弹，力不从心，无能为力。山本信玄勃然大怒，又用头撞赵驹，赵驹却将头一偏，躲开了攻击。

两人互锁缠斗，像紧紧厮咬在一起的野兽。

阳光浓烈，天空湛蓝。

突然，从赵驹胸前被割开的衣服里，掉出来了一团东西，落在了地上。

赵驹一愣。

这，是丽云的那束断发。

山本信玄即将一脚踩到这头发上。

赵驹一把推开了山本信玄。

没有人踩到这束头发。

赵驹弯下腰，去捡丽云的头发。

山本信玄拔出了手枪。

“砰——”一枪。

山本信玄的子弹，穿过了赵驹的肚子。

赵驹吐着血，痴痴地看着丽云的头发，喃喃地说：“对不起，丽云，我一定让你失望了……”

“砰——”又一枪。赵驹的左大腿中弹。

赵驹血流如注地，单膝跪在了地上。

赵驹颤抖着，小心翼翼地，将丽云的头发重新放进了怀中的衣袋里。他将丽云的头发轻轻往心口上贴了贴，痴情地说：“我们再也不会分开了……”

鲜血，像泉水一样，从赵驹体内往外奔涌。

山本信玄的枪口，顶在了赵驹的额头上。

赵驹深吸一口气，重新站了起来。

赵驹平静地说：你敢不敢赤手空拳地和我来一场生死格斗，我们这次不分胜负，只决生死，至死方休。

山本信玄犹豫不决，无法回答。

赵驹嘲讽与轻蔑地大笑了起来，说：难道你竟然不敢与我这个将死之人决战吗，难道你们引以为傲的武士道精神只是一个软弱的谎言吗。

渡边大声说："山本！别给我们大日本皇军丢脸！"

士兵们也开始起哄。

山本信玄一咬牙，丢开了手里的军刀与手枪。他握紧了拳，说：来吧，东亚病夫！

赵驹怒啸一声，纵身跃起。

热血喷涌生死一决，龙腾虎跃慷慨悲绝，排山倒海气势恢宏，舍生忘死意志如虹。秋风萧瑟生绚烂，黄叶缤纷起轻寒，悲舞人间几番看，血泪哀恸红尘暗。怒发冲冠天崩地裂，仰天长啸壮怀激烈，沧海横流天涯呜咽，生为英雄死亦鬼杰。霜染苍鬓泪斑驳，一片痴情哀难休，莫问明月几时有，生死大爱悲欢破。

那一天，看见过赵驹终极一战的人都说，赵驹像极了当年最威风时的赵三牛，他，没有辱没江南赵家在武林中的赫赫威名。只是，在赵驹死后，赵家八极拳，便从此绝迹于江湖。而赵驹，也像他父亲一样，成为一个永远的传说。

山本信玄被打得骨骼尽碎，内脏破裂。

赵驹像个血人似的，一步一步，走向着最后的山本信玄。

山本信玄躺在地上，哭爹喊娘地大叫了起来："救命！救命！快开枪打死赵驹！快！！"

有日本兵端起了枪。渡边赶紧大声说："不许开枪！武士就要遵守武士的约定，贪生怕死的人，只会丢尽我们大日本帝国武士的脸！真正的武士宁可死，也不能破坏武士的荣誉！"

"渡边！你这条老狗！"山本信玄大骂。

赵驹一拳砸下，山本信玄的脑袋开了花。脑浆四迸。

现场一片肃静。

说时迟那时快，赵驹一下子捡起了地上那把山本信玄的手枪。

"砰砰砰砰——"

赵驹打死了护在渡边身前的几名卫兵。

卫兵倒下，露出了渡边。

渡边大骇。

“砰砰砰砰砰——”

日本兵们举枪齐射。

赵驹全身中弹。血如泉涌。

赵驹向渡边开枪。但是，枪里已无子弹。

赵驹垂死挣扎地，又去捡起了地上的那把日本军刀。他拼尽全力地，想要将刀向渡边掷出，可是，他的双臂不可抗拒地一软。军刀，掉在了地上。

渡边向赵驹开枪。

赵驹倒在了地上。

赵驹看见了赵宏伟，他向赵宏伟伸出了手。

赵宏伟跑到了赵驹的身边。他强忍着泪，抱起了浑身都是血窟窿的赵驹。

赵驹说：“帮我杀……杀……”

赵驹断了气。

赵驹大张着眼，两行泪，从他的眼眶里滑落了出来，滚烫滚烫。

赵驹最后的眼泪里，有湛蓝的天空，灿烂的阳光，还有永逝的丽云。

赵宏伟，合上了赵驹的双眼。

渡边走过来，问赵宏伟：赵驹最后说了什么？

赵宏伟说：他说，我恨日本人。

渡边笑笑。

渡边交给了赵宏伟一把手枪，让他去枪毙方远梦。

刑架上的方远梦，已奄奄一息。

赵宏伟走到了方远梦的面前，问：方兄，你可还有什么心愿未了？

方远梦笑了笑，摇了摇头，说：此生已无其他心愿，只是未见王师北定中原，赵兄，将来要是有一天，全国解放了，建立了新中国，请你一定要给我报声喜。

赵宏伟含着泪说，放心。

赵宏伟开枪，打死了方远梦。

渡边没忘记桥本想将赵驹千刀万剐的请求。渡边命现场的所有日本兵，每人从赵驹的身上割下一两片肉来。

很快，赵驹就被削尽了全身的皮肉，只剩下了骨头和内脏。渡边命人将赵驹的内脏拿去喂狗，另外，渡边还要将赵驹的骨架悬挂在广场的旗杆上示众。

只是，发生了一件很奇怪的事情。那一束女人的头发，不知怎么，竟然死死地缠绕在了赵驹的白骨上，不管如何拉扯，也拉扯不下来。

赵驹的白骨，被高悬在旗杆上，丽云的头发，紧紧地陪伴着他，宛如，生生世世不分离的誓言。

悲哀无限。

时间过得很快，马上就要到一九四〇年的元旦了。

江南的冬天，凄凉入骨。悲冷的风，像永恒的呜咽。

新四军向江南日军发起了新一轮进攻，日军节节败退。

渡边被升为了大佐，据说不久便将离开江庆县，去往南京。

赵宏伟光荣地成为江庆县的县长。日本人还将已故的那个汉奸县长的一处宅子送给了赵宏伟。

赵宏伟把吹捧渡边的书给写好了，中日双语，渡边看完非常满意。十二月底的时候，渡边还给赵宏伟办了一个新书印成庆祝仪式。据说，渡边会将这本书分送给日军中的各级将领，以求扩大自身的影响力。

在那天庆祝仪式结束的时候，赵宏伟向渡边及桥本发出了邀请。赵宏伟说，元旦那天是他生日，他想办十桌酒席，宴请渡边、桥本以及诸位日本勇士，而且，他刚搬进新宅，也算是顺便庆祝乔迁之喜。他要渡边和桥本届时千万赏脸出席。

渡边春风满面地应允，他说：我就要离开江庆县了，本也想与你畅谈一番，这样最好。

赵宏伟感激不尽。

一九四〇年元旦。阳光灿烂。

中午，渡边、桥本如约而至。他们还带来了许多日本兵。

渡边笑问赵宏伟：会不会嫌我带的人太多？

赵宏伟说：太君开玩笑，皇军赏脸，鄙人寒舍蓬荜增辉，人来得越多越好。

进了宅子，却并无看见其他宾客，也无厨子、佣人等人。赵宏伟解释说，今日只宴请太君与皇军，所以并无其他宾客，而菜肴，皆是鄙人亲自下厨，美味堪比大厨。

日本兵们皆在院中酒席落座。而渡边和桥本，则都被请入了雅致精美的堂屋。

赵宏伟拿出了那坛状元红。酒坛一开，香气四溢。

赵宏伟给渡边和桥本斟酒。

赵宏伟先自喝了一碗酒，然后，每盘菜自尝了一口。这样之后，渡边与桥本才笑吟吟地动起了筷，饮起了酒。

渡边喝了一口状元红，赞叹得连连啧啧。他说，果然好酒，与众不同。

赵宏伟说，此酒与鄙人同寿，饱览人世沧桑，风味自然别具一格。

渡边笑对赵宏伟说，还记得当初，我说，总有一天，这酒会自己跑到我嘴里来，你看，我所言非虚。

赵宏伟说，太君高瞻远瞩，料事如神，一切，都逃不出您的掌握。

渡边哈哈大笑。

渡边、桥本、赵宏伟三人推杯换盏，谈笑风生，交谈得不亦乐乎。

渡边感叹地说：这样美好的时光，真的是难得呀，只可惜，这世上所有美好的东西，都是那样短暂，稍纵即逝，无法挽留。

赵宏伟说：太君此言差矣，这世上的一切都是过眼云烟，除了那些曾经美好的时光，因为，美好的东西，会永远刻在人的心底，不管人是活着还是死了，都将被人的灵魂带向永恒。

渡边笑说：你果然是文才出众，不愧为江南才子，人中龙凤。

赵宏伟说：百无一用是书生，我惭愧至极。

酒过三巡，菜过五味。那坛美妙的状元红，已被渡边和桥本喝了个干干净净，一滴不剩。

渡边放下了筷子，说：今天是你的生日，只可惜，明年今日，将会是你的忌日了。

说罢，渡边和桥本一起掏出了手枪。

赵宏伟一笑，问：两位太君何意？

桥本说：从赵驹暴露的那天起，我们就知道，你必定是有问题的，因为，以前，一直都是由赵驹在负责监视你，另外，那一天，方远梦在离你那么近的地方向你开枪，居然都没打中你，这不是太可疑了吗。

渡边说：本来，我一早就该杀了你，只可惜，你是我发掘并提拔起来的，一个赵驹已让我颜面扫地，我若再公开揭穿你，岂不是自己打自己耳光，另外，你的文笔也确实精妙，我需要你给我写一本歌功颂德的书，现在好了，你大功告成，可以功成身退了，我们今天杀了你，会告诉外界，你是被军统特工所杀，你在名誉上，仍然是我们皇军的好朋友，而我，也不会被人指责为昏庸无能、引狼入室。

赵宏伟看了看表，然后，心平气和地笑了笑。

赵宏伟说：真好，你们终于说穿了一切，我可以再也不用低声下气地演戏了，你们说得都对，包括你们说的明年今日是我的忌日也对，但是，有一件事，你们说错了，今天，不是我赵宏伟的生日。

渡边和桥本一脸讶异。

赵宏伟说：共产党的手枪队，留下了一批炸药和一枚定时炸弹，今天，这批炸药就埋在这座宅子的下面，遍布每个角落，只要时间一到，定时炸弹就会爆炸，引爆这里的全部炸药！你们，这群灭绝人性的禽兽，就会灰飞烟灭！！现在只剩下两分钟了！！哈哈哈！！！

渡边和桥本急忙起身想逃，却脚底发软，胸口发闷，疼痛无比。

赵宏伟说：你们无论如何也走不了了，刚才那坛状元红里，我已下了毒。

说完，赵宏伟从桌底下抽出了手枪。

渡边和桥本一齐向赵宏伟开枪。赵宏伟也向渡边和桥本开枪。

院子里的日本兵们听到枪声，纷纷往堂屋方向跑去。

浑身是血的赵宏伟走出堂屋，向日本兵们猛烈射击。

日本兵们集体向赵宏伟开枪。

赵宏伟，万弹穿身。血如泉涌。

时间到。

赵宏伟最后说了一句："中国万岁！！！"

"嘭——嘭嘭嘭——轰隆隆——"

滔天巨浪般的爆炸，山呼海啸般拔地而起。

烈焰如涛，火海无涯。

血红的火光烧红了苍茫的天际。

一切，都在爆炸与烈火中化为了彻底的灰烬。一切，烟消云散。

只留下一滴滚烫的英雄之泪，在不灭的天空中，悲伤洇开，流连徘徊。

江南的冬天，寒风凛冽，哀冷入骨。

2013 年 11 月 12 日至 2017 年 1 月 7 日